D0054827

What the Media Are Saying About Gideon's Torch

"*Gideon's Torch* is a watershed 'evangelical novel' that articulates the commitments and frustrations of the heirs of Francis Schaeffer in the nineties in a way no piece of Christian fiction has done."

Christianity Today

"Colson and Vaughn present every warring faction fairly; the portraits of the president and attorney general are particularly sensitive . . . quite movingly done."

Booklist

"There is more to this political thriller than blood, dirty tricks, and movie script editing. The cover needs a warning sticker: 'Warning—this book contains disturbing moral messages.'"

Scripps Howard News Service

Charles Colson does not blaze new trails. He constructs new continents . . . Colson uses the book as a mirror, both on society and on the reader."

Christian Retailing

"Readers get a behind-the-scenes glimpse into America's most powerful issues and people."

Bookstore Journal

"This is an important book because it will cause conservatives and liberals alike to consider their thoughts, words, and actions. For that reason alone, *Gideon's Torch* is a worth addition to any Christian's collection, but fiction readers will devour it."

Charisma Magazine

"Compelling reading that unfortunately rings too true for today."

Contact Magazine

GIDEON'S TORCH

GIDEON'S TORCH

CHARLES COLSON &
ELLEN VAUGHN

WORD PUBLISHING
Dallas•London•Vancouver•Melbourne

PUBLISHED BY WORD PUBLISHING
DALLAS, TEXAS

Copyright © 1995 by Charles Colson and Ellen Vaughn.
All rights reserved. No part of this publication may be
reproduced, stored in a retrieval system, or transmitted in any form or by any
means—electronic, mechanical, photocopy, recording, or any other—
except for brief quotations in printed reviews, without the
prior permission of the publisher.

LIBRARY OF CONGRESS CATALOGING-IN-PUBLICATION DATA
Colson, Charles W.
Gideon's Torch / Charles Colson and Ellen Vaughn.
p. cm.
ISBN 0-8499-3977-1
I. Vaughn, Ellen. II. Title.
PS3553.04767G5   1995   95-21744
813'. 54 DC20
CIP
PRINTED IN THE UNITED STATES OF AMERICA
6789 QKP 987654321

To the heroes of Eastern Europe, known and unknown: the believers of every confession who defended the Truth, overcame evil with good, and toppled the greatest tyranny of the twentieth century. May their lives both inspire and caution us in the tumultuous times in which we live.

". . . A Christian must be a sign of contradiction in the world . . . A Christian is one who all his life chooses between good and evil, lies and truth, love and hatred, God and Satan . . . Today more than ever there is a need for our light to shine, so that through us, through our deeds, through our choices, people can see the Father who is in Heaven."

JERZY POPIELUSZKO, 1947–1984

PREFACE

THIS IS A WORK OF FICTION. Apart from obvious historical references to public figures and events, all characters and incidents in this novel are the products of the authors' imaginations. Any similarities to people living or dead are purely coincidental.

Writing this book has proved to be an eerie experience for us. While it might appear to the reader that a number of the incidents included in *Gideon's Torch* have been taken from real newspaper headlines—including the suicide of White House counsel Vincent Foster, the murders at several abortion clinics, and, most recently, the tragic bombing of the Alfred P. Murrah Federal Building in Oklahoma City—our fictional episodes were conceived and written long before those actual events took place.

The truth *is* stranger than fiction.

Do not repay anyone evil for evil. Be careful to do what is right in the eyes of everybody. If it is possible, as far as it depends on you, live at peace with everyone. . . . Do not be overcome by evil, but overcome evil with good.

ROMANS 12:17–18, 21

1

A LL CLEAR FOR YOUR APPROACH, United 6031," said the crisp voice from the control tower. "Runway number thirty-five cleared for visual approach. Come on down, and welcome to Fargo."

As the twin-engine Beechcraft 1900 slowed and bobbled toward landing, the thin, rumpled, dark-haired woman in seat 3-A looked absently out the window, then checked her watch: 8:35. They were coming in about ten minutes early. Unusual, but good. She had a full day of appointments at the clinic.

Hope John is there to meet me, she thought, putting her newspaper back into her leather satchel. She stretched her legs, rubbed her eyes, and flexed her long, narrow hands, then settled back as the plane touched down, braked, and headed toward the terminal.

Dr. Ann Sloan was exhausted. She felt like she had fur on her tongue and grit in her eyelids. For five years now she had been a "circuit rider," shuttling between abortion clinics in three states. Fargo was her busiest stop. The approval last year of RU-486 had slowed early-trimester abortions, but there was still a booming business in later-term procedures. Since no doctor in North Dakota would perform them, Ann and another out-of-state physician

1

took turns servicing the women who traveled for eight and ten hours from all over the state in order to terminate their pregnancies.

Ann earned more than $100,000 a year, but it wasn't easy work. The travel was draining, and then there was the harassment. She had received more death threats and horrifying messages than she cared to remember; as a result, her teenage daughter knew never to listen to their answering machine unless Ann had previewed the tape first. Their home in Minnesota had been the target of routine harassment over the last few years: blood-colored paint on their driveway, grisly photos of aborted fetuses stuffed in their mailbox, "wanted" posters of Ann nailed to trees in the neighborhood.

This had only deepened her resolve. She hated the anti-abortion movement, hated its smug self-righteousness, hated these terroristic fundamentalists who were always trying to intimidate women from exercising their constitutional right to reproductive choice. She hated the songs, the sidewalk prayers, the taunts, the harassment of patients. It made her so angry that she felt the only reasonable response was to continue to supply the needs of North Dakota women, no matter what.

The "no matter what" had escalated over the years. After two doctors and several clinic staffers were shot, the FBI had paid her a formal call. A dispassionate agent, speaking in stiff, bureaucratic language, had let her know that though federal marshals and other officers had stepped up their protection of the clinics and their investigations of anti-abortion groups, the agents were spread too thin to cover every abortion facility all the time. It would be in her best interest, he said, to endure various "inconveniences."

She took his advice.

Now she never took the same route anywhere for two days in a row. She constantly checked her rearview mirrors. Her car phone was programmed to dial both 911 and a special FBI number. And if an unfamiliar car passed her house twice in an evening, she recorded its license plate. The FBI kept a file of those numbers.

She had even started checking underneath her car for bombs, using a special mirror the police had given her.

At the airport she always positioned herself near clumps of other commuters, taking comfort in the cluster of the crowd. And though she hated it, she had begun to wear a Kevlar vest. It was hot and bulky, but at least she was doing all she could reasonably do to protect herself. It was up to the government to do the rest.

But come what may, she was not going to let the "antis" win. She was not going to quit her practice. She was not going to be intimidated into abandoning these women who needed her help.

Today, however, she wasn't thinking much about any of this. She was worried about her daughter. Lindsay, a junior in high school, was in love for the first time, and the object of her affections was a freshman at the nearby university. Her daughter's apparent obsession with this young man was pulling her in over her head, but she just would not listen to Ann's warnings to take it slow.

The plane had rolled to a stop near the small commuter terminal, and Ann could see men in bulky parkas, their breath frosty in the cold air, pulling luggage from the plane's underbelly. As the copilot wrestled the cabin door open and positioned the portable stairs, Ann belted her heavy trenchcoat, picked up her satchel, and made her way to the door. The copilot nodded at her.

"Thanks, Greg, good flight," Ann said and headed down the stairs. When she reached the ground, she looked toward the waiting area in the terminal. She could see John, one of the clinic volunteers, waving to her. Good. She'd have time to have a cup of coffee before she began her appointments.

AS THEY NEARED THE CLINIC, a large old house that had been rehabbed, Ann groaned. She always hoped the protesters might take a break one Friday, but it never happened. Today there were at least seventy of them. Their numbers always swelled in January as it got closer to the anniversary of *Roe v. Wade*. Ann had also noticed that there had been more protesters since November's election, probably because President-elect Griswold was aggressively pro-choice. Or else they were venting their frustration with the defeat of Martin Masterson, the anti-choice candidate.

"Why can't these people just march on Washington and leave us alone?" she said to John.

Today there were reporters on the scene as well. *Must be a slow news day*, Ann thought as she noticed a van from Channel 11 parked out front and a smaller white van from Channel 4 at the curb near the side entrance. She could see Channel 11's crew already filming out front. She dreaded the sight of them, too. The media's presence always made the protesters louder and more aggressive. Fortunately, the reporters usually gave the clinic personnel an opportunity to advance their point of view as well.

John gunned the car toward the narrow driveway. Simultaneously, two clinic workers appeared at the door and came down the front steps gripping a large sheet of white canvas, moving quickly toward the car door on Ann's side. She unlocked the door and stepped out, ducking behind the sheet. John slid across the seat and followed her.

The protesters' chants turned into vicious shouts.

"Baby killer!"

"Cursed are the hands that shed innocent blood!"

Ann stumbled up the steps and through the clinic doors. Inside its haven, past the metal detectors, she looked at her watch. Still running a bit ahead of schedule. Great.

"Good morning!" she said to her colleagues, who were folding the canvas as if it were a flag. "I see our friends outside are in full form today. Do we have enough volunteer escorts to handle all of today's appointments?"

"I think so," said Diane Brook, the clinic's administrator. "We've got twenty-four clients scheduled, and the first three are already inside. One of them is a basket case. She got here early, but the antis were already here and harassed her on the way in. She asked if she could talk to the doctor before the procedure, just to ease her mind. We told her she could if you got here in time."

Diane took Ann's coat. "Let me hang that up for you, and I'll get you a mug of coffee. Anyway, this girl is twenty-one. By herself. Boyfriend left, family not supportive. She's been in the bathroom for a while. Said she was nervous."

"I'll talk with her," Ann said. "Just get me that coffee first. I need it bad today."

Ann walked down the narrow hallway toward the small room that served both as her office and as the clinic's file room. Ann took out her keys, but the door was already unlocked. Diane must have been in there for some files; her key was stuck in the deadbolt on the inside of the door.

ANN HAD JUST DROPPED her satchel on the desk when Diane came in carrying a big blue mug of coffee and leading a petite girl in jeans and round, dark sunglasses, the kind Ann's daughter favored. Her hair was swept up under a baseball cap, and she was huddled in a too-big leather bomber jacket, her hands jammed in the pockets. Underneath the jacket Ann could see an EarthFirst! T-shirt. *Poor thing*, thought Ann. *That jacket is probably all she has left—that she wants—from her boyfriend.*

"Here's your coffee," said Diane. "I'm going outside and have a word with those antis while the guys from Channel 11 are still filming."

Ann went around to her side of the desk and scanned the open appointment book. She sipped the hot coffee gratefully.

"Please sit down," she said to the girl, gesturing toward a metal folding chair in front of the desk. "I'm Doctor Sloan. I understand you were given a hard time this morning."

The girl perched nervously on the edge of the chair, hands still in her pockets, head down. "It was awful," she said softly. "They said not to murder my baby. They said there was still time to change my mind. They had big bloody posters of tiny babies . . ."

Ann flushed, the familiar anger rising in her chest. It was one thing to harass the strong, she thought. It was a pain, but she could handle it. But here was this young girl, all alone, vulnerable. It made Ann crazy. This was a medical procedure, for heaven's sake, perfectly legal, affordable, safe . . . and yet women across the country faced every obstacle these fanatics could think of to keep them from exercising their rights. It infuriated her every time she thought about her own daughter and the future *she* faced . . . all of the advances feminists had fought for, and women still couldn't freely control their own bodies and lives. It was insane.

"What's your name?" she asked.

"Sherry," the girl said, her head still down.

"Sherry, those people are living in the Dark Ages. They're just trying to impose *their* morality on you. They don't even care about you; all they care about is their own agenda. But this is still America. You have the right to make your own choices."

The girl looked up for the first time, and Ann was struck by how much she reminded her of Lindsay.

"They just made me feel so bad," Sherry said. "It's not like I'm so crazy about having this done. It's just that I don't know what else to do. I'm in school, I don't have much money, I don't have anyone to fall back on."

"I can understand if you're not happy about having an abortion right now," Ann said. "I've dealt with thousands of women over the years, and believe me, what you're feeling is normal. But you do have a right to make this decision. It's your choice—nobody else's. Probably now isn't the right time for you to continue a pregnancy. But it's up to you. Not a bunch of terrorists shoving posters in your face."

Sherry sighed. "You said you've dealt with lots of women," she said hesitantly. "How many of these do you think you've done? Abortions, I mean."

Ann paused for a moment. She had left her gynecology practice during Lindsay's last year in elementary school. Now she served three clinics in three states—about six thousand procedures a year.

"I've done this about thirty thousand times," she said. "And I can't begin to tell you how many of those women told me that it was the best choice they ever made for themselves." She lowered her eyes as she took another big swallow of coffee.

THE GIRL SLID THE GUN FROM HER POCKET. The safety was off; the silencer was on. She kept it and her hands below the edge of the desk.

"Thirty thousand babies," she said slowly, taking a deep breath. "Then your own lips have condemned you."

The doctor looked up, startled.

Both of her gloved hands on the gun, the girl stood, raised the barrel quickly, and aimed at the quarter-sized round of skin between the woman's dark eyebrows.

She gently squeezed the trigger, just as she had been taught. There was a spitting sound and, simultaneously, the doctor's head exploded against the wall behind the desk. A pink mist hung in the air; the coffee cup dropped to the desk, spreading a brown stain across the appointment book. The doctor's body slid down in the chair and to the floor.

The girl turned, as she had practiced, slipped the gun back in her pocket, and ran the few steps toward the door. She took the key hanging from the deadbolt, closed the office door behind her, and locked it. Hands back in her pockets, she moved quickly down the hall.

The woman who had escorted her into the clinic earlier looked at her questioningly.

"I'm sorry," the girl said. "I just can't go through with it. I've got to get out of here." She moved toward the doors.

The woman shrugged. Sometimes it happened; patients panicked. Well, that made one less on the schedule.

The girl burst through the front doors and pushed through the protesters. They were still trading insults with the woman who had brought the doctor her coffee. The cameras were rolling, and the woman kept talking, jabbing her finger at the pro-lifers.

The girl made her way through the crowd and around the corner. The white van was waiting, its motor running. The side door slid open, she jumped inside, and the van pulled away from the curb, the Channel 4 logo on its side just a bit off-center.

2

IRA LEVITZ sat at his computer, his fingers darting across the keyboard. Usually he wrote his newspaper columns at home, relishing the privacy of his book-strewn office and the silent companionship of his cat, Josephus, who loved to lie in the wide windowsill adjacent to his desk, flicking his tail, while Ira pondered and pounded the keys.

Now and then, however, Ira liked to come into the newsroom, so the *Post* reserved this cubicle for him. As usual, it was cluttered with Styrofoam cups, books, and unanswered mail. Dozens of his colleagues milled around in the huge room, phones to their ears, drinking coffee, arguing with one another, and clattering away at their computers.

Writing in the midst of this newsroom furor always gave him a satisfying sense of power: He really could block out the chaos and force clean, organized thoughts onto the computer screen. And he loved the energy, the camaraderie, that flowed from the network of people, all striving toward the same goals: Get the story. Make the deadline. It reminded him of his early days as a journalist, before syndication had beckoned.

Now he was nationally known, with regular invitations to give speeches, appear on talk shows, and kibitz with Washington's inside-the-Beltway powerbrokers. All this because he hammered out his blunt, hard-edged opinions twice a week. It never ceased to amaze him. He was forty-eight years old, but he would never lose his childlike delight in his work and the fact that, somehow, he was well-paid and well-regarded just for the privilege of doing what he loved.

Ira Levitz was an anomaly. He was Jewish, liberal, a watchdog on constitutional issues, bombastic, aggressive . . . and pro-life. His colleagues put up with him because he was a good liberal and exuded an eccentric charm. The pro-life community liked him because he was a straight shooter and had the guts to believe and write about constitutional protection for the unborn. And both sides were drawn to the large, lumpy man because of his unmistakable air of compassion.

Nine years earlier, when his marriage had fallen apart, Ira had fallen into clinical depression. He still went to therapy once a month, but the Prozac his psychiatrist had prescribed kept him on a fairly even keel. His experience with the dark side, however, had given him an aura of empathy that was unusual among journalists. Ira knew the numbness, the helplessness of deep-rooted despair. So in spite of his talent, his privilege, and his sophisticated lifestyle, he had compassion for the weak and helpless. And that fact, paradoxically, made him very attractive to the strong and powerful.

Ira paused in the middle of a paragraph. He ran his hands through his thick mat of unkempt black hair. This particular column—musings on the upcoming Griswold presidency—had been giving him fits. That's why he was working in the newsroom today, hoping that inspiration would seep by osmosis into his work. But he was stuck—not just on ideas, which always came hard, but on words, which usually came easily.

He leaned back in his chair, pressing his palms against his eyebrows. What was another word for "aggravate"? His software thesaurus listed ten perfectly good synonyms, but Ira had an innate distaste for the computer's automatic wordsmithing options. It seemed so lazy. He possessed a perfectly good brain; surely he could come up with the right word.

Besides, choosing a term spat out by software seemed so technical. No heart, no passion, no sweat. He used to feel the same way about writing at a computer, preferring the tactile sense of hand gripping pen, ink mapping paper, words arranged in rows on yellow legal pads. But now here he was, banging his hands on his forehead, driven in desperation to the auto-thesaurus. Maybe he was just getting soft.

As he sat there, thinking that maybe he should go walk around the block or get an early lunch at the deli around the corner—feed the muse—he suddenly heard the soft, urgent tone of two short bells.

The *Post's* satellite dish constantly received news stories, personality profiles, sports information, digitized photographs, and sophisticated graphics of everything from cutaway drawings of the latest space technology to the eldest Supreme Court justice's recent prostate surgery. Hundreds of stories, photos, and graphics streamed from the receiver on top of the building right into the newspaper's computer system, neatly organized by directories.

The computer software was designed to notify writers and editors when the satellite had picked up a story of particular interest. Five bells meant "huge" news: a presidential assassination. Three bells tolled plane crashes and other such disasters. And today's two bells, according to the information just now spilling onto Ira Levitz's computer screen, meant that an abortion doctor had been killed in North Dakota.

10:30 AM Inches: BULLETIN PM-Killing-AbortionDoc 1st
<B>PM-Killing-Abortion Doctor, 1st Ld-Writethru, 4236<D>

FARGO N.D. (AP)—A Minnesota abortion provider who serves North Dakota's only reproductive choice clinic was shot and killed this morning, evidently by a woman posing as a patient.

Ira stared at the screen and took a long swig of coffee. A minute later the first writethru came through with a fuller account of the story.

. . . Assistants found Dr. Ann Sloan, 47, in her office, dead of a head wound apparently caused by a high-velocity bullet shot at close range. Sloan had been conferring with a patient, who left the scene shortly before the doctor's body was discovered.

"Dr. Sloan was tireless, utterly committed to the needs of women," said Diane Brook, administrator of the Fargo clinic. "She gave her life so that women in North Dakota could have access to reproductive rights."

Sloan, a gynecologist who left private practice five years ago in order to provide abortion services in three states, had been the target of numerous death threats and harassment by antiabortion forces. She had obtained a standing court order barring protesters from entering her residential neighborhood.

The Fargo clinic is the regular site of demonstrations; antiabortionists were protesting outside the clinic at the time of the shooting. It is not known if Sloan's attacker was associated with any particular anti-choice group, but many of the clinic protesters, detained at the scene by police, seemed less than sympathetic when told of Dr. Sloan's murder.

"What goes around comes around," said a protester who identified himself as John Smith. "This woman was a coldblooded baby killer. Maybe it's shocking that somebody went in there and blew her away, but isn't it more shocking that dozens of babies die in there every day and nobody seems to care?"

North Dakota police have launched a full-scale alert for Dr. Sloan's assailant. Fargo detective Mike Boyle said that officers are circulating descriptions of a young woman in her teens or early twenties who may have fled in what appeared to be a local Channel 4 news van. Channel 4 reporters who appeared on the scene in response to reports of the attack informed police that they had no van at the clinic at the time of the shooting.

Clinic personnel informed police that Dr. Sloan had complied

with FBI recommendations to purchase a bullet-proof vest in response to threats on her life. She was wearing it at the time of her
attack. AP-DS-01-10 1115 CST

Ira Levitz looked at his watch. Given the time difference, it
had been about two hours since the shooting. He could imagine
the scene: reporters scrambling over each other, screaming their
stories into cellular phones so the fragments could go up onto
the satellite.

Ira was ideologically opposed to abortion; he also empathized
with the pro-life cause. Perhaps his own broken marriage had
softened him in this regard. Precious things were so fragile. And
the feelings of abortion—a stronger being asserting its will over
a weaker being . . . the elimination of the most defenseless—
sickened him.

Ira had talked with many in the pro-life movement who articulated their position with wit and·grace. Their arguments, he
believed, could not effectively be rebutted by the pro-choicers.

Yet he had also seen the crazies at work, the fundamentalists
dressed in their Grim Reaper garb shoving pickled fetuses in
politicians' faces. Ira knew the minds of the Washington circuit:
Such demonstrations only steeled the resolve of even the least
committed pro-choicer.

Their cause is just, he thought. *But they ravage their cause by the
tactics they use.*

As he stared at the story on the screen, the buzz in the newsroom increased. His colleagues were reading the account, too.

"Mr. Levitz." He looked up. Threading his way between the
cubicles, waving a large, thin brown envelope, was one of the
earnest journalism students who served as interns at the *Post*.
"This came for you, sir. By messenger to the front desk. Marked
extremely urgent."

"Thanks," said Ira. He unfolded the fat paper clip he had
been playing with and used it to raggedly slit open the envelope.
The brown paper tore. He pulled out a single typed sheet, and
his stomach tensed as he read:

Ira Levitz,

You have shown yourself to be a responsible journalist on the issue of the human right to life. We ask that you pass this letter on to our president-elect.

AN OPEN LETTER TO J. WHITNEY GRISWOLD

Mr. President-elect,

In a few days you will assume the highest office in what used to be called the civilized world. To whom much is given, much is required. Let the actions of this day serve notice as to what is required of you.

For now you must read the writing on the blood-soaked walls of our nation. An individual who takes the lives of the defenseless has no defense; she brings judgment upon herself. A nation that devours its young digests its own future. A leader who allows lambs to be led to the slaughter will be held responsible.

It appears that our nation is no longer content merely to spill the blood of the unborn, to turn human blood into profit, but will now begin, in large numbers, to extract the brains of the near-born. Turn from these evil policies while there is still time.

Perhaps you find it shocking that in Fargo, North Dakota, a woman took the life of a woman. In cold blood. Well, consider that you have helped to create a nation where every day women kill their own young.

Surely you have not forgotten the horror of the millions of Jews and others who lost their lives in the killing centers of the Nazis.

Turn while there is still time, Mr. President-elect. If you do not, no clinic will be spared, no hospital operating room will be immune. We will not stop until the innocents are safe, until this nation has turned from its wicked ways. Otherwise you will find your administration undermined at every turn, thwarted by those who answer to a higher law than your own.

The Holocaust Resistance

In the midst of his reading, Ira had risen to his feet. He reread the sheet quickly as he walked toward the glass-walled office of the A-section editor. He entered without knocking.

"Larry," he said. "Here's something you should see."

3

J. WHITNEY GRISWOLD stood at the window of his temporary offices on the top floor of the New Executive Office Building. Outside, far below in Lafayette Park, he could see a ragged man perched on the edge of a bench feeding the pigeons from a plastic bag he had just dug out of the nearby trash can. Dozens of the fat, ugly birds clustered around his feet, jabbing their purple beaks at crumbs of corn chips.

"I don't get it, Bernie," said Griswold. "Why doesn't that homeless guy eat the Doritos himself? Why isn't he in a shelter anyway? Why don't they enforce some order around here—we're across the street from the White House, and we've got a park full of crazy people and pigeons!"

Bernard O'Keefe, sitting in a leather chair next to the desk and buried in a pile of documents, didn't even look up. "This is Washington, Whit. It wouldn't be Washington without homeless people and pigeons. We'll look into clearing the park once you're president, but right now we've got a few more important things on our plate."

Whitney Griswold restlessly returned to the rosewood desk and stood behind its black leather chair. In spite of the thick navy blue carpet, the rich cream-colored walls, and the grouping of bright flags on stands behind the desk, the office seemed cold. The walls were bare, save for an enormous seal of the president of the United States on the wall behind the desk. Whitney looked at it for a moment, then sank into the chair and stretched out his long legs.

Yes, the huge office was sterile, as was the whole New Executive Office Building. Built in the 1960s, its flaming red bricks had been chosen by Jacqueline Kennedy to match the style of the Federal period. Instead, it looked like art deco. Across the street, next to the White House, stood the Old Executive Office Building, a lofty gray edifice that had gained a certain whimsical grandeur over the years, despite the fact that when it was erected there had been so much criticism of its flamboyant designs that its architect had committed suicide.

Whitney Griswold, president-elect, had just moved his transition office from New York to Washington a few days earlier. He had waited this long because he felt much more at home in New York than in this capital city, which seemed so strangely small town and southern, this place that would be his home—if all went well—for the next eight years.

Griswold was a tall, athletic man in a loose-fitting Brooks Brothers suit—rumpled yet attractive. His clear gray-blue eyes changed according to his circumstances. With his wife or constituents they were usually a serious shade of gray, but with Bernie or other close friends they were often a warm blue. He had longish still-blond hair that started out each day neatly in place but was tousled before his first public appearance was half over. The effect made him look unconcerned with personal image, and that unselfconsciousness, along with his privileged family position and immense personal wealth, had proved a seductive combination with the voters. Here was a man, they believed, who could be independent, above politics as usual.

Bernie O'Keefe, Boston trial lawyer and, in ten more days, counsel to the president, was Whitney Griswold's oldest friend, but the two men could not have been more different. They had, however, three common bonds: law school, their mutual ambition for J.Whitney Griswold, and an old secret, long-buried by the years.

Whitney Griswold had been born to wealth. His father was one of New York's most successful lawyers; his grandfathers and uncles had been establishment pillars and among Connecticut's earliest land owners. Bernie O'Keefe's father, grandson of Irish immigrants, had worked for Boston Edison in the construction division.

Whitney Griswold always noted "Episcopalian" on any form or questionnaire that required a religious affiliation; beyond that, he thought little about it. Bernie's family was devout Roman Catholic. Bernie himself regarded his Catholicism the same way he regarded his rust-red hair: it was simply part of who he was. He had noticed the hair was thinning lately. He hadn't thought much about the religion.

After graduating with honors from Groton, Griswold had been accepted at Harvard, Yale, and Brown. He had chosen Brown, which at the time was considered the most exclusive of the Ivies. O'Keefe, a top honors graduate of Sacred Heart High School, had earned a full scholarship to Boston College, lived at home, and worked thirty-four hours a week at two jobs to help his family.

Griswold, an ardent sailor since he was nine years old, had captained Brown's championship crew team, rowed at Henley, and won the cup. He and his family spent every summer at their nine bedroom Martha's Vineyard oceanfront home, golfing, sailing, and playing endless, graceful sets of tennis. O'Keefe had never been to Martha's Vineyard until Griswold took him when they were in law school. Bernie was not much of a sailor, but with his fire hydrant build he had been a fierce linebacker for BC.

The two had met at Yale. "It was fate," Griswold would joke later, winking at his friend. Bernie was the brightest new student in the law school, with top scores on his aptitude tests. Griswold's performance had been mediocre, but Yale could not turn down someone named Griswold.

Their relationship in school soon found the pattern that would define it for the next two decades. Bernie was broke most of the time; Griswold always had money. Bernie briefed the cases, Griswold bought the beer, and they both lived the experience to the hilt.

J. Whitney Griswold had first felt political stirrings during his Groton days while staring at the school's photo homages to Franklin Delano Roosevelt. Then at Brown he had studied economics under George Borts, a renowned free marketer. Griswold read and mastered the writings of Frederick Hayek and Milton Friedman. He even subscribed, while an undergraduate, to *The Freeman* and soon became absorbed in classic libertarian arguments.

This fit the Griswold view of life. His great-great-grandfather had helped Andrew Carnegie in many of his bold enterprises, one of which was forging a railroad across Pennsylvania, eventually linking the railroad across the continent. Some historians derided his ancestors as robber barons, but Whitney Griswold was proud of their entrepreneurial spirit, so classically American— the energy that had opened the land from sea to sea and prepared the way for the Industrial Revolution.

While at Brown, he had begun to dream that that same spirit could unleash market forces and bring about yet another revolution. One that would end poverty and usher in an age of peace based on knowledge, education, and true human autonomy. The more he thought about it, the more optimistic he became. And the more he dreamed about his own political future.

At Yale, these views began to gel, and for the very first time, J. Whitney Griswold imagined he might be president of the United States. That thought had initially entered his head when someone boasted that three out of five presidents since the mid-seventies had been Yale men: Jerry Ford, George Bush, and Bill Clinton. It could be fate, thought Griswold.

Then one day, after class, fate took a hand in an unexpected form. It had been a deadly session on civil procedure. He and Bernie had been out late the night before, and Griswold's head kept bobbing down throughout the lecture. Eventually he fell into a deep sleep. The professor let him doze, but called him over after class.

"What do you plan to do, assuming you graduate from here, Mr. Griswold?"

"Practice law, of course," he replied, startled at the question.

"Some branch other than civil law I should imagine, Mr. Griswold, though that rather narrows your choices."

Griswold was flustered. He had done badly on his midterms and hated this course. "I'm sorry, sir," he stammered. "I just didn't get much sleep last night."

The professor jabbed his index finger into Griswold's chest. "Mr. Griswold, for every student we accept, thirty are turned away. If you are not going to apply yourself with diligence, you might at least have the decency to make way for one of the other thirty."

That stung. "I'm sorry," Griswold repeated. "It won't happen again."

The professor continued as if he hadn't heard. "Remember, Mr. Griswold," he said, "to whom much is given, much is required."

Griswold nodded, not sure what to say. He had heard the phrase before; he didn't remember where, but its principle made sense to him. For generations, the Griswolds had lived well. He had much, by anyone's standards, and there was a certain responsibility for him to give it back. He should serve. It was his duty. Perhaps the state legislature, perhaps the governor's office. Or why not, like those other Yale men, the presidency?

When he told Bernie, his friend did not laugh. They were standing in the sun-warmed quadrangle at Yale one afternoon in front of Harkness, the old Gothic stone clock tower.

"It's weird, Whit," said Bernie, "but I've been thinking—you really could go a long way. You've got everything you need. I don't see why you couldn't be president one day. I mean, somebody's got to do it . . ." Bernie trailed off as the carillon above their heads began to peal, the bells tolling five o'clock.

"Why not you, Whit?" Bernie continued with a grin. "You've got money, looks, charisma, connections, you'll end up with a decent background in law . . . and you've got an asset that no one else coming up the ladder has. Me!"

THERE WAS A KNOCK at the transition office door, and it swung open. "Robbie," Griswold said, without looking up. His chief of staff was the only person, other than Bernie, who didn't wait for an invitation. Besides, the Secret Service wouldn't let anyone else come in like that.

Harvey Robbins, known to all as Robbie because he hated the name Harvey, was cold, efficient, and brusque to an irritating degree, but his colleagues put up with it. It didn't matter that he rarely smiled, rarely seemed remotely human. After all, in every office someone had to make the trains run on time. And Robbie did.

"Mr. President-elect," he said, even more imperiously than usual. "We have something unexpected on our hands. There's been a shooting in North Dakota. One Dr. Ann Sloan, who performed late-term abortions."

Robbie proceeded in his usual staccato style, information bites designed for Griswold's easy digestion. "Point-blank, one shot to the head, dead at the scene. Suspect is a woman posing as a patient, fled in a fake news truck. Police are all over Fargo and surrounding areas, but no hard leads at the moment. Happened about 10:30 our time. FBI is on the move.

"But here's the wrinkle. Ira Levitz, over at the *Post*, is writing his column at about noon, courier brings him a letter from the anti-abortion terrorists claiming responsibility. Open letter to J. Whitney Griswold. *Post* sent it over here, confidentially—but it's gonna break on the front page tomorrow. Above the fold."

Griswold's face flushed with anger. Bernie sat straight in his chair, his mind already considering and rejecting various courses of action.

"Here's the letter, sir." Robbie placed a copy of the single sheet at precise right angles in front of Griswold's nose.

Griswold read it quickly, then spun it across the polished rosewood toward Bernie.

"Those cockroaches," he said quietly. "They're crawling out of the ground all over the country. Stamp 'em out one place, they breed and come out somewhere else. These anti-abortion bigots break up the party, turn the nation upside down, execute doctors, and smile all the way to the electric chair. I can't stand it, and we are not gonna let them get away with this. This administration is not going to be held hostage to religious terrorists.

"Last November the nation voted for decency. People are sick of this. We have got to root it out once and for all."

Bernie, holding the letter in his hand, shook his head. "I knew things were too easy," he said. "Here I thought all we had to worry about was the economy, the international balance of peace, taxes, education, health care . . . you know, the basics. But before we're even out of the gate, here come the crazies. Look at this: They're not just going to shoot up clinics, but hospitals too."

"Let me see that," said Griswold.

Bernie handed the paper back and Griswold stood up. "The country's going to be in a panic if this stuff spreads. We've got to get the attorney general on the job at 12:01 on January 20."

"We've got to get her confirmed first," said Bernie. "We need to get her confirmation hearings moved up fast so she can get on this right away."

"Right," said Griswold. "Get hold of the chairman of the Judiciary Committee. We're dealing with extraordinary circumstances here, and we need those hearings immediately."

"I'll take care of it," Bernie said. "But right now, we need to get a statement out, and it's always a good touch to call the victim's family. What was the doctor's name again?"

"Sloan," said Robbie. "Ann Sloan. Divorced. One teenaged daughter."

Griswold jotted the name on a pad with his heavy gold pen. "Well, let's get Caroline in here and work up a statement for the press. And let's get that daughter on the phone. People need to see that their president cares."

4

WHILE HE MIGHT THINK IT FATE, it was actually a bizarre series of events several years earlier that had catapulted J.Whitney Griswold to power. And, like many historical watersheds, it all began with a small leak: an overheard conversation in a Washington, D.C., office elevator.

Bill Rudnick, gray eminence of the mid-1990s Republican resurgence and respected neo-conservative, was clutching a sheaf of papers and explaining one of them in a whisper to his aide. "If we can just keep the Dillman crowd quiet, I think we've got a deal here. We won't announce it until the convention."

The paper was a compromise pro-life plank, and the Dillman to whom Rudnick referred was Jason Dillman, conservative evangelical radio preacher whose program reached seven million homes a day—a force to be reckoned with by conservative power brokers.

The amended platform just might have slipped by. It was, after all, a ringing affirmation of the GOP as the pro-life party, asserting the party's historic commitment to the defense of the unborn. It also spoke of sparking a renewed moral dialogue leading to change in public attitudes and reforms gained by returning power to the states.

But in the back of the elevator, unnoticed by the bulky Rudnick, was a young writer who had just been hired by the leader of an evangelical ministry located in Washington. He eagerly passed the tidbit on to his new boss, who called Dillman immediately.

It was still almost a year before the Republican Convention. But Rudnick had been working feverishly to come up with a "big tent" platform, one that the pro-choicers in the GOP would tolerate, but one that wouldn't alienate the religious right—what the press saw as the anti-choice wing of the party. The religious conservatives were 20 percent of the party, maybe 10 percent of the electorate. Problem was, the Republicans couldn't win with their platform, and conventional wisdom said the party couldn't win *without* their votes. A major dilemma.

The radio preacher's aides saw immediately what Rudnick was doing. The plank was strong in its defense of the pro-life position, but Rudnick had pulled its teeth by extracting any support for a human life amendment. By relegating it to the states for decision, the party was effectively surrendering the abortion issue.

A few years earlier, in *Casey v. Planned Parenthood*, the Supreme Court had declared the right to an abortion a fundamental constitutional liberty protected under the Fourteenth Amendment. No state law, therefore, could interfere. You could win the moral debate over abortion, change the minds of 90 percent of the voters in a state, and it would make no difference. They couldn't overrule the court. Thus, a constitutional amendment regarding human life was about the only way to stop the widespread practice of abortion.

Dillman wasted no time. In a broadcast heard by millions, he exposed Rudnick's plank as a "covert conspiracy of cynical Republicans who would trade lives of the unborn to get elected."

The evangelical grapevine surged to life. Technology had done for them what the printing press had done five centuries earlier for the Reformers. While secular minds still controlled the major media, by the mid-1990s talk radio, fax machines, and the Internet and other online services had created a whole new world of alternative communication. So even without a mention in the *New York Times*, the *Washington Post*, *Time* magazine, or the four major networks, within a week, ten million evangelical families were hopping mad.

And the news hit more than the grapevine. Within four days, Phil Calvin, evangelical commentator and widely read syndicated columnist, captured the irony in his column.

The Republican Party, he wrote, had been born out of just such a divisive moral debate. In the 1840s, Democrats advocated non-interference with slavery. The other major party, the Whigs, were too timid to touch it. But by 1852, 20 percent of the delegates to the Whig Convention were outspoken opponents of slavery. The majority turned them back on the grounds that raising the slavery issue would be "dangerous and agitating."

But for the minority, the moral issue was non-negotiable. That 20 percent split away and in 1856 called their first national convention, under the banner "Republicans of the Union." Thus the Republican Party was born—out of a principled defense of unalienable rights, Calvin reminded his twentieth-century readers.

Then, in the 1858 Illinois senate race, Stephen A. Douglas argued that slavery was a state issue. A matter of choice. His opponent, Abraham Lincoln, defended the Republican position that slavery was a moral wrong, that human rights were unalienable. Douglas won the debates and the election. But two years later Abraham Lincoln was elected president, and the Whigs were finished.

"Today's Republicans are selling their birthright for a mess of pottage," Phil Calvin thundered from the pages of 250 major papers.

The ruckus over the Rudnick plank only furthered the already-growing rift between mainstream Republicans and the religious right.

Old-line Republicans had grown accustomed to big government. Some governors boasted that they could be tax-slashing economic conservatives and social liberals at the same time.

The evangelicals countered that social liberalism—more welfare, education, pensions, and the like—inevitably led to more spending and made economic conservatism impossible. The new breed was anti-establishment, disgusted with the failed, big-government, liberal dream.

Several Republican governors courted the gay vote and championed gay rights initiatives, as if openly challenging the religious right.

Fundamentalists and evangelicals were latecomers to the Republican Party. Traditionally, fundamentalists didn't vote, and evangelicals, for the most part from the South, were Democrats. But during the Reagan years, millions had moved into the Republican Party. Yet there was always an uneasy tension in the alliance. The mainstreamers slammed the door on Pat Robertson's 1988 campaign bid, and the Republican establishment battled hard in state after state to keep Christian activists from taking over the party machinery.

Had the evangelicals read their history books, they would have recognized that they were barely tolerated guests at the GOP's big tent party. Historic American conservatism had precious little room for the religious activism of these unsophisticated interlopers. So the Dillman broadcast and the Calvin columns simply accelerated the inevitable.

Bill Rudnick had already figured that the party overlords had had enough. Give the back of the hand to the noisy and demanding activists, and the Republicans could shed the negative image of the 1992 Houston convention and then, with their enormously popular tax-cutting promises, move to the center, scooping up millions of Independents and disaffected Democrats, more than making up for the loss of hardcore evangelicals.

Besides, Rudnick thought, millions of these evangelicals would put pocketbooks ahead of principles. Only the extremists would stamp out of the tent. And good riddance.

It was these events that brought Martin Masterson to center stage.

CENTRAL CASTING couldn t have picked a more perfect candidate for the Religious Right. A former history professor at

Furman, in Greenville, South Carolina, Masterson had catapulted into South Carolina state politics by age thirty-eight after he headed a commission to reform welfare. By age forty, he had been elected governor.

Masterson, a tall, energetic man with a shock of prematurely silver-gray hair, blue eyes, and a winsome smile, coupled his personal charisma with populist policies, slashing taxes and downsizing government. He was unabashedly pro-life, uncompromisingly against special rights for homosexuals, and was the darling of the pro-family movement.

His campaign ignited. First, South Carolina conservative activists announced Masterson would be their favorite son as an Independent. Petition campaigns began in neighboring states and then, as with Ross Perot's independent campaign in 1992, organizing groups sprang up across the country. In some states there were six or more state chairmen, and confusion reigned until the Christian Alliance, almost reluctantly, assumed central command. In fact, the Alliance, whose leadership had become more concerned with the overall conservative fiscal agenda than with social issues, had been surprised by the grassroots intensity for Masterson. They had planned to play a kingmaker role in the primaries and at the Republican Convention. Now they were being forced to bypass it.

While the abortion issue was rewriting the American political script, it had also convulsed American life in a more incendiary way. The most passionate pro-lifers concluded, in light of the *Casey* decision, that there was no hope for change through the courts or the political system. Driven to the fringes, all other strategies exhausted, some openly concluded that violence was the only recourse left.

So, as murders of doctors and clinic workers, bombings, harassment, and other threats escalated, abortion rights activists demanded protection, and federal forces began guarding clinics. The Freedom of Access to Clinic Entrances Act measured off justice in inches: Protesters could sing and pray thirty-five feet from a clinic, but do so at thirty-four feet and you were guilty of a federal offense.

As the anti-abortion activists' frustration erupted into further violence, columnists condemned not only the pro-life movement, but all conservative evangelicals and Catholics. Incidents of overt intolerance against believers mounted.

Federal grand juries convened, police powers unleashed. The more moderate elements of the pro-life movement were intimidated and called for an end to protests. Dependable political allies fled. Many moderates lost heart.

Energized by this harsh opposition, however, new cells mutated from the pro-life movement. Some advocated violence. Some proposed blowing up empty clinics. Others simply stepped up their efforts in every creative though illegal way possible, short of violence.

The decentralized nature of the pro-life movement made it impossible for authorities to control it. Just when the government thought it knew all of the threats and had everyone identified, new groups emerged. It was like the French Resistance in World War II: an underground, spidery web of activists spun through every level of society.

THE REPUBLICANS, meanwhile, freed from any obligation to the intolerant Religious Right, slid quickly to the center. The party's abortion plank became a placebo: Republicans were officially pro-life—who, after all, was *against* life?—and would work to discourage abortion, while at the same time fully respecting individual liberty, the "bulwark of historic Republicanism." This liberty included the right to make one's own informed decisions about life's most intimate matters. The party moved aggressively on the same reasoning—individual liberty—to court the gay vote. Above all, the GOP concentrated on tax-cutting, welfare reform, downsizing government, and tough crime-fighting policies. Polls showed big gains, particularly among Independents and centrist Democrats disillusioned by their party's identity crisis.

A divided field of candidates emerged from the primaries,

and the surprise front-runner was J. Whitney Griswold, governor of Connecticut. In any other year a candidate from the Northeast would be unimaginable, but the emergence of Martin Masterson reduced the South's influence, and the field was generally fractured with five candidates from west of the Mississippi. Moreover, Griswold was very appealing. He had slashed individual taxes by 40 percent in Connecticut, had reduced the size of the bureaucracy in Hartford by over one-third, had a surplus in the treasury, and was presiding over the state's economic renaissance.

On the Republican Convention's fourth ballot, he went over the top. The polls showed him an instant front-runner in the campaign, and the GOP faithful were jubilant.

As Griswold appeared on the platform for his acceptance speech at the convention, the crowd roared. They smelled victory. Balloons dropped; confetti swirled. Griswold stood grinning broadly, clutching his wife's hand, arms raised in the traditional V.

Beside him, Anne Griswold grinned and waved. They would never know how much she hated this whole thing, how tired she was of huge campaign buttons, stupid hats, and even the eager faces of the campaign workers who lined up to shake her hand and fling their arms around her as if she and Whitney were their best friends.

Anne, tall and well-tailored, her short, straight hair framing the planes of her aristocratic face, was, like her husband, from an old New England family. She was more reserved than he but smiled enthusiastically at the milling throng. Behind them stood their son, Robert, and their daughter, Elizabeth.

Gripping Griswold's other hand was vice presidential candidate, Stuart Potter, the conservative senior senator from Virginia, chosen to blunt Masterson's appeal and to hold on to some support in the South.

As the Griswolds and Potters waved to the crowd, Harvey Robbins paced back and forth, just behind the entrance to the platform. Robbie had picked the optimum moment for television coverage of Griswold's speech, and he was worried that the thunderous, endless ovation would upset his timing. Any later and they might start to lose some of the East Coast audience. And, he noted with irritation, Griswold had unbuttoned his suit jacket. Robbie had warned him about that a thousand times; it looked unpresidential. Little things like that made a difference.

As Robbie paced, shaking his watch and peering out through the curtains, Griswold cleared his throat to speak.

"About time!" Robbie muttered. "Let's get on with it."

"My fellow Republicans, my fellow Americans. Tonight we launch a great crusade on behalf of all Americans who want this once again to be the land of liberty, opportunity, and decency . . ."

On the word "decency," the crowd broke into a frenzy.

"No more bigots!" they began chanting. "No more bigots! No more bigots!"

Griswold took Anne's hand and raised it high. The crowd thundered its approval.

"For America, this has been a long night," Griswold said, "but that means the dawn is much nearer. And it is. A bright, new dawn for America . . ."

The crowd roared, but he plowed ahead.

"A new dawn with fresh economic opportunities for every American; a new dawn of social enlightenment in which the last vestiges of bigotry and bias are finally rooted out of our midst, and tolerance, respect, and civility restored."

Griswold's jaw was set. He meant it. He was not a great orator, but he understood passion and momentum in a speech. He knew how to pace his words; he knew, intuitively, how to connect with a crowd.

Glancing at the 3" x 5" card in his palm, he continued. "In this past century, we have witnessed a world transformed. My Republican predecessors, Ronald Reagan and George Bush, were unshakable in their commitment to liberty. They faced down the Communist tyrants . . . and we won. Millions were set free from their ideological chains."

The crowd roared.

"And now, we must finish the job. Ironically, in this era of human freedom, there are those who would use uninformed prejudice to oppress us. But we will unshackle hearts and minds from the blind biases of darker times gone by. We will usher in a new era of enlightenment in which all people—regardless of the color of their skin, their station in life, or the lifestyle they freely choose—can live together with dignity and mutual respect.

"We will celebrate our diversity, the source of true greatness; and we will rise up on the wings of eagles to new heights, and from those heights, we will see the dawn's light from sea to shining sea, a land of true liberty . . . Yes, my fellow Americans, that new dawn is coming. I promise it."

THE CAMPAIGN WAS GRUELING, but the Republicans gained weekly in the polls. The incumbent president, with only the Democratic ideologues still behind him, slipped badly. Masterson, the Independent, however, was close on Griswold's heels.

The election itself was a cliff-hanger. But by one o'clock in the morning, California made Whitney Griswold president. He had just 40 percent of the popular vote but managed to get 286 electoral votes, sparing an electoral deadlock that would have thrown the election into the House. First the lame-duck president, then Masterson, conceded.

OVERNIGHT THE GRISWOLDS' lives changed. The day after the election, the family was flown to Hobe Sound, Florida, in a backup presidential jet. The Cabots, in whose guest house the Griswolds had regularly stayed in the past, now moved into the guest quarters themselves, giving the Griswolds the main house. The neighbors on the quiet, exclusive island were not pleased with the Secret Service roadblocks, the helicopters buzzing overhead, and the Coast Guard patrol boats that ignored the "no wake" signs as they crisscrossed the usually tranquil sound.

The sudden change was hardest on the children. Robert, thirteen and already self-conscious because of the miseries of acne

and a changing voice, was a middle classman at Groton, an oars-
man like his dad. Though his wire-rimmed glasses gave him a
bookish appearance, he was only a modest student. Robert had
enjoyed the fact that at Groton, being a governor's son was not
all that noteworthy. But being the son of the president-elect of
the United States now made him the uncomfortable center of
attention.

It was even tougher on Elizabeth, a perky eleven-year-old
with wide blue eyes, a sprinkling of freckles, and shoulder-length
blonde hair. Elizabeth was in the sixth grade, or "form" as it was
called at Hotchkiss, another exclusive New England prep school,
and two Secret Service agents now followed her everywhere.
Some of the older girls teased her about them—"Wish I had a
hunk like that following me around"—but Elizabeth, at the age
where everything was mortally embarrassing, hated the fact that
the men were always with her. She called her mother and asked
to come home.

"Griswolds," her mother reminded her, sympathetic but unyielding, "do their duty."

FOR ANNE THE DAYS glided by. She began packing personal
items, negotiating with the lieutenant governor's wife for the continued loan to the governor's mansion of Griswold family art
treasures, scheduling State Department protocol sessions, and
tendering her resignation from the boards she had served as
Connecticut's first lady. There were eight, including the Hartford
Hospice, the Sierra Club, and, of course, the Junior League. All
quite worthy, she thought, satisfied that she had spent her time
well. Still, she would have to be more selective in the White House.

Meanwhile, Griswold set up his transition office in New York
City, more convenient for his closest advisors and of symbolic
importance. New York was, after all, still the financial capital of
the world. There, each day, delegations from the National Security Council, the Defense and State Departments, and the CIA
briefed him on policies and trouble spots around the world.

He learned much he'd never known before; for example, there were two governments continuing to vie for the sympathies of the Angolan people, and at various times U.S. policy had favored one, then the other. "One policy for Angola," he jotted in his notes.

The Middle East left him utterly perplexed. Israeli intelligence was once again fearful of a secret nuclear capacity in Damascus. China was sending military aid to Iraq in exchange for oil. And the CIA presented a worrisome intelligence analysis indicating that the ultra-right party might make big gains in the Knesset in Israel's upcoming election. That could well precipitate attacks on West Bank Arabs.

Griswold's stomach knotted every time he thought about Middle East policies—and soon it would all be in his lap. He hadn't even mentioned the Middle East on the campaign trail except for the obligatory pledges to the Jewish community of unyielding support for Israel. "The brave people of Israel will have no greater friend in the world than Whitney Griswold in the White House," he had assured the United Jewish Appeal banquet six weeks earlier in New York. It had sounded fine then, but what if the extremists gained control?

After these briefing sessions, Griswold found himself retreating to the men's room, the only place he had any privacy these days. There, besides the essential bodily functions, he would practice the relaxation response a doctor friend at the University Club had recommended: "For sixty seconds, let your mind focus on some desirable thing and take deep breaths, exhaling slowly." He usually thought of his daughter, Elizabeth, or a perfect summer day sailing off Martha's Vineyard. That helped, but still his stomach churned.

On January 3, the Griswold team had moved to Washington and taken up residence in the New Executive Office Building. And there, as in New York, every afternoon at precisely four o'clock—Robbie was ruthless about the schedule—Griswold met with his inner circle. Robbie and Bernie; investment banker Nicholas Berger, a Brown classmate; his personnel chief, J. Stuart

Upham, former managing partner of an internationally renowned headhunting firm; his chief domestic advisor from the campaign, Geraldine Klein, on leave from the Hoover Institution at Stanford; Marine General George Maloney, a Pentagon whiz kid and old friend of Bernie's from Boston; and Griswold's long-time press secretary, Caroline Atwater, known by the Hartford press corps to be coolly efficient and unflappable. Caroline was a tall brunette in her early thirties, attractive and unmarried, which had given rise to unsubstantiated rumors of something more than a professional attachment to Griswold.

These meetings would last until seven in the evening, at which point, mercifully from Bernie's perspective, the bar was opened. Discussions were orderly and civil, agreement on policies and appointments almost always unanimous—a sign of orderly minds at work, men and women groomed and chosen for this kind of service.

The new appointments to the Griswold administration had been announced each Friday morning at the New York press center by Atwater or, in the case of cabinet announcements, Griswold himself. This gave the news magazines thirty-six hours before their deadlines and assured Sunday feature articles and some discussions on the weekend talk shows.

The appointments were, to Griswold's delight, received well. His cabinet, after all, was a model of diversity: eight men, five women; one Hispanic, three African Americans, and a secretary of interior-designate who was a Native American. The secretary of health and human services was an avowed lesbian with two adopted children, and the secretary of agriculture, wheelchairbound, had written a biographical bestseller on how his New Age beliefs had carried him through physical adversity. Griswold had made a note to read it.

HIS ATTORNEY GENERAL designate was the last nomination announced, and now, only ten days before his inauguration, that appointment had become the most crucial.

Lafayette Park looked cold and frosty, but the men in blankets and the perennial protesters of every stripe were still there.

"Bernie," said the president-elect from his place at the window, "we need to start planning now. No time to waste. These people are putting us to the test, and we're not going to let them get away with it. Where is our attorney general anyway—do you know?"

"I think she's still up at Harvard," said Bernie. "We're working on it."

5

T HIN WINTER SUNLIGHT dappled the bare trees of Harvard Yard as Emily Gineen took what would be her last stroll there for quite some time. Everything was packed and in order for the move. Emily liked order, demanded it in fact, but this morning she needed to get away from the boxes, the lists, the telephone, the aides, the memoranda already flowing in a fat stream from Washington.

The square was quiet. It was reading period, before exams, and most students were huddled away somewhere reviewing last fall's material. She relished the solitude. The past few weeks had been a frenzied blur of people.

She jammed her gloved hands in her coat pockets. The frosty air stung her cheeks, and she was glad she had grabbed the old wool hat off the top shelf of the hall closet at the last minute. The hat smelled like the dog had been wearing it, but she had pulled it on over her chin-length dark hair, put on a pair of sunglasses, and left the house. Swaddled in a heavy sweater, pants, coat, and a long scarf that belonged to her son, she didn't look like the urbane constitutional law professor her students admired. Nor did she look like the attorney general-designate of the United States.

She exhaled, watching her breath flow out in the cold air. She had wrestled horribly with the decision to accept Whitney Griswold's offer. Her life at Harvard was just about perfect. She loved the detached, peaceful life of academia, and between her law professorship, board memberships, consulting fees, and the occasional constitutional case she carefully selected, she was earning $800,000 a year. She was devoted to her family as well: a son and a daughter, twelve and fourteen, in a Cambridge prep school, and her husband, Frederick, also on the Harvard faculty at the Kennedy School of Government.

They took lavish vacations whenever she and Fred could get away at the same time, and their large old Victorian home was a haven of books, dogs, teenagers, and Rosemary, a rather corpulent live-in housekeeper who ruled the roost with a firm hand. Along with all this, she and Fred had made great friends in the Harvard community, spending many a pleasant evening brimming with pasta, red wine, and simmering discussion.

That circle of friends had encouraged Emily to work with Governor Griswold when he had first called her, back during the campaign. "He needs your help, Emily," they had teased. "He's a good guy, about as charismatic as you get these days, but he doesn't have a clue about the tough issues. You can serve a strategic role right now. You're the woman of the hour."

Usually at that point in the dinner discussion she would throw a sourdough roll at someone, but she knew that what they were saying was partially true. She did have something to offer. She had a good brain, good ideas, and good law experience. But she also had a gut sense of how to strip layers of rhetoric, bureaucracy, and spume to get to the essence of an issue. In short, she could discern the heart of a matter. Which was an instinct that J. Whitney Griswold, for all his breeding, charisma, and political clout, didn't have. She had noticed, however, that he surrounded himself with a few good men and women who did, so perhaps he at least realized his own limitations and compensated for them.

After Griswold won the presidential election, however, she

figured her association with him was finished. Then had come the formal phone call regarding the attorney general appointment.

Frederick knew how much she loved their comfortable life at Harvard, but he had encouraged her to consider the president-elect's offer. After all, he said, a stint in the new administration would mean a commitment of only a few years, not a lifetime. (Though it would probably seem like a lifetime, he had teased.)

"Besides, you need something new," he had said. "You're comfortable here, but I know you. You get too comfortable, and then you get uncomfortable. You need a new challenge. Think of it as a temporary teaching post. The kids and I will weather it just fine. Do your duty."

That phrase was a mantra for her. During her childhood in Alabama, Emily's father, an attorney, and her mother, a social services counselor, had always stressed duty: One did one's best in order to give one's best to others. So Emily had excelled in academics, won a Princeton scholarship, went on to Harvard Law, edited the *Law Review*, spent her first year out clerking at the First Circuit in Boston, then her second year clerking at the Supreme Court.

She had her father's head, people used to say, and so she had carved out a career even more illustrious than his. But she also had her mother's heart and had grown up visiting the women's shelters where her mother counseled young women toward new lives. Emily had seen how few arrived at those new lives. Too many were drawn back to the men and addictions that eventually destroyed them.

She had also seen her mother drained, her health wasted, by the effort of pouring herself into individual lives, and so Emily had, almost subconsciously, gravitated toward systemic cures. Surely government could do more than the thwarted efforts of the too few committed volunteers like her mother.

She became the U.S. attorney from Alabama, known as a fearless, utterly efficient prosecutor. Then later, while at Harvard, she had filed an amicus brief in *Casey v. Planned Parenthood*. For this and her committed defense of women's issues, Emily Gineen was a heroine to feminist groups; because of her prosecution work, she was a favorite of the law-and-order crowd.

She was proud of her work on *Casey*. But at Harvard she had also taken pride in equipping a new generation of lawyers, feeling it was one of the best means of doing her duty and shaping the future. She thought of the comments she had recently given her students on *Marbury v. Madison*, cornerstone of every constitutional law course.

"The final thought to keep in mind regarding *Marbury*," she told the class on the last day of the term as they capped pens and stuffed books into backpacks, "is also the most basic: *Marbury* establishes the Court's right of judicial review, its authority to rule on the constitutionality of laws enacted by Congress. But the Supreme Court has no enforcing mechanism of its own, no militia or troops to execute those rulings.

"As we have discussed, at certain points in our nation's history, the civil rights movement key among them, when a state refused to comply with a Court ruling, the federal branch of government had to call in troops. Mercifully, those occasions have been rare. The continuing success of our democratic experiment in America today depends on the consent of the governed, the compliance of not only the citizenry but the various branches of government itself, to submit to the checks and balances intrinsic to our system. Otherwise we could well find ourselves, civilized people though we are, on the brink of anarchy, in constitutional crisis. I leave you with that sobering thought."

NOW SHE WOULD HAVE A CHANCE to make it work, she thought, as she pulled her coat tighter around her. The sharp air stung the inside of her nose as she inhaled, and something in the smell of the cold courtyard reminded her of Januaries gone by.

She had always loved January's sense of beginnings: fat new calendars, the smell of new textbooks, fresh snow not yet tracked. But now, as she took a deep breath, there was almost a pang, a hint of melancholy. A sense of something half-remembered, something known but lost.

It's Proust, she thought. The French writer had called it "the remembrance of things past."

Or C.S. Lewis, the British writer whose autobiography she had read after she and Frederick had seen the movie *Shadowlands* some years back. Lewis had called it the intense desire of something never to be described, the near-realization, then loss, of something from another dimension. The longing for Joy.

She kicked a cluster of dead leaves, watching them skitter across the pavement in a flurry of cold wind. Life would never be the same again, she realized. Soon they would be off to Washington, far from the familiar, constrained rhythms of academic life. She hated what she knew of politics, but it was the next challenge.

She looked up and saw a figure running toward her. *I knew this was too nice to last*, she thought. It was Jerry Kirkbride, the aide who was managing her transition to Washington. He had an odd look on his face.

"There's been a shooting," he gasped, coming right beside her and looking around to make sure no one else was close enough to hear. "An abortion doctor at a clinic in North Dakota. Griswold wants you in Washington, wants to get the big guns on this right away. They're pulling some moves to get your confirmation hearings ASAP."

6

WINTER IS USUALLY QUIET in Fargo, North Dakota. The wheat, corn, and sugar beet farms are under snow, and activity ebbs until spring, when the agricultural cycle begins again. But within hours of the clinic shooting and the leaked news of the open letter to President-elect Griswold, Fargo's Radisson, downtown at the corner of Second Avenue and First Street, was fully booked. Even the old Holiday Inn out by the mall at Route 29 was sold out. Avis, Hertz, and Budget had rented everything in stock. The four-wheel-drive vehicles went first. And to make matters worse, it began snowing at dusk. The bartenders in town grinned and replenished their stock.

Reporters weren't the only people milling around. Law enforcement officials were everywhere, sometimes creating more confusion than order.

At 10:00 A.M. Chief Walter Larson of the Fargo Police Department assured Channel 11's live coverage that he and his men were on top of the investigation.

One hour later, the governor announced that the North Dakota state police, headed by Colonel Tollefson, had been ordered to conduct a statewide manhunt for the party or parties involved in the murder.

Thirty minutes after that, the FBI special agent from Minneapolis, Jim Grady, arrived by King Air and held an impromptu news conference in the Radisson lobby. The Freedom of Access to Clinic Entrances Act of 1994 and the RICO statutes, as interpreted by the courts, made the killing of an abortionist a federal crime, and the federal government would assume jurisdiction from the outset. The director of the FBI, Anthony Frizzell, had authorized him to say that the bureau's full resources would be committed to this case. Grady added, however, that the federal government would, of course, welcome and indeed expect the state's full cooperation.

State trooper patrols fanned out to Grand Forks in the north, Jamestown in the west, and Watertown to the south. In the east, Minnesota state police joined in the hunt. Before the snow arrived, the civil air patrol, along with police helicopters, had covered a one-hundred-square-mile area. Though it was easy to see great distances across the wide-open spaces, a white van had the best camouflage possible. Everything was white—roads, rooftops, fields, and the light reflecting off them.

By 5:00 that afternoon, reports came in that a van rented from Hertz in Bismarck, 180 miles away, had not been returned; police, who were checking all car rental agencies, discovered that this van had been rented to Jerome Nordland, 320 Sixth Street South, who had presented a valid North Dakota license and paid cash. But police found no Jerome Nordland at the address on the license. It was clear that the young woman who had shot Dr. Sloan had not acted alone.

Pictures of the missing van were faxed to law enforcement officials in five states as well as to the Royal Canadian Mounted Police along the border.

IN THE FIRST TWENTY-FOUR HOURS after the shooting, eighteen agents, including latent-fingerprint experts (those who can, through powder, chemical, and laser, find even fragments of prints), combed every inch of Dr. Sloan's office. They made over seven hundred separate impressions of full or partial prints, each one placed on a small card, then carefully catalogued and boxed. Footprint impressions were made throughout the clinic, along with tire impressions outside.

Another team of forensic experts flown in from Washington worked over Dr. Sloan's body at the morgue and in the clinic office. Hair and blood samples were extracted for DNA analysis. Skin fragments, particularly around the wound area, were carefully put in plastic bags, all marked. Every piece of clothing was carefully examined by agents wearing plastic gloves, marked and individually wrapped.

The ballistic experts found the spent round, dug out the bullet, and did elaborate calculations about direction and velocity of the bullet fired.

Other agents visited Channel 11 and obtained a copy of all the footage shot that day. Very likely the killer would have been caught on camera either entering or leaving the clinic.

It snowed heavily the second day. Though the roads stayed open, thanks to the heroic efforts of removal crews, air operations had to be suspended. Out-of-state federal agents spent more of their day digging their vehicles out of snowbanks than they did patrolling. The reporters congregating in the Radisson and Holiday Inn bars took it all in stride.

EVERY SCRAP OF POTENTIAL EVIDENCE was assembled, catalogued, boxed, and loaded aboard a small FBI jet, which got airborne as soon as the runways were cleared from the latest storm.

The fingerprints were taken to the bureau's facility in Clarksburg, West Virginia, where over two hundred million fingerprint cards are in the center's fingerprint identification services. When the boxes arrived from Fargo, they were instantly entered on an encoding terminal, and technicians began a high-speed search. Laser readers scanned the impressions and, by computer, compared them to the millions of fingerprints in the agency's information banks.

By the end of the third day, the prints of Dr. Sloan and every clinic employee had been identified and eliminated. Sixty-two prints were unidentified, and these were encoded; one of them could possibly belong to the suspect.

Meanwhile, Dr. Sloan's clothing, hair samples, blood, and skin fragments had been delivered to the FBI laboratory, which occupies 145,000 square feet on the first basement level and the third floor of the J. Edgar Hoover Building, the gargantuan FBI headquarters complex at the corner of Pennsylvania Avenue and Ninth Street Northwest in Washington.

Each year this lab handled 20,000 cases with 170,000 pieces of evidence and 900,000 examinations. But the evidence from Fargo, on Frizzell's direct orders, was moved to the head of the list.

The blood, hair, and skin samples were taken to a laboratory inner sanctum, the DNA analysis unit. The chances of one person having the same deoxyribonucleic acid analysis as another is one in one hundred million. Since there had been no signs of a struggle, there was little chance that the killer's blood would show up, but the possibility had to be eliminated. Hair samples, on the other hand, offered more promise, and every speck of human hair found in that office had been scooped up and catalogued. The agent in charge of that detail speculated that no one had vacuumed the floor in months.

Ballistics experts had the easiest time. The murder weapon appeared to be a .45; the bullet fired from six feet away and from slightly above the victim's head was a soft-nosed, hollow point. That's why it had virtually ripped off the back half of Dr. Sloan's skull.

Agents had also figured out how the killer had gotten the gun past the clinic's metal detectors and security. In the rest room across the hall from Dr. Sloan's office they found traces of electricians' tape, and a waterproof bag was recovered from the trashcan. Evidently the killer had retrieved the gun from the toilet tank, where it had been placed earlier, the agents surmised, by some accomplice—possibly a supplier or even a member of the cleaning crew. The custodians were interrogated first.

A team of handwriting and document analysis experts was hard at work on the letter delivered to Ira Levitz. With computer analysis and laser, they identified the machine on which it had been printed, but it yielded no fingerprints other than those of Levitz and *Post* personnel.

Meanwhile, from across North Dakota and, indeed, across the country, written reports by agents were being faxed to the Minneapolis field office, distilled, and in turn sent to the situation room on the seventh floor of the Hoover Building.

ON THE FIFTH DAY they found the van, buried in a snow drift behind a deserted barn in the tiny town of Hamilton, approximately ten miles from the Canadian border. With so much fresh snow, it was impossible to check tire tracks or footprints, but agents descended on the vehicle, dusting every piece of metal and plastic for fingerprints. Not one good print was found inside; in the North Dakota winter, everyone wears gloves.

Frizzell called his Canadian counterpart to ask for intensified efforts on the other side of the border, though both men knew the task was next to hopeless. Whoever was in that van had not likely passed through one of the numerous border stations. There were a hundred ways to avoid detection, including snowmobile or private plane. And, of course, the killer and her accomplices could have fled east, south, or west after dumping the van.

A TEAM OF FBI AGENTS, with sketch artists, interviewed clinic personnel trying to get a description, in this case a painfully frustrating process. The killer was young, her hair tucked up under a baseball cap, and she was wearing sunglasses. Nothing distinguishing about her. No visible moles, birthmarks, or scars. No one had noted anything distinctive; One witness said her nose turned up; another said it was straight.

The Channel 11 film had offered some help. In a two-second clip, someone meeting the assailant's description could be seen, side view, exiting the building. Lab technicians did exhaustive enhancement on the individual frames, then fed it into computers used to reconstruct visual images.

The final composite lacked any distinguishing details, but it was the best they could do. The sketch was pumped out all over North America on the law enforcement fax line.

Within minutes, the calls began. One came from a student at Concordia College, a conservative Lutheran school in Moorhead, Minnesota. There was a strong pro-life group on the campus, the anonymous caller claimed, and one of its members looked "exactly like the girl in the poster."

In less than an hour, two agents waiting outside a classroom met nineteen-year-old Dorothy Wilkinson and escorted her into the college administrator's conference room. The picture could fit her, but it also could fit at least 20 percent of the student population.

Wilkinson was chairperson of "Concordians for Life." Her hands shook as she admitted to the G-men that she had picketed that very clinic. "But I was at home in Minneapolis on Friday morning," she quavered. "I h-h-had four wisdom teeth removed." The agents rolled their eyes and called her dentist. It was true.

In the first four days, thirty-two similar young women were investigated, some the result of crank calls, others from people settling a score. There were no serious leads.

Whitney Griswold could do nothing officially, but he did get written reports from Director Frizzell about the progress, or lack thereof, on the shooting. Much of Griswold's frustration with the case came from the fact that apart from the economy, crime had been his biggest campaign issue. He had advocated stiffer sentences, repeal of the Miranda rule, random roadblocks, and other extraordinary measures in the cities, as well as expanded federal police powers. The promises had struck a responsive chord in a public gripped by fear: Violent crime was up 16 percent in just the past twelve months. Some cities were like no-man's lands; random violence was epidemic.

The murder of Dr. Ann Sloan was the worst kind of crime and social disorder and a direct affront to the decency and order Griswold had promised. And thanks to the open letter, published by the *Post*, it was also a direct assault on his administration. On him. So it deserved top priority.

7

J. WHITNEY GRISWOLD didn't actually think about abortion itself very often. And when he did hear the word, it did not evoke mental images of a medical procedure; instead, it immediately conjured up notions of choice, autonomy, freedom, and tolerance. In fact, abortion had gradually, unconsciously, become a metaphor for matters near and dear to what it meant to Griswold to be an American. So when those so-called pro-lifers waved their bloody posters, all he could see were the ugly tactics of sensationalism; when they shouted about life for the unborn, all he could hear was the fanatical clamor of bigots who would trample other Americans' freedoms to advance their own agenda. What Griswold called a "direct threat to the nation's domestic tranquility, an assault on the Constitution itself."

During his campaign he had spoken freely about using "whatever measures are necessary to protect a woman's right to choose, her sacred right of privacy." And he often spoke of wanting young women like his daughter, Elizabeth, to live in a land that enjoyed true liberty so they could experience, unfettered, the "full flower of their personhood."

The president-elect was a champion for all the political messages that "choice" had come to represent. In this, he was not unlike most Americans.

And he, like many, was dismayed and somewhat bemused as to why the abortion issue itself would not just lie down and die. Hadn't the right to choice been affirmed since 1973? Weren't we now living in a society in which diversity and tolerance had become accepted standards of civilized behavior?

For years Griswold, like many progressive Republicans, had ignored the issue as best he could, maintaining a fair degree of uncomfortable silence and hoping it would just go away. But in the early 1990s angered by the "indecency" of it all, he had begun to speak out, and found his words resonating with many who were sick and tired of the "anti-choice zealots."

But then the tide had turned. After the first abortion doctor was murdered in 1992 a wave of fury swept the nation, and a similar wave of revulsion swept through the pro-life movement. Its leaders condemned any use of violence as a means to advance their cause. The more radical cells of the movement, however, stepped up their harassment, intimidation, and violence.

Then, with FDA approval of the American version of RU-486—"the abortion pill"—there was a lull in the violence. The pill still required a doctor's oversight, of course, but it removed a focal point for prolife protest. Since any gynecologist could prescribe the drug, there was no way to know which patients were seeing the doctor for a pregnancy checkup, which were there for a pap smear and physical exam, and which were seeking the abortion drug. Even the most aggressive pro-lifers had a hard time identifying appropriate targets for demonstration.

In addition, swallowing the RU-486 tablets was an utterly private act, and revulsion against the invasion of that kind of privacy was an integral part of the American fiber. Many who might have been sympathetic to the pro-life cause revolted at the thought of taking away such personal privilege.

But it wasn't long before the pendulum swung back—for two reasons. First, RU-486 was too complicated to use for second trimester abortions, so abortion clinics that had done the procedure at eight to twelve weeks were now routinely performing much later abortions. And second, through new technologies and discoveries in fetal tissue research it had become apparent that fetal tissue might hold the key to a cure for the most dreaded epidemic of the century.

AIDS.

Throughout the history of medicine, each new advance in science had been yoked with an accompanying ethical debate. Modern medicine's early history, for example, had been marked by a reluctance to disturb the dignity of the deceased, bringing strict statutes against the dissection of human cadavers. (Some of these remained on the law books longer than most people might suppose. In 1975 four Boston doctors were indicted for performing an experiment to determine if antibiotics to combat fetal syphilis could breach the placenta in therapeutic concentrations. They were charged with "illegal dissection," as defined by an 1814 Massachusetts graverobbing statute.)

In the 1960s the ability to actually transplant human organs brought new debates. When the news broke on December 3, 1967 in Cape Town, South Africa, that the heart of a twenty-five-year-old woman killed in a car accident had been sutured into the chest of a fifty-three-year-old grocer named Louis Washkansky, commentators questioned everything from the permission granted by the family of the deceased, to the location of the human soul, to the formal definition of death.

By the 1980s and 1990s organ transplants were routine. But the questions regarding donors had shifted: The ethical debates no longer revolved around how to treat the dead with dignity, but when it was permissible to remove organs from the living.

As medical advances made organ transplants possible even in the tiniest of infants, the lack of organs small enough for that age group could not keep up with demand. That was when medical researchers turned to anencephalic infants. Since these babies were born without most of their brains, they had no hope of survival. Most lived only a few hours or days.

But there was a problem.

Because these infants demonstrated brain-stem activity, they did not meet the legal requirements for total brain death called for by the Uniform Determination of Death Act. Hospitals were therefore legally bound to care for them until brain-stem activity ceased. But by the time they could be declared legally dead, their vital organs had usually undergone irreversible hypoxic injury and were unsuitable for organ donation.

Some advocates of this procedure lobbied for changes in the laws to allow the organs of live-born anencephalic infants to be used without a requirement of total brain death. In California, Senate Bill 2018 was introduced in 1986 but was subsequently withdrawn. Still, there were few who were willing to suggest out loud that organs be taken from anencephalic infants while they were still alive.

But for the pre-born, a different movement was afoot.

Research involving human fetal tissue had become the source of debate almost immediately after the Supreme Court handed down *Roe v. Wade*. In 1974 Congress created the National Commission for the Protection of Human Subjects of Biomedical and Behavioral Research and made the formulation of regulations on fetal research the first item on its agenda.

Some on the commission sidestepped the question of elective abortion by recommending that only tissue from spontaneous abortions be considered. But half of those spontaneously aborted in the first trimester were chromosomally abnormal, and most spontaneous abortions were subject to a variety of microorganisms, including cytomegalovirus, herpes simplex types 1 and 2, rubella, and toxoplasma. Thus, relying on miscarriages for fetal tissue was not a viable option.

For a number of years the ethical dilemma simmered on the back burner, for during the Reagan and Bush administrations, federal monies were blocked from tissue research on fetuses obtained by elective abortion.

Then, in 1993, in one of the first official acts of his presidency, Bill Clinton ended the moratorium on federal funding for research on transplants of fetal tissue. Many researchers breathed a sigh of relief and set to work.

The first grant was awarded to a doctor who had made headlines in 1988 when he used private funding to perform the first fetal tissue transplant on a human in the United States. Now this $4.5 million grant, funded by the National Institutes of Health's National Institute of Neurological Disorders and Stroke, afforded him the opportunity to conduct large-scale testing of the effectiveness of fetal tissue as a treatment for Parkinson's disease. Though controversial, the study opened the floodgates.

Fetal tissue offered doctors distinct advantages over adult tissue: It lived longer than adult tissue in a graft, had low immunogenicity, and was still differentiating into mature cells. Now dozens of research teams vied for a piece of the multimillion-dollar grant action, considering proposals for using implanted neurological fetal tissue in diseases from Alzheimer's to diabetes to severe immune deficiencies.

The immune deficiency studies, however, carried the most political clout. By the mid-1990s, researchers had determined that fetal tissue held what might well be the only hope to disarm the AIDS epidemic. Other hopes for a cure or a vaccination had come up short. The fetal proteins held the key. Members of populations at risk for HIV could have government-funded testing every three months; if the virus was present, injections of fetal tissue seemed to stop its spread.

The studies were not fully conclusive, and doctors had been careful not to reveal the extent of the procedures required to extract the tissue. For in the frantic atmosphere created by the urgent search for a cure for AIDS, some of the standard ethical questions about tissue procurement were falling by the wayside.

Doctors had found that the more mature the tissue, the better its immunogenicity; and if any deterioration of the cells set in, its effectiveness was severely affected. Consequently, they were working more and more with second-trimester abortions: fetuses that were more mature than those of an earlier gestation but that could not yet sustain life outside the womb.

Once viability became a factor, the questions about uniform determination of death and legal limits of brain-stem activity became part of the equation. But before viability, doctors had fewer concerns about removing tissue from a living organism.

As word of the tissue's potential effectiveness leaked out to a sympathetic press, there was a tidal wave of euphoric public reaction. Thrilled homosexual groups organized benefits and lobbied Capitol Hill to speed the FDA approvals process. Hollywood entertainers threw lavish fund-raising galas.

The new technology was still in its testing stages, but pressure from the homosexual community was so great that government-funded programs, matched by private funds, were already fueling a series of new centers for harvesting fetal tissue. The umbrella for all this, the Regeneration Foundation, underwrote a series of public service announcements to introduce the notion to the public.

"Life to Life," a thirty-second, slow-motion advertisement, showed children and young men, old people and teenagers, all holding hands and dancing on a grassy mountain meadow while passing flowers to one another.

The focus was fuzzy, and so was the message: These images of dancing people somehow had something to do with the coming "regeneration centers," to be announced later. These centers would be built in six key cities across the nation, and Washington, D.C. would host the first, which was even now under construction on a site across the street from the George Washington University Hospital.

THE REGENERATION CENTERS caught many in the prolife community unawares. But for those who read medical journals and for those who read between the lines of the exultant news reports, the regeneration centers meant nothing less than a national holocaust of the unborn.

And the pro-life grapevine had it on good authority that the National Institutes of Health were already producing a video for mass distribution in training hospitals: "Correct Procedures for Removing Fetal Cranial Contents."

Now, with this looming threat of fetal tissue transplantation on a broad scale, a new movement appeared on the scene. Calling themselves The Life Network, these Christians, who had long been committed to the pro-life cause, had formed a network of twenty cells across the country, with a total membership of just under four hundred people.

Their goal was twofold: first, to uphold an unwavering policy of nonviolence, and second, to hold an unwavering spotlight on the new reality of abortion in America. To strip away the benign political messages that hid the reality of fetal tissue harvesting and to illuminate the fact that, in modern America, doctors in sterile white lab coats were suctioning brain tissue from the skulls of live, unborn babies.

The Network's organizers purposely kept their network small. Members were chosen on the basis of their ability to infiltrate communities of influence. Pro-life journalists, for example, would quietly try to persuade their colleagues in the press of the patent injustice of the regeneration centers; businessmen and women did the same in their spheres. Each cell was directed by a small executive committee whose members were determined to keep the Network a tight, disciplined, and nonviolent movement.

Members were asked to read a booklet prepared by a senior member, who didn't hesitate to draw chilling parallels between their existence as an "underground" resistance in abortion-plentiful America and the activities of those who, compelled by conscience, resisted the tide of ideology that took the lives of millions of Jews and others during the Nazi reign of terror.

"During the Nazi Holocaust," the booklet asserted, "an entire nation of otherwise civilized people allowed a malevolent insanity to rule them, not by becoming insane themselves, but simply by looking the other way. They refused to recognize the evil for what it was.

"They said nothing when their neighbors disappeared without a trace. When ashes from the crematoria rained on their neighborhoods, soiling their sidewalks, they simply went inside their homes.

"The ugly spectacle of those mass rallies of the Nazis, the banners, those thousands of voices shouting 'Seig hiel!' in the night . . . that ugliness was far surpassed by the monstrous horror of silence.

"In the same way, if we don't speak out today against this holocaust of the unborn, against this gruesome medical experimentation reminiscent of the worst the death camps had to offer, then we bear the blood of these helpless infants on our hands."

The author of this booklet, leader of the Washington cell of The Life Network, was a cheerful, unassuming pastor named Daniel Seaton.

8

DANIEL SEATON threw his head back and laughed loudly as his four-year-old daughter shone the flashlight under her bed. They could both hear thumps and yowls as the kitten chased the beam of light, crashing into the legs of the bed and making the ruffled bedskirt twitch.

"Daddy, she's so silly," Abigail giggled, bringing the light out from under the bed and shining its beam on the opposite wall of her bedroom. The little cat flew out from under the bed like a furry rocket, her paws flailing after the circle of light. "Doesn't she know she can't catch the light?"

Daniel laughed again as the yellow kitten circled round and round, chasing the light on its own stubby tail. "No, honey, she thinks she can get it. I don't know what she'd do with it if she could catch it."

He straightened up and kissed his daughter on the top of her head. "Okay, now, you need to settle down. Try not to kill the cat. She's still little, and you're going to wear her out. Why don't you read her a book?"

Abigail snapped off the flashlight, unusually compliant. "Okay, Daddy. Dan and Mark and me are going to build something with Legos."

"That's great," Daniel said. "We have a lot of people coming over, so you guys need to be quiet. Dan is in charge, okay?"

"Okay," Abigail said, hugging her dad's knees just as the cat pounced on the cuff of his khaki pants. Daniel winced. The little bugger's claws were like tiny needles. He disengaged the kitten from his ankle and tossed it gently on his daughter's bed, where it bounced a few times and started attacking the pillow furiously, obviously hallucinating tiny mice.

Daniel went into the hall bathroom off Abigail's room to brush his teeth. Downstairs he could hear Mary moving chairs around, pushing the dining room table against the wall, getting ready for the buffet dinner. He had wanted to get his colleagues together to talk about the shooting in Fargo, and a potluck supper seemed the best, and most outwardly innocuous, way to do it.

The Reverend Daniel Seaton was about six feet tall, an earthy, stocky man with an easy grin. He wore his bushy, dark-brown hair rather short, lest it sprout out of his head in all directions, but allowed himself the luxury of a lush mustache. When he read late at night, at home, he also allowed himself the luxury of a pipe. Mary told him he looked more like an Oxford don than the pastor of a suburban American church. He rather liked that.

After college graduation, eighteen years earlier, Daniel had toured Europe with a backpack. He had taken odd jobs here and there, eaten vast quantities of pasta in Italy, considered a master's program in English literature at Oxford, and lingered at a Christian study center in Switzerland, partially because he loved the mountains and the courses offered there, but mostly because he had met an engaging, independent young woman named Mary.

Then his money had run out. Reality invaded. He had come home, considered his options, and ended up, with Mary's encouragement, in seminary. They had married after his first year, and she had supported them through her work as a nurse while Daniel took on odd jobs, as his study schedule allowed working as a carpenter.

Now, three children and many years later, the Seatons lived in a modest home in Falls Church, but their rooms were graced by the most intricate wainscotting in the Washington area. And for the past four years Daniel had pastored a small church that had sprung off from a larger congregation in McLean.

Daniel brushed his teeth, splashed water on his face, and combed his hair, then descended the stairs to the living/dining room. When they had bought the old house, it had been cordoned off into a small, dark warren of rooms. Daniel had knocked out walls with abandon, and now the airy great room was a frequent gathering place for people from their church, as well as the twenty or so local members of The Life Network.

Mary looked up and smiled at him as he entered the room. Tonight, Daniel thought, in her trim jeans and faded denim shirt, she looked about eighteen. Her long, heavy, glossy dark hair was clipped back with a tortoise shell barrette, revealing dangling silver earrings.

At the moment, she was talking with Amy O'Neil and Jennifer Barrett, two early arrivals who were helping her set out plates and silverware.

Amy and Mary had been friends for five or six years. Just before they met, Amy had been six months out of college, working as a receptionist for a congressman on Capitol Hill, and eight weeks pregnant. Her boyfriend was in law school at Georgetown, and when she had told him the news, which had coincided with his midterms, his entire demeanor had changed. His face had hardened, and he had told her in a cold voice, as if he were already an attorney dispassionately arguing a rather distasteful case, that their lives were really on separate tracks and the next few months were going to be extremely busy for him in terms of his study schedule.

"Listen," he had concluded. "I care about you. But we've got our own lives to live. It's not fair for you to look to me for something I can't give. I want to do the right thing in this situation, though. I'll split the cost of an abortion with you."

Shaken by both his attitude and the farewell in his voice, Amy had declined his offer.

Alone with her fears in the middle of the night, struggling to concentrate on her work during the day, Amy became more and more panicked. Her family was on the West Coast, she had to support herself, and the only way to do that was to keep working. And besides, a baby would squelch every dream she'd ever had. So she had made an appointment for an abortion.

A friend offered to drive her to the clinic, but she said no; this was not a day she wanted to share with anyone. She took a taxi, thankful for the anonymity provided by the typical Washington cabby, who barely spoke English.

Then, her worst fears were realized. Anti-abortionists were protesting at the clinic, waving signs and shouting slogans, while a group of pro-choicers in yellow T-shirts stood inside the yellow police tape, guarding the clinic and shouting through megaphones at the pro-lifers.

Dazed by the din, Amy hesitantly raised her arm to attract one of the yellow team's attention, and a small group of them burst through the barricades toward her. Surrounding her with their bodies, they escorted her toward the clinic.

The pro-lifers intensified their screaming, pressing toward her, thrusting their signs into the air. "Jesus loves the unborn," read one. "Abortion stops a beating heart," said another.

Then the shouts began.

"Murderer!" some of them shrieked. "Murderer!"

Amy put her head down and hung on to the arms of the women dragging her through the crowd.

"Murderer!"

Finally, they were at the clinic doors. A security guard held them open as Amy half-walked, was half-dragged through. As the doors shut, the screams dimmed slightly.

Afterward, she could remember little of the procedure itself. The doctor had offered general anesthesia, and she had taken it, inhaling hungrily through the mask, vaguely afraid that she would never wake up but desperate for the oblivion it offered.

She awoke in a crowded clinic room. All around her were women stretched and huddled on narrow cots. She felt nauseated and groggy from the anesthetic, and powerful cramps rolled through her lower body in waves. She felt like she had to go to the bathroom, but she couldn't get up. The cramps kept coming. With each one, she could hear the echo of the people outside: *Murderer! Murderer!*

After several hours, she was free to go.

The clinic was quiet now; the protesters had left, and so had most of the yellow-shirted pro-choice squad. A woman pressed open the double doors for her, and Amy walked slowly down the steps, still bleeding a little and feeling woozy.

She looked for a cab. There were usually a lot of them here on Sixteenth Street, across from the Capitol Hilton hotel and only about four blocks from the White House. Now there were none in sight.

As she waited, an attractive woman, dressed neatly in a denim skirt and long-sleeved plaid shirt, approached her.

"Hello," she said. "I noticed you when you went into the clinic. I know this must be a very hard day for you. Is there any way I can help you? Do you need a ride home?"

Amy stared at the woman, still groggy. "Are you with the clinic defenders?" she asked.

"No," said the woman. "I was here with the demonstration. I come here every Saturday to pray in front of this clinic. But I'm afraid some of my colleagues allowed their emotions to get out of hand. I saw them shouting at you. I've been waiting for you to come out so I could apologize for their behavior. I'm really sorry they were so hateful.

"My name is Mary," she continued. "And I'd be glad to take you home, or buy you a cup of coffee or something to eat, if you like. I just want you to know that not all Christians are so hurtful."

Amy felt dazed. She looked out at Sixteenth Street again. Still no cab in sight. This woman looked safe enough; and the way she felt, she didn't care if anything bad happened to her anyway. All she wanted to do was go home and go to bed.

"I'm Amy," she said. "If you wouldn't mind, it would be great if you could take me home. I don't live too far from here. And I feel horrible."

Mary had driven Amy to the townhouse she shared with several friends on Capitol Hill. No one else was home, so Mary had walked Amy up the stairs, gotten her into bed, made her drink a cup of hot tea, and left. When Amy woke from her deep, death-like sleep hours later, she found a note propped on her dresser.

"Hope you feel better soon," it said. "Please give me a call if I can be of any help to you. I'll be thinking of you." She had left her phone number and her name. "Mary Seaton."

A month later, Amy still couldn't shake off the abortion. Maybe it was all in her mind, but she felt hollow. The medical term for the procedure kept running through her mind: dilation and curettage. That was exactly how she felt: swollen, then scraped out. Empty.

Meanwhile, at work, she answered phones, arranged appointments for the congressman, and issued White House tour tickets to eager constituents visiting Washington for the first time. The business of her days exacerbated the emptiness she felt whenever she was alone, but she didn't feel like going out with friends to the usual distractions of movies, restaurants, and parties. Few of her friends knew about the abortion, but all of them knew about Brad's abrupt departure from her life. She hated the feeling that they pitied her.

She found herself watching more television than usual, reading magazines she had read before. Drinking a couple of glasses of wine every evening helped her go to sleep—but then she often woke in the middle of the night, exhausted and terrified, alone with her thoughts.

Finally one evening as she finished up at her office, she pulled Mary Seaton's number from her wallet and dialed.

"Amy!" said Mary. "I'm so glad you called. I've been thinking about you. How are you doing?"

Amy could hear the clamor of a toddler in the background.

"I'm sorry to bother you," she said. "This probably isn't a convenient time, but I was just wondering if you would mind getting together tonight for a cup of coffee or something."

Mary hesitated for only a moment. "That would be great," she said. "I'll have to get my kids' dinner on the table, but my husband will be home any minute, and he can watch them for the evening. I could probably leave here in forty-five minutes or so. Where would you like to meet?"

The two had met for coffee many times after that evening and had become close friends. Amy spilled out her feelings about the abortion—about feeling like she had hurt not only herself, but someone so small and defenseless that she couldn't even begin to think about it, about Brad's desertion, about the empty feeling inside.

For the most part, especially at first, Mary just listened. When she did talk, she spoke of forgiveness and second chances, of grace—a word Amy vaguely remembered from her childhood Sunday school. Mary talked without embarrassment about Jesus, about His love and the fact that He alone could offer new beginnings.

Then, one evening, it all broke through in Amy's mind. She prayed with Mary. She began attending Daniel Seaton's church. She was baptized.

And now, several years later, though she still had sad memories of the ghost-child she had aborted, the awful weight of guilt was gone. She had special empathy for women who felt trapped, women who felt they had no choice *but* abortion. She had a special horror about the procedure itself. And she was one of the most fervent members of The Life Network. As a congressional staffer she was well-positioned to distribute literature to key Capitol Hill offices.

Jennifer Barrett was newer to their group. Daniel didn't know much about her, but now, as he watched her talking with his wife and Amy, he was glad she had come. Physically, she was the opposite of petite, blonde, blue-eyed Amy. Jennifer had a no-nonsense look about her; she was tall, with short-cropped black hair and the healthy, thin-skinned look of a regular runner.

She was also very articulate. In the few conversations they had shared, Daniel had found her to be an utterly confident person. She didn't speak often, but when she did, she was quite insightful. She had just started coming to their church, and though she wasn't yet a full-fledged member of the Network movement, she seemed seriously interested in their cause.

The doorbell rang again and again as others arrived. John Jenkins was a member of Daniel's church, a quiet man with his own printing business, who, for no charge, produced the article reprints the group distributed. Jan James was a public-relations contract writer with good press contacts. Melissa Brett, whose husband owned a chain of successful restaurants, devoted a significant proportion of her wealth and energies to the pro-life cause. Linda Demmers was a nurse; her husband, Mark, was working on his doctorate in genetics. They both had excellent access to the latest in medical developments. Chris Smith was a carpenter who had worked with Daniel on building projects years before. He often spoke to area church groups about their cause.

Many in the group were from Daniel's church; others were members of various evangelical churches in the D.C. area. But none of them were the wild-eyed religious bigots and crazies so derided by the media.

They were a group of ordinary people who paid their taxes, voted, worked in their local PTAs, contributed to the Boy Scouts and disabled veterans, brought Meals on Wheels to homebound sufferers of AIDS and cancer, and gave themselves to dozens of other worthy causes. They just happened to hold uncompromising views about abortion and had been drawn into The Life Network because of their conviction that the abortion battle in America was entering a new, more ominous, phase. They sought to inform and educate opinionmakers, to calmly and reasonably expose the horrors of the coming regeneration centers.

WHILE DANIEL, MARY, AND THEIR FRIENDS were enjoying lasagna, bread, and salad, Alex Seaton was rounding the last bend in his evening run, his Nikes pounding the cold pavement. The hill before he got home was always the worst; but tired as he was, he always tried to speed up as he ran the final incline.

The streets were quiet; most people were probably inside watching the final play-off game before the Super Bowl. Alex's breath came in deep gasps, but he disregarded the pain in his chest. The chilled air felt fresh on his face as he ran up the long hill, fixing his mind on the goal. Then, finally, he hit the plateau where the street evened out.

He slowed to a walk and glanced at his watch. Not bad. The six miles had taken him a little less than thirty-eight minutes; his pace was consistent, day after day. He hadn't wanted to miss the dinner at Daniel's, but his run came first. No problem. He'd take a quick shower and be there in time for the meeting itself. He didn't need the lasagna anyway.

Alex Seaton was two inches taller, four years younger, and a good deal leaner than his brother. He was dark-haired, like Daniel, but lacked both the lush mustache and the robust good will his brother exuded, although he had always followed his brother's example. Daniel was the first to focus in on the pro-life cause, but Alex, with characteristic intensity, had elevated it to the primary cause in his life.

He had long since run through the inheritance that had come to him and his brother when their parents were killed in a plane crash, and he had bounced between a variety of jobs over the past few years. He borrowed money from Daniel all the time. But, as he had told Daniel rather stiffly, his part-time construction work was perfect; it allowed him the freedom to spend more time on the pro-life movement.

"If you're so pro-life," Daniel had responded cheerfully to his bachelor brother, "you need to get more of a life of your own!"

FORTY-FIVE MINUTES LATER, Daniel came back downstairs after checking on the kids. While he was talking to Mark Demmers he had heard thumps and scuffling upstairs and had gone up to find all three of them jumping on Abigail's bed and throwing pillows at one another and the kitten, who had then fled under the bed again.

Daniel had separated them, made them put on their pajamas, heard their prayers, and was now ready to get back to adult conversations. Usually Mary refereed bedtimes, but she had seemed so engrossed in conversation—or maybe she was just pretending not to hear the ruckus upstairs—that he had taken care of things himself.

Downstairs again, he saw that Alex and Lance Thompson had arrived. They stood by themselves in a corner, both holding mugs of coffee, looking over the group. Lance, a disciplined, private man who was cordial when approached but always restrained, had been part of The Life Network for some months now.

With his powerful build, his bulky arms, and his wide, thick neck, Lance was the epitome of the Special Forces officer he had been during the Gulf War. Daniel had learned through his brother that Lance had worked with a team of civilian demolitions experts commissioned to defuse the network of mines and booby traps the Iraqis had left in the desert, and had seen fellow team members blown to pieces in the millisecond after a moment of carelessness.

Lance lived in the District and felt more comfortable in the worship style of the all-black church he attended there, though he had visited Daniel's church. He had for years been deeply concerned about what he called the "genocide" of African-Americans because of Planned Parenthood's pervasive presence in the inner cities, and had enlisted many influential black pastors in the Network's cause.

On Saturdays, Lance usually could be found in front of the Women's Reproductive Health Clinic of D.C., simply standing the requisite number of feet from the clinic entrance, holding a placard depicting an aborted fetus and the black-and-white photo of a 1920s-era lynching of a young black man. "Abortion: the new black lynching," read the poster.

Lance kept to himself most of the time, unless he was with Alex. The two had spent a lot of time together in recent months, and to Daniel it seemed they had both grown increasingly paranoid.

Two days ago, when they'd heard of the Fargo shooting, Alex

had told Daniel there was a possibility that leaders within various pro-life groups were being monitored by the FBI. Daniel had rolled his eyes.

"You've been listening to Lance too much," he said. "This isn't the mine fields of Kuwait or the back alleys of Baghdad. Leave the cloak-and-dagger stuff for Lance's war stories."

And, Daniel realized, they were both potentially dangerous men. Their commitment to the pro-life cause was linked with their reactions against powerful ideologies. Daniel agreed with Lance that it was clear that Planned Parenthood targeted the poor. But for Lance, slavery was just a few generations in the past, lynching only a few decades removed, and the goals of the civil rights movement still largely unrealized. To him the politics of abortion were simply the most recent threat to true equality for African Americans.

And though Daniel shared his brother's fascination with Nazi Germany and the forces that had allowed Hitler to seize and retain power, it seemed that Alex's interest now bordered on obsession. He often read late into the night, reviewing again and again the details of the Nazis' crimes against humanity, the capitulation of many German Christians, and the underground attempts to assassinate Adolf Hitler. The evil they faced in America was similar. But Alex, without the stabilizing influence of a wife and children, seemed to be more willing to go to extreme lengths to fight it.

Looking around at the group now, Daniel cleared his throat. "Well, why don't we come to order," he said. "I don't have a big agenda here—most of our projects are proceeding well and all of you know what you're to be doing—but I thought it would be good if we got together to talk just a little about recent events and the potential fallout."

People found chairs, settled down, and looked up at him with the same expressions he usually saw when he was preaching from the pulpit.

"I'm not preaching tonight, folks!" He smiled. "So let's cut to the chase. This Fargo thing, coming right at the same time as

Whitney Griswold's coming into office, means that some ugly forces are on the move. You've seen the news reports. Pro-lifers are going to be blamed for anything and everything. No matter what we say—assuming we're still allowed the right to free speech, which I sometimes wonder—it will be twisted.

"So we have to be absolutely clear about what we're doing here in Network. No violence. No ugly demonstrations. We just need to keep up the pressure of exposing the regeneration centers for what they really are. Through every creative means available."

He paused and looked around. Most were nodding, sipping coffee, tracking with him.

Inside his head, he counted to five. He knew who was going to speak up first.

There was a movement in the corner, and Alex cleared his throat. "Look," he said, "I hear what you're saying. But I don't think you're saying enough. That shooting in Fargo is neither here nor there. One abortion doctor down. Good riddance. But we don't have enough time to shoot every abortionist in the country, though that's not a bad idea. In about six months, those regeneration centers are gonna be up and running.

"How long are we going to sit here? Right now we've got millions of early abortions because of RU-486—and even worse, babies are being killed in the womb, their brains sucked out for research studies. Dilation and extraction. D and X for short. They don't have enough doctors trained in the procedure; it takes a high level of surgical skill. So do you know what they're doing? Producing training videos! Government-funded snuff movies . . . and people don't even care. Now women are being told that they're not only exercising 'reproductive choice'—the most glorious of all human rights—they're at the same time saving human lives. Women who hesitated about abortion before won't waste a minute now."

"I've been there, Alex," Amy O'Neil interrupted quietly as Alex took a breath. "No woman can feel good about getting an abortion. I don't care how much bull you feed her about helping others. It's a death. It's a vacuum. It stays with you."

Alex paused, then continued as if no one had spoken. "I don't think we should exclude any means of action available. If a sniper was shooting people at random on the street, wouldn't we stop him?

"Why are we sitting here, going on with our everyday lives, when the Auschwitz camps of our day are under construction right now? We ought to bomb every center they build."

"Wait a minute, Alex," interrupted Chris Smith, the carpenter. "Do you hear what you're saying? People just don't realize what these regeneration centers are all about. We need to find ways to expose them for what they are. People aren't so far gone that they won't recognize that it's wrong to suck the brains from a live fetus. Our job is to reveal the truth, however we can. Letters to the editor. Nonviolent protests. Get on the talk shows. Pictures. Be reasonable, so people can see we're not crazy. Our cause is *reasonable*: People in a civilized society do not behave this way."

"But that's just it!" exploded Alex. "*Who* is the epitome of a civilized, utterly sophisticated human being in America today? I'll tell you: It's our new president, J. Whitney Griswold, who talks all the time about 'bringing decency back to America!' Meanwhile he's gonna make sure that every neighborhood in the country has its own private fetus-harvesting center by the end of his administration.

"We can't reason with people anymore," Alex continued. "What we should do is show up at the inauguration and pour buckets of blood on the Capitol steps. Griswold is just another Adolf Hitler."

Mark Demmers sipped his coffee and let Alex's energy dissipate for a moment before he asked, dryly, "So you want us to get out our buckets, Alex?"

Alex raised his eyebrows. "I'm not proposing anything to this group right now except that we don't bury our heads in the sand and think our little tiny efforts here and there are going to accomplish anything. The time has passed for sitting around and having meetings. We've got to do something. We've got to be ready to give our lives for this cause. Millions and millions have already been slaughtered, and more are on the way!"

"Skip the rhetoric," somebody muttered.

Daniel held up his hand. "The main thing I'm concerned about is that we don't get carried away," he said mildly. "When people are frustrated—it sounds like we all are—they don't think clearly. As long as I'm involved with this group, we will not consider any action that involves violence. We cannot use evil means for 'good' ends. That's too easy. We have to do the hard thing. We have to overcome evil with good.

"If I were preaching," he said, "I would say that God ordained government. In America, however dark it seems, we've still got the best thing going. And if the apostle Paul could sit in a jail cell and write that believers were to be in subjection to the governing authorities, who were 'established by God,' when the guy on the throne in *his* day was totally insane Nero, then certainly we can respect Whitney Griswold.

"And we need to pray for him. We're supposed to love our enemies. No matter what. And I'm not trying to be the heavy here, but if I hear of anyone in this group planning anything that has to do with violence, we'll have to disband. Period."

There was a general shift in the room as people moved in their chairs, exhaled, and several stood up to get more coffee. At Daniel's last words, Alex and Lance exchanged a quick look—just a tightening of the mouth and a blink of the eyes that nobody else noticed.

9

S ENATOR BYRON LANGER leaned back in his old black
leather chair and thumbed through the fourteen-inch-
thick sheaf of papers on Emily Gineen. The FBI had
completed its background check in record time, and as ranking
member of the Judiciary Committee, Langer was entitled to the
full report, background interviews included.

"Quite a woman," he muttered, as he flipped page after page.

Professor Gineen's record was unblemished. Not so much as
a traffic violation, and her finances were beyond reproach. She'd
paid Social Security taxes on nannies and household employees.
Her own taxes had been audited twice, and in both cases, it
turned out the government owed her money.

Her personal life was as flawless as her public record. She
had married her first serious boyfriend, a Princeton classmate. The couple had been devoted to one another for
eighteen years, with never a hint of indiscretion. She drank
wine only with meals. No one remembered her ever making
an insensitive or politically incorrect remark or losing her
temper.

One former neighbor, whose name had been blocked out on
the report, summed up the general attitude about Emily Gineen:

"I didn't think I'd like her when she moved in next door. Here comes this famous Harvard couple with their twin BMWs, the television crews setting up in their front yard now and then, the articles and interviews and the whole bit . . . I didn't think we'd have much in common. My husband does very well with his software company, but I didn't even finish college. I've devoted my whole life to being a wife and mother.

"But the first night, she came over and introduced herself, wearing jeans and an old sweatshirt. She asked if she could use our phone since hers wasn't hooked up yet. They'd forgotten to get that taken care of. That shocked me. Later, when my son was in the hospital, Emily helped with our younger kids, visited the hospital, cooked casseroles. I've never heard her raise her voice with her own kids. They're great. And she's almost always cheerful too, just about the best person I've ever known. She couldn't do anything wrong if her life depended on it."

Langer sat forward and scribbled some notes on his yellow pad. "Admirable character . . . Probably self-righteous." He knew he would keep his questions to the issues only. With a sigh, he looked at the stack of articles, books, and volumes of the court reports that his aides had piled on the left side of his desk.

Tall, vigorous, and once athletic, Langer was now thirty pounds overweight. Most of it had settled around his middle so that when his coat was open, his bulging, wrinkled shirt obscured his belt; the rest was in his puffy jowls which, along with his large lips and drooping eyelids, cast him as the stereotypical good ol' boy one could find at noontimes eating biscuits and sausage gravy at the Elite Cafe across from the Jackson Courthouse.

Langer was given to quoting Scripture in his deep Mississippi drawl which had somehow deepened since he came to Washington. With his flowing, wavy hair, he looked the part of a filibustering, Bible-quoting, segregationist senator from the South of two generations past.

But appearances were deceiving. His detractors believed that Langer cultivated this image, often shrewdly using it to lure his opponents into his trap. Honors graduate of Ole Miss and former editor of the *Vanderbilt Law Review*, Langer was a formidable intellect with a prodigious memory.

His public record read like an old school politician's: decorated Green Beret officer in Vietnam, distinguished attorney, state supreme court justice, and now in his third term in the U.S. Senate. He and his wife, Lily, along with their four children, always pictured together on Langer's campaign posters, were a tight-knit family. He was untouchable in Mississippi politics, and had he been a little more photogenic and from a larger state, he would have been a national contender.

Langer sighed and shoved away from his desk. It was 7:30, time to go home for dinner with Lily. Then after dinner he'd read cases. There was still time before the hearings, and he wanted to be ready.

He picked up his briefcase, stuck his old leather Bible in the side, and thought about the psalm he'd read that morning. Psalm 139. "You wove me in my mother's womb," the psalmist had said. It was one his favorites, and spoke to the main issue he had to deal with when it came to the appointment of Emily Gineen. The view of human life that he held wasn't politics; it was something he knew deep in his soul. Emily Gineen did not. Nothing personal, but she simply didn't know.

SURROUNDED BY PUSHING REPORTERS, trailing cords, and popping flashbulbs, Emily Gineen, carrying a large lawyer's file case, made her way slowly to the entrance of the Senate Caucus Room. The Judiciary Committee was in the Dirksen Building, but the demand for seats and press credentials had been so great that the chairman had elected to hold Dr. Gineen's hearing in the most illustrious room in the Capitol, the room where the McCarthy, Watergate, and Iran Contra hearings had been held.

Byron Langer had not been happy with this change. It would put too much attention on Gineen and would give Griswold too big a victory when, as was all but inevitable, she was confirmed.

Dr. Gineen was smiling until the moment she was asked to raise her right hand and repeat the oath. Then her blue eyes were sober as she repeated, "I do, so help me God." Her dark-brown hair was swept back, her makeup understated, just enough to emphasize her clear eyes and even smile, and she wore an unremarkable dark blue suit with a soft cream blouse.

Langer noted her calm manner. He had seen many at that witness table start to come apart even before the questioning began, rattled by the pomp, the press, and the procedures. But the Harvard professor sat easily, even eagerly, as if she looked forward to the session.

The chairman invited her opening statement. Some witnesses took far too long to say far too little, reading slowly from dull documents, their hands trembling. But Dr. Gineen spoke briefly, animatedly, and without notes about her understanding of the role of attorney general, her sense of the historical context in which this administration found itself, and her commitment to discharge her duties faithfully, in accordance with the law and the Constitution.

She finished and smiled at the chairman, who seemed nervous himself, perhaps because he had been roasted some years earlier for his insensitivity in questioning a woman. His counsel handed him a page of typed questions, which were notably timid and quickly dispatched by Dr. Gineen. Predictably, she was asked about the situation in Fargo; if she was confirmed, she said, she would vigorously prosecute the investigation and provide more resources for clinic protection.

Before long, the chairman announced, "I yield to my colleague, the ranking majority member and distinguished senior senator from Mississippi," and leaned back, relieved.

"Professor Gineen," Langer paused, adjusting his dark-rimmed glasses, "let me commend you on a very direct and forthright presentation and for illuminating this committee on the role of attorney general. Let me say also that I find your record admirable, particularly your history of prosecuting criminal offenders.

"But I do have some concern that you have made it sound as if you are just a high-priced functionary, enforcing the law my colleagues enact and the Court interprets. Would you not agree, Professor, that the attorney general has a policy role as head of the department and of course as advisor to the president?"

"Of course that is so, Senator."

"Then, Professor, may I assume you are able and willing to discuss your views on the great policy issues that confront our Republic?"

"Of course, Senator, I am prepared to do so." Emily's grin masked her impatience. *Get to it, Senator, we all know what's coming.*

"To begin, let us turn to your arguments so eloquently advanced in *Casey v. Planned Parenthood*. You wrote, and I quote," he pushed his glasses to the end of his nose, 'The ability of women to share equally in the civic social life of the nation depends on their ability to control their reproductive lives.'"

Gineen nodded.

"You should be complimented that the Court adopted your language almost verbatim in its decision."

"Every lawyer is gratified, Senator, when the high Court endorses his or her arguments," she said softly.

"This is, or I should say was, a rather novel argument. Do I understand this means that abortion is a necessary right in order to assure gender equality for jobs and that sort of thing?"

"Yes, Senator, for 'that sort of thing.' Indeed. A woman's right to control her reproductive life is a matter of her liberty protected under the Fourteenth Amendment. This case, sir, was a very important step in the process of emancipating women."

Hard as she tried not to, Emily allowed a slightly defiant tone to slip into her last sentence, but it was drowned out by the applause from the women who had packed the spectators' seats.

"Order, order," the chairman cracked the gavel. "We will maintain proper decorum here."

Langer resumed. "I am familiar of course with the arguments in *Roe v. Wade*," he said, "the implied right of privacy. And I am familiar with the Court's application of the Fourteenth Amendment to this issue, distressing though I find it. But what I was getting at was your reasoning. Do we abort children to achieve gender equality? Was that your argument, Professor?"

"No, sir. The argument turned on questions of liberty. Equal rights was a consequence."

"But you advanced it as a reason, Professor, to assure women's economic and social rights. I don't know anyone who argues that abortion is a desirable thing. It is taking a life, or if you prefer, a potential life, and it is offensive to the deepest-held convictions of conscience for millions. But you would advocate it as permissible to help someone get a job? And if so, what other difficult and painful things would you allow in order to secure 'social and economic equality'?"

"I think we may be confused here, Senator. We are talking about liberty." Gineen, for the first time, appeared flustered, repeating her answer.

"The question is not difficult, Professor." Langer paused after "Professor" as if for emphasis. "What else do we offer up to achieve gender equality—the gentle, loving syringe for those burdensome and dying patients whose care prevents us from sharing equally in the economic and social life of our nation?"

"That's inflammatory, Senator. I've never proposed any such thing, and you know that."

"But how far do you go? Would you sterilize welfare mothers who refuse abortions and bear children repeatedly? This disposition on their part denies them full economic equality. Costs us a lot too."

"Many women choose sterilization, Senator."

"Or lose their welfare checks . . . but my question, Professor, goes much beyond this."

Langer paused, took off his glasses, held them at a distance, and stared through them; then, with what Emily found to be maddening deliberation, he began cleaning them with his handkerchief. Langer's capacity to unsettle witnesses was legendary.

After what seemed like minutes to her, he continued. "It might seem somewhat philosophical, but the question is: What is liberty and who defines it? One person's liberty can be another person's bondage."

"Liberty is well defined in a long series of cases, sir." Emily started to reach for her notebook, but Langer never gave her a chance.

"Let me read what the Court said in *Casey*, again I believe relying on your brief. 'At the heart of liberty is the right to define one's own concept of existence, of meaning, of the universe, and of the mystery of human life.' Do you agree with that?"

"I recall the wording."

"Do you agree?"

"I think I argued it slightly differently. But it does, certainly, define liberty of conscience."

"Ah yes, quite so, Professor. I would defend with my life a person's right to his or her deepest personal convictions. But there is a difference between holding convictions and acting on them. Certainly the state, to preserve order and domestic tranquility, can limit one from acting on his thoughts."

"Of course, Senator."

"Then there are limits on liberty. So I come back to my question. How do we define those limits?"

"The legislature, you and your colleagues, sir, make the laws. The Court interprets and enforces."

"Indeed, Professor. I'm familiar with the process." Langer tried not to be condescending, but he was no more successful than Gineen was in disguising her impatience. Two different cultures were facing each other across the witness table.

"But my question goes to the basis on which our legislatures and courts determine what is liberty and what is to be restrained. It is not a new question, of course. It is the one Plato asked and then attempted to answer in *The Republic*: What is justice?"

"It is the rule of law, sir, which protects liberty, secures the peace, and promotes the greatest good," said Emily. "Law is sustained by the plain language of the Constitution and by the laws and decisions of the courts over the years."

Langer looked up, fixing his gaze on the fresco around the

ceiling edge. "Yes, indeed," he said slowly, "the greatest good . . . Bentham, of course, of course."

There was another of those painful delays, but this time it hit Emily. Suddenly she sensed where he was taking her. *I might have known he'd pull this*, she thought, *the one impossible dilemma*. She braced for his next question, annoyed that she hadn't seen it coming earlier.

"What then do we do, Professor, in the case of a law that benefits the greatest number but is manifestly unjust—might I even say one that is self-evidently unjust?"

"The Court would have to declare it unconstitutional, sir."

"And if it did not?"

She knew the trap was set and there was no way to escape. "Well, sir, we trust our system to work."

"But let me invite your attention to an historical episode that is painful still to some in my region of America, Professor Gineen. The majority in America once believed that slavery was in the best interest of the greatest number. The majority approved slavery when the Kansas Nebraska Act was passed by the Congress. And the Court in the Dred Scott decision then affirmed it on the grounds that the black slave was not a person under the Constitution. Now as you well know, President Lincoln held a very different view."

"It is a good example of an unjust law, sir. And of course it took extreme courage to resist it. But America's heritage is rich in that characteristic, sir." Emily wanted to divert him from this issue in the worst way.

"Courage? Courage indeed, my dear Professor. Courage that ran crimson, draining the life from 600,000 men and boys. The system didn't remedy itself, Professor, did it?"

"Dred Scott was reversed, sir, by the Thirteenth and Fourteenth Amendments."

"Amendments enacted by an army of occupation. This was after a war, Professor, a war that almost destroyed us. So I come back to my question. How do we deal with an unjust law today? Another war?"

"No, Senator, the majority ultimately favored the abolition of slavery. I trust the majority today to see and do what is right."

"Majorities create tyrannies, Professor. You need only look at what the Germans in the thirties thought was just. No, my question is: How do you measure justice? Do you believe, as Lincoln did, that there is a higher law beyond the law?"

"In our social contract, sir, the majority determines the law. We rule by the consent of the governed. Sovereignty is in the people."

"Our founders spoke of certain self-evident truths and unalienable rights that are not given by government and thus cannot be taken away by government but rather are endowed by our Creator," said Langer. "It is a government under God, Professor Gineen . . . or perhaps you prefer Jefferson's formulation that the nation was governed by 'laws of nature and nature's God.' This is what Lincoln relied on. Without that, perhaps I'd own slaves, as my great-granddaddy did."

"I'm glad to have the assurance you do not, sir, though from what I hear, I'm not sure your staff would agree." Emily tried levity, and for a moment it worked.

But Byron Langer knew just where she was headed, and he knew what he wanted on the record. He chuckled, made a half bow in her direction, and resumed.

"Are there no truths by which the state is bound? After all, there are physical laws governing the universe. Are there not also moral laws binding us? Are there not binding truths that limit the state?"

"Truth? I believe truth, sir, is, as the great Justice Oliver Wendell Holmes once wrote, the majority will. In fact, Judge Robert Bork, whom you so enthusiastically supported, once said, 'Truth is what the majority thinks it is at any given moment, precisely because the majority is permitted to govern and to redefine its values constantly.'"

Emily had been on the defensive, but she had him on that one. Her grin gave her away. The crowd chuckled.

The senator showed no emotion but once again removed his glasses and leaned forward.

"Well now, Professor, no one is perfect. Judge Bork was an eminent jurist who was crucified by this very committee—to its shame." He glanced at the Democrats, only one of whom had been sitting when Bork was nominated. "And he was, to his great credit, a strict constructionist, looking at what the framers meant. He clearly would have voted to overturn *Roe v. Wade.* But he was, I will confess, a bit myopic on the broader question of whether the laws of men and nations are judged by a higher law. I think Judge Bork in time would have come to see that."

"Truth, sir," Gineen said, her eyes sparkling, now on the offensive, "is when a government sees to it that every individual can enjoy his or her full and equal opportunity; when every man and woman, following the dictates of conscience, is not just tolerated but respected in their lifestyle choices; when bigotry is banished from our common life."

There was a sprinkling of applause and the chairman gaveled for quiet. He turned to Langer. "The gentleman from Mississippi has exhausted his time. One more question, sir."

Langer nodded, propped his glasses on the end of his nose, and leaned back in his chair. For several seconds he simply stared at Gineen, without rancor.

"May I simply say, Professor Gineen, that I respect your intellect and ability and your record of public service. But good people, particularly those who are smart and can't imagine that they can do anything wrong, frighten me. For in their zeal and idealism, they can often become the very thing they most deplore. To guarantee your definition of liberty, Professor, will ultimately make us oppressors of liberty."

Emily stared at him, caught in the web of his riddle. Then a photographer knelt in front of the witness table; she smiled, and the web was broken.

Emily remained in command throughout the rest of the hearing. Most of the questions dealt with her views on law enforcement and fighting crime, and she was eloquent, armed with facts, statistics, and studies that she rattled off without looking at a sheet of paper.

Late in the day, however, shortly before the hearing ended, a Langer aide handed her an envelope containing a handwritten note.

"I'd be greatly obliged if you will meet me in my office at the conclusion of the hearings. Byron Langer."

Emily read it twice. Nothing good could come of this, she thought.

DESPITE HIS SENIORITY, Byron Langer chose to remain in the Russell Building, the oldest of the three Senate office buildings. He liked the older architecture, the ten-foot-high, dark-stained doors, the ornate moldings, and the well-worn black-and-white tile corridors.

It was after 6:00 when Emily arrived at room 141 accompanied by Jerry Kirkbride, the young Washington lawyer assigned to her by the presidential transition team. The office was ablaze with lights, people still hard at work at each of the old mahogany desks that lined both walls. The smiling receptionist jumped to her feet, took Emily's coat, nodded Jerry to a waiting-room chair, and immediately escorted Emily through two more crowded offices.

Senator Langer was standing in his office door, putting on his jacket. "Come in, Professor, come in," he said.

As she entered, she gave the senator's crowded office a quick scan. One wall was floor-to-ceiling books; the other three were covered with pictures, plaques, degrees, and certificates. Langer showed off a few favorites.

"This is my family last Christmas. This is my granddaughter, little Eugenia, here." He jabbed a finger at a blonde toddler who was laughing right into the camera. "She's a pistol."

"And over here was my first visit with President Reagan, years ago . . . here's my Green Beret company in Vietnam. The sergeant beside me, what a guy. For forty-one days the unit was behind enemy lines taking a pounding. He got three Bronze Stars for saving men under fire."

"You did too, didn't you Senator?" Emily had read up on her adversary.

"Well, one does one's duty. I was proud to serve my country. Still am."

He pointed to an overstuffed leather chair. "May I offer you a seat?"

"Do you mind if I sit here?" Emily asked, pulling over a black lacquered armchair with the Ole Miss seal on the back. "If I sat there, I'd be too relaxed. And for you, Senator, I need all my faculties."

"Well now, Professor, I wasn't all that rough on you today—at least I hope not." He took the leather chair himself. "Just a friendly exchange between two people who care about the law."

"Of course, Senator, entirely so." She smiled like she always did when she had to lie. She hated politics—one of the reasons she was already regretting that she'd accepted this job. But she couldn't go back now. And she knew she had to get along with the man. Bernie O'Keefe, in one of her briefing sessions, had told her the senator was the key to making her life here bearable or unbearable. He could be a fierce adversary. He could also be eccentric and sometimes talked in enigmas, a throwback to an earlier time. Not an easy man to deal with.

"Ms. Gineen," the senator said, gently twirling his glasses, "I thought we should have this discussion alone simply so that I could be completely forthright with you, as is my habit.

"You are remarkably well-qualified to be attorney general of the United States. Much about your life and professional career I find extraordinary and admirable. The president is indeed fortunate you agreed to serve."

Emily nodded while adjusting her cuffs. "Thank you, Senator," she said, waiting for the other shoe to drop.

"And you will, of course, be confirmed."

She smiled, beginning to relax slightly.

"This means you and I will have to work very closely together, being that I am the ranking member."

"It will be a pleasure, sir. After all, we are both committed to stopping crime and we are both Republicans."

"Yes, ma'am," he said. "But I was a Masterson Republican—and you, of course, were with Griswold."

"The election is over, Senator. We need to bring the party and the country together."

"Of course, of course. The election is over. But there is still a great gulf that divides us, Professor."

"I've not been in politics as long as you, Senator, but I understand it to be the art of the possible. That means compromise and consensus. People have to work to understand each other and arrive at prudential judgments." Emily was annoyed to find that she sounded as if she were pleading.

"That's just it. Political judgments, like anything else, are mere reflections of deeper beliefs. The real issue today is truth. It's not the rot that passes for political discourse in this place." Langer swung his arm as if to embrace the whole Capitol. "I mean the real questions are of life and existence, of meaning, of ultimate things. Truth itself—that's the great issue of our age."

Emily was groping for an answer. Just when she thought she was engaging the man, he'd slip away into philosophical issues. What was his game? She detested abstract discussions. *Just give me the cases, the citations, and the holdings to support your point. I want the law*, she would tell her students at Harvard.

She started to answer, but the senator cut her off. "That's the gulf: We're from two very different cities; we both speak the same language, but the words mean different things.

"It's like driving in England. I always tell my British friends that they drive on the wrong side of the road; but, of course, to them, it's the right side. They tell me I drive on the wrong side. Right means two different things to us—opposite things. And if we carried it far enough, we'd create chaos in each other's cities."

"I think I understand your point, Senator. We've been talking about culture wars in America now for a long time. Different fundamental values honestly held by different factions with different presuppositions. But that tension is nothing new; it's part of the dialectic of American life."

Emily took a tissue from her purse, pretending to blow her nose, but actually wanting to dry her palms and give her something to do besides stare into Langer's piercing eyes.

"No," he said decisively. "It's different than that. If you have two cities, separated by this great gulf, you can no longer communicate, unless you have an interpreter who knows the rules of the other city." He seemed to stare past her at something on the wall over her right shoulder, and for a moment he was quiet, reflective.

She decided to wait him out. Maybe he's gone around the bend, she thought. Early Alzheimer's. Or, more likely, he's after something.

"Oh, forgive me," he exclaimed suddenly. "No southern hospitality here. I'm so sorry. May I offer you coffee or a soft drink?"

She seized at anything to break the conversation. "A Coke, if you have it. Thank you, Senator."

Langer hit a button and in seconds the door swung open. "Two Cokes, if you would, Joan. Thank you very much." And then continued as if there had been no interruption.

"Truth is the issue. You see that, don't you, Ms. Gineen?" He was staring at her again.

"I think I understand, sir," she nodded, still waiting him out.

"I believe in absolute truth," he said. "I believe that there is a point of ultimate reality, an absolute from which all truth as we know it flows. You don't, of course. I've read your articles."

"I believe in truth, Senator, but it is a truth we discover through debate and consensus. We find it in our collective wisdom."

"But truth is not subjective. It is not relative. It is truth. You see, I'm afraid this makes my point," he said. "We use the same word and mean something totally different.

"And this, Ms. Gineen, affects our entire view of life, and, of course, government. I believe, as most of our founders did, in a transcendent, binding absolute by which men and nations are judged. God, of course. I say 'of course' because I believe. Others call it natural law, as some of the founders did. Russell Kirk, in fact, said one cannot be a conservative without believing in natural law."

"I'm quite familiar with that, Senator. I've studied Kirk, and I read Leo Strauss when I was at Princeton. And, of course, I'm familiar with the founders' debates."

"But you don't agree with them either, do you?" Langer stared at her intently.

"No, sir, I do not. I believe our government was founded on the principles of a social contract, with ultimate sovereignty in the people. That's what consent of the governed means."

Langer continued to stare as he said, "So the people can do what they want. Each generation sets the terms of the contract anew and defines what truth is for their times?"

Emily nodded.

"But that's the rub. I can't accept that as a matter of conscience. Perhaps I should explain, Ms. Gineen, that I'm a Christian. I was saved as a very young man, taking Jesus as my Savior many, many years ago. Though I'm not as good a Christian as I should be perhaps, I take it all quite seriously. I believe Jesus when He says He is *the* truth. In Him is ultimate reality."

Gineen felt her cheeks flush. She shifted uncomfortably. She didn't enjoy talking about something so intimate as one's faith, and she hated the term "saved"—so smug and southern and Baptist, reminding her of her childhood in Alabama.

"Now not to pry—there's of course no religious test for public office—but I imagine you don't believe that the way I do."

"Well, I'm a Christian, Senator. I attend the Episcopal Church. Or, well, I used to. I haven't for some time . . . there are many reasons . . . but I believe faith is very important. It's also very personal."

"Of course. But I believe that if God is God, faith cannot be simply personal. God has spoken the universe into being. He has given a concrete, moral prescription for life. All law ultimately finds its roots in God's Word. All legitimate law, that is. That's where our natural law comes from."

Gineen took her tissue out again. *Oh no*, she thought. *And the*

White House tells me I need to work with this guy? I'm not gonna get out of here till he ties me down and converts me.

"Of course I'm not trying to convert you." It was as if he had read her mind. "I simply want you to see how different our basic presuppositions are. And why, as a matter of conscience, I do not think that I will be able to vote for your confirmation, Ms. Gineen."

His blunt words came unexpectedly, and Emily felt her face flush again. What a terrible way to start. And the White House had told her Langer would take six or eight senators with him. This would be a terrible symbolic defeat for the incoming president, coming from his own party.

"I understand, sir," was the best she could get out.

"Of course I will explain that you are eminently qualified. It's simply a matter of conscience over deeply held beliefs. And it won't matter; you'll be confirmed anyway, of course. But at least I will have been true to my convictions. I'm sorry. I truly am sorry."

He's either a great actor or he really is sorry, Emily thought as she gazed into his eyes. "I wish, sir, I could persuade you otherwise. I approach these issues on their merits. I'm sure we'll be able to do that."

"Oh, of course we will try. We have to. But we'll really never understand each other. We'll never be able to communicate, because our words mean different things. And there are no interpreters—I mean, there's no one around you to explain what I mean, what I and maybe thirty or forty million Americans believe."

Langer let the words hang in the air. He took off his glasses and smiled benignly.

He can't be. He can't be, Emily told herself. Despite all of his pious philosophy, could he be angling to get her to appoint one of his people? Was this deal time—politics plain and simple? She detested this, but like it or not, she was in it.

She took a deep breath and stared at him, her blue eyes hard. "Would you happen to know any interpreter, Senator? Someone I might consider?"

"Oh heavens, there are many, of course, but I wouldn't be so presumptuous."

"No, please, Senator. If we are to work together, we must be able to deal the cards face up."

"I don't play cards, Ms. Gineen. Threw them away when I was saved, like the preacher told me to. Good thing, too. I'd have lost my shirt at poker. I'm just a transparent southern boy."

Emily had to catch herself to keep from rolling her eyes. Right. *This good ol' boy is a master manipulator. He could take your socks off without touching your shoes.*

"No, please, Senator. You must know some capable attorneys I might appoint to the Justice Department to, as you put it, be interpreters."

"Well, I'm not urging this, you understand, but the chief counsel on this committee—judiciary—is a very able man. His name is Paul Clarkson, and he's a brilliant attorney. He's smart, full of energy, committed . . . but I don't want to put you in a difficult position, Ms. Gineen."

"Not at all, sir. I know Clarkson. He's impressive. But he's rather young, isn't he?"

"He's thirty-eight but has a lot of wisdom for his years."

"Perhaps I could find a good position in the Office of Legal Counsel."

"Of course, of course. But I don't think he'd leave here for that. Who have you picked as associate attorney general?"

No poker player, huh. He's going for the number three position in the department.

"We have many candidates, sir. That's, of course, a critical position since the AAG runs the department."

"Paul has run this committee. I don't know how we'd do it without him . . . but I suppose, well, I wouldn't stand in his way, of course."

She stared at Langer, not caring if her anger showed. There it was—the deal, the horse trade—shamelessly laid on the table. And she determined, at that moment, that she would not sacrifice her honor. If she could not rise above this sort of thing, she'd simply go back to Harvard. Griswold had promised her her independence.

"I'm afraid he would not be mature enough for that position, Senator. But I will consider him for some post, I assure you."

"Well, of course, of course. You do whatever is right. But not mature enough? Hmmm. How old are you, Ms. Gineen? Ten years ago I wouldn't ask a woman that question, but things have changed a lot."

"I'm forty-two, Senator, and sitting in here with you has aged me well beyond that," she snapped.

"Well, that's right.We do a lot of maturing from thirty-eight to forty-two. But now I want you as attorney general to do what you think is right."

Gineen, furious, looked at her watch. She refused to sit here and be this wacko's prisoner any longer. "I appreciate your time, Senator. I must go.Will you have Clarkson call me?"

"Yes, indeed.Very important to have a strong associate, someone who understands Washington and, of course, this end of Pennsylvania Avenue. He'd be a good interpreter."

Langer escorted her to the door, and she willed herself to say goodbye calmly.

STILL FUMING, Emily called Bernie O'Keefe from the phone in her limousine and told him what had happened.

"This is Washington," he said. She could hear his chair squeaking as he leaned back. His feet were probably on the desk.

"I know where I am, Bernie," she said sharply. It infuriated her that he sounded so cavalier. "I'd like to see Griswold on this. He told me I would be independent, and I want him to back me up. I can't be held hostage to this kind of horse-trading."

"Look, Emily, you're the attorney general-designate. If you want to see Whitney Griswold, you can see him. I'll put you on the calendar for tomorrow morning. But I'll tell you exactly what he will do. He'll listen politely, tell you he wants to think about it, and then he'll call me and have me call you and tell you to hire Clarkson. So why don't we save all of us a lot of trouble."

Emily rolled her eyes and picked at a piece of lint on the

leather car seat. How in the world had she ever gotten herself into this situation?

"Besides," O'Keefe continued, "it's a good move. You're the only southerner in the cabinet, and Clarkson will help you reach out to the Masterson people."

Emily leaned back and sighed. "That hypocrite Langer. All that rambling about truth, philosophy, and religion. He's one of those born-again types. All that stuff was just to get his boy a job."

"Or maybe, Emily, it was for power. He wants his man where he can be an influence. I can't blame him. This is politics. Get used to it. Look, small concession now and you'll be confirmed with a unanimous vote; stand on principle and the president's attorney general gets ten negative votes, the president gets slapped in the face, and the attorney general is crippled. Face it. You don't have much of a choice here."

Emily hit her palm against the armrest. "Right," she said sarcastically. "This stinks, Bernie. And stop smiling."

He laughed into her ear. "Yes, ma'am, Madam Attorney General, sir. Go home. Have a drink. Relax."

THE NEXT MORNING Bernie and Emily interviewed Paul Clarkson for two hours. The FBI completed their check on him within forty-eight hours, and by week's end the announcement had been made.

Two days before the inauguration, the Senate voted ninety-eight to nothing, with two absences, to confirm Emily Gineen as attorney general of the United States. Byron Langer gave an impassioned speech, assuring his colleagues that while there had been differences in the campaign, "This brilliant woman shows a profound understanding of the democratic process; we'll work together productively." Paul Clarkson's confirmation went without a hitch as well.

10

WHITNEY GRISWOLD'S cheeks smarted from the fresh wind sweeping in from the northwest across the open spaces of the Mall. A cold front had moved through only hours before the Inauguration, clearing the skies and dropping the temperature into the high thirties.

The president-elect, dressed in the traditional formal cutaway, had just stepped through the door leading from the west front of the Capitol building to the huge wooden platform constructed to hold the VIPs. He stood for a moment soaking in the incredible spectacle, shaking more from excitement than from the cold as the military band launched into "Ruffles and Flourishes."

Immediately before him were the platform participants, all turned toward him, smiling and applauding—the entire Congress, the diplomatic corps, the members of his government to be. Television cameras were everywhere; around the world, more than a billion people were watching.

And beyond the stands was the sea of faces. Over one hundred thousand. Like colored dots on a vast blue-gray background. The applause came in waves. He could see hands moving seconds before he was engulfed in the thunderous sound.

Beyond the Mall, in the distance, stood the Washington

Monument, tall, erect, and proud. And beyond that the stately edifice of the Lincoln Memorial.

Step firmly, he reminded himself. *This is the picture the whole world will see.*

He had dreamed of this for twenty years but hadn't dared think about it since his big victory in New Hampshire. Against all odds, the pundits had said. *Well, we showed them.*

Remember, he told himself, *walk erect, not casual like Bush, no loping stroll like Clinton. People want a leader, firmly in charge, someone bigger than life.*

When Griswold was finally seated in the cupola at the front of the platform, the Episcopal bishop of Washington moved to the podium to give the invocation. As he did so, Griswold rehearsed his speech in his mind. The printed words of the address would flow across three sheets of nonreflecting, bulletproof glass surrounding the podium. If he paused, the words paused; if he speeded up, they speeded up. He could read and no one would be the wiser. But he had rehearsed his speech so many times that he had most of it committed to memory.

He scanned the crowd. They trusted him with their dreams for their children, their hopes for a better job or for decent medical care, or for just the freedom to walk around safely in their own communities. The American dream. Another president—the dream rekindled.

Overwhelmed by his own thoughts, Griswold almost missed the cue to take Anne by the hand and walk toward the chief justice. His knees felt wobbly, his heart was thumping, and a sudden sensation clutched the pit of his stomach. He raised his right hand, trying to stop it from shaking; then the roar of the crowd slowly faded. "I, John Whitney Griswold, do solemnly swear. . . ."

Within moments he was the president of the United States.

Griswold's speech was an unusual blend of philosophies of government. On the one hand, he committed his administration to free market, supply-side economics. That meant lower taxes, free trade, allout economic growth. "Opportunity" and "empowerment" were words he frequently invoked. But there was paternalism as well: He promised that government would fulfill its duty to preserve order and justice, that more police and sterner punishment would make the streets safe again, and that more medical and social programs would help the needy and the homeless.

But his strongest theme was social libertarianism. In fact, the line that drew the most sustained applause was his promise to "not only get the government out of your pockets but out of your bedroom as well."

"We will achieve the concord of which Cicero wrote," he thundered," so that we can truly enjoy the rich life of a civil community. Decency and tolerance will once again be the distinguishing hallmarks of American life."

The crowd thundered back its approval.

Suddenly a surge of passion welled up within him; his face flushed. "But one thing we will not tolerate are those who would subvert our domestic tranquility. So help me God, we will do what we need to in order to protect the domestic order for the good and decent and caring people of our land."

His finger jabbed the air as he warned, "Let there be no mistake. Let those who would deny our most sacred birthright take notice: There is no price too high, no exertion too great, to safeguard our liberty. And I solemnly promise you I will do precisely that.

As he ended the speech and turned toward the door leading back to the Capitol, outstretched palms jutted toward him from the senators, congressmen and women, judges, and other dignitaries lining the steps. He basked in the glow of the sun and the thunderous roar from the crowd.

Capitol police and Secret Service agents elbowed one another to guide the first family to a brief reception in the rotunda. From there they were taken to their limousine which would lead the inaugural parade from the Capitol, down Pennsylvania Avenue, and on to the White House.

The Griswolds, for the first time, stepped into the long black Cadillac with its bulletproof glass and half-ton of armor plating. One front fender bore a flag with the Great Seal of the United

States, the other the Stars and Stripes. Four agents wearing sunglasses and earphones climbed on the running boards, two on either side. A cordon of forty motorcycle police moved ahead, the rumble of their engines filling the air, and two station wagons full of agents and the president's doctor trailed close behind.

The parade route was lined with temporary bleachers, four hundred thousand board feet of lumber, all constructed for this one moment. But all Griswold could see were the faces, all colors and shapes, all smiling and waving flags and banners. Such genuine jubilation. *They trusted him.* He waved from side to side as did Anne. Robert and Elizabeth, however, sat stiffly in the jumpseats along with Major George Hughes, the marine aide, who was wearing dress blues with a gold epaulet draped from his shoulder.

The Secret Service had warned Griswold not to get out of the car. There had been more than the usual number of threats, and the police had spotted two suspicious-looking men in a car near Rockville, Maryland; they had found a high-powered rifle with telescopic sight in the trunk. The men were being detained in a suburban jail. One anti-abortion group was reported to be planning to throw human blood on the president's limousine. Then there were all the usual crazies the agents kept files on, more than two thousand of them.

As the motorcade slowed the first time, Griswold noticed a group of school girls, probably from a parochial school because they were all wearing blue jackets, white shirts, and dark blue skirts. They reminded him of Elizabeth. They were standing just behind the barricades carrying "We Trust You" signs.

"Oh, Whitney," Anne sighed as he hit the door handle and jumped into the street. Major Hughes followed.

Instantly Robbie barked into his radio and four agents from the wagon in back surrounded the president, even as Griswold vainly attempted to wave them away. Taking long strides, he moved toward the girls and started grabbing hands. Television crews were running to catch up.

Just then Griswold looked up and saw two men, wearing black

jackets and black watch caps, elbowing toward him through the crowd in front of the bleachers. When they were not more than twenty feet away, they unfurled a huge banner lettered in red: "Stop Killing Babies." The television cameras caught the scene of Griswold staring at the sign.

The crowd began to press in, and the police were having trouble holding the barricades. Troops in dress uniforms now closed the line. Finally, Griswold waved broadly to the cheering crowd and, just as the motorcade turned onto Fifteenth Street, walked briskly back to the limousine.

"For goodness sakes, Whitney, think of us if nothing else. You know the dangers," Anne said angrily, but the president just kept waving to the crowds as the limousine moved onto Pennsylvania Avenue, whose barricades had been removed for the occasion, and past the White House, where the driver turned through the northwest gates onto the grounds.

There, the first family was escorted behind the great reviewing stand, up steps covered with red carpet, and into a heated, bulletproof glass-enclosed presidential box.

Robert's eyes lighted, "All right! Just like the owner's box at Shea Stadium."

Elizabeth also brightened at the spectacle. There were marching bands from every state, and floats with banners proclaiming Griswold's themes: "Bring Us Together," "We Trust Griswold," "The New Enlightenment," "Decency Again."

For the president, the most impressive display was the U. S. Marine Corps Marching Band led by the drill team of forty men marching in perfect precision without a command, spinning their rifles in the air, bayonets unsheathed and gleaming in the sun.

"Flawless, flawless! Bravo!" Griswold applauded. "Remember Tocqueville," he said to no one in particular, overwhelmed by the sentiment of the moment. This was the world's wealthiest and most powerful nation on parade, celebrating the oldest constitutional democracy on earth. "'America is great because America is good.' What's the rest of that quote?"

"'If America ever ceases to be good, she will no longer be great,'" said Robbie.

"Yes, that's it," the president said, rubbing his hands together after returning the salute of passing troops. "We will keep her good and great. That's why we're here."

FOLLOWING THE WHIRL of inaugural balls, the Griswolds, exhausted, arrived back at the White House for one last reception for close supporters held in the diplomatic receiving room in the basement. Then Major Hughes escorted the first family to the main floor where the head usher, Rex Leonard, two agents, and Juan Garcia, the navy steward assigned as the president's valet, were waiting.

After a day of bands and roaring crowds, the White House seemed eerily serene, and Robert and Elizabeth examined the portraits in the Great Hall as Leonard steered them to the family elevator at the west end of the hall.

"Welcome to our new home, kids," Griswold sighed. "We made it."

The agents explained that one of them would remain on duty on the main floor, one in the basement, and another was in the control room in the west wing. In addition, executive police were at their positions all around the grounds. The president thanked them, and the usher led the family into the elevator to the second floor.

The quiet now was almost unsettling. All alone in this huge place, thought Anne, you could almost imagine that all the stories about Lincoln's ghost were true. Elizabeth squeezed her mother's hand as Leonard led them to the right toward the west hall, where a beautiful living room separated the president's bedroom from the first lady's.

Most first families had kept the same, somewhat impersonal arrangement, and with good reason: the president often had to be awakened in the night. Some presidents, like Lyndon Johnson, roamed the corridors when, as was often the case, they couldn't sleep. Nixon had made a habit of sleeping from 11 :00 P.M. to

2:00 A.M., then waking up to work for two hours in the Lincoln sitting room, then sleeping again from 4:00 until 7:00. Others, who had taken a more liberal view of marriage, had found the arrangement convenient for other reasons.

At the west end of the hall, the usher opened the door to the spacious room with its elegant Palladian windows, through which the flag, illuminated by a spotlight on the roof of the west wing, could be seen unfurled in the night breeze. Elizabeth let go of her mother's hand and, with a grin, dropped into the downy cushions of one of the bright yellow-and-cream brocade sofas. Robert walked around the room, then went over and peered out the window.

The Griswolds, who had stayed the night before in Blair House, had been given an earlier tour of their new home and thorough briefings by the Secret Service. All of their clothing and personal belongings had been delivered to the mansion precisely at noon that day, and the staff had already placed them neatly in closets and bureau drawers.

"Both the stairs and the elevator will take you to the children's bedrooms on the third floor. Would you like me to show you the way?" Rex Leonard asked.

"We're not children," Robert grumbled, just loud enough for his father to hear him and frown at him.

"No, Mr. Leonard, we've been through all the rooms," Griswold said. "We're fine. Juan, here," he said, nodding at his valet, "can help us, but you've been very helpful."

"Thank you, Mr. President. And remember, an agent will be at his station in the Great Hall downstairs all night. Any of the staff is, of course, available at your call."

"Yes, yes, much obliged, but we are just fine," Griswold assured him as the usher closed the door and left.

"Juan, the Dom Perignon, please—and Cokes for Robert and Elizabeth." The president grinned at his valet, who turned and headed for the kitchen just beyond the family dining room on the north side of the living room.

"I'm so tired, Whitney," said Anne. "I'm not sure I can stay up another minute."

"Just one glass, Anne! This is a night we'll always remember. A historic night for the nation—and for our family!"

Anne smiled and nodded, but Elizabeth was not impressed. "I don't like it here, Daddy," she broke in.

Garcia returned just then with a magnificent silver tray and a bucket full of ice with the neck of the champagne bottle just visible. Bowing slightly, he quietly retreated.

"You will, darling, you'll get used to it, and you'll make new friends." Griswold pulled off his tie and unbuttoned his collar.

"I like my old friends. Besides, it's creepy here. "

Anne moved over and sat next to her daughter, putting her arm around her. "Everything will be fine, dear. You'll see."

Elizabeth ignored her mother. "Daddy, you promised if I didn't like it here I could go back to Hotchkiss. You promised."

They had made the decision to move Elizabeth to Washington, where she would attend the all-female National Cathedral School. Better for security, among other reasons. Robert, however, would stay at Groton. To Elizabeth, it didn't seem fair that she had to leave her old school.

"Elizabeth, you and I will talk about it tomorrow," said Anne while Griswold bent the wires back from the cork. "But you need to give the Cathedral School a chance."

"I can tell you why she wants to stay at Hotchkiss, Dad," Robert chimed in.

"Shut up, Robert." Elizabeth glared at her brother.

"She's got a boyfriend at school," Robert announced just as the cork flew out of the champagne and foam ran down over his father's dress pants and the handsome floral-patterned rug.

"Well, why haven't you told me about this, honey?" her father asked as he swung the foaming bottle back over the silver tray.

Elizabeth blushed, and her mother said, "We'll talk about it tomorrow, Whitney. Pour the champagne, please."

Griswold filled two crystal glasses to the rim and handed one to Anne. The children got their Cokes.

"To our beloved country." He raised his glass. "To keeping

our trust. May we do everything we can—as a family—to make this a better and safer nation."

Anne took a sip. Griswold downed half the glass, then sat down and kicked off his black patent leather shoes.

"Well, well," he said. "A boyfriend. My little girl." He shook his head.

"She's not a little girl, Whitney," Anne said, slipping her arm around her silent daughter's shoulder. "She's a young lady."

"Well, we'll talk about that later, too. Great champagne, isn't it?" he said as he filled his glass a second time. He hit a buzzer beside the chair and Garcia appeared in the doorway.

"Juan, would you escort the children to their rooms and be sure they have everything they need?" He turned to the children, "It's very late. You get ready for bed, and your mother and I will be right up."

As Robert and Elizabeth followed Garcia out of the room, Anne walked over to her husband, leaned down, and kissed him lightly. "She'll be fine, dear. I'm going up to help her. We just need a little girl talk. You come in a few minutes. "

"Good, Anne, thank you." Griswold was already reaching for the red folder the agent in charge had given him on security procedures.

ANNE HAD CHOSEN SMALLER ROOMS on the third floor for Robert and Elizabeth. They were adjacent to each other on the south side, across from the Washington Monument. There was plenty of space on the main floor, but she wanted them to have their own area, a more normal environment, away from all the guests and traffic. Besides, the third floor reminded her of their home in Greenwich, Connecticut. The ceilings weren't nearly so high as downstairs, and it had a homey feel.

Anne sat on the edge of Elizabeth's bed. "This button here, just press it, and Juan or Daddy will be here before you can blink an eye."

"Mom, this place is weird." Elizabeth's lip was quivering. The excitement of the day, the strangeness of the White House, away from all her friends and facing a new school . . . Anne knew her daughter was feeling overwhelmed and frightened, and she hugged her hard.

"I hear a noise outside the window," Elizabeth said.

"It's the wind, honey, just the wind."

"No, Mom, I hear something."

Anne stood up, walked to the window, drew the drapes to the side, and looked out. "There's nothing out there," she said, "nothing except the most beautiful view in the whole world."

Anne reached up to unlatch the window and open it so Elizabeth could see that it was only the wind, forgetting that she had been told never to stand in the window at night, silhouetted against the light. There was no bulletproof glass on the third floor.

IN W-16, the Secret Service headquarters located in the basement directly under the Oval Office, Agent Callahan saw the red light flash before he heard the buzzer. He had been leaning back in his chair, sipping coffee, and watching a thirteen-inch television set on the back of his desk.

He jumped up, spilling coffee while yelling into his hand-held radio, "Alert, alert, red one, third floor residence, station six." A giant electronic map of the White House pinpointed the precise location of the alarm.

Oh, no, he thought. *The first night—just my luck. Only Matthews and Brown here with me.*

"Come in, Matthews. Where are you?" he snapped into the radio. "Move, man."

"I'm headed for the quarters, chief," came back the reply. "Brown's behind me."

Searchlights strategically placed around the White House grounds activated automatically. The executive police at the gate were alerted, and several drew their weapons. At the kennel across from the tennis court, two officers brought out two German shepherds. Executive police stepped out onto an Executive Office Building balcony, handheld stinger surface-to-air missiles at the ready. They had practiced so many times it was almost a reflex reaction.

Griswold had heard the bell and bolted out of his chair. He needed an instant to orient himself, then realized the alarm was upstairs. He headed for the kitchen stairwell, bounded up the circular staircase three steps at a time, and turned into the corridor. But he was not as fast as Brown and Matthews, who were running directly toward him from the center stairwell, both with submachine guns at the ready.

The president froze as the two agents reached Elizabeth's door and swung it open so hard it smashed against the wall.

Elizabeth sat up in bed, screaming. Anne stood helplessly, a telephone receiver in hand.

"False alarm, chief," Brown spoke into his wrist radio. "All secure."

Griswold came in wide-eyed and breathless.

"I'm sorry, ma'am," Matthews said. "Did you open that window?"

Anne nodded.

"See that key there on the side?" he said and pointed. "That has to be deactivated first. It will turn green when you turn it to the right. You should have been briefed ma'am. "

Robert was standing in the door, rolling his eyes upward and shaking his head. Elizabeth was sobbing.

"I'm sorry," Anne said. "We went over so many things in the briefing. I just forgot."

"You gentlemen are good. I'm impressed," said Griswold. "We're sorry for the alarm."

The agents returned to their stations, and Anne took Elizabeth down to her room for the night.

LATER, WHITNEY GRISWOLD still could not sleep. He tossed for an hour, then got up, put on his camel-colored bathrobe and leather slippers, and walked down the hall to the Lincoln sitting room.

From this room, Abraham Lincoln had directed the Civil War. Griswold felt his cheeks flush and his stomach churn at the thought. Maybe he hadn't been kidding the family. Maybe ghosts did roam these corridors. He gingerly ran his fingers over the tufted yellow velvet chair in the corner before sitting down.

He stared for a long moment at the painting of Lincoln on the wall just inside the door. Then he checked his watch. 2:15. Doubtless there would be many nights like this. He'd been briefed by four of his predecessors, and all had warned him of the terrible pressures, the need for discipline and stamina.

"Only do those things that only the president can do," they had cautioned. "But even that is job enough for six strong people."

Though the problems seemed great at the time, he thought, being governor of a state with three million people was nothing by comparison.

The strange burning sensation in his stomach continued, and for a fleeting moment, Griswold found himself almost praying for wisdom. He'd never done anything like that before. He scribbled a little note on the pad next to his chair to ask the rector of St. John's to make that point—the need for prayer—in the service he would attend on Sunday. St. John's, directly across Lafayette Park from the White House, was known as the church of the presidents.

Still he felt that strange sensation. Might he, somehow, be the kind of leader who could heal the nation? Surely he was no Lincoln, but the nation needed healing. His own party was divided. The evangelicals who had supported Masterson had no use for him, and the feelings were mutual. The country was bitterly divided; abortion foes were increasingly militant. Homosexual groups were angry that the government hadn't done enough for AIDS, even with the new technologies coming down the pike. Minorities were increasingly restless, and the condition of the inner cities was horrible.

What was it Masterson had written to him, late on election

night, after he had conceded? Griswold had a gift for remembering precise words; now parts of Masterson's fax came back to him. He had cast it aside at the time, laughing about it with Bernie. But now he remembered.

"You can with reason, love, and compassion begin to end the terrible divisions that are rending the very fabric of our common life," Masterson had written. "But it will take courage the nation has not known since Lincoln."

Griswold stared again at the great president's portrait. He remembered, too, that Masterson had promised to pray for him. He hoped he was doing so.

For several moments he sat quietly, contemplating all that lay ahead. The enormity of his own responsibility was overwhelming. But he remembered the old Yale professor's words: "to whom much is given, much is required." The time had come to fulfill his life's destiny. And that meant, now, in every decision he faced, every day, he had to do the right thing. People trusted him. He could not let them down. That meant pure politics was behind him now. He had to do his best to be a good president. Even a great one.

TWO MILES AWAY in a red brick federal townhouse in Georgetown, Bernie O'Keefe sat alone with his thoughts as well, sipping what he vowed would be his final Dewars on the rocks for the evening. He had had more than he wanted to count. Marilyn and the kids had gone to bed hours ago.

It had been a momentous day. His kids had loved it, but they were all returning to Boston that weekend—with Marilyn. She had insisted that the children finish their school year in Wellesley. They would decide later if they should all move to Washington.

His wife had inherited her Italian father's jet-black hair and her Irish mother's blue eyes. And from both she'd gotten a fiery temper and a stubbornness even more iron-willed than his.

Bernie had been making $700,000 a year practicing law and dabbling in politics. His $140,000 government salary would not support the mortgages on two homes, the pricey summer rental on Martha's Vineyard, and three kids in private school. And Marilyn wouldn't even think of public schools in D. C.

No doubt about it, politics had put more distance between them, Bernie thought, not that things had ever really been that good. He was always preoccupied—if not on the phone, then deep in thought. So Marilyn had made her own life, playing golf during the day, bridge at night, active in several charities. Even on this jubilant evening they had exchanged bitter words.

Bernie stirred his drink with his index finger. Good thing Marilyn was in bed; she hated that habit. She also thought he drank too much. Nothing new. Bernie took another sip.

Tomorrow we begin running the government, he thought. I still can't believe it. We've made it, and we're gonna make a difference. We're gonna bring things together, help the people, heal the nation.

For now, though, his drink was drained, and so was he. Bernie put his glass down, staggered out of the box-cluttered study, and made his way upstairs to the bedroom. Marilyn rolled over, looked at Bernie, then at the clock, shook her head, and went back to sleep.

11

THE MARINE SENTRY at the door under the portico
of the west wing entrance to the White House looked
like he had just stepped out of a recruiting poster. He
stood ramrod straight, his forearm snapped into a perfect forty-
five degree angle so that his white glove just touched the tip of
his polished black visor.

Emily Gineen noted that Anthony Frizzell, who had been
the FBI director for five years, barely nodded in response to the
sentry's salute. To be so preoccupied with the weighty matters
of state that one hardly noticed others was one of the most visible marks of the Washington powerful; she had learned that
already. Today, however, neither of them needed to feign the
appearance of being weighed down by responsibilities. The president had summoned them to the Oval Office to discuss the
Fargo killing.

The two were ushered immediately through the reception
room, down the corridor running from the press room past the
cabinet room, and into a small office where the two secretaries
barely nodded, then returned to their word processors. A Secret
Service agent motioned for them to wait just behind a door
which, except for its bare, pencil-thin outline, looked like part

of the wall; it was the side entrance used mostly by staff. There was a faint buzz, then a click, and the agent swung the door open.

For Emily, this citadel of power was as dazzling as it had been yesterday when she was sworn in. Though the day outside was gray and wintry, the room seemed flooded with light, illuminating the Great Seal of the United States embroidered in the large, deep-blue, oval rug that covered all but a narrow border of wood running around the room. To the right was a fireplace with birch logs crackling in the flames, and at the other end of the room, flanked by flags, Whitney Griswold sat at his desk.

The president, his half-circle reading glasses perched on the end of his nose, was studying a single sheet of paper. Harvey Robbins and Bernie O'Keefe sat quietly in two straight-backed Chippendale chairs on either side of the desk. The president bounded to his feet as they entered.

"Emily, come in. Good, good. And Director Frizzell. Thank you for coming." He shook their hands and pointed them to two empty chairs in front of the desk. Robbins and O'Keefe stood up, smiled, nodded, and sat down without saying a word.

"Getting settled in all right, Emily?" Griswold grinned.

"Yes, Mr. President. All twenty-four hours' worth. But everything is under control, sir." Emily feigned confidence. In truth, she had barely found her way around her new office.

"Good, good," the president nodded. Then his demeanor abruptly shifted as he leaned forward.

"Now, this is my first official meeting, except for yesterday's formalities, of course, and the CIA defense briefing—the spook community is all over a new president like a blanket." It was Griswold's way of impressing on the attorney general and FBI director the gravity of the Fargo killing.

"So let's get right to it. This is the first real crisis we have to face, and I want to hit it hard. Rotten way to start, but here it is." There was a stern intensity in Griswold's voice that surprised Emily. She nodded, as did Frizzell.

"I've, of course, read all your reports, Mr. Director, but I want it firsthand. I've got to make the decisions now." Emily's heart was pounding, and she was relieved that Griswold was staring at Frizzell, rather than at her.

"Let's begin with this letter." The president pulled from the sheaf of papers before him a copy of the open letter that had been sent to Levitz at the *Post*.

"What is this Holocaust Resistance? I want to know everything you know about these murderers—everything."

Frizzell hardly waited for the president to finish. "Well, sir, the bureau has been right on top of this since the shooting. There is no Holocaust Resistance as such. We're quite sure of that. It's got to be some person or persons who are part of the pro-life movement. This letter was to send you a message, sir, from the movement."

"Well, I've gotten their message. And they're going to get mine. My answer is act fast and stamp this thing out, or we'll have a new wave of violence like we had a few years ago."

"Yes sir," Frizzell said. "You've analyzed it precisely right, Mr. President. It's a warning shot. More to follow. But we'll beat them to the punch, I can assure you of that, sir."

Emily watched as the president nodded appreciatively. Frizzell, whose bureaucratic skills, particularly in promoting the FBI's image of invincibility were legendary, was in total control. She hadn't opened her mouth yet.

"All right then, Mr. Director, what leads do we have?" asked Griswold.

"We've got a hunt under way with a lot of good leads, sir. We'll get the killer. Rest assured of that. But I want something more. I want the whole conspiracy this time. We're spreading the net wide." Frizzell grinned.

"What do you mean 'this time'?" Griswold was leaning forward in his chair, one fist propped under his chin.

"Well, before, sir, like in the John Salvi or Paul Hill cases, we got just the gunman. But we suspected there were others involved. Grand juries were impaneled back then, but they botched it. We want them all this time . . . if we can get the prosecutors with us, that is." He glanced at Emily and smiled.

"Good, good," the president nodded.

"And we'll do it this time, sir, because we now have assets throughout the militant parts of the movement."

"Assets?"

Frizzell smiled, hesitated a moment, glancing at Robbins and O'Keefe.

"It's all right," the president assured him. "What do you mean?"

"An asset's an informer—an agent in their ranks. We've infiltrated most of the groups, including one here in Washington that is very interesting. They call themselves The Life Network and are supposedly nonviolent, merely wanting to expose the horrors of abortion, as they put it. But you never know. Then there's another group in Chicago. Actually there are eight or ten major ones across the country that we're certain of. Some are very, very dangerous, Mr. President, but we're inside."

Gineen watched Frizzell with admiration. According to his record, the FBI director had begun right out of Fordham as a street agent. A tough cookie who'd survived a big drug-bust shootout, he'd been decorated, promoted, and become special agent in charge in Memphis at age thirty-five. He'd made it onto the federal bench at thirty-nine and been named head of the bureau five years ago at age forty-two. Seemingly overnight he'd remade it in his own no-nonsense image. The street boys loved him, and no one in Justice ever crossed him. She could see why. He had taken over the meeting, knew more than the president, proved that the FBI was on the job, and made the situation sound so dangerous the president couldn't afford not to listen to him, all in three minutes. Yes, he was good, and this was Washington.

"Now, Director, is all this infiltration, this asset business, within the law? I want no wanton searches or other shortcuts in my presidency." Griswold tapped the desk with his index finger. The idea of stealing the other side's signals bothered him a little.

"Everything done in due process, sir. We have plenty of authority. These groups fall under the terrorist categories of the statute Congress passed after the World Trade Center bombing.

With groups like this we can do almost anything—all within the law." He grinned. "So we just have agents doing their job, sir."

"If the agents were doing their job, Director, how come we didn't know that these people were going to attack Fargo a week before I came into this office?"

Frizzell didn't miss a beat. Most of the pro-life movement, he explained, had remained nonviolent. "That's changing, though," he warned. "The problem is, these groups are loosely connected, relatively independent cells spread around the country. Some simply run around carrying signs. Others, like this The Life Network group in Washington, simply seem to be making information public. And some of them are clearly trying to intimidate abortion clinic workers. Even though we have the authority, our resources are spread pretty thin. We just need more enforcement."

But the bureau was after them, he said. Like all zealot movements, there were very dangerous individuals spread throughout. Frizzell used the word "terrorist" continuously.

While the FBI director was giving his detailed briefing, Griswold leaned forward with his elbow on the desk and his chin cupped in his left palm. His questions were sharp and quick: What could be done to monitor the movement more effectively? Could a conspiracy be proved? How would anti-racketeering statutes apply? What was being done to search for the killer? Robbins and O'Keefe were also listening intently, taking notes.

Griswold leaned back in his chair. "All right, then, we all understand the facts. Let's get on with the job—fast. I realize these people are testing me; the timing is deliberate, of course. But our job is to get them before they strike again.

"What the nation has to know is that we're in charge. It was, I think, 1918 or 1919 . . . check that Robbie . . . when Calvin Coolidge, governor of Massachusetts, called out the National Guard to break a police strike. Didn't say much, Coolidge didn't, but he was quick and tough. Made him a national figure and got him seated at this desk in short order. Well, there's a lesson here. We need to act fast and tough . . . but by the rules. Is that understood?"

There was a chorus of "Yes sirs."

"All right, Emily, you're in charge." Griswold's directive startled her. It was the first time he had addressed her since his initial greeting, but he was apparently well aware of the protocol. "I want marshals stationed at every clinic."

"We've got them spread around the country as best we're able, sir," she said. "We've got more marshals at abortion clinics than we do in the courtrooms."

"Get more if you have to, Emily. Whatever it takes. And I want the Freedom of Access to Clinic Entrances Act enforced. I mean tough. Get rough."

"Yes sir. The department has been using it in every instance over the past few years."

"Well, use it everywhere. You see, Emily, I want you to go after the whole movement here. These people claim that they're exercising peaceful protest, but by their violent language they are inciting violence. Wasn't it Oliver Wendell Holmes who talked about that?"

"Yes sir," Emily agreed. "There's a limit on free speech. You can't shout fire in a crowded movie theater."

"Yes, that's it. We're going after this whole movement. But I must tell you: We're to observe every statutory restraint and constitutional protection." Then he smiled. "But I don't have to tell you that. You're the professor of constitutional law."

Gineen nodded, but before she could reply, Griswold moved to Frizzell. "Director, put your best men and women on this. Spare nothing. We want to know what they're going to do before they do it."

"Yes sir, we will." Frizzell grinned.

"You call Robbie day or night if you need me. And from our end, Bernie here is my man. He knows me. He knows the law. You can deal with him as if you're dealing with me. Understood?"

Griswold didn't wait for the chorus but kept right on, the captain giving his oarsmen a pep talk. "And remember, firm action. Decisive. Quick. We nip this in the bud. Has to be done in days, not months. Understood?"

As there was another chorus of "Yes sirs," and Emily and Frizzell were going out the door, the president called out, "One more thing, Emily. We'll make a brief statement here, of course, in the press room. Any problem if we say we'll seek the death penalty for the criminal when apprehended?"

Emily stared at him for an instant while searching her mental casebook. Could it be prejudice? Could defense counsel use it? But before she finished her search, Frizzell assured the president that the bureau would have no objection.

Emily glared at him, then spoke firmly, "I'm the prosecutor, Mr. President, and I want a conviction. For the president of the United States to refer to the death penalty might be considered prejudicial—attempting to influence a jury. I'd recommend, sir, you just say we will prosecute to the fullest extent of the law."

"All right," the president nodded. "Got that, Robbie?"

AS FRIZZELL and Gineen left by the side door, Griswold turned to his aides. "Well, what do you think?"

Robbie, who had hardly opened his mouth during the meeting, broke into a grin. "Mr. President, this is more than we could have hoped for. Look at this latest poll I got just before the meeting began." He laid a single sheet of paper on the president's desk.

Griswold put his glasses on, sat back, and scanned the figures, pursing his lips and exhaling a whistling sound. "Well, well, Robbie. Good work. We've been doing something right, I gather." The poll was almost double the percentage by which he had been elected. "Sixty-seven percent," Griswold grinned.

"But look at the break-out of your personal qualities, sir," said Robbie. "Eighty percent list your decisiveness, 76 percent your integrity, 72 percent strength of character. You see, just what our focus group tells us. People are worried about crime and what they perceive as the breakup of our society. What they want more than anything else is a strong leader. They want order."

Griswold nodded. "But this killing will unsettle them. That can hurt us."

"No, I don't think so, sir, and if we work fast, I see it as an opportunity. You take charge. Crack down. These are the bad guys. I say we go for them. Not just the murderer in this particular case, but the whole network, wherever we can find them," Robbie said. "Remember your history, Mr. President. Franklin Roosevelt. He became hugely popular by making the National Association of Manufacturers his public enemy number one."

Griswold nodded.

"And these are the fundamentalists, tops on everyone's bad-guy list—45 percent in Gallup's poll didn't want one living next door. It's a natural, sir."

Griswold nodded again.

"And I think you should put Frizzell right out front. He's so eager to please you, he'll be out in the streets with his Uzi blazing. I mean this character was born for this part. You think of a racketbusting cop, and you've got Frizzell, Eliot Ness reincarnated. Perfect. Besides, Bernie will like him. He's half Irish."

"That's all fine, Robbie, I understand the politics," said Griswold, "but remember, we must do the right thing. The campaign is over now."

"The right thing? Yes sir. These people are evil. They kill people. They must be stopped. And it happens to be the right politics." Robbie kept running his hand through his close-cropped hair, which he did on those rare occasions when he got really excited.

"Robbie's right, Mr. President." Bernie spoke slowly, subduing his natural impulsiveness to create the aura of the deliberate, thoughtful lawyer-philosopher. "You cannot separate politics from the art of governing. Your task, sir, is one of moral suasion. We're not interested in polls just to get re-elected," he paused with a wry grin, "but because they measure how well your persona and policies are moving this country."

"So what are you saying, Bernie? Be a lawyer now." Griswold was twirling his glasses by one stem.

"Go after them, Mr. President. Simple as that. I knew little about these groups before we came into this meeting. I thought this was one crazy knocking off one money-grubbing abortionist—neither one any good in my book. But this pro-life movement—what's left of it anyway—is dedicated to your defeat. They'll be nothing but trouble for four years. I've been worried how we're going to deal with them. But now, with incredible stupidity, they've handed you the sword with which you slay them," Bernie said, grinning widely.

"We're not just after a murderer here; we have a movement claiming credit. So you strike now, go for the movement, discredit it, break it up. The people are with you. They'll cheer you for it. Right now we can do anything—and we'll be rid of them—that will make life easier from here on out. Not to mention what it will do to show up the Mastersons and the rest of those renegades."

Bernie shook his head. "I can't believe their stupidity. If I didn't know that Robbie here was a man of exemplary integrity, I'd think maybe he wrote the letter himself."

The three men roared with laughter.

What had started out as an unpleasant intrusion into Griswold's first days in office didn't look so bad after all. Thoughts of what breaking the police strike had done for Coolidge and what campaigning against big business had done for Roosevelt danced in Griswold's mind. Yes, clearly this was an opportunity.

As Robbie left to brief Caroline Atwater and prepare a press statement, Griswold turned to Bernie.

"You call Gineen and emphasize how important swift, tough, decisive action is. We may need to do more here. Maybe wiretaps, more informers. She needs to understand that the job is not just to prosecute but to break a movement. These are subversives, really. Dangerous people."

Bernie was nodding.

"You know what to say. I obviously can't be quite so blunt, and of course you keep me out of it. But take care of it, Bernie."

His friend smiled and nodded. He knew exactly what

Griswold wanted. Use whatever it takes, shove the other guy's face in the mud. This was the way Yankee Brahmins played the game. They used tough Irish boys to do their dirty work. Bernie had been faithfully doing this for J. Whitney Griswold for more than twenty years.

CAROLINE ATWATER called a special press briefing at 5:00 P. M. that day. The Griswold team already knew the tricks of the trade: 5:00 was perfect, just enough time for the networks to make their 6:30 or 7:00 feed but not quite enough for the commentators or critics to organize a rebuttal. This story would be covered, and it would get just the spin the White House wanted. Atwater, standing before the blue screen with the rendering of the White House behind her, reviewed the day's events, referring to government intelligence reports indicating that the assailant in North Dakota had not been acting alone but as part of an organized conspiracy. She announced that more U. S. marshals would be dispatched to guard clinics and that all government agencies would cooperate with the Justice Department.

She concluded her prepared text: "The president has authorized me to say that he has ordered the attorney general to use every means at this government's disposal to bring the guilty to justice with the maximum penalty the law allows. But beyond that, this administration will not tolerate such terrorist acts. An action like this declares war on peace-loving Americans, and whenever that has happened in the past, Americans have responded. Let those who would challenge our freedoms know of our resolve: We will take whatever steps are necessary in defense of liberty."

"Who's declared war?"

"What conspiracy?"

The reporters stood waving their notebooks in the air, bombarding the press secretary with questions. But she smiled, folded up her briefing book, turned and walked off the platform without a word. Bernie had programmed her perfectly.

AT THE JUSTICE DEPARTMENT, Emily Gineen was handed a fax of Atwater's statement only moments before 5:00. She shook her head as she read. This didn't sound like the cool, carefully calculated Griswold she had met with only hours earlier. But then the call from O'Keefe hadn't made sense either. His instructions about "getting tough, breaking the movement" sounded more like overzealous aides than Whitney Griswold. The government clearly could overplay this.

Emily made a mental note to raise her cautions with the president the next time they spoke.

AT 5:20 P.M., Ben Thomas, Capitol Hill reporter for ABC, reached room 141 of the Russell Senate Office Building. It was worth a try to get a reaction from the ranking Judiciary Committee Republican.

Thomas was in luck. Langer was in and agreed. So the reporter's cameraman set up in the corridor with the door to the senator's office in the background, his nameplate perfectly framed in the lens.

Langer was used to the twenty-second rule and kept his remarks short and blunt. "Whoever did this despicable act must be brought to justice. But we should keep things in perspective. In the long and emotional struggle over abortion, there have been relatively few such incidents. So I would hope the government would not use this as an excuse to suppress legitimate dissent. In this city, there remain some who take the words of the Constitution quite seriously."

Perfect. One-third of a minute to the second.

Thomas sent his cameramen rushing to the Senate gallery where the tape would be fed instantaneously to New York. The editors would slide such sound bites in right up until the last minute, and it was a good take. New York always liked a little confrontation, and Langer was a pro. He was also a friend.

"All right, Byron, we're off camera now," Thomas said when they were alone. "What do you make of Atwater's statement?

What's the White House angle here?"

Langer frowned, tightening his lips and folding his arms across his chest. "I don't know, Ben; I don't know. But it doesn't feel right. Doesn't feel right at all. We're heading for trouble, I think."

Langer looked up as if he had been caught in his own thoughts. Then he shook his head and said it again. "Big trouble."

12

I 'M READY, if you'd like to take my order," Jennifer Barrett said to the young woman behind the deli counter. "I'll have the vegetable pita sandwich, hold the cheese, extra cucumber instead."

"As long as you're making one, you might as well make two of those," Alex Seaton added. "I'll have the same."

He took the bottle of seltzer Jennifer was holding and picked up two red apples from the straw basket on the counter. "Let me take care of this."

"No," Jennifer said. "Come on, let me pay. I invited you."

"You can take me next time." Alex grinned. *If there was a next time,* he thought.

They picked up their paper-wrapped sandwiches and headed to a table near the deli's picture window, which overlooked an ice-skating rink where wool-bundled children swooped and slid on the ice while their mothers hovered nearby, clumped in conversational knots. Jennifer unwrapped her sandwich and neatly smoothed out the white paper, folding it into a square. She paused, and Alex said a short blessing over their food.

"Thanks for buying lunch, Alex," she said when he finished. "I just thought I'd be bold and see if we could get together. I've moved around so much over the last few years, I've found that the best way to get to know people is to go ahead and take the initiative. If you wait for people to come to you, you end up waiting for a long time."

"I appreciate you giving me a call," Alex said. "Some people seem to think everyone should come to them; they're not willing to be the first to reach out. Do you feel like you're getting settled in Washington?"

Jennifer picked up a sprout that had fallen out of her sandwich. "I love it here," she said. "There's always so much going on. I haven't been able to find a full-time job yet, so I've been temping. I've worked at offices all over the city, and in some of the suburbs too. I really like it here in Weston, though—so many trees, and the bike paths are great.

"And some days I don't have work, so I just take the Metro downtown and walk around. The Smithsonian is tremendous, and I can't get over the fact that the museums are free. I lived in Philadelphia before this, and you have to pay to get in anywhere there. Even the zoo. "

"Your federal tax dollars at work," said Alex. "Have you been to the Holocaust Museum?"

"I went right after I came," Jennifer said. "It was one of the most incredible experiences of my life. I think every adult in America should go there. It sears your conscience."

Across the room three young businessmen were looking for a table, balancing steak-and-cheese subs and Cokes on plastic trays heaped high with bags of potato chips. They made their way to the table next to Alex and Jennifer.

"Excuse me," said one as he bumped past Jennifer's chair. "You've got a nice view of the ice skaters." He smiled, and his eyes lingered just a little too long on her legs.

Jennifer's startling blue gaze was often so direct it was disconcerting, but now she broke eye contact with the young man almost immediately. "No problem," she said, then turned back to Alex.

"Have you been there?"

"Where?" he asked, momentarily distracted by the Neanderthal at the next table.

"The Holocaust Museum," she said, smiling and taking a bite of her sandwich.

"Oh, yes, I went there right after it opened," he said. "I've been back a number of times. When I look at the model of the crematorium at Auschwitz, sometimes I wonder if people in the future will one day look back at a model of an abortion facility, or one of these regeneration centers they're building now, and wonder how in the world it could have happened. Maybe they'll be as disgusted at the abortion holocaust as we are that the Nazis managed to murder six million Jews."

"Is that why you started the Network group?" she asked.

Alex took a long swallow of seltzer. "Daniel's the one who really started it," he said. "We've both been in the pro-life cause for a long time, but Daniel felt there needed to be a new organization with a more specific purpose than just being another protest group. He said we needed to expose the inner workings of the abortion industry: that if people see what's really going on, there's still enough of a core of common decency in our country that people would stand up against the regeneration centers. I kind of doubt it, though," he added. "And I wonder if it's really enough just to expose the evil."

Jennifer leaned forward slightly. "What about the shooting in Fargo?" she asked. "Do you support that kind of thing?"

"Of course not," Alex said quickly. He picked up his sandwich again. "What about you? Why did you get involved with us?"

She leaned back. "It's sort of a long story," she said.

"I grew up south of here, in Richmond. My father was an insurance executive, very successful. On the surface our family looked fine. We had a nice home, nice clothes, nice friends.

"But my dad was an alcoholic. He drank every night, but on the weekends he really went around the bend. And when he drank beyond a certain point, he was violent.

"My mother just took it. She was a classic enabler, if you're into those kind of tags. Didn't want to upset the applecart. My older sister compensated. She started looking for father figures everywhere. When she was a teenager, any older man would do. She was always getting involved with married men. And by the time she was twenty-five, she'd had three abortions.

"They were convenient, but they didn't help her at all. They just perpetuated the cycle she was on. No personal responsibility for her actions. More self-destructive behaviors. No self-respect. She just dwindled and dwindled as a person.

"The situation at home made me go the other way. When I was about sixteen, I decided that when women are weak, they get preyed upon one way or another. So I would be self-sufficient. I would be strong. I would take care of myself. By the time I left home for college, my dad knew better than to harass me, even verbally. Let alone physically.

"So I've always been in control, master of my own destiny, whatever. But about two years ago I realized I had over-compensated, that I did have needs I couldn't meet on my own. I worked with a woman who ended up inviting me to church, and I went with her. I decided I needed God. I take my faith very seriously. But now I'm not quite so self-sufficient."

Her smile gave Alex a strange feeling for a moment. He hadn't dated anyone since he and Sarah had broken up nearly a year ago, and he had forgotten that feeling.

"What are you waiting for?" Daniel had teased him. "You're a bachelor in your thirties. If you're planning to be a monk, then let me tell you something: You're in the wrong church."

At the time, Alex had told his brother, rather awkwardly, that maybe it was better for him to be free and unhindered, maybe he wasn't cut out to be in a relationship. Women took so much time, so much care and feeding.

Jennifer had finished her sandwich and was looking out the window at the skaters.

"Why don't we walk for a few minutes?" Alex said. "Do you have some time before you have to get back to your office? I've got the afternoon free. That's the great thing about being in construction: The winter months are lighter, business-wise, which gives me more time for the cause. Or, sometimes, for other things." He caught her eye, then immediately felt ridiculous.

But she smiled, looking at her watch. "I saw an espresso cart out there near the rink," she said. "Let's get some coffee and watch the skaters for a few minutes."

AS HE WATCHED THE PRESS CONFERENCE clip on the evening news, Daniel Seaton thought about William Butler Yeats's poem again. The same four lines had been turning over in his mind ever since he'd heard about the shooting in Fargo:

> *The blood-dimmed tide is loosed, and everywhere*
> *Else ceremony of innocence is drowned;*
> *The best lack all conviction, while the worst*
> *Are full of passionate intensity. . . .*

It was passionate intensity of the worst kind that had led to the murder in Fargo; now he could see it spilling over into official reactions here in Washington. *We have to be so careful*, he thought. *Violence begets violence.*

When Daniel and Alex had first discussed the idea of the The Life Network, they had talked at length about the narrow line they needed to walk. At the beginning they had brainstormed about whether there was any effective way to assault RU-486. Many pro-life groups had urged boycotts. The two of them had concurred but felt them to be of limited effectiveness.

Then had come the first clouds on the horizon regarding the regeneration centers. With the help of Lance and others, they had collected every article and clue they could find. Sympathetic doctors at Johns Hopkins, NIH, and other facilities had helped. Many medical professionals were shocked by the prospect of live-fetal brain suctioning, and their group had gradually built a substantial network of friends in high and useful places.

After hearing the president's remarks, Daniel had gone into his office and deleted several key files from his computer. He had also pulled out his address book, a few manila file folders, and a list of phone numbers. Better to be prudent, he had thought. The time might well come when any concrete information and connections would need to be destroyed.

He didn't have time to memorize all the names and numbers tonight, though; Alex and the others would be here soon. So he sealed all the papers in a Ziploc bag and stowed the bag, for safekeeping, in the bottom of his toddler son's diaper pail. When he showed Mary, she rolled her eyes but said nothing.

They would have to be extra careful as they made their next moves to fulfill their purpose. *Expose the deeds of darkness*, he thought. Right now the D and X procedure was going on behind closed operating-room doors, cloaked in secrecy by white-coated professionals with clean fingernails, eased by the complicity of many in the media. Dark deeds in a bright, sterile, enlightened environment. And those deeds were about to be multiplied many times over, destined to take place not just in research hospitals or laboratories but in well-funded, well-received processing centers across the country. The centers would somehow legitimize what would take place within them simply by the fact that they existed.

Still, they would have to be extremely careful. Daniel sighed. He knew he'd have to keep his eye on Alex.

AN HOUR LATER, Daniel and Alex, along with Mark Demmers, John Jenkins, and Lance Thompson, were on their way west out of the suburbs. The traffic was still heavy on Route 7, through the congestion of Tyson's Corner, past dozens of housing developments on the edges of Great Falls, Sterling, Ashburn, and through the town of Leesburg. On its outskirts, they had pulled off Route 15 and parked in the yard of a small complex known as Doggett's Garage.

Frank Doggett was a former navy pilot, now retired. He and his wife, Ida, owned this twenty-acre plot of land where Ida cultivated her garden and Frank had built up a small foreign-car repair business. He ran it more to keep himself out of trouble, his wife said, than for the income it brought in.

Frank and Ida had known Daniel and Alex's parents, and after their deaths, Frank had looked out for the two boys, ready to help if they had financial needs, ready to offer crusty advice whether they wanted it or not. Frank had also funneled a fair amount of money into the Network, underwriting various costs as they came up. He had even given Daniel a lovingly buffed, burnished, and cherished 1992 BMW 535i.

"I feel guilty keeping it," Frank had said. "It's just a toy. You use it for good." So Daniel had sold the car for $17,000 to a middle-aged attorney in Great Falls and put the money in a special fund earmarked for a special project he had in mind.

Now on this January evening, Frank welcomed Daniel and the other men at the front door of his comfortable home, almost as if he had been expecting them.

"Hello, gentlemen," he said, wiping his hands with a dinner napkin. "We've been listening to the news. That's some statement the president's press secretary put out. You guys need a place to talk, I bet. Just don't let me hear anything."

He led them over the frosty rutted mud past the back of his garage to a cinder-block outbuilding with a bathroom, a kitchenette, an old television set, and a few mismatched plaid sofas and folding chairs. When Frank's kids were teenagers, they had used it as a gathering place; now it stood empty most of the time.

Frank pulled two large metal space heaters out of the closet and flicked on a thermostat in the corner. "This'll warm up in a few minutes," he said. "But Ida will want you to have some coffee. I'll bring it over in a few minutes. Have you had dinner?"

"Yes, Frank, thanks," said Daniel. "But coffee would be great."

The older man grinned and lowered the miniblinds on the large front window, then pulled the door shut behind him.

"Cozy," said Mark Demmers. "I feel like I'm in a CIA safe house or something." The men took off their coats and pulled the space heaters closer to the couch and easy chairs.

"Do we have any idea who was behind the killing in Fargo?" John Jenkins asked.

"Absolutely not," Daniel said. He pulled out a faded orange

Frisbee that had been lodged between the plaid sofa cushions. "Whoever did it got angry and antsy and did the worst thing they could have done. You can't fight evil with evil. It doesn't work, it's stupid, and it's not Christian."

"I just can't believe that anyone would do this now," Mark Demmers said. "Shooting people does nothing but hurt us. Look at all the backlash after each killing over the past few years. Abortion doctors have become martyrs, and now, if you listen to the news, people in the pro-life movement are all terrorists."

"That's why our approach is right," Daniel said. "That's why we've got to keep going with our plans. No violence. Just exposing the abortion industry for what it is. More articles, more information in the right hands. People don't know what goes on in those places. If they see it—if we expose it—the public can't help but be revolted."

"Don't you think the time has passed for that approach?" Alex said. "Our hands are tied. I think we need to rethink some strategies."

"I've gathered that," Daniel said. "That's why I thought we should talk here tonight."

There was a noise at the door, and Mark got up to let Frank in. He was carrying a large teak tray balanced with a big thermos pitcher of coffee, five pottery mugs, and a napkin-wrapped basket.

"Hot cornbread," he said.

"Ida is amazing," said Daniel. "Tell her thanks."

He bent the Frisbee back and forth between his hands. "You know, when I was on the phone with Howard Fay in Chicago the other night, he alluded to something big coming down. I thought he was talking about the regeneration centers. But then he said something strange: 'Thank God for snow.' I let it go by, thought I must have missed something in the conversation."

Lance smiled and took a mug of coffee from Mark. "I don't think the snow in Fargo is a coincidence, do you?"

"I don't think anything is ever really a coincidence," said Daniel. "But we can't justify violence by the fact that the killer's tracks are being covered. Why? Do you think that's proof that God is on her side?"

Lance shrugged and smiled slightly.

"I'm telling you, guys, if this killing is traced to anyone we know, or the cousin's sister's aunt of anybody we know, then we're in for the type of times we've only read about in bad novels," said Daniel. "Judging from Griswold's press statement, he's going to use this to strike a blow for law and order. That means mostly order. The feds are gonna crack down in a big way. Now, more than ever, we have absolutely got to stick together."

"Well," Alex broke in. "That's fine. That's great. But all I know is that the first regeneration center is going to open in a few months. It's not enough to expose the evil, Daniel. You gotta explode it. And once that center's open they're gonna have so much security we won't get near it. We've got to go after it before it's opened."

Daniel rubbed his face in his hands.

"I'm not talking about people," said Alex. "Just take out the building. Blow it up. Disassemble the killing center. We can't just sit here."

Lance cleared his throat. "I know just the guy who can help us with that."

"Hold it," Daniel said, unusually abrupt. "Put the brakes on. I've got another plan here, a perfect opportunity for us, if everything goes right."

"I've been talking with some people in New York, and we think if everything breaks for us just right, we can pull something off that's pretty incredible. We've got a friend at NIH who says that they're moving forward with the training video there. You know about it, Alex. It's designed to train medical personnel who will work in the regeneration centers how to do the dilation and extraction procedure—shows the actual D and X. It's unbelievable, like a snuff film. From what I hear, they show the baby's head positioned in the birth canal, and then the doctor takes a pair of scissors and jabs its brains out. There's a voiceover, telling just how and where to do what in order to extract the brain tissue neatly and dispose of the corpse properly. It's absolutely unbelievable.

"Anyway, here's the deal. If a few things go right for us, we can get a copy of that video. And if about four thousand things go just right for us, we can get that video onto millions of television screens in America. We just have to knock off the evening news in order to do it."

By now, all of them were staring at Daniel, who was grinning with excitement. "I can't really tell you anything more about it at the moment," he said. "It's the New York group's baby. We'll just be helping in D. C. with a detail or two. We're calling it Gideon's Torch."

13

WELL, I SAY they should line up all these people who say they're pro-life and haul 'em off to jail," an angry man yelled into the microphone from the front row. "All of 'em!"

"Thank you," said talk-show host Bill Donnell, spinning on his heel and running up the steps of the studio audience to poke the mike at a woman gesturing to him from the top row.

"He's right," she screeched. "They're all guilty by association. They've made it so every crazy out there thinks it's okay to take out a gun and blow somebody away. This has been going on for too long." She paused to take a breath, then added loudly, "These people should all be locked up."

The studio audience burst into applause, and Donnell cut to a commercial break.

MR. PRESIDENT, you might want to look at Helen Jackson's editorial this morning," said Robbie. "She makes some good points here. It's the old argument—you know, just the act of protesting at a clinic or hospital incites people to violence. But she lays it out well: When these anti-abortionists call abortion 'murder,' they're leading people to believe that killing abortionists is justified."

"Let me see that," said Griswold. He skimmed the column quickly. Then he swung his chair around and stared out the thick windows overlooking the south lawn toward the Washington Monument in the distance.

"Maybe," he muttered, running his finger over his chin; he had shaved too hurriedly this morning. "Just maybe. We'll see what Bernie says."

DRINKING HIS THIRD CUP OF COFFEE of the morning, Ira Levitz scanned Jackson's column. He shook his head angrily and scribbled a few notes on a pad for his own column. *Hannah Arendt*, he wrote, so he'd remember later to make the point that Arendt, the German Jew who'd escaped the Holocaust, had written that whenever a nation suppresses moral debates or attempts to silence those who assert positions based on deeply held moral convictions, the inevitable result is violence.

And what was it JFK had said? Ira tried to remember, tapping the pad with the end of his pen. Right. When peaceful revolution is suppressed, violent revolution is inevitable. Thomas Jefferson's point.

If Griswold listens to the Helen Jacksons, we're in big trouble, thought Levitz. If they clamp down too hard on the pro-lifers, stifle all dissent, they're just going to have more murders on their hands.

ANTHONY FRIZZELL STUDIED the latest intelligence summaries on the most ominous of the anti-abortion groups. According to some fairly fuzzy information, Dr. Sloan's killer was rumored to be from the Chicago area, but the informant had no hard evidence. Frizzell's eyes sped from line to line.

"Nothing hard here, Toby." He turned to his special assistant, long-time agent Toby Hunter.

"No sir. Sorry. Our people have to be very careful. We're doing well, under the circumstances, to get this much. "

"This much?" Frizzell echoed derisively, then swung around in his chair to stare out the window at Pennsylvania Avenue. "Well, beef up our office in Chicago."

"Yes sir. We can put forty extra street agents there."

"And, Toby, for now at least, don't put this in the daily report to the attorney general. Let's save it for a pleasant surprise later," Frizzell said with a slight smile.

Toby returned the smile. He knew his boss well. He would crack the case and then be there when the bust was made. Above all, he'd want to keep the politicians out. It was important not to share the spotlight. Not for his own advantage, of course. All for the bureau's good.

THE ATTORNEY GENERAL'S OFFICE is located on the fifth floor of the Justice Department, occupying the southwest corner of the massive old building. Many Washington powerbrokers measure the influence of their peers by the square footage and splendor of the office space they occupy; by that standard, the attorney general surely has power. The reception room is large and handsomely furnished, with ample leather sofas for visitors. The reception area, presided over by two secretaries, opens into the main office, which might pass for a great hall in a feudal manor house: long and high-ceilinged, with dark, burnished, mahogany paneling and portraits of former attorneys general lining the wall. A huge conference table occupies the center.

At the far end is a door leading into the attorney general's private suite, a more modest working office, and a generous private dining room.

Emily Gineen had been in this office only a few days, so she still found it somewhat overwhelming. The conscious and somewhat exaggerated splendor, the private stewards to attend every need, the young, bright-eyed interns from Harvard, Yale, and

Stanford hovering, waiting to bring a brief or case at the snap of a finger.

As she had expected, the transition to her new role had not been particularly easy. Frederick was commuting back and forth to Harvard, their new home in Spring Valley was still crammed with unpacked boxes, and the children were not happy with their new schools. Just last evening, Kathy had sobbed as Emily tucked her into bed. She just didn't like Sidwell Friends, she told her mother, and she missed her friends at home. When were they going home?

Emily had stroked her daughter's curly hair and commiserated. "Just give it a little time," she said. "This is a great place to live. We're just having a bumpy time settling in. Are there any girls in your class you'd like to have over for dinner and a movie on the weekend?"

"No!" Kathy had sobbed.

At this point, her job was just as frustrating. Emily was used to an attorney's routine, examining cases, delegating research, pondering issues, consulting clients, and preparing arguments. She had never been in a position in which the amount of work to be done was absolutely limitless. It was triage: She delegated madly, judged in seconds what had to be done and what could be refused, and staggered home at the end of each day knowing she had just barely avoided total disaster for one more day.

The next morning she would emerge from her front door at 7:30 to find the limousine waiting, engine idling, in the driveway. Spread out on the back seat was *The Washington Post*, a White House news summary, and urgent faxes or memos that the Justice Control Unit had received during the night. By 8:00 she was at her desk, already fighting off the unrelenting series of demands: "The Civil Rights Division wants you to sign off on this proposed settlement,". . . "the Criminal Division needs a budget fix,". . . "Personnel has questions,". . . "Senator so and so demands to talk with you personally,". . . "This report needs your okay to go to the White House . . ."

By 7:00 in the evening Emily was reeling. Each day her

briefcase grew larger with reading material, and after spending an hour or two with the children, she'd pore through papers until 2:00 A.M.

And on top of all this was the shooting of the abortionist in North Dakota. Griswold seemed obsessed with it. Bernie O'Keefe had called three times. The FBI had turned up only bits and scraps of information, though Frizzell had told her this morning that more problems could be in store for the future. But she was dubious about his agenda and skeptical about his motives. If his Oval Office performance was any indication, she knew this guy could operate.

Emily called O'Keefe about Fargo and the government's response. He didn't have any great insights for her. Then she'd sent an "eyes only" intelligence fax for the president, a single sheet that sounded very impressive but said next to nothing. She could imagine Griswold's reaction; he just wanted results. Period. Problem was, she had to walk a very fine line here, with pressure from the White House on one side but big trouble if she tried to cut any corners. Politicians like Byron Langer would love any excuse to nail the administration. He and others were already issuing high-sounding statements about not repressing the pro-life movement.

Maybe she should consult Paul Clarkson, she thought. She had met him only once, a perfunctory session at that. But he at least would understand Langer's camp. After all, wasn't he supposed to be "the interpreter"? Of course he was in Langer's pocket, but she'd take what she needed from what he said.

Emily picked up the phone line that automatically rang on her assistant's desk.

"Pamela, could you ask the associate attorney general to come in here—that is, if he isn't busy. Let me know if it's not convenient."

"GOOD MORNING, General," Paul smiled as he moved slowly from the doorway toward Emily's desk.

Paul Clarkson was almost impossible not to like—the kind

of man every father prays will ask to marry his daughter, and he was the type who would ask, not announce. Unfailingly courteous but also smart and quick, he never seemed to press his intellectual advantage with others. His humility could be deceiving, however. With his curly auburn hair and a grin that accented two deep dimples, he was disarming.

It was impossible also not to feel sympathy for the man. Though only 5'11" and 170 pounds, he had been a star linebacker on the Duke Blue Devils football team, making up for his lack of size with speed, agility, and a certain fearless abandon on the playing field. Then, in a big game against navy his junior year, he had met a bruising running back head-on. Paul had stopped him, but had been carried off the field on a stretcher. He had spent almost a month in the hospital, and doctors had to fuse his spine. Ever since he could walk only slowly, often painfully, with a cane or walker. He would never again bend his back or gain full use of his legs.

Turning his determination and energy into training, Paul used his mind the same way he had his body. In three years at Duke Law School, despite taking public issue with most of his professors whom he regarded as incorrigibly liberal, he never got less than an A. He graduated at the head of his class, winner of the moot court competition, editor of the *Law Review*, and Order of Coif, the legal honor society. He had his pick of the nation's best law firms but chose to clerk for a Fifth Circuit judge for two years then spent two years as a public defender in Atlanta. From there he moved to Washington, joined the Senate judiciary staff, and before he was thirty-three had become chief minority counsel.

"Sit down, Paul. And by the way, you needn't call me General or Professor or Mrs. Gineen, at least not when we work together in private. Just call me Emily."

"I'll try." Paul smiled and then nodded somewhat deferentially. "Thank you."

"I'm sorry that we've not really talked much thus far," Emily said. "I need to delegate more, I'm realizing. You're responsible for administration here, so I want to pass over a number of things in the administrative area to you."

"Certainly," he said eagerly. "I want to be as much help as I can to you." He paused, then added with a slight smile, "Emily."

"Right," she said. "Now, there are a few key areas I'd like to rely on you to handle." It was a modest list, but Paul nodded appreciatively as he took notes.

"Of course," she paused, staring intently at him, "you'll want to recuse yourself from anything involving the abortionist killing, I'm sure."

Clarkson looked startled. "Why?" he replied.

"Well," she said, feeling uncharacteristically awkward, "I thought that in light of your, uh, convictions and your close friendship with Senator Langer, I would not want to put you in an awkward position. I do not question your objectivity, of course."

Paul bristled. "No," he said firmly. "I took the same oath you did, and like you, I take it seriously. My job is to uphold the law, and I mean to do just that."

"I don't doubt that, Paul," she said, "but I understand that you are firmly committed to the pro-life cause, and our work right now very much involves anti-abortion issues."

Clarkson's face muscles tightened. "Well, you're right. My views are very much pro-life. That means I'm against the taking of innocent lives, but it also means I'm against the taking of an abortionist's life. What happened in Fargo is a heinous crime. I'll do my job."

Emily was relieved. Maybe Langer had done her a good turn after all. "I respect that, Paul. Some people—I don't mean any offense here—who are very conservative, religiously speaking, don't make the distinction you do. They can't separate their religious view from their private duties."

"Nor can I." His jaw was set. "If you mean those who say they are personally opposed but do it as part of their office, that's not me. That's hypocrisy. It's a cop-out. My faith affects all of my life. If you asked me to run an abortion clinic or order someone to have an abortion, I'd resign and be out of here in thirty seconds—"

"But that's exactly what I mean," Emily interjected. "I'm not interfering in your religious convictions. I just don't want to put you in an awkward position."

Paul seemed to relax just slightly. "I realize it sounds confusing. Let me just explain. I'm a Christian. No equivocation, no excuses. I know that makes some people in public office very nervous. But the fact is it shouldn't. Because it makes me a better public official. I can do nothing contrary to my deepest convictions, but those convictions include not lying, not cheating, not bearing false witness—not altogether bad attributes for a person in the public trust.

"And if people understood, they'd realize that Christians believe government has been given the God-ordained job of preserving order and justice. So I view discharging that responsibility as my duty as a Christian as well as my duty as associate attorney general. So in the Fargo case, and in any others like it that may come along, I want those responsible prosecuted."

Emily sat back, tenting her fingertips beneath her chin, gazing at him intently. *He's really unusual*, she thought. *He's sincere about this. He's not just posturing to make himself look good.* She thought about Frizzell again.

"Well, just how would you go about prosecuting these unknown perpetrators in Fargo, Paul?" she asked.

As he gave her his lucid summary of the situation, Emily realized that he had already thought about the question and prepared his answer. His analysis was not only impressive but a challenge to conventional wisdom. The FBI, Paul argued, shouldn't have ultimate responsibility.

"They still play Eliot Ness games, want to rush in with guns blazing, get the bad guys, and haul them into court. That's the way the bureau thinks. They're cops, the best there are, but still cops. What we need here is a strategy," Paul argued, "to break the leaders, get to the higher-ups. This is a master political struggle." He ticked off various techniques for breaking conspiracies.

"Where did you get your criminal experience?" Emily asked.

"On the Committee we worked with Justice strike forces in cracking down on drug cartels and organized crime. It's the same thing. But you can't rely on Frizzell . . . you, Emily, need to take charge."

For the next forty minutes Paul laid out options: wiretaps, reviews of Secret Service lists of known dangerous criminals or those who had made wild charges, obtaining search warrants after choosing the judge carefully.

"The right judge can be lenient on probable cause," Paul explained. He also advocated "questioning" various leaders around the country, trying to get someone scared into testifying.

"Remember the killing of the three civil rights workers in 1964 down in Mississippi? Those three bodies were buried in a levee, and nobody would have found them to this day had not the bureau and Justice moved in, followed witnesses, knocked on doors in the middle of the night. They bullied it out of the Klan, and good thing they did. All within the law, but justice was done. Same kind of thing here."

Paul talked about the strategy almost clinically, like a lawyer advising a client, cautioning Emily on the limits of the law, the kinds of things Langer and others on the Hill would be sensitive to. Throughout, she took notes, smiling occasionally.

"Please understand," he said at one point, "I'm only offering alternatives, not making recommendations. I realize that the situation, as it develops, will dictate the course to follow." Emily agreed.

Before the meeting adjourned, Emily had unloaded other projects on Paul. He would handle the budget and personnel, call staff meetings, and perhaps deal with other parts of the Justice Department that weren't so sensitive.

"I'll want to get together again soon so we can assess progress on the Fargo case," Emily said as Paul got up to leave, rising from his chair with some difficulty. "And let me state once more, Paul, how impressed I am with your knowledge of the law. I'm looking forward to working with you."

After Clarkson left, Emily tucked her notes in her briefcase— just what she would need when O'Keefe called, as no doubt he would, around 10:00 this evening, probably with a thick tongue. She would give him quite an earful.

14

WHITNEY GRISWOLD walked briskly along the covered passageway from the Oval Office to the family quarters, looking forward to a quiet evening with his family, the first since his inauguration fourteen days ago. As he entered the living room, Elizabeth jumped off the sofa where she and her mother were watching the news together and ran to give him a hug.

"How was your day, dear?" Anne asked, rolling her eyes slightly as she bowed to convention. It seemed ludicrous to ask such a mundane question in the White House.

He rolled his eyes back, connecting with her playfully. "Oh, just the usual things, darling. Issues of national security, nuclear threats from Third World crazies with First World weapons, terrorists alive and well in the U. S. . . . . and how was your day?"

She smiled and nodded toward Elizabeth. "Your daughter had a big day."

Elizabeth smiled and straightened up proudly. "I made the basketball team!" she said loudly. "Coach Bell says he'll start me in the next game or maybe the one after that. Can you come? You've got to watch us!"

"Wonderful, Elizabeth!" he said, clapping his hands. "I'm so proud of you!"

"But will you come see me?"

"Well, we'll see," Griswold stalled as they all made their way together toward the dining room. He looked at Anne for support. It wasn't like the president of the United States could slip into the bleachers unnoticed. Just to set up the communications gear and do the security checks would cost about $100,000 and paralyze the school for a week.

They took their seats in the small family dining room just down the hall from the west end sitting room. Griswold sat at one end, Anne at the other, Elizabeth in the middle. The centerpiece was a large bouquet of fresh-cut flowers, and the table was set with the family china, not the official set used at state dinners. Anne had been clear about wanting a family feeling in this room.

"What a shame Robert can't be here," Griswold said. He smiled at Elizabeth, but the diversion didn't work.

"Daddy, you will come see me play, won't you?" She smiled at him. She had inherited both her mother's stubbornness and her father's appeal.

Anne took him off the hook. "We'll see, dear. I'll be there for sure, but you know Daddy has big responsibilities right now. But we'll work on it."

"Tell me about your schoolwork, dear." Griswold tried again to detour Elizabeth. "How about English? Do you like your teacher?"

"Okay, I guess, but Mrs. Martin is a drag." She was frowning, still thinking about the game, one more reason she didn't like what had happened to her life.

"How about history then? That was always a favorite for me. What are you studying?" he asked as the stewards were serving the first course, a chilled vegetable pate.

"Oh, it's okay. We're studying the Civil War. You know, Daddy, two of the big battles were fought right near here. We talked about Manassas today. Can we go see it sometime?"

"Absolutely," Griswold quickly assured her. It would be easy for a president to visit a historical site.

"Daddy, my teacher said the Civil War was fought for moral reasons. To end slavery. But who would think slavery was moral? Why did people have to fight and kill over that?"

"At that time, there were people who believed that slavery was moral, just as there were others who saw it as horribly immoral," he said. "Today we can't imagine that anyone would condone slavery, but at that time, they did. The South believed that slavery was right; the North did not. And those two points of view led to a war. A terrible war."

Elizabeth listened. "But how do you tell which point of view is right?" she said slowly. "By which army wins?"

Griswold stared at his daughter, and the French bread stuck in his throat. He had to take a sip of water before he could continue. "Not necessarily," he said. "The moral point of view is the right point of view. What's right."

"How do you know what's right, Daddy?" his daughter pressed. Griswold looked at Anne. She was grinning slightly.

"You've been raised to know what is moral, Elizabeth," he said. "It's inside of you. You know when something is right, and you know what is wrong. Some people call it conscience—and families like ours understand that. We try to do right things, help others. That's why we're in this place."

Elizabeth nodded, but came up with one more zinger, just as the main course was served. "One of the kids in class asked if it's right to kill someone else for 'moral' reasons? I don't get it."

"Of course," the president muttered, cutting into his salmon.

"Whitney, did you hear the question?" Anne asked sternly.

Griswold looked up and smiled. "Sorry, sorry. I was thinking of something else. Ask me again, dear."

Elizabeth did.

"Decisions about war, where there is killing, are made by a majority in our society. When the majority votes to go to war and the government acts on it, then it becomes all right. I suppose you'd say that government decides that it's moral. It depends on the situation."

Just then Juan entered the dining room carrying a packet that had just arrived from Robbie.

"Thank you, Juan," Griswold said. "Just put it on my stand in the living room." It was, he was certain, more late dispatches from the National Security Council on the situation in Nigeria. The coup there was endangering the oil supply for several European nations, and American allies were concerned.

Glad for the interruption, he leaned back in his chair and turned to Anne. "And how was your day, dear?"

"We're getting organized, I think." Anne was, above all, organized. "Tea with the congressional leadership wives group. Sort of tedious, actually. And I've contacted the hospice national executive office. Their director is coming in next week. I think I'll give them a boost if you agree."

"That's a great idea, dear," Griswold said enthusiastically.

"And there's a new group called the Peacemakers. It sounds very interesting—helping people who are at the end of their lives leave peacefully and with dignity."

"Oh?" Griswold looked up. Assisted suicide was still not legal. The Supreme Court had decided that, but not whether the right to die was a protected liberty under the Fourteenth Amendment. So there were groups quietly helping suffering people find a dignified and compassionate solution. Despite the progress the country had made, it was still a controversial issue for many, particularly the Masterson crowd, the Religious Right.

"Look it over carefully, please," he said to Anne. "It's a noble enough work, I'm sure, but we don't want needless controversy."

Glancing at his daughter, he could tell she was still smarting because he had not promised to come to her basketball game.

"Listen," he said, reaching out a hand toward her. "How would you like to go to Camp David for the weekend? It's beautiful in winter. There's sledding, fires in the fireplace, cross-country skiing. We'll just get away, the three of us in the mountains. What do you say?"

"I guess it would be fun," she said, sounding less than enthused.

"Would you like to bring a friend along, someone from school perhaps?" Anne asked.

"Yeah," Elizabeth's face brightened. "Molly is my really good friend. She'd love it. Yeah."

Anne promised to call Molly's mother.

"I'll even leave here Friday noon," Griswold announced as he waved off the chocolate mousse dessert. He had weighed in at 210 this morning. No more sweets for a while.

"We can't. I've got basketball practice, Daddy."

Griswold nodded. "Okay, after school then." That was that. The president of the United States, whose every wish was someone's command, would, in this room at least, have to defer to the Cathedral School's basketball team.

AFTER DINNER, while Anne sat down in the living room with her folder of correspondence to be signed and Elizabeth stretched out on the rug with her schoolwork, Griswold headed for the Lincoln sitting room and his own "homework."

He settled into the comfortable chair in the corner and slid open the envelope. He skimmed the memos. Included just behind Nigeria was the attorney general's report on the Fargo shooting. Two hundred fifty words to say next to nothing. Killing for moral reasons indeed. These people were nothing but self-appointed executioners.

Moments later he was on the phone to Bernie O'Keefe, who was sitting in his study at home.

"You doing all right, Bernie?" Griswold asked. His friend sounded tired. No surprise.

"Fine. Fine. Just cleaning up a few loose ends, sitting here at the desk with a cup of coffee." Bernie grinned as he stirred his Dewars with his finger.

"Yeah, I hear the coffee's ice cubes tinkling," Griswold said dryly. "How are Marilyn and the kids?"

There was a pause. "They're back in Wellesley. Marilyn said they won't be down this weekend."

"I'm sorry. Anything I can do?" Griswold asked. "What about the box at the Kennedy Center, you know, the president's box? Why don't you use it this weekend? Call Marilyn. She can't turn that one down."

"Thanks, Whit," Bernie said. "I really appreciate it. I'm not sure I can get Marilyn to come down if she doesn't want to, even for that. You know how she can be. But I'll give it a try." Bernie knew his friend knew just how stubborn Marilyn could be.

"Bernie, I've been thinking about this Fargo business," Griswold said after a slight pause. "It's been some time now, and I don't see that we know one thing today we didn't know the day of the shooting. Frizzell talks a good game, but that's it. I'd like you to call Emily and—"

"I'm one up on you tonight, for a change. I just hung up from talking with her. She's got some great ideas. We need to watch things, but if there are no breaks in the next few days, she's got a plan. A good one. She's sharp, and she's got style. I think you'll be pleased."

"Good. That's what we need, initiative. But now listen, Bernie, you keep on top of it. The only disturbing thing in Frizzell's report is the indication that there might be other things in the works. These are zealots, remember. People who will kill for moral reasons tend to be a little unbalanced. So we need to nip this thing in the bud.

"But remember Waco, the Koresh case, Bernie." Griswold stopped, letting the point sink in.

"Indeed I do," Bernie replied.

"Well, Janet Reno went bonkers, overreacted. We can't do that either. Of course we need to find them first."

"We'll find them. Gineen has some good strategies in mind. We'll watch things though, and I'll take care of it. You worry about Nigeria."

"Yes, Bernie, you take care of it."

Take care of it, Bernie thought after he'd hung up. He'd been taking care of it for years. Then he thought back to the first time, the time he doubted Griswold even remembered anymore. . . .

IT BEGAN LIKE COUNTLESS OTHER Wednesday nights in law school. It ended with the secret that cemented the bond between Whitney Griswold and Bernie O'Keefe for life.

At Yale, Whit and Bernie had fallen into a fairly disciplined routine.

Weekends were reserved for civilized dates with their girlfriends, both conveniently out of town. On Friday evenings, Whit usually went home. Anne would often meet him there, and they would go out to dinner parties, sailing if the weather allowed, and Sunday morning brunch with his family. He would get back to New Haven early on Sunday afternoon and study until early evening, when he'd meet Bernie for beer and pizza. Bernie usually stayed in New Haven on the weekend.

Both Whit and Bernie had come to assumptions about marriage to Anne and Marilyn, respectively, but wanted to wait until they finished law school. And until that happened, they weren't going to be totally fettered by relationships that would likely constrain them the rest of their lives.

Mondays, Tuesdays, and Thursdays were reserved for study, but Wednesdays were hump nights at their favorite local bar, with half-price drinks and free hors d'oeuvres.

So this particular Wednesday in April, near the end of their second year at Yale, found the two men working their way through their second Dewars and discussing the evening ahead. Two fellow students—female—had invited them over for a cookout later that night.

"I think it's okay to go," said Bernie. "It's not like it's a major commitment or anything. Just burgers on the grill and polite conversation with two law school colleagues who happen to be of the feminine gender. I don't think Anne or Marilyn would mind. . . even if they did ever find out, which they won't."

Whitney grinned. "Bull," he said. "If Anne finds out, she won't talk to me for a month."

"Do you really think that would be such a loss?" asked Bernie. He liked Anne as little as she liked him.

Whitney rolled his eyes and took another sip.

"Well, then," said Bernie, "let's make sure they don't find out. It's not a big deal." He drained his drink, signaled the bartender for another, and yelled down the bar to a friend five stools away.

"Hey, Tom! What you gonna do this summer?"

"Hogan and Hartson in D. C.," Tom shouted back. "It's a three-month internship. I'll check out the bars on Capitol Hill for you, Bernie. You want me to deliver any personal messages to Jimmy Carter?"

"Ask him what kind of dental floss he uses," responded Bernie. "Good luck!"

He turned back to Whitney. "He's smart," he said. "It's not a bad idea to do the D. C. thing. I've heard it takes awhile to get the feel of things there, and you're going to need that. Eventually."

Griswold laughed and swirled the ice cubes in his glass. "You're more ambitious than I am," he said. "Maybe we should just stay here, practice law, sail on the weekends, keep it simple. Maybe we should forget about politics. Too tiring." He smiled at a young woman two stools down.

"It is tiring," said Bernie. "That's why we've got to relax a little while we can. The package store is open till seven. Let's get a bottle to take with us to Jane's house. "

Six hours later, the bottle was empty, and they were on their way home. Whitney was at the wheel as the April night rushed through the open windows of his Audi. Bernie was slouched in the passenger seat, clutching a beer in his right hand and singing the theme song from *Gilligan's Island* at the top of his lungs.

". . . The weather started getting rough, the tiny ship was tossed. If not for the courage of the fearless crew, the *Minnow* would be lost . . ."

"The *Minnow* would be lost," echoed Whitney, squinting into the darkness ahead.

"You know, they just don't make television shows like they used to," reflected Bernie. "I mean, our generation grew up on great stuff . . . *The Dick Van Dyke Show, Bonanza, Mr. Ed, I Dream of Jeannie . . . My Mother, The Car.*

"Think of it! It's our common heritage, the ideas that made America great! A talking horse. A car that was somebody's mother. Four dudes living in the wilderness with a Chinese cook named Hop Sing. An astronaut who has a genie as a personal housekeeper . . . and her name just happens to be Jeannie! . . . What a great country!"

"You're raving," said Whitney. Usually Bernie drove them home, but tonight he had seemed unusually soused, so Whit was at the wheel of his own car.

The women had turned up with not only burgers on the grill but some sort of concoction they had called oyster shooters.

"Good for virility," they had teased. "Good for the brain, too. These really help you absorb the intricacies of the American system of jurisprudence."

"Why should we care about prudence?" Bernie had responded.

The shooters consisted of raw oysters shoved into the bottom of shot glasses, doused with a dash of cocktail sauce, then drowned in a combination of vodka and champagne and crowned with a pickled jalapeno pepper. The women were downing them with wild abandon.

Whitney couldn't stomach oysters very well, and the jalapeno didn't help any. He'd only had one and then stuck to Dewars. Bernie, who could eat anything, had raved over the combination of flavors and downed about six of them. So had Jane and Mindy. It had ended up being a far wilder evening than the mellow night on the patio they had expected.

But now the evening air felt so sweet and fresh, a promise of the springtime to come, and the two of them felt relaxed and confident. As Bernie continued singing off-key, Whit pushed the accelerator slightly and watched, detached, as the needle on the dashboard climbed.

The curve came too quickly. The car rushed into the turn,

there was a sudden squeal of brakes as Griswold tried by reflex to adjust, and then everything spun out of control. There was the clipping thuds of the mailbox, the street sign, and then the telephone pole.

Bernie was out of his seat belt as soon as the car stopped. The shock and adrenaline somehow overcame the alcohol in his brain, and he assessed the situation quickly. The car was sideways in the street, wrapped against a telephone poll. Whit was slumped against the wheel, a little trickle of blood running down his temple.

Bernie clicked to attention. He opened the car door and deliberately crumpled the empty beer can in his hand, flinging it as far as he could into the trees. Then he ran around the car to the driver's side, forced the door open, punched open Whitney's seat belt, and dragged him from the car. The motion caused his friend to stir.

"What happened?" he said.

"Are you okay?" asked Bernie.

"I'm all right," said Whitney. "It's just that there's a telephone pole around my car."

"That's a small problem at this point," said Bernie. "Just keep quiet. Let me talk. I was driving. It's your car, but you were tired. Is your registration in the glove compartment?"

"Yes," said Whitney, who always kept everything in its place. "But are you okay?"

"I'm fine," said Bernie, licking his lips, rubbing his eyes, and bending down to look into the driver's side mirror. "I shouldn't have let you drive in the first place. I should have known you couldn't even handle the Dewars."

"A lot better than you could handle those oyster things," said Whitney. "Why are you doing this?"

"You're going to be a lawyer," said Bernie. "Think like one. You know the cops are going to come. You know we're both way over the top on the Breathalyzer. You know where we want to go in terms of your future. Somebody has to fix this mess, and I'm the only one here to save your butt on this one. Let's just say you'll owe me one."

Bernie raked his fingers through his hair, combing it back from his face. "I've got some Certs in the glove compartment," Whitney said, impressed that he had remembered this detail.

"Oh, those'll be a big help," said Bernie sarcastically. "Well, let's get 'em out."

He peeled a white mint and sucked on it. "We'll say I was driving, I had a few beers, and I'm so sorry. At the worst I'll go to jail for a night or two and lose my license for a while. Maybe the experience will help me when we get to criminal law. But we can't afford all that on your record. I'm sure your dad will take care of the car"

Bernie paused, looking at his tall friend now standing by the side of the smashed Audi. Whitney nodded toward the passenger seat, then rubbed his head with his shirttail.

"Okay," he said. "You know better than I do what to do." He paused. "And thanks."

Thus it had begun. That particular matter, as investigated by the New Haven police department, had resulted in a night in jail, a DUI citation, and a suspended driver's license for Bernard O'Keefe. It had also cemented the friendship—and commitment—of J. Whitney Griswold toward Bernie O'Keefe for a long, long, time.

15

THE RECESSED, round lights flashed along the edge of the subway platform, and a moment later the train thundered into the station. Late commuters hurried through the automatic doors, stuffing rumpled *Washington Posts* into fat briefcases, jangling car keys as they rushed toward the Metro parking lots and home. A group of students entered the train, settling into the padded orange seats and chatting casually.

As the lights flashed again and a bell sounded, warning of the train's departure, Alex Seaton darted between its doors. The train pulled out of the station, gathering speed.

Alex looked around, satisfied: No one had followed his last-minute jump onto the subway. The students and a few weary women who looked like maids or nannies, returning home to the city after a day in the suburbs, looked up for a moment without much interest.

Alex walked the aisle, steadying himself as the train rocked, and sat down with his back to the connecting door to the next car. He didn't put his briefcase on the floor, as most businessmen did, but placed the large, boxlike case gently on his knees then folded his hands over its flat surface, like a man contemplating evening prayers.

The train pitched and rolled to the next stops. Ballston. Clarendon. At the Courthouse stop, Alex rose abruptly as the departure bell chimed, then jumped off the train, excusing himself as he passed through a group of attorneys clustered on the platform.

Eight minutes later, another D. C.-bound train arrived. Alex walked to the far end of the tracks, entered the first car behind the driver, and chose a seat adjacent to the section reserved for handicapped and elderly riders. The car's only other occupant, a middle-aged woman reading a paperback novel, looked up to register his arrival, then returned to her book.

Alex carefully opened his thick case and removed the A section of the *Washington Post*, turning to the story on page A-6. "Despite Construction Delays, Regeneration Center Moves Toward Completion." It was a small article, buried among the usual trash about Whitney Griswold's latest cabinet appointment and reports on the earthquake in California. Alex eyed it briefly, though he had already read it so many times he had nearly memorized it, then turned the page.

The train stopped in Rosslyn. "Last stop in Virginia," the driver announced. The lights flashed, then there was a muffled roar as the train passed under the Potomac River.

Alex stared into the darkness of the tunnel, feeling the irrational need to hold his breath. It was an odd sensation: the sense of being in a tube, tons of pressure outside, this fragile shell rushing along the canal in the darkness. Then a subtle change in the air, a breath, and they burst into the light again.

"Foggy Bottom—George Washington University," the PA system announced. "You are now in the District of Columbia. Doors open on the right."

Alex walked out onto the platform, carefully carrying his briefcase. He strolled to a pillar and looked at his watch, then eyed the platform again. A Metro security guard nodded in his direction as he glided up the escalator.

Alex walked to the elevator, entered, and waited inside for three minutes. He didn't want to be paranoid, but Lance had said that from here on out, they would need to assume they were being followed. He pushed the "ground-level" button. When he emerged on the surface, he walked quickly toward his destination.

Across the street, an ambulance sat in the curved emergency entrance of George Washington Hospital, siren off but its red lights still flashing. The hospital complex sprawled over several blocks adjacent to the mix of brick townhouses, nondescript dorms, and classroom buildings that made up the university.

Near the Metro stop, where its parking lot had once been, was the complex's newest addition: a long, three-story building, connected to the hospital by a second-floor glass walkway arching across Twenty-third Street. "Future Site of George Washington University Hospital's New Regeneration Center," read the sign affixed to the wooden wall next to the sidewalk. Development by Hughes and Crown." Dumpsters full of trashed construction materials rested on the bare ground in front of the main entrance.

This was the first time Alex had come downtown to see the building itself, but he knew about the forty well-appointed patient rooms, the four comfortable lounges, the snack area, the reception area, the doctors' conference rooms and offices, the counseling facilities, and the "staging areas," as the operating rooms where the procedure would actually be performed were called. He also knew what seven hundred pounds of high explosives, resting in the proper spot, could do to the center's concrete-and-steel reinforced construction.

He turned and walked several blocks down Twenty-third Street. Though there were people on the street, he knew instinctively he was not being followed. So he paused for only a moment when he reached Sam's Deli.

A bell strung on the back of the old-fashioned wood-and-glass door tinkled as he pushed it open. Sam's was a neighborhood hangout with eight booths, a counter, and a smattering of groceries and other essentials of college life: a self-serve coffee bar, plastic-wrapped packages of Nabs, Pop-Tarts, aspirin, deodorant, newspapers, magazines, and a big, glass-doored refrigerator full of cold beer.

The man behind the counter, known to the neighborhood as Sam though his name was Yasmir, nodded to Alex as he entered then went on wiping down the counter and watching the basketball game on the small TV mounted on a bracket near the ceiling.

Holding his briefcase with his left hand, Alex poured himself a cup of coffee with his right, fished seventy-five cents out of his pocket, and left it on the counter.

He moved toward the booth in the back, holding the Styrofoam cup carefully.

"Hey, how are you?" he said to the man in the booth, like any businessman meeting a friend after work. "Sorry I'm late."

Lance Thompson, sitting with his back to the door, looked up and grinned at Alex. "Hey, man," he said. "I'm fine. You owe me a cup of coffee, though. Make it decaf."

Alex sat down, placing his case between them on the table. "I'll get that for you in just a minute," he said, satisfied that no one was paying them any particular attention.

The basketball game was so loud it would drown out most of their conversation, and he had discovered that college students were so self-involved that their curiosity was rarely piqued by anything outside their own experience. The kids in the other booths and at the counter were intent on their books or their beers.

Nevertheless, Lance lowered his voice. "Do you have it?" he asked.

Alex nodded, his eyes indicating the briefcase between them. "Right here," he said. "I passed the center on the way in. The *Post* says it's due for completion by the beginning of September. It's too bad for them to go to all that trouble for nothing, isn't it?"

Lance nodded, then glanced at his watch. "I've got the van in that alley in the back," he said. "Let's go."

Alex gulped down the rest of his coffee, crunched the cup, and threw it in the plastic trashcan near their booth. He stood aside as Lance headed toward the rest room in the back of the deli; from there he would go out the back door that led toward the alley.

Alex went out the front door. Sam was still wiping the same

section of the counter, mesmerized by the Knicks and the Bulls, and didn't even register his departure.

A few moments later, Lance's nondescript white vehicle, the sort favored by electricians and carpenters, slowed near the curb, and Alex jumped into the front passenger seat. Lance headed back to the Metro stop, where he idled the van at the curb as if waiting for someone to emerge from the subway.

Alex stared out the darkened windows at the regeneration center. He noted the high fences, the checkpoint outbuilding between the narrow driveways awaiting security gates still to be installed. He balanced the briefcase on his lap as Lance pointed toward the checkpoint.

"I talked to a guy named Nick," he said. "He says that the plan is to hire an outside security company. Twenty-four-hour surveillance, sweeping guard patrol three times an hour, a canine unit on call. The whole building will be wired; the fence around the grounds will be electrified. It'll be like a prison camp, or maybe the White House. Nobody goes in or out except patients, staff, and doctors. They'll have armed security guards at the walkway between the center and the hospital. Once it's operational, there's no real way to get in . . . unless we get somebody on the inside working with us. I'm working on that."

Alex nodded. He knew that Lance's past had taught him that survival depended on uncovering every detail. He also knew that once those details were in hand, his friend would hesitate at nothing in order to execute their plan.

"Let's take a look at this," he said. "I used some of the treasury to get hold of these." He dialed the combination lock then snapped open the latches of his briefcase. Inside was a thick sheaf of blueprints.

"I looked for the load-bearing pillars in the parking garage," he said. "We can do it, once we have the supplies in order. I'm working on that. We can set them back a few million dollars and at least a year or so in time. And we'll give our friend Griswold another chance to read the writing on the wall."

Lance bent his head over the plans. "Our best hope is getting a plant inside," he said. "But if I can't make that happen, the other option is to use a woman. It's just that that gets a lot more complicated. And since Fargo, they're more suspicious of women posing as patients. If this was the Middle East, we'd just send in a suicide bomber."

"We're not the Middle East," said Alex. "Not quite yet."

Lance rolled the blueprints again, securing them with a rubber band. "I'll take these," he said. "And thanks for the briefcase. You'd better get out now. I'll call you later, once I've checked out a few things."

Alex climbed down from the van and watched it pull off into traffic. Then he stood on the sidewalk for a moment, gazing at the regeneration center.

He looked at the large color placard the architectural firm had put up, with its pretty pastel trees and vague figures strolling the walks of the center as if it were an English garden. The artist had drawn in extensive landscaping; large, curving flower beds filled with bright blooms lined the walkways to the main entrance.

Petunias, Alex thought with disgust. *Well, Auschwitz had flower beds, too. They always find a way to mask the truth.*

He looked again at the security gate then turned and walked back toward the Metro.

16

Thursday, February 20

O N SATURDAY MORNING, February 15, Emily
Gineen and Anthony Frizzell had been summoned
to the White House to meet with Bernie O'Keefe.
For over an hour, the three huddled around a small conference
table in O'Keefe's spacious, paneled office located directly above
the Oval Office. There they reached the decision, which O'Keefe
assured them he would clear with Griswold. Frizzell called the
plan "Operation Steamroller." O'Keefe chose a more apt title:
"Plan B."

Whatever it was called, it was simple enough. On February
20 agents would fan out to eight cities, all hotbeds of anti-abortion activity, and simultaneously at 4:00 P.M. EST (good for
network coverage), would "visit" known leaders of the pro-life
movement. No warrants needed; the agents were simply fact-
finding. They would pound loudly on doors, flash badges, and
make enough ruckus that as many neighbors and coworkers as
possible would see them. They would "invite" the leaders to
accompany them to the FBI offices. They'd also read them
their rights, even though, unknown to them, their rights weren't
in jeopardy. They weren't suspects; the agents would simply
treat them that way.

It was the bully approach, and it had been used many times and to good effect in the civil rights days. With enough pressure, someone breaks. And at the very least, the pro-lifers would get the message that the government was not going to mess around with them anymore.

It was 7:45 on Thursday morning, February 20 however, that the first big break came. An urgent e-mail message from Chicago said that the Chicago office had a serious suspect and needed headquarters approval before acting. The agent in charge of the message center immediately called the situation room on the fifth floor and was given approval to route the message simultaneously to the assistant director for operations and to the director.

Seconds later, the screen in Toby Hunter's office started flashing, sign of an urgent transmission. Frizzell had just arrived at his desk and was lifting two thick leatherbound briefing books from his case.

"Chicago office, Chief," was all Hunter said. The Chicago office could mean only one thing.

"Get me Kane," Frizzell snapped, then grinned.

In seconds, special agent in charge Matthew J. Kane, a twenty-two-year veteran, highly regarded for his work busting the Cleveland mob, was on the line. He was one of Frizzell's favorites.

"Chief, we have a strong suspect. Very strong. A young Loyola College student, anti-abortion activist. Took this semester off. Fits the description, no one can account for her during the week of the shooting, and she has been talking quite a bit about saving lives of the unborn—"

"Any forensic evidence, ballistics, handwriting, any of the checks?" Frizzell cut in.

"No, but we've been following her for five days, and she certainly acts the part. She bought a large suitcase, and, get this, she has tickets—bought them three weeks ago—for a flight to Frankfurt, on to Warsaw, leaving tonight."

"Poland?"

"Yup. She's Polish-American. And she has a big man with her, also Polish. Maybe fiftyish. She calls him 'Dad'—but I think he's protecting her, or maybe there's some fooling around going on. Can't tell. Surveillance can't get a good view into the bedroom."

"You have to move fast if you're sure."

"I'm moving. Her flight leaves O'Hare tonight at 7:00, and after that, bye-bye. We'd be dealing with Polish authorities for months. You know what that means."

"Do you want to just question her, or do you have enough for an arrest?"

"Close call, Chief. If we just try to question her, she could tell us to buzz off. With a warrant, we can take her in and shake her up."

Frizzell was already repacking his briefcase. "See Judge Antonelli, no one else—only Antonelli—before court goes into session. We'll call him first, but he'll give us the papers we need. He always does."

Frizzell glanced at Hunter, who was on the extension phone. He nodded as he took notes.

"And don't move," Frizzell continued, "until I get there." He checked his watch. "We can have wheels up before 9:00 . . . where is she now?"

"Home packing in a basement apartment, south side of Evanston," Kane replied.

"Okay, okay, let's see . . . Glenview, no, Meigs Field. Have an unmarked car there—no limo—at 9:45 your time. Don't talk to anybody."

Frizzell made a sweeping gesture with his arm toward Hunter, who immediately moved off the extension and called Administrative Services. The Justice Department Lear 35 with nothing but FAA markings would be fueled and ready to go at National.

"No press until we're sure, Matt," Frizzell warned. "You understand. But alert a friend or two. We want them at the scene right after the bust. You know how. Go to it."

"I've got you, Chief. See you at Meigs."

Minutes later, Frizzell and Hunter and one security agent were in the director's private elevator descending from the seventh floor to the garage where a black Chrysler was waiting.

Even with morning rush hour traffic, they would make it to the FAA hanger at National Airport before 8:45. And before Frizzell even left headquarters, the copilot of FAA 79TD was already on board, doing his cockpit check, while the pilot was inside filing his flight plan.

SIPPING COFFEE at forty-one thousand feet, Frizzell and Hunter planned their day. They would drive immediately to the location, already staked out. Frizzell would stay in the car, within sight, and be signaled in when the suspect was securely in hand. Just a precaution in case anything went askew. The press was to be notified the moment they were certain they had the right person. She would be detained in the apartment until the press arrived, then escorted out, at which point Frizzell would make his appearance, preferably on the front steps.

"What have we missed here?" Frizzell asked as he handed the steward his cup for a refill.

Toby Hunter was a perfectionist with the kind of mind that seemed to have a built-in checklist. He was no strategist, but never missed a detail. Perfect aide.

"Just one thing, Chief. Should we notify the attorney general?"

"Good, Toby, of course notify. That's all, however. Nothing specific." He grinned. "Use the plane's fax and do it as we're landing. Anything else?"

"Nope, we're covered, Chief. Except for Murphy's Law. If something can go wrong, it will."

Frizzell tried not to show his irritation. That was Hunter's weakness. He was a fretter, too negative. But then the world must need negative people to keep the checks and balances going, Frizzell thought, because God certainly made a lot of them.

It was a dreary day in Chicago. The skyline did not break into sight until they reached six hundred feet on their glide path over Lake Michigan into Meigs. Everything looked gray, including the slushy remains of last week's snowstorm. Two cars were waiting beside the runway.

Frizzell, Hunter, and the security agent stepped down the plane's self-contained stairway. Frizzell nodded at Kane, shook hands quickly, and slid into the backseat of the second car, a dark gray Ford Crown Victoria. At 9:56 CST the two vehicles sped away.

DORRIE KISTIAKOWSKY was a twenty-two-year-old graduate nursing student at Loyola. She lived in a basement apartment in an older area of three-story brownstones, vintage 1920. Most of the lower windows in the building were barred, testimony to the decline of the once fashionable neighborhood.

Frizzell's car was parked half a block away but with a clear view of the suspect's house. Across the street, facing the other way, was Kane's car.

The plan was for Kane and two other agents to go to the front while two more agents staked out the back door of the building. Having studied the blueprints on file in the city's building department, the agents knew the suspect's apartment consisted of two rooms in the front and that there was an emergency door off the kitchen leading into the furnace room, and thence to a door opening to a back alley. No escape.

Kane half-saluted Frizzell, got out of the car, and walked alone down the street. When he was in front of the girl's brownstone, he nodded, then turned and opened a waist-high, wrought-iron gate. Two agents bounded from another parked car and followed. They walked down eight steps and turned to the right to the apartment's front door, partially obscured by the steps leading up to the main entrance. Kane stood in the center, the two street agents on either side. Kistiakowsky was classified as a dangerous suspect, so both men had weapons drawn.

The plan was to startle those inside, so Kane pounded his fist on the door several times. "Open up, FBI! Open up immediately!" he shouted, then pounded hard again.

INSIDE THE APARTMENT, Dorrie Kistiakowsky ran out of her bedroom toward her father, who was gasping and holding his chest.

"Be quiet!" she whispered, grabbing him by the arm. There had been two robberies and one rape in this very block over the past six months, in broad daylight. It could well be a trick.

The door was vibrating under the heavy pounding. Dorrie crept toward it, checked the dead-bolt, and activated the security alarm her father had insisted she install after the rape episode.

She pointed at the phone. "Dial 911!" she shouted. "Dad! Dial 911!"

Her father, who had been frozen for a moment, headed toward the phone, but then, clutching his chest, stumbled over a small footstool, knocking a lamp off its stand, and crashed to the floor.

Kane, hearing the noise, assumed the suspect was heading through the emergency exit.

"Hit it," he shouted, and the bigger of the two agents pulled out a crowbar, wedged it into the doorjamb by the dead bolt, and pulled violently. At the same time, the other agent hit the door with his left shoulder. The door shattered, and the men burst through. The girl was screaming hysterically; the older man was on the floor.

SEVEN BLOCKS AWAY at the South Side substation a loud buzzer sounded at a computer control station. Officer Shick stared at the screen.

"Oh, man, another one! Down on Dodge Street. Probably another false alarm; we've had three in the past four days. But it's not a good area. Better check it out," he said, looking over at the only other officer in the station house.

Officer Bell, who had just completed his morning rounds, would have waited to finish his coffee, but this morning he had to be diligent. They had a visitor.

"And take Mr. McCartney here with you," said Shick. "He

can see how taxpayer funds are used when these idiots don't know how to run their security systems."

Jim McCartney was a young *Tribune* reporter just assigned to the police beat, spending his very first day at this station in order to get indoctrinated. He grabbed his pad and followed the officer out the door.

MAT KANE approached the girl, his gun drawn and his badge flipped open. She was crying uncontrollably, leaning over the man's prostrate body and holding his wrist, obviously checking his pulse.

"Daddy!" she shouted.

Kane saw blood flowing from a gash on the man's forehead He nodded at the phone, and one of the agents called 911. Just then two more agents burst through the rear door, and Kane waved them back.

"I'm sorry, ma'am," Kane said, "but I must ask you some questions. We'll call for medical help, and we'll take care of him."

"What are you talking about?" she shouted. "This is my father. You've killed him. He has a heart condition."

She ripped open the man's shirt, placed the heel of her hand over his heart, and began plunging her hand up and down, administering CPR. The agents hovered around her awkwardly; one got a damp towel from the kitchen and held it over the man's bleeding forehead.

Outside, the ambulance arrived, sirens blasting, at about the same time the police car did. A large group of neighbors was clustered around the front door. The paramedics rushed through them and loaded the unconscious man onto a gurney.

Officer Bell and the rookie reporter pushed their way through the crowd. McCartney pulled out a small thirty-five millimeter camera at about the same time Bell realized he was the only uniformed person in camera range. He accosted the men in suits; they flashed their FBI badges. Bell watched as they stopped the girl, who was trying to leave with the paramedics as they loaded her father into the ambulance.

"Wait a minute here!" Bell said to the agents. "What are you people doing?"

Kane, backpedaling madly, retreated to the kitchen and radioed Frizzell. "Get out!" he said simply.

The dark gray car, unnoticed, slid quietly down the street, and back toward Meigs Field.

SHOULD WE ABORT Plan B, sir?" Hunter asked during the flight back to Washington.

"Of course not, Toby. The AG herself ordered it. Why would you ask?"

"Well, we may not look too good this morning."

"No one will care. It only matters if we get the killer. Let's just pray Kane was right."

Toby noticed that the decision had now become Kane's.

"So why should we call off the AG's fireworks?"

"Murphy's Law, sir. "

"Toby, stop that," Frizzell snapped and returned to the reports he had been scanning.

Even as they spoke, the wire services were carrying the story that the FBI had taken into custody a prime suspect in the Fargo abortionist doctor murder. Special Agent Matthew Kane acknowledged that some force had been used and that one innocent bystander, the suspect's father, was in intensive care from a myocardial infarction.

LATE THAT AFTERNOON, Emily, Paul, and Ted Foran, assistant AG for the criminal division, gathered in Emily's office as the field reports came in.

At precisely 4:00 P.M. EST, FBI and Justice teams had visited the homes and offices of anti-abortion activists in eight cities: Pensacola and Melbourne, Florida; Wichita, Kansas; Minneapolis, Minnesota; Tacoma, Washington; Portland, Oregon; Los Angeles, California; and Falls Church, Virginia.

The officials were meticulous, loud, and obvious. But courteous. These were simply fact-finding interviews. They apologized carelessly for neglecting to call and arrange the visits, though that was usual FBI procedure. They asked about pro-life opinions and activities, their questions blunt, their voices often weighted with suspicion. In several instances the agents left with a warning that they very well might return, and if the questioned parties were to take any trips, they should let the local FBI office know.

This countrywide barrage was intended as a shot across the bow, a chilling signal that the government was cracking down on pro-life leaders. It succeeded. It was also intended to reassure the press and public that the government was on the job. It did that—and much more.

Foran, an aggressive ex-Texas prosecutor, was jubilant at the incoming reports. Paul was more subdued, Emily cautious and anxious. The big story was Chicago, marred only by the heart attack of the suspect's father. But by late that afternoon, though he was still in intensive care, Dorrie Kistiakowsky's father was out of critical condition. The *Chicago Tribune*, however, the public information officer reported, was preparing a savage story that the bureau had disregarded the suspect's constitutional rights and botched the job completely.

The bureau was being less than helpful, Frizzell offering no information about the suspect. When Emily called him at 5:00 P.M. he informed her that the interrogation was still under way. He warned her that no information should be given to the press lest it be considered prejudicial at a later time.

Emily in turn called O'Keefe. He was with the president, she was told, but a few minutes later he called back from the Oval Office.

"Hold on," he said. Then Emily heard Griswold's familiar voice.

"Good show, Emily. We were elected to get tough on criminals, and we're doing just that."

"Yes sir."

"And don't let a little flak you'll take over that Chicago business throw you. The people trust the bureau. Let them handle it. They're the pros. This too will pass. How are your kids doing?"

"Fine," she sputtered with surprise. "Uh, thank you for asking, sir."

"Now look, you go home and spend an evening with them. We've got three years and eleven months, at least, in this place. We're going to make this government work. So stay strong for the long haul . . . and tell your kids their mom earned her pay today. Good show. Good show. That's what I like. Action."

Emily reported to her colleagues that the president was euphoric. "He likes action," she said dryly.

"I don't know," Paul shook his head. "We'll see."

He was more subdued than usual, Emily thought, and she wondered what he was thinking.

"Well, gentlemen," she said, "I have a presidential order to see my children, and I always obey the president. Paul, good job. Call me at home if there are any developments. Good job, Ted— and you tell your field people that for me as well."

She turned, scooped up papers into her case, and buzzed her secretary to order her car. For the previous two nights she hadn't seen the kids at all; they'd been asleep by the time she got home. Tonight would be different.

IT WAS 8:00 P.M. before Kane called on the secure line with the first real report. It confirmed the awful feeling Frizzell had had in his gut for hours.

"Not too promising, Chief. Our Miss Kistiakowsky says she was at a Christian conference when the Fargo incident took place, and so far it seems to check out. And she was getting ready to go to Poland all right, but she says it was to be part of a Catholic relief agency's work in some gypsy camps near the Slovakian border—"

"And that, I suppose, checks out as well," Frizzell sighed.

"So far it does. Of course, all this could be a cover. But I don't think we should hold her. We let her go over to the hospital to see her father, agents with her of course, and she got so angry she was nearly hysterical. "

"What about getting the witnesses at Fargo to make ID?"

"They've seen her picture. They say she looks like the one. We're bringing them down in the morning. But it's real shaky. We can't book her, Chief; there's not enough. The magistrate would laugh us out."

"Has she got a lawyer?"

"Yeah, some buddy from the pro-life movement who doesn't know where the courthouse is, but I'm sure he could file a habeas writ."

"What's happening with the press?"

"All over us like flies in a pasture, but we've said nothing—not a word."

"Good. Say only that this is a major capital case, the usual stuff. Just buy some time."

"But she'll talk," Kane warned. "When we let her loose, she's gonna be all over the papers. She's that type. Probably sue us, too, if she gets a decent lawyer."

"Tell her we won't book her, but for her protection, until the witnesses come, we'll put her in a good hotel near the hospital, pay all the bills, cover the hospital expenses too. We've got to get some time here, Matt. Use your charm. Do what it takes."

"I'm sorry, Chief. We should have interviewed her first, but it looked like she was getting ready to take off—and who would figure the old man would have a heart attack?"

"Well, just keep the lid on, Matt, as long as you can." Frizzell hung up the receiver and sent Toby home. Then he called Clarkson since no one wanted to bother the attorney general at home with her kids and her husband, who had come back a day early from Harvard. Clarkson had passed the director's report on to O'Keefe, who had called Frizzell back immediately. Though it looked like the woman might not be the one, Bernie didn't think it cause for alarm. Certainly no need to bother the president. As for Robbie, he loved it. The government was acting. His tracking polls would show a blip-up the next morning, he was certain.

No one seemed concerned. The network coverage had been straight, the story about Mr. Kistiakowsky the only off-key note in a generally favorable report.

Frizzell sat there under the silent gaze of J. Edgar Hoover, whose portrait dominated the far wall of his office. He angrily threw his pen on the desk. So meticulous he was, prided himself on details. To botch this was unforgivable. Kane had misled him, of course.

He'll have to go, and fast, when the press hits, he thought.

He stared at the portrait. The old man seemed to be staring right back. What would he have done? That's a joke. He would have called the president and said, "We all screw up, don't we, sir?" And he'd have on his desk a file a foot thick on every indiscretion and dalliance his boss had ever committed since he was a teenager. In those days the president knew full well what Hoover had. So the president would tell him he was a great American, and Hoover would pick up the phone, call three buddies in the press, and the whole thing would disappear.

But things weren't like that anymore. Too bad. Frizzell picked up his dictating machine, instructing his secretary to get a larger picture of Griswold on the wall behind his desk—and one of the new attorney general. Her predecessor's was still hanging. That kind of ineptness could be costly.

17

N O O N E, not even Frizzell, who knew the worst, expected the firestorm that swept across the next
morning's newspapers. The *Chicago Tribune* started it with
a banner of the story, and the *Post*, for its final edition, moved it
above the fold. The wire services were feeding new material hourly:
stories from unnamed hospital sources about the grave condition of
Dorrie's father, then from sources close to the investigation who
admitted that the FBI had arrested the wrong woman, then from
other cities with reports of bullying tactics by the bureau. By 11:00
A.M. the ACLU's Washington office had issued a statement with a
cautious denunciation. When Congress opened at noon, a procession of speakers took to the microphones and cameras, chastising
the administration for ineptitude at the very least.

By that time, Frizzell had worked out public statements so
positive that it made the agents look like death-defying heroes.
If the story worked, fine; if not, Kane would take the fall.

The bureau's public information office was working feverishly,
calling in chits. The agent in charge kept a lengthy list of all news
sources to whom they had leaked before, and these were the first
called. Even the most scrupulous reporters were reluctant to bite
the hand that fed them.

At the White House, Robbie coached Press Secretary Atwater, who put a reasonably good spin on the story at her 12:00 briefing in the White House press room—and behind the scenes was frantically giving background briefings to friendly reporters. There was, she told them, evidence implicating Dorrie Kistiakowsky that couldn't be publicly discussed. No question, in time the case would be cracked.

Griswold called Robbins and O'Keefe to the Oval Office. Robbie, who, more than anyone else, had been goading the president to act, was unfazed by it all.

"Looks like a two-day story to me, sir," he told Griswold as Bernie sat slightly slumped in the chair, frowning, uncharacteristically quiet. The lawyer in him was always more tentative than the politician, and it was a tension he struggled with.

"But if the father dies . . ." Griswold said.

"A downer, but it wouldn't last . . . and he won't die." Robbie smiled. The polls had shown a tic up overnight.

"And we can fire an agent or two," Bernie chimed in. "The important thing is, we have the initiative. You were acting. It's what people expect. Leadership." Bernie was leaning forward in his chair as if to add some momentum of his own to the campaign.

"Yes, yes, these things are going to happen, of course, gentlemen. We have to learn to take it in stride and not be thrown off. We'll keep the pressure on, Bernie. Don't let them use this as an excuse to back off. The sooner we shut down these terrorists, the better."

ONE PERSON NOT SHARING in the self-induced euphoria was Paul Clarkson. He met with Emily for an hour, carefully reviewing all the information from the field. She was most worried about Mr. Kistiakowsky: first about his health and survival, and second about the possible civil rights violations. But on the whole, she said, the work in the eight cities had gone smoothly. The prolife network was shaken, she was sure, and if they kept the pressure on them, someone would break. Somebody would talk.

Afterward, Paul walked the length of the south corridor to his own office to wait. He knew Langer would call. And he did.

"Paul, I sent you down to that swampland to keep the alligators tamed. What, for heaven's sake, is going on?"

"I understand, Senator. Chicago was a bad break. The FBI may have jumped the gun a bit. "

"No, no. That's bad enough, but I understand. But these other eight cities, Paul. It looks to me—no, it smells to me like you people are trying to intimidate and break a movement. Can't you restrain those wild-eyed bureaucrats?"

"Senator, in fairness I have to tell you that this was my idea."

"What! I sent you there to convert them, and they've converted you. Paul, Paul, you listen to me. These are our folks out around the country. Good, honest, God-fearing people who want to save babies from having their skulls crushed. That's all. One nut in Fargo doesn't taint the whole movement."

"There are elements in the pro-life network that are what could be called a terrorist operation, sir," said Paul. "I've seen the intelligence, and we have to bring them to justice. We need to do it before they discredit the good people."

"Paul, you and I need to talk. If you go after the killer, that's fine. Use the Eighty-second Airborne for all I care. But I'm warning you and your boss, you start trampling on civil rights or you use this as an excuse to stamp out legitimate dissent, and you'll have a real war on your hands right here at this end of Constitution Avenue where the people's representatives have the power.

"And listen, Paul, don't let your boss forget that all of her judges have to come past me—and all of her crime bills—and even her appropriations." Langer was steamed. Paul had worked for him long enough to know that the senator's cheeks would be flushed, his brow furrowed.

"And don't you forget," Langer's passion came through the phone lines, "that the right of civil dissent is at the very heart of a free society. Look at the civil rights movement: It wasn't so popular down home, but it was the essence of how a free society works. Or Vietnam. There's irony, for heaven's sake. I was prepared to die in the jungle—almost did—to protect the right of my peers at home to protest what I was doing. Sounds strange, I know. I hated them, but I'd die for their right."

"I respect you for that, Senator, and I agree with you." Paul could barely get any words in.

"But remember, the pro-life movement is the first one in the history of this republic to have its rights restricted—like what's coming down now." Langer paused for breath, and Paul spoke quickly.

"Senator, I share your convictions; you know that. But we have to enforce the law. It's different here than it was on the Hill."

"Never fails," Langer sighed, "send a politician to the executive branch and he becomes a statesman. The bureaucracy swallows even the best of them. You see here, Paul; you just get my message to the attorney general."

"Yes, sir, I'll do it today. "

Paul hung up, chastened. He did live between two worlds. And in his heart he agreed with Langer. But as associate attorney general he had his duty to do. He picked up the phone to call Emily.

IRA LEVITZ sat in his cubicle at the *Post*, sipping coffee and scanning news accounts of the administration's campaign against the pro-life network. Turning in his chair, he knocked an empty Domino's pizza box on the floor. Crumbs and scraps of hardened cheese showered his lap.

It wasn't what he read that troubled him so much; he'd seen thousands of instances of bureaucratic overreaching and bungling. He and others in the press would rap their knuckles hard, and then the bureaucrats would draw their grubby hands back under their shells.

Maybe it was uncertainty about what to write. Usually he would mull over the ideas for a column for a day or two; then he'd sit down at the word processor and the words would pour out of him. But today, with only an hour to go, the words simply weren't there.

What was bothering Levitz was something he couldn't identify, a nagging sense that things were just not quite right. Over
the years, he had learned to trust his feelings as much as his
head. That's where the passion came from. And he didn't like
his feelings today. He knew, deep down inside, that the country,
without even realizing it, was crossing an invisible line.

Suddenly his fingers started moving on the keyboard.

Only thirty days in office, and Whitney Griswold has arrived
at the defining moment of his presidency. It started with a gun-
shot in Fargo and now hangs in the balance in a Chicago intensive
care unit.

At the risk of overstating, a common complaint about this
profession, it may well be a defining moment for the nation.
For in the Griswold administration's reaction to this wretched
abortion clinic violence, we may discover that the defense of
liberty costs us our liberty.

He stopped and rubbed his eyes. *That line's too cute*, he thought.
*People simply won't see this. Don't want to. Crime is so bad in America
that they'll welcome a police state. Anything for personal peace.*

The signs were everywhere, Levitz realized. Government
SWAT teams, without regard for the Fourth Amendment protection against unreasonable search and seizures, were kicking
down doors at night in public housing projects. Random roadblocks in Miami, Los Angeles, Detroit, and Atlanta. Threats to
free speech. Curfews—nothing but martial law—in a thousand
American communities.

He ran his hands through his hair and started again.

When challenged by reports this week that the gestapo-style
raids . . .

He went back, moved his cursor to the "gestapo-style" and
struck out the words . . .

. . . on pro-life leaders might violate civil liberty, Griswold
looked startled. "Why of course not," he said. "The first freedom is freedom from fear, and we are going to do what we must

to guarantee that, for people in their homes, walking the streets, or exercising their constitutional rights in an abortion clinic."

Well, thank you, Mr. President. But perhaps you should study your history. Some seventy years ago another leader said almost exactly the same thing, and the people loved it. They welcomed fascism. It's an unfair comparison perhaps. Griswold is a decent man; Hitler was evil incarnate. But the fact remains: People will always choose order over liberty. And the most ghastly transgressions are often committed by decent, well-meaning people sitting in well-lighted offices, doing what they believe is right and noble.

Levitz sighed, drew back, saved the draft, and decided to come back to it in a few minutes. It was a wonderful, sunny day outside, brisk, clean air, maybe in the mid-forties. He'd walk to the park at the end of Connecticut Avenue, stop at his favorite cigar store on the way and indulge himself. And he'd clear his head.

Deep in his own thoughts, Levitz walked through the *Post* lobby, his trench coat swinging open. He hardly noticed the guard with the big grin until he heard, "Have a good day, Mr. Levitz." He grinned and waved back.

He made his way along L Street to Connecticut Avenue, passing the shining white edifice of the Mayflower Hotel, its bright flags snapping in the cool breeze. He thought how he must be careful not to let his own experiences distort his thinking. The passion for human freedom and human rights was, after all, in his genes. His mind moved back, as it had thousands of times before: He could see his grandfather, once a tall, stately gentleman—or so the pictures made him appear when he was professor of physics at Tubingen—being shoved from the train as it pulled into Auschwitz. He and Ira's grandmother were never heard from again. His own father had narrowly escaped.

America didn't have to worry about Hitler, or some madman plotting to exterminate Jews. But the moral vacuum of the '80s and '90s, had left people without any inner restraints.

And when there are no inner restraints, he thought, government has to increase force. But it's never enough. So it keeps increasing. And eventually comes the Faustian bargain: You give up your liberties, says the government, and I'll provide you security. And the next thing you know, you end up killing Jews after all. Or something like it.

Levitz stopped in Farragut Square where Connecticut Avenue and K Street intersect, a beautiful patch of green in the middle of the busiest part of the city. He looked around, taking a deep breath. It was such a beautiful day.

He noticed a young couple sitting on a bench. The man looked like a lawyer; so did the young woman. Both had short, glossy hair and wore matching horn-rims that clicked as they laughed and leaned together, talking quietly. Love blooming in the park on this faux-spring day.

What do they care about order and liberty and social contracts and the Bill of Rights and writing deadlines? thought Levitz illogically. He felt an irrational impulse to walk over, grab them both hard, and ask them if they realized that the social consensus in America was unraveling and that they might someday, like his grandfather, be on a train to a gulag or a camp. He had a perverse sense of humor, so it took all his self-restraint not to do it. He could just see them jumping up, screaming, running away, and then telling their friends about the psycho who'd accosted them in the park.

And maybe they'd be right. Coat flying, slightly hunched over, chuckling to himself, with cigar smoke billowing over his head, Ira Levitz walked east on K Street, back to the *Post* to finish his column.

18

O N THE VIRGINIA HILLS sloping down toward the
Potomac River, underneath the noisy path of jets thundering along the river toward National Airport, lie
the green slopes housing Washington's quietest neighbors: the
235,000 graves of Arlington National Cemetery.

The cemetery's formal entrance lies at the end of Memorial
Bridge, the gleaming white span over the Potomac River guarded
by huge statues of naked men with flaming swords and golden
horses. The cemetery itself rises up a steep hillside to the lawns
of the Custis-Lee Mansion, where the Stars and Stripes always
fly at half-mast. Not far away is the celebrated grave of John F.
Kennedy, its eternal flame still burning; and the grave of Robert
Kennedy, interred near his brother five years later; and the Tomb
of the Unknown, guarded night and day by the Honor Guard
Ceremonial Unit of Fort Myer's Third Infantry.

Despite its tourmobiles and visitors' center, Arlington main-
tains its quiet dignity as the final resting place of presidents,
generals, admirals, astronauts, and thousands upon thousands
of ordinary men and women who gave their lives in the service
of their country. The nation's history is marked and measured in
its headstones: The Civil War. The Spanish-American War.

World War I. World War II. The Korean Conflict. Vietnam. And then there are the less celebrated skirmishes that claimed much smaller numbers, but still demanded the ultimate sacrifice: Beirut. Granada. Kuwait. Somalia. The simple, rounded white-granite stones stretch out in uniform, heartbreaking rows, dotting silent hillsides and guarding grassy meadows.

On this particular morning, a slow procession wound its way up one of the cemetery's quiet drives to a green canopy draped above a freshly dug, perfect rectangle of red Virginia clay. Beside it were three precise rows of folding chairs. At a discreet distance, atop a small rise, an army band waited, along with four soldiers at attention, bearing flags.

The cortege topped a hill near the gravesite. An army officer walked slowly, leading a large, glossy chestnut horse who strode the familiar road, occasionally snorting and shaking his head from side to side. Its saddle was empty; a gleaming pair of high black boots were turned backward in the stirrups.

All was quiet save the measured clop of the riderless horse's hooves on the pavement—and the echo of four more horses behind, pulling an open, large-wheeled cart bearing the flag-draped coffin: Colonel Carl Lee Miller was coming home to Arlington for his final rest. Behind the caisson walked his widow, children, and grandchildren.

On a hillside nearby, two men stood erect near a copse of trees and a grouping of graves. Their arms angled in salute as the caisson rolled by. Then, as they watched the funeral procession move to the gravesite, the two resumed their conversation.

"Thanks for meeting with me, man," said Lance Thompson. "This was the best place I could think of where we could talk in private. But I forgot they would be having funerals. It sure brings back the memories."

His colleague was a tall black man with close-shaven salt-and-pepper hair. He wore round wire-rimmed spectacles, had a large, rather flat nose, and when he grinned, a gap between his teeth offset his otherwise rather forbidding appearance.

James Jones had served with Lance in the army's Special Forces in the Gulf War. Though the two had not been in the same unit, the unique challenges of the deserts of Iraq and Kuwait had drawn them together in a way they hadn't anticipated: They had been part of a tiny, top-secret, multioperational force chosen to infiltrate Baghdad and neutralize Saddam Hussein.

The two men had dropped into the dark skies above Baghdad in camouflage chutes, made their way to the Iraqi leader's hidden compound, slit the throats of the guards at the entrance, used a minute amount of plastic explosive to blow their way into Hussein's bunker, and there had found the Iraqi leader engaged in an interview with an American journalist.

Before they could recover from the shock, an entire squad of armed-to-the-teeth Revolutionary Guards had sprung into action. The two infiltrators had thrown smoke bombs, sprayed the room generously with their Uzis, and barely escaped in the resulting firefight. But as they were running toward the door, James had returned to break the news camera, still rolling, and destroy the film. Lance had then torn back through the wall of troops and dragged his friend out of the bunker.

From there they had fled by foot through the streets, hiding in garbage dumps until dawn, when they had connected with their helicopter unit and been spirited out of Iraq.

The bizarre scene had been buried. The western journalist's memoirs, helped along by a large and anonymous financial contribution, had not mentioned the incident; neither had any reports to the joint chiefs and the president. But ever since, Jones had said he and Lance were blood brothers for life.

After the war, Jones had retired from the military and started a small security company. Aided by loans extended to minority-owned businesses, he had built his company, even in the security-saturated Washington area, into a scrappy, good-bargain agency whose employees combined military-style precision with an unusual ability to blend into the background. Many diplomats and government attaches used their services, and, increasingly, so did private companies looking for top security at a good package price.

For all these reasons, it had seemed only natural that his company would bid for a new contract on a soon-to-be-completed building in D. C.'s Foggy Bottom area. The owners seemed unusually skittish, and several other security groups had already been screened out of the action for one reason or another. Now, essentially, it was down to his company and one other. But James Jones was determined to get this contract. He had special, personal reasons for wanting to be in charge of security for the regeneration center.

"I think it's all just about in place," he told Lance. "We bid as low as we could without making it suspicious. And we've thrown in a goodie they seem to like: additional checks and sweeps based on information we obtain ourselves from subcontracts with private investigators and networking with police units. You can tell they've gotten more jittery since the Fargo thing. They liked the idea of additional intelligence and information gathering on possible threats to security."

"I guess there's nothing more we can do, then," said Lance. "It sounds like you guys have everything in place. We just gotta hope they sign you."

"Right," said Jones. "And I think they will. Hey, you remember my boy Justin? He's graduating from college in May—"

"No way," said Lance. "He was a high school football player last time I saw him."

"Well, he finished out as right tackle this year at Maryland," said Jones. "He's a big boy. But he's coming into the business with me after he graduates, and he's starting from the ground up. That means if we get this contract, he'll be working the night shift at the center this summer—"

"That's perfect," said Lance. "You are too smooth, my man." He looked at the funeral canopy in the distance. "I don't know quite when we're going to be ready to move. But I know we gotta do it. All the talk these people do isn't accomplishing anything. People are dying. Little people. I just need a little more time to work on the white brothers—they're a little slow, if you know what I mean."

Jones laughed. It was a longstanding joke between them.

"It's because they've never been in war," he said. "Sometimes people wait until the situation hits 'em right over the head before they understand where they are. And usually by the time they understand where they are, it's too late."

"Right," said Lance. "And this *is* war. It has been for some time, but now it's too far gone to ever go back. That's why things are heating up. We can't talk on the phone anymore unless we're both at pay phones. There can't be any traceable connection between us . . . so don't call me. It's too chancy. If I need you, I'll put an ad in the personals section of the *Fairfax Journal*: 'Gay black man seeks same for discreet, explosive good times.' Check every day. If you see that ad, meet me here at noon."

Jones sighed. " 'Gay black man seeks same'?" he said. "It was easier in Iraq, dealing with terrorists . . . but I'm with you, brother."

They looked around for a moment, then hugged vigorously, clapping each other on the back. For good measure, in case anyone was watching, they each looked down, touched the headstone nearest them, crossed themselves, then headed in opposite directions down two different cemetery paths.

Suddenly the hills echoed with the final tribute to Colonel Carl Lee Miller: the three sharp explosions of the salute—seven guns fired perfectly in unison—then a trembling moment of silence; then the clear, throbbing notes of "Taps" filling the quiet air of the cemetery.

Lance Thompson's eyes filled with tears, as always, and he turned, hand over his heart, then saluted a farewell to the fellow soldier he had never known.

19

EMILY GINEEN guarded her weekends. With Frederick home from Harvard and the kids home from school, weekends were family times at their large brick Georgian-style Rockwood Parkway home in the Spring Valley section of northwest Washington. On Saturday evening they usually cooked up a huge batch of chili or pizza and watched videos or played board games.

But on this Saturday morning she made an exception. Director Frizzell had sounded so insistent on the phone the night before: issues of grave national concern, he said, that were better not put in writing. So Emily had invited Paul to join the two of them at her home, 9:00 A.M. for one hour only.

Paul was first to arrive, wheeling into the circular driveway in his old red Volvo. Emily watched from the window as he swung his legs out first, grasping the door handle firmly, and then thrust himself upright; at almost the same instant, he clutched the two canes just behind the seat. It required perfect balance, but she imagined he'd had lots of practice.

A few moments later, at exactly 9:00, a black Chrysler arrived. The security agent in the passenger seat bounded out to open the rear door for Director Frizzell. He strode up the front walk in his suit and tie.

Emily shrugged to herself and opened the door. She was wearing jeans, a turtleneck, and a gray sweatshirt with a black Labrador stenciled on the front; Paul had on khakis and an Irish knit pullover. She escorted her two visitors to her cherry-paneled library, a spacious room at the far end of the first floor.

"Help yourselves, gentlemen," she said, pointing to the pot of coffee and stoneware mugs on the coffee table. She then sat in one corner of her brown-leather sofa, the kind one finds in musty Boston law firms. Frizzell took the leather wingback chair that looked new and didn't match the sofa; Paul chose the upright, lacquered, Hitchcock chair with the Harvard seal on the backrest.

"I felt it extremely important," Frizzell began, "to share the latest intelligence with you, much of which lends itself to some interpretation. This room is secure I assume?"

Emily nodded. Security checked it at random times but at least every month.

"Good. First let me show you this." He picked up a large folder. "We've had psychological profiles prepared on the more notable anti-abortion leaders. A lot of the observations here are, of course, quite predictable, but what I found interesting was a pattern that emerges. Interesting and, I must say, disturbing."

Emily resisted the urge to fidget as Frizzell explained the bureau's facility for psychological analysis. "So reliable that the CIA even asked for help."

Why are bureaucrats so obsessed with proving their own importance? Emily wondered as she sipped her coffee. Insecurity perhaps, or to justify budgets? After all, the bigger the budget, the more important the job is perceived to be.

"And what did you find?" she asked, glancing at her watch.

Frizzell cleared his throat. All of these leaders, to no one's great surprise, seemed to be single-minded, zealous in their cause, and, in some cases, exhibited behavior bordering on obsessive/compulsive, he said. They were generally without fear for themselves and evidenced definite psychopathic tendencies. The report was filled with technical jargon, but Frizzell frequently interjected a layman's interpretation.

"In short," he laid the report on the coffee table, "very dangerous people, prone to violence, with Messianic complexes. The CIA tells us that these profiles are not unlike Muslim terrorists who want to die for Allah. It's their ticket to paradise."

"The CIA has read these? It's against the law for them to spy on American citizens."

"Oh, they're not involved, other than to give us technical advice, sort of an informal understanding," Frizzell shrugged.

"But clearly here," he continued, "we have certain signs of imbalance. For example, we understand that some of these people actually claim to hear voices they believe are divine messages."

Paul frowned slightly. He wondered what Frizzell would say if he told him that God had spoken to him at times. Not audibly, but in distinct inner convictions. Like the time he had sensed God's clear leading about spending two years in Atlanta as a public defender. He decided to say nothing.

"Nothing surprising, Director." Emily smiled, nodding, her eyebrows up, as if to ask what else.

"The urgency, you see, is that I think they're about to strike again. These types of people could do just about anything. They hate the president, and I fear they might go to any lengths to embarrass or discredit him to make their point."

Emily nodded again.

"The most critical information is contained in one informant's report. One group seems to have a plan. They've even named it."

"Plan B?" Emily interjected. "Operation Steamroller?" She couldn't help herself.

Frizzell looked at her coldly. "An operation they're calling 'Gideon's Torch.' We don't know anything specific. They're very security conscious. Some of the conversations, though, have alluded to 'lighting the darkness and exposing evil deeds.' Our analysts say this could be violence, perhaps even spectacular violence to make a point . . . I mean, lighting the darkness could refer to some violent explosion."

Frizzell then explained the grave possibilities. Four and a half pounds of highly enriched uranium, capable of being used in a nuclear weapon, had recently been stolen in St. Petersburg, Russia. Intelligence reported that organized crime groups there had the components to construct nuclear weapons and were offering them for sale. Just a year earlier, a nuclear weapon produced in North Korea had been intercepted on its way to Iran. The CIA, he pointed out, was diligent, as were the other intelligence organizations. But this kind of thing could always slip through. And there were plenty of less exotic ways to concoct huge lethal explosives. Messianic zealots talking about "torching" something could not be ignored.

"Which group is it that's developed the plan?" Emily asked.

"That's another part of our concern," said Frizzell. "It's the one right here in Washington. The one called The Life Network."

"Why all the torch stuff?" she asked.

"We've looked into that. You can tell a lot about these types by the imagery they choose. Our analysts presume the metaphor comes from the Old Testament, where there's an account about an ancient battle between the Israelis and the Midianites. The Israeli commander was a man named Gideon. His army was overwhelmingly outnumbered, but he won the battle. Used torches as weapons."

Paul started to say something, then thought better of it. Frizzell had his facts skewed, but perhaps now was not the time to correct the FBI director, nor the time to seem overly familiar with the biblical text in question.

"So what do you propose?" Emily asked Frizzell.

A laundry list, he said. Authority to put bureau agents or marshals in selected major hospitals across the country, in addition to those already posted at clinics; authority for "deeper" surveillance and wiretaps; and a "supplemental budget allocation of perhaps fifty million dollars to pay the bills." And the president needed to be apprised of the profiles, Frizzell added.

It was 9:45. Emily thanked the director and assured him she would read the profiles and weigh all he had said carefully over the weekend.

"Please do not underestimate the gravity of this situation," he said. "My experience over the years tells me that this is a matter not to be taken lightly."

Frizzell left first, and Emily motioned for Paul to remain. She was learning to trust his judgment.

"Well," she said when they were alone, "what do you think?"

"I dunno. He's very shrewd. And remember, he was badly stung by the Chicago fiasco. I think he's covering his butt. Then again, he may be genuinely concerned. Still, I can't help but wonder if he isn't seeing this as a chance to puff his budget—and his own importance."

"But he's got informers. He wouldn't dare misrepresent the intelligence," Emily pressed.

"But he might also not understand everything quite right. 'Gideon's Torch' for example. It comes from the Book of Judges, chapter 7. It's a great story: Gideon's men, three hundred of them, blew their trumpets and shined their torches in the night—and their enemies fled. The torches weren't weapons. That's pretty mild stuff by Old Testament standards."

Emily smiled. "I knew your Bible knowledge would come in handy one of these days. Anyway, I don't think we'll rush into the Oval Office with this one yet. But we will consider wiretaps and surveillance."

Paul looked surprised. Emily didn't notice this, but she did think he was showing a little more pain than usual as she walked him to the front door.

20

DANIEL SEATON woke groggily, feeling as if some one was calling his name. Even as he swam to the surface of consciousness, the fragments of the dream still clung to him, like seaweed from the depths.

He sat up in bed, looking over at Mary, who was on her side, one knee raised up to her chest as if she were running in her sleep. He looked at the clock. Nearly four o'clock.

The dream was slipping away even as his mind cleared. It had been a mixture of Old Testament and modern times, the type of dream he'd often had during his seminary days. Moses on the Metro. Noah at the National Zoo. His brain had no problem pairing biblical characters and twentieth-century Washington, D. C. Sometimes, in fact, the former seemed more real than the latter.

And this dream in particular had seemed so real, even though it didn't make sense. In it, he and Mary and Alex and Lance and the others had been marching in a line around the White House. He could still see the pointed tips of the wrought-iron fence separating the sidewalk from the green lawn. They had been carrying pro-life protest signs in one hand, torches in the other.

Then the president and the first lady had come out to the

fence, and the president had reached through, his hand extended toward Daniel's.

"You're right," he had said. "I've changed my mind." And Daniel was nodding.

Suddenly the Secret Service were all around the president, so Daniel backed up slightly. There was an enormous terracotta pot positioned on the sidewalk, full of red geraniums; Daniel backed into it and knocked it over. There was a huge crash. And then he woke up.

He wasn't into literal dream analysis, but this dream made sense. The FBI invasion of their home a month earlier had shaken him. Four men, pounding loudly and flashing badges, had charged in without warning and begun reading them their rights, even though he had assured them there was no need for that. He and Mary would answer truthfully anything they were asked.

At first he had been surprised when the agents had asked about the Network by name. But he had answered deliberately, without restraint, telling them that the The Life Network was an informal, voluntary group of like-minded and seriously committed Christians sworn to nonviolence.

No, he said, they knew nothing of the open letter to President Griswold or of anyone involved in the abortionist killing in North Dakota. He often preached vigorously against anything of this sort, he said.

He and Mary had been exhausted by the time the agents left their home after warning them, in so many words, not to leave town.

The other elements were equally recognizable. He had been so focused on Gideon's Torch for so long the dream had mixed the biblical account with the desires of his heart.

WHEN DANIEL WAS A CHILD, one of his favorite Bible heroes was Gideon, a man who had used cunning, not violence, to outwit and defeat the enemies of Israel in a thrilling story of psychological warfare.

In 1150 the armies of the Midianites had amassed in the great valley adjacent to Mount Moreh, south of the Sea of Galilee and just north of the borders of modern-day Israel's West Bank. The Midianites had allied themselves with the Amalekites and other eastern, nomadic armies and settled into a seven-year occupation of the nation of Israel, devastating their crops, possessions, and storehouses.

Now 135,000 troops were camped in the valley, their tents billowing in an occasional breeze, which also carried the odors of roasted goat, human sewage, and strange Oriental anointing oils to the nostrils of the men of Israel, peering down upon them from the heights of Mount Gilead. The Jewish soldiers could hear the rough shouts of drunken soldiers, the barking of dogs, even the chatter of the women and children accompanying the camp.

The Israelite commander, Gideon, was young but not untested. His reputation and his devotion to the strange God of Israel were well known to the Midianite leaders. They had heard tales of this Jehovah's delivering power against Israel's enemies. They believed the stories enough to be unnerved by them, but not quite enough to quit the fertile land.

Gideon's command had initially consisted of thirty-two thousand troops—hardly a reasonable hope against the vast eastern army. And yet God had told him to reduce his fighting force, so it would be absolutely clear that their victory over the Midianites was the work of God, not men.

Thus, Gideon had informed his soldiers that whoever was afraid was free to leave. Twenty-two thousand Israelites, hearts pounding in their chests from the sight of the vast opposing force, clutched their cloaks and gratefully returned to their tents.

But the ten thousand remaining were still too many. God told Gideon to winnow down his fighting unit even further, and soon there were but three hundred men left.

As the darkness deepened, each man was given a ram's horn trumpet, a clay pitcher, and a torch. The pitchers were inverted over the torches to protect them from the wind and to hide the light from the Midianites until Gideon's men were all in place.

But just before the battle was joined, Gideon and an assistant named Purah had crept from rock to rock until they reached an outcropping where the last patrol of the Midianite advance guard kept watch around a crackling campfire. Here they heard one soldier tell another of his strange dream of a loaf of barley bread rolling into the camp and upending the general's tent. His comrade, raising his eyebrows and thinking of the strange stories from the past about the Jewish God, had no question about the interpretation: It was the army of Gideon, the Israelite commander, he said. Their God was going to cause the Israelites to prevail.

Grinning with tense exultation, Gideon and Purah crept back to the waiting Israeli troops. And even as they did so, the strange dream and its chilling interpretation were repeated from watch to watch, carried via couriers throughout the camp, building into a common premonition of disaster that fed on the dark edges of the Midianites' pagan fears.

Before midnight that evening, the three hundred Israelites, now divided into three companies, crept silently into position above the valley where the Midianites slept. By now the sentries had all heard the strange dream and jumped at every crackle in the dry desert grass.

Suddenly the night exploded. On signal Gideon's troops all blew their trumpets, broke open their clay pitchers, and raised their torches in the darkness. The abrupt convulsion of light and noise terrified the jittery sentries, who leaped to their feet, drew their swords, screamed, and slew one another in the chaos. Meanwhile, the soldiers in their tents, groggy with sleep and fermented drink, stampeded in panic. Those who weren't cut down by their own troops fled, shrieking and stumbling, into the hills.

Daniel loved the strange story of Gideon's battle. He loved the parallels between the ancient victory and their modern mission—the victory of light over darkness, of truth over fear. It was fitting that they had named their project Gideon's Torch.

PAUL CLARKSON arrived at his office a few minutes after 7:00 Monday morning. He liked to use the limited-access highway in from Virginia that was closed to vehicles with fewer than two occupants after 7:00 A.M.; he also liked to get a headstart on the paperwork while things were quiet.

As he glanced through the agency summary for the day, his eyes stopped on a criminal division report recommending that a proposed prosecution be dropped.

Eight Act-Up protestors had smashed vials of contaminated blood on the door of the Senate Appropriations Committee to protest inadequate funding for the regeneration centers. The Capitol police had arrested them, and the protesters were then released on their own recognizance.

The event had been widely covered on the networks and in the press. The U. S. attorney first announced he would prosecute for criminal trespass and assault with a deadly weapon (the blood tested HIV-positive), but on review, the department was now contending that they could not make the charges stick; even if they could, it wouldn't be good policy. A prudential call, the assistant AG argued.

Clarkson remembered an earlier case that had outraged him when he was on the committee. Over a hundred Act-Up activists had hurled condoms and desecrated the sacramental elements at St. Patrick's Cathedral in New York. Judge JoAnn Ferdinand sentenced four of them to seventy hours of community service. She was the same judge who had sentenced pro-life rescuers charged under the same disorderly conduct statutes to fifteen-day prison terms.

Act-Up had used such tactics for years. In 1989 protesters invaded the headquarters of the Burroughs-Wellcome pharmaceutical firm, protesting the price charged for the AIDS drug AZT; some even chained themselves to desks in the offices. Later, other demonstrators disrupted the New York Stock Exchange for trading Burroughs-Wellcome stock. The response: With much fanfare, Burroughs-Wellcome gave a million-dollar donation to the AIDS cause.

Clarkson finished the report and stared at it a moment. He thought about the Saturday morning meeting and Frizzell's information and comments.

Gideon's Torch, he thought. *Exposing the darkness. No doubt there is darkness.* He added the report to a small pile on the right side of his desk

21

"M R. SMITH, I think I'm gonna get what you want," Alfonzo Rojas said into the pay phone. "I got a call from NIH early this morning. They've got a big videotape duplication order for me. From the gynecology unit. I'm gonna pick it up at three o'clock this afternoon."

The long-distance wires from Bethesda to New York crackled for a moment, and Alfonzo watched the cars roar past on Wisconsin Avenue as he strained to hear.

"That's great," said "Mr. Smith," whose real name was Bill Waters. "I'll catch the next shuttle and meet you at 3:30 at the pickup point."

"Right," said Rojas.

After he hung up the phone, he crossed Wisconsin Avenue, retrieved his old, rust-colored Honda Civic from its parking meter, and headed back to his office.

IN A RESIDENTIAL SECTION of Bethesda, Maryland, not far from the busy downtown grid of restaurants and shops, sprawl the 260 acres of the National Institutes of Health. The disjointed campus includes high-rise apartments housing doctors and their families; the Children's House, where children with cancer play on the green grass; a low, white building with what appears to be a crumpled UFO on its roof, housing the national medical library . . . and on it goes.

Federally funded, the hospital complex welcomes patients from all over the world, patients whose conditions have defied conventional treatment, patients who are willing to engage in experimental therapies. Sterile testing laboratories adjoin chaotic offices resembling a cross between a clinical research facility and the back room of a fraternity house.

Ringing faxes and phones compete with the visual displays of computer monitors; beside these, piles of open books and pamphlets are half-hidden by scribbled notes and half-eaten sandwiches and bottles of Evian water. Nearby are the patient wings where critically ill men, women, and children receive test protocols developed by the enthusiastic, blue-jeaned young researchers who live in the labs.

One of the most secure buildings on campus houses the animal research laboratories. Staff and doctors entering the building must wear proper identification. Vendors and civilians are not allowed in at all, for on the top two floors live a colony of meticulously maintained, exotically diseased mice, dogs, rabbits, and research monkeys costing $20,000 apiece, all locked carefully away from the rabid denizens of the People for the Ethical Treatment of Animals, who have vehemently vowed to free their fellow mammals.

Security for the human mammals at Building 10, an ugly glass-and-brick high-rise, is not so stringent. Marked by a grotesque black-metal sculpture at its entrance, Building 10 houses inpatients, outpatients, hordes of researchers, and, in its patient wings, any number of critically ill individuals. It is a hubbub of activity at nearly any hour, day or night. So no one took any particular notice of Alfonzo Rojas as he stepped onto the central elevator and pressed the button for level B-2.

The car descended into the bowels of NIH, and Rojas stepped off into an underground labyrinth of wide, dark corridors with stained, spotted floors. Occasional double doors opened into grimy, subterranean boiler rooms; as always, he half-expected to see shackled, slave labor manning the boilers in the darkness.

He eventually emerged into the medical arts and photography branch. Here the doorways were painted shocking pink and other bright colors to create an illusion of cheerfulness.

Whistling slightly, Rojas tapped on one of the pink doors. A receptionist let him into the television production offices, a well lit area, with plants, a few padded chairs, and cream-colored dividers separating a claustrophobic warren of cubicles crammed with videotaping equipment. Here a media staff produced training videos, from script to finished product, for the various institutes of the NIH, as well as medical facilities throughout the country.

The videos, generally about twenty minutes in length, gave overview information on anything from the proper care of laboratory animals, to procedures for new surgical techniques, to the correct procedure for filling out the laborious paperwork needed to apply for an NIH grant. The media office also provided stock video clips for news affiliates' use when they ran NIH-related stories: photography of cancer cells, backgrounders on various laboratories, and quotes from NIH officials. The production offices also had monitoring devices for taping network and local newscasts so any mentions of NIH could be culled for the files.

"How're you doin' this afternoon, Cindy?" Rojas said warmly to the receptionist. "I'm here to pick up a master video to be copied for distribution. Some kind of training video. Beth called earlier this morning."

The receptionist smiled. "Yeah, this is a big order," she said. "They're in a big hurry for it, too. I'll get Beth for you."

She picked up the phone and buzzed an extension. "Beth," she said. "The gentleman from TapeMasters is here."

Almost immediately Beth emerged from the cubicles in the back and extended her hand. "Hi, Alfonzo! How're those babies of yours? Got any new pictures?"

Rojas gave her a huge smile and reached for his wallet. He pulled out a plastic sheaf featuring a small, dark-haired boy and a tiny girl with huge brown eyes and gold pierced earrings.

"They're doing beautiful," he said. "Things are a little tight for us on the money end, if you know what I mean. But we wouldn't trade our twins for anything."

"I know what you mean," said Beth. "But I don't know how your wife does it. We've just got one, and she keeps us going all the time."

She put a videotape on the counter of the receptionist's cubicle as Rojas pulled a clipboard out of his soft-sided briefcase.

"This is a big order, right?" he said as he began filling in the work order.

"Right," said Beth. "I usually make these training video copies here myself, but I can't handle this many very easily. They want fifty dupes, and I need them in three days."

"Okay," he said. "Here's the work order. Just sign here. We'll get these back to you by Thursday."

Beth handed him the video, a one-inch Beta cassette in a dark blue-and-gray jacket with the NIH seal on the spine. Rojas glanced at the long, official title quickly—fetal tissue something or other. This was it.

He gave Beth a copy of the work order, initialed it, and stuck the video and the clipboard into his briefcase.

"Thanks," he said, smiling. "We'll get right on this. I'll call you when it's done. You all have a great day. "

"You, too," the two women echoed as the door swung shut behind him. "Thanks a lot."

ROJAS ASCENDED the elevator, exited past the ugly black sculpture, and got into his Honda. At the corner of Center Drive and Cedar Lane, a few blocks down, he turned right. A big, unmarked van was idling there. He parked at the curb and walked up to the passenger door. There was a stocky young black man at the wheel and a slender white man on the passenger side. In the back, Rojas could see snaked cables, sophisticated-looking video equipment, and a small pile of video cassettes.

"Did you get it?" asked the white guy, the one Rojas knew as Mr. Smith.

"No problem," said Rojas. "It's the one you want."

He handed his briefcase to the man, who extracted the video and looked at the spine, smiling. "Great!" he said simply. He reached into his rear pocket, pulled out a thick sheaf of twenty dollar bills, and tucked them into the side flap of the briefcase.

"Alfonzo," he said. "Here's a thousand dollars. Why don't you go get yourself a cup of coffee and come back in forty-five minutes?"

Rojas's eyes widened at the bulge in his briefcase flap, and he thought of the twins. This was the best thing that had happened to him in a long time. He took the briefcase and looked at his watch.

"Thanks," he said. "I'll be back at about 4:15."

"Great," said the man. "I'll have the rest of your payment and the master for you when you come back. Enjoy your coffee—make it an espresso."

As Rojas headed back to his Honda, Bill Waters smiled again, looking at the video in disbelief. Getting it had been almost too easy; but what it would eventually unleash would be hard indeed.

22

S PRING IS SOMETHING you not only see but feel in Washington. And for Whitney Griswold it felt very good. His tax overhaul had won editorial plaudits and was enormously popular in the opinion polls. People seemed to like his leadership style—his no-nonsense approach to issues. Crime continued to dominate public concern, but he and his attorney general had positioned themselves well, having sent a tough new sentencing bill to Congress and recommended federal jurisdiction for more capital offenses.

The polls showed him riding almost as high as he had been right after his inauguration. Robbie's grin as he entered the Oval Office each day assured the president that things were on track.

The only sour note remained the unsolved Fargo killing, and in that regard Griswold was discovering the sobering truth about the presidency: The chief executive sits in the most powerful office in the world, atop a bureaucracy employing more than 3 million civilian employees, 1.75 million military personnel, millions of offices, resources, budgets, and brain power . . . but it is not unlike sitting atop a huge, cold-blooded dinosaur, massive, obstinate, and sluggish. The president can kick, cajole, scream, pound on its armor-coated skin, but though it may occasionally stick up its head and stare back at him blankly, it moves at its own deliberate pace, one enormous plodding foot at a time.

Though Frizzell dutifully provided a daily intelligence report on the progress in the case, it contained less information than Griswold could pick up on any television broadcast.

"FBI and Justice are doing their best," Emily Gineen assured him. "They just haven't gotten the break they need yet."

Each morning, during his session with his senior advisors, the same ritual was repeated. Irked by the media drumbeat—the leaks and sensationalized stories and editorials demanding action—Griswold would lean forward, tap his desk, and order Bernie to order the FBI to step up its work. Bernie would agree and call Frizzell, who in turn would notify his field offices of "intense interest at the highest levels." And then the bureaucracy did what it would have done anyway.

On the foreign policy front, things seemed to be going smoothly. Then, in early April, new Arab-Israeli tensions erupted, thrusting Griswold into long sessions in the Cabinet Room with his national security team. General George Maloney, a square-jawed, battle-decorated hero, was proving to be one of the best of Griswold's appointees. He was tough, taciturn, but fluent in six languages and with a versatile mind that could wrestle with three major problems at once without missing a beat. Griswold liked his take-charge, can-do attitude.

This time, the problem was on the Israeli side. Right-wing factions had wrested concessions from the ruling party, and there was serious talk about renouncing the pact with the PLO and cracking down on infractions of the Gaza Strip agreements.

Some groups in Israel, Griswold thought, always wanted war. They were no better than the Islamic zealots or, for that matter, the zealots here at home.

"This must have been a great job when Calvin Coolidge had it," Griswold grinned to Robbie after a particularly long day. Still, his morale was good.

Buoyed by the polls and the fresh beauty of the cherry blossoms, Griswold decided to keep a month-old promise to his family: a long Easter weekend at Camp David. Robert was home on spring break, Elizabeth had Good Friday off, and basketball was finally over, to his enormous relief.

Aware that things were not going well in Bernie's family life, Griswold invited him and his family to join them for the weekend at Camp David. To Bernie's surprise, Marilyn agreed, and his kids were excited. Griswold had even sweetened the offer by proposing to send a special air mission King Air to Hanscom Field in Bedford, Massachusetts, to pick them up. Not really within the rules, but he wanted to help patch things up for his old buddy.

Late on Friday morning, *Marine One*, the big, specially fitted CH56 helicopter, painted olive green with the telltale white engine housing, swooped in over the Mall, approached the White House across the south lawn just above the treetops, and then reined back, its nose jutting upward, and hovered clumsily to the ground.

While the awkward bird sat on the landing pad, motor whirring and blade spinning, members of the White House press corps were ushered to the usual observation position in front of the rose garden on the walkway between the mansion and the west wing. Unless the president chose to come over and talk to them, not a very common event, they had only one reason to stand there: to observe and write about the crash if the president's helicopter went down.

The Griswolds walked briskly out of the south diplomatic entrance on the first floor, escorted by Juan, two Secret Service agents, and General Maloney, who was carrying a large briefcase. Captain Slattery, naval aide to the president, also carrying bags, and the president's doctor were close behind. Griswold held Anne's hand with his left and waved to the reporters with his right, flashing an even broader grin than usual.

The family filed across the red carpet rolled out from the chopper's steps, and Griswold returned the marine sergeant's stiff salute—something he still felt awkward about, never having served in the military—and then turned and waved once more for the cameras, ducked his head quickly, and went through the door, which swung shut seconds later. With its twin turbos whining, the machine, vibrating hard, rose, banked to the right, and swooped back over the south lawn, leaving the reporters to return to the press room empty-handed once again.

Marine One followed the Potomac River west and north across Chain Bridge, the Beltway, then Great Falls. In less than thirty minutes, a thousand feet in the air and fifty miles from the capital, they approached the foothills. Soon the heavily wooded Catoctin mountaintop came into view.

As the chopper descended, armed marines in fatigues waited at the edge of the landing area. A navy commander wearing a field jacket with the presidential seal saluted smartly when the front door was let down and the president and his family descended. The Griswolds got into golf carts driven by Secret Service agents and headed down a winding road.

"This place is creepy," Elizabeth said. Men with guns were everywhere, behind trees and along the roads and paths of the mountaintop retreat.

Other Secret Service agents scrambled ahead. At the first bend in the road, an agent lifted his radio. "Amos to control. Searchlight and party on road to Aspen." "Searchlight" was the president's code name.

"Control to Amos: Stay on the air."

"Searchlight now in Aspen. All secure."

"Roger, Amos. All secure. Out."

Two agents took their positions in Elm, a small building camouflaged in the foliage with an eight-foot wide darkened window from which all approaches were visible. From these quarters, packed with electronics, including closed circuit TV, they could watch both the front and rear of Aspen, the big presidential cabin, a rambling cottage with a huge stone fireplace, a rustic great room, cozy down sofas, and a picture window overlooking the pool and woods. The agents in Elm could also monitor the main gates, the helicopter pad, and every path within the fenced compound.

Griswold called to be sure Bernie had arrived and was being well cared for in Sycamore, one of the nicer cottages scattered through the woods. Built in the '70s when Richard Nixon had brought many world leaders there, the newer lodges were rustic on the outside, luxurious inside.

"Listen, Bernie," said the president. "You and Marilyn just take some time together. This isn't a working weekend. Just have some fun."

"Thanks," Bernie responded. "We've needed something like this for quite a while."

"We'll leave you alone tonight—but we'll have dinner together tomorrow night, okay? Just like old times."

"Like old times," Bernie echoed. "Thanks, Whit."

THE FIRST AFTERNOON, the first family enjoyed a walk in the woods, a game of horseshoes, and an informal dinner. Anne had given them a reprieve from their usual low-fat diet and granted the children's wish: a cookout. Big, fat hamburgers on the grill, "the way Daddy used to cook them," were Elizabeth's words.

The president would cook? The stewards scurried to locate a charcoal grill and lighter fluid, while the Secret Service hurriedly secreted fire extinguishers in the woods just to the side of Aspen.

"Like old times," Griswold grinned, pulling Elizabeth to his side as he lined eight half-pounders on the grill over the fiery coals. All at once, he felt a bubbly sensation in his stomach. He realized what a great moment this was. He was enjoying being president and he was enjoying even more, at this moment, being a father. He looked into his daughter's face, radiant in the glow from the embers. So innocent and pure. And Robert—what a great kid, doing well in school. And Anne was a wonderful woman. He was fortunate to have her. Life was good, Whitney Griswold thought as he sipped his glass of chilled Sauvignon Blanc.

"Daddy, why is today called Good Friday?" Elizabeth broke her father's reverie.

"Well, honey, it marks the day long ago that Jesus Christ was crucified."

"But what's good about that?"

Where does she come up with these questions? Griswold wondered. He'd never really thought about that himself.

"Well, it has religious significance. But I don't know why it's called that," he answered slowly, hoping his daughter would change the subject but knowing she wouldn't.

"We went to the cathedral this week to listen to a lecture. The man said it was good because Jesus paid for our sins. But why did he have to die?"

Griswold shoved his spatula under the hamburgers where the fire was hottest. "It's a religious symbol. It's like He had to suffer in our place."

"Why?"

"It's part of the story. The people didn't like what Jesus taught: that we should love one another. And that's the important thing. Our family are Christians, so we do the good things Jesus taught, like loving one another. Do you understand that?"

"No, Daddy. The man said we are sinners, all of us. And that Jesus died for us, in our place."

"Who was this man?"

"His name was Mr. Greene. Michael Greene, I think. And he said that crime and all the bad things—and wars and everything—happen because of our own human nature. Is that so, Daddy?"

"Michael Greene . . . from where?" Griswold asked, trying to place the name.

"England," Elizabeth said. "From some place where the Archbishop of Cadbury lives."

"Wait," said Griswold as the information clicked into place. "You mean the Archbishop of Canterbury, dear. Michael Greene is at Lambeth Palace there. Well-regarded, I'm sure, but if he was being so negative about human nature, he must be terribly out of date. Old-fashioned, like the Middle Ages. People are good, dear. We know that today."

"Mr. Greene said we are born in sin. I don't get it."

Griswold frowned. "Of course not. What a terrible thing to say."

Why would they teach such things? he wondered, nodding at Anne and making a mental note to have her check with Elizabeth's teacher.

"But why *do* bad things happen then, Daddy? Why do people kill each other and all the crime and everything?"

"That's what we're doing something about in the White House, dear. Your mother and I, and you and Robert, are very fortunate. We have a good family, good parents, good training, good homes. But many people just never have a chance. They're poor, or their parents didn't help them. Or they never got a good education. It's really not their fault. Then there are some people who are bad, and we have to arrest them and put them in prison and try to teach them to do good things with their lives. We're working very hard on that right now."

Elizabeth nodded.

"You see, with the right policies in our government, we can end a lot of bad things. We can cure a lot of the conditions that cause people to do wrong things in the first place."

"What about war, Daddy?"

"Well now, honey, that's a very good question and happens to be exactly what I'm spending most of my time on these days. And if we could just learn to trust other people—I mean look them in the eye and tell them the truth—I believe we wouldn't have any wars." Griswold was gesturing with the spatula now as he talked. "Like what I'm doing right now in the Middle East. I look straight into those Arab and Israeli leaders' eyes—"

"Whitney!"

Robert, bored, had drifted over to the fish pond, so Anne saw it first—the flames shooting up and the shriveled hamburgers looking like hockey pucks. In the trees, an agent rechecked the location of the hidden extinguishers.

"Oh, oh, sorry. I'd better turn these." Griswold struggled to turn the charred burgers, but they stuck to the grill and broke apart.

Anne cleared her throat. "Juan," she called. "Could you bring out some more hamburgers, please? We seem to have worked our way through the first batch already."

Then she smiled, and Elizabeth laughed as she watched her father fling the burgers into the woods and then scrape down the grill with the metal spatula.

"Do you think squirrels like burned hamburgers?" he asked.

"They're vegetarians, Dad," Robert volunteered.

"Thanks for that insight, son."

Elizabeth started up again. "So what does Easter mean, then, Daddy?"

"Well, dear, it means we should all be like Jesus. Good people, kind and patient." He gritted his teeth slightly. "Very patient."

Just then Juan arrived with a hastily assembled platter of plump pink burgers.

"Okay, now," said the president, "let's try this again." He slid the spatula under the first burger; it wobbled, and he promptly dropped it into the black dust next to the grill.

Elizabeth laughed again, and Griswold pretended to smile.

SATURDAY WAS A GREAT DAY for the president. With his Camp David windbreaker zipped to the top, he took a long, early morning walk alone in the woods. (As alone, that is, as any president ever can be; two agents with radios flanked him, tramping through the woods, and a third followed on the path a respectable distance behind.) He whipped Bernie soundly in three rounds of tennis during the morning, took the kids all around Camp David on one of the electric carts, and bowled with Robert before dinner, all without an interruption. (General Maloney was in the main office, just down the road from Aspen, ready to alert the president should anything of importance occur.)

That night the Griswolds and O'Keefes dined together around the large oak table at Aspen. The kids were off at Laurel in the staff mess, eating hot dogs, French fries, and enormous amounts of ketchup, settling in for an evening of first-run films in the private theater. Anne was back in control of the adult menu: sauteed Dover sole and steamed vegetables.

Anne couldn't remember the last time the four of them had sat down like this and had a leisurely dinner. The wine flowed, along with Bernie's Dewars, and the combination of the relaxed schedule, the alcohol, and the crisp air reminded her of days long gone, back when they were in school and their dreams were young. She and Marilyn leaned their elbows on the table and started reminiscing.

"Remember Barb Brookstone?" Anne said, using a pair of silver shears to cut a cluster of grapes. "Try these, they're perfect." Marilyn took the grapes and then passed the fruit tray to Bernie without looking at him. The men were preoccupied in some hot discussion about the Middle East.

"How could I forget her?" Marilyn said. "Remember when she got her skirt stuck in the top of her pantyhose and no one told her until the party was almost over?"

Anne laughed. "Well, I'd lost track of her over the years, but she sent me a wedding invitation. Funny how when you're in the White House everyone comes out of the woodwork. She's getting married—third time—to this Viennese count or something whose bloodlines go back to the last czar of Russia. So she'll be related to the English royal family and the new Russian aristocracy . . . great career move, right?"

Marilyn smiled. She vaguely remembered Barb as the sort of woman who always had to have a man at her side. She had traded them in often, and she always traded up. Once Barb had said something to Marilyn at a party, something about Bernie, appraising him with her cool blue eyes. He wasn't great-looking, but he had great potential, Barb had said. "He's going somewhere."

At the time Marilyn had loved Bernie for his laugh, his heart, his wit, his energy, his Bernie-ness. She'd never thought much about where he was going; she just knew she wanted to be with him. She'd shot back a barb at Barb. Something about feeling reassured about the caliber of the O'Keefe gene pool, and that she'd stick with him for the sake of future generations.

But now those future generations were eating hot dogs, Bernie was two sheets to the wind, as usual, and he and Whit were laughing as if they were fraternity boys.

Maybe I could compete with just the alcohol, Marilyn thought. *Or just the White House. But I sure can't compete with them both. I haven't had Bernie's full, sober attention in a long time.*

Just then the president leaned across the table. "Listen," he said. "I've got a great idea! This has been tremendous, just the four of us together again. Why don't we go horseback riding tomorrow morning? The kitchen will pack us a picnic breakfast. Champagne, orange juice, croissants, fruit . . . it'll be great!"

Bernie grinned and nodded. Anne smiled, too; the weekend had really relaxed Whitney already.

But Marilyn frowned, a well-worn vertical crease coming between her eyebrows. "I'm sorry, but I'll have to respectfully decline, I'm afraid."

Bernie flushed. No one turned down the president.

Whitney looked surprised, then smiled winsomely at Marilyn. "But why?" he said. "The weather report says it's going to be a perfect day, Marilyn. The trails are safe. The horses are great."

Marilyn smiled. He really did sound sincere. "I really appreciate the invitation. It sounds wonderful. But tomorrow is Easter, and the children and I will be going to Mass. We always do."

Bernie sputtered. "But Marilyn—"

She turned toward him, her eyes steady. "Won't you be coming with us, Bernie?"

MUCH LATER THAT NIGHT, Whitney Griswold shook his head as he thought about the dinner. "And I thought tensions were tough in the Middle East," he said, as he leaned down to take off his slippers. "Tough times for Bernie."

"Well, I'm not so sure about that," Anne said, raising her eyebrows. She was sitting in bed reading a copy of the new definitive biography of Eleanor Roosevelt. "I'd say tough times for Marilyn."

23

BILL WATERS looked up from the editing machine. It had been a simple job. So far. Getting his hands on the NIH training video had proved easier than expected. Extracting its visceral contents, recording an additional message, and splicing the two together had also gone smoothly. The new tape timed out at four and a half minutes.

Though Gideon's Torch was an ambitious plan, it was also reasonably feasible, providing everything broke just right. Though it sounded preposterous, bumping ABC News's satellite uplink and interrupting their programming wouldn't really be too difficult, given the resources they had in place. What would be difficult would be getting their own message up and keeping it going for four and a half minutes—an eternity in the world of television.

But their people were at their posts. The tape was ready. All they needed now was a disaster of some sort within a hundred miles of Washington on a Saturday or Sunday so that *ABC World News Tonight*, which was broadcast from D.C. on the weekends, would send out a certain satellite news-gathering—or SNG—truck manned by a certain operator for an on-site report.

The truck in question—a white van with a satellite dish on

top, with uplink capacity to any transponders the networks used and a phone that could reach anywhere in the world—was privately owned, as were many contracted for news reports. It had been designed to provide news-gathering capacity at crisis spots, but with much more ease than the huge network vans with their towering radio mast transmitters, huge white dishes, and megatonnage. The networks tended to contract the smaller trucks for short-notice projects in confined spaces, such as Amtrak train wrecks on the Boston-to-Washington line, row-house fires in Philadelphia or Washington, and inner-city drug busts.

Fortunately for Gideon's Torch—absolutely providential, thought Bill—the operator of an SNG truck based in D.C. had proven himself a friend to their pro-life ideals. Only at the lower levels of the operation had they paid people for services rendered. Like Alfonzo Rojas at TapeMasters. A good guy, focused on the concerns of his own life, worried about providing for his family, he didn't mind taking some money for what in his mind was an insignificant action—getting one extra copy of some dull medical training video. But at the higher end of the operation, you couldn't depend on hired guns; you had to have people in place who were committed not because of dollars but because of ideology.

Hired guns can be rehired by a higher bidder, thought Bill, and their opposition would always have more money than they did. But the people now in place at ABC in New York and Washington believed in the cause. So much so that they were devoting considerable creative effort, at considerable risk, to get their message on the air. One of them was a promising young man Bill had met at a church-sponsored building-renovation project in Harlem. His name was Reginald Warner.

Washington, D. C.
Everything about Reginald Warner was huge. He carried about 275 pounds on his 6' 3" frame and walked with the characteristic pigeon-toed gait of a linebacker, his giant thighs rubbing

against each other like enormous twin hams. His head was shaved on the sides, with his curly black hair two and a half inches long on top, tightly coiled yet erect, a buzz cut with an attitude. His dark, clear eyes were spiked with lashes so thick and curly they looked like tight spirals on his lids. His big white teeth split his good-natured face whenever he smiled, which was often.

Reginald would have been even more imposing were he not just seventeen years old, finishing his junior year of high school. When he was older he might seem more like a bulldog, but for now he was an enormous, big-footed puppy—friendly, sweet, and bumping into whatever was remotely near his path.

Reginald had been raised in Harlem in a home that defied the statistics: his no-nonsense mother exacted obedience from him and his five brothers and sisters in everything from the length and care of their fingernails to the status of their homework. And the Warners were the only family for blocks around with a father in the home. Reginald's dad worked for the New York transit system, and the scheduled comings and goings of buses and subway trains gave a grid, a backdrop of consistency, to the home.

Their spiritual structure came from the family's second home. Almost all day Sunday, and on Wednesday evenings and Friday nights, the entire Warner family was lined up, overflowing their worn pew at the Faith, Hope, and Love Missionary Baptist Church on the corner of Grady Avenue and Stokes Street.

The Warners had cultivated a fruitful life in Harlem's barren blocks by avoiding shades of gray about the temptations of modern society. Consequently, Reginald thought about life in terms of absolute right and wrong. He wasn't narrow; it was just that rules and structures had provided a bastion of protection for his family in a neighborhood where too many young people confused liberty with license. He had seen many friends pay the consequences of that confusion.

Given his mindset, it was not surprising that Reginald had developed an affinity for short-subject black-and-white documentaries. His teachers marveled at their young student's proficiency with a video camera. Despite his natural clumsiness, he had a deft ability to juxtapose visual images to communicate truths that were more than the sum of their parts. He had a way of capturing the realities and the unfulfilled potentials of urban life in the crosscutting of a few living portraits, a few simple words on a script.

Assisted by a grant that supplied news-making resources to the inner city, his teachers had encouraged Reginald in his documentaries, and eventually a three-part series had made its way to a local news affiliate, then to the network. This had resulted in Reginald winning a six-month internship at ABC News in New York and Washington, D.C. Only too glad to give wings to their precocious student, his teachers and principal had granted a special dispensation, and Reginald was now spending the last term of the school year learning the ropes of network news.

He was having an especially good time with the network staff in Washington, where ABC's weekend news broadcast originated. It was the first time he had traveled beyond New York, and he loved being in the capital city. He marveled at Washington's clean streets, its marble monuments, its manageable crisscross of important streets. And though its delis weren't up to New York standards, there were still plenty of places that made a mean steak-and-cheese sub. Reginald ate them two and three at a time.

24

I DREAMED ABOUT my baby last night," Amy O Neil said to Mary Seaton. It was a Saturday afternoon, and the two women were sitting on a park bench at the playground just a few blocks from Mary's home.

"Right after my abortion I used to dream about her all the time. It doesn't happen that often anymore, but I guess things lately have dredged up a lot of memories . . .

"I dreamed that the baby was tiny, about as big as a sparrow. I carried her in my pocket. I'd check on her every once in a while to make sure she was okay, but then it was like I was at a football game, and there were all these people in the stands, and then the stands started to cave in, and people were running against each other, pushing and shoving, and I was running, trying to get outside the stadium through this long, dark tunnel.

"In the tunnel I was terrified, but I couldn't run fast enough. My legs were like lead. But I got to a quiet place, and then I realized that I had forgotten to keep my hand on my pocket, and I looked, and my baby was gone.

"I panicked and started screaming, and no one would help me, and I was trying to run back into the stadium against this huge wall of people, and I couldn't get in and I couldn't find my baby. It was horrible."

Amy's blue eyes filled with tears, and Mary put her arm around her shoulder. "That sounds awful," she said, "but it was just a dream. God is taking care of your baby. She's safe with Him. You'll see her later."

It was at times like this that Mary realized how vulnerable Amy was. In some ways she seemed self-assured, at peace, despite all she had been through. In other ways, she seemed much younger than her years, prone to emotional mood swings that made her just a bit volatile.

Amy dabbed at her eyes, ineffectively, with the sleeve of her cotton sweater. "I know," she said. "It's just that sometimes late at night, or in nightmares, it seems so overwhelming. She was so little, so vulnerable, so helpless. And now everything is all upside down: This abortionist in Fargo gets shot, and the newspapers and the television and the police and everyone are acting like it's the crime of the century. I mean, it's awful. But what about the babies?

"I don't understand why they're cracking down so much on the pro-life movement. Don't they see who's at stake here—the babies who can't defend themselves?"

Mary rolled her eyes, shook her head, and focused on the playground. They had brought the children here to run off steam; she figured that maybe an hour of swinging, leaping, and sliding might begin to wear down the edge of their seemingly boundless energy. At home they had been bouncing off the walls, driving Daniel, herself, and anyone else who happened to visit their home slightly crazy.

"Abigail!" she shouted at her four-year-old daughter. "Give your brother a turn on the swing. You push him for a while. He doesn't know how to pump his legs yet."

Abigail looked up, waved, and leapt off the still-moving swing. "Sure, Mommy!" she shouted.

Wonder what she's plotting, Mary wondered. *That's a little too cooperative.*

She turned back toward Amy. "We just have to keep moving forward, carefully," she said. "The way the government is cracking down means we have to conduct ourselves as prudently as possible. It doesn't change our agenda, though."

Amy bent down to retie her tennis shoe. "Well, what is our agenda at this point?" she asked. "I feel like we're kind of in a holding pattern."

"Sometimes being in a holding pattern is the smartest thing you can do," said Mary. "We don't want to act rashly."

"But what are we going to do?" asked Amy. "Thousands of babies are being killed every day we wait. And the regeneration centers will be up and running soon. Aren't we going to do something? I heard Alex say something to Daniel about Gideon's Torch . . . is that the code name for something?"

Mary looked at Amy sharply, a bit surprised by all her questions. She had noticed, though, that Amy would sometimes swing just a bit between depression on one hand and excess energy on the other. Nothing major, but maybe she was a bit manic.

"I don't know," said Mary rather unconvincingly. "If we all knew everything there was to know these days, none of us would get anything else done. I have a family to raise; you have a job to do. We have to fulfill those responsibilities first. Our roles within the Network group are going to ebb and flow, depending on how we can best be useful for different tasks. We're not in charge of this thing; we're the foot soldiers. John Jenkins was on the Hill all week, gave out some articles to congressmen. That sort of thing is going on all the time. We just perform our duties when we get the orders from the commanding officers."

She said it all rather lightly, wincing to herself; her analogy sounded so sexist. Women doing what men assigned them to do. But it was true; they weren't in charge. Daniel and Alex and others were orchestrating the big plans. Especially the one that would be coming down next.

She watched Abigail pushing Mark on the swing, her small mouth set in a straight line.

"I think you know a lot more than you're telling me," Amy said, a bit petulantly. "You're not just a foot soldier; you're married to the general. You've got to know what's going on! What about pillow talk and all that?"

Mary laughed, trying to steer away from the issue. "You wait until you've been married twelve years and have three children," she teased. "By the time our heads hit the pillow at night we are out, snoring like banshees."

Amy smiled, evidently deciding to pull herself into a better mood. "Remind me not to get old and gray and have three children, then," she said. "When I'm married, I'm going for *amour*. Surprises. Negligees. Keep the romance alive."

Mary sighed. "Great. You can be the Total Woman for your generation."

"Who's the Total Woman?" asked Amy.

"Never mind," said Mary. "She was before your time."

In the distance, Abigail swung her little brother too high and too far, and Mark sailed out of the swing into a weeping heap on the mulched playground surface. Mary could tell it was an angry cry rather than a pained or panicked one.

"I'll be right there," she shouted. "Abigail, you tell your brother that you're sorry!"

She turned back toward Amy. "Listen," she said. "If any operations come up, you'll know what you need to know when you need to know it. Until then, we'll all just stay at our posts and keep our mouths shut." She smiled to take the sting out of her statement, then ran toward Mark before Amy had a chance to respond.

25

A T ANY GIVEN MOMENT, dozens of domestic, unmanned communications spacecraft gently orbit the earth like a ring of miniature moons 22,500 miles above the equator. Tin cans with wings, they serve as sophisticated shortstops, receiving the signals thrown to them on transponders that amplify and transmit the messages, then throwing them back to earth within a fraction of a second.

It's an impersonal process for the stuff of daily life: telephone conversations, bank transactions, financial and business information, and, of course, television programming—all broken down into digitalized bits of information, crammed together to save space in a process called multiplexing, and beamed into space.

Those signals take the form of electric and magnetic fields vibrating at right angles to each other at the same frequency, traveling at the speed of light. And anyone with the right tools— a transmitter and dish antennae—can create a satellite uplink, sending a message to the orbiting parking lot in space. One need only identify an empty transponder of the hundreds available, call one's recipient and have him turn his receiver dish to the right coordinates, and beam up the information. The transaction would take only seconds, and the satellite's owner would never know. And even if the unauthorized use was noticed, it would be difficult to locate the perpetrator: an uplink beam is extremely narrow, and a search plane with radio-monitoring equipment might take weeks to find it. By then the bootleggers would be long gone.

So using empty transponders for information uplinking is not particularly difficult. But sabotaging television programming is: in order to get a message out to a broad audience, one has to ensure that people are watching. That means bumping and replacing scheduled television programming.

THE METAL BIRD floating in the cold reaches of space, mechanically processing the signals from earth, was not subject to human passions, which was fortunate, for such passions abounded at the Washington headquarters of ABC News on DeSales Street, just around the corner from the heart of Connecticut Avenue and the Mayflower Hotel. According to the red digital numbers on the clock dominating the control room wall, it was 6:28:44 P.M. with the network news broadcast due to air at 6:30 P.M. EST. The air in underground Studio B and its adjacent control room sparked with electricity, primed to ignite at any moment.

In the studio, ABC weekend anchor Amanda Dawson sat in the swivel chair behind the large gray anchor desk on the set. Leaning against the walls were the backdrops for the sets for such programs as *Nightline*, as well as the wall-size photo of the Capitol dome used for remotes from Washington for New York's *Good Morning America*. But for this broadcast, the familiar newsroom backdrop was set up.

Dawson sipped coffee from a white Styrofoam cup, leaving huge red lipstick marks on its rim; through long practice, she managed not to smear her teeth in the process. She was already wired for sound, a microphone clipped to her lapel. A coil of clear thin cable snaked up her back and connected to an earpiece that linked her by audio to Hal Humsler, the executive producer in the control room. Before her lay the news script, timed to the second by a small army of writers, producers, and technicians.

A few feet away, out of camera range, the TelePrompTer scrolled down through the first report. On it, sentences were broken into three-and four-word fragments, the typewritten periods and other punctuation augmented by big, black-marker, handwritten additions to emphasize the potently stilted style that was the trademark of the anchor's delivery.

The lights on the set, automatically set by computer, were remarkably low, thanks to the sensitive Fuji boom cameras the network used. The lowered lights kept the heat down in the studio and also lowered the tension level on the set to some degree. Or so the technicians thought.

MEANWHILE THOUGH the control room was almost dark— so the directors, producers, and assistants could better see the lighted computer displays and the forty-nine video monitors lining the walls—the tension level was anything but low.

The control room felt like something between the austere expertise of the space program's Mission Control and the escalating desperation of a party of people trapped together in a large freight elevator. It was built on two levels: a higher room, perhaps fifteen by twenty feet, separated from the lower level by sliding glass windows.

In the lower room, technicians orchestrated everything from sound, to dissolves between video images, to the graphic titles appearing on the screen. They could also, by means of the digitized D-2 machines and quick human sweat, call up standard video footage such as shots of the floor of the House of Representatives, should the producer call for such last-second augmentations to the newscast.

Down a step and out the door, past the red "on the air" light, was the entrance to the studio. And a few steps down the narrow hall from that was the submarinelike confines of Master

Control, the brains of the whole operation, manned by two grizzled network veterans named Dutch and Mike. Mike ran audio; Dutch ran video.

Orange cables hung like intestines from the belly of the control panels stretching from floor to ceiling on both sides of the narrow rectangle. The two men, evidently immune to claustrophobia, sat side by side at a small desklike area extending from the middle of the long wall of panels. From there they monitored everything beaming up from the satellite dish at the top of the building on the uplink, determining frequencies, wattage, and other technical considerations.

During periods of bad weather or thick cloud cover, they blasted their signal up to the satellite at eighty-three watts, though normally they illuminated the bird at about seventy-five watts—what the techies called "full saturation." The satellite would take a hundred-watt hit, but such a strong signal normally wasn't necessary. From D.C.'s heading position—a near-semi-circle from about twenty degrees above the terrain to twenty degrees in the opposite direction—there were fifty-four satellites in range, with between twenty-four and thirty-six transponders on each.

Dutch knew he could easily knock his competition off the air. All he would have to do would be uplink to the same coordinates, same transponder, as NBC or CBS. But the result would simply be competing signals—double illumination—and a lot of snow on viewers' screens. A gentlemen's agreement between the networks, not to mention a 1986 federal statute, kept that from happening. Dutch had no particular desire to mess with the other networks nor go to jail—particularly so near retirement.

ON THE FORTY-NINE screens of the control room were transmissions of those rival networks, NBC, CBS, and CNN; the scrolling script of the TelePrompTer; various camera angles; the net return—the actual downlink of the news coming from New York to Washington via a fiber-optic line; video footage of the correspondents' taped reports; and, at this particular moment, closeup shots of Amanda Dawson's nostrils.

On a standard evening, the only live element of the news was the anchor's script-reading, usually about 230 seconds of the whole, or less than four minutes of air time. Commercial messages took more than six minutes of the broadcast. That left about seventeen minutes for the correspondents' reports, which were taped—usually perilously close to broadcast time—unless news was breaking even as the news was airing. In that case, a correspondent would wait at his or her site and do live interaction with the anchor, usually in the form of short questions and answers.

Though these live interchanges amounted to just seconds, they often caused problems and added to the tension level of the control room. Tonight, because writers were still gathering intelligence regarding Senate reaction to the president's proposed crime bill, the broadcast would have a short live tag at the end from Capitol Hill correspondent Rob Bickhert.

Typically the news was broadcast live for those on Eastern Standard and Central Standard Time, then the tape replayed later for Mountain and Pacific—unless there was breaking news, in which case the anchor remained on site to redo the broadcast for the West. When that happened—like tonight, because of the crime bill—everyone had to stick around, and the network was contractually bound to provide dinner for the entire crew. For Reginald Warner, sitting in his usual spot on a stool in the back row of the control room, these were his favorite nights.

"AMANDA," said the executive producer into the microphone built into the control panel at his station.

Hal Humsler was a tall, thin, intense man in his late forties, his hairline receding and his sharp, hooked nose protruding. He habitually bobbed his head when he was angry, which was fairly often, particularly when he neglected to take his medication. Because of his beak, his bobs, his long, thin legs, and his rather widely spaced pale-blue eyes, some of the less respectful crew members called him the "Blue Heron." But never to his face.

Hal had produced the weekend news for several years, and though deep down he enjoyed the work and the people, his habitual intensity usually got the best of him. *ABC World News* had held its number one spot for some years now, but the weekend post made Hal feel like he was on second string. Ratings couldn't help but decline on the weekends; that was a fact of life. Their advertising time sold for only $40,000 for a thirty-second spot, compared with as much as $75,000 for a comparable weekday slot. And he couldn't help but notice that their advertisers catered to the older segment of the population, the La-Z-Boy folks who stayed home on the weekends and watched the news, then settled in for the Saturday night lineup.

Just look at tonight's sponsor, he thought. The company that had paid more to get the billboard slot and their logo on screen near the top of the program, as well as the first commercial, was Attends. *Great*, thought Hal. *Diapers for adults.*

He scanned the program sheet in his hand. Typical. Here were Attends, Listerine, Centrum Silver, Dr. Scholl's, Efferdent, and Metamucil. It read like the pharmacy shelves at the home for seniors where his mother lived. *What I wouldn't give for a good condom ad on the weekend*, he thought.

But the commercials weren't as bad as the fact that real news just seemed to wait for the Monday-to-Friday shift before it happened. Earthquakes, hostage situations, assassinations—none of the good stuff ever happened on Hal's watch. Even those now-classic mesmerizing hours of live television, the celebrated O. J. Simpson white Bronco police chase on the freeways of L.A., had happened on a Friday. Hal kept waiting for a Saturday or Sunday disaster of some sort . . . anything to spike his ratings.

He bobbed his head and drummed his fingers on the desk where he sat, just in back of the glass window at the control desk. Before him was a complicated panel of switches and buttons, a video monitor, and a bank of sophisticated controls. His senior producer sat to his right, the timer/researcher to his left on a stool before a computer monitor crammed with files, a production manager and an operations manager to her left, and in the corner, a frazzled technician in front of a vertical video monitor and controls.

Behind them was a flat table manned by two technicians and a small flock of assistants who served as runners to the studio and the operations deck. Behind them were two interns: the kid from New York and a young girl from Florida.

As Hal spoke into his microphone, which fed into the clear coil snaking into the anchor's ear, Amanda Dawson continued to sip coffee, then rubbed her tongue over her gums and used a long red fingernail to floss between her two front teeth.

"Amanda!" he said again. Louder.

Oblivious, she laughed, apparently at something a lighting technician had said, and closed her eyes while a makeup person dabbed powder on her face.

"People!" said Hal to the crew in the control room in a measured, clenched tone, "Amanda cannot hear me. I cannot hear Amanda. We need to hear each other. We are going on the air in two minutes. DO SOMETHING!"

The sweating technician in the corner, with multiple cords coming out of his ears, began punching buttons on a side monitor.

"Amanda!" said Hal again. "Wave if you can hear me!"

Amanda looked up and waved, her lips moving. No sound came out.

Humsler took a deep breath and exhaled slowly, a relaxation technique his therapist had recommended. He turned to the frantic man in the corner, who was flipping buttons madly.

"We are halfway there," Hal said calmly, even as he snapped a pencil in two between the clenched fingers of his right hand. "It's nice that Amanda can hear me. But perhaps I need to point out that I also need to be able to hear Amanda, so I can direct this broadcast. Maybe I would not be so concerned if this did not happen rather often, LIKE EVERY SINGLE WEEKEND!"

His scream was cut short by Amanda's voice coming through his earpiece.

"All right," he said, as everyone exhaled together. "That's much better. Thank you. Why don't we do the news now?"

The technician in the corner popped a Rolaids in his mouth and kept hitting buttons.

"Thirty seconds," said someone in the lower control room.

Amanda took a last swig of coffee, put the cup behind her, straightened her blouse, and pulled on the sleeves of her jacket.

The control room population watched the clock. Then came the countdown . . . six, five, four, three, two, one . . .

"From ABC," the announcer intoned as the dramatic trademark music throbbed, "this is World News Saturday . . . here's Amanda Dawson."

"Good evening," she said, nodding crisply toward the camera. "With America's crime rate up 16 percent over a year ago, the president's long-awaited crime bill is at the forefront of focus in our nation's capital tonight."

"Though the president's plan has received the endorsement of many, conservatives and liberals alike, it must still overcome tough opposition on Capitol Hill."

"As ABC's Rob Bickhert reports, Senator Byron Langer is leading a movement of those who believe the president's plan may lead to infringements of individual liberty. Some have even suggested that the plan is motivated by retribution against a very few and endangers classic American civil rights for the many."

"Twenty-nine seconds," said the assistant in the control room.

As the monitors switched to Bickhert's report from Capitol Hill, taped only fifteen minutes before air time, Dawson reached behind her for more coffee.

Hal spoke into his mouthpiece. "Amanda, your hair is sticking up a little on the right side." She reached up and patted the right side of her head. "No," he said. "Sorry. I meant your left side. My right; your left." She smoothed the other side as the makeup person rushed to assist. "Great," said Hal.

Bickhert's report ran for two minutes. Amanda wet her teeth as the studio cameras rolled at 2:39 into the broadcast for the second story, an augmentation to the first.

"The president's desire to get tough on crime echoes his campaign promises to restore order to American society. But President Griswold's actual plan is a far cry from the niceties espoused by Candidate Griswold last fall. David Bawman reports."

"Eighteen seconds," said the control room as Bawman's taped piece, a commentary on the disparity between the then-candidate's remarks and the now-president's actions, began to roll.

As it did, talk in the control room turned to the consuming issue of sandwiches. An operations person in the corner hung up from booking additional satellite time for the extra West Coast broadcast and punched the automatic-dial button for Arnie's Deli.

"Sandwiches for fifty," she said. "Just like last time . . . chicken salad, tuna salad, ham, turkey, roast beef, on mixed breads. Then do about a dozen vegetable and cheese combos on pita . . . and six steak-and-cheese subs."

Reginald Warner grinned in the semi-darkness of the back row.

"Amanda," said Hal into his microphone. "We're running about four seconds over now. Just speed up the thing about the vice president slightly."

Amanda nodded just as Bawman's taped report ended and they went live again. A square stock photo of the vice president floated in the air just above her left shoulder. If she were to lean too far toward it, it would block her face.

"Vice President Stuart Potter is recovering from surgery at Bethesda Naval Hospital," she said briskly. "Potter tore his Achilles tendon yesterday morning while playing basketball at the House of Representatives gym. He underwent more than an hour of surgery . . . and is expected to be released from the hospital tomorrow."

"She picked it up perfectly," said the assistant in the control room. "We're right at five minutes for bumper one."

"Coming up," said Amanda, "the fired head of the American Civil Liberties Union meets the press . . . a southern town rebuilds itself a year after a tornado reduced its dreams to rubble . . . and later in this broadcast a high school athlete shoots for the Olympics . . . from her wheelchair."

The announcer's smooth voice took over as the ABC music came up. "*World News Saturday*," he said, "brought to you by Attends."

There was a general groan in the control room. "Attends again?" said an assistant director.

Meanwhile, Hal and the senior producer were conferring on the phone with a writer. "We're going to a live feed from Bickhert at the end of the broadcast. Amanda will need to ask him a question. Something like, 'What's happening now on the Hill, Rob, with this unusual Saturday session?' Then Bickhert needs to respond with something tentative, like, 'Well, Amanda, Senator Langer is caucusing, even as we speak, with aides and colleagues in the Senate. Their plan of action is not yet determined. But one thing is certain: Langer and like-minded legislators are not going to let the president off easily on this one.'"

"Something like that, okay? Tentative, but still teasing the fact that there's going to be a war on this issue. Just write it up; we'll have a runner there in a minute."

Hal looked at the clock. The Listerine commercial was just finishing. They were due up again at 6:40. The only other live element in the broadcast was the sports report: Jack Tyler live from New York before he introed the tape on the high school basketball player . . . not a big thing.

Tyler was usually reliable, though the chemistry between him and Amanda was absolutely nil, so Hal kept the interplay between the two pretty minimal. All Amanda had to say was, "Now to New York . . . here's Jack Tyler . . . good evening, Jack." No joshing back and forth.

And then the live thing at the end, maybe fifty-five seconds of wrap-up between Amanda and Rob Bickhert. Shouldn't be a problem. He wasn't going to run any accompanying video, just Bickhert standing up live at the Capitol. And Bickhert was a pro.

Hal's stomach was settling down. He breathed in and out a few times. It looked like it was going to be okay. For tonight.

26

E MILY MET Paul Clarkson at her private elevator in the Justice Department building.

"Hate to ask you to go with me, Paul, but these guys on the Hill . . . well, I need my interpreter. I think Langer was right."

"I'm happy to do it." Paul said. "Crime bill, huh?"

The elevator descended into the underground parking area, and they walked to the waiting Lincoln town car. As Paul swung himself into the car, laying his canes on the floor, Emily pulled papers from her case.

"Rayburn Building," she told the driver, who already had explicit typed instructions. The car accelerated up the ramp onto Tenth Street into blinding sheets of spring rain.

"This statement, Paul, I should have given it to you sooner, but I've been pressed. Here, check it. I don't want to sound high-handed to the Democrats. Congressman Peyton can be a bear."

"Sure can. Let me see it." Paul took Emily's statement and immediately underlined two sentences at the beginning. Then his eyes skimmed down the pages of the document. "Here, on page four, I'd leave this out altogether."

Paul suggested several more changes, and Emily nodded

appreciatively. Then the limousine stopped on Constitution Avenue, at least a block from the jammed intersection of Constitution, Pennsylvania, and Third Street at the base of Capitol Hill. One by one, cars were timidly navigating through the huge wading pools that had collected at the corner.

"Frizzell's done it to us again." Emily shook her head and arched her eyebrows in a look of resignation.

"Not another Chicago," Paul frowned.

"No, no. But get this: He goes to the White House last night for the dinner for President Landos . . . then at one this morning, who calls me, wakes me out of the beginnings of a very sound sleep?" Emily didn't wait for an answer. "The president . . . 'Uh, hope I didn't wake you, Emily.'" She lowered her voice several octaves in a rather remarkable imitation of Whitney Griswold. "'Didn't disturb you, I hope,' he says. 'Oh, no, Mr. President,' I said, rubbing my eyes and slapping my cheeks."

Paul chuckled and nodded sympathetically.

"He's in the Lincoln sitting room, he tells me, and just thinking about the terrorists. Frizzell just happened to mention in passing at the state dinner that something big was about to pop. Could be very serious. 'What are we doing?' he asks. Must be prepared—and all that. Hopes we'll do whatever it takes: more agents, task force, surveillance."

"That Frizzell is a piece of work," Paul said, stroking his chin. "He's going to get his budget one way or another."

"You don't take advantage of a social event like that. The man is power mad, if you ask me." Emily sighed.

"The old Plato quote is right," said Paul. "'Only those who don't seek power are fit to hold it.'"

"Problem is, if we applied that criterion, Washington would be a ghost town," Emily replied. The limousine inched forward, its front wheels entering surging water up to the hubcaps. The rain was pelting hard on the roof.

"But the fact remains, Paul, we've got to do more. The president is right, we can't afford any more political heat on this. People are screaming out there."

"We've got over twelve hundred men and women assigned right now," Paul said. "It's overreaction."

"The president wants it."

"He's the boss," Paul said, but shook his head.

"And he asked if we are doing enough with wiretaps and surveillance—wants us to use the conspiracy laws to widen the net. I mean to head off any new incidents. Just legitimate security."

"Frizzell really got to him good." Paul stared straight ahead as the rain began pounding even harder, driven by a rising wind.

"Robbie and the others are pushing on the president too. They say he can't get hurt, can't get tough enough to suit the public."

Paul smiled.

"Okay, what is it? Your old comrades that you're worried about?"

"No, Emily, my job is to enforce the law. My personal views aren't at issue here," he said. "You know that. But when public passions dictate like this, we're headed for trouble. 'Get tough, hang them, just leave me and mine alone.' That's what people want."

"Well, that's our job, isn't it? To secure our citizens' right to live peaceful lives?"

"Yes, sure. But you can't do it with naked force. You need the willingness of people to be governed. That's what self-government is all about. The founders called it republican virtue, the idea of duty and responsibility."

"Save that for the philosophy class, Paul. Right now we've got a real-life problem."

"No, Emily. *This* is the real-life problem. People want to do their own thing. They see liberty as the right to do what they want, but it isn't. Liberty is the right to do what you *ought* to do. So now we have chaos because we have no moral consensus—which, I might add, has always been supplied by our religious beliefs." He paused, then added, "It was Aquinas who once said that 'without a moral consensus, there can be no law.'"

"Very trenchant."

"Yeah—and very true. In a free society that honors virtue,

you have 270 million policemen; in a society that mocks virtue, you can't hire enough policemen."

"Maybe," she shook her head. "But we have the rule of law in this country that protects us. For heaven's sake, Paul, you need to sit in on one of my classes at Harvard."

"What's the rule of law? Is it what these people on the Hill say it is . . . ?"

Emily feigned a cough and groaned.

". . . Or does it rest on truth—truth that is true because it is true, not because someone votes it in?"

Emily looked out the window.

"You've got to see where this is leading us, Emily. Griswold never will. There are only two restraints on human behavior. One in here," he pointed to his heart, "the inner restraint of conscience. Moral. And the other out there," he pointed to the street, "the outer restraint of force. Police. The less you have of the inner, the more you need of the outer. Take away people's Bibles and you will replace them with bayonets."

Emily's eyes met Paul's. She saw his passion and intensity and realized that he had really thought these issues through; she, for all her legal training, had never thought a lot about them.

"And remember that Levitz column? He was right. When the restraints of conscience break down, when there is chaos, people welcome force. They'll do what every society in history has done. They'll trade in their liberties—oh, just a little at first, then everything."

Emily shook her head, mostly amused. "That's not about to happen here, Paul. You know that."

"Yes it is, Emily. We could put on wiretaps, call out the troops to guard clinics and neighborhoods—the president would love that idea—we could arrest suspects, intercept mail—all to enforce the law—and they'd line those streets." He pointed out toward Independence Avenue as the limousine slowly climbed the House side of Capitol Hill.

"They'll line those streets waving their flags, cheering . . . then we can put on our armbands and take them to the camps."

"Paul, you're being melodramatic," she laughed.

"Emily, I am associate attorney general, I'm loyal, I'll do my job. But I want you to think about where things can lead us."

"Think? How much time do I have to think in this job?" Emily said dryly as the limousine pulled into the wet circular drive on South Capitol Street.

"Emily." Paul put his hand on her arm, which startled her momentarily. "The issue here is truth. If truth retreats, tyranny advances. A democracy cannot survive if the law has no other authority than force."

Emily stared at him a moment then again sought to dismiss the strange conversation. The driver held an umbrella over the open door. Then she grinned, relenting. "Well, Paul, let's go give these honorable representatives some lessons in truth."

Flashbulbs popped as Emily was escorted through the main door. Paul followed slowly, getting very wet.

27

R EGINALD WARNER stood at a phone booth on Connecticut Avenue, just outside the Metro stop. During the week the area was clogged with commuters, but late on Sunday afternoon there weren't many people around.

He dialed the number he'd been given. Area code 212 . . . New York. He wondered how his parents were. He missed his family. They would appreciate what he was doing; it was like he was a spy for the underground railroad or something . . .

Bill Waters answered on the third ring. "Yes?"

"The truck has been activated," Reginald said. "There's been a disturbance at Lorton prison. It's a hostage situation. They've called for the SNG truck. It should be there in forty-five minutes. They'll be doing a live feed on the news tonight."

"Right," said Bill. "Thanks, Reginald."

Waters hung up and looked at the briefcase on the desk before him. Inside it was the tape . . . or, actually, just a copy. The original he'd made had been taken to D.C. three weeks ago and was now on its way to Lorton prison in a white satellite truck.

He smiled. God *had* provided a way to get His message out.

5:09 P.M.

Agent Thomas Pilch at the FBI command center picked up the special phone line set aside for incoming information from assets in the field.

"This is Orange 2," said the woman's voice. "I expect to be able to confirm soon. It is New York. Something big is coming down. More later."

6:12 P.M.

Finally, thought Hal Humsler as he sat at his control room post, his feet drumming the carpet under the desk. The air around him was electric with activity, but Hal felt less than his usual stress. He hadn't even taken his medication today, but he had an unusual sense of well-being. Finally, a break from the humdrum Mickey Mouse exchanges with New York! Finally, a Washington-based crisis—on the weekend!

If there is a God, thank You! he thought. A voice in his head was saying that it probably wasn't really much, just a prison riot at Lorton; maybe it would just be arbitrated down to nothing in a few hours. *But at least they have hostages*, he thought. None injured yet, but there was potential for tension and drama. Finally! Some breaking news!

6:20 P.M.

At the small house behind Doggett's Garage, in spite of the warm spring evening, the windows were closed and the blinds tightly drawn. Inside, Daniel Seaton and his friends had gathered. Some sat on the old plaid sofas, sipping coffee; some paced the room. A television set, sitting on an old brown TV cart on wheels, was on, its volume low.

"I can't believe they're really gonna pull this off," said Alex, the tension evident in his voice.

Daniel, too, was wound tight. He sat on the sofa, tapping his fingers on the water-ringed surface of the wooden coffee table.

He felt a mixture of things, his stomach in a knot and his mouth dry. It reminded him of a long-ago debut in a college theater production . . . or his feeling just before he stepped out in front of the church the day he and Mary were married. He thought of the scramble in his brain just before his oral comprehensives in seminary. And he remembered how he had felt on that long-ago day when he had heard that Ronald Reagan had just been shot outside the Washington Hilton.

It was an odd pastiche of memories, but they all shared the stomach-churning sense of significance that he felt inside.

As he looked around the room, he could tell the others were feeling something similar. Lance stood in the corner, occasionally peering out the window blinds, calm but at full military alert. Alex paced, stopping periodically to stretch his legs, the way he did before a big race. John Jenkins sat quietly on the sofa, cracking his knuckles. Mark Demmers guzzled coffee from a thermos.

The television droned on. The local ABC affiliate was winding down its Washington-area newscast before the national news came on at 6:30. The sportscaster finished his golf coverage. Next was the entertainment critic's review of a new action film starring an aging Arnold Schwarzenegger teamed with a child actor from Singapore. Then they were teasing reports on the Lorton situation: update to come on *ABC World News Sunday*, next.

6:25 P.M.

Up in the family quarters at 1600 Pennsylvania Avenue, Anne Griswold was relaxing with her daughter. It had been an unusually quiet Sunday, and the beautiful spring afternoon had coaxed her from her usual preoccupation with schedule and protocol. An hour ago she and Elizabeth had walked the White House grounds, looking for purple violets in the lush emerald grass.

Though Secret Service agents had trailed behind and she

knew there was a video camera in every tree, she had felt a sense of freedom. Perhaps it was the scent of wisteria blossoms in the air, an elusive link to springtimes past, before life had gotten so complicated.

Elizabeth had had three friends over for Sunday lunch; she was fitting in more and more with her classmates at the Cathedral School. And, she confided to her mother, her friend Molly—one of the girls who had come for lunch—had told her that her brother thought Elizabeth was beautiful. Half the girls in her class had crushes on Molly's brother. Anne had smiled, vaguely remembering that feeling from a hundred years ago when she was eleven going on sixteen.

And now, best of all, they had the evening off. No official events, and tomorrow seemed far away. So she and Elizabeth were sitting on the tufted yellow sofa before the mammoth entertainment center in the White House family quarters. They would dine later, hopefully with Whitney. He was in a meeting, something about the Middle East. But for now Anne sipped a glass of Chardonnay, Elizabeth a Coke; they shared a bowl of popcorn while they watched the evening news together.

6:30 P.M.

Hal Humsler tapped his pencil on the panel before him as he watched the control room clock tick down the seconds.

Amanda was wired, in more ways than one, her revised script before her and the TelePrompTer poised with her opening lines.

"Six, five, four, three, two, one," chanted the assistant. It was 6:30:00.

ANNE GRISWOLD brought the sound up on the remote control. The familiar theme music sounded. "From ABC," said the announcer, "this is *World News Sunday* . . . here's Amanda Dawson."

Elizabeth pointed at the anchor. She dreamed sometimes

about going into broadcasting. "I like her suit, don't you, Mom? It's such a pretty color."

Anne nodded, smiling, and popped a cluster of popcorn into her mouth.

"Good evening," said Amanda Dawson, looking more serious than usual. "An inmate uprising rages this evening at the District of Columbia's Lorton prison complex, located in the Virginia suburbs. A group of prisoners has taken control of part of the institution.

"The inmates are holding an unknown number of guards hostage and are armed with weapons that were evidently smuggled into the facility. They have not yet issued any demands. For more on this tense situation, we turn to ABC's Jim Warren."

"TOO LONG," said the assistant in the control room. "We're already running over, right out of the gate."

It was 6:30:34. In Master Control, Dutch punched a button and switched the uplink feed loop to the SNG satellite truck remote at the prison.

Standing fifteen feet from the white truck at Lorton, correspondent Jim Warren took his customary breath before the camera's red light went on and he would begin his report on the hostage situation.

Inside the truck, at precisely the same moment, the operator flipped a switch and popped the altered NIH videotape into the uplink drive. The standard encryptions the network used as a protection against such sabotage posed no problem: a week before, Reginald Warner had gotten hold of a digitized decoder card. Effusive with questions about just how the signals were scrambled and unscrambled, he had engaged in a conversation so innocent and enthusiastic that the operations person who had explained it all to him had felt gratified that she could help such a nice young intern learn the ropes.

Outside the truck, oblivious, Jim Warren continued his report as the cameraman filmed.

BACK AT THE TELEVISION STUDIO, no one had noticed when Reginald Warner left his customary observation spot on the back row at precisely 6:30:30 and wandered into Master Control. Part of his internship involved lots of question-asking, and Dutch and Mike usually welcomed his visits. Tonight things were hot because of the live feed at the top of the broadcast, but that didn't affect Dutch and Mike as much as it did the producers and directors. Especially the Blue Heron, who, according to reports from the control room, was flying high.

So Dutch and Mike smiled when the gregarious young intern came into their submarine carrying a tray balanced with steaming 16 ounce cups of coffee, then frowned a little as he negotiated his huge bulk in the narrow confines of Master Control, then shouted in horror as Reggie tangled himself up in some of the cables, twisted, and crashed on top of them, knocking them both to the floor.

The scalding coffee flew up in the air, suspended in space for a horrifying moment, then splashed over the central part of the control panel, as well as on Dutch, Mike, and Reggie himself. They all yelled in pain; what they were feeling would turn out to be first degree burns, according to the emergency room medics who would see them later. Some of the coffee even splashed up on Dutch's glasses; with his eyes squeezed shut in panic, it would take a few moments for him to realize that they weren't burned. Meanwhile, the three were a shouting, tangled mass of arms and legs. It took a full minute for Reggie to untangle himself and get his 275 pounds off the other two.

Reggie's maneuver didn't divert Master Control for the full four and a half minutes. But it was a start.

ANNE GRISWOLD stared at the television screen. There was a moment of snow and static, and she wondered if the transmission had somehow been affected by the situation at Lorton. Things must certainly be in upheaval there.

Then a picture came into focus. But it wasn't the ABC

correspondent, and it wasn't the anchor desk in the studio. It was something entirely different. It looked like an operating room scene.

Then Anne slowly realized what she was looking at. A patient was lying on a gurney, draped in white sheets. It was a woman. Her legs were straddled wide, feet resting in stirrups, as if she was going to deliver a baby. The camera was pointed directly into her cervix, which was fully dilated.

Anne froze, her wine glass halfway to her lips.

There was a pause, and then the sound—the voice of an off camera narrator—caught up with the picture.

". . . Candidates for this elective procedure are placed on the operating table in a sterile, yet pleasantly nonclinical setting. Nurses stand by to reassure the patient.

"The surgical assistant places an ultrasound probe on the patient's abdomen and scans the fetus, locating the lower extremities.

"Once these are found, the surgeon introduces a large grasping forceps through the vaginal and cervical canals into the corpus of the uterus.

"Based on the image on the sonogram screen, the surgeon is able to open the instrument's jaws to firmly grasp a lower extremity. The surgeon then provides firm traction to the instrument and pulls the extremity into the vagina. . . .

"At this point, the right-handed surgeon slides the fingers of the left hand along the back of the fetus and 'hooks' the shoulders of the fetus with the index and ring fingers (palm down). Next the surgeon slides the tip of the middle finger along the spine toward the skull while applying traction to the shoulders and lower extremities.

"While maintaining this tension, the surgeon takes a pair of blunt curved Metzenbaum scissors in the right hand. The surgeon carefully advances the tip, curved down, along the spine and under his or her middle finger until he or she feels it contact the base of the skull under the tip of the middle finger.

"The surgeon then forces the scissors into the base of the

skull. Having safely entered the skull, the surgeon spreads the scissors to enlarge the opening.

"The surgeon removes the scissors and introduces a suction catheter into this hole and evacuates the skull contents. With the catheter still in place, the surgeon applies traction to the fetus, removing it completely from the patient."

The film had been edited to mesh clips from the actual procedure with the narrator's description. Anne saw the fetus's tiny body positioned in the birth canal, its thin leg grasped firmly by the surgeon's forceps like an animal caught in a trap.

She remembered how it had felt as Elizabeth and Robert had slipped out of her, how even then their little bodies had had tone and resistance. She had touched Elizabeth's tiny fingers just after she was born; she had gently pushed her little arm, and her daughter had pushed back. Anne had been so proud. Even a few seconds after birth, her daughter was a fighter.

This fetus appeared to be a fighter as well. She seemed to resist a little as the gloved hands of the doctor positioned her, hanging out from the birth canal. The doctor held the scissors, then jabbed them through the base of the soft skull. The fetus jerked, then hung still. The tube sucked out the brain. Then the tiny limp body slid from its mother, broken and bloody in the jaws of the doctor's forceps.

Next to her, Elizabeth broke out in a huge sob, her hands over her eyes.

Anne jumped. She had forgotten her daughter was right there. She put down her wine glass, pulled Elizabeth toward her, put her daughter's head in her lap, and turned her away from the television screen. She rubbed Elizabeth's head gently but continued to watch, mesmerized.

THE CONTROL ROOM was in a state of suspension. Dutch and Mike hadn't shut down the sabotaged uplink; Hal wasn't sure where they were or what was going on in Master Control down the hall. New York was on the phone, the producer there screaming that something was wrong with their switching system and they couldn't bump the broadcast off the air.

"Get it off, get if off, GET IT OFF!" New York shouted into Hal's ear.

Maybe that was when he snapped.

He was still feeling great, with that crisp-edged clarity that often came on the manic side of his mood swings, enhanced by the fact that he hadn't taken his lithium. He felt a delectable sense of power: New York was begging him to do something. He also had an idea beginning to form on the fringes of his brain.

As the video progressed, the control room was eerily silent. People's mouths were open, everyone frozen in position, looking back and forth from the video to Hal. Only the senior producer was shouting at him, echoing New York: "Get it off, get it off, get it off!"

In that second, it all came together for Hal. The first commercial break wasn't due until almost five minutes into the broadcast, and this thing, whatever it was, might well be the best thing that had happened to weekend ratings in years. He looked at the switchboard. All the phone lines were lit up.

He looked over to the upper row of video monitors: NBC and CBS and CNN were still blathering on with their regular scheduled programming. Whoever was doing this, whatever it was, the saboteurs had chosen ABC. On the weekend. On his watch. It was the chance of a lifetime!

He flipped the microphone switch so everyone in the control room, the studio, and down the hall in Master Control—whatever in the world was going on there—could hear him.

"LEAVE IT ON!" he shouted, his eyes bugging out of his head. "I don't know what it is, but leave it on. At least until the first commercial break! Trust me, people. If anyone goes down on this one, it'll be me."

ANNE GRISWOLD continued to watch in disbelief as the grisly video dissolved to a new scene.

A man faced the camera, his face in total shadow. As he began to speak, it was clear that his voice had been electronically altered.

"What you have just witnessed is not footage recovered from the files of Nazi Germany," he said.

"This actual video is currently in use in medical schools across America, equipping doctors to suck the brains from live, unborn babies in ever-expanding numbers. This is what the coming regeneration centers are all about.

"Americans are being told that the regeneration centers are the great new hope for cures for cancer and AIDS. That is a lie. The regeneration centers are nothing but killing centers.

"Mothers who once aborted their children at ten or twelve weeks are now being encouraged—and even paid—to wait until the third trimester of their pregnancy, when the unborn baby, if born, could live outside the womb.

"Instead, these babies are tortured to death in the most gruesome manner possible, as you have just seen.

"These deeds of darkness must be exposed to the light. Americans must not allow their so-called freedom of choice to open the door to the greatest holocaust in human history.

"We must reject the regeneration centers and turn back this bloody tide before it is too late. Surely Americans can look within themselves to a core of common decency and stop this grisly killing!"

The television screen went snowy again, and the next thing Anne saw was a bewildered Jim Warren, limply holding the microphone in his hand. He was still standing there as the scene flipped back to the studio in Washington. Amanda Dawson was pale and strained, a strand of hair hanging over her forehead as she prepared to deal with the utterly unscripted challenge before her.

"Ladies and gentlemen," she began, but Anne Griswold had heard enough. She hit the mute button on the remote and, still holding Elizabeth, picked up the phone on the end table.

"Nancy," she said when her assistant answered, "get me the president." Her voice shook with anger and shock. "I don't care what meeting he's in. Just get him for me. Now."

28

A CCORDING TO OLD World War II movies, the White House situation room is a hubbub of activity, with fleets and armies arrayed on huge charts, and screens with troop movements descending from the ceiling. But the National Security Command Center, known as the situation room, is, in fact, an ordinary cluster of offices in the west wing basement, entered through a small door just across from the White House senior staff dining room.

Normally, the White House was quiet on Sunday. Tonight, however, it was abuzz with senior staff in meetings and the press room on full alert. The president, General Maloney, and the secretaries of defense and state were gathered in the situation room, along with assorted aides and note takers, though the latter were superfluous since everything in the room was automatically taped.

The president had just taken the secretary of defense's recommendation to order a task force consisting of the *JFK*, escorted by six frigates and one cruiser, along with two LPHs, amphibious ships loaded with a regiment of marines, to steam toward the Israeli coast. The move might enflame hotheads on both sides, but Griswold felt the risk was worth it. Today's bombing violence could make it necessary to evacuate American citizens in the Middle East in a hurry.

"All right," Griswold said, the decision made, "what's next on the list?"

The secretary of state was starting to suggest a personal call to the Israeli prime minister when Captain Slattery walked into the room, moved quietly around behind the president's chair, and passed him a single sheet of paper folded over. Griswold shook his head, then Slattery leaned over and whispered in his ear.

"Excuse me, please," Griswold said to the group, but looked annoyed as he took a portable phone Slattery handed him. He cupped his hand over the mouthpiece as the others around the table engaged in obvious conversation to give him some privacy.

Anne sounded nearly hysterical. He had never heard her like this.

"Now calm down, Anne. I can't help what's on the evening news. I've just sent an attack force to the coast of Lebanon."

"Well, tell them to turn around and come back here to ABC!" Anne shrieked. "Don't you hear me? It was a live abortion!"

"I'll get someone to call the network, dear."

"No! No! You don't understand! Elizabeth is so traumatized she can't even talk."

"What do you mean?" he asked. "Elizabeth saw this?"

Suddenly the president's face flushed with anger as he held his hand over the receiver and told Slattery, "Get O'Keefe on the phone right now."

BERNIE O'KEEFE stood in his mahogany-paneled office wearing only a starched white shirt and blue-and-white-striped boxer shorts, fumbling with the suspender buttons of his tuxedo trousers. He was supposed to host the president's box at the Kennedy Center that night, a black-tie symphony benefit for AIDS research. He was already running late for the dinner before the concert, an event featuring a blue-ribbon bevy of Hollywood stars and producers.

The loud persistent buzzer on the president's direct line went off just as the final thread holding the button holding the suspenders to the trousers popped. With a string of expletives he hurled the trousers onto the tufted corner sofa and headed for the phone.

"Yes sir."

Griswold was on a fast boil. A live abortion on the evening news . . . his daughter traumatized . . . get troops moving . . . take over the studio.

"Let me get this straight, sir." Bernie was seated now at his small conference table, scribbling across a yellow pad with his maroon Mont Blanc pen.

Caroline Atwater, who had seen the broadcast in the press room, had run up the main west wing stairway and down the long corridor to Bernie's reception room, arriving only moments after he picked up the president's call. Bernie's secretary, Barbara Shannon, a plump, gray-haired woman who had taken care of her boss through every conceivable crisis for more than a decade, tried to fend her off.

"Please, Ms. Atwater, don't go in," she said, jumping up from her desk. "Mr. O'Keefe is on with the president . . . see the red light is on . . . and besides—"

"That's exactly who I want, the president." Caroline threw her head back. "I'm sorry, move aside."

She swung the door open, and there was Bernie O'Keefe sitting at a small conference table, his shirt draped open exposing a hairy chest and rumpled layers of flesh, his white legs punctuated by boxer shorts and dark socks.

Caroline shrieked. Bernie held his hand up, pointed at the door, and shouted, "Shut that!"

"No, no, sir, I wasn't saying 'shut that' to you, Mr. President. It was to Caroline . . . Yes, sir, I understand, yes, sir." Bernie was nodding, waving off both Caroline, who was somewhere between shock and revulsion, and Barbara, who had tried to get to the door before Caroline.

Bernie hung up, darted to the sofa, and threw his pants to

Barbara. "Can you get that button back on for me?" he asked in a lather. "National emergency!"

"What? The button?" asked Barbara.

"No!" Bernie shouted at Caroline. "Terrorists on television!" He grabbed his jacket and draped it around his middle.

Barbara took the pants and went off looking for the sewing kit she kept in her desk for such emergencies.

"Come in, Caroline; maybe you can tell me what's going on," said Bernie. "The president didn't see it, but he's out of control. Have you called the network?"

"I can't get through," she said. "Their phone lines are jammed, and their correspondents downstairs are as much in the dark as we are."

"That's hard to believe," said Bernie drily. "Sit down while I call the attorney general. Would you like a drink?"

The press secretary glanced over her shoulder. "Desperately," she said. "What do you have?"

Bernie pointed at the credenza. "And make me one too—a double on the rocks."

Emily Gineen hadn't seen the broadcast, so Bernie recounted as much as he knew. It sounded even less believable than when the president had told him about it, so he took refuge in talking tough.

"Look, Emily, the president of the United States is in orbit. The first lady is in shock. What is this, some kind of banana republic where rebels take over the country by seizing radio and TV stations? We give you $10 billion a year, armies of FBI agents, and somebody can hijack a television network and you don't even know it? Maybe I should call the Defense Department and get the army out."

He bulldozed ahead, ignoring her questions, mostly because he had no answers himself.

"Now, I suggest you get back to the department and get your butt in gear. Call me as soon as you do, if that's not too much to ask. The president would like to know what's going on. He'd also like to get a SWAT team to the ABC studios on DeSales Street."

Bernie felt better after he'd vented for a moment.

"Get on it, Emily! I don't mean to sound harsh, but this is absolutely unbelievable. Thank you. Yes. Yes."

Bernie dropped the receiver hard in the cradle, muttered some more expletives, and took a large gulp from the glass Caroline had set on his desk.

"Welcome to Nicaragua," he sighed.

At that very moment Sharon Holmland, Caroline's special assistant, fresh out of Columbia University Journalism School, arrived breathless in the outer office with urgent news.

Barbara, pants and needle in hand, shrugged and opened the office door for her. Sharon froze at the sight of a half-naked Bernie O'Keefe, jacket wrapped around his ample waist, sipping scotch, and her boss sitting across from him, drink in her hand as well.

"ABC has just announced that it appears that someone hijacked their satellite transmission," Sharon spoke to her boss, trying not to look at the president's counsel.

"Wonderful!" Bernie exclaimed. "We'll call out the air force, not the army." Then he turned to Caroline. "You schedule a press briefing right away. We've got to get a presidential statement and avert a panic here."

ACTUAL EVENTS DID LITTLE to avert a panic. Two vans filled with an FBI anti-terrorist team roared to the network's studio, where ambulances were already on the curb. The agents, wearing black jackets and carrying H&K MP5s and sawed-off shotguns, stormed the building, which was already in utter chaos.

Griswold left the situation room and the fast-breaking developments in the Middle East to return to the family quarters in the mansion. He was sitting with one arm around Anne, the other gently stroking Elizabeth's hair, when Bernie arrived. The two men adjourned to the Lincoln sitting room and talked to the attorney general, now in her office. The president also called Frizzell, who gave him the most thorough report he'd received so far while resisting the temptation to say "I told you so."

"Bernie," Griswold said somberly, "this is close to anarchy. An assault upon the established order that no responsible government can tolerate. We must toughen up my statement."

Robbie, who had appeared out of the woodwork, had already drafted something stronger.

Caroline Atwater announced to the White House press corps that there would be a special 8:30 briefing so she could read a statement from the president. The networks would carry it live— "providing," Griswold muttered to Bernie, "they can keep control of their own satellites!"

The phone lines were jammed. Statements cascaded from Capitol Hill with senators and representatives calling for congressional hearings, demands for Griswold to act, scathing denunciations of anti-abortion terrorists and the "religious bigots who spawned them," and one hapless Pennsylvania congressman who demanded the air force "shoot down" the offending satellite.

Platoons of young marines in battle dress, M-16s in their laps, sat in the Marine barracks at Eighth and I Southeast awaiting a command. At Fayetteville, North Carolina, the eightieth battalion of the Eighty-second Airborne were put on standby. Somewhere in the jumbled first moments of the crisis, O'Keefe had called the deputy secretary of defense, asking that units be put on alert. No one had bothered to call them off when it was discovered that there hadn't been an attack by terrorists after all.

"LADIES AND GENTLEMEN, please." Caroline Atwater stood before the blue screen with the drawing of the White House behind it. The red lights indicated the networks were on live, but in the back of the room the buzz continued.

"Please," she intoned pleadingly. "Before I read the president's statement, let me simply explain what we know at this point."

She then referred to an ABC press release from corporate headquarters in New York, explaining that the evening news, like all programming, was transmitted to a preassigned target frequency received by a satellite leased to the network; the signal was in turn transmitted back to receiving units on the ground across the country which in turn transmitted them either by transmitters or by cable to individual receivers. No one had yet determined how, but it appeared that someone had displaced the regular uplink and replaced it with the abortion video.

Atwater then explained the actions Griswold had ordered for Justice, the FBI, and other investigative arms of the government.

"The president is committed," she put emphasis on every word, "to exposing and bringing to justice those responsible for this act of piracy."

"'I deplore this act of terrorism,'" she read, "'which offends the sensibilities of every law-abiding, decent citizen in this land. It is an outrageous invasion of our privacy to bring such an offensive, grotesque scene into our living rooms.'"

"'I know what it means: My own daughter was deeply wounded emotionally. This is a direct attack on the authority and legitimacy of the American government, no less seditious than a physical assault upon our elected leaders or institutions.'"

"'It is, in short, insurrection, which will not be tolerated. This government will act swiftly and decisively, of that the American people can rest assured.'"

When the press secretary finished reading Griswold's statement, the room erupted, several dozen journalists shouting at her at once.

Caroline sputtered for a moment; then Bernie O'Keefe walked over from the doorway, took her gently by the arm, and led her off the platform and back to her office. The networks were then forced to cut away to their own studios, where their anchors gave their interpretations of this profoundly unsettling assault on the collective national psyche.

29

BERNIE O'KEEFE passionately hated his buzzer alarm, but it was the only thing that really roused him. He either slept right through the clock radio's music or news reports, or else he hit the snooze bar and went back to sleep. But the horrible shrill ring of the old windup alarm always got him. Now he knocked over two magazines and an empty glass to get to it: 6:30 A.M. after a long, surreal night.

He rubbed his eyes and raised himself on one elbow. What he could see—and it was all still blurred—looked terrible, reminiscent of his room at Yale where there was always total disorder, clothes strewn everywhere, a big towel draped over the dresser top. And his head throbbed horribly.

Not that he had the usual excuse. He'd been in the Lincoln sitting room all evening with the president, who'd offered nothing stronger than decaf. So he'd had only a couple in the office and one big one before going to bed.

His legs felt heavy as he steered them toward the bathroom. *The forties are cruel,* he thought, staring into the mirror. Sagging jowls, puffy sacs under each eye, the right one slightly bloodshot. He still thought of himself as the kid at the top of the class, son of a construction worker who had made it to the White

House, always the youngest in any group of peers and surely the smartest. He didn't look it today.

Bernie splashed cold water on his face and ran his hands through his auburn hair. He needed a haircut. When Marilyn was here she nagged about such things, but now his hair, like everything else, was out of control. Actually, though, he liked it longer; it reminded him of his courtroom days.

Now, that was fun, he thought. There was nothing like standing there matching wits with your opposing counsel, like two gladiators going into combat, and only one could survive. He'd almost always won, and even when he didn't, he was in charge. It was his show. He missed it.

TWENTY MINUTES LATER Bernie was shaved, showered, dressed, and in the kitchen washing down his aspirin and handful of vitamins with a large glass of orange juice. The coffee was brewing, the beans freshly ground and the water slowly dripping through. The stronger the better.

He stared out of the kitchen window at the bricked-in court-yard at the rear of the house. The sun was still low, the yard still cast in long, deep shadows. When they had looked at the house, Bernie had imagined a little oriental garden and patio furniture, maybe with a trellis full of vines along the wall of the carriage house behind.

But all he saw today were two patches of green, with unruly grass sprouting out in corners of the yard. The bricked path-ways were uninviting, covered with green moss. And the kitchen, as he looked around, seemed no more inviting. Empty bottles— dead soldiers, Bernie called them—filled a brown grocery bag in the corner, an empty peanut butter jar and mounds of crumbs on the countertop, and a sink piled with dirty dishes. Good thing the maid came tomorrow.

All at once he missed Marilyn and the kids and the big open lawns of their Wellesley home. He and Marilyn had had their share of difficulties, both of them with explosive tempers, but the house was always neat and full of cheerful noises with kids running in and out. Often at night, in years past anyway, he and Marilyn would linger over the kitchen table and talk about the kids and school and his cases. Bernie would have his Dewars and maybe a hunk of cheese and some grapes, Marilyn a glass of white wine.

That was all before the politics, which Marilyn detested. Also, though she never said it in so many words, Bernie knew she resented Griswold. She thought he used people, especially her husband. Bernie knew she was right.

She still said she'd be moving down when the kids were out of school in June, but Bernie knew about that too. She wouldn't. And he really couldn't blame her. There was nothing for her here.

Life moves on, doesn't it? You can't go back; it never works. He sighed and poured his coffee, black and steaming. He took great gulps, rolling the hot liquid down his throat. He loved the sensation of that first strong cup in the morning, almost as much as he loved that first tinkling glass of Dewars in the evening.

Bernie cleared a space on the cluttered kitchen table and spread out the *Washington Post.* The headlines screamed: "Antiabortionists Hijack Network." He gulped more coffee. His head throbbed. "Public Outraged" was the smaller headline over a background piece by the *Post's* national political editor.

"Pro-choice Leaders Demand Griswold Act," was the second lead. O'Keefe read fast: The heads of six national organizations, including Act-Up, NOW, and Planned Parenthood, were demanding greatly expanded federal efforts. "Muslim terrorists have been deported," argued Jade Worthy of NOW. "Why shouldn't these equally dangerous individuals be locked away for good where they can do no harm?"

The newspaper confirmed what Bernie already knew: his agenda for the next few weeks. He would be chasing a bunch of wackos, putting out statements, putting out fires, calming the president, writing legal opinions, studying polls—and all for what? Had these people really thought they would change anyone's mind?

He flipped quickly to the back of the A section to see if Levitz's column would be in today's edition. Yes, there it was. He must have written it late last night in order to get it in. *He's Washington's conscience*, thought Bernie. *Though that's a contradiction in terms.*

Last night anti-abortion extremists set back their own cause by an act of terrorism. Now they have not just committed murder, as in Fargo, nor merely attacked the rule of law, but assaulted the very means by which what the founders called domestic tranquility is sustained in our nation.

Strange paragraph construction, thought Bernie. Levitz must have written quickly.

Like it or not, television is the one instrument that provides national cohesion. In earlier days, Americans met in town halls for political discourse; today our town hall is in everyone's living room. Television has become the lifeline of the late twentieth century community. It is the tie that binds us together.

"Scary thought," Bernie muttered.

Free societies cannot survive without free civil discourse. Only with the open exchange of ideas can we form shared values and assumptions about life—what philosophers call the moral consensus.

The extremists who stole last night's broadcast stole free discourse as well, attempting, one supposes, to achieve ends they believe good by evil means. They would do well to heed Solomon's words: "He who pursues evil will bring about his own death."

"To pursue evil is to bring about one's own death." Bernie repeated the words to himself, then heard his driver rapping on the front door. His limo had arrived.

JUST A FEW MILES TO THE WEST in Spring Valley, Emily Gineen crisscrossed her spacious kitchen, grabbing milk from the refrigerator, hauling boxes of cereal from cupboards, boiling eggs on the stove, and anxiously staring at the coffeepot. Each time she passed the table, she would stop for a spoonful of strawberry yogurt, her own breakfast staple.

Before she had time to finish the kids' breakfast or hers, her limo pulled in the drive. She kissed each of the children as she headed to the front door.

"Mom!" said Kathy, pulling her back for a moment and giving her a strong hug. "Have a great day. Hang in there!" Emily hugged her back fiercely. So sweet, she thought. Both of them knew she was under the gun. She picked up the *Post* and poured herself a big mug of coffee to go. Rosemary would see that the kids ate their breakfast and got off to school.

As she passed the dining room window, Emily was struck by the incredible beauty: explosions of pink and vivid red and white from the banks of azaleas. It was a glorious day. She was glad she could soak that in; somehow she knew she would need it later in the day to offset all the ugliness awaiting her.

There were, after all, no precedents to draw upon; no attorney general before her had had to face an issue quite like this because no terrorist group had ever hijacked a television network.

In the back of her limousine, Emily spread open the newspaper. She scanned the front page and stopped on the background piece headlined "Public Outraged." The *Post's* national political editor had an uncanny sense for what people were thinking.

> No event in recent memory has created such instant indignation. Americans take in stride the garbage strikes, poor postal service, power outages, tornadoes, yes, even wars, but the message today is clear: don't fool with our television.
>
> That was what pollsters discovered in an evening survey of 320 homes. It will no doubt disappoint the hijackers to learn that far less outrage was directed at what was shown on the film than at those who interfered with the broadcast. According to recent surveys, television is the prime source of news for 70 percent of Americans. . . .

Emily chuckled at the irony. Paul really had a point the other day when he said that Americans just wanted to be left alone to live their contented lives, and they expected government to provide that privacy. No great passion over great issues, no raging national debate over policies or the nation's future. Just let me get my sixpack and watch the tube, get my kids into a halfway decent school, and be able to walk around the block without getting mugged.

Maybe that's all we should shoot for, Emily thought for a moment. Then she turned to Ira Levitz. Most of the column scolded the terrorists who had hijacked the network. But near the end, the pundit called for moderation in the government's response. The closing paragraph, in fact, sounded like Paul Clarkson himself might have written it.

As president, Whitney Griswold must also be a moral leader. For only he can break this ugly downward spiral of repression and violence.

To be sure, Mr. President, enforce the law. But at the same time rebuild our nation's sense of decency and civility. Our moral values are in tatters.

When people feel they cannot speak, their frustration spills over into violence. The president must choose: He can seek to restore free and open moral discourse in which those with minority views are not driven to the margins—or he can continue the current crackdown and watch as the violence continues.

The president would do well to heed the words from the prophet of old: "Come, let us reason together."

Nice phrase, Emily thought. But columnists make it all sound so easy. They don't have to make it happen. They just sit at their word processors and pontificate. Still, a good point.

THREE LEVELS BENEATH the White House is the old World War II bomb shelter, a subterranean labyrinth of gray hallways punctuated by rooms with triple-thick steel doors, used for miscellaneous secure and secretive purposes, including the dental chair used for filling presidential cavities.

Whitney Griswold had chosen one of the larger rooms to

house his elaborate physical fitness equipment, primarily an antique rowing machine equipped with an ergometer. The year he graduated from Brown, the university was replacing its ancient, one-ton, castiron machines with sleek, lighter, and cheaper ones. Griswold, sentimentally attached to the monstrous old machine and the heroic memories it evoked, had bought one.

After his election, the navy had lugged the thing to the White House basement, and at 6:30 every morning, Griswold would strap his feet in, adjust himself on the seat, and grip an oar handle.

The oar, on the starboard side because it was the same position he had rowed, was cut off halfway and connected to a large, mechanical pivot, which in turn, drove a cast-iron flywheel two feet in diameter and weighing eight hundred pounds. There was a crude brake to create resistance, consisting of a strap wound around the wheel and attached to several two-pound weights called stones—a reference, oarsmen always said, to the age in which the machine was invented.

The object was to set the flywheel counter to zero and then row as hard as possible for six minutes. One's score was measured by the number of rotations clocked in the wheel. It took incredible fortitude to overcome the intense physical pain, but Griswold had learned, as champions do, how to best the system.

With exactly the right cadence and an extra push, the brake strap would begin to bounce at its resonant frequency, thus releasing some of the load. The only problem was that the noise from the weights clanging as they swung wildly was ear-splitting, so much so that the more senior Secret Service agents always managed to avoid the early morning detail, laying it off on junior agents.

But for Griswold, it was pure exhilaration. Sweat streaming down his face and soaking his shirt, breathing hard but perfectly synchronized with his legs and arms, the man and the machine became one. He could almost feel the shell gliding through the rippling waters of the Narragansett River. Pain would give way to euphoria as he reached his full stroke—and then there was a deliriously joyful sound of iron and steel colliding as the stones flew through the air.

The old machine was important to Griswold. It reminded him of his own golden days, affirmed his belief that some things in life had permanence, stability, connection to the past. And the challenge was fresh every day.

"Crew is a sport of the mind," he frequently told his young agents, who stood silently cursing their ringing ears. It was a challenge to the will to ignore pain and persevere to the finish line. Bernie, the old football player, used to kid Griswold that crew, the sport of the select few, was the only one in which the participants moved backwards, since they always sat facing the rear of the boat.

The doctors had told the president that he should taper off because eventually the strain would be too great and he couldn't stop all at once. But Griswold was not only disciplined, he was compulsive.

After his exercise, he would take alternating hot and cold showers, wrap himself in a terry-cloth robe, and use his private elevator to go to the second floor quarters. There Juan had his suits and shirts and shoes arranged so that Griswold could dress quickly and be in the hall in time to kiss Elizabeth good-bye as she was escorted to school. By 7:15, not a moment later, Griswold was at his place at the end of the table in the family dining room for his breakfast of orange juice, yogurt, and coffee.

Other than weekends at Camp David and his two trips out of Washington, this was the first morning of the nearly four months into his presidency that Griswold had missed the routine.

Elizabeth who, complaining of horrible dreams, had come in to sleep with her mother during the night, then awoke early, still visibly disturbed over the television broadcast. Anne had summoned him early, and instead of his morning routine, he sat with Elizabeth in the small breakfast room while she ate.

He tried to get her talking about school and soccer, but Elizabeth's thoughts were elsewhere.

"Daddy, was that film real?" she asked. "I mean real people, not actors?"

"I think so, dear. I haven't seen it. But remember, this is a medical film. It is meant for doctors to help them do their work better. It has to be very realistic."

"It was totally gross. Blood and everything."

"Any operation would be very sickening to watch, dear. But that's what doctors and nurses must do to save lives and make people well. But you should just put it out of your mind."

"Daddy, do babies feel it when they're killed?"

Griswold felt his heart pound and that heavy sensation come into his stomach that he always felt after a fight with Anne or when some very bad thing happened. "No, no, dear, and they really aren't babies. They are not born. They aren't persons. So you needn't even think of that."

"It looked like a baby."

"I know, dear, but the age of consciousness comes much later. Like you—what's the earliest you can remember anything?"

"Hmmm." Elizabeth thought for a moment. "I think when I fell and cut my forehead and you took me to the hospital. I remember lying on the table."

"Of course. And you were three, almost four at the time. So these babies . . . er . . . I mean fetuses, they are not babies. They don't know or feel anything."

"But Daddy, this baby wiggled around. It jerked. The doctor stuck a pair of scissors in its head." Elizabeth shook her head, put her spoon down, and pushed her cereal away. "It was horrible."

She looked up. "Since you haven't seen it, why don't you watch it, Dad?"

"Well, I've got a very busy schedule. A meeting at 9:00 this morning with all of my advisors to discuss the film, in fact."

"Promise me you'll watch it so you can tell me what you think."

Griswold hesitated, but knew he couldn't avoid it. "Yes, dear, I promise."

"Cross your heart."

Griswold made a cross over his heart, and though it wasn't easy, forced a big grin. "All right, Elizabeth, get your books. And remember, guard that goal in the soccer game today."

"Yes, Daddy." Elizabeth started toward the hall, then turned.

"And you remember, you watch that film. You promised."

More tired than if he had rowed six minutes, the president went to the breakfast table where Juan had arranged in a neat pile beside his place the *Washington Post*, the *Wall Street Journal* and two folders, a red-leather binder marked "Intelligence Summary—For the President's Eyes Only," which contained overnight dispatches compiled by General Maloney, and a black binder containing the president's news summary. The red folder, as always, was on top, the first thing the president read.

This morning he fished down, picked out the *Post*, scanned the front page, and then turned to Ira Levitz.

30

J. WHITNEY GRISWOLD considered tardiness the moral equivalent of slothfulness, one of the seven deadly sins. It was 9:04. Robbie, Emily, and Frizzell were seated in front of the president's desk. Griswold was reaching for the phone when Bernie O'Keefe, slightly out of breath, came through the side door.

The president's half smile and voice evidenced his irritation. "I'm happy, Counselor, that you could grace us with your presence."

"Sorry, Mr. President, a very important call, getting the latest intelligence."

In truth, Bernie had been talking with Marilyn, who had called him at his desk about their eldest son's failing grades, and she was mad at him, too, when he had to cut the conversation short to get to the president's office. This had been a double loser.

"You know, obviously, why I have called this meeting," Griswold began somberly. "We must in the next hour assess what has happened, review our options, and I will also expect your recommendations. We must be decisive.

"I should warn you that the National Security Council is meeting now, so we may be interrupted by an emergency—like

251

the outbreak of war in Israel—which some of us might perhaps find a welcome diversion from the rather bizarre matter at hand."

The group chuckled.

"Emily, you get us started here. What are the grounds for criminal action? I don't remember reading any cases in law school about theft of a network's air time." Griswold leaned back, resting his elbow on the chair arm and propping his fist under his chin.

"No, Mr. President, it is somewhat novel. But my people have found the pertinent statute." She looked at her notes. "It is 18 USC 1367, the Electronic Communications Privacy Act passed in 1986. Twenty-five-thousand-dollar fine and a ten-year sentence."

Griswold leaned forward and made a note as his lawyer's mind kicked in. "Any precedents?"

"Yes sir," Emily grinned. "You'll love this one. In 1987 a technician at the Christian Broadcasting Network was apparently sitting in the control room with nothing to do. *Lassie* or *The Waltons* or some other rerun was going out of CBN. So he started scanning satellite transmissions and came across a hard-core pornographic movie being beamed in on the Playboy channel. He sat down at a scripting machine and made a few biblical graphics; you know, terse little messages like 'Repent, the kingdom of God is at hand.' Then he beamed them up from CBN's transmitter and superimposed the words over the Playboy broadcast . . ."

Bernie let out a huge laugh. "Can you imagine? In all those homes and bars, people watching a couple go at it on the screen and then all of the sudden there's writing on the wall screaming, REPENT! Aaauuuggghhh! Probably had people on their knees or rubbing their eyes all over America!" Bernie slammed his hand on the chair arm, almost doubling over.

Even Griswold couldn't contain his laughter. Then he asked, "What did they do to him?"

"Jury convicted, $1,000 fine, and 150 hours community service." Emily looked again at her notes.

"Not enough." Griswold shook his head. "No deterrent there. Do you suppose that's what happened in this case?"

"We can only speculate," Emily replied. "But the FCC tells

us that a hijack like this is relatively simple to do. There are three hundred earth stations that can transmit and no way to tell where the signal comes from. In this case, it was probably from a mobile satellite van. You can even rent them for a few grand."

"Clever," Griswold said thoughtfully. "But too easy, too dangerous."

He stared at Emily. "If we don't come down hard and fast, every nut in America will be doing the same thing. We've got to prosecute to the hilt."

"Yes, sir," Emily nodded.

Then he turned to Frizzell. "And you, Director, you find those who did this."

Frizzell could hardly wait to answer. Information from assets had pretty well pinpointed those responsible, he told the president. Arrests could be made quickly, probably within twenty-four hours.

"Good! Go to it!" Griswold leaned forward. "Okay, Robbie, my speech to the nation will be tonight. I'd like to wait until tomorrow, after the arrests, but the country needs to hear from me quickly. I'll say that we know the perpetrators—"

"No, sir, mustn't tip them off," Frizzell interjected.

"And be sure to always say 'alleged perpetrators,'" Emily added.

"Yes, yes, of course. Be careful of the language. You watch that, Bernie."

"Right. We'll just say that 'the FBI is diligently pursuing the investigation and we expect swift action. Justice will be done.' Are we agreed?"

Everyone nodded.

"So much for that," Griswold said. "But we must now examine some broader questions. Robbie has given me a very disturbing report." He held up a sheet of paper. "You explain, Robbie."

Harvey Robbins's power had increased dramatically in the first four months of the Griswold presidency. Viewed initially as a coldblooded campaign technician and administrator, he had slowly but surely gained influence over policy. Whoever controls the president's schedule, Robbins had discovered, controlled the issues agenda.

But Robbins was also winning sometimes grudging admiration for his computerlike mind and shrewd political insights, which included mastery of poll data and demographic research. A polling service headed by J. D. Sindberg reached six hundred homes between 6:00 P.M. and midnight every night so that issues and attitudes could be tracked day to day. The service was located in Sioux Falls, South Dakota, but Robbie had a direct line installed in his office so that he could often listen in as interviewers were questioning respondents. He'd learned that he could sense the intensity of issues simply from the tone of voice of the people being polled.

"The events last evening," Robbins began, "precipitated a dramatic change in public opinion. For example, the percentage responding in the affirmative to the question, 'Is America on the right track?' dropped from 57 percent to 44 percent; the percentage giving approval to the president, from 59 percent to 51 percent. That is the greatest single movement in one night that J. D. remembers since the market crash in '87. And the voices are angry, impatient."

"For heaven's sake, one interruption in the network news for five minutes wouldn't do that," O'Keefe, never a great fan of the pollsters, scoffed.

"It sure has, Bernie. Maybe in some ways it was a minor incident, but it had a big symbolic effect. It's like the last straw— proof that life is really out of control, that this is an ugly society, that people can't feel secure even watching television in their own living rooms."

Robbie adjusted his chair, turning to face the others as well as the president. He squinted, creating deep furrows in his brow, then gestured toward them with his pen. "This presidency is at a grave crisis point. All our backup data shows the public wants someone to take charge. Last night's broadcast and the Fargo shooting are being seen, quite correctly, as a direct assault on the authority of this office. The American people will watch very closely, and what they decide now may stick with us for the rest of this term."

"What are you saying, Robbie?" Emily asked. "We'll move immediately. Director Frizzell here says we can have arrests in twenty-four hours; the president will be on TV tonight."

"Not enough." Robbie stood and paced to the left side of the president's desk, adjusting his rep silk tie and looking very stern. The sun, reflecting in from the french doors leading to the rose garden behind him, silhouetted his short blond hair.

Bernie knew Robbins well enough to know his agenda: He was testing his new-found authority, and he was also plowing the dirty political soil so the president could be the statesman. Bernie'd seen the one two routine before.

"Not enough," Robbie repeated. "We have to break this movement. Finish it off. The people want this president to take charge. They want order."

Just what Paul was talking about in the car, Emily thought to herself. *We must keep all this in perspective.*

"All right, Bernie, Emily, you tell me what steps we can take under existing statutes to bring this violence to a halt." Griswold pointed to each one. Robbie had set him up perfectly.

Bernie liked feeling like a lawyer again. He traced the statutes in case law, beginning with *NOW v. Scheidler*, in which the Supreme Court had held that anti-abortion protesters, even if they had no economic motive, could be considered "racketeers" under RICO, the tough laws enacted to break organized crime. The anti-abortion movement as a whole could be considered a conspiracy, and anyone could be drawn in if they had any connection to a "racketeer influenced corrupt organization," as the New Covenant Church in Pompano, Florida, discovered when its church building was confiscated because it had allowed Operation Rescue workers to meet there before rescues. And under FACE, the Freedom of Access to Clinic Entrances Act, any interference with abortion facilities was a federal offense.

"Tie those in with federal civil rights statutes," Emily interjected, "or the new anti-terrorist laws. You, Mr. President, just have to make a finding as to who *is* a terrorist. Then we can do anything we want. We can spread the net to anyone who has ever been involved in an abortion protest. We can go as far as you want legally. As a law professor, I question whether these statutes go too far. As attorney general, I have to say they are the law, and I'll enforce them."

"Good. We'll start to crack down on the known activists first. Agreed?" The president looked around. O'Keefe seemed troubled, but Frizzell was enthusiastic.

"Absolutely, sir." Emily nodded. Robbie grinned.

"I'll announce this evening," the president said to them, "that I am directing the attorney general to treat as conspirators all those who have aided, abetted, or assisted *in any way* those whose conduct violates the law, that grand juries will be impaneled in each major city, and that we will prosecute to the fullest extent of the law. We must be very clear in our intentions. Do you agree?"

"Yes sir," said Emily. "I understand your point. We'll draft the language carefully."

"All right, but be clear."

Bernie sat silently. *Just because a law can be enforced*, he was thinking, *doesn't mean it's prudent to do so*. As a litigator, he had always counseled clients to be sure they knew what they were getting into before they rushed into the courtroom. Once in, he would say, it's hard to get out; and it can be bloody. His advice was always to try to settle first.

"Mr. President, remember that letter Martin Masterson faxed you on election night?" Bernie asked.

"Of course I do."

"Well, do you suppose we could invite him in, along with Senator Langer and a few others? See if we couldn't get the responsible elements on our side. *Reason together.* Maybe build a little consensus before we get too far down this road. It's just a thought."

Robbie didn't give the president a chance to answer. "No one has heard two peeps from Masterson since the election.

Langer . . . well, I wouldn't trust him if he came in here on his hands and knees carrying an olive branch between his teeth.

"Come on now, Bernie." Robbie's eyes were darting. "These are the 'responsible elements'—is that what you call them? They've called us 'baby killers' and worse. Their speeches are what caused the crazies to go off the edge. No, it's too late for that."

"I like to be a peacemaker, Bernie, but Robbie's right," said Griswold. "It would be a sign of weakness. I've shown restraint. My door has been open. But now the train is out of the station, and they've missed it."

The president turned to Frizzell. "Director Frizzell, I've read how the FBI destroyed the Klan in the 60s. Glorious chapter in your bureau's history. Wiretaps, infiltration, some heavy-handed stuff—but it brought an end to that evil. It's unbelievable, but less than half a century ago we were lynching African Americans in this country." Griswold shook his head.

"I want you to go after these people in the same way," he said. "It may sound extreme, but these people are extreme. Wiretaps, infiltration, whatever it takes—but you go after the leaders. Hard!" He startled Emily by smashing a fist in his open palm.

Frizzell sounded gleeful. "Yes, sir, we will."

Bernie remembered what Levitz had said in the paper that morning: *The extremists . . attempting . . . to achieve ends they believe good by evil means . . would do well to heed Solomon's words: "He who pursues evil will bring about his own death." . . . The president can seek to restore free and open moral discourse . . . or he can continue the current crackdown and watch as the violence continues.*

"Now, Robbie has another recommendation we need to consider," the president continued, turning to his chief of staff. "Go ahead, Robbie."

Oh, boy, Bernie thought. *Old Robbie set this one up. He's been lobbying for weeks.*

For years, Robbins said, the mayor of the District of Columbia had urgently requested authority to call out the National Guard to help patrol some of the gang-ridden combat zones in the capital. The White House had always said no. But the truth was that crime was out of control in D. C.: eight hundred homicides a year, 60 percent of the African-American males between nineteen and thirty-one in jail or on parole, and the statistics were getting worse by the day.

People had debated why it was getting worse. Some said it was part of a general moral breakdown; this administration believed it was the lack of educational and economic opportunities and that its empowerment programs in time would bring change. But for now there was a crisis. The police couldn't handle it. Just two thousand Guardsmen could bring an immediate sense of order.

"But what's that got to do with this TV business or the abortion controversy?" Emily asked, looking perplexed.

"The breakdown of order. All part of the same general problem. It's time to act, and if we do it all at once," Robbie replied, "the public will be overjoyed."

"I may include a declaration of national emergency in my statement tonight," said Griswold. "Robbie has come up with a statute that I think covers us on national emergency powers, one that was passed in 1976. What would you think of that, Emily?"

"I want to reflect on it, Mr. President, study the law." She frowned. "It's an extraordinary measure to take, and, of course, that statute—I happen to be familiar with it—closely regulates what you can do. For one thing, Congress can overrule you."

"Well, there are plenty of good precedents." Griswold had obviously thought about this. "Nixon activated the reserves to move the mail during the 1971 postal strike—and there was even emergency detention of anti-war protesters. Bush brought in the army during the L.A. riots. No, I think the constitutional power under Article II is clearly there—even without a statute."

"I'll need to look carefully, sir. It's a major step."

"But let's look what it would do," Griswold said. "It would send an important signal and give us all some added authority. And we should give the guardsmen police powers. Let them make arrests," he continued. "It may be our best chance to finally break the back of street violence—at least here in D.C. where we are responsible."

"We have to do something. I'll certainly agree with that, sir," Emily said. "The statistics are horrible. It's a vicious cycle, really. There's no law and order in the big cities, so criminals know they can do whatever they want. And I'll admit, doing this would send a signal that we mean business."

"Even if Congress raises a howl—and they will—think what we're saying: The president has this situation in hand." Griswold set his jaw, ready for battle.

"Let Congress scream." Robbie rubbed his hands together. "Who do you suppose the public will back in that fight? Ha! Joe Sixpack wants safe streets—and he doesn't want some crazies invading his television set. No, we need to draw the line."

What is it about this room? Bernie wondered, looking around at the flags behind the president, the exquisite rose garden through the Drench doors, the rug with the Great Seal of the United States in the center. *People come in here with good, clear, level heads and within a few months they become raving powermongers.* He should, he realized, raise all the warning flags, but so far no one had talked of breaking the law, and the political analysis was unassailable. Bernie decided he'd talk later with Griswold.

"Let's remember that those who have preceded me in this chair have had to take extraordinary measures in times of great national crisis," said Griswold, standing to indicate the meeting was over. He scooped up two folders, one red and one gray.

"Roosevelt faced the problem, of course, of the Japanese Americans—citizens put in detention camps without trials. What he did sounds repugnant now, but at the time it was the only thing he could do. Lincoln suspended habeas corpus. It was a measure of their greatness that they acted to avert what imperiled the republic," Griswold said. "What we're facing is no less a challenge than what those men faced. We have to act accordingly. Are we agreed?"

"Yes sir." Frizzell was first, then Emily, who said, "I agree with your analysis, sir. I'm satisfied. We have no choice."

Griswold looked at Bernie. "And you?"

"Yes, I think so, sir. I want to work on the language of your speech very carefully, however—and look at the statutes."

"Good, good." Griswold picked up his folders and headed for the situation room.

THE PRESIDENT spent the next two hours closeted with his National Security advisors. Meanwhile, Bernie informed Caroline Atwater of the president's plan, and she called each of the network's liaison executives, requesting that five minutes be cleared at 8:00 P.M. EST, for a major presidential announcement. Bernie then contacted the president's top speech writer, Jack Carmichael, who assigned two of his assistants to begin drafting the president's statement.

Emily returned to the Justice Department, where she asked the Office of Legal Council for draft language for an executive order declaring a state of emergency. Impossible to do adequate research by 5:00 P.M. she was told, to which she replied, do it anyway; it's for the president. Then she summoned Paul to her office.

By 3:00, they had looked over the first drafts and returned them for rework. Then an idea flashed across Emily's mind. She leaned back in her chair and looked at Paul. "What would you think if the FBI were to break the Fargo case today? I mean, make the busts and let Griswold announce it tonight?"

"Terrific, Emily. Of course, the president and his palace guard would be euphoric. But the bureau's not ready—unless you know something I don't. I mean, they've got some good leads to that one woman—the one in Chicago—but according to Frizzell's latest report it's not a sure thing."

"Let's see." Emily grinned as she reached for her phone. In a matter of seconds Frizzell was on the line.

"Director, I've been thinking . . . this report you gave us last week about the Fargo suspect in Chicago . . . we just might be able to do something for the well-being of this nation."

Emily swung her chair around and explained what an arrest

might mean, how Griswold could announce it, with the FBI moving in even as the president spoke.

"Sounds good, General." Frizzell would like nothing better than to be part of Griswold's address to the nation. "But there are just a few problems. We haven't nailed this one down yet."

"Like what?" Emily said as Paul quickly slipped the bureau's latest summary under her nose. "Says here your lab got some positive tests, physical description fits to a T, travel records establish that Ms. Pignato was in the area at the time, and we've got an informant's report that she boasted about having done a 'big job.' What more do you need?"

"We have no motive and no connection to the movement." Frizzell did not sound his exuberant self.

"There must be something. People like this don't come in from Mars." Emily was surprised at her own enthusiasm. It was a real role reversal. Here she was, the thoughtful and deliberate attorney general pushing the trigger-happy FBI director.

"We've looked, believe me. Not even a scrap of literature lying around. No testimony, nothing, nada."

"Remember John Salvi? I mean he had no ties to the movement, but they found some pro-life stuff in his apartment."

"We've looked. Nothing."

"You've searched thoroughly?"

"Yes, ma'am."

"With a warrant I suppose? No, forget I asked."

"We have our ways."

"Well, perhaps your agents could *find* some literature when they visit the suspect again?"

There was a pause.

"If I understand you, the answer is yes," said Frizzell, "but there are great risks you may want to consider."

"I was a prosecutor, you may recall, Mr. Director," Emily responded coldly.

"Yes ma'am. There are some other things that trouble us however. She's only twenty-five but has a rap sheet as long as your arm. Spent two years at Dwight in the Illinois system. Numbers stuff. Lots of family ties."

"Good, good. The record helps . . . casts suspicion."

"No, not really," he said. "Because in this case it just doesn't fit the anti-abortion zealot profile."

"Neither did Salvi. He was nuts, but he did it."

"You're the attorney general. If you tell me to do it, I will. But we have her under surveillance. Eventually she'll slip and lead us to others. Then we will have a conspiracy. If we move now, we may never know. It could compromise the case."

Emily shook her head and bit her lip. Griswold needed a break; she could just see him announcing it on television with just a touch of a smile. But compromise the case? She knew better. What in the world had gotten into her?

"In addition, General, I think we're going to bust the New York gang in the morning. That's great timing. The president says tonight we're going to get them, and in the morning, we do."

"That's good, Director. You just sit tight. I want to think about this, and I'll call you."

"We'll need time to set it up."

"I know, I know." She hung up.

Looking down, Emily could feel Paul's stare. He was smart enough to figure out from her end of the conversation what was going on. She was angry at herself; she had never suggested anything remotely like planting evidence before, and now Frizzell had one on her. She had gotten carried away.

"So, it's not such a good idea?" Paul broke the silence and smiled, giving her a reprieve.

"Well," she said, feeling uncharacteristically awkward, "we won't complicate the president's task tonight. It'll be hard enough as it is. And we'll continue investigating to find the connection. We know there has to be a conspiracy. Break the case prematurely and we could lose it."

"Right," said Paul. "Let's just get through tonight. We'll talk later."

"Let's get to work then," Emily agreed, visibly relieved.

ANTHONY FRIZZELL leaned back in his big chair and placed a call at 7:20.

"Bernie," he said. "Tell the president that we'll make the bust in the morning. Everything's going fine. And tell him to stick it to 'em in his speech tonight."

He paused, relishing the moment. On the issues that mattered, he knew a lot more than Bernie O'Keefe.

"Bernie," he continued. "Griswold may take some heat for what's coming down, especially from some of our favorite friends on the Hill. The whole Langer crowd. If you run into any trouble, feel free to give me a call."

He heard a quick, deep, impatient sigh from Bernie.

"Well, I know you need to go," said Frizzell. "But just remember, I've got some information on tap that may be of help to you in the near future."

Frizzell hung up, leaned back with his hands behind his head, and smiled at the picture of J. Edgar Hoover.

AT 7:45, the president was escorted into the small dining room adjacent to the Oval Office, where a cosmetician wielded pancake makeup and powders. As she swabbed away at his face, he joked, "It's like getting a corpse ready for showing, isn't it?" It was an old line, but she laughed.

At 7:55, Griswold took his seat behind the desk with a thin sheaf of papers before him. The Oval Office looked like a Hollywood set. Two cameras on large rollers were positioned in front of the desk, with lights beaming down from both sides. Behind the cameras were reflector lights illuminating the ceiling and bathing the room in a chill white light, which caused the walls to sparkle. Thick black cables snaked across the rug and into junction boxes in the hall. There was a backup system for everything and a generator on standby in the basement.

Behind the president were the two traditional stands of flags and a table between them with a bust of Lincoln prominently on one side. On the other side was a picture of the Griswold family in a burled walnut frame and a picture of Griswold at the helm of his sailboat. Robbie had wanted that photo moved, on the grounds that only one-quarter of 1 percent of the American people sailed; but Griswold was adamant. There was also a framed letter he had received during the campaign from an eight-year-old dying of cancer. "Heal our nation," proclaimed the crayoned letters.

At 8:01 the red light flashed on camera number one, directly in front of the president's desk, and the senior technician nodded and pointed at Griswold, who cleared his throat and began.

"My fellow Americans. This is the first time since I took the oath as your president nearly four months ago that I have believed it important to address you directly from this office. Events of the last twenty-four hours have moved me to do so.

"For just as evil forces have threatened our national security at various times during our history, so now have unwholesome forces, hostile to free democratic society, threatened our domestic security. We have always risen to these challenges, and we will do so now."

He reminded viewers of Fargo and explained that these same forces, "bent on subverting the democratic process," had now hijacked a network broadcast. He told of the effect it had had on his own daughter. Then he assured the watching millions that he had directed the attorney general and the director of the FBI to "swiftly bring to justice those responsible."

In the back of the Oval Office Robbie was watching on the monitor. "Perfect, perfect," he kept muttering. Griswold had mastered the timing, the pauses, the modulation of his voice. Robbie could already see the polls rising.

As he had been coached, Griswold exuded self-assurance, firmness but no hint of alarm. The nonverbal message was clear: The situation was under control because Griswold was in control.

"The anti-abortion movement may have started with deeply held personal goals. But no longer. They have become dangerous terrorists, and their random acts of violence are undermining respect for the law, so much so that other reckless forces in our culture are being unleashed, threatening the very security of our neighborhoods and homes.

"The first freedom," Griswold said, nodding directly into the lens, "is freedom from fear. This administration, I assure you, will do what must be done to guarantee that freedom for every American.

"And to that end I am signing an executive order tonight." He reached for the black folder to his right, opened it, then took his thick, black pen from his inside jacket pocket and scrawled his signature on the open page.

He looked up again, speaking softly, reassuringly.

"This order declares a state of national emergency."

"It's necessary to augment the police force of the District of Columbia which is, after all, the seat of government. Accordingly, two thousand National Guard troops will be called to active duty in the morning. This is secondarily necessary to reenforce the authority of law enforcement officials who may have to make very quick decisions in emergency circumstances. This is not new: Similar authority has been invested in America's peacekeepers by my predecessors when the national interest was similarly threatened."

"You elected me president, and I swore on my oath to uphold the Constitution and faithfully discharge the laws of this great country. Let no one be mistaken. This is precisely what I will do."

"Together we will meet this challenge and do our duty with the same courage and resolve previous generations of Americans have demonstrated."

"God bless you, and God bless this great land of liberty."

Robbie and other staff members standing in the doorway burst into applause the moment the red light went off. Griswold stood, grinned, and gave a thumbs-up sign.

IN HIS NORTH ARLINGTON HOME, Senator Byron Langer slumped back in his chair.

"I knew it. I felt it coming," he said, staring at the screen as the network anchor appeared, standing under the lights on the White House lawn, ready to debrief the nation.

"Mark this day, Lily," he said to his wife. "One day this will be remembered as a very dark moment in the history of our republic."

31

THANKS SO MUCH, Dawn," Mary Seaton called up the stairs to the baby-sitter. "We really appreciate your help. They can each have *one*—I repeat, one story. Then into bed. No negotiating. Daniel and I will just be gone for an hour or so."

Mary paused. Daniel was at the front door, his hand on the knob, impatient to go. Upstairs she could hear muffled chaos; the children must be bouncing on the beds—or off the walls—while they got ready for bed. But Dawn could handle it. She was only fifteen, the daughter of a neighbor, but she was great with kids. Mary decided she wouldn't worry; she and Daniel should escape while they could.

They eased out the front door and down the front walk. She and Daniel needed to talk, but things had gotten to the point where they felt they could not speak freely in their own home. Mary remembered a friend telling her years before about living in Iran as undercover missionaries. She and her husband had had to whisper in their home, had been followed when they went out to the market, and an Iranian member of their little Christian community had actually been killed by government agents. It had sounded surreal, but Mary now understood, at least somewhat, how her friend must have felt.

Daniel grabbed her hand and pulled her down the sidewalk, walking quickly, as he always did when he was upset. They both looked behind them, all around them. No one seemed to be following; in fact, the neighborhood was unusually quiet.

After they had walked in silence for a block or two, Daniel sighed, then spoke softly.

"This thing is really getting to me," he said. "I absolutely cannot believe the response during these past twenty-four hours. It's like a bad dream. I have not seen one thing in the media about the video itself. Everyone is just screeching about network sabotage and if your TV can be violated, then the nation is going down the tubes. Never mind that babies' skulls are being crushed and their brains sucked out. No, just don't mess with our TV!"

Mary's stomach turned over sickeningly. "It's still so early," she whispered. "This is just the first wave of reaction. People will come to their senses."

"That's what I thought!" he hissed back at her. "I thought the video would be the bucket of cold water that would shock people out of their stupor. But all they seem to care about is to find and prosecute the terrorists who dared to mess with their regularly scheduled programming. It's ludicrous!"

"I think that'll still happen," said Mary. "People *have* been shocked. But they're in denial. That's why they're all overreacting. They're shifting the focus to the TV issue because they aren't willing to face the regeneration-center issue. Maybe it'll just take a while for people to face facts."

"That's a nice psychological analysis," Daniel said. "But I'm afraid. What if Gideon's Torch ends up backfiring? It seems to me that all it's accomplished so far is that we now live in a police state. I mean, we've got the National Guard patrolling D.C. like this is Haiti or some Third World dictatorship. There's probably a tank formation rolling down Route 7 toward Falls Church even as we speak . . ."

Daniel sighed and clutched Mary's hand tighter. "I believed

the video was the clearest way possible to expose the regeneration centers. We showed them what will happen; people actually saw the procedure, right in their living rooms. I thought no one could watch it and turn away. Evidently I was wrong."

A FEW MILES AWAY, Alex Seaton and Jennifer Barrett were also walking in the darkness, strolling the bikepath in Reston. Usually they ran this route, their conversation carried on in short, breathy bursts, but tonight they didn't want to risk being overheard by other joggers on the trail.

While Daniel was mourning people's lack of response to the video, Alex was angry. He was furious that Americans could look at a baby's death on television—a murder committed coldbloodedly by those sworn to save lives—and not rise up in indignation against the perpetrators of that death. He was furious that President Griswold—hypocritical co-conspirator that he was—was self-righteously loosing troops on the streets. Griswold was the criminal.

Alex was also mad at himself. He was furious that he had allowed himself to be cajoled into even believing that something so benign as putting a video on television could work. He was angry, too, that his strategies had been ignored. Lance was right. This was war, and you don't win wars by hoping the bad guys change their minds. You win by taking out enemy targets. One by one.

In spite of his inner turmoil, Alex was silent. Jennifer walked beside him, also quiet. He appreciated that about her; she didn't need to be constantly chatting in order to feel secure. Their relationship had moved along rather well, he thought. She didn't require some of the mysterious attentions, gratuitous phone calls, and constant affirmations that had mystified him in earlier relationships with women. She obviously enjoyed his company, but she didn't pressure him. As a result, he was moving faster with this relationship than he ordinarily would. They had spent a lot of time together lately. They ran together nearly every day, had gone to a few movies, and had spent several very nice quiet Sunday afternoons in one another's company.

He took her hand in the darkness. Her fingers were cool and dry. "What's on your mind?" she asked.

"I just can't believe everything that has happened in the last twenty four hours," he said.

"I don't think anyone could have imagined how much of a stir the video would cause," she said.

"Not the right kind of stir," Alex said. "It's all turned into a huge mess. The pro-lifers are the villains in people's minds. Not the butchers who carve up defenseless babies. I don't get it."

"No one gets it," she said. "How's your brother doing?"

"He's devastated," said Alex. "I mean, it's not like he had anything to do with it," he added awkwardly. "But he can't believe people's reaction. I guess he's sort of naive about human nature."

"What about the people in New York?" she asked. "I mean, they're the ones who did it, right?"

"We don't know who did it," Alex said quickly. "We don't want to know."

"Alex, you can be a little more open with me, you know," she said. "There's more information floating around than you seem to realize. I heard Mary and Amy talking after church yesterday, and one of them mentioned something about a big project in New York. You need to be really careful with security; the feds are going to be on your tail from now on, and the less anyone knows, the better. Especially the people on the fringes—like Amy. She's too young and too volatile. She could easily let something slip."

Alex felt a twist in his gut. Amy had been acting sort of strange lately, he thought, especially in the past week or so. He'd thought that maybe she was jealous because he had been spending time with Jennifer. She'd seemed a little evasive, a little abrupt, a little cool. "Hell hath no fury like a woman scorned," suddenly popped into his mind. But Amy hadn't been scorned; he hadn't really made any overtures toward her before Jennifer appeared on the scene. But maybe she somehow felt slighted. She was one of those mysterious emotional women he didn't understand.

32

ANTHONY FRIZZELL stood, hands clutched behind his back, staring from his office window at the mass of cars crawling slowly in both directions along Pennsylvania Avenue. He had spent the night in his office so he could stay in touch with the field, getting only four hours sleep on the daybed in the side room, but he felt exhilarated. He was made for battle, and he knew it. Probably would have been a great general if he had lived in a different era.

He checked his watch: 7:20 A.M.

"It's amazing, Toby," he said without turning his head. "Every year the traffic starts earlier and earlier. All these people hurrying to get to their desks and make all the machinery work. Worker ants." He gestured grandly toward the Capitol to the left, then toward the White House to the right.

"Most of them don't have a clue," he concluded, swinging around toward his assistant. "Are you sure everything's in place?" Frizzell stood with arms folded, leaning on the back of his overstuffed, black-leather chair.

"Yes, Chief. I've gone through the checklist with Martin himself. Every item is covered. Solid. They should be calling in here in, let's see . . ." Toby Hunter looked at his watch, compared it

271

with the digital clock on the wall. "In eight minutes, thirty seconds."

"Everything covered?" Frizzell said again.

"Yes sir. No more Chicagos."

"Let's go then, Toby."

The two men strode down the hall to the command center. The duty officer and the assistant director for operations both stood as they entered.

"Thought we'd come down here where we can watch," said Frizzell. "All set for 7:30 gentlemen?"

"Yes sir. Enjoy the show, sir," the assistant director said, flipping on a huge TV screen that took up most of one wall. It was connected by closed circuit to cameras in the back of a mobile control van parked near the corner of Broadway and Roosevelt Avenue, not far from LaGuardia Airport.

The camera panned the busy intersection; cars heading west jammed the roads. Then the camera swung back to a side road off Roosevelt, to a tavern just to the right, then down the street to a long string of townhouses, 1920s vintage, most of them in need of paint and repair. The camera zoomed to the front door of number 1246. Through the speakers overhead in the command room came live transmissions. Frizzell could hear a voice counting down the seconds, "Ten, nine, eight . . . three, two, one, go."

The back doors of a parked van marked "Perucci's Bakery" burst open, and twelve men, some carrying H&K MP5 subguns, others riot shotguns, and one leading the way waving a .45 pistol in the air. They were wearing Kevlar helmets and black, heavily padded sweatsuits with FBI in huge white letters on their backs.

Twelve more poured from another van, then two groups from parked cars. Within seconds, FBI sharpshooters with highpowered rifles had taken up positions behind parked cars and in two doorways across the street. Roaring past the cameras, with lights flashing, came a herd of New York City police squad cars and one wagon.

It all happened so fast that only trained eyes like Frizzell's could follow the action. The alleys were covered, men with rifles peered down from rooftops, a helicopter swept into view. Two agents knocked on the door, then swung themselves back against the wood columns of the front porch. The agents waited to the count of five, then used a battering ram on the door. It collapsed into the room, shattering the glass panels, and, with bulletproof shields in front of them, they burst through the doorway.

A few minutes later, four men and three women, all hand-cuffed, were being led down the front steps. Then, one by one, they were herded into the back of the police van.

Frizzell grinned and gave a thumbs-up. It was a textbook operation, surgically clean and quick, over in seven minutes, start to finish.

While the vans and their escorts sped off away from the camera, the New York police pushed back curious bystanders and began blocking off the area with sawhorses and yellow tape while FBI crews moved in to examine every nook and cranny of the building.

"Get me Martin," Frizzell ordered. "I want a confirm on this before I call the AG or the president." He strode out of the room, headed for his office. Toby trotted ahead to put through the call.

By 8:15 seven suspects had been taken into the Jackson Heights headquarters; two others, including a priest, had been picked up on the lower east side of Manhattan; and three had been arrested in Yonkers. It was the New York cell of the The Life Network, at least all known members. In Washington, D. C., Reginald Warner and the satellite news-gathering operator had also been detained.

Emily Gineen had just arrived at her office when Frizzell called.

"Congratulations, Director," she said. "That's faster than I thought possible. Good work."

Emily picked up her direct White House line. "Get me the president, please."

All in all, this might turn out to be a pretty good day, she thought. *Probably not,* her gut responded.

BY 9:30 A.M., Senator Byron Langer had spread out on his desk four statute books, a well-worn little volume containing the Constitution, and a long memorandum from the Library of Congress detailing every invocation of extraordinary powers by any president since Washington had called the troops out for the Whiskey Rebellion in 1794—when farmers in western Pennsylvania, Virginia, and Carolina fought off the feds collecting their excise tax on whiskey. There were, to Langer's surprise, hundreds of such precedents; there were fifteen national emergency declarations in the relatively tranquil years of 1979 to 1993 alone.

He reread Article II of the Constitution, under which many presidents, including Lincoln, Roosevelt, and Nixon, had declared national emergencies: the so-called implied powers of the presidency. *Dangerous if abused,* he thought. It was a small miracle indeed that through all these years this delicate balance of government powers had been maintained when there was so much latent power in the executive. *The system is so fragile; it depends entirely upon men and women of good will to protect it.*

Then he reread the act Congress had passed in 1976 attempting to regulate the statutory declarations of national emergency that have been authorized under 470 separate provisions. Congress had attempted to rein in the power of the executive branch by determining that presidential declarations could be overturned by a joint resolution of the Congress.

If Griswold decided to act under Article 2 Congress had no specific authority to overrule him, and he might well get away with it. Even mild-mannered George Bush had called out marines and soldiers to put down the L.A. riots in 1992—forty-five hundred of them with orders to shoot if fired upon. The crisis was so grave that very few people had ever questioned him.

Langer leaned back in his chair. Presidents had acted unilaterally before. So why did Griswold's actions bother him so much?

The man had no consistent convictions, that was the problem. And he wasn't a conservative. Oh, sure, Griswold talked like a conservative on economic issues; he was pro-business and free market and railed against big government. But he was also a social libertarian, bending with the breezes on social issues and political judgments. In Langer's mind no one could subscribe to social liberalism and at the same time be a true economic conservative. Somebody had to pay the bills, after all, for the libertine lifestyle such liberalism unleashed. You eliminate all social conventions, people go on welfare or get AIDS, and the government ends up paying the bill. So inevitably one philosophy destroys the other.

And the social liberal ended up, no matter what he said, supporting big government. This was what happened to men like Griswold. No matter what they said, whether they were right or left, they were utopians. Ideologues, in fact. These kind always figured you could create incentives, social engineering really, and thereby create the so-called good society.

But it was nonsense. No matter how good the policies, government can never create the good society. That comes only from people *being* good. *By a change of heart*, Langer thought. Public virtue depends on private virtue, the moral life, the very thing Griswold so disdained.

No, Griswold was a utopian ideologue, like so many who called themselves conservatives these days. But Langer considered ideology and utopianism the real enemies of true conservatism. He believed in the established order of things, of wisdom handed from generation to generation. He was especially fond of T. S. Eliot's description of the "society of permanent things." He believed in a tradition of republican virtue based on respect for covenants of the past; he believed that citizens were moved to their own civic responsibility not because of some political decree but because of gratitude for the liberty their forefathers made possible.

In Langer's view, one took hold of such enduring truths and guarded them with everything one had. And that's why, he realized, Griswold frightened him so much. The man was a good politician, keen, quick, and articulate, able and well-meaning. But he had no tie to things enduring, no belief system bred in the bone. Of course he had descended from umpteen generations of New Englanders. But roots did not go deep in New

England's rocky soil. As Langer saw it, Yankee aristocrats believed they were born to govern and therefore had the instincts to do so. Their reliance was in themselves, not in enduring truths.

Griswold was decent but not deep. And surely not of Langer's school of conservatism.

Langer stared at the pile of papers on his desk. The laws, the precedents, the Constitution—they were one thing. But in today's environment, how could written statutes stand against an opportunist who fanned public passions and preyed on people's fears?

Byron Langer sighed and closed his eyes. He had a foreboding sense of doom, like watching from a distance as two locomotives hurtled toward a railway junction.

He shook his head, then leaned forward and hit his intercom button. "Get me the attorney general, please."

EMILY WAS WORKING in ner inner office. Spread out before her were the same four statute books Langer had on his desk, along with a memorandum of precedents the Office of Legal Council had hurriedly assembled. Around the desk were her four most trusted assistants, including Paul Clarkson. She was expecting Langer's call, and had, in fact, told her secretary to put it through immediately.

Emily had slept only four hours, but she did her best to sound bright, chipper, and confident.

"Madam Attorney General, I have a question," Langer began, "which I ask in a most constructive spirit. My deepest desire, I assure you, is to avoid a constitutional crisis."

"It's my deepest desire as well, Senator."

"Well then, tell me please, what are the specific extraordinary measures the president and you contemplate under this executive order?" he asked calmly.

"We will allow the National Guard to make arrests. There are many precedents for it, Senator, as in Los Angeles with George Bush or during the '60s anti-war and civil rights riots."

"Yes, I understand, though I have difficulty seeing that this crisis begins to approach those."

"We have reasons, Senator."

"Oh, yes, of course. You'll tell me it's your intelligence reports, I suppose. That's usually the case. What else?"

"We will put marshals or deputized guardsmen on duty at earth station transmitters. We can't have a repeat of the other night."

"Oh, my," Langer gasped. "Like Nicaragua, where the military guard the communications. Apart from the symbolism, don't you think that has some ominous First Amendment implications?"

"No, Senator. It's a mere precaution."

"And what about search and seizures?"

"We are looking at all the authorities at this moment. We may, as President Clinton did, take some extraordinary measures in this regard. I hope you realize, Senator, that this is a very dangerous national conspiracy we're up against. Very dangerous."

"No, Madam Attorney General, this is a very dangerous response. It is an unwarranted usurpation of power that cannot help but pose a grave constitutional threat, and I will oppose it with all the strength at my command."

"I'm sorry you feel that way, Senator." Emily was not surprised, but she paused a moment, wondering whether to attempt to persuade him. She decided it was pointless. "We, of course, respect your right to dissent."

"May I ask under what authority the president has made this decision?" Langer spoke slowly, deliberately.

"Well, we have thus far concluded it is within his implied powers under Article II of the Constitution."

"There are 470 statutes giving him emergency authorities. Why not one of them?"

"Well, sir, we considered the 1976 act but decided it wasn't necessary—"

Langer cut her off sharply. "Under the 1976 act, of course, Congress can overrule the president. That probably never entered your deliberation. But let me assure you, this will not stop us. The Congress will not have its authority disregarded. Before we head down that road, I beg you to reconsider."

"We'll consider your views, certainly, Senator, but we've studied this issue very carefully."

"Mrs. Gineen, I have come to respect you, but I must say that I believe you are reading from a different Constitution than the one on my desk. In any event, we will soon see. I must as a courtesy tell you that at noon today I will file a joint resolution to override the president's order. He has his implied authority under Article II; the Congress has its explicit authority under Article I—and we will not shirk our responsibilities."

Emily hung up and looked at her associates. "Well, he's against us. No surprise there, of course. But he says he'll file a resolution to block the president's order." She looked quizzically at Paul, whose expression was grim.

"We're playing this one on his home field, Emily, and he seldom loses at home," Paul said somberly. "This will be bloody."

Emily called Bernie O'Keefe, and within thirty minutes six White House congressional liaison assistants were leaving West Executive Avenue, their limousines headed for Capitol Hill.

AS SOON AS THE SENATOR finished his call to the attorney general, he summoned his speech writer, legislative assistant, and personal secretary. Still a judge by temperament, Langer dictated the outlines of the case while his aides scribbled notes furiously.

First he framed the issues: Could a president be stopped from asserting extraordinary powers under Article II? There were 470 specific situations giving the president emergency powers; didn't that mean Congress intended to define such emergencies? In which case, Congress could block him. Finally, what would happen in the event of a constitutional confrontation?

Then he began to recite just a few of the precedents, going back to Washington. There were hundreds to study; he told his legislative assistant to put absolutely everyone to work on this one.

At that point, Langer drew himself up straight in his chair. This would be, he said, a principled defense of the Constitution. No politics, no petty vindictive feelings.

"Take the high ground here, Josh," he exhorted his speech writer. "The very viability of our government is at stake here. This goes to the very heart of our republic."

With his staff at work, Langer set out for the minority leader's hideaway office in the Capitol; from there he went to the majority leader's expansive office just off the ornate Senate reception room. With the latter sympathetic and the former passionately pledging support, he then strode through the corridors, confronting colleagues and visiting offices in the three Senate office buildings. Since senators seldom drop in on one another, he created quite a stir and also managed to see many of his colleagues. Few wanted to turn him down face to face, especially when the issue he championed had to do with the protection of senatorial prerogatives.

By noon, Langer had lined up an impressive list of twenty-six cosponsors for his resolution, an unusual alliance of liberal Democrats, civil libertarians who relished the thought of embarrassing a Republican president, and evangelical Christian conservatives who distrusted Griswold and saw his power grab as a not-so-subtle attempt to break what remained of the pro-life movement.

Langer checked with his office and was told that legislative counsel had drafted the resolution and research was nearly completed. The senator then phoned the majority leader and was granted permission to introduce the resolution and speak for thirty minutes at noon the next day. By then he might have close to a Senate majority on his side.

Langer's strategy was announced to the Senate press gallery, and the news arrived in newsrooms around the country minutes later, about the same time it hit at 1600 Pennsylvania Avenue.

DESPITE THE DOMESTIC CRISIS, Whitney Griswold had maintained his scheduled activities for the day. This included a National Security Council meeting, a carry-over from the day before, to deal with the fast-developing events in the Middle East. The 10:00 meeting included the secretary of state, the secretary of defense, the director of the CIA, and top NSC staffers.

CIA director James Quarles's briefing included voluminous information about the inner workings of the Israeli government, provided by CIA assets—Israeli officials sympathetic to Americans, if not by ideology then by augmentation of their numbered Zurich bank accounts.

As Quarles spoke, Griswold doodled on his scratch pad, centered on the black-leather desk pad with "The President" engraved in blue. Months earlier he had realized that Quarles, a career intelligence officer, gave more information than anyone needed simply to prove how proficient his agency was. Besides, Griswold's mind was not on the maneuverings in the Knesset, but on his daughter. Elizabeth had had another bad night's sleep.

Griswold had learned from early childhood to maintain a cool and dignified composure under all circumstances, but inside his anger raged. He'd like to get his hands on those terrorists who had traumatized his little girl. Or at least get them behind bars. Good work on Frizzell's part, hauling in the New York gang this morning. He scribbled a note to call Frizzell and congratulate him. Coax him on. Do more. Get the rest of the bunch. Suddenly anger gave way to a burst of enthusiasm: He, Whitney Griswold, would have a role in cleaning up this kind of pernicious influence in American life.

The meeting ended at 11:30. Griswold started for the south door, which led directly through the secretaries' spaces and into the Oval Office. Then he paused and, impulsively, walked to the right into the hallway, startling both the Secret Service agents at the main Oval Office entrance and two low-level staffers passing by, one of whom backed up against the wall, flushed and flustered. Griswold shook hands with both. Then he turned right and walked straight down the corridor to the door at the end and into his press secretary's office.

Caroline Atwater was on the phone; she quickly hung up and stood behind her desk. Griswold thought she looked particularly attractive this morning, with the light streaming in the windows giving a lustrous sheen to her soft glossy hair. Such a wholesome look.

He walked to the front windows and looked across the north lawn. "Good view," he chuckled. "You can watch the sharks swim by, can't you?"

Caroline laughed. There was a pathway right past her windows where the members of the press could walk from the press room to the front lawn. Just off the path outside her windows was the place where television correspondents often stood for network reports from the White House.

"Are we getting beaten up?" Griswold asked.

"Too early for editorials. The ACLU issued a rather tepid disapproval. Most others seem supportive, although there is some restlessness on the Hill. But not bad so far, sir," Caroline replied.

"Good, good." Griswold turned and looked her in the eye. "But it doesn't matter. We'll do what we have to do—do what is right—and not let these armchair journalists intimidate us. You stand out there, Caroline, and face them down," he commanded, pointing at the press room. With that, he gave her a thumbs-up sign, a pat on the shoulder, and marched out.

It was time, Griswold reasoned, to buck up the troops. The leader has to be firm, strong, self-assured. Others sense it if he isn't.

This was the first time the president had walked randomly through the corridors, opening doors to the wide-eyed gaze of secretaries. Griswold gave each the thumbs-up sign, a word of encouragement, and then moved on, two agents now trailing behind him. He ended up at the southwest corner suite of his chief of staff.

Robbie, also on the phone, stood, but kept the conversation going. Griswold took a seat at the conference table and watched his assistant. Robbie never skipped a beat in his conversation, showed no emotion, let alone signs of stress.

"Well, what does your stargazer tell us, Robbie?" the president asked when he'd hung up.

"Wonderful, Mr. President. Almost brought you a note in

the NSC meeting. Your approval is up ten points—biggest one-day jump yet—and it more than makes up for yesterday morning's drop. The speech was a home run, sir, nothing but glowing comments. All positive. Calls and faxes are coming in by the thousands, overwhelmingly supportive."

"Good, good," Griswold grinned, visibly relieved. He rubbed his face with his large, bony hands.

"Only concern Sindberg picked up—and not really a negative—was a little uncertainty, people worried about what will happen next. It's understandable. This thing is volatile. But they sure hate the antiabortionists. We've picked a good enemy."

"We won't let up, Robbie, until they're all in jail. The country will be better off without that movement. They're terrorists."

Robbie answered his intercom. "Yes, bring it right in." He turned to Griswold. "A statement by Langer. Better get a grip on your seat, Mr. President."

After his secretary had brought in the statement and left, Robbie read it aloud: the announcement of the resolution to be filed the next day, one quarter of the Senate already in favor, the speech planned. It was all there, and it ended with a bite, "The Congress of the United States will not be intimidated. The Constitution will be defended."

"Sounds like he's at the Alamo, but he won't get thirty votes," Robbie scoffed.

"The Democrats might see this as a chance to embarrass me." Griswold frowned thoughtfully.

"They're not going to get on the side of the religious right—not even for partisan politics."

"I don't know. I don't know." Griswold started to get up. "Call Bernie. He told me he knew about some things that might come in handy with Langer sometime. Don't tell me about it though . . . just see what you and Bernie can do."

"I understand." Robbie grinned.

Griswold held his head high and marched into the corridor. Then came the self-assured grin and the thumbs-up sign again as he passed more startled staffers and one visitor who was so unsettled he couldn't respond when the president said hello.

Griswold headed past the Roosevelt room and into the Oval Office, but not before greeting the Secret Service agent guarding the door with a punch on the arm and a "Good job, good job."

AFTER THE CALL from Robbie, Bernie O' Keefe called Frizzell. "Yesterday you told me if I ever needed a little information on Senator Langer to let you know."

"It doesn't involve the bureau, you understand," Frizzell said. "We're not into that. That went out with Hoover."

"Okay, but what is it?"

"Call William Johnson, assistant secretary of defense, personnel and readiness. Tell him you understand he has a sensitive file that you would like to see. The Langer file. He'll know. He may insist that you make it a presidential directive."

"Thanks, Tony."

"No, no thanks to me. We never talked. Wipe your recorder clean. I'll do the same here."

"Understood."

"Oh, and by the way, if you can't get the file, call me. I just might know where a copy is."

"You're a good man, Mr. Director. A good man." O'Keefe could almost see Frizzell's smile.

THE MARKET TOOK Griswold's speech well, opening twenty-eight points up. By 10:30 it was up fifty-two points. The big traders already loved Griswold's tax package; now it appeared he might get domestic unrest under control. Wall Street liked nothing better than churning markets and quiet streets.

At 1:00 P.M. when Langer's statement became public, the market reacted to uncertainty by beginning erratic movements. Within thirty minutes, the gains were almost erased. Minutes before closing, it plunged thirty points—an eighty-point swing in four hours.

By 6:00 P.M., 2,000 D.C. National Guard troops arrived at the D.C. armory in full gear. There, routine drug screening eliminated 175; another 190 had legitimate reasons to be excused. By 7:00 P.M., nearly 1,600 were mustered in, but it was a disorderly lot, looking less like an army than a crowd laughing, shoving, and pushing, waiting to get into a football game.

The battalion commander, Colonel Pierce, and the D.C. police captain, briefed the officers and non-coms then broke the battalion into squad size units assigned to police details across the District.

The first unit arrived at 9:30 P.M. in two Humvees to take up their position at the corner of Sixteenth and R Streets, a turf ruled by drug dealers and prostitutes. The D.C. police normally only drove through the area, usually looking straight ahead, allowing the dealers to duck into the shadows, though most didn't even bother to do that.

The guardsmen didn't know the rules. They parked both Humvees on R Street and began to unload. One young guardsman, a Corporal Jefferson, heard some commotion in a doorway on R Street and started toward it, his M-16 at the ready.

Jefferson had never had riot training, so he hadn't been warned that one can see out of darkened doorways but not into them. Six loud shots cracked through the darkness. Several rounds embedded themselves in Jefferson's Kevlar jacket, but one went clean through his Adam's apple, and he crumpled to the ground, blood gushing from the severed main artery. He was dead within a minute.

The other guardsmen, twelve in all, scattered behind street posts, cars, and fences. All at once, a volley of fire erupted, lighting even the darkened recesses of the streets.

There was no return fire, the drug dealers having fled through the rear, but by the time the squad leader, Sergeant Chambers, had restored order, two prostitutes were dead, two bystanders wounded by ricocheting bullets, and one guardsman had been shot through the arm by friendly fire.

Across town, two armored personnel carriers loaded with two squads of men pulled into an RFK Stadium parking lot. The back doors burst open and troops jumped out and immediately dispersed to patrol the Anacostia riverbanks. The shadows under the East Capitol Street Bridge usually sheltered an assortment of homeless folk and cokeheads. This night, as four scared young guardsmen moved along the bank, peering into the darkness under the bridge, a fusillade of rocks suddenly showered down on them, launched from a group of kids atop the bridge.

Most bounced along the bank, but some hit the troops, and one landed on a guardsman's helmet, making a nerve-shattering noise. In pure reflex, the guardsmen fired blindly at the bridge. One thirteen-year-old was killed outright; another, only ten, was gravely wounded and taken to D.C. General Hospital.

Six other shootings were reported that night, three involving the Guard. In an Anacostia bar, three individuals were stabbed, two fatally.

"SOME NIGHT!" D.C'.s mayor looked grimly at the report the next morning. "We call out the Guard, and instead of our usual quota of two dead, we have seven killed, one gravely wounded, and three others hospitalized, not to mention about $300,000 in reported property damage. And that's only because the lawyers haven't gotten into it yet."

"It'll get better," his aide said stiffly.

"Sure it will," the mayor said dryly, shaking his head. "No problem. Next we'll just bring in the Eighty-second Airborne and clean out the Guard."

33

WILLIAM JOHNSON was a tall, bookish man with unkempt brown hair. Squinting through thick glasses and wearing rumpled tweeds, he looked more like a college professor than a high-ranking government official. In fact, he had graduated at the top of his class when earning a doctorate at Stanford University Business School and had been a human resources whiz for Apple Computer. Apart from his involvement as a community activist in Marin County and head of the Audubon Society for northern California, Johnson had had no experience in politics before coming to Washington. Thus, Bernie O'Keefe's call sent him scurrying to his agency's general counsel's office, where he was advised to accede to White House directions regarding a matter as sensitive as a personnel file only if issued with the president's authorization. There were standard procedures for such things.

At 9:00 A.M. as instructed, carrying a small, black-leather bag under his arm, Johnson entered the northwest portico, was saluted by the marine sentry and shown to the main reception area. The smiling secretary quickly checked his ID and showed him to a blue damask sofa. Out of nowhere a redjacketed steward appeared with a silver coffee service. The china cup had a narrow silver rim and, on the side etched in silver, the seal of the president.

Moments later, two cabinet members breezed by into the corridor to the chief of staff's office.

The Israeli ambassador soon arrived, and General Maloney came into the reception area to escort him back to his office.

Johnson watched through the window as a camera crew set up just in front of the portico and two senators were escorted to the cameras.

Upstairs in his corner office, well aware of what was transpiring a floor below, Bernie O'Keefe rifled through morning reports, occasionally checking his watch. *We'll warm him up for ten minutes,* Bernie mused, smiling slightly.

But then the report of the Guard's first night in D.C. wiped away the smile. Bernie had had doubts, expressed them to Griswold in fact, but no one was thinking in terms of restraint these days. "Show action. Get hold of things," Robbie had said, and the president had followed his lead.

O'Keefe called Barbara Shannon in and instructed her to go downstairs and get Johnson.

"Don't bring him up in the elevator," Bernie said to his secretary. Rather, she should walk him by the cabinet room, where the doors were always open, stop in front of the closed doors to the Oval Office and whisper that the president was in, then pass the Roosevelt room, where some of the senior staff might still be lingering from the 8:00 meeting. She should then walk him upstairs, pointing out General Maloney's office in the northwest corner on the way. It was a circuitous route, but Johnson would not know the difference; and by the time he got to Bernie his eyes should be popping.

The president's counsel was on the phone when his secretary showed Johnson in; he waved his visitor to the straight-back leather chair in front of his desk and kept talking, taking notes, and then said, "Yes, sir, I'll do it, sir."

There was only one person from whom O'Keefe would be taking orders, Johnson realized. He tried to glance unobtrusively around the room; the walls were covered with photos of O'Keefe and the president, some dressed informally. William Johnson was, indirectly at least, in the presence of the president.

"Dr. Johnson. Your reputation precedes you, sir." Bernie bounced out of his chair and thrust his hand across the desk as soon as he hung up the phone. Johnson rose awkwardly, smiled, and nodded.

"Coffee, Coke, anything?" Bernie looked up over his gold-rimmed reading glasses as he moved some papers off his desk, clearing the pad in front of him and taking out his Mont Blanc pen. Johnson, clutching the briefcase in his lap, declined.

"We are both very busy, so we'll waste no time here, Mr. Secretary," Bernie began, removing his glasses and setting them on the desk. Assistant secretaries liked being called "Mr. Secretary."

"The matter of which we spoke on the phone has been discussed, I should assure you, at the highest levels. It is also, I should add, a matter of utmost security and sensitivity. I'm sure we can trust you to respect that?"

Suddenly, unexpectedly, Johnson felt defensive. "Why, of course, sensitive indeed."

"So I would suggest, Mr. Secretary, that we not request that file which is in your briefcase. It is there, I assume?"

Johnson nodded.

"Not officially, that is. It needn't be logged in or anything of the sort." O'Keefe spoke so reassuringly that Johnson could feel his tightened muscles relax.

"As counsel to the president, at this point I should merely like to glance through the file. I cannot decide unless I see it whether it warrants a formal request. Should we decide to make such a request, it would have, I assure you, full authorization. I understand the protocol, of course."

O'Keefe seemed to have anticipated Johnson's well-rehearsed objections, and he certainly sounded eminently reasonable, more so than Johnson had expected. And he could hardly deny the president's counsel a look at any government document.

"Of course, sir. If you just want to skim through it. You are acting, of course, as counsel."

"Of course."

Johnson opened the case and pulled out a legal-size, yellowed folder with a large metal bar clip across the top. He handed it gingerly to O'Keefe, who smiled reassuringly and leaned back in his chair, perched his reading glasses on the end of his nose, and started to thumb through the pages, almost as if indifferent to the contents.

"Must be tedious work wading through all this bureaucratese. They must have a course over there that teaches bureaucrats how to say one page's worth of information in six," O'Keefe laughed.

Johnson chuckled and relaxed another notch.

Suddenly the door opened, and Barbara was standing in the doorway. "Mr. O'Keefe," she said in a matter-of-fact tone, "the president is on line two. Israeli matter." Then she walked over and tapped Johnson gently on the arm. "National security, if you don't mind," she whispered.

Johnson did, but he followed her meekly. He heard O'Keefe pick up the phone and say, "Yes, sir, Mr. President," before the door closed.

Barbara showed Johnson to a large armchair, offered him a copy of the president's news summary, and gave him more coffee in another of those china cups with the silver seal.

Inside his office, Bernie laid the receiver on the desk, turned to the fax machine on the table behind him, removed the clip from the folder, inserted the papers he needed in the machine, and punched the green button marked "copy." In just over three minutes, he slid the copies into his desk drawer. Then he carefully reassembled the folder and laid it on his desk under a large blue folder marked "For the President," which he laid open. In less than five minutes, he buzzed Barbara to show Johnson back in.

"I'm so sorry, Mr. Secretary," Bernie said. "Simply one of the hazards of this office."

"I understand, of course. I have the same problem with the secretary of defense," Johnson lied. The secretary hadn't called him in four months.

"Now let's see." Bernie lifted the folder marked "For the President" and slowly closed it, laying it almost under Johnson's nose. "Where was that file? . . . oh yes, right here." He leaned back and began thumbing through it as casually as before. "Can't be too careful, can we?" he asked, looking over his glasses.

"No," Johnson said. Then, "In what way do you mean that?" Now he was curious.

"Well, it appears here that there is some evidence of, shall we say, instability. We must know these things because, of course, we share information with Congress that is, well, actually above top secret classification."

Johnson immediately agreed. "Indeed we must be careful."

"Thank you, Mr. Secretary," O'Keefe said, closing the folder, handing it across the desk, and standing all in one quick motion. Johnson instinctively stood also.

"It will not be necessary to take this any further, Mr. Johnson; nor do we need to trouble the president with this. He has so much on his mind these days, and as I look through this, I see no need for us to have this folder," Bernie said.

O'Keefe had established what in the White House is called "deniability": The matter could not be traced to the president.

Johnson seemed almost disappointed, as if his visit had somehow been diminished in importance. But he left clutching the pair of gold-plated presidential cufflinks that Bernie had given him rather effusively. The White House bought them for $2.49 a set.

As the door shut behind Johnson, O'Keefe picked up the phone. "See if the president can take this call, please," he directed the operator. Seconds later, Griswold was on the line.

"I've got it. Dynamite."

"Good. Bernie, you take care of it."

34

PAUL CLARKSON was in conference with Emily when the call came from O'Keefe. They were both surprised by the demand that Paul come to the White House immediately. O'Keefe would normally have called for the attorney general. Furthermore, he sounded insistent, almost angry. "Drop everything; be here in ten minutes," he had said.

Emily dispatched Paul in her limousine, and shortly after 10:00 the black Lincoln was waved through the southwest gates.

There was no delay in the reception room this time; Paul was immediately taken to the elevator and escorted down the long corridor as fast as his canes would allow. Barbara showed him into O'Keefe's office, where Bernie was eagerly awaiting him, the papers on his desk now neatly arranged, with only one file sitting in the center.

"We have exactly two hours, Paul," Bernie said, unsmiling, "so let me get right to the point. This administration naturally respects the right of any senator or representative to dissent from its policies. But your friend, Senator Langer, is going beyond the bounds. He is threatening to undermine the government's sworn duty to maintain domestic order. That is government's first task, as I know you agree."

"I understand, Mr. O'Keefe, but you don't know Senator Langer. This isn't politics. He's a man of real conscience and conviction. I spoke with him last night and—"

"Conscience? Conviction? I don't think you know him as well as you think, my friend. And please, call me Bernie."

"Oh, no. I'd stake my life on that. I know him as well as any man can. I worked for him closely for five years, remember."

"All of us, I suppose, have secret hiding places, inner recesses that we never open to others, maybe not even to ourselves, Paul. Your friend, the good senator, was quite a war hero, wasn't he? I'll bet he sat around regaling you with great war stories."

"What are you getting at?" Paul said angrily. "Don't beat around the bush with me."

"All right. Fair enough. Let's see here," Bernie said, opening the file in front of him and picking up the top sheet. "First Lieutenant Byron Langer 0622873, commissioned ROTC, June 6, 1966. OCS, Fort Benning. Qualified for Airborne, good officer." Bernie looked up and saw Paul glaring at him, deep furrows on his brow.

"After jump school, assigned to Eighty-second Airborne, then qualified for Ranger School, from which he graduated. Hot stuff, a regular Rambo, top of his class.

"Arrived in Da Nang in July 1967, just when things were getting very hairy over there. Eager young man—he volunteered for behind-the-lines stuff. Military advisory group in Laos, working with Montagnard fighters. They were mean little devils in the highlands who would cut out the enemy's heart and eat it, literally—"

"Could we get to the point here?" Whatever O'Keefe had, he was relishing the moment, Paul thought. This man was cruel.

"Well, our good friend here is choppered in to a Montagnard camp just in time for an attack by the North Vietnam regulars. They shoot the place up pretty good—so good that Langer's platoon is decimated. He's petrified, loses his men, and goes bonkers. He runs away. The platoon sergeant saves the day, rescues the men and Langer. The sergeant gets the Silver Star, and

Langer gets an army hospital at Clark Field in the Philippines for two months—'battle fatigue,' or, in layman's terms, a nervous breakdown."

"I don't believe it." Paul was angry. Langer had told him stories about Vietnam for years.

"Right here in black and white. Got his commanding officer's statement in front of me."

"What about his medal? I've seen it. It's in a case on the bookshelf in his office."

"Oh, that's the best part. Lieutenant Langer goes back to Vietnam, to a supply depot near Saigon. No more boom-booms for him. He works his butt off and comes up with a system to get supplies of cold beer to Khe Sanh and other hot spots during the Tet offensive. The doggies in the field are so happy, General Westmoreland gives him the Legion of Merit . . . for, it turns out, getting beer to the troops." Bernie leaned back in his chair and laughed loudly. "Isn't that rich?"

Paul stared at him, furious. "So you want to blackmail Langer and get him off your back. That's the little plan here, right?"

"Whoa!" Bernie leaned forward in his chair and raised his hand, palm out like a traffic cop. "Not so fast, my friend. We would never do something like that. We just thought . . . rather, I just thought . . . you might simply explain to your old boss the wisdom of the president's action here—"

"Bull." Paul knocked over one of the canes that had been leaning against the arm of his chair. "You want to shut him up. Well, I'm not gonna play ball with you."

"That's fine. I just thought you might like to spare your esteemed senator some embarrassment. Just an act of Christian charity, you know. He doesn't exactly occupy the high moral ground here. And it seems to me a good lawyer could certainly be able to explain why it's in everyone's best interest that he get behind the president."

Paul leaned over and recovered the cane, lifting himself slowly from the chair. Bernie thought he was leaving, but instead he walked to the narrow window that looked over the parapets of the west wing roofline toward the mansion. He stared out for a few minutes. Bernie waited. Finally he turned.

"I'll talk to him, because I care about him. He's my friend. That's the only reason. I want him to have a chance to spare himself if he chooses to. He's entitled to that," Clarkson said. "But I can't tell you how badly I feel for you. Sitting in this beautiful office, day after day, doing the president's dirty work for him. It stinks in here, but you're so full of yourself, you can't even smell your own odor." He paused, then added, "How do you sleep at night?"

Bernie sat still, startled, for a moment. No one had talked to him this way since sixth grade in parochial school. Then he shook his head, dismissing the thought. Clarkson's little lecture was a small price to pay for what they were about to gain. The fate of the nation—or at least the fate of Whitney Griswold's presidency—hung in the balance, and there was one hour and forty minutes to keep it from tipping over the edge.

"We'll talk about things like that some other time," he said, trying to sound gracious. This guy was so black and white. "Why don't you call the senator from here? You may not see it now, but it's for the good of the country. Stop him from filing his resolution. The nation can't afford that kind of constitutional crisis." He stood and extended his hand.

"Right. I understand," Paul said, ignoring Bernie's outstretched hand. "I'll call from your secretary's desk, if you don't mind." He gathered his canes and made his way to the door, then turned to look at Bernie. "Listen, if you ever need to talk about something more than garbage like this, give me a call. It must get pretty rancid up here sometimes." He opened the door and left.

Bernie, still standing behind the desk, watched as the door closed. The guy's got spunk, he thought. He's better than the pompous 'war hero' he's trying to defend. Langer had it coming. Pretending to be something he's not. Clarkson may say it stinks here, but at least we shoot straight about who we are.

Right, his conscience echoed, ever so slightly. *And you, the great constitutional lawyer, are gleefully bending the Bill of Rights for J. Whitney Griswold?*

Bernie stood for a moment, shrugged, and picked up the phone. There was work to be done.

AT 11:15 THAT MORNING, several guardsmen and a D.C. police officer stumbled onto a drug deal near the intersection of Columbia Road and Eighteenth NW, an area surrounded by hot Latin restaurants and lively sidewalk cafes. The policeman was unscathed, but both guardsmen were hit, one seriously. Again a bystander caught a ricocheting bullet. Colonel Pierce issued a bulletin to all units to withhold fire unless fired upon. In each of the incidents the night before and this morning, the troops had shot first.

By 11:30 as news flashed over the wires, the market was down another sixty points.

PAUL CLARKSON could not remember ever feeling more uncomfortable. It was like he had eaten a huge meal and it simply wouldn't digest. A huge lump, just sitting in his gut. He fought back touches of nausea.

Langer's secretary escorted him into the senator's office to wait. The senator was still in a meeting at the Capitol, she said, lining up more supporters for his resolution. Paul glanced around the room at the familiar books and pictures. He had great memories of this office, when he and the senator had teamed up to fight for the causes they so passionately shared.

Paul walked to the bookshelf. It was there, all right, in the glass case: a small bronze medallion hanging from a pin by a red silk ribbon. The Legion of Merit. For the first time Paul realized there was no printed citation under it. Beside it was another medal with purple silk, the Purple Heart. Not far away were pictures of Lieutenant, later Captain, Byron Langer, with his men, a happy looking band of warriors in their combat gear.

"Well, Paul, I'm glad you came today." Langer smiled broadly as he walked through the door. He took off his coat and came over to Paul, placing both hands on his shoulders, a near embrace. Paul knew he had at least fifty-one votes in his pocket. He'd seen him this way only a few times before.

"I'm afraid I'm going to have to challenge your president, Paul. Teach him a lesson, in fact. But it is very important for the country," Langer effused. He was in high form. "The Constitution judges us, we don't judge it."

"He's not my president, sir," Paul said so bitterly that Langer stopped abruptly.

"What's going on?" he asked.

"It's you, sir," Paul said, then paused, not knowing how to begin. "Sir, I respect you more than any man I've known other than my father. And my feelings are unaffected by what I must tell you. We're up against people without principle or conscience. Hollow men. They'll do anything right now to stop you—"

"Of course. Don't you think I know that? I've been in this swamp a long time—"

"This is something else, sir. Believe me, whatever they call it, I call it blackmail. They want you to back off this resolution—and if you don't do it right now, they're going to smear your military record."

"Smear what? What are you saying, Paul? Come out with it." The senator's eyes darted to the string of photos on the wall.

"The White House has a file, Senator. I cannot vouch for its authenticity, of course, but they say you didn't get your medal in combat—"

"Bull," said Langer abruptly. "What else did they say?" His heart was racing; he could feel the flush in his cheeks and the heavy weight in his stomach.

"That you broke down in combat, sir. Battle fatigue. Not that anyone would blame you . . ."

Langer's heart was thumping so hard he wondered if Paul could hear it. He rolled his eyes back and looked up. *Thump, thump, thump . . .*

THUMP, *thump, thump.* The noise of the chopper was deafening, blades rotating loudly against the steady whine of the Huey's turbines. Lieutenant Langer could feel his heart thump as well, straining against the huge nylon harness fastening him into his bucket seat. The machine seemed to be brushing the tops of dense green foliage. In the open doorway, a sergeant with linked bandoliers of 7.62 mm shells over his shoulder straddled an M-60 machine gun, one of his boots actually hanging out the door. The gun was trained at a forty-five degree angle, ready to spew its lethal load at the first sign of life on the ground.

Langer glanced at his platoon sergeant, Jim Howard, an old Vietnam hand on his second tour, sitting next to him. He could show no anxiety; Howard would pick it up in a heartbeat.

Thump, thump, thump. The Huey was vibrating so hard you wondered why the rivets didn't fly off in all directions. It bore its battle scars proudly, metal patches all over the fuselage.

Suddenly the machine lurched upward. It wasn't easy to see ahead, hard to move with a steel helmet rubbing on the padded collar of his flak jacket and a fifty-pound pack on his lap, with canteens and ammo belts dangling from it. But Langer could lean forward far enough to see a small mountain not five hundred feet ahead. The Huey strained and pulled, nose pointed down, as it scaled the side, thrusting ahead as it reached the top.

They were in Laos, he figured, probably fifty miles west of Con Thien and the DMZ, and they were heading north. This was not only illegal—the politicians in Washington created absurd artificial boundaries for this war that sure didn't bind the North Vietnamese regulars—but exceedingly dangerous, way behind enemy lines. That's why the major at the controls was hugging the tops of the banyan trees.

Suddenly the jungle was behind them and they were over open, rocky terrain; even at this higher altitude, they were an inviting target. Oh God, protect us, Langer breathed. He glanced around at the ten men, most of them silent; some, he was certain, were praying as well.

For twenty minutes the Huey roared up over the hilltops and

glided down the slopes; then the thumping intensified, and the machine shook and quivered. The gunner stiffened. The crew chief, a master sergeant doubling as copilot, turned around in the cockpit and screamed some command which no one could hear, but they had done it so often, everyone knew instantly what to do. As the skids hit, Langer and his men released their harnesses, grabbed their packs and weapons, and nearly dove through the open hatch, hitting the dirt and falling forward. By doing this, the chopper, never more vulnerable to enemy fire than at that moment when it was immobile, could lift off without waiting for the troops to get away from the spinning blades. It was a discipline troops learned fast; stand up and you could be decapitated.

The bird lifted, and Langer signaled his sergeant to send hand signals to the two other squads, one to the left and the other to the right, that had been similarly disgorged by two other Hueys.

Langer and his platoon were reinforcing a Green Beret company, advisors to a small Montagnard army in the Laotian hills. Each night Montagnard patrols, along with their U.S. advisors, ranged the eastern slopes of the mountains setting ambushes for North Vietnamese troops coming down the Ho Chi Minh Trail. Of late, however, this company had been taking some heavy casualties, and Langer's troops were there to give the veterans a break.

The choppers had come into the compound at dusk when visibility was reduced for the enemy snipers and mortar men. At the north and south ends were two forty-foot-high observation towers, assembled with rough hewn jungle wood. The entire perimeter, perhaps six hundred feet square, was protected by electrified fences and rolls of razor wire. Outside, the area was studded with land mines; inside, bunkers were strategically placed so that machine-gun and automatic-weapon fire could saturate every direction, defending against an attack.

The base gave a great sense of security. Each night the enemy, scattered throughout the area, would lob in mortar shells, but the troops almost became used to them. Seven months earlier a North Vietnamese regiment had assaulted the base, but the Montagnards repelled them, then pursued them down the slopes, killing every single attacker. They had sliced the heads off the dead and wounded and carried them back on sticks.

By 11:00 that night, Langer had dropped off into a deep sleep in his bunker when the sirens blared. He had already been briefed that the siren was only to signal a massive assault. As he grabbed his helmet and came up out of the bunker, the first waves of North Vietnamese troops were assaulting the east fence.

Langer was completely disoriented; he started running, he thought, toward his platoon area. Two mortar rounds landed just behind him, hurling him forward into the soft dirt. He came up with a mouthful, shaking his head and recovering his helmet. Everything seemed to be in slow motion and sounded far away; only later would he discover that his right eardrum had been blown out.

Everything was ablaze. The defenders fired flares that arched high over the camp; shells exploded all around. As he recovered his balance, Langer ran toward his platoon stationed on the northeast corner. He stumbled over the bodies of two soldiers. One was groaning, his entrails protruding from a huge gash in his gut.

"Medic, medic!" Langer screamed, but his shouts were lost in the explosions of mortar shells on either side. As he turned away, reeling, a shell hit the two soldiers. Too late for the medic.

Dazed and shaking violently, Langer reached his position. A radioman was kneeling next to his commanding officer, calling for help. Langer heard the steady rat-tat-tat of automatic weapons and saw dozens of men in khaki suits running straight at him. His position had been overrun. Langer pulled out his .45 and emptied the magazine. Two bodies fell to the ground. Another GI came up out of his hole, blasting his M-16 on automatic, cutting down the others.

Langer was crouched down, reloading, when the mortar shell hit to his right. The soldier next to him caught the full blast. His arm flew past Langer's head and pieces of flesh splattered against his face; he looked down and saw blood all over his tattered uniform. The last thing he saw was more men in khaki coming at him. . . .

He woke up in a hospital bed at Clark Air Force Base. Padded leather straps held his wrists and ankles. Two doctors, one with a used syringe in his hand, were standing over him. For nearly two months, it turned out, he had been in some twilight zone. Except for superficial wounds and a punctured eardrum, he was unhurt—physically.

They told him what had happened. The base had held out, somehow. Half the Americans had been butchered. They had found him in the fetal position under some rubble. There were only sixteen survivors from his platoon; they had been rallied by the platoon sergeant. He had been treated both with electroshock and heavy doses of antidepressants.

THUMP, THUMP, THUMP ... "Senator, are you all right?" Paul was standing over him holding his chin cupped in his hand. He sounded far away. "Are you all right, sir?"

He shook himself, loosened his tie, and ran both hands through his hair. He had to get control. "I'm sorry, Paul. I'm okay. Some sort of flashback or something."

Langer took a deep breath. "I guess I always knew it would come to this at some point," he said without looking at Paul. "I can't believe it, though. I was negligent to leave myself so vulnerable, stupid to allow it to happen in the first place."

"Senator, you don't have to explain," Paul said. "I can't imagine what you went through in Vietnam. None of us know what we'll do till we're put to the test. No one could hold that against you."

"But that's not it," said Langer. "I let this myth kind of grow on its own. When I came home, I just wanted to forget it all. I never talked about Vietnam.

"But then when I ran for office the first time, somebody put 'decorated Vietnam vet' on the campaign literature. That was true enough, so I didn't object; I didn't even think much about it at the time. I should have. But then on the stump, well, you know, the story got a little better and better. Not so much by me as by all those well-meaning, wonderful people who want you to succeed so desperately so they can get a job or a favor. Pretty soon you begin to believe it all yourself."

"Senator, you don't have to explain," Paul repeated.

"No, Paul, it's a relief to talk about it. Even Lily doesn't know it all," he said. "So these kind and decent gentlemen in the White House want to make it all public?"

"They didn't say it in so many words, but that's the threat."

"Well, I have to do what I have to do. I couldn't live with myself if I didn't. Those gentlemen in the White House are going to bring down this country. They have no respect for the Constitution. I have to do it."

"Yes, sir, you do." Paul was being disloyal to his present position, and he knew it. But he was in such anguish for Langer, he could not resist. Besides, he wondered if Langer wasn't right.

"Anyway," he added, "people are much more forgiving than you think."

"Maybe," said Langer. "But you know who'll chew me up will be my own constituency—the Christian Alliance. I've noticed they're not very forgiving when one of their own falls."

Paul winced. He had noticed that too. "You're human, sir. Some Christians are so smug and self-righteous, they put everyone off, and they're usually hypocrites anyway. If a person who is known as a Christian falls, and admits it, then people can identify with him. The people who matter will stick with you."

"Sounds good, but can't you see the press, too? They hate us 'rightwing Ayatollahs.' They'll crucify me. And the worst thing is—I deserve it. I broke the first rule: Never hand your enemy the sword with which to kill you. Stupid. Stupid." He shook his head then got up and walked to the window.

"Senator, just face right into it. Tell exactly what happened. The people will understand."

Langer continued to shake his head as he gazed over the green park in front of Union Station. A limousine pulled up at the Russell Building's First and D Street entrance, letting out an obscure subcabinet official Langer knew vaguely. The man walked as if he was the president himself. *Washington*, thought Langer.

"They'll call me a hypocrite, Paul—number one hypocrite. I've been the hawk on military issues, and now it comes out that in battle I cut and run. I can't face it."

"Hypocrisy, Senator, is the tribute vice pays to virtue. Hypocrisy is better than men like Griswold and O'Keefe who don't know there's any difference."

"Good philosophy. Try it on the editorial board of the *Post*." Langer walked back to his chair. Then he turned back.

"Thank you, Paul. Whatever happens, you've been a good and decent friend. You go back and tell them you really twisted the screws on me. Protect yourself. I need thirty minutes alone to think it over. What time is it?"

"It's 11:30, sir." Paul answered, disturbed. Langer was staring straight ahead at the wall, not even bothering to look at his watch, the wall clock, or the chronometer sitting on his desk.

"You sure you're all right, sir?"

"Yes, yes, thank you." Langer managed a faint smile. "You go on now.

After Clarkson left, Langer buzzed his secretary. "No interruptions, please, for the next few minutes." Then he sat, continuing to stare at the wall.

O'KEEFE was with the president in the small dining room off the Oval Office when the dispatch came in at 12:30. Juan passed the paper to Griswold who scanned it, jumped up, threw his napkin down, came around the table, and grabbed Bernie's hand, pumping it hard.

"Listen to this, Bernie! 'Senator Byron Langer, who until noon today had vowed to block President Griswold's declaration of emergency, has had a sudden change of heart. Briefed in the last hour by administration aides, Langer says he has been made aware of sensitive information convincing him of the gravity of the national crisis. He has concluded that President Griswold's actions are justified.'

"And listen to this, Bernie: 'Leading senators expressed consternation at the dramatic turn of events. Majority Leader Keenan announced that consideration of the resolution will be delayed. According to informed Senate sources, Langer's decision throws into doubt the Senate's ability to veto the president.'

"Have we got a team? Good work, Bernie. And call that AAG over at Justice. We ought to promote him. Make a note of that, Bernie. The next slot is his, or maybe he wants the bench."

O'Keefe pushed his plate aside as Griswold smashed his fist into his palm. "Good job. Leadership, that's what it is."

Robbie joined them seconds later, grinning broadly. "This is the way things are going to work around here," he enthused.

"The trains are running on time," Griswold said, slamming Robbie on the back.

35

I RA LEVITZ dined at Dick Morton's at least three times a week. He usually hit the Washington landmark about noon, where one of Dick's minions, or often Dick himself, would lead Levitz to his favorite table, already stocked with half dills and matzo crackers. Here, he would hold forth with assorted Washington insiders.

Today, however, his meal was interrupted when Dick brought the phone to him at 12:45. Levitz's guest, Chief Judge Satterfield of the D.C. Court of Appeals, an authority on constitutional law, made a rather obvious effort to look away while Levitz gripped the receiver to his ear.

"What?" he exclaimed. "You're not serious. That's incredible. Incredible!" The judge glanced at him, noting the columnist's neck turning an odd shade of purple.

Levitz threw his napkin on the table, where it landed in his plate of chicken livers and coleslaw. "Impossible," he yelled. Those at surrounding tables were now listening. "Impossible!"

He clicked off the phone and lowered his voice. "Do you know what Langer has done?" he said to the judge. "Withdrawn his resolution. He's backing Griswold!"

Satterfield looked startled. "Why?"

"Who knows! I'm heading for the Hill. You'd better finish your soup and get back to your courthouse fast. The way things are going, the army may have gotten there ahead of you."

In minutes, Levitz was downstairs, raincoat under his arm, three steps off the curb on Connecticut Avenue, hailing a cab. He brushed right ahead of two middle-aged women to grab the first taxi that stopped.

"Russell Office Building," he barked.

LEVITZ BOUNDED up the steps of the Russell Building at the First and D Street entrance, then turned right to the first office.

"Ira Levitz to see the senator," he growled.

"How are you, Mr. Levitz?" Langer's receptionist stood immediately. "Let me take your coat. I'll see if he's in."

"He's in. Otherwise you would have said he was out," he snapped, hanging on to his raincoat.

"Yes sir," she answered patiently, then made her way through the large mahogany door into the next office.

Levitz lit up a long, dark cigar, ignoring the smoke-free environment of the Senate, then pulled his small notepad out of his raincoat pocket and started scribbling.

Less than a minute later, a bright-eyed aide in his early twenties came through the door, asking if he could help. The senator simply wasn't available, he said, much as he was sure Senator Langer would have wanted to see Mr. Levitz.

"Young man, you go right back through that door and tell the senator I am here to see him and him only. Tell him I know why he changed his position, and I'm waiting." It was a tactic that had worked before, as it did now.

Two minutes later, the same young man returned. "Follow me, please, sir."

THE FIRST THING that struck Levitz was how ghostly Langer appeared. His skin had a grayish tone. His eyes looked reddened like he had an allergy. His hair was limp, as was his handshake. But he was as courtly as ever.

"Please sit down, Mr. Levitz," said Langer. He stepped around behind his desk and sat in his high-backed leather chair, then pulled an ashtray from his drawer and pushed it toward Levitz.

Levitz dropped into the nearest chair, folded his raincoat across his lap, and propped his notepad on top.

"I know why you're here, Mr. Levitz, and all I can say is that I have come to understand the urgency of our domestic crisis in ways that I had not before. I felt my decision was the only one I could make as a responsible public official." Langer spoke slowly.

"Just what information do you have today at"—Levitz glanced at the wall clock—"1:30 that you didn't have at 9:00 this morning when your office confirmed your speech plans? What in the world changed your mind, Senator?"

Langer's mind was moving slowly. Was Levitz bluffing to dig for information, or did he already know what had happened?

He decided to chance it. "I'm not at liberty to explain in great detail, but I can say that I know a great deal more about this conspiracy than I did before. I'm also aware of intelligence about the general breakdown of order in our cities that is of grave concern, Mr. Levitz."

"That's an old dodge, Senator," Levitz said bluntly. "What did they offer you? The Supreme Court? Air force planes at your disposal? A few million in pork?"

"Nothing," Langer said with conviction.

"Well, whatever it is, I want to tell you, man to man, you are betraying your trust, Senator, and I will say so in my column tomorrow—unless you can persuade me otherwise," Levitz said angrily. "Frankly, I'm shocked. How could you do this? You must see where those people in the White House are taking us!"

"It's the only responsible decision," said Langer dismissively.

"Bull," shouted Levitz. "It's a sellout. I don't know for what or why, but it is absolutely unconscionable. For years you've shown courage and a respect for the Constitution, for the law, for truth—and now you're no better than they are. What in the world happened to you?"

Levitz waited for Langer to speak, but the senator just sat there, staring vacantly at him.

"In fact, Senator, you're lower than they are. They're unprincipled, self-centered pragmatists who do whatever it takes to get what they want. They're amoral! We've known that for a long time. But you know right from wrong . . ." Ira trailed off, then picked up again. "And if we lose our liberties—God forbid—it will be because people who knew better did nothing. Don't you care?"

Levitz waited again, certain that Langer would reply this time and he'd at least get a quote or two . . . something, anything.

"I'm sorry you can't see my position, Mr. Levitz. I'm truly sorry." Langer's words were perfunctory, and his eyes seemed to stare past Levitz. His flesh looked almost transparent. Levitz wondered if he was ill.

Angry and confused, Levitz jumped up, flapped past the secretary, and flew down the corridor to see the majority leader. Somewhere he'd find someone with some honor and conviction.

AT 2:00 P.M. the White House announced that National Guard units would be activated in Miami, Baltimore, New York, Los Angeles, Detroit, Atlanta, Houston, and Dallas.

Because of the "success in the District," Caroline Atwater told the press corps, this additional action was deemed advisable and fulfilled this administration's pledge "to make the nation's streets safe again for every American."

She reminded the press that for the past three years Guard units had been detailed to the Miami police to help curb the epidemic of tourist killings. This action, therefore, should be viewed in context as "administrative escalation," a nice phrase Atwater herself had invented.

The press secretary had no comment on Senator Langer's announcement, except to say the president had phoned the senator to express gratitude for his putting the public's interest first.

EMILY GINEEN had scheduled lunch from 12:00 to 1:30 with the House Judiciary Committee. The subject was the crime bill, and she couldn't cut it short.

Paul had not returned to the Justice Department after his visit with Langer but had sent the limousine back for Emily to use. He had then walked to his old office in the Capitol. It hadn't been reassigned yet, and he went in and sat at his old, scarred mahogany desk for a long time. He wasn't sure why; he just knew he needed to. After a while he took a cab to the Justice Department.

AT A FEW MINUTES after 2:00 Emily made her way to Paul's office. She hadn't been there before, and she immediately noticed the photo of his family on the desk. "What a beautiful family, Paul. Beautiful!" She leaned against the desk corner. "What did Bernie want?" she asked cheerily.

Like a doctor describing a particularly painful operation, Paul clinically repeated exactly what had transpired: the meeting with O'Keefe and the confrontation with Langer. He left out only the references in the report to Langer "cutting and running" and being "found in the fetal position." All the while he talked, he avoided eye contact, staring out the window. Emily watched him intently, concentrating on the whole ugly story.

When he finished, there was a long silence. Then Emily pushed herself away from the desk and walked toward Paul's bookshelves, staring at the neat rows of volumes in the case, then at a framed quote penned in flowing calligraphy hanging on the wall . . . "Civil authority is a calling, not only holy and lawful before God, but also the most sacred and by far the most honorable of all callings in the whole life of mortal men."

Emily cast her eyes down to see the quote's source. John Calvin . . . who obviously wasn't well acquainted with the dirty tricks of civil service in Washington, D.C., she thought bitterly.

"I can't stand this," Emily said, whirling back to face Paul. "I hate politics. Griswold told me this office would be removed from politics, that we'd be able to work above all of this stuff— and now here we are, in garbage up to our necks.

"I mean, I've never agreed with Langer, and I never particularly trusted him; I felt like he was always manipulating things to get his way. But I knew he was a decent human being. I knew he had convictions. That he cared about something besides himself."

Emily slumped in the chair opposite Paul's desk and looked at her fingernails as if she had never seen them before. She didn't say anything for a while. Neither did Paul.

Finally, she looked up. "Paul," she said, "you are associate attorney general. You did your job. There is a higher interest here. The very heart of government is to maintain order and justice. This hurt, but it's a personal matter. Don't let it affect you so much that you feel like you didn't do the right thing. There's more at stake here than one man. It's the government."

Paul nodded, not knowing what else to do.

"As for me, well, I guess I've got to get used to this. It was so easy at Harvard; I could just look at cases and facts and opinions, all so stable and uncluttered. But that wasn't reality, I guess."

"Reality?" Paul echoed. He looked at Emily and raised his hands, palms up.

AT 2:45, a rumor swept Wall Street, already unsettled by the announcement of further Guard call-ups: The administration was readying a plan to limit the independence of the Federal Reserve Board—something that had been kicked around for years. It was one of those Washington secrets everyone knew:

Griswold felt the Fed was being too tough on interest rates. The market closed fifteen minutes later, down 270 points.

Robbie walked into the Oval Office shortly after 3:00 with the alarming news. Griswold, who two hours earlier had sailed the heights of elation, now felt the crushing weight of his position. Except for dealing with his wife and daughter, he wasn't accustomed to such mood swings.

"Alan tells me that Nixon faced a crisis like this in '71," Robbie said clinically to his boss. "Bottom fell out, a 10 percent drop in one day, all over the reaction to Vietnam. Nixon called every big money man on Wall Street, a hundred of them, to dinner in the state dining room. Wowed them. Next day the market soared one hundred points and then some."

Griswold stared for a moment, then tapped his fingers on the desk. "Hmmm," he said. "Good thinking. You call Lucy in the social office. I'll call my wife. She'll get the menu and all that. Good, good. When do we do it?"

"Tomorrow night," Robbie replied.

Griswold arched his eyebrows. "Impossible."

"Lucy says she can pull it off."

"You've already talked to her?"

"Of course, sir. I knew you'd agree. I have the invitation list being put together right now. We'll get on the phones, and by 6:00 tonight we'll have a hundred leaders invited. No spouses. Working dinner."

"Robbie, you're amazing," said the president. "All right, let's go. I suppose you've called my wife too."

"No, sir, I leave the hard jobs for you."

Griswold laughed. He felt better already.

AT 4:00, Senator Byron Langer's office issued a two-sentence announcement: The Senator, suffering from exhaustion, had been admitted to Walter Reed Army Hospital. His condition was stable, although he was undergoing cardiac examination.

The president called Mrs. Langer to express his concern and wish the senator a speedy recovery.

AT 7:15 Bernie O' Keefe, leather attache case in hand, exited the west wing through the basement door onto West Executive Avenue, where his limousine, a black Chrysler, was waiting. The driver, Scott Hubbard, an army sergeant, hustled around to open the door.

"Home, sir?" he asked.

"No," Bernie said. "Kelly's tonight."

Hubbard always suggested "home," hoping he'd influence the answer. Going home meant he'd be through for the night. But Kelly's, a Georgetown bar and eatery, meant he'd have to either wait or return for O'Keefe later, usually much later. Recently, however, Kelly's was the regular destination.

Kelly's was a Georgetown landmark, a cozy Irish pub and Washington watering hole since the Kennedy administration. On weekends the bar featured live Irish music and attracted throngs of singles; on weeknights Kelly's drew professionals in post-work recovery from all over the city.

Bernie pushed through the crowd, waving to a few regulars, and stood at the end of the long curved bar, waiting for a stool. He was in luck. A couple who obviously had been at the bar for some time were just coming to the climax of a long-simmering argument. The young woman leaped up and flung a couple of dollars on the bar.

"If *that's* the extent you're willing to commit, then forget it!" she shouted. "I'm outta here!"

The young man, abashed, picked up his car keys from the bar and threw a few dollars down as well. "You're being totally irrational!" he hissed. But she was already plunging into the crowd.

"So sue me!" she shouted.

He leaped off the stool and followed her.

Bernie raised his eyebrows at Henry, the bartender who had been at Kelly's for twenty years. "Makes me feel at home—like the old days with Marilyn," he joked.

Henry picked up the crumpled bills and wiped down the bar where the couple had been. "They'll be in here later this week," he said. "They love to fight."

Reminds me of Marilyn, Bernie said again, this time to himself.

"What do you want tonight, Bernie?" Henry asked. "Anything to eat, or just some Dewars?"

Wonderful, Bernie thought. He doubted that the bartender even knew his last name; to Henry, he would always be just Bernie. The fact that he was counsel to the president of the United States didn't mean a whit. *They say that only in church is the ground level, everyone equal at the foot of the cross*, Bernie thought. But he'd seen those religious people operate, with their head tables and their power cliques. Where the ground was really level was in a good bar.

"Thanks, Henry," Bernie said. "Yeah, I'd like a menu."

The bartender handed him a menu, left for a moment, and came back with a double Dewars on the rocks. Bernie sipped, then loosened his tie. The laundry had put too much starch in his shirt, and it had irritated his neck.

"Good job today, Bernie. That old coot on the Hill saw the light, huh? 'Bout time. Imagine trying to block the troops. Give us more, I say."

"You like the Guard on the street, Henry?"

"Sure do. Guy left here the other night with his girlfriend, got up onto P Street where they'd left their car, and two jerks with a gun waited till they got into the Mercedes, then held them up and took the car. The guy resisted. They shot him twice in the head. If I could get away with it, I'd have an M-16 right behind the bar here and blow 'em away myself, like I did in 'Nam."

"That's right, you were in Vietnam," Bernie said. "I forgot." He passed his glass back for a refill.

"On the DMZ, Third Marines. We took a pounding and then came home to the real enemy."

Henry poured another generous drink and handed it back. "Let me tell you, Bernie, and you tell your boss. I talk to people all day long, and folks out here like what he's doing. Keep it up."

Bernie thought about Robbie and his obsession with Sindberg and his polls. He could see why Robbie listened in to the live calls; there was something energizing about hearing what real people thought, instead of just staffers and bureaucrats and politicos.

"I'll tell him, Henry."

"I mean it. You knock heads out here, put these animals away, clean up these streets. Lock 'em up. Fry 'em. We've had it. You do that and we're with you."

"Thanks, Henry." Bernie had heard the man's political views before, but he was surprised at the intensity in Henry's expression tonight.

The bartender left to wait on some customers at the other end of the bar, and Bernie stared into the mellow golden fluid in his glass. The pain was lessening.

Henry came back a few minutes later and refilled Bernie's glass. "What do you want to eat?" he asked. "You gotta eat when you're putting away this stuff like that." He had seen a lot of people drink a lot of alcohol over the years, but few of them could hold it like Bernie.

"I'm not really hungry," said Bernie.

"You gotta eat," said Henry again. "Just have some soup and a burger or salad or something. The onion soup is good tonight."

"Right, Mom," said Bernie. "You order something for me."

Henry left again and returned with a steaming crock of soup and some French bread.

"You seem a little quiet tonight, Bernie," he said as he laid the meal out on the bar. "Tired?"

"Henry, have you ever killed a boar?" Bernie asked abruptly.

"A bore? Yeah, we get 'em here all the time. I wouldn't kill 'em just for that, though."

"No, I mean the animal—the wild pig."

"No, don't know that I've ever even seen one, aside from my wife's mother, of course. Have you ever hunted boar?"

"Yeah," said Bernie, looking into his drink. "A real little one. Last animal I ever shot."

"That's a shame. I go to a farm in West Virginia after wild turkeys. I love it. What's wrong with hunting?"

"Oh, it's fine. Just not for me. Forget it." Bernie took a big gulp of scotch, and Henry left for another customer.

But the moment was still stuck in Bernie's thoughts. It had

started as a wonderful weekend, right after he and Marilyn were married and before the kids. A client belonged to a private hunting preserve in New Hampshire, thousands of acres stocked with elk, deer, and wild boar.

The first morning, Bernie and his client, a big game hunter, were stalking an elk. They moved up the tree line silently and came to a clearing with a view to a distant field. Bernie's client spotted him first, the boar trotting across the field. "Too far away," he said. "Can't be sure how big he is, and you couldn't hit him anyway."

But Bernie eagerly leaned against a tree, got the animal in the crosshairs of his scope, lifted the high-powered .30 caliber just slightly to compensate for trajectory, and squeezed ever so gently. *Poom*, the rifle butt recoiled into his shoulder.

"Bull's-eye!" his companion shouted as the boar rolled over.

The two men walked briskly toward the fallen animal, which proved to be well over three hundred yards away. When they approached the animal, they could see he was lying helpless but in great agony, flailing his left front paw in the air. As they closed in, they could also see he was very young, maybe only fifty pounds. Though arguably the ugliest creature on the face of the earth, the boar's face had a pathetic expression, as if he were asking for help.

Bernie's companion drew his .38 pistol and shot the animal through the head. Then he gutted it, except for the liver, tied its feet together, and dragged it back to the camp.

Bernie had never hunted again.

"Another one, Bernie?" Henry asked. His glass was empty.

"Yeah, sure, one more," said Bernie, shaking his head. "And Henry . . . never kill a boar."

36

ROBBIE LOOKED at his watch. Only 8:30. Which meant the phones had been going at Sindberg's headquarters in Sioux Falls for only two and a half hours. Yet already the pattern was clear, and it was startling. So much so that J. D. Sindberg himself had called. People were rallying behind the president in astonishing numbers. They didn't care what he did as long as he cracked down on extremists and terrorists and criminals. Get rid of 'em.

Robbie jumped up from his desk in his McLean home, rubbed his hands together, and paced around the room. He couldn't contain his exuberance. He picked up the phone and asked the operator for the president.

"I'm sorry, sir," she replied. "He's on the tennis court with Mrs. Griswold."

Robbie then asked to be patched in to the army's signal corps network. "Get me the military aide with Searchlight," he ordered.

Seconds later, the aide on duty, Commander Hall, was on the line. "Have Searchlight call me at home," Robbie instructed him. "In between sets, of course. There's no crisis."

Minutes later Griswold called, struggling for breath. "What's up, Robbie?"

"You are, sir. Sindberg thinks you could be up five to eight more points in approval ratings tonight. He says the respondents all sound the same: Knock heads. They're with you, sir."

"Excellent!" The president was still gasping. "And oh, Robbie . . . thank you."

IRA LEVITZ had never felt worse. For one thing, his column was due at 9:00 P.M. precisely thirty minutes from now. It was an inflexible deadline; any later, and he'd be bumped from his regular space, replaced by a gushy background piece written by David Johnson about how Griswold had reached his momentous decision. That kind of soft journalism revolted Levitz.

For another thing, he was hungry. He'd had nothing for dinner but Heath bars and an old piece of pizza he'd found in the microwave. And he was angry—at Langer, Griswold, and the whole crazy world of Washington and its currency of pride and power and puffery. And his legs hurt. Cramps from sitting too long.

All of this added up to an apparently terminal case of writer's block. So he did what he often did when this happened: don't wait for grand inspirations; just write. Get it on paper. Then you can fix it.

Levitz took several deep breaths and stared at the screen, hating it, hating Washington, hating the *Post* because they wouldn't let him smoke in the building. Then his fingers began to move on the keyboard.

> Once again J. Whitney Griswold has proven himself the consummate politician. Someone evidently opened the Oval Office windows, and the president has wet his finger to the wind and knows which way it's blowing. If the people want action, crackdowns on criminals, then J. Whitney Griswold is ready to give them what they want in the circus called Washington.

"Yes, the president has asked not for whom the polls toll; he knows they poll for him," Levitz wrote wickedly. "So too apparently do a group of suddenly weak-kneed, compliant senators.

But President Griswold and company should learn from history, lest they be doomed to repeat it."

Doomed. Did he really believe that? Yes, and then some. Once you give up liberty, the process begins to feed on itself. And there is never enough. Much is never satisfied with less than more. The obsession with order, with power, with control, always leads to the same end. The despots of every century end up on the ash heap of history.

> Providing the Guard learns to shoot straight, some measure of order may be restored to our nation's troubled streets. Though it will be at an awful price. A people who cannot govern their own behavior are incapable of self-government. Troops in the streets are but a signal of the death of the American experiment.
>
> But Griswold's second objective may be even more frightening. For the government to believe that it can suppress by brute force a movement driven by the deepest convictions of conscience is to ignore the most dramatic testimony of the twentieth century.

The words were flowing now. But was he being too supportive of those maniacs who had hijacked the network news? Two days ago he'd denounced them. Was he reversing himself? Would readers be confused?

No, he thought. His position had been consistent. It was Griswold who'd flipped, virtually declaring martial law.

He started writing again.

> What has sustained American democracy has been the most fragile, yet the most enduring of all its qualities—its moral consensus. The values held in common that inform our consciences, restrain our behavior, and encourage virtue. These come at the very deepest level from the religious impulse, the conviction of a higher power which calls us to live righteously and compassionately. The impulse to be good and do good. It is the weakening of this impulse and the resulting collapse of private virtue that has led to the loss of civic virtue.
>
> But tanks in the streets will not restore it. Force leads only to

further tyranny. Or, perhaps, to an equally frightening prospect: revolution.

The essence of a free society is that different points of view can contend openly and freely in the democratic process. People have to believe that the system works, that they can make a difference. But when those doors are closed, when different points of view are declared out of bounds, frustration mounts. People move from the mainstream to the fringes. Violence erupts. And then, from somewhere in the heartland of this great nation, will arise a modern Oliver Cromwell.

Levitz's leg cramps increased along with his sense of frustration. Did it matter? Who really cared? Would anyone even get the reference to Cromwell and the overthrow of the British monarchy?

"Call off the troops, Mr. President," Levitz concluded. "Before it's too late."

He looked at his watch. Five minutes to nine.

He read through the column quickly. It was bumpy but passionate. Had some life to it. He keyed in a few changes, ran his spell check, and copied the file to the managing editor's terminal. Within fifteen minutes it would be read, checked for libel, and in type, just as the giant presses began rolling. The earliest edition would be off the press at precisely 10:30.

Levitz pushed back in his chair and rubbed his thighs. A White House messenger would be at the L Street entrance of the *Post* to pick up a copy at 10:35. It was the same every night. Griswold's aides would be poring through the paper within two hours.

"I hope he looks to the lessons of history," Levitz said to himself as he got up and stretched. "Well, at least I hope it scorches his butt."

He reached for his raincoat. Time to go home.

37

MRS. BROWNSON, Please cancel my appointments tomorrow afternoon. I'll be dining with the president," the managing partner of Goldman Sachs had ordered on Wednesday afternoon, his effort to sound casual betrayed by the slightly elevated level of his voice. He was not alone. The White House invitations had come by phone, and in New York, Chicago, and elsewhere across the nation, America's financial movers and shakers got ready to move. Personal and company pilots were alerted to get their Gulf Streams ready and flight plans filed; in more frugal circles, first-class reservations were hastily confirmed.

Meanwhile, Harvey Robbins called out the marines. The marine lieutenants, that is; those stationed in the honor units whose job it was to make Washington properly Washingtonian. In dress blue, gold braid, and white gloves, they were individually dispatched in White House cars to meet each arriving guest at National Airport.

Everything went flawlessly until 4:00 P. M. when Lucy Cabot, the White House social secretary and long-time friend of the Griswolds, discovered something suspicious. She knew New York City well and was surprised to see that the address of Herbert

Greenberg, managing partner of the investment banking firm of Baer and Morgan, was listed as Seventh Avenue and West Thirty fifth, the heart of New York City's garment district.

Angry with herself for not noting it sooner, Lucy called Robbie, who immediately called the secretary of the treasury, Josh Wainwright, who had recommended Greenberg. Minutes later the information came back to Lucy: Wainwright's secretary had mistaken the Herbert Greenberg of Greenberg Garments, a cut-and-stitch sweatshop, for the Herbert Greenberg of the prestigious Wall Street firm.

"We'd better get word to Greenberg immediately that he's not invited," Lucy advised flatly.

But Robbie, aware that the press would seize the story as a potentially embarrassing tidbit, vetoed that. A hasty strategy conference convened in his office and a plan was designed. Two White House assistants would stay with Greenberg at all times, keeping him away from the other guests as much as possible and also keeping him at great distances from the president— and light-years away from the White House press corps who would be let in once during dinner for a photo opportunity. Beyond that, Robbie suggested prayer.

THE HIGH-CEILINGED state dining room on the west end of the main floor of the White House is dominated by an extraordinary brass chandelier hanging in the center and the portrait of a pensive Abraham Lincoln sitting with his chin supported by his right hand. The portrait hangs over the fireplace whose original mantel design called for a lion's head; Theodore Roosevelt changed that, appropriately, to an American bison. The deep gold in the draperies is accented by the gold brocade chairs and gold tones in the muted patterned carpet.

Normally for a state dinner the room was set with twelve round tables seating ten each. But Robbie wanted a working boardroom feel for this group, so straight tables had been arranged in a giant square, with the center empty and twenty-five chairs on each side. The president's place was with his back to the fireplace. Two seats away to his right would be the attorney general and two seats to his left, Secretary of Treasury Wainwright. Wall Street loved Wainwright, a zealous supply-sider and tax-cutter. Then around the tables, scattered among the Wall Street guests, would be other cabinet officers and White House aides.

Herbert Greenberg, sandwiched between the two aides, would sit in the corner closest to the president, where he would be most obscured from Griswold's view. As it turned out, his short body was barely visible anyway, his round face peeping over the wine glasses, his shoes barely touching the floor.

The guests arrived at 6:30 and were ushered upstairs, where they were greeted by members of the cabinet. After everyone was seated in the dining room, the head usher appeared at the door and announced grandly, "The president of the United States," and Whitney Griswold strode into the room, smiling and shaking hands left and right as a marine band contingent played "Hail to the Chief."

Dinner was a feast of regional American dishes topped off by a selection of Hawaiian sorbets. Over demitasses of coffee the president spoke informally with the guests seated near him. Several were old friends from Brown and Yale, a number had been Greenwich, Connecticut constituents, and others frequented the same clubs Griswold had belonged to in New York City.

Then the president began the evening's program with a glowing introduction of Emily Gineen, who, he said, would describe the character of the crime crisis and terrorist threats that had prompted the White House's current course of action.

Emily, wearing a simple black linen dress and pearls, stood, her back to the draped southwest window, and spoke easily for several minutes, profiling the situation: Violent crime was up 700 percent since the 1960s and police were so overtaxed that law enforcement had effectively broken down in the inner cities. She then traced every major historical instance of the invocation of emergency powers since Abraham Lincoln.

"This administration," she concluded, "with scrupulous

adherence to our fundamental constitutional liberties, will restore order to our streets. It is government's first obligation, one that demands courage and boldness, but we will not shrink from the task." She smiled as she looked around the room, connecting directly with her audience, then sat down as the bankers, investors, and money gurus applauded her warmly.

Wainwright followed with a less-inspiring speech, but he pushed all the right tax and growth buttons so important to this crowd.

Then it was Griswold's turn. He began as relaxed as Emily had been, but with a firm, direct, even blunt tone.

He first reassured the crowd that the rumors about limiting the Fed's independence were totally unfounded. The group applauded heartily. Griswold then turned to domestic matters. "Our crime bill puts real teeth in our laws, giving police and prosecutors the weapons they have long been denied," he said, and was again interrupted by a burst of applause. Robbie, watching, smiled and checked his watch.

Then Griswold spoke of the missing ingredients in American life, the qualities he had learned on "the playing fields of Groton and Brown," the things many in the room believed they had acquired in similar settings: decency, tolerance, civility.

"These religious bigots—who are, in fact, quite unchristian by my definition—will not be allowed to pollute our social environment," he said. "Free religious expression, always. Violence and obstruction of the rights of other law-abiding citizens, never."

On that line, delivered powerfully as Griswold jabbed his index finger in the air, the powerbrokers of Wall Street rose to their feet in enthusiastic applause.

Emboldened by the response, Griswold ignored his typed 3" x 5" cards and leaned toward the group. "Let me say something that I trust will not be misunderstood. I probably could not say this in a more public setting for fear of being called racist, which, as you all know, I most certainly am not . . ."

Emily tried not to look as startled as she felt.

". . . but the truth is," continued Griswold, "the crime crisis in America is quite localized. If one were to remove the African-American crime rate from the overall statistics, our national crime rate would be lower than the Belgians', lower than most of Europe, and below average for industrialized nations."

Around the room of mostly white faces there were raised eyebrows, quiet gasps, then nods of understanding. Emily was horrified. The figures were true, but the crime rate had to do with the breakdown of the family, which was epidemic in the inner cities—which happened to be predominantly black. For Griswold to use the stats the way he was doing was exploitative, fueling prejudices of the worst kind.

But it worked. Though a few faces were still frowning, most of the crowd had locked in with Griswold. He had merely articulated what they had thought all along. Robbie was grinning.

Griswold went on to explain that the National Guard was, therefore, the only feasible solution. Many of the soldiers, after all, were minorities, so racial tensions would be minimized. The troops also could be targeted exactly where the problem was: the inner cities. This was further grounds for their support for the president's inner-city empowerment legislation.

"Once we cure the root problem—that is, jobs, education, better housing—then we will no longer need the Guard," he concluded.

Once again the applause rang out from the bulls and bears of Wall Street; they had just experienced Whitney Griswold at his most adroit, skillfully manipulating the crowd. But Bernie O'Keefe, watching them, thought they reminded him more of sheep, baaing on command of the shepherd. *It worked, but it's a cheap shot at the blacks. Robbie must've cooked that one up.* He shifted uncomfortably in his seat.

Robbie, too, was uncomfortable, but for a wholly different reason. His eyes were trained on Herbert Greenberg, who had enjoyed his meal with great relish, had sipped appreciatively on the wine selection, and now was nodding gravely and moving his lips as if he wanted to speak.

Robbie, who had watched him carefully throughout the

evening, willed the little round man to silence. *You may not open your mouth . . . you may not open your mouth*, he repeated silently. The press had just been let in, the evening had gone perfectly, and this man must not be allowed to say or do anything to call attention to his presence.

But then it happened. Robbie had the sensation he was in a dream, everything in slow motion; he couldn't move fast enough to stop the horrible thing from happening.

Herbert Greenberg raised his hand, signaling a question.

The aide to his left, eyes wild, wrestled his arm down, hissing in Greenberg's ear. Startled, the short, stocky man stood up. The aide on the other side attempted to pull Greenberg down by the back of his jacket but succeeded only in rolling him backward on his heels, off balance . . . Greenberg clutched the tablecloth desperately, and plates, silverware, and wine glasses rolled and tipped to the floor.

Robbie knew at once he had made a crucial tactical error by not alerting Griswold. He had hoped that Greenberg would not be noticed so there would be no need to concern the president, who had a tendency to fret over such things, and who, incidentally, would blame Robbie for not being more careful.

Griswold started toward Greenberg just in time to collide with the secretary of treasury, who had thrust his chair backward to avoid the splatter of wine from the tumbling glasses. Robbie winced when the president got to Greenberg first and helped steady him as the waiters converged on the scene.

"I'm so sorry," Griswold said with instinctive graciousness. "You have a question, sir?"

"Yes, sir, I do," Greenberg said, still wiping the melange of pineapple, mango, and papaya sorbets from the front of his jacket and pants. "First, thank you for inviting me and having me met at the airport."

The president nodded.

"I haven't been in Washington since the wife and me drove through here twenty-two years ago on our way to Miami Beach. On my fiftieth birthday, in fact. Now we own a condo on the beach and we fly. You can do it cheaper than driving, you know."

By now Griswold's eyes were wide, his mouth frozen open in a half smile. Robbie knew what he was thinking—and it wasn't good.

"My partner and me," Greenberg continued, "we started our business forty-two years ago. Just the two of us, it used to be. Back then you could go uptown on the subway for a nickel and it's $1.25 today, which you should do something about." He looked sternly at the president.

"But we've worked hard, twelve to fifteen hours a day, and because of that we now employ forty people. About half Spanish and half black—on two shifts. That's forty off the welfare rolls that you don't have to worry about."

Robbie could feel the knots in his stomach. Bernie caught his eye and sliced his finger across his throat. Some of the guests were looking at each other with arched eyebrows, shaking their heads. Griswold stood motionless, arms folded, a dreadful, sickly smile on his face. And Greenberg kept going, telling the president his whole business history, while the television cameras kept grinding, the flashbulbs popping.

Robbie gestured for Caroline to get the press out. Envisioning herself herding some horrible stampede, the press secretary knew that was impossible. Now the other guests were clapping for Greenberg, a few calling for him to sit down.

But the applause snapped Griswold out of his trance.

"Now, now, gentlemen and ladies," he said, raising both hands, palms outward. "We've just heard a very sincere account of how from humble beginnings one man built a good, successful business. We thank you, sir, for creating those jobs by your ingenuity, enterprise, and hard work. This is the American dream, which we are pledged and determined to keep alive."

Greenberg was still standing, trying to ask his question, which was about minority job quotas, but the crowd drowned him out with sustained applause for the president. The two aides, gently this time, got Greenberg back into his chair. Robbie, breathing heavily, took his napkin and wiped his brow as Griswold asked if anyone else had a question.

"Mr. President," a middle-aged man whom Robbie knew to be the head of one of the largest mutual funds in America, rose to his feet. "Michael Novak has written, sir, that the American system is like a three-legged stool; one leg is the free economic system, the second is our free political system, and the third, our moral base. And clearly, Mr. President, there is an ethical collapse in this country. What can you do to strengthen the moral leg?"

Griswold could answer policy questions all day with one hand tied behind his back. But no one had asked him a question quite like this in a very long time. He hesitated just a moment, searching to recall Novak's thesis, but showed no emotion.

Then he grinned. "Good question, good question. I see it as government's first task to punish wrongdoers and reward right behavior. That establishes the moral norms. Beyond that, we must create a climate of economic and political freedom, the first two legs of the stool, which will in turn encourage the full creativity of the American people. If we provide the freedom, we will allow the basic goodness and decency of Americans to flourish. That's precisely why we are pursuing our present policies: to achieve order and preserve freedom so decent people—and Americans are that—can live decently. That's the moral answer."

The man who asked the question did not applaud, but the rest of the room did. The sound signaled the end of the evening, and the Marine Corps band began to play. The press people were ushered out, and Griswold started around the table pumping hands.

Robbie's knees were still a bit weak, but he knew all was well. Everyone was smiling.

THE NEXT MORNING, the market opened 140 points up and kept rising. Sindberg himself called Robbie to tell him that the president was now at the highest point of his presidency: 67 percent approval. In his euphoria Griswold apparently had forgotten about Greenberg. Robbie, not a religious man, thanked God.

"Just one thing, Robbie," Griswold said, twirling his reading glasses by their stems and leaning back in his chair, propping one leg on his bottom desk drawer. "That Novak question. I've been thinking about it. I've got to be a little better prepared on stuff like that. Government can create virtue by the right policies; I've always believed that, and I still do. But I don't think I convinced that fellow—who was he anyway?"

"President of Federated Investors. Very devout Catholic."

"I see. Of course. Probably a religious right-winger. Still, we ought to be ready. Have you read Novak?"

Robbie shook his head. Conservative Catholics weren't on his reading list.

"Well, I haven't lately. It's pretty right-wing stuff, I remember." Griswold kept twirling his glasses and half smiled. Robbie knew he had not read him either.

"Have Carmichael's boys do a little analysis for me. Put someone on this, Robbie. Read his stuff and give me a summary."

"Yes sir."

"That's it for now, I guess." Griswold sat upright, a signal he wanted time alone. Robbie gathered his papers.

"And, uh, Robbie, good job last night."

"Thank you, Mr. President. But you made it, sir. You were brilliant."

"Yes, yes . . . and, uh, Robbie," he said, just as his assistant reached the side door. "Give my warm regards to our friend Herbert Greenberg."

Robbie blanched, nodded, and went out the door. Griswold reached for the direct line to the private quarters in the mansion. Anne answered.

"A terrific morning," Griswold said, then proceeded to tell her about the polls, the feedback from the dinner.

She listened without response until he finished, then said, "That's wonderful, Whitney."

"So I've got an idea. It's a beautiful day. My schedule isn't too bad. Why don't we pick Elizabeth up after school and drive out to Middleburg. No big fuss, just two cars. We can have dinner at the Red Fox Inn. They won't advertise I'm coming."

"But, Whitney, you know wherever we go, it creates a fuss."

"No, we can do this."

"And I'm in the middle of packing. Everything is spread out on the bed. Maria's helping me. I'll be at it all day."

On Saturday Anne would be flying to Martha's Vineyard to supervise the opening of their twenty-two-room summer home on Starbuck Point, an exclusive enclave on a neck of land at the entrance to Edgartown Harbor. As soon as school was out in June, the family would spend as much time there as they could squeeze out of the schedule. The Secret Service and military had already taken over the basement, built a guard post, installed electronic devices and communications gear, and Anne wanted to get it all back in order. She hated mess.

"But, dear, that can wait. This is a great day for us and the country. We should celebrate, like the old days." Griswold was almost pleading.

"Oh, Whitney, of course. How insensitive of me. Whatever you'd like."

Anne put the phone down and stared out the bedroom window at the Washington monument in the distance. It was a gorgeous day, her husband was in a wonderful mood, she was looking forward to Martha's Vineyard, and yet she had this awful feeling. She remembered when she was a small girl, putting the furniture back in her dollhouse one day. Everything was in place perfectly; she was kneeling, reaching into the bedroom with a tiny rocking chair, and then she lost her balance and knocked the house over, scattering all the furniture.

Should she say anything to Whitney? Certainly not. He'd probably dismiss it anyway. But it was real; it wouldn't go away. She thought of Elizabeth, then realized she was tearing her cuticle, something she hadn't done for years.

Maybe a ride in the country would be good for them.

38

B ERNIE O'KEEFE couldn't remember a morning when he had felt more miserable, at least not since the awful time five years ago, a time he had almost totally blocked out of his memory.

He opened the top drawer of his dresser and fumbled through piles of handkerchiefs, a traveling iron, a box of buttons, three packs of hemorrhoidal suppositories, and miscellaneous luggage tags. In the corner, behind some old used airline tickets, he found the small round vial filled with pills, five milligrams each of Xanax. The label had a red warning sticker: "Avoid alcoholic beverages while taking this medication." Bernie shook his head slightly—he never drank in the morning—and threw two pills in his mouth, swallowing them without water.

Dr. Nikkels had told him to take one at the first sign that stress was getting the better of him. Maybe he'd waited too long. The black veil had descended. For four hours in the night he had clutched his pillow and tossed fitfully, his heart racing, his thoughts dark and clouded, in the grip of that awful feeling of helplessness he remembered from before. Around dawn, he had fallen into an hour of sleep; then the horrible alarm had rung. His temples throbbed, his head felt like it was an eighty-pound ball of iron.

And the awful thing was that he was alone. Marilyn had held him in her arms the time before, stroked his head while he had sobbed in the night. Now she was in Wellesley, and the way things were going, she probably wouldn't be particularly sympathetic if he called her. He couldn't talk to any of his colleagues at the White House, or even the White House doctor. He knew the rule there: Walk the corridors with your back to the wall. Somebody was always waiting to sink the knife in and take your place in the inner circle. He could think of a number of people who would be overjoyed at the thought of Bernie O'Keefe having a nervous breakdown.

Bernie tried to absorb himself in the intelligence summary awaiting him on the back seat of his limousine, but he couldn't concentrate. He could focus his eyes, and he saw the words, but he couldn't process the thoughts. It made him angry, and he was already raging inside.

At the dinner last night he had put his finger on what had been troubling him for weeks. Robbie was now totally controlling Whitney Griswold, manipulating him with his polls and his little divisive bits of information, exploiting the man's darker side. It was infuriating, and as Bernie's limo worked its way through the morning traffic, he got angrier and angrier.

When his car arrived at the west wing at 7:45, Bernie leaped out and headed straight for Robbie's office. It was time to set a few things straight. He walked by Robbie's secretary with hardly a glance and through the big mahogany door. Robbie was at the conference table, his back to his desk, his two young assistants seated on either side, scribbling instructions into their notebooks.

"Bernie, come in, come in." Robbie could be irritatingly cheerful in the morning. He waved Bernie to a chair at the table.

"Got more good news from Sindberg. The boss is staying right up there in the polls. Look at this, Bernie." He slid a paper across the table.

By now the Xanax had made its way into Bernie's central nervous system, numbing it slightly. He took a look at the paper: The approval was holding near 70 percent.

"Impressive, all right, impressive." He handed it back to Robbie. "Could we have a minute?" he asked.

Robbie motioned to his assistants, who were both wearing almost identical gray suits and red silk ties. Bernie called them the beaver patrol: young and eager, obsequious around Robbie, brusque with most everyone else. They got up after Robbie nodded and quietly slipped out.

"Jeez, you look rough this morning, Bernie. You all right?"

"I'm fine," said Bernie quickly. "Just a short night's sleep. But there's something I need to say to you . . . I don't want you to forget, Robbie, that Whitney Griswold and I go back together a long way—twenty-five years. I know this man, his good side and his bad side, and I know when someone is manipulating—"

"Wait a minute. What are you talking about? Look at these polls. We're playing this thing like a violin—"

"Live by the polls, and you die by the polls. This is the president of the United States, Robbie. He's not a marionette. You can't just put him on stage, pull his strings, and make him dance."

"Bernie, are you sure you're okay? This is the way every White House is run. The president's out front. That's his job. He's the public face; he's scripted according to the game plan that's already set. You can't run the modern presidency any other way. Not with the media in your face. Look what happened to Clinton when he tried to wing it."

"Yeah, I know. But Whitney Griswold is a good man, Robbie. Let him be president. I trust his instincts."

"What's eating you?"

"Last night at the dinner. That crack he made about the black crime rate. Emily didn't give him that; I know, because I've talked to her. I didn't give it to him, it wasn't in the briefing material, and it's not Whitney Griswold. It was a cheap shot, Robbie. Those fat boys from New York loved it, but it was a cheap shot. The cause of crime doesn't have to do with race, and you know it."

"Maybe he read it somewhere. Maybe he isn't scripted all the time."

"You planted that one, Robbie. Don't manipulate him."

"Right. And who are you to moralize? Politics is a rough game. Just ask Byron Langer."

Bernie's cheeks flushed. "That's different," he snapped. "That hypocrite had it coming. He lied about his war record, he blackmailed us into hiring his man, and don't forget that he was just about to launch a major torpedo right at us."

"Listen, Bernie," Robbie's eyes narrowed as he glared, "my job is to keep this man in this chair for the country's good. What do you want? The bigots cramming their narrow-minded values down our throats—or the Democrats who will bankrupt us? Whitney Griswold is this country's hope."

Bernie got up. It was almost time for the 8:00 staff meeting. "I believe that," he nodded. "Let's just remember that it's Whitney Griswold who is president. We aren't running a puppet show here."

Bernie stopped in the men's room before the meeting. As he splashed water on his face, he was disgusted to see that his hands were shaking.

Later that morning, he found Dr. Nikkels's card in his desk drawer and placed the call. He couldn't face what he'd gone through before: the deep black holes, the long counseling sessions, the Prozac. The doctors had called it clinical depression. It had been so bad, there were times he'd wished he was dead. He couldn't go through all that again. He'd have to see if Nikkels could just send down some pills.

While he waited for Nikkels's nurse to get the doctor, he rubbed his temples. He felt exhausted.

39

PAUL CLARKSON arrived at the attorney general's office a few minutes before 4:00 and found the other assistant AGs already gathering around the big table in the conference room. Director Frizzell was setting up a chart board, and Lieutenant General Childers, assistant chief of staff for the army reserve and the Guard, was also on hand.

Paul was making his way to his chair just as Emily entered from her private office at the other end of the room. She slid quickly into her place at the head of the table.

For the next twenty minutes Frizzell briefed the assembled executive team on the progress of the bureau's investigation of the anti-abortion groups. All those who had been involved in the Gideon's Torch operation had been apprehended, he assured them, including a young broadcast intern and the man from TapeMasters who had "loaned" them the original tape to copy. The suspects were being held, awaiting preliminary hearings and arraignment. None had been able to meet the $500,000 bail set by a government-friendly judge.

Furthermore, five churches in the New York area at which the Gideon's Torch people had held meetings were being charged under RICO statutes as part of the conspiracy. The civil division was moving aggressively to confiscate assets. Several businesses that allegedly had supported the members were being vigorously investigated and would likely be charged as well.

Undercover assets were still in place, and more anti-abortion leaders were being "visited"—Frizzell smiled when he used the word—and interrogated extensively.

"Our only problem at this point," he explained, "is in knowing who could be tied in by overt acts, but we're casting the conspiracy net wide. Extensive phone taps. Physical surveillance. Particularly where we can't infiltrate. If anything is coming down the pike, we'll know about it."

He warned them, however, that more terrorist acts were possible, even likely, and security at the White House was being significantly augmented. But violent acts were possible anywhere.

"These are dangerous people," he reminded the group.

Agents in each field office would soon begin visiting anyone visibly involved in the pro-life movement. It was a huge task and would take months.

"Won't that, at the very least, border on harassment?" asked the assistant attorney general for civil rights.

Frizzell grinned. "Sure. We're dealing with terrorists."

Any clinics that had ever been targets of protest at any time were being given round-the-clock protection by U.S. marshals and FBI personnel. Even the regeneration centers, still under construction, would receive federal protective security in the weeks ahead, just as soon as more personnel became available. "Our resources," Frizzell said, looking pointedly at Clarkson, "are being taxed to the limit. I have submitted a supplementary budget request to the associate attorney general's office."

As for progress in the Fargo case, Frizzell concluded, the bureau had a very strong suspect but had to be careful not to act precipitously; she was being kept under active surveillance, and it was hoped would lead them to others involved in the conspiracy.

General Childers, a tall man with rugged features, a one-time West Point all-American fullback and a decorated veteran, followed. He lacked the adroitness of Frizzell and occasionally stumbled as he read from his briefing papers.

The report was also anything but inspiring: thirty-two shooting incidents involving guardsmen; a number of the victims were innocent bystanders. Arrests were up in each city where the Guard was working, but also, surprisingly, were homicides—sharply up in D.C. and L.A. There were no questions for Childers.

As the briefing concluded and the staff assembled their papers to leave, Emily signaled Paul to her office. "Let's talk a few minutes," she said, leading him toward the doorway.

"Of course," he said. "But I do have a little time problem."

"Oh? Well, I guess it could wait until tomorrow."

"If it could wait, that would be great. I really need to go. I'm sorry, but I promised Paul Jr. I'd be at his Little League game tonight, and it starts early, at six o'clock."

The bottom was falling out in the country, terrorists were on the rampage, and the associate attorney general was heading to a Little League game? Emily raised her eyebrows.

Paul smiled. "A long time ago, I promised June that whatever happened in my work, I would not neglect my family. I promised my son I would come to his game tonight, and if I break that promise, he'll never forget it—"

Emily stopped him. "I really do understand. That's great. It helps to cut through the garbage and distinguish between the important and the urgent. I should get home too. Where's the game?"

"In Great Falls, near where I live."

"Good, I'll drive you out. We can talk in the car. I'd like to see your son."

"It's way out of your way, Emily," he said.

"Well, that'll give us a chance to talk. No problem."

AS THE BLACK Lincoln wound along the George Washington Parkway in bursts of speed and abrupt stops—traffic was at its worst before six—Emily seemed unusually reflective.

"It's beautiful," she said, looking at the spring growth, the wildflowers, and lush green embankments. To the right they could see the Potomac, its waters higher than usual.

"Paul, what do you think?" She turned toward him. "Is all this we're doing going to work?"

Paul smiled and shrugged his shoulders slightly. "Maybe, for a while at least, if we can get the Guard not to shoot everything that moves—and if there are enough of them."

"But only for a while?"

"Yup. Levitz's last column was right on."

"What would it take to really stop crime, Paul? What do you think would really work for the long run?" she asked.

"Put kids in Sunday school."

"Oh," Emily shook her head, annoyed, "you religious people are all alike with your simplistic, cute answers. Langer did that with me too. Be serious."

"I am being serious," Paul said. "There was a study done in England by a professor at the University of Reading. He found that when Sunday school attendance was at its peak, crime was lowest. When Sunday school attendance declined, crime went up, in direct proportion. A group of scholars studied the data and came up with the answer: Put kids back in Sunday school."

"Look, that all sounds very nice, but we were elected to lock 'em up. The criminals, I mean. You don't want the government to get into the Bible school business, do you?"

"No, I sure don't," Paul said. "Government can only do so much. I mean, we can help in little ways by the standards we set in the laws we pass. But government can't create virtue, Emily. That has to come from within the people themselves. Individual lives changed. That's what God alone can do."

Emily stared at Paul for a moment, then shook her head. "So we're just keeping our finger in the dike, trying to hold it all back, right?" she asked tiredly. "Trying to keep the troops from killing innocent citizens. Trying to keep Frizzell's storm troopers from taking over the Capitol. Right?"

"Just about," he sighed.

"Got any constructive ideas, Paul? Any good news?"

"I can tell you where the really good news is, Emily."

"You going to get your Bible out?"

"Sure," he chuckled. "You ready?"

"No, not today."

A FEW MINUTES BEFORE SIX, they pulled up behind a chain-link fence. Beyond it, groups of parents were standing or sitting on the wooden bleachers, chatting, watching their kids warm up around the softball diamond.

As Paul got out of the car, a boy spotted them. "Hey, Dad!" he shouted with a grin, tossing the ball to a teammate and running around the fence.

"You remember Attorney General Gineen, son," said Paul. The boy took off his hat and shook Emily's hand.

Emily had seen him the day Paul took his oath of office, but now looked him over more carefully. With his close-cropped, curly hair and beautiful smile, Paul Jr. was a copy of his father.

"Thanks for the ride, Emily," Paul said. "I'll see you on Monday."

She watched them for a moment as they walked away. Paul walked slowly, leaning on one cane, his other arm around his son's shoulders. Paul Jr. was carrying his father's briefcase.

It's incredible, she thought. Most of the politicos she had come to know in Washington never got home from the office before midnight and prided themselves on their "commitment." *I know one thing*, she thought. *Paul Clarkson does have his priorities straight.*

Emily got back in the limousine. "Home, please," she said to the driver.

KELLY'S WAS JAMMED, as it was every Friday night. Bernie couldn't get a stool at the bar; he had to stand behind somebody else.

"Hey, Bernie, how's it going?" Henry grinned, waved, and headed for the Dewars.

"Great," Bernie yelled. *No problem*, he thought. He'd popped his last two Xanax hours ago, before lunch. Dr. Nikkels had prescribed some sleeping pills and recommended Valium. Nothing stronger, he said, until he could examine Bernie.

In any event, he was feeling better, and the first sips of scotch were soothing. Bernie always liked the feeling when the 86 proof hit his stomach. On an empty stomach it took only seconds for the alcohol to penetrate the walls of the intestinal lining and enter the bloodstream. He could feel the warm glow before his second sip. It was comforting; life was really bearable after all.

He'd fly to Boston tomorrow night, see the kids, and then Nikkels had agreed to see him at his home on Sunday. With a plane from Andrews, he'd be gone less than twenty-four hours.

Within a few minutes he had edged his way into an open spot next to a young man with a ponytail and an earring in his right ear. Henry was wiping down the counter.

"Good day, Henry?" Bernie asked.

"Yeah, no complaints."

"Big weekend?"

"You bet. We're taking the boat to Lake Anna tomorrow. Can't beat it." Henry smiled. "The kids love to go down there."

"What kind of boat?" Bernie asked.

"Century 21. Nothing fancy. Fast, though. Kids like to waterski. Me, I just float around with a few cool ones."

"Is it worth it?" Bernie asked suddenly.

"Is what worth it?"

"Life. You work your tail off in this place, full of smoke and noise, listening to everyone's gripes—you hear more than most shrinks do. You work all week so you can zip around on a lake on Saturday. Is it worth it?"

"I never thought about it, Bernie. It's what I do. I mean, I might like a bigger boat. And my wife wants a bigger house. I don't know why. We've got four bedrooms and three kids. But I wouldn't trade with most of the people who come in here every night," he said. "No, I guess I've got it okay. Why do you ask?"

O'Keefe drained his glass and put it on the counter. "Just wondering," he said. "I'm doing a poll." He shoved the glass toward Henry. "Get me one more, would you?"

Henry knew he never meant only one more.

40

I T W A S S T I L L Q U I E T in Rehoboth Beach in mid-May. The big crowds didn't start coming until Memorial Day weekend, when the summer season kicked off with a bang. Then all the boardwalk shops opened, beach umbrellas sprouted like colorful mushrooms in the sand, coconut suntan lotion wafted in the breeze, and the waves were dotted with bobbing heads, while children built sand castles and adults lay nearby, baking and basking in the latest Tom Clancy or John Grisham novel.

Incorporated in 1891 as an alcohol-free Methodist retreat town, by the 1990s Rehoboth's well was no longer dry, most of the Methodists were gone, and three distinct populations worshiped at the shrine of sun and sand. Each had its own particular amusements and hangouts.

First were the families, who staggered onto the beaches in landing parties carrying more equipment than the troops at D-Day. They set up elaborate camps stocked with coolers, umbrellas, chairs, sipper cups, playpens, strollers, sunblock, plastic shovels, buckets . . . and when they tired of the ocean, they made their way across the sand and up the wooden stairs to the boardwalk's dubious delights: miniature golf, Wack-a-Mole, cotton candy, fudge, and funnel cakes.

Rehoboth was also a magnet for D.C.-area single professionals. They traveled lighter than the families yet still made the two-and-a-half-hour trek from the city each weekend with solemn ritual. To avoid the bottlenecks on the Chesapeake Bay Bridge, they would linger downtown after work on Friday evenings, waiting for the traffic to die down. Many gathered in groups at the rooftop bar of the Washington Hotel, whose breezy clusters of comfortable sofas and low tables overlooked the Treasury Department and the White House. It was one of the best views in Washington.

By nine or ten at night, they would head east for the beach, stopping sometimes at the landmark Red, Hot, and Blue restaurant on Route 50 just before the Bay Bridge. The Memphis barbecue was a Washington ritual: pulled pig sandwiches to go.

FINALLY, in recent years Rehoboth also had built up a substantial homosexual community. They kept mostly to themselves, sunning on what the locals had called Poodle Beach until a city ordinance prohibited the nickname as a hate crime.

The locals were still allowed to note that the gays had the lock on the best restaurants in Rehoboth. If you wanted a really good meal, the best places to go were the Blue Moon or Syndey's or LaLa Land.

But the undisputed king of Rehoboth cuisine drew from all three of the town's populations: the legendary Grotto's Pizza, with multiple locations in Rehoboth and its next-door neighbors, Dewey and Bethany Beaches. A trip to Rehoboth was not complete without the experience of sitting on one of the ancient white benches on the boardwalk with noisy seagulls circling above and a huge, hot, triangle of Grotto's extra-cheese pizza in your hand, oozing oil down your chin with each bite.

DANIEL AND ALEX SEATON had come to Rehoboth Beach every summer of their lives. After their parents had died in the plane crash, the boys had held on to the family's summer home on Columbia Avenue, a pine-lined residential neighborhood near the heart of town. Number 31 was modest yet comfortable, a snug bungalow with a generous screened porch.

Whenever Daniel and Alex were there, childhood memories merged with recollections from the years since, especially all their latenight discussions on the porch with friends. Such conversations usually came after an evening spent laughing and pounding the redseasoned shells of blue crabs with wooden mallets, then plucking out the tender meat.

Most of the memories were from an earlier, more innocent time. Before J. Whitney Griswold. Before Gideon's Torch. Before violence and ugly confrontations. Before things had gotten so complicated.

This evening found the two brothers, along with Lance Thompson and John Jenkins, sitting on the beach in the light of the setting sun, a Grotto's pepperoni pizza between them, the grease seeping through the cardboard box and into the big old bedspread spread out beneath them.

Recent events and the arrest of their friends in New York had made Washington feel too alien. The walls seemed to be closing in. So Alex had suggested that the four of them, the inner circle of the D.C. cell, take an overnight and go up to Rehoboth.

"Staring at the ocean is always therapeutic," he'd said. "And I can't think straight with federal troops on the streets of D.C. I feel like I'm in a movie."

Even as they ate the pizza, however, he found himself looking around to see if they had been followed. The public beach off Columbia Avenue was about a quarter mile from the end of the boardwalk; he could see the big street lights just beginning to come on, spiking the wooden walkway at intervals.

As they faced the ocean, behind them were several hundred yards of sand dunes, and to the northwest, the quiet, exclusive neighborhoods of Henlopen Acres. If anyone wanted to overhear their conversation, they would have to march across open sand and plop down on the blanket with them.

DANIEL TOOK another bite of pizza and stared at the sea. The sun was setting, and the pink glow from the clouds reflected slightly on the foamy curl of the cresting waves. It was his favorite time of day.

He thought of how many summers he had sat on this sand and stared at the ocean. Sometimes he had prayed and struggled with decisions here. Like whether or not to go to seminary. And he had come here and gazed at the sea, in a grinning daze, before he had asked Mary to marry him.

He and Mary had come here when Dan Jr. was a baby; he had slept under an umbrella in his mesh playpen while they stretched out on the sand, relaxed, and dreamed about the future. The fall after their parents had been killed, he and Alex and the rest of the family had come here for Thanksgiving; it had seemed appropriate to gather together in a place that had brought them so much joy.

Constant yet changing, the ocean was Daniel's touchstone, the place that tied him to his past and freed him for his future.

But he had never been at the beach in such turmoil. Even as they ate this ordinary pizza, looking like any average group of guys relaxing and talking, he noticed that Lance was not facing the ocean, but toward the west, like a sentry. And driving Route 50 east, headed to the beach, well under the speed limit, Daniel had noticed that he himself had flinched each time he saw a police car. *Why do I feel like a fugitive?* he wondered.

Lance startled him; the usually silent sentry spoke. "I think the time has come to do something," he said simply.

"We have done something," Daniel responded.

"It didn't work."

"We don't know that," Daniel said tentatively. He was talking like Mary, though without much conviction. "Changing people's minds takes time."

Alex wadded up his paper plate and napkin and thrust them into their trash bag. "We're out of time," he said. "The video didn't do anything but make people mad. At us. The government has cracked down like we're Colombian drug dealers, except they treat the drug dealers better.

"Look, Daniel, let's just lay it all out. We've done everything we could over the past two years. We've protested peacefully. We've sent mailings to people who influence public opinion. We've called legislators. We've protested some more. Written articles.

"And we've gone the extra mile to accomplish something unprecedented in the history of broadcasting: We actually showed a third of the nation what will happen in the regeneration centers. We've taken every conceivable route within the system—and then some—to expose the evil. Gideon's Torch: We lit up the darkness, right?"

Alex turned toward John Jenkins, who was watching Daniel. "John, you're a businessman. Would you continue a project that had failed on every single count? No. You'd learn from the failure, cut your losses, and take another strategy."

Daniel thought of Bill Waters. They had gone to school together. He had seen his friend's familiar face, briefly, on the network news. Two federal agents were leading Bill, manacled. There had been a million reporters, all shouting questions. It was chaos, and yet Bill had had his head up, looking directly into the television cameras, his expression neither defiant nor cowed. Then one of the agents had put his hand on the crown of Bill's head and pushed him down into the unmarked car . . . he wondered when he'd see Bill again.

Lance spoke again with his characteristic brevity. "Alex is right."

Daniel sighed and started digging a hole in the sand with his fingers. "I've always argued against Christians working outside the system. No one ever thought this would be easy. But we have to exhaust every avenue of reasonable nonviolent action."

"They're exhausted, man," Lance said. He was beginning to sound like the chorus in a Greek tragedy.

"I'm exhausted, too," said Daniel. "Maybe Gideon's Torch hasn't worked. I don't want to sound holier-than-thou, but I've never been too concerned about what works; I've tried to think in terms of what's right."

"But it's gotten a lot more complicated," Alex responded. "We haven't gone outside the system; the government has prevented us from working in the system, blocked our access. The courts for years have enshrined abortion as the one sacred right of American life. Congress won't act, and the politicians have all left us. You can go to jail for simply protesting. And if you look at some of the bills in Congress now, even expressing our views is going to be a crime. Writing a letter to the editor will be called inciting violence. And on top of it all, the president is out to crush every pro-life group in the country. They're acting like we're the Ku Klux Klan."

"We may as well *be* the Klan, according to the public opinion polls," John interrupted.

Then Alex turned to Daniel. "You remember what Levitz just wrote? When a government stifles legal dissent, it invites violence. He's right."

Daniel rolled his eyes upward as if carefully weighing the point, then spoke deliberately. "I'll admit that this government has lost its moral authority," he said. "The White House is acting like a police state. And people out there are loving it. But I have to read Romans 13 literally. Government wields the sword for our good. I don't like it any better than you do. And I realize these guys care only about polls and elections and shutting up those who disagree. Okay, it's getting a lot harder to honor those in authority, but that's what the Bible says to do."

"So what do we do?" Alex asked, egging his brother on toward the natural conclusion of his reasoning.

"Well, the church has to act as the conscience of society. God knows no one else will. We have to resist."

"We have been resisting," said Lance, playing off Alex to make sure Daniel kept going.

"I know," Daniel said. "And when we break the law to make our protest public—like Gideon's Torch—we should pay the consequences and go to jail. Our guys in New York were all committed to that. Maybe the four of us belong there too. We knew about it." He paused. "We've had it easy on our end."

They were all silent for a few moments. Then Daniel continued thoughtfully. "But now I wonder if future generations will judge us," he said, "like the church in Germany in the '30s. It was silent. We haven't been silent, but maybe we haven't done everything that we should do." He rubbed his eyes.

"Proportionate response," said Jenkins. He knew his friend well. The phrase from Augustine clicked in Daniel's brain.

"I know," Daniel responded automatically. "Right. Just war theory says you use the reasonable force necessary to counter the evil. But only the minimum."

"Oh, great!" Lance said. "This isn't Sunday morning. You don't need to preach. This isn't theory. I've been in wars, just and unjust. I know how much force you need in order to survive.

"But we aren't talking about our own survival," Lance pressed on. "We're talking about thousands and then millions of unborn babies. The regeneration centers are like the slave ships, bringing in helpless people about to be tortured. They're like the trains bringing the Jews to Auschwitz. We can't just stand by with our little cardboard protest signs anymore."

Daniel stared at Lance. His comparisons caught in Daniel's throat. *Maybe it's not that complicated after all*, he thought. *We've tried everything within the system, and they just keep delivering up helpless people to the slaughter. So we try to stop them.*

He looked at Alex, who was making a road in the sand, just like he used to when they were boys. Daniel realized that over the past year or two he had tended to dismiss his brother more often than not: too impetuous, not well-read or well-reasoned enough. *Maybe there's a certain wisdom to such simplicity*, he thought.

And it didn't take much to understand that there were two sets of rules being applied. For years, abortion protesters had had to answer to a different standard than, say, animal rights protesters.

In Maryland a few years earlier, a group of PETA activists had thrown vials of their own blood on the sidewalk and blockaded the entrance to the building housing the animal labs at

Bethesda's National Institutes of Health. They had gotten a free-for-all of media attention, appearances on the *Today* show, a thirty-day sentence in jail—suspended—and a $500 fine.

The same week a group of pro-lifers at the Planned Parenthood clinic at the corner of Sixteenth and L in downtown Washington had stood in the rain, quietly praying as the clinic opened. A ten-year-old girl with them had strayed into the legal "bubble zone" in front of the clinic entrance. Her mother, trying to retrieve her daughter, had gotten into a shouting match with the pro-choicers, been arrested, thrown into jail, and fined $10,000. The story—eighteen lines—appeared on page three of the *Post's* Metro section.

Daniel had visited the woman when she was released to her home. She was pale and shaken, her arm still blistered from where a group of aggressive inmates in her cellblock had burned her with cigarettes before the guards had dragged them off her.

Her husband had stood with his back to Daniel, looking out the window. "There is no justice," he had said quietly, though his shoulders were shaking with anger. "We have no recourse. They've stripped us of dignity, they're mocking God's law, and no one cares." Daniel had nodded awkwardly, unsure of what to say or do. He felt impotent, a pastor offering nothing but carrion comfort.

Six months later, the man had been arrested in Bethesda, an explosive device in the trunk of his car and a map with a penciled circle around the home of the doctor who performed abortions at the Planned Parenthood clinic. He was in prison now, and his wife and child were living with her parents. Daniel had written the man a letter. He had gotten back only a rambling note, ending with the old quote from Edmund Burke: "All that is necessary for the triumph of evil is for good men to do nothing."

DANIEL STARED into the darkening ocean and sighed. He felt like he was slipping out with the tide.

"But wait. I still say—we mustn't fall into the tactics of the other side," he said suddenly. "You don't overcome evil with evil. You overcome their evil with good."

"I've been thinking about that," said Jenkins. "It's true. But we're not talking about defending ourselves, or about aggression. We're talking about defending the defenseless. For their good, we choose to break a lesser law. A lesser evil, for a greater good. We need to respond with a proportionate response. Some kind of surgical strike."

Alex couldn't help himself. "That's what we've been saying for months now," he exploded, though he kept his voice low. "We take the obvious target. The first regeneration center. I've got a munitions expert who'll help us. This is not a public relations campaign. This is practical. The center is due to open in the fall. We're not talking about taking people out, though getting rid of a few dozen of these doctors who do the D and X wouldn't be a bad idea. We're talking about a *building*.

"And once that building is open, at least a hundred babies a week will die there. If we take it out, that saves five thousand babies in a year. That might not sound like much, but it makes a difference—particularly to those five thousand babies. Oskar Schindler saved twelve hundred Jews; today their children's children's children play on the streets of Jerusalem."

Daniel sighed again. He had seen *Schindler's List* three times when the film had come out a few years earlier. Its images burned into his brain, particularly the ending, in which art and reality had merged and the Schindler Jews—the actual people whose lives had been saved, along with the actors—had walked in droves, topping the crest of a green hill in Jerusalem, wrinkled old men and women, their eyes full of life, their faces full of dignity, bringing flowers to the grave of Oskar Schindler.

Daniel thought about Schindler. He was a flawed man, but a man compelled by conscience to do what he could do. He hadn't sat around and debated the fine points of civil disobedience. He hadn't circulated petitions. The death trains were moving too quickly. He had acted.

Daniel looked out at the ocean again. It was dark now, and

the waves seemed louder as they crashed into the cool sand. Alex and Lance and John were vague shapes in the darkness.

Daniel shook his head. "I'm sorry," he said. "I can't be part of something like that." He felt very tired. "But I can't tell you what to do. We all have to follow our own consciences. But don't do anything that hurts anyone."

Alex knew when not to push his brother further. He and Lance stood up together, picking up the pizza box, the trash bag, and their Coke cans.

"You coming?" Jenkins asked when Daniel didn't move.

"No, you all go on back to the house. I'm going to stay here for a while," Daniel said. "I need to pray."

41

I N WHAT HAD BECOME his usual morning ritual, James Jones flipped open the *Fairfax Journal*. His wife had teased him that he was going to leave her as soon as he found who or what he was looking for in the personal ads. He had responded that he was just checking up on her to make sure she wasn't advertising for a younger man. Across the breakfast table, Justin, home from college, just grinned at his parents and attacked a huge plate of bacon and eggs.

It was in the fourth column, under the "Men Seeking Men" section. "Black man seeks same for discreet, explosive, good times."

Jones looked at it again, slowly, to make sure, took another swallow of coffee, and looked over at Justin. "I'll take you to the office this morning, son," he said. "Then I've got to go on a little errand in Arlington."

ACCORDING TO the upper-left-hand corner of the front page of today's *Washington Post*, sunset was due at 8:06. As the shadows lengthened at the site of the nearly completed regeneration center, the crowds of commuters at the George Washington

University Metro stop began to thin. Every booth at Sam's Deli was full. At the GW library, summer students settled into their study carrels. In the hospital, groups of doctors and interns had just concluded their nightly rounds.

Lance Thompson turned right onto Twenty-third Street off Washington Circle and slowly drew near to the regeneration center in the van he had rented. He was calm, composed, and dangerously quiet as he examined his target.

The center's first floor was lit, like a model home beckoning buyers. The second floor was dark, except for a few dull glows that looked like security lighting and the lighted glass walkway that arched over Twenty-third Street, connecting the center with the hospital. Its decorative glasswork made it look like a high-tech amusement park tunnel. According to the blueprints Lance had studied, the center was secured from the walkway by an electronic door that could only be opened by a keycard, and a checkpoint that would later be manned by a guard.

Where's Alex? he wondered. Their plan depended on split-second timing. He would take the van under the building, and Alex would have the getaway car ready for their exit. They'd ditch it somewhere at the airport and get the 9:30 flight to Miami, then go on to Costa Rica. He had their fake passports, tickets, and everything else they needed.

Relieved, Lance saw Alex's brown Toyota edging up behind him in the rearview mirror. Then he watched as a police car whizzed past, made a U-turn at the next traffic light, and came back by, siren blaring. Maybe the National Guard just shot somebody else, Lance thought. Well, at least the cops weren't hanging around here at the moment. Good thing.

IN THE George Washington University Hospital's Tandy Pavilion, a theaterlike arena within the hospital that was used for teaching sessions, press conferences, and the like, the private cocktail reception was in full swing.

The regeneration center wasn't due to open for three more

weeks, when there would be a major ribbon-cutting ceremony, speeches, and a big splash of media coverage. Tonight's event, however, smaller and absolutely private, with no reporters present, represented the real power base behind the center's creation: key AIDS activists from around the country and a few wealthy supporters whose names would grace the main wings of the center; they had kicked in big dollars to the private foundation piggybacking the center's federal funding. The center's senior staff were there as well, along with a few key guests from Capitol Hill.

The center's executive director, Dr. Barbara LaMar, had taken the group of thirty or so for a tour of the new building. Then they had returned to the Tandy Pavilion, where caterers had set up an open bar and waiters strolled with silver platters of hors d'oeuvres. There LaMar had delivered remarks, as had the chairman of the fundraising matching campaign.

Congressman Peter Meyer had concluded the formal program, ending his short speech with the well-known personal odyssey of his own family and their struggle with AIDS.

"As many of you know," he said, "my wife was one of three siblings. She worshiped her oldest brother—his life, in fact, inspired her own decision to pursue public service. Doug's term in the Peace Corps, his bold campaign to save the rain forest, his tireless efforts for antibigotry legislation against those who would incite an atmosphere of hate and fear of diversity are shining examples of his ongoing contributions to society.

"Many of you know my wife, and April wanted me to express to you her regret at not being able to be with us tonight. But her decision to pursue law and her subsequent career on the bench came directly from the example of her brother's tireless dedication to justice and the service of others.

"We will never forget the pain of Doug's HIV diagnosis, nor the false hopes raised by AZT and other medications. We will never recover from the pain of watching April's brother wither, week by week, into a pale shadow. The loss of bodily functions, the loss of hope, the loss of life itself. Yet Doug died with dignity, the entire family by his side.

"Tonight, however, we gather with new hope, for perhaps our long national nightmare is almost over. Just around the corner is a whole new beginning, a new dawn when out of life new life can spring, when the sacrifice of women willing to exercise their reproductive rights for the good of others can bring about a new birth of hope for us all."

Meyer's unctuous speaking style was relieved by his striking good looks. He had not had much use for his wife's brother while he was alive, but in death Doug had served him well, providing an anecdotal verity and emotion to his otherwise predictable language. That emotion had resonated well with voters, and, it turned out, with people who held the purse strings for the "regen cen," as he liked to call it.

The alliance with the center had also helped Meyer's reelection campaign the past fall. He had faced a tough race and had needed as much television air time as possible to put his handsome face and resonant voice directly into voters' living rooms. That was expensive, but he had found that raising money for the center had put him in touch with celebrities and liberal corporate heads who didn't mind spilling a few extra thousand into his private coffer in exchange for political and legislative favors.

Another advantage of his association with the center was that it had brought him into contact with Barbara LaMar for the first time. He had heard about her long before he met her; the former NIH administrator and new head of the regeneration center was known in Washington circles as a tough, bright, sexy powerbroker. Meyer liked that trinity in a woman. His wife was tough and bright, but she failed decidedly in the third area. Barbara LaMar had it all.

Meyer finished his speech with the request that they all observe a moment of silence for the AIDS victims of the past and a moment of hope for those who would be saved in the future. He had found that that moment of spirituality worked well with audiences—even somewhat cynical ones like this small, powerful group. When the silence ended, most people made their way to the bar for fresh drinks, and the silver platters of smoked salmon and sushi circulated again.

Meyer popped a cube of fish in his mouth and drained the Chivas the bartender had just poured him. Even as he chatted most sincerely with one of the center's wealthiest benefactors, he watched Barbara LaMar working her way through the crowd, nodding, smiling, calculating, and, it seemed, making a bead right toward him. He smiled and ordered another Chivas. It was only 9:30, and April would be working very late tonight. Perhaps he wouldn't get home until late himself.

AT 9:30, in the regeneration center's security control room, Justin Jones flipped the center's automated security alarm—the one that rang automatically at the nearest D.C. police station—to its off position.

James Jones, sitting at the control panel at his company's offices, saw the center's monitor glow, meaning electronic security was down at the facility. His heart pounded. Please, Justin, just get yourself outta there in time, he thought.

LANCE LOOKED at his watch. By now Justin would have deactivated the automatic electronic surveillance. And traffic was light. He drove slowly to the center's entrance and slid the passcard Justin had given him into the front-gate monitor.

The electric gate slid open silently, and Lance drove through, down the curving drive past the central drop-off area and around the back of the building toward the underground parking garage. There, he inserted a second computer-coded card into the monitor standing like a small sentry outside the big double-bay doors to the garage. There was a rumble, and the huge doors rolled upward.

The garage was empty and dark except for the twin beams of the van's headlights. Lance drove toward the center of the garage, near the entrances to the elevators, and parked the van next to one of the huge, concrete, load-bearing pillars of the regeneration center.

JUSTIN JONES, making his rounds on the first floor, heard the rumble of the garage doors and looked at his watch. Lance was right on time.

LANCE OPENED the van door to shed some light, then went around to the back to deal with the job at hand. Most of his work had been done in advance; now it was just a matter of positioning the fuse igniter, then pulling its metal ring.

The van's two rear seats had been removed, and in the shell where they had been were now ten tidy stacks of military-issue explosive—seven hundred pounds of dense sticks of off-white material wrapped in olive-colored Saran wrap and stored in army haversacks. Lance prepared to prime one of the sticks in the bottom layer of the explosives so the explosion, when it came, would go straight up.

He pulled what looked like a pair of pliers from his pocket, opened the tool, and pierced one of the sticks of C-4, rotating slowly to create a narrow hole. He slid the time fuse into the hollow blasting cap, then crimped its neck and secured the blasting cap in the C-4, unrolling a length of black electrician's tape and taping the deadly package so the device wouldn't fall out of the explosive. When the thing blew, in roughly five minutes, a spark would spit from the igniter into the concave end of the blasting cap, which would in turn create a shaped charge, focusing the explosion in a bubble that would shatter the regeneration center's floors right up through the building and on out the roof. An immense, voracious fireball would incinerate just about everything in the facility, including, Lance thought with satisfaction, the operating suites above his head.

He brushed his hands lightly against one another. He knew the C-4's deadly potential, but he moved deliberately and without panic. It was one of the easiest explosives in the world to work with; in fact, you could even set it on fire, and it would burn, but it would not detonate. In order to blow, it needed the small shock of the blasting cap. And in just a few more minutes, it would have it.

BARBARA LAMAR and Peter Meyer sat in the front row of the Tandy Pavilion, slouched a little in the padded blue leather seats. Barbara had taken off her red-linen jacket; underneath it she was wearing a thin, soft, cream-colored blouse with satin buttons. She had also kicked off her black heels. Peter had abandoned his jacket as well, loosened his tie, and they were near the bottom of the bottle of Chivas they had lifted from the bar just before the caterers packed up and left.

Peter twirled his short glass, expecting by habit to hear the clink of cubes. He had forgotten they were out of ice.

"So why didn't you stay with him?" he asked. They had gotten off on a tangent about travels in Europe and had figured out that they had both spent the same summer in Italy, years ago.

"It would have screwed up everything," she said. "I was just starting medical school. That summer in Europe was a last fling before I settled down for the long haul. It was a great affair and he would have left his wife for me, but I couldn't really see staying in Florence. What would I have done over the years? Get fat eating pasta and gelato? I needed something a little more fulfilling than being the armpiece of some rich Italian count. I'm sure he just got bald and died anyway."

"Your tenderness knows no bounds," said Peter.

"I'm as tender as you are, Congressman," she said sarcastically. "Why don't you show me your soft underbelly?"

"It's not my best feature," Peter said.

"I've been thinking about your features," she said, leaning toward him slightly. "None of them are too bad."

He liked her directness. He looked around the big empty room. Not exactly a private place for two public figures.

"Listen," she said, reading his mind. "I've got a private office already set up over in the center. It wasn't on the public tour earlier, but I think I can arrange a private showing. It's a little more comfortable than this."

"Is anyone over there?" he asked.

"In three weeks there will be a veritable army over there," she said, stumbling ever so slightly over the word veritable. "We've spared no expense on security. With those crazies out there, I wouldn't be surprised at anything, once the center's up and running. But right now all we've got is electronic surveillance, an electrified fence, and a lonely security guard making regular rounds."

"How lonely is he?" Peter asked.

"Not as lonely as you are," she responded. "So wouldn't you like to see it?"

"See what?" he said.

"My office!" she laughed. She picked up the bottle of Chivas and dropped it into her large Armani leather bag on the floor. It sloshed a little.

Peter Meyer laughed too and stood up, pulling her to her feet. "Yes, Dr. LaMar," he said. "I'd like to see it very much."

IN THE EMPTY echoing underground garage, Lance breathed again. He had checked the device three times. It was right, and now the alarm was set. The thing would blow in four more minutes.

Lance turned and trotted across the expanse of the garage, exiting through the doorway to the right of the big doors. He walked briskly up the curving driveway, along the sidewalk, and then used Justin's security card to open the gate at the side entrance to the center. He hoped Justin was getting out according to plan.

The brown Toyota slowed next to the curb. He looked in, and saw that Alex looked like he was about to explode. His eyes were wide, and he was drumming the wheel wildly with his fingers.

I shouldn't have brought him in here, Lance thought. *I should have known he couldn't take it.*

He ran around the front of the car and opened the driver's side door. "Move over," he said.

"I'm supposed to drive," Alex hissed at him.

"I know, but trust me, man," Lance said calmly, noting the seconds ticking by on his watch. "I'll drive."

Alex started to protest, then shut up and scooted across the vinyl seat. Lance got in, started to accelerate, and saw that the traffic light on I Street had turned red.

As they waited for the light, both looked back toward the regeneration center. It looked just as it had when they arrived. The first floor was lit, the second dark except for the glass walkway connecting the center to the hospital. Lance turned back to watch the traffic light, and Alex made a choking sound. Lance looked back again. Two figures were strolling through the lighted walkway.

"No!" Alex said.

"They can't get in," said Lance. "It's locked. They'll just turn around."

The traffic light turned green.

"Pull over!" Alex shouted. Lance eased over to the curb.

Inside the glass tunnel, the figures stopped at the door. One had a big satchel; it was a woman. She reached in her bag and fumbled for something. The man leaned over her, wobbling slightly.

"No! No!" Alex cried again.

Lance looked at his watch. Thirty seconds. "We gotta go," he said.

THE MAN AND WOMAN had turned the big purse upside down and were rummaging through its scattered contents on the floor. As they did so, in the dark on the other side of the door, where no one could see him, Justin Jones was panicking. He had seen the man and woman on the security monitor on his side of the door. They weren't supposed to be there. How was he going to get out? He'd lost track of time, but he figured he still had a minute or so. Enough time to get to another exit. He turned and sprinted down the dark hallway in the opposite direction.

DOWN in the street, Alex watched as the woman in the walkway stood, triumphantly waving a card of some sort in her hand.

"What do we do?" he quavered.

"There's no time to go back," Lance said. "Just think of this as war, 'cause that's what it is. And in war, this kind of stuff happens."

"But we can't just let them get blown up!" Alex cried.

"There's no time," Lance shouted, the tension finally breaking through in his voice. "We've got to get out of here!"

He pulled away from the curb, but the traffic light was red again. A police cruiser pulled up on the opposite side of the intersection and sat facing them, waiting for the light. A thin woman with a huge dog waited on the corner. Lance gritted his teeth, counting the seconds. Up in the glass walkway, the woman unsteadily tried to jam the card into a slot near the secured entrance into the regeneration center.

Just then Alex lost it. Lance saw it coming, but not fast enough. He popped down the automatic locks on the car, but Alex had already yanked up on his door handle and was out and running back toward the center, arms flailing.

Lance jerked the car into park and jumped out to get his friend. His brain counted down, even as he ran . . . three, two, one . . .

The flash was huge, the sound crashing down on top of them. Alex was thrown to the pavement. Lance, tripping, falling, got to him a second later and grabbed him under the armpits, dragging him back toward the car.

As he did so, he could sense, rather than see, the floors of the center thundering down on one another, crashing into the parking garage . . . tons of cement tumbling into the ground . . . shards of glass flying everywhere . . . screaming people on the street . . . smoke . . . flames . . .

Lance threw open the car door and thrust Alex onto the front seat. He was mumbling, and blood was streaming from his head. Lance scrambled around the car, into the driver's seat. He sent the Toyota hurtling away from the curb.

The last thing he saw as he screeched away was the D.C. policeman, out of his car, screaming into his radio, his face a mask of horror.

42

B ERNIE FELT IT before he heard it, a shiver running along the heavy wooden bar, just enough to make the golden fluid in his glass swirl slightly. Then, within seconds, came an enormous jarring thump, like a fist slamming on the bar.

As the rumble echoed in the summer night, people at the bar looked quizzically at one another. A few at tables near the door walked out onto the sidewalk, then shook their heads. Nothing in sight.

Bernie's first thought was the White House. Pointing at the television above the bar, tuned to a Cubs and Cardinals game on ESPN, he shouted at Henry, "Flip to Channel 5!"

The Fox network was first on with the late news at 10:00, so their news team, already set up at the studio, might know something. But the regular programming was still just blathering on. Bernie grabbed his portable phone out of his attache case and dialed 456-1414.

Almost instantly he heard the familiar voice. "White House."

"Bernie O'Keefe just checking in, Mary. Everything okay?"

"Yes sir. We didn't page you, did we?"

"No, no, but give me W-16. Thank you."

359

The Secret Service duty officer answered on the first ring and quickly assured Bernie that everything was secure at 1600 Pennsylvania Avenue. But after volunteering to call the police and find out what was happening, he put Bernie on hold. While he waited for what seemed like minutes before the agent returned to the line, Bernie felt uncharacteristically uneasy.

"It's bad, sir. An explosion of some sort at GW Hospital. The police say a real big blast—looks like a whole wing is gone."

"What wing?"

"The regeneration center, whatever that is. Apparently something new, sir."

"Okay, okay, thanks. No, wait a minute. Call the president and inform him. Tell him I'm on my way back."

Bernie dropped a twenty on the bar and headed for the street, annoyed at himself for letting his driver go back to the motor pool. He didn't like the limousine sitting in front of Kelly's and had assumed he'd have plenty of time to call it back. No time now, though. He'd have to hail a cab.

The sidewalks were packed with people, and the traffic on M Street was bumper to bumper, the usual carnival atmosphere on a summer night in Georgetown. No cabs. Bernie turned right out of Kelly's front door and ran along the crowded sidewalk, jostling people along the way.

At the corner of Wisconsin and M, in front of Nathan's, a couple was just getting out of a yellow cab. Bernie ran toward the taxi, his arms waving, tie flapping. "The White House! This is an emergency!" he shouted. Bernie grabbed the door and jumped into the cab. "The White House!" he repeated.

Traffic was horrible. It took almost twenty minutes to get there. But finally Bernie was being escorted by Agent Ferguson up the main stairway in the executive mansion. The agent knocked on the door of the Lincoln sitting room and they heard the president growl impatiently, "Come in, come in."

Whitney Griswold's tie was loose and he was pacing, hands behind his back, a furious expression on his face. On the ottoman in front of his chair was an open briefing book which Bernie recognized as being from the National Security Council. The rebel government in Nigeria was creating huge problems, withholding oil shipments to Europe; prices were soaring, and the Germans were particularly upset.

"Bernie, they've done it now. Off come the gloves. All the way. Time to knock heads. We've been too easy, soft in fact. They're misreading us if they think they can do this. Blowing up a building ten blocks from the White House! Do we have no intelligence in this government? What in heaven's name are we spending thirty two billion dollars for?"

Bernie had not heard Griswold this upset in a long time. There was a half-finished drink on the table next to his reading glasses. He was not a happy drinker.

Griswold didn't wait for Bernie's answer, since he knew there wasn't one.

"Bernie, call the Pentagon. If we need more troops, let's get 'em. And get on Gineen and Frizzell. I've already talked to Frizzell—told him to kick butt, get those agents out from behind their desks and on the streets. I want those responsible nailed." He turned toward Bernie and pointed. "You understand me? Cordon off this city. Roadblocks. I don't give a rip about all the pussyfooting civil liberties types. Just get 'em. You understand? Get them!"

The president was sizzling, and Bernie realized it was more than the scotch talking. Griswold was taking this as an armed assault. Revolution.

"I'll take care of it, Mr. President," Bernie said. "Don't worry about this. You concentrate on the important things—Nigeria."

Griswold nodded. "Okay, Bernie, you take care of it." He forced a half smile.

BERNIE WENT TO HIS DESK, where for the next several hours he was in almost continuous communication with the bureau, local police, and the attorney general, except for the interruptions from Griswold, who called every thirty minutes. The last call was at 1 :00 A.M., when Bernie could tell he had almost calmed down enough to sleep.

At 2:00 A.M., Bernie called for his car. He needed some rest as well. He stopped in the washroom on his way to the elevator and then threw two Xanax in his mouth. One, he had discovered, didn't do enough.

"Yeah, I'll take care of it," he muttered, shaking his head. "Some job."

43

B EADS OF SWEAT clotted Lance Thompson's lined forehead as he gripped the steering wheel and propelled the car away from the city. Alex slumped in the front seat next to him, moaning, bleeding steadily into the red, sodden wad of paper towels he was holding against the back of his head. It was clear they couldn't make the 9:30 flight to Miami; Alex's head was bleeding too much for them to even think about getting onto a commercial airplane. So they'd have to get to Frank Doggett's and put plan B into effect. But first he had to get Alex stitched up. He knew where he could go for that.

It was a miracle, Lance thought, that they hadn't been challenged. Even as the screams of sirens echoed all over the city, they had careened away from Foggy Bottom, onto Constitution Avenue, and west on Route 66, toward the suburbs.

He tuned the radio to WTOP, the all-news station, as the first breathless reports of the bombing came over the air. "A scene of total devastation," the reporter said, obviously relying on reports coming out over the police radio. "Police and fire personnel are searching the area for casualties. They are also reporting that witnesses saw a brown four-door Toyota sedan near the scene just prior to the bombing . . ."

Lance bit his lip and glanced in the rearview mirror as he exited from Route 66 and made his way toward Falls Church and Daniel Seaton's neighborhood. He turned off the lights as he pulled into the Seatons' driveway, then drove around Mary's mulched flowerbeds at the side of the house and into the grassy backyard. He killed the engine.

Lance ran up three steps to the back door and rapped a few times, then swung it open. The Seatons never locked their doors until they went to bed.

Mary whirled around from the kitchen stove. The kettle was whistling; she was brewing tea.

"Lance! What's going on?"

Daniel rushed through the arched doorway from the living room. The television was on, and Lance could hear snatches of the news reports.

"What have you done?" Daniel stammered, ashen and trembling. "Where's Alex?"

Lance flicked his eyes toward the backyard. "He'll be okay," he said. "Got caught in the flash. We need some bandages. Maybe Mary can sew him up, and then we need to get out of here."

Daniel ran out the back door, and Mary froze, staring at Lance, then turned and ran upstairs. She was back seconds later, a plastic box full of medical supplies in her hands.

Outside, Daniel flung the car door open. His brother's dark hair was thick with blood, and his face was smeared with blood where he had wiped his eyes and forehead with the back of his sleeve. He was conscious, but barely coherent. Daniel ripped a handkerchief out of his jeans pocket and dabbed his brother's face. "Alex!" he cried. "I'm here!"

Alex groaned and looked at his brother. "We did it," he said. "We took it out. I saw it fall. Fire in the night. The walls came tumblin' down."

Daniel looked around the car. The vinyl seats were smeared with blood. *Stupid! Stupid!* he thought. *How did I let them get to this point?*

Mary rushed down the back steps from the kitchen with her medical kit, Lance behind her.

"Alex!" she said. "Let me help you." She caressed his face lightly with her hands, looked into his eyes, felt around his head, and probed the injury. It was a long, slightly curved laceration, an eight-inch slice in the back of his scalp.

"What happened?" she said.

"There was a flash," said Alex. "It knocked me down. I woke up in the car with Lance."

"Concussion, isn't it?" Lance asked Mary.

"I think so," she said. "And he's got a long cut in his scalp; it's pretty deep, I think. But head wounds always bleed like this. Help me get him to the kitchen table. You can't leave here till I sew this up, or he's going to have problems later."

"Just patch him up and get us out of here," Lance said. He and Daniel hoisted Alex up the stairs to the back door.

Daniel closed the kitchen curtains while Mary positioned Alex in a chair facing the table, head forward on his arms. She swabbed his head wound with peroxide and saline solution then popped the plastic off a new Bic razor and quickly, evenly shaved the hair from around the gash. From her kit she took a 10-cc syringe, armed it with a 24-gauge needle, and injected lidocaine into the skin adjacent to the wound.

Alex moaned.

"That will deaden the area," Mary said, placing a comforting hand on his shoulder. "I'll have you fixed up in just a minute."

"Who're you calling?" Daniel asked.

Mary looked up. Lance had pulled a cellular phone from his pants pocket. He jerked his eyes toward the Seatons' kitchen phone. "It's tapped," he said. "I've gotta set something up."

He punched in a number, said simply, "B as in boy," and hung up.

In Leesburg, Frank Doggett sighed heavily and prepared for Plan B

MARY OPENED a small box, pulled out a curved needle, threaded it with a small skein of 5–0 silk that she had stuck in her uniform pocket just last week after she had assisted Dr. Fortney when he stitched up a toddler who had fallen off a playground swing. She had never sutured a wound herself.

Pretend it's counted cross-stitch, she told herself as she plunged the needle into the thin skin of Alex's scalp. The gash was long, but there was no time for small, neat stitches. She tied off the knots and kept going, pulling the wound closed with ten long running stitches. It wasn't a great job, but at least the wound was closed. It would probably heal all right. And Alex's hair would grow back and cover the ugly scar it would become.

Mary smeared Neosporin over the bumpy, stitched cut, then stuck two 4 by 4 bandages over the mess, securing them with several lengths of silk tape. It wasn't exactly plastic surgery, but it would do.

"He's probably got a concussion," she told Lance. "But he should be okay." She thrust two sample bottles of Ceclor into his hand. "These are antibiotics. Make him take two with lots of water every four hours."

"We've got to get out of here," Lance said, pocketing the vials.

"Look," said Daniel, who had hovered and paced while Mary sewed his brother's scalp. "Where are you going? You're not gonna be able to get away. The FBI, the National Guard, the ATF—everybody is mobilizing. The news reports are already talking about a brown Toyota with Virginia plates. Give yourselves up! You've done what you wanted. You took out the center. Thank God no one was killed."

Alex moaned and began to say something, but Lance cut in. "We don't give ourselves up," he exclaimed. "They'll kill us—one way or another—if we do. I've had a plan for months. We have people in place. We can wait this thing out."

Daniel looked at Alex. Mary was talking gently to him now, the way she talked to the children when they were sick. He was looking up at her in the vulnerable, trusting way he had looked up at their mother when they were young. Daniel knew his brother wouldn't last a minute in prison. If he didn't get himself killed first. Lance was probably right. He was trapped.

"Okay," he said. "This isn't right, but you've got to get out of here. God forgive us." He plunged his hand in his jeans pocket and fumbled as he pulled a key off his key ring. "Take my car. Just get out of here."

"Thanks, brother," Lance said.

"You take care of my brother," said Daniel.

He leaned down and put his hands on Alex's shoulders. Mary had wiped Alex's face clean, but the fresh white bandage on his head was already oozing red again. Lance would have to redress the wound when they got wherever they were going.

Mary had fresh bandages in one hand and a big tumbler of orange juice in the other. She handed the gauze to Lance and held the glass against Alex's lips, popping two white tablets on his swollen tongue. "Drink this," she said. Alex tipped his head back like a child and swallowed.

"Alex," Daniel said. "It's time to go with Lance now. Be careful."

He and Lance lifted Alex from the chair, half-carrying him from the kitchen and down the steps. Lance backed the Seatons' white Honda out of the garage, and Daniel gently lowered Alex into the front seat. He pulled the seat belt around him, clicking it into place. "Be careful," he said again. "You know I love you."

Alex looked up at his brother, still dazed. "I'm sorry," he said. "I didn't mean to."

The Honda backed out of the driveway, no lights on, paused, and then roared down the quiet street. The last thing Daniel saw, by the dim street light, was Alex, staring straight ahead.

AS LANCE AND ALEX drew closer to Doggett's Garage, they both slipped into a state of mind that was somewhere past fear.

Lance was back in Baghdad. There, discovery by the authorities would have meant death, and he had thrived on the thrill of eluding them. He felt the same way now. So he kept his foot steady on the accelerator, eating up the dark miles along Route 7 west by staying within the speed limit, using his signals, and behaving like a model driver. He had seen a police car or two in the distance, but the fragmented news reports weren't yet talking about a white four-door Honda sedan. No roadblocks yet. We're gonna make it, he thought.

Alex was in a world of his own. He watched the dark trees rush by in the night, silent, reliving over and over the brilliant flash of the huge fireball, the flying glass, the crash of concrete. Like the end of the world. He still clutched Daniel's handkerchief, wadded and bloodstained, tight in his hand.

When the white Honda pulled into Doggett's Garage in Leesburg, Frank Doggett was ready. Lance jumped out of the driver's seat and into the back; Frank slid behind the steering wheel and swung the car toward Godfrey Field, Leesburg's small municipal airport. The Honda had been in Doggett's driveway for less than fifteen seconds.

At Godfrey, Frank used his keycard to enter the unmanned front security gate. Though the airport was usually quiet at this hour, it was not unusual for private pilots and businessmen to take off at odd hours of the night. Freedom from conventional airline schedules was one of the privileges of private plane ownership.

The Honda crept silently into hangar number two. Frank cut off the engine, and he and Lance jumped out of the car. They guided Alex toward Frank's plane, a Cessna 172. Alex could walk, but he was disoriented—cooperative when they gave him instructions, but unable to focus on the situation unfolding around them.

"The blast knocked his head into the pavement," Lance said quietly to Frank. "But he'll be okay."

The Cessna, built in 1962, had nearly eight thousand hours of flying time on her and was on her fourth engine. The brown seats were cracked, their foamy lining showing between the splits in the leather. The paint, inside and out, was worn, the instrument panels cracked in a few places. It could carry four people, two seats in the front and two in the back. Lance didn't want Alex near the controls, so he strapped him into the right-rear seat.

The two men pushed the chocks away from the three wheels and rolled the small plane out to the taxiway. Frank handed Lance a tiny flashlight and a hand-held Global Positioning System.

"It's all programmed," said Frank. "You stay low, don't fly over the mountains; you're going in between 'em. We don't want you popping up on radar screens if we can help it. I've put in your course; just trust this thing. Don't deviate from the coordinates."

Lance tucked the flashlight under his arm, took the satellite positioning device and the flashlight in his left hand and shook Frank's with his right. Then he swung up into the pilot's seat on the left and shone the tiny light on the control panel. He had flown small surveillance aircraft in the Special Forces; he was familiar enough with the design of the Cessna.

He pulled the knob regulating the plane's fuel mixture, opening it all the way and pumping the throttle several times. Gas flowed into the carburetor. Then he turned the battery switch on, kicking in the plane's electrical system, and pumped the throttle again. He knew Frank had been out here earlier this afternoon, double-checking everything, just in case they had to go to plan B; though the engine was cold, it was priming well.

Lance turned the key to start the engine then looked out the window and down through the struts supporting the wing. He nodded at Frank and saluted. "We'll see you in Costa Rica," Lance called, "if all goes well. Good luck!" Frank nodded, and Lance turned away for a moment to check on Alex. When he looked back, Frank was gone.

The little plane shook and sputtered. The four-cylinder, 145-horsepower engine was screwed on rubber mounts, but they weren't absorbing the shock. The plane's body popped and cracked, rocked and rolled. In the backseat, in spite of his lethargy, Alex's eyes were wide.

"Just relax and stay calm," Lance said. "We're gonna be fine."

Frank was an old pilot of the cowboy school; it didn't surprise Lance that his plane wasn't exactly a smooth ride. But it would get them where they needed to go.

He taxied toward the main runway. The lights were off, but there was enough glow from the moon and the pinkish haze of the distant lights of Washington and Tyson's Corner that he could make out contours and direction. The runway was five thousand feet long, and the little Cessna needed only about eight hundred of those feet to get up.

Lance pushed the knob all the way in. Full throttle, to the fire wall. Due north. He didn't want to get any closer to Dulles Airport, just ten miles to the south. He eased his feet off the brakes and began to roll down the runway, bouncing and jostling as the plane gained speed. The hangars on one side and the woods on the other whooshed by; inside the tiny cockpit, the roaring of the engine and the moaning and creaking of the structure precluded any conversation with Alex, who wasn't talking anyway. At seventy miles per hour, Lance pulled back on the wheel slightly; the wheels lifted, and the small plane was airborne. He did not turn on the transponder, the device at the bottom of the aircraft that would emit an identifying signal for traffic controllers.

Lance exhaled, loving the familiar rush of the plane's transition from ground to air, the freedom of the wind rushing by and the horizon beckoning ahead. At one thousand feet, he banked northwest toward Martinsburg. The landing gear was stationary, so he didn't need to worry about retraction; he made the fuel mixture leaner, but kept the rpms at about twenty-six hundred in order to keep the speed as fast as possible.

They were still below fifteen hundred feet, at the range that air traffic controllers didn't even need to hear from him; local jet traffic came in at five thousand feet.

AT THE WASHINGTON Air Traffic Control center in Leesburg, controller Jerry Leach sat at his Raytheon radar console, sipping from his old "Ollie for Senate" coffee mug. In the northwest quadrant of his 360-degree black screen, a green blip appeared. It was not a commercial airliner, just a small plane heading out of Godfrey and not in the Dulles traffic area. Not that there were many flights coming in or out of Dulles at this hour.

Leach paused for a moment, then flicked his radio switch to the frequency private pilots in the area used most frequently.

"Aircraft off Godfrey Field, please identify yourself," he said.

He waited a few moments, drained some more coffee from his cup, and passed a US Air flight bound for Pittsburgh off to the air traffic controllers at the Cleveland center.

It was quiet. Usually he listened to the radio late at night, but his wife, Holly, had gotten a new set of promotional tapes for the vitamin sales distributorship she had started in their home. He had the cassette player plugged in, ready to go, with tape number one: "Be Well, Breathe Well, Sell Well." Holly thought that after Jerry's retirement the vitamin business might provide some income on the side. As long as she was excited about it, he was willing to go along.

No response from the little plane. That wasn't unusual. Sometimes the private pilots forgot to turn their transponders on or ignored the radio contact with Leesburg if they were headed toward West Virginia. Late-night private planes didn't follow the same technical strictures that bound the commercial pilots, and Jerry didn't blame them. If he was flying late, he probably wouldn't bother with all the bureaucracy either.

Anyway, the plane was small and slow and heading toward Martinsburg. He decided not to worry about it. He took another swig of coffee and hit the tape player's play button.

ALEX'S MOMENTARY FEELING of comfort from Mary's care was long gone. He stared out of the plane's windows in terror. The blue-black ridges of West Virginia were nearing; the plane was too low to go over them, and it was too dark to go between them. His stomach had been clenched ever since the explosion; now the nausea rose into his throat. He leaned forward toward the front seat, bile in his mouth.

Lance looked back for a second. "Don't do it!" he shouted, reaching back and pushing Alex's face to the side. Alex's stomach heaved, and the bitter citrus of the orange juice splashed all over the empty seat next to him.

He wiped his mouth with Daniel's handkerchief and put his head down as near to his knees as he could get it in the tiny space, so he couldn't see.

Lance looked at the dim outline of the mountains. He, too, was disoriented. It had been awhile since he'd flown, but he knew he couldn't trust what he saw. He looked down at the GPS Frank had given him. Arrows on either side of a center line would flash, telling you to adjust to the left or right; when the arrows didn't show, you were right on course. Good thing they'd had Doggett; he had planned this alternate escape as carefully as if it was the primary plan. Doggett had actually flown the route himself in the daylight, weaving through the mountain passes, entering in the correct GPS locations at each point.

Location A-1 was the first, A-2 would be the big turn south, and the others would take them all the way to the destination—ten station readings in all. He could fly blind if he trusted Doggett and this little box with its bleeping light. He did.

According to the chart, the first ridge was twenty-two hundred feet away. Lance knew if he climbed a couple of thousand feet he could clear the ridges easily. But he had no idea if the FBI had by now launched an all-points bulletin or if the FAA had been alerted. He didn't know what was going on. It had been over two hours since the explosion; anything was possible. So he would stay low, trust Doggett's GPS calculations, and wind his way between the mountains out of radar range. It would be pretty hairy, he thought.

Alex still had his head down. His eyes were throbbing, his mouth was sour, his head ached horribly. In his mind was a picture from a movie he had seen years earlier. Sweet Dreams. The story of country singer Patsy Cline, who, with her entire band, had died in a small-plane crash.

The climactic scene kept replaying itself in Alex's mind: Cline and her friends had been laughing; then, suddenly, the plane broke through a cloud and they saw the sheer rock face of the mountain looming before them. Then the impact: The small plane burst into flames. Then silence.

Just like tonight, thought Alex. *The explosion, the flames, the fireball . . . then the silence.*

LANCE FELT the familiar rush in his gut. He looked down at the GPS. The right arrow was flashing; he moved the wheel ever so gently to the left. Coming up on A-1. No radar was going to pick him up here between the mountains. He peered out to the side; it was black out there, but in the darkness he could still sense vague shapes whooshing by in the night. He realized these were pine trees—and they were higher than he was. He was annoyed to see that his hands were trembling. But no arrows were showing. He breathed easier.

Minutes later, he came to point A-2. He rose, banked left, just south of Martinsburg, he figured, and then dropped below twelve hundred feet; they were now in the quiet well of the Shenandoah Valley. He couldn't see, but the GPS was clicking off the points. He was right on course and should be approaching the mowed field where, if Frank had called them in time, friends would be waiting.

The Cessna dropped. Alex still had his head down. For the past half-hour he had been moaning about explosions, Sweet Dreams, Gideon's Torch . . . Lance had ignored him. He opened the fuel mixture, slowly lowered the flaps, and dropped toward the field he could not see. The GPS, A-8, told him it was there, and Lance had learned long ago that equipment was usually more trustworthy than people. Alex was proof of that.

Then he saw them: two tiny, faint lights, below and ahead in the darkness. It was unbelievable. They were there! The green light marking where he needed to touch down, the red one where he needed to stop.

He decreased his speed, the needle on the speedometer dropping alarmingly . . . 100, 90, 80, 70, 60 . . . The little plane would stall around 50. At 60 he flared the Cessna's nose up slightly and let her stall. He had done it a thousand times, but not recently.

But Frank's old plane responded to his touch. He dropped to what he thought was about a foot or two off the ground; no way of telling, really. The speed was still 60 when the plane banged hard against the ground. Lance flew up against the ceiling of the cockpit, and Alex screamed in pain as his head hit the wall. They jostled and hurtled down the expanse of field, plunging and jerking into ruts and running straight toward the second little light in the darkness. Lance held his breath and held on, his thoughts too blurred for prayer. Alex clutched his oozing head and moaned.

The Cessna rolled to a stop, and Lance exhaled, exhilarated. He released his seat belt, opened the tiny door, and leaped to the ground. Ned Keener was running toward him, his flashlight already off. Together they pulled Alex from the plane; then Lance climbed back up and taxied the plane toward the crumbling wooden barn at the end of the field. Ken Jordan had opened the big double doors and was shining his light so Lance could see. He pulled the Cessna into the far corner of the barn where a huge mound of hay bales stood waiting.

Lance jumped down, grasped Jordan's hand, and then ran toward Keener's waiting truck. Alex was already in the middle of the front bench seat, leaning against Ned. Lance climbed in and shut the door, and seconds later they were slowly jostling across the field, heading toward the cabin in the hills.

44

C AMOUFLAGE-CLAD troops with M-16s stood at barricades erected at Washington Circle, Twenty-second Street, and G Street, creating an armed perimeter around George Washington University Hospital and the remains of the regeneration center. Hundreds of students and other area residents stood at the checkpoints, watching the small army of earthmovers, troops, and armored equipment passing through.

The east end of what had been the regeneration center was now a huge mound of jagged, smoking concrete blocks. Metal rods protruded from the moundlike spears. On the west end, there was still some shape to the collapsed structure, with concrete pillars thrusting in the air like smokestacks; the walkway to the hospital was smashed, part of it still dangling in the air.

Giant searchlights suspended from cranes illuminated the entire area as rescue crews began ripping through the deadly mound in search of life. Ambulances, trucks, and army personnel carriers lined the block.

An unshaven Anthony Frizzell arrived at the FBI's command-control trailer just before dawn. He let out a low whistle as he surveyed the damage.

"A real pro. Yes sir, this took a real pro. Army demo man is my guess," he mumbled. Toby Hunter nodded his head, as he did whenever his boss spoke.

Frizzell strode into the trailer where four agents sat at small desks, computers clattering. "Okay, give me everything you know," he barked.

The agents knew what that meant: though members of the press were being held half a block back from the bomb site, the networks would be ravenous for live reports for their 7:00 A.M. broadcasts. If they had anything good, Frizzell would be ready for those morning news show interviews. If there was nothing promising, someone else would do them.

Toby handed Frizzell a small black sack from which the director extracted a mirror and an electric razor.

"Excuse me," Frizzell said to one agent as he leaned past him to plug it in.

Over the buzz of the razor, the agents gave their report. A bystander had given the FBI a description of a car seen leaving the scene after the explosion; it corroborated what the D.C. policeman had seen. Despite checkpoints around the city and officers patrolling the major arteries, however, the car had not been located.

"I already know that," Frizzell snapped, shaving his right cheek.

The agents continued. There were still no leads, but the bureau and local police were "fine-combing" the area. The perpetrators would never be able to escape the net. In an hour or two, bureau operations would print out a complete list of potential suspects. Agents would "visit" them, and it would be fairly quick work to determine who could not be accounted for. The director stopped shaving. Toby knew what this meant. Someone else would brief the media.

But the most alarming news involved persons not yet accounted for who might have been victims of the bombing. Congressman Peter Meyer had last been seen by a member of the hospital cleaning crew heading toward the glass walkway connecting the hospital to the regeneration center. His wife had informed agents that her husband had not yet arrived home.

Frizzell rolled his eyes. What else was new?

And, said the agents, Dr. Barbara LaMar was also missing.

ABOUT 5:00 A.M., a rescue worker found in the collapsed walkway part of a human hand, blackened and shredded by the blast. Two fingers were wholly intact, with long nails that had been painted with enamel, probably once red.

By 6:00, more remains had been discovered. No definitive IDs yet, but preliminary reports suggested that the blast might have claimed at least three victims, most likely Meyer, LaMar, and the security guard on duty at the center.

Frizzell called Emily Gineen, who called Bernie O'Keefe. He was groggy but alert enough to groan loudly at the grim news—news that was certain to inflame Whitney Griswold. Now, on his watch, a congressman had been killed.

Frizzell was not pleased either. Not because of any personal love for Meyer; Congress would be better off without him. But unless the bureau got the bombers within, say, a week, Frizzell thought, his job would be on the line. No time to mess around.

"Assemble the press at the west corner of Twentieth Street," he ordered. Then he turned to Toby. "Have the agent in charge of D.C.—Duffy—brief them. Short, sweet, to the point. Assure them the bureau will get those responsible. 'The director has ordered a nationwide manhunt,' et cetera, et cetera—you know what to tell them, Toby. Get to it."

Seconds later, the red phone rang, the direct line from the bureau's command center. It was the assistant director of operations.

"Good news, Chief," he told Frizzell. "Informant has finally checked in. It's Lance Thompson—the black guy we've been worried about, ex-Special Forces—and Alex Seaton. We've got an 'all points' out on these two. We'll get 'em."

"You listen to me," Frizzell interrupted. "Get those guys and get them now. Shake every one of their buddies loose. Somebody knows where they're hiding. Use whatever force you need. Just get 'em."

DANIEL SEATON sat at the kitchen table, drinking another cup of coffee. It all seemed like a bad dream, but his aching eyes and jumpy stomach attested to the realities of the night. After Alex and Lance had sped away into the darkness, he and Mary had sponged Alex's blood off their kitchen table, put away the medical supplies, and drunk a cup of tea while they figured out what to do next. There weren't any answers. In the end, Mary had collapsed into bed, exhausted.

Daniel had gone into each of his children's bedrooms, tenderly tucking the covers around Abigail, Dan, and Mark, and marveling, as always, at their absolute, trusting abandon as they slept, their small, warm bodies sprawled freely in their beds. He bent and kissed Abby, and she rustled for a moment, half-awake.

"Daddy, where's Kensington?" she asked. Daniel reached under the comforter and pulled out the well-worn brown plush bear. "He's right here, honey," he said. "You go back to sleep."

Now, just before seven o'clock, the children were still sleeping as he downed three extra-strength Tylenol with his third cup of coffee. Mary was downstairs again, and the two of them moved into the living room and flicked on the *Today* show.

It's ironic, Daniel thought. *I'm tuning in to national television to see if my brother made it out of town. How did it come to this?*

The camera zoomed in on Rockefeller Center, and anchor Rick Smith's voice was more somber than usual as he led with the morning's headlines.

"A huge explosion engulfed the soon-to-be-opened regeneration center in Washington, D.C., late last night, totally destroying the building," he announced. "The structure, which was due to open in September, was thought to be empty at the time of the explosion. But as investigators sifted through the rubble early this morning, they discovered two victims killed in the blast. These have now been identified as the center's executive director, Dr.

Barbara LaMar, and Congressman Peter Meyer. The building's security guard is still missing. Federal investigators are moving quickly to apprehend suspects. For more on this tragic story, we'll go live now to . . ."

"Oh, no!" Mary gasped, clutching her hands to her face.

Daniel felt as if someone had kicked him in the stomach, and tears stung the back of his eyes. *How could this have happened? Lance and Alex didn't say anything about anyone being in the building . . . why would a congressman be there at night?* His thoughts swirled, and he reached out for Mary. They huddled on the sofa, holding on to each other like children.

Suddenly, the doorbell rang. Daniel jumped, first worrying out of habit that it would wake the children, then moved toward the door with an awful sense of foreboding. He opened the door and saw four somber men standing on their small front porch.

"Good morning," said one of the men in the center. "I'm Carl Pratt, FBI." He flipped open a wallet and dangled a laminated card where Daniel could see it. "Are you Daniel Seaton?"

Daniel nodded, his throat dry. "Come in," he croaked. Mary was standing behind him, her hand on his shoulder. "This is my wife, Mary." He held open the screen door awkwardly, and Pratt and one of the men entered the living room. The other two men stayed on the front porch, like sentries.

"Please sit down," Mary said, gesturing toward the sofa. It was amazing, she thought, how social conventions still took over, even in the midst of chaos.

"Thank you," said Pratt. "We have a few questions for you, and they will necessitate your coming with us. Both of you."

"What about our children?" Mary asked. "They're sleeping upstairs."

"I'd suggest you call a neighbor or family member, ma'am. We'll need you for several hours."

Just then Daniel heard a familiar thump on the stairs and looked up to the landing. Abigail sat on the top stair, her hair tousled and Kensington Bear clutched under one arm.

"What's happening, Daddy?" she said.

Before Daniel could answer, there was a rap on the front door and one of the agents stuck his head in to address Pratt.

"Sir, we've found something in the garage we think you ought to see."

AFTER THE ATTORNEY general's call with the news from Frizzell, Bernie O'Keefe put the phone back in its cradle and rubbed both hands over his aching forehead. He must wake up, he thought. A congressman dead. He fumbled for the clock. 6:15. In fifteen minutes, Griswold would be on his infernal contraption in the White House catacombs. He had to get the information to him before he saw it on the 7:00 news.

Bernie stumbled only once on his way to the bathroom, when he almost tripped on his bathrobe wadded up on the floor. The throbbing over his eyes was intense; it seemed to have gotten much worse lately. Two ibuprofen and one Xanax would gently ease him back to the world of the living.

The hot shower helped too, and with surprising speed, he was dressed and downstairs in his library, waiting for his limousine, which he had summoned to come early. This library could be such a handsome room, he thought distractedly, if he could ever unpack. Every wall was floor-to-ceiling bookshelves and paneling. He ran his hand over the open-grained oak. It felt strong, reassuring.

Then he turned and faced the bay windows that looked out over the front yard, a small patch of grass boxed by a Victorian iron fence. He imagined what this room had been like when the man who sold it to him, a lawyer, lived here. Full of wonderful rich books, a great place to think about cases and arguments.

Bernie checked his watch. 6:50. Thank goodness Griswold was so predictably punctual; he picked up the direct line to the White House switchboard and asked for the president. Bernie figured he would just about be stepping out of the shower after his workout and Juan would bring him the phone.

Two minutes later Griswold came on the line. "Hey, Bernie, I'm dripping wet. What's up now?"

Your blood pressure is about to be, Bernie thought. He briefed the president in his most matter-of-fact voice.

Griswold instructed him to be in the Oval Office with Robbie at 8:00 sharp and to have the attorney general on standby. He sounded calm and deliberate. But Bernie knew this was not a good sign. When Griswold was really angry, he spoke more slowly in a voice lower than normal, carefully measuring words, carefully showing that he was absolutely in control.

AT 7:59, Bernie arrived at the staff entrance of the Oval Office, with Robbie a second or two behind him. They were nodded in by the Secret Service agent.

Bernie was surprised to see Griswold in shirt sleeves—uncharacteristic informality for this office. His face seemed somewhat flushed, as it often was after exercise, but he looked warmer than usual. Bernie knew his old friend well. Beneath the calm surface, he suspected, was a frothing caldron.

Griswold was reading the news summary but looked up, half-smiled, and motioned them into the straight-backed chairs on either side of the desk.

"Well, gentlemen, we have quite a situation on our hands. I assume you've gathered your thoughts as to what we should say. That's our first order of business, since Caroline tells me the press room is a madhouse; the animals there are all very restless in their cages. So, Robbie, you go first . . ."

"Yes sir. I'm of the opinion, Mr. President, that you need to be seen as in immediate and complete control. Reassure people that there is no cause for panic. I think you should come out to the press room at 10:00 and make a brief statement. We've already been assured the nets will carry it live."

Griswold's eyes pierced laserlike through Robbie, but his voice remained calm. "Let people know the president is right on top of things, is that it, Robbie?"

"Yes, sir. Caroline agrees, by the way."

"And I should explain," the president continued calmly, "how

five thousand federal agents and ten thousand National Guardsmen could not keep some jackass terrorist from blowing sky-high
a huge building built with millions of federal tax dollars not ten
blocks from the White House, and then they threw in a congressman for good measure. In control, did you say, Robbie?
Who, may I ask, is in control of this government?"

"Well, sir, the polls tell us the people need—"

"No, no, I've thought this over. You're overexposing me, Robbie,
and it's going to hurt my credibility. What about you, Bernie?
You want to trot me out to the cameras as well, I suppose?"

Bernie was about to answer when to his relief Juan came in
with a pot of coffee and three cups on a silver tray. At the same
moment, the intercom rang.

"No one is to interrupt here." Griswold was plainly irritated.
"I told Susan . . . yes . . . oh, yes, yes, . . . yes dear . . ."

Griswold stood and turned to look out the window while he
listened to the only person who could interrupt matters of state,
his wife.

"Yes, dear, I agree with the Secret Service. Tell Elizabeth she
shouldn't go . . . Is that so? Are they sure?"

As he began to pace, the phone cord slid under the saucer. Robbie
saw it happening but couldn't move fast enough. With a snapping
motion, the cord flipped the coffee and china into the air, and they
crashed down on the desktop. Griswold jumped at the crash and
the fact that hot coffee had splattered all over his back.

"Ahhhhhh," he screamed into the phone. "No, no, Anne, I'm
fine. Just spilled my coffee."

Bernie was out of his chair immediately, rescuing brownstained
papers on the president's desk. Griswold was leaning over the
desk when Robbie came around behind him and started rubbing his handkerchief on the president's backside, blotting the
coffee that had stained the seat of his tan, worsted suit pants.
Griswold, startled, swung around and almost knocked Robbie
over. Juan came running with towels and clutched the Nigerian
briefing book marked "President's Eyes Only." Griswold, still
trying to talk to his wife, grunted, "I'll take that."

The whole scene was enough to test even the sturdiest person's self-control. Griswold, Bernie could see, was about to lose his.

He hung up the phone. "My wife just told me that the bureau has identified the bombers—came over ABC a few minutes ago. Good thing Anne was watching television. Otherwise, I suppose, I would never have known. And my daughter is being told she can't go to school because the Secret Service thinks it is unsafe. Imagine that."

Griswold scowled, cursing as he sat down, then bolted upright again. "Seat's wet." He stared at Robbie and Bernie for a moment, then called for his valet. "Juan. Bring in a banana, no three bananas." Bernie and Robbie exchanged glances.

"If we're going to preside over a banana republic, we might as well eat bananas." Griswold laughed loudly.

"Bernie," Griswold stood behind his desk chair, pointing. "No more excuses. I want these guys. Get 'em. You tell Gineen and Frizzell that their jobs are on the line here. I want them to get these killers and get them fast. Twenty-four hours. No excuses."

"Yes sir," Bernie replied quickly. He had never seen Griswold this uptight, not even the time he thought Anne was on to one of his weeknight dalliances in New Haven. The stress was clearly affecting him.

"You see, Bernie, this is war. There are people determined to destroy this presidency. We are under attack, and blood is flowing. Their blood must flow too."

Bernie shouldn't have said anything, but he couldn't resist. "We are not at war with our own people, for heaven's sake. We're talking about a few criminals here, sir."

"What do you want, men with AK-47s running through the streets? That would be cleaner and easier. This is guerilla warfare—harder to fight, but it's warfare. Don't think it's not, Bernie."

"And Robbie," Griswold turned to his chief of staff coldly, "this president is not going to that press room. Why don't you go and face the lions in there? Do I have to do everything around here myself?"

Griswold shook his head, clutched his hands behind his back, and walked toward the french doors leading to the rose garden. The summer sun streamed into the room. For a moment he was silent, as if deep in thought. Robbie and Bernie sat quietly. Then Bernie spoke.

"Well, sir, every president has moments like this. It's an awesome weight on your shoulders. No one knows."

"That's it, Bernie. That's certainly it. No one knows. What a mess. And these terrorists—they're trying to destroy us. We have to stiffen up." He was pacing once more. "Nobody knows," he said. It seemed like minutes before he spun around and walked toward his desk.

"Well, gentlemen, it's clear then. Caroline will brief the press with the latest information. Advise them that the president is fully informed and in constant touch with the attorney general . . . that we will enforce the law to the fullest . . . and oh, yes, some nice words about Peter Meyer . . . now there's a challenge for you," Griswold chuckled. "What can we say? 'Crooked as a corkscrew, so we'll screw him into the ground at Arlington Cemetery.'" The three men laughed shallowly.

"And, somebody, please make sure Caroline explains that I'm in meetings regarding Nigeria. Does anyone realize what a madman we're dealing with in General Haoud? Holding Europe hostage, that's what he's doing. Crazy people in Nigeria and on the streets of Washington. No difference. The president has to be firm . . . anything else?"

Griswold grinned as his two aides nodded and headed for the door.

Robbie walked straight to the press room to give Caroline her instructions. His head still throbbing, Bernie was relieved just to be in the corridor.

He stopped for a moment and stared into the Roosevelt room, serene and quiet. He felt rotten; and now, for the first time, he was worried about his friend.

Bernie looked at the massive painting of Teddy Roosevelt charging the hill at San Juan. *Presidents had power then*, he thought. *The nation was small. Cohesive. Presidents could really lead back then.*

You couldn't do that anymore. People thought the president, the government, had so much power, but it was all smoke and mirrors, Bernie said to himself. Oh, you could make laws and issue statements and tell people you were going to enforce the law, but you couldn't do anything about chaos in the streets—let alone influence what people talked about over their breakfast tables in the morning. And it was those tens of millions of little decisions that ordinary people made that determined the habits and dispositions and decisions that defined a nation.

So what's the use? he thought, then caught himself. He couldn't afford to fall into another downward spell this morning. He'd better get another pill when he got to his office.

"COULD YOU PASS ME one of those jelly doughnuts?" Paul Vincent asked. He was sitting on his desk at the *Washington Post*, a cellular phone cradled on one shoulder; he was on hold, waiting for a friend who worked in George Washington Hospital's pathology department. "Raspberry, not the grape."

Jeanne Jasper fished a fat doughnut out of the white cardboard box and handed it to him on a paper napkin. They were both a little punchy; neither had gotten much sleep last night. The entire newsroom had scrambled madly to get the bombing on the front page of the final edition, but facts had been sketchy. Today they could start playing the story out with as many gory details as possible.

"Meyer's wife didn't even realize he was missing," Jeanne said to Paul, biting into her second doughnut and spurting red jelly onto her napkin. "Evidently it wasn't too unusual for him to stay out rather late. Like all night. Pressing congressional business, you know."

"Well, if he was pressing with Barbara LaMar, he wasn't the first," Paul said. "She's pressed half of Capitol Hill."

"Now, let's not exaggerate," said Jeanne. "She was a woman of principle. She only engaged in public relations with people who held purse strings."

"Barry's checking into the pathology reports," Paul said, nodding toward the phone perched on his shoulder. "They're still doing tests at the morgue, but it looks like LaMar and Meyer were both pretty pickled by the time of the explosion. Their blood alcohols were over the top. They were feeling no pain."

"That's good," Jeanne said. "From what I gather, there wasn't much of them left."

"Nope. But it's too bad for Meyer. He's going to get dissected all over the place. We were already starting to poke around into some of his campaign financing. Seems like his relationship with the regeneration center and some of its backers was ever so slightly incestuous."

"It'll be a great story," Jeanne said, popping the last bite of doughnut into her mouth. "It's got it all. Sex. Violence. Mysterious terrorists. Washington powerbrokers. Murky financial wheeling and dealing. And a mourning widow who just happens to be a federal judge."

45

THE DAY AFTER the bombing, FBI teams rapped on the front doors of anti-abortion activists in Pensacola, Wichita, Chicago, Minneapolis, Tacoma, Portland, and Los Angeles. Some of those targeted had been involved with civil disobedience activities in the past; others were simply contributors to mainstream groups such as Americans United for Life and the National Right to Life.

In most cases, agents found their quarry at their breakfast tables, groggily listening to news of the bombing; many were bundled off for interrogation in their pajamas. Plain-clothes personnel stayed behind to search activists' homes, dredging up everything from computer files to study notes in people's Bibles.

Meanwhile, local phone company records had been requested, bank records subpoenaed, passports seized, and neighbors questioned about suspicious meetings or behavior. Nearly a hundred people were taken in for questioning.

In Falls Church, Virginia, agents were absolutely tight-lipped with the media regarding the arrest of Daniel Seaton and the search of his home. Mary Seaton had been detained for six hours then released to care for her children; Daniel was now being held without bail at the Arlington County Jail.

Amy O'Neil, Mark Demmers, and several other Networkers were questioned for hours by the FBI. After determining they knew nothing about the bombing, agents released them. Amy returned to her congressional office to find her desk cleaned out and her personal possessions in a cardboard box by the door. The congressman would not see her.

Shaken, Amy called her parents in California; her mother flew to Washington the next day to help her pack her things and come back home.

In Leesburg, agents discovered Daniel Seaton's white Honda in Frank Doggett's garage, but Frank and Ida Doggett were nowhere to be found. All-points bulletins had been issued for Lance Thompson and Alex Seaton as well as the Doggetts, and their pictures were being shown on special news bulletins and hourly newscasts.

At the site of the explosion, agents continued sifting through the rubble of the regeneration center, reading the telltale residue. Twelve hours after the blast, the experts—many of them veterans of the World Trade Center bombing investigation—knew roughly the make of the van that had housed the explosives, the approximate amount of explosives used, and the fact that the blast had been caused by military-issue C-4, a high explosive with medium-to high-range brisance favored by the army.

Agents were dispatched to investigate army installations on the East Coast, starting with those within a day's drive of Washington.

Friaay, June 5
Arlington County Jail
Mary Seaton sat nervously at the cubicle in the visiting room, perched on the edge of an orange plastic chair. She had been patted down by a female officer and scanned with a hand-held metal detector before she entered the main part of the jail. Now she had nothing with her but her driver's license in her jeans-skirt pocket and a crayoned sign the children had made for their

father. She wasn't allowed to give it to Daniel, she had been told, but she would be permitted to hold it up to the glass partition separating them.

She looked up at the big clock on the cinder-block wall, angrily coveting the minutes ticking by; she would have only ten minutes' visiting time, and they still hadn't even brought him out from the cell. Then she heard the far door on the prisoners' side of the partition opening; a bulky officer held it open while Daniel shuffled through awkwardly.

Standing up so she could peer over the waist-high counter in her cubicle, she could see that his legs were manacled, each ankle wound with a thick circlet of steel and bound together on a three-foot length of chain. He wore an ill-fitting, bright-orange, one-piece jumpsuit. The suit and the manacles made him look like every piece of television footage she had ever seen of serial killers. It was unbelievable.

I mustn't let him see me angry, Mary thought. *There's time for that later. I need to be absolutely positive, so I don't add to the struggles he's already going through.*

Mary smiled brightly and stood as Daniel shuffled toward her. She stretched both of her arms wide, as if to hug him, then sat down while the guard assisted him into the plastic seat on the other side of the glass.

Daniel nodded toward her, and they simultaneously picked up the black telephones hanging on the partition wall. She knew she had to keep the conversation as ordinary as possible; the guards were watching them carefully, and agents were probably listening in on the telephone connection.

"Daniel, I love you so much! Are you all right?" she whispered into the phone, willing warmth and encouragement into his ear.

He smiled, looking at her carefully and taking in her dark shining hair, her steady gray eyes, the color in her cheeks. "I'm fine," he said. "I'll never complain about your cooking again, though. You are an absolute Julia Child compared to the chefs who concoct my prison cuisine."

She laughed. "Thanks for the encouragement."

"How are the children doing?" he asked quietly.

"They're doing fine," she said quickly. "They miss you, and they keep asking when Daddy is coming home. I keep telling them that it will be soon, that Daddy has done nothing wrong."

He raised his eyebrows, and she kept going.

"They drew you this picture. The officers wouldn't let me give it to you, but can you see it?" She held the drawing up to the glass, which had thin gray wires woven between its double thickness.

Daniel smiled as he looked at the crayoned field of green, the gray castle—their conception of the jail, he assumed—and the bright yellow-and-orange butterflies escaping near the top turret window.

"Tell them it's beautiful," he said. "I can see they all worked very hard on it."

Mary hesitated. "Otherwise, things are pretty quiet at home without you. There's not much to tell. We haven't heard anything from anyone . . . people from the church have been really kind, though, bringing meals over and helping with the kids—stuff like that."

Daniel watched her eyes. So Alex was still out there somewhere. He cleared his throat. "Please tell everyone hello. Tell them I'm doing fine, and I hope I'll be home soon—as soon as these gentlemen decide they've extended their hospitality to me long enough." He nodded toward the officers standing against the wall.

He reached his hand up to the glass, and Mary put her right hand up as well, so they were palm to palm, separated by the wall of glass. "I love you so much," he said.

"I love you too," said Mary. "Please don't worry about us; we're doing fine. We pray for you all the time, and we know you'll be home soon."

Friday, June 5
The National Cathedral

Judge April Meyer took a deep breath to compose herself as the long black limousine pulled into the circular drive in front of the National Cathedral. Her chin-length dark hair was streaked with gray, and deep lines etched her cheeks and forehead. In her black knee-length suit she looked as severe as she did in her usual black calf-length robes. But today she didn't have on the tortoiseshell half-glasses she usually wore on the bench. And though she had taken more care than usual with her hair and makeup, she looked exactly how she felt: exhausted, embarrassed, and angry.

It was one thing for Peter to betray their marriage in private. But for him to go out like this, drunk on his butt with a bottom-feeder like Barbara LaMar . . . it was absolutely humiliating, and she had no recourse. Before, she could just hide in her work, ignore it, get on with her own life . . . but now their private lives were all over the front pages. It hurt.

She took her sunglasses out of her purse, put them on, lifted her chin, and swung out of the limo. Her younger brother, John, and her mother were with her. John took her elbow to escort her up the warm white steps to the cathedral's magnificent center doorway. The limo behind them had pulled up as well; in it were Peter's parents and his two brothers, clones of her husband in looks and attitude. She would rather not deal with them today if she could help it.

Mourners on either side cleared a path for her. Looking slightly to the left and right behind her dark glasses, she could see people's faces. Some looked sorry for her. A few wore small, tucked-in smiles, the catty look she had seen so many times at cocktail parties when Peter was off somewhere in a corner with the hostess or some other man's wife. But most of the faces were reserved, respectful, lined with genuine shock. Whoever he had been in life, Peter had gone to a hideous death, his life blown away at the most casual, unexpected moment. It was everyone's nightmare.

The nightmare was evident, too, in the extraordinary security around the building. As they pulled up in front, she had noticed agents armed with automatic weapons. Metal detectors had been set up for all the mourners to pass through, and there were Secret Service personnel everywhere.

Just inside the door, waiting for her, was her escort, John Edward Stevenson, chief justice of the Supreme Court, his silver hair shining in the morning light. She took off her sunglasses, smiled at him, and took his arm.

As they moved forward, she felt an odd echo of her own wedding, when she had held her father's arm and walked the long aisle to meet Peter, so handsome, smiling, waiting for her by the altar. She looked down the immense path of marble before her. Peter was at the end of the huge cathedral, waiting for her again. Except this time he was in a long, burnished box, closed forever, hidden by huge sprays of yellow roses. Her steps faltered, and Edward patted her hand on his arm.

She looked up. The rose windows on the right side of the massive church flooded warm color on the stone pillars that marked her path toward the front. Magnificent strains of Bach floated from the organ pipes, echoing off the vaulted roof.

Suddenly there was a slight commotion at the front. With so many people pressed into the rows of wooden chairs on either side of the center aisle, it was hard to tell at first what was happening. Then she could see the Episcopal bishop of Washington waiting in the front. His head turned toward a swirl of Secret Service agents entering from the side, and in their midst she could see the tall form of J. Whitney Griswold.

The president moved to the front row, agents fanned out around him, and then he turned and smiled at her, holding out his hand as she moved toward the empty seat next to him and the first lady. Griswold smiled gently at her and embraced her quickly. April clasped the president's warm hand.

"How are you doing, April?" he asked quietly.

She paused and looked up into his blue eyes. "I don't know, Mr. President," she said.

"These are strange times," he said. "What happened to your husband is absolutely horrible, and Anne and I both want you to know you have our deepest sympathies."

The Bach prelude swelled to its final chords and the bishop moved toward the pulpit. The television cameras, positioned next to the great pillars at the front, rolled as the service began.

Griswold leaned toward her again, and the cameras caught the image for the evening news: the president of the United States whispering encouragement to the grieving widow.

"You have my word," he told her in a low voice, "we are doing everything in our power to obliterate the animals who did this."

46

A LEX SEATON gingerly touched the back of his head. Little bristles were sprouting where Mary had shaved him. They were immensely irritating. Lance had changed his bandage several times since they had arrived at the little mountain cabin, but now they had run out of bandages, and Lance had told him the air on his wound would be good for him. "Just don't touch it!" he'd commanded, as if Alex was three years old. Alex had tried not to touch it, but the bumpy scab and prickly hairs felt so strange that his hand kept straying back there, as if his fingertips would help it heal.

The three days he and Lance had been in the cabin might as well have been three weeks. The cottage had a small front porch with a cord of firewood stacked near the door, a small living/dining room dominated by a large fireplace, a cramped kitchen with a door to the back, and two narrow bedrooms, one with a double bed, the other a single. Ken Jordan had been kind enough to stock the dressers with a few changes of clothing for each of them, and though the pants were too big and the legs too short for Alex, he cinched his belt tight and wore them up around his waist.

"You look like Jethro Clampett," Lance had told him.

There was also a bathroom with a shower and a medicine cabinet stocked with a few essentials—toothpaste, brushes, soap, shampoo. Old-fashioned braided-cotton rugs covered most of the floors, except in the kitchen, and there were several plaid easy chairs in the living room, along with large woven baskets stuffed with dozens of back issues of *Field and Stream* and *Popular Mechanics*. Mounted on the wall was a gun rack holding two 12 gauge over-and-under shotguns, a .30 caliber high-powered hunting rifle, and a smaller caliber rifle.

The place was certainly cozy enough, if you were here for a quiet weekend getaway. But it was beginning to drive Alex crazy. Neither he nor Lance had been outside since they were dropped off in the middle of the night after their hair-raising flight through the mountains. And after dark they dared not use the lamps, lest someone notice that the old cabin was inhabited.

The kitchen was stocked with cans of pork and beans, corned beef hash, green beans, corn, and, fortunately, a can opener. There was also an industrial-size box of peanut butter crackers and a case of Coke. Aside from that, they had the metallic-tasting tap water, an old green teakettle, and some dusty Red Rose tea bags. Alex longed for a pitcher of orange juice.

The time passed slowly.

For his part, Lance had settled into his soldier routine. He did pushups three times a day on the living room floor, ran in place, and had read almost every magazine in the cabin already, sitting erect in one of the easy chairs, absorbing them as if preparing for an exam. At night he paced the cabin like a sentry, checking doors, adjusting curtains, staring out into the darkness beyond the windows. Alex didn't know when he slept.

Alex himself slept a lot. Maybe it was the concussion; or perhaps it was an automatic response to the confinement. His dreams were consistent and strange: replays of the explosion, the quick visit at his brother's house, the plane escape. He kept Daniel's handkerchief underneath his pillow. It was a blood-stained mess, but it felt like a physical link with his brother and the faraway world of normal life.

Their only connection to the outside world was a radio, and they left it on all day. The news reports were full of the bombing investigation, the search for the perpetrators, and the arrest of dozens of suspected conspirators. They knew Daniel's car had been found at Doggett's Garage, but it sounded like Frank and Ida had slipped through the net somehow. Hopefully they had made it to Costa Rica.

They knew, too, that Mary had been questioned and released. And they knew that Daniel was in the Arlington County Jail, held under highest security. Alex stared into the empty fireplace, wondering how Daniel felt, how the other inmates and guards were treating him, and thinking about how much he must miss his family.

If it hadn't been for his injury, Alex thought, they would never have had to involve Mary and Daniel. They would have made the 9:30 flight to Miami and caught the next morning's flight to Costa Rica with the phony passports from an old friend of Doggett's in Baton Rouge. They even had backup fake passports, and the eyeglasses, scissors, a Clairol hair-coloring kit, and other materials necessary to alter their appearances accordingly.

Unknown to Alex, Lance also had two military-issue handguns and ammunition, along with several thousand dollars folded into the compartment in the thick belt around his waist.

Now, on the third afternoon after the bombing, they were sitting in the kitchen, listening to the little radio. Thank goodness they had electricity, Alex thought. He dipped his tea bag into one of the mugs he had found in the cabinet. The brownish water was faintly tea-flavored. Trying to conserve, he had already used the bag three times.

"Don't touch your head!" Lance snouted suddenly. Alex jumped, and tea sloshed on the old wooden table.

"Sorry," he said."I can't help it."

"You can help it. If you break open those stitches, you'll be sorry."

Alex fished the bag from his weak tea, then turned the volume up a little on the radio. "Congressman Peter Meyer has been laid to rest following services at the National Cathedral. . . ."

"Turn it down!" Lance hissed at him, grabbing the radio away. "You don't seem to understand what's going on here. No one must hear us, no one must see us, no one must know we're here, or we could end up in prison for a very long time—if not death row. You think you feel penned up in here? Just think about what prison is like!"

"I have been," Alex said, spilling his tea again as he raised the cup to his lips. "How can I not think about it? Daniel is sitting in prison right now. Because of us."

"He's not in prison. He's in jail. There's a difference."

Lance looked at Alex's thin, pale face. He never should have been on this mission. James had been right. A long time ago he had warned Lance. "Just use military men," he'd said. "You can't expect a civilian to be able to handle a special op like this." Alex was falling apart in front of him, looking to Lance for every move, totally dependent, thinking too much, missing too much, shaking too much.

Well, it adds to the challenge, he thought. *People are working on it, and if we can get out of here, we're doing all right.*

Alex broke into his thoughts. "It's our fault," he said again. "Daniel never wanted it to come to this. He got frustrated, but he never wanted violence. And we didn't mean for anyone to get killed. But now he's sitting there getting questioned every day about things he doesn't know anything about."

"That's good," Lance broke in.

"Why are you so cold?" Alex exploded. "This isn't Vietnam or Iraq or some military mission. This is my brother!"

"Look," Lance said. "I can't expect you to understand, but you've broken the first rule of military engagement. You've gotten personally involved because somebody in your family is hurting. Don't you remember everything you were saying a month ago? This is war! You said it didn't matter if you were killed; we had to take out the regeneration center. We had to save babies from execution. And we did it!"

"So get hold of yourself. Daniel is a grown man. He can take care of himself. He doesn't know anything. They'll have to release him eventually. Don't worry about him. Right now we've got to concentrate on hanging tight here and then getting ourselves away from the heat. It's all going to be fine."

Alex stared at him, biting his lip. He reached up and probed the back of his head again then looked at his watch. Four o'clock. Time for news on the hour. Time to hear how his brother was doing.

47

T HE DAY AFTER the bombing, Emily announced that there would be a crisis management team meeting at 7:00 every morning. This morning, FBI Director Frizzell had done most of the talking as the assistant attorney general for the criminal division, Frizzell's two operational directors, the head of the office of legal counsel, Paul Clarkson, and Emily listened.

Frizzell always managed to project an air of authority. Part of it was his dress—the trademark blue pinstripe suit, heavily starched white shirt, bright silk tie, and pocket handkerchief to match. And part of it was the intensity of his mannerisms and expression, in spite of the fact that today he had little new information to impart.

When he had completed his briefing, Emily thanked him, then addressed the group. "I need not remind you that bringing these guilty parties to justice is the very highest priority of this government." Her voice sounded tired and, Paul thought, she seemed distracted.

"Thank you, gentlemen," she said with a slight wave as she assembled her notes. The group left, but Paul remained.

"Are you all right, Emily?" he asked.

"Of course. Why would you ask?" she snapped, then immediately caught herself. "Yes, just fine. I'm sorry, Paul, I just haven't had much sleep."

"The FBI will find them. Don't worry. Frizzell will make sure of that. His whole career's at stake."

"No, no, it's not that. I'm sure they will. But what's happening to this country? There's such anger and hatred and fury. The newscasters are foaming at the mouth. People on the streets are mad. It's so ugly out there."

Emily was standing behind her chair at the end of the massive table. Paul knew she had an 8:00 meeting scheduled, and she didn't look in any mood for long philosophical discussions. But he thought it worth a try.

"I think we're going at it all wrong, Emily. The answer isn't troops and cops; it's making people believe that the system works. I know I sound like a broken record, but it's a moral problem. People don't know what to believe in—or even what's appropriate."

"Appropriate? Bombing? Don't give me that stuff, Paul," she cut him off, her eyes cold. "Don't stand there and tell me moral values, or lack of them, even excuse or justify this kind of thing. We're talking about people blowing up hospitals, killing people. This is anarchy—revolution. And if we don't stamp it out, this society will come apart." She paused, took a breath. "And that's what these people really want—these anti-abortion terrorists. Your people, right? They want to bring the government down. Admit it."

Before he could reply, she shook her head. "I'm sorry, Paul. That wasn't fair. I'm beat. And I shouldn't take it out on you. I just don't understand what's going on. What moves these people? I'm serious."

"Emily, don't apologize. Sometimes I think you're the one person in this government who has her head screwed on right. This is very bad stuff. But you, of all people, need to see why."

"Okay, then," she sighed. "Go ahead."

"Right now there's tremendous frustration out there. People just don't think the system works. They don't believe the political elite—that's people like us, inside the Beltway—that we hear them or care. And without the confidence of the people, democracy just doesn't work. Our system depends on the consent of the governed. It's a fragile thing."

"I know, Paul. I used to lecture on this at Harvard . . . the Social Contract. I'm well aware, but—"

"I know you are, Emily, but the contract has been broken. Look at it through the eyes of ordinary people out there. A majority of voters in Cincinnati pass an anti-pornography statute. Majority will. And a judge overrules them. Twenty-three states pass term limits. The Court says no. Same thing in Washington State. People pass a referendum outlawing assisted suicide. Judge overrules it, citing *Casey v. Planned Parenthood* . . ." Paul paused, half-smiling.

"You needn't be cute," she said defensively. "That's mine. I'm proud of it. It's a matter of liberty."

"Maybe. But think how ordinary citizens see it. They thought their vote counted—that they made the laws, that they decided how they were going to live together—and along comes some judge or bureaucrat who says he knows better. The people get squeezed. They feel they're not part of things. And they get angry. And that's what you're seeing."

"Maybe. Some judges have gone too far. But it doesn't justify this." Emily tapped vigorously on the briefing memo she was clutching. "This is violent revolution."

"Of course not. But when people feel the system isn't working, when all the political doors have been slammed in their faces and they know babies are being killed, it pushes them over the edge," Paul said. "I'm not justifying violence, Emily. But you have to understand the way they think. And that's why troops and cops and tanks only push them further."

Emily shook her head, more in despair than disagreement. She looked tired, vulnerable, her cheeks pale.

"What we've got to do is let people have some room to vent their feelings; we have to let them know we understand, that we hear them, that their government works. You're the one person who can do something. Griswold and his gang, they'll never see this."

Emily smiled wanly. She knew when she was being flattered. It felt good. Then she nodded again. "But the system does work, Paul."

"Are you sure, Emily?"

Outside the windows they heard the sudden shriek of sirens as several police cars raced by on the street below. Emily sighed and shook her head.

Friday, June 5
FBI Headquarters

"Yes sir," FBI dispatcher John Pascoe said to Toby Hunter. "The calls came in within a few minutes of each other. Maybe the weather is clearing people's minds out there in Virginia."

Hunter grinned. The humidity had dropped overnight, and it was a clear, bright June day, rare in muggy Washington. He and Director Frizzell had had no doubts they'd crack this case, but it certainly helped to finally have some specific leads. The white Honda and the Seatons' home had yielded nothing in terms of specific clues as to where they should concentrate the search for Alex Seaton and Lance Thompson.

He scrawled some notes on the pad in front of them. "So tell me about the call from the FAA guy."

"Name's Jerry Leach," the dispatcher responded. "He called first thing this morning. Said that he's worked at the FAA Leesburg facility for twenty-two years and doesn't usually think much about unidentified small aircraft in the area of Godfrey Field; a lot of pilots there seem to take off at odd hours without many formalities.

"So on the night of the bombing, at 22:15 hours, he noted an unidentified radar presence on the screen. Small plane. He radioed a request for ID, but the pilot didn't respond. Leach didn't think much of it at the time, but he didn't know about the bombing yet. Then, he figured, since the bureau hadn't located the perpetrators yet, maybe the radar blip was something to report. So I was getting ready to send that up to you, sir, and then the second call came in.

"This one was a guy down in Warren County, near Front

Royal. Stonewall J. Dinkins. These people still fly Confederate flags from their barns. Anyway, Dinkins owns a well-drilling business and has a hundred acres of apple orchards on the side. He's a real piece of work. Seems he and wife Loretta were sleepin' the other night and Loretta woke up and started punchin' him in the belly. Evidently his belly is rather ample or that's not too unusual, 'cause he just keeps sleepin'; but then Loretta starts pullin' his hair and tellin' him she hears a plane comin' in real low."

Toby Hunter grinned again, though he was tapping his pen impatiently on the desk. The dispatcher was doing pretty well laying on the accent.

"Okay, Mr. Pascoe, so then what?"

"So Loretta's havin' a tizzy, Dinkins tells me, because she had read about a plane crashin' into a house in New York a month or so ago, and she jumps out of the bed and is lookin' out the windows, but she can't see anything 'cause it's dark. Then they both hear the plane comin' lower, lower, lower, and then the motor sounds like it's about to stall, according to Dinkins, and then it cuts out. And they're still alive, their house is still there, they still can't see anything, and he's tired, so he just tells Loretta to hop back into bed, that it's probably just some boys playin' around with their daddy's plane. That's what he said. Then Loretta takes a snort of Jack Daniels to calm her nerves and they both go back to sleep.

"He said it was a little before midnight. He and Loretta go to bed early; they were sound asleep by then. And he wasn't gonna call, but Loretta's been readin' about the bombing in the papers and kept buggin' him to call. So he did."

"Sounds like Loretta's not someone to mess with," said Toby Hunter.

"You got it, sir," the dispatcher replied.

WITHIN THE HOUR, a swarm of FBI agents descended in Leesburg. Jerry Leach, interviewed at home, repeated what he had told the dispatcher.

A search of Frank Doggett's records revealed his ownership of an old Cessna 172, and agents made their way to Godfrey Field, where the nervous airport manager escorted them to hangar number two. Doggett's plane was gone, but agents sealed off the area and called in a team of forensic technicians. The technicians picked up several bags of evidence—most notably, several small splotches of dried blood on the hangar floor near where the plane would have been parked.

Meanwhile, at FBI headquarters downtown, a team of agents gathered around a long conference room table, looking over a detailed Virginia state map. Using a large compass, Special Agent McCrane drew a red circle passing through part of West Virginia, the Shenandoah valley, and the Blue Ridge mountains.

"The Cessna's tank holds forty-two gallons of fuel," he said to the men around him. Their shirt sleeves were rolled up, their suit jackets off, and their weapons draped under their armpits and around their shoulders in leather holsters.

"Leach must have spotted the plane on radar just after take-off, heading north toward Martinsburg. The Dinkinses heard the plane right here." He marked an X about midway between Front Royal and Winchester.

"So, gentlemen, I think this makes it fairly straightforward for all of us. They've got a few days on us, but they can't have gotten too far without a lot of help, and we can shake that down. I want teams here, here, here, and here." He jabbed the map again, this time with a green pen.

"Command center will be set up in White Post. I want two SWAT team companies, and we've requisitioned a regiment of army Rangers to lend a hand. We'll search every barn, every house, every cabin, every field, every outhouse, every apple tree. We will bring these boys in, and we will consider them armed and extremely dangerous. If they can blow up a building in downtown Washington, they have resources and weapons on hand. They've already killed three people, including a United States congressman.

"Any questions?"

48

F BI'S ON OUR TRAIL," Lance said to Alex as he came out of the bathroom. "I just heard it on the radio. 'Unnamed officials confirm that a tip from the FAA has concentrated their search along the Virginia/West Virginia border.'"

"I guess we don't have a plan C, do we?" Alex asked, sighing and walking slowly into the living room.

"I'm working on it."

"Well, I'm going to take a nap," Alex said. "I'm exhausted, and it's not like there's anything we can do here. Have you ever thought about just giving ourselves up?"

"We didn't come this far to give ourselves up," Lance said quietly. "Why are you sleeping so much? It's not good for you."

"You're not getting any sleep at all. You're pacing all night long. That's not good for you either. You're wound so tight you don't even sound like yourself anymore."

Lance let that pass. "Look," he said. "The radio says the FBI has launched a full-scale search, concentrating in Martinsburg. That gives us some time; they won't get this far south for a while. We need to get to Ken and Ned before the FBI does. Tonight, after dark. They can give us a car, and maybe we can get through, just keep moving south, get to Miami."

THE BLACK GOVERNMENT CAR looked incongruous, parked slightly askew on the freshly mowed farm field. In his gray windowpane tropical wool suit and shiny wing tips, Toby Hunter looked equally out of place. A piece of hay clung to his right sock, and he leaned down to brush it away then shielded his eyes from the sun as he straightened up and looked at the barn.

"Good work, men," he said. "You make working for the United States government a pleasure."

The SWAT personnel and a small cluster of Rangers lifted their eyebrows at that but cleared a path leading toward the barn. Its big, red double doors were propped open with piles of cinder blocks; inside, straw and hay were strewn everywhere. And in the far corner, the little Cessna rested like a baby bird in the nest, its wings still partially covered with hay, its tail bearing the ID number they were looking for.

"Good work," Hunter said again. "If we could just find our friend Mr. Doggett, he would be so delighted to hear that his plane has been safely located."

An assistant with a cellular phone trailed behind Hunter, and he turned toward her. "Patti, keep the media thing going. Get our guys in Martinsburg to leak that there's a promising find up there. A gun, or two changes of clothing, or something. We just need a little more time down here, I think, and I'd like our friends in hiding to feel like we're not as close as we are. I'm sure they're listening to the radio."

"Yes sir," said Patti.

Hunter saluted the Rangers and the SWAT team leader. "Go ahead and pick the plane apart," he said. "I want fingerprints, blood samples, whatever we'll need when this thing comes to court. And let's pay a visit to the man who owns this barn."

ALEX LEANED OVER the small bathroom sink, plastic gloves on his hands. His hair, under a cap of clear plastic, was smeared with light brownish-gold goop. "'Loving Care,'" he said to Lance.

"'Covers the gray' . . . 'ash blond' . . . I never thought it would come to this. It'd be funny if it wasn't so awful."

Lance felt slightly encouraged. Alex was still acting like an automaton, but at least he was doing what Lance told him. And having a plan in place had given him a small burst of energy. Maybe once he got out of the cabin he'd be all right. But before then, they had to alter their appearances as much as possible. Then they'd wait for darkness, make their way to Jordan's house, get his car, and head south. Lance had the guns and ammunition in an old suitcase he had found under the bed—ready, just in case.

"You're doing a good job," Lance said. "Rub just a little more into your eyebrows. Once you've got these glasses and a baseball cap on, you won't even look like the same person. And once we get clear of Virginia, we can even stop and get you some pants that fit."

Alex obediently smeared goop into his brows. "The directions say to leave it on for about half an hour," he said. "I'll just sit in here so I don't get this stuff on Ken's furniture." He flipped the toilet lid down and perched on the edge. "Could you get me a magazine?"

"Sure," said Lance. "*Field and Stream* okay?"

"That's great," said Alex. "Maybe you could bring the radio in here, too."

"Why, yes sir. And would you like a cup of cappuccino and a slice of apple pie with that?"

Alex's eyes widened for a second until he realized Lance was kidding. "Don't torture me," he said.

"I won't," Lance said. "You wouldn't last a minute under real torture anyway."

AT THE WHITE POST command center, Patti Ward looked up at Toby Hunter.

"Ken Jordan works in Front Royal," she said. "He sells insurance in a little storefront office on Main Street downtown. His secretary says he usually goes home right at five unless he's out on the road. Today he had an appointment in Winchester at four o'clock. He told her he'd go straight home after that."

ALEX LOOKED in the mirror. It was incredible. He really did look different. He tried the glasses on again. Maybe it was his imagination, but he looked more nondescript now. Less noticeable.

Lance wasn't less noticeable, but he looked different too. He had shaved his entire head, then carefully glued a short mustache to his upper lip. He looked forbidding and streetwise.

Alex moved into the kitchen, where Lance was heating some beans. They planned to eat early, then wait for darkness. The radio was on, low. It was almost 6:00; Alex sat down to listen to the news on the hour.

"Mutual News," the announcer said. "Federal investigators report no breakthrough developments in their search for the terrorists who bombed Washington's regeneration center three days ago. Though Rev. Daniel Seaton has been in custody for almost four days, he has shed no new light on the bombing.

"And today, as Seaton's wife, Mary, visited her husband in the Arlington County Jail, she was accosted by a self-described militant AIDS activist who said that the destruction of the regeneration center had signed his death warrant. A man named Hugh Ripken approached Mrs. Seaton as she prepared to enter the jail and doused her with a vial of what he said was HIV-contaminated human blood. Mrs. Seaton was shaken but unharmed by the incident . . ."

"Oh, man!" Alex moaned. "It just gets worse and worse. Mary didn't do anything. Daniel didn't do anything. We did it, and they're the ones taking the heat for it all. I should be there, in jail, instead of Daniel, not sitting here getting ready to run away."

"You're not there. We have to deal with the situation we're in," Lance said calmly, continuing to stir the beans on the stove though his hand tightened in anger on the wooden spoon. "We've just got to get ourselves out of here."

"When will that be?" Alex shouted, jumping to his feet. "This is never going to end. I'll never see them again."

"Quiet!" Lance turned and grabbed Alex by the arm, wrenching him back into his chair. Lance spoke through clenched teeth. "Listen to me and get a grip on yourself. We are going to get out of here as soon as it gets dark. We are going to get a car. We are going to get to Miami. If you ever want to see your brother and Mary again, you do everything I say exactly when I say it. There's no other way."

Alex just sat at the table, holding his arm where Lance had wrenched it. Lance looked so different, so sinister, with his head shaved and the dark mustache positioned above his lip.

"I'm sorry," he said meekly. "Maybe I'll just take a nap for an hour or so, if that's all right."

Lance nodded. "You can eat later. You'll need your sleep, anyway. I can't drive the whole way."

Alex headed back toward the small bedroom, rubbing the back of his head. Lance looked at his watch, then at the shadows of the trees outside. The sun was sinking, and they were just beginning to lengthen.

AN EIGHT-MAN SWAT TEAM, heavily armed, lay in the tall grass and bushes around Ken Jordan's small garage. They nudged one another as Jordan's pickup topped the small hill on the approach to his property, raising a cloud of reddish dust as he turned onto the long, unpaved road leading to his house.

The team leader spoke very quietly into his radio. "Subject is on his way."

ALEX'S HEAD THROBBED as he lay on the old bed. He was asleep but thought he was awake, back in Falls Church. He and Mary were eating apple pie at the kitchen table. "I'm sorry," he was telling her. "It's okay," she said. "Did you know that there weren't really any people in the building? It was just a dream. No one was hurt."

Then the doorbell rang, and Mary and Alex went to answer it together. Daniel stood on the front porch. "It's all over," he said. "They set me free!" Then there was the sound of running feet, and Abigail was scampering down the stairs, running toward her dad . . .

The running feet sounded heavy. Alex started, then realized where he was. The feet were Lance's, running back and forth from room to room. What was happening?

LANCE HAD BEEN STARING out between the drawn curtains of the front window. *If I could just get some sleep, I'd be okay*, he was thinking. But he couldn't sleep. Not until they were well on their way to Florida. It was just like a special op; the mind had to overcome the body's weakness and do the undoable . . .

Then he saw them. Six of them. Four in green fatigues and two in black jumpsuits. They were coming up the gravel road from Jordan's house, and if he was seeing right, they had semiautomatics in their arms. The way they were coming meant two things: There must be more of them in the woods, and Ken Jordan must already have been arrested.

Lance whirled from the window and back toward his bedroom. He split open the old clasps on the suitcase and shoved a loaded weapon in both of his big front pockets. Then he ran back to the living room and ripped open the gun rack on the wall. Two nights ago, while Alex was sleeping, he had carefully oiled and loaded each weapon. They were in good shape.

He ran to the back door, through the kitchen, and looked out into the thick woods in the back. In the shadows from the trees, he saw more shadows; the blurry shapes of men stealthily approaching the cabin. He bit his lip; they were surrounded.

He ran to the front door again, his mind racing through options. There weren't any good ones. He thought of the men in the rear, and his mind slipped off its tracks; he was back in the narrow alleys of Baghdad, caught in the web of Revolutionary Guards. They had approached in the same way, picking their way from point to point until they were almost upon him.

The Iraqis had been careful, but they had seemed arrogant, as if they knew they had this renegade black American in their grasp. They had been less insolent when he blew them all away . . . Now Lance thought he saw that same arrogance on the white faces out the front window. The SWAT teams were just sauntering up the road in their bulletproof vests, cautious but confident, as if he was just a boy, like Alex.

Lance bit the inside of his cheeks so hard that blood filled his mouth. He wasn't going to let them take him. He took the high-powered rifle and prepared to break the window and take aim.

"No!" Alex screamed, charging out of the bedroom. He clutched his brother's blood-stained handkerchief in his hand and lurched toward the door like a crazy person.

"Get out of here," Lance screamed back. "Get back in the bedroom! It's too late! It's all over!"

"No!" Alex screamed again, throwing himself toward the front door.

Lance used the gun stock to push him to the floor. "Get back in the bedroom!"

Alex scrambled backward on all fours, like a crab, then suddenly rolled and catapulted himself toward the kitchen.

Lance pulled the .38 from his right pocket. He snapped it up like a gunfighter and pulled the trigger, firing over Alex's head. There was a loud explosion, and Alex shrieked as he slipped on the linoleum floor; he scrabbled desperately with his fingers at the back lock.

"No!" Lance shouted, the rifle in one hand and the .38 in the other. He rounded the corner just as Alex wrenched the door open and ran down the two back steps, screaming and waving his arms, the handkerchief trailing off his right hand like a dingy flag. "No!"

It all happened within five seconds.

Alex sprinted toward the woods, focusing on one army Ranger in the distance, not even seeing the SWAT men who had dropped to a firing position on the ground, weapons trained on him. As Alex ran, waving the handkerchief, Lance blew out the glass on the kitchen window.

There was a deafening blast, and the man in front of Alex dropped to the ground like a dead squirrel. Then there was another explosion from the men on the ground, and crashing thunder from the cabin, and Alex suddenly realized that he wasn't running anymore. He was on the ground, and the sound of gunfire was all around him, deafening, the ground shaking like the end of the world . . . and then the sounds grew fainter, fainter, and he realized the pine needles around him were wet and sticky and warm, and he felt cold . . . and then he felt nothing at all.

49

REVEREND SEATON?" the guard called. Daniel Seaton was still huddled on his cot, face down, shoulders shaking. He had been that way for hours.

"Go away," Seaton responded, his voice husky and thick. "Please go away."

Thomas Chambers peered through the cell bars a moment longer then shrugged and turned away. Nothing he could do. But he felt for the man. Daniel Seaton was a nice guy, even if his brother had been a crackpot.

Thomas knew what it felt like to lose a brother, though. His own little bro had been gunned down three years earlier, popped off execution style by a rival druggie down on Fourteenth and R. It hurt to lose a brother, even a bad one. He patted the bars for a moment then turned away. He'd see if he could find some coffee for the reverend.

DANIEL'S THIN PILLOWCASE was wet, and his head ached. He turned on his side and swung his feet to the floor, then sat there, head down and cradled in his hands. His thoughts swirled, the same ones over and over.

Stupid, stupid. It was my fault. He didn't know any better, and I let it all go on and on until it came to this. I should have known. I kept hoping things would somehow get better.

"It is your fault," his conscience echoed, kicking in like a prosecutor. "You just let it go. You assumed that things would get better? Since when does good come out of bad? Alex and Lance were out of control, and you knew it."

He got up slowly and made his way to the far end of his cell, ten feet from the bars, staring at the wall.

"It was my fault!" he shouted, anger surging inside of him and taking control. Suddenly he lashed out, slamming his fists on the concrete, beating the wall again and again, until the sharp pain in his hands and the blood on his knuckles made him stop. He staggered unsteadily back to his bunk.

I shouldn't have let him get so involved with Lance, Daniel moaned to himself. He clutched the pillow so tightly that his raw hands trembled. Blood splotched the sheets. For the first time he felt thankful that his parents weren't alive so they didn't have to feel what he was feeling. He tried to pray, but his mind was too scrambled. Forgive me, was all he could manage. Forgive me.

THOMAS CHAMBERS gingerly approached the cell again, a Styrofoam cup of coffee sloshing in his big hand. Reverend Seaton was curled on the bed in a ball. He was saying something out loud, and Thomas leaned near the bars to hear.

"My brother," Daniel Seaton sobbed. "My little brother!"

THE BLACK GOVERNMENT car idled outside the two-story brick condo in Reston. In the bedroom, Jennifer Barrett zipped shut a hanging bag and a small suitcase; the agent waiting in the living room had already carried down the rest of her things. Later other agents would pay off her lease, scrub the apartment of fingerprints and any other identifying information, and leave it as she had found it when she began the assignment. Her higher-ups had determined that her usefulness within the Network movement was over. She'd have a short break then be prepared to testify at the trials to come—and then another assignment.

I wouldn't mind a drug case, she thought. Infiltrating narcotics smugglers was extremely dangerous, but at least with the druggies she knew what she was dealing with. These religious terrorists were something else. She'd been briefed to expect a cult rallying around one charismatic figure; the FBI had taken as its models the cases of Jim Jones, David Koresh, and even the Swiss extremist leader of the Order of the Solar Temple.

Jennifer had been a natural for the assignment. Having grown up attending church twice every Sunday, and every Wednesday night for seventeen years, she knew not only the religious jargon, but a fair amount about the way these people tended to think.

But the cult model had been all wrong, she thought. She had found Daniel Seaton a self-effacing though vigorous personality. The women in the movement had not been a gaggle of mindless groupies but had distinct personalities and views of their own. The men had listened to her ideas. Their prayers and practices had been similar to the home she grew up in, but their attitudes had been markedly different. For the most part, they had treated her with real warmth and compassion; in some ways it hadn't been a hard assignment at all.

On the other hand, she'd had a job to do, and even if most of these people were rather likeable, not at all like the caricatures for which the bureau had briefed her, they still had their dangerous elements.

Alex Seaton: classic case of someone whose passions overcame his reason. Her stomach turned when she thought of all her lunches and afternoon runs with him. His touch had reminded her of those thin, tentative, yet invasive young men she had met during her freshmen year at Bob Jones, before she woke up, escaped, and started a new life far away from the strictures of fundamentalism. And Lance Thompson: another classic case. A veteran who had gotten unhinged somewhere in the midst of enemy fire. She was sorry she'd had to deceive the women, but such men needed to be exposed and stopped. Absolutely.

Jennifer called to the agent in the living room. "Could you carry these suitcases down? I want to get the potted palm. I brought it from home."

She hoisted the palm and hugged the big plastic planter with both arms as her eyes swept the room one last time for any personal items.

Well, it's over, she thought. *I did it.* But there wasn't the sense of accomplishment and closure that she usually felt when she finished a job. Just a dull sense that there was something she'd missed.

50

IR FORCE ONE touched down precisely at 5:00 P.M. and taxied to its berth at Andrews Air Force Base. The giant walkway was wheeled up to the front door, and within seconds, the president, who had that day spoken to the Chicago Economic Club, appeared in the doorway. Immediately behind him were Harvey Robbins, the secretary of treasury, and the secretary of commerce. Blue-uniformed air force officers snapped salutes, which Griswold returned with a casual nod.

He waved quickly to the press pool assembled to the side of the ramp, stopped at the bottom of the steps to wave to the small crowd clustered behind the chain-link fence, and then, with Robbie walking two steps behind, was passed quickly from the air force to the marines.

Marine One was less than a hundred feet away, its door open and red carpet unfurled. A marine in dress blues with white gloves saluted smartly as Griswold, Robbie, two Secret Service agents, and the president's doctor climbed inside.

Air Force One had glided gracefully onto the runway; *Marine One*, its engines groaning noisily, lifted slowly straight up forty feet in the air in direct defiance of the laws of gravity, jerked its nose downward, turned to starboard, and shot across the taxiways.

On board, the president sat in his leather-padded chair on the port side. Robbie sat facing him across a desk folded out under the large window, taking notes as Griswold issued rapid-fire instructions about the upcoming state dinner for the king of Spain and the agenda for the cabinet meeting. In spite of the helicopter's plush padding and heavy insulation, the engines were deafening. Robbie could barely hear the president, and the desk table was vibrating so badly, his notes were almost illegible.

"And Robbie, we didn't have a chance on the plane to talk about the Seaton case. Poor George Norton—I thought he'd never shut up. You'd think the Commerce Department was the only agency in the government. If I heard once more about his plans for a new digital oceanographic survey, I thought I'd get up and push him out the cabin door—right at thirty thousand feet."

"He was the same way at Brown," Griswold continued. "Insufferable when he got involved in something—thought everybody ought to be as excited as he was . . . still, he's a good secretary, don't you think?"

"Yes, sir, the business community thinks he walks on water," Robbie smiled.

"Well, I don't know if he walks on it, but he certainly carries water for them. They ought to like him. He sucks right up to them. Not too much though, do you think?"

"No, sir, he handles it well."

"And we want to keep him happy. He raised a ton of money in the campaign. And next time he'll be scooping it in with both hands."

"Yes sir, he's very important," Robbie nodded.

"So we'll give him a chance to prove how brilliant he is—at least as long as it isn't too often . . . Now, Robbie, the regeneration center bombing. The polls still showing the same thing?"

"Yes sir, numbers rising."

"People want capital punishment, right?"

"Seventy-eight percent think those who did it should be executed. They believe Daniel Seaton was responsible for the bombing," Robbie chuckled.

"What do people say that you talk to? What are our friends saying, Robbie?"

"The same thing, sir. The only thing that will settle this country down right now is to nail these people. Lock 'em up. Execute Seaton."

"And do you agree?"

"Yes sir, you've got to restore public confidence, Mr. President. You were elected to do this. And these people are directly challenging the office of the president. You do it for the sake of the country and for the sake of protecting the integrity of this office."

"Now listen, Robbie," Griswold leaned across the table, "when we land, you get hold of O'Keefe. Tell him 'no ifs, ands, or buts, no fine points in the law books.' I want Bernie to understand how important it is for us to get Seaton. I mean all the way. Every statute we can use, every way we can tie him into a conspiracy. Go the whole way. You understand?" The president sat back in his chair. Then he turned to stare out the window.

"Absolutely, sir. It will be done." Robbie sensed the president's anger. Griswold seldom showed rage; it was part of his stoic Yankee reserve not to show strong emotion. But Robbie could tell.

"Execute this man Seaton. Yes, he must be executed," Griswold muttered, his words barely audible over the whine of the engines and the thump of the spinning blades. He continued to stare at the river as the chopper crossed over the Fourteenth Street Bridge and swept alongside the Jefferson Memorial. Near the Reflecting Pool, the pilot banked sharply to the north.

"It's merciful to them. Of course most people don't understand. They never do. But that hijacking of the American Airlines flight in Miami two years ago. You remember that, Robbie?" Griswold turned and looked at his assistant, who nodded.

"Well, that bureau marksman did the right thing. Shot to kill. Brought the guy down with one shot between the eyes. That was right, Robbie. People like that are better off dead . . . It's the natural way societies have of weeding out dangerous influences. Right?" The president did not wait for a reply. "And it's the same with this crowd. I mean these people are really crazy, don't you think, Robbie?"

"Yes sir, they are obviously unbalanced. Probably have a death wish."

"Well, we'll take care of that." Griswold arched his eyebrows and smiled faintly.

ROBBINS PHONED O'Keefe in his office immediately after the chopper landed. Bernie was not pleased with the curt orders.

"Look, Robbie, you take care of the schedule and the polls and parading the president around, and keeping the state dinners straight—don't get yourself into this. Justice has to work its course. This is a very sensitive business."

"I'm just relaying the orders of the president who, the last time I checked the Constitution, had the oversight of faithful execution of the laws of the United States."

"Yeah, yeah, that's all well and good, but we're talking about a highly charged, emotional atmosphere here, and the justice system can't be played with. Any sign of prejudice or political pressure, and you'll mess up this case. Leave this one to the pros, Robbie."

"The president said you'd cite cases and throw the law books at him."

"Well, he's right. But it's for his protection and for the country's."

"Remember, Bernie, the president has to look at the big picture. There are some grave issues at stake here—public confidence that he's got to have in order to handle problems in Nigeria and Europe and the Middle East. You won't find anything like that in your law books. We're dealing with the balance of peace in the world. Just take care of it, Bernie."

"'Take care of it.' Yeah, I understand." Bernie hung up the phone, chucked his glasses on the desk, and turned in his chair to stare out at the south lawn behind him. He sighed deeply.

ROB KNIGHT had known Daniel Seaton for several years. Rob's sister and her husband were members of his church. And while Rob was well-known to the Washington pro-life community for his defense of pro-lifers who had trespassed on clinic property or been arrested for blocking access to the clinics, he had certainly never expected to represent Daniel Seaton in a court of law.

Knight was a tall, thin man who never stopped moving; he was always beating his fingers on a table, tapping his feet, pacing about the room. He was in his mid-thirties but looked younger, and when he wasn't in court, he usually wore jeans and casual cotton shirts rather than the power suits of the Washington legal elite. His sandybrown hair hung over his collar in the back, and he wore a pair of gold wire-rim glasses that he ripped on and off as the spirit moved.

Rob loved a good challenge, and his friend's situation certainly presented one. But he didn't want Daniel to take him on with any rosy illusions.

Right now he was pacing, at least as much as the confines of the jail conference room would allow. By contrast, Daniel Seaton sat unmoving, quiet, hands folded, docilely watching him roam the room. Daniel's short time in jail had already accentuated his introspective demeanor, making him seem passive and emotionless. Rob was worried about that.

"Rob," Daniel said, "I want you to represent me. I know you haven't exactly been doing this kind of case . . . I know I could find somebody more high-profile; all kinds of lawyers out there would salivate at the publicity this case will bring . . . but I want you. I want someone who thinks the way I think, somebody who's going to bring the same moral perspective into the courtroom. That's more important to me than your legal experience."

Rob stopped and leaned over one of the orange-plastic chairs, draping his elbows on the back, turning his glasses in his hands.

"I'll do anything to help you, Daniel," he said. "This thing is a nightmare, and I want to help. But I want to be sure that you get the kind of representation you deserve. I don't think you realize how serious this is."

Daniel looked down. "Look, I've lost my brother, I'm locked up away from my family, I'm in jail with the wildest group of characters you'd ever want to meet, and, yes, I do understand that the government wants to burn me at the stake. I know I need help. But I don't want some flashy hired gun. I want you."

Rob jumped back up, put his glasses on, and started pacing again while Daniel continued.

"I don't want to sound naive, but I can't imagine that it's going to be that bad. I didn't do what they're charging me with; I wasn't part of any conspiracy to blow up the regeneration center, I had nothing to do with the deaths of the congressman and the others. I've always preached nonviolence. We can get dozens of people to testify to my character. . . . All I did was bandage Alex's head and let him go on his way. I realize that was wrong in the eyes of the prosecutors, but what would anyone do if their brother came to them with his scalp sliced open?"

Rob ripped his glasses off again and rubbed his eyes, hard, with his hand. Controlling himself, he sank down in the chair opposite Daniel.

"This is exactly what I am worried about," he said. "You are naive. It is *not* simple. We are dealing here with a situation where the public is absolutely screaming for your blood. The perpetrators of a terrorist bombing in the heart of Washington are now dead. The one other member of the conspiracy alive is John Jenkins, but the government doesn't care about him. I'll tell you what will happen. They'll offer him a plea bargain he can't refuse, and he'll say anything the prosecutor tells him to. It'll be your neck to save his skin. At the U.S. attorney's office they're already talking.

"Listen, Daniel, they want you. Bad. They are going to bring down every ounce of energy and venom and expertise they have to convict you. Remember the scapegoat? Very biblical, right? You are about to become one, in a big way."

"Well, at least I'm not pleading guilty," Daniel said. "At first, I thought that was the right thing to do. You've talked me out of that. I'm guilty of a few things here, and I know what they are, and I've asked God to forgive me for them. I've repented of what I did wrong. But I'm not guilty of what they're accusing me of."

Rob pulled out a thick sheaf of legal papers.

"Think about your charges. Murder . . . including the killing of a congressman. It's murder in the first degree because the perpetrators of this crime had reasonable cause to believe the building might have people in it; so the crime was done with malice aforethought, willful, deliberate, malicious, premeditated. Explosion . . . knowledge that the circumstances existed to cause the death or bodily injury to any person or substantial damage to property. Conspiracy to commit a crime of violence. Aiding and abetting these crimes. And, of course, accessory after the fact.

"And the thing is, if Alex and Lance were alive, the government would offer you a deal. They'd want information, and they'd go light on you."

"I would never testify against my brother," Daniel said.

"The prosecutors would find a way to make you feel like it wasn't ratting—that you were offering up truthful testimony to the government rather than concealing the facts. And I know you. You would have to tell the truth to those in authority, as much as you knew."

"That's just it. I didn't, I don't, know anything!"

"Well, it's moot," Rob said. "Alex and Lance are gone, so it's all gonna fall on you. What the government will do is, in effect, try Alex and Lance in absentia for the bombing, the deaths of Meyer and LaMar and Justin Jones, and the destruction of the center . . . then they'll tie you into aiding the execution of these crimes and harboring and helping them after the fact.

"Accessory after the fact wouldn't be so bad. They couldn't nail you for much; that is, if five years isn't considered much. But what the 'aiding and abetting' and conspiracy charges mean is that you will be, in the eyes of the law, equally culpable as the perpetrators of these crimes.

"And when it comes down, who's the jury going to believe?

This isn't a jury of your peers; this will be a motley crew of District of Columbia residents who will find great pleasure in convicting a naive white guy from the suburbs."

Daniel sputtered, but Rob kept talking through clenched teeth.

"And if you're found guilty, you will receive the same penalties Alex and Lance would have if they were convicted, which they would have been in a heartbeat. There's no death penalty in D.C., unless they try to pull this under one of the crazy federal statutes. There you can get the chair for killing a poultry inspector. And they might try. They gave it to Paul Hill, remember?"

"Anyway, the least you are looking at it is between twenty years and life in prison. Not much difference. And the federal sentencing guidelines mean that that sentence is absolute. The judge has no discretion to mitigate it because of your unblemished record or your family life or your pastorate or your rugged good looks—"

"But I'm not guilty!" Daniel protested. For the first time he seemed agitated. "The jury will have to believe me."

"Listen, Daniel. That jury will never hear from you. As I see it right now, I'll never put you on the stand. Our best chance is to let the government stew in its own juice. They can't corroborate their facts."

"But—"

"But nothing. You need to understand one thing. From here on out, I'm in charge. I run the case. That's the way it is. The lawyer calls the shots. Otherwise you can get somebody else."

Rob could see that Daniel wanted to object, and he kept going to drive his point home.

"This isn't *Perry Mason* or *Matlock* . . . no one is going to jump up in the courtroom at the last minute and confess and you'll go free, a hero. This is the real thing, and it's going to be nasty."

51

PAUL CLARKSON stretched his aching legs and looked out over his backyard. The grass needed mowing and was a little dry; he'd need to remind Paul Jr. to stick with his yard work. But the cascading mounds of pink and white impatiens edging the flower beds were full and bright, the mulch was fresh . . . things looked pretty good on the whole, he thought.

He had slept in a bit this morning, and now he and June were having their coffee on the back deck. It felt strange to be sitting here at 7:30 on a weekday morning, but he was going to take June to a doctor's appointment at 9:00. He had told Emily that he would be coming in to the office late. His wife's health came first this morning, and the two of them were enjoying an unusual few minutes of quiet.

The Washington Post lay spread out on the round glass table under the green-striped patio umbrella. Paul had usually digested the news, editorial, business, and federal sections by this hour, but today he couldn't get past the story that began on page one: "Senator Langer Announces Retirement: Mississippi Statesman Cites Poor Health, Fatigue."

"He didn't even call to tell me," Paul said.

June sighed and watched a mockingbird chase interlopers away from the Bradford pear tree adjacent to the deck. "You need to call him, Paul. He needs you now more than ever."

"He's hung in there all these years; he's been through all kinds of attacks," Paul said. "But this thing really cut him to the quick. I hope Bernie O'Keefe realizes what he's done."

"He'd have to have a conscience to do that," June said dryly. "I don't think Bernie O'Keefe has a conscience."

52

BERNIE LIFTED his briefcase onto his desk, ready to pack it in for the day. *If only this bag could talk*, he thought, running his hands over the supple, golden-brown leather worn to a smooth patina. What tales it could tell. Stories of long hours in the most exalted courtrooms of Boston, Washington, and New York. Journeys on the backseats of limousines or in the overhead racks on sleek jets, including *Air Force One.*

A surge of nostalgia swept through him, and he looked over at the huge, white, beautifully calligraphied parchment that hung behind his desk: "J. Whitney Griswold, President of the United States of America to Bernard Jerome O'Keefe . . . Reposing special trust and confidence in your integrity, prudence, and ability, I do hereby appoint you Counsel to the President of the United States of America." His commission. The most coveted possession in Washington.

Then he shook his head; he didn't need any more play on his emotions today. He began stuffing files and papers into the soft-sided case that opened at the top and easily held, along with his files, extra shirts, shaving gear, even a laptop. He knew he wouldn't read any of this stuff tonight; he just needed the security of having it. Then he shut the bag, headed through the door, and into the outer office, trying to decide whether to go home or stop at Kelly's. It was already nearly 8:00 P.M.; he and Barbara had put in a long, brutal day. Stopping at Kelly's would probably help.

He was still stewing over the message Clarkson had sent by e-mail, chastising him for his part in bringing down "a good and decent man, a man who wanted nothing more than to serve his country." The charge had stung because it was true. Langer had flinched in battle, then covered it up. So what? Who knew what he'd have done with Vietnamese crawling all over him and shells exploding.

"Bernie . . . Bernie . . . are you all right?"

The words jolted him. He looked down and saw his hand on the knob to the outer door. He had walked right past Barbara—his secretary and faithful friend who had mothered him for the past twelve years. He hadn't even looked at her, let alone said good night.

"I'm sorry, Barbara," he said. "I'm fine. Never better. A rough day, you know, but you can't keep the sons of the old sod down for long," he said with an Irish brogue and a broad grin.

But it was a lie. An hour earlier he had felt the familiar sinking feeling in his chest and stomach, the sensation that everything was senseless . . . the awful, inexorable feeling of deep despair.

When he felt it coming, Bernie had taken a double dose of the pills Dr. Nikkels had prescribed, and they had stabilized things a little, though he still had difficulty getting energy into his legs. His brain was giving the commands, but his joints and muscles were ignoring them. Insubordination.

Nikkels had told him to call if he began slipping into what he had called the dark tunnel. Bernie needed professional attention at once during such periods, the doctor had warned. But Bernie never liked to ask anyone for help; he could handle things himself. He had the scars to prove it.

Besides, he usually disdained psychiatrists, at least in public, even though he liked and needed Nikkels in private. "A lot of them are quacks," he'd once told a colleague after calling a psychiatrist as an expert witness. The doctor's testimony had succeeded in getting off one of Bernie's most celebrated defendants, a man Bernie knew perfectly well to be guilty. He also knew that the doctor would say anything he wanted him to for a price. He'd had little respect for psychiatry since then—until he hit the black tunnel five years ago. Then it was Nikkels—almost as much as Marilyn—who had pulled him through it.

KELLY'S EASILY WON the tug-of-war, and by 8:15 Bernie was at his favorite spot at the bar. Maybe it wasn't going to end up such a bad day after all. Tonight there was even an empty stool.

Henry greeted him warmly and was starting to pour his usual when Bernie stopped him. "Henry, tonight I need a Bud Lite—nice and cold."

The bartender stared. He'd never seen Bernie O'Keefe drink anything but scotch, always Dewars and always on the rocks. "Bud Lite, draft?"

"Yup," Bernie grinned. "A little change."

Dr. Nikkels had been insistent. "Remember, Bernie, absolutely no alcohol while you're on this medication." But a beer wouldn't hurt, Bernie reasoned. The slight alcohol content would wash right out before it could do any harm. Besides, beer was made for the Irish, their national tonic. No one ever saw a depressed Irishman.

Bernie downed almost half of the first mug in one swallow, then rested both elbows on the bar as the familiar, comforting sensation coursed through his body; he could feel muscles relaxing and his mind clearing. He wasn't really responsible for Langer, he reassured himself; somebody would have exposed the guy. He was living a lie after all; it wasn't as if they had made something up about him. Simply the truth coming out. Mr. Military Hero had been impaled on his own spear. That's life—justice actually.

Whitney Griswold was another matter, though. Bernie gulped down the rest of the beer and rapped the mug on the bar for a refill.

Probably Whit's just blowing off steam, Bernie told himself. *But I want no part in executing a criminal defendant.*

Memories of his deep-seated opposition to capital punishment filtered through his mind, starting back when he was a kid at Sacred Heart and had argued passionately against the topic in debate: too many innocent men wrongly convicted, and no real deterrent to crime. Later, a professor at Boston College, Father Sheehan, had tutored Bernie in moral philosophy and drilled into him the anti-capital-punishment arguments at a philosophical level. His study of capital cases at Yale only deepened his commitment. Now the president of the United States wanted to take Seaton and hang him, just to appease public anger.

Bernie shook his head. What had his old friend come to? Where was the noble Yankee gentleman called to the highest ideals of service to others? Corrupted, that's where, and Bernie was being corrupted right along with him. No decency or truth, or tolerance, for that matter, in their administration. He swallowed deeply. He'd have to find a way to back Whit off, make him listen, regain their balance.

Bernie finished the second mug and beckoned to Henry. Thank goodness for malt and hops and the Irish. It was the first time he'd felt alive all day. He even found himself cracking jokes with the bartender in between swigs from the third mug. The cold liquid soothed his throat, a pleasant contrast with the warm flush he felt in his cheeks. His limbs felt lighter, buoyed by an unseen force. *Ah, the relief.*

"Fill it up again, Henry," Bernie said. "I'll be right back." He headed for the men's room, a familiar-enough route. Around the bar it was . . . no, not that side. He made two false turns, then found the hallway, his legs a little rubbery.

BACK AT THE BAR, Henry was waiting with the fourth round. "You sure you want another?" he asked sternly.

Bernie reached out. "Of course. You ever seen me drunk, Henry? I've never in my life lost control."

"You aren't walking too straight, Bernie." Henry was scowling.

"Give me that glass. No Irishman quits with two beers," Bernie grinned.

"This is number four."

"It's only beer, Henry."

"Last one." Henry handed it over cautiously, then smiled. "Well, with all the pressures you got, guess I can't blame you."

Bernie nodded, wiping the foam from his lips.

"Hope you guys are going to nail that maniac Seaton." Henry scowled again.

"If he's guilty we will." There was a coolness in Bernie's voice now.

"Guilty? Of course he's guilty. These are bad guys, Bernie. Oughtta fry 'em."

"Yeah, I know." Bernie stared into his beer. Why should Robbie bother with all those expensive pollsters? Just come into Kelly's and ask Henry. Fry Seaton. Sure. Why not? Who gives a rip? Guilty or not. What's one sacrificial lamb anyway? Griswold's got it right. He knows.

At that moment, as the toxin level in Bernie's blood rose, the uninhibited, almost giddy feeling began to fade. For just an instant he felt a touch of nausea, though it quickly passed; but he could sense the tunnel, that he was nearing it, about to enter its vacuum. The awful thing about the tunnel was that there was no way out, and the walls closed in.

"Thanks, Henry. I'll see you. I'm going to take a walk." Bernie slid a bill out of his wallet, then slid off the stool, bumping hard into the man on his left, and walked unsteadily to the front entrance.

"Bernie, you sure you're okay?" Henry called after him.

Bernie turned back for a moment. "Of course," he said, then saluted and went out the door.

OUTSIDE HE TOOK several deep breaths and looked around, absorbing the sights and sounds of the warm summer night. Spanish music floated over from an outdoor cafe, a man was selling bouquets of fresh red roses on the street, and couples strolled past him arm in arm.

Bernie had already decided not to call for his car; he would walk home. He had done it twice before and enjoyed it. So he turned left out of Kelly's front door, listing slightly to the right under the weight of the overstuffed briefcase swinging at his side.

He waited at the light then nearly tripped on the curb as he crossed M and headed up Thirty-fourth Street, walking quickly up the small hill, enjoying the exercise. Just like the old days, he thought. When he was on the BC football team he could drink half the night and still play hard the next afternoon, hurling his muscular body at opposing players, grinding them into the ground. Those were great days. Carefree days.

Hey, he thought. He was only four blocks from Georgetown University. Why not walk through the campus? There'd be summer students there, maybe even some pretty ones. It was such a beautiful night. Maybe he could walk away from the tunnel.

N Street dead-ended into the university at Thirty-first Street. Bernie climbed several flights of steps up to the main level of the campus, which, like most older, eastern, urban schools, was an eclectic mix of Victorian, Gothic, and Colonial architecture surrounding rectangles of green. To his left he saw book-laden students streaming in and out of what was obviously the library. In front and to the right of him was Healy Hall, Georgetown's distinctive landmark, a gray Gothic structure with narrow spires soaring into the night sky.

Awash in memories, Bernie drifted past the library, stopping to admire the collection of whiskey bottles some party-loving student had lined in his dormitory window, fondly remembering his own undergrad days. Another window held a lighted neon "Lite on Tap" sign. The campus was serene, though, a few students sitting on benches talking quietly. The lampposts that lighted the path seemed to flicker in the gentle breeze.

Bernie staggered right and made his way up a brick walkway bordered by beds of ivy and boxwood hedges and eventually came to a central square hidden behind Healy. This was evidently the heart of the campus. If it weren't for the jets roaring overhead on their landing approach down the Potomac River to National Airport, Bernie could have imagined himself transported back into the nineteenth century.

At the center of the square was a charming brick building with curved steps leading to its entrance. Two students were sitting on the steps, talking loud enough for him to hear, something about some Jesuit retreat or something. They looked up at him quizzically. As he walked closer, he realized this was the chapel, and he walked up the three steps to read the signs posted on the board. Several masses were scheduled, he noted, the last one at 10:15 P.M.

Bernie looked at his watch—9:40. He always joked about being a three-Sundays-a-month Catholic, but that was stretching it. More like once every few months, and only then when Marilyn absolutely insisted. In fact, he hadn't been to Mass at all since he'd come to Washington.

Church held no meaning for him anymore, if it ever had. Church was the nuns who used to whack his knuckles at Sacred Heart, or the priests who droned on in Latin when he was a kid—even when they'd switched to English, he couldn't understand them. Church was his mother holding him by the scruff of the neck and scrubbing his face on Sunday morning; it was his brief time as an altar boy before the priest discharged him— to his father's horror—for laughing during Mass; it was his father locking him in his room. Church was rules and pain.

The two students left, and Bernie stood alone on the front steps watching the bubbling fountain in the middle of the green and the towers behind, stretching straight and narrow into the night sky. His head throbbed; though the air and exercise had helped, the tunnel was not far away. He could sense its nearness in the cramped feeling that gripped his chest and stomach. He took several deep breaths and sighed.

Then he felt an odd prompting to go into the chapel. *Why?* He chuckled to himself. Here he was, Bernie O'Keefe, one of the most powerful men in the United States, clutching a bag full of sensitive government papers, standing on the steps of a chapel in the middle of a campus full of twenty-year-old summer-school students. But he was also feeling wretched and angry, maybe even frightened. He couldn't sort out the jumble of emotions raging inside.

Bernie turned and went through the doors. He was struck immediately by the inviting warmth and informality of the large room. Not a cold, sterile cathedral—more like a library. There were blond wooden chairs with worn red cushions, linked in rows, with red-leather kneeling pads under each one. Wooden beams arched across the white-plaster ceiling, all bathed in soft light from the sconces on the walls.

The altar was a simple table with candles on either end. Behind it was a piano, and to the right the most unusual crucifix he had ever seen. At least eight feet high, made of gray iron with a silvery statue of Christ impaled on it. It was starkly compelling, and Bernie found himself slowing walking toward it. At the second row, by reflex, he genuflected and slid into a chair, putting the briefcase down at his side. He bowed his head.

If only it were all true. But even if there were a God, what would He care about someone like a Bernie O'Keefe and these clutching demons, he thought. The indictments began to sear his mind like hot irons.

Bernie O'Keefe, you are a wretched husband. Marilyn left you and with good reason. Even if she didn't know about the other women—and she probably did—she knew you cared only about yourself. Not about her, not about the kids.

And you have been a total failure as a father, never even getting to one of Matt's games last fall. Not one. You don't know your kids, and your kids certainly don't know you. *Failure.* It stung.

You put your whole life on the line for Whitney Griswold, a pompous ass who has used you and will discard you like a used Kleenex if it suits him. That is, if his whole government doesn't collapse in a heap first. The army in the streets and chaos in the country—nice work for only six months in office.

And now, to top it all off, you've destroyed a decent man's career and are about to try to get the death penalty for another.

Surely any good God would banish such a man to the lowest reaches of hell. Bernie's chest was heaving with huge sighs. He thought he might break into tears.

"If I can help in any way, I'd like to," said a voice, and Bernie felt a hand rest lightly on his shoulder for a moment. At first he thought he was imagining it, probably losing his mind by now anyway. Then he slowly looked up into the face of a man with penetrating deep-blue eyes.

"No, no," Bernie said. "Just thinking through some things."

He was startled by the man's directness, but that attracted him as well. He'd always liked straight shooters. The man was dressed in a white polo shirt and khaki pants. Over his arm were some white sheets. *Maybe a choir robe*, Bernie thought.

"I'm just fine." Bernie said, his defense mechanism back at work. "Just needed a little space. You know how it is. Are you a graduate student here?"

"No." The man stuck out his hand. "I'm Bob Garrison."

"Oh, well, good to meet you." Bernie shook his hand.

"And you are?"

"Bernie."

"I noticed you staring at the crucifix, Bernie. Interesting, isn't it? I do the same thing myself all the time."

"I've never seen one quite like it. Do you know who the artist was?"

"Oh, someone pretty well-known, actually. But the significance is what you see in it. A lot of people see themselves. Crucified, suffering, death to self. I see myself in it often," the man said as he stared at the cross." And, of course, I see Christ, suffering for us."

The man, probably in his early thirties, was handsome, but it was his smile and his air of confidence that were so compelling. As he talked, he threw his head back slightly and ran his hand through the spears of light-brown hair that had fallen over his forehead.

"You're a Christian, are you, Bernie?"

"I was raised Catholic."

"That wasn't what I asked," the man said. "Do you believe?"

"I don't know." Bernie shook his head. "Right now I don't know what I believe."

"It's all right. You can find answers here. Something's really bothering you, isn't it?"

Bernie paused. "Well, you could say I've been through some things. Who are you, anyway, if you don't mind my asking? Campus thought police?" He grinned at his own stupid joke.

"Oh, I'm sorry. Of course. I'm Father Bob Garrison. I'll be celebrating Mass here in a few minutes."

"But you're so—"

"Casual?" The priest chuckled. "Well, this is a campus, you know. I've just come from a student Bible study."

Bernie nodded. A priest leading a Bible study?

"But don't worry, I'll be dressed properly." He held the white robe and chasuble up before him and smiled. "See? I turn into a priest at 10:15."

Bernie smiled.

"Why don't you stay, Bernie?" Garrison looked at him directly again.

There was a long moment of silence.

"No, thank you," Bernie replied. "I just came in here to sort some things out, clear my head, get a load off."

"Well, you're carrying a heavy load. I can see that. Christ said that His burdens are light. Why not take Him at His word? "The priest pointed toward the cross. "The Lamb of God who takes away the sins of the world."

"Father, I haven't been to confession in ten years." Bernie put his hand up, palm outward. "And you don't have time to listen. We'd be here all night and into some time next week."

"I have all the time you'd need—but it's not a matter of time, is it?"

Bernie suddenly felt trapped. "I'll be honest, Father. I used to believe . . . I guess. But I'm afraid I'm a long way from where you are."

"No, you aren't. You're here. And you're not here by accident, you know. Something, or I should say Someone, compelled you to come here. All you have to do is receive—"

"No," Bernie broke in. He couldn't believe that God had somehow compelled him, after a day like this, to end up in this chapel talking to this priest. God must have other things on His mind. "I just came here by accident. It's a beautiful evening. I wanted to walk around. I was curious about the chapel."

The priest simply smiled.

Bernie could feel the beads of sweat on his forehead. He was torn. The priests he had known were never like this kind, yet strong young man. He wanted to cry out, "Yes, I'm here! Help me! I'm going down the tubes!" But he was Bernie O'Keefe, successful and important and in no position to open his messed-up life to some obscure priest on a college campus. What if it ever got out?

"Look, Father, I can't say I believe if I don't. Most religious people are hypocrites anyway. They don't really believe, I mean way down deep inside."

"Ah, yes," the priest laughed. "We all have doubts and we all fall short. I suggest you come, join us for Mass. You'll probably feel right at home."

Then he stopped and looked at Bernie, hard. "Listen," he said. "You must believe so you can understand, and when you understand, you will believe."

Bernie stared, trying to sort through the words. He couldn't make sense of them.

"Thank you, Father. I think I'll just sit here and think it through."

"Great. Stay through the Mass, and then we'll talk more. Let me buy you a cup of coffee down the street. But stay. Whether you realize it or not, you've come here because God has brought you. Stay and meet Him. Celebrate with me." Father Bob locked eyes with him for a moment then turned and went through a door in the back of the chapel into the sacristy.

A few minutes later, as the pianist began playing, he reappeared in a flowing white robe with a light stole draped over his shoulders, on it a green-and-gold embroidered cross. He moved slowly now, deliberately, his hands together, palm to palm. His face was peaceful, composed.

Bernie looked around. A few dozen people had slipped in while he and the priest had been talking. An odd mix: a few older people, some faculty types, a street person, and a surprising number of students. And also, squirming in discomfort, the counsel to the president of the United States.

FATHER BOB GARRISON looked at his troubled visitor several times during the liturgy. The man's bloodshot eyes were fixed on him, and the priest almost felt distracted: Where had he seen this man before? He read the familiar words, but as he did so, his heart swelled and hurt for the silent soul before him.

He held up the silver chalice, saying softly to the people and himself the amazing words of Christ: "This is the cup of My blood, the blood of the new and everlasting covenant. It will be shed for you and all so that sins may be forgiven. Do this in memory of Me."

He looked at the crucifix. In memory of Christ, yet celebrating with the risen Christ even now, alive and present this warm summer night. He smiled and looked back at the people who were acknowledging: "Christ has died, Christ is risen, Christ will come again."

His eyes stopped where the man had been sitting. The chair was empty.

HOME. Sort of. Bernie entered his library and rubbed his open palms over the oak paneling. So rugged and enduring. This room with oak everywhere reminded him of the first law office he'd clerked for, one of the last of the big firms to remain in an old turn-of-the-century, granite-faced building in downtown Boston, the kind that still had elevators with steel-meshed doors and worn black-and-white marble-tiled corridors. Lawyers today chose mahogany or rosewood or sleek, exotic furniture; but in those days, when lawyers were lawyers, not smooth-talking techno-crats, it was oak and big desks and overstuffed leather.

If only he had a chance to unpack, he'd make something of this room, he thought for the umpteenth time, something solid and stable. "Which I could use right now," he startled himself, saying it aloud into the silence. Something like he had felt in that chapel—a feeling he hadn't had in a long while.

Bernie pushed his briefcase under the desk, chucked his coat onto a large packing crate, and kicked off his tasseled loafers. The walk home had tired him, and he slumped into the big black leather desk chair, the one his partners had given him when he left the firm.

Yes, there was something about that chapel. Bernie rubbed his eyes, even as the images passed through his mind. The crucifix was so striking. The aluminum stark, yet in the figure was all the agony and passion it represented, that good and decent and inno-cent man being executed to satisfy the anger of the mob.

Nothing has really changed in two thousand years, Bernie thought. We'll kill today to satisfy the mob. Even a decent man like Griswold will—and without blinking an eye.

But could it be true? he wondered. Did Jesus really die for others? The priest had spoken of Him with such familiarity. And he had looked right into Bernie as if he knew him—and loved him anyway. The priest had seemed . . . so good, so de-cent, so kind, and yet strong. Not a patsy. Not beholden to anyone. Bernie hadn't met anyone like him since he'd been in Washington.

And why should he have? Think of those buttheads in the government . . . Robbie, the cold, calculating vampire who probably slept in a refrigerated vault. Frizzell, just a gutter-fighter. Many of those jokers on the Hill would turn in their own mothers to get elected, not to mention the little power-mongers who strutted around the corridors of the White House, and their junior clones-in-training, the beaver patrol. And then there was Griswold himself . . . Bernie tried to remember back to how they had first become friends. Why? Maybe he'd never really known the man, or maybe he'd changed. Could Washington have done this to him—or worse, was it something in him?

Probably all of us are the same, Bernie thought. *So prideful and powerful and self-assured on the outside, rotten and whimpering within.*

Bernie didn't like being so honest. But how could he ever face his law partners who had sent him off to save the republic? He thought of their admiring, envious grins, their strong hands clapping him on the back. He shook his head, staring at the empty bookshelves. All those grand dreams and plans, unraveling now, he thought. The country is in absolute turmoil, we have how many more years of this to go, and our administration is crumbling. An absolute failure. *I can never go back.*

The images rolled in his mind, tossing his emotions. One moment he felt better, lifted with a surge of hope; the next he crashed in despair, dashed to the sand. His head hurt worse than it had in a long time. The beers had worn off, and the darkness was still there. His limbs felt heavy, his mouth was dry, his vision slightly blurred, and that awful, sinking sensation was back in his abdomen.

Bernie got up quickly and walked down the hallway to the kitchen where he took an unopened bottle from the twelve neatly stacked on the pantry shelf. General Dewars was there to serve. Then, tucking the bottle under one arm, he filled a glass with ice. He returned to the front of the house, checked the security system, then turned back into his library, stepping over a pile of mail on the floor.

Bernie never used a shot glass, boasting that he could measure two ounces exactly with his eye. Maybe once that was true, but the two ounces looked suspiciously like four as he filled the tumbler three-quarters full and sat down again at his desk.

Dr. Nikkels had also warned him to beware of the signs of alcoholism, and lying about how much he drank was the first sign. The next was when he felt he had to have a drink. Bernie told the doc that never happened, but that was a lie too. The truth was that Bernie refused to believe he was addicted or ever could be. Yet tonight he watched his hand tremble as he lifted the glass and took several swallows.

If only it were true. Bernie couldn't shake off that thought, nor could he clear his mind of the image of the cross or the appealing expression on the priest's face. "The Lamb of God who takes away the sins of the world," the man had said. Something else came back to Bernie, something from childhood. "Seek and ye shall find." Could it be true? If only . . .

It was less than a minute before the familiar relief returned, starting with the warm sensation in his stomach, and he suddenly remembered he hadn't eaten since lunch. Then came the numbing of his nerve endings and a sudden release of tension.

Dr. Nikkels had warned him against even one drink when he was taking Xanax or lithium; it would release inhibitions faster than normal, he said, and there would be no resistance to the second, third, and fourth drinks. On top of the drugs, that amount of alcohol could almost shut down the central nervous system and possibly be lethal.

But it had been six hours since the last pill, Bernie thought. The beer hadn't killed him, and anyway, how he felt now was such a relief that it was worth it, no matter what.

Bernie leaned back in his chair, breathed in deeply, and massaged his temples. The pain was easing but not the images. He should have stayed for the Eucharist. "The blood of Christ, shed for you and for all, that sins may be forgiven." Memories of childhood, his first communion, his mother's hug. He felt a moistening in his eyes.

Whoa! Get yourself together, O'Keefe, he commanded. Annoyed, he took out his handkerchief and dried his eyes. Maybe he could call the priest.

The phone book, a huge gray-and-yellow volume, was on the floor. With some effort he found a listing for Georgetown University.

An operator picked up on the second ring. "Georgetown University."

"May I have the chapel, please?"

"Is this a joke?"

"No, no. Connect me to the chapel. I don't know the name."

"You mean Dahlgren?"

"I don't know. Is there more than one?"

"Look, sir, it's nearly midnight. I'm sorry. I can't connect you with the chaplaincy services until office hours tomorrow morning."

"This is an emergency. I need to find Father Bob."

"Do you know his last name? I can look in the directory if he lives on campus."

Bernie stopped. He thought. He could not remember the priest's last name.

"Sir?"

Bernie gently put the receiver down and wiped his eyes dry. He finished his drink and poured another generous portion.

Bernie had always thought of himself as one of the more fortunate people in life. He had been either lucky enough, or smart enough, to seize the moment as the winds of fate blew past, finding his destiny by being clever enough to recognize the opportunity and take it.

Had he just missed such a moment?

Within a few minutes the second drink was gone, and Bernie poured a third. All inhibitions removed now, he experienced a momentary euphoria. But only momentarily. The surge of alcohol in Bernie's blood, coupled with the residue of Xanax, was dramatically depressing the functions of his central nervous system, which acts as a command center for the body. Its signals exert control of every nerve and muscle, including the automatic functions of the lungs and heart. As the signals dim and the body begins shutting down, fatigue and ennui set in.

"So what," he muttered aloud. "So what. Nobody cares about me. Mr. Big Shot Lawyer. Hah! Oh sure, they all look up to Bernie, the president's right-hand man. And what happens? The whole blasted country is up in arms. Cops, National Guard, FBI. People shooting each other. And we're going to end up throwing the Constitution down the tubes . . . Hah! What would Professor Friedman think of me now, his prize student in constitutional law!

"It doesn't matter." Bernie was crying uncontrollably but made no attempt to dry his eyes. He was breathing harder, and the head throbbing returned with a vengeance.

"And Marilyn. What a hero she's hung around with all these years. She's right. I've failed her and failed the kids," he sobbed.

All the veneer and bluster were stripped away, and what Bernie saw revolted him. He hated himself.

Then an alien thought fought its way through the fog of his memory. *Paul Clarkson*. He once offered to help me. He's a religious guy. Sort of like that priest tonight . . . Father what's-his-name. Maybe I could talk to him.

"Hah!" As quickly as the thought came, he dismissed it as ridiculously funny. He had destroyed Clarkson's hero. Imagine calling him at midnight. "Excuse me. Could you tell me how this religion thing works?"

Bernie laughed, almost hysterically. "He'd slam the phone in my ear. No, I'd do that to him; he probably wouldn't do that to me. That's the difference between us . . .

"I've got his number somewhere," he exclaimed, pulling his wallet from his hip pocket. It was jammed full with money, receipts, scraps of paper with expense information, dry cleaning tickets. He tore the money out and started through the wads of paper. He took two big gulps, finishing his third drink, frantically pulling paper out of his wallet, balling up piece after piece and throwing them on the floor.

He flung the wallet to the corner of the desk. The paper was not there.

He checked his watch. Moving toward midnight. The White House operator could find Clarkson; she'd get anyone, anytime. No, the Secret Service might be monitoring the phones, as they did randomly. He didn't want them nosing into anything.

It didn't matter anyway, he thought; the darkness was here . . . the tunnel . . . waiting to swallow him. He swallowed another drink, but the alcohol only intensified his feelings of rejection . . . aloneness . . . hopelessness . . . danger.

I can't do it, he thought. *Nobody cares . . . and why should they?* His self-loathing was almost overwhelming.

The answer suddenly seemed clear. He reached for a sheet of paper from the center drawer of the desk. He scrawled some words on it, folded it neatly, and laid his pen on top of it.

He took another quick shot of the Dewars, then reached into the bottom drawer of his desk, behind a thick file folder. His hand closed around the cold blue metal of the Smith and Wesson .38 caliber revolver the Secret Service had issued him for emergency security at home.

Suddenly he felt a surge of confidence, an odd assurance that he was in charge again. He could get out of this on his terms.

He was breathing hard, but the tears had stopped.

There is a way out of the tunnel, he thought. He could control it.

He loaded one soft-nosed bullet into the chamber and snapped the cylinder shut.

Then, holding the gun with both hands, he placed the barrel in his mouth and pulled the trigger.

53

WHITNEY GRISWOLD's long form was draped over a spindly nineteenth-century chair in the Lincoln sitting room. It was almost midnight and he was alone. A Secret Service agent stood outside the door and others were down the hall, but here in this room he was alone. Alone with his thoughts as the nightmare day drew to a close.

After the news broke about Bernie's suicide, the media had been absolutely out of control, and his own shock had been so great that he couldn't rally the strength to even issue a statement. This was a scenario he and Bernie had never anticipated.

He wasn't even sure who to be. The tough president, striding into the press room, assertive and confident? The competent president, announcing a plan of action that others might follow? The grieving-but-in-control president, issuing poignant statements of condolence and comfort?

In the end, Caroline Atwater had simply put out a terse announcement that the Griswolds were mourning the loss of their close friend in private . . . and now J. Whitney Griswold was simply the wounded president, sitting in an uncomfortable chair and reading, over and over, the copy of the note Bernie had left for him. The Secret Service had confiscated the original from Bernie's desk, but the photocopy was cruelly clear.

The president was drinking Dewars. It felt like the right thing to do, in memory of Bernie, but it also felt exactly wrong without his old friend slouched on the sofa opposite him, red-faced and enthusiastically trading barbs, relishing their successes, laughing at something some pompous bureaucrat had done, brainstorming their next political victory.

The shots of Dewars weren't helping. His mind felt as clear as ever, the pain still there like a razor. How could Bernie be gone? He had clapped Bernie on the back just hours ago, telling him to buck up, things were going to be all right. He couldn't be gone.

Griswold looked down at the single sheet of paper in his hand. It had come in a White House envelope marked "For the President's Eyes Only," and he vaguely hoped the staff had honored that plea for privacy.

On it, scrawled in the bold handwriting he had known so well for more than twenty years, was but a single sentence: "Whit, I'm not going to be able to take care of this one for you.—B"

54

ANNE GRISWOLD and Marilyn O'Keefe had never been soul mates. But as her limousine headed toward the O'Keefe's Georgetown home, Anne realized that the years of their husbands' friendship had bound them together more closely than she'd thought.

Anne rarely did anything apart from a carefully considered strategic plan, but she had simply felt compelled to visit Marilyn. The younger O'Keefe children were being cared for by their aunt, and now Marilyn was at the house with her oldest son, Matt, and her parents, going through things, planning Bernie's funeral, doing whatever one does after a shock like that.

I hope she has some Valium or something, Anne thought. *There's just no way to cope with something like this otherwise.*

Secret Service personnel had restricted other cars from parking on the narrow Georgetown street around the O'Keefe townhouse, so Anne's limo was able to pull right up in front. Marilyn must have been watching from the window because the front door opened just as Anne got to the top step.

"Come on in," Marilyn said.

Anne stepped into the foyer. One of her agents stayed on the front porch; the other stepped discretely into the living room.

The two women paused for a second, then hugged.

"I'm so sorry," Anne said. "I don't know what to say."

"I don't know either," Marilyn said. "Let's go in the kitchen. My parents are upstairs packing boxes for me. I can't face that just yet."

Anne couldn't help glancing toward the library that Bernie had used as his study. The doors were shut; she could only imagine what it had looked like when they found him.

"Would you like some tea?" Marilyn asked. She gestured toward the tiled counter, piled with gift baskets, flowers, and tins. "The neighbors have been bringing food. There's some wonderful apple bread here."

"Thank you, a cup of tea would be nice," said Anne.

Marilyn looked thin and exhausted. When they were younger, the fullness in her face had disguised the sharpness of her features, but now Anne could see deep lines etched around her eyes, the thin skin stretched tight over her cheekbones, the sharp line of her narrow lips. *How did we get so old?* Anne wondered vaguely.

"I don't know what to say," she said again. "We had no idea Bernie was so depressed."

Marilyn looked up from the teakettle. "How could you not?" she asked. "I don't mean to be rude, but you knew we were separated. Whitney must have known how much Bernie was drinking . . ."

Anne felt a flush of irritation. "Whitney is very busy. He has a thousand things on his mind every day. Everything's top priority. He's the president! How could he know what Bernie was doing after he left the office?"

"I'm sorry," said Marilyn. "It's just that we all should have known. There were plenty of clues, and we didn't pick up on them. I just knew that I'd had it; I needed to get my children into a normal lifestyle . . . how could he have done this?"

Anne picked up her tea cup. "I don't know." This visit was going badly; after all, she needed to comfort Marilyn, not get into some blame exchange. A phrase from the California spiritualist whose book was on the best-seller list popped into her mind.

"They say that when someone takes his own life, it's actually a great catharsis," she said. "Maybe Bernie's inner pain was so great that this was the only way out. He had the courage to recognize his choice and take it, and now he's at peace. And I'm sure his life energy is with you and the children now, but now he's free of all his pain . . . It was his choice, his right."

Marilyn stared at Anne, her face harsh. "His right? What about my children's right to a father? You don't really believe that garbage, do you?"

Anne looked into her tea cup. "I don't know what to believe," she said with rare candor. "I just want you to feel better."

EMILY GINEEN slumped in the leather chair behind her office desk, alternately twirling a Flair fine-point pen between her fingers and dabbing her nose with a Kleenex. Paul Clarkson sat opposite her in the blue wing chair facing the desk, sipping a cup of coffee.

Usually their Justice Department schedule did not allow time for slumping, but a flu bug and laryngitis had caused Emily to cancel her plans for the day, a speech at the University of Virginia. *Just as well*, she thought. The idea of giving a speech on the pursuit of justice while her mind was reeling with the news of Bernie O'Keefe's suicide seemed more than she could handle.

She sneezed, dabbed her nose, and popped another menthol eucalyptus lozenge into her mouth.

"Did you know Bernie was so depressed?" she whispered.

"Bernie and I weren't exactly confidants," Paul said.

"Maybe I've been insulated all my life, but I've never known anybody who committed suicide," said Emily. "Why would he do this? There had to be some terrible thing in his life, some deep dark secret we knew nothing about, something he just couldn't deal with. But what a tragedy. He had so much going for him, so many opportunities ahead. He's . . . he was . . . much smarter than the president."

"Maybe he was so smart he saw he was running out of options," Paul said.

"What do you mean?"

Paul paused a moment. "People like Bernie are on the fast track. They make a lot of compromises. Bernie had a conscience—we all do, even if we bury it sometimes. Maybe he just got tired . . . and it's not like he could just drown out his conscience and stay drunk all the time."

Emily stared at Paul. She had never heard him sound so harsh. "That sounds so self-righteous," she said bluntly. "I know you're a straight arrow, but you can't tell me you've never done anything to offend your conscience."

"Of course I have, Emily. Every day. But I know there's an answer. That's the heart of Christianity. Christ died for my sins so I can be forgiven. So I can go on. So I can know that life has meaning. I couldn't go on without that."

"Yeah, but not everyone has it put together like you do, Paul," she croaked. "You've got a wonderful family and a good profession and your faith gives you comfort. If Bernie's whole life was falling apart, and on top of that he had all of Griswold's problems on his shoulders . . . I guess that's enough to make anyone depressed—even without any dirty little secrets."

"Don't you think I was depressed when this happened to me?" Paul asked, gesturing toward his legs. "I was depressed when we lost our first baby at three months. I'm like anyone else—I get depressed. But your state of mind isn't dependent on what you have or don't have. It depends on who you are."

"If anybody had self-confidence, it was Bernie," Emily whispered, coughing into her Kleenex.

"I don't mean confidence in oneself," Paul said. "I mean confidence in something outside oneself. The self-confident person has the biggest problem of all. When he looks at himself and doesn't like what he sees, if that's where his confidence is, he's done. No, there's got to be something beyond ourselves that we have confidence, or faith, in; otherwise we'd all commit suicide."

"Bernie was a Catholic," Emily said. "He had faith in God."

"I don't just mean believing that God exists. I mean a personal faith, the kind that—"

"I know about that," Emily interrupted. "I walked the aisle when I was a kid. Every summer I'd give my life to Jesus again at Bible camp. I'm born again. Just like most of the American public."

"No, I'm not talking about the cliches. I mean down deep—a real commitment. One you'd stake your life on," Paul replied.

"That sounds so sanctimonious," Emily rasped, "as if you have the corner on truth, and anyone who doesn't phrase things just the way you do is out in the cold. Or out in the heat, going to hell."

"I'm sorry," Paul said. He hated conversations like this. "I'm not judging anyone. But I believe that Christ is God; that He gave His life for me, and so my life is not my own. It belongs to Him. And that shapes my beliefs about everything else."

"You make it sound so simple." Emily snapped her fingers. "Come on, Paul, faith is fine, but life is more complicated than that."

"No, Emily, when you think about it, there are only three logical choices in life. The first is to accept the Truth. It's not easy, but it is what gives life meaning. The second choice is to reject the Truth, to believe life has no meaning; and so you do the only honest thing—you get it over with. You put a gun in your mouth. Remember what Camus said, if God is dead, the only philosophical question is suicide.

"Or," he continued, "you can avoid the question altogether and just keep yourself anesthetized with booze or TV or sex or power. But if you don't keep yourself distracted all the time, if you get involved in the contradictions of life and try to struggle with them, you eventually go nuts. That's it, three options: life, death or madness."

Paul paused. He could see that Emily was listening, processing, the way he had seen her evaluate dozens of briefings during the months they had worked together. He knew he couldn't argue his faith as if it was a legal case; certainly faith was logical, but it couldn't be boxed. If Emily was going to understand, he thought, it would have to come from more than any clever arguments he might make.

"Listen," he said. "Bernie's suicide is a terrible shock. It's a nightmare for his family and for this administration. We don't know what he went through at the end. We're just left to deal with what he did. And we need to pull ourselves together now. You'll need to be there for the president. He'll be leaning more on you now, so the country needs you to be strong. And the first thing we need to do is work on your cold. Can I get you some hot tea?"

Emily nodded, glad to get him out of the room for a moment. As Paul limped out the door, she sighed. What he had said made sense, but it also scared her. It reminded her of those smug Christians she had known in her youth, that Sunday school world where emotion ruled over reason and anything deemed too hard to figure out intellectually was simply glossed over as a matter of faith.

But Paul wasn't like that, she had to admit. He wasn't smug. Everything she had ever seen him do spoke of dedication, commitment, excellence, even humor. He had served her, and this administration, well. He hadn't nagged or bugged anyone in the office about his faith. He was different. And he was consistent.

There was a tap on the door, and then it bumped open. Paul leaned on his cane with one hand and in the other he had a big mug of steaming tea balanced on a small plate, with a white napkin and two fat wedges of yellow lemon on it.

"Where in the world did you find that?" she asked.

Paul grinned and shrugged. "The Lord provides," he teased.

Emily grinned back. "I'm sure He does," she said. "I'll think about what you said. But right now we need to get back to work."

Thursday, June 25

The motorcade slowly pulled away from the cemetery gravesite. The private service earlier had been in the Catholic

Church in Wellesley Hills, a Victorian-era, stone structure filled with mourners for Bernie O'Keefe. The crowds outside had been held back by the Wellesley police under the watchful eye of the Secret Service.

A strong northwest front had moved through the night before. Even in June there were occasional cold days in New England—and this was one. As the president's limousine passed through the cemetery gates, a few pieces of paper scuttled across the narrow road, then swirled in a sudden gust of wind.

In the back of the heavy, black limousine, the Griswolds said nothing, but sat closer together than usual. Anne reached out to take Whitney's hand. It was cold. He had refused to wear a coat.

The graveside ceremony had been rather brief. At the end they had left Bernie's coffin next to the rectangular hole in the earth, and Whitney had escorted Marilyn and the children to their car. Then Anne had watched as he turned to look back at the coffin, resting on the pulleys that would lower it into the grave. His face showed nothing as he turned, silently put his hand under her elbow, and escorted her to their own car.

Now, as the motorcade turned onto the main road, Whitney stared out the window at the cemetery and the old parish church next to it. And then the bells began to toll.

55

DANIEL SEATON stood beside Rob Knight as the judge strode through the door of U.S. District Court room number six, his black robes swirling around him. The words of the bailiff were still ringing in Daniel's ears: "Oyez, oyez. The U.S. District Court for the District of Columbia is now in session, the Honorable Randolph Green, presiding. All persons having business before this court will please rise . . ."

Rob Knight looked at the table to the left. There were six lawyers from the U.S. attorney's office flanking the U.S. attorney himself, Sam Gilquist. *Press hound*, he thought. The U.S. attorney rarely appeared in court, and certainly never for a simple arraignment.

Judge Green sat down, and the lawyers, clerks, stenographers, and rows of spectators—mostly press who had clamored for credentials—did the same thing. Except for the rustling of the bodies, the room was quiet as the judge sat staring sternly at a sheaf of papers. Known for his no-frills style, this was a judge who had little patience with the self-indulgent rhetorical excesses of bombastic attorneys; he ran a tight ship.

Green's wife had been killed three years earlier, when, under the influence of alcohol, she had collided head-on with a teenaged driver on his way home from high school band practice. Judge

Green rarely spoke about the horrible incident, but his staff and those who appeared in his courtroom had found that the experience had softened the once-stringent technocrat. Since the accident, he had shown more compassion for the human lives touched by the strictures of the law. Some might say his justice had been tempered with mercy.

Now the judge smiled and nodded toward the prosecution's table. "Ah, I see the government is represented this morning by its senior counsel. We welcome you to our courtroom, Mr. Gilquist. And the defendant is represented by his counsel, Mr. . . . ah, yes, Knight—good to see you also."

The lawyers and Daniel rose and moved a few steps forward. Daniel had lost so much weight that his suit hung limply, but he was grateful for it; Rob had arranged with the U.S. attorney's office for him to change from his orange jumper into his regular suit in a holding cell just outside of the courtroom. It was the first time he had been out of prison garb since his arrest.

He was struck by how sterile the court seemed. Just a big cubeshaped room with light paneled walls. The furniture was austere, upscale government issue. It all seemed cold and clinical, like an operating room, and he was the body now being wheeled in.

It was difficult for him to follow what was happening. The judged fired questions at the prosecutor about the grand jury and the papers that had been prepared. Rob interjected some comments and asked about motions. Then the docket clerk walked forward and began to read very stiffly and dramatically: "The United States of America versus Daniel Seaton . . ."

That hurt. He loved his country, always had. And now here it was, the United States against him, as if he had betrayed her.

Rob had agreed to waive the reading of the indictment, but the prosecutor had insisted, so the clerk droned through it. Daniel knew he was being charged with everything in the book, from aiding and abetting the destruction of the regeneration center, to homicide of a U.S. congressman, a doctor, and a security guard, to conspiracy, to accessory after the fact. It was written like a verdict, like all of these things had been proven. It was a good thing Rob was gripping his arm; he needed steadying.

As the clerk cited each statute—18 USC Section 831, 18 USC Section 841, 18 USC Section 371, 18 USC Section 3, 18 USC Section 351—Daniel winced. It was like salt in a wound. He thought he heard Mary sobbing somewhere behind him.

"How does the defendant plead?" the judged peered down after the indictment was read. Rob nudged Daniel, who spoke clearly, "Not guilty, Your Honor."

Then the haranguing began. The lawyers sparred over preliminary hearings, scheduling of motions. Judge Green kept interrupting. There was an extended argument over the time for the trial, the prosecutors arguing for sixty days. Rob, knowing the government wanted the trial while passions were highly charged, was balking.

Finally Judge Green hit the gavel. Barring unforeseen delays, he pronounced, the case would begin in ninety days. He whacked the gavel again and stood up, walking off the platform to the side door. There was a loud buzzing in the courtroom as people broke into conversations.

Rob turned to him and said only, "Okay. Round one is over. It's just technical. The indictment."

Then two armed marshals grasped Daniel firmly under each elbow and began moving him toward the side door to the right. He almost stumbled trying to see Mary. She was looking straight at him, her eyes steady, smiling, nodding her head slightly, willing him her love and support and strength.

"It'll be all right," she mouthed toward him through the confusion. "We love you!"

Wednesday, July 22

Harvey Robbins took no responsibility more seriously than the plotting and protection of Whitney Griswold's schedule. To that end, each night he mapped out the next day for the president, minute by minute, like a theatrical script. Then he would attach file cards for every event—crib sheets for the president, who had grown totally dependent on the technique.

And Griswold was very good at it. Before a meeting he would glance at the cards, memorize them quickly, and then sound wonderfully spontaneous and informed with his visitor.

Robbie remembered the time when Max Wendell, an old Nixon aide, now CEO of a major international conglomerate, whom Griswold had made chairman of a commission to study Head Start programs, came into the office to present an interim report on the commission's work. Wendell's wife was with him. The two had not been back to the White House for several years, and Wendell was obviously moved as he walked into the Oval Office. Griswold greeted him warmly and walked him around the room, explaining each change that he had made and what had been in its place when Nixon had sat at the same desk so many years before.

Then Griswold stopped, put one hand on the older man's shoulder, and recited four paragraphs from Nixon's first inaugural address. He didn't miss a word. Wendell listened raptly.

"I was, of course, just a youngster at the time," said Griswold, "but it made an impression on me that has remained to this day. Those words were so filled with vision and passion . . . They gave me the inspiration to pursue a career in politics. Those words are part of the reason that I'm standing here today as president of the United States."

Wendell nodded. His wife dabbed a tear from her eye. Robbie smiled slightly. Griswold had followed his instructions to the letter.

But now Robbie was frustrated. In the weeks since Bernie's death, Griswold had been uncontrollable. He ignored the program sheets, couldn't or wouldn't bother to memorize the cards, got consistently behind schedule, something neither he nor Robbie would have tolerated in the past.

And by ignoring his briefing materials, he had made some substantial gaffes. He had given a framed picture of the White House—one of the gifts, like the boxed cufflinks, that he often gave important visitors—to a leader of a Native American tribe, suggesting it would look good on his tepee wall. Another time he told the muscular dystrophy poster girl how much his daughter, Elizabeth, liked to play basketball.

Much of the time the president simply seemed detached and disengaged, just going through the motions. Robbie had even talked to the White House physician, who said these were normal reactions to deep grief and that they would pass in time.

But now Robbie was sitting in his office, waiting for Griswold's call to start a senior staff meeting, a meeting Griswold himself had requested to set out their legislative agenda before Congress adjourned in August. It was 8:55, already ten minutes late, utterly unlike the president. Busy people were cooling their heels, and the entire day was getting backed up.

Robbie tapped his pencil on his desk impatiently. He had nothing to read at the moment because he had arrived this morning at 7:00, as usual, to clean every memorandum off his desk. It was a strict discipline—the only way, he believed, to stay ahead of things. And the 8:00 senior staff meeting had adjourned at 8:30 promptly, as scheduled; and he'd signed off on every action paper for the day.

Just as his irritation was increasing, his secretary buzzed over the intercom. "The president is ready."

"Good thing," he mumbled, tucking his black, leather-bound folder under his arm and bounding out of the chair.

GRISWOLD WAS SEATED behind his desk, writing. He looked up just long enough to wave the staff in. Six men and one woman took their regular seats around his desk.

Forbes Carlton, a lanky, angular man whom Bernie had, under some pressure from Griswold, appointed his deputy, sat in what had been Bernie O'Keefe's regular chair. Griswold had pushed Carlton, a Harvard graduate and partner in Dewey Ballantine in New York, only because his father and Griswold's father were best friends and polo partners. It was the one favor Griswold's father had asked.

But the president felt some irritation as he looked up and saw the studious Carlton, his lips tightly pursed as if he had just eaten a dill pickle and a shock of brown hair dangling over his forehead, staring at him through thick lenses and, of all things, sitting in Bernie's seat.

"Well, good morning," Griswold smiled, putting the cap on his pen and straightening up in his chair.

"Good morning, Mr. President," came the chorus.

"Robbie will first review very briefly my schedule for the next ten days so you'll know what we are working with here." Griswold nodded at Robbie, who reviewed in detail upcoming commitments. Griswold grimaced. Something every minute, it seemed, and worst of all, no time for Camp David on the weekend.

"Now let's look at each legislative agenda; that is, what we must accomplish before the distinguished members of Congress go home for August—and what a wonderful day that will be," he grinned. "National Security first, General."

Maloney had only one item, the Gatt III Treaty, but it was assured passage, with a vote coming within the week.

Each senior staffer followed with options and requests for the president—a call to a key fence-sitting congresswoman, a public works project awarded for another. Robbie was pleased. The staff was well prepared and organized, and, most important, Griswold seemed to be tracking with them.

Robbie checked his watch—thirteen minutes left. They might even recover lost time and keep the day on schedule, particularly important today because every minute was planned until lunch when Griswold would eat his cottage cheese and apples, then take his daily twenty-minute nap. From 2:00 until 6:00 was tightly scheduled with key representatives and senators, one after another, most of it arm-twisting on the crime bill—and important.

Griswold had been listening to John Parker, former congressman from Pennsylvania and now the legislative liaison chief.

The president was taking notes and, without looking up, nodded toward Carlton. "All right, Bernie, clean this up for us . . . oh." The president jerked his head up, looking angry and startled. "Oh, my, I'm sorry . . . go ahead, Carlton, I mean Forbes."

Robbie thought Griswold's complexion looked unusually sallow, and his face seemed creased and sharp. His eyes never met Carlton's—although that might have been partly because Carlton was reading a very bureaucratic and lengthy explanation of the effort by liberal members in the Appropriations Committee to cut off funds for the National Guard. Having failed to override the Declaration of Emergency on the floor, they were now working a back-door approach. As Robbie watched, he could see Griswold's impatience grow.

"Oh, forget it, Carlton. Forget it. Those jackasses will never get it out of committee. Don't waste your time with it." Griswold made a great sweeping motion with his hand as if to dispense with the entire Congress—and maybe Forbes Carlton at the same time.

But Carlton persisted. "But, Mr. President, sir, there could be a basis to argue under—"

"Oh, put it in their ear, Carlton . . . I mean Forbes . . . it's drivel. They're like little red ants, and you can just step on them. As a matter of fact, you should go up to the Hill and moon them." But Griswold wasn't laughing. He was scowling, and Caroline Atwater looked startled. "You know what I mean. That's what they deserve."

Robbie made an effort to get things back on track. "Well, that's a good morning's work. I'll put the action sheets together, have them in your office in an hour." But Griswold wasn't finished.

"What you've got to learn, Carlton, or Forbes, whatever—I had a friend at Brown named Carlton—is not to let the little people get under your skin." Griswold had an almost sickly grin on his face, an expression Robbie had only seen once or twice—when the president was very upset.

"So don't give them the time of day. There are people out there who want to take down the presidency. We've got to defend this office . . . all of you. You need to understand that. But no one does really, I suppose . . ." Griswold suddenly turned reflective. "Nobody understands, nobody."

Then he turned away, stood up, and walked to the table behind his desk, and slowly began rearranging the pictures of his family.

Everyone sat silently. They weren't dismissed, and the president might be thinking some great thought. So they sat uncomfortably for what seemed a full two minutes before Griswold turned back and faced them. He still had that odd grin on his face.

"Yes, Carlton. That's fine. Good work. Now the Seaton case. I'll need a full report. By tonight. I want you to tell me in detail what is going on. I'm a lawyer; I understand it. You are not to let Justice drag their feet. They do that, you know. You'll find out. All of them are the same. They just don't see the big picture. Most people don't. Never do. Well, let's get to work . . ."

The senior aides all nodded, filing out one by one. The president remained standing behind his desk, smiling faintly and gripping a picture of his daughter.

PRISON LIFE both mocks and mirrors the human condition. The soul is stuck, thwarted, wings beating against the bars of the cage, sick, pacing, alone, and sad. The walls close in, assaulting the spirit. The mind longs for a fresh scent, a flower, a glimpse of blue sky above.

And yet for some, the mind and body embrace the rigid constraints of life in the box. Some inmates abandon themselves altogether, sleeping up to twenty hours a day, lost in the nether world of dreams beyond the wall. Others come to so rely on the quarantine of choice that they begin to depend upon it. They are told when and what to eat, when to sleep, when to shower, when to exercise; upon release, the free world seems overwhelming in its dazzling array of options. Most ex-prisoners commit new crimes. They just cannot deal with life outside the box.

Daniel Seaton's confinement had not yet progressed to the monotony of the full-fledged prison experience. Though he chafed at the routine, he'd had regular visits from Mary and the few friends who were allowed in. Mary's parents had come from Florida for an extended visit, and her mother was now staying at the house, helping with the children.

And he spent many hours with Rob Knight in the special visiting room set aside for attorneys. These meetings were often painful and at cross-purposes. They kept going over the same ground, exhaustively, and Rob seemed to be looking to Daniel for ideas about how to cross-examine the government's witnesses, especially John Jenkins . . . Daniel had no idea. And Rob was jubilant that he was forcing delays in the government's case while Daniel simply wanted it all over.

But the days were all right—except for the ceaseless noise: the clanging of steel, blaring of radios, and inmates shouting at the guards and one another. It was the nights Daniel dreaded. Even though the cellblocks were finally quiet, in the dark he was alone with the ghosts of his thoughts about Alex and the sick sense of shame. He re-examined his motives; he anguished again and again. He had not meant to do evil, but he had been naive. And evil had been the result.

Over and over again he saw Alex at his kitchen table on the night of the bombing, bowing his head while Mary stitched his scalp. He thought of the mad rush away in the night and imagined the chaos that had followed. The FBI hadn't revealed much about how Alex and Lance had died, but he had pieced the scene together in his mind. All he could think of was Alex as a child, Alex leaping the waves at Rehoboth Beach when they were young, Alex's rising anger in the pro-life cause, escalating to the point where his rage had overrun his reason.

For his part, Daniel realized that he had been like Alex. Not that passion had overtaken him; he wasn't that sort of person. He had allowed himself to be overcome—to slide, inch by inch, into the sin of despair. He had given up, relinquished the battle. Back at Rehoboth Beach, when he sat on the sand with Alex and the others and had, in essence, let them go, he had done so because he had lost hope. He realized he had come to believe, ever so unconsciously, that the only way left to stop the regeneration centers was the path of violence. Just as long as he didn't really know what was happening. He had compromised, vaguely assenting to ugly means in order to achieve the godly end he so desired. He had passed off his personal responsibility, he had lost hope, and the bars now penning him in seemed a fair price to pay for that sin. Alex's death did not.

Daniel had not been allowed to go to his brother's funeral, a small and private affair attended by Mary and the children, Mary's parents, and a few members of their church. The police had provided security for the family and kept the media at a distance, but they hadn't been able to shield Mary from the taunts and threats she received each day when she visited the jail.

Daniel marveled at his wife's strength; she seemed to take it all with such dignity, even when things got ugly. When she had been splattered with blood by the AIDS protester, her response had defused the situation. Ira Levitz had written about it in his newspaper column—something about grace quenching rage—and it seemed there had been a wave of sympathy for her since.

Not so for Daniel. If his wife was now perceived as a good woman drawn under the influence of a crazed cult of extremists, according to the papers, he was still the villain, the mastermind of a conspiracy that had now taken the lives of five people.

In the jail, though, he wasn't seen that way. Most of the inmates knew well the pitfalls of blood ties and betrayal; they knew how an innocent man could get caught in a legal vise that could pull him all the way down. And most of them operated by the convict code of ethics: Those who would have marked Daniel for death if he was accused of child molestation didn't find killing a congressman a particularly heinous crime.

"Way to go," one old guy with vacant, watery blue eyes had whispered to Daniel in the shower room. "Blow 'em all up! That's the only way things'll ever change."

In the world of the haves and the have-nots, where life's

inequities were chalked up to a "crooked system," where the rich got rich and the poor got poorer, none of the cons had particular sympathy for the likes of Peter Meyer and Barbara LaMar. Whether Daniel had anything to do with the bombing or not.

And Daniel's attitude toward them didn't hurt either. He had found that the parishioners to whom he was now called had common enough needs. Car thieves, drug dealers, burglars, muggers, drunks, and illegal aliens—they all needed someone to listen. He tried to hear the needs behind their words, to gently expose the flaws in their thinking: They were all innocent, even the man who admitted he had shot his wife in a drunken rage.

Daniel began to realize that he hadn't listened, really listened, to Alex. And though Alex was no longer with him, these men were.

56

As autumn fell into winter, the atmosphere in Washington felt as bleak as the frigid breezes. At George Washington Hospital, the windows broken by the bomb blast had been replaced, but the site of the regeneration center was still cordoned off. On the wooden fence that had been erected around it, someone had spray-painted, "death to the anti-choice hypocrites." Officials removed the graffiti on six separate occasions, but by the next morning, the message was always there again. Eventually they just left it.

Every day, news reports brought more grisly headlines. Some of the violence, like the graffiti, was directed against anyone perceived to be a "religious extremist" or connected with the Seaton case. In Virginia, someone left a dead lamb on the Seatons' front porch. In St. Louis, a group of homosexual activists conducted a march outside a Presbyterian church hosting a prayer meeting; later, hundreds of condoms filled with mayonnaise were found scattered throughout the church's Sunday school classrooms. In Minneapolis, three nuns sitting on a bench in front of a doctor's office were harassed and spat upon.

Most of the violence was random. But it was also rampant.

On October 31, the annual Halloween parade in Georgetown

evolved into a full-blown riot. As usual, the police had cordoned off the main thoroughfare for the parade; in deference to the curfew, they had mandated that the streets be emptied by 10:00 P.M. By 9:00, the crowd had swelled to several thousand at the corner of Wisconsin Avenue and M Street, milling around the gold-domed Riggs Bank on the corner and down the hill toward the Potomac River, where the waterfront restaurants were doing a desultory business; most of the Halloweeners didn't have the money or interest to be good customers, and the usual business-and-government clientele stayed away, put off by the devils and the undead.

With good reason. At 9:30, chaos erupted at the corner of Wisconsin and M when a gang of teenagers dressed as Hell's Angels started harassing a group dressed as SS officers. A witch and a werewolf who'd had too much to drink got into the act and joined in the obscenities raining down on the Nazis. A local TV crew, taping an interview with a vampire, turned its cameras to cover the scene.

People started pushing and shoving, and even as two D.C. police officers on the sidelines started to move through the crowd toward the fight, one of the Nazi officers pulled out a real gun from under his uniform and started firing into the cluster of Hell's Angels.

People ran in every direction, but they were hemmed in by the mass of bodies, and so many were so drunk that they stumbled to the pavement and were trampled . . . and as the policemen closed in on the shooter, with another officer on the side barking into his radio for National Guard backup, the dark night turned into a nightmare. So many in the crowd were smeared with fake blood, made up as ghouls, that as the ambulances started arriving, it was difficult to discern whose wounds were real and who should be treated first.

In the end, armored personnel carriers bristling with machine guns rolled down M Street, and more than seventy-five people were taken to local hospitals, with a final body count of three dead.

Washington was not the only site of civil unrest. In Chicago, an arsonist torched three of the apartment blocks in the Cabrini-Green housing project. Fifteen residents died, mostly young children. Since government housing and social services agencies were already stretched beyond their limits, there was nowhere for the survivors to go.

After the most recent earthquake in L.A., 6.8 on the Richter, riots erupted in the south central sector of the city, chalked up to allegations that rescue units had responded quicker to wealthier sections of the city.

In New York, a freak storm in early December knocked out electrical power for seven hundred thousand people. The governor declared a state of emergency within half an hour of the outage, but in spite of armed federal troops patrolling the streets of Manhattan, looters broke into Fifth Avenue's most exclusive half mile. Merchants later reported $60 million worth of damage and lost merchandise.

"HAPPY HOLIDAYS," Emily Gineen said grimly to Paul Clarkson. Government employees had been restricted from saying "Merry Christmas" for several years now, but the generic holiday greeting still didn't feel natural to Emily. She sighed; in five minutes they needed to adjourn to the conference room for the AG's annual "winter celebration"—what used to be known as the office Christmas party. Her two secretaries' desks were lined with tinsel, and there was a holly garland on the fireplace in Emily's office, but she felt anything but festive.

"I hate parties," she said to Paul. "I particularly hate parties where I have to personally greet and mingle with 150 of my closest professional friends. Isn't there some national emergency just about to break that will necessitate a quick trip to the White House? I don't want to go to this party."

"I think we've had enough national emergencies to do us for quite a while," said Paul. "I can't ever remember a time like these past months."

"It's like the whole country is in a horrible mood," Emily said, turning to stare out of her fifth-floor window to the wet, gray scene below. "You'd think things would be coming together. We've clamped down like never before, we've got troops on the streets and a policeman on every corner, just about, and—the crime rate continues to *climb*. That's why I can't go into this party and smile and pretend everything is all right in the halls of justice. Everything is not all right."

"No, it isn't," Paul said. "And what we're doing is not going to fix it."

Emily frowned.

"You and I have talked about this. When people lose their inner restraints—conscience . . . religion—you have to keep putting more and more outer restraints on them. They get more and more frustrated. And you end up with troops and tanks in the streets."

"You make it sound so simplistic, Paul."

Paul shrugged. "Lord Acton had it right. You've seen that quote on my office wall. 'The greater the strength of duty'—and he meant *religious* duty—'the greater the liberty.'"

"If people aren't moved by a sense of religious responsibility, something above themselves, then the only way you can restrain or control their behavior is by fear. The more fear, the less freedom. That's what's happening."

There was an awkward silence for a moment, then Emily turned from the window to face him. "Thank you so much for that encouraging word," she said, adjusting the cuffs of her blouse and buttoning her double-breasted red jacket. "Perhaps you'd like to deliver a short speech at the party?"

"I'm sorry," Paul said. "I shouldn't be adding to the mood here. Things will probably get better after Christmas and after Daniel Seaton's trial. Let's hope so—until it's over, people aren't going to settle down. They've made him into the biggest national villain since Saddam Hussein. It's ridiculous."

But Emily wasn't listening. She had switched gears, and Paul watched her as she leaned over her desk, intently studying the typed list of those who would be attending the party as if it were a legal brief. She had a remarkable ability to compartmentalize. Right now, if duty called for her to shove aside personal feelings and host a party, then she would do it. And by the time she entered the conference room, Paul knew she would be greeting people right and left, never stumbling over a name, charming and gracious and witty. She was amazing.

She looked up and grinned at him, connecting again for half a second. "Okay," she said. "Let's get in there and have a good time, even if democracy as we know it is heading right down the tubes."

She strode to the door, flung it open, and moved briskly toward the conference room, where people were already milling about, balancing punch cups and plates of smoked salmon and crackers. "Rodney!" Paul heard her exclaim warmly to someone whose name she would not have remembered five minutes earlier. "It's so good to see you here!"

57

A S THE NEW YEAR BEGAN, a pass to the Seaton trial was the hottest ticket in Washington. Thanks to Rob Knight's legal machinations, the trial had been delayed several times, but by the first week in January, he could hold it off no longer.

On Thursday morning, January 7, crowds began to gather behind cordoned areas on the street leading up to the steps on the United States Courthouse, the sand-colored fortress sprawling across the corner of Constitution Avenue and Third Street NW in downtownWashington. Despite the slushy sidewalks and plowed piles of dirty snow, there was almost a festive atmosphere. Vendors were soon sold out of hot coffee and bagels. Others hawked Tshirts.Television cameras zoomed in on the array of posters and placards. "Abort Seaton," read one. "Pro-life Hypocrites Deserve Justice—Gay and Lesbian Alliance," said another. And there was the usual, terse, "Fry him!"

Daniel Seaton escaped the maddened crowd; at 7:00 A.M., marshals had driven him in an armored wagon through the garage entrance to the courthouse. Since then he had been pacing a six-by-nine holding cell in the basement.

Mary Seaton was not so fortunate. Following Rob and

surrounded by friends from church, she braved the gauntlet at 9:30. There was a clamor from the crowd, and uniformed officers formed a human barrier in front of the police saw-horses.

Rob, weighed down with fat briefcases and legal folders, pushed past the camera crews hanging over the barricades near the main door. Mary picked up a folder he dropped and fol-lowed him through the door.

Every seat in the courtroom had been assigned. Family and friends were in the first two rows on the right side behind the defense table; the media, along with the courtroom artists down front, occupied most of the left-side seats. Behind the family, seats were reserved for government officials, researchers, some graduate students, and even representatives of the diplomatic corps. Tickets had been handled by the chief judge's office with the same care as if it were a state occasion.

AT PRECISELY 10:00 A.M., the bailiff announced the court in session. The room hushed, and Judge Randolph Green entered from the door to the left of his desk. He pulled his black robe together and walked solemnly to his seat.

Rob Knight and Assistant U.S. Attorney Jack Barnes moved toward the bench as Judge Green asked, "Are we ready to call for a jury?"

Fifty potential jurors were in the pool, and the first two days of the trial were occupied with winnowing them down to the twelve jurors and six alternates who would ultimately hear the case. Rob Knight knew that in the District of Columbia the majority of the jurors would be black, probably suspicious of any white suburbanite. On the plus side, of course, he only needed one dissenting vote to hang a jury, and he could count on the odds that at least one of the African Americans on the jury would likely be a member of an inner-city Baptist church.

But Jack Barnes had done his best to winnow out anyone with religious inclinations. Counsel couldn't ask a juror's religion, of course, but he fished around; one potential juror who admitted listening to WAVA, the Christian radio station, was quickly dropped.

The jury was impaneled by Friday evening. Seven women and five men. Ten blacks, one white, one Asian. Four worked for government agencies, two were unemployed, one was a schoolteacher.

BY MONDAY, the court was ready for opening statements. Judge Green looked over his immense desk and down to Jack Barnes and Rob Knight. "I don't want to hear any inferences or advocacy in these statements," he said. "Stick to the facts you can prove, gentlemen. Thank you."

Jack Barnes was a tall, handsome man, smooth and deferential in his approach, a political player who knew how to grease the wheels of the system. He strode slowly to the counsels' podium.

"Your Honor," he said in a deep, confident voice, "ladies and gentlemen of the jury. We come to this court of law to see to it that justice is done—justice in the face of a most extraordinary assault on our system of justice itself.

"We will demonstrate to the court that Mr. Seaton— though no doubt before his involvement in this plot a decent and wellintentioned man—was part of an insidious conspiracy attacking the very foundations of our American democracy and our national order.

"This case involves a conspiracy by people, including the defendant, who held themselves above the law. They violated not only the civil rights of those they slaughtered by means of deadly, overwhelming force, but also in so doing they violated the peace of mind of every American . . . for if religious extremists can strike down a federal officer, a congressman, in the heart of our nation's capital, how then can Americans trust in the safety of their streets across the nation?"

Rob Knight, scratching notes on a yellow pad, whipped off his glasses and rubbed his eyes. He had known it would be like this. But now the drama of the courtroom—the clerk taking down every word, those same words hanging in the air for a moment, then digested by the media and the jury—suddenly felt overwhelming. Rob's stomach turned over, and he clenched and unclenched his hands, then his jaw, trying to relieve the tension. The prosecutor was making it sound like Daniel had personally pulled the trigger and killed one of the Founding Fathers.

"It is too late for the other conspirators," Barnes continued, "the perpetrators of this bombing, murder, and mayhem to stand before us in this court of law and be held accountable for their crimes. But the proceedings of this court will signal that this nation will not tolerate Mr. Seaton or others like him setting themselves up according to what they call a higher law but which is, in fact, a law unto themselves.

"The government will prove that these men, including the defendant, did knowingly and willfully plan to bomb the regeneration center in Washington, D.C., a place designed, ironically enough, to save lives." Barnes looked disdainfully toward Daniel and then proceeded to outline his case: Alex Seaton and Lance Thompson, with the aid of the other named co-conspirators, including John Jenkins and Daniel Seaton, did plan for the destruction of the center, plant and detonate the explosives, and take the lives of Congressman Peter Meyer, Dr. Barbara La Mar, and security guard Justin Jones.

Barnes continued, clinically, "Said defendant did aid and abet the perpetrators by providing medical help after the bombing, failing to tell the authorities of their whereabouts and assisting in their escape."

The outline was clear, Rob noted with a sigh. The government would take weeks proving the bombing, the deaths, all of the horrors, just to get to two points of fact: whether Daniel had foreknowledge and whether he assisted, with an overt act, in the bombing.

On both counts the evidence was shaky and circumstantial. Inferences would have to be drawn. But would the jurors see how narrow it was? He'd have to rely on the judge to keep instructing them.

Barnes moved slowly away from the podium and walked toward the rail behind which the jurors were seated in two rows. He leaned on the rail and smiled.

"Ladies and gentlemen, you know, as I do, that our country began as a place where liberty-loving people found freedom to practice their particular beliefs.

"Today it is a place brimming with the diversity of such beliefs, a place where people must be allowed not only their freedom to choose their own way, but the freedom to live their lives without the interference of those who believe they have the corner on what they call 'absolute truth.'

"In this anti-choice movement, this group on trial, we see those who would impose their particular beliefs, by means of violence, on others. This trial allows us the opportunity to assert that America is still a place of liberty and freedom."

Rob Knight looked down at the floor, tapping his feet. Next to him, Daniel seemed unmoved by the sweeping charges coming down.

"The anti-choice movement has a very dangerous wing," Barnes continued, "an extremist and fractured faction within it that will stop at nothing to accomplish its goals. Daniel Seaton is the leader of such a faction.

"Murder itself is not off-limits to these so-called 'pro-lifers.' They, and anarchy-minded extremists like them, must be sent a message. This trial constitutes a powerful means to not only convict Daniel Seaton of the crimes for which he is guilty but also to send that message.

"Thank you."

Barnes, who had started his speech in an understated style, had by now come to a crescendo. He concluded by looking directly into the faces of the jurors, establishing the sort of intense eye contact that made it clear to everyone in the courtroom that the fate of the nation and the future of democracy itself hung on the twelve men and women in the jury box.

It seemed that everyone in the crowded room exhaled at once, and Rob Knight got slowly to his feet. He didn't want to be dependent on notes, so he had memorized most of his statement as if it were a part in a theatrical production. He would improvise a bit now, leaning on his instinct that many of the people in the jury box were probably suspicious of someone too smooth. That was, in fact, the reason he had worn an old suit—not that he had any new ones— a plain tie, and, to his wife's consternation, a pair of brown suede oxfords that he usually wore on Saturday mornings to do errands.

"Why those shoes?" Lisa had said when he left the house that morning. "They look so unprofessional."

"That's exactly the point," he had told her as he kissed her and headed out the front door. "Those government lawyers will look like big money, big guns; they'll have on their power ties and every hair in place. Barnes has probably already put on his pancake makeup for the TV cameras. I need to look like a real guy, not some corporate attorney."

He groaned as he spilled a few drops of coffee from his travel mug onto his pants and tried ineffectually to scrub them with a napkin that still had bagel crumbs on it. "I've gotta get out of here," he said. "Pray for me!"

Lisa rolled her eyes. "Of course I will . . . you'll need it!" she shouted cheerfully. "I'll be watching you on the news—let's hope the cameras don't pan down and show your shoes!"

But in spite of her teasing, his wife knew him well. Earlier that morning she had told him, "Just be careful. Don't get too worked up. Don't get too dramatic. Don't overplay your hand. The other side will be very careful; you have to watch out that you don't get carried away by the passion of the moment. You do that sometimes, you know."

Don't get carried away, Rob reminded himself now. He had already decided not to bother contesting Alex and Lance's culpability; no need to expend energy on that or use up any of the jurors' goodwill fighting about the deceased perpetrators. Just set Daniel apart from them—and create reasonable doubt in the minds of the jurors.

"Your honor, Mr. Barnes, and ladies and gentlemen of the jury," Rob said, nodding to the government's attorneys and then focusing his attention on the people in the jury box.

"Mr. Barnes has spoken to you from the government's perspective. He speaks for dozens and dozens of attorneys, an army of legal minds who have carefully constructed and crafted a case to make you believe that Pastor Daniel Seaton is the evil mastermind behind an entire chain of events designed to bring democracy itself crumbling down around us.

"Mr. Barnes has postulated and inferred and obfuscated and conjectured so much that it is difficult to clearly focus on the facts. Let me speak plainly. He is doing that because the government does not have a case against Daniel Seaton.

"Here is the matter at hand. We are here to consider the innocence or guilt of Pastor Seaton. We cannot try his younger brother, Alex; Alex Seaton is dead. But if we could try Alex, we would have an entirely different case before us.

"Daniel Seaton does not contest the horror of the events that Alex Seaton and Lance Thompson set in motion. Daniel is not some kind of religious zealot. He is like you, and me, and every American who grieves with the families of those who were killed. He decries the destruction of property, the wanton violence of the bombing, the events of the night of last June 3.

"And what the evidence will demonstrate is that Daniel Seaton was in no way responsible. He is no terrorist. He is the pastor of a small church. He has always preached nonviolence to his congregation. He has always lived a productive, peaceful life with his wife, his children, his neighbors. He put himself through seminary as a carpenter; he continues to work hard and live simply. And he has spent far more time helping others, working with the hungry, the homeless, the hurting, with sufferers of AIDS—real people with real needs—than he has engaging in political debates. He has been steadfastly pro-life in the truest sense of the word, helping people live their lives in peace and dignity.

"As this trial proceeds, however, you will see that the prosecution would desperately like to punish *someone* for the bombing of the regeneration center and the deaths of Congressman Meyer, Dr. LaMar, and Justin Jones. The leaders of the government are angry, and their attorneys are desperate. So they have seized upon Pastor Seaton, whose chief connection with these crimes is the fact that his brother committed them.

"I would submit to you that if we have come to the point in America where a person can be tried for a crime committed by his brother, then perhaps Mr. Barnes is right, and our democratic system of justice is in jeopardy."

Rob was jarred by the crashing of the gavel. "Mr. Knight, let me gently remind you that arguments will come later. Stick to the evidence you will establish, sir. There will be time later for inferences." Green spoke gently, like an instructor in a beginners' class.

Rob tried to show no reaction. "Of course, Your Honor," he smiled. "I was simply responding to Mr. Barnes."

Rob continued, but with less passion in his voice. "Ladies and gentlemen of the jury, we will demonstrate that Daniel Seaton is no extremist, no terrorist. He is not a bomber and a murderer and a conspirator.

"Of course, we will not contest that Daniel Seaton is guilty of one thing. He is guilty of loving his younger brother. And when his brother came to him in the night, bruised and bleeding, he helped him. He bandaged him. He washed his face with a damp towel and gave him a glass of orange juice.

"Who among us would not do the same for our brother or sister? The evidence will be clear: Daniel Seaton did not know what his brother had just been involved in . . . he knew only that he was hurting. He ministered to his brother's pain. This is not a heinous crime. Yet because they cannot convict Alex Seaton, the government and its armies of attorneys want their pound of flesh. So they want to take a decent, kind human being and destroy his life, just to make a point. You must not allow them to do that.

"Thank you."

Rob turned and returned to the table. His lower back was killing him; he had been holding the muscles contracted, clenched, in his concentration to make his points to the jury. It was a relief to sit down. As he took his seat, he noticed that Daniel was looking at him with an expression he couldn't quite read.

DURING THE LUNCH BREAK many spectators stayed in their seats, afraid they might lose them. But Ira Levitz left the courtroom and headed for Constitution Avenue. He had been trying to take a brisk walk every day at lunchtime; his doctor had told him some fresh air and moving his legs vigorously were the least he could do to combat the cigar smoking, the inactivity behind the computer screen, and the big lunches at his favorite restaurants.

Ira chewed his unlit cigar as he walked, his overcoat flapping behind him in the winter wind. There was no way the government was going to convict Seaton, unless they had some major surprise ahead. They just didn't have the evidence, and the conspiracy charge seemed absolutely ridiculous, the type of inept legal action more reminiscent of Communist courts of the 1960s than of the U.S. government in the 1990s.

He sighed. The picture fit, though: tanks on the streets and trumped-up charges in the courts.

BEGINNING WITH the second day of testimony, the forensics experts were on the stand.

"Yes," a specialist named Lynn Mickey said in a strong voice. "This is the photograph taken at the scene of the bombing. It's hard to recognize what one is looking at, but this is the wreckage near the hospital entrance leading to the regeneration center."

Using a pointer, Jack Barnes indicated the center left of the large, blown-up photograph displayed on the easel at the front of the courtroom. "And would you be kind enough to tell us what this is?"

Dr. Mickey cleared his throat. "Human remains in a bombing of this type are almost always unrecognizable as having been human. This photo indicates a mass of blood and tissue, here, and a general area of fragments and matter, here, that were the largest single identifiable remains of the deceased."

Just like an abortion, Daniel Seaton couldn't help thinking.

"Dr. Mickey, were you able to reassemble the bodies of Congressman Meyer and Dr. LaMar?" asked Barnes.

"Yes, after combing the area, including the street below the walkway, where quite a bit was found actually, we were able to make positive identification."

"What was the cause of death?"

"Death would have been instantaneous. The body would be hit first by the concussive blast, then by shrapnel—that is, the glass and other debris. But the acoustic injuries from the blast would kill the victim instantly, tearing apart the lungs and arteries. Although it might not be of any comfort to the families of the deceased, I would add that the victims of this bombing did not suffer. It was too quick."

"Would an explosion of this type have been survivable, Dr. Mickey?"

"There are always cases that defy the odds, so I hesitate to call something absolutely unsurvivable. But an explosion of this type, in a relatively small building of this type, would almost inevitably lead to the deaths of anyone in the building. Particularly in the walkway."

"Thank you, Dr. Mickey. Your witness, Mr. Knight."

"Thank you. We have no questions, Your Honor."

A RATHER LOQUACIOUS demolitions expert named John Spout was next on the stand.

"Commander Spout, how many bombing sites have you examined?" asked Jack Barnes.

The lieutenant commander, a massive, square man in his late forties with a tanned, lined face and bright blue eyes, sat erect in the witness chair.

"Over the years it would be hard to say, but I would say I

have been on site for at least twenty-five post-explosive incidents."

"Have you also had experience with planting explosives?"

"Oh, yes. I've had extensive experience in military demolitions—be glad to outline that for you, sir."

"There's no need for that at this point, Commander. We're interested right now in the forensics of the regeneration center blast."

"Yes sir." Spout cleared his throat. "All explosives leave some form of residue after they've been exploded," he said. "The residue is like a fingerprint almost . . . with the right chemistry you can determine its origin. Even to the point of international origin, if the explosives didn't come from this country.

"You can also tell the rate of detonation—and the higher that is, the more shattering effect it has. We call it brisance—that's the French word for the breaking or shattering effect of the sudden release of energy. Another defining characteristic is the nitrogen level. All explosives have a high concentration of complex nitrogen molecules; if you can determine the types, by analyzing the residue, you can also determine what kind of high explosives were used."

Spout gushed forth for some time regarding rates of detonation, plastic explosives, and the like.

Rob Knight sat and doodled. All of this was simply dragging the case out. It didn't matter. Everyone knew these guys blew the place sky high.

Spout surmised that Alex and Lance must have filled a van with between seven hundred and one thousand pounds of military-issue C-4 explosive, rigged it with a non-electric timer, pulled the fuse igniter, then skedaddled out of the parking garage.

Fine, thought Rob. Point was, Daniel was on trial here. But, of course, the government was going to great lengths to paint the horrors of the bombing; they'd also go to great lengths to establish a conspiracy. Rob shifted uncomfortably in his chair.

Spout kept spouting. As the time went by and the courtroom got warmer, Rob noted one juror's head bobbing. The temptation to snooze was strong. Now the judge was cutting in.

"Counselor," Judge Green addressed Jack Barnes. "This testimony regarding the explosives, is, of course, quite interesting, but how much do you need to establish here? Where are you going, may I ask? No aspersions on your testimony, of course, Commander."

"Your Honor, this expert will demonstrate the ease, if you will, with which this building was exploded. How, in fact, any amateur—or anyone familiar with standard military-issue explosives—could do it, which the government believes is important to its proof."

"Well," said Green dryly. "I would hope the government would not advertise it as being so easy, or you'll have every aggrieved lawyer coming in here with haversacks full of C-4."

The courtroom erupted in laughter. The jury woke up.

"I'll let you go until 4:30, Counselor. Then this court will recess."

"Thank you, sir."

Jack Barnes prodded his witness, and eventually came down to his final question. "In your expert opinion, sir, would it take a high degree of professional expertise to set up a bomb like the one that destroyed the regeneration center?"

"That's just it," said Spout firmly. "It's not that difficult. Anyone with a little military explosives training could do this in a heartbeat. C-4 is one of the easiest explosives in the world to work with. All someone would need is a little bit of knowledge, a lot of explosives, and a little chutzpah."

"Thank you, Commander. Your witness, Mr. Knight."

Rob stood. "We have no questions, your honor."

The jury was nodding, whether in understanding or in relief was anyone's guess. Judge Green dismissed his court. It had been a long day.

REPORTS REGARDING Spout's testimony headlined the evening news. Since federal courts allowed no TV cameras in the courtroom, the trial itself was not televised. But its progress was duly reported, day after day, with the networks breaking into scheduled programming throughout the day if anything juicy came up.

After the trial each afternoon, Daniel was returned to the holding cell in the courthouse basement; there, he changed into his jail-issue orange jumper for transfer back to the Arlington jail. With processing and security, it was often 7:00 P.M. before he was back in his cell, and later if he and Rob met in the jail conference room to discuss the case.

THE NEXT DAY, the prosecution called Mabel Watkins to the stand. The small, slightly built woman with dark, graying hair stepped into the witness box and raised her right hand to take the oath. She wore a navy blue suit, severely cut, with a white blouse and sensible, low-heeled pumps. Her only concession to jewelry was the round gold National Association of University Librarians pin on her lapel; her only concession to makeup was some startling red lipstick slashed haphazardly across her thin, pursed lips. She wore a pair of half-glasses on a thin cord around her neck.

"Please state your name and occupation, Ms. Watkins."

"Mabel Watkins. I'm a librarian at the George Washington University main library. I've worked there for twenty-three years and seven months."

"Could you please tell the court what you witnessed on the night of last June 3?"

"Yes, I can. It's my regular practice to walk my dog each night before I go to bed. I feel safe as long as I stay in my neighborhood; everyone knows Fifi."

I bet Fiji is a miniature black poodle who looks just like the dog version of Mabel Watkins, Rob Knight thought as he drummed his fingers on the table.

"What kind of dog is Fifi, Ms. Watkins?" Jack Barnes asked solicitously.

"Fifi is a Great Dane."

Well, I missed that one, Rob said to himself.

"My brother gave her to me five years ago," Mabel Watkins continued. "He was worried about me living alone in the city. I've never had any trouble since I've had Fifi."

"So please continue," said Jack Barnes. "You and Fifi walk each evening."

"Yes, we do. I have her on a leash, of course, and I carry a pooper scooper and a plastic bag. The city is pretty strict about these things."

"Yes, it is," said Jack Barnes, grinning for a moment as a chuckle went through the courtroom. "A good thing, too. Well, please tell us, if you would, what happened as you walked Fifi near the university hospital."

"Certainly. I had just rounded the corner across the street from the building that was under construction, the regeneration center."

"So you were directly across the street from the regeneration center?"

"Yes. I looked at my watch; we were right on schedule. Fifi had relieved herself, and I had put her waste into a trash can on the corner of Twenty-third and I Streets. I was standing there for a moment, waiting for the light to turn, and then all of the sudden, Fifi started acting very strangely."

"Strangely?"

"The only thing I can compare it to is how she acts during a thunderstorm. She was pacing back and forth, whining, pulling on the leash, her ears pricked up. She was upset, and I didn't know why. I looked around. There was no one nearby. Then I looked across the street, and there was a car next to the curb with its motor running, and two men acting strangely."

"What did these men look like? And, if you could, please tell us what you mean when you say they were acting strangely," Jack Barnes said.

"Well, one was tall and thin; he was Caucasian. Then the other man was shorter but stockier, heavier looking. He was African American. I could see them because of the streetlights. The thin man was running toward the center; the other man seemed to be chasing after him. They were shouting, but I couldn't really hear what they were saying. Then Fifi pulled on the leash again, and I looked down at her, and then I looked up at the men again, and suddenly there was the sound of a huge explosion, and a huge flash. I've never heard anything like it."

"Could you describe it for us the best you can, Ms. Watkins?"

"It was like a huge fireball. The flash was so bright in the night that it was like when a camera flashes in your eyes and you see red reflections afterward. I closed my eyes, of course, and then it was all confusing. The building was crashing down, there was black smoke, and fire, and the sound of shattering glass everywhere, and I fell down on my knees, hugging Fifi."

"When I looked up again a second later, still holding Fifi, there was smoke everywhere, and fire, but I saw the two men again. The bigger one was dragging the tall man under his armpits, pulling him toward the car on the curb. Then he pushed him in, got behind the wheel, and drove away. It was very strange. First all the noise of the explosion, and then this moment of silence . . . then crashing and screaming, and then sirens and horns and total chaos."

"It must have been terribly frightening," said Jack Barnes.

"It was horrible," Mabel Watkins said. "But I just thank the stars that Fifi was all right."

"Ms. Watkins, do you believe you could identify the two men you saw leaving the scene of the bombing?"

"Yes, I could."

Jack Barnes held up a large foam-backed posterboard with a blown-up photograph of Alex Seaton.

"That was the thin man I saw that night," Mabel Watkins said.

"And what about this man?" Jack Barnes asked, holding up a large photo of Lance Thompson.

"Yes, that was the African American, the larger man who dragged the other man away from the explosion."

"Thank you, Ms. Watkins. No further questions. Your witness."

Rob Knight stood up. He had anticipated casting a little reasonable doubt on Mabel Watkins's self-important testimony. He just hoped it worked.

"Ms. Watkins, you say you saw two men the night of the bombing?"

"That's correct."

"Let me understand. It was dark outside?"

"Yes, of course. But I could see by the light of the streetlights."

"And you were across the street, approximately thirty yards away from the car you say the men drove away in?"

"Yes, that's about right."

"You said that the explosion caused your eyes to see red flashes afterward?"

"Yes, like after someone takes your picture in the dark with a bright flash."

"So your eyesight was not, shall we say, at its optimum after the flash of the explosion?"

"Just for a moment, I guess, you could say that."

"And you have stated that the entire incident, from the time you noticed Fifi acting strangely until the time of the explosion and the car driving away, was just a few moments long?"

"Well, it seemed longer. A traumatic thing like that stretches out in time."

"I would suggest, Ms. Watkins, that the duress of that trauma might have affected both your eyesight, as you have stated, and your impressions, adversely. Can you be sure that these men you saw at a distance, in the dark, in the midst of a very traumatic incident, were the same men Mr. Barnes has so selectively shown you in these photographs?"

"Well, I have a very good memory," said Mabel Watkins defensively. Rob had gotten her where it hurt. "In fact, I have a photographic memory. I can read a printed page and practically memorize it, because I can see it in my mind's eye. That's why I love being a librarian."

"And you are saying that you can remember faces the way you remember the printed page?" Rob asked.

"Oh, yes. I never forget a face."

"That's certainly admirable," Rob said. "Let me ask you a question. Look at the second row on the left side of the courtroom. Do you see any faces you recognize there?"

Mabel Watkins took ninety seconds before she answered, carefully scanning each person on the row. "No, sir, there is no one there whom I have seen before."

Rob turned. "Ms. Watkins, I would beg to differ. My wife, Lisa, there in the red dress, second from the end of the row . . . Lisa came to your library and used her GW alumna card to check a book out from you last Tuesday, five days ago. In fact, she was wearing the same red dress she's wearing today. And you initialed her copying expense receipt for her. I have it right here."

CUTE, thought Ira Levitz. He liked Rob Knight, thought he was refreshingly spunky, even though Knight occasionally got too excited for his own good. It was okay this time to show off his stuff and play Perry Mason if it helped break the tedium. It really didn't matter anyway; everybody knew these guys blew up the center.

But Knight had better be careful, Ira thought. He's the kind of person who could trip up if he doesn't watch out.

THE FOLLOWING MORNING, the government called an army NCO named Bruce Pearson, who had cut a deal with prosecutors. Pearson had had responsibility for maintaining ammunition and demolitions security at Fort A. P. Hill, near Fredericksburg, Virginia, an hour's drive south of Washington. Since demolitions training was routinely conducted at Fort A. P. Hill, Pearson had, over a number of months, routinely checked out slightly more demolitions than needed for training exercises.

The standard C-4 explosives came in twenty-pound haversacks. Pearson had stockpiled the extra haversacks in which the pliable sticks of explosives were stored, slipping them out of the base regularly on days he knew he could breach security. The haversacks were fairly easy to conceal and came equipped with handy carrying straps, almost like a backpack, about twelve inches wide, four inches deep, fifteen inches high. Over the months, Pearson had managed to assemble a considerable amount of explosives, as well as non-electrical blasting caps, time fuses, and fuse igniters.

Pearson hadn't been part of the pro-life movement. Ideologically, he didn't care much about the fetal tissue issue. He had been well paid for his services. The final payment had been a thousand dollars, the week before the bombing, he said matter-of-factly. But the main reason he had gotten involved in the plot was out of loyalty to an old army buddy, Lance Thompson, who had set up the scheme and brought him into it.

Pearson would have died to save Lance; but now that his friend was gone, he owed no similar loyalty to anyone else involved in the case. When investigators started administering lie detector tests to all personnel with access to explosives, Pearson knew his time was short. He volunteered: his court martial for the lesser charge of misappropriation of government funds in exchange for his testimony.

Rob Knight didn't consider the Pearson testimony particularly compelling or relevant, one way or the other. But Jack Barnes took a long time establishing Lance's connection with the NCO. It seemed a psychological boost for the other side to convict a dead man. But Rob was focused on his client, alive and well, though pale, in the chair next to him.

BY THE TWELFTH DAY of the trial, Jack Barnes was questioning Jennifer Barrett.

"Ms. Barrett, you have told us that you had cause to observe Alex Seaton and Lance Thompson for a period of several months while you were part of the The Life Network group as an undercover federal agent. You have established that they planned the bombing of the regeneration center and were involved, as well, in the sabotage of the network news broadcast in order to air the anti-abortion video. Did you also have cause to observe Daniel Seaton during that same period of time?"

"Yes," said Jennifer Barrett. Her long legs were crossed and her hands folded in her lap. She was cool, dispassionate, and reserved on the witness stand. "I didn't see Daniel Seaton as much as I did his brother and Mr. Thompson, but I attended his church and saw him and his wife at least once a week, often more."

"In what circumstances would you see the Seatons?"

"The church was a small congregation. People tended to spend a lot of time together. They were like a little community. I became part of that community, so to speak, so I shared meals with the Seatons, and I worked with them on some of the church's outreach projects."

Jack Barnes chose not to pursue the image of shared suppers and ministry to the poor and needy. "Did you ever discuss the issue of abortion with Daniel Seaton?"

"Yes, we talked about a number of issues over the months. We spoke about abortion a lot. We also talked about the harvesting of fetal brain tissue."

"What was Daniel Seaton's disposition about this issue?"

"Oh, he was extremely passionate about it. He said that the harvesting of fetal brain tissue represented the most grievous slaughter of the innocent since the Nazi Holocaust."

"Those are strong words, Ms. Barrett. Are you sure that you remember them correctly?"

"Yes. The comparison with the Nazi Holocaust stuck in my mind, particularly since I heard Alex Seaton say the same things, and that taking out the regeneration centers was the only way to stop the holocaust."

Rob jumped to his feet. "I object, Your Honor. The witness is volunteering a connection here that can only prejudice the jury. That proves nothing."

"Sustained. The jury will disregard the answer."

"Let me ask this, Ms. Barrett. Would you say that the Seaton brothers had similar views regarding the regeneration center?"

"Yes. I remember Daniel Seaton saying once that it was ironic that the president was spending all his time dealing with crises in Africa and Korea instead of focusing on the scourge of his own nation. He said the regeneration centers were immoral, that our leaders would one day be held to account for their carnage against defenseless human life."

Daniel Seaton, sitting at the defense table, bowed his head for a moment. He remembered saying that. He had said a thousand similar things, all in light of the coming judgment of God . . . not the judgment of taking matters into his own hands and bombing the center. But in court, stripped of its biblical context, his words sounded harsh, crazy, and violent. Exactly the way Jack Barnes wanted them to sound.

Jennifer Barrett's testimony, all in similar vein and all obviously well-rehearsed, went on for another hour. Rob Knight's cross-examination of her was disorganized but helped to defray the damaging picture she had painted.

"Ms. Barrett, it must have been hard to pretend to be something you are not, living with a group of unsuspecting people as if you were their friend, as if you shared their deepest-held beliefs, when in fact you were an informant for the federal government."

"I object, Your Honor. That's not a question. It's a statement," Jack Barnes called out.

"Mr. Knight, why don't you rephrase your question?" said Judge Green mildly.

"I'm sorry, Your Honor. Ms. Barrett, according to all concerned, you fit in remarkably well with Pastor Seaton's church. You knew all the old hymns. You 'talked the talk,' if you know what I mean. Do you have a Christian background?"

Jennifer Barrett raised her eyebrows but shrugged slightly. "I grew up in a fundamentalist religious home," she said.

Rob paused for a moment. "You told people in Pastor Seaton's church that your father was an insurance salesman. But a little checking reveals that your father was a minister. Isn't that true?"

"It's not uncommon to alter one's life details when one is undercover," Jennifer Barrett said. "Yes, my father was a minister."

"Did you get along with your father?"

Jack Barnes objected again, but Judge Green allowed the question.

"No, Mr. Knight, I didn't get along with my father. He was an abusive, rigid, cruel man. I left home when I was a teenager."

"Have you attended church regularly since, Ms. Barrett?"

"No, I have not." In spite of her training, Jennifer Barrett was getting angry. "The example of Christianity I grew up with wasn't exactly the type of thing I'd want to be part of ever again."

"So you are, shall we say, hostile toward conservative Christianity?"

"I wouldn't put it that way."

"Some might think, Ms. Barrett, that you were settling a score."

"I object, Your Honor."

"Sustained."

"Let me ask one last question. Were you chosen for this assignment to infiltrate Pastor Seaton's church, or did you volunteer?"

Jennifer Barrett looked down for a moment, then raised her chin just a little too high as she met the defense attorney's eyes. "I volunteered, Mr. Knight."

"Just so. Thank you, Ms. Barrett. No more questions."

ON SATURDAY NIGHT, Rob and Lisa had Mary Seaton over to their home for dinner. The previous day, the FBI men who had found the getaway vehicle in the Seatons' garage the morning after the bombing had testified. The court had also heard testimony from the agents who had found Daniel's car at Frank Doggett's house in Leesburg.

It had been the most direct testimony thus far tying Daniel to any aspect of the actual crime, and it was damaging. Rob, of course, had known it would come. But it was still circumstantial and after the fact. It did not tie Daniel to the bombing itself, a point Rob hammered home in his cross-examination.

Over linguine and sauteed chicken breasts, the Knights and

Mary talked about other things for a while, chatting rather distractedly about the Seaton kids, the church, and a mutual friend who had just lost her husband to cancer. After dinner, Lisa carried the dishes into the kitchen, piled them up in the sink, and returned with three mugs of steaming coffee.

"How do you really think it's going?" Mary asked Rob quietly.

Rob swirled some milk into his coffee. "I get in trouble with Lisa if I seem too enthusiastic, but I would say that things are really going pretty well. Yesterday was a little squirrely, but unless the prosecutors have some ace up their sleeve that we don't know about, we're doing okay. The other side is intimidating—after all, it's 'The United States of America' versus Daniel Seaton. But they've got some big holes."

"What about the car thing?" Mary asked. "Looking back, I can't believe we were so naive, but Daniel did loan Alex our car.

"We had no idea anyone had been hurt in the bombing. We were upset, Alex was hurt, we just wanted to help him. But he was a fugitive, and we helped him escape in a different car than the one the police were looking for . . . all of that is bound to look pretty bad to the jury."

"Not on the major charge, that Daniel was part of the bombing conspiracy. Remember, in order to convict, the jury has to believe beyond a reasonable doubt that Daniel is culpable, that he had guilty intent," said Rob. "They have to believe that Daniel was involved, that he was really part of an evil conspiracy and that he took some action—one act is what they would have to prove—to further the conspiracy."

"The prosecutors have hung a few little pieces of things out there, but nothing that really establishes guilty intent or aiding and abetting or conspiracy. Now, on the other front—accessory after the fact—that's where we're weak, but that's a much lighter charge."

Mary shook her head. She knew that "much lighter" charge still meant several years in prison for Daniel. But she smiled at Rob as she said, "There's just one thing. I do wish you'd let me testify. I mean, who knows Daniel better—and I know he wasn't part of this. Why not, Rob?"

"Mary, you know why. You'd be great on the stand—believable, articulate. But don't you see? I can't put you on and not put Daniel on. It would look like he was hiding behind Mama's skirts. It would be death with the jury."

"And you aren't putting Daniel on, for sure?"

"Not in a million years. They've got a real job to prove intent except from inference, and I'm going to impeach their witnesses. If I put him on the stand, Barnes eats him alive on cross-examination. He would get enough, I am positive, to put your husband away for good. No, no, no." Rob tapped hard on the table with his fingertips; the coffee cups jumped.

Mary smiled at Lisa and put her hand on Rob's arm. "Thank you for everything you're doing," she said. "My husband's life is in your hands. You've been such a good friend to us through all this. We trust you."

AS ROB LOOKED over the government's witness list, he thought that the only tough one ahead of them was John Jenkins, who, like Bruce Pearson, had made a deal with the prosecutors. Rob hadn't been worried about Pearson, but Jenkins might be a loose cannon. The government had evidently done a good job of scaring him.

AFTER THE BOMBING of the regeneration center, it had taken only a matter of hours for John Jenkins to make his decision. The FBI had interrogated him the next morning, and he was surprised by the degree of terror he felt. He hadn't even thought about how he would react once Alex and Lance really carried through with the bombing. Now he realized he certainly wasn't willing to give up his family, freedom, and business for the cause. In spite of his fear, Jenkins had been composed enough to refuse to answer any of the agents' questions. Then, after they left, he'd called Dick Kingman, one of the hottest criminal lawyers in Washington. By that afternoon, Kingman had contacted Jack Barnes. It had taken only hours for Kingman to cut a deal with prosecutors, an arrangement that would, as Kingman put it in-delicately, "save Jenkins's butt."

And indeed he had. Kingman got him a grant of full immu-nity in exchange for the testimony the government wanted. Jenkins, whose fear of prison had escalated with each passing day since the bombing, thought Kingman's retainer of $25,000 was eminently reasonable.

FROM THE MOMENT Jenkins took the stand, Rob marveled at how well-coached he was. He had a pleasant smile, which he occasionally showed the jury. He scrupulously avoided eye con-tact with Daniel, even when he was asked to identify the defendant.

Barnes did not drag out the testimony but simply established Jenkins's clean record and admirable family life. Then, the jury's interest piqued, he moved in for the kill.

"On May 16 of last year, did you visit Rehoboth Beach, Delaware?"

"Yes sir."

"Who were you with?"

"Lance Thompson, Alex Seaton, and Daniel Seaton."

"What was the purpose of the trip?"

"Well, we needed some time to get away from Washington and relax. Also, to think about our next strategic move regard-ing the abortion industry."

"Whose idea was the trip?"

"It was Alex's, I guess, or Lance's. They thought it would be good for us to have some time alone. And they were worried too about security. We didn't feel it was safe to talk back in Wash-ington. We knew the FBI was monitoring us. We just didn't know how."

"What did you discuss during the weekend?"

"Well, we talked about what had happened so far. We talked about people's response to the abortion video on television—that people didn't care. Alex and Lance argued very hard that we had to do more."

"Like what?"

"Specifically, to destroy the regeneration center."

Jenkins spoke so firmly, almost defiantly, that a murmur went through the courtroom.

"And why was Daniel Seaton included in this trip?"

"Alex said he couldn't do it, wouldn't, unless Daniel approved."

Now another murmur rippled through the court. Almost everyone could sense what was coming. Rob's stomach turned over. Daniel was just staring at John Jenkins as if he couldn't believe what was happening.

"Did Daniel know of the plans that were being discussed to bomb the regeneration center?"

"Certainly."

"Did he approve of these plans?"

"Not before we went to Rehoboth. No." John Jenkins looked straight at the jury. "But at Rehoboth he did."

A loud stir went through the courtroom, mostly from the press. Judge Green hit the gavel, calling for order. Some reporters slid through the back door, obviously to get the jump on the rest.

Barnes continued. "I'd like you to be specific. Exactly what did Daniel Seaton say?"

"There was a very spirited discussion. Alex and Lance were pressing for action—that is, to bomb the center. Daniel listened carefully, and then at the end of the discussion he told them that they would have to follow their consciences, that if they felt that was the right thing to do, they should."

"Are you saying, Mr. Jenkins, that he told them to go ahead?"

"There was yet another stir, and this time one of the jurors exclaimed, "'Jeez." Green hit the gavel again.

"Mr. Jenkins, were you with the others the entire time?" Barnes asked.

"I believe I was. I was part of every conversation. We left Daniel alone once at the beach. He said he wanted to pray. But I'm certain I heard everything said."

Barnes smiled, turned toward Rob Knight, who was furiously scribbling notes, and said, "Your witness."

Rob knew he couldn't immediately attack Jenkins's credibility. At that moment, the jury wouldn't even hear it. For two hours, Jenkins had been well-spoken, personable, reasonable, dispassionate.

Rob knew he had to slowly change the jury's perception, and then, at the end, move in to destroy him. This was absolutely crucial; the fate of his client would ultimately turn on whether the jury believed Jenkins. At least so he thought.

Rob took thirty minutes establishing the relationship of Jenkins and the others, how close they were, how much they trusted one another, trips they took together, prayer sessions together, meals shared . . . Throughout, Jenkins kept his pleasant disposition.

Jack Barnes, watching from the prosecution table, knew exactly what Knight was doing: putting all of the conspirators together, painting them with the same brush. Clever, he thought. It showed maturity on Knight's part that he wasn't jumping down Jenkins's throat.

Then Rob stopped pacing and stood directly in front of the witness.

"Mr. Jenkins," he said, "you have testified that Daniel Seaton was an adamant foe of the regeneration centers."

"Yes, that's true," said John Jenkins.

"That fact is well-known," Rob said. "Pastor Seaton hates the regeneration centers and what they are designed to do . . . that is, the harvesting of brain tissue from mature fetuses while they are still alive. Do you support the regeneration centers?"

"No, I do not."

"So you are against them?"

"That's correct."

"And you have made statements regarding your feelings about them? Again, there are a number of people who have heard you speak out against them."

"Yes, I've spoken about my feelings."

"It strikes me, Mr. Jenkins, that your testimony about Pastor Seaton's animosity toward the regeneration centers could apply equally toward yourself or any other individual who disagrees with the morality of cutting open the soft skulls of the unborn and suctioning out their brains. Yet you have gone further in your testimony against Pastor Seaton, a friend who has supported you in difficult times in your life. You have seemed to put all the responsibility on him."

John Jenkins's composure was fraying slightly. It was obvious that he was a man caught between his instinct for self-preservation and a fair degree of self-loathing for his own efforts to save himself.

"I've simply answered the questions," he said.

"Well, that's appropriate, Mr. Jenkins. But it seems to me that you are all equally involved—or not involved."

John Jenkins was silent.

"Did you favor the bombing of the regeneration center, Mr. Jenkins?"

"I didn't object."

"That's not my question. Did you favor it?"

"Yes, when I was asked my opinion, I did."

"Just like you say Daniel Seaton favored it, though I think you also said he was very reluctant."

"That's true." Jenkins looked rattled.

"And yet, Mr. Jenkins, you are not on trial. Would you explain to us why that is so?"

"I have been granted immunity, as the prosecutor said at the beginning."

"Of course, of course. I think we call it making a deal, do we not?"

"Your Honor, I object." Jack Barnes jumped to his feet. "This line of questioning is intended only to damage Mr. Jenkins before this jury. There's no question of fact here. The government has made it clear from the beginning that John Jenkins is a government witness who has been granted immunity—a standard practice in conspiracy cases."

Green stared down from the bench. "Now, Mr. Barnes, I understand your point, but I am going to allow counsel to pursue this line of questioning. It does, after all, go to the believability of the witness, a proper area for examination."

For the next ten minutes, Rob Knight performed masterfully. And Jenkins squirmed. Rob asked about briefing sessions with the prosecutors, whether they had suggested testimony, whether Jenkins's lawyer had made any offers at the time the deal was struck. Barnes objected frequently, to no avail. Jenkins consistently answered that while he had made a deal, everything he had said today was true.

During much of the questioning, Rob did not look at Jenkins. Instead, he positioned himself in front of the jury box and stood leaning against the jury rail. His tactic was to get the jury to identify with his questions.

"Mr. Jenkins," Rob said finally, after a long pause. "I have no further questions. And I am sure you don't either because you know the oath you have taken today is one made not only in this court but before God. You understand, I am sure?"

Jenkins sat staring, saying nothing, his face now ashen.

The government rested its case. The court adjourned, to resume in the morning.

58

R ANDOLPH GREEN had begun his career as a sole prac-
titioner hanging around the courthouse waiting for some
judge to assign him a case. Anything to pay the bills.
Though he was now the Honorable Judge Green, he had not forgotten what it was like to work alone and scrounge for evidence,
comb through law books, and sometimes improvise in court. The
judge had therefore agreed to Rob's request to use his conference
room for preparation time with the defendant. It would be a particular help during the presentation of the defense, sparing Rob the
drive to the Arlington County Jail and all the security hassles there.

The afternoon after the prosecution rested, marshals led
Daniel into the judge's chambers to a large rectangular room
with a window at one end, floor-to-ceiling bookshelves on either side, and a huge conference table in the center. The marshals
guarded both entrances, nervous only about the window, although it would trigger an alarm if opened.

As Rob and Daniel faced each other across the table, Rob
was grinning, his leg bouncing incessantly under the table. "Well,
let me sum it up, Daniel." he began. "First, we've made it through
with no surprises. That's very good. Most lawsuits that get lost
do so because of surprises.

"Second, Jenkins hurt us, but it's only a surface wound. His credibility was pretty badly damaged on cross. I think I did as well as I could—"

"Rob, you did a great job." Daniel smiled reassuringly.

"Well, good enough, I hope. But the big thing is that there is no overt act. Even if the jury believes you gave them your permission, agreed with their plan—and I don't think they will—but even if they do, that isn't an act furthering the conspiracy. They can't get you on aiding and abetting without an act. Like handing them the bomb or something. Or, actually, any little thing before the crime."

"On that score," Rob continued, "they've come up empty-handed. In fact, in the morning I intend to move for a directed verdict. That is, ask the judge to direct the jury to find you 'not guilty.'"

"Now, don't get your hopes up. There's only one chance in a hundred—judges don't like to take cases away from the jury. But this judge just might. And at least I'm going to let everybody know that the government hasn't made the case. I can plant some doubts."

"But whatever happens on that motion, there's always the accessory after the fact. There we don't look so good. But even if we lose that, remember, the maximum is five years. Not good, but it's not life."

Daniel was standing, stretching his legs. "So then we go with our defense, right?"

Rob began to list witnesses and what each would say to establish Daniel's good character, his consistent position against violence, the sermons he preached about obeying the law, work he had done with local government officials indicating his respect for the political process. Rob had seven witnesses planned, five of whom were members of the church and two local government officials in Falls Church.

Daniel walked toward the window while Rob was outlining the defense and jotting notes on a pad. Not much of a view, just an inside courtyard, but better than three walls of concrete and bars in prison. He was staring distantly, showing no emotion; in fact, Rob wondered if he was listening. It was understandable. After the shock of the bombing, Alex's death, his own arrest and imprisonment, now this ordeal, he was probably numb.

"Rob," Daniel said quietly, turning to look at him.

Something in his voice made Rob put down his pen. "What is it?" he asked.

"I've been thinking a lot over the past few days. You're not going to like this, I know, but I feel convicted that I have to take the stand."

"No way," said Rob. "We've been through that before." He picked up his pen again.

"I mean it. I've got to take the stand," said Daniel.

"Why?" Rob looked at Daniel carefully, then jumped up and walked over toward him. "Why?"

"When you lie on a prison cot at night, you think a lot," Daniel said. "I've thought so much about Alex, about this whole mess. I've missed my children, I've died inside wanting to be next to my wife. But the main thing that has happened to me is that I've realized that all this is so much fluff. Chaff. I can't put the earthly things above the heavenly things. What would it profit me to win this case but lose my own soul? . . . So I have to do what is absolutely right according to my conscience."

"What are you talking about?" Rob said, his voice shaking.

"I have to testify. I have to tell this court what I did and said. Honestly face the charges and answer. And I am innocent, at least as you explain it, but I will leave that to the justice of the court."

"What are you talking about?" Rob said again. "Have you gotten some Messianic complex going here? Have you gone nuts?"

"No. You and I both know the truth. I did some things wrong—and I'm willing to face those. But I sure didn't bomb the regeneration center, and I didn't agree to anybody else bombing it. The jury will believe me."

"Besides, remember how all this began, Rob. We wanted to expose the horrors of abortion. That's why I started The Life Network in the first place. So maybe this could be the greatest opportunity yet. There's much I can say that could affect the conscience of this court. I think."

"You're insane. I think I can have you certified and put away. Don't you realize Barnes will tear you apart on cross-examination? He'll take every little thing you say innocently and make it sound guilty. The only hope they have of winning this case will be if you take the stand, and there's no way I'm handing that to them on a silver platter. And if you're convicted, we won't have a chance of appeal, because you did it to yourself. There's no need to do this!"

Daniel looked at him with a trace of anger. "You can't tell me there's no need if I'm sensing a conviction from God that there is a need! You can't dictate my conscience!"

Rob beat his hands on the conference table. "I'm your attorney! I'm your friend! You can't do this! I'll quit, and you'll have no defense at all!"

"Look," Daniel said, his calm demeanor returning, "you are my friend. So you won't quit. And besides, you're my attorney— and you can't quit unless I perjure myself. I looked that up in the jail library. And perjury is exactly what I won't be doing."

Rob was holding the sides of his head. "Okay, tell me again why you want to do this. I understand about your conscience. But why is your conscience affected?"

"I really started thinking about how I needed to testify after Jenkins was on the stand today," Daniel said.

"That lying weasel?"

"Well, he was afraid, and he made a deal. That's his problem. But I have to testify now."

"Why?"

"He was right about one thing," Daniel said. "I told them they had to follow their conscience. And now I have to follow mine. I have to say exactly what happened as I know it. I can't run away from this "

OVER THE NEXT FOUR DAYS, Rob Knight produced each of his witnesses. Their answers could not have been better if he had scripted them. Barnes made only a perfunctory cross-examination, knowing that this would, in the end, have little influence on the case.

Rob had waited until the last moment to announce that he was calling the defendant as a witness. He had hoped, right down to the end, that he could persuade Daniel that it was utterly rash, but Daniel was resolute.

The morning he announced that Daniel Seaton would be the defense's final witness, Jack Barnes struggled to keep the smile off his face. Members of the press murmured to one another and grabbed their notebooks. Green had to pound the gavel several times to restore order.

TWELVE BLOCKS AWAY at the Justice Department, where Emily Gineen was presiding over a senior staff meeting, one of her office interns brought her a note reporting the latest development from the courthouse.

Emily interrupted the assistant attorney general for administration's report.

"Ladies and gentlemen, you are, of course, all following the events in Judge Green's court in the matter of Daniel Seaton. You might wish to know that the defense has just announced that Seaton will testify in his own behalf."

There were gasps around the table.

The assistant attorney general for the criminal division interjected, "I knew it. It's another case like Paul Hill. He's got a death wish."

Emily sat back in her chair and looked pensive. "I don't know. I don't know," she muttered. "I simply do not understand this man."

DANIEL'S TESTIMONY went better than Rob had expected. He concentrated on Daniel's view of nonviolence, his lack of involvement in meetings with Lance and Alex, and his view of the evils of abortion and why he felt that the general nonviolent activities were so essential.

Barnes objected several times on the grounds of irrelevancy, but Green was not about to curtail anything the defendant wanted to say in his own defense. Each objection was overruled.

Rob felt he actually made some headway in the case by pointing out the childhood relationship between the two brothers and Daniel's history of protecting Alex; this just might help on the lesser charges.

When Rob announced that he had finished his questioning, Judge Green recessed court for the day. They would resume at 10:00 the next morning, he said, with cross-examination of Daniel Seaton.

Back in the judge's conference room, Rob acknowledged that Daniel had helped his cause.

"But tomorrow, Daniel, you're in for the most brutal day of your life, and I want you prepared. So right now I'm going to ask you every difficult question I can think of. Remember, on Barnes's cross, he'll try to lead you down the primrose path with yes and no answers. Answer fully, but only answer the question he asks. Never volunteer. Stay on the point."

For the next four hours, Rob paced the room, his tie loosened, shirt sleeves rolled up. He was as brutal as he knew Jack Barnes would be. But Daniel stood up to the assault so well that when Rob finished, he walked around the table, helped Daniel up out of the chair, and threw his arms around him.

"There's just one thing left," Rob said, looking into Daniel's reddened eyes. Both men were exhausted.

"What's that?" Daniel asked.

"Pray."

THREE FLOORS BELOW in the prosecutor's chambers, Jack Barnes sat alone in his office going through volumes of transcripts of Daniel Seaton's sermons and writings—material he had never expected to have the pleasure of asking the defendant about.

It was 11:00 that night when he finally flipped off his office light and started down the long corridor. He noticed the lights on and some noise coming from the third office down on the right. He went to the door, knocked, and swung it open. Inside, six of his assistants and two paralegals were sitting around a small table in shirt sleeves, laughing and joking. On the center of the table were two bottles of champagne.

"Get that out of here immediately," Barnes scolded furiously.

"Sorry, Chief," one of the young lawyers responded, "but this is a night to celebrate."

"No," Barnes snapped. "Prosecutors don't celebrate. We don't seek victories, only justice . . . and we don't have that yet. We still have a lot of work to do."

THE SILENCE in the courtroom was almost unnerving as Daniel Seaton took the stand. He was wearing a dark-blue suit that showed up his prison pallor, a bright tie that Mary had selected, and he seemed relaxed as he took his oath.

Jack Barnes began with basic questions to put the defendant at ease and draw him out. Then came the questions Rob Knight had dreaded.

"Reverend Seaton, you have been adamant in your anti-abortion views for quite some time, have you not?"

"That's true. Since I became a Christian in high school."

"You have testified that you do not support violence as a means of protesting abortion, that homicide is never justifiable in the cause of saving the unborn."

"That's true," Daniel said.

"But have you, in fact, supported the rather radical notion that revolution is justifiable in certain situations?"

Daniel, concentrating hard, didn't see what Jack Barnes was getting at, but Rob Knight could see it coming.

"Well, that's a rather complicated question. I think that in certain conditions, revolution could be warranted. I would have to apply just war criteria to evaluate such conditions. But revolution would only be a last resort after all other forms of civil disobedience have failed."

"Have you not written on this matter of revolution and civil disobedience, Mr. Seaton?"

"I could have . . ."

"Allow me to refresh your memory with these words: 'There are two realms, and Caesar is not to usurp that which belongs to God. When a government violates the law that is higher than its own, God's law, it exceeds its legitimate authority. When a government destroys life and order, rather than protecting and establishing them, the church must resist. In such cases Christians must rise up against godless leaders.'"

"I think I wrote that a long time ago," said Daniel. "You're taking it out of context."

"I have here also the tape of a sermon you delivered eleven months ago. In it you say that 'governments are established by God, but the Christian must discern when it is time to resist godless leaders who forfeit their authority by ruling contrary to the higher law, God's law'. . . Do you believe there are two sets of laws, Mr. Seaton?"

"That's a theological question," Daniel said.

"Still within the prosecutor's power to ask you. Please answer," Judge Green leaned across his desk.

"Yes, I believe there are two laws. There is man's law—that is, the legal codes we all live by, ranging from everything from the law that we must wear seat belts to the laws prohibiting murder. In many cases, man's law complies with God's law; it reflects God's law as it was handed down on Mount Sinai in the Old Testament account. But in some cases, man's law violates God's law; I believe that the Supreme Court decision that opened the doors to legal abortion all those years ago is a prime example. It was an immoral decision because it sanctioned violation of the sixth commandment, 'Thou shalt not kill.'"

"So you have taught your congregation that when push comes to shove, God's law is supreme?"

"I'm not quite sure what you mean by that. When man's law

conflicts with God's law, the Christian's higher allegiance is to the law of God."

Jack Barnes switched gears again.

"In your writings and sermons you have referred repeatedly to 'ungodly leaders.' How would you define an ungodly leader?"

"One who flagrantly defies and disdains the laws of God."

"Do you believe that President Griswold is an ungodly leader?"

"Well, I don't know the condition of his heart."

"You seem to be avoiding the question. Have you not said from the pulpit that Whitney Griswold was ungodly?"

"I may have, not as a political statement, but in the sense that nothing in President Griswold's public policy record would indicate to me that he considers God the ultimate authority."

"So you have, in fact, called President Griswold an ungodly leader?"

"Yes, I suppose I have."

"Let's see," said Jack Barnes. "We have covered my questions about your thoughts about revolution and civil disobedience, and your thoughts about what you call a higher law that requires you to disobey civil law, and your analysis of President Griswold . . . let me ask you if you recognize another piece of writing."

Rob Knight felt sick. It was impossible for ordinary citizens to put theological truths in context. Still, Barnes was only dealing with state of mind, not action.

"This is from an article you wrote, I believe, a year and a half ago, for a conservative journal, but I understand that you never sent it in for publication." Barnes paused and then read from the photocopy John Jenkins had given him. "I quote:

> We must read the writing on the blood-soaked walls of our nation. An individual who takes the lives of the defenseless has no defense; he brings judgment upon himself. A nation that devours its young digests its own future. A leader that allows lambs to be led to the slaughter will be held responsible.
>
> It appears that our nation is no longer content merely to spill

the blood of the unborn, but will now begin, in large numbers, to extract the brains of the near-born. The regeneration centers represent, in fact, the new Holocaust of our own day, the killing centers where the slaughter of the innocents will be accelerated to new heights of horror. We can only pray that our new administration, whichever one it is, will turn while there is still time, before judgment comes upon it, and us.

"Do you recognize those words?"

"Yes, I think I may have engaged in some rhetorical excess."

Jack Barnes took a sheaf of paper off the prosecution table and held it up before the judge. "Your Honor, I would like to call for prosecution exhibit number 3-A a copy of the open letter sent to President Griswold on January 24 of last year and published in the *Washington Post*. Would you, Reverend Seaton, read the first two paragraphs?"

Daniel read the beginning of the open letter sent to Griswold in the wake of the Fargo shooting. With a few small alterations, the wording was exactly the same as Daniel Seaton's unpublished article.

There was a gasp in the courtroom. Mary Seaton, sitting in the front row, clenched her hands so tightly that her fingernails dug into her palms.

Daniel paused, trying to regain his equilibrium. "So what is your question? I didn't write the letter to President Griswold. I was as surprised as anyone else when I saw it in the paper."

"It's odd, though, Mr. Seaton," said Jack Barnes smoothly. "I find it hard to believe that the exact same language is a coincidence. Do you?"

"Alex sometimes looked to me for ideas," said Daniel. He paused and looked down at his hands for a moment trying to recover. "Perhaps someone lifted some of the language from my article. I don't think Alex did it," he continued. "But I certainly did not write that letter to President Griswold."

"Did you at any time discuss the bombing of an abortion facility with your brother?"

"Certainly. Since the 1980s we've talked about it a lot. That's when clinic bombings first started happening. Everyone talked about them. But I consistently opposed it."

"What about more recently?"

"Yes, I think we've talked about the issue in recent times."

Rob was surprised. This was the first time he had heard Daniel shade an answer, even slightly.

"Mr. Seaton," Jack Barnes said loudly, "did your brother at any time discuss with you the possibility of bombing the regeneration center? Mr. Jenkins has testified that he did at Rehoboth on May 16 and 17 of last year."

Daniel took a deep breath. "Yes, Mr. Jenkins was correct. Alex did discuss it with me."

There was a loud murmur in the courtroom.

"And what did you say?"

"You need to understand the context, Mr. Barnes." Daniel's voice shook with emotion. "It was an intense conversation. We were all very frustrated, absolutely sick about unborn children being killed and harvested—"

Barnes cut in. "What did you tell your brother?"

"I told him that he had to follow his conscience."

"Did you think your brother capable of such violence?"

Daniel paused. He had reviewed all this in his mind, but was he sure? He thought about the look in Alex's eyes when the abortionist was shot in North Dakota. He thought about the glow on his brother's face when he had talked about taking down the regeneration center.

"Yes," he said tiredly, "to be absolutely truthful, I believed Alex to be capable of blowing up the center."

"And yet you did not warn the authorities, Mr. Seaton? Even though you have preached that one must respect and obey the governing authorities?"

"No, I did not."

"Thank you, Reverend Seaton. I have no further questions, Your Honor."

Judge Green started to nod, then Barnes cut in. "Oh, no,

I'm sorry, Your Honor, I have just one more question, if I may?"

"Go ahead, Mr. Barnes," said the judge.

"Mr. Seaton," Jack Barnes said deliberately, "how much money did you give your brother, Alex, in the week before the bombing?"

Rob was out of his chair almost before Barnes had finished asking the question. "I object, Your Honor. There was no matter of this sort raised on direct."

Green rolled his eyes upward, thought a moment, and then said, "The objection is premature. I'd like to see what the prosecutor has in mind. Overruled."

"I'll repeat the question, Mr. Seaton," Jack Barnes said. "How much money did you give your brother in the week before the regeneration center was bombed?"

"I'm not sure," he replied. "I was in the habit of giving Alex money often. He was in the construction business, you know; his income went up and down. He always paid me back eventually."

"That's understandable, Reverend Seaton. But just tell us what you gave him in the week prior to the bombing of the regeneration center."

"I don't recall . . ."

Rob Knight had his head bent over the table, muttering to himself. *Don't remember, don't remember. Oh, please God, don't let him remember.*

"Well, wait," Daniel said slowly. "I think I'd have to check to be sure, but I believe I gave Alex money right around that time."

"How much money, Reverend Seaton?" Jack Barnes asked.

"I remember now," Daniel said. "Alex said he needed some cash, and I was busy with other things so I didn't think much about it. I borrowed it from Melissa Brett for him. It was a thousand dollars."

A gasp went through the court. One of the jurors, apparently sympathetic, exclaimed, "Oh, no." Jack Barnes looked at the jury, shaking his head as if saddened by this news while Green pounded the gavel to restore order.

Barnes then turned to the judge. "We have no further questions, Your Honor."

IN THE JUDGE'S CHAMBERS, Rob Knight was furious. "You should have told me . . . you should have told me," he exclaimed.

Daniel looked hurt. "It never occurred to me. Rob, you've got to believe me. I gave Alex money all the time. He was always in trouble, and he always paid it back. I didn't even remember until Barnes prodded me about it."

"But you knew. You should have known. Pearson already testified that his last payment for the explosives was a thousand dollars. Didn't you remember? Don't you see? This is an overt act."

Daniel said nothing.

Rob shook his head. "I don't think anything I can say will make any difference. But I'll do my best."

THREE FLOORS BELOW, Jack Barnes walked into his office, followed by his assistants. He was laughing. "Break out that champagne after all," he said.

They all laughed, but one young attorney looked puzzled. "I didn't see any reference to money in any of the papers we all went through. I mean, there was one thing about Alex borrowing money from Daniel all the time . . . but how did you know he gave him money before the bombing?"

"I didn't," Barnes grinned. "Just a hunch. I got lucky. Very lucky."

THE PROSECUTION'S closing arguments went quickly. Jack Barnes simply reviewed the evidence: The conspiracy for the bombing was established, and each of the conspirators, including those now dead, had played their own role. Daniel Seaton's role was clear. He knew in advance of the bombing, encouraged his brother, gave him the thousand dollars needed to finish paying for the explosives, knew full well what it was being used for, then provided the escape vehicle. He was just as responsible as those who had rigged the bomb and set it off.

"Your deliberations," Barnes told the jury, "carry great weight. Not only is the fate of a man at stake, but so is the fate of justice in this nation.

"By finding Daniel Seaton guilty, you will send a message to all Americans that this remains a nation under the rule of law, that those who take the law into their own hands—for whatever reason, matters of conscience or otherwise—must nonetheless pay the price under that law. I trust each one of you to uphold the laws of this nation." He met each juror's eyes, then turned and walked back to his seat.

Rob Knight's closing arguments went much longer. He had not gotten much sleep, and though he had knocked himself out to pull it all together, he felt conscious that he was truly on the defensive, now forced to answer charges and suspicions that hadn't even been in the jury members' minds when he made his opening arguments. He felt like he was going around and around, desperate, circling back on his own rabbit trails. Then, finally, he closed.

"Again, ladies and gentlemen of the jury, please don't let the passion of the moment, the current atmosphere around us, cloud your reason. The prosecution has shown no compelling evidence that Daniel Seaton is a murderer and a conspirator; they have dredged up old papers and chance comments that mean nothing."

"Surely you know in your hearts from Mr. Seaton's own testimony that any involvement he had with the events cited in this case were wholly innocent, compelled by his love for his brother. Mr. Seaton believes enough in a system of justice that he testified before you, knowing you would have the wisdom to discern his innocence."

Rob walked back to the rail in front of the jury box and leaned on it. "Ladies and gentlemen, you have in your hands the fate of a good and decent, caring human being whose principal failing, as happens so often in history with noble figures, is that he cared too much. He cared too much for his congregation, for unborn babies, for his brother. If he stands convicted of anything, it is of zeal for what is right and just and truthful."

Rob walked back to his seat, feeling weak in the knees, his back stabbing him in the usual place. Lisa was looking at him, her brows knitted; Mary Seaton had a similar look on her face.

But Daniel seemed buoyed by some invisible force. He put his arm around Rob's shoulder. "Thank you, Rob," he said. "We've done our part. Now let them do theirs."

AFTER JUDGE GREEN had charged the jury and dismissed them to deliberate, he allowed Rob to take both Daniel and Mary into the conference room.

"The longer they're out, the better for us," Rob grinned, trying to encourage them.

Less than two hours later, the jury sent the message that they had reached a verdict.

As the jurors filed back into their box, their demeanor gave Rob no cause for hope. No encouraging smiles at his client. Each juror was looking straight ahead.

Daniel seemed oblivious. He just watched the bailiff bring the white piece of paper to the judge. Judge Green read it, then nodded. The white piece of paper then traveled back to the foreman of the jury. The foreman, a portly black man in his mid-fifties, cleared his throat.

"As to count one, the charge of conspiracy, we the jury find the defendant guilty as charged."

There was a huge gasp in the courtroom and then a muffled cry from the first row. The murmur continued as the foreman continued reading.

"As to count two, aiding and abetting in the act of homicide, we find the defendant guilty as charged."

Rob Knight closed his eyes. He couldn't watch. He knew every other count would be the same, and the words "guilty, guilty, guilty" echoed in his head. He had his arm around Daniel and turned toward his client with a look of absolute agony. Daniel had his lips pressed together, and he was looking back toward Mary, straining to connect with her.

But when he turned back to Rob, his eyes were clear. "It's all right, Rob," he whispered. "It's the court's will, and the Lord's will. My conscience is clear. I told the truth."

Judge Randolph Green banged his gavel. "Thank you," he said to the jury. "You are dismissed. Sentence will be pronounced in three weeks. This court is adjourned."

59

AS PAUL CLARKSON entered the attorney general's office, Emily Gineen was behind her big desk, her suit jacket off, focused on a thick pile of papers. She looked up and smiled, gesturing Paul toward his usual chair.

"I've been looking at the Seaton trial transcripts," she said, "trying to understand why this guy did what he did. I talked with Jack Barnes, and he is one grateful prosecutor. He's probably never prayed before in his life, but he's been thanking the Man Upstairs ever since Seaton took the stand. He said it was like the guy had a death wish."

"Well," Paul said, "I've seen defendants give up before, just throw in the towel and plead guilty. This wasn't like that; he didn't have a death wish. From what I've heard, evidently he had gone over it all in his mind, and he wanted to make sure that the court knew every detail of the whole story. Just the facts . . . judge for yourself. No spin."

Emily nodded. "I don't mean to offend, but I had assumed Seaton was a religious wacko until all this happened. But reading the transcript, he sounds like a decent person. He sounds too smart to get sucked into something this stupid. I don't know why, but I'd like to meet him. His sentence is pretty well determined by the federal guidelines, but the government still has to make its recommendation to the judge. And this is such a high-profile case, Barnes wants us to concur. But he wants the full extent of the guidelines; and I want to be sure that's right. I want to know more about what kind of person Seaton really is, what makes him tick."

Paul, in his shirt sleeves, ran his hand through his hair. "Why?" he said. "You know what we have to do—demand the maximum. If it gets out in the media that the attorney general met with Daniel Seaton . . ." He let out a low whistle. "People aren't in a pretty mood about this thing."

"On this one, I just have to follow my gut," she said. "I'm not sure what it is, but I need to meet him face to face. We'll keep it quiet, and if it is leaked, well, I would think the press would appreciate a hands-on attorney general. Out of the ivory tower and into the prison—it makes a nice spin, don't you think?"

Paul raised his eyebrows. "No, but I'll get it set up," he said. Then he smiled slightly. "And I'll go with you. You might need an interpreter."

AS IT WORKED OUT, Paul was able to keep the visit quiet. The Arlington County sheriff, Burt Kloster, was a friend and a member of Paul's church; he arranged the extraordinary clandestine meeting between the attorney general and the convicted felon. It was no small feat; Seaton was probably the most publicized defendant since O. J. Simpson.

Emily and Paul, traveling in Paul's old Volvo, arrived at the jail's back entrance at 6:00 P.M. The sheriff and an aide met them and escorted them quietly through narrow cinder-block hallways to the sheriff's inner office, where, in deference to protocol, both were frisked with a hand-held metal detector and Emily had her handbag searched.

Emily accepted a Styrofoam cup of weak coffee from the sheriff's secretary. It tasted as if it had been brewed from old socks, but it was something to hold on to. She hadn't been in a correctional facility for more than a decade.

It's shocking, she thought. *Here I am, the senior criminal justice administrator in the nation, and I haven't even set foot in one of these institutions. More than a million and a half people in prisons across the country, and I haven't been near one for ten years.*

It was the smell that took her back. Years ago, as a young prosecutor, she had visited a few miserable jails to take depositions from defendants. They had all smelled this way—a muddled but distinctive mixture of close stuffy air, unwashed bodies, unbrushed teeth, unwashed hair . . .

But the smell took her back even further, to something she hadn't thought about or even remembered for years. As a teenager, she had loved to sing—and she, at fourteen, had also had a crush on a sixteen-year-old named Will Sizeman, one of the few boys who could sing bass. So she had joined her Baptist church's youth choir. That Easter, the choir had accepted an invitation to sing at a nearby prison's sunrise service. It was a minimum-security institution for women, so the youth group was allowed in; Emily's parents had encouraged her to go, to broaden her horizons.

She didn't remember much about the prison itself. Except for the razor-wire fences, it had looked like a drab college campus. The service had been held in the cinder-block chapel. After the choir had arranged themselves on rickety risers at the front, the inmates had filed in, filling most of the small chapel.

The inmates had responded warmly. They had clapped after each song, and on some numbers had sung along with the choir; all in all, it had been a surprisingly pleasant experience, except that the place had been stuffy and smelled bad. But what Emily now remembered, for the first time in years, was the reaction of one woman as they did their closing song, the traditional Easter anthem, "He Lives."

Emily was singing her part, watching the women and the choir director at the same time, and also thinking about Will Sizeman on the back row behind her, wondering if they would sit together on the bus on the way home. Then, when they got to the chorus, suddenly this big black woman on the front row stood up, hands swaying in the air, singing along with them.

"He lives!" she was shouting. "He lives! Christ Jesus lives today!" She was weeping, tears running down her face and dripping onto her wrinkled smock.

Emily had stopped singing, aching with adolescent embarrassment at the open display of emotion. Why is she crying? Emily had wondered.

THE SOUND OF shuffling footsteps in the corridor brought her back to the present. The door to the outer office opened, and an officer entered, then another escorted Daniel Seaton into the room. His legs were shackled, and his wrists cuffed in front of him. His prison jumpsuit hung on his tall frame, and his face was gaunt. There were pale, fleshy puffs under his eyes, and his hair stood up in little spikes in the back, courtesy of the jail barber. His lush mustache had been shaved off before the trial, but some photos the newspapers had been using for months had showed him with the mustache. He certainly didn't look like the robust, stocky man she had seen in the newspapers.

"Reverend Seaton," Sheriff Kloster said, "we weren't able to tell you the nature of this special visit until you arrived in my office, and we would ask that you yourself keep this matter confidential as well. The attorney general asked to meet with you personally, and while this is highly unusual, we of course honored her wishes."

Emily stepped forward. "Good evening, Mr. Seaton," she said, feeling awkward because she couldn't shake his hand as she normally would. "I'm Emily Gineen, and this is the associate attorney general, Paul Clarkson. Thank you for meeting with us."

Daniel extended his shackled hands toward her. "I'm honored to meet you, Mrs. Gineen," he said. "I must say, when they told me I had a special visitor, I was hoping it was my wife. But in her absence, it is a great pleasure to make your acquaintance . . . and yours, too, sir," he said to Paul.

Surprised, Emily smiled. "I'm told that your wife is a very courageous woman," she said.

"That she is," Daniel said. "I never realized how amazing she is until all this happened."

"Well, that's what I would like to talk with you about, Mr. Seaton," Emily said. " 'All this.'" She took charge. "And I'd like to ask you gentlemen," she nodded to Paul, the sheriff, and the officer next to Daniel, "if you would excuse us, so we might talk in privacy."

Paul jerked his head, and the sheriff started to protest, but Emily cut them off. "Sheriff, as you know, I have brought no picks or files to assist Mr. Seaton in an escape. Perhaps he and I could adjourn to your office, and you could stand by here in the anteroom. Have some coffee. Maybe you and Paul can talk about church business. This officer can also stand by, and we will leave the door open, so you can be assured that everything will be all right."

Paul looked at Emily carefully, then he and the sheriff nodded.

Emily and Daniel walked slowly to the sheriff's inner office, where she gestured toward two vinyl chairs next to the file cabinets. He sank awkwardly into one, and she took the other.

"We don't have much time, so I want to speak with you as directly as possible, Mr. Seaton," she said, leaning forward in her chair. "I sense from your statements at your trial that you are a direct person as well. As you probably know, the U.S. attorney makes a sentencing recommendation to the judge in your case about the range within the federal guidelines. Normally that would be handled by others, but I wanted to get directly involved in your situation, because I want to understand what is at the heart of it."

Emily shifted in her chair. Daniel was sitting slightly bowed but looked directly into her eyes while she spoke.

"The crimes for which you have been convicted have struck an exposed nerve with the American public. Understandably. They have done great damage. They have contributed to, if not created, a dangerously ugly mood in our nation. Terrorism always does. And yet in your court statements I found you to be a man of reason and some civility. We are not retrying your case right now. But I want to know: What were you trying to accomplish with The Life Network group?"

Daniel waited a moment, as if expecting her to say more, then took a breath. "First, I want to say that I fully accept the judgment of the court. I had no intention to cause anyone's death or any damage to property, but I inadvertently allowed others to pursue a path that led to those ends."

"I understand that," Emily interrupted. "I'm asking something more basic than that. Why did all this get started?"

"I started The Life Network because I believe that abortion kills unborn human life. We've fought that for decades now. But I knew that as soon as the regeneration centers opened, the demand for fetal tissue would increase dramatically. I knew that the immorality of abortion would be compounded and multiplied even further.

"But the public was being led down a rosy path: The centers were to be our new national hope—lifesaving facilities for AIDS sufferers . . . but they are, in fact, killing facilities for the defenseless. I had to shine a light on them, expose the evil. I could not see any difference between them and the extermination camps of Nazi Germany. Can you?"

"Abortion is a constitutional right," Emily said. "These matters have been settled in the courts for years. It is legal. Millions of Americans find it personally acceptable. Those who don't, don't have to have one. It's a matter of personal choice."

"With all due respect, Mrs. Gineen, if we're going to engage in a political argument, we might as well save our breath and you can go somewhere where the coffee is better," Daniel said. "You asked why I did what I did. Because abortion—and the harvesting of live fetal tissue, which I notice you didn't mention—may be legal according to human law, but it is wrong according to God's law."

"Laws are based on the will of the people," said Emily.

"Cultures change. America is not a theocracy; our laws don't come from the Old Testament Jewish code."

"I agree with you. We can't impose God's law, even though some people say that we want to. But the Christian has to work in the democratic system, trying to influence the process, so that human laws conform to God's character. And God hates the murder of the defenseless. He is the ultimate Judge. And God doesn't change, no matter how much we change."

Emily refrained from rolling her eyes, but she found herself absolutely frustrated, the same way she felt sometimes in arguments with her husband . . . impossible to resolve, no way out. Why can't relational conflicts be like legal arguments, both sides present their case and then the judge rules? She paused in her thinking. The analogy felt uncomfortably like where Daniel's language was leading.

"Look," she said. "You're right; we don't want to argue political issues here. So let's argue theological ones. How can you purport to know the mind of God? How do you know what God thinks about a particular issue? There are plenty of clergy who disagree with you about abortion. Do you have the corner on truth?"

Daniel looked down at his manacled hands. "Please forgive me if I sounded self-righteous," he said. "Being in jail has caused me to realize how weak I am. I've made terrible mistakes. And I'm paying for them. But it's also made me realize more deeply than I've ever known that God does not make mistakes. God is God. He has spoken. His word is Truth."

"What do you mean?" Emily said bluntly. " It sounds so presumptuous, almost arrogant. How can you be so sure—how can you even know there is truth?"

"First of all, because you asked that question," Daniel responded. "Something in you causes you to ask it. We have a mind, a consciousness . . . there is something, some ultimate reality, and the mind and soul are restless for it."

Emily frowned. "But even if there is some ultimate reality, one can't know it with certainty."

"Ah," said Daniel, "but that's the search. Look at the order of the universe. Think about its physical realities." He lifted his manacled arms high and let them drop; the chains rattled. "Gravity is a physical law; without support, anything will fall. Every time. If there are known physical laws, why would we even suggest that there aren't known moral laws? Certain behavior produces certain predictable consequences. Every time. And if there are physical and moral laws, there has to be a Lawgiver. That's what I mean by ultimate reality. It is God."

"I've always believed in God," Emily said defensively. "He set things in motion. He made people able to discover the truths about things on their own—"

"But a Christian believes Jesus," Daniel interrupted, not even conscious he was doing so. "Jesus said 'I am the Truth.' He holds together the universe—all that we know and can understand flows from Him. I know it's hard to take, but it's the only certainty we have. We call what we see around us the 'real life,' as if life was nothing but buses and budgets and newspaper headlines. But how many times have you experienced the fact that the real is the unseen? Do you have children?"

His abrupt question startled her. "Yes," she said.

"So do I," he said. "I love them. My love for them is real—I would die for them—but you can't see my love. You can just see its effects. And it is there whether you accept it or not. Or let me think of another example . . .

"Maybe you've been sailing at night. We used to do that when I was a kid, my dad and Alex and me, and we would sleep on the boat . . ." He paused and looked away for a moment, then swallowed. "But there would be times on moonless nights when you couldn't see ten yards ahead of the boat. There was a light positioned at the top of our mast, but if we had tried to navigate from our own light, which was moving with us, that would have been no help. So my dad would navigate by the stars. Fixed points, shining out in the darkness above a spinning world.

"Now, if the stars moved, or if I believed the stars were in one place and you believed they were in another and we were both supposed to be right, how could anyone navigate? Truth has to be fixed in order for us to know how to live. In order for it to be truth. God is real. Certain. Even though we can't see Him, we see the effects of His presence. Like the wind. And one day we will see Him. Face to face."

Emily felt a tightening in her throat. Daniel's homey analogies made intellectual sense, but they also stirred something in her imagination that hadn't been touched since she was a small girl. A longing for a fixed point above a world spinning out of control. A warm hand on her shoulder in the cold. A light on a dark path. She wished it were true. She longed for it to be true.

"I would like to believe with that kind of certainty," she said slowly, feeling very tired. "But I don't know how. It can't be true."

"If it weren't true," he said. "I wouldn't be sitting here in jail with handcuffs on. I'd be at home with my family, because I would have lied in court faster than anything you ever saw."

"You wouldn't have had to lie," Emily said, her legal demeanor returning. "You didn't have to take the stand."

"But that's just it," Daniel said. "I got myself into this. And once I did, I couldn't lie to get out. Maybe I might have been cleared by the earthly judge. But I would have done wrong in the eyes of the heavenly Judge."

TWENTY MINUTES LATER, Emily and Daniel emerged from the office. Paul and the sheriff stood up, looking puzzled. They had heard the constant buzz of voices but hadn't been able to hear any of the conversation.

As the officers escorted Daniel out the anteroom door, Emily whispered something to the sheriff. He nodded, and followed the group out the door.

Paul looked at Emily. "Well? How was it? What did he say?"

Emily opened her purse and took out a roll of mints, offering one to Paul. He shook his head.

"He said what you said before," she told Paul. "Same message. Different messenger."

Paul looked at her sharply.

"I've asked Sheriff Kloster to arrange for a car to take me

back to the office," Emily said, peeling off a mint and putting it in her mouth. "You go on home. It's late."

"What—"

"Paul, I'll see you tomorrow," Emily said with unusual abruptness. "Thank you for setting this up. Good night."

60

D ANIEL SEATON'S sentencing was, like his trial, a huge media event. Though the federal sentencing guidelines had little flexibility, they allowed for a range, and so the courtroom was crowded with reporters waiting to hear Judge Randolph Green's pronouncement—as well as the Seatons' friends and parishioners, who had been praying for some sort of miracle.

Daniel himself had prayed for one. He had felt peaceful ever since he had testified, in spite of the outcome. But he also could not help but hope that God would somehow deliver him back to his family. At one point he had even found himself praying the prayer of Gethsemane: "If You are willing, Lord, remove this cup from me; yet not my will, but Yours be done"—and then he had felt ashamed. He wasn't exactly going to the cross.

So on the morning of February 22, Daniel sat as peacefully as any man could who was awaiting a decision that might take most of the rest of his life away. Beside him was Rob Knight. Jack Barnes and his team sat across from them. The courtroom was hushed, expectant, when the door opened and the judge entered the room.

Daniel and Rob approached the bench and stood as Judge

Green began to address them. He was to the point, but surprisingly personal.

"I am not ordinarily an angry man," the judge said in even, measured tones. "But I have been for some time enraged to find myself in the ironic position of being an alleged agent of justice, and yet having, in some cases, to dispense gross injustice. This is, I fear, such an occasion.

"Reverend Daniel Seaton, as I read the probation officer's report, you are a good and decent man. The history of your life has been previously unblemished, without so much as a parking ticket on record. You give every evidence of having been a productive and exemplary citizen, and you have consistently helped others in a way we can all admire.

"Yet you made a serious mistake. You became involved in the violent business of the tragically misguided effort to expose and stop the regeneration center, so you have been found guilty by a jury of your peers—on rather circumstantial evidence, I might add. I must abide by that decision; it is the way our system has worked since the beginnings of this nation.

"But in the matter of determining punishment for Reverend Seaton," the judge continued, looking out at the packed courtroom, "I have little discretion. I am not allowed to exercise the very justice of my office in considering the nature of the crimes, the likelihood of future danger to society, nor the commendable history of the defendant. Instead, because of the rubber-stamp nature of the federal sentencing 'guidelines,' as they are called..." Green spat out the words. "I must, against my will, judgment, and discernment, issue push-button, mechanical 'justice.' It is the judgment of the court that the defendant, Daniel John Seaton, be hereby committed to the custody of the Bureau of Prisons, to serve not less than twenty years."

He leaned down and spoke directly to Daniel. "I am very sorry, Mr. Seaton. May God go with you."

Then the gavel fell.

61

BUT MR. PRESIDENT, sir, it doesn't seem appropriate for Daniel Seaton to be in Newton," Emily Gineen said into her office phone. Usually she did whatever the president wanted when he wanted it. But Whitney Griswold was being utterly unreasonable. "He's not a threat to others, and we've got to get him into a safer institution. Newton is one of the most violent prisons in the country."

"Seaton is a terrorist!" Griswold shouted into Emily's ear.

He's really losing it, she thought—a thought that had confronted her with unsettling frequency in recent encounters with the man.

"He blew up a building, killed people, and he belongs in maximum security, not in some cushy institution," Griswold continued. "People out there want him locked up. They'd want him in the electric chair if we could do it. I will not tolerate a person like him anywhere but in Newton . . . and Emily, if I hear about any more quiet moves on your part to put him in a different prison, it will raise very serious questions in my mind. I am not going to have the authority of this office undermined by my own attorney general. Do you understand?"

Emily had been gripping the phone so hard that it was hot.

She forced herself to unclench, took a breath, and said, "Yes, Mr. President. I understand you." She hung up, restraining her desire to smash the receiver down.

I understand you, Mr. President, she repeated to herself. *You hate bigots and zealots? Well, you've become the very thing you hate most.*

RISING ABOVE THE ROLLING HILLS and flat farmlands south of Philadelphia and north of Wilmington is a medieval fortress little known to the outside world, but notorious within the netherworld of the federal institutions of corrections. Named for a colonel who died defending his post in an Indian uprising, Fort Newton traces its origins to the early 1700s, when it was an outpost for the embattled colonists who settled there. Since then, many more men have died within its bounds.

The Indians burned the wooden fort to the ground, but it was reclaimed and rebuilt by the colonists. Some years later it served as a holding facility for those found guilty of criminal offenses in the brutal environment of pre-Revolutionary America. Prisons, as such, had not yet made their debut, but early chronicles of the fort detail an execution held there in 1758: the offender was disemboweled, then his entrails thrown upon a fire while he was still conscious enough to watch; he was then decapitated and his body quartered. The offense: horse stealing.

The first American prisons were established in Pennsylvania in 1790 and in New York two decades later, championed by Quakers and others who believed that, given a place of solitude and enforced reflection, a criminal would contemplate his sins and penitently seek to reform his errant ways. Hence the felicitous language of "penitentiaries" and "reformatories"—myths that endured, in spite of the reality that those early humanitarian experiments failed miserably. Many offenders did not quietly reform; instead, the solitude, inactivity, and despair drove them utterly insane.

Yet the fantasy of rehabilitation behind prison walls persisted, and by the late twentieth century, America's "correctional" facilities hosted a million and a half offenders of every degree. The expensive, unwieldy system, a behemoth of government ineptitude, had succeeded only in evolving into a huge tax burden and a separate society with its own language, values, and code of conduct for the culture's most violent.

Ironically, the inmates who complied with the official system were the most likely to be victimized, and the prisoners who ruled this upside-down world were the absolute rabble of a vicious society.

By the time Daniel Seaton arrived at its gates, Newton had become a federal concrete fortress encircled by hundred-year-old thirty-five-foot-tall stone walls. Gun towers that were even taller bulged out from the walls at each corner of the fifteen-acre compound. Approached from the narrow highway that led toward it, Newton looked like a gray, medieval citadel, rising like a nightmare in the middle of pleasant farmlands.

Inside, six wings—concrete corridors lined with barred cells—jutted offfrom the main prison. One wing housed the most dangerous inmates, allowed out of their cells only an hour each day. Another housed protective custody, the no-man's land where snitches, child molesters, and other vulnerable prisoners sought the dubious protection of solitary confinement. Other wings housed the crazies, the druggies, and the gangs, and there was one open dormitory in which inmates deemed less dangerous slept in gray rows of bunks. Even there, though, stabbings were frequent. On average, there was a serious assault every week at Newton.

Between the spokes of the main structure and the wall was an exercise yard, a gray, forbidding place without grass. In the past, inmates had used the turf to conceal weapons: shanks made from scissors, sharpened shards of metal snapped from cots, shivs made from wooden dowels inlaid with pieces of metal slowly ground to a cutting edge by furtive, endless scraping on the concrete floor. When the guards found such weapons, they always marveled that men of such volatile, murderous impulses possessed the patience it took to make a prison knife. After many such weapons were found hidden in the grass, prison officials had poured a huge slab of concrete that lapped to the very edges of the towering walls. The slab made the yard blistering hot in the humid Maryland summers and dismally gray and cold in wintertime. And the prisoners found other places to hide their weapons.

But even though it was a concrete plateau rimmed by walls of stone, walking the yard was a coveted privilege that relieved the endless, mind-numbing tedium of prison life. There the prisoners could at least breathe relatively fresh air and see the sky.

Monday, March 14

This was the world to which Daniel Seaton arrived, shackled and chained, on a gray prison bus. As the bus topped a small rise on the ribbon of highway slicing the cornfields and he saw the dark stronghold with its immense walls, his stomach had tightened.

Nothing in his experience had prepared him for life in a maximum-security institution. He had tried to mentally prepare himself. He had resolved to relinquish, as best he could, any holds on life beyond the walls. He realized that living for his family's visits could drive him to despair, so he would live one day at a time, meeting the challenges and troubles as they came. God is with me, he told himself over and over.

He shared a two-man cell with a lifer named Don who painted and wrote odd, Zenlike poetry. Twenty years ago, Don had killed his ex-wife and her fiance with a mail bomb disguised as a wedding present. Don was quiet, reflective, and a little bit crazy, but he kept out of Daniel's face and occasionally enlightened him with bits of wisdom about prison life.

For his part, Daniel read his Bible furiously, focusing in particular on Paul's letters, relishing the kinship of incarceration, a link he had never expected to share with the great apostle. If Paul had survived prison—that is, until he was executed, Daniel thought wryly—then he could do the same. God was with him.

A FAIR NUMBER of D. C. drug-gang members were incarcerated at Newton. Though the gangs had been popping off one another with great regularity for years, there seemed to be an endless supply of young men rising up in the drug ranks to take their places.

With each generation, the loss of conscience had grown greater, until the young men in their late teens and early twenties now at Newton made no distinction between right and wrong and knew only violence as a means to prove their manhood. They were a pitiless lot, and many of them were housed on Daniel Seaton's wing. From there they ran a busy clandestine smuggling operation within the prison, where drugs and other contraband were astonishingly plentiful.

One officer who had looked the other way for them a few times was now driving a champagne-colored Lexus. Another, who had thrown three of them into solitary confinement when he had found drugs on them after visits from their old ladies, had been surrounded one morning and stabbed repeatedly with homemade prison knives. He had recovered, but had been forced to retire on disability, having lost the use of his right arm.

IN THE MIDST OF ALL THIS, Daniel prayed vehemently to keep his expectations and emotions at a stable level. He got involved with the chaplaincy program, one of the various educational and work opportunities offered to inmates, depending on security clearance, and found a small but vigorous Christian community. There was a chapel meeting once a week with volunteers from the outside, and against his best efforts, Daniel found himself living for that Thursday night Bible study and Mary's weekly visits on Saturdays.

On her last visit, Mary had told him, a little breathlessly, that she had received a phone call from the attorney general herself, woman to woman, telling Mary that she was thinking about a way that she just might be able to get Daniel moved. He would be farther from home but in a federal institution with a less-violent reputation, one that housed mostly white-collar criminals.

"Keep this absolutely quiet," Mary had said. "Mrs. Gineen said she was thinking about doing something fairly radical to get you out. I don't know quite what she meant."

Daniel had tried to thrust that particular hope to the back of his mind . . . but despite his most vigorous efforts, it became a lifeline for him through the cold, damp days of March.

Thursday, April 14

It happened on a Thursday evening.

That morning a busload of new inmates had arrived, and, as always, the older cons had looked over the young guys stepping uncertainly into their cell blocks. Some inmates were welcomed with backslapping and shouts, as if it were a big, happy family reumon.

"Been waitin' for you, man," the shout came down as one muscular new arrival with a shaved head entered the wing. "What's the word on the street?"

Others entered the blocks with less confidence. New inmates, or "fish," were vulnerable; most would have to align themselves with a group for protection in order to survive. Some new prisoners found that the price for protection was their own bodies; some became prison prostitutes or the property of older inmates, called dockers" or "wolves." Young or physically weak inmates were particularly vulnerable. In the all-male environment of prison, many otherwise heterosexual prisoners met their sexual needs with "queens"—gay inmates who adopted a feminine role—or by preying on "punks," weak inmates who performed sexual acts in order to stay alive.

So it was that a stream of catcalls and whistles greeted a slender, smooth-faced boy named Terrence Watson. Watson was borderline retarded, one of six children, who had no idea who his father was. One summer night, his seventeenth birthday, he had drunk a bottle of MD 20-20 with a sixteen-year-old friend then decided to rob a small Korean grocery store on Capitol Hill, armed with handguns they had "borrowed" from the sixteenyear-old's older brother.

The boys had gotten angry when the clerk had locked the register and reached for the police alarm button, then panicked when a second clerk burst out of the storeroom in the back of the shop. They had wildly sprayed the two men with gunfire then fled on foot. Police had found them hiding in the scraggly bushes of Lincoln Park.

The two clerks had died, and now Terrence Watson, who still didn't quite know why he had done what he did, was looking at a life sentence in Newton Federal Correctional Institution.

Watson's eyes were wide with fright as he looked over the dark rows of barred cells. Calls filtered toward him.

"Hey there, darling I want some of that."

"Need a place to sleep tonight, sweetheart?"

Daniel Seaton, who had drawn the job of cleaning the walkways of his cell block, kept swabbing the concrete floor with a fat gray mop, but inside he was burning with disgust.

That evening, as Daniel was on his way to the chapel for the Bible study, he turned a corner and found three inmates surrounding the new kid. He recognized the three as members of one of D.C.'s drug gangs; Don had pointed them out to him during his first week at Newton. Two were huge men; they had been convicted of murdering five members of a rival gang in just one night of drive-by shootings and execution-style murders. They were bodyguards, of a sort, to the third, a convicted murderer named Shaqqar Redding, who had a reputation as the mastermind behind some of D.C.'s dirtiest drug business. It was Redding who was harassing the kid.

"You gonna need some protection while you here, sweet boy," he was saying. "What's your name?"

"Terrence W-w-watson," the kid stuttered.

"My friends and me, here, we'll be glad to take care of you, Terrence," said Redding. "We hear you like to drink sweet wine, and we've got a little something you might enjoy."

"I dunno," said Terrence. "I got to get to my cell. I don't wanna mess up on my first day."

"We'll take care of you," the older man said smoothly, laying his hand on the boy's arm. "You just come with us. We got a little time before the next count. You won't mess up."

Daniel's stomach pitched with fear, but he stepped forward.

"Why don't you leave him alone?" he said mildly. "He's just a kid."

The three men turned slowly, deliberately, toward Daniel.

"It's the preacher," the bigger bodyguard said to Redding.

Shaqqar Redding looked Daniel over, his grip tightening on Terrence Watson's thin arm.

"You might want to just mind your own business," Redding said with exaggerated courtesy. "This doesn't involve you."

For a flicker of a second, Daniel agreed. The cardinal rule, every halfway friendly inmate had told him ever since he had arrived at Newton, was "Don't get involved." Period. Stay to yourself, see nothing, hear nothing, say nothing, and maybe nothing will happen to you.

He looked at the kid again. The boy's eyes were wide. The bigger man's fingers pressed deeper into his arm. He looked at Daniel, wincing a little bit.

Daniel took a deep breath and looked both ways down the corridor. He could see an officer about a hundred feet away, rounding a corner, heading slowly in their direction.

"Listen," he said again, "why don't you just leave him alone? Give him a break. Think of him as your younger brother."

Redding's muscles tightened in his jaw, and as he turned fully toward Daniel, Daniel saw his eyes for the first time in the fluorescent light. His pupils were dilated. Daniel realized belatedly that the man was high on something, probably smuggled amphetamines.

Redding looked at his lieutenants, then shrugged and dropped Terrence Watson's arm. "Sure," he said to Daniel. "Fine. We'll just leave him alone. Come on, boys."

Daniel exhaled, not sure what to think. The two bodyguards

clustered around Redding for a moment as he turned and began to walk away, and Terrence looked at Daniel questioningly. Then, suddenly, Redding whirled around, his right hand clenched tight in a fist. Extending from the fist was a six-inch narrow blade with a needlelike point on the end.

The stiletto caught Daniel in the upper left chest and pierced his heart. The muscle continued to pump for a moment, tearing itself further with each beat, and blood flooded Daniel's chest cavity even though the small hole in his shirt barely bled.

Daniel looked down at himself in disbelief for just a moment, then sank to his knees on the concrete. The three men walked rapidly in the opposite direction. Terrence Watson stared down for a moment, not even sure what had happened—he had seen only the fist, not the stiletto. Then he began to scrabble away as well, following the three, who by now had vanished around a corner.

The officer, in the distance, had seen only a clump of inmates talking, then saw one of them pitch to the ground. He ripped his radio off his belt and called for backup, then ran toward the fallen inmate.

Daniel Seaton lay in a heap, facedown on the cold concrete floor. The officer turned him over and saw the small red tear in his shirt. A slender river of blood ran out of his mouth, but his eyes were already fixed and dimming. He was dead.

62

MILY GINEEN pressed her forehead against the cool glass of her library window, looking out into the dark night, seeing nothing but the faint shadow of her own reflection. She felt sick.

The kids were in bed, and she had been sitting at her desk, sipping a mug of tea and working her way through a stack of papers, when the call came. She was alone; there was no one to confirm that the ghastly call had really happened, so she found herself actually checking reality again.

Yes, she thought slowly, the phone had rung; Mort Cranston, head of the Bureau of Prisons, had told her tersely that Daniel Seaton had been murdered at Newton earlier tonight. There were several suspects, but details were sketchy at the moment. They would find out more and call her back in the morning with a full briefing. She looked at her scribbled notes on the pad next to the phone. It hadn't been a dream.

She looked at her watch. She dreaded the 11:00 news, but the media might have a detail or two about Daniel's death that Cranston had not. She had to watch. Then she would call Frederick. Then Paul. And maybe Mary Seaton.

Monday, April 18

Four days later, Emily was back at her desk, the doors to her office shut, Paul Clarkson sitting opposite her. She had canceled all appointments for the afternoon and blocked an hour of time with him. No calls except the White House, she'd told her secretary, absolutely no interruptions.

"I went to see Mary Seaton late last night," Emily told Paul. "I drove myself, got there after her children were in bed, after the media had left for the night."

Paul nodded. Emily looked terrible. She was as tailored and crisp as ever, but there were deep circles under her eyes and her face was pale, tired, older.

"She's an incredible woman," Emily continued. "I wanted to tell her myself about Terrence Watson's testimony about the situation surrounding Daniel's death. I wanted to tell her that I felt responsible for that situation. He probably should not have been convicted in the first place—well, that was out of our hands—but he never should have been sent to Newton. This administration has created such an ugly atmosphere, Paul. It was like Daniel was a scapegoat for all that. People were hungry for blood, and they got it.

"I wanted to understand how Mary was dealing with everything that has happened," she said. "I didn't comfort her much; it was almost like she was a priest, and I was there for confession. Once we got started, I couldn't stop talking."

Paul nodded again. Emily had been coming apart at the edges ever since the news about Daniel's murder. She hadn't been herself. He could almost—but not quite—imagine the torrent of words that must have confronted Mary Seaton.

"I told her that Watson said Daniel was trying to keep the other guys from hurting him. He said it all happened so fast, but it was like Daniel turned their attention away from him and toward himself. He was protecting him. And they killed him."

She looked down while she said this, then looked up again at Paul. "Watson has been in protective custody since he talked to the officers. I've given the order for him to be moved this afternoon to another institution. I am not repeating the same mistake that happened with Daniel Seaton.

"I have also given quite a lot of thought and consideration to the other matter I want to share with you," she said, speaking more like her usual self. "I've prepared a letter to the president— typed it up myself early this morning. It is my formal resignation from the office of attorney general."

She slid a single sheet of paper across the desk toward Paul. He read it quickly.

"This is a draft, I trust?" he asked, catching her by surprise.

"Why?" she asked, teasing for a moment. "Did I spell something wrong?"

"Something bigger than that. Why are you doing this?"

"For the first time in my life, I have absolutely had it. I'm a fixer by nature. Usually I can see how to make a situation better, how to win . . . but not this time. This time I see no way out but out. I've been thinking about it a lot. From the very beginning—actually, from even before the inauguration, when that abortionist was shot—this administration has missed the boat."

"I shouldn't have expected the president to really be able to see it; I realize he's not a particularly discerning person when it comes to moral issues. Far from it. But I should have seen it. It was like I had blinders on. At every step, in response to every crisis, we made policy without any understanding of human nature or the moral issues. You made some good points along the way, but I guess I wasn't really listening. Until the last few months."

"Now I look back, and everything is one huge mess. The most powerful government on earth, and we are running on fumes. Over at the White House, the president has turned into an automaton. Ever since Bernie's death. He doesn't know what to do next unless some pollster tells him it'll be popular. This is not the type of work I signed on to do."

She paused to take a breath.

Paul inhaled deeply, gathering his thoughts. He was exhausted, too. He hadn't slept much the past few nights. But he also hadn't realized what a toll recent events had taken on Emily. Ever since she met with Daniel Seaton in the jail, she had pulled back from him a little, in subtle ways. They still had a great working relationship, but it was as if she had become more private with her personal assessments. Now they were spilling out in a flood.

"Emily. Please reconsider," he said. "If you resign, what in the world will Whitney Griswold do? You've said it yourself: The administration is in a shambles; the cabinet is on autopilot—"

She broke in. "You told me before, right after Bernie's death, that people have three choices. They accept Christ as the Truth, they reject Him, or they go insane. You tell me what you think will happen to Whitney Griswold."

Paul stared at her. "Wait a minute," he said. "We were talking about your resignation. Where did that come from?"

"Look," she said. "I'm sorry. I guess I am jumping around a bit. I haven't slept much. One thing at a time. What did you want to say about my resignation?"

"You can't pull out," he said bluntly. "This government needs you. Some of the problems we have right now have come because the government—actually, I should say the people who make up the government—have not understood some basic principles. A government can't govern wisely unless it's made up of people of virtue. Government is not some mega-nanny or huge computer technocracy. It has to be the means by which justice is maintained for the people. For that to happen, it needs people within it who understand right and wrong, people who determine to restrain evil and promote good within the populace at large. People who have the confidence of the governed."

"If you leave your post in this government, Emily, who will do that? The person who takes your place? Not very likely."

"Unless it was you," Emily broke in.

Paul stopped for a moment. That thought had never entered his mind. "Are you kidding?" he asked. "They would never even consider me. I'm here because of a horse trade with Langer, remember?"

Emily raised her eyebrows. Her private conversation with Senator Langer about Paul's appointment seemed like a hundred years ago. It had made her so angry at the time. She couldn't quite remember why.

"I've thought about resigning a dozen times over the past few months," Paul said. "I've been tremendously frustrated. But I've felt like I had to stay, to be a Christian influence where it's desperately needed. Any government, but particularly this administration, needs people who recognize moral standards in positions of influence, Emily." He paused for a moment, fumbling for words. "And even though you don't call yourself a Christian in the same way I do, you need to be at your post as well."

"How do you know I don't call myself a Christian the same way you do?" Emily said. "Isn't that a little bit presumptuous?"

Paul waved his hands. "You know by now I don't mean to offend. We've had that conversation before. I just didn't want to label you in a way that you've told me in the past you don't appreciate. You've said you don't consider yourself one of those 'wild, extremist born-againers.'"

Emily grinned at him, looking for the first time in days like her old self, but still a little different. "Well, maybe I've become one."

"What do you mean?" Paul said, thoroughly confused by the course of the entire conversation.

"I'm still not an extremist. And I still don't like labels. But I've been realizing something ever since I talked to Daniel Seaton. It's like I've been remembering something I knew once but had forgotten. The remembrance of things past, something half-known but buried like a dream, a longing for something permanent, fixed, absolute, something that I once hoped existed, but for which I had lost hope.

"But when I talked to Mary Seaton last night, it all came together for me. I can't put it into religious terminology for you, but it's like what Daniel Seaton said, and something you said earlier: You either believe that Jesus is the Truth, or you don't. Well, I believe it."

63

IN RESPONSE to the Orwellian events around them, the president's advisors had taken a decidedly Norman Rockwellian turn, studding Whitney Griswold's schedule with all kinds of old-fashioned, cheerfullly contrived pieces ot vintage political Americana.

The president had appeared at the outdoor wedding of his brother-in-law's niece, grinning and dancing with the blushing bride, a relative he had last seen when was she was six and missing two front teeth. He could still barely remember her name.

He had dedicated a new track on the D.C.-to-New York Metroliner run, cutting a fat red, white, and blue ribbon and then boarding the train, waving and chatting casually, yet presidentially, with a select crop of commuters.

He had taken a group of underprivileged children to the circus, muttering under his breath to his aides the entire time about the stupid acts, the dirty animals, and the obnoxious vendors with their sticky cotton candy and hot dogs. But he had still managed to grin and point to the elephants, laughing with the big-eyed kids. That night, at the White House, he had drunk more than usual.

Some of the photo ops were more substantive: meetings with

foreign leaders in the rose garden, convening a conference on crime with experts from around the country, chairing Cabinet meetings. In such settings, J.Whitney Griswold's tall, graceful demeanor appeared utterly presidential, and the pictures looked good on the evening news and in the papers. Robbie was beginning to hope that maybe, just maybe, their string of bad luck was over.

In late April, Griswold visited Washington, D.C.'s Woodrow Wilson High School for an assembly. The school gymnasium had been transformed into a town-meeting setting, with the less trustworthy elements of the student population arrayed on bleachers. A handpicked group of several dozen students sat in folding chairs on the newly polished gym floor in a semicircle around the president.

Secret Service personnel patroled the building, which had been sealed off. Everyone had passed through metal detectors; everyone had submitted to extensive searches of their persons and book bags. Along with the students, the gym was crowded with members of the print and television media.

Things got off to a decent start. The president had been briefed thoroughly, and the day's topic, "Rights and Responsibilities of the Coming Generation," actually yielded an interesting discussion. The students brought screened questions for the president on higher education, the quest for democracy in central Africa, yet another baseball strike, and his own decision to pursue a law career while he was in high school.

Then a sixteen-year-old named Vidalia Perkins stood up. Vidalia was an honors student chosen to ask a key question about healthcare reform for the inner city, a centerpiece of the president's legislative package on its way to Congress. She walked to the standing microphone and bent it down toward her face. The slip of paper with her question typed on it was in her hand, but she didn't refer to it. Good poise, Whitney Griswold thought as she looked him directly in the eye.

"Mr. President," Vidalia said, clearing her throat and stumbling for a second, then regaining her composure. "My name is

Vidalia Perkins, and I had a question about healthcare all planned for you, but there's something else on my mind. May I ask you that instead?" The news cameras turned toward Whitney Griswold, and he nodded smoothly. "Sure, Vidalia," he said. "You go right ahead."

The reporters' recorders and video cameras picked up every word.

"Well," Vidalia said, "I've seen a lot of my friends die here in the city. They've gotten into trouble with drugs. My girlfriend killed herself last week. She left me a note that said she just couldn't go on. I know you had somebody on your staff who killed himself, and I've been wondering how you dealt with it. I mean, what's the point? What kind of hope can you give people in my generation? Many of us feel like there just doesn't seem to be any meaning to life . . ."

She trailed off, and the president's easy smile took on the look of an animal frozen in a truck's approaching headlights. He quickly assumed a brow-furrowed look of compassion.

"That's a great question, Vidalia," he said, stalling for a moment. "Bright young people like you have asked that in every generation. I'm really sorry about your friend; I know how much it hurts to lose a friend. Believe me." He shook his head in obvious pain. "But even when the going gets tough, those of us who are tough have to just keep going. It's kids like you who make the future bright for the rest of us . . . and this government is pledged to do all we can to create a society in which you can have hope and opportunity. Together we can do that. Look at the programs like our voluntary service and youth corps.

"As you get involved in things like this, you'll feel good about yourself—you know, get in touch with your feelings and realize who you are. That's it. Because when you feel good, when you have high self-esteem, then you'll help others."

TWO DAYS LATER, Ira Levitz"s column blistered the editorial page of the *Washington Post*.

"Feel good?" A bottle of cheap wine can make you feel good. If this is the best response the leader of the free world can offer a questioning teenager, we are in far more trouble than any of us ever realized.

The problem is, President Griswold not only missed the answer, he didn't even understand the question. Vidalia Perkins was speaking for a generation of young people who are far smarter than we give them credit, a generation that has seen the situation in America and found it wanting.

I would suggest, in response to Ms. Perkins's question about untimely death and the meaning of life, that perhaps there is far more to be found in the death of convicted conspirator Daniel Seaton than in the death of presidential counsel Bernie O'Keefe.

By all accounts, O'Keefe struggled with a growing sense of despair. Many of us have faced that same black void, and my sympathies are with the man in his last, tortured moments, as well as with his family, left behind to deal with his loss. But his death took place in a vacuum. What meaning can one derive from it? "Don't do this"? Why not?

By contrast, I can't help but take the rather unpopular view of admiring Daniel Seaton. Seaton's naivete hooked him into a conspiracy that took him, unjustly in my opinion, to the pit of one of our worst federal correctional facilities. There, Seaton died defending a young, handicapped inmate from the depraved designs of a group of criminals. In essence, Daniel Seaton gave his life for another. Never mind that the man for whom he died was a convicted murderer, an impaired young man who will never see free society agam.

Seaton died defending someone weaker than himself. O'Keefe died escaping from himself.

There is a lesson for Vidalia Perkins—and all of us—in Mr. Seaton's death. The "meaning to life," as Ms. Perkins put it, is to be found more in the ancient notion of giving oneself for others than in the modern concept of feeling good about oneself. If this president ever knew that fact, he has forgotten it.

Perhaps, through the death of a good man in the nexus of

evil, we will begin to find that the moral malaise of the past year can begin to be purged. Perhaps, when the despair goes deep enough, something within us responds, saying "this far, and no farther."

Perhaps, as we confront the mayhem, we are compelled to return to the hope of permanent truths long abandoned. Perhaps we are compelled to look to something beyond ourselves . . .

LEVITZ LEFT THAT LAST SENTENCE of his piece unfinished. He couldn't think of a time, ever in his life, when he had concluded a column with an ellipsis, but this time it felt wrong to end with a declarative summation. No, better, just this once, to leave it open.

BY THE MIDDLE OF JUNE, as summer officially arrived, there were small signs of change in the warm, fragrant air.

The hydrangea was flowering in Mary Seaton's garden just a few days after she received a surprising phone call from Jennifer Barrett, who expressed her condolences and asked if she might visit. Soon after, Mary also received an ebullient letter from Amy, who had married the youth pastor at her parents' church in California. She was expecting twins. In Mississippi, Byron Langer, who was preparing to open a law office after the elections and the end of his Senate term, presided over the first birthday party of his sixth grandchild.

In North Dakota, a young woman named Sherry Sullivan, a long-time friend of Alex Seaton, turned herself in for the murder of Dr. Ann Sloan and implicated two others in the conspiracy. Meanwhile, the FBI pursued a tip that Frank Doggett had been sighted in a small village forty miles from San José, Costa Rica.

John Jenkins and his family moved from Washington to Southern California. Anne Griswold resigned four of her board memberships and made plans for an extended summer stay at Martha's Vineyard.

Hal Humsler became the manager of a video rental store in Spartanburg, South Carolina, and always remembered to take his medication. Reginald Warner completed his community service sentence and prepared to enter Columbia University's media communications program.

Influenced by his friendship with Father Bob Garrison, Marilyn O'Keefe's eldest son, Matt, made plans to go to Georgetown University, where attendance at Mass and student-led prayer meetings had been so high that even the *Washington Post* had sent a reporter to cover the story.

Rob and Lisa Knight welcomed a baby boy into their family. They named him Daniel.

And, pressured by his own Justice Department, J. Whitney Griswold withdrew the National Guard from the streets of several of the nation's major cities. Ironically, statistics showed a slight drop in the crime rate in those cities the following month. To the surprise of many, a move was begun in the Congress to block the regeneration centers. Though it fell short of a majority, sponsors promised a renewed effort. Shortly after, an ABC News poll found a significant shift in public sentiment, with the majority of respondents opposing the centers. And a Newsweek national poll found an unexpected slight upturn in people's confidence regarding the future for the nation.

ON JULY 4, Attorney General Emily Gineen hosted a catered picnic at her home for her staff and their families. After feasting on grilled chicken, hamburgers, pasta salad, watermelon, and double-chocolate brownies, Paul Clarkson packed his family and a few leftover balloons into their Volvo. Before he swung into the driver's seat, Paul paused to shake Emily's hand.

"Thanks so much, Emily. This was the best idea anybody at Justice has had in a long time. Everyone has been saying what a boost it's been."

Emily grinned. "It's good to get away from the office and stop and appreciate one another now and then. Thanks for all your help." She leaned down and waved through the window. "Bye, June. See you Sunday."

64

Saturday morning, July 9

THE SUN WAS BARELY ABOVE THE HORIZON, a blazing orange ball shooting its fiery glow across the churning ocean. A glorious moment, and Whitney Griswold breathed deeply of the fresh, salty air, enraptured by the splendor of the setting. A brisk southwest breeze was raking the waters just off Martha's Vineyard. He could see across Nantucket Sound to the shoreline of Cape Cod. A great day for sailing.

Yessir, perfect sailing, thought Griswold, and he was ready for it, dressed in khaki slacks and a blue turtleneck sweater. Draped over his left arm was a dark blue windbreaker with the presidential seal embroidered over the left breast. The windbreaker was a standard White House perk for senior staff—but only Griswold, of course, had "The President" embroidered over the seal.

The President. Griswold smiled to himself. *Yes, indeed.* He used to stand right on this spot as a kid and think of his destiny, the greatness he knew he would attain. He lifted his foot onto the thick rail that surrounded the enormous veranda running across the front and around the side of his cedar-shingled Starbuck Point home. Then, with folded arms, he leaned forward on his raised knee and looked across the generous green lawn that stretched level, then sloped gently down to the ocean. Perhaps this evening the family would play croquet at sunset, just like they used to years ago.

Griswold took in huge gulps of the salt air and exhaled slowly. The doctor had told him that deep breathing was not only good for tension but for cleansing the oxygen in one's body. Gazing into the distance, he could see small boats already pushing into the waves across the harbor on the other island, Chappaquiddick. He sipped his coffee—made with six scoops for eight cups of water, just the way he liked it—and checked his watch. 7:45. In fifteen minutes the launch would take him to his boat, the *Sea Hawk*.

Oh, how he'd longed for this moment for months; to be here and on the water. It would give him a fresh perspective. He needed that, with only four months to the mid-term elections.

Not even two years in office, he thought, and already it had aged him. He breathed deeply again as he ran his right hand over the deep creases in his cheeks. In the mirror this morning, while he was shaving, he'd noticed how hollow his eyes looked, dark and a bit sunken.

He had been too idealistic. He'd had such high hopes when he became president, such noble ideals about public service. But his dreams had been shattered by that assassin's bullet in Fargo, splintered even before his inauguration. It had been downhill ever since. He'd had to use force to suppress attacks on legitimate authority. It was his duty. But the more he applied force, the more the terrorists fought back. It was like fighting a guerrilla war, and the guerrilla always had the advantage.

Terrorism. Violence poisoning our society. Upsetting our balance as a nation. Griswold clenched his fists, breathing harder, faster. Crime and ugliness rampant. And now look at us! The National Guard in the streets . . . people angry and fearful. Whatever became of the American dream? *Whatever became of my dream?*

Why has all this happened? No doubt it's the fault of radicals who want to bring down our system, he thought angrily. *Like the Seaton brothers—dangerous men, better off dead.*

But then there are some signs things may be turning around,

he thought. Just maybe. Robbie says attitudes are different, a little more peaceful since that sanctimonious Daniel Seaton was killed. The polls show it; 60 percent still say America is on the wrong track, but a few months ago it was 80 percent. And whatever happens in the short run, this will all be put in perspective by historians. Remember, Lincoln wasn't popular during the Civil War. Historians are always more charitable. Look at Nixon. Still, we have to get through the November elections.

But people will give us high marks in foreign policy, he thought. No thanks to the State Department, that striped-pants, little-pinky, tea-set crowd. Griswold sipped his coffee and breathed in more of the fresh morning air. Yes, the public would give him credit for the tax cut too; Wall Street certainly liked it. And the Fed—his buddy Roger, now chairman, was coming through—loosening money just in time before the elections. Just like he'd asked him to do. The trade negotiation was good for business, and the crime bill should make people feel safer.

If only the jackasses in the press would give us half a break. They don't want to, of course—that's the problem. They're only happy when they're tearing someone down. A rotten lot—like the rest of the critics. Doesn't matter whether it's the Congress—that slimy, self-seeking bunch of hypocrites—or the lobbyists sucking around sniping at everything you do. Problem is, they're all in the bleachers watching. Only the man in the arena, sweat streaming down his face, bloodied but unbowed, only he understands. That's where the real honor is, not on the sidelines. Teddy Roosevelt understood when he wrote those words. Only the man in the arena.

He smashed his fist into his palm. "We'll show them," he muttered.

But today all that didn't matter. What counts is this twenty-mile-an-hour wind right out of the southwest, he thought, lifting his face to taste the salt breeze. A perfect day to sail. He checked his watch again—five minutes to go—and began to pace the long veranda, past the big wooden rockers with the fresh white cushions tied over the seats and backs. This grand old home, its white trim and balustrades shining against the weathered cedar shingles, was a proud place. For eighty years it had stood with its jaw set against the fiercest nor'easters Mother Nature hurled its way; like the man in the arena, it was unbowed, its honor unsullied. That's the real measure of character: to stand against the best they could hurl at you and keep going. Chin up. Thirty-two percent approval in the polls—so what? They're not in the arena.

Anne, wearing a blue and green rugby-striped sweater and white shorts, came through the screen door with Elizabeth and Robert following behind. bike his father, Robert loved the water and was dressed for sailing; Elizabeth was still in her Mickey Mouse nightshirt.

"You sure you ladies won't come?" Griswold said, putting one arm around Anne and drawing her close. "It's a great day to sail."

"No," said Anne. "I've got a tennis game this morning, and Elizabeth's going into town with the Tate girls."

With his other arm he drew Elizabeth to his side, kissing her on the cheek.

"Whitney, please be careful today. Watch the rocks at West Chop," Anne frowned.

"Really now, Anne. I've sailed that point a hundred, no, two hundred times," he grinned.

"I know, dear, but concentrate on your sailing. You've been very . . . well, forgetful lately, Whit."

"Nonsense." He put his index finger to her lips. "Just a lot on my mind, you know. But today Robert and I will sail. That's all I'm going to think about."

"The launch is ready, sir," Captain Slattery, the president's naval aide, announced from the foot of the six wide steps leading to the huge oceanfront lawn. He was carrying two bags. One was "the football," the brown bag that contained the code cards for launching a nuclear strike—an anachronism in the post-ColdWar world, Griswold had thought, but the military insisted. With terrorists and rogue nations like North Korea, the world was still an uncertain place. In the other bag was the battery-powered communications equipment, a direct satellite uplink courtesy of the army signal corps, enabling him to talk to anyone, anywhere in the world, at any time, almost instantaneously. His doctor along with two Secret Service agents and navy enlisted personnel would be waiting at the launch.

Two other agents, wires from their earpieces threaded under their dark windbreakers, were stationed on the fence line at both corners of the property. They watched as Griswold, Robert, and Slattery walked down to the pier and the launch.

The chief boatswain's mate saluted as Griswold stepped aboard the forty-five-foot, high-powered vessel. The navy called it an admiral's barge, a fiberglass boat accented with generous amounts of mahogany. In the center was an enclosed cabin with bulletproof glass windows. On the bow were two men, their submachine guns held just below the gunwales, and two others were stationed in the stern.

The boat's engines were throbbing as Griswold stepped into the cabin after returning the boatswain's salute and waving to the lieutenant at the wheel. Its lines cast off, the boat pulled gently from the dock; then its engines roared as it turned northeast to begin the swing around Starbuck Point and then south into Edgartown harbor. Griswold came out of the cabin once the boat was under way, his hair blowing straight back in the wind.

Before he was president he used to have to walk down North Water Street past the Daggard House, then into a narrow street leading to the harbor and the yacht club launch that would take him out to his boat. He missed the sights and sounds and smells of Edgartown harbor. But security was a big consideration, and the navy made it so easy; he could be under way fifteen minutes after leaving his front porch.

As the launch threaded its way into the harbor, Griswold watched the current surging out. A good sign. It would be going with him when he sailed out of the harbor.

He glanced ahead at the two navy patrol boats clearing their way through the harbor; on shore he could see the armed marines. Griswold felt uncomfortable disrupting the tranquil life of Martha's Vineyard. He knew the locals resented it, even though he was a hometown boy, so to speak—but the tourists and shopkeepers loved it.

The *Sea Hawk* came into view, its gleaming black hull looking sleek and graceful at its mooring. Shrewd fellow, his grandfather, to have laid a cast-iron mushroom in the late 1920s right in the choicest mooring spot in this harbor. The *Sea Hawk*, a forty-three-foot wooden ketch, was twenty-three years old but lovingly maintained, its mahogany and brightwork polished and its rails covered with varnish so thick you could see your reflection in them. It had the best pedigree in the harbor, designed by Sparkman and Stephens and built at the Hinkley yard in Southwest Harbor, Maine, the finest yacht craftsmen in the world.

The launch pulled alongside and Whitney scrambled aboard, followed by Robert, Captain Slattery, the doctor, and two Secret Service agents wearing thick sunglasses. Two boatswain's mates who would help crew, along with Lieutenant Coughlin, a communications specialist, were already on board. So was Jeff Springer, a Boston investment banker and an old sailing friend of the president's from boyhood.

Jeff grinned and saluted loosely, and Griswold slammed him on the back. "Great day, huh, Jeff. We'll make the old girl fly today."

Griswold went directly to the cockpit and unfastened the lines holding the boom; then he nodded to Jeff, who went to the base of the main mast and began pulling on the halyard, slowly hoisting the main as Griswold held the boat into the wind.

He grinned as the giant sail fluttered in the breeze. Less proficient or more cautious sorts would motor off the buoy and out of the harbor before setting sail. But the tides were right, so he'd sail off like any good old salt should do. He didn't even turn on the engine, though he noticed one of the boatswain's mates was standing near the switch.

"Secure this," he said, handing the line to Robert after he'd pulled in the mainsheet. Then he turned the helm hard to star-board, and a puff of wind filled the sail just as Jeff, now on the bow, released the mooring.

"Perfect timing," Griswold yelled, grinning triumphantly.

The *Sea Hawk* sliced through the blue water as other boaters cheered. So did a small cluster of people standing on a nearby pier, held back by a wide rope stretched in front of them.

Jeff and Robert unfurled the jib as they glided north, and a cheer went up from another cluster of townsfolk standing on Memorial Wharf. Griswold glanced to the left and waved. A quaint picture it was, the town of Edgartown with its gray, cedar-shingled, colonial buildings decorated with white trim, a church steeple or two, some gingerbread decoration on a few of the build-ings, piers, and docks lined along the water. Boats everywhere.

Griswold felt a sudden exhilaration. Home. His harbor. His beloved boat. The salt air. He was positively giddy.

The *Sea Hawk*, jib and main full, began to heel as they left the harbor headed for Marker 8. A puff of wind raised spray, the cold salt water smarting Griswold's cheeks.

At Marker 8 Griswold brought the boat around to a port tack.

"Let it out, son," he shouted, and Robert released the mainsheet, letting the boom way out so that the ail could catch the full breeze coming off the port stern quarter. The boat be-gan to pick up speed, gradually reaching eight knots.

Griswold grinned broadly as he set the course past West Chop, a point of land dotted with homes owned over the years by ce-lebrities like Mike Wallace and Carly Simon, and then took a straight 330-degree bearing, right for Woods Hole. With the wind like this, they'd be there in an hour and a half, and from there through the narrow cut off Nonamesset Island into Buzzard's Bay.

JEFF OPENED A BEER for himself and asked Griswold if he wanted a Coke; he knew his friend never drank while sailing.

The president nodded and smiled.

Jeff thought Whit was unusually quiet today. He'd said nothing other than to call for sail changes. But Jeff waited for him to initiate any conversation, out of deference to the position his friend now held.

Finally Griswold turned to him and said, "Great day."

"Yes, it is," Jeff answered. And then for another twenty minutes Griswold said nothing. He simply gripped the wheel with an almost childlike smile on his face, seemingly unaware of anything or anyone around him.

Finally Jeff could hold back no longer. He had to break the silence.

"Wonderful, isn't it, Whit?"

"What?" Griswold looked startled, then quickly recovered. "Yes, beautiful, beautiful, nothing like it."

"You're quiet today. Everything okay?" Jeff said.

"Just fine, just fine," Griswold grinned. "You know, the great thing about this boat is that the captain controls it. It's right here in my hands." He gripped the wheel and continued to stare straight ahead.

"You turn to the right, it responds. To the left . . . there, see." He jerked the wheel. "Maybe the only thing left in life that a person can control."

"You need to do this more often, Whit. Get away from Washington."

"And how. You know, Bernie, it's a sick town."

Jeff bit his tongue. Better not correct him; he knew Whitney was still haunted by the suicide of his old friend.

"Positively sick. Full of power-mad people who want to destroy us—the presidency. But we're not going to let those no good . . . oh, sorry, Jeff . . . hard to shake it all off. Yes, this is wonderful, the greatest pleasure I have. Here, Robert, take the helm. Hold this course. We're two miles off Woods Hole."

Robert bounded up to the wheel, and Jeff sat back, relieved.

"This is like old times," Jeff chuckled.

"Sure is." The president pushed up his sleeves and sat back

on the cockpit seat, but he still looked somewhat distant.

"Steady on course, Son," Griswold commanded, staring straight ahead, the breeze blowing his hair in all directions.

They were a mile off Woods Hole, headed for the entrance to Buzzard's Bay, when the water darkened ahead.

"Looks like the wind's picking up," Jeff said. "Maybe we should reef the main."

Griswold didn't respond.

"Dad!" Robert said, "I think we've got too much sail up."

Griswold was still staring into space. Jeff and Robert looked at each other, uncertain what to do.

Then, just as Jeff stood up to dig out the reefing lines, they hit the first gust and the boat heeled sharply, digging the starboard rail into the water.

"Dad!" Robert yelled, and as Jeff and Griswold were thrown against each other, the president finally snapped out of his daze.

But even after they'd pulled in some sail and Griswold was back at the wheel again, Jeff still couldn't make eye contact with the man.

The pressures must be awful, he thought to himself.

"A beautiful sound, isn't it?" Griswold asked suddenly.

"What?" Jeff asked. "The waves?"

"No, no. The bells, Bernie, the church bells. Must be coming from Falmouth. "The president brushed the hair out of his eyes, staring straight ahead.

"I don't hear any church bells, Whit. Can't be. This is Saturday. Maybe it's a bell buoy."

"No, no. Church bells. Listen, clear as can be, and beautiful."

"I don't hear them either, Dad." Robert said, glancing at his father.

"Of course you do," Griswold snapped, finally looking at them, first at his son and then at Jeff with steely eyes and an expression so intense it made Jeff shiver.

"Whit, are you all right?"

"Ah, yes," Griswold sighed. "Bells, beautiful bells. Hear them ring."

ACKNOWLEDGMENTS

We are profoundly grateful to a number of people who have so graciously helped to make this book possible.

We owe heartfelt thanks to: Grace McCrane and Nancy Niemeyer, administrative support; Kim Robbins and Roberto Rivera, as well as Jean Epley and Gordon Barnes, research help; Bessie Cool, interview transcriptions; Emily Murray, Scott Sforza, and Kathy Doyle, ABC News; Ed Wright, Harry Mahon, and their colleague, satellite communications information; Lyn Mickley, the National Institutes of Health; Captain John Sandoz, explosives expertise; Rob Showers, Gammon and Grange, legal help; Father Bob Tabbert; Ted Collins, piloting expertise; Dr. Joseph Spano and Dr. Paul Hoehner, medical information; Nat Belz, *World* magazine; and Wendell Colson, former captain of his crew-team at Princeton, for the details regarding Whitney Griswold's antique rowing machine.

We appreciate Steve and Sandy Smallman, Wallace and Cynthia Zellmer, General William Maloney, and Dr. Gary Pileggi for taking the time to give critiques of an early draft of the manuscript. Chuck is grateful to Dick and Dottie McPherson and Jack and Ruth Eckerd for the creative time spent in their guest houses. And Ellen extends hearty thanks to Jan O'Kelley, Jan Pascoe, Mildred Santilli, and Norma Vaughn for their kind help with baby-sitting.

Thank you to our faithful, fearless editor, and long-time friend, Judith Markham.

And, as always, we thank our spouses, Patty Colson and Lee Vaughn, for their steadfast love, support, and patience.

ABOUT THE AUTHORS

CHARLES COLSON writes from his rich, unique experiences as a Washington insider who served as a chief Senate assistant on Capitol Hill, and as counsel to President Richard Nixon. He is the recipient of the 1993 Templeton Prize for Progress in Religion, a highly regarded speaker and columnist, and the founder and chairman of Prison Fellowship Ministries. Mr. Colson has authored numerous best-selling books, including *Born Again*, *The Body* (with Ellen Vaughn), *Why America Doesn't Work*, (with Jack Eckerd), and *A Dangerous Grace* (with Nancy R. Pearcey).

ELLEN VAUGHN, a talented, accomplished writer in her own right and former vice president of executive communications for Prison Fellowship, has worked with Charles Colson since 1980, collaborating with him on seven previous books. A Washington D.C. native, she, too, is intimately familiar with the capital city settings of *Gideon's Torch*. Ms. Vaughn earned a bachelor's degree from the University of Richmond and a master's from Georgetown University.

Read The Colson Classic That Has The World Talking...And Thinking.

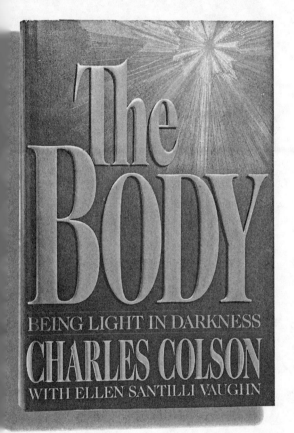

"With punchy prose and haunting stories, Colson challenges, humbles, and inspires."
–J.I. Packer, professor of theology, Regent College

"A deeply moving and significant work."
–John Cardinal O'Connor, Archbishop of New York

"This book will provoke discussion and debate for years to come."
–*Enrichment* Magazine

O nce every generation, a book comes along that defines debate, shapes attitudes, and changes society. *The Body* is such a book.

- *The Body* has been covered and excerpted everywhere from *USA Today* to "Larry King Live Radio" to *Focus on the Family*.
- In *Christianity Today* poll, readers named *The Body* one of the Top 10 books of the year and Charles Colson their "Favorite Living Author."
- Colson was awarded the prestigious, worldwide 1993 Templeton Prize for Progress in Religion as reported in *Time*, *Newsweek*, and *The New York Times*.
- *The Body* was awarded ECPA Gold Medallion as 1993 Book of the Year.

Available in book and audio format.

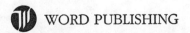 WORD PUBLISHING

CITIZEN

OF THE

VINTAGE CANADA

Praise for *Citizen of the World*

"[A] magisterial biography drawing on many previously unpublished letters and diaries."   —*National Post*

"*Citizen of the World* is more than just another volume on an already overcrowded shelf. It offers the most intimate look at the most dominant of Canadian political figures in modern times."
—*The Gazette* (Montreal)

"The most illuminating Trudeau portrait. . . . John English was given full access to the gold mine—all of Mr. Trudeau's diaries, letters, and papers. It is from that kind of entree that truths emerge. The Trudeau story is more wondrous than imagined."
—*The Globe and Mail*

"English's work is very readable, balanced in judgment and of course deeply informed. . . . Trudeau's energy, passion, ambition, wit, and intellectuality leap off the page, leaving this reader once again with a sense of the extraordinary nature of his life and character."   —*Winnipeg Free Press*

"John English has written a brilliant biography of the early life of Pierre Elliott Trudeau . . . *Citizen of the World* will be as commanding a book as Trudeau was himself."
—Dafoe Book Prize jury citation

"*Citizen of the World* . . . is one of the most fascinating and revealing books I have encountered in years. . . . Sensitively, thoughtfully, and absorbingly written."
—*The Owen Sound Sun Times*

"The most complete version yet of Trudeau's life, and one of the most revealing biographies of any Canadian prime minister. . . . [T]he definitive Trudeau biography."
—*The Record* (Kitchener-Waterloo)

"Brilliant, so perceptive about Trudeau, so well informed on the context, so beautifully written."
—Ramsay Cook, former General Editor of the
Dictionary of Canadian Biography

JOHN ENGLISH

WORLD

THE LIFE OF PIERRE ELLIOTT TRUDEAU

VOLUME ONE: 1919–1968

VINTAGE CANADA EDITION, 2007

Copyright © 2006 John English

All rights reserved under International and Pan-American Copyright
Conventions. No part of this book may be reproduced in any form or by any
electronic or mechanical means, including information storage and retrieval
systems, without permission in writing from the publisher, except by a reviewer,
who may quote brief passages in a review.

Published in Canada by Vintage Canada, a division of Random House of
Canada Limited, Toronto, in 2007. Originally published in hardcover
in Canada by Alfred A. Knopf Canada, a division of Random House of
Canada Limited, Toronto, in 2006, and simultaneously in Quebec by
Les Éditions de l'Homme, Montreal. Distributed by Random House
of Canada Limited, Toronto.

Vintage Canada and colophon are registered trademarks of
Random House of Canada Limited.

www.randomhouse.ca

Pages 545 to 546 constitute a continuation of the copyright page.

Library and Archives Canada Cataloguing in Publication

English, John, 1945–
Citizen of the world : the life of Pierre Elliott Trudeau / John English.

Contents: v. 1. 1919–1968.
ISBN 978-0-676-97522-2 (v. 1)

1. Trudeau, Pierre Elliott, 1919–2000. 2. Canada—Politics and
government—1968–1979. 3. Canada—Politics and government—1980–1984.
4. Prime ministers—Canada—Biography. I. Title.

FC626.T7E53 2007   971.064'4092   C2007-900752-X

Book design by CS Richardson
Printed and bound in the United States of America

4 6 8 9 7 5

To Hilde, without whom this book and so much else
would never have been possible

CONTENTS

—

PREFACE

Pierre Trudeau is the prime minister who intrigues, enthralls, and outrages Canadians most. Remarkably intelligent, highly disciplined, yet seemingly spontaneous and a constant risk-taker, he made his life an adventure. The outline of the story is well known. Born into a wealthy French-English family in Montreal, he was educated in the city's best Catholic schools and at university in Montreal, followed by graduate work first at Harvard, then in Paris and in London. When he returned to Canada in the late forties after an extensive journey through Europe, the Middle East, and Asia, he spent the next decade and a half seemingly as a dilettante, writing articles for newspapers and journals, driving fast cars and a Harley-Davidson motorbike, escorting beautiful women to concerts and restaurants, travelling the globe whenever he wished, founding political groupings that went nowhere, and finally getting a teaching position at the Université de Montréal. Then, suddenly, or so it seemed, in 1965 he stood as a Liberal candidate in the federal election, won his seat, and quickly gained national attention as a constitutional expert and an innovative minister of justice. Three years later, he became leader of the Liberal Party of Canada amid a media frenzy usually reserved for rock stars, not politicians. How did it all happen?

This first volume of *The Life of Pierre Elliott Trudeau* offers a key to this mystery. Soon after Trudeau's death, his executors asked me if I would be interested in writing a definitive biography, based on unique, full access to his papers and including both his personal and his public life. I had doubts, knowing how private Trudeau had been and how little he had revealed of his life in his memoirs, even though his public career ranks among the most influential in Canada. While I admired Trudeau, supported him during his political career and after, and shared many mutual friends and acquaintances, I had met him only a few times, nearly always in political settings, where sometimes he was superb but, at other moments, visibly uncomfortable.

Yet the enigma of Trudeau intrigued me. Moreover, when I learned from some of his executors—Alexandre Trudeau, Jim Coutts, Marc Lalonde, Roy Heenan, and Jacques Hébert—that he had kept a huge trove of letters and personal documents in his famous Art Deco home in Montreal, I realized I had a rare opportunity and agreed to accept their challenge. These papers, which are now mostly housed in the ancient Tunney's Pasture research centre of Library and Archives Canada, provide an extraordinary record of his private life. I am the only biographer who has had full access to these papers and to the closed room in which they are preserved. In addition, through the Trudeau family and others, I have had access to other papers that have been ignored, restricted, and absent to earlier scholars. Together these papers form an extraordinary collection that reveals the private hopes, fears, loves, and loathings of Trudeau from his earliest years until his death.

The personal papers, which were assembled by Grace Trudeau and by Trudeau himself, give a detailed record of his early life. Until the 1960s Trudeau, a literary perfectionist, drafted every letter he wrote and kept most of the drafts—in some cases several drafts of the same letter. In this sense, Trudeau's papers

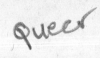

are more complete than those of Mackenzie King, his only rival in maintaining a full record of his life. Moreover, Grace Trudeau was even more diligent than Isabel King in saving the school records of her favourite son. Virtually every report card, school notebook, award notice, and school essay was preserved. Trudeau also kept materials in his papers that were highly controversial, notably the evidence of his nationalist and secret activities during the early 1940s.

In reading Trudeau's own words, I came to realize that the seeming contradictions in his life were more often consistencies, and that this man of reserve to his male colleagues and friends was astonishingly open and honest with women. I uncovered youthful allegiances he hoped to keep secret, yet saw how completely he changed from a socially conservative Catholic to Catholic socialist once he was exposed to different ideas and influences at Harvard and the London School of Economics. I also discovered that his move into political life in middle age was no surprise at all, but something he had planned since his adolescence. He had merely been waiting for the right moment to make it happen. And the playboy who was photographed with one stunning blonde after another had, I found, enjoyed deeply rewarding relationships with a few extraordinary women. His letters to his female friends and his mother are the most frequently quoted in this volume, not because they are sensational but because they reveal most fully the private self that Trudeau quietly cloaked.

As a youth, Trudeau wrote in his journal that mystery was essential to defining identity and that he wanted to be a friend to all but an intimate to none. It was an intention he held to for the rest of his life. Although he read through many of his papers in his later years, he did not use them in his own brief memoir published in 1993. Nor did he succumb to the temptation to edit or destroy them. Fortunately, he chose the course of integrity and truth, and he retained controversial or intimate items in his archive. Once I had read through the collection, many of his close friends who are still alive generously agreed to discuss these letters with me, and, as we talked, they told me more of their memories of Pierre (I thank them in specific detail in the Acknowledgments to this book). As a result of their generosity and support, my text in several instances revises and even contradicts Trudeau's own account of his life and other earlier biographies of him. Trudeau, as he emerges in these pages, is a far more complex, conflicted, and challenging character than we have ever known before.

The first volume of this biography takes Trudeau through the crucial formative years, from his birth in 1919 (a year of disappointment in Canada) to the Liberal leadership convention of 1968 (a year of abundance and promise in the nation he was soon to lead). The second volume will cover his fifteen controversial years as prime minister, his role as husband and devoted father, and his often tumultuous public and private life until his death in the opening year of the twenty-first century.

—

CHAPTER ONE

TWO WORLDS

The Great War was over; the times tasted bitter. Influenza came back with the soldiers and killed more at home than had died in the trenches. Like the war, it preferred the young to the old. Death usually came quickly as the victims suffocated in a blood-tinged froth that sometimes gushed grotesquely from their faces.[1] As winter became spring in 1919, theatres stayed empty. Men and women entered public places warily, concealing their faces behind gauze masks. The plague invaded private spaces, compelling isolation and reflection. What, then, did Grace Elliott Trudeau and her husband, Joseph-Charles-Émile, think when she learned she was pregnant in Montreal in mid-winter 1919? Pregnancy was dangerous in normal times, but the influenza surely terrified her as her body began to swell with her second child.

The twentieth century had so far been a great disappointment—especially for francophone Canadians. There was some excitement and hope when it began with Canada's first French-speaking prime minister, Wilfrid Laurier, in power, and an increasingly prosperous economy. The great transformation of Western society that occurred as electricity, steamships, telephones, railways, and automobiles upset the balance of the

Victorian age profoundly affected the world of the young Trudeaus. In Quebec, as elsewhere, people were in motion, leaving the familiar fields of rural life and traditional crafts for the cities that were exploding beyond their pre-industrial core. In Montreal, the population rose from 267,730 in 1901 to 618,506 in 1921. The rich had clustered together, initially in mansions in the "Golden Square Mile" along Sherbrooke Street and north up the southern slope of Mount Royal, while the poor spread out below them and in the east end. It was said in 1900 that the Square Mile contained three-quarters of Canada's millionaires. Stephen Leacock, who knew them well, commented, "The rich in Montreal enjoyed a prestige in that era that not even the rich deserve."[2]

Unfortunately, the rich were nearly entirely English; the poor, overwhelmingly French. When the French lived mainly in the villages, the gap was less obvious. In the city, it sowed the seeds of deep discontent. And, as new immigrants, mainly Jewish, flowed in from continental Europe, new tensions emerged in the more diverse city.[3]

Even before the war, foreign visitors sensed trouble. In 1911 the Austrian writer Stefan Zweig, after a visit to Montreal, said that all reasonable men should advise the French to abandon their resistance to assimilation. They were fast becoming simply an episode in history.[4] Among francophones in Quebec, the challenge of the new century brought an increasingly nationalist response, particularly when English-Canadian politicians became entangled in the British imperialism that marked the years before the Great War. By then there was a new prime minister, Robert Borden, and the voice of French Canada in the federal government became faint. And in 1914 the war divided the country as never before between the French and the others.

Once again, it seemed that a bargain had been broken.

Now leader of the official Opposition, Wilfrid Laurier supported the war, along with the French Catholic Church. Even Henri Bourassa, who had founded the nationalist newspaper *Le Devoir* and become the vocal spokesperson for francophone rights throughout Canada, kept his silence. He and the bishops went along because Borden promised there would be no conscription, but, three years later, conscription was proclaimed, accompanied by vitriolic attacks in English Canada on the French in Quebec. In the bitter and violent Canadian election in 1917, francophones voted overwhelmingly for Laurier's Liberals, who opposed conscription, while anglophones responded by backing a coalition composed of English-speaking Liberals and Conservatives. There were riots in Montreal and deaths in Quebec City. In 1919 Laurier died, then depression struck, while, at Versailles, the victors divided the spoils even as the world began to understand that the war to end all wars had not done so.

In their modest but comfortable row home at 5779 Durocher Avenue in the new suburb of Outremont, the Trudeaus could find some comfort. Outremont was neighbour to Mount Royal and, in population, split between residents of French and British origin, along with a substantial number of Jews. They lived far from the crowded tenements of the city below the hill, where death often came for both mother and child during pregnancy.[5] Charles and Grace had married on May 11, 1915, and she had become pregnant soon after with an infant who did not survive.[6] In 1918 she gave birth to a daughter, Suzette. Charles already had good reason not to enlist and, after the *Military Service Act* became law in 1917, to avoid conscription.

When the Trudeaus married, Grace, in common with other Quebec women of the time, acquired the same legal rights as minors and idiots. Her husband owed her protection in return for her submission.[7] Yet Grace had her own sources of strength. Her father, a substantial businessman of United Empire Loyalist stock, had sent his daughter to Dunham Ladies' College in the Eastern Townships, where she had acquired an education in literature, classics, and etiquette that few girls in Quebec possessed. She knew French, her mother's tongue, as well as English, which she and Charles chose to speak most often at home. Like Charles, she was Roman Catholic and devout.* Though not wealthy in the first years of their marriage, the Trudeaus had the means to hire country girls to help with household tasks.

Assisted by a midwife at home, Grace gave birth to Joseph-Philippe-Pierre-Yves-Elliott Trudeau on a warm fall day, October 18, 1919.[8] The parents immediately chose Pierre from his multiple names, though he, later, took a long time to make up his mind which name he favoured. His mother probably reflected the original intention when she wrote in his "Baby Book" Joseph Pierre Yves Philip Elliott Trudeau. Years later, when he was quizzed about it, Trudeau himself could not recall the correct order.[9] He weighed eight pounds four ounces and, from the beginning, suffered from colic. The crying finally stopped when he had an operation for adenoids in May

---

* Grace's mother was a Catholic and, in the practice of the day, she took her mother's religion. She also spoke fluent French, even though her mother died when she was ten years old. Trudeau later explained, "Obviously she always spoke French too because otherwise she wouldn't have met the gang that my father was hanging around with in the time of his studies in Montreal." Trudeau also said that they met at a church attached to Collège Sainte-Marie, adding, "It's a good place to meet, I suppose, at least in the stories you tell your kids." Interview between Pierre Trudeau and Ron Graham, April 28, 1992, TP, vol. 23, file 3.

1920. Along with Pierre's physical health, Grace recorded his spiritual growth in a diary. It began with his baptism, followed by the moment in October 1921 when two-year-old "Pierre made the sign of the cross." In December he began to say his prayers alone and "blessed Papa, Mama, Suzette etc."[10] Six months later the proud mother recorded that her precociously bilingual child knew "Sing a Song of Sixpence," "Little Jack Horner," "Au clair de la lune," and "Dans sa cabane." She continued dutifully to collect mementos of Pierre's life—school essays, marks, news clippings, and letters—until he finally left her home in the 1960s as a middle-aged man.

Grace kept only a few documentary fragments revealing the lives of herself and her husband. We have one intriguing letter from Charles in 1921, when he was working in Montreal and Grace, pregnant with Charles Junior (nicknamed "Tip"), was with Pierre and Suzette at Lac Tremblant, where the family had a cottage. He began with an apology for not being in touch but claimed that his daily tasks were overwhelming. Then his emotions flowed freely as he anxiously asked after the children in a hastily written letter:

> How are the "babies"? Always watch them most attentively; and I urge you not to think of me but of them. Watch their steps, their games, their fights, their health. It appears that the little brother [Pierre] is on the right path. This should make you happy, enjoy it; but you must remember that the two of them, the couple, are young and an accident can always happen. If we had to lose one . . . They are so sweet, so nice—both of them—and you know the proverb: "if you are too nice, you'll die young." These words are so true that they make me frightened for those two; a third, and a fourth etc. . . . would be very welcome if only the good Lord would provide more like those we

have. I believe now that I am a "garage man" I can use the expression: more of them would make good "spares."

After this lame attempt at humour in which he referred to the service stations he had recently purchased, Charles returned to his didactic style, telling Grace to watch their children's character closely and to correct their faults. Such correction, he urged, was always for the children's good. After a few more homilies, he closed with kisses and hugs to all: "Salut à Madame, un bon baiser à toi et des caresses aux petits" [Bye Madame, a good kiss for you and hugs for the little ones].[11]

Affectionate obviously, hierarchical certainly, Charles has remained elusive, even in the descriptions given by his children and friends.[12] He moved outside the familiar categories of his time and place, much as his son would later do. In the beginning, however, his path was familiar. Like most nineteenth-century francophones in Quebec, he grew up on a farm. His father, Joseph Trudeau, was a semi-literate but fairly prosperous farmer at St-Michel de Napierville, south of Montreal. He was a descendant of Étienne Truteau, a carpenter from La Rochelle, France, who had arrived in 1659. Three years later, according to a now vanished plaque that was once affixed to a building on the corner of La Gauchetière and St-André in Montreal: "Here Truteau, Roulier, and Langevin-Lacroix resisted 50 Iroquois, May 6, 1662."[13] By the time of Charles's birth in 1889, the challenge to the French presence came not from the Iroquois or the British soldiers who had conquered Quebec but from the impersonal forces arising from the transformation of a commercial and agrarian society into one that was urban and industrial.

Charles's parents, especially his mother, Malvina, a mayor's daughter and a doctor's sister, knew that their world of the farm, parish, and family would soon be lost. They were determined that the boys among their eight children would have a chance in the new world they faced. They sent Charles to Collège Sainte-Marie, an eminent classical college in Montreal established by the Jesuits in 1848, once the previously banned powerful religious order was allowed to return to Canada. Although situated in the heart of the city, the college was—at least in the later view of some students—a place apart. Its discipline, beginning in the morning with prayers at 5:30, followed by study at 6:00 and Mass at 6:30, took the students "away from the daily realities and the concerns of the day."[14]

Paradoxically, by stepping out of the world, these boys became part of a privileged elite that would eventually dominate the fields of law, politics, religion, and medicine in twentieth-century Quebec. Those areas, however, were the traditional ones for francophones in the province, and, in the new industrial age, they increasingly brought fewer material rewards than did the world of finance and industrial capitalism, where the English dominated. Moreover, politics seemed increasingly beholden to wealth, and the francophone politicians of the time catered to the English capitalists. Just as some leading Quebecers, especially in the Roman Catholic Church, developed a critique of modern capitalism, others came to terms with its needs—including Charles Trudeau.

A few notebooks survive from Charles's years at Collège Sainte-Marie, and they cast a faint light on his education and personality. Warned by his parents that failure meant a return to the farm, he was diligent. In his final year, 1908–9, he wrote and defended his thesis in Latin in a class on philosophy given in that language. He also copied out quotations to memorize and reflected negatively on the issues of the early years of the twentieth century—revolution, alcoholism, and war. "War kills the arts, the sciences, the civilization," he wrote and then transcribed quotations supporting that cryptic declaration. On the key question of imperialism, he was not yet a stern critic of Britain. One of his quotations suggests it would be dangerous to separate from "Albion": "We would be incomparably weaker, isolated as we are in a nation of five million facing an immense country of sixty million." Moreover, Quebec needed foreign investment. But he had some doubts: "The authority of the mother country and the decisions of the Privy Council are not sufficient protection for the rights of Catholics in a province." The seeds of nationalism had taken root. After Charles left the college, where he won many prizes despite a reputation as a troublemaker, he studied law for three years at the Montreal campus of Laval University (which became the University of Montreal in 1919).[15]

Charles seems to have been a good student: his notes are impressive in their organization and detail; he wrote in a fine and even elegant hand; and his classical education provided a strong intellectual base. Yet, in the accounts of those who knew him later, he changed radically at this time. He became an extrovert who loved games, gambling, and the high life. At home, though, it was different. In interviews, both Suzette and Pierre recalled him as a strict father who, though often absent, was intense and dynamic when present. He taught Pierre boxing, shooting, and even wrestling tricks. He also made him independent. Trudeau later told how disappointed he was that his friend Gerald O'Connor was put in the second grade and he in the first. He complained to his father, begging him to ask the principal to promote him. "No!" his father said. "It's your problem. Knock on his door and ask him yourself." Pierre did—and he happily joined Gerald in the second grade. In the seventies George Radwanski described how, when Trudeau spoke of his father, his eyes lit up and his gestures became more animated. He got "the impression of a child who may have been unknowingly overawed by an exceptionally dynamic father, perhaps in ways that contributed to his childhood sensitivity, insecurity, and later self-testing and rebellious."[16]

Trudeau himself wrote more openly about how his father was "very extroverted. He spoke loudly and expressed himself vigorously. His friends were the same."[17] On weekends at Lac Tremblant, he invited guests, sometimes as many as twenty, and expected Grace to cook for them. "They liked to get involved in our games," Trudeau recalled; "they liked to play cards, and they liked to drink and feast." Sometimes the parties were organized in the basement of their Montreal home, but normally, he explained, "the only time in the whole day that we got to enjoy his company" was when Charles came home for dinner, took a quick look at the children's schoolwork, and disappeared into the night to work or play. Although Pierre credited his father with teaching him sports, he claimed, despite visits from the flamboyant Montreal mayor, Camillien Houde, that they did not discuss politics: "I never asked my father any questions on the subject, and he for his part made no attempt to arouse my interest." But, at the very least, he did so indirectly.

Others have painted a darker picture of Charles as "Charlie" or "Charley," the bon vivant who played poker with rough-edged friends. Stephen Clarkson, co-author with Christina McCall of a study of Pierre Trudeau, has speculated that Charles was sometimes abusive towards Grace. They quote a family friend who said that Charles was brutal with his own friends and made things difficult when he came home drunk.[18] There is no documentary evidence to support these suggestions. The family strongly denies the rumours of abuse towards Grace, though not of loud partying late in the night.

A small, wiry man, Charles's energy and drive for success soon made him tire of petty legal affairs in his reasonably prosperous three-person law firm, Trudeau & Guérin, on St. James Street.

In the fashion of the times, Charles-Émile Guérin was a Liberal, while Charles and his brother Cléophas were identified as *bleus*, or Conservatives. He took big chances; his son's papers contain an undated notebook detailing his gambling wins and losses, nightly sums that often exceeded the yearly earnings of a Montreal worker. But in 1921, with two children and another, Charles, on the way, he completely changed course. He had noticed how automobiles were increasingly common on city streets and wondered who fixed and fuelled them. In 1910 there were only 786 automobiles in Quebec; in 1915, 10,112; in 1920, 41,562—and, within five years, there would be almost 100,000. By the 1920s, roads had become the largest item in the Quebec budget.[19] Sensing the future, Charles opened a garage near his home, and soon he owned several others offering gasoline as well as the maintenance so often needed by the automobiles of the time—a "garage man," as he had described himself to Grace—and he called his operation the Automobile Owners' Association, with offices at 1216 St-Denis. The business quickly succeeded, and he ingeniously expanded the association into a club in which car owners signed on for an annual fee in return for guaranteed service.[20]

By the early 1930s the association had approximately 15,000 members, and Charles owned thirty garages. Imperial Oil noticed his success and offered him $1.2 million for the business in 1932. He accepted and then invested the funds in mining (mainly Sullivan Mines), Belmont Park (a large amusement park in Montreal), and even the Montreal Royals baseball team, of which he became the vice-president. Mining and entertainment were the best investments for the 1930s, and the stock market moved briskly upward immediately after Charles received his funds. Charles's fortune was, Pierre Trudeau wrote modestly later, a sum that was "quite respectable for the time." He became a member of the Cercle Universitaire, the Club Canadien, and several golf clubs. In truth, their affluence brought financial security for Grace and her children for the rest of their lives.[21] They became and remained members of the *haute bourgeoisie* of Quebec.

Perhaps what impressed Pierre about his father was the way in which he so cleverly beat the English at their own games. His father had left law early, although he did tell Pierre that it was a "useful" degree. More interesting and rewarding was business, and his extroverted personality fitted it well. Charles had an excellent Jesuit and French education, but he was determined to learn English, and he insisted that his children write to him in that language. He even signed some of his letters to them "Papa Charley." He knew they must learn English to succeed in the Quebec of that time, and he sent them to French schools only after he was certain they were fluent in English. Although Pierre later recalled that the workers in his garages were French, the company name on its stationery was in English alone, and probably the majority of customers were anglophones.[22]

Yet Charles was committed to the French presence in Quebec. He chose to live in Outremont, not Westmount — his wealth would have gained him easy entry. His club was the St-Denis, the "French" club founded in the 1870s; and his office on St-Denis was far from the centre of bourgeois wealth in Montreal. He was generous to many French Catholic charities, particularly the hospitals. His politics were Conservative and nationalist. Very tellingly, his newspaper was the nationalist bible *Le Devoir*, and he was even a member of its operating board. Unlike many Quebec francophones of the day, Charles relished modern times and its wonders. The family's increasing prosperity brought a move from the row house on Durocher to a more substantial Outremont home at 84 McCulloch (sometime McCullough) Street, with a large veranda and rooms for the maid and the chauffeur, Elzéar Grenier. It was also near the great park on Mount Royal, away from the city's slums, and close to the best schools for the children. The brick house, while not pretentious, was impressive in its three storeys, large rooms, stately furnishings, and easy access to the verdant surroundings on the mountain.

When Charles was not at his garage or his club, he travelled sometimes to Europe and often to the United States. In one letter that Pierre sent to his father, Grace added a postscript: "Will write you in Los Angeles—at Biltmore Hotel. I don't know of any other."[23] Clearly, Charles was always difficult to follow, a trait his son inherited, yet his presence was strong, sentimental, and loving with, or away from, his family. On September 28, 1926, he sent a postcard with a photograph of an airplane to Pierre and wrote over the picture: "There I was for nearly 3 hours." On the back he informed his young son: "Whatever you do when you grow to be a man, Pierre, don't be an aviator. Your Papa would be too much afraid. 3000 feet high, a speed of 125 miles an hour for 3 hours. Gee that's long!" From New York City in May 1930 he sent another postcard, with a cartoon of a young boy who is being rebuked by his mother for spitting on the floor: "Hello there, Pierre! Are you the papa at home just now? Tell them they have to take orders from you. Love & kisses, Pa." He wrote from San Francisco a few months later, "My own Pierrot," and told him, "Glad to see that you can do anything when you want."[24]

Pierre was equally warm in his letters to his father—which were normally written in English. He wrote in the summer of 1929, when the children and Grace were at their summer home at Old Orchard Beach in Maine:

Dear Papa
How are you? We are having a good time. We are doing
our exercises three times a day. Tippy [brother Charles]

is learning how to swim pretty good. I can float and I like it. We went on a picnic yesterday afternoon—ten kids. We played around and when it was time to eat we had to open our bottles on a barbwire fence! There were lots of mosquitoes so we came home. I would like to have my bike down here and Tippy would his also. Did mamma tell you about it? Hope you come back soon.

> Your loving son, Pierre
>
> (P.S.) don't forget the bike.

Pierre's plea was gently rebuked. On July 19 Charles replied to "Mon cher petit Pierre":

I am very glad to see that you're having a good time, that you are doing your exercises and you are good "kids" because Mamma told me so in her last letter . . .

Being the oldest I hope you are showing Tippy how to swim and you yourself are watching him: the biggest brother should always do that.

I like to see that you have learned how to float and I bet you have also improved your swimming. Now, is Suzette doing her exercises good and is she practicing swinging? I wish I had an eye on her too and show her how to get strong and healthy and wise.

Yes, Mamma told me about your "bike," Pierre and you may be sure Mamma does not forget anything when she thinks it can please her "kids" but my opinion is that out there you don't need the "bike" because you can play all sorts of games on the beach, have all sorts of exercises etc., which is much better, I think, than promenading on the streets with a "bike." Never mind, Pierre, if the other guy gets one: he won't be any better off and then you have things that he does not have and besides there are very few boys that have a bike over there. In fact I don't think I saw one.

Now tell Suzette that I expect a letter from her by return mail and I don't see why she has let you write before her.

Tell Tippy too that he can at least write a postal card and sign his name.

Tell Mamma that I'll write tonight or tomorrow. Keep on having a good time and be good. Don't forget your exercises and your swing and listening to Mamma and by doing all that you'll be working as hard as your papa and work is what makes a man out of one.

Kisses to all, Papa Charley

There would be no bikes on Old Orchard Beach that summer.[25]

Charles's frequent absences brought a flow of postcards, and ten-year-old Pierre responded with banter and warmth. In an undated letter of the late 1920s he assured his father that he did "not mind staying till half past five every afternoon" at school because, when he got home, he had all his homework done. After saying that he had not missed his 5BX exercises, a military calisthenics drill, and had missed piano practice only once, he concluded: "I have nothing more to say so I will close up my letter giving lots of xxxxxx and love." In the summers they went to the Laurentians, followed by a long stay at Old Orchard Beach. In their Lac Tremblant cottage, the children "would listen for the faraway sound of tires on the bridge across the outlet of the lake that would mean [Charles] was arriving." Pierre often became playful in his signoff, once declaring himself J P E Trudeau and another time mimicking the end of radio programs: "We are now signing off. Please stand by for station announcement. Your loving son, Pierre."

In 1933 Charles decided to take the entire family and

Grace's father to Europe. Sixty years later, Pierre said that he retained "a thousand vivid images of it" in his mind. For the first time, he said, they (presumably the children) "experienced the remarkable feeling of being almost totally out of our element." He enjoyed that feeling and always would. He developed an abiding wanderlust. One story that Trudeau retold many times was how his father stopped the car in front of a German hotel and said, "Pierre, rent us the rooms." Faced with the challenge and possessing limited German, the thirteen-year-old lad nevertheless made the deal.

Although Charles gave his older son adult tasks, Pierre retained a childlike tone when dealing with his father in his early teenage years. He wrote to his father from Old Orchard Beach in the summer of 1934. He and Tippy, who seems to have become the subordinate younger brother, had just enjoyed the Marx Brothers in *Duck Soup*, and he reported on the arrival and departure of friends and relatives. The latest group did not "interest me much as there are only girls in both families," he said, but the complaint was almost certainly a fib. Beach photographs from the period suggest that Pierre's already penetrating eyes were constantly fixed on the girls, who were often grouped around him. Once again he reported on his exercises and concluded: "I hope you come up and see us sometime soon. Now I must be signing off as everybody is on the beach and I must go too. Kisses (xxx), Pierre."[26] Pierre treasured these summer months and yearned for his father's presence.

On March 30, 1935, he complained to his parents, who were then vacationing in Florida as the Montreal Royals began their spring training, about the "disagreeable" winter season in Montreal. He eagerly awaited the coming Easter vacation, but even more the summer holiday that was only three months away. At school he had received a "Bene," but the most interesting event of the month was the visit of "Antoni, the famous

Canadian magician," who had mystified the students with his extraordinary tricks. His mother returned from the South on April 8, and Pierre immediately wrote to his father:

> Dear Papa,
> As Maman has decided to send you my report card [from Brébeuf] which came today, I've decided to add a few words:
> When I got home this evening, Maman told me you were ill and I hasten to wish you a speedy recovery. I'm relieved to know it is apparently nothing serious.

He expressed hope that his father would write soon, noted that he had obtained another "Bene," and suggested that the results of his essays should also please him. Then he concluded:

> Don't stay away too long and try to be with us for Easter at least!
> We're all well here. Goodbye!
> Your loving son,
> Pierre

But Charles did not come home for Easter.

The pneumonia that had not been "serious" had caused a heart attack. When Grace heard that Charles's condition was quickly worsening, she and Suzette flew down to Florida, leaving Tip and Pierre with an aunt. Before Pierre could send his letter, the telephone rang. From the landing in the stairwell, he saw his aunt turn towards him. "Your father is dead, Pierre," she said.[27] "In a split second," he recalled later, "I felt the whole world go empty. His death truly felt like the end of the world." And forty years later he said: "It was traumatic, very traumatic . . . I still can't go to a funeral without crying."[28] Death had come quickly for Charles, who was only forty-six, and it traumatized the whole family.* Grace told Suzette: "I'll never be able to bring up the boys alone."[29] Pierre himself recalled that, at fifteen years of age, "all of a sudden, I was more or less the head of a family; with him gone, it seemed to me that I had to take over."[30] Brébeuf's rector wrote to him: "Poor little one! But you are a little Christian, Pierre, and you have the consolation of our beautiful Catholic faith."[31] It helped, but the distraught boy tore up the letter he had written to his father.

When Grace came home, she found its pieces in the wastebasket, along with a draft of the earlier letter he had sent to his parents in Florida. She carefully pasted the pages together. They were among the documents she kept until her death, when they passed to Pierre—and into his collection of papers. He preserved another item too. In the celebrated portrait of Trudeau in the Parliament Buildings, just outside the House of Commons, he wears, as a final homage, Charles's cape, which he had kept for over half a century.[32] Clearly there was intense grief, but did he also feel "ambivalence" towards his father, thus

------

* Charles Trudeau's death attracted considerable attention in the Montreal press, with similar responses. *The Montreal Star*, April 12, 1935, mourned the death of a major sports figure, the owner of Belmont Park and the major investor in the Montreal Royals, while *La Patrie*, April 11, lamented, in a key editorial, the loss of a French-Canadian businessman who had attained "the prestige and influence of the rich," yet did not lose his friends even when he reached the highest steps on the ladder of success. Trudeau, *Le Devoir* claimed, had served superbly on its board as a financial consultant. The April 11–12 issue even speculated that although Charles Trudeau had become disillusioned with politics, he might some day have entered politics as a reformer.

complicating the grief, as some have suggested? That is less certain. I will return to the psychological impact of Charles's life and death on Pierre later. The documentary records of the time support his sister Suzette's comment that "[Pierre] didn't shock or disturb us or react in a way that I would think was because my father was gone . . . Perhaps he took on a certain responsibility."[33] He never ceased to miss him profoundly, however.*

Camillien Houde, the Conservative and nationalist mayor of Montreal; J.-A. Bernier, the president of the nationalist Société Saint-Jean-Baptiste; and Georges Pelletier, the editor of *Le Devoir*, joined the family as Charles's remains arrived in Windsor Station early on the following Saturday morning. At the funeral there were thirteen priests, several judges, and seven cars carrying the flowers.[34] The funeral became etched forever in Pierre's memory, but he was away from school only briefly and his marks, which were recorded weekly, remained remarkably high. He wrote rather formally to his mother on April 28 and again on May 2, less than a month after his father's death, saying in both letters that he knew she was "in good health" and hoped that she

---

* On April 10, 1938, the third anniversary of Charles's death, Pierre went to Mass and took communion for the sake of his father's soul. He wrote in his diary: "Time heals all. Maybe it's true that you are able to become accustomed to an absence, but the more time passes, the more I miss his firm but kind goodness, his advice so full of wisdom. Without doubt, he guides me from Heaven still but it would be so good to be able to talk with him and discuss things with him once again." He lamented that he had been given only fifteen years to profit from his father's wisdom. He accepted that it was God's will that Charles was with Him. The loss is expressed constantly in the diaries he kept from 1938 to 1940. Journal 1938, April 10, 1938, TP, vol. 39, file 9.

remained so. Occasionally he stayed in school as a boarder and, in the first letter, he noted that he missed the charm of home and the caresses of his mother. In the second he reported that his marks were the highest in the class, a total of 292 out of 300. He then wrote out "April's fool" in Greek, Latin, English, French, and another script. It was a good academic year. He wrote again to his mother on June 10 and told her that he expected to win prizes. Thanks to his excellent teachers, "we have all had a good year." He ended by thanking his mother for sending him to such a fine school.[35]

Several of Pierre's classmates have said that it was a different boy who returned to the school after his father died. He became more nonconformist, more eager to shock teachers and students alike.[36] Certainly his father was missed at Brébeuf, where the Jesuit priests later remembered how "Charlie" would "offer to buy them Havana cigars to pass around at a college dinner in honour of a visiting papal delegate or to send them a case of whisky for their own pleasure any time they liked."[37] Small wonder so many of them attended his funeral. The atmosphere at home also changed. Trudeau said later: "When my father was around, there was a great deal of effusiveness and laughter and kissing and hugging. But after he died, it was a little bit more the English mores which took over, and we used to even joke about, or laugh at, some of our cousins or neighbours or friends—French Canadians—who'd always be very effusive within the family and towards their mother and so on."[38] Pierre began to use the hyphenated surname Elliott-Trudeau, suggesting a new orientation towards the English side of the family, though in 1931–32 he had briefly favoured J.P. Elliott Trudeau.[39] It seems that he became more rebellious in class, while, in the less playful atmosphere at home, he increasingly strove to please Grace. His letters and notebooks indicate a more complex pattern after his father's death: he became more like a stone whose colours radiated differently, depending on the angle from which it was viewed. He concealed more, but, paradoxically, what he did reveal briefly illuminated his core.

To be sure, Pierre doted on his mother, expressing constant concern for her health. Although we have no written records of what Grace thought, Charles's death profoundly affected her. Her life had focused on her husband's career and, most of all, the children. Years after, Grace Pitfield, who was related by birth or marriage to many of the British elite of Montreal (and was the mother of Trudeau's friend and later colleague Michael Pitfield), told a journalist how Grace Elliott, who had Loyalist roots and a minor inheritance, had simply disappeared. She had friends who "had been at school with Grace Elliott," she explained. "They heard later that she had married a Frenchman. But nobody knew who he was, and of course they never saw her afterwards."[40] It was not surprising, given this divide in Montreal society at the time, that Grace—having cut herself off from her background—craved the affection and attention of her children. And they responded. The reserve that had marked her when the exuberant and extroverted Charles was alive disappeared when she was the sole parent, and she became more assertive, more playful. But that was Grace's private side. "'Formidable' is the word Trudeau sometimes uses to describe his father," quipped the journalist Richard Gwyn. "Everyone else applies it to his mother." After Charles's death, Grace Trudeau gained presence.[41]

Pierre seemed to become both son and companion, an emotional combination that has its charms and its dangers. He took more responsibility for family affairs, according to both Suzette and Pierre himself. His father's death brought financial independence and security, and Pierre cherished this freedom. Each of the children apparently received $5,000 a year, more than the average annual income for doctors and lawyers in the late 1930s. And there were reserves if needed.[42] In his late teenage years, Pierre became directly involved in managing a large inheritance. For her part, Grace divided the long remainder of her life among travel, charitable work, and the Roman Catholic Church, and she paid little attention to the management of the funds. In 1939 she even managed to lose some of the many stock certificates the family possessed.[43] She loved music and played the piano very well, to the envy of Pierre, who did so in an amateur way. She seldom missed a classical concert and even brought some of the leading artists of the day to her home, to perform for friends and family. At one time she persuaded the great Artur Rubinstein to come to McCulloch and perform.[44] Some thought the Trudeau home darkened after Charles died; it did, her children sometimes joked, because Grace was on the road so much. She travelled frequently to New York, Florida, Europe, and her beloved Maine, occasionally with the children but, increasingly, with female friends. Suzette, an amiable and uncomplicated daughter, became a consolation and companion to her, but she doted on Pierre.

—

When Charles died, Pierre was a day student at the Collège Jean-de-Brébeuf on St. Catherine Street in Montreal. His parents had initially sent him when he was six years old to Académie Querbes, a Catholic school for both English and French Catholics, and he stayed there until 1932. He first enrolled in the English section "for reasons I do not know," he claimed in his memoir. He had forgotten: his father had once written that, in the world in which "they" lived, the advantages came to those who learned English.[45] And so his children did.

Querbes, which boasted both a bowling alley and a swimming pool, was located at 215 Bloomfield Street in Outremont, and Pierre had only seven classmates in his first year. His report gave him perfect marks for conduct, application, politeness, and cleanliness. He stood first in the class nearly every month except for March, when he was sick. The size of the class grew to sixteen by third year, when he stood second. The following year he began in English, but then changed to French. He stood first in his last month in English, and he retained that place in his first month in French. He again graduated at the top, overall, with a percentage of 92.5 in June 1930. Grace had signed the reports when the courses were in English; Charles signed most of them when Pierre switched to French.

In school, Pierre became immersed in the Catholic faith and in the debate about mortal sin, while on the streets, he fought as boys seemed to do in those days. Michel Chartrand, a fellow Querbes student and future labour activist, recalled that Pierre got into brawls on the streets of Outremont, where the poorer kids liked to take on the precious sons of the well-to-do.[46] In his final year, when he stood first in a class of twenty-six students with a percentage of 95.4, his best classes were mathematics and religion—and that pattern continued throughout his academic career.[47] Several of his essays are preserved in his papers. They reflect both his mind and the times in which he lived. He received "Beau travail" for an essay on the fabled French soldier Dollard des Ormeaux, who, in 1660, held off the Iroquois on the Ottawa River. Pierre concluded that Dollard and his companions were martyrs and saints without whose sacrifices "the colony would have been completely destroyed" by the barbarians. In an essay on guns, he told how he had asked "Papa" if he could go hunting with him. His father replied, "No, Pierre, you are only eleven years old and not old enough." When Pierre persisted, Charles gave examples of how accidents happen with firearms, and Pierre finally agreed with him. In an essay on the polite child, Pierre emphasized kindness to others, including the servants. In church, no one should speak or shuffle about but simply pray. The overall lesson he derived from the exercise was that a polite child becomes popular in society.[48] For this essay, he received his highest mark: 9.5 out of 10.

From Querbes, Pierre moved to the new classical college, Collège Jean-de-Brébeuf, which was within walking distance of his home in Outremont. It had been established in 1928 as one of the five Jesuit colleges explicitly devoted to the education of a French elite in Quebec. Discipline was quick, short, and brutal. The priests frequently expelled troublesome students, and the strap and other forms of discipline were always available. Pierre soon established himself as an outstanding student, but he developed a sharp edge during his eight-year stay there. He brought friends with him from Querbes and the streets of Outremont, notably Pierre Vadeboncoeur, who would follow him through Brébeuf, law school, and political activities for three decades. Brébeuf was a decisive experience in Trudeau's life, endowing him with a remarkable self-discipline, a profound interest in ideas and politics, and a cadre of friends and acquaintances who would play major roles in his life and career. He later claimed that he had little interest in politics while he was at Brébeuf, but, again, his memory failed him.[49]

Trudeau's account of his involvement in contemporary politics during his Brébeuf years is contradictory. He also said on occasion that Father Robert Bernier, who was "the most cultivated man I had met . . . talked politics to me."[50] His notebooks of the time are full of "politics," both in the sense of political theory, beginning with the classical tradition, and in the narrower sense of the political events of the 1930s. He entered Brébeuf at the height of the Great Depression, "la Grande Crise" in Quebec, just before Roosevelt's presidency and Hitler's chancellorship. Students disappeared from his class as their parents fell into abject poverty, and the Catholic Church in Quebec and elsewhere was in turmoil as it tried to understand what the collapse of democracy in Europe, and capitalism everywhere, meant for the faithful. In Quebec a critique of Canadian capitalism and democracy emerged most strongly in the writings of Abbé Lionel Groulx. In 1919, the year of Pierre's birth, Groulx had given a historic lecture, "If Dollard Were Alive Today." His argument already had a deep impact on the young Pierre when he wrote his essay on Dollard at Querbes. The Abbé held the first chair in Canadian history at the Montreal branch of Laval University and went on to edit the highly influential journal *L'Action française*. In short order it became the catalyst for a new nationalism that linked the Catholic faith, the French language, and the family, while calling for autonomous institutions that would protect these key elements from Anglicization, Americanization, secularization, and a corrupt political class.[51]

The Abbé responded to the conscription crisis and the First World War by turning to the past: the Conquest of New France in 1760 became a decisive event, God's test of Quebec's defeated people; the pact of Confederation, a broken promise. Dollard's first battles with the Iroquois, or, for that matter, Étienne Truteau's, led to the origins of the parish, where the germ of the nation appeared and where common institutions and memories formed. In his eyes, during the Conquest, the Rebellions of the French against the English in 1837–38, the betrayals of Confederation, and the conscription crisis of 1917, a Quebec nation was forged in a fire of constant struggle and within the enduring bond of Catholicism. According to Groulx, the nation had become a reality through this continual battle with "the others."[52] The aggressiveness of English Canada during wartime; the continuing flow of rural francophones to Montreal, where the symbols of power were English; the drop in the birthrate of francophones in the city and of the French population in Canada (31% in 1867, but only 27% in 1921); and the economic inferiority of the francophone professional class created "the call of the race," or *L'appel de la race*, the title of Groulx's bestselling novel of 1922, about the difficulties of a mixed marriage between a French Catholic lawyer and a converted Protestant English mother. The jacket of the first edition carried a quotation: "All of the descendants of the valiant 65,000 who were conquered must act as one."[53] It was a powerful nationalist argument, one that roiled Quebec society in the interwar years.

In the 1930s, with bourgeois liberal democracy in danger and Communism, socialism, and fascism contesting for dominance in Europe, the winds that blew strongly from Europe reached Quebec. For Quebec Catholics, Communism was simply evil, and liberalism was tainted with its anti-clerical past and enervated present. Within the Quebec church, an angry debate developed between those who believed that the first task was to "rechristianize" the population and others who, with Groulx, thought that "national action" must coincide with "Catholic action" and with what he termed the refrancization of Quebec. On his return from France in 1937, André Laurendeau, later the co-chair of the Royal Commission on Bilingualism and Biculturalism, attacked the supporters of bilingualism in Quebec. An admirer of Abbé Groulx, he warned: "When all French Canadians have become bilingual, they will all speak English . . . and French itself will soon be useless."[54] The debate raged within the numerous Catholic youth groups that proliferated in Quebec in the 1930s, especially in response to a report on the subject by the Dominican priest Georges-Henri Lévesque which said the first concern must be the individual in society, not the national question.[55] When these debates left the classrooms and church buildings and arrived on the streets, they sometimes took a vulgar form in the creation of a Quebec fascist movement, the National Socialist Christian Party (Parti national social chrétien), whose emblem was a swastika surrounded by maple leaves, with a curious beaver as its crown. Its leader, Adrien Arcand, was a vicious anti-Semite who condoned attacks on Jewish businesses in Montreal and urged the deportation of Jews to Hudson Bay.

The times were clearly important in the formation of Pierre Trudeau, with the breakdown of the European order, the emergence of new nationalist movements in Quebec (especially the Action libérale nationale, or ALN), and the continuing economic crisis. Although there is no direct evidence that Charles Trudeau had urged political beliefs on his son, his own nationalism, as reflected in his association with Le Devoir and his friendship with men such as Camillien Houde, surely left its mark. And Pierre, until he turned twenty-one in 1940, was sheltered within the cocoon of Brébeuf, where the atmosphere was decidedly nationalist. In his first years there, Pierre concentrated on his studies and on sports. He usually began in the morning with prayers at 5:30, followed by early morning Mass. He did not shirk his religious duties, sometimes participating in Mass three times in one day. He attended retreats frequently, although at times he complained about the number of religious observances offered there.

About sports, he never complained. He became the captain of the hockey team, played lacrosse, and went on ski excursions.* And he exercised. In photographs, he is always lean and his body is hard, not in the fashion of modern weightlifters but similar to Clark Gable and other film stars of the time. His love

---

* Trudeau also liked to go to Montreal Royals' baseball games, and he tracked the scores. He won some popularity among the priests at Brébeuf by using the family interest in the Royals to get opening-day tickets. He was rewarded with a day off school when he accompanied Father Toupin to the game. Personal Journal, 1937–40, TP, vol. 39, file 9.

of competition was reflected in his academic work: he carefully followed his own marks along with those of his fellow students. He had to be first—in 1935, despite his father's death, he won numerous prizes and excelled. He also developed the reputation of being devilish in class: during a presentation on navigation, for example, he took a glass of water out of his inside coat pocket. He later interpreted these tricks as "opposing conventional wisdoms and challenging prevailing opinions," but they apparently did not greatly offend his teachers—or his mother, whom he regaled with some of the stories. And, it seems, they did not irritate fellow students as much as some of them later recalled. He was elected to several positions, including vice-president of the student assembly, and chosen to be editor of the student newspaper.[56] He was disappointed that he was not elected president but counted himself lucky, considering he had no particular group of friends, to finish second in the vote out of a class of fifty.[57]

Pierre's pranks and mocking comments were forgiven by his teachers because he became increasingly committed to the school, to the Catholic faith, and to understanding the "national question." The commitment intensified after the death of his father. Trudeau's son Alexandre (Sacha) believes that one major consequence of Charles-Émile's death on Trudeau was a distrust of business and commercial life and a suspicion of law. He came to identify business with late nights, heavy drinking, smoking, and boozy argument. In Alexandre's words, Pierre thought business killed his father. He never smoked, drank to excess, swore vigorously, or argued long into the night, even though he adored his father, who did.[58]

Oddly, although several Brébeuf priests influenced Pierre, notably Father Robert Bernier, the one who would have the strongest impact never taught him. Father Rodolphe Dubé, a Jesuit priest and novelist, wrote under the pen name François Hertel—the actual name of a ferocious and brutal opponent of the English and the Aboriginal enemies of New France. Trudeau's papers suggest that Hertel was probably the major intellectual influence in his life until the mid-1940s—explaining, perhaps, the lavish but oblique praise for him in his memoirs. However, the priest was a remarkably charismatic leader of the young, and his views on politics and the arts deeply influenced Catholic youth in the late thirties and early forties. He first attracted attention when he wrote a study in 1936 entitled *Leur inquiétude,* in which he talked about the restlessness of youth in Quebec, with their "desire to evade reality, their dissatisfaction with the present, their dolorous focus on the past, and their anxious view of the future."[59] Later scholars have reinforced Hertel's views and have argued that the anxiety that marked students in the classical colleges in the thirties—in the form of pranks, demonstrations, and misbehaviour—was a response to the colleges' emphasis on chastity, asceticism, and submission. In these male institutions, such teachings represented a threat to the sexual identity of the students at a time when modern attitudes provided so many distractions and temptations.[60]

Pierre was never dolorous, like the students Hertel describes, but he was increasingly restless. In February 1935 the fifteen-year-old wrote a spirited but juvenile essay for his English class, "My Interview with King George of England," in which he went to visit the monarch because there was so much disorder in his class at school. Arriving at the court, he was escorted in:

> Then amidst the sounds of trumpets and cries of "The King! The King!" a dignified old gentleman entered, escorted by many brilliantly colored soldiers.
> "How do you do Sir?" I said.
> "Fine, thank you, except for a little trouble with my teeth," he answered. "I am pleased to meet you."

"The pleasure is all mine," said I, "but come let us get down to business, and I would like to see you alone."

"Very well, you may leave, Captain," and after a brief argument in which the King proved he could take care of himself, the captain left. [An increasingly angry teacher writes, "Nonsense."]

Seeing the gentleman was beginning to sweat under his uniform, I bade him take off his coat; having done so I began. [Teacher: "Nonsense."]

Pierre went on to say that Governor General Lord Bessborough had urged him to see the King because the teacher was "English." He described the total disorder in his classroom at home:

"They are even setting off matches, no doubt to burn the college, and also stink bombs, the odors of which are very disagreeable. Now our professor, M. Gosling, being from England, I thought you might have some sympathy for him (for he finds it trying on his nerves)."

King George replied that he was very sad, for he "thought that all the boys in the British Empire on which the sun never sets were perfect gentlemen. It must be looked after at once." He promised to come down to speak to the class at Brébeuf. Then Pierre concluded:

"Thanks very much, George, I knew you would do it. Well, so long, I will be seeing you."

"Good-bye, Pierre."

"Good-bye. I think I shall go to Rome now and see if I can convince Pope Pius to come up and see us over in Canada too."

The teacher wrote: "As a writer of nonsense you may achieve fame but try to become a little more serious and do not use slang." A gentle caution, but more criticism would follow.[61]

As Pierre Trudeau became increasingly nationalist in his views, along with his classmates and teachers, his growing enthusiasm was reflected both in his academic work and in the books he read. He focused in particular on Abbé Groulx, apparently finding some of his interpretations congenial. On a copy of an article the Abbé published in *L'Action nationale*, he underlined a passage stating that some men dream for Canada of "total independence; for their province [Quebec] total autonomy; and for their nationality, a noble future." He also read one of Groulx's pamphlets and declared it "very interesting," adding, "It is necessary to make total preparations," although it is unclear what those preparations might have been.[62]

At the same time that he became more interested in national questions, his conservative Catholicism also deepened. The two commitments became inextricably intertwined for him, as they did for many other students too. While he had earlier complained to his parents about the frequency of religious observances, he now began to seek out retreats and discussions about the faith. Still, probably because of his independent spirit and Brébeuf's elitist ways, he did not become involved in the Jeunesse étudiante catholique, the best-known Catholic youth group of the day. When he edited the school newspaper, *Brébeuf*, he took strong issue with a request that all student newspapers take a common view. Rather, he read widely in Catholic literature and became especially interested in the Catholic revival in France in the twenties. In the fashion of the times, he vigorously condemned Communists: for example, he denounced André Gide as a Communist who, from a moral point of view, was "one of the most pernicious authors who ever existed." It was "a matter of life," of how Catholic faith penetrated all thought.[63]

In his notebooks, the adolescent Pierre reflected his times and his environment as he groped to understand a complex world. He blamed the Treaty of Versailles and, bizarrely, the British insistence on Germany giving up its colonies for the troubles of the 1930s. And his father's views found a place with his son. He expressed a traditional view of the difference between men and women: "God made the sexes, that of woman for the work in the house and that of man for the things outside." Men's robust bodies suited them for war and voyages, but women's weaker physique meant that "God has destined them to work at home and bear children."[64] In an October 1937 story he described a soapbox orator who talked about the conscription of twenty years before and warned that another war would mean automatic conscription.[65] In a Brébeuf debate he argued against intervention in the Sino-Japanese conflict because "China is infested with strangers, so Japan has a noble aim wanting the yellow race to survive." He also blamed the "Reds" for causing troubles in China.[66]

He wrote a short story in Father Robert Bernier's class in 1936 in which he deplored the isolation of the college and dreamed of what he might do as a sailor on some future adventure. In his fantasy, he travelled the world, joined the air force, engaged in "numerous dangerous exploits, blew up some enemy factories," and won the war. He then returned to Montreal "about 1976, when the time was ripe to declare Quebec independence." The Maritimes and Manitoba joined with Quebec to confront the enemies, and "at the head of the troops, I lead the army to victory" over the English Protestant infidels. "I live now," he fantasized, "in a Catholic and Canadian country."[67] He was the modern Dollard of the fabled "Laurentie" of Groulx and other nationalists of the day.

Like many of Pierre's intellectual meanderings at this time, this fantasy—that he would lead an army that won independence for Quebec in the same year that the Parti Québécois actually came to power—is simply juvenile trivia. In some essays, he favoured anti-Semitic, elitist, and conservative Catholic writers. In others, he merely took positions in a school where debate was strongly encouraged. He even praised the misogynist and elitist *L'homme, cet inconnu* by Alexis Carrel, as well as other works of a similar conservative Catholic character.[68] And, in a speech he gave on the survival of French Canadians in November 1937, he took his approach directly from nationalists like Groulx. "To save our French civilization," he said, "we must keep our language and flee American civilization." The "revenge of the cradle," he predicted, whereby French Catholics had large familes while English Protestants had few children, would soon allow the French population to exceed the English. He attacked immigration, because it tended to increase the English population, but rejoiced that the government had cut off most immigrants during the Great Depression. French Canada, he said, had a precise and even divine role—to propagate "French and Catholic ideas in the New World."

Yet the young Trudeau was also inconsistent at this time. In his 1936–37 notes, he made favourable references to Jacques Maritain, an eminent Catholic philosopher who opposed fascism and supported liberal democracy. He paraphrased his idea that "if the author is good, he will spontaneously criticize vice and approve good," and he strongly agreed with this liberal sentiment. He also proudly reported to his mother that he joined with other students in honouring not only the nationalist hero Dollard but also May 24, "la fête de la reine," the Queen's birthday, which was "another excellent occasion to display patriotism."[69] Contradictions abound.

Trudeau attended a "semaine sociale" at Brébeuf from November 28 to December 4, 1937, where they discussed a variety of social questions. The diet was strongly nationalist and conservative, and he learned about the "error of economic liberalism," "the necessity of corporatism," and "the illusion of communism and socialism."* To his nationalist teachers and friends there, he could deny strongly that he was "Americanized." Yet in 1937 he tried to establish a liaison between the student newspaper *Brébeuf* and its counterpart at the New York Catholic Fordham College. He told the U.S. editors that "you will come more directly in contact with the French and French Canadians, and the object of Mr. Roosevelt in establishing relations of goodwill and friendship between the American people will be greatly helped."[70] And, on the language question generally, unlike André Laurendeau, Trudeau rejected the popular nationalist cause of unilingualism, following, instead, his father's view that "because of the advantages which knowledge of the English language presents, the majority of 'Canadiens' are compelled to learn English. Far from blaming them, I find them to be perfectly reasonable"— except when they introduced anglicisms into French.[71]

Pierre could never identify with the element of extreme nationalism that attacked the brothels and nightclubs of Montreal and detested American music and movies. He continued to visit

---

* While the fare was highly nationalist and, in economics, corporatist in the fashion of Catholic economic thought at the time, there was some diversity and balance. André Laurendeau, for example, condemned Communism strongly, but said that all collective property—"propriété collective"—was not bad, giving the examples of electricity and railways. Father Omer Jenest, SJ, said that the church's support for corporatism distinguished it from fascism. He argued that the imposition by force of corporatism in Italy must be condemned. Gérard Filion, the future editor of *Le Devoir*, spoke on cooperatives and said they were most advanced in the Nordic countries. He added that Italy, because of fascism, was better off than France. Trudeau's notes are in TP, vol. 4, file 6.

New York, go to the theatre, and adore the Marx Brothers and the sirens of Hollywood. He made a pledge to himself in 1937: "I don't want to go out with girls before I am twenty years old because they would distract me," especially frivolous American girls.[72] But that summer at Old Orchard he met an American student, Camille Corriveau, "whose beauty I had admired for 4 years."[73] She finally spoke to him on August 18, his resolve melted, and within a week he fell in love. In October she told him he should choose any profession except the priesthood. "Even the life of a policeman would be more exciting," she thought. Then he returned to Brébeuf.

It was a different world. Father Brossard taught him Canadian history. He was, said Pierre, a patriot but not a fanatic. On October 20 the young Trudeau shaved for the first time. The next day he stood for the "autonomists" in the student parliament and heard Henri Bourassa, the nationalist founder of *Le Devoir*, speak in the evening. On October 22 he and other students demonstrated against "Communists." Then he joined the family at Christmas, went skiing for a week before New Year's, and refused an invitation from his sister, Suzette, to attend a New Year's Eve dance with her and her friends. The proffered date, "Olga Zabler," was very pretty, but he was still shy. "I am always timid around women," he mused, though that reserve frequently made him exaggerate his self-assurance in their presence. In short, he was awkward. Reflecting his frustrations, he made a New Year's resolution to "cultivate the strongest possible sense of honour" and to avoid any act that would cause him embarrassment. Without doubt, the "exalted patriots," as Pierre called the fervent nationalists, would not have thought much of his ideas and activities during this holiday season.

Tip tagged along with his brother on a trip to New York on January 2, 1938. They went immediately to a Broadway musical, the next day to see the American Jewish comedian Ed Wynn, the following day to Rockefeller Center—"c'est colossal!" Pierre wrote—and, in the evening, to the fabled Cotton Club. There, "the orchestra and the comedians were good," but there was a touch of Brébeuf in his comment that "the review was rather immoral and vulgar." Far more satisfying was Radio City Music Hall, where he saw the Rockettes kick their legs high. They were "very good," and the theatre itself "a marvel." When he got home, he continued to go to movies and to write to Camille, all the while trying to resist his strong urges to approach attractive young women.[74]

When Pierre returned to Montreal on January 8, Brébeuf enclosed him within its capacious bosom. He was ambitious academically and athletically, although he remarked that a pretty girl could capture his attention "despite my coldness and independence."[75] His ambitions included standing for the school elections and participating in a drama contest. He worried about his popularity because of his shyness and his tendency to be "contrary." At times he was troubled. He wrote to his mother: "Temperature uncertain, like adolescence." And, in his notebooks, there is a draft of what is perhaps a poem: "My adolescent heart is like nature / Everything is upset. The temperature of sadness."[76]

Father Bernier had reassured him in the fall of 1937 that he had "a Canadien mentality mixed with English," a combination, in Pierre's own view, that was "not bad for broadening one's outlook." Brébeuf was French, however, and he resolved to improve his French diction, to read more widely, and to attend Mass often. Still, he had pride in his bicultural background, even if many critics of the time deplored the mixing of French and English. He determined that he would continue to sign "Elliott" as part of his name: it was an indication of "good stock and distinction."[77]

Then came a brutal blow to this bicultural calm. Just after the early February 1938 elections for the Academic Council,

where his great rival Jean de Grandpré narrowly beat him for
the presidency, "Laurin" told Pierre that a fellow student had
declared he had no confidence in him—"that I was mediocre,
Americanized, and Anglicized, in short, I would betray my race.
I made it seem that I wasn't bothered, but it was a profound
shock." "Perhaps I seem superficial about certain things," Pierre
wrote in his journal. "But the truth is that I work. And I would
never betray the French Canadians." If he was accused directly,
he would punch the accuser in his face. Then he paused:
"However, I am proud of my English blood, which comes from
my mother. At least it tempers my boiling French blood. It leaves
me calmer and more insightful and perspicacious." The incident
made him more determined than ever to finish first at Brébeuf,
the educational jewel of French education in Montreal.[78]

Four days later, on February 9, the results of yet another
election were announced, this time for the Conventum—the
class council. Pierre had initially not wanted to run but did so
when he discovered that his father had been on the secretariat of
the Conventum at his school. He again ran behind Jean de
Grandpré, but he won the run-off election and became vice-
president. "Oh, inexpressible happiness!" he exclaimed in his
diary. He added that he was very pleased that his bilingual name,
Pierre Elliott Trudeau, had not hurt him much in the election.
In March the issue still bothered him. In English class he pretended to be Irish and, "for a joke," dared other students to take
him on. No battle followed, although Father Landry threatened
him with expulsion. However, he wrote in his diary after the
class that he was content to have his English blood mixed with
his French blood. The blend, he concluded, made him less fearful of going against "the popular spirit."

Some have claimed that Trudeau was the model for François
Hertel's 1939 novel, *Le beau risque*—a story about "Pierre Martel,"
a young student at a classical college who loses his restlessness

as his "soul" becomes thoroughly French. The novel takes the form of a memoir by a priest-professor who is going to Asia. He says that Pierre lacks confidence, despite his intelligence and a successful surgeon father he admires. The narrator, Father Berthier, soon discovers that the father is empty and lacks depth, concerned as he is only with appearance. Like Pierre Trudeau, Pierre Martel has acne, lives in a large house in Outremont, has a wealthy father, takes trips to New York, gratuitously irritates his teachers, prefers individual sports to team sports, loves poetry, and, most tellingly perhaps, spends his summers at Old Orchard Beach. The novel traces how Pierre turns away from the materialist and Americanized world of his father and finds strength in Boucherville, in the traditional world of his grandparents. He confronts his father for his scepticism, his Anglicisms, and his materialism, while, at the same time, he comes to admire his grandfather's respect for the past and, in particular, the way he has retained the spirit of the 1837 Rebellions. Pierre senses the call of the blood and angrily refuses to go to Old Orchard or to visit a Quebec "inn," which, he tells his father, must be called an "auberge." He takes up the continuing struggles of his people, becomes devoted to a renewed Catholicism, and expresses commitment to a world where "we will be more ourselves."[79] Trudeau read the book when it appeared, as did many young Quebecers, but his short review in his journal does not indicate that he identified himself with Martel. Nevertheless, the evidence suggests that Pierre Trudeau, like Martel, was a divided soul in those troubled times.

In the spring of 1938, while Pierre contemplated the comments about his "Americanization and Anglicization," he wrote a play entitled *Dupés*, about a Montreal tailor. In itself a disappointing, slight confection, it won a competition at Brébeuf and was performed there, with Pierre as one of the actors. Jean de Grandpré, Trudeau's greatest academic rival and a future prominent business executive, played the lead. At the time it was written, nationalists in Quebec were urging a "Buy from our own" campaign, which the Jewish community in Montreal condemned as anti-Semitic. Trudeau's "comedy of manners" is laced with sarcasm and some bitterness. The main character is a tailor, Jean-Baptiste Couture, who, in the first draft, is described as a good father of a French-Canadian family, honest but sometimes violent. Another character, Jean Ditreau, is interested in Couture's daughter, Camille, a name Trudeau devilishly chose in honour of his American girlfriend. Others in the play include a few customers, notably the dubious Paul Shick.

Ditreau has a diploma in "commercial psychology" from McKill University, and he offers to help Couture assess his clients. "Your business," he explains, is in a French-Canadian area, but francophones "prefer to buy from Jews, firstly because they don't want to enrich one of their own and then because they believe they will get a better price." His solution: Put up the sign "Goldenburg, tailor" in place of "Chez Couture." He also advises Couture to sell "American magazines" and to install a "soda-fountain"; people will then come after Mass to drink "Coke." While he is speaking, Ditreau tears down a sign that reads "Help our own" and replaces it with a new English sign that says: "We sell for less—Goldenburg, fine goods. Open for business."

Once all the signs have been changed, Couture tells his first customer, in the "manner of a Jew," that he has the latest fashions from Paris, New York, and London and then whispers, "in spite of our repugnance [for Hitler] we even follow the fashions of Berlin."[80] The deals continue—and the confusion mounts. Ditreau is finally rejected as a suitor by Camille because he is a politician, the lowest of all professions. The evil ways of politicians are also demonstrated by another customer, Maurice Lesousflé, clearly modelled on Quebec premier Maurice Duplessis, who proposes having six "heroic" Canadians split the vote so a "Hebrew" candidate can win an election.

Dupés was a great triumph for Pierre Trudeau at Brébeuf, and the priests, parents, and students who attended the performance vigorously applauded its young author—youthful but complicated. It reflected not only the mood of Outremont but also a time when the Canadian prime minister could compare Hitler to Joan of Arc; when his major adviser, O.D. Skelton, an eminent liberal, could fret about the "Jewish" influence that was pushing Britain towards war; and when Vincent Massey, the high commissioner to Britain and future governor general, could declare that Canada needed no Jewish immigrants.

Like most students, Pierre Trudeau responded to what his teachers, his peers, and his family wanted of him—most of the time. But certain unresolved contradictions appear in his personal journal, where his private activities and views are expressed. On the surface, he seemed to conform to the nationalist, anti-Semitic, and anti-English environment of the time. Yet, just a few days before *Dupés* was performed, after careful supervision by the Brébeuf staff, Trudeau had his "encounter" with Laurin about his mixed blood and his American and English ways. Without doubt, this incident made the final text of *Dupés* more reflective of the general mood at Brébeuf. Pierre had written to his mother on January 24, 1938: "One of the qualities of the letter is tact. That is to say that when one writes, one should take account of the circumstances and adapt the letter to the one who will read it."[81] It was meant to apply to a specific letter, but the comment describes well how Trudeau believed he must adapt to particular circumstances. Yet, as he told his mother, he found it a "complex" task. He conformed, yes, but in his heart he often rebelled, and in his acts he sometimes contradicted.[82]

Three days before Pierre wrote *Dupés*, he made some notes about the "pros and cons" of the religious life. Here doubt and belief abound. The pro side emphasized how the priesthood would always lead him towards perfection and closer to Christ. It would grant him a better place in heaven and, more generally, make him a better man. But the cons won. He was not much attracted to the vocation. He was not humble enough; he was too proud and too independent. He liked an active life, and he would not be good at confessions because he lacked the necessary spirit. Moreover, he would not be a good teacher: "I'm not open enough," he concluded. It was a shrewd assessment.[83] Pierre Trudeau was a good Catholic, but he would have made a poor priest.

—

CHAPTER 2

LA GUERRE, NO SIR!

I n the late spring of 1938, after the success of *Dupés* with the students and their parents at Brébeuf and his decision not to enter the priesthood, Pierre Trudeau began to wonder, as older adolescents often do, what his fate might be. He disliked business, and his father's career and death had left him ambivalent towards law. He wrote in his diary as the school year came to an end in June 1938: "I wonder whether I will be able to do something for my God and my country. I would like so much to be a great politician and to guide my nation."[1] This dream never died, though his conception of both his nation and its politics certainly changed.

When Pierre began the quest for his destiny at Brébeuf in the 1930s, the stream of world events quickly turned into rapids. The Great Depression altered its direction, Hitler's Germany disrupted its flow, and the confluence of war in China and in Spain created a torrent that crested in September 1939 when the world burst apart once more. Like others, Canadians became immersed in the flood of current events. Some were swept away by the martial spirit. Farley Mowat, the son of a soldier who gloried in memories of the First World War, saw his gleeful father come down the country lane bearing news of war, and the dutiful son set out to fight through six cruel years of war.[2] In the poor parts of Montreal, recruiting centres were clogged as the unemployed and the young with few prospects (including the future hockey star Maurice Richard) viewed the dangers of war as more alluring than the pain of their present plight. Among Pierre's classmates at Brébeuf, however, few answered the call, and most of this young elite probably opposed the war as a British imperial conflict that would spill Canadian blood and bitterly divide the country. Charles Trudeau's close friend Mayor Camillien Houde did not hide his agreement with that view.

Pierre was nineteen years old when the Germans stormed across the German-Polish border that September. His own attitude towards the war was not predictable, and he understood its bloodiness. In the debate at school on the Sino-Japanese conflict in which he took the Japanese side, he admitted they were ruthless: "But in war can such things be avoided?" he asked. "Did not Germany use gas in 1914 and bomb the Red Cross of the Allies? Did not Italy use very crude means in Ethiopia, did not China massacre Europeans in the Boxer rebellion, did not Franco render thousands of Spanish children orphans, did not France execute unscrupulously certain of her enemies in the last war, did not Great Britain herself use the inhuman explosive bullets against the Boer?"[3] Trudeau obviously knew much about war, but he displayed none of the generous views towards Mussolini's Italy and Franco's Spain that were common among the clergy and the commentators in Quebec at the time.

Camille Corriveau, his American girlfriend, wrote to him at the outbreak of war, begging him not to enlist. He did not answer directly but described the immediate signs of war in Montreal: "Soldiers guard the Jacques Cartier bridge; airplanes often survey the city. The regiments hunt for recruits. Parliament is now sitting to decide if there will be conscription.

There are some anti-conscription gatherings across the city. One hears some threats." He admitted he had not read any newspapers and was not well informed, but he confided that he personally believed Hitler was near the end.[4] Many who had read the newspapers shared this view when Hitler's war machine halted during the "phony war" of that first winter. But they were wrong.

Pierre could have enlisted, but he did not. There was no military tradition in his family, despite Étienne Truteau's celebrated seventeenth-century triumph over the Iroquois, and he later recalled that only one of his cousins enlisted.[5] In general, francophones were poorly represented within the Canadian military. French was spoken only in the famed Royal 22e Régiment, and military administration in Quebec was conducted in English despite the controversies of the First World War. Among the higher ranks, francophones were scarce, and not one of the brigade commanders of the First Canadian Division was francophone.[6] In Pierre's last year at Brébeuf, 1939–40, he concentrated on his studies for his bachelor's degree, on editing the school newspaper, and on his future plans. Meanwhile, he carefully guarded his opinions about the war.

"I'm not open enough," he had decided when pondering a religious life in his future. Certainly, Pierre had become less open as his teenage years progressed and as his own sense of identity reacted to his understanding of external events. He told his mother in the fall of 1935 that the priests at Brébeuf might be worried about the election results, but he expanded no further and passed quickly on to another subject.[7] He also grumbled that there were three Masses each day and no fewer than fifty-six religious exercises of various kinds in the Brébeuf regimen. But despite his complaints, his Catholic piety was increasingly and devoutly expressed: with exhilaration he told her how the lights were turned out at a retreat so they could better see the magnificent cross that loomed above them on Mount Royal. At another retreat house, in modest rooms near a quiet river, he told her he enjoyed the sermons but valued most the silence during meals—and, after the experience of those few days, he began his lifelong practice of meditation.

Pierre wrote this letter to his mother on November 26, one day after Quebec politics changed completely with the near defeat of the corrupt and capitalist Liberal government of Louis-Alexandre Taschereau; six weeks after the victory of Mackenzie King's Liberals in Ottawa; three months after Mussolini's dive bombers, in attacking Abyssinia, demolished the fragile hopes of collective security through the League of Nations; and nine months after Germany denounced the disarmament clauses of the Treaty of Versailles and introduced conscription. It was also only eight months after the death of Charles Trudeau. Quebec turned inward as it confronted the new realities; so, for a while, did Pierre.[8]

Although he turned inward, Pierre, contrary to his frequent later statements, remained deeply immersed in politics in two important ways: in the sense, set out by Aristotle, that the end of the science of politics must be human good; and in the specific Quebec context where the rights of francophone and Catholic citizens must be upheld. The cross on Mount Royal, after all, symbolically linked Roman Catholicism with the national mission of the descendants of New France in North America. Pierre's Jesuit education mediated his understanding of contemporary politics in the 1930s, and his youthful play Dupés illustrates how closely he followed political events despite his later claims of ignorance. His views, as expressed publicly, were conventionally nationalist—what one would expect of an adolescent Brébeuf student in 1938. He supported the "Buy from our own" movement that arose as Jewish shopkeepers proliferated in the francophone districts of

Montreal. He deplored the tendency to create constituency boundaries so that Jews could have electoral representation, although he wrongly blamed Maurice Duplessis rather than the federal Liberals for that chicanery. In common with most Quebec nationalists of the time, he portrayed active politicians as corrupt and craven, a view that he expressed bluntly in a Brébeuf essay that year where he said that anyone who entered politics risked acquiring "the reputation of an imbecile." Yet he and many others dreamed of a new kind of politics, not so corrupt, and he fancied a future political career for himself.[9]

Much later, in minimizing his nationalist views, Trudeau recalled that he had joined students at a demonstration against the French writer André Malraux, who was touring Canada to advocate the Republican cause in the Spanish Civil War.[10] Similarly, his views on international affairs, as expressed in his schoolbooks—which the priests read—followed the line taken by Quebec Catholic nationalists. For an English rhetoric class, he wrote in October 1937: "Do we want to go to war? We do not. Ask those who have been if they enjoyed the horrors, if they enjoyed the terrors, the misery and the uncertainty of war."[11] The memories of the last war and the bitter divisions it caused were still strong in the province.

The anti-Semitism of *Dupés* was as conventional in its time as it seems deplorable today. It lacks the ferocity of Quebec fascist leader Adrien Arcand or, for that matter, the Canadian-born Catholic priest Father Charles Coughlin, who spread hatred and fear of Jews in Roosevelt's America—a fear that grew rapidly as he denounced American Jews for drawing the United States into a European war. It was less extreme than the exaggerated view of Jewish economic power expressed in 1933 by Les Jeunes-Canada, a Quebec Catholic youth group that in a famous April rally, "Politicians and Jews," heard speakers denounce the "Jewish plutocracy" and argue that

Canadian politicians were quicker to condemn discrimination against Jews in distant Germany than against French Canadians in Ontario or the West.[12]

Pierre's anti-war sentiments echoed the strong isolationist sentiment not only in Quebec but also among English-Canadian intellectuals in the 1930s. His rhetoric pales beside that of University of Toronto history professor and war veteran Frank Underhill, who called on the Canadian government to make clear to the world, "and especially to Great Britain, that poppies blooming in Flanders fields have no further interest for us . . . European troubles are not worth the bones of a Toronto grenadier"—or, Pierre would have added, a Brébeuf student.[13] The conventional, history reminds us, is frequently badly wrong. The moral quandaries of the time lay elsewhere, and Pierre's manuscript for *Dupés* was revised several times not for its anti-Semitism but for its suspected sexual nuance.*

After 1935, Pierre began that period of adolescence when, in psychologist Erik Erikson's well-known phrase, individuals ask, "Who am I?" The voices he most often heard after the death of his father were those within Brébeuf—his teachers and

---

* The revisions were made at the insistence of Father Brossard, who was the censor for the occasion. After the play, leading Outremont figures such as "le juge Thouin" and Mesdames de Grandpré and Vaillancourt congratulated Pierre. The play was, Pierre wrote, "a great success," judging by "the congratulations and the laughter." The only objection was to a section of the play where Jean Couture speaks to his daughter, Camille, and uses the word *grosse* to describe her. One of the priests thought it might mean "pregnant" and condemned the "double sense." Pierre wrote in his diary that it was not his intention at all. When the hint of sex brought horror to the hallways of Brébeuf, he noted: "One can't please everyone." Journal 1938, May 17, 1938, TP, vol. 39, file 9.

his classmates. He immersed himself in books, especially in the Catholic religion, French literature, and Catholic philosophy. In a more general sense, he followed the outline, or *ratio*, established by the Jesuit founder Ignatius of Loyola in the sixteenth century. It laid out the first international system of education, one whose method and content were similar in Peru, Poland, or Quebec. For its time, it was utilitarian, a method to provide the human resources for good government and to create a Catholic elite. Its design was "intended to ensure an immersion into classical culture, mastery of material, quickness of mind, sensitivity to individual ability, and personal discipline."[14]

In this sense, Pierre Trudeau was an exceptional student. His discipline, a quality that Jesuit education inculcated, was extraordinary, and it remained so throughout his life. His notebooks are remarkable in their detail and conscientiousness; even when he was writing the compulsory letter to his mother, he made numerous corrections to individual phrases so as to find exactly the right word. He wrote reviews of every book he read while at Brébeuf, and the commentaries were perceptive beyond his adolescent years. He maintained his enthusiasm as he studied the differences between Aristotle and Plato, Rome and Athens, Jerusalem and Rome. He mastered his academic material in every class, whether classical Greek or, in 1939, political economy. His record was outstanding: in competition with an elite student body, he stood first in most of his classes, won more prizes than anyone else (to his delight, they were often in cash), and, in his final year, he bested his strongest competition, Jean de Grandpré, and stood first overall. He was extremely ambitious, a quality Ignatius of Loyola also valued: he carefully recorded de Grandpré's marks and cheered those occasions when his rival finished second.

In the world of the later 1930s, as Pierre contemplated the question of his identity, Brébeuf created the context where he found most of the answers. It differed from some of the other classical colleges, which concentrated on producing priests, and self-consciously viewed itself as the vanguard of intellectual Catholicism in Quebec. It already stood at the apex of a structure of classical colleges that Maurice Duplessis regarded as "our fortresses, indispensable bastions that are essential to preserve our patriotic and religious traditions."[15] As he remarked in one of his school essays, the "fortress" of Brébeuf was a closed world where daily rituals and duties defined his days.[16] Among his teachers, Father Robert Bernier, a Franco-Manitoban, was important in inspiring Pierre's literary interest, and they certainly had great respect for each other. At one Easter retreat, the priest advised him to develop a broader cultural interest, which, he said, most Canadians lacked. Above all, he added, "you must avoid all contact with the vulgar, even if it is under the pretext of a distraction." Pierre apologized for raising the subject but told Bernier he had no intimate friend who could give such advice.[17]

Bernier continued to counsel Pierre so long as he was at Brébeuf, but he was traditional in his views and self-effacing in manner. Gradually, Father Rodolphe Dubé, better known as the author François Hertel, became the greater influence. Hertel, Trudeau wrote later, "naturally gravitated towards everything that was new or contrary to the tastes of the day" and carried his students far beyond the thick stone walls of the fortress and the classroom.[18] In the words of one of Pierre's closest Brébeuf friends, Hertel was "a truly revolutionary force" among the sons of the bourgeoisie who predominated at the college, and he saved them from "the mediocrity and congenital folly of our condition."[19] Hertel's biographer has argued convincingly that the success of this charismatic and humorous priest derived in large part from the solemn atmosphere and rigorous discipline of Brébeuf in those times. A brilliant teacher and a clever comedian, he would begin his classes with a joke that often shocked the students and dramatically pierced the greyness in the classrooms.[20]

Deeply anti-capitalist, profoundly distrustful of the influence of Britain and the United States, but also a critic of racism in Germany and of "British imperialism," François Hertel admired the nationalist interpretation of history put forward by Abbé Groulx. In a 1939 article in *L'Action nationale*, the Abbé, in turn, responded with enthusiasm to Hertel's novel, *Le beau risque*. He said it provided a penetrating exposé of the empty soul of bourgeois French Canadians, who had cut themselves off from their nationalist roots, and he focused on one short passage which noted that the francophone bourgeoisie always raised the "national question" hesitantly with their children. In his view, the new generation had to break away from the compromises of earlier generations if the national question was to be seriously addressed.[21] Then a true democracy could exist, one based on a national faith that resided in the hearts and minds of the people.[22]

Pierre made no mention of this article in his journal, but his school writings contain similar anti-bourgeois and nationalist sentiments. Although there are several references in his papers to works by the Abbé, he seems to have had only one personal encounter with him during his Brébeuf years. On February 18, 1938, he went to a lecture Groulx gave on the intendant Jean Talon, who, in the latter seventeenth century, had tried to consolidate the prosperity of New France, and he reported: "The subject is interesting and was treated well, but the poor Abbé does not have a good voice or oratorical talent." Moreover, whether or not Trudeau was the model for the character Pierre Martel in Hertel's *Le beau risque*, the message of the novel—the dangers of Americanization and Anglicization, the obligations to the past, the limitations of bourgeois capitalism, the importance of national sentiment among youth—resonated loudly for him, despite his later denials in interviews that they did.*

Like Hertel and the other Brébeuf teachers, Pierre Trudeau shared the excitement that came from the reinvigoration of French Catholicism in the twentieth century, especially after the First World War. France, so secular and revolutionary in the nineteenth century, had become the centre of a remarkable revival of Catholic faith in the twentieth century. Leading Catholic thinkers and theologians such as the liberal Jacques Maritain, the "personalist" Emmanuel Mounier, and the conservative, elitist Charles Maurras came to dominate French intellectual life in the interwar years and began a process of seeking to "bare the human condition utterly."[23] Among the subjects they bared was the relationship between the citizen and the state. "Personalism"—a philosophical approach to the Catholic faith that emphasized the individual while linking individual action with broader purposes within society—would have a profound impact on Trudeau and on Quebec intellectual life.

----

* In an interview with Ron Graham in 1992, Trudeau gave this answer to a question about Groulx's influence on him. "I used to get some of his books as prizes at the end of the year when I'd get a first or something like that. He was quite revered as a historian. I don't think any of us at the time understood some of the analysis which has been made later that he was perhaps somewhat inclined to racism or fascism and so on, so I don't remember him as that, but he used to be talked about and he had quite a few disciples and followers, of which I was not one as I say; he wouldn't have liked me for applauding the defeat of the French at the Plains of Abraham." Although Trudeau encountered Groulx only once while he was at Brébeuf, the Abbé's work formed the basis of Canadian history teaching at the college. Interview between Pierre Trudeau and Ron Graham, April 28, 1992, TP, vol. 23, file 3.

Son of a bourgeois father and an English-speaking mother, rich, charmed by the New York theatre, at ease with American wealth, intrigued by American women, and infatuated with the movies, Trudeau's words and convictions as a Brébeuf student seem to belie his own past, present, and future actions and beliefs. And it is precisely these contradictions that shape the emotional and intellectual growth of Pierre Trudeau. He had internalized deeply the death of his father, but the source of his inquietude seems to have been the tension between the Catholic nationalism of Brébeuf and his own personal experience and developing convictions. Brébeuf was immersed in nationalism from the mid-thirties on. The college priests detested the Liberal government of Premier Louis-Alexandre Taschereau, who had compromised with the Americans and the capitalists, and they welcomed the rise of the Action libérale nationale—a rebel group that expressed the nationalism and social action which they and the Catholic youth groups found attractive as a response to the Depression and the discontents of the time. However, after the ALN formed a coalition with the Conservatives to form a new party, the Union nationale, the ALN's leader, Paul Gouin, lost the leadership to Maurice Duplessis, a conservative nationalist tied to rural Quebec. And, in 1936, the Union nationale won the election. In *Dupés*, Pierre had revealed his politics and those of the play's audience when he mocked Duplessis as Maurice Lesoufflé. Nationalism in itself was not enough.

—

In 1938 Pierre Trudeau began a journal, which he continued through his last two years in school. It is detailed, frank, and extraordinarily revealing. It is the only diary in his papers, apart from less personal travel diaries and an agenda for 1937 that contains some commentary, and it expresses his own need to chronicle the moments of late adolescence as he tried to find his identity. It begins on New Year's Day 1938 with the intriguing advice: "If you want to know my thoughts, read between the lines!"

The lines themselves tell a great deal about this tumultuous time in his life. He recounts how he lamented his father's absence on the third anniversary of his death; at other times, he says that things would be different and, presumably, better if his father were still with him. He does not mean that the Trudeaus would be wealthier. Here the pages abound with evidence of the Trudeau family's considerable wealth—a Buick for Suzette, who enjoyed bourgeois pleasures; a grand Packard that bears Pierre, Tip, and some priests to a retreat; the chauffeur, Grenier; the tickets for friends and teachers for Royals' games and the Belmont amusement park; and the good hotels and restaurants the family frequented when they visited New York City. Above all, the entries reveal two aspects of his character: first, his goals, as his ambition for a public life at the highest level becomes a constant refrain; and, second, his extraordinary intellectual curiosity and commitment to hard work. On February 17, 1938, the eighteen-year-old student even thanks God for the good health that allows him to work to midnight almost every night on his studies. Rarely does God receive such thanks from schoolboys.

His mother encouraged but did not direct. Grace Trudeau continued to spend summers at Lac Tremblant and Old Orchard Beach in Maine, while travelling frequently to New York in the fall and spring and to Florida in the winter. Grace, though a strong personality, gave her children surprising freedom. In his journal, it is the "eyes" of Brébeuf that watch the young Trudeau throughout these pages. He complained about this constant attention not only in the diary pages but even in an article he wrote in May 1939 for *Brébeuf*, the student newspaper, where he suggested that the departing class will rejoice at the end of the constant "surveillance" and the need to ask, "Father, may I . . . ?[24] There were endless permissions, perpetual denials, and eclectic censorship. In March 1938 the censor forbade the presentation of a play after Trudeau and others had rehearsed it many times. And a few of the priests used the threat of expulsion for even trivial misdemeanours. Pierre was always diligent and fundamentally shy, but he sought popularity and gained attention by clever, rebellious distractions that infuriated some of his teachers. After a snowball fight and a couple of other incidents, Father Landry warned him in a menacing fashion that he was a millimetre from being kicked out of the college: the rector would no longer tolerate the "insolence of Pierre Elliott Trudeau," he said, and the next offence would mean a trip to the rector's office. Throughout the reprimand, Pierre smiled, to the certain annoyance of Landry. The next day the clever student found "an excuse" to call upon the rector, and there he discovered that everything was fine so far as the top man was concerned. Pierre already possessed political wiles.

Landry continued to pester him, but Pierre found allies in other teachers, notably Fathers Bernier, Sauvé, d'Anjou, and Toupin. Despite their counsel to avoid jazz, movies, and American popular culture, he travelled to New York in the spring of 1939 in his sister's Buick, which his mother agreed he could drive after an excellent academic year. Suzette had spent four months in France and, very much the young sophisticate, was returning on June 16 on the art deco gem the *Normandie*. Grace and the boys stayed on Central Park South at the elegant Barbizon Plaza, attended the New York World's Fair, and, with a friend of Suzette's, Pierre danced the night away at the Rainbow Grill on the roof of Rockefeller Center. The fair initially disappointed Pierre: "The first good effect is spoiled by all the common people, the crowd, and especially because nearly all the buildings are made of beaver board and the columns are of cardboard. And inside you see only a bunch of merchandise." It was, he concluded in best Brébeuf fashion, too vulgar. He found the Soviet pavilion an impressive exception with its marble, but he deplored the "marvellous Communist propaganda" it represented. He approved of the monumental Italian pavilion, however, though he made no political comments about it or Mussolini. On another evening he was deeply moved when he saw Raymond Massey star in *Abraham Lincoln in Illinois*. The aspiring politician was no doubt assured to discover that young Lincoln had been "troubled, timid, overwhelmed, and a misanthrope."[25]

The world beckoned, yet Brébeuf's pull persisted. There, Pierre increasingly wrestled with questions of faith, nationality, and vocation. Outside the college walls, he enjoyed experiences that his school notebooks often condemn. The tensions between experience and education, belief and practice, nationalism and cosmopolitanism, ambition and timidity created the dynamic that drove his personal growth in these critical years. As the international situation worsened and nationalist currents flowed more strongly, he built up his own internal protections against the pressures that suddenly confronted him. The eminent psychologist Jerome Kagan has explained that adolescents tend to categorize people and endow them with certain characteristics. If an adolescent who believes he belongs to a particular category suddenly behaves in ways that violate those expectations, he experiences considerable uncertainty.[26] Discontinuities compel resolution. In the late 1930s and early 1940s, Pierre Trudeau sensed such discontinuities, and he, too, sought their resolution.

One huge discontinuity occurred when Grace Trudeau registered both her sons at Camp Ahmek, the Taylor Statten summer camp on the shore of Canoe Lake in Algonquin Park, which was a favourite of the Ontario English elite. When he arrived on July 2, 1938, Pierre discovered that he had four English-Canadian roommates. Since he had left Querbes, his companions had been almost exclusively French. Sensing the foreign environment, he promised his diary that he would seize every occasion to declare that he was a "French Canadian and a Catholic." He quickly made his mark, not least in boxing, where his skills and well-developed body resulted in bloody noses for several of the other campers. He also excelled in acting, receiving the highest marks for performances that were, of course, entirely in English. In the sole English entry in his diary that summer he wrote: "It's good to hear 'He is Pierre Trudeau, the best actor in camp!'"[27]

—

The Brébeuf priests would also have been upset to learn that their prize eighteen-year-old student had fallen in love. Camille Corriveau, one year older than Trudeau, was a student at Smith College, and photographs indicate she was very pretty, with a full figure. Certainly Trudeau found her as attractive as Vivien Leigh and Jean Harlow, the actresses he admired in the movies. He was annoyed when the photograph she sent did not catch her stunning beauty. As he opened the envelope, he wrote in reply, the radio began to play the song "You must have been a beautiful baby." He wanted more than this unsatisfactory photo, he complained, "so I keep thinking of the beautiful soft hair that was left out of the picture, the delicate ear [he stroked out 'I am kissing'], a feminine shoulder, a graceful arm, a few charming curves, here and there [stroked out 'a lovely leg'], and so many other things I am missing. Truly, you have been holding out on me, you little iconoclast you!" We cannot be sure Camille received exactly the words in this draft letter, but it does convey the allure she held for him.[28]

A Franco-American, Camille vacationed in Orchard Beach every year with the many other francophones who gathered on the Maine beaches. Although a good dancer, Pierre was still shy with women, and he often turned down invitations thrust at him by his sister. When Suzette was presented as a debutante at Rideau Hall in Ottawa on January 28, 1938, he described himself, as he reflected on the occasion, as a bit of a misogynist. Still, he admitted that, for "esthetic" reasons, he could admire a beautiful woman. That would suffice for now, he concluded. It didn't.[29]

A few days after they met, Camille sent him a warm letter that stirred him despite his "coldness and . . . independence." At least, he opined, Camille was more serious than the majority of women he encountered in Montreal. The memory of her lingered and he was soon looking forward with anticipation to their coming summer meeting. There was a moment of doubt in April when he went to a religious retreat. Father Tobin, the American priest for whom he had procured Montreal Royals tickets, took him aside to talk about universities in the United States. Pierre had been considering American schools for graduate work himself, but Father Tobin was firm in rejecting this option. The universities, he declared, were mostly co-educational and had become veritable dens of immorality. The male-only universities were equally bad because students would sneak women into their rooms. Worst of all were women's colleges such as Vassar and Smith, which were "schools of immorality." Indeed, the mother of a Smith student had confessed to Tobin that contraceptives were to be found everywhere at the school. The reason—the immoral cinema. But even more influential were the professors who openly professed free love.

A shocked Pierre apparently did not argue with Tobin, who was his "guardian angel" for the retreat, but in his diary he wrote: "I am convinced that my Camille is an exception.

However, the atmosphere can have an influence." Fortunately, "she is Catholic," a commitment that was, in his still innocent mind, an impregnable shield against the forces of lust and the availability of condoms.[30]

The conversation lingered in the recesses of Pierre's conscience as the summer of 1938 and Camille's presence approached. Unfortunately, Pierre and Camille had not connived to make their stays coincident, and he went off to Camp Ahmek again in July. After lamenting to his diary that Camille was in Old Orchard while he was in the wilds of Ontario, he broke down in tears when he finished reading Edmond Rostand's 1897 play *Cyrano de Bergerac*. Cyrano spoke to his sense of romance and became his model. The greatest compliment, he wrote to Camille, would be to hear someone say, "You have won because you are Cyrano!"[31] Throughout his life Trudeau identified with Cyrano, who appealed to his romantic spirit. The daring seventeenth-century swordsman believed that, because of his ugly nose, the beautiful Roxane would never accept him — and, in the end, his handsome but dull friend Christian won her heart.[32] Pierre, who constantly worried about his acne and thought women did not find him appealing, clearly identified with the brilliant poet but tragic lover Cyrano. Four decades later, Trudeau also recalled the importance for him of Cyrano's famous "tirade" about walking alone to the heights: "I found there an expression of who I was and what I wanted to be: I don't care if I don't make it, providing I don't need anyone else's help, providing what I do make I make alone."[33]

Pierre enjoyed Camp Ahmek, but when the month was up on July 29, he was impatient to get to Old Orchard Beach.[34] The family chauffeur immediately drove him and Tip to Maine to join Grace and Suzette. Camille had agreed to stay a few more days. Alas, when he arrived, he discovered that she had not been able to find a room and might have to leave. Grace and

Suzette quickly responded to the crisis with an invitation for Camille to stay with them. For Pierre, "utopia had arrived!"[35] They had five glorious days in which, like Cyrano with Roxane, he read poetry to Camille, they watched the stars at night on the pier, and they went to confession together. Then they parted sadly on August 6, vowing to stay in touch.

They met again the next year in August at Old Orchard Beach, and the external world that was falling apart was far distant from the young lovers. Camille had spent part of the academic year in France, and Pierre found her aloof at first, but soon enchantment returned. They went to Hollywood films almost every night, then walked on the pier and talked—he about law school, which he had begun to consider, and she about becoming a schoolteacher. On the 17th they had their first fight, when he wanted to pass the evening reading and she wanted him to spend it with her. He finally agreed, and, the following night, they went dancing with Suzette and her boyfriend to celebrate the second anniversary of their meeting. Afterwards, the moon over the water was especially bewitching and, for the first time, they kissed.

At month's end, however, they fought again. She sent him a note telling him to meet her on the pier if he was not tired; her tone was cold. Pierre noted in his journal: "I found the proposal comic and I would have responded to her in the same tone, but I wasn't able to do so because I was in the bath." Resentfully, he met her and reproached her for her bad mood. They went to Camille's summer place, where he told her that she was beautiful and enchanting but he would not be pulled along by "the end of the nose." He confessed to himself that his behaviour might have been impolite, but, he reasoned, "it seems to me that the woman should not push the man around."[36] The next evening, as the Second World War began, she begged him not to do anything dangerous. Rather, she asked him to visit her at Smith in the autumn and to attend her graduation the following June. As she wept, he kissed her tears and whispered poetry in her ear before they finally parted at 2:45 a.m.[37]

The summer of 1939 was the best, he told his diary: "I read little, but I kissed a woman."[38] In September, school resumed: Pierre became the editor of the college newspaper, *Brébeuf*, and prepared to wrest class leadership away from Jean de Grandpré. He thought constantly of Camille, but among his peers the news of war incited considerable debate in the college corridors. He avoided the discussions and deliberately cloaked himself with ambiguity. On October 9 he wrote in his diary: "It's true that there is a certain charm to surrounding oneself with mystery." He preferred to have people say "Trudeau? No one knows him. Friend of all; intimate of none."

Pierre remained publicly aloof from the controversies about conscription. His journal provides convincing repudiation to anyone who argues that his nationalism made him an immediate opponent of the "British war." He found the declarations of many students—that they would resist conscription and flee into the bush—simply foolish. "Everyone is talking for and against conscription," he noted in one entry. "It is a sad thing but I would not do what many others are promising to do: hide themselves in the bush. I would sign up and go and come back for the sake of adventure." Then he hesitated: his own preference was to avoid the war and go to England—not as a soldier but as a Rhodes Scholar—or maybe to the States.[39]

Within the next months, war, as it so often does, changed everything, notably Canadian politics. Trudeau attended two election rallies in the fall as Duplessis challenged the federal government's war authority under the *War Measures Act*. On October 20 he went with his mother to the Montreal Forum for a Liberal rally. A family friend had given them tickets, but Pierre, whose father had been a Conservative, was offended by the Liberal crowd, which "cried like babies with each invective against the *bleus.*"[40] Still, he found Mackenzie King's French lieutenant, Ernest Lapointe, very impressive. The federal Liberals had warned francophone Quebec that the re-election of Duplessis would mean the resignation of the Quebec Liberal ministers and, inevitably, the emergence of a conscription coalition, as in the First World War.

Six days later he attended yet another Liberal rally with his mother, where he heard the brilliant orator Athanase David speak. Pierre could not yet vote, but in his first *Brébeuf* article dealing with the war he cast a plague on all the older parties and expressed his belief that Quebec needed a new movement that was neither *bleu* nor *rouge*, conservative nor liberal. About the war, he was remarkably taciturn. He made no comments on the defeat of Poland or on the alliance of Communism and Nazism in its destruction. He attacked the tyranny of public opinion, where "soldiers dare not say they would like to halt war . . . and generals dare not call for peace."[41] Camille and plans for his future career preoccupied him more than politics, and he said nothing publicly when the provincial Liberals defeated Duplessis.

Camille had asked him to visit her at Smith. He hesitated, writing in his diary: "2,000 women. Ouf!" He admitted that he understood neither her nor women generally. He was jealous; he was suspicious. Perhaps recalling Father Tobin's warnings, he wondered about the summer day when Camille had revealed a "naughty" character. He finally decided that he would go to Smith, and he borrowed Suzette's impressive Buick for the occasion. Once again they went to the movies, where they saw *All Quiet on the Western Front*, the film based on Erich Maria Remarque's novel. Its anti-war message impressed Pierre, but this time Camille did not. She was too materialistic and too independent. She was, to be sure, charming and pretty, but "My God," he exclaimed, "I am too much an idealist and an intellectual for her." Although Catholic and French, she was, regrettably, too American.[42] He returned home, worried about the war, and with one goal in mind: to win the prestigious Rhodes Scholarship and go to Oxford.

—

If the Rhodes had been granted, Pierre Trudeau would have embarked on a path that took him away from his companions and the whirlwind of Quebec political life. His teachers at Brébeuf recommended him strongly for the award and, in January 1940, his chances seemed excellent. Indeed, the letter from Father Boulin, the head, or prefect, of the college, listed the astonishing number of prizes that Pierre had won (a hundred prizes and honourable mentions in seven years) and stated that he had performed with great distinction in all fields. Pierre was, he added, diligent and intelligent, though a bit timid and his own most severe critic. He was "a manly character, a desired companion, and a perfect gentleman." His determination was exceptional: in the past year, when he broke his leg in a skiing accident, Boulin continued, Pierre chose not to take a comfortable break at home; "instead, he became a boarder at the college, prepared for classes in the sick room and went to each course in a wheelchair. The decision was entirely his," he explained, "because his mother and his sister had not yet returned from a trip to Europe." He had demonstrated the manliness that Cecil Rhodes so prized, and he was developing a strong personality and character little by little. Boulin sent the letter to Grace, requesting that she not reveal its contents to Pierre. One suspects she did.

The family's Liberal friend Alex Gourd was asked to supply a letter of support for Trudeau's nomination for the scholarship. In it he listed the many awards Pierre had won and drew particular notice to *Dupés*, the work by the young playwright. After mentioning the numerous sports in which Pierre participated, he noted that he was fluently bilingual, his mother being "Scottish"—a description increasingly used by Pierre himself. Like Boulin, Gourd also suggested that the young man was "timid," but, in his view, the reserve derived from a lack of life experience. A final letter came from a Montreal city official, who emphasized the "affection mixed with respect" that Pierre showed towards his family, particularly his mother.

Pierre had to compose an essay for the Rhodes Committee. He offered to write it in English, but "being a French-Canadian student of a French-Canadian college," he thought the committee would prefer that he present it in French. He began by admitting the difficulty of writing about his interests and hopes, and then he continued with a defence of his education. First in his life came religion, which had universal application; then came study at Brébeuf, which had prepared him well for future public life. He pointed to the diversity of his studies and to his own tendency to grasp new experiences. He was, he noted in English, a "Jack of all trades." After listing an exhausting number of extracurricular activities, he said that this thirst for diversity had affected his career choice. Very simply, he stated, "I have chosen a political career." He defined politics broadly and indicated that both his own capacity and his particular circumstances would determine whether such a career was in politics itself, in the diplomatic service, or even in journalism. In any case, Pierre said that he was choosing his educational path so he might prepare quickly for public life.

To this end, he continued, he had studied public speaking and had published many articles in *Brébeuf*. He rejected demagoguery and political jobbery, arguing that the politician must have "a perfect understanding of men and a knowledge of their rights and duties." That was a tall order and good reason to study "Philosophy-Politics-Economics" at Oxford and, if it was not too much, modern history as well. His ultimate goal was a law degree. Finally, after raising the issue of what Oxford would mean for his "French self," he provided his own answer that the intimate contact with English culture would serve to broaden him. Rhodes himself had famously said, "So much to do, so little time in which to do it." Like Rhodes, Pierre Trudeau stated that he, too, possessed "an inextinguishable passion for action."[43]

But it was not to be. In January 1940 the Rhodes officials awarded the scholarship to another applicant. If Trudeau had won the Rhodes and gone to England, he would have become much less French and more a part of the Anglo-American world. He seemed to anticipate that fate. As editor of *Brébeuf*, he wrote that the journal had decided not to express any defined opinion on the subject of the war during the fall of 1939.[44] That public position echoed the private thoughts expressed in his diary. He did not initially oppose the war, reflecting the attitude of his church and probably that of most of his teachers. The archbishop of Quebec, Cardinal Villeneuve, took a clear stand for the Allies by asking God "to hear our supplications and that the forces of evil may be overthrown and peace restored to a distracted world."[45] Trudeau's presence at Liberal rallies with his mother and Liberal family friends suggests that he probably would have voted Liberal against Maurice Duplessis—as his mother surely did. But because he was not yet twenty-one, the voting age, he did not have to make that choice.

Everything changed in 1940. Jerome Kagan has noted how "adolescents, who are beginning to synthesize the assumptions they will rely on for the rest of their lives, are unusually receptive to historical events that challenge existing beliefs." Whether in Ireland at Easter 1916, Prague or Paris in spring 1968, or Montreal in 1940, adolescents are keen witnesses as history "tears a hole in the fabric of consensual assumptions." Young minds fly through that hole, Kagan wrote, "into a space free of hoary myth to invent a new conception of self, ethics, and society." With Pierre, some myths lingered, but in 1940 the conception changed.[46]

His contemporary and friend of the 1950s, the sociologist Marcel Rioux, later wrote that, for him and his generation, the war completely changed the direction of their lives. Their understanding of society and, especially, of the relationship between the economically dominant anglophone minority and the poorer francophone majority altered dramatically. Rebellion took many forms, whether at classical colleges or in the working-class areas of Montreal. For Pierre Trudeau, son of a French businessman and an English (now always termed Scottish) mother, this transformation was very turbulent.

—

The war made Trudeau into a Quebec nationalist. The ambiguities that had marked his writings and thought in the 1930s began slowly to disappear. He was well prepared: he knew the nationalist arguments and had repeated them to the nationalist priests at Brébeuf and to a broader audience in *Dupés*. Although he had serious reservations about the stronger nationalist arguments made by "our exalted patriots," he increasingly regarded his heritage as primarily French, and his education constantly strengthened that belief. When the Canadian government imposed the Defence of Canada Regulations that limited free speech and invoked conscription for Home Defence in 1940, Pierre suddenly saw history differently. He became, in his own phrase, deeply concerned about the fate of his "French self."

But the change came gradually, as he worked diligently to stand first at Brébeuf and as he edited, rather eccentrically, the student newspaper. As editor, he took a "hands-off" approach and put much energy into a "Tribune libre" edition where free expression was permitted. He was too busy to write to Camille very often, but at last on March 30, 1940, he sent her a long letter to fill her in on his activities. He wrote in English, even though Camille's French had improved after her time in Paris, but he took her to task for her earlier comment that his meanings were often obscure and his prose too complex. He admitted, however, that others at Brébeuf had made the same complaint. The letter gives the flavour of his life at the time and contrasts with the impression presented in his notebooks, where he concentrates on philosophical works and ignores the movies and concerts he attended and the popular books he read. After a long apology for the delay in writing, he began:

> And to make a long story less long, you find me with a pen in my hand, a happy Easter on my lips, and very little in the back of my head. But shall we get down to facts?
>
> During the past month I have done a great deal of most anything. Naturally we were overworked in school. As we finish a month ahead of the other classes, our teachers want to cram everything in at once.
>
> Then I have been reading quite a bit of "Dominique" by Eugène Fromentin [a French author and painter]. In the line of plays, I was at [Canadian director and actor] Maurice Evans' staging of Hamlet. It was a masterpiece of producing. I found his playing very comprehensive yet too declaratory. I saw Rostand's "Aiglon" which had some very high spots.

He went on to say that he had read Charles Péguy's *Notre jeunesse* and *Frivolimus '40*, a good example of Montreal low humour. He also saw French director Sacha Guitry's movie *Le roman d'un tricheur*, which he declared "insipid." He went to two concerts, one a Red Cross benefit which combined "the two Montreal Symphonic Orchestras," but "it was remarkable by its lack of anything remarkable." To all that, he told Camille, "you can add a few conferences [lectures] by the French philosopher [Jacques] Maritain," who strongly supported the Allied war effort. Given Trudeau's increasing nationalism and opposition to war, it's interesting that he listened carefully to the liberal and pro-Allied Maritain at this time.[47]

Pierre told Camille that his hockey team was in the play-offs and that he was simply "crazy" about skiing. He boasted that he had bought "jumping skis" (which, unhappily, were soon to break his leg). He said that the whole family had skied during the Christmas holiday and he and Tip had spent time together on the "superb" hills at Mont Tremblant. He went on to describe the controversies he had proudly stirred at Brébeuf:

> And now to end this one topic (myself conversation), I will please you by admitting that you are not alone to find my style obscure and incoherent: the last edition of "Brébeuf" had a "Tribune libre" in which several fellows took a few cracks at my essays. Evidently I could not let them have the last word, so I answered right back with good style . . .
>
> By the way I also published an article on Rut-thinking and standardized education that we have discussed together. It caused a scandal in the cloister, and I was called up to explain my views. It was even funnier because Tippy at the same time wrote an article on individualism. But I leave this to some other time for I am anxious to talk about you, my dear Camille.

After inquiring about her college, how she looked, and what she planned to do, he made a characteristically lame joke: "I think I'll have my graduation diploma pickled; that's because

I can't get stewed." In France, Camille had developed an interest in philosophy and in Freud and Proust.* Suddenly, Pierre, in a pattern that he followed later in his relationships with women, became earnest with her:

> Such deep thinking brings me to the subject of Philosophy and to your concept of philosophical ethics. Honestly, I think we could have a peach of an argument on the subject. Firstly, I would tell you to read [Alexis Carrel's] "L'homme, cet inconnu" to find out how bad it is to always do what pleases you. Secondly I should ask you to demonstrate, either by examples of metaphysics, your theory on how "one thing that might be wrong for the whole world to do, might be perfectly alright in one particular case." In other words, if all men are participants of the human nature, why shouldn't all men obey one universal natural law? Thirdly, I should inquire why you say it took over 2000 years for society to catch on to

---

* Camille introduced Pierre to Proust in a serious way. He told her: I will "always remain indebted to you for having set me under Proust's influence." He had "heard much about him" but much "was naught in comparison with what I found in reality. What power of expression, what penetration in his observations, what suppleness of a style that can follow a concept into its most subtle relations, explore the secrets of its development and verily track it down to its birth in the proudest depths of the soul as surely as a hound will track a bleeding prey." As this sentence indicates, Proust had affected his prose style, and not for the better. The fact that Trudeau had not encountered the giant Proust until he was almost twenty-one reflects upon the deficiencies in his education—it had extensive French literary content, but only selectively so. Trudeau to Corriveau, Oct. 29, 1940, TP, vol. 45, file 5.

itself. Do you mean that the birth of Christ marked the beginning of the period when society misunderstood itself, or of the period when it understood itself? But don't bother answering; true to your sex, you have probably changed your mind about everything in the past month, exchanging Freud's theories for Aristotle's.

Camille must have read Freud's *Civilization and Its Discontents*, a study that had its faults but was infinitely superior to Carrel's book. *L'homme, cet inconnu* is highly elitist and racist and, because of Carrel's repute as a Nobel Prize winner in medicine, his argument gave intellectual weight to Hitler's extermination policies. The book's "woman is weaker" strain is also reflected in Pierre's comments to Camille. He indicated no understanding of how Carrel conflicted with Jacques Maritain or, for that matter, Tip's article on individualism.

In an addendum to his letter, he signalled his confusion about himself and his beliefs. Apologizing for failing to write to an apparent mutual friend, Pierre wrote: "I should like to call it laziness; yet it truthfully is nothing but lack of genius. I, who always believed myself simple and 'like unto a little child,' have realized that I am, unfortunately, a complicated adult unable to speak a simple thought, without forethought and afterthought." He was, very slowly, becoming an adult, but a complicated one.[48] Given that Trudeau would turn twenty-one that year, he appears astonishingly adolescent in this letter. He wants to be a contrarian, to escape the "ruts," but his education seems to have left him adrift as powerful new waves swept over his world. He was well read but not yet well educated.

—

After he lost the Rhodes competition, Pierre Trudeau decided to stay in Quebec and to study law at the Université de Montréal—with the intention of entering politics. He had consulted widely, asking even Henri Bourassa for direction. Edmond Montpetit, the most prominent Quebec economist, advised him to study law, followed by economics and the social sciences. Father Bernier was involved in the final decision, in mid-June 1940. Trudeau told him that he had considered a career in chemistry or in medicine, with a psychiatric speciality, or, alternatively, in "politics," which he believed required a legal degree. When Pierre decided to rule out chemistry, on the grounds that it was "as good to govern men as atoms," Bernier accepted his final decision in favour of politics, but insisted that his former student should always maintain his interest in the arts. He explained, as Pierre noted in his journal: "So many worthy men, like Papa, had been compelled to work to earn their living" that they were unable to enjoy the fruits of their earlier studies. They both agreed that a man of principle should "have a mystique," and Pierre resolved to give fifteen to twenty minutes every day to "meditate on the goals of man, the Creator, the tasks to do, morality etc. and then conclude with a true prayer, a conversation with God." They also concurred on the need to maintain an ascetic life. Pierre recorded but did not comment on Bernier's advice that, in relationships with young women, one should not make "the least sensual concession." However, he agreed that "it was bad to work too much," no doubt recalling his father's early death. He concluded his entry on their discussion with a pledge to read literature more widely and to continue to study theology.[49]

A few weeks earlier, Pierre had expressed the same sentiments to a Camp Ahmek friend, Hugh Kenner, who, later, became an eminent literary critic. As he prepared to leave Brébeuf, Trudeau told Kenner that it had been "such fun probing into the mysteries uncovered by the study of metaphysics and ethics . . . Personally," he added, "it was with great awe that I came to the conclusion that space was only limited by God himself; that somewhere beyond our universe and all the universes, millions of light years away, out where matter ceased to be possible, there exists space conceivable, that is to say the Conceiver." Cosmology, Trudeau declared, would become his second focus; the first, of course, remained literature. And, as for so many others, literature would play a major role in making Trudeau a revolutionary nationalist at this time.[50]

In June, the same month Trudeau graduated, France fell. Immediately, the call for conscription echoed throughout English Canada as the British, the Free French, and a few Canadians fled Dunkirk in the famous defeat that became "their finest hour." In France itself many attributed the defeat to the secularism and socialism of the Republic and saw the creation of Vichy, the German puppet government under First World War hero Marshal Pétain, as a base from which to build a new France—one more Catholic and less corrupt than the previous regime. These views found strong support in conservative circles in Quebec, to the annoyance of many in Ottawa who were concentrating on the threat of invasion to Britain. Paul Gérin-Lajoie, the scion of one of Quebec's leading families, Trudeau's predecessor as editor of *Brébeuf*, and later an eminent public servant, wrote in the college newspaper in February 1941 that French democracy had been hopeless and that it must be replaced by a corporatist state based on the family—a system that recognized the French people's obvious need for authority. Drawing on the papal encyclical *Quadragesimo Anno* and, in Quebec, on traditional nationalist distrust of the impact of modernization, corporatism was a rejection of capitalism, socialism, and liberalism in favour of a more Catholic, authoritarian, and self-sufficient state. Mussolini's Italy, Salazar's Portugal, and, after 1940, Pétain's Vichy were sometimes cited as models of a corporatist state.* Trudeau came to share most of these views, and he kept Gérin-Lajoie's article among his papers.

The historian Esther Delisle has argued that, as early as 1937, Trudeau was secretly an ardent nationalist dedicated to Quebec independence, and that, while still at Brébeuf, he became a member of Les Frères Chausseurs, or LX, a secret revolutionary cell plotting the overthrow of the existing government. Although evidence of his early nationalism and even his sympathies for independence began to emerge before Trudeau wrote his own memoirs, he never responded to this charge. In the memoirs, he portrays himself as an anti-nationalist throughout the earlier period and depicts the war as a mild deviation from that path, one caused by the wrongs of wartime. "The war," he wrote, "was an undeniably important reality, but a very distant one. Moreover, it was part of current events, and, as I have explained, they did not interest me very much."

That account is disingenuous at best. The information about Trudeau's involvement in a secret revolutionary cell came initially

---

* Corporatist thought, the standard text on modern Quebec rightly declares, "is not easy to summarize." Essentially, "its vision was of all social groups, organized in 'corporations' or '[intermediate] bodies' dedicated to the pursuit of the common good, working together in harmony to ensure order and social peace. In this way, class 'collaboration would replace class struggle: employers and workers in the same economic sector would belong to the same corporation and work together for the advancement both of their sector and of the nation as a whole . . . Parliamentary democracy was a source of dissension, and corporatism would replace it with a unanimous society in which each person, imbued with the national mystique, would work towards—and at the same time benefit from—the general harmony and prosperity.'" Paul-André Linteau, René Durocher, Jean-Claude Robert, and François Ricard, *Quebec since 1930*, trans. Robert Chodos and Ellen Garmaise (Toronto: James Lorimer, 1991), 79.

from two sources: from his contemporary François-Joseph Lessard, an important member of Les Frères Chausseurs, who claimed in a book published in 1979 that Hertel had introduced Trudeau to the group in 1937 as the Simón Bolívar of French Canada; and from François Hertel himself, who said in 1977 that Trudeau was a founder of the group and, at that time, an angry nationalist who had battled with the police in 1937–38 during the centennial celebrations of the earlier Rebellions.[51] Trudeau did admit to interviewers that he was present at student protests against André Malraux and the representatives of the Spanish Republic, but he claimed it was the noise of the crowd that had attracted him to the event.[52] His journal clearly refutes that explanation.

Without doubt, Trudeau would later deceive interviewers who asked him where he was and what he believed when the Second World War was fought. Surprisingly, much of the evidence was already in the public domain, though Delisle was the first to put it all together: the testimony of Hertel and Lessard; press clippings about a speech and a trial following an anti-Semitic riot; and articles in the Université de Montréal student newspaper, *Le Quartier Latin*, where Trudeau's virulent opposition to the war was publicly expressed. There was even a question in the House of Commons from a Social Credit MP on April 5, 1977, when Trudeau seemed to admit that he had been a member of a "separatist" secret society. Yet before Delisle and, more recently, Max and Monique Nemni drew attention to this evidence, there was no public discussion about it, and, astonishingly, no journalist "followed up" on the question asked in the House.[53]

Based on Trudeau's complete personal papers, the evidence is overwhelming that Trudeau did become a strong Quebec nationalist and that, during the war, he associated with supporters of "Laurentie," who espoused an independent French Catholic state. How did the fan of American movies, the participant in Liberal rallies in the 1939 Quebec election, the student who was suspicious of "exalted patriots" and proud of both his "English" blood and his "Elliott" name so quickly become a revolutionary separatist? The path, as always with Trudeau, has unexpected turns.

Trudeau's papers suggest that, in the pre-war years, because of his education and experience, Pierre was capable at certain moments of being strongly nationalist. Conversely, he reacted against that same nationalism when it touched on those of mixed English/French blood. He correctly told biographers that, at Brébeuf, he had shocked the priests and his classmates when he applauded Wolfe's victory over Montcalm on the Plains of Abraham. At other times, he was a strong defender of nationalist positions—on one occasion burning the Union Jack with a bunch of Brébeuf boys. In his own mind, he had established a sense of balance that occasionally tilted when, on the one hand, he attended an English-Canadian camp or, on the other, when a student accused him of betraying the French "race." Still, his heritage was primarily French and Catholic.

As France fell and the Canadian government introduced conscription for home defence, the Trudeau family was on its way to Old Orchard Beach. There they received a telegram from Grace's brother, Gordon, who lived in France and now asked for money to help him flee from the Nazis. Pierre recorded this "bad news" but, by the next morning, paid little attention to the crisis in Europe and the anti-conscription marches in Montreal as he slept in, did some oil painting, and remarked on the "perfect tranquility" with so few people on the beach. A few days later the full force of what was happening in Europe struck Pierre—perhaps because Camille was fiercely anti-Nazi and pro-Allies, even though she was an American. He wrote in his journal that the Germans were now in Paris. "Ah! the pigs," he exclaimed. He saw a newsreel on the fall of Paris that infuriated him; it was, he wrote, the work of "the dirty Boche." He decided he would join the Canadian Army to fight. In the meantime, he had to return for graduation.[54]

This evidence decisively disproves the claims made later by Hertel and some later historians that Trudeau had early anti-war or even pro-fascist sympathies. However, it is true that his attitude in June 1940 is surprising, given some of his notebook jottings on works by Alexis Carrel and others. Very simply, he is contradictory and conflicted.

—

Meanwhile, the Trudeau family had decided to take a train and car trip across Canada and down the west coast of the United States. It began on June 26, and Pierre's admiration for what he saw is clear in his notes. North of Superior, he wrote, "Quel pays admirable!" as he watched a splendid sunset. On arrival in Winnipeg, he described the city as "a drop of oil on the plains." As he surveyed the vastness of the land, he again pondered whether law and politics was the right career choice: "Would I be capable of leading the people of Canada," he asked, "or even the people of my own family?" In any event, he would follow where God led him, though, he added accurately, he would not be surprised if "the road has many forks, ditches and detours."

He had vowed to keep a psychological journal during the trip, but the demands of daily travel were too much. Still, he thought about what fate had in store for him. He worried about his timidity with women, in particular, and humanity, in general, and resolved to look people directly in the eye — something he apparently had found difficult earlier. But he did not lack self-confidence:

> I must become a great man. It's amusing to say that! I'm often surprised to think, as I walk alone, do others not see the signs, don't they sense that I bear within me, the makings of a future head of state or a well-known diplomat or an eminent lawyer? I am frankly astonished that those things

do not shine through. And I have compassion for those who will not be able to boast in ten or twenty years of having seen me a single time.

He believed he had made the right career choice but recognized that he might change course. For a man, he noted, career is essential. "In a young woman you admire what she is; in the case of a young man, you admire what he will become." He fretted about his strong attraction to women, although he admitted that the list of those he knew was "perplexingly short." Camille came first, followed by "Micheline, Myrna, and Alice Ann." Obviously, in his choice of women, Trudeau was—and remained—thoroughly multicultural. The danger, he warned himself, was that he would fall in love and marry before he completed his education. He concluded his self-assessment: "The moral of all this is that I must continually work for perfection and become likable, obliging, and gallant (what a word!)."

The trip continued, and, as he realized, it was as difficult to rule his family as Canada itself. In Edmonton they stayed at the grand Macdonald Hotel, where they met up with his Brébeuf friend Jean-Baptiste Boulanger and his family. The encounter was important because Jean-Baptiste, a Franco-Albertan, later became part of the secret society advocating a separatist state for Quebec. Together, they toured the cathedral at St. Albert, realizing, first hand, how far the French presence had extended. There was no talk of independence at that time, of course, and Trudeau passed on through the mountains at Jasper: "The first impression was profoundly moving," he wrote. He remained deeply impressed after they unloaded Suzette's Buick and drove through the Columbia Ice Fields to Lake Louise—where, on July 1, they celebrated Dominion Day.

There Suzette became sick, so Pierre had to drive through the mountains. It terrified him, not least because the car had faulty shock absorbers. Finally they reached Vancouver, where the natural setting impressed him but the university did not. Then, on July 9, they set off to drive down the Pacific Coast and have the car repaired. Pierre reflected upon the trip one day and pronounced it very worthwhile, especially from the point of view of the family. "We discussed a range of things," he noted in his journal, "assayed our faults, and recalled old times." He was more candid with Camille, telling her: "We are still having a riotous time, what with the scenery and the family arguments (some of them are honeys)." In his own case, he used the trip to develop "conversational arts," which he believed he lacked. He deliberately tried to draw strangers into conversation with him and looked them in the eye as he had planned. It was, of course, all good training for politics.

Finally, on July 22, they reached Los Angeles. The family went to the Hollywood Bowl, where they saw Paul Robeson in an "unforgettable" performance. But that was the best of Los Angeles for Pierre, who betrayed his Brébeuf training in his assessment of the entertainment capital: "I can't wait to escape this city," he complained. "I'm sweltering." There was no "ozone" in the air and too much carbon dioxide. "The people have the appearance of a dead fish," while the women did not look natural—all of them seemed to be waiting for a director to pass by. At this point in the trip he was tired of writing, so he brought his account to an end. At least, he noted, he had served "the needs of my biographers." Indeed, he had.

—

America was still neutral in the war, and the conflict seemed distant in Pierre's account as June turned into July. Still, he remained strongly opposed to the fascists, writing on July 19 that Gordon Elliott had finally reached England as the war continued "its hideous advance." Despite some later claims that Trudeau admired Hitler, he expressed loathing for him in his private journal. Hitler, he wrote, threatened to "exterminate the English," who were nevertheless putting up a brave fight. He had heard little of what had happened in France. "What an affair! But good night: that's my solution." He learned that there would be a "mobilization" on August 23 and wondered whether it would "spoil our trip."[55]

It did not spoil the trip, but Montreal was a changed city on his return. After the fall of France in June 1940 and the imposition of conscription for home defence, Camillien Houde, the Montreal mayor and his father's old friend, was interned for the duration of the war under the Defence of Canada Regulations because he had called for resistance to conscription. Before Charles Trudeau's death, when Houde, then the Quebec Conservative leader, had come to the Lac Tremblant cottage, Pierre would hear their loud voices complaining about the "Liberal machine." According to an accountant who had worked for Charles, Houde would drive into one of the Trudeau gas stations and say he needed "oxygen." The accountant would go to the safe and hand over one hundred dollars in cash.[56] The arrest of Houde and others shocked Pierre and his friends, and the war that had been so distant while he was on the Pacific shores became much closer.

It was not a war they wanted to fight. Of his 1939–40 class at Brébeuf, only one out of forty entered the Canadian military, in comparison with three who entered the priesthood, six who studied law, and nine who went into medicine.[57] At the Université de Montréal in March 1940, a poll showed that 900 opposed any form of conscription and only 35 approved; in the law school Trudeau entered that fall, the vote was 53 to 3. Daniel Johnson, a student leader (and future Quebec premier), had already declared in the student newspaper his strong opposition to a future war where Canada's interests were not involved. Now, with the "phony war" ending and conscription for home defence near, a young law student, Jean Drapeau, the future mayor of Montreal, also wrote an article in which he warned that another fight against conscription must begin, and he issued a call for vigilance.[58]

Once the *National Resources Mobilization Act* was passed, Trudeau and his friends were compelled to enrol in the Canadian Officers Training Corps and to engage in regular drill and summer training. He had been eager to join up as German tanks entered Paris, but things changed after he began law school. In the fall of 1940, when he entered the Université de Montréal, Trudeau immediately attended Abbé Groulx's history lectures. Of course, he had read Groulx's numerous books and articles, but his earlier comments did not suggest that the Abbé impressed him greatly. His decision to take this class reflected both his revived nationalism and the influence of Hertel, who was increasingly a guest at the family home. Trudeau never told interviewers later that he had studied with the Abbé, yet his detailed notes for the lectures exist among his papers. And, although his early encounter with Groulx had left him with the impression that the esteemed historian lacked oratorical skills, the content of the course intrigued him now. His notes indicate that Groulx was characteristically silent on questions such as separation and, seemingly, the war. Like any good historian, he provoked students to think about consequences—in his case, the consequences of the Conquest of New France. It was the will of God for the heirs of the defeated in 1760 to maintain French Catholic culture in North America.[59]

The Abbé left another clear mark on Trudeau: in his lectures, he emphasized the importance of the Statute of Westminster, giving it an exceptional constitutional significance in granting Canada freedom from the British Empire—an interpretation that went far beyond what the government of the day accepted. For many years afterwards, on December 11, Trudeau wrote "Statute of Westminster Day" on letters instead of the actual date. And, as he attended Groulx's lectures, his life at school became associated with nationalist causes. For example, in the fall of 1940 he took part in a satirical farce at the university that ridiculed politicians and denounced conscription. Among the players were Jean Drapeau and Jean-Jacques Bertrand, who later became premier of Quebec while Trudeau was prime minister.

Even his social life became buoyantly nationalist: Pierre kept a dance card from December 1940 on which he wrote, on the front, "Praise to liberty," and, on the back, "Long live liberty and the debutants."[60] To Camille, he wrote in French for the first time, thanking her for calling him "my dearest friend" and saying, "It is impossible to know fully the value of a friend, of someone who penetrates our inescapable solitude." But their romance was chilling, perhaps because of his new attitudes. He objected strongly when she ridiculed the decision of his friend "Roland" to become a monk, especially as she had always thought he was a "Don Juan." "The idea of getting up in the middle of the night to sing is perfectly ridiculous," Camille declared. An angry Trudeau found her remark "shocking."[61]

By the spring of 1941 he was complaining to her not only about law school — "A genuine lawyer is only supposed to study six times longer than what I have; no wonder most of them are idiots" — but also about the Officers Training Corps, which he had earlier told her he was eager to join. Now it would be "more thrilling to go to the Concentration Camp* or to the Front."[62] But he joined the Corps and, with resentment, did his service with many of his Brébeuf friends. Charles Lussier, a fellow nationalist then and a distinguished Canadian public servant later, remembered a revealing incident from that time: "One day our cadet captain marched us over to a depot where we were

* A camp for war protestors in Canada.

to move some shells. The officer in charge was English and gave instructions entirely in that language." The eight trainees were all French Canadians and all obeyed except one — Pierre Trudeau — who refused to move because, he said in French, he did not understand the command. After an officer repeated the order in very bad French, Trudeau replied in unaccented English, "Good, now I understand you."[63]

Liberty meant resistance, and resist Trudeau did, whether it was a unilingual officer or a bureaucratic directive. Yet his rebellion had limits. When, for example, he wanted to read Marx's *Das Kapital* and other works on "the Index" (the Catholic restricted list), including Rousseau's *Social Contract*, he dutifully asked the archbishop of Montreal for permission. After an initial refusal, he received the approval, although "His Excellency" urged him to treat the books with great care and guard them closely.[64] No doubt he did, but in other respects neither he nor some of his friends heeded the archbishop's counsel in 1941 and 1942 that French Catholics in Quebec should show restraint in opposing conscription and the war effort.

François Hertel was now openly separatist, and his 1942 study of personalism called for "men of action" who would make a free choice "to live." Trudeau took the advice. He became ever more drawn to the widening circle around the priest and wrote him several admiring letters. Hertel, who was an enthusiastic patron of modernism in the arts, introduced the Trudeau family to the surrealist and cubist artist Alfred Pellan, who had returned to Montreal from Paris after the Nazi invasion. Highly cultured, Hertel impressed Grace and her children, and they frequently invited him to their home and wisely took his advice on purchasing art. Hertel paid Grace the highest compliment in August 1941 when he wrote to Pierre that she was "the least bourgeois woman he had encountered in his life."[65] He encouraged Tip's growing interest in architecture and music, as well as Pierre's in literature. In this complex man, religion, literature, and politics mingled with romantic notions of revolution. Although he admired the French liberal philosopher Jacques Maritain, he did not follow his politics. Like many European personalists, including Emmanuel Mounier himself initially, Hertel saw much in Vichy to commend—particularly its "Catholic" sense of order, anti-capitalism, and corporatist rhetoric.

In 1941, when the Jesuit hierarchy exiled him to Sudbury for having a negative influence on the young, Hertel became Trudeau's confidant.* He encouraged Trudeau to work with a fellow student, Roger Rolland, to produce a literary review, while also expressing his firm opinions against conscription and the Catholic hierarchy and in favour of Pétain. Roger, the son of a major French-Canadian entrepreneur, had first captured Trudeau's attention when he lit a cigarette with a two-dollar bill, reminding him of the flamboyant ways of his father. He soon became Pierre's close friend (and, later, his speech writer when Trudeau was prime minister).[66] Hertel approved thoroughly of François-Joseph Lessard's "revolutionary" activities through his secret society, though he considered him a bit

---

* In July 1942 Hertel was told that his writings under his pseudonym did not bring credit to the Jesuit Order. While his influence on the young and his knowledge of theological doctrine were admitted to be great, his teaching was dangerous: "It is not by light talks on love or jokes or similar ways that one gives the young a taste for the serious, the profound, and the solid nor do they become aware of the gravity of the problems they face in their individual, family and social life." He threatened to quit the order but remained until 1946, when Trudeau encountered him once more in Paris. E. Papillon, sj, to Rodolphe Dubé, sj, July 18, 1942, Fonds Hertel, Archives Nationales du Québec-Montréal.

intense — as when Lessard suggested that Winston Churchill himself had intervened to send Hertel to Sudbury.[67]

The correspondence between Hertel and Trudeau began rather formally, with Hertel signing his name Rodolphe Dubé, SJ, but soon he developed a remarkable candour. Hertel was clearly Lessard's patron, and he asked Trudeau to be patient with his excitable colleague. Both men believed that Trudeau's major contribution to the revolutionary movement would be intellectual, and in October 1941 Trudeau mocked Lessard's political espionage in a letter to Hertel which clearly indicates that he was already a part of Lessard's secret society: "Meanwhile Lessard constantly has some missions of extreme delicacy to be undertaken, some deeply serious events to announce. I have some regret that he has taken me to be a confidant. I feel a certain embarrassment in displaying gushing enthusiasm when he reveals the exact number of fire hydrants in Ste-Hyacinthe." The revolutionary was well-meaning, the activities intriguing — but Lessard was too earnest.[68]

As their relationship developed, Trudeau flattered Hertel, calling him "un grand homme," a great man, while Hertel, in turn, told Pierre he now had the opportunity to be the man of action that Hertel himself had always wanted to be. In this sense, Lessard, however irritating, offered opportunity. In response to a letter from Pierre asking Hertel to explain who he really was, the priest wrote an extraordinary reply — distancing himself by using the third person:

> His friends are largely young men. And yet he's in no way homosexual. He differs in this respect from a certain number of the *Amérique française* [review established by Rolland and others] collaborators. Have no fear, it's not about the two Trudeaus and Père Bernier and [the unidentified] Jacqueline.
>
> And so this strange character is a softy deep down. He possesses a sensitivity that was once touchiness. He now

knows how to forgive and forget everything, and even fails to notice [insults] when it comes to his friends. The others he can forgive also. As often as possible he simply forgets. Above all, he has resolved to ignore petty reprisals.

Loving his friends is his life. Yet this love—and that's as far as it goes—however platonic and platonist, is demanding as Hell. To his friends, this "pilgrim of the Absolute" . . . desires the highest good more than anything. He would be much sorrier—I'm sincere here—to learn of Pierre Trudeau's death than to learn he was living common-law. And this is why, however broad-minded and tolerant of the tolerable he may be, the said Hertel's ears perk up when he foresees any potential danger that could be lethal to his friends' souls. That is why he doesn't like Gide [whose tolerance of homosexuality was controversial in Catholic circles], and dreads this elegant and naively perverse man because he may remove the fresh blossoms of those of his friends who are still blossoming. As far as a certain Pierre Trudeau is concerned, he believes his cynicism and maturity are sufficiently developed to keep him from being adversely affected by Gide. However, he would not like the said Trudeau to think that all his friends have reached the necessary degree of shamelessness to assimilate Gide without allowing themselves to be spoiled.

Hertel, in fact, doesn't like revolution the way Trudeau does. The latter loves it as one does a mistress. Hertel married revolution out of duty, because he had first given her children, and he does not wish to abandon them . . .

All in all, the moral portrait of the said Hertel—which we are currently sketching—is quite handsome. However, the hero is aware he is more handsome in his dreams than in reality. While on this subject, today this strange individual has chosen to add to this moral portrait his physical portrait. There are two. One for Pierre—which shows the tense, hardened Hertel, so fond of the "coups d'état" (although he has never himself seen or executed one); and [the other photo], Hertel, *par excellence*, the great Hertel.

Egads! I almost forgot the third: one for Madame Trudeau, in which she will easily recognize Hertel "à l'américaine," the one who offered to take her to a baseball game last year, while her two sons studied (the studious one) and tinkled away at the piano (the artistic one). A strong mother whose sons have been made effeminate by legal and literary hairsplitting was worthy to accompany the strong man from the Mauricie to these virile games.[69]

This letter makes several points clear. Whatever his faults, Lessard and his fellow revolutionaries were "Hertel's children," a fact the hierarchy recognized in moving him to Sudbury. The other references to homosexuality are obscure, but Hertel, though clearly regarding homosexuality as sinful, banters here and later about the physical appearance of young men. When he received a photograph of Trudeau in December, for instance, one he called a "physical photograph," he said it was "great. It could be Tahiti! Ah! If only Gauguin had known you." In the same letter his definition of his "revolutionary creed" had echoes of French Catholic thinkers of the thirties:

God is strong and pure and lucid. We are weak, carnal, and blind as bats. But do we blindly throw ourselves to God in order that he might give us all that we radically lack? The only great originality of my peculiar thinking is to have understood this: the close alliance between Christianity and Revolution. The all-embracing Christian revolutionary, practising and devout, this is the product I am striving to create and protect. This, because I have understood that he who may give his life is he, he alone, who knows how to give it without losing [its essence]; that he who is completely sincere, he alone can free himself of anti-revolutionary and bourgeois prejudices . . . The church is, at the present moment, the only possible source of revolution.

"Revolution" was a term used very casually at the time not only by the political left and right and but also by the Protestant and Catholic churches.* The Quebec Catholic hierarchy certainly did not share Hertel's views on "revolution," but the priest had allies.

Father Marie d'Anjou—one of Trudeau's four favourite teachers at Brébeuf—was even more supportive of the "revolution." The Catholic hierarchy had removed him too from Montreal, and his resentment was profound. Hertel believed that his fellow priest was his closest ally in confronting these church leaders. In his correspondence, d'Anjou always called Montreal "Ville-Marie," and he cherished the dream of Laurentie, the independent French Catholic state.[70] During his absence from Montreal, he wrote often

---

* French intellectual debates had a great influence during these years on the rhetoric of revolution in Quebec. In his history of postwar Europe, the historian Tony Judt has emphasized how the "bipolar" politics of France, along with the myth of revolution and the acceptance of "violence," was at the centre of public policy. He cites the postwar example of the radical politician Edouard Herriot, who announced in 1944 that normal politics could not be re-established until France passed through a "bloodbath." His language, Judt adds, "did not sound out of the ordinary to French ears, even coming as it did from a pot-bellied provincial parliamentarian of the political center." Within French intellectual and political circles, there was general if vague acceptance of the idea that "historical change and purgative bloodshed go hand in hand." Hertel clearly was part of this heritage in both his language and his concept of historical change. Tony Judt, *Postwar: A History of Europe since 1945* (New York: Penguin, 2005), 211.

to Lessard, and he recommended young Trudeau as the one most able to undertake various tasks for his "group."[71]

In his papers for the 1941–42 period, Pierre Trudeau has copies of a "plan" that describes a secret society which had been created some years before by three "guys" who were tired of half measures while "the people" slid downwards into the crevasse. They had read "Groulx, Péguy, Blois, Hertel, Istrati, Savard," and they believed in the immortal lessons of both history and Catholicism. The glories of New France must live beyond the granite of the monuments, they said, and the fearful, the down and out, the prostitutes, the blasphemers, and the drunkards who besmirch that tradition must be destroyed. Revolution is the daughter of "the Fatherland," the plan writers noted:

> Political and military revolution is but a stage, an accident of Revolution, as wars are but cataclysms of history. This is what the revolutionaries are, philosophers and doctrinaires. Of the philosophers of the Laurentian Revolution, one preached to the people the dogma of homeland, the other promulgated the dogma of hope to the desperate. Revolution, in this common view, of which we are the proof, is mankind who, in spite of everything, his selfishness, his cowardice, his passions, his flaws, the number and power of his adversaries, his failures, his mistakes, advances relentlessly. He, in the midst of all, sword in hand, despite obstacles, strikes again and again, until they fall.[72]

The plan identifies three "types" who had met together and organized this revolutionary cell. They were Lessard, Trudeau, and Jean-Baptiste Boulanger, the Brébeuf friend Trudeau had met on his cross-Canada tour in Edmonton. In his memoirs, Trudeau says that Boulanger and he "decided together to read over one summer the great works of political writing—Aristotle,

Plato, Rousseau's *Social Contract*, Montesquieu, and others . . . Boulanger knew more than me in this field, and that was why I hung around with him." In fact, Boulanger's course of studies included Georges Sorel, Leon Trotsky, and other theorists of revolution. Both also read the French authoritarian Charles Maurras, whose works became the pillars of Vichy.[73]

The barricades beckoned—and Trudeau rushed to the defence of the cause. The first battle came with the referendum on conscription. After the Japanese attack on Pearl Harbor on December 7, the Canadian government moved quickly to full mobilization. Ernest Lapointe, who had promised no conscription, had died, and the English newspapers demanded that Canada now respond as America and Britain already had. The wily Prime Minister Mackenzie King decided he should call for a referendum that would ask Canadians not a direct question on conscription itself but whether they would release the government from the pledge that there would be no conscription for overseas service. The date was set for April 27, 1942.

In Quebec, André Laurendeau organized the No side quickly under the banner of the significantly named Ligue pour la défense du Canada. Trudeau's anger was deep. He had written some rough notes twelve days after Pearl Harbor. "Is it necessary to be pro-British or anti-?" The answer was clear. He boasted to Camille about a "revolution" he was planning and, in 1942, asked her to obtain for him a copy of Malaparte's *Coup d'Etat: The Technique of Revolution*. Fearing censorship at the border, he cautioned: "I am anxious to read it as soon as possible; but I doubt it would be wise to mail it to me. I seriously wonder if the officials of this pharisaic puritan government would let the thing be delivered." He concluded with the words "Thanks for your trouble, and long live liberty."[74] Out of Trotsky and other revolutionary theorists, Trudeau, Boulanger, and Lessard took the lesson that a small cell could carry out revolution effectively if it was cohesive and its plans were clear. It was, Trudeau suggested, the wave of the future. The old were the imperialists; the young, the separatists. The old did not belong to the future; they sought a solution that would maintain the status quo and allow them to play out their hand. It was already too late for that.[75]

Trudeau wrote to Hertel in January 1942 to say that the plan was moving forward, although not so effectively as he would have liked. As he had indicated earlier, he thought he could serve best intellectually—a position Hertel strongly supported. The anti-conscription movement continued to unite behind André Laurendeau, who, Hertel wrote in December 1941, was "a good man. Lots of sangfroid and vision." However, being too cerebral, he was "not a leader." Trudeau perhaps took the advice and told Hertel that "we" are trying to organize a study circle, which, under Laurendeau's direction, will examine social questions. Then he continued in a passage that, while illustrating his participation in a secret cell, revealed his doubts:

> I've told Arsenault, who is very understanding. He agrees that my work should be almost exclusively one of study . . . (with a touch of the spectacular anarchy I find indispensable). Lessard doesn't understand quite so well and is more inclined to have me play the role of mailman.
>
> I think the whole business is going badly in all respects. Too few are believers. Too weak an organization to fortify the tottering. Missed demonstrations. Too many clergy from the meek bourgeoisie . . . If it is impossible to make them see good sense and understand what's important, there must be some other way to force their hand. We'll have to see about that.

And so the "revolution" tottered forward, with Trudeau reading furiously, demonstrating regularly, and somehow crowding in his legal studies.[76]

Montreal seethed with discontent. Mayor Houde wore his prison garb; the Italians, whose main church honoured Mussolini, were adrift; the sailors fought furious battles over women in the bars near the port; and restaurants could serve only one cup of coffee or tea to each patron. On March 24, 1942, anti-conscriptionists gathered for a rally where the dissident Liberal Jean-François Pouliot was to speak with the support of the Université de Montréal student association at Jean-Talon market.[77] After the rally, a group of forty students got together at the corner of Saint-Laurent and Napoléon, in the centre of the city. Suddenly, windows shattered as young demonstrators threw stones, shouting, "Down with the Jews! Down with conscription!" The police quickly appeared and the demonstrators fled, but one fell and could not escape. In April this arrested demonstrator, Maurice Riel, a law student at the Université de Montréal, appeared in court charged with vagrancy—a favourite of Canadian police in those times. Trudeau spoke as a witness for the defence, and Riel—a Trudeau appointment to the Senate of Canada in 1973—was acquitted.[78] Meanwhile, the plan for an uprising went forward.

There were protests, even riots, and overwhelming francophone opposition to conscription. To Trudeau's despair on referendum day, Outremont stood out among the francophone population, with 15,746 voting Yes and only 9,957, No. There is no record whether Grace voted No with her son.

In his reading at this time, Trudeau focused on biographies of mystics and individuals who had confronted danger in support of Christ.[79] And many of his friends noted this sudden abstraction and mysticism in him. Already in the spring of 1941, Camille had told him that he was avoiding reality. A year later, ten days before the plebiscite, "your friend, the Great Hertel" wrote to him warning that he was becoming too abstract:

You are definitely a difficult guy to fit into day-to-day life.
It seems that you are frightened to death of coming close
to the quotidian and, therefore, the banal. Would you not,
by chance, be some type of misunderstood romantic?
Like Julien Sorel. Yet you haven't read, o chaste young
man, [Stendhal's] *Le Rouge et le Noir*. Misunderstood
romantic means, according to my worthy pen, unbalanced
by choice, in love with tension. Don't you try to avoid,
through energy and resolve, anything that could turn you
away from your beautiful spirit? Do you not seek to escape
to the higher levels than the barn floor upon which we
must keep, at whatever cost, one foot of our being?

Hertel says he [Trudeau] has both feet in the blue skies:
from time to time you come down to where mortals live to
attend embryonic riots.[80]

Through the summer, the plan continued to spin out, with
the hope that there would soon be a decisive event. Trudeau
signed his letters to Hertel "Citoyen" and to Boulanger
"Anarchiste," and he used the language of the French Revolution.
During those warm months, even his travels testified to his nationalism. In 1941 he had joined his Brébeuf classmate Guy Viau and
two others in retracing the path by canoe of the great coureurs du
bois, Pierre-Esprit Radisson and Médard Des Groseilliers. They
went along the Ottawa River, crossed Lake Timiskaming, and
eventually reached Moosonee. The journey through the wilds
of the Canadian Shield was described by a journalist as a group of
students on a "planned trip." Trudeau was enraged: he wrote to
Hertel, "Imagine then my mood when I learned that this
'arranged excursion' about which I had long dreamed, and which
was a little *my* plan . . . should take on a thoroughly bourgeois
allure. Merde!" In his description of his voyage, he emphasized
the challenge and his brave response—a pattern he followed

throughout his life. He emphasized how he ran the rapids while others portaged. As dangers mounted, rain poured, and harsh winds blew, he became stronger. "In fact, life began to be beautiful."[81]

By the following summer, Trudeau had a Harley-Davidson motorbike—already a symbol of youthful rebellion and reckless-ness long before the Hell's Angels and Marlon Brando gave the machine its swagger. Its speed was legendary; its exhaust explo-sive. For the timid Trudeau, it was the perfect accessory. He even wrote a short tribute, "Pritt Zoum Bing," for the Université de Montréal student newspaper, *Le Quartier Latin*, to the freedom motorcycles offered. During the long vacation, he decided to take two trips between sessions for his compulsory COTC training. Gabriel Filion, who accompanied him on the Harley, recalls that, on the first, they travelled "some five thousand kilometres through New Brunswick, Nova Scotia, and Prince Edward Island, sleeping in barns at night and sometimes in churches, or in houses that were being built. Most often, however, we slept in the countryside, pitching our tent in the fields or in the forest. We ate in small restaurants, and Pierre always paid the bill." On the other, they "retraced the route taken by François Paradis, the hero of *Maria Chapdelaine.*" Here the nationalist motivation seems clear as Trudeau, Filion, and another friend, Carl Dubuc, followed the path of Paradis—in the novel, he left La Tuque and sought to join his love, Maria, on the shore of Lac St-Jean, only to die of exposure. The travellers escaped this tragic fate, but Filion injured his right leg badly on the second day. They decided to carry on and, in Filion's words, "every day, Pierre tended to my injured leg."[82]

When the trio returned to Montreal, Mackenzie King's Liberal government decided not to impose conscription imme-diately. But that did not still the anti-conscriptionist sentiment. In November 1942 a law-school classmate, Jean Drapeau, became an independent candidate in a by-election in Outremont, supported by both the Ligue and the Bloc populaire canadien, a new nationalist party that had supplanted the weak Action libérale nationale. At twenty-six, he was a fiery orator with strong connections to Catholic and other nationalist groups. It was Trudeau's own constituency, and he fought the battle furiously on streets he knew well. The Liberal candidate was General Léo Laflèche, who was endorsed not only by the English papers but also by *L'Action catholique* and several major French papers. *Le Devoir*, however, dissented and supported Drapeau. Trudeau spent most of his time in the fall of 1942 on that campaign, so much so that he told a business colleague that he had little time for other activities.

At a major rally during the campaign's last week, Trudeau gave such a spirited speech for Drapeau that *Le Devoir* published almost all of it. He began by denouncing the Liberals for running a military officer as their candidate; in a democracy, the military had no place in politics. He minimized the German threat, ridiculed the King government, and, according to *Le Devoir*, said that "he feared the peaceful invasion of immigrants more than the armed invasion by the enemy." The French of North America would fight when threatened, just as they had against the Iroquois; "today," he scorned, "it is against other savages." Then Trudeau stated dramatically: the government had irresponsibly declared war even though North America faced no direct threat of an invasion, "at the moment when Hitler had not yet had his lightning victories." The newspaper quoted his dramatic conclusion in full: "Citizens of Quebec, don't be content to whine. Long live the flag [*drapeau*] of liberty. Enough of Band-Aids; bring on the revolution."[83]

Two days after this demagogic speech, which seemed to equate the King government with savages, minimized the Nazi threat, and attacked immigrants (who, in Montreal, were mainly Jewish), *Le Devoir* ran another story about a polite heckler at a Laflèche rally who had been beaten by a thug. Trudeau kept the clipping and identified the heckler as his friend Pierre

Vaillancourt.[84] After the election, which Drapeau lost, Trudeau explained the reasons for the Liberal victory to a friend. There was no need for "lamentations," he said: "We know that in a constituency two-thirds Jewish and English, a nationalist and anti-bourgeois candidate would not have great appeal. Drapeau did not lose his deposit. And especially if Mr. King gives consideration to the polling statistics, he will understand that the votes for Laflèche are owed [?] almost uniquely to the Jewish and English areas and . . . to a powerful Liberal machine." He concluded by arguing that they had not really lost the election; rather, he blamed the "dishonesty" of what would later be called the "ethnic vote." The Bloc could well take the riding the next time.[85]

Trudeau's dramatic contribution to the Drapeau campaign contrasts with his relative silence at the university, where he published only one article in Le Quartier Latin that dealt directly with the war. This article, "Nothing Matters Save the Victory," mocked war propaganda and dripped with sarcasm about the rights the British were fighting to preserve. Although no fan of Hitler, Trudeau ridiculed the British regard for the rights of minorities. The Nazi hordes, he declared, would take away language rights, deny the rights of minorities in other provinces, capture the economic heights, and make the French population hewers of wood and drawers of water. Not even the dullest reader could miss Trudeau's comparison with the English treatment of the French after 1763. The editors indicated that its publication in the fateful month of November 1942 barely escaped the censors.[86]

One incident that has continually stirred controversy occurred in the summer of 1943 and involved Roger Rolland. In The Secret Mulroney Tapes, journalist Peter Newman complains that "journalists . . . seldom [mentioned] the fact that during the Second World War he [Trudeau] had cruised around Montreal on a motorcycle wearing a German helmet." The cruising was not in

Montreal, and the helmet was probably French, not German. In his memoirs, Trudeau explained how he and Roger had found some old German uniforms from the Franco-Prussian War of 1870 in the Rolland attic. Rolland's wealthy father had collected military souvenirs, including memorabilia from both the French and the Prussian side in this conflict. According to Rolland, Trudeau chose a French helmet when they decided to don the ancient military gear and surprise their friends, Jean-Louis Roux and Jean Gascon, who were members of the comedy troupe Les Compagnons de Saint-Laurent. The troupe was spending the summer season at a chalet at Saint-Adolphe-de-Howard in the Laurentians, quite some distance from Montreal.

As the pranksters headed north on their Harleys, Trudeau caught up to Rolland near Sainte-Agathe and told him that a villager had hailed him down to inform him that "a German soldier had just gone by heading north." That dramatic reaction spurred them on to even more tricks. They stopped at an imposing house and knocked on the back door. When a servant answered, Pierre demanded water, and the terrified woman brought a large glass out to him. But he signalled his suspicion of the contents, handed the glass to Roger, and demanded that he drink his share of it first. Once Roger had taken a few sips, he suddenly collapsed, screaming with pain. The servant quickly bolted the door, and the "soldiers" fled. When they reached their friends, they found only one of the actors there. He was "petrified" as he encountered the bizarre invaders and thought he was hallucinating. It took him a few minutes and a strong shot of cognac "to recover his senses." Trudeau later dismissed the whole incident as simply a prank, but, when interviewer Jean Lépine told him in the early 1990s that Rolland had admitted that they scared some people, Trudeau agreed.[87]

Curiously, the *Quartier Latin* article (although not the motorbike incident) escaped the attention of Canadian journalists, politicians, and writers when Trudeau was prime minister, even though it contained political dynamite. In 1972 a clever opposition party could have used Trudeau's angry anti-British rhetoric to win a few Ontario seats where "Queen and country" still mattered. Rumours constantly swirled around Trudeau, but surprisingly little effort was made to clear away the mists when, in some cases, they could have been easily dispersed. Jean-Louis Roux was not so lucky. After a brilliant career as one of Quebec's finest actors, he was appointed lieutenant-governor of Quebec. When the press revealed that he had worn a swastika on his lab coat five decades earlier at the Université de Montréal, he responded that, like other students fiercely opposed to conscription, he had simply wanted to be noticed. He apologized for his youthful deeds and explained that the context of the time had skewed his understanding of evil.[88] The appointment, however, was aborted.[89]

Trudeau, too, was a clever actor. In the summer of 1942, for example, he took part alongside Roux and Gascon in a play, *Le Jeu de Dollard*, in front of the statue of Cartier at the base of Mount Royal. And throughout this period, he changed roles quickly. The bland young essayist of Brébeuf became a biting polemicist at the Université de Montréal, as the caution that had marked his adolescent escapades disappeared. He was daring. In a debate on gallantry that took place the following January 8 in the presence of the federal minister of fisheries, Ernest Bertrand, Trudeau was outrageous, just as everyone expected him to be. The program romantically described him as "chevalier des nobles causes." Pierre, it declared, "cuts the figure of a revolutionary in our time." He told George Radwanski that, in his defence of gallantry, he pulled a gun, pointed it at one of the judges, and fired it. A puff of smoke appeared, but it was a blank. The judge ducked; the crowd was stunned. Not surprisingly, Trudeau and his partner lost the debate, in which they argued that gallantry belonged to the past, not the present, where gallantry was a fake.[90]

That winter night Trudeau received poor marks for gallantry—
and common sense—from many in the crowd.

—

What are we to make of Trudeau in these exuberant, troubled
times? His correspondence with François Hertel leaves no doubt
that he was deeply involved with François-Joseph Lessard's revolutionary activity and that his politics were not only anti-war and
anti-Liberal but also clandestine, highly nationalist, and, at least
momentarily, separatist and even violent. Hertel was, as Lessard
himself said, the major recruiter for the secret cell, and Trudeau
was involved with Lessard well before the summer of 1942. His
letter after the Drapeau defeat in which he blamed the Jews and
the English, and the speech in favour of Drapeau where he
announced his fear of immigrants, are both appalling. So too are
some of the comments he made in his notebooks on works that
were anti-Semitic or racist. After he read Charles Maurras's pro-
Pétain and anti-Semitic volume *La seule France*, for instance,
he told Hertel it pleased him very much, just as the "political
jobbery" of Canada in 1942 disgusted him.

Trudeau's education, his friendships, and even more his participation in the summer military training exercises took him
briefly to the barricades in 1941 and 1942. He deeply resented
the military training, and his colleagues shared that resentment.
Their attitude is clear in the remarkable photograph of the
commandos "without zeal," and it's easy to imagine the pranks
they contemplated as they "trained" together—pranks such as
stealing their military kit and weapons.

Trudeau's opposition to conscription is understandable, and
his political activities in the referendum campaign and in campaigning for Drapeau are expressions of his democratic rights.
Under Hertel's spell, however, when he was bored with law

school, entranced with the mystique of revolution, and freed by fortune to make his own choices, Trudeau did and said some foolish things. Yet perspective is needed.* He regarded Les Frères Chausseurs, or LX, as hopelessly disorganized and François-Joseph Lessard as a great bother. He did read Charles Maurras, Alexis Carrel, and others, but Hertel also introduced him to Alfred Pellan and Paul-Émile Borduas, and he spent far more time in salons listening to symphonies than in the streets calling for revolution. He, Lessard, and Jean-Baptiste Boulanger, who later became a prominent psychiatrist and disapproved strongly of Trudeau's dismissal of their separatist activities in his memoirs, seem strikingly immature. But then, many are in wartime.

Throughout this period, Trudeau lived at the family home, with its chauffeur and servants, while denouncing the bourgeois life. He invited his fellow students there for evenings of classical music, where his mother graciously entertained them. It seems

---

* In his memoir, Trudeau's friend and political colleague Gérard Pelletier describes their future colleague Jean Marchand's disillusionment with violent political nationalism in the forties in terms that could also apply to Trudeau: "[Marchand] had been recruited into one of the innumerable leagues that existed at the time (each one with twelve or fifteen members), all of which wanted to overthrow the government and put an end to democracy. That was the spirit of the age. Of course, the half-baked leaders of these little groups had no precise notion of what political action meant. They dreamed, they grew intoxicated with words, and in the basements of middle-class houses they cooked up heady plots which no one ever dreamt of acting on." Trudeau was far from alone in "trying out" these "heady" plots, but he later treated them with the disdain that Marchand and Pelletier did. Pelletier, *Years of Impatience, 1950–1960*, trans. Alan Brown (Toronto: Methuen, 1984), 9.

that he told her nothing about his nights on the streets or his notorious motorbike jaunt. These secrets he kept from her, and it surely would have jarred and distressed her had she known. And that, most assuredly, he was loath to do. It was a troubled time, and, as Camille Corriveau and even Hertel recognized, Pierre Trudeau, who had dreamed of being Canadian prime minister as he travelled across the country in the summer of 1940, had become a troubled young man.

Despite the daring of his political involvement (which was mentioned in the Université de Montréal debate program) and the boredom of his legal studies, Trudeau once again excelled in the classroom. He stood first at university even more often than he had at Brébeuf. Sure, he complained about the drill of law classes, but his remarkable discipline prevailed. His marks in civil law, for example, were 40 out of 40 in January 1941; 38 out of 40 in June 1941; and 38.5 out of 40 in June 1942, when he received 28 out of 30 in criminal law, 20 out of 20 for constitutional law, 17.5 out of 20 for international law, and 24.8 out of 25 for notarial procedure. Evidently, the plebiscite and politics made little difference to his grades.

The following year, in June 1943, Trudeau graduated first in law "with great distinction." He won the Governor General's Medal for overall excellence as well as the Lieutenant-Governor's Medal for standing first in the licensing examination. He personally wrote a letter of thanks to Their Excellencies for the medals. The response from the office of the Governor General thanked him for the information that he had won the medal—a gesture that surely confirmed Trudeau's contempt for the British nobles who then occupied the office.[91] When his sister, Suzette, read the results in *La Presse*, she wrote from Old Orchard Beach and congratulated him on "his latest achievements." She hoped he could use the publicity "in obtaining what you would like for next year."[92]

Trudeau, however, was still unsure what he liked. The five years between 1938 and 1943 were, nonetheless, decisive for him and, most historians argue, for Canada and Quebec too. He had to make a choice: Would he be a French or an English Canadian?[93] When he lost the Rhodes Scholarship and chose the Université de Montréal, Trudeau became Québécois. The term itself had no meaning in 1940, apart from being a resident of Quebec City. But Trudeau decided during those years that he was "French," a choice that was almost inevitable given the intensity of his education and the great events of the time. In making that choice, he became entangled in those events. And there was another factor: as Brébeuf's top student in a period when French-Canadian excellence was prized, he became a magnet for those who sought a leader for difficult times.

The debates, the battles fought by the young, and the relationships that were forged in the early 1940s echoed loudly in Quebec and Canadian political life for the next half century. The bodies aged and nuances emerged, but the names endured: Daniel Johnson, Jean-Jacques Bertrand, Jean Drapeau, Jean-Louis Roux, Paul Gérin-Lajoie, Charles Lussier, and so many more. When Trudeau spoke in the Outremont by-election, the other speakers for future mayor Drapeau's candidacy were Michel Chartrand, later a prominent labour leader and separatist in Quebec, and D'Iberville Fortier, one of the most eminent federal public servants forty years later. André Laurendeau, who worked closely with Trudeau in these battles, became the most respected Quebec journalist of his age. His best friend in the 1930s, Pierre Vadeboncoeur, became a major literary figure in Quebec; and Jean-Louis Roux and Jean Gascon were among the key personalities in the French and English theatre in the last half of the twentieth century. Most of these principal actors in the "revolutionary" moments of the early 1940s kept their silence about themselves—and about Pierre Trudeau.

At Brébeuf, Trudeau had stood a resented second to Jean de Grandpré until his final year. In another fateful decision, his rival chose to attend McGill University. As he explained:

> [Trudeau] could afford to search for his identity. People like me . . . were forced by economic necessity to get on with our careers, to go to McGill to improve our English because English was the language of business, to get a law degree and enter a practice immediately. Most of us married fairly early and started to raise a family and you had to earn money for that. As a rich bachelor, Pierre was able to spend years "finding himself."[94]

De Grandpré, whom Trudeau himself thought the most polished and articulate among his classmates at Brébeuf, rose to the top of the business world and became wealthy as the head of Bell Canada. There is much resentment in de Grandpré's comment, but also some truth in his charge that Trudeau, because of his personal wealth and independent circumstances, could search for his identity, experience adventure, try out anarchy, and delay finding himself. It was easier to be anti-bourgeois when your circumstances were thoroughly bourgeois.

Because Trudeau chose Université de Montréal for law and because he became involved in the conscription crisis as a leading opponent, he was immersed in the debate about the future of French-speaking Canadians in a way that he never could or would have been had he won the Rhodes Scholarship or gone to McGill. In a particular sense, he was correct in stating that the politics of wartime passed him by. Those great tides that turned in 1942 and 1943 did not sweep over his life, his classroom, or his friends as the Americans won the Battle of Midway, the Soviets held their ground at Stalingrad, and the Allies—with Canadians among them—set out on a bloody path up the boot of Italy. Trudeau and his associates stood on separate ground, avoiding the battles in Europe while furiously debating what their future as francophone professionals would be in a modern North America. They knew that there could be no return to the past, but in the early 1940s they saw the outline of their future only dimly. Yet the debate that dominated Canadian politics from the 1960s through the 1990s began among Trudeau's classmates in the university corridors and the Montreal streets in the 1940s. Those times cast the die.

For Trudeau, the times were exhilarating, confusing, and dangerous. He swam in the same stream as others, opposing conscription, favouring Vichy and Pétain, outrageously equating Hitler's Reich with British policy towards Quebec, and even contemplating and plotting Quebec independence. Yet, in some important personal ways, he remained apart, a self-declared independent who often donned a cloak of mystery. He wrote to his mother in English about how well he worked with his military superiors, and he vacationed at Old Orchard, enjoyed American nightlife, and thought about a future political career. What career, and even what country, remained an open question in 1943 as democracy, so threatened in the 1930s, began its march forward towards its greatest victories. Despite his later denials, he swam with the currents that flowed strongly through his university. Yet, because of his background—his mother, his wealth, and his intense search for free intellectual choice—he sometimes took refuge on the shore, as when he apparently told Gabriel Filion, his travelling companion on the *Maria Chapdelaine* route, that he dreamed of a united Canada, or when he told his diary that he was proud that his English blood tempered his boiling French blood.

In the 1940s, as conscription loomed, Pierre Trudeau's French blood boiled; as times changed, so would the man. He would forget much of his youth, as all of us do. Yet in the attic that preserves memory, fragments of the friends, the games, the debates, the Harley, and the wilderness endured—as did, ineffably, Camille's first kiss.

—

CHAPTER 3

IDENTITY AND ITS DISCONTENTS

Twenty-one can be the cruellest year. Pierre Trudeau had drifted away from infatuation with Camille Corriveau by the spring of 1941, but, as with other significant women in his life, he clung to the intimacy they once had shared. With her and several women who followed, he peeled away the layers of hardened bark that enclosed the core where emotions flow. With men, he consistently refused to show weakness, whether in the classroom, the canoe, or the political forum. Among men, he sought uniqueness or, as he put it in his Brébeuf diary, to stand apart. This impulse created its greatest tension for him as he passed from adolescence to adulthood, that period when friendship is deeply craved and when, in twentieth-century North American society, identity becomes a pre-eminent concern. For Trudeau, the times were particularly difficult because he was determined to shape his own identity and to make choices freely, away from the direction of others.

In 1940 Pierre sent Camille a list of nine authors he felt he should master: it included René Descartes and Adam Smith, as well as Aristotle, Pascal, Montesquieu, Kant, Marx, and Bergson.[1] Many years later, in 1962, Germain Lesage, a Quebec journalist, asked ninety-seven Quebec clergy, writers, academics, and dramatic and visual artists to identify those who had influenced them most. Overwhelmingly, they chose French writers or philosophers, with Blaise Pascal and Paul Claudel—the French diplomat-writer—receiving the most mentions (thirteen times). Out of step with the others, Pierre Trudeau chose only one French author, Descartes, who appeared on no other list. His other choices were Adam Smith, Cardinal Newman, Sigmund Freud, and Harold Laski. Three were British, two were Jewish, and only Freud was mentioned by more than two of the others questioned.[2] Was Trudeau being playful in challenging the contemporary ethos or was he reflecting the unusual diversity of his intellectual mentors—particularly with his selection of Descartes and Smith? Still, it's worth remembering that 1962 was the year when the Quebec Liberal government stoked nationalist fires by nationalizing Quebec's private electricity companies. Descartes, of course, represented reason, and Smith the case for minimalist government intervention. At that moment Descartes and Smith made more sense to Trudeau than the passionate arguments for nationalization put forward by his friend the Quebec Cabinet minister René Lévesque. His choice of British thinkers was also provocative, a deliberate attempt to "shock the intellectuals" in Quebec. They also represented Trudeau's cosmopolitanism, a value and a term he had actively embraced as he matured intellectually in the mid-forties.

Because of his restricted education up to that point, Freud and Laski were virtually unknown to Trudeau when he graduated in law from the Université de Montréal in 1943. Like his peers, he had had his mind crammed with Jacques Maritain, Abbé Groulx, Paul Claudel, and the other names on the lists. Freud had already begun to interest him, and that prepared him for the intense personal encounter he had with Freudianism later in the decade. Harold Laski, a professor at the London School of Economics and a socialist thinker of renown and influence in those times, would also profoundly influence Trudeau's conception of the state and public life.[3] In the details of his playfulness with the poll lay some truths, however, the major one being the fundamental importance of the period 1943 to 1948 in the intellectual, personal, and public life of Pierre Trudeau. Let us begin, as Trudeau would have preferred, with his mind.

When Trudeau was denied the Rhodes Scholarship and forced to remain at the Université de Montréal in 1940, he gained an enduring voice in the long debate among French Canadians about their place in Canada. When he left Canada to study abroad, first at Harvard in 1944–46, then in Paris in 1946–47, and finally in London in 1947–48, Trudeau, to use one of his best-known metaphors, opened the windows to fresh currents of thought and action. Like many others, he unloaded some baggage that had become offensive or superfluous: the former included the casual anti-Semitism of his youth; the latter his close study of religious thought. As Father Bernier had counselled, he continued to read theological works, but religious references quickly disappeared from his prose. Unlike many other Quebecers, such as the eminent journalist and sometime politician André Laurendeau, Trudeau would remain a believer, deeply interested in debates about the character of faith and observant of Roman Catholic sacraments. In this respect, his mention of Cardinal Newman rather than Jacques Maritain, Teilhard de Chardin, or Emmanuel Mounier is fascinating.

At Harvard and later at the London School of Economics, Trudeau participated in the Newman societies that were the centre of Catholic life in the Protestant milieus of those universities and, typically, immersed himself in Newman's life and thought. What attracted him to Newman, the great Anglican intellectual of the early nineteenth century? In part it was surely Newman's intellectual passage that he had detailed so brilliantly in *Apologia pro vita sua*. When the English theologian sought to dispute the legitimacy of the Roman Catholic Church, he concluded that, contrary to his task and his own beliefs, the church "had preserved unbroken her continuity with the Primitive Church, the Church set up by Christ, and founded on the Twelve."[4] At a moment in British history when anti-Catholicism was intense, Newman followed his conscience and converted to the Roman Catholic Church. He was no social reformer, but his intellect guided his actions, and his faith emerged from reason. An individualist, Newman chafed at the emerging doctrine of papal infallibility. Always, though, he found truth through reason, and Trudeau searched for the same grail. Trudeau's growing focus on individual choice within the structure of the Catholic faith stems directly from Newman, as does his willingness to challenge orthodoxies.

In commenting on the choices of the Quebec intellectuals he interviewed, Germain Lesage made two significant points: first, the fact that Paul Claudel and Georges Bernanos trumped Aquinas (named by only six of the ninety-seven interviewed) indicated that the intellectuals chose those who had influenced them most "beyond their formal academic training"; and, second, the choices reflected "loyalty to France" and "devotion to Christianity."[5] In this respect, Trudeau's political activism and his attacks on clericalism were not a rejection of Catholicism or religion itself; rather, like Quebec's Quiet Revolution in the sixties more generally, they were deeply rooted in "the grand ideas of European Christian renewal" among Catholics such as Jacques Maritain and Emmanuel Mounier.[6] Revolutions once begun find their own paths, and Trudeau eventually found the taste bitter. In the 1940s, however, he frequently savoured its flavour.

Trudeau consciously fashioned his identity in this decade, creating a recognizable shape from the elements provided by his past, his family, and his education. In his study of the "sources of the self" in modern times, Trudeau's friend and, later, political opponent, the philosopher Charles Taylor, emphasized how the modern Western quest for self differs from earlier Christian and other traditions in which "what I want and where I stand" is defined by others and by a set of beliefs and practices. In contrast, he said, the modern search for identity requires "leaving home"; it stresses self-reliance and, above all else, individualism. As we strive to orient ourselves to the good, however, we must try to "understand our lives in narrative form, as a 'quest.'"[7] In these words, Taylor, who was also a Catholic Montrealer, captures the sense of "quest" that pervades Trudeau's own understanding of his identity.

Trudeau was indelibly shaped by his childhood and adolescence, but he also exhibited a profound sense of individualism. "Ah! Liberty, independence," he wrote in his diary in February 1940. "Don't bend [your] knees before anyone; keep [your] head high before the powerful."[8] We see this spirit in his choice of intellectual influences, especially Newman and Freud. We understand its romantic origins in the tears that flowed from his eyes when he read how Cyrano de Bergerac strove to break free of the restraints of time and place. Yet, like the great nineteenth-century romantics, Trudeau had to bring his individualist instinct in line with his well-defined ambitions, which could be realized only within a mannered and ordered society. For Trudeau, writing that life narrative was an enduring struggle, one that brought periodic silences and curious forays, but never malingering.

There were delays: Stephen Clarkson and Christina McCall turn to psychology when they discuss Trudeau in the forties and conclude that he was a *puer*, a condition marked by delayed adulthood and prolonged adolescence. It's true that Trudeau did prolong the ease of adolescence and delay the trappings of adulthood, but he did so not only because he could, in material terms, but because he struggled continually with his past, his beliefs, and his quest.

In a very real sense, Trudeau mirrored Quebec itself in the forties as it wrestled with modern technology and politics and its relationship to its past and its traditions. The parallels are striking. Women in Quebec obtained the vote in April 1940, the same spring that Trudeau was wrestling with his strong sexual urges and his traditional Catholic conception of female chastity. Trudeau chose law over philosophy or the priesthood because he wanted to have an active part in public life, just as his province similarly came to terms with modern industrial capitalism despite the enormous impact it would have on traditional ways. When Trudeau talked in the forties about becoming a leader in his country, there was an ambiguity that is familiar to students of Quebec history in the twentieth century. He deeply resented British domination and was unsure what "la patrie," the fatherland, meant, but he did not commit fully to the concept of a separate Quebec state even while musing of revolution. It's a curious but common tradition at the time in Quebec, one that's reflected in the name of the nationalist groups Ligue pour la défense du *Canada* and the Bloc populaire *canadien*. Finally, he sought validation through external recognition—study at Harvard, Paris, and London—much as Quebec itself did, first by engaging in the "renewal" of Catholicism in the thirties and forties and in the lively European debates, and then by injecting modernism into culture and government in the fifties and the sixties. Trudeau was very much "a Québécois" Catholic; but, as with Cardinal Newman, his quest took unexpected turns.

When Pierre first began to ask, "Who am I?" at Brébeuf, he turned to his clerical teachers, notably Fathers Robert Bernier and Marie d'Anjou, for guidance. After many intense conversations, he took their advice very seriously and began to read the classics, to learn about art, and to listen to the finest classical music; in short, he immersed himself in the Western canon, though with a strongly European flavour. When he left Brébeuf for the Université de Montréal, he brought an extraordinary foundation of linguistic skills, knowledge of philosophy and religious thought, and, above all, intellectual discipline. At Montréal he quickly discovered that he was bored by law. He studied only what was "barely necessary" and despised lawyers but not his classmates. Instead, he devoted his time to politics and the arts and immersed himself in culture: reading books, attending concerts, studying the piano, painting in oil, and learning ballet, his favourite art. Still he stood first in his class. More than anything, he wrote to Camille earlier, he felt that his task in his early twenties was to "master" Pierre Trudeau.[9]

The correspondence continued mostly in English despite Camille's Parisian stay, and in March 1941 he reiterated that he was "still aiming to be accomplished in every field." This enormous goal meant constant challenges and tension, introspection, and even isolation as he tried to figure out his future:

> I seem to be slowly, surely and peacefully drifting away from the human world. I have forsaken every possible organization which might rob me of my time, and although I make an effort once in a while to go to a dance or a movie they profoundly bore me for the most part. Most of my law professors nauseate me, so I just study as much as is barely necessary . . .
>
> These different circumstances cause me to envelope myself in a world apart, where I crazily read and wrote, and dreamt about music and beauty and revolutions and blood and dynamite. It was most contradictory this combined desire of action and thought.[10]

His intensity frightened Camille, who, now in love with another man, warned him that he had fallen into "a terrible rut . . . You have shut yourself up in a room, and you are brooding and meditating on the future, and wondering how it will all come out." He should learn patience, she wisely counselled: "My dear Pierre, do you realize that 99% of the people with whom you will come into contact will be much more stupid and unintelligent, and you shall have to be patient with them because they will be the people on whom you will depend. You want and shall be successful, and whatever you do, either in law or the political field, you will find that people are not of your mental caliber." Still, she advised, he must learn to be patient with those "who are less fortunate and less endowed than you are."[11]

He infuriated her and others when they tried to grow close, yet at the same time he worked constantly to make himself ever more intriguing and attractive. In his notebooks, complaints about his appearance became fewer as excitement about women glancing his way grew. His graduation photograph captures the deep blue eyes and the fashionably parted dark wavy hair. He claimed that it was "brown" on a passport application in June 1940 and that he stood 5 foot 10—probably an exaggeration. At the university he honed the acting skills he had first developed at Camp Ahmek and Brébeuf and became a brilliant debater. He kept reminding himself that he must lose his timidity and always seek originality. He knew that humility was a virtue, but, he admitted to his journal, it was "sometimes difficult to reconcile ambition with such humility."[12] He practised different ways of relating with others, carefully noting their reactions to him. He committed himself to the healthy life, engaging in a variety of fitness exercises and testing his physical prowess on ski hills and, even more ambitiously, on wilderness trips.

In his confessional correspondence with François Hertel, he responded to the priest's observation that the "man of action" was a special and valued type.[13] Hertel ended an October 1941 letter with the words "Long live the France of Pétain. There was a man of action"—one who was undertaking challenging but necessary deeds even though he was over eighty years old. "Act, act, act," he counselled, advice that the young Trudeau believed he must heed.[14] Already acutely aware of his physicality, his presence as an actor and athlete, his attraction to women and beauty, he desperately tried to efface the acne blemishes on his face. His mother urged him to go to a chiropractor in the hope of finding a cure.[15] Time did end the acne, but the youthful affliction left him with mild scars that did not detract from the compelling intensity of his narrow face, piercing eyes, and remarkably high cheekbones. When he graduated from the Université de Montréal in the spring of 1943, he was very much an original and, to a large extent, his own creation.

But what to do? The war had disrupted all his plans to study abroad when he graduated from Brébeuf. Now, as he was completing his law degree, he applied to Harvard, Columbia, and Georgetown universities. The law school, apparently unaware of Trudeau's opinion that the professors were idiots, tried to secure a scholarship for its best student. He was, the dean wrote, "particularly outstanding, not only by his academic excellence but also by his assiduity and application."[16] Trudeau, however, could not get permission to leave Canada and his military obligations.

Fearing correctly that the practice of law would bore him, he sought other escapes, ones that suggest his revolutionary activities of 1942 were somewhat more playful than seriously considered. He wrote to a friend who had become a Canadian diplomat in South America and asked if he could get a diplomatic position in Rio de Janeiro: "I will be a lawyer within two months, old friend; that is to say, I'm almost a diplomat." The friend offered him little hope. He applied to the Experiment in International Living for a study trip to Mexico, but once again permission was denied. He spent part of the summer at a military camp in the Maritimes, after which he went on a trip "with his moto," telling his worried mother that, whatever happened, "be reassured, I will be prudent."[17]

The motorbike liberated him from the routine of practising law and released a side of him that his friends knew well—his playfulness and love of adventure. His close friend Jacques Hébert says that these were his most endearing qualities and that they redeemed his seriousness. In his article "Pritt Zoum Bing" in *Le Quartier Latin*, Trudeau claimed that the human species was made for the motorbike: "Man was conceived with the motorcycle already in mind: the nostrils open towards the back, the ears push back against the head, allowing the greatest acceleration without being overwhelmed by wind and dust." Above all, the roar of the bike as it swept through the countryside and crowded city streets served to "liberate the spirit; the body is turned over to its own resources and you think new thoughts again." [18]

Indeed, Trudeau was thinking new thoughts once more.

—

On his return to Montreal in the fall, he became a lawyer at 112 St. James Street West. He joined the firm of Hyde and Ahern, where he was paid $2.50 a day. For those apprentice wages, Trudeau handled simple files, most of them involving car accidents and evictions from apartments. As a landlord himself of a property at 1247 Bishop Street in central Montreal, which earned him $50 a month, Trudeau had no fondness for deadbeat tenants. He pursued one particular delinquent mercilessly through the courts that year.[19] Gordon Hyde and John Ahern were both King's Counsel, and Ahern was the grandson of Charles Marcil, a Liberal MP for thirty-seven years. In typical bicultural fashion, he was a member of the Reform Club as well as the francophone Club St-Denis, Charles Trudeau's old favourite.[20] Trudeau's rough files, still retained in his personal papers, reveal him to be a careful lawyer, extremely attentive to detail and thorough in his approach to cases. But however much his work pleased his employers, his politics in 1943–44 surely did not.

Trudeau remained active in politics, still firmly opposing Canadian war policy and the possibility of conscription—as did his friends.[21] The whiff of revolution quickly passed in 1943, leaving behind the nationalist and anti-conscriptionist Bloc populaire canadien. Trudeau participated in Bloc affairs, as did many of the other activists from Jean Drapeau's by-election and the conscription plebiscite. He sat on the organizational committee of the Bloc and agreed to be the secretary of the committee on education and policy. He even saved his badge from the Bloc Congress at the Windsor Hotel on February 3–6, 1944. It was signed by André Laurendeau, the man chosen because of his earlier role in the anti-conscription campaign to lead the Bloc in the upcoming provincial election.[22] Laurendeau denounced the federal and provincial Liberals and took his stand on the left. The Liberals, he declared in his inaugural speech, "gave us hypocritical governments which taught the proletariat much more effectively than any Marxist that the only way to triumph over a liberal capitalist state is through revolution."[23] The term "revolution" was used frequently by Quebec nationalists at this time, including Trudeau. Its meaning was broad and remarkably imprecise. So was the Bloc, which included right-wing Catholics, social reform Catholics, and others who simply despised both the Liberals and the Union nationale. Trudeau did not run in the election that summer, but he contributed financially to the impoverished party. Despite early hopes, however, it won only four seats. Maurice Duplessis used the nationalism card effectively during the campaign and defeated the Liberal government.

Trudeau remained loyal to the Bloc, but the fires of nationalism had begun to burn less intensely for him. Unlike Jean Drapeau, Michel Chartrand, and others who cast themselves energetically into the summer 1944 provincial election, Trudeau disappeared. He had applied again to the Mexican program of the Experiment in International Living and had spent the year studying Spanish. When he learned of certain restrictions the Experiment faced, he attached himself to a group of Canadian students who left Montreal on June 15 on a forty-day "goodwill" trip to Mexico. On June 7 Trudeau gave notice to his law firm and to the National Service registration. On the National Service form he first wrote "lawyer," then stroked it out and wrote "avocat," and provocatively added that the reason he was leaving was "La Bohème."[24]

Bohemian life in Montreal revealed itself to Trudeau in the late 1940s, mainly through Hertel. A mutual interest in the arts had initially brought him close to the Trudeau family, and he began introducing Grace and her children to some of the leading young artists of the time. Grace's brother Gordon Elliott had long been a friend and neighbour of the great French painter Georges Braque, and the Trudeau home already possessed one of his works. When the Canadian abstract painter Alfred Pellan returned to Canada after fourteen years in Paris, determined to break the shackles of traditionalism in Quebec artistic circles, Hertel became his champion. He arranged to hang a few modern paintings in the Trudeau home, which became, in effect, a salon where artists mingled with potential patrons in a time of political and artistic ferment. Pierre himself purchased three paintings—including a Pellan—from Hertel, who acted as an intermediary for some of the artists. He told a friend to pick up "a very fine [Léon] Bellefleur . . . from Pierre's room" which, he confirmed, Madame Trudeau would give to him.[25] Hertel, who occasionally wrote art critiques for *Le Devoir*, enthusiastically welcomed the European influences that Pellan brought back with him. He also encouraged Paul-Émile Borduas in 1941 as he moved from religiously centred representational art and portraiture to abstraction, when "the echo of an ideology more global" was first heard in Montreal salons—and in Pierre's bedroom, where the walls became adorned with modernism.[26]

Trudeau met Borduas through Hertel, and, in 1942, he often visited Paul-Émile and his wife, Gabrielle, and mesmerized

them—especially Gabrielle. She apparently went to a performance by Pierre in a play and was captivated by the younger man's
comic sensibility and dramatic presence. Like her husband, she
saw Pierre as a young revolutionary, albeit a peculiar one who
signed his entirely proper letters, addressed to "Madame Borduas,"
with "Citoyen." The following year her attraction moved to a
different level. "Good evening, my dear Pierre," she wrote most
familiarly on December 14, 1943, offering him "le plus grand
amour de la terre," the greatest love on earth. She was jealous, she
told him openly, adding that she hoped other women "would know
how to love you as fully as I could." She would not write more
for several reasons, one truly essential: "I deeply fear that I would
trouble your mother and, through her, Hertel, who is probably
her counsellor." She loved Grace because Pierre was her son,
because her son had her qualities, and because she had allowed
"an almost impossible friendship between us." However bohemian
he aspired to be, such a love affair—or such a future for the two of
them—surely was impossible. The relationship remained platonic
yet adoring.[27]

As Gabrielle knew, Trudeau had to take other paths. He
applied to Harvard, got his military service deferred, and went off
to Mexico for most of the summer. Camille had married Bill
Aubuchon Junior, a Franco-American businessman, in May 1943.
His family business was hardware, and the stores were found in
most cities and towns in the American Northeast. She invited
Pierre to the wedding. He did not go but replied, elegantly, that
he hoped "the man with whom you have agreed to share your
destiny . . . will show you all the concern that your tenderness
deserves." Over the years, he and other members of the Trudeau
family kept up some connection with the Aubuchons. Still,
although they had parted ways, Camille understood Pierre and,
as early as 1941, she had told him that he, too, needed to find
someone he could confide in and trust.[28] Obviously, Gabrielle

Borduas was not the answer, but, as she had recognized, he had begun to fall in love again.

Pierre had met Thérèse Gouin, the daughter of the eminent Liberal senator, Léon-Mercier Gouin, in 1943, when his friend Roger Rolland brought her to one of the classical music gatherings which Grace Trudeau held during the war years. Sometimes there would be a pianist; most often, young friends of Pierre, Tip, and Suzette would come to hear the best records on the expensive phonograph. Four years younger than Pierre, Thérèse, with her quick mind and glowing face, immediately caught Pierre's competitive eye, and he began to court her. When he left for Mexico in the summer of 1944, she was in second place on the list of people with whom he intended to correspond. There he wrote his first missive to her, in which he posed a question: Which was the greater civilization, the one Cortés founded or the one he destroyed? The brief postcard ended, "Amitiés du citoyen," Regards of the citizen. The language of revolution still persisted; so did Pierre's pranks.

In the late summer of 1944 as Canada faced a conscription crisis, the impish Pierre tried to attach a "No to conscription" label to the back of her father's jacket, just before he went off to his office. Thérèse stopped Pierre before he comitted this possibly fatal joke very early in their romance. That same summer, when Thérèse and Pierre were out together in a rowboat, he suddenly bolted to his feet and proclaimed, "I want to be the prime minister of Quebec."[29]

As Pierre courted Thérèse, he was attending plays and concerts and reading books in an eclectic fashion. Although his proposed course of study at Harvard was Political Economy, he read mainly literature, notably Paul Claudel, Stéphane Mallarmé, Arthur Rimbaud, Feodor Dostoevsky, and G.K. Chesterton. He also read and enjoyed James Hilton's *Lost Horizon*, whose exotic Shangri-La intrigued the adventurous

Trudeau. Law practice interested him little, military training irritated him, and political passions had waned despite his continued association with the Bloc populaire. In response to drift, Trudeau wrote a brilliant and revealing essay in 1943, "The Ascetic in a Canoe."

First published in the journal of the Jeunesse étudiante catholique , the essay was profoundly biographical and is a wonderful blend of descriptive writing and cultural analysis:

> I would not know how to instil a taste for adventure in those who have not acquired it. (Anyway, who can ever prove the necessity for the gypsy life?) And yet there are people who suddenly tear themselves away from their comfortable existence and, using the energy of their bodies as an example to their brains, apply themselves to the discovery of unsuspected pleasures and places.

A canoeing expedition is a beginning more than a parting, he said. Recalling his own search for the trails of the voyageurs between Montreal and Hudson Bay, Trudeau declared that "its purpose is not to destroy the past, but to lay a foundation for the future." He insisted that a canoeing expedition purifies one more than any other experience: "Travel a thousand miles by train and you are a brute; pedal five hundred on a bicycle and you remain basically a bourgeois; paddle a hundred in a canoe and you are already a child of nature . . . Canoe and paddle, blanket and knife, salt pork and flour, fishing rod and rifle; that is about the extent of your wealth."

On a trip by canoe, he wrote, there is a new morality, one where God can be gently chided, where one's best friend is not a rifle but the person who shares a night's sleep after ten hours of paddling. How does it affect the personality? The mind works in the way that nature intended, and the body, "by demonstrating the true meaning of sensual pleasure," serves the mind. "You feel the beauty of animal pleasure when you draw a deep breath of rich morning air right through your body, which has been carried by the cold night, curled up like an unborn child." Sometimes exhaustion triumphs over reason, and the mumbled verses of the first hours "become brutal grunts of 'uh! uh! uh!'" The humility one gains becomes a future treasure when one confronts the great moral and philosophical questions. He concluded, significantly: "I know a man who had never learned 'nationalism' in school, but who contracted this virtue when he felt the immensity of his country ('patrie') and saw how great the country's creators had been."

That man was Pierre Trudeau, and in 1944 that country, or "patrie," was Quebec, or "Laurentie."* His loyalty to its "founders" remained strong when he left Quebec in 1944 at the age of twenty-four. That October, before he embarked by train for Harvard and Boston, Thérèse visited him at home. She discovered

---

* The translation of this concluding sentence is by Professor Ramsay Cook. In the famous translation in Border Spears, ed., *Wilderness in Canada* (Toronto: Clarke Irwin, 1970), reprinted in Gérard Pelletier, ed., *Against the Current: Selected Writings, 1939–1996* (Toronto: McClelland & Stewart, 1996), 12, the nationalism vanishes: "I know a man whose school could never teach him patriotism, but who acquired the virtue when he felt in his bones the vastness of his land and the greatness of its founders." Professors Ramsay and Eleanor Cook had translated the original French for the Spears book, but when it was published, "nationalism" became "patriotism" and the "patrie" vanished. The Prime Minister's Office made the change, reflecting the Trudeau of the seventies, not of the fifties. Trudeau told Cook that he was the "man" who had not learned "nationalism" in school. Thanks to Ramsay Cook for this fascinating information.

that his strong sense of the past resonated deeply. He asked her to come to his bedroom, where he guided her towards a portrait of his father. Then, before his image, they prayed.[30]

—

Harvard University was an entirely different environment for Trudeau when he arrived in Cambridge, Massachusetts, that fall. A citadel of the English Puritan tradition, it had become a refuge for some of the finest Central European minds as they escaped fascist persecution. The university was filled with the wounded, the weak, and the foreign—but there were few women, except at the distant Radcliffe College. Yet it remained profoundly American, the self-confident expression of the swelling American sense of superiority in the late war years. Liberal democracy, after its failures in the 1930s, was winning a second chance on the battlefields of Western Europe and the islands of the South Pacific.

Trudeau, whose teachers in the late thirties had been frequent critics of bourgeois democracy, was now exposed to new arguments that profoundly challenged him. Although he had a law degree and a year of legal practice, he felt adrift. "The majors in political science at Harvard had read more about Roman law and Montesquieu than I had as a lawyer," he explained later. "I realized then that we were being taught law as a trade in Quebec and not as a discipline."[31] If his legal training was deficient, his knowledge of economics was pathetic. He knew nothing of John Maynard Keynes, whose economic theories were transforming not only the discipline of economics but also the role of the state in postwar economic life. Quebec academics and leading journalists knew that the province desperately needed a better knowledge of the revolution in economics that was occurring. In his memoirs, Trudeau says that his decision to study economics at Harvard followed a conversation with André Laurendeau, who told him that there were only two economists in Quebec and that the province lacked economic expertise. Trudeau had already met both of them, the academics Édouard Montpetit and Esdras Minville, and they, too, had strongly encouraged him in this direction, particularly when he told them that he wanted to enter public life.[32]

The great intellectual migration of the 1930s and 1940s from a disintegrating Europe recreated Harvard from a Protestant American cradle of the economic and political elite into a major intellectual centre through which flowed the stormy yet stimulating currents of twentieth-century thought. Very soon, and for the first time, Trudeau encountered Jewish intellectuals. Other professors, including Heinrich Brüning, the last German chancellor before Hitler, possessed thick European accents and deep wounds. Far more than the outer limits of the Canadian Shield, this new environment tested Trudeau. Domesticity and Montreal tempted him often. Suzette was marrying; his young brother, Tip, was soon to follow.[33] Fortunately, Thérèse, as she gradually captured his heart, helped him to endure Harvard.

Trudeau's Harvard experience was, in retrospect, intellectually rich; in his own words, Harvard was "an extraordinary window on the world" in which "he felt like being in symbiosis with the five continents."[34] He began his study of economics with the future Nobel laureate Wassily Leontief, who recalled bullets whizzing by his head in St. Petersburg in 1917 as the Russian Revolution began, who had studied in Weimar Germany, and who, in his twenties, had worked as an adviser to China's national railways before taking refuge in the United States in 1932. Within a decade he developed the first input-output tables for the American economy and made early use of a computer for economic research. He was a generation

ahead of what passed for the discipline of economics in
Canada in the early forties. In his class, Trudeau read Keynes,
Kenneth Boulding, John Hicks, and Joan Robinson, although he
remained respectful of Catholic practice when he asked the
Boston archbishop if he could read books proscribed on the
Index for his academic courses.[35] He learned quickly what was old
(J.M. Clark and his long-winded descriptions) and what was
new, notably Keynes's theory of general equilibrium.

But if some were charmed by Keynes, Trudeau's course in
economic theory taught by the Austrian Gottfried Haberler
clearly set out the case for the other side. Haberler, later a leading
scholar at the conservative American Enterprise Institute,
introduced him to more traditional views of what the state
could and should do. The professor who left the most indelible
impression was the Austrian Joseph Schumpeter, who fitted no
categories but dominated a brilliant group of scholars at
Harvard at the time. The gifted writer's 1942 classic, *Capitalism,
Socialism, and Democracy*, argued that democracy's success,
particularly its creation of an intellectual class, assured its
doom, as the entrepreneurial spirit so essential for capitalistic
renewal drowned in the doubting footnotes of intellectual
debate in an advanced capitalist society.

Trudeau did well in his economics courses. His notebooks reveal that he was a serious student of economics: he soon
mastered both the new approaches that were transforming the
profession and the increasingly high mathematical requirements
of the field. Harvard economist John Kenneth Galbraith, who
met frequently with Trudeau later, described him as a "first-
rate economics mind of postwar vintage," a judgment his
Harvard marks confirmed.[36] And here lies an enigma: Trudeau
rarely reflected his economics training in his writings and,
once he became prime minister, not only his enemies on Bay
Street but also many of his colleagues and friends complained

that he paid no attention to economics. Yet his training and even the lectures he gave to trade unionists in the fifties show clearly that he had a solid graduate education in economics. What he said was not original, but he was thoroughly aware of what the best students must know. Indeed, among Canadian politicians of his time, he ranked at the peak in terms of formal academic training in economics. Why, then, did he seem to put it to the side?

There are probably several reasons. First, Trudeau's Harvard training reflected a diversity of approach to economics that made the discipline much less confident than it had been earlier and than it was to become later. Keynes had created a tempest at Harvard, but traditionalists and the Austrian School, notably Schumpeter and Haberler, had battened down and resisted. From these two men he learned, in his own words, that Keynes had "expressed himself too vaguely, and can't be fitted to everyone's particular needs." Haberler, a strong personality ("Thus spake Haberler, May 3, 1946," Trudeau wrote on his notes), introduced Trudeau to Friedrich Hayek's conservative opposition to political Keynesianism.

Trudeau's comments on the texts he read reveal his intellectual excitement but also a growing understanding that economics was a debate, not a science, one that is grounded in political positions, economic circumstances, and the psychology of the crowd. "From Sept '29 to Aug '33 great losses were incurred," he wrote in his notes about Schumpeter's course. "Capitalists themselves lost faith in the system to a contemptible extent, and the Roosevelt administration had to cope with this psychological attitude." No fan of Schumpeter, John Kenneth Galbraith later reflected on the views he shared with Trudeau, notably "a consistent view of the inadequacy of those qualified simply by their possession of money or motivated only by the hope of pecuniary reward." Economics was, for Trudeau, not a mystical wand that

the wealthy could wave before the politician. Economic judgments were not the product of a science but more often the
result of special interests. It was a Harvard lesson he did not
forget. It moved Trudeau, who was himself a wealthy man, to
the political left.[37]

The second reason Trudeau moved away from economics
may seem paradoxical: by studying political economy, he finally
came to understand the significance of law. After his initial
encounter with the finest minds in economics, he moved on to
political science, which, initially for him, lacked the intellectual
excitement of economics. His course on comparative government offered by the distinguished British academic Samuel Finer
was, in Trudeau's view, too opinionated. More interesting was
Merle Fainsod's course on the Soviet Union, where he quickly
concluded that the British socialists Sidney and Beatrice Webb
were hopelessly naïve. Trudeau reached an important conclusion about political science and, perhaps, academic life: "The
more you read of [the Webbs'] seemingly thorough and detailed
analysis, the more you realize that respectable political scientists
can also indulge in pseudo-science."[38]

Trudeau also read several important contemporary works
on European fascism, and was profoundly troubled. He read
Franz Neumann's *Behemoth* sometime in 1945 and realized what
horrors Hitler had wrought. "Powerful work," Trudeau wrote in
his diary, "by an honest scientist, exceedingly well documented;
though written by a violent anti-Nazi, there is remarkably little
prejudice. The book in consequence is all the more convincing.
Shows all the power of Nazism, its awe-inspiring accomplishments; and yet analyses so thoroughly its cynicism, its militarism,
its fundamental, irrefutable irrationality." From Neumann's
work, Trudeau took an important lesson: liberal democracies
must prove that "efficiency" is compatible with liberty and that
"democracy is not synonymous with capitalistic exploitation."[39]

This important conclusion was the germ of his later beliefs that politics in a democracy must be "functional" and that romantic and unrealistic notions such as nationalism could be deeply damaging. Law is important not in the landlord-tenant disputes he had worked on in Montreal but in establishing the covenant between a ruler and a people. Positivist social science itself was insufficient because statistics cannot establish values. After reading Auguste Comte, he concluded: "The spiritual should have a decisive voice in education, but it should be only consultative in action."[40] This assessment marked a profound break with some of his earlier assumptions, and it remained a belief that was to animate his future public life.

Harvard and its professors made Trudeau rethink what he had learned and done. His past suddenly seemed parochial; all the excitement of Jean Drapeau's by-election, the plebiscite, and the debates in *Quartier Latin* seemed very different viewed through the prism of the violent history of the twentieth century. He realized, just as the Third Reich fell in the spring 1945, that he had been wrong.

> Will this be my great regret? In all my life, never to have raised my eyes from work of questionable value, tied to a hypothetical future, when the greatest cataclysm of all time was occurring ten hours from my desk. Or, does listening to one's conscience bring its own compensations for the losses it inflicts? And incidentally, what is true conscience, that which comes from reason or that which one feels intuitively?

Pierre had written these words to Thérèse Gouin in Montreal, and she asked for clarification: What cataclysm do you mean? He curtly answered on May 25, 1945, just as the Third Reich fell: "PS–The cataclysm? It was the war, the war, the WAR!"[41]

First baby picture, Pierre with his mother, Grace Elliott Trudeau.

On the boat to Europe. Front to back: Charles-Émile, "Tippy," Grace, and Pierre.

Grace Elliott Trudeau,
Pierre's beloved mother.

Pierre and his brother, Tip, already liked fast cars.

Pierre's last class at Querbes. Pierre is fourth from the right in second row; Pierre Vandeboncoeur is between the two priests on the left.

Class photo of the Belles-Lettres class at Brébeuf in 1936: Father Bernier is in the middle, front row; Jean de Grandpré is fourth from the right in the fourth row from the back, Pierre stands fourth from the left in the third row from the back and his face is turned away from the camera.

"Pour Pierre." The photograph that François Hertel, the influential mentor at Brébeuf, sent the young Trudeau.

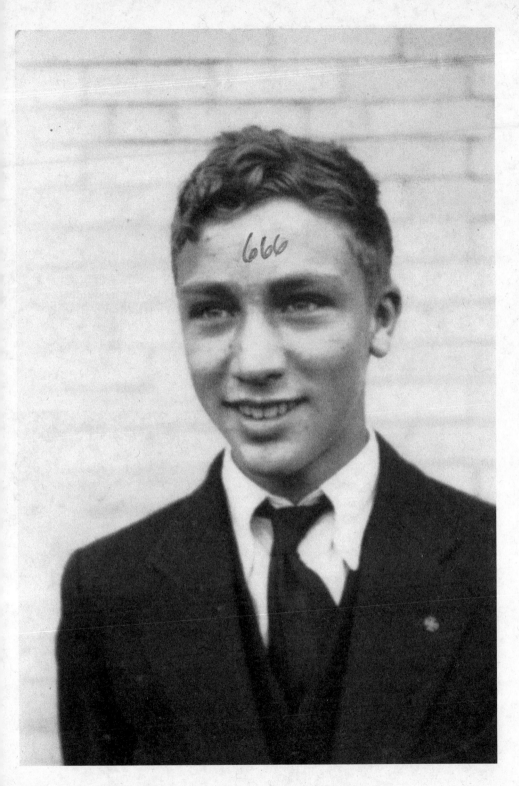

The young Brébeuf scholar with his school badge in his lapel.

Throwing snowballs.
Winter, Montreal, 1935.

Pierre the team captain. Lacrosse, 1936. He stands in the middle of the second row.

Pierre (at back) at Old Orchard Beach. He had told his father he was not interested in girls!

Pierre with his first love, Camille Corriveau, at Old Orchard Beach, Maine.

Camille in 1940. Pierre found her as attractive as Vivien Leigh and Jean Harlow, his favourite movie stars, but this demure portrait disappointed him.

Camille and Pierre on the beach again. Camille introduced Pierre to both Proust and the kiss.

This exchange had a long life. George Radwanski was troubled when Trudeau spoke to him in the seventies about the war. He said, simply, that he had been "taught to keep away from imperialistic wars"—an explanation Radwanski found not "entirely convincing."[42] More tellingly, in his own memoirs, Trudeau seems to have an almost exact memory of the exchange with Thérèse. "It was only at Harvard, in the autumn of 1944," he wrote, "that I came to appreciate fully the historic importance of the war that was ending." Of course, it was not in 1944 that he wrote his letter to Thérèse but in May 1945, which was the actual date for the end of the war in Europe. He continued: "In that super-informed environment, it was impossible for me not to grasp the true dimensions of the war, despite my continued indifference towards the news media." Again, in almost exact parallel to his comment in May 1945, he wrote: "I realized then that I had, as it were, missed one of the major events of the century in which I was living."

Thérèse Gouin later recalled accurately that Trudeau had expressed doubts to her about the way the war had passed him by, but he never raised the issue again in his more than two hundred letters to her. Moreover, in his memoirs he refused to express any regrets for "missing" the "historic importance" of the war. "I have always regarded regret as a useless emotion," he said. At Harvard, he had "no time to indulge such moods."[43] The exchange reveals much about Trudeau: his exceptional memory, which retained exact details of his earlier thoughts and actions; his quick reactions to great events and his tendency to cast them in terms of his own personal narrative; and his willingness to change his views without pausing to admit he had been wrong. He had little patience with those who remained mired in the past, and, despite his great memory for detail, he could also close his mind to events and experiences that he deemed "chaff," a waste of time.[44]

In one powerful way, Trudeau's memory is correct: he did change at Harvard. From the debris he found around him in 1945, Trudeau, like the West itself, began a process of reconstruction. He realized that the law was not what he had learned in the "horrible" civil procedure class at the Université de Montréal or in the landlord-tenant tiffs he had handled in his practice. Rather, it was a conceptual framework through which he could understand change and help to shape it. His notes, particularly in his classes on political thought with constitutional scholar Carl Friedrich* and legal historian Charles McIlwain, reveal a curious and exceptional intelligence actively engaged in organizing his experience and his previous learning into categories of modern legal and political thought.[45]

The courses in general celebrated liberal democracy and were very different from what Trudeau had heard at Brébeuf. He recognized the contrast in intellectual climate and was sometimes uncomfortable. He "did not see the traces of fanaticism and ultra-democratic sentiment" in Samuel Finer's textbook, he said, that were sometimes present in his course.[46] Similarly, he had reservations about Friedrich's support of the Nuremberg trials, saying that "the present trials only give more legal appearance to things that could be done without them." Friedrich argued that the trials were important, even if "they deny positive law," because when a new "community" is created "it often overrules legal concepts." Trudeau was not convinced: "But if the emerging community imposed duties on the Germans, it did too on the

---

* On one occasion Trudeau took issue with Carl Friedrich on a question of philosophical definition. Friedrich apparently dismissed his comments, but then asked to see him and apologized for his brusqueness. Trudeau, as he told Thérèse, appreciated the gesture. Trudeau to Thérèse Gouin, Feb. 14, 1946, TP, vol. 48, file 17.

Allies. Shouldn't they be punished for having created a state of affairs conducive to war? Etc."* He himself was sceptical of the positivist and secular tone he found in many of his professors.

Trudeau did not become an American liberal democrat, but neither was he any longer the corporatist Catholic of Brébeuf days. Harvard, along with the success of the democracies in wartime, greatly altered his political thinking. Moreover, it focused his mind on the importance of the rule of law and its embodiment in constitutions—documents that could be used to protect minority rights. He remained deeply sceptical of the celebrations of British tradition at Harvard. He also retained a Quebec nationalist's resentment of the British impact on his people.

One professor, William Yandell Elliott, an anglophile, deeply offended him, and he responded by challenging him, at one time murmuring "son of a bitch" in class. When Elliott said that Robert Borden seemed an imperialist to French Canadians but a liberal to foreigners, and that R.B. Bennett put

---

* Trudeau was deeply troubled by another book, *The Day of Reckoning* (New York: Knopf, 1943), by Max Radin, a law professor, who had argued for international war-crimes courts. "Far from realizing its goal of making the trials for war criminals seem justified," Trudeau argued, "it raises a great many doubts—if not on humane grounds—surely on legal ones. I think it certain that if the (hypothetical) accusation was of an individual crime-murder-the trial should have been before ordinary tribunals of the state where the crime was committed. Before an international court, you can only try international crimes, e.g., who caused the war? But such a question can only be answered by history. The court's refusal of trial before German courts on grounds that it would take too much time is surely spurious." Trudeau continued to hold these views as prime minister when he argued against "correcting" history by compensating Japanese Canadians and in favour of trials of war criminals in Canadian courts. TP, vol. 7, file 21.

Canada first, Trudeau wrote: "But both would rush to defend Britain! . . . maybe their Canada First was Canadian pockets first." He put an exclamation mark in Elliott's statement that "G.B. prestige [came] as center of spiritual values[!] of freedom and toleration." The course profoundly annoyed him, as did the required readings. On one work he wrote: "There are any number of tedious repetitions and re-repetitions. But this seems to be the English way . . . Rather poor style; and many boring precautions, introductions, forewarnings etc. that the author thinks marks of a conscientious thinker."[47] Alas, Trudeau had the ill fortune to have two courses with Elliott and to write his major paper for him. One of these courses had considerable Canadian content, including F.R. Scott, J.B Brebner, and Stephen Leacock. Scott had impressed Trudeau very much when he spoke at the Université de Montréal in 1943 in opposition to conscription and the infringement of civil liberties in Quebec, but he was only a brief respite from Trudeau's general irritation with the course. Elliott assigned his own book on the British Empire as a text, even though it had been published in 1932. Trudeau was rightly contemptuous: "The Chapters were originally delivered as lectures, it seems. Which would account for the loose structure and loose style throughout. For all the rest would be forgiven, even a certain supercilious humor, if facts were not 14 years old."[48]

Trudeau submitted his major essay, "A Theory of Political Violence," to Elliott on January 20, 1946. He had consulted with him about sources several times, as well as with a new friend, Louis Hartz, who was to become a major theorist of American liberalism. Hartz, who was Jewish, had suggested that Trudeau study Mussolini, and Elliott had recommended, sensibly, that Trudeau look at Harold Laski, Tolstoy, and Gandhi. The essay, it seems, was written deliberately to offend Elliott. Trudeau, for example, said that the 1837 Rebellions should not be called by that term because "the 'Canadiens' were too realistic to believe their shooting would have much more effect than scaring the rulers into being a little less iniquitous." He wrote also of "our North-west Rebellion" as an uprising that aimed only "at getting a little more justice out of the Federal Government." One sees traces here of the debates in 1942 and Trudeau's flirtation with violent protest and demonstrations. He returned to Brébeuf form when he denounced the "liberal bourgeoisie" as "lovers of vicarious experience." Then came a remarkable paragraph:

> So I will say very little of [propaganda], else that I always feel a touch of hypochondria when I see how propaganda of a stupid sort can succeed in making people swear by absurdities one day, and die for the contrary absurdities the next day. "The sacred and worthless Atlantic Charter. The impossibility and necessity of conscription. Roosevelt for peace and for war too. Our friend Russia, the arch fiend. Beloved, execrable Finland Etc." Where mendacity in former times had to be whispered from mouth to ear, now that it is coupled with propaganda, every one in the land can be made to change his mind quicker than his shirt.

On the returned paper, Trudeau wrote beside this paragraph: "Probably the reason for my mark 'B.'"[49] Surely it was, but only in part. There were other reasons too. The essay, apart from its eccentricities, is weak. It drips with contempt for Elliott's anglophile views and for the man himself. Elliott was pompous but not entirely a fool. The paper merits his complaint that "it misses the systematic analysis and application of concepts." Too often it prefers the quip and the rhetorical flourish to the sustained development of its thoughts.

In Harvard's inflated mark system, the B meant trouble for Trudeau just before his general examinations, which, if passed successfully, would permit him to continue for a doctorate. He had done well in other courses, notably Merle Fainsod's course on Russia. Typically, he responded to the challenge. In May 1946 Trudeau passed his examinations with distinction — and left with an "A.M.," as Harvard eccentrically abbreviates its master's degree.

—

Trudeau did not like Harvard, even though he recognized that the experience and the education were intellectually valuable. Several of his classmates from his Harvard years have described him as "holed up in his room at Perkins Hall [the drab graduate residence], working ceaselessly to master the mysteries of economics and to cope with the heavy readings and essay assignments prescribed by his professors."[50] Unlike earlier student days, he did not participate in extracurricular events, and he made few friends. Traces of his Brébeuf flamboyance remained: the sign that he posted on the door of his room read "Pierre Trudeau, Citizen of the World" — though at Harvard its meaning was very different from what it would have meant at Brébeuf. His values were now increasingly cosmopolitan, a concept shunned by many of his teachers in the 1930s. His outlook changed. In many ways, Trudeau later minimized Harvard's influence. In an interview for the New Yorker in 1969, he spoke barely of Harvard but said, "I have probably read more of Dostoevski, Stendhal, and Tolstoy than the average statesman, and less of Keynes, Mill, and Marx."[51] The statement is absurdly modest and untrue.

Politics or, more accurately, the relationship between political action and political thought preoccupied him at Harvard. In his letters to Thérèse Gouin, he spoke almost never of literature but frequently of politics and, obsessively, of himself.* Trudeau, as Camille Corriveau earlier sensed, considered himself a loner and found intimacy difficult. Whether consciously or not, he took her advice that he must find someone he could trust and, with her, share his fears and hopes. He and his friends were invariably flirtatious in their relations with women, a trait that was common among young males at the time. Trudeau himself had become congenitally flirtatious, much like Clark Gable and Humphrey Bogart, the current movie stars. Yet proprieties were still often rigorous. After Tip's marriage, his wife, Andrée, wrote to Trudeau: "Pierre you are not supposed to write Xs to me because I'm married. They are for your girlfriends. Besides, they make me shy."[52]

In his isolation at Harvard, Thérèse Gouin seemed the ideal answer to his prayers. She had an eminent political lineage. Her

---

* The remarkable collection of letters between Thérèse Gouin and Pierre Trudeau is an archival treasure that reveals brilliantly two extraordinary young people as they fall in love and debate their times, dreams, and future. When their relationship ended, Thérèse returned his letters to Pierre, and he kept them in his personal archive. Madame Gouin Décarie did not expect that these letters would become available to any researcher during her lifetime. Pierre promised her they would not when they met during the 1970s. At that time he told her he had recently re-read the letters, and his comments about the war in his memoirs suggest that he also read them again in the early 1990s.

When the Trudeau private archive was transferred to Library and Archives Canada, the Gouin-Trudeau correspondence formed part of the donation. Because I had full access to the papers, I was able to consult the correspondence. I immediately recognized that, for a Trudeau biographer, it was the most significant portion of the entire archive. Moreover, Madame Gouin Décarie was one of the two or three most important influences on the young Trudeau. When I met with her to discuss these letters and her relationship great-grandfather Honoré Mercier was the founder of the Parti national and had become premier of Quebec in 1887 after a nationalist campaign that followed the hanging of Louis Riel. His son-in-law Sir Lomer Gouin, Thérèse's grandfather, became premier in 1905 and steered Quebec through the difficult war years; he opposed conscription in 1917 but then, in 1918, eloquently defended Confederation in a historic debate on a Quebec legislative resolution which stated that Quebec should leave Canada. After retiring in 1920, he became a minister in Mackenzie King's federal government from 1921 to 1924. His son Paul Gouin formed the radical Action libérale nationale in the thirties, the party that was popular with Brébeuf students, including Pierre

---

with Trudeau, she stated that she never expected that the letters would be read by anyone except Trudeau before her death. She had always refused to speak about her relationship with Pierre except with her husband, who admired Pierre. She said her reticence was, in part, a reflection of the agreement she had made with Pierre years before.

Once she became aware that her letters were in Library and Archives Canada, she travelled to Ottawa to read them. She wants them to remain private, but she recognizes the great significance of the correspondence for a biographer and has graciously allowed me to use the information I found in them. Her extraordinary generosity and warmth became evident as soon as I met her, and I immediately grasped why Pierre had become enthralled with this highly intelligent and sensitive woman. She and her husband, the distinguished philosopher Vianney Décarie, spoke freely of their enduring affection for "Pierre." They laughed easily about his pranks, complexity, and zest for experience. Of course, the "break-up" between Thérèse and Pierre created initial distance, but, eventually, both Thérèse and Pierre came to recognize that her decision in 1947 was correct, even though they retained deep affection for each other. When the Gouin-Trudeau correspondence does become public, readers will understand well why they did.

Trudeau, at the time. Pierre had heard him speak at the college in 1937, where he told the students and priests that he thought it his duty to battle Communism. He ended with the words "We are the sons of heroic Canadians and do not retreat before the sons of Stalin."[53] Lomer Gouin's other son, Léon-Mercier Gouin, a prominent Montreal lawyer and Thérèse's father, accepted an appointment to the Senate as a Liberal in 1940 and served as a deliberate Liberal contrast to Paul, who opposed the war and became associated with the Bloc populaire canadien in 1942. Rich, brilliant, attractive, and a student of psychology, Thérèse responded to Pierre's loneliness. She was a godsend to him during his two years in Cambridge, Massachusetts.

In the spring of 1945, just as his despair about Harvard deepened, Thérèse replied to a despondent letter from Pierre by telling him that she would see him in Boston on a study trip in early June. He was always careful when he wrote to her and sometimes produced multiple drafts of his letter. In his letter of response, he told her that, although he could speak to her more honestly than to other women, he had hesitated to write openly for several months.[54] That summer in Montreal, Pierre's springtime invitation to become "a friend" deepened into love. "Forgive me," he wrote on July 5, 1945, "for having slipped away without a gesture, Thursday evening. You appeared to be sleeping, and why should I awaken you?"[55] The formal *vous* became the personal *tu* by September, when he wrote from Boston, "this city of strangers," asking her for a photograph or a letter. He even attended some lectures on psychology so he could report to her on Harvard's Psychology Department.[56] She turned twenty-two that September; Pierre, twenty-six in October.

He began to write letters of remarkable intensity to her. The previous year, he wrote on September 26, 1945, he did not wish her happy birthday because of his natural reserve. But in 1945 he would wish her happy birthday knowing that she was ready to accept the joy and the worries and this strange being that was called Pierre Elliott Trudeau. And that was how he ended this early love letter.[57]

They soon became deeply affectionate, but the price for Thérèse was bitter complaints about his Harvard life. All was going badly, he wrote in October:

> I'm a misanthrope. I hate the Americans, their jazz, their cigarettes, their elevators.
>
> For almost three weeks now I've been trying to learn the virtue you recommended: flexibility.
>
> One has to be as flexible in life . . . Well, damn it, madam! I'm now in a room where you can hear all the neighbours' noises, the radios across the hall, the pianos downstairs, the elevators next door, the bands in the night-club, the kids in the street, the pacing upstairs, and the racket of the garbage men.[58]

The complaints continued: his work was "going to hell." In restaurants, thoughtless women sitting beside him blew hated cigarette smoke; in seminars, there were the abominable pipes. "I embrace you," he concludes this very long letter of complaint.

A few days later, on the eve of his birthday, his mood was better: "And so I am Pierre, I am 26 years old, I have passed my quarter-century, and for the first time [on a birthday] I have received an extraordinary and almost frightening gift." Her love had saved him from the arid and lifeless atmosphere in which he was imprisoned.[59] Yet, he protested, she did not write as often as she should. And there was the matter of the photograph. It was rather strange, he wrote on November 15, 1945, that almost every-one had a photo of his girlfriend except for him: "I who is—or you pretend is—one of your favourite admirers."[60] In reply, she play-fully dismissed his doubts and declared her love. In their letters, she became "Tess"; he, "my love" or, sometimes, "my little one."

He was demanding, complaining in one letter that she did not care enough about her physical health and that she should "work out" and not breathe the bad air on St. Catherine Street. Among his laments about his work and school, there were boasts about his own physical prowess, such as when he noted that he alone at the Harvard pool could do the swan half-twist.[61]

Despite his doubts about Harvard, he encouraged Tip to study architecture there with the German exile Walter Gropius. Tip, who clearly deferred to his older brother, took his advice after his marriage in June 1945.[62] The many contradictions in Pierre sometimes troubled Thérèse, and she chastised him often for being evasive. Their caution and Catholicism mixed oddly with the Freudian psychology that Thérèse studied and Pierre found intriguing. In planning their Christmas together in 1945, he wrote: "It would be so charming if we could celebrate the Nativity side by side." He dreamed of a midnight Mass together in the northern countryside, "but such plans perhaps assume an intimacy that is not appropriate or correct for us in the circumstances. Alas!"[63] He asked that his mother be involved in their plans together. And so she was.

Grace was, probably, present too often. Trudeau would later say that she "was a great respecter of the freedom of her children and was always prepared to take a chance." She allowed them to make their own decisions and did not impose her wishes.[64] Yet we sense in the letters how powerful her presence was to Pierre and how he yearned for her approval. Clarkson and McCall comment astutely that Thérèse "seemed eligible even to Grace Trudeau, who was notoriously sniffy about her son's female friends."[65] The freedom she granted created its own constraints. And she could be so intimidating. Thérèse told Pierre that she found Grace formidable. She said they talked often on the telephone, but "in front of your mother, I'm always afraid to show affection and to tell her how much I like her."[66] Yet neither her presence nor the eminence of Thérèse's father (whose Liberal politics Trudeau certainly did not share) inhibited the growth of their love. After he returned to Boston, he yearned for her presence:

> I've read your letter which had been waiting for me [in Boston] since before Christmas. I've found new reasons to love you, and thus to be even sadder. I don't yet dare take out your photograph because your real face is still freshly imprinted on my memory. But I think despairingly that just a few days will erase these ineffable features, that the taste of your mouth will elude me, that your heartbeat will vanish along with the soft warmth of your body. And so will begin my meditation before your image.

In conclusion, he quoted Walt Whitman:

> Passage, immediate passage! The blood burns in my veins
> Have we not darken'd and dazed ourselves with books
>   long enough?
> Sail forth—steer for the deep waters only
> Reckless O soul, exploring, I with thee, and thou with me.[67]

Trudeau desperately wanted to see her in the latter half of January, but his schoolwork was overwhelming; moreover, his mother wanted him to join her, Tip, and Andrée in New York at the end of the month. Thérèse also had school work, but he told her not to worry so much about her thesis. It was a means, not an end: "I want you to be a woman, Thérèse," he pleaded; "I don't want you to be an intellectual." Moreover, he was jealous of her associates at the psychology clinic who were allowed to dissect her soul, who knew more of "*my* Thérèse" than he, who talked with her about sex, masturbation, and other matters that he and she did not dare to raise. He was jealous of the way she turned herself over to "those who didn't truly care about her," while to him, who loved her, she pretended to "pacify" him with the assurance that he was "not neurotic." And she, he continued his rant, carried the blood of the daughter of a senator "and of the great Mercier! O shame, shame, shame!"[68] The tensions in this exchange— about her career, his ambitions, psychology, politics, and sex— intruded on the deep affection developing between Thérèse and Pierre. The strain reflected their place and their era.

Despite his desire for her presence, Trudeau had already begun applying to European universities for the fall term in 1946. He would attend classes abroad while continuing to work on a dissertation for Harvard, although he had not established a supervisor there for the work. In the end, he won two scholarships, one from the Quebec government to go to Oxford and one from the French government to study in Paris. With the war's end, the plans he had long ago made for study in Europe could finally be fulfilled, and he chose Paris. The French capital attracted him because he believed, correctly, that its spirit was markedly different from Harvard. Just before his general examinations, he complained to Thérèse: "The method of instruction at Harvard is the worst you can imagine. Everybody complains but nobody rebels. The teaching staff is recruited nearly exclusively of tyrants or megalomaniacs, with the result being a servile student body. Everyone simply follows the course because otherwise the professors will punish you. One does not study to learn something useful but simply to get the grades." He admitted that many of the professors were brilliant but deplored the fact that equally brilliant students were so servile.[69] Happily, his close friend Roger Rolland was also heading to Paris.

Thérèse and Pierre had begun to dream of touring the world, of transforming Quebec, of spending their lives together. She told him she would come to Boston at Easter with a friend. Her letter, with its news and its vision of a shared life, delighted

him, "for [he wrote in English] it was not the letter of the intellectual, nor of the psychologist, nor of the mystic, nor even of the
childish romanticist; but that of the *woman I love*." He found a
place for the two girls for thirty-five cents a day, near Perkins Hall,
and warned her that if she arrived with any of her "far-fetched,
incongruous, high-sounding and unconvincing complications of
the soul," he would have no patience.[70] At Harvard he showed her
off, and she was "wonderful advertising for Canada." Her sweet
presence still graced Harvard, the restaurant where they dined,
and his room after she left. Yet there were some problems among
the rush of expressions of love. It seemed to him that there was a
part of her that remained closed to him.[71] He admitted he was
often rude, complaining about her supervisor Father Mailloux,
snapping at her over dinner, but, then, "Thérèse, understand me,
I ask you on bended knee and with wet eyes to stop me from
becoming someone 'who loved not wisely, but too well.' I love
you too much to love you wisely."[72]

In May, after successfully passing his general examinations,
Trudeau delayed his return to Montreal for several days because
his mother had decided to come to Boston, which meant that
Thérèse and Pierre would see each other for but one week in
June. He had to return to Boston to receive his degree on June 26,
and she had to leave on a study trip. Although both their schedules caused the problem, he said she was too caught up in her
psychology courses.[73] Just before he went to Harvard for graduation, he and Thérèse went to the annual meeting of the Quebec
bar, which was held, serendipitously, at the Manoir Richelieu,
close to the Gouin summer home. Along with her mother, they
all dressed up for the grand banquet. He returned to Montreal on
his fabled Harley-Davidson late on a Sunday night.

Surprisingly, after graduation, he went to work in the
Sullivan gold mines at Val d'Or, Abitibi—the company Charles
Trudeau had invested in after he sold his garages to Imperial

Oil. There Pierre truly went underground for a short time, and emerged with stories of hard labour that he used thereafter as the occasion arose, particularly with his sons.[74] His pay book indicates that he began on July 9 and ended on August 2, sufficient time to dirty his hands. "The work is hard," he wrote Thérèse, "the men tough, the food plentiful, the night cold, the flies bad . . . and," he added suggestively, "my arms are empty every night."[75] His pay was $5.65 for an eight-hour day, more than he had been paid as a very junior lawyer. His fellow miners probably did not know that the Trudeau family owned many shares in the company.[76] He concluded that, despite his hopes of getting to know and understand the workers, he remained different from them: "I am not assimilable. I don't speak like them, I don't think like them." Their drinking habits bothered the young ascetic, but he was more troubled, he said, by the emotional distance between him and the other men.[77]

The brief and solitary experience of hard manual labour does not seem to fit with the young intellectual he had become. What took him underground as a miner in the summer of 1946? He gave no answers then or later, but we can surmise that the purpose was similar to the journeys to the wilds of earlier summers. He possessed a profound desire to know "the other," and in the postwar world where labour and socialist parties thrived, the "worker" was an "other" that Trudeau believed he must know. In this instance, his disappointment was keen when he discovered that he stood apart.

That summer, before he left for Paris, Thérèse and Pierre talked often about marriage and about going to Paris together. Thérèse's mother whispered in her ear that Pierre was "a strange man," but Thérèse reassured her that even though he was, she still loved him madly. Moreover, the mother had come to adore her daughter's brilliant and rich beau, however strange he sometimes could be.[78] Pierre tried to get Thérèse more interested in politics, and he gave her a recent book by Harold Laski to read—agreeing, in return, to read one on psychology.[79] While he worked in the mine, she travelled to the Gaspé. In the end, they spent only a few weeks together in this summer they had long dreamed of sharing.

—

Trudeau left Montreal in September and arrived in France on the 29th, Thérèse's birthday. She wrote to him the previous day, asking where he was: "Today, I am 22 years old and I love you; tomorrow I will be 23 and I will love you still."[80] He did not respond until October 9, his excuse being that he had no paper and had lost some of his considerable baggage. Among the items he took to France were a beret, a Grenfell parka, a tuxedo, five suits, five sports jackets, eleven "chemises de ville," eight sport shirts, four sweaters, eleven jockey shorts, skis, his Harley (a treasured machine on Paris boulevards after the war), chocolate, jam, sugar, coffee—and cigarettes for his uncle, Gordon Elliott, who had returned to France after the Liberation.[81] Mocking himself and Thérèse's psychology studies, he said he had already lost his analism in Paris. In truth, he admitted he had lost himself in the quartiers, the courtyards, the grand boulevards, and the bistros of Paris.[82] In those times, so did many others.

Perhaps there was, in fact, no paper on which Pierre could have written. There was still rationing in Paris in the early fall of 1946, and the streets had few taxis, many military vehicles, and an emptiness that allowed a rich young Canadian student to race his Harley "across Paris at speeds that under other circumstances would have cost me my life—or at least my freedom."[83] Pétain, whom Trudeau had defended at Harvard, was in jail, his death sentence for treason having been commuted to life imprisonment. Charles de Gaulle, France's president after the Liberation, had resigned dramatically in January 1946, leaving an uneasy provisional government, including Communists, Socialists, and the right-wing group, over which the socialist Félix Gouin briefly presided. Soon after Trudeau's arrival, the French narrowly approved a draft constitution that gave women the vote. In the elections that followed on November 10, the Communists came first, but the third party, the Socialists, again provided the premier because the right quarrelled with the Communists. In the grand hotels, diplomats and journalists gossiped long into the nights as the Allies tried to agree on the shape of the postwar world, while prostitutes outside the peace conference offered delegates "an atomic bomb" experience.

Paris came alive after the Liberation. The clash of ideas between East and West, left and right, the modern and the traditional played out on a front along the Left Bank of the Seine, around the dining tables of the Café de Flore, or in cramped apartments crammed with books and Picassos. Jean-Paul Sartre, Albert Camus, Simone de Beauvoir, Maurice Merleau-Ponty, and others who came to dominate the footnotes of postwar Western academic journals created one of the great moments of the intellectual life of the twentieth century in Paris in these years. For Trudeau, the atmosphere was familiar in its uniquely French blend of the literary with the philosophical. As a Catholic, he became intellectually engaged in the attempt to reconcile Catholicism, modernism, and Communism, and this endeavour left a lasting intellectual imprint upon him. He was present, as one critic later said, in Paris during its "heyday."[84]

After staying at the Maison des étudiants canadiens, a student residence built in 1926 at the initiative of Canadians, Trudeau and Roger Rolland moved in the spring into L'Hôtel Square, a small but charming Left Bank hotel on St-Julien-le-Pauvre. There François Hertel, Pierre's former mentor and confidant, soon joined them. They had, as the hotel correctly advertises, "the finest view" of the magnificent Notre Dame Cathedral, and they all enjoyed their proximity to the intellectual and social turmoil of St-Germain-des-Près. The church on their street had become a Greek Orthodox Church late in the nineteenth century when secularism thrived in Paris.[85] Unlike Harvard, where Trudeau had no friends from Montreal, Paris had attracted seven other students from his years at Brébeuf, including Guy Viau, with whom he had canoed the Canadian Shield. Most of them, like Rolland, were studying literature and the arts, but Trudeau alone among former Brébeuf students opted for political science at the École libre des sciences politiques.[86] Other Montrealers, notably Jean Gascon and Jean-Louis Roux, guided their compatriots through the experimental theatre of Paris, while a future Trudeau minister, Jean-Luc Pepin, also studied politics.[87]

Aware of his presence in the city at a remarkable moment in the arts, Trudeau retained a pile of ticket stubs that indicate he saw, among other performances, Jean-Paul Sartre's *Huis-Clos*, Paul Claudel's *L'échange*, a private "Hommage à Jean Cocteau," as well as events with Walter Damrosrch, Artur Rubinstein, Jascha Heifetz, Leopold Stokowski, and Harry James. He also attended the opening of the celebrated Automatism exhibit at the Galerie du Luxembourg which featured Paul-Émile Borduas, Jean-Paul Riopelle, and other Quebec artists.[88]

With relatively light academic requirements, given his limited goal of gaining background information for his proposed Harvard dissertation on the vaguely defined but important theme of Communism and Christianity, Trudeau had freedom to indulge once again his love of the arts and, simply, to enjoy Paris. Now that Trudeau was united with François Hertel and Roger Rolland, the three quickly recalled an old trick they had learned together in Montreal. "Les Agonisants," or "The Dying," as Hertel, Rolland, and Trudeau dubbed themselves, performed their remarkable feat of suddenly going rigid, falling forward, and catching themselves with their hands only at the last second. In the salons and cafés of Paris they would appear to drop dead, one after another, before astonished Parisian innocents.[89] Trudeau comes alive in the photos from France, most tellingly in the images sent back to Canada by the French information service. Trudeau's brilliant eyes begin to dominate photos, and his physicality is obvious in the lithe contortions evident even in the still photography.

After his immersion in contemporary liberal democratic theory at Harvard, France took him back to familiar subjects in his personal history—most notably, religion. The postwar period proved to be a turning point in French Catholicism, and most of the contemporary French theologians Trudeau had encountered earlier at Brébeuf were themselves coming to terms with the war and its aftermath. In the lecture halls and churches of Paris during those years, the historic path to Vatican II was being paved as the Catholic Church modernized its liturgy, broke down barriers to dialogue with other faiths, and created a greater role for the laity. In early 1947 Trudeau attended lectures with Étienne Gilson, the great neo-Thomist philosopher, and, within a period of five weeks, he met the personalist Emmanuel Mounier, the Christian existentialist Gabriel Marcel, and the Jesuit Teilhard de Chardin, whose visionary linkage of evolution with Christianity deeply influenced modern Catholic thought.[90] He reported to Thérèse that he had met Teilhard, whom he found "formidable," but added that "Hertel was also formidable in his own way."[91] However, it was Mounier who left the deepest mark on Trudeau as the student linked his religious beliefs with his own sense of individual identity.

"It was [in Paris]," Trudeau later wrote, "that I became a follower of personalism, a philosophy that reconciles the individual and society. The person . . . is the individual enriched with a social conscience, integrated into the life of the communities around him and the economic context of his time." Although he had encountered personalism through Hertel and Maritain in the late thirties and forties, the war had fundamentally affected the concept of what personalism meant. In the courses he chose and the lectures and conferences he attended in Paris in 1946–47, Trudeau began to shape his personalist approach to religion.[92] He was, as always, a diligent student and, as before, he received permission from the church to read some proscribed books on the Index, so long as he kept them to himself. Among his courses, he studied with the renowned historian Pierre Renouvin and the sociologist André Siegfried, who had written two major works on Canada. He went on a student pilgrimage to Chartres in May 1947 and attended many other lectures on religious thought, especially with Hertel.[93]

These interests and activities captured the attention of his earlier acquaintance Gérard Pelletier, who was travelling through Europe for a Catholic fund for student victims of war. He had asked Trudeau in March to head a seminar on American civilization at Salzburg, Austria, that summer and to take an active part in the international Catholic youth movement.[94] Though Trudeau refused, he, Pelletier, and the other young Quebec students in France had begun to contrast the intellectual atmosphere in Canada with the passionate and open debates among Catholics, socialists, existentialists, and Communists that occurred in France and Europe more generally. Together, a group of these students wrote a bitter letter of protest home objecting to Premier Duplessis's banning of the celebrated French film Les enfants du paradis,[95] whose frank treatment of sexuality offended the church, but only one newspaper published it. Marcel Rioux, one of the Canadian students in Paris, recalls that "a negative unanimity" developed among these young intellectuals in this period against both the political regime and the hardened and ritualistic

Catholicism in Quebec.[96] It was a negativity that created the passion of positive commitment.

—

While Trudeau was wrestling successfully with his problems of religious and intellectual identity, his absence was creating difficulties in his relationship with Thérèse, problems that made him seek help to understand why he acted as he did. Paradoxically, Montreal seemed far away from Paris, despite the presence of many, like Guy Viau and Roger Rolland, who were part of the circle of friends they had shared in Montreal. Paris, where the left and especially the Communists occupied the postwar intellectual mainstream, radicalized Trudeau, who, like Emmanuel Mounier, sought to discover the intersection between Catholic thought and the egalitarianism of Communism. In these circumstances, Trudeau made little apparent use of the letters of introduction written by Senator Gouin to important Paris friends in which he described Trudeau as "a little like an adopted son."[97] Thérèse began to sense quickly that Paris was changing Pierre and that the rush of emotion that had overflowed in his letters from his lonely Harvard room did not flow quite so freely in Paris. Still, he began a letter on October 21, 1946: "This morning just before I woke up, I dreamt that you came into my bedroom and, to make me wake up, kissed me warmly on the mouth . . . it was so real, so beautiful, so good."[98]

But it was only a dream. He wrote less frequently than she expected; he asked how she found the time to write so often. He worried that she did too much, for "you are weak, a woman, delicate, precious and so petite. How are you able to prepare your course, your thesis, and the conference presentation and the evening course and [simultaneously] go through psychoanalysis, go to Mass, and do your exercises?"[99] But the bonds between them remained very strong: although he loved Paris, he said he loved her more. He wrote her on November 6 after looking at her latest photos: "Your last photo is stunning; with your hair swept back and your open mouth, you have a fire around you with the style of an Irish lass—and I love you always with all my heart."[100]

Thérèse expressed some doubt when she replied, indicating that their friend "D.D." (Andrée Desautels) thought Pierre should have a woman who was tall, thin, and fair, not one with the dark complexion and full figure that Thérèse possessed. She missed his presence profoundly, but with the reserve that marked young Quebec Catholics of their station, she added: "No, what I have to say has no sense and maybe cannot be said. I just feel like loving you. I think that if you were near me tonight, my darling, I would be 'coy,' resist you, play with you, evade you and then kiss you so hard and so well that you would feel faint. Therefore it is much better, my darling, that you are not near me."[101] How, after only two months apart, could they endure ten months? But for conservative young Roman Catholics of the time, the sexual revolution was far in the future. Courtship was prolonged, restricted, and titillating simply because sexual intercourse itself was inconceivable.

Despite their yearnings, they continued to disagree about her work and about the psychoanalysis she was undergoing as part of her academic course. He went to hear the psychologist Anna Freud, Sigmund Freud's daughter, speak at UNESCO and attended a seminar on love and marriage as a mark of his good will.[102] She told him—helpfully, she hoped—that her psychoanalysis made her realize that she was guilty because she had concealed some things from him. She did so, she added perhaps unhelpfully, because she felt in him "an insatiable curiosity" to know everything about her. She had no desire to live with Pierre "under a system of rules with exchanges and obligations," an attitude that obviously ruled out marriage soon. They should rather maintain an "essential" friendship.[103] Pierre responded to her in early December, saying he was not really bothered by the suggestion that she should keep some of what occurred in her psychoanalytic sessions private. However, he did not like her letter: "It's the tone in which you speak to me, a tone that is cold, strange, and even defiant." He admitted to being possessive, but added that being together meant sharing thoughts, hopes, and events.[104]

Then, on December 10, Trudeau was rushed to the American hospital in Paris for an emergency appendectomy. The cost of the stay was meagre, about the price of a stay in a modest Paris hotel at the time, but the anaesthetic was in short supply. The operation was painful and the food scarce. On December 13 he had to eat meat on a Friday, probably for the first time in his life.[105]

From his hospital bed he wrote to Thérèse. He had thought about their love and had come to realize that jealousy was a deadly emotion. He apologized. Moreover, she should now become his fiancée. On his back in the hospital, he had realized that life without her would be impossible. He signed off, "Poor Pierre."[106] She sent a message of love at Christmas, but he had already left for Mégève, in the Alps, to recuperate. There, his mood changed. He wrote her a letter a few days later in which he returned to her earlier letter that had irritated him. He again questioned her course of psychoanalysis. Once more he was jealous, apparently because their mutual friend Pierre Vadeboncoeur had passed on some news that displeased him about the company she was keeping. He hinted that "André Lussier" is more than "a friend"—but only the draft of this letter remains; he never sent the final copy. However, in a letter he did send on December 29 he admitted what he had intended to write: "At this morning's Mass, I prayed for you. And I was ashamed of myself, profoundly ashamed because yesterday I wrote you a harsh letter that I knew would deeply hurt my 'Katsi,'" a pet name for her. He apologized, but he remained anxious about her associates and asked specifically about a friend with whom she went to a concert.[107] These fits of jealousy occurred even though Pierre and Thérèse had agreed that both could go to social events with others during their separation.[108]

The worm had entered the bud. Their letters alternated between abundant expressions of love and querulous doubts. On February 15 she was exasperated, not least because he had hinted he was enjoying the presence of a blonde. Indeed, he was. He had met Sylvia Priestley, and his agenda reveals that he saw her often that month. Thérèse called Pierre "cette étrange construction," this strange construction, and recommended that he consider psychoanalysis himself. In fact, he had already begun to visit a Paris psychoanalyst. He told her it was "cette dernière concession," his last concession.[109]

What survives of the consultations are the bills, which are high; the hours of consultation, which modern psychoanalysts tell me are unusually long; and Trudeau's transcript of his dream diary and his own notes of the sessions where he associated freely.* Psychoanalysis in the postwar period was thoroughly grounded in Freudian theory, and Trudeau's psychoanalyst, Georges Parcheminey, used Freudian categories to describe the process of

---

* I deliberately chose not to read these notes in full until I reached this point in my story of Trudeau's life, fearing they would influence the earlier chapters and sharing, I admit, some of Trudeau's doubts about overdependence on Freudian psychoanalysis for understanding the formation of identity. Once I did read them, I decided that the notes have great value, particularly because they confirm much of what Trudeau's teachers, school friends, and some scholars have surmised about him. But they also reveal subtle and even major amendments to the standard version of Trudeau presented in his own memoirs and in other studies of him. Still, there are problems with the document.

identity formation. Though a poor empiricist himself, Freud believed that psychoanalysis required a series of sustained sessions, and Trudeau's psychoanalysis reflected that belief. He went three or more times each week for appointments that sometimes lasted several hours. Fortunately, he found a psychoanalyst who mixed solid common sense with the heavy doses of Freudianism. He often told Trudeau not to take himself, his problems, or psychoanalysis as a science too seriously. Trudeau grew fond of the fifty-nine-year-old psychiatrist, whose commitment to Freud was so strong that he had courageously paid tribute to the Viennese Jew during the German occupation of Paris, and before German officers.[110]

The notes on the psychiatric sessions provide a snapshot of Trudeau at a particular and emotional time, February to June 1947.[111] They reflect those circumstances, particularly in their many references to his closest friend at that moment, Roger Rolland, and to Hertel, who lived in the same hotel room. They confirm Rolland's penchant for pranks and excursions but suggest little else about him. They substantiate Trudeau's close relationship with Hertel, but also his doubts about Hertel's fights with the church. He mentions Pierre Vadeboncoeur (nicknamed "the Pott") frequently, though in the context of his fondness for a friend whom he regarded as wonderfully eccentric. Unfortunately, some of the document is illegible, especially the part where Trudeau was scribbling down his psychiatrist's interpretation of his dreams or free associations.

The first dream, the night of February 11–12, sees him at the gold mine where he had worked the previous summer. A worker speaks to him about a nationalist book, which has been reissued in a deluxe edition. The worker explains that such writings displease the company management. Trudeau says he will buy the book, but not in the deluxe edition. The doctor gave this sensible interpretation to the dream: Trudeau's nationalism conflicts with his professional ambitions. In another dream that describes a speech by Henri Bourassa, Trudeau becomes troubled when someone he did not invite shows up. Similarly, when someone tells him that a Co-operative Commonwealth Federation candidate lost an election, he says, "Too bad," but then, when told that this candidate "got beaten in King's constituency," he approves, even though, earlier, he seems to have the contrary view. Ambition, nationalism, and socialism clearly clashed. There was, however, surprisingly little politics in his dreams.

In many dreams, his father was strikingly present and was regarded fondly and rather sweetly, such as when "Papa, on his return from Europe, ordered a 'frou-frou' cake, but a 'Canadien' brought him a half 'tarte' with whipped cream." In one session of free association with the doctor, he spoke of "great admiration" for his father but of impatience with certain of his mother's characteristics. His brother, Tip, and sister, Suzette, appear often in the dreams, without particular comments, but Parcheminey told Trudeau, who agreed, that he envied their more settled state, especially the fact they were married. Throughout the sessions, Trudeau talked about his fear of choice and the conflict between his wishes to tour the world and to have a "place." He saw a contention between his desire to be independent, which sometimes led to aggressiveness, and the contrary quality of caring about what other people think. Parcheminey told him it was a response to his timidity—a normal reaction when growing up.

On another occasion Trudeau described a dream in which he was walking along a beach with his mother when her brother Gordon appeared. Trudeau left them and went off with a young woman who was somewhat common and who told him he was good for nothing except skiing—a comment that pleased him. He then took a taxi, but the driver annoyed him by speaking English. He refused to pay him because he had not put on the meter. He concluded that this dream showed his dependency towards familial duty, his possessiveness towards money, and his sense of inferiority, which he manifested in his reaction to the skiing comment and his aggressiveness with the driver. In psychiatric terms, he wrote: "It is the combination of timidity and aggressiveness. I was not able to reveal myself openly in the genital phase because of restrictions. We saw, therefore, a regression towards the preceding phase, the anal phase. This frustration causes timidity and aggressiveness. [I show] possessiveness in the case of some things (money, adventures, and reputation, etc.) And these compensate for a genital phase that had not been achieved." When Parcheminey heard this interpretation, he warned Trudeau not to make too much of his own analysis and to avoid so much self-criticism—surely good advice.

When Trudeau talked about the development of his religious convictions, Parcheminey explained that they had become a restraint made even stronger by the sense of duty instilled during his childhood. He said that he had not found any particular castration complex in Trudeau which had been traumatizing, though there was "a certain blockage at the doorstep to virility" that had created compensation mechanisms through regression. In one of Trudeau's early dreams he leaves his friends to go in a car that has some beautiful women as passengers; another dream has him at a church, dressed in a bathing suit; and yet another has him finding a crucifix on a table and removing the linen that covers it. The psychiatrist explained that these dreams revealed how his religion conflicted with his "élan vital" and how he sublimated his strong sexual desires through his religious and intellectual activities as well as through sports and adventures. In the story of the cross, Parcheminey found a tendency to "asexuer le Christ." The genitals in these dreams are "dirty, unacceptable things."

Trudeau's mind whirled with these different comments. At that moment, he received a letter from Thérèse, who was at a retreat and fasting for Lent. Psychoanalysis, she told him, helps an individual to understand the self but not to change the self.[112] Pierre appeared to agree: after his many hesitations on the value of Thérèse's own psychoanalysis, he now seemed to develop a belief that the process could be helpful in fathoming himself.

Despite the costs in money and time, Trudeau persisted in his frequent trips to the psychiatric couch, where, his notes indicate, he hoped to gain insight into his timidity, aggressiveness, and sexuality. Parcheminey and Trudeau talked about homosexuality (which the psychiatrist said was curable, unlike schizophrenia), and he assured Trudeau that his absence of sexual intercourse with women did not mean that he had homosexual tendencies. He agreed with Trudeau, to use Freudian terms, that he often "regressed" to the anal phase, with its characteristic timidity, possessiveness, and occasional aggressiveness. Still, in Parcheminey's view, Trudeau's sexuality, although he remained a virgin at twenty-seven, was "normal." He had sublimated his strong sexual drive successfully because he was a believing Catholic, and marriage therefore had a special importance for him. In his own observations, Trudeau noted that abstinence and marital fidelity were much less common in France than in Quebec, even among believers.[113]

After a break at Easter, where patient and doctor agreed that Trudeau had no neurosis but that the sessions were nonetheless helpful, he returned for the final set that began in mid-May and ended on June 14, just before he left France. On his return, Trudeau said he wanted to focus on career and personal development, and both Parcheminey and Trudeau agreed that controlling his aggressiveness and impetuosity were important in that respect. They were, in the doctor's view, perhaps the result of his timidity and his lack of "visibility." The psychiatrist reassured him, after further discussion of a series of dreams, that there were mechanisms to cope: in Trudeau's case, marriage. "One or two years of married life, where the vital spirits would be able to find expression, where your virility would find its expression in the responsibility of the marital home, the contact with feminine softness, and the satisfaction of your sexual appetite."

After this discussion, the meetings continued for two more weeks, with marriage a central topic. Trudeau had a dream where a friend described a marriage gone bad, and another where his father confided in him how he had proposed to his mother. Parcheminey told Trudeau that it was probably true that his school and the strong moral authority of his home and his father were barriers to an "affirmation of self," but, step by step, adolescence and adulthood would lead to the solution of his problem, especially when he finally had intercourse within marriage. And so, to end the sense of inferiority and to achieve his desired virility, he must become "a man with a wife." The alternative was sublimation of his sexuality.

Parcheminey advised Trudeau that he considered the analysis ended. "One or two years after marriage, all should go well," he said.[114]

It would not be so easy.

CHAPTER 4

—

COMING HOME

During the winter months, Pierre and Thérèse had begun to consider spending their lives together. Senator Léon-Mercier Gouin, Thérèse's father, had even raised the question of a possible journalistic career for Trudeau in discussion with some publishers; and, in early March, Thérèse overcame her timidity in the presence of Grace Trudeau and attended a concert with her.[1] It appeared that, in Parcheminey's parting words, all would work out. And, sometimes, it seemed it would.

Thérèse finished her thesis, graduating *summa cum laude* and winning the major prize. Pierre rejected Gérard Pelletier's tempting invitation to lead a Harvard summer school in Salzburg and instead made plans for the summer with Thérèse in Quebec.[2] Yet jealousies stirred in Pierre, and doubts arose with Thérèse. Pierre went to dances in Paris; Thérèse, to concerts in Montreal. He yearned for her presence, but there were lapses in the letters and too many abject apologies. Although he complained about Thérèse's many friends and what he termed her silences, his own life was filled with parties, dances, and some other women in the spring of 1947. "If I wanted to make you jealous," he wrote to her in March, "I would tell you of a certain American or of Sylvia,* the daughter of the English writer [J.B.] Priestley."[3]

Grace Trudeau met up with Pierre in Paris in April, and mother and son toured the French Riviera together, sometimes on his Harley-Davidson, with the grande dame of Outremont riding behind her daredevil son. They saw the Ballets russes at the Casino de Monaco during the Easter break. She remained in France until June 6, only a few days before Pierre himself embarked for Canada.[4]

In Montreal's dreary spring, Thérèse dreamed that she, too, was in Paris, walking with Pierre along the Champs Élysées in the night, guided by the light of the fountains and the monuments while the fragrance of spring blossoms lingered in the air. As their hands softly embraced, she turned towards him, "his clear profile lost in the stars." She told him that she loved him and, she whispered, "I believe that you, too, are stepping towards love." In this letter, written shortly after Easter, she thanked Pierre for the chocolate rabbit he had sent but even more for his "love letter" and, above all, for his "great love."[5] On May 21 he told her of the romantic hotel where he dwelt and added: "If you would be my mistress, we would share the room together beneath the garret, between the dusty walls. The bed is low and rough, but your arms would be soft and your mouth welcoming . . . Every morning we would find a lost corner of Notre Dame and ask for pardon."[6] His desires were clear.

Yet tensions abounded. In his sessions with Parcheminey, Trudeau spoke surprisingly seldom about Thérèse but did have

* Priestley was second only to Churchill in his influence on the BBC in wartime. His broadcasts appealed enormously to the British working class. Trudeau told Thérèse that her father would not approve of Priestley's socialism.

visions of other women, including Thérèse's friend Andrée
Desautels, or D.D., who herself came to Paris in the spring. The
correspondence became intense yet less frequent, especially from
Thérèse. He wrote to her on April 16, begging her to write more
often, but before he sent the letter, he received one from her in
which she yearned for his return, while promising to meet him
wearing a hat of flowers when he arrived in July on the *Empress
of Canada*. Soon they quarrelled again about psychoanalysis,
and he protested strongly that she had revealed in Catholic confession that he was seeing a psychoanalyst: "a secret ought to
remain a secret," he bitterly complained.[7] On June 1, 1947, the
mood was different when he wrote to "My love Therese, my love-
able child, my crazy wise virgin." Still doubts persisted. He said
that "D.D." had spoken with difficulty about Thérèse. What did
D.D.'s silences mean? Why should he learn about her academic
success from others? A week later, after a bad dream about
Thérèse and an odd dream about "D.D.,"[8] he wrote an angry
letter, addressing her ambivalently as "My foolish love."[9]

> My very difficult darling, I have to rebuke you for being so
> worried, for being so full of fear and anguish. I pray for you
> often, as you have asked; but God is not pleased with you.
> He has told me that you were somewhat idolatrous and
> that you now find yourself being punished for worship-
> ping science above Him. You are playing God, and are
> becoming caught up in your own game. Beware that your
> game does not first trap you and, then, strangle you.
>
> My love, continue with your analysis, pursue it seriously
> and honestly. But don't take *tragically* that which should
> only be taken *seriously*. Believe me, Péguy's advice is impor-
> tant for you. Out of love for me—if you still have any such
> love left—do not try to do too much good. Remember that
> the arrival of this letter precedes my own arrival by only

three weeks; be tamer in those few days that remain. Your soul is peaceful; your spirit should be so as well. Do not fight, do not yell (I am using your own expressions). Do not inquire so persistently: you have not lost anything and you are not yet lost yourself. You are in my heart, I am holding your heart; yet I cannot embrace your spirit; it should be a more calm and more loving one.

Believe me, out of love for me I ask you to believe me; can you do so out of love for me? Don't take your analysis or [your analyst Father Noël] Mailloux so seriously in these few remaining days. You are so sad, and I hate myself because I am not there with you now. But give me only one half-moon, and I will be with you in Montreal. In the meantime, I urge you, at any cost, don't finish the analysis. You will have all summer and all of next year, and your whole life to do what you wish. But right now, ask Mailloux for permission not to worry so much: perhaps you can go to Malbaie for a few days, and, then, maybe you will see my ship go by in the distance, past the whistling buoy.

Parch[eminey] often warns against needless fears, against unscientific inductions, and against generalizations and systematizations. One must be calm and patient. You shouldn't believe in the bogeyman. Apparently, psychology students [like you] don't heed such advice.

We must not destroy all that time has slowly created. Above all, we must not systematize. My friend, my friend, my love, I wish so dearly that you would not be so sad.

~~Pierre~~ Me

P.S. I am leaving Paris on the 21st; you have time to send me a letter if you feel up to it.

Thérèse, I have just reread my letter, and I fear you will ignore all my words, instead choosing to portray me as ill-disposed towards psychoanalysis. You should not read my letter as such; I like your psychoanalysis, but I want you to do it better, in a way that is less caricatured. Either stop, or move forward "very cautiously."

The letter arrived just before Pierre reached Montreal, not on the *Empress of Canada* to be greeted by Thérèse in her hat of flowers but by air from Paris at 6 a.m. on June 22. They met again nine days later, and their love affair began to end. Years later Thérèse reminisced that, in the spring of 1947, she had decided that "if she and Pierre were to marry, they would have endured marital misery of a monumental order, 'un grand malheur.'"[10] Perhaps. Certainly, if the two privileged and brilliant children of the francophone elite had wed, their lives together would have been very different from the lives they did in fact lead.[11] Thérèse became an eminent psychologist.* Pierre would probably have become a university professor, a lawyer, or even a rich businessman. Again, perhaps.

What we do know is that he was most willing to marry Thérèse in the fall of 1946 and the spring of 1947 and that their relationship soured because of his jealousy, their professional ambitions, his suspicion of her psychiatric analysis — and his demand that she prematurely end it. We also know that, for a long time, they loved each other intensely in the peculiar fashion

---

* Thérèse became one of Canada's best-known psychologists, the author of several important works on the psychology of children, and an interpreter of the experimental psychology of Jean Piaget. An outstanding researcher and academic, she became an Officer of the Order of Canada in 1977 and served as president of several psychology associations.

of their different time and place. Theirs was not a physical relationship but it was intensely emotional. For that reason, we know that when Thérèse ended their love affair, the disappointment shattered Trudeau more than any other event since the loss of his father. He wrote to her brother Lomer on July 10: "It is exactly 24 hours ago that your sister removed all reason for me to live." Men, he said, cannot survive such deep wounds. And because he sensed there was a certain empathy between Lomer and himself, he asked him to discover whether Thérèse could even "bear my presence." Could they meet just once more? He ended with the signature, "Your lamentable, etc. Pierre."[12]

Brothers, of course, are seldom useful in such cases, but Pierre did try to meet "Tess" once more at the Gouins' summer home in Malbaie on the St. Lawrence, but Thérèse, to her mother's distress, would not see him. Trudeau stayed the night but left the morning of July 27, without talking to her. The next year she fell in love with Trudeau's friend Vianney Décarie, a young philosopher. In the late spring of 1948, as Vianney and Thérèse were dining at the apartment of Jean-Luc Pepin in Paris, there was a knock at the door. It was Pierre, Jean-Luc's former classmate, but he had come to see Thérèse. This time they did speak, but when Thérèse told him she was now engaged, he simply shrugged. In that case, he said, he would tour the world alone.[13]

Their paths crossed often in the future, Trudeau saved press clippings about the increasingly eminent psychologist Thérèse Décarie,[14] and Vianney published in Cité libre—the journal Trudeau edited for several years. In 1968 the Décaries, both then professors at the Université de Montréal, circulated a petition soliciting support for the candidacy of Pierre Trudeau for the leadership of the Liberal Party.[15] There's also a story, repeated by Stephen Clarkson and Christina McCall, that, after Trudeau became prime minister, Thérèse went to Ottawa and asked a staff member in the Prime Minister's Office if she could see him and offer her congratulations. Trudeau was not there, but she asked for a sheet of paper, wrote *Thérèse* on it, kissed it, and left the lipstick-stained note on the desk.

Madame Gouin Décarie laughs when asked about the story. There was neither the visit nor the lipstick on the paper: it was a prank by their mutual friend and congenital prankster, Roger Rolland, who was then a speechwriter for Trudeau. There is only one note from Thérèse in Trudeau's papers after their love affair ended. It is undated, but was surely written in 1969 when his political fortunes began to fall after the triumphant election of 1968. "Pierre, our Pierre, what has happened to you? You always seem angry. Your eyes are spiteful, and you appear mean." She cautioned him that those around him and those he must rely on would not understand. She ended gracefully: "We think so often of you. Thérèse."[17] The note lacks lipstick but not affection and dignity.

Thoroughly romantic, Trudeau deeply mourned the end of their relationship. It was, admittedly, an affair that seemed to flourish best when they were apart and one that faced many constraints. Still, its end was a decisive moment in the career of Pierre Trudeau. That summer in Montreal he seemed adrift. He saw a few old friends, including some women. In his quest for solitude, he journeyed by foot the hundred miles from Montreal to Lac St-Jean, experiencing the rough charms of La Mauricie, its surging rapids, deep forests, and high waterfalls.[18] In early August he took his first flying lesson, and continued the classes every day for two weeks in a Curtiss-Reid plane. He managed to fly solo on September 3, but he does not appear to have earned a permanent flying licence, although in the early fifties he did take up gliding.

During the remaining few weeks of the summer and early fall, Trudeau did not sulk as jilted lovers sometimes do. His calendar was full and interesting. On July 7 he had lunch with his friend Gérard Pelletier, and he spent the evening with his erstwhile revolutionary companion François Lessard and his wife. In mid-August he went to Toronto with Catholic youth leader Claude Ryan, who would later become a rival and a Quebec Liberal leader — they were hoping to found a coordinating committee of Canadian Catholic associations. Pelletier, a key organizer, was unable to accompany them because he lost his train ticket. In Toronto, Trudeau met Ted McNichols, whom he described as a Protestant and a Communist. The meeting featured "lively discussions on democracy and the possibility of reconciling [democratic] life with Communism." On his return, he went north on his motorbike, where he met an acquaintance whose girlfriend reminded him poignantly of Thérèse. He spent an evening with François Hertel, who was also back in Montreal, and visited Abbé Groulx. He spoke to Claude Ryan on Hertel's behalf, probably to explore whether his old mentor, who had by now left the Jesuits but not the church, could find work with the groups Ryan was organizing.

—

In September, Trudeau left Montreal once more for study abroad, this time at the London School of Economics (LSE). Within a month he would celebrate his twenty-eighth birthday. He travelled in a first-class berth on the *Empress of Canada*, and among his fellow passengers were Allan Blakeney, the future Saskatchewan premier, and Marcel Lambert, later Speaker of the House of Commons, both in tourist class.[19] Significantly, before he departed, he made certain that his Quebec links were strong. On September 8 he had lunch with Lomer Gouin; met at 3:30 with Gérard Filion, who became editor of *Le Devoir* in 1947; and followed with a call on the conservative nationalist Léopold Richer, with whom he spoke about possible articles for the journal *Notre Temps*. The following day he saw Claude Ryan again and had dinner with Hertel in the evening. Hertel was, in that month, his closest companion. He also had lunch with his classmate

Charles Lussier, now a promising lawyer, at the home of Paul Gouin, Thérèse's uncle, the former radical Liberal politician. And just before his departure, he met with the eminent civil libertarian, law professor, and poet F.R. Scott at the McGill Faculty Club.[20] Altogether, Trudeau's agenda for the summer of 1947 confirms his strong political interests and his continuing links with Catholic youth groups (Pelletier and Ryan), with Liberals (Gouin), with socialists (Scott), and with older and more traditional Quebec nationalists (Groulx, Hertel, Lessard, and Richer). Already he was preparing for his future. He was keeping many options open.

What did he discuss at these meetings? Career most likely, his education probably, politics certainly. Some hint of Trudeau's mood in these times is given in a letter to him from Lomer Gouin in the fall. Lomer, who had begun practising law, told Trudeau that he reminded him of "a bit of champagne that had turned into vinegar: you are full of effervescence, of young courage, but the taste is bitter." He would never make a good saint, but he was "ripe" for politics, a profession where saints, apparently, did not thrive. Gouin encouraged him to halt his travelling and his studies and return home. There would be elections in the spring, and Pierre should run, presumably as a Liberal candidate.[21]

Confusion and contradiction more than emptiness seemed to mark Trudeau's life in late 1947. He entered a doctoral program in political science at LSE in October, even though his Harvard doctoral thesis remained undone. And London, he soon found, was not Paris. The cluster of intense, madcap Brébeuf and Montreal friends was missing, and Trudeau stayed aloof, just as he had at Harvard. Paul Fox, a classmate and later an eminent Canadian political scientist, recalled that Trudeau seemed like a "young nobleman on a Grand Tour, very intelligent but quite disengaged."[22] As at Brébeuf, Trudeau deliberately concealed parts of himself, revealing only what seemed appropriate to the circumstances. His past, however, had made him, and the traces

were clear: some he followed fitfully; others he began systematically to efface.

One trace was indelible: his commitment to Roman Catholic
Christianity. But the nature of that commitment was changing. He
could still write a letter that would have satisfied the most traditional of his Brébeuf teachers. At Easter 1947, for example, he had
written to Thérèse about "the Christ of the Passion," who had come
to represent for him the fundamental humanity of Christ. Christ's
last days, he continued, were filled with uncertainty, betrayal, and
defeat. He was no more than a poor fisher, and that humility bore
His essential message to us. To the ever devout François Lessard, he
sent a postcard that same Easter that ended with the words "Christ
is King!"[23] In Paris he had paid scant attention to the atheist existentialism of Jean-Paul Sartre, Albert Camus, and Simone de Beauvoir,
but Paris had nevertheless jolted him loose from the restraints on
behaviour that Catholic devotion had previously entailed. In particular, his extended encounter with Freudian psychology at the dawn
of the age of Kinsey began to loosen the religious bindings on his
sexual behaviour.* Trudeau's faith was becoming more personal
and less responsive to ecclesiastical authority and tradition, and in
this respect he reflected his more fully defined personalist approach
to religion and Catholic belief. While remaining a believer, he was

------

* The Toronto conference of young leaders that Trudeau, Claude Ryan, and
others attended in August 1947 indicates that most Canadian young people
were conservative in their personal behaviour. The meeting discussed a poll
taken in 1945 of 57 Catholics, 56 of whom went to church every week. They
were all opposed to gambling; 40 were opposed to drinking; and only 26 were
supportive of "kisses and caresses" between unmarried men and women. All
said they were opposed to going further than kisses and caresses—a frontier
Trudeau was soon to cross. TP, vol. 8, file 16.

becoming a sceptic towards the Quebec Catholic Church, which, in his opinion, lacked the breath of contemporary life.

Some critics have pointed to contradictions in Trudeau's beliefs at this time. They certainly exist, as is to be expected in a man of his age, though his papers make it clear that they derived less from uncertainty on his part than from the influence of old friendships and relationships. He maintained close ties with the increasingly conservative and nationalist Quebec journal *Notre Temps*, in which he had invested the considerable sum of $1,000 in 1945. It had emerged from the rubble of the Bloc populaire canadien, where conservative and leftist nationalists had briefly embraced during the war. Subsequently, it had become increasingly supportive of the conservative provincial government of Maurice Duplessis and his Union nationale party.[24]

In the spring of 1947, Trudeau had told Thérèse that he felt angry with Canada and that he intended to write a critical essay about his country. And, soon after he arrived in London, he produced a long article, "Citadelles d'orthodoxie," which *Notre Temps* published in its October issue. As the title implies, Trudeau attacked the "orthodoxies" of contemporary Quebec society. While acknowledging that the conservatism of Quebec society had been essential in the resistance to assimilation, he deplored the way religion and nationalism had become stale "orthodoxies" that suffocated citizens who sought to be free, "without a system." The article is curiously vague and refers to only two individuals, the nationalists Henri Bourassa and Paul Gouin. Trudeau linked both of them with the "courageous" initiatives of the Bloc populaire. On the whole, the article lacks clarity, detail, and force; it reflects a mind in motion, but one whose direction is still unclear.[25]

Another major change came in Trudeau's political understanding and outlook. Both the classrooms and the streets of Paris had taken him on paths that led towards the political left. At

Harvard he had attended a couple of "socialist" gatherings, mainly out of curiosity. In Paris the Communists carried the cachet of wartime resistance and the promise of a revolutionary future. Trudeau was intrigued, particularly by the attempts of French Catholics to come to terms with the challenge of Communism. The eminent philosopher Emmanuel Mounier cast away the remnants of corporatist thought, which Vichy and wartime Belgium had discredited, and took up the cause of Christian socialism and opposition to the role of American capitalism in the postwar world. In his journal, *Esprit*, he linked personalism and Marxism, pointing out that both were concerned with alienation in modern industrial society. He saw the Communist revolution that was stirring in postwar France as a means of rejuvenating Christianity itself.[26]

These thoughts intrigued Trudeau. When the excitement of the Parisian streets drew him into the mass movements of the left, he had related to Thérèse how a demonstration had carried over from the revolutionary cafés of the Left Bank to the government institutions on the Right Bank; how he had been surrounded by police but managed to escape, then waved "bye-bye" in the depths of a Métro station.[27] More seriously, he listened attentively as Mounier and other French Catholics turned to socialism to reinvigorate Christianity.

While still in Paris, Trudeau had begun to tell friends that the thesis he would finally write would not focus on a narrow academic subject but would make a major contribution to the grand debate about the reconciliation of Catholicism and Communism. Long into the nights that year he debated with Gérard Pelletier whether anyone could reconcile Communism and the Catholic faith. Later, before the Iron Curtain crumbled, Pelletier candidly admitted the attraction Communism offered in those years. His French friend at the time, Jean Chesneaux, said that the logic of Christianity compelled a Christian to be a Communist in the postwar years. Trudeau, Pelletier continued, was more informed, more rational, yet in those times, in "the pile of rubble Europe had become . . . with neighbourhoods . . . flattened by bombs, and where Auschwitz and Dachau were horrible testimony to the bankruptcy not only of fascism but also of pre-war conservatism, Communism was a temptation or, at the very least, intriguing to a young practising Catholic."[28]

The London School of Economics was poorly suited for the study of Catholicism but ideal for academic work on Communism. Although it already had some eminent conservative thinkers, notably Friedrich Hayek, whose 1944 classic, *The Road to Serfdom*, was a brilliant attack on state planning, the school was rightly identified with the British Labour Party and with socialism. Sidney Webb, whose admiring work on the Soviet Union Trudeau had scorned at Harvard, had founded the LSE in 1896 to advance "socialist" education. Britain's postwar Labour prime minister, Clement Attlee, had taught there, but its most noted faculty member when Trudeau arrived was Harold Laski, a political scientist and Labour Party adviser. Laski had taught at McGill during the First World War, knew the United States well, and was a highly controversial public figure because of his continued praise for the Soviet Union as the Cold War began. He was, moreover, a brilliant lecturer—Trudeau described him as having an "absolutely outstanding mind"—who encouraged debate among his adoring students. Ralph Miliband, a British Marxist political scientist, recalled how Laski came up by train during the war to lecture in Cambridge:

> The winter was bitter and train carriages unheated. He would appear in his blue overcoat and grotesquely shaped black hat, his cheeks blue with cold, teeth chattering, and queue up with the rest of us for a cup of foul but hot coffee, go up to the seminar room, crack a joke at the gathering of students who were waiting for him, sit down, light a cigarette

and plunge into controversy and argument; and a dreary stuffy room would come to life and there would only be a group of people bent on the elucidation of ideas. We did not feel overwhelmed by his knowledge and learning, and we did not feel so because he did not know the meaning of condescension. We never felt compelled to agree with him, because it was so obvious that he loved a good fight and did not hide behind his years and experience.[29]

Trudeau cared little for London but very much for Laski. He became a major intellectual and, to a lesser degree, personal influence on the young Canadian. A decade after Trudeau had written the anti-Semitic *Dupés*, only five years after he had questioned Jewish immigration and participated in a riot where Jewish windows were smashed, his mentor was a Jew and a socialist.

In the formal ways of even the socialist English, Laski required students to send him a letter requesting their first appointment. Trudeau saw him at 3:15 on October 8, and he asked Laski to be his thesis supervisor and told him he would like to research the relationship between Communism and Christianity. Trudeau, it seems, impressed Laski immediately: he agreed to supervise his thesis and allowed him to attend several of his seminars. Trudeau's schedule indicates that he had classes with Laski on "Democracy and the British Constitution" for over three hours every Monday afternoon, another seminar on "Liberalism" every Tuesday, and a final one on "Revolution" every Thursday.[30] Trudeau claimed later that, when he left London, "everything I had learned until then of law, economics, political science, and political philosophy came together for me."[31] Certainly it was not "together" when he arrived, as the prolix and opaque "Citadelles" article demonstrates. Harold Laski became, for Trudeau, a model: an engaged intellectual whose philosophical and political thought had influenced one of the major movements of the twentieth century—the British socialist movement as embodied in the Labour Party. Laski and the experience of the postwar Labour government was, he wrote to a friend, "excellent training" that made him anxious to return to Canada and to play his own part in politics.[32]

Laski may have influenced Trudeau in another way. He wrote superb accessible prose that Labour backbenchers, trade unionists, and Oxford dons could all appreciate. He began his work on the state with this gem: "We argue, as with Aristotle, that the state exists to promote the good life. We insist, as with Hobbes, that there can be no civilization without the security it provides by its power over life and death. We agree, as with Locke, that only a common rule-making organ, to the operations of which men consent, can give us those rights to life and liberty and property without the peaceful enjoyment of which we are condemned to a miserable existence."[33] In London, Trudeau's mind became clearer, his prose sharper, and his political ambitions more strongly defined.

Trudeau brought from France his interest in the reconciliation of Christianity and Communism. But as the Labour Party under Foreign Minister Ernest Bevin joined the Western alliance against the Soviet Union, Laski became a critic of his own party, believing that it was Labour's first interest to come to terms with Soviet Communism, which, even though corrupted by power, represented the ideal of economic equality and justice without which there could be no true democracy. These views influenced Trudeau deeply, and he quickly moved outside the North American liberal mainstream represented by men such as Arthur Schlesinger and Lester Pearson, both of whom argued that Soviet Communism represented a fundamental threat to the principles of individual liberty and the practice of democracy. Laski's views on the Soviet Union and his later writings have aged badly; indeed, critics at the time said that his work seemed "very old-fashioned," especially in his insistence, after the Nazi catastrophe and the evidence of Soviet imperialism, that capitalism was the greatest enemy of human freedom.[34] Still, Laski's views found echoes on the French Catholic left, where Communism was a political force, and they resonated with the young Trudeau, who followed those debates closely.

Laski also influenced Trudeau's interest in federalism, a topic of paramount importance in his later writings. He was a major theorist on federalism who argued, much like the later Trudeau, that authority should reside where "it can be most wisely exercised for social purposes." Later he shifted to the view that the central government should have primacy because of broader social needs.[35] In this respect, trade unions have a fundamental obligation to become directly involved in political activity, both for the workers as individuals and for the working class in a pluralist democracy. Laski lamented the fact that American unions stood apart from the political process.

Trudeau had demonstrated little interest previously in the Canadian labour movement, which had advanced quickly in wartime, but in France and now in Britain he was witnessing first hand a different model, one he came to believe could be adapted to the political circumstances of Quebec. When he eventually returned to Canada, he immediately sought out labour leaders and spoke to the leaders of the Co-operative Commonwealth Federation, Canada's socialist party, which was slowly moving towards a close embrace of the Canadian labour movement.[36]

The impact of his work with Laski was already evident in an article he wrote for *Notre Temps* in November 1947. He followed his professor in emphasizing that a system of law bestows "a certain order of things that guarantees sufficient justice that no revolution occurs." Similarly, he criticized the previous Liberal government of Joseph-Adélard Godbout because it had relied on the federal government to correct social and economic abuses, but in a way that abused the distribution of powers set out in the

Canadian Constitution. The present Duplessis government, in contrast, abused the people of Quebec by refusing to enact social reforms, arguing that the Constitution prevented it from acting in these areas. Still, there was a chance for Quebec to act. It was not too late if Quebec rejected orthodoxy and if the people showed their disgust for the elites and their rigidity. If they did not, he would not hold much hope "for our Christian and French civilization which our ancestors created with so many hopes." However, if Trudeau came to agree with Laski on the importance of a politicized and active trade union movement, he disagreed on one major item.

Unlike the atheist Laski, Trudeau was very active in Catholic circles in England. In early January he attended a conference on "Existentialism and Personalism" in which the French intellectuals Emmanuel Mounier and Gabriel Marcel participated. It was also at this time that he began to study the works of Cardinal Newman and to participate in Catholic youth discussion groups. He joined the Union of Catholic Students and helped to collect books to ship to Catholic universities in Germany.[37]

Otherwise, he fraternized little with other Canadian students, who mostly lived in crammed student rooms. He, in contrast, could afford better accommodation—he lived at 48 Leith Manor in the tony Kensington section of London, met with the great names of academic life,* and raced his motorbike around

---

* Modern students can only envy Trudeau, because it is unusual for students to meet the great names of academic life. In London, Trudeau met with the famed Fabian socialist G.D.H. Cole (an "anti-papist") and Harold Laski on October 8, soon after his arrival. The next morning he met with Ritchie Calder, a celebrated journalist and politician. Within two months, he had attended lectures by the Labour intellectual Richard Crossman, the historian Arnold Toynbee, and the philosopher Bertrand Russell.

the city and through the narrow trails of the British country-side.[38] On the Harley-Davidson, he travelled 1,725 miles through England and Scotland, apparently following the shoreline as much as possible and staying in youth hostels when he could. On some weekends he disappeared to Paris, memorably when his wild, good-looking friend Roger Rolland married there on March 20, 1948. Suzette, who had a taste for gossip, reported to her brother that Madame Rolland had told her she was astonished at the marriage because she did not know her son was interested in women.* Pierre, the best man, was overcome at the wedding and could not find the words he wanted to say at the reception after-wards.[39] It was an unusual lapse, but, given his own recent loss of Thérèse, completely understandable.

The spring brought uncertainty and illness. In February, he contracted a virus, accompanied by diarrhea, which led to several trips to a Harley Street doctor and a stay in the Charing Cross Hospital. He thought about returning home, and his family, partic-ularly Suzette, who fretted about Pierre as older sisters often do, urged him to do so. He wrote to a "Monsieur Caron" about a teach-ing position at the Université de Montréal, adding in his letter that he had always aspired to be in "active politics one day or another."[40]

At the same time, unknown countries far away from home still beckoned. Trudeau had dreamed of a world tour while at Brébeuf, had tantalized Thérèse with the romance of travelling together around the globe, and had developed contacts with diverse people in several countries who might assist his passage. He had met the young Jacques Hébert at a Catholic gathering in

---

* Roger Rolland denies Suzette's tale, pointing out that his mother knew of his many girlfriends (including Thérèse Gouin). She was upset that she had not met Roger's fiancée. Letter from M. Rolland, June 7, 2006.

the summer of 1946, and the two quickly became friends after
Hébert regaled Trudeau with tales of his travels to exotic locales.
A rebellious student like Trudeau, Hébert, four years his junior,
had been sent by his father to Prince Edward Island to learn
English after he was expelled from a classical college. Hébert then
began a life of travel, and his tales intrigued Trudeau.[41] After he had
recovered from the intestinal illness in June, Trudeau went to
Harold Laski and asked for a letter of recommendation, telling him
he wanted to finish his thesis on Christianity and Communism by
travelling through Communist lands as well as the birthplaces of
the great religions in the Middle East and Asia.[42] Jules Léger, later
the Governor General of Canada but now a first secretary at the
High Commission in London, and Paul Beaulieu, the Canadian
cultural attaché in Paris, provided Canadian government letters of
reference for Trudeau's wanderings.[43]

He was only twenty-eight, but his family remained troubled
about his failure to "settle down." Suzette had complained to
him even before he went to Paris in 1946 that he "had enough
studying for one lifetime: that's what your friends and I have
decided anyhow!" He should, she warned, not force himself to
occupy every minute of his life with a "studied program—Learn
to live and let yourself go," she advised, "otherwise it will soon
be too late." More than two years later, in the fall of 1948, Tip
gave the same message to his brother, urging him to settle down
as he and Suzette had done earlier. Trudeau replied candidly,
mildly rebuking his younger brother for the criticism:

> You have chosen marriage, a home, the quiet life, the work
> you enjoy, and moderation. I'm a nomad by inclination, but
> also by necessity, for academic pursuits alone haven't
> brought me wisdom. As I discover the world, I discover
> myself. This no doubt seems terribly trite, but I now accept
> the trite along with all the rest.[44]

Trudeau wanted to strip down to the essentials. He would travel like "Everyman: on foot with a backpack, in third-class coaches on trains, on buses in China and elsewhere, and aboard cargo boats on rivers and seas." Then, he would rebuild, taking the strongest materials he had found in his education and experience, and bonding them to the enduring pillars of his heritage.[45]

—

Trudeau left London on a fine summer day in 1948 and headed east, determined to pierce the darkness that had fallen over Eastern Europe. Despite letters of introduction from Canadian officials, he encountered sullen border guards, machine guns, and barriers as he passed through Poland, Czechoslovakia, Austria, Hungary, Yugoslavia, and Bulgaria. Soot darkened the elegant mansions of the Hapsburg Empire, and the remains of war were everywhere. In Poland he saw Auschwitz, where, he wrote not entirely accurately, "5 million were killed by the Nazis (1/2 being Jews)." He seemed not to ponder then what Auschwitz meant, but he had long ago left behind the casual anti-Semitism of his adolescence.[46]

What he retained was his intense curiosity, his sharp blue eyes that scrutinized all he encountered, and his lean, muscled physique. He sometimes shaped himself to his environment, wearing a full, albeit thin beard through the Middle East and donning native garb when appropriate. At other times, he was defiant, wearing North American shorts where none had been seen before. When he failed in his plan to visit the Soviet Union, he passed in the company of some students from Bulgaria into Turkey and the Middle East, where stability had been shattered first by war and then by the establishment of the State of Israel. In May 1948 five Arab armies had attacked Israel, but the better-disciplined Israelis defeated them and seized most of the lands the British had held as Palestine under the League of Nations mandate. When Trudeau came in the fall of 1948, the war had not officially ended, and tensions and suspicions abounded. Borders were in doubt; gunfire sounded throughout the nights.

After he was told in Amman, Jordan, that all the roads to Jerusalem were closed, Trudeau joined a group of Arab soldiers and crossed over the Allenby Bridge to Israel, making his way up to the Old City of Jerusalem. Through gunfire, he sought refuge in a Dominican monastery. As he left, however, the pale-skinned, bearded Trudeau attracted the attention of Arab Legion soldiers, who promptly arrested him as a spy. He was briefly imprisoned in the Antonina Tower, where Pontius Pilate suppos-edly judged Christ. Fortunately, a Dominican priest, who, like most Arab Christians, probably sympathized with the Arab cause, convinced the jailers that Trudeau was simply a Canadian stu-dent, not a Jewish spy. A group of Arab soldiers returned him to Amman, no doubt convinced that the peculiar Canadian student was certainly a spy. In Jordan, where the government remained closely linked with Great Britain, the British passport that Trudeau had wisely procured in Turkey convinced the local authorities that he should be released.[47]

In the turbulent Middle East, Trudeau constantly encoun-tered new adventures and troubles of one sort or another. From Jordan he travelled to Iraq to visit Ur, Abraham's birthplace, and the fabled Babylon. When he stepped off the train, he asked to be directed to Ur and was immediately sent to the great ziggurat. He left his baggage at the station and wandered through the ruins of the city, collecting a few shattered tiles inscribed with Sumerian characters before climbing to the top of the ziggurat. As he did so, he encountered some bandits:

> They made it clear that they wanted money. One of them indicated by gesture: "Let's see your watch." Since I wasn't wearing one, I replied, "Let's see your knife"—and

snatched it from his belt. They persisted: "We want whatever you've got. Hand it all over."

But Trudeau now had the knife, and he persuaded them to
go down the stairs to discuss matters. Meanwhile, he tricked them
and stayed at the top, shouting down: "Now come and get me."
They stood transfixed while he began to scream "to the skies all
the poems I have memorized, beginning with Cocteau's verse
about antiquity. I spewed octosyllables and alexandrines by the
dozens. I accompanied them with dramatic gestures." They
quickly and understandably concluded he was "dangerously
deranged." He descended the stairs, "still yelling." As the brigands
disappeared into the desert, Trudeau suddenly realized that his
study of poetry had brought him unimagined benefits.[48] He was
alone in Ur, which was surprisingly pristine. After seeing the vast
mausoleum, he climbed the ziggurat once again and reflected on
the history that surrounded him and what it meant. To be sure, he
wrote to his mother, some of the greatest treasures were now in the
museums of the many conquerors:

> But digging will always obsess archaeologists, and the compul-
> sive ritual of the dig will continue to reward them mainly with
> frustration. Every bump may hide treasures, but every pit may
> also. Nothing is ever finished, even if you have to keep digging
> another six inches. And by removing soil, they make other
> mounds, and forget a shovel here and there, leading archaeol-
> ogists of the year 10,000 to establish that 20th-century man had
> made little progress since his Paleolithic ancestor . . .
>
> Having reached the top of the ziggurat, I saw an enor-
> mous black bird fly slowly away after defecating on the
> column whose offerings had once been made to the moon
> goddess . . . *Vanitas vanitatum, et omnia vanitas.*

Alone, five days after his twenty-ninth birthday, he saw the burning sun create his shadow, the only human form where once a great civilization had thrived.[49] He felt mortality.

With his prized British passport, Trudeau set off on the fabled Silk Road that carried him through Samarkand to India and Afghanistan. He had already developed a lifelong dislike of Canada's Department of External Affairs, whose representatives, he claimed, had treated the bearded backpacker with disdain — in sharp contrast with the friendly reception given by British diplomats. He wrote to his mother and sister on December 2 that, in India, the "people at the Canadian High Commission were quite nice for a change."[50] In general, however, he sought out priests when he needed counsel and refuge, and they welcomed the ascetic of New Testament appearance who knocked on their doors. Curiously, although he had made no formal arrangements with any Harvard professor to supervise his proposed thesis on Communism and Christianity, he used the pretext of thesis research for Harvard to gain entry to political offices and to journalists and professors.[51] As a result, the letters he wrote to his family from Asia present a remarkable portrait of a continent in turmoil and a young man in the process of finding himself.

Although Trudeau gloried the scantness of possessions and in the meagre cost of his trip ($800, he later claimed), he mingled with the mighty as well as the derelict and the desperate as he passed through the Middle East and on to India, China, and Japan, before returning to Canada in the spring of 1949, after almost a year on the road. He wrote several letters to his family as his adventure progressed. What they reveal is his fondness for his mother, whose travelling passion he inherited; his keen eye for the variety of human experiences; and his passion for understanding the basis of political action. In their own right, the letters are important as descriptions of Asia at this critical time, as the

British Raj dissolved, India divided violently into separate pieces, and a new united China bloodily emerged.

He wrote from Kabul in early December, having passed through the Punjab, where he saw the Golden Temple at Amritsar. There he discovered few who spoke English and concluded that the Indians "seem to be getting even against all foreigners for 150 years of foreign domination." Imperialism became a constant theme in his writings home. Stranded with only his knapsack, Trudeau found himself in the no man's land between India and the new state of Pakistan. He was rescued from a walk of twenty miles to the Pakistani frontier by "a Muslim Punjab Police Captain," who whisked him through police cordons in a private car. That night he went "to bed with a huge glass of sweetened warm buffalo milk" and "slept like an angel." The next morning, he continued, "I bid this hospitable family good-bye, despite the invitation to remain longer; for the wife had to remain in purda all the time a foreign man was in the house, and I couldn't bear keeping the man from his wife all the time I was there."[52]

He moved on to Peshawar in new Pakistan, which had a fascinating bazaar, "by no means pretty, and a hopeless jumble, but [with] the atmosphere of a frontier town, various races seem to mingle, the Mongolian with the Indian and with the white." As he watched, "a troop of frontier tribesmen marched down the street, beating their tumtums obviously on their way to the fight in Kashmir, blowing their bagpipes and shooting in the air, something out of a movie." Trudeau said he "wandered about at random," and "dusk found me lost in the maze of lanes. I was too enchanted to be disturbed, except that my eyes stung with the heavy acrid smoke which hung about the place, smoke of that particular kind which comes from cooking over cow dung fuel." Once again, the police picked him up, but his British passport secured his release.

He finally managed to get a ride with an American diplomat who took him through the Khyber Pass, where he saw on the mountainsides the plaques commemorating British battles long ago in the great game to win Asia. He reported the stories of refugees who were fleeing their ancestral homes as Hindus and Muslims set upon each other in the bloody aftermath to Indian independence:

> We had a welcome breakfast at the outpost of the famous Khyber Rifles, high up in the pass. Wild honey was on the menu. Then on to Jahalabad: all along the way we passed endless caravans; these were the nomads of the heartland which I had thought had ceased to exist, but here they were, hundreds, thousands of them, men, women and children, all trekking south into Pakistan, through the Khyber Pass, coming from way beyond Kabul, whence the cold of the winter had driven them. The newborn babes ride on top of the camels with the chickens, perched high up on top of the huge load. I could write a book on these people, so much was I impressed by their features, their dress, their behaviours, their beasts of burden, their history, their inner mind; however I won't write it now for I would never get you to Kabul, the city a mile above sea level . . . We crossed the final pass at sunset and the pink and purple mountains, stretching away to infinity, is something to behold. And as a cadre, on either side, higher mountains snowcapped and formidable. Then the descent into the valley of Kabul, where the crisp winter air and smell of wood fires awakened many longings within me; despite my crude room in the only hotel in the place, I slept happily. Here was a taste of winter, and of Laurentian air, a change from the six months of summer I had enjoyed by going gradually south all the way from England, as I went east.

In Kabul, time seemed frozen. The bazaars stood "as they

have stood for centuries, all selling the same spices, silver jew-
ellery, colourful silks, beautiful cloths, artistically worked shoes
with pointed upturned toes, heavy woollens and brightly designed
skullcaps, to wear under turbans, as they have done for centuries."
But he could see clearly that the twentieth century would bring
changes as no other century ever had.

Later in December he returned to India, where he took a
boat through the twisted bayous at the mouth of the Ganges. He
passed through "lush jungles where tigers hunt the deer and
gazelle, betwixt banks with their many villages of grass houses,
whence primitive natives drive their sacred bulls and water buffalo towards rich prairies." Surrounded by Hindus and some
Muslims, Trudeau spent a pious Christmas Day: "I read the
masses, sang the hymns and generally spent the day in deep
meditation." It was, he claimed, "good for the inners." Then he
discovered a priest from Quebec who had been in India since
1922 and was overjoyed, he told Suzette, to encounter a young
guy from Montreal—a "petit gars de Montréal."[53]

"Do you remember the song we used to sing around you at
the piano?" Trudeau wrote to his mother from Bangkok on January
18, 1949. The song included the lines "North to Mandalay . . .
South to Singapore," and, thanks to the Dutch and "their outrageous imperialistic policy" in Indonesia, Trudeau was forced to go
north to Mandalay and, then, to China. Bangkok beckoned,
because Trudeau believed it was the best "listening post" in the
area. In Indochina, too, French colonial policy was "undergoing a
very critical test," though Trudeau was more sympathetic to it than
to the British brand. He quickly passed through Burma, where
"armed bandits" were everywhere. "I have seen no country," he
told his mother, "where chaos, bribery, looting, smuggling, insurrection and political assassination have been so prevalent and to so
little avail. There is perhaps no weaker government in the world
today; but there is no more divided and purposeless opposition, so

the government still stands. But that is all it does, it stands . . . at a standstill." He stayed, as so often, with priests and even gave a lecture to Catholic girls in a convent.[54]

Then he arrived in Siam (now Thailand), a country that bewitched him and from which he drew important lessons. "If anyone ever called upon me in argument to give him evidence of the beneficial effects of Freedom upon the evolution of a nation," he wrote to his mother on January 28, "I should suggest that he settle in Siam awhile." There he found cordiality, grace, and a basic truth:

> Practically alone in the East, this country ignores the vicissitudes of domination by an imperialistic power (the Japanese stay was too short-lived to have left an imprint). In consequence, hate, suspicion, envy and arrogance, which follow from the inferiority complex of colonies, or former ones, are entirely absent from the psychological make up of the Siamese; instead you find a good-natured curiosity and a genuine desire to live and let live—at worst, add a dose of disguised condescendence. The spoken word is superfluous here, you can smile and gesticulate your way to anything, bow, clasp your hands before your face and you are at peace with everyone.

As an added benefit, he said, "tipping, soaking the foreigner, begging, shoe shining, 'guiding,' and other forms of disguised servility are practically unknown here."* In Siam, he admired the way

---

* Tipping was a practice Trudeau despised. Some of his later dinner companions sometimes discreetly left additional cash on the table as Trudeau walked out of the restaurant.

everyone went his own way in a population that was "hybrid, part Thai (ancient Chinese), part Laotian, part indigenous (of the same ethnical branch as the Polynesian)." He regretted that he had brought no camera to record the "fairy-like splendour, the stupendous colour, the tireless worship, the unthinkable shapes," though the "very abundance of exotic form could not possibly fit into a camera." Oh, he exclaimed to his mother, "that I could blindfold you and instantly transport you within some sacred precinct, and leave you sitting on the matting of some pagoda; you would find no single familiar form with which to gauge reality, and you would swear you were dreaming."[55] Pierre, truly, had become his mother's son; there is a warm, settled, and satisfying quality in their banter.

He also took a trip to the old Siamese capital of Chiang Mai with an unexpectedly distinguished group, including a Thai prince and princess, the American cultural attaché, the French military attaché, and assorted judges, bankers, and other dignitaries. His own attention, he admitted, was fully diverted between "a pretty fraulein and a jolie demoiselle," although he did manage to talk to some missionaries and one of the "rare Communists" for the purposes of his thesis.[56] From Thailand he went to French Indochina, then in the first battles of a thirty years' war. In Saigon he found "hate, strife and inevitable waste of men, money and morals." Once again the youth of France were in uniform, fighting a war that was going "nowhere fast." Soldiers were everywhere, and people could travel only in convoys. The French held the towns and main highways, the rebels ruled the countryside, and "nobody holds the peace, though on both sides men die, [are] wounded, suffer and atrocities are committed in the name of elusive righteousness and honor." On the one side were patriots, "coupled together with cynical Stalinists and bloodthirsty thieves." On the other side, "you find bewildered idealists joined together with greedy Imperialists and disgusting knaves." Politics, Trudeau concluded, "thy name is mud."

He managed to find a bus to the legendary Angkor Wat, but he thought it such "a disgusting trip" that "at times [he] was hoping that the convoy would be attacked and a few of us killed off, to make room for the rest." Angkor, by chance, proved to be safe thanks to the presence of a *Life* photographer for whom French troops cleared out the beggars and bandits who normally lurked nearby. The grandeur and scale seemed to Trudeau to represent the "confused aspirations of an awesome builder, obsessed by the need to accumulate idol upon idol, height upon height, hallway upon hallway, in endless and fearful mountains of stone." Surrounded by French troops, the photographer and sundry others toured the ruins by torchlight and listened to an aged conservator tell the history of the monuments and how, among other things, the French novelist and future culture minister André Malraux, against whose "Communist" presence in Montreal Trudeau had protested in 1937, had stolen some of the artifacts.

Trudeau returned in an all-day convoy to Saigon, where he managed to get an admission card to an elite private club. There, enjoying the swimming pool, were women whose "bathing suits have gone one better" than those in France. At this "Club sportif," Trudeau sipped the forbidden absinthe and supped in regal splendour. The city itself was crammed, and he dwelt "in a makeshift dormitory, hot, noisy and crowded, only bearable because there are a few other shifty fellows like myself, foreign legionnaires, etc." He asked his mother to tell his friends that he would eventually write, but, he concluded, "when I settle down on a side-walk café, I don't seem to get much work done."[57]

From Saigon, Trudeau went to China, just as Mao's Long March was ending in triumph. At the edge of chaos and conflict, he saw a society and a polity in the throes of death. From the safety of British-ruled Hong Kong, Trudeau went to Canton, a city crammed with "all types," from "the escapists to the hardboiled sewers of mankind." Then he set out for Shanghai. Refugees and wounded soldiers were everywhere, and the value of money changed by the hour. There were still many missionaries, and they frequently gave the wandering Canadian refuge. The devout Catholic also found welcome in the Protestant YMCA, and, thereafter, he always had great admiration for it as an institution. The road to Shanghai was unforgettable:

> I saw something of the real China; rambling mountains, wide rivers, endless rice fields in tiers along the hillsides or into gulches, poor villages, walled hamlets. I shivered at the poor peasant plowing his paddy fields with water buffalo, knee deep in the cold water. I slept in a tiny Chinese hotel and helped the daughter of the house with her English home work. I sat on a stool at a round table with many other famished travellers and learned to warm my fingers, numbed, on the boiling teacup, that I might be more agile with the chop sticks. Indeed, agility was an essential if I were not to go hungry; for there is no time to lose when everyone begins digging in at the common bowls.

When Trudeau left the crowded bus for a final journey by train to Shanghai, he noticed signs of a brilliant spring all around:

> A warm breeze rolls through the mountain gaps, and sweeps along the broad valleys, carrying the fragrance of the exquisite peach blossoms. Flooded paddy fields alternate with Yu-tsai crops in flower. The shimmering silver and pure gold squares form a heavenly checkerboard. Broad rivers and swift streams chase wildly through lush green expanses, young wheat under quaint, steep, Chinese stone bridges. Peasant women in bright blue pajamas stand on the threshold of their mud or brick houses. Old men in their long blue gowns and silver chin beards, smoke their silver pipes.

Coolies with conical straw hats bustle along with that quaint gait, synchronized with the oscillation of a double load dangling at either end of their bamboo yoke. Rolly-polly children in their over stuffed clothes look as wide as they are high. With mitigated attention, the sun beams benevolently on the glistening world. Yes it is truly great to be alive![58]

He told Grace on March 10 that he dreamed of being home for the three great events the next month: "your birthday, Easter and the sugar shack—la cabane à sucre." China, however, delayed him. The ancient city of Hangzhou, the "noblest city in the world" to Marco Polo, so intrigued him that he decided to return to it one late afternoon by climbing a mountain rather than following the valley. With the earth drenched by rain, he climbed into the dark towards a Taoist monastery but, on reaching it, he discovered its entry heavily barred:

I pounded on the doors, exchanged foreign words with voices inside, but to no avail. They would not risk unbarring their gates to any weird devil of the stormy night. So I turned away, quite downcast. However I had discounted oriental curiosity, and when they heard my heavy boots begin to clang down the steep, flag-stoned path, a monk and several servants opened the gates to get a peep at the marauder. I brazenly (but with appearance of dignity) walked through the monastery, caught a glimpse of the Taoist monks in black silken gowns and silken cornered head-dress, sipping their tea, made my way to the temple where I was guided by the pounding of a drum. There I stood, shielded by a few candles against impending, incense laden darkness, and as I peered through the shadows towards the eerie idols, the drum beats quickened and suddenly gave away to a weird rhythm tapped out on loud gongs, against a background of howling wind and beating rain. I stood there

as in a trance, feet together and hands joined, with a feeling
of many eyes peering at me, hardly daring to bat an eyelid.
Slowly the realization came to me that my hands had begun
to tremble, and I awoke to the thought: enough of this foolish-
ness. I hastened (walk, don't run) through the halls and courtyards to the door of the domain, and out into the rainy but
familiar night.

After this disturbing escape, Trudeau met the dean of the
law faculty at the university in Hangzhou and discussed "politics at great length with the professors," some of whom had
attended Harvard or London in earlier and better days. He then
left for Shanghai, where he immediately got into a fight "with a
gang of rickshaw coolies." He soon learned how to deal with the
throng of "swindlers, pimps, coolies, rickshaw coolies, shoe-shine
boys, down-and-outers, thugs and pests" that abounded in that
city. Refusing to speak French or English, he broke silence only
to shriek a few "ominous Russian words," to which they immediately responded by slinking away.[59]

In Shanghai he once more sought the company of Jesuit
priests, with whom he had "several jolly get-togethers." Refugees
from nearby battles were flowing into the city with tales of the
Communist army's approach. "I sure would like to be here for
the kill and see their operations first hand," Trudeau wrote, no
doubt to his family's despair. As hundreds of thousands fled the
looming battles, space was scarce on the ships leaving Shanghai,
but Trudeau managed to find passage to Yokohama in Japan. There
the Canadian government official* initially barred the bearded

---

* Likely Herbert Norman, who was later accused by the Americans of being
a Communist agent of influence and driven to suicide.

backpacker from leaving the ship and further increased his animosity towards Canadian diplomats. Once released, Trudeau
asked Grace if she wanted to join him on a tour through Japan,
as she had the previous spring, when they travelled through
Provence and the French Riviera on his motorbike. She apparently declined, so he left Japan on a ship crowded with refugees,
most of them Eastern Europeans, who were once again fleeing
Communist revolution.[60]

—

At the age of twenty-nine, Trudeau returned to a home that he
anticipated with uncertainty and ambivalence. He wrote much
later in his memoirs that his return "threatened to be a nasty
shock. It was."[61] In this respect he was referring to politics in the
province of Quebec, but to others he also emphasized the personal doubts he had at the time. "But what did the wanderlust correspond to? Was it a basic loneliness? . . . I think the best answer
would be that I was really completing the pedagogy of Pierre
Trudeau, the growing up of Pierre Trudeau."[62] But had he yet
grown up? Did Trudeau finally know who he was?

George Radwanski speculated that the trip and its deliberate
"risk-taking" and "self-imposed hardships" reflected, on the one
hand, his asceticism and, on the other, his desire to experience
poverty, a "reality" that had eluded the wealthy young man.[63]
Gérard Pelletier credited Trudeau's travels with developing an
"international" sense that others then lacked. He deliberately
sought out political ideas that could be applied to Canada and
Quebec.[64] Trudeau's own letters and documents provide new
answers to some of these questions. He did "miss" the war; and,
during his political years, he expressed some regrets; he had told
Thérèse Gouin in 1945 that he was too lost in his books as the war
ended to understand the great "cataclysm" that had exploded

around him. Yet there is little in his writings of 1948–49 to confirm that he regretted he had not fought in the war. In *Notre Temps* on Valentine's Day, 1948, he wrote a scathing attack on the policies of the King government in wartime, indicating that his views had not changed since the war. There he listed the multitudinous sins of the King government:

> Government by decree; suspension of habeas corpus, the Arcand, Houde, and Chaloult incidents. The lies of [Ernest] Lapointe. The joke of moderate participation. The farce of bilingualism and French-Canadian advancement in the army. The forced "voluntary" enrolment. The Drew letter and the scandal of Hong Kong. The fraud of the plebiscite, featuring the king of the frauds, Mackenzie King, the intimidating propaganda, and the no that meant yes.

The war, he said, had brought "the end of civil liberty" in Canada, and he vigorously denounced the wartime incarceration of fascist leader Adrien Arcand. This support led Arcand to write to Trudeau's mother praising the article and asking for Trudeau's address.[65] Probably shocked, she appears not to have replied. If some old grievances endured, others vanished, however, as Trudeau completed what he perceptively termed his "pedagogy."

What is striking is how deliberately and systematically he sought perfection in himself. The Jesuits and the classics rightly received credit for this emphasis on excellence in all parts of his person. He was demanding of himself and, very often, too demanding of others. In terms of education, he was fully "grown up" by the third decade of his life. Whether on the steps of the ziggurat at Ur, where he hurled unending stanzas of poetry at bandits, or on the streets of Shanghai, where he shouted abusive Russian phrases to repel street thugs, or in Harold Laski's office at LSE, where he defended his views, Trudeau demonstrated that he had an extraordinary range of knowledge. Fluently bilingual in French and English, comfortable in Spanish, understood in German, and with reading and writing knowledge of Latin and Greek, he knew the classics of Western thought in literature, economics, political science, and history. His travel writing drew on a deep understanding of historical and societal change, and his learning derived from his diligence in the classroom and in his private study. His receptive mind, with its unusually good memory, contained a deep reservoir from which he could draw as few others of his time could do.*

But to what end? In the late 1940s, Trudeau was still not clear about his destiny. Rather, he was wrestling with the direction his erudition and experience would lead him in and what his future public career might be. His article in *Notre Temps* illustrates the contradictions that existed in his understanding of the future of Quebec. The journal was a conservative and nationalist publication, and Trudeau's bitter attack on the wartime policies of Mackenzie King undoubtedly pleased most of its readers. At the

---

* John Crosbie, who possessed both a Newfoundlander's gift of gab and a fine education, had a grudging respect for Trudeau which transcended their profound political differences. He wrote in his memoirs that Trudeau "was a worthy adversary. Duelling with him was always risky, but it was very tempting." On one occasion, Trudeau was challenged about corruption in government and responded: "Quad semper, quad ubique, quad ab omnibus." Crosbie heckled, "That's the Jesuit coming out in you," to which Trudeau replied that Crosbie clearly did not understand what he had said. Crosbie replied with the lawyer's standard "Res ipsa loquitur," to which Trudeau replied in Greek. A frustrated Crosbie could only mouth the Greek motto of St. Andrew's College, the private school he had attended in Ontario. John Crosbie with Geoffrey Stevens, *No Holds Barred: My Life in Politics* (Toronto: McClelland & Stewart, 1997), 236–37.

same time, he also maintained some of his friendships from the days when he and others, enraged by the incarceration of Camillien Houde during the war and the betrayal on conscription, mused about revolution and separation. To two such friends, François and Lise Lessard, he sent a postcard on October 19, 1948, from Mesopotamia. Striking a strongly nationalist note, he wrote: "Here is a place which has known a bit more history than the island at the confluence of the Ottawa and the St. Lawrence. But what's five thousand years; perhaps the next five thousand will belong to us. Mesopotamia, the birthplace of the human race; Laurentie, the birthplace of the new world." He ended with a request that best wishes be sent to other nationalist friends.[66] It was a strangely discordant note for one who styled himself a "citizen of the world," but it was a reminder of how much had changed since Lessard and Trudeau had dreamed of revolution in the streets of wartime Montreal. His chords were not yet in tune.

Some friends and themes persisted, but much had changed in Pierre Trudeau during his absence from Quebec. His *Notre Temps* article uneasily combined a defence of the rights of fascists and nationalists with a strong defence of liberal and popular democracy, one that had rarely been heard earlier. He argued that the governors believed in government for the people but not by the people. Some might object that, in wartime, democratic rights can be suspended. "Quite the contrary," he asserted; "if there is any law upon which the individual citizen has the right to pass judgment, it is one that would expose him to death." What is more important in the article is evidence that he had rejected the corporatism that he had learnt at Brébeuf in favour of popular democracy. Similarly, he had rejected the formalist approach to law in favour of the emerging American positivist approach: that law must express changes within society, "for the world marching forward continuously creates new needs."[67] Among those needs in Canada was a more explicit understanding

923.271
TRU
ENG
v. 1

of ... a term that was becoming increasingly current in the postwar world.[68] These rights were to be grounded in a democratic society—"no other form of government safeguards those values better"—where the dignity of the individual person was most completely fulfilled.

Although the absence of ideology based on religion is striking here, Trudeau found grounds for his argument in a passage from Saint Paul that held that each human being was justified in obeying his own conscience. The study of Cardinal Newman had left a clear mark, as had Emmanuel Mounier and the French personalists, who stressed the role of lay Catholics as opposed to the clergy. In this case, diverse streams met and formed a stronger current in Trudeau in the wake of his travels, one that began to swell after he returned to Quebec and confronted the conservative government of Maurice Duplessis. Although he had become liberal, however, he was certainly not a Canadian Liberal—he believed the party had, among other sins, too poorly defended the rights of minorities.

In his letter to his mother from Siam, Trudeau's comments on the absence of "domination by an imperialistic power" are significant, particularly because they illuminate his detestation of colonial rule and minority intimidation. The result of colonial imperialism was, he claimed, "hate, suspicion, envy, and arrogance," all the product of the "inferiority complex of colonies, or former ones." Colonialism breeds suspicion and envy, qualities that are fundamentally destructive. From his travels and studies, Trudeau adapted this lesson to Canadian circumstances, as he and others began to draw parallels between the sullen anger of the Indians and the Indochinese emerging from colonial rule and the resentments of French Canadians. The killing of millions in the break-up of India, some of which he witnessed at close range, had an impact. Separation had brought massive bloodshed, and a federal solution was obviously the better alternative. Trudeau's fascination with the emergence of former colonies remained in his later writings. It was also reflected in his approach to international politics after he became prime minister, when he regarded the end of the colonial empires and the establishment of new states as the most significant historical event of the second half of the twentieth century.

Most of the world Trudeau saw on his travels was poor beyond his expectations. His decision to strip himself of worldly goods on his trip derived only in part from asceticism; it also reflected a rich man's attempt to enter into the life around him in all its facets. Like George Orwell's ventures into the world of the down and out, Trudeau linked his experiences with his education, which both in Paris and in London had awakened him to egalitarian philosophies. In postwar France, he gravitated naturally towards the socialist left and, like Emmanuel Mounier, recognized that Communism's greatest appeal came from its assertion of economic equality. His proposed thesis was based on the premise that the egalitarian character of Communism found echoes in the papal encyclicals that had long deplored the great material inequalities in modern industrial capitalism.

In Britain he encountered Laski, a controversial figure because of his defence of the Soviet system as one that attempted to create the economic equality he believed was the foundation of true democracy. Laski struggled both with Stalinism and with the obvious strengths and attractions of postwar American democracy. He prompted Trudeau to look at federalism, a subject Laski had long studied as a means of finding a balance between minority interests and an active central state that would be the strongest force in achieving the economic justice he regarded as essential. When he left London, Trudeau told a Harvard friend, he was "more and more preoccupied with problems of authority, obedience, the foundations of law etc." Harold Laski had left his mark.[69]

So had politics in Britain, where the Labour Party was creating a modern welfare state—something yet to take form in Canada. The importance of the trade-union movement in the Labour Party and, in a broader sense, in drawing workers into politics affected Trudeau's perception of how change might occur in Quebec. No doubt recalling the workers in the Abitibi gold mines with whom he had shared so little in 1946, he determined to focus more closely on what trade unions did. He began to see the trade-union movement as a highly effective method of expressing the workers' voice in politics. It was, he wrote in 1948, "the duty of all to participate in the body politic and to express one's conscience in guarding the common good and in all things to bear full witness to the truth."[70] The Welsh labour politician Aneurin Bevan, whom Trudeau came to admire during his year in Britain, would have strongly agreed.

Wearing a thin beard, Trudeau returned to Montreal in May 1949 with traces of the intense Middle Eastern and Asian sun on his hardened and lean body. He had acquired a broad knowledge of international politics and, through his education, of contemporary political economy. That knowledge formed the basis for political views that had become more secular, liberal, and egalitarian, and that co-existed with a renewed yet different Roman Catholic faith. He was less interested in nationalism and, indeed, in history and more concerned with what he was beginning to describe as "effective" and "rational" approaches to politics. He had, most definitely, grown up in respect to his "pedagogy" and his social and political views, although there remained an unpredictability and elusiveness about him.

And had he matured emotionally? He had outgrown the sophomoric hyperbole that he displayed in his major essay for the despised William Yandell Elliott at Harvard. His encounter with Freudian psychiatry seemed to be helpful in clarifying his adolescent fears about women and sex and in fortifying his belief in the importance of individualism. Freudian terms pervaded his prose over the next few years; and, although there is no definite evidence, it appears that the restraints on sex outside of marriage disappeared for Trudeau. Freud, personalism, and probably impatience apparently combined to do the trick. However, other restraints were accepted. The cascade of emotionalism and the regular outbursts of anger that had marked Trudeau in the early forties and, indeed, in his letters to Thérèse Gouin were tempered. Although he became a superb polemicist, his pen accepted limits, ones that eliminated the anti-American rants while at Harvard or the anti-English tirades whenever he had encountered the Union Jack. In fact, soon after his return he wrote a letter to the editor of Le Devoir, Gérard Filion, in which he dismissed Filion's call for a republican "social" movement. Republicanism, Trudeau declared, would be a waste of scarce political time; the "social" revolution must come first.[71]

Trudeau had changed; but, despite his claims that, in Quebec, "nothing had changed," it had, in fact, altered a lot.* He recognized that change on May 19, when he bought a painting

---

* In his Memoirs, written in the early 1990s, Trudeau makes this claim and adds that "Quebec had stayed provincial in every sense of the word, that is to say marginal, isolated, out of step with the evolution of the world." He quotes the chansonnier Jacques Norman, who predicted that "when the Soviets invade, they'll rename Montreal; they'll call it Retrograd" (61). Scholars now tend to emphasize the forces of change that were strongly felt in Quebec in the 1940s. Social and economic historians stress the impact of war on even relatively isolated areas of Quebec. In Quelques arpents d'Amérique: Population, économie, famille au Saguenay, 1838-1971 (Montreal: Les Éditions du Boréal, 1996), Gérard Bouchard indicates that the period after 1941 saw decisive shifts in major indicators such as the use of contraception, age of marriage, and,

by Paul-Émile Borduas for \$200.[72] In August 1948 Borduas, then an instructor at the École du meuble, wrote a scathing indictment of Quebec society and its major institutions, *Refus global*, which he and fifteen other younger artists signed. Decades later, its anger still erupts from the page as Borduas attacks a society where feelings were "shamefully smothered and repressed by the most wretched among us." The past could no longer beat down the present and the future: "To hell with Church blessings and parochial life! They have been repaid a hundredfold for what they originally granted." Now was the moment for magic, for love, for passionate action, and a world where "the ways of society must be abandoned once and for all."[73] Borduas set off a firestorm of criticism for his negativism and his tone. He lost his job and left Quebec within a few years, but the artist who had begun as a church painter had signalled the fundamental changes in Quebec society that were taking place. So had Trudeau, by his purchase of a Borduas canvas.

Gérard Pelletier did not approve of Borduas's statement. Returning to Quebec to become a journalist at *Le Devoir*, he

---

most important, literacy, where the rise was dramatic (455). In the area of intellectual history, Michael Behiels published a study of Quebec liberalism and nationalism which stressed how much change had occurred before 1949. Writing of the impact of war and depression in *Prelude to Quebec's Quiet Revolution: Liberalism versus Neo-nationalism, 1945–1960* (Montreal and Kingston: McGill-Queen's University Press, 1985), he argued: "Shattered beyond repair was the belief that Quebec was a society where nothing changed or would change." Despite the book's extensive and largely favourable treatment of him, Trudeau did not acknowledge its arguments in his memoirs. He did admit, however, that there was "a bubbling of ideas that already, in a very timid way, presaged the changes to come" (62).

condemned the document as adolescent, adding that "Mr. Borduas is not a young man. This is a mature man."[74] Yet Pelletier, too, was caught up in the sudden changes in Quebec society, and, when Trudeau sought out his old friend shortly after his return, Pelletier persuaded him to join the cause of the asbestos workers, who had been on strike since mid-February.

—

Trudeau had paid little attention to trade unions before his departure from Quebec in 1944, even though Thérèse's father was the author of the major text on labour law in Quebec. Now, however, he was interested in the potential of trade unionism to effect political and economic change and, even before his return, he had contacted Canadian Labour Congress officials about a possible job with them in Ottawa. Nothing eventuated, so, still uncertain of his own future, he quickly accepted Gérard Pelletier's invitation to join him in the Asbestos Strike, in the town of Asbestos, in the Eastern Townships.

This strike is a fabled moment in Quebec history because it illuminates the class and ethnic differences that fuelled the resentment and dissent in the province. The companies were overwhelmingly foreign-owned, and the managers spoke only English. The miners simply took the asbestos from the ground, loaded it on freight cars, and shipped it away. Less than 5 percent was processed in Canada. On the great rolling hills of the Eastern Townships where it was extracted, large gaping holes remained as testimony to their work. Although the postwar boom benefited the industry, and workers' wages rose, they knew the rewards went mainly to the foreign owners and the English-speaking managers. Gradually, too, the miners became aware that the material they extracted daily was destroying their lungs. All this knowledge gave force to the strike that exploded when Jean

Marchand, the secretary-treasurer of the Confédération des travailleurs Catholiques du Canada (CTCC or Canadian Catholic Confederation of Labour), first met with the workers about their grievances in February 1949. Spontaneously, the workers in their caps took to the streets, along with Marchand in his beret. The strike was illegal, passionate, and immediately controversial.

Trudeau and Pelletier set out to drive from Montreal to the strike sites in Pelletier's decrepit British-made Singer. Along the way, the police stopped this suspicious-looking vehicle and took both occupants to the police station for questioning. When the officer asked Trudeau, who had been sitting in the left front seat, for his licence, he replied, defiantly, "I have none," even though he had it in his pocket. The police were set to arrest him when Pelletier, in his typically calm fashion, asked the officers to come to the car. There they saw that the Singer's controls were on the right, in the British fashion. After an exchange of barbed words, the police resentfully let them go.

Once they arrived at Asbestos, Trudeau met Jean Marchand, a social scientist who had become a brilliant labour organizer in the fashion of the American Walter Reuther. Personally striking, with an uncontrollable thatch of dark hair and a voice that easily reached the back of union halls, Marchand was an impassioned orator who moved to action the men (and the few women) who came to hear him talk. Four decades later, Trudeau's boyhood friend Pierre Vadeboncoeur recalled Marchand in those days. "He had qualities that were truly exceptional," he said: "a lively intelligence, sure judgement, a critical spirit, a passionate temperament, obvious sincerity, combined with the extraordinary eloquence of a popular champion that one encounters only two or three times in a century in a single country."[75]

Trudeau's role in the strike was minor. He marched with the strikers, who called him Saint Joseph because of the oriental headgear, North American shorts, and straggly dark beard he still wore. But he made his mark when he gave a fiery speech attacking the Quebec police to five thousand miners. Jacques Hébert thought he spoke emotionally and well about the importance "of democracy, justice, and liberty in language they understood,"[76] but Marchand, more experienced with crowds, had a different take on the event. "Miners are not schoolchildren," he warned, "and while students might steal pencils, the miners steal dynamite. I had managed to defuse two or three cute little plots by the boys which would have blown up the mine manager and most of his staff. So you can imagine that when Trudeau urged physical resistance by the strikers, I got a little worried." All calmed down, but Marchand had discovered a valuable new colleague, and Trudeau had discovered where he belonged.[77]

At Asbestos, Trudeau, Pelletier, and Marchand bonded together—and they stayed together for the rest of their lives. They seemed to understand their mutual strengths, interests, and beliefs. Jean Marchand was the organizer, who travelled the highways and backroads of Quebec and became one of the workers' own. He slept in their bedrooms and spoke in their church basements, where he thrilled them as his emotions boiled on the tip of his tongue. He never had notes, but his thoughts suddenly exploded into the air. Sometimes, he would break into song, as he did in an Asbestos café one evening with "Les lumières de ma ville," a ballad made famous that year by the young Quebec chanteuse Monique Leyrac in the film of the same name.[78] Gérard Pelletier was not a singer or even much of an orator, but he listened well, as the finest journalists do. He quickly provided stories for the press that helped to make Marchand's case in the dailies.

Initially, Pierre Trudeau struck both Pelletier and Marchand as different but also remarkable, a man who brought the intellectual depth and international experience that Quebec labour badly needed in the forties. Pelletier's father was a stationmaster, Marchand's a worker, while Trudeau's had been a millionaire businessman. Both Pelletier and Marchand had developed a contempt for the sons of Brébeuf and Outremont, with their "smart" clothes and special banter, but when they saw Trudeau speak directly to the workers about justice and democracy in ways that the workers listened to and understood, they realized he possessed the gifts and commitment they needed. As Pelletier remarked later, Trudeau "made no show either of his money or his muscles. Nor of his intelligence. But despite a strange shyness that [would] never leave him, and which made him less than talkative on first acquaintance, he aroused one's curiosity."[79] Beginning at Asbestos, Trudeau began to link the world of Christian personalism he had discovered in Paris, and the socialism he had encountered in Laski's classrooms, with the needs of the Quebec working class. The workers became for him the best hope in a Quebec that had disappointed him on his return.

What Trudeau found there was, in his later words, "a Quebec I did not really know, that of workers exploited by management, denounced by government, clubbed by police, and yet burning with fervent militancy." It was, in many ways, a new Quebec, a fact he recognized in his finest publication—the introduction and conclusion to a 1956 book he edited on the strike. Although there had been other strikes, he wrote, the Asbestos Strike "was significant because it occurred at a time when we were witnessing the passing of a world, precisely at a moment when our social framework—the worm-eaten remnants of a bygone age—were ready to come apart."[80]

Trudeau did not forget the smoke-filled union halls or the workers in checked flannel shirts, their faces lined from years of hard and unhealthy work. After he went back to Montreal, he took on their case against the provincial government and the police, who had broken into workers' homes, falsely imprisoned many of them, and generally intimidated their towns and villages. He did not charge his clients a penny.[81]

But the strike was illegal and the workers were violent, destroying the property of the "scabs" who replaced them. The Duplessis government opposed the strikers on the legitimate basis of illegality, but it went much too far, breaking its own laws with impunity. The Catholic Church was divided on the strike, with parish priests rallying to their parishioners while most of the hierarchy backed the government—as they normally did. There were, however, notable exceptions: Archbishop Charbonneau of Montreal strongly supported the strikers' cause, and dozens of truckloads of food went from working-class Montreal parishes to feed the miners' families. Charbonneau's vigorous support of the strike became a principal factor in Duplessis's decision to have "a showdown with elements of the Church that he considered were subverting his authority and working iniquity with his constituents."[82] With prodding from conservative elements of the church and from the government of Quebec, the Vatican persuaded Charbonneau to resign his archbishopric on the grounds of "ill health," and he spent the rest of his life in Victoria, British Columbia. Pelletier realized that he and the others who had supported the strikers so vociferously had also become "marked men." Trudeau could no longer get a university job. Jean Marchand therefore offered him a position with the labour movement in Quebec, where he could continue to fight Duplessis.

But, in one of the surprising moves that mark Trudeau's life, he left Quebec just when, in his own words, the strike brought "a turning point in the entire religious, political, social, and economic history of the Province of Quebec."[83] To the shock of Pelletier and other friends, Pierre Trudeau departed for Ottawa and became a civil servant.

CHAPTER 5

—

HEARTH, HOME, AND NATION

Pierre Trudeau's decision to go to Ottawa perplexed some of his friends, who sought a rational explanation for this sudden change in direction. Gérard Pelletier, for example, later claimed that he never understood why Trudeau became a federal public servant when the challenges in Quebec were so great.[1] But when people make a choice, the rational and the emotional, the private and the public normally mingle together, and there were profound reasons why Trudeau found working in Montreal difficult in 1949. Several are obvious.

First, he had not liked his student experience at the Université de Montréal and probably had little desire to teach there, even if clerical and political conservatives had permitted him to do so. After his involvement with the Asbestos Strike, they would not. Second, many friends had married, including his closest male companion of the time, Roger Rolland, and Thérèse had married another friend, Vianney Décarie. Third, his brother and sister were married, and Suzette now lived close by her mother and could keep an eye on her, so he could leave secure in the knowledge that she would be cared for. Then again, the swarm of family and old friends must have seemed overwhelming after his solitary wanderings of the previous year.

Moreover, in the five years Trudeau had essentially been abroad, the world had changed. Liberal democracy, so troubled in the 1930s, had risen to the challenge of fascism during the Second World War, and Canadians now eagerly entered what *Time* magazine publisher Henry Luce had named the American century. In the stones and the forests of Quebec, American enterprise extended its claims, and church, state, and citizens responded to both its energy and its consequences. Some of Trudeau's former classmates, including his greatest Brébeuf rival, Jean de Grandpré, began to find their place within the Canadian corporate world, which was moving rapidly from its traditional link with the British-Canadian imperial tradition to welcome the flow of precious American dollars available to Canadians in the post-war years. Other classmates, such as Pierre Vadeboncoeur, were deeply suspicious of the impact of American economic and cultural influence on Quebec society, even though they recognized that the future world imagined in the Catholic classrooms of their childhood was undeniably lost.[2]

Outside Canada, a Cold War was emerging in the confrontation between the Soviet Union and the West or, as it was more often expressed, between Communism and democracy. In 1949 a new chill appeared in international affairs as the Soviet Union exploded an atomic bomb, thus ending the American monopoly, and Mao Tse-tung's armies passed through Peking's Gate of Heavenly Peace in triumph, not long after Trudeau left Shanghai. In the 1949 Canadian election, Conservative leader George Drew campaigned in Quebec on a strong anti-Communist platform, but he convinced few that Prime Minister Louis St. Laurent was "soft" on Communists. Both St. Laurent and his popular foreign minister, Lester Pearson, joined in stern jeremiads against the Communists. Indeed, even at the height of the Second World War, many Catholic leaders in Quebec had attacked the alliance with the Soviet Union. When Cardinal

Villeneuve and Premier Joseph-Adélard Godbout had called for assistance to Russia after Hitler's attack, the great nationalist Henri Bourassa had bitterly complained: "How can they not see that, some years from now, Russia will be the nightmare of the world?"[3] In 1949, for most people in Canada and Quebec, it was.

Pierre Trudeau, in many ways, was a bad fit for Quebec in the spring of 1949. During his long educational absence and world travels, he had carefully maintained links through correspondence with friends, family, and other individuals who kept him informed about events at home. The articles he published in *Notre Temps* clearly reflected this aim, as did an article in *Le Devoir* which appeared just as he returned: "Five minutes with Pierre Trudeau—Around the world in 580 days."[4] He immediately re-established old links and made pronouncements on a range of issues both in private and in public. His exchange on republicanism in *Le Devoir* attracted attention among the intellectual elite, for whom the nationalist newspaper was essential daily reading.

After the Asbestos Strike, Trudeau and Pelletier began to discuss the creation of an intellectual journal, which would be modelled on Emmanuel Mounier's *Esprit*. At the invitation of Claude Ryan, now the general secretary of Action catholique canadienne, Trudeau also spoke to a group of students on June 20. The West, he lamented, lacked economic liberty and was too materialistic. Marxism failed because it restricted liberty, but a better alternative lay in the blend of socialism and Christianity. He echoed the French diplomat-writer Paul Claudel in calling on students "to be sensitive to the world which surrounds us, the international community."[5] At a time when both the Canadian press and politicians were issuing clarion calls to confront global Communism, Trudeau's comments reflected his profound doubts about such a crusade.

The state of Quebec nationalism similarly made him

uneasy. His own public and private writings in the late 1940s possessed ambiguities that confused readers about what he actually believed. His old friend Pierre Vadeboncoeur, with whom he had re-established a close relationship, even wrote to *Le Devoir* on July 14, 1949, in an effort to clarify what Trudeau had meant in a letter he had written attacking Gérard Filion's call for a new nationalist political party. With considerable presumption, Vadeboncoeur stated that any party that he "and Pierre Trudeau" founded would not emerge in a nationalist cradle. "The nationalist should not integrate the social but the social should integrate nationalism, which currently has a traditional character."[6]

Trudeau knew that Quebec nationalism had a traditional, or conservative, character; reflecting that character, the Duplessis government rejected the social needs of society. Yet the Liberal Party in both Quebec and Ottawa represented neither the national nor the social needs of French-speaking Canadians. The federal CCF had no provincial counterpart, and its attentiveness to the demands of workers and economic inequality was not accompanied by a sensitivity to Quebec's heritage and postwar cultural challenges. Later, Trudeau told an interviewer that he had not looked for an active political career on his return because, very simply, "I did not agree with any of the major parties." He probably would have fitted well into a British Labour Party or a French Socialist Party, where the temptations of power balanced a commitment to social programs based on economic equality and progressive social action. In Canada, however, he found no defined political channel through which he could express the ideas he held and the facts he had learned in his five years of absence from Quebec.[7]

He was not alone. Many other Canadians, including the sociologist John Porter, the novelist Norman Levine, and the painter Paul-Émile Borduas, found Canada unresponsive to the dynamics of postwar progressive currents, whether in the arts or in politics.

In 1949 Canada remained distant from the ideal society that postwar social thought offered and economic prosperity seemed to secure.[8] What had begun with thunderous election declarations in 1944 and 1945 promising national health care and new social programs had ended with the conservative nationalism of Maurice Duplessis in Quebec and the business-oriented liberalism of Louis St. Laurent's Liberals in Ottawa. Despite some changes, Trudeau believed that the Old Regime still prevailed in Canada and Quebec, just as it did in the Roman Catholic Church.

A political career, then, was not an option in 1949, and Trudeau found his old friends adrift in a world where the mists of past debates too often clouded the form of the future. Other young intellectuals shared his alienation and uncertainty. When the sociologist Marcel Rioux returned to Quebec from Paris, he discovered no professional opportunities and took employment with the National Museum of Canada in Ottawa, a city which became, in his own words, "a refuge for the opponents to the [Duplessis] regime" in Quebec.[9] Trudeau, similarly, had no political outlet in Montreal, detested the regime in Quebec City, had limited professional opportunities as an academic in Quebec, and did not want to practise law.

No sooner was he back, it seemed, than others prepared to leave. For Trudeau and many of his friends, the most upsetting departure was that of François Hertel. In the spring of 1949, Hertel began, in his own words, his "exile" in France. He believed that his readers in the new world could no longer respond to what he taught and wrote, and, for that reason, "it became essential, almost a duty . . . to disown or leave that milieu."[10] Grace had warned Pierre that his friend was disconsolate. After a dinner with Hertel as he prepared to leave the priesthood and Canada, she reported that he said: "I'm returning to the new world because I'm weary of the old one, and contrary to geological and geographical opinion, I claim that America is the old world." The cultural renewal in France in particular, but in Europe more generally, he told Grace Trudeau, "makes America look old and decayed."[11] For the Quebec intellectuals of the postwar period, "troubled by the future of their own land, the ideological landscape of Paris was seductive."[12] For Trudeau, however, a return to Paris would have been exile from family, friends, and, not least, his own ambition. Ottawa, then, offered a convenient detour.*

—

Grace Trudeau was another factor in her son's decision to go to Ottawa. If Trudeau was to consolidate his new-found independence, he no doubt sensed that he should not return to live in the family home. He and his mother had always had an exceptionally close relationship. In the spring of 1947 she had clung to him like a youthful date while his Harley-Davidson careered at high speed through the corniche roads above Monte Carlo. In other photographs, the middle-aged matron and her adult son cavort on the beach just as they had done as young mother and child. When

---

* On his return in 1949, Trudeau spoke to two lawyers who were fast-rising francophones in External Affairs—Marcel Cadieux and Michel Gauvin. Both men were conservative Roman Catholics who had served with distinction in the war—the former as a public servant; the latter as a Canadian officer on the battlefields of Western Europe. Both were blunt. Cadieux said he would do everything to prevent the iconoclastic and capricious Trudeau from entering the department. Trudeau himself recalled that Cadieux was upset with his beard, which was not considered proper for young men in "External in those days." Interestingly, in 1968, when Trudeau became prime minister, Cadieux was undersecretary of state for external affairs; the

they were apart, they both wrote or phoned often. Her home was always his. Sometimes they misunderstood each other, but they shared their thoughts, their impressions, and, occasionally, their decisions. In 1949, when Trudeau returned, Grace was understandably relieved and welcoming, but she knew her son was more fraught than he would admit. More than anyone else, she was aware of the difficulties Pierre faced in Montreal that spring.

"Every time the postman comes I make a rush for the letters, hoping to hear from you," she had written to Pierre in January 1947 during his Paris sojourn. Pierre had been ill but had sought recuperation in the French Alps. How much better his boldness, she told him, than the complaints of Suzette's husband, Pierre Rouleau, who stayed in bed after a minor hemorrhoid operation. He is not, she declared, "of the Elliott stock! As Aunt Annie used to say." Although Grace adored her charming son-in-law, she sometimes could be a critical mother-in-law. Constantly she worried whether Pierre had enough "cash" and regularly enclosed British pounds or treasured American dollars to "help out." As mothers do, she worried about his health and appearance, writing to him on January 17: "Be good to yourself—take

---

less guilty Gauvin was ambassador to Ethiopia. But Trudeau bore no grudges: he made Cadieux the first francophone ambassador to the United States, Canada's most important diplomatic position, and he gave Gauvin several choice assignments, including ambassador to China. Interview with Michel Gauvin, May 1995. Cadieux's strong personal views on Canadian politicians can be glimpsed in John Bosher, *The Gaullist Attack on Canada, 1967–1977* (Montreal and Kingston: McGill-Queen's University Press, 1999), in which Bosher quotes extensively from Cadieux's very opinionated diary. Interview with Michel Gauvin, April 1994; interview of Pierre Trudeau by Jean Lépine, April 27, 1992, TP, vol. 23, file 2.

the pills. How is your hair behaving, losing any? Beware of hard soap on it." The hair became a lasting concern, and photographs of Pierre as he aged provide genuine grounds for her worries. She regularly sent news of his friends, past and present. While visiting Tip at Harvard, she called on Pierre's past love, Camille Corriveau, and reported that she was "kept busy all day with two young ones." Even worse, she has "no help from outside—does all her own work"—as most American mothers did.

In response to Pierre's letters about Paris, she wrote: "You are in a social whirl, as much, if not more than your mom." She always shared his enthusiasm for French ways, although both were thoroughly North American in most of their tastes. A friend of hers had a guest from France who behaved badly and burnt a hole in a treasured Persian rug. "I can't but think," Grace wrote, "there is something French in this way of acting, giving one the impression they are our lords and masters." If her faith in the French was lacking, she had much confidence in her son. On February 20, 1947, she asked what Pierre thought of the world "upside down," with the British leaving India and the "Jews in Jerusalem [wanting] to get out and return to Germany." Concerned, she wrote: "It will take some intelligent people and strong minds to unravel the future. Will you be amongst them?"[13] Perhaps even more than Pierre, she was determined he would be.

In late February 1947, as Trudeau was in the midst of psychoanalysis, Grace was preparing for her trip to France. "Dear big boy," she wrote from the "Land of Snow": "Hurray! You are coming to meet me I heard today—what fun—provided I don't look all washed up when I step off the ship." To her son, if no one else, she did not. When she met up with Pierre again in April, she brought copious amounts of food to a France where heavy rationing still prevailed.[14] She had first visited her brother in Normandy and then rejoined Pierre, to sweep through the south of France on the Harley-Davidson as spring warmed the Côte d'Azur. There is no suggestion that he told her of his psychiatric sessions in Paris, and she appears not to have been aware of the intense correspondence between him and Thérèse in those weeks. Yet, as a mother, she surely knew something had gone badly wrong.

On her—and Pierre's—return to Montreal, Grace learned that Thérèse, great-granddaughter and granddaughter of pre-miers, niece of a political giant, daughter of a senator, and, in the view of many of the leaders of Montreal society, the ideal life partner for her brilliant son, had decided not to marry him. On July 16 she reacted with distress and concern to the news as Pierre began his trek by foot to the remote parts of Quebec. "My dear coureur des bois," she wrote:

> It was a good opportunity to get away and clear the sombre thoughts that have haunted you for the past few days. If I could only have consoled my poor boy in *those* moments—you know a mother's heart is much upset when she sees the unhappy situations that often arise in the course of her children's lives. It was something of a shock to me as well as to you. When I realized how serious was the rift, especially as I had begun to take the girl to heart—which requires time for such an adjustment! Blood is thicker than water you know I often say.
>
> However, I still believe that perhaps within a short time all may be well again between you two. I'm sure the girl must be unhappy—it is impossible to think otherwise. Since she had led you to believe—or I can imagine so—that you were the only man in her life—just be patient—she will have time to think things over and no doubt one of these days you may receive a note asking to meet her half way—I can speak from experience my dear—and when both parties concerned are proud and unwilling to make the first step—it means unhappiness for two people who are

really in love. Are you quite sure that you are *not* to blame
in showing any lack of affection? Or in being brusque? I know
that when a man makes up his mind to marry the woman of
his choice he can't stand or comprehend why there should
be any delay or seeming hesitation on the girl's side—of
course I'm surmising incidents which may have no bearing
on the whole situation. I feel so sorry for you my dear boy
that I can only pray the dear Lord may console and be your
guide and always mom will be there by your side to give
what comfort she can. All my love to you, Mom.[15]

It was, from a mother to a distraught son, a sensitive and
wonderful letter.

As with most sons, some parts of Pierre Trudeau's life
remained closed to his mother, but most did not. She had gently
chided him about the "tricks" that he and Roger Rolland were up
to in Paris and wondered, when Pierre was in London, whether
he missed the "street fighting" in which he and Roger had par-
taken. She anxiously worried whether he was healthy and
whether he had friends. In November 1947 she told him that
when people inquired about him, she replied that he was making
the most of his stay in London, "getting about to listen in on lectures, conferences as well as communist meetings." Perhaps, she
speculated, he was "freer to go about not having many friends or
am I wrong and do you have a circle? You never mention anyone." For good reason, of course, Grace had quickly realized that,
in London, there was no "circle."[16]

As Trudeau published his articles in *Notre Temps*, Grace
carefully monitored reactions. She told him that some of "the
clergy" said that one article was a "deep and well-sounding
piece," although she did seem a bit troubled that the former
Quebec fascist leader Adrien Arcand "wanted to write to" him with
compliments about the other article. However, "Dr. Turgeon

was tickled that you knocked [Prime Minister Mackenzie] King" in yet another essay. Surely, she remarked, "by the time you enter journalism in this town your name will be a byword." Wherever she went she heard praise for her exceptional son. Madame Décarie predicted a great future for Pierre, "just as we all think! Naturally—me especially."[17]

She fretted that he lacked money and, occasionally, operated on the black market for him, especially when postwar Canadian currency restrictions were put in place in 1947. In February 1948 she offered to get some funds in Boston if he ran short during his studies at the London School of Economics. And she made certain that he was well prepared for his adventures. Later, when he was short of funds after a trip to Africa, she sent him $500 by cable immediately and, when she heard nothing, sent $200 more a month later and told him not to "wait until the last minute" for further requests.[18] These were large sums for the time, equal to almost $6,000 today; in 1948 a decent meal could be had in a Left Bank bistro for twenty-five cents. When he proposed to tour Britain, she wrote: "I shall send you socks, army ones? Also shirt, long sleeves? I bought one a khaki color, perhaps it is not heavy enough—a gabardine cotton would be best, I shall look around altho' for hiking it might be the right weight. I also bought a short sleeved cotton jersey—dark blue—you could use for underwear—instead of wearing pyjamas if you get cold." Then she concluded, typically: "Thinking of you every day dear boy and praying the Lord to keep you safely. My love to you and God bless you. Mom. Enclosing $10." When he sent her saris from India, she proudly showed them off to her friends. She wore them for Pierre on his return, and the two of them hosted an "Oriental afternoon." She also reassured some priests, who wondered about his articles, that he was, most definitely, a strong Roman Catholic.[19]

Grace understood well his urge to wander. She even quoted Whitman to him: "O farther, farther, farther sail!" and told him that she, like him, "early in life . . . felt imbued with the desire to forever seek unknown worlds." Yet she advised him that he must come home and forget the wounds he bore, though she knew they would not heal soon.[20] She was wary as he began once again to introduce new female friends to his family. When she received a few photographs from a woman whom he had spent some time with after the relationship with Thérèse ended, Grace wrote to Pierre about his great love affair. Like mothers generally, she was unfair to the one who had rejected her son:

> I sincerely hope—and I am much in earnest, that you won't
> go out of your way for her—from things I learned in the
> *past year* my sympathy for her has completely turned . . .
> Perhaps I shouldn't have said so much—but you know how
> mothers feel when they could fight for their children's hap-
> piness—and I don't want you going through once more—
> the agony of last summer—we were all very much affected,
> in spite of saying little about the episode.

Grace worried about these strong words she had written to her son, concluding, "I hope you won't take offence at all this."[21]

Trudeau did not, but Grace's letters now lacked the sensitivity of her letter a year earlier when she had first learned of the break-up with Thérèse. Gone are the hints that Trudeau may have been "brusque" or that he was not always "affectionate." Grace, as always, came down strongly on her son's side. Trudeau likely believed that his mother's words reflected the continuing gossip in Montreal about what had happened between the couple. Many of his old friendships must have been affected by the end of his close relationship with Thérèse. In one letter Grace reflected on his future after he told her he had danced "socially" in Asia. "By the time you return and begin looking about for a 'wife,' many comparisons will be made—certain standards must be met—but then you have your ideal no doubt—the older one grows the more difficult one becomes—but I couldn't say or accuse you of having those bachelor ways which are hard to deal with—you still are the young enthusiastic youth I am sure."[22]

Grace Trudeau deeply affected her son, not least because he lived with her for most of her adult years. After his move to Ottawa, when he returned to Montreal on weekends, he brought his laundry. "I noticed you didn't bring your towel along this time," she wrote in October 1950, telling him that he should not send it to the laundry.[23] She became an authority on foreign currency rates as she made certain that he had the necessary funds for travel and study. She supervised cooking in their home—a skill that her epicure son, who cultivated his knowledge of fine wines and restaurants, never mastered. A later female companion recalled that, after several elegant dinners together, she visited his country home in the Laurentians, where she discovered that, if a meal was not cooked by someone else, dinner was spaghetti out of a can.[24] In his mother's home, Grace or her staff served him.

On a more positive side, they travelled together often and maintained into the sixties their custom of attending concerts and gallery openings. "My dear boy," she wrote in 1951, "once more we had to say good-bye—after such an enjoyable trip in Italy—for myself at any rate. It will remain one of the highlights in my late life."[25] Her support for him was generous financially and emotionally, and their relationship had an astonishing familiarity. For his thirty-first birthday, for example, she sent him a card with an attractive woman on it and wrote: "Hurrah—it's Pierre's birthday—many happy returns of the day dear boy. We must celebrate over the weekend. All my love, Mom." Then in a small note that could be detached, she wrote: "Happy birthday to the best son in all the world." She did, after all, have two sons.

The coureur des bois on the canoe trip to Hudson Bay, 1941.

At the officers training camp at Farnham, "21 juin au 4 juillet" 1942. "Les guerres commanos de la tente 'sans-zèle.'" This revealing photo was taken at the exact time when Jean-Baptiste Boulanger and Trudeau were musing about a coup. The rifles may have been taken from the base by these soldiers "without zeal." From left to right: Charles Lussier (future director of the Canada Council); Gaby Filion (prominent artist and Trudeau boarder); Robert Pager; Jean-Baptiste Boulanger (member of the LX with Trudeau); Trudeau; Jean Gascon (future Companion of the Order of Canada and artistic director of the Stratford Festival); and Jacques Lavigne, who apparently was in a neighbouring tent.

At twenty-two, stylish on the boulevard, May 1942.

The archer, 1944, the year after Pierre graduated in law.

Grace and Suzette skiing
at Ste-Adèle, May 1945.

Pierre and his friends get a moose, 1946–47.

Harvard, jeudi soir, 3 janvier, 1946.

Thérèse bien-aimée,

Les chevaliers d'antan saluaient leurs Belle avant de chevaucher au combat, et je pitoyable contre-façon ne me sens pas le courage de m'engager dans cette longue et morne étape qui s'ouvre sans avoir préalablement adressé un dernier mot.

J'ai pu prendre l'avion ce midi, et ce n'est pas Mozart mais toi que j'ai vue là-haut. Je me suis endormi dans les airs, et j'ai rêvé à toi, non seulement de toi "... Belle, ô Mortels, comme un rêve de Pierre".

Les premières heures dans Cambridge sont très dures. J'ai l'âme égarée, un creux au cœur, et les jambes un peu molles.

An example of Pierre's romantic correspondence with Thérèse Gouin, 1946.

Pierre and Thérèse just before their "engagement,"
at Samovar, a Russian restaurant in Montreal, 1946.

Pierre recovering from his appendix operation in Mégève, Switzerland, December 1946.

Pierre "studying" in Paris. This photograph, and the next three, were commissioned by the French government educational office to show how Canadian students enjoyed Paris.

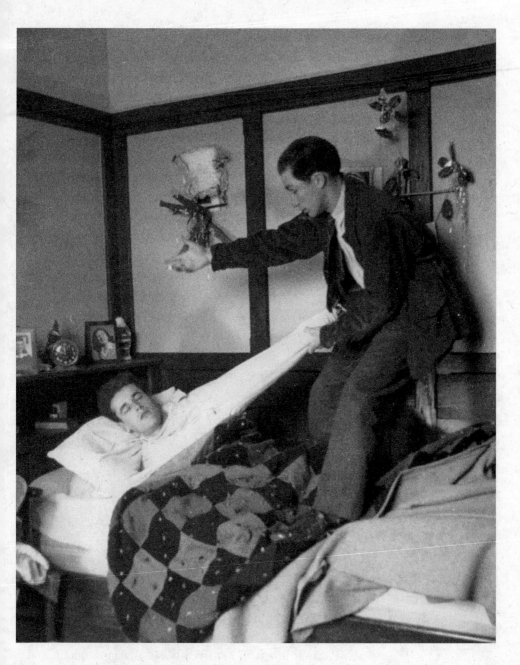

Pierre awakening Roger Rolland in Paris, 1947.

Pierre scaling Parisian Heights as Canadian students look on. His future Cabinet colleague Jean-Luc Pepin is at the back, apparently ready to catch him.

Dinner at a Paris restaurant: "Pierre, D.D. (Andrée
Désautels), Hertel, 'Chanteuse,' Roger Rolland, 'Chanteur.'"

In 1949 Pierre visited the Middle East and adopted the area's traditional garb.

Pierre often stayed with priests on his world tour. Here he resists their attentions, 1949.

"He used to go from country to country with only a packsack on his back," said his brother, Charles. He was once arrested by the Arabs as an Israeli spy.

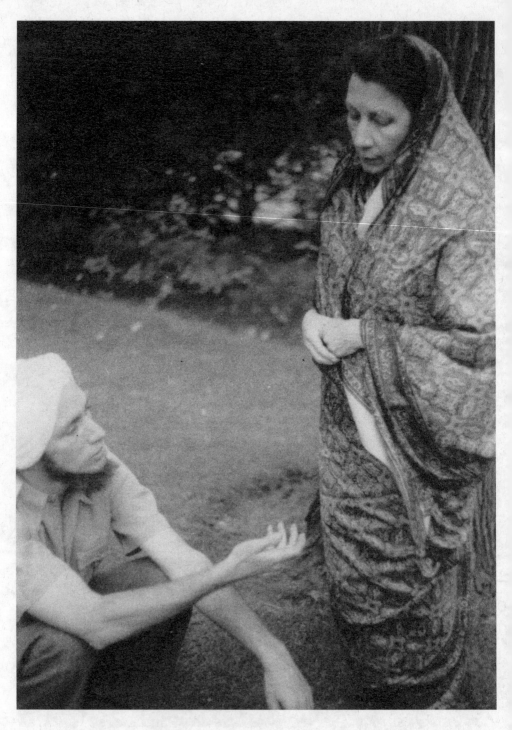

Pierre brought home a sari for his mother. This was, he wrote, their Oriental moment, 1949.

Hélène Segerstrale: It was a photograph of her in the *Ottawa Citizen* that first attracted Pierre.

Pierre and Hélène at "Ottawa's only caberet," the Copacabana, 1950.

Malaga, Spain, 1952. Trudeau on a roadtrip with his glamorous motorcyle.

When Pierre despaired, Grace, more than anyone else, was the rock upon which he built his hopes.

But she may also have been the reef on which his romances sometimes foundered. Certainly, Thérèse came to believe that she was, even though, like Madeleine Gobeil, she admired the way Trudeau softened in Grace's presence, and the devotion mother and son felt for each other.[26] In his psychiatric sessions in Paris, he portrayed his father, Charles, as almost Apollonian, distant and heroic, but, like the Greek gods, indifferent to the world in which humans live. Grace, however, troubled Trudeau. He required her approval; and, because of her strong presence, she represented forces such as the church and the social approval he occasionally and impetuously struck out against in a way that others found puzzling or inconsistent. Although, on the surface, his mother often had good relationships with Pierre's female companions, the women themselves, beginning with Camille Corriveau, came to believe, first, that she was a formidable individual not easily challenged and, second, that she had an enormous, perhaps decisive, influence on her son. Though Grace sometimes grumbled about her son-in-law, despite a good personal relationship with him, she forgave Pierre many flaws. Interestingly, Pierre Trudeau delayed marriage until he moved out of his mother's house and, indeed, until she was virtually an invalid, no longer fully aware of events around her.

In her memoirs, Margaret Trudeau wrote that, for her husband, women fell into three categories: "There were his female colleagues, and these he saw only as working companions and not as women, though many were also close friends. Then there were possible dates and here, like Edward VIII, he preferred actresses and starlets, glamorous women who were perfect for flirtations and candlelight dinners. Then there was his wife, and she had to be dependent, at home, and available." The last of these roles, she and others suggest, was an impossible one played most effectively by Pierre's own mother. Trudeau, Henry Kissinger once quipped to Richard Nixon, was best understood as a "mommy's boy."[27]

In a very real sense he was, but Kissinger's dismissal is a cheap shot. To her timid son, Grace Trudeau brought confidence and a belief that he had few limits on what he could accomplish. He adored her because of her exceptional combination of playfulness and discipline, both qualities he inherited, and the strong sense of family that carried her children through first the turbulence of Charles's death and then the religious and social change in Quebec. She introduced him gracefully to the arts and provided stability as he moved into different worlds. She wrote to Pierre on May 11, 1948, her thirty-third anniversary:

> Tuesday, May 11, 1915—our wedding day, your father and I—strange that I happened to write it down just to-night— Since 13 years I like to think I have forgotten or at least over-look it—and you three children helped me carry on. What a blessing you have been to me—what would I have become without you—looking after your needs when you were young filled my life and now that you are all older and capable of carrying on without me—I still like to think I can be of help somehow.[28]

And in so many ways, she surely was.

Grace influenced Trudeau's relationships in two key ways. Obviously, she was a model of the domesticity he championed from the forties, when he quarrelled with Thérèse about her plans for a career and further study, to the seventies, when he opposed Margaret Trudeau's decision to work or return to school. His attitude troubled not only Thérèse and Margaret but also the other women to whom he talked of marriage. More subtly, and also more positively, his close relationship with his mother, their easy bantering and affectionate exchanges, made him seek out women as his confidantes. In his early days at Brébeuf he had resolved to stand apart from his classmates, and his correspondence with even his closest male friends tends to be brief, impersonal, and surprisingly rare. Always the disciplined correspondent, he kept lists of those with whom he corresponded while he was absent, and women were consistently at the top. Moreover, with male friends he tended to write about public or even philosophical matters; with women, he blended these topics with intimate discussions of his own feelings and ambitions—just as he did with his mother.

Anecdotes bear out the same impression presented in his private papers. Jacques Hébert, with whom he travelled frequently, said that Trudeau never spoke with him about religion, a view echoed by the devout Catholic Allan MacEachen, his House of Commons seatmate. MacEachen also reported a conversation with Jean Marchand in which he indicated, to MacEachen's surprise, that he and Trudeau had not spoken for several months. Marc Lalonde, Trudeau's closest adviser, said in the early 1970s that Trudeau spoke to him only once about a personal matter—the break-up of his marriage. He was, Lalonde added, like an oyster that opened with great difficulty. Yet with women, from Camille Corriveau in the early forties to the celebrity Kim Cattrall in the late eighties, he often bared his soul. To Cattrall, Trudeau was "epicurean." The actor Margot Kidder, with whom he later had an affair, described him as "the gentlest, sweetest little boy you'd ever known . . . When you realized this (as he eagerly handed you the simple-minded dinner of pork and beans and bacon out of a can that he'd cooked; or when he held you in his arms in the morning, beaming and enormously pleased with himself), it felt as if you knew a secret no one else knew, and in knowing it, you'd been anointed keeper of his flame."[29]

From de Grandpré at school in 1940, through his closest male colleagues in succeeding decades—Pelletier, Hébert, and

Lalonde—the private Trudeau remained a secret they never really knew.

—

Trudeau kept many secrets in Ottawa after he arrived in the late summer of 1949. After briefly considering External Affairs and the Finance Department, he opted for the Privy Council Office because, he later wrote, it was "the key decision-making centre, and because I wanted to observe in practice what I had just been studying in theory." His initial salary was a decent $2,880 per year, with a 5 percent deduction for his pension, and his office was in the historic abode of prime ministers, the East Block of the Parliament Buildings. A Victorian Gothic classic with high ceilings, impressive vaulted windows, and elegant fireplaces in the major offices but cubbyholes for junior clerks like Trudeau, the edifice was sufficiently small for Trudeau to encounter the "key decision-makers," including External Affairs Minister Lester Pearson and Prime Minister St. Laurent. In those days, however, to encounter was not to meet. The British traditions of formality and rank had formed a hardened crust around the so-called mandarins, whose sway in Ottawa was decisive in the postwar years. Even though St. Laurent was a francophone, he brought the manners of Quebec City's Grande Allée to an Ottawa that warmly embraced his almost regal bearing. His style contrasted strongly with the rough *bonhomie* of Premier Maurice Duplessis in Quebec. Despite their propinquity, there is no evidence that Trudeau and St. Laurent ever had a conversation during his time in Ottawa. Trudeau had considerable respect for St. Laurent, however, particularly for his work when, as justice minister, he made the Canadian Supreme Court the final court of appeal for Canadians.[30]

Ottawa at mid-century was very different from London or Paris. In contrast to London's West End, where the great thespians

performed nightly, there was only sporadic amateur theatre in
Ottawa. Paris bistros, with their excellent cheap Chablis and fine
fare, were another distant fantasy. Junior civil servants normally
brought bag lunches to work, while senior officials dined at the
cafeteria of the Château Laurier. Across the river in Hull, alcohol
flowed more freely, but few bureaucrats dared risk any hint of
the bohemian life. Trudeau correctly described mid-twentieth-
century Ottawa as "an English capital" where English was the
only working language.

Later studies confirmed this view; the Royal Commission on
Bilingualism and Biculturalism pointed out that the recruitment of francophones actually decreased considerably in the
Department of External Affairs after the Second World War. In
his account of Ottawa's mandarins at the time, historian J.L.
Granatstein is scathing in his description of the "cultural blind-
ness" that "has to be seen as an unconscious expression of the
English-Canadian view of Quebec as a land of happy (if slightly
disloyal) peasants, notaries, and priests." Pauline Vanier, the wife of
the pre-eminent francophone Canadian diplomat of the time, told
him that her husband's francophone compatriots were treated no
better than "natives." Trudeau's experiences as a public servant testify to these criticisms: most of his lunches were with the relatively
few francophones in Ottawa, while his memoranda are nearly all
in English.* His most frequent luncheon partner was his old friend
Marcel Rioux.[31] However, he was completely bicultural — indeed,
multicultural — in his choice of female companions in Ottawa.

---

* Recruitment of francophones after the war brought the francophone
percentage of the public service to the lowest level in Canadian history,
even though the prime minister was francophone. The Interdepartmental
Committee on External Trade, of which Trudeau was a member, had

As always, Trudeau was extraordinarily diligent. Although he was eligible for twenty days of leave in his first sixteen months, he took only seven of them. His supervisor was the similarly industrious Gordon Robertson, perhaps the finest Canadian public servant of his generation. Robertson, who was only two years older than Trudeau, recognized that a well-educated young francophone was a precious asset in federal-provincial relations and assigned Trudeau major responsibilities in that area. Trudeau, in turn, approached the arcane details of the Canadian Constitution with a zest for the subject that he retained until his death. In a climate where the correction of grammar and prose style was usual, Robertson rarely found fault with Trudeau, and in most cases he responded with such comments as "Thanks, very interesting."[32]

Both the quality and the quantity of Trudeau's work were remarkable, even though some of it was surely not congenial. As in law school, Trudeau may have resented the unimaginative tasks, such as the list of over fifty pages of federal-provincial agreements he was asked to compile, but he completed it quickly and thoroughly. When he finally went on vacation in October 1950, he described how all his major responsibilities were being fulfilled. His duties included such diverse subjects as civil aviation, territorial waters, peace treaty implementation, loans to immigrants, and the Sub-Committee on Coastal Trade. He gently chided Norman Robertson, the clerk of the Privy Council, over this last project, indicating in a note to his supervisor—Gordon Robertson—that the most senior public servant had

---

only two francophones among twenty-two members. Frequently, as the sole bilingual member, he became the secretary to various committees—in case some committee member momentarily lapsed into French. TP, vol. 9, file 13.

not responded to Trudeau's memorandum on the subject: "Presumably there is no urgent business."[33]

Trudeau himself attended promptly to business, a quality that impressed and sometimes surprised his superiors. Obviously, they did not expect the opinionated and spirited intellectual to carry out menial tasks with dispatch. Like a seasoned lawyer, he could argue a case where his own opinions were different. This fierce foe of conscription and wartime registration dispassionately analyzed "national registration" between 1940 and 1946, concluding that it might serve to "locate individuals who had been separated from one another during an evacuation."

He even asked Gordon Robertson whether he should draw up a summary of arguments for and against banning Communists.* His memoranda reflected the government's concern that foreign-language publications were often Communist in sympathy, but he concluded by pointing to Prime Minister St. Laurent's view that legislating against opinion was wrong. While noting Conservative leader George Drew's stern anti-Communism, he also observed the young Saskatchewan MP John Diefenbaker's strong attachment to the principles of human rights. In the tradition of the public service, he presented choices objectively, carefully analyzing the impact of decisions. It is small wonder that Gordon Robertson wrote to him: "Your note outlining government and opposition statements . . . is just what

---

* On matters relating to the Catholic Church, however, he was less open-minded and still observant of certain restrictions. On January 20, 1950, he wrote to Archbishop Vachon of Ottawa indicating that, because of his professional responsibilities, it was necessary for him to read Marxist works that were on the Index. The archbishop gave him the permission he sought eight days later. TP, vol. 14, file 12.

I wanted and should be very helpful"—helpful, of course, to the Liberal government of Louis St. Laurent.[34]

Although Trudeau's Ottawa memoranda fit the requisite blend of clear prose and well-reasoned argument, occasionally his strong streak of independence and caustic impishness broke through bureaucratic restraint, as when he wrote about national registration: "Having done very little to prevent man from being anything but a number in a series of numbers, we have no right to object when the government institutionalizes that philosophy through national registration." His advice, though carefully measured, normally expressed his own views. National registration, he suggested, might be appropriate in wartime but not in peacetime. Communism was a threat, but existing legislation was sufficient to meet it. Only on one subject—federalism—did his own opinions break through the usual official Ottawa wisdom.[35]

Trudeau's time in Ottawa made him extremely interested in the character of federalism, in both the theoretical and the practical sense. His far-ranging education had often dealt with the subject, and Emmanuel Mounier, Harold Laski, and Frank Scott had probably become the pre-eminent influences on him, despite their own very different approaches. Still, until he began working in the Privy Council Office, Trudeau was more likely to write about democracy or economic and political equality than about federalism.

Ottawa clinched his fascination with the various theories of federalism and its application in Canada. Pierre Vadeboncoeur, one of his closest friends at the time, later described Trudeau as one who approached political questions "through his legalistic side." François Hertel similarly emphasized that, to understand Pierre, you had to realize that he was essentially "a lawyer." While it is true that both men were bitterly estranged from Trudeau when they made these remarks, their comments have validity.[36] Once in Ottawa, Trudeau drew increasingly on his legal training and his conception of the importance of law, statutes, legislation, and, implicitly, political order. The legal structures of Canadian federalism began to fascinate him — in the way that a young pianist experiences his first lessons in counterpoint and harmony and finally understands how beautiful chords are made. In a setting where surprisingly few officials had a legal education, Trudeau's training in the law and in philosophy gave him advantages, especially in debate.

There was one additional legacy of his Ottawa years: he became much more interested in Canada, in how it worked and how it could fail. He attended the Dominion-Provincial Conference of 1950 and took copious notes on the discussions of possible constitutional change. He also revised official documents, as the government took advantage of his fluent bilingualism. To his superior's delight, he used his lawyer's skills to undermine provincial arguments. His views on Maurice Duplessis did not echo the harsh opinions of his superiors, who thought the Quebec premier a destructive and devious boor in federal-provincial meetings. In his opinion, Duplessis did not represent his province well because he was too narrowly nationalist and too blind to the forces of change. After one exchange, Trudeau remarked that Duplessis's intervention was "interesting but Supreme Court would have to be changed." F.R. Scott, then an adviser to the Saskatchewan CCF government, impressed him most with his arguments that the best way to break through constitutional impasses was to begin with fiscal issues and social security. It was the same view that Pierre Vadeboncoeur had expressed on Trudeau's behalf the previous summer in *Le Devoir.*

Throughout the next decade, Trudeau developed this position more precisely.[37] His Ottawa experience began to persuade him that the problems he observed in Quebec could be confronted through a more effective Canadian federalism:

But there is yet another reason why co-operation is indispensable to a federation. What is popularly referred to as division of powers is in reality division of legislative jurisdiction. And since legislative jurisdiction does not always ideally correspond to divisions of administrative jurisdiction, it so happens that very often the government most apt to legislate on a given subject cannot be relied upon to administer the laws most efficiently. Thus the legislative power of one government will have to seek co-operation with the executive or judicial power of another; which in short means that federal and provincial governments, far from seeking efficiency through complete independence in their spheres, will resort to agreement and understanding.[38]

While increasingly persuaded that federal government initiative in social and fiscal realms was essential, Trudeau argued that the provinces should maintain authority where they had clear constitutional responsibilities. He therefore vigorously attacked a bill on civil defence that came forward in 1951. "The most offensive provisions," he told his supervisor, Gordon Robertson, were "those which appear to be based on a fantastic conception of federalism." Some parts of the bill extend the "peace, order, and good government" clause of the British North America Act far beyond what its drafters intended. "It is preposterous," he declared, for the federal government "to claim jurisdiction over the provincial governments themselves." Cooperation, he wrote in another memorandum, "is indispensable to a federation," and neither jurisdiction can proceed "with complete disregard" of the other.[39] His view of the federation differed from that of some Canadian officials who were, in the postwar era, strongly centralist. Those views derived from his past—and they would affect the future.

If Trudeau was dutiful and restrained in his first year in Ottawa, he nevertheless chafed at the restraints that the government of Canada placed on its civil servants. He impatiently drafted a letter to *Le Devoir* in May 1950, complaining that "public servants do not have the right to have opinions." He never sent it. However, his differences with the St. Laurent government became significantly greater when Canada decided to enter the Korean War during the summer of 1950, after the North Koreans invaded the South, and the United Nations, through the General Assembly, authorized an America-led intervention.

Trudeau disapproved of that decision and, especially, of Lester Pearson's strong advocacy of Canadian participation. Pearson believed that the North Korean attack represented the same threat to the young United Nations as the Italian attack on Abyssinia (Ethiopia) had been in 1935 to the League of Nations. Just as Canada announced an expansion of its earlier participation, Trudeau wrote hastily to Jules Léger, who was then a middle-rank officer in External Affairs:

Dear Jules,
I've just heard Pearson's speech on Korea in the House. Not a single original thought. A little current history, a lot of propaganda . . . Asia is heading down hill. There is still time to save Europe, at least by introducing the European division [of External Affairs] to that study on neutralism you spoke to me about.[40]

Trudeau was a rare dissenter on Canadian foreign policy at a time when even the socialist CCF had joined the Cold War consensus on the need to confront the Soviet Union in Europe and in Asia. Grace Trudeau was also caught up in the fervour. She had written to her son during his world travels in February 1949:

Does world news reach you fresh? What do you think of Cardinal Mindszenty's trial, Hungarian. It is the talk of the

whole world. Prayers have been recited in all churches; now
it is the Protestants who are being persecuted, those Reds
are infiltrating themselves at an alarming rate, and no doubt
we Americans of this continent are too willing to close our
eyes, and not be on guard to the subtleness of their smooth
ways. Everyone repeats that there exists a large number of
communists in Canada. Are you going to be able to exterminate them with all your knowledge?[41]

In this case, Trudeau did not heed Grace's advice or share her
views.

On a copy of one of Pearson's speeches on December 5,
1950, in which he claimed that Canada had urged moderation
and a sense of global strategy, Trudeau scrawled: "Not very
really."[42] Five months later he sent private notes to Douglas
LePan and Pierre Trottier, both of External Affairs, attacking
another of Pearson's speeches. In his note to LePan deploring
Pearson's attack on the "hard-faced despots in the Kremlin,"
Trudeau pointed out that the cultured Canadian diplomat John
Watkins* had "pictured Soviet Russia as a country of war-weary,
peace-loving people, naïvely proud of their primitively democratic institutions; whose government was mainly engaged in
improving the civilian economy, and was even proceeding with
a certain amount of demobilization." Similarly, Trudeau said
that the Canadian mission head in China, Chester Ronning,
who sympathized with Mao's side, had indicated that "progress
is being made in their solution for the benefit of the Chinese

---

* John Watkins was later accused of being compromised by his close personal
friendship with a Soviet agent, but he died of a heart attack during the long and
secret RCMP interrogation in Montreal.

people as a whole." Given these reports, Trudeau concluded (in somewhat flawed English):

> Either Mr. Pearson is unacquainted with such reports, then he is not doing his job; or, being acquainted with them, he discounts their veracity, then he is guilty of retaining the services of two foreign service officers who are gullible soviet stooges; or, believing in their veracity, he still prefers to spread the belief that the Communists are intent on starting a war, then he is misleading the people. Wars are fought with physical courage, but in these times courage of a finer temper is required to affirm one's belief in truth and justice. If Mr. Pearson had that courage, would he not acquaint the public with facts which might tend to open an avenue of comprehension and sympathy towards the potential enemy?

He wickedly signed the letter "Comrade Trudeau."[43]

In his note to Jules Léger complaining about Pearson, Trudeau had recommended that Léger read the latest *Esprit*, some articles by Étienne Gilson in *Le Monde*, and a piece by Hubert Beuve-Méry of *Le Monde* which pondered neutralism in Europe. He did not hide his dissent from the consensus, and his colleagues began to mock his stance in a friendly way, calling him "Citizen" as a mark of his left-wing rebelliousness.

While Trudeau remained cordial, it soon became clear that neither his opinions on international affairs nor his personality were suited to the puritanical and earnest ways of St. Laurent's Ottawa. Still, he continued to work on his files and did not turn down social invitations. "It was very kind of you to have me in for dinner last Monday," he wrote to Norman Robertson a couple of months later, on June 5, adding, "Wine excellent."[44] At this dinner, his host apparently gave him an article that had appeared in the *Partisan Review* by Lionel

Trilling, the Columbia University English professor who had abandoned earlier Marxist and radical left positions during the first stages of the Cold War. Clearly, Robertson wanted to draw the clever young francophone away from the European temptation of neutralism in the increasingly fierce battle between the West and the East.* Trudeau, however, held tightly to the arguments against both the Korean War and the rapid strengthening of North Atlantic Treaty Organization troops in Europe—forces that included a significant Canadian presence. In both cases, he believed that Canada was simply following American policy towards the Soviet Union and China—policy he deemed too uncompromising and aggressive.

—

Although there was a cadre of talented young francophones in External Affairs, there were few in the Privy Council Office where Trudeau worked. Moreover, the women in the office

---

* Trudeau did not often attend dinner parties, mainly because he spent many weekends in Montreal. However, the family of the eminent journalist Blair Fraser was linked with the Trudeau family through a mutual acquaintance, and they entertained him several times while he was in Ottawa. He responded gracefully after one such dinner. "That was an extremely pleasant evening I spent at your house on Thursday. Not only was the dinner excellent, the sherry stimulating, and the conversation informative, but I was able to confirm by scientific experience a principle which had long been laid down, 'the Frasers are very nice.'" He claimed that he was fortunate to meet all the family and felt "privileged that even little Graham [later another eminent Canadian journalist] should have condescended to see us after the ominous interest of the tam-tam." Trudeau to Mrs. Fraser, nd [1950], TP, vol. 9, file 12.

were exclusively secretaries. As Margaret Trudeau commented, he treated these women professionally, as working colleagues; and they responded to his charm and invariable courtesy with an admiration that is still quickly evident when they speak of him. He was considerate, familiar yet respectful, and polite. When some of these female employees were interviewed shortly after his death, they expressed deep admiration mingled with fondness. Words like "gracious," "thoughtful," "shy and charming" were frequently used.[45] Yet Margaret mentioned another category—"the dates"—who were often "celebrities" in the seventies and the eighties.

In the fifties, Ottawa had few celebrities, but Trudeau's attention was captured one September morning in 1950 by a front-page article in the *Ottawa Citizen* which featured a large photograph of Helen Segerstrale. "Your attention Men," the article began. "May we introduce Miss Helen Segerstrale, 20 years of age, accomplished and beautiful. She's just out from Sweden to take over a clerk's job in the Swedish Embassy." She had studied at Lausanne, where she specialized in French literature, and spoke five languages. The dark blonde, strong-featured Swede would, the *Citizen* proclaimed, be "Sweden's antidote to the 'crisis blues.'" Interestingly, Trudeau, a relatively small, very thin, though strongly muscled man, was attracted to beautiful, full-figured, and tall women. He kept photographs of most of the women in his life, and they usually fit this description. He clipped out the newspaper column, quickly forgetting his "blues" as Canadian troops prepared to go to Korea, and began his pursuit of Ottawa's newest celebrity.[46]

By Christmas, Trudeau had managed an introduction and set out, intensely, to win her heart. No doubt Helen, who became Hélène to Pierre as they became more intimate, was immediately intrigued by the unlikely civil servant who drove a Harley-Davidson and a Jaguar, dived and swam like the Olympian movie star Johnny Weissmuller, bought expensive Italian-tailored suits and wore them elegantly (in a town where Eaton's department store set the fashion standard), and could converse about a Rodgers and Hammerstein opening in New York and a recent performance of Sartre's *Huis Clos* in Paris.* Their letters mingle polylingual banter (including some Swedish), ceaseless repetition of love's language, tales of travel planned or finished, and philosophical reflections.

In diplomatic mail delivered "by hand" to the East Block from the Swedish Embassy the following summer, notes arrived bearing such unofficial messages as "You made me sooooo happy . . . you are the most wonderful person on this side of the globe . . . no, even on both sides (though I don't know any Chinese yet, I'll have to find out." And, on another occasion: "I feel like a young debutante, who has the love of a young man who must write sentimental things to the object of his great desire." She signed her letters "Puss." Beaches beckoned, and candlelight dinners at twilight were followed by intimacy. His Catholic commitment to chastity had disappeared sometime in the fifties, as it apparently did for many others of the faith. Yet he, like many who wavered from the official teachings, remained committed to the church.

Pierre and Helen began to talk about spending their lives together. Grace Trudeau had come to know her well during her frequent weekend visits to Montreal with Pierre, and she began

---

* In February 1950 he bought two suits for $183, and, in June, a sports jacket for $35, at Tobia Felli, a Montreal Italian bespoke tailor. He had another suit made for $74 in November 1949. A suit at Eaton's in 1950 cost about $20. TP, vol. 9, file 5. Before he resigned, his salary had increased to $3,696, a reflection more of the rise in the cost of living than of a generous government.

to guide Helen on a critical path towards marriage: her conversion to Roman Catholicism. Like most Swedes, Helen wore her traditional Lutheran faith lightly and did not resist change. The process, however, became complicated when she received different messages from the parish priests and from Pierre's Montreal friends. She told him how she had explained to her own mother that it was not he who was imposing Catholicism on her, but that she was finding Catholicism an attractive way to live:

> On the contrary, you always told me how important it is to be free, to follow your nature, and that religion is a question between oneself and God. And then I told her [her mother] that the clerical atmosphere in Quebec could hardly have led me to Catholicism, on the contrary; I explained how you and your Cité-Libre friends at the meetings made me understand the problems and trouble the Catholic priests can cause. But it's always the same thing that is difficult for us, "free Vikings of the north": to feel humble and to keep faith precious and essential, and to disregard man's imperfections as having nothing to do with faith.

With Pierre's help, Helen wrote several times over the following few months, she would find the humility that was the prerequisite to Catholic belief, commitment, and marriage.[47]

Now over thirty, Pierre was anxious to marry. Still, he was an exacting lover, demanding in the attention he craved yet fiercely independent in his own allocation of time. And, to complicate matters, by the late summer of 1951 he had decided to leave the civil service, travel in Europe and other exotic places, and then return to find his future in Montreal. Ottawa, he realized, was not a congenial place for him to accomplish his goals, and he craved the freedom he had earlier possessed. Amid Pierre and Helen's declarations of profound love that fall, there were frequent arguments. Still, they continued making plans to marry.

Then, in December, Trudeau wrote Helen a brusque letter complaining about her "manner." Baffled at his anger, she responded: "My love, I love you, I always have and always will to the end of the world. My love, is this itself not enough? Evidently not, because you seem to say that I don't express my love well enough or often enough." He apologized and asked her to meet him in Gibraltar in January 1952, enclosing with his letter a collection of Rimbaud's poems.[48]

Like Thérèse, Helen had decided that the relationship would not work. On January 26, 1952, she wrote and told him she had decided they should not marry. There were, very simply, too many crises and too much torment in their relationship. It was now necessary to "see things as they are." Among the problems was religion, which had concerned her "constantly during your absence." The leap of faith required to become Catholic was proving to be difficult. His absence had not made her love stronger. Indeed, she had met someone shortly after Trudeau left on his trip the previous October, someone he probably knew. In one week with him she had found more "harmony and peace" than she had ever known before.[49]

Trudeau was deeply wounded, especially when she refused to meet him in Europe in the spring of 1952. He begged to see her, accused her of being cruel, and promised to silently withdraw from her life forever if she so desired. Later, he begged forgiveness for his conduct: "I cannot take leave of you without adding that my present grief has permitted me to fully understand the anguish beyond endurance that in the past year I have inflicted upon one who loved me more deeply than seems humanly possible, and one whose pardon I can at last most humbly seek . . . Fare thee well, sweet, sweet Hélène."[50] The old pattern was repeating itself.*

—

Once Trudeau had decided to leave Ottawa by October 1951, he openly chafed against the restrictions of the Canadian public service, just as he had earlier reacted against the transatlantic alliance of Britain, the United States, and Canada in which Lester Pearson's foreign policy fitted so well. Against the conventional views followed in Ottawa, he presented those proclaimed by the French Catholic left in *Esprit* and *Le Monde*—ideas that argued for conciliation rather than confrontation in the Cold War and that supported decolonization in countries such as Indochina, where smouldering embers had become raging flames.

In keeping with this contentious mood, he had an interesting exchange with Norman Robertson when he returned the magazine in which Lionel Trilling had argued the liberal case

---

* Grace Trudeau had liked Helen, whom she too called "Hélène," and she comforted Trudeau: "My dear boy it is needless to say how I feel about the turn of events—my heart aches for you–Why oh why, are you put to such suffering? I shall keep on praying that the future holds promise of happiness for you who are so kind and good—but these are God's people whom He puts to severe tests." In a letter a month later, Grace pointed to religious beliefs as the major difficulty: "It is always necessary to meet and iron out various opinions during the normal span of married life—let alone religious beliefs which are principles and foundations one should share." Grace to Pierre Trudeau, Feb. 24 and March 9, 1952, TP, vol. 46, file 20. Trudeau did not write to his mother for several weeks at this time.

against Soviet Communism. He told Robertson that the article did not impress him, although he did agree that it was an anachronism to look at "labour as an oppressed cause." He objected strongly to Trilling's description of the idealist as "someone who finds virtue only where he is not." Far more convincing to Trudeau would be the definition "someone who finds not only virtue where he is." To the rather intellectually pretentious Robertson, Trudeau responded in kind: "Both these brands of idealists are poor material for totalitarianism of either extreme. The true totalitarian is an idealist who finds only virtue where he is, or a realist or an agnostic* who pretends to do so in order to avoid the fate of Buridan's ass." This medieval ass faced starvation when he could not choose between two equally attractive piles of hay. Trudeau continued: "Incidentally the ass might not have starved had there been more than two hay stacks to sway between. Which makes me feel that if free men ever let the world be divided in two, they will have to die like asses to avoid living like slaves. Another argument for the third force!"[51] The "third force" was a popular concept in *Esprit* and *Le Monde* in which Europe, under French leadership, stood aside from the Soviet-American confrontation and established an alternative social democratic society. Robertson, a former socialist himself, had little patience with such views, but he and Trudeau parted on good terms.

---

* Robertson was an atheist, which Trudeau probably knew. In pious Ottawa, Robertson insisted that the census record him as "atheist," a category which the Canadian census did not then have. On Robertson, see J.L. Granatstein, *A Man of Influence: Norman A. Robertson and Canadian Statecraft, 1939-1968* (Ottawa: Deneau, 1981).

Trudeau invited Norman Robertson and his wife, Jetty, to drop in on Saturday night, and then he drafted his letter of resignation, which he sent on September 28. His first draft began with "Dear Great Man," which eventually became, in mock revolutionary fashion, "Dear Citizen." His secretary told him he had to send a written resignation, and he did so in a letter that mixed polite sarcasm with a modest degree of gratefulness for an experience where he had been able to put his ample learning into practice:

> My work with the Privy Council has been to me a constant source of satisfaction, and not infrequently of delight. As for fellow workers, I cannot imagine a more sympathetic lot. I have never ceased to be aware of the precedence in your mind of human beings over institutions, and this in itself has been a valuable lesson . . .
>
> I dare to hope that the structure of the central government will not be too badly shattered by my departure. But however that may be, any sense of despair should be tempered by the knowledge that I will probably return to the Bar from which I once so impetuously resigned.

He departed from Ottawa on October 6, 1951, took five days of statutory leave, and formally left the civil service on October 14, 1951.[52]

—

While Trudeau was still in Ottawa working as a civil servant, he had become intrigued by discussions with his friend Gérard Pelletier, who had now left journalism to work for the Catholic trade-union movement. During these talks, the idea came up of a Canadian journal, to be called *Cité libre*, similar to the review *Esprit* published by the French philosopher Emmanuel Mounier. It would link progressive Catholic faith with analysis of contemporary political and social issues, just as *Esprit* had done in France.

According to Pelletier, *Cité libre* emerged from the Catholic youth movement and his own admiration for Mounier. In 1950 he took the lead, because of Trudeau's absence in Ottawa, and worked with others, notably the teacher Guy Cormier and the trade-unionist Jean-Paul Geoffroy, to create a journal that would be Catholic yet dissident. Another *Cité libre* founder, the literary critic and notary Maurice Blain, has perceptively noted the impact that the Great Depression and the Second World War made on the generation that founded the journal: "This generation without masters is seeking a humanism," he said, "and is anxiously asking on what kind of spiritual foundation this humanism should be based."[53] Those were the central questions that Trudeau, too, had asked himself in the forties, although he, as a Brébeuf student, had not done so within the Catholic youth movement.

After riding his motorbike to Montreal, Trudeau would join in the long night debates about the shape the journal should take. Pelletier cemented Trudeau's participation with the suggestion that *Cité libre* would fundamentally challenge the status quo in Quebec. But, he recalled, he had to convince others to accept Trudeau:

> On the one hand, he really was a novice among us, still grudgingly accepted by our team, several of whom barely knew him. On the other hand, he was vitally interested in our undertaking, which was to allow him, after several years' absence, to find his place in his generation, and in a circle that was broader than the one to which he belonged.

Neither his personality nor his wealth* (or his continuing references to Cardinal Newman as a source of inspiration) made Trudeau popular among some of Pelletier's colleagues, and they told Pelletier their complaints:

> Four or five of us were standing in the middle of the large kitchen, glasses in hand. It was well past midnight, closer, in fact, to dawn. We were having a quiet post-mortem on the evening's discussion when, suddenly, the thing that had been incubating for months gave the conversation an unexpected turn. It was not Trudeau's ideas that were questioned by my friends, but his origins, his circle, his society connections.

Although fascinated by his intelligence and strength, many found him, in Pelletier's words, "a disturbing influence." And, as Pelletier added wryly in the 1980s, "he has continued to be throughout his life."[54]

---

* In 1992 Ron Graham asked Trudeau whether it was true that Claude Ryan had once told him to give up his wealth and that he had considered renouncing his inheritance at Harvard. He dismissed the rumour, though he added that, at Brébeuf, he had realized it was unfair that some students "were doing their homework . . . on the kitchen table with mother cooking the food and the rest of the family milling around and so on. And I felt it was a bit unfair that I should have a private room in my house to do work." Citing a story by Antoine de Saint Exupéry, Trudeau said that it was wrong that a Mozart could not have a piano because of poverty. "So," he concluded, "I think there's more sense of fairness than of guilt on my part." Interview between Pierre Trudeau and Ron Graham, May 4, 1992, TP, vol. 23, file 7.

Guy Cormier, reporting the same conversation, said that when the first issue of *Cité libre* was passed around on the evening of July 14, 1950, at a cottage on Île Perrot, the editors had a "courteous but very lively discussion" about Trudeau's participation. The former Young Catholics were especially critical, with one of them saying: "I don't want to see Trudeau on the team. He's not with our people; he never will be with our people." On that and so many other occasions, Pelletier strongly defended his friend.[55]

This account is unconvincing, not because of the details of the discussion but because the first issue was ready well before Bastille Day, 1950, and because Trudeau was essential to its production. While it is undoubtedly true that his wealth caused hesitations, Trudeau is probably wrong to think it was the major source of the opposition to him. His financial support was, in fact, a large ingredient in the journal's success. Pelletier's Young Catholics predominated and Pelletier's wife, Alec, not Trudeau, signed the bank note to guarantee funding, but Trudeau and his friends brought resources and relationships that were crucial for its early success. The journal depended on money from nine people: Réginald Boisvert, Maurice Blain, Guy Cormier, Jean-Paul Geoffroy, Pierre Juneau, Charles Lussier, Pelletier, Roger Rolland, and Trudeau. Pelletier and Trudeau gave the largest contributions, $250.32, while the others gave much less. Cormier contributed only $31.09, and Geoffroy, $47.09. Trudeau covered debts when necessary, and he regularly paid the costs for the impecunious Pierre Vadeboncoeur and for Geoffroy.[56] He was, admirably, always silent about his private charity.

Moreover, Trudeau's meticulous address book provided buyers for the journal, which had only 225 subscriptions on its second issue. Among the names on Trudeau's list are female friends (including Jacqueline Côté, later the wife of Professor Blair Neatby, Mackenzie King's biographer, and his sister, Suzette), the great Catholic philosopher Étienne Gilson, and

Marcel Cadieux, Jean-Louis Delisle, Mario Lavoie, Georges Charpentier, and Jean Langlois of the Department of External Affairs. Trudeau's reach, both financial and personal, considerably exceeded his colleagues' grasp. He also bought up thirty-three copies to send to François Hertel to distribute in France, in the hope of increasing their readers abroad.[57] The initial price asked of subscribers was a lofty $2, at a time when the popular weekly *Le Petit Journal* sold for 10 cents.

Trudeau's presence was dominant from the first issue on. And, significantly, Trudeau began to find his place among his generation in Quebec through *Cité libre*. In the June 1950 premier issue, Trudeau wrote tributes to three giants who had recently died: the French socialist leader Léon Blum and his own intellectual mentors Emmanuel Mounier and Harold Laski. "Emmanuel Mounier has gone," he began his tribute to the founder of *Esprit*, whose influence touched every page of *Cité libre*'s first issue. So great was his impact that the journal's founders had hoped to give him the first copy of the new review. The other obituaries have more substance, and they also indicate why Trudeau did not share the opinions of Lester Pearson and the Ottawa mandarins in the summer of 1950 as Canada joined the United States and the United Nations in responding to the invasion of South Korea by the Communist North.

There were, Trudeau wrote, two systems that divided humanity in a dangerous way, with each one able to annihilate the other. There were, however, some who had "refused to be signed up in one or the other of the totalitarianisms. They have instead devoted their lives to interpreting and acting upon a belief which holds that liberty, justice and peace must be pre-eminent. As is inevitable, they are hysterically denounced and hatefully censured by both orthodox Marxists and official Christianity." Among the "circle of the just" (to use Dante's phrase linking eternal and temporal justice) who maintain the principles of Christianity and human dignity, Trudeau found it "astonishing" that "two Jewish Marxists have without pause distinguished themselves by their intelligence, their courage, and their unending generosity": Harold Laski and Léon Blum. Laski, he wrote, received heads of states and poor students with equal simplicity, and his work would endure as humans built the "free city" where they were able to live in tolerance and eventually in love. That, he continued, was why both capitalists and Stalinists were sworn enemies of the principled Laski and of the admirable Blum.[58] And that was why Trudeau was increasingly uncomfortable in Ottawa.

Trudeau did not sign his name to those tributes, understandably, given his civil service position. In the same issue, he wrote a major article whose title became an emblem of his approach to politics, one which, before that summer, had lacked coherence. "Politique fonctionnelle" (functional politics) became a term that he bore with him as he navigated the rapids of political change in Quebec in the fifties and sixties. Right from the first issue of Cité libre, Trudeau demonstrated that his experience with the practical side of politics in Ottawa had left a mark, while, simultaneously, he recognized the uniqueness of the Quebec Catholic experience of his past. A church, he wrote, "would be an impostor if it stayed forever in the catacombs. Similarly, in politics, you cannot stay below ground too long." French Canada, it seemed, might be heading for a dead end where its leaders exaggerated the dangers of religious and linguistic assimilation while brandishing threats from supposed enemies—"the English, Jews, imperialists, centralizers, demons, free-thinkers, and I don't know what else." While slaying imaginary enemies, he cautioned, "our language has become so impoverished that we no longer notice how badly we speak," and clerics discouraged students from going abroad lest their faith be challenged.

Another passage in the article became celebrated as Trudeau's political credo:

We want to bear witness to the Christian and French fact in America. Fine; so be it. But let's get rid of all the rest. We should subject to methodical doubt all the political categories relegated to us by the previous generation; the strategy of resistance is no longer conducive to the fulfillment of our society. The time has come to borrow the "functional" discipline from architecture, to throw to the winds those many prejudices with which the past has encumbered the present, and to build for the new man. Let's batter down the totems, let's break the taboos. Better yet, let's consider them null and void. Let us be coolly intelligent.

It is, in retrospect, a remarkable paragraph. It gave no offence to his Ottawa superiors, yet it initiated the definition of a new program.* Indeed, although there were no senior public servants on *Cité libre*'s subscription list, Trudeau's criticism of the high-handed way the Duplessis government acted at the federal-provincial conference of January 1950 would have pleased them immensely. When presented with concrete offers, Quebec remained stupidly silent. In concluding, Trudeau argued that the nationalism of the past and its intimate link with the clergy

---

* Another unsigned article in June 1951 would certainly have offended his superiors. In it he argued strongly against Canadian participation in the Korean War. He complained, as Canadian diplomats themselves did, about American policy towards Formosa (Taiwan) and the decision of the American general, Douglas MacArthur, to cross the 38th parallel and enter North Korea. However, he went beyond those complaints to attack the policies of the West towards Asia more generally and those of the United States more specifically. Everywhere, he claimed, the hallucinating fear of socialism guided American policy. Can they not understand, he asked, that their free-enterprise policies protect the most

no longer served the interests of a Catholic and French people who must confront a new world where old barnacles had to be scraped away.[59]

The importance of *Cité libre* for Trudeau was enormous. When he left Ottawa, he asked Jean Marchand whether there was a position for him in the trade-union movement, but he took no permanent job.[60] Through *Cité libre* he developed close contacts with the emerging media, especially television, where several of his friends, including Alec Pelletier and Roger Rolland, were finding positions. Although the journal's subscription list remained small, its influence among the intellectual and political elite of Quebec was considerable. The conservative historian Robert Rumilly warned Maurice Duplessis that "the people at *Cité libre* are extremely dangerous; they have international affiliations with the review *Esprit* in France; they are subversives and you must be wary of them. In the long term, it is very dangerous for your government."[61] Duplessis accepted the advice, which had merit, and cast an increasingly suspicious eye on the "*Cité libre* crowd."

Historians more recently have criticized the oversimplification that *Cité libre* was the overwhelming centre of opposition

reactionary feudalism and that their evangelical promotion of democracy "refuses to the oppressed [Asians] the right to use their new liberty to create an economic system different from *the biggest and the best?*" "Positions sur la présente guerre," *Cité libre*, May 1951, 3–11 [English and italics in the original]. In the case of Canada, he pointed out that it was always faithful to its tradition of defending the strong against the weak and "in matters of external policy, it has followed, it does follow, and it will follow." It is not surprising that External Affairs was an early target of Prime Minister Pierre Trudeau in 1968 or that Lester Pearson so strongly objected to Trudeau's Foreign Policy Review.

to Duplessis. It was not, but, in the words of the leading text on modern Quebec history, "*Cité libre*, despite its small circulation, represented a major gathering place and channel of expression for reform liberals."[62] It stood out because it championed two predominant themes that resonated widely at the time: traditionalist nationalism was outmoded, and the socioeconomic reality of Quebec required new approaches that emphasized democracy and individual freedom. In defining and refining those themes, Pierre Trudeau was to play a principal role in Quebec after the mid-century.

—

CHAPTER 6

NATIONALISM AND SOCIALISM

Trudeau returned to Canada to play the part in public life he had long planned and for which he had conscientiously trained at Harvard and in Paris and London. He discovered that his legal and social scientific training had value in public policy debates within the national government, but Ottawa was then too distant from Quebec—the province where he wanted to play a part. He told a later interviewer: "I had searched for a way to put [intellectual change] in motion in Quebec in order to renew ideas, old habits of thought, and old cultural customs. *Cité libre* was a path. Ottawa was not."[1]

Those were grand hopes for a journal that had fewer than 250 subscribers, including some in Ottawa, girlfriends and relatives of the editorial team, and the former priest François Hertel, who peddled copies in Paris. Yet in Quebec in the 1950s the Catholic Index still survived, intellectual life among francophones remained centred within the church (which dominated both the colleges and the universities), and classical colleges like Brébeuf had created an elite whose members closely followed the activities of their peers. The debates occurred within this context—one Trudeau recognized in his article on functional politics in *Cité libre*'s first issue. Although he called there for demolition of the "totems," he still bore witness to the Catholic and French fact in North America. The church, according to the historian Michael Behiels, "remained, even in 1950, one of the most powerful social institutions in Quebec, sharing power with the predominantly anglophone commercial and industrial institutions and the francophone political institutions. Through its diocesan and parish administrations, educational institutions at all levels, farmers' and workers' organizations, social service institutions, national associations of every variety, and its enormous fiscal power, the Quebec Catholic Church permeated all of the conscious and unconscious social, cultural, and political behaviour of the vast majority of French Canadians."[2]

In this context the journal had attracted clerical attention almost immediately—something the editorial team had fully expected. Trudeau and Pelletier, the co-editors, shared a profound intellectual and emotional commitment to Roman Catholicism, but their criticism of the Catholic Church in Quebec was "that it preached an overly theocratic social and political philosophy which had spawned a corrupting form of clericalism." This clericalism brought a religious dogmatism and an authoritarianism that stifled intellectual freedom in the province. Young Catholics like Trudeau and Pelletier, who had thrilled to the intellectual openness of the church in France in the postwar years, were determined to challenge it, though they had to work within the well-defined and narrow world of Quebec Catholicism.

And so, from the beginning, *Cité libre* tested the limits. On international matters, where Trudeau's training and travels gained him immediate pre-eminence at the fortnightly editorial meetings, there was considerable freedom. His article opposing the Korean War, for example, reflected the opinion of many influential people in the church, the newspaper *Le Devoir*, and, according to the polls, the French-speaking population at large. Although it created a modest stir in Ottawa, it was largely ignored in Montreal. The real problems came for the journal when it touched on the power and the glory of the church within Quebec.[3]

Not surprisingly, Trudeau's combination of playful mischief and personal independence got him into trouble first. He wrote an article attacking clericalism and, in particular, interference by the Catholic Church in secular affairs where the opinion of the priest, he argued, should count for no more than anyone else's. He even referred mockingly to the "divine right of bishops." Trudeau's friends warned him that he had gone too far. Father Richard Arès, the eminent editor of the Jesuit journal *Relations*, indicated that Paul-Émile Léger, the archbishop of Montreal and brother of Trudeau's friend Jules, was very concerned about the orthodoxy of *Cité libre* and of Trudeau personally. Monsignor Lussier, whose brother Charles was active in *Cité libre*, was even more troubled.[4] In *Relations*, Trudeau's comments provoked a harsh attack from Father Marie d'Anjou which startled Trudeau. D'Anjou had been one of his four favourite teachers at Brébeuf and, in the extreme nationalism of the war years, d'Anjou had collaborated with him in the creation of the secret revolutionary cell and promoted Trudeau as the natural leader among the group. When Trudeau questioned why he had published the article without first telling him, d'Anjou sent this reply:

But objectively, I think you deserved the criticism. Yet, I will always distinguish between your errors and you as a person. And you were very much mistaken when you wrote that prime ministers have no more divine right than do bishops. True as far as prime ministers are concerned but heresy when you apply it to bishops. You knew that, Pierre, I'm certain. Why did you risk this pointless and inappropriate bravado in your otherwise sound and dispassionate article?

Perhaps you will think I am coming to the defence of a bad cause, that of the clergy you no longer trust. Pierre, this needs to be qualified! You know me too well—even some aspects of my personal religious experiences—to suspect me of blind loyalty. If I intervene here, it is because there are principles at stake which go infinitely beyond the cause of certain members of the clergy (however many there may be). My despair would be that you not recognize my point of view. But that is not my fear.

Then, suddenly, he changed topic:

> Have you given your alms for Lent? If not I have a proposition to make, similar to the one you sent me from London three or four years ago. Once again I am coming to the assistance of an unwed mother. You know what that means. My cashbox is empty. If your finances allow it, I wonder if you could make a contribution . . . You need not apologize if my request arrives at an inopportune time. Thanks in any event.[5]

Despite his anger, Trudeau responded to d'Anjou's request for the contribution. D'Anjou thanked him "in the name of the individual who has benefited from your wonderful charity" and promised that he would say a Mass for him during Easter week. However, he added that he had chatted with Archbishop Léger, who expressed his concerns about *Cité libre*.[6]

In the spring of 1951, Archbishop Léger summoned Gérard Pelletier and Trudeau to his office. Trudeau was still working in Ottawa and had to make a special trip to Montreal for the appointment, which finally took place in the late summer. Pelletier had already warned him that Léger had told Claude Ryan, a prominent official in the Catholic Church and then an admirer of Trudeau, that he was concerned—and that it had something to do with *Cité libre*.* The mood was tense for the early evening meeting.

The Archbishop made his entrance. There were the usual greetings and handshakes, then . . . nothing. An embarrassed silence on both sides. A bad start. Why was our host, normally at no loss for words, sitting there and smiling at us? Was he expecting explanations from us before they were even asked for? As Trudeau didn't let out a peep, I screwed up my courage and said:

"You called us in, your Grace . . ."

He shifted in his chair.

"I invited you," he corrected me. "This is not a summons, I invited you, first of all to make your acquaintance and then to draw your attention to certain points . . . of doctrine raised by your articles."

After some discussion, it became clear that Trudeau had been the main offender by his comments about the "divine right of bishops," but he did not back down. He even said that if he and *Cité libre* were condemned, "we would appeal to the universal Church, as is our right." The archbishop, in response, "stared strangely" at Trudeau. Then, he passed to the next point. In "those few seconds," Pelletier wrote later, "the fate of *Cité libre* was decided in the incredible atmosphere of a medieval dispute."[7]

---

* Ryan reported that he said to Léger that "the group at *Cité libre* are Christians and their intentions are sound," that they were among his friends. He advised the archbishop to see Trudeau and Pelletier before he acted, but nothing happened. When Ryan next met Léger, the archbishop asked why they had not come. Ryan replied that "they were probably waiting for their invitation." After some time sorting out how it should be handled, the meeting was arranged. Pelletier to Trudeau, Feb. 28, 1951, TP, vol. 21, file 21.

But Quebec in the fifties was no longer medieval, even if some knights of the church and state wished it to be.

—

When Trudeau returned to Canada in 1949 after his world trip, he found that the Quebec nationalism that had thrust him towards the barricades earlier in the decade was no longer intellectually compelling or emotionally consuming. The Quebec Catholic Church, which had absorbed him earlier, now seemed marginalized from the engrossing debates he had encountered on his travels, particularly in France. There was, for him, a striking dissonance in his home province. In many ways Quebec was part of the general North American prosperity, with its new highways, stores crammed with merchandise, telephones that worked, and electricity that no longer flickered or disappeared. Yet in other ways it lagged, and, for Trudeau and his colleagues at *Cité libre*, the church had become the barrier not only to progress but to a richer spiritual life. In the diverse countries he visited, Trudeau had seen the boundaries changing, and he was becoming convinced that the essence of freedom for groups and individuals alike was the right to choose their identity.

Yet in defining his own identity he was still, at this time, preeminently French and Catholic, and he sought change within that mould. In his two years in Ottawa, his relationship with Helen Segerstrale is revealing: he wrote to her in French, they escaped to Montreal whenever they could, and his commitment to the Catholic faith became an obstacle between them. He did not wear British woollens or read the *New Yorker* magazine as his fellow mandarins did. Although he learned a lot about the Canadian political system through his work, his emotional and intellectual commitment to Canada's national political system remained weak.

As the 1950s progressed, however, Trudeau would develop an intellectual appreciation of Canada as a potentially successful state. Gradually this cerebral admiration would win over his emotional loyalty too. In these years he began to form the sense of Canadian identity that he later expressed eloquently in his political life, as both an author and an actor in the Quebec and the Canadian political process. The route he followed at this time, however, has perplexed scholars who objectively study his career, just as it did his closest personal friends.

In the fifties Trudeau often appeared to be aimless, if not dilettantish. The conservative nationalists with whom he had worked in the early forties, such as the Union nationale politician Daniel Johnson, dismissed him as a "dandy," a rich, unreliable playboy who made no serious contribution to the political scene. Even Pelletier became so frustrated by Trudeau's eclectic ways and frequent journeys to exotic destinations that he inquired: "Pierre, isn't it a catastrophe to be born rich?" Another friend bluntly asked, "What are you going to do when you grow up, Trudeau?" Thérèse Casgrain, the leading Quebec feminist and socialist who worked closely with him in the 1950s, also expressed impatience with his habit of "launching ideas or movements, only to lose interest or turn to something else." Reporters impressed by his quick intelligence and articulate arguments frequently qualified their praise by remarking on his lack of perseverance and sustained focus. An irritated Maurice Duplessis dismissed his old friend Charlie Trudeau's son as "lazy, spoiled, and subversive."[8]

True, Trudeau was single, and it did give him a freedom that Pelletier, for instance, who had a wife and children, did not possess. Some of his other colleagues, even if they were bachelors, had jobs at universities or colleges or with Catholic trade unions, and they feared losing positions and salaries because of clerical wrath. Trudeau also had the independence that wealth brings. His net worth in the early fifties remains unclear, but Belmont

Park, one of his principal investments, flourished, and the stock market and real estate provided handsome returns. His mother's money was available to him if he needed it, but, clearly, he did not. He derived enough from his trust, and, as the elder brother, he managed the estate with the assistance of an accountant and bankers. At that time, travellers needed banker's drafts for extended periods abroad. They were not automatic and most had limits placed on amounts that could be withdrawn. Trudeau, however, quickly obtained letters that allowed him to draw on funds in Canada, and most of them specified no limit.

To many observers, it seemed that Trudeau lived like a hedonist. Gérard Filion of *Le Devoir* called him a bohemian, but it was a peculiar bohemianism. He lived in his mother's gracious house, where she or the servants looked after all his daily needs. He wore expensive clothes, drove a Jaguar first and then a treasured Mercedes 300SL convertible, courted stunningly beautiful young women, and travelled to foreign locales whenever he felt like it. He frequented the bars on Crescent and the galleries on Sherbrooke, and, after his mother became president of the Montreal Symphony women's association in 1951, he often joined her in the finest seats at the concerts. With his colleagues, however, he often appeared indifferent to money—and understandably so, given that nearly all his youthful friends, except for Roger Rolland, lacked it.*

Yet Trudeau did not hesitate to appear ostentatious when the mood struck. Jean Fournier, a witty and charming External Affairs officer Trudeau sometimes socialized with in his Ottawa

---

* Rolland, whose family owned a large paper company, said later that they enjoyed being outrageous together, getting into pranks that made their families furious. Grace's letters reveal, however, that she, at least, enjoyed hearing about their escapades.

days, recalled that, one icy winter day, he and his wife urged Trudeau not to risk the motorbike trip to Montreal. Instead, Trudeau appeared at their house the following Monday morning "behind the wheel of a brand-new American car." Their young sons shrieked with pleasure when Trudeau scooped them up and drove them to school. The story reveals not only Trudeau's wealth and independence but his remarkable ways with children—who always loved his own childlike playfulness.[9]

Youngsters also appreciated his generosity. His brother, Tip, who remained a close friend, shared his family with his bachelor brother. Tip's wife, Andrée, who adored Trudeau, gently chastised him for the abundance of gifts he bestowed on his nieces and nephews at Christmas and when he returned from exotic locales. A cottage neighbour said his five young daughters often heard complaints about Pierre's arrogance or distance but could not believe it of the older man, who charmed with his many tricks and listened to each of them as if there were no one else on earth. The stories about Trudeau's interaction with children are absolutely consistent.[10]

The criticism of the adults, however, left its mark. Deemed unreliable by some of his friends, lazy and ineffective by his enemies, Trudeau himself seemed to view the fifties later as a lost decade. When he published his memoirs in 1993, he allotted only five of the 368 pages to the period between his departure from the Privy Council Office in October 1951 and the election of Jean Lesage in 1960. He knew about the comments of his friends—Casgrain wrote in the early 1970s and Pelletier in the 1980s—yet he did not bother to refute them, much less the harsher comments of his enemies. He seemed to treat politics as a plaything, flirting with the Co-operative Commonwealth Federation (CCF), skewering Louis St. Laurent and Duplessis in the media, and periodically announcing a bold initiative for a new political grouping. It is hardly surprising that the blondes, the cars, the clothes, and the travel made even his friends wonder whether this extraordinarily gifted young man was truly "serious." But he was.

Trudeau's papers and writings indicate that the 1950s were fundamental in shaping the role he would later play so dramatically in both Quebec and Canada. That was the decade when he did become serious and consistent. Moreover, he began very ably to shape his adolescent thoughts of a public life into an adult reality. It was not an easy task. In his memoirs, he says that "people have often asked me whether, in the 1950s, I already had political ambitions. I have always answered in the negative, which was the truth."[11] It is a partial truth: only if you take an extremely narrow view of political ambition—specifically, election to a legislature—is the statement true. Even then, he did consider such a political career as early as 1952.

These personal papers also reveal a disconnect in this decade between the image of the brilliant but erratic bohemian and the reality of his life. Even more than the forties, when he moved from being a conservative Quebec Catholic nationalist to a cosmopolitan francophone on the left, the fifties was a transformative decade for him. He became deeply grounded within the political life of Quebec, and he gained political skills as he participated in the protracted assault by Quebec intellectuals and the liberal media on Maurice Duplessis's government. Simultaneously, he began his fateful encounters with the English-Canadian intellectuals in person and with the broader English-Canadian public through the media.

There are certainly moments of insouciant bohemianism in Trudeau's life in the fifties. But there is also great ambition, diligence, and a deliberate attempt to create a public presence that confronted not only Duplessis's Union nationale government but also Canada's lazy sense of conformity. Although Trudeau had no regular job, he worked hard on labour arbitration boards and on his journalistic writing, which appeared not only in *Cité libre* but also in *Vrai*, a newspaper edited by his crusading friend Jacques Hébert. There were letters to the editor, travel pieces for *Le Devoir*, attacks on various wrongs, and piles of handwritten letters to friends and foes. He was a painfully careful writer, revising drafts several times as he sought the perfect word. Usually, he found it. Pelletier later recalled how Trudeau would labour over a minor piece for *Vrai* and submit it at the last possible minute for publication. And he worked for several years on his major intellectual effort, an edited study of the Asbestos Strike. When it finally appeared in 1956, it immediately set off intellectual explosions in classrooms, editorial pages, and secular and religious chapels.

Books mattered, but Trudeau realized in the fifties that the new media—initially the radio, then television—were becoming fundamental to shaping public debate. On radio his quick repartee, distinctive voice, and immediate expression of emotion brought frequent invitations to participate in debates and discussions. Not so on television, where, initially, he was wary, hesitant, and not very good. Soon he mastered his presentation, however, and it became the medium that carried his message and personality far beyond the intellectual crowd at *Cité libre*. The proportion of Quebec homes with television grew from only 9.7 percent in 1953 to 38.6 percent in 1955, to 79.4 percent in 1957, and 88.0 percent in 1960—a higher number than for Canada as a whole. Very quickly, the audience that mattered most were the groups of people surrounding the black and white box every evening in Quebec homes.[12] Trudeau's face became familiar; his voice, compelling, as television aerials sprouted at astonishing speed above homes not only in Montreal and Quebec City but in the small towns and villages of Quebec. And he made sure he maintained close ties with television producers and personalities. Alec Pelletier was a producer; his former roommate Roger Rolland worked for Radio-Canada and his *Cité libre* colleague Pierre Juneau for the National Film Board; and several other acquaintances had employment or other ties in the field. He ceased to search for university jobs that would place him in classrooms rather than in living rooms.[13] He wanted a defined and carefully constructed public presence. He also wanted his independence and privacy. The tension between these competing desires remained until his death.

Trudeau learned to play to the camera. His compelling eyes, even white teeth, and high cheekbones captured the attention of his viewers, who became fascinated with his remarkable ability to shift his expression in an instant from withering contempt to an engaging, bashful smile. He used the debating skills he had honed so well at Brébeuf and in hundreds of evenings in Paris, in Pelletier's home, and "on the road." Marshall McLuhan, the celebrated Canadian media analyst and gifted phrase-maker, soon noticed this new talent on the "cool" medium of television and wrote to Trudeau, "You've got the cool image, the mask." There was an almost mystical link between Trudeau and television, he said: "The story of Pierre Trudeau is the story of the Man in the Mask. That is why he came into his own with TV."

McLuhan's comments intrigued Trudeau, and the ambitious young Quebecer struck up a friendship with the professor, often making unannounced visits to his home in Wychwood Park in Toronto. "The medium shapes the message," McLuhan quipped, and, in this electronic age, television was the medium for politics and campaigning—politicians, henceforth, would need to have charisma. Trudeau should not worry about possible contradictions in his developing ideas, he advised, but should "probe" wherever his thoughts led him. "It freed me up," Trudeau reminisced later, after this mentor's death. In McLuhan's view, Canada, and especially French Canada, possessed a profound "cultural gap." French Canada "leapt into the 20th century without ever having had a 19th century. Like all backward and tribal societies, it is very much 'turned on' or at home in the new electric world of the 20th century."[14] The statement oversimplifies, but it also emphasizes, rightly, the enormous impact television had on Quebec, as well as Trudeau's warm relationship with the camera.

The mystical mingled with simple good luck and crafty planning to make Trudeau's television presence so striking. He consciously created an aura of intrigue, adventure, and intellectual brilliance about him. The last came easily to Trudeau, although, characteristically, he sometimes had private doubts.*

---

* In 1954 Trudeau took an IQ test at the University of Ottawa. The Wechsler Test had seven categories and Trudeau was measured against the francophone population of Ottawa between the age of fifteen and sixty years. The results, interestingly, reflected his marks at Brébeuf. He ranked highest in mathematical and abstract reasoning (excellent) and lower in visual motor tasks (average and above average). His "average" ranking in attention and short-term memory was surely wrong. In any event, his overall ranking was the highest possible (excellent). Maurice Chagnon, University of Ottawa, to Pierre Trudeau, Feb. 1954, TP, vol.14, file 37.

He also had a "Miss Parsons," who appears to have been a female colleague, analyze his handwriting. She told him that his mind was "extraordinary. Brilliant, searching, certainly above the average." In a remarkably perceptive analysis, she wrote: "You are methodical in procedure, accurate and dependable . . . You may give the appearance of not noticing people and their actions, or what is going on around you to any great extent, but you intuitively understand and observe more, in five minutes, than the ordinary individual would observe in a day." She noted that he was shy but could also be "the life of any party." He had a quick temper and a tongue that could bite. He gave the appearance "for the most part of a gentle nature, and you probably are, but you can certainly be the opposite at will." She concluded, perhaps expressing a personal experience, that his interest in women was "nil." He admired beauty, "but it does not go any deeper, either by intent or nature." She concluded that there was "a great deal more to this writing of yours than meets the eye." One suspects that personal contact as much as Trudeau's unremarkable handwriting guided Ms. Parsons's analysis. D.L. Parsons to Trudeau, nd, ibid.

The mystery, so important to the culture of celebrity in the twentieth century, became part of the Trudeau image that he and others created in the fifties. Although his travels often inconvenienced his collaborators, they initially dominated the content of his public appearances on radio and television. As his critics noted, he romanticized his voyages.

On Radio-Canada on May 5, 1950, for example, the broadcaster Jean Sarrazin painted a "Portrait of Pierre Trudeau" that Trudeau corrected himself before the broadcast—one of the changes being his addition of "Elliott" to the title. Sarrazin began the broadcast by noting how "French Canadians like to travel." He then proceeded to describe how Trudeau had toured the world with only a backpack, a few dollars, and a beard. He "clandestinely" created "some ultra-official documents" that permitted him to penetrate the Iron Curtain. The most beautiful women in Europe were in Budapest, and he spent "voluptuous nights on the Danube!" The voyage continued in breathless prose as Trudeau became a postwar blend of Phileas Fogg and James Bond, fearing none, confronting evil, and meeting gorgeous women at unexpected moments. There was, for example, the time in Turkey when he was offered a bath: "Tragedy! He did not understand the sign and entered the women's section entirely nude . . . the beautiful Ottomans cried and sighed." Once again, he was expelled from the country.

The tale of dash and daring forged on, of the young Canadian with the backpack who went "behind the Iron Curtain . . . encountered Greek guerrillas, the war in Palestine, the troubles in Afghanistan, the war between India and Pakistan, the Burmese revolution, the battles in Indochina, and civil war in China. He was in prison ten times, shot at three times . . . And yet survived to tell the story." The last word on the broadcast belonged to Trudeau: no matter how perilous the journey, he said, it had been worthwhile because he "saw how human beings are good when you present yourself without pretension."[15] The story, of course, bore only passing resemblance to the accounts in his letters home. Altogether, it indicated that Pierre Trudeau had already learned how to make himself a lively story. He knew that presentation mattered as much as content.

Part of the presentation involved his clothes, hand tailored not at Eaton's or Holt Renfrew, but by an Italian tailor working with the finest imported cloth and sometimes even silk. Occasionally, he would wear his father's dramatic black cape. Accessories such as scarves or gloves he often bought on European trips, where he also purchased some vintage wines unknown in Quebec, even though he was abstemious where alcohol was concerned. In the photographs of the early fifties, Gérard Pelletier, Jean Marchand, and most of the others have cigarettes in their fingers, tousled hair, and jackets a bit askew. Trudeau, in contrast, has a short haircut, never a cigarette (although he had tried smoking in the early forties), and, even in casual wear, clothes that seem to fit perfectly. He bought the best but, as Marc Lalonde later pointed out, he kept it for a long time, depending on an excellent sense of personal style in his clothing.[16]

Certainly, he is fit himself: the enormous stock of photographs of Trudeau in a bathing suit, surprisingly bikini-like for the times, reveals an adolescent's lean, well-muscled body. He tended it carefully, to the point of taking ballet lessons to learn how artists control their movement.* Similarly, he supplemented the boxing skills learned from his father with the Japanese self-defence system of

---

* The ballet lessons he took with Sylvia Knelman, later the eminent economist Sylvia Ostry. Conversation with Dr. Ostry.

karate. All these acquired abilities created a shield, along with the personal self-confidence that sometimes seemed "swagger" to others. René Lévesque, for example, once said that Trudeau had an "inborn talent for making you want to slap his face." As Pelletier remarked, René would have "taken good care to avoid a dust-up with Pierre . . . because he [Lévesque] was gifted for boxing the way Muhammad Ali is for embroidery."[17] Despite his average stature, Trudeau intimidated physically.*

Once he returned to Montreal, Quebec politics quickly became his main preoccupation. His Ottawa experience had soured him on federal politics, though it had intrigued him in terms of the potential he now saw in federalism. Still, he was annoyed by the dull, anglophile style of the capital and by the government's integration of Canadian defence and foreign policy with that of the United States. He respected Louis St. Laurent, but the francophone prime minister disappointed him because he expected him to be another charismatic Laurier and not a "chairman of the board," while Lester Pearson, the external affairs minister and the most popular politician in the Canadian media, did not impress him much. He now also detested the Duplessis government and thought little of the Liberal opposition in Quebec City. He could not abide the anonymity of being a civil servant, particularly the requirement that he remain silent on public issues. Freed of such restraints and home in Montreal, he expressed his political interests through his pen and his media presentations and, to a much lesser extent, through membership in the CCF.

---

* Although the 5'10" height he always listed for his passports may be in doubt, his tailor's records indicate that, in 1955, at age thirty-six, his neck size was a well-muscled 15 inches, his chest 38, and his waist only 32. TP, vol. 14, file 1.

Among the *Cité libre* crowd, Trudeau's specialization quickly became politics and international affairs—areas that fitted in well with his desire to travel.*

But the team was not amused when, on October 24, 1951, just a few weeks after his return to Montreal from Ottawa, he set off on yet another grand tour for the winter and spring to Europe, Africa, and the Middle East—including a visit to the Soviet Union.

—

Trudeau's decision to attend the International Economic Conference in Moscow in the spring of 1952 so soon after his

---

* Trudeau had been deeply influenced by dreams of a "middle way" between Communism and capitalism. His experience around the world had made him sympathetic to national liberation movements in colonial empires—developments the Soviet Union ostensibly championed and many Western states opposed. In Ottawa there had already been an example of this interest.

During his world tour in 1949, French Indochina, as it then was, had charmed him. He admired the people and the mingling of French and Asian culture. Now a public servant, on October 2, 1950, he took two "Annamite gentlemen" to call on the External Affairs' Asian specialist, Arthur Menzies: Peter Martin Ngo Dinh Thuc, the archbishop in Hué, Indochina, and his brother Ngo Dinh Diem. Five years later, Ngo Dinh Diem would become president of an independent South Vietnam, only to be killed by the Central Intelligence Agency in 1963, just as the Vietnam War entered its bloodiest years and three weeks before the assassination of President John Kennedy. In the External Affairs memorandum on the meeting, Trudeau is reported as saying little, but he expressed scepticism in a later marginal note he wrote about "American weapons" being an appropriate response to the challenge of Vietnamese departure from the Privy Council Office troubled his former Ottawa colleagues. As a civil servant working in the Privy Council, he had been granted the highest security clearance and access to top-secret diplomatic dispatches. Meanwhile, in Washington, Senator Joe McCarthy and his henchmen were hounding suspected Communists, and, ever since the Gouzenko spy affair of 1945–46, Canada had been a favourite hunting ground. When Igor Gouzenko, a cipher clerk in the Soviet Embassy in Ottawa, defected, he revealed the existence of a spy network within the Canadian government. It was a dreadful time—one of paranoia and fear. The Canadian diplomat Herbert Norman, who had been linked with Asian Communists while

---

Communist leader Ho Chi Minh. "Like building up Chiang Kai Shek!" he scribbled. Although he believed deeply in decolonization, he knew that the process could be difficult, and he thought the Americans were usually clumsy in their attempt to preserve capitalist interests during the decolonization process. In his conversation that day, Diem was adamant that France should not fight to keep Indochina; indeed, he said that French culture, which the Vietnamese treasured, should be maintained through French Canada, whose missionaries were highly respected in Indochina. Trudeau agreed: whether in Algeria or Indochina, he opposed the French Empire but supported a French cultural presence.

This belief was ultimately the basis for later Canadian efforts to create a community of francophone-speaking countries. The incident reveals how Trudeau's international politics drew deeply on his European education and possessed neither the anti-Communism of the Catholic Church nor the American suspicion that led the United States into Indochina and the Vietnam War. "Visit of Monseigneur Thuc and Mr. Ngo-Dinh-Diem," Oct. 2, 1950, TP, vol. 10, file 11. Dr. Greg Donaghy, the Foreign Affairs historian, informs me that the record of this meeting is missing in departmental papers.

a student and teacher at Harvard, was already in McCarthy's sights, and FBI director J. Edgar Hoover even expressed doubts about Lester Pearson. Trudeau, moreover, had made no secret of his strong opposition to American foreign policy.

When Norman Robertson, the clerk of the Privy Council, heard about Trudeau's imminent departure, he recalled his former officer's arguments against the Korean War and in favour of reconciliation with the Communists.[18] He was concerned that Trudeau was setting off to Moscow just as the Soviet Union was imposing even greater restrictions on the freedom of Canadian diplomats in the capital. As a result, Trudeau's path was carefully followed by External Affairs personnel, and they assured Canada's allies that Trudeau had guaranteed them he would reveal no secrets.

After an initial disagreement with Robertson about his even attending the conference, Trudeau obtained credentials as a reporter for *Le Devoir*. The other members of the Canadian delegation were well-known figures on the left, including Morris Miller, who had been a classmate at Harvard and at the London School of Economics. As Trudeau departed from Prague on his way to Moscow, he told journalists (according to a report from a Canadian Embassy official) that the conference "would provide the first step for the establishment of economic and trade relations between capitalist states and countries with planned economies." It did not. He also claimed that the conference had attracted "lively interest" in Canada. Again it had not, except, perhaps, in the East Block and the Communist Party of Canada.

On March 31, 1952, *Pravda* announced the arrival in Moscow of Pierre Trudeau, "lawyer and adviser on trade-union questions." The Canadian Embassy contacted him and he met the chargé d'affaires, Robert Ford—a poet and perhaps the shrewdest diplomat ever to serve in Moscow during the Cold

War. Ford dismissed the conference as propaganda and paid little attention to Canadian delegation members apart from Trudeau. He reported to Ottawa that Trudeau, unlike the other delegates, continued to check into the embassy "for advice and also to inform us of what was going on." He was "useful" as he gave them copies of the conference proceedings. Ford soon realized that Trudeau was not the usual "fellow traveller" from the West. He quickly irritated his Russian "guide," for example, by asking why there were so many portraits of Stalin and none of Trotsky. The two men seem to have had fun together: Ford introduced him to caviar at the embassy, where Trudeau spent more and more of his time as he quickly became fed up with the conference itself. Still, Ford found him "puzzling" and wondered what "his real attitude to this country is."

There, in the darkest days of the Cold War, with madness insinuating its effects even more deeply into Stalin's aged mind, Ford and Trudeau argued about the meaning of Soviet Communism. Trudeau, according to Ford's memoranda to Ottawa, had been greatly impressed by the conference sessions on Soviet living conditions. He described conversations with three Soviet academic economists, and he took those exchanges as support for his belief that people could associate freely in Moscow. Trudeau, Ford continued, "claims his position is that of a neutralist-idealist and that it is possible for men of good will to try to act as a centre group which will gradually widen and prevent the two extremes from clashing." Ford strongly disagreed: "I am willing to believe that his feelings on this subject are genuinely idealistic, but I am afraid that he fails to realize that being neutral in the present struggle seems inevitably to involve leaning over backward to justify Russian actions, on the one hand, and to criticize the Western position, and particularly the United States, on the other." This idealistic strain was, in Ford's words, accompanied by "a kind of infantile desire to shock"—one that would not matter in Montreal but did very much in Stalin's Moscow.*

Trudeau went to the American Embassy chapel to attend Easter Mass. There, at midnight, he met the wife of the American chargé. In a provocative mood, he told her, yes, he was Catholic but a Communist too, "after which he proceeded to heap praises on the U.S.S.R. and attack the United States." Or so the dispatch to Ottawa reported. Ford encountered an angry American diplomat the next day: "I thought you said Trudeau was not a Red?"

---

* In his memoirs published in 1989, Ford was forgetful, discreet, or exceedingly diplomatic about this incident. He said he met Trudeau when he "unexpectedly turned up in Moscow at a mysterious economic conference organized by the Soviets and attended mostly by representatives of communist front organizations," and that Trudeau also became fed up with Russian lodgings and food. Strangely, given the story told by the U.S. envoy, he concluded his account: "Nor did he hesitate to accompany my wife and myself to Easter mass in the impromptu chapel of the American embassy." Robert A.D. Ford, *Our Man in Moscow: A Diplomat's Reflections on the Soviet Union* (Toronto: University of Toronto Press, 1989), 113. However, he was more caustic in an interview with Professor Robert Bothwell on October 15, 1987. "Going off the record," Ford asked: "What should one make of a prime minister who in 1952 had visited Moscow to attend the conference of a front organization? He'd enjoyed Hotel Rossiya food for a week before he came to the embassy for relief dinners—after which he ate well enough and clung to the embassy. But no explanation of why he was there." Then he said to Professor Bothwell, at the embassy "he liked us and we liked him." He discovered caviar there and always contrasted the treatment in Moscow with the bad treatment he received at other Canadian missions. Really, Ford said, Trudeau was "one of the brightest and most attractive people" he had ever met. Interview with Robert Ford, Oct. 15, 1987, Robert Bothwell Papers, University of Toronto Archives.

Ford denied he was, but then the American repeated Trudeau's remarks to his wife. Ford responded that Trudeau was simply joking. Nevertheless, he told Ottawa that he was sure a report would "go back to the State Department that a man who only six months ago was employed in a confidential job in the Privy Council is now in Moscow . . . and has openly stated that he is a Communist."

Not for the first time, Trudeau knew he had gone too far. He sent a handwritten letter to Norman Robertson, copied to several desks in External Affairs, in which he said that he had "half heeded" his advice not to go by gaining his press credentials. Claiming he held "few men in higher regard" than Robertson, he defended his decision to attend because of his urge to travel. Then, unctuously, he concluded: "I trust that Spring is finding Mrs. Robertson and your daughters in the best of health, and that you are finding life in the Privy Council Office as pleasant and as stimulating as I always did." Indeed.[19]

Trudeau was subsequently denied a visa to travel to China via Tashkent, but he did manage to obtain permission to visit Tbilisi, Georgia, after obtaining some extra rubles from British economist Alex Cairncross. When he arrived at the train station in Moscow, he met a beautiful young woman who addressed him in excellent English and shared his mixed-sex compartment for the three-day journey. She was, of course, a spy, but a welcome one. To know a country, Trudeau later wrote, one must take a long voyage on a train . . .

Farther away from Moscow, the Soviets became "nice and friendly, they walk around in pyjamas every day, exchanging jibes with the vendors in the train stations, before buying their roast chicken and their cheap wine; they could not care less about the propaganda being spouted out all day, but rush in to hear the football scores. In short, it's a normal society, with the normal sampling of swindlers, drunks, beggars and loose women. They're human, in other words."[20] Trudeau visited the grave of Stalin's mother, where his interpreter wept. He returned to Moscow and tried to travel to Leningrad, but his activities, notably his throwing snowballs at Soviet monuments, had caught the attention of the authorities. One early morning there was a bang at the door and "these burly policemen came in," told him to go, packed his bags, took him to the airport, and placed him on a plane. Leningrad would await a later journey.[21]

On his return to Canada on July 23, 1952, Trudeau declared publicly what he had told Ford privately: "I felt that people must use every possible means to get to know each other better. For, on either side, it is precisely the fear of the stranger which is at the root of this pathological hatred that is bringing us relentlessly closer to the third and final world war. So at last I would be able to throw a little light on this stranger . . ."[22] And in a later broadcast he denied that the secret police were terrifying. He mentioned how a Bolshevik Party member told a joke that mocked the police and the military, who, Trudeau claimed, seemed too preoccupied with exchanging salutes "to have the time to terrorize the population." He also ridiculed those in the West who claimed he was "followed" at every moment when he was in the Soviet Union.[23]

Trudeau's reports quickly brought criticism, most notably from Father Léopold Braun. The priest had been in Moscow during the purges and famines of the 1930s and he now condemned Trudeau's articles in Le Devoir and other Catholic publications as hopelessly naïve, ill informed, and even dangerous. Trudeau reacted with surprising vigour. He told André Laurendeau at Le Devoir that Father Braun was "an imbecile" and demanded full right of reply. "If Le Devoir does not give me a half page, I will pay for it," he threatened.[24] Braun pointed out that he had lived in the Soviet Union, endured the persecution of the Catholic Church, and witnessed church members disappearing into the Gulag.[25]

Trudeau responded strongly, but his tone was too harsh. The editor of Le Droit told him that although Braun might be wrong, he should treat the issue seriously, not dismissively and crudely. In the journal *Nos Cours*, where Braun and Trudeau exchanged attacks, the editor, J.-B. Desrosiers, took Braun's side, telling Trudeau that if he had damaged his reputation, it was his own fault. Trudeau again demanded a right to respond and approached Archbishop Paul-Émile Léger (soon to become a cardinal) to assist him, even though his articles in *Cité libre*, quite apart from the Soviet trip, had upset the Catholic hierarchy. Others, including the respected Université de Montréal economist Esdras Minville, said the Braun attack on Trudeau was a "serious" matter. With some desperation, Trudeau wrote to a Father Florent, a priest with whom he had enjoyed long discussions about the Soviet Union in Paris in 1947, and enclosed his exchanges with Braun. He told Father Florent that his reputation had been hurt in Quebec, and he asked him to openly declare his support. It would, Trudeau declared, be "an act of charity and justice."[26]

Braun then went too far and labelled Trudeau a Stalinist mouthpiece, which he definitely was not. Trudeau's reaction to Braun reflects his deep opposition to clerics using their position to pronounce on political affairs. This reaction was consistent with his writings in the period. Yet Trudeau too readily dismissed Braun's descriptions of Stalinist atrocities. Solzhenitsyn, Khrushchev, scholars of the Soviet regime, and history itself have all revealed the enormity of Stalin's crimes. Appalled by the exaggerations and excesses of Senator Joe McCarthy and the use of anti-Communism by the Duplessis government against its opponents, Trudeau in response found some virtue on the streets of Moscow. In the Université de Montréal *Quartier Latin* report of his visit, he permitted himself to be called "Comrade Trudeau."

His writings and his associations with the many "fellow travellers" soon caught the eye of various intelligence agencies and

their media colleagues.[27] In March 1954 Trudeau was denied
entry to the United States—as were other eminent individuals at
the time, including Graham Greene and Charlie Chaplin. He
moved quickly to remedy the problem. Questioned about his visit
to Moscow, he responded that he had gone to the conference to
see if international trade would break down the Iron Curtain. On
March 9 he learned that he was temporarily excluded because
his entry might be "prejudicial to the interests of the United
States." But after an appeal to American consular officials, the
decision was soon reversed. He was allowed to travel through
the United States on his way to a Commonwealth Conference in
Pakistan, which he attended at the invitation of the Canadian
Institute of International Affairs. Still, Trudeau's trip to Moscow,
his favourable comments about the Soviet Union, and his other
journeys behind the Iron Curtain and to China made him a
target for extreme anti-Communist groups such as the Canadian
Intelligence Service. Henceforth he also drew the ire of fierce
nationalist journalists and writers such as Duplessis supporter
Robert Rumilly in Quebec, and the militant anti-Communist
Lubor Zink in the conservative *Toronto Telegram*.

A close reading of Trudeau's many reports on his visit
reveals his scepticism about the Soviet system and its accomplishments and his commitment to Western democratic values.
Unfortunately, his tendency to shock and to provide "colour"
often grabbed the attention of his readers and distorted his
meaning. As ever, he enjoyed being a contrarian and, when
pushed, he would defend his position passionately. Still, the
analytical portions of his travel accounts yield a more subtle
and balanced view. For example, he probably attracted the
attention of the student audience at the Université de Montréal
when he praised the Soviet educational system and, bizarrely,
Soviet architecture. Nevertheless, his remarks strongly criticized
the "capitalism of the state" created by Soviet Communists, and

he contrasted the proletariat's control of political parties and unions in the West with the closed system in the Soviet Union.[28] Although he lavished praise on the Bolshoi Ballet and on Soviet support for the arts, he recognized that the government there supported the "extérieur" of artistic expression but suppressed the internal spirit—the composers Shostakovich and Khachaturian, for instance, were reduced to writing mere melodies, while the great film director Eisenstein had simply been tossed aside. "Perhaps," he wrote, "it is not wise in the USSR to cast a glance inwards. There is a warning at the frontier of the world of the spirit: Do not enter."

Trudeau told a Soviet Communist acquaintance that he should not be surprised that the Catholic Church was opposed to Communism. He too was opposed to a system that was anti-religious. Although he ridiculed the claims of the extreme "anti-Soviet camp"—Rumilly and Zink—that the great Russian authors were banned in schools (he had seen Dostoevsky in the libraries, he said), he commented in his writings on the void at the core of the system, one where the brilliant Russian composer Stravinsky and the great Russian painter Chagall were as unknown as Maynard Keynes and Alfred Marshall. And, he said, there was no doubt in his mind that "the worker has, in effect, more importance and much more influence in our democratic countries than in the USSR."

The strongest indication of his views is Trudeau's description of the evening in a popular Moscow restaurant where he met three Russians. They recognized him as a foreigner, and two of the three spoke with him. They left, and the silent one remained for a moment. Then, in a voice "which did not tremble in spite of the danger, this perfect stranger told me that he was neither Bolshevik nor Communist but a democrat." The effect was electric: "He seemed to have released a truth that had long been buried in his heart, for he shot up and strode to the exit like a visionary. If poetry is this man's art, I thought, this evening he will write his greatest poem, because his inspiration has just been set free." In Russia as in Canada, Trudeau knew, liberty was the most precious individual good.[29] These were not the words of a duped fellow traveller.

—

Trudeau's travels were fundamental to his broader purposes throughout these tumultuous years, and reflected both his ambitions and his doubts. First, he believed, correctly, that his journeys—especially to remote and challenging regions—provided him with the intellectual capital on which he could draw for his analysis of his own society. In some ways he resembled other intellectuals in the early years of that decade who "welcomed the television rays that illuminated the integration of Quebec into North America."[30] While welcoming assimilation into a more "efficient" and "modern" society, Trudeau recognized that francophone Quebecers had to learn about the world beyond North America. More specifically, they had to locate their own experience within the context of the "winds of change" that were quickly sweeping away the old colonial empires in the postwar decades.

Although he later had a reputation for inattention to Canada's role in the world, his articles and media appearances in this period certainly focused more often on international than domestic events. He also realized that the rise to celebrity of René Lévesque came from *Point de mire*, a television series in which the irrepressible Lévesque, hands darting and smoke billowing, introduced viewers to the cascade of international changes in those times. The shrewd Gérard Pelletier, who knew Lévesque well because his wife also worked for Radio-Canada, recalled how, in their meetings together, Trudeau would cast a sceptical and mocking glance at Lévesque as he started "on one of his usual long tirades, riddled with hasty judgments, brilliant, profound or superficial."[31] Trudeau was convinced that his analysis of international affairs had a profundity that Lévesque's stream of consciousness lacked—yet both knew that events outside Quebec now mattered more than ever.

Second, Trudeau knew that his own comparative advantage in the intense debates among Quebec intellectuals came from his far-ranging education, now bolstered by the layers of exotic detail and intriguing anecdote he had gleaned through his travels. The stunning Russian on the train to Tbilisi, the mysterious dark monastery on a Chinese hill, the bandits on the ziggurat of Ur provided the colour that listeners and viewers would remember. His articles and Radio-Canada presentations are crammed with stories to illustrate his arguments, and, as radio broadcasts of his world tour indicate, he did not mind embellishing his tales for dramatic effect. In a remarkably insightful article on Trudeau, Jim Coutts, his long-time principal secretary, pointed out that, contrary to general opinion, Trudeau "did and said little publicly that was not carefully rehearsed in advance."[32] His presence and his charisma were carefully constructed; his "cosmopolitanism" was a fundamental building block. At times he went too far, secure, perhaps, in his wealth and independence. Gérard Filion, publisher of *Le Devoir*, believed that Trudeau occasionally hurt rather than helped his cause, and he sometimes refused to publish his letters, even though he had visited Moscow himself soon after Trudeau did, and they agreed on the need for reconciliation between East and West.

Third, Trudeau's cosmopolitanism reflected the unease he felt about Quebec and Canada in the early fifties. He felt more assured about his beliefs on international relations than on domestic Quebec and Canadian politics. And his return home brought a hard landing. His romance with Helen had burnt out suddenly, although he had tried to relight the flame during his months in Europe in the spring of 1952. Then he told her in late summer that he had no permanent work in Montreal. Tip, who was a precise but not very profitable architect, was leaving to live in Europe, and he would follow if things did not work out in Quebec. "Have you left Canada," she asked on December 18, 1952, or had he made a final commitment to "Quebec's social issues?" Trudeau was grumpy.[33] Things were not working out well in Quebec, he replied, especially for one who had "social causes."

On July 16, 1952, exactly a week before Trudeau returned to Canada, the Duplessis government had been re-elected, even though the Liberals under their new leader, Georges-Émile Lapalme, had initially led in the polls.[34] Duplessis, as always, had campaigned brilliantly, albeit often demagogically. His biographer Conrad Black describes the raucous election day, when the mayor of Quebec asked for the intervention of the Royal 22nd Regiment to protect a Liberal victor in Lévis from a mob and, later, to prevent the assault on Liberal committee rooms in Montreal by gangs armed with "bottles, brickbats and revolvers." In one case, hooligans threw a Liberal campaign worker and a police constable out of a first-storey window.[35] In a later broadcast on the election, Trudeau declared that democracy is a form of government that works when everyone agrees on counting heads, not breaking them. In *Cité libre*, he warned:

> Our deep-seated immorality must be explained. After all, we claim to be a Christian people. We subscribe to ethics that rigorously define our duties towards society and our neighbour. We do not fail to respect civil authority, and we generally live in a climate of obedience to law. We punish treason and assault in the name of the common weal and of natural law; we explain Communism in terms of the faltering of faith; we consider war to be the ransom of sin.

While "our ideas on the order of society are shaped by Catholic theology," Trudeau continued, there was one exception. In the case of the state, "we are really quite immoral; we corrupt bureaucrats, we blackmail members of the Assembly, we put pressure on the courts, we cheat the tax-collector, we turn a blind eye when it seems profitable to do so. And when it comes to electoral matters, our immoralism is absolutely appalling. The peasant who would be ashamed to enter a brothel sells his conscience." With a glance to his own experience only a decade earlier, perhaps, he wrote: "We have to admit that Catholics, collectively, have rarely been pillars of democracy. I say that to our shame, and without seeking to prejudge the future . . . In countries with a large Catholic majority . . . Catholics often avoid anarchy only by means of authoritarian rule." He went on to express a theme he expanded on continuously in future years: pluralist societies do not turn to authoritarianism, but there was a danger that they might devote too much of their civic energies "to the pursuit of the Catholic weal." The product of this pursuit was a narrow nationalism that created immorality and undermined the greater "public weal."[36] Trudeau had travelled far along the liberal democratic path since those nights on the streets in 1942.

Despite these views, Trudeau did not bother to rush back from Europe to work in the coming election campaign. His absence betrayed the weakness of the intellectuals opposed to Maurice Duplessis, and of the Quebec labour movement, which had failed to build politically on the Asbestos Strike. Gérard Pelletier, Jean Marchand, and others had briefly considered running labour candidates in working-class ridings in 1952, a policy that would have broken the traditional policy of formal neutrality espoused by the Confédération des travailleurs catholiques du Canada (CTCC) while, at the same time, "punishing our enemies and rewarding our friends." To that end, Pelletier wrote to Trudeau, asking him to consider being one of the labour candidates. Trudeau replied from Paris on March 16, 1952. Yes, he said, "it would interest me because I have never in my life felt so unattached, physically and morally; because I am ready to commit the greatest follies; and because, all in all, I am in a rather pitiable state." Perhaps he was still recovering from Helen's rejection. Whatever the cause, he told Pelletier that he had intended to "vegetate in the Sicilian sun," but he would consider a candidacy if certain conditions were met. His conditions were impossible but appropriate: such a "labour" campaign would need organization, money, a platform, and "total support of the unions." However, the unions were split; there was no platform; and no other candidates had yet been chosen. Wisely, Trudeau declined. Yet he was intrigued by the offer and, tellingly, asked if his candidacy would exclude "the possibility of my becoming a 'technical adviser' to the CTCC (the job Marchand offered me)?"[37]

Trudeau never took the job, but, the following year, he did become more directly involved in the labour movement. In a broader sense, his focus began to shift from international politics, the subject of most of his writings since 1949, towards domestic politics. He had proudly told Helen back in the summer of 1952 that he had been asked to speak at the prestigious annual Couchiching Conference of the Canadian Institute of International Affairs on the topic "The Adequacy of Canadian Foreign Policy." Of course, he found it inadequate.

What is striking is the self-confidence of his presentation at Couchiching, and the consistency of his views. With some revisions created by current events, the ideas he expressed on the shores of Lake Simcoe that summer remained his opinions throughout his life. He was publicly and scathingly critical of Lester Pearson, who, he said, thought the role of Canadian policy was to interpret "London to Washington & vice versa, as if they needed a despicable mouthpiece." To confirm his point, he mentioned a recent speech Pearson had given in New York where he said that Canada's tutors were the United Kingdom and the United States. He suggested that Pearson sounded like an Albanian speaking in Moscow. Trudeau agreed with Pearson that Canada's foreign policy should follow from Canada's "Anglo-Saxon political thoughts and institutions," but he held that it should also reflect our "bi-ethnical and bi-lingual character" and the fact that Canada was a young, small, but economically powerful country. Yet Anglo-Saxonism "drowned" out everything else. There was no independent Canadian public opinion. Ottawa read and heard only American and, to a lesser extent, British news. Why not read *Le Monde* or even the Paris *Herald Tribune?* Canada needed to develop a public opinion that truly reflected its bicultural and bilingual character and to build a foreign service that could "construct" truly Canadian policies in those many areas where there was not "a determined U.S.–U.K. axis." How could that be done, he asked, when "we had not formulated political theory about Canada itself" and when Quebec was not integrated into Canada's international presence?[38]

—

Trudeau's journeyings became less frequent and earnest, even though he gave a long radio broadcast on "Techniques du voyage" in which he said he travelled not to bring home tales of three-star restaurants or, like diplomats, of meetings with kings and presidents, but to know humanity in its richness. To do so, he needed to mix with the people, travel light, and abandon airs and luxury— only then did he encounter the saints, the wandering philosophers, poets, and scoundrels who form the human fraternity.[39]

By the fall of 1952 he realized that his adventures in Palestine and Moscow were richer than his recent experiences in Quebec or in the remainder of Canada. If he was to fulfill his goals for a public life in Canada, he would have to change direction.

So he began to clarify his domestic political program. In personal terms, he identified three specific actions: deeper involvement in the trade-union movement in Quebec; more political activity in Quebec; and interaction with English-Canadian intellectuals who were "waking up" to Quebec and who shared many of his political ideas about civil liberties and the dangers of unbridled capitalism.

Trudeau's contact with anglophone intellectuals, notably his growing friendship with F.R. Scott, a McGill University law professor, CCF activist, and well-known poet, was undoubtedly a significant factor in his closer identification with liberal democratic thought—especially as it was embodied in the English-Canadian socialist tradition.[40] Yet Trudeau was always his own man, deriving his approach to domestic affairs from diverse influences ranging from personalism and *Le Monde* to Maynard Keynes and Paul Claudel. He reflected these varied streams in his involvement with *Cité libre*, and, during the fifties, his experience in teaching workers in the mine and mill towns of Quebec also influenced him strongly. As his address to the Couchiching Conference reveals, Trudeau knew and, in many ways, admired the Anglo-Saxon political tradition, but he had profound doubts about the manner in which it had developed in the former British North American colonies.

During his long absences in Europe and in Africa and Asia, Trudeau had remained in contact with his *Cité libre* colleagues, and he missed those nights where the group came with their wives, girlfriends, and manuscripts to obey, in the words of one of the members, Jean Le Moyne, "no orders of the day but only the disorders of the night."[41] He realized that he must immerse himself more deeply in the life of his city and his province or risk losing the influence his intellect and imagination had gained for him since those first gatherings in Gérard Pelletier's stone house on Lac des Deux Montagnes. The election of 1952 in

Quebec, which he had conspicuously missed, had stirred dissent and opposition to Maurice Duplessis among intellectuals and the professional classes in Montreal. *Le Devoir,* which had generally supported Duplessis in 1948, had become an opponent of the government by 1952, and it followed the election with ever stronger attacks on the ruling party. One rallying point was the dismissal of the reformist archbishop Joseph Charbonneau in Montreal (who actually controlled some shares of *Le Devoir*) and his replacement by Paul-Émile Léger. The new archbishop "sought to reassert the influence of the Church on the faithful and to stimulate religious faith while opposing the growing materialism of Montreal." [42] Yet the schools, the hospitals, and the social services that the church had controlled for so long were overwhelmed by the material and spiritual needs of the postwar flood of people to the factories and shops of Montreal, whose metropolitan population grew from 1,139,921 in 1941 to 1,620,758 in 1956. The Catholic urban voice in the Quebec capital was fainter than that of the rural counties where Duplessis's Union nationale held sway.

Tensions grew. In the fall of 1952 a strike of textile workers at Louiseville had brought police intervention, violence, and bloodshed. Duplessis declared the government response justified, arguing that society rested on two pillars—religious authority and civil authority—which must not erode. A threat to one undermined the other. In the pages of *Le Devoir,* André Laurendeau had already decided that the government no longer defended the common good and, in the eyes of the workers, had become no more than "the ally of the bosses." Laurendeau's niece later recalled that she had the impression that "the Laurendeau living room became the staging ground for the warriors on the left," gathering their forces to defeat Duplessis. [43] The CTCC, the Catholic union, called a meeting just before Christmas, 1952, to discuss a general strike, but it was a confession of weakness rather than strength. The CTCC was only part of organized labour in Quebec, where the Fédération des unions industrielles du Québec (FUIQ) and the Fédération provincial du travail du Québec (FPTQ) competed for membership and authority. Although the CTCC had grown faster than any other union, it lacked the financial support of international unionism that its rivals possessed. That financial weakness was one reason why the CTCC decided not to enter directly into politics.

That December, in *Cité libre*, Trudeau attacked the decision, claiming that Quebec workers would cleanse the political system and that the old parties offered no prospects of real change.[44] On a Radio-Canada broadcast early in the new year he explained his beliefs in more detail. In a democracy, he said, a police force must not be allowed to beat up a union member's family, blow up a bus, and break a legal strike. Yet a general strike was not an answer either. Equally ineffective were the solutions offered by some well-meaning church officials—a volley of prayers in one instance and, in another, a quasi-fascist dictatorship that would act against evil factory owners. These responses, he stated, betrayed the political illiteracy of French Canadians: "It is a notorious truth that the English Canadians have healthier political reflexes than we do. But this superiority has not come by chance: it derives from a civic education that is continuous from schooldays through daily life and is expressed by those English Canadians who think, write and discuss civic affairs." Quebec, he said, must first choose democracy; then social good would follow. If it did not, hatred for the "rules" would grow, civil disobedience would stir, and violence would follow that would make the "massacre" of the textile workers at Louiseville seem like a picnic.[45]

Some aspects of Trudeau's views were naïve, but his gibes about the excellence of English-Canadian democracy were deliberately provocative. Nevertheless, he was increasingly excited about Quebec, its future, and his participation in the debates that swirled around the changes taking place. Another participant in those debates, André Malavoy, recalled the "astonishing" intellectual clashes of the fifties:

> All shrewd observers sensed imminent change, a real upheaval in the structure of politics, our way of life and our thoughts. As in all pre-revolutionary periods, the intellectuals at last engaged and were drawn into political action. In truth, they were not numerous—perhaps no more than two hundred people who knew each other and met often.
>
>   But how enriching were those meetings, those long nights of discussions, those projects and dreams.[46]

Emmanuel Mounier, the French Catholic personalist and founder of *Esprit*, had taught Trudeau to "see, judge, act." It was now the time to act.

That summer, Trudeau began to encounter workers directly for the first time since his brief stint in the Sullivan mines in Abitibi seven years previously and his 1949 foray to Asbestos. Yet, theoretically, he and the *Cité libre* group had decided it was the workers who, through democratic means, were the best hope to overthrow the Duplessis regime and give birth to a modern, secular Quebec state whose leaders would be young francophone intellectuals like themselves. Trudeau was well prepared to act as the major players took their place in the public forum. His training as a lawyer and an economist provided him with the tools to take apart many of the arguments of the Duplessis government and the conservative nationalists, and he did so with a rapier that often cut quickly and deeply.

—

Two events deeply affected Trudeau's activities in the mid-fifties, and defined his views of Quebec's place in Canada as well as his own position in Quebec and Canadian intellectual life. The first was the decision of the province of Ontario to accept a tax-rental agreement with the federal government, thereby breaking the alliance between Canada's two largest provinces against the federal government's assertive centralism. This decision caught Duplessis by surprise and forced him, and his opponents, to consider not only the revenue sources for the province but also Quebec's response to the federal government's increasing presence in the social and economic life of Canadians. In February 1953, when Maurice Duplessis created a Royal Commission on Federal-Provincial Relations, under Judge Thomas Tremblay, Trudeau was appointed to draft the brief of the Féderation des unions industrielles du Québec for the commission. The second event (as described in the next chapter) was the 1954 decision by Pelletier to pass over to his friend the long-delayed editing of a book on the Asbestos Strike. This task gave Trudeau a leadership role among a group of respected intellectuals and, most important, the opportunity to write the introduction and the conclusion to the book. Fate had made a choice.

Trudeau complained later that his acquaintances did not believe that he "worked" during the fifties. The comments angered him: "But, you know," he replied, "I'd be working bloody hard— at writing articles and preparing my dossiers for whatever conciliation procedure I had or at administering my father's estate, which my brother and sister had no inclination to do, or at receiving clients or visiting the labour groups."[47] His complaints are justified. His personal papers are crammed with arbitrations where he acted for the labour side. He carefully prepared notes for his summer visits to labour classes. He gave lectures or talks to labour groups in church basements or union halls. He would spend a week or a long weekend giving a more sustained series of presentations in educational sessions for workers. There are also numerous broadcasts, meetings, and articles that he drafted and redrafted.

The creation of the newspaper *Vrai* by his friend Jacques Hébert brought new deadlines. His agendas are full, and, when travelling, he brought his work with him.

Trudeau rode his motorbike to the labour colleges, wore open shirts under his leather jacket, and appeared very much the rural teacher. His presentations were conventional explanations of the operations of the economic system, with particular attention to the place of the worker and the union. Although he was a member of the CCF, his lectures lacked ideology, and he accepted the idea that owners should have their profits. Of course, he was an owner himself who carefully monitored the profits from his family's stake in the Belmont amusement park in Montreal. Even when dealing with trade unionism, he did not speak of nationalization—the subject that dominated British Labour Party Congresses in those times. In a course given at a school of metallurgy in January 1954, he neatly set out the principles of Keynesian economics without ever mentioning Keynes: budgetary surpluses in times of inflation compensate for deficits in times of unemployment, thus assuring the long-run prosperity of the nation. He was offered $25 for his course, but he returned the cheque—perhaps to the surprise of the organizers, who might have heard many stories about Trudeau's careful ways with money.[48] In another course in 1956 he spoke about politics rather than economics, although economics indirectly entered his discourse when he talked about the respective duties and jurisdictions of the federal and the provincial governments.

Trudeau's work for the Tremblay Royal Commission on Federal-Provincial Relations made him a major figure both in Quebec and in Canada, a recognized authority on the Canadian Constitution and the division of powers. Because he wrote the brief for the international Fédération des unions industrielles du Québec, he worked closely with the Canadian Congress of Labour and its research director, Eugene Forsey—a charming and influential labour historian. At the time he wrote the brief, the debate on the economics of Canadian federalism had been stirred by the publication of *Le fédéralisme canadien: Évolutions et problèmes*, by Maurice Lamontagne. Its message, coming from a leading Quebec economist, brought enthusiastic approval in Ottawa and denunciation from nationalists in Quebec. Accepting the Keynesian argument Trudeau had presented to the workers, Lamontagne argued that only a strong central government could assure the prosperity and economic security that postwar policies had produced. From this point, he concluded that only a fuller integration into Canadian society could assure Quebec of the fiscal resources needed to modernize its society and provide economic security to French Canadians.[49] Trudeau did not know Lamontagne, one of the organizers, with Father Georges-Henri Lévesque, of the Social Sciences faculty at the Université de Laval (which irritated Duplessis even more than *Cité libre* did), but he recognized the similarity of Lamontagne's views to his own.[50] So did Duplessis and traditional nationalists in Quebec. The battle formed around the Tremblay Commission.

Like Trudeau, Lamontagne called for a functional approach, one grounded in the new social sciences and in a better understanding of the way economic levels could be manipulated by experts to guarantee economic growth and equality. *Le Devoir,* so critical of Duplessis in many areas, nevertheless rejected Lamontagne's claims, arguing that an "Ottawa-inspired social welfare state would result in a technocratic and bureaucratic nightmare of statistics, reports, and programs all unsuitable to the complex and ever-changing socioeconomic realities at the regional and local level. Ottawa's social welfare state would lead to the regimentation of everyone, making them dependent upon a distant bureaucracy, 'not eager to come to life, grow, study, work, suffer, age and die.'"[51] For Trudeau, this attack on Lamontagne went too far, yet, despite similarities in language and approach, he disagreed with Lamontagne in many respects. In doing so, he drew on his own experience in Ottawa, where he had come to believe that the St. Laurent Liberal government was too careless about treading in provincial fields. That experience, along with his recognition as an economist, gave authority to his voice.

When the Fédération des unions industrielles du Québec presented its brief to the Tremblay Commission in March 1954, it attracted immediate attention because of its content and also because of its clear and sometimes eloquent prose: "The Federation is made up of men and women who use all of their earnings and energies to assure their material security and that of their family," Trudeau declared. "They know that they are influenced more by the imperious need to earn their daily bread than [by] constitutional guarantees of their religious, cultural, and political evolution, for it is necessary to live before philosophizing . . ." The survival of the French language and culture depended neither on the law nor on literary conferences; rather, in an industrial age, he continued, it rested on the hard work of, and proper rewards to, the working class. He followed with a detailed analysis of the economic condition of Quebec's working class and the economic inferiority of Quebec workers, compared with their Ontario counterparts.

The analysis, if not the approach, reflected Lamontagne. But when it came to specifics, the differences appeared. Trudeau believed that the federal government needed to possess adequate powers to secure economic stability and growth, but it did not require (as Lamontagne recommended) the replacement of tax-rental agreements with subsidies. Nor did the weakness of Quebec labour legislation justify a constitutional amendment transferring that authority to the federal government. In a federation, he said, such authority normally resided at the regional level. Closer cooperation among jurisdictions was essential, but each one should respect boundaries that were rational. Rather than reduce or eliminate areas where the provinces held responsibility, the provinces should make sure that they had the revenue necessary to carry out the services required at the regional level: "In effect, the unity of a political society depends on the will to assure the vital minimum to all members of the society, wherever they may live."

The role of the federal government was clear: it had responsibility for economic stability. At the same time, Trudeau stressed, the provincial governments had to have taxation power and responsibility for education and the family—areas that were strictly in the provincial jurisdiction. The federal government must cease payments to universities and direct grants to families; in such cases, the funds should pass to the provinces.[52]

Eugene Forsey scribbled large question marks on this passage of the draft Trudeau sent to him. Trudeau was never predictable. At a time when many reformers in Quebec, especially professors and college administrators, were ridiculing Duplessis's refusal to accept federal government grants to universities, Trudeau took his side, a stance that would have important repercussions later. His attitude surprised many, but it reflected his increasingly defined views on Canadian federalism and his wariness about Ottawa. Why, he asked, should Quebecers or other Canadians put "the future of Canadian federalism entirely into the hands of federal economists"? Other traces of his scepticism towards Ottawa in the 1950s came in a *Cité libre* article in which he attacked, along with André Laurendeau and traditional nationalists, Ottawa's refusal to consider tax deductibility for Quebec taxes on federal taxes: "The federal government and its clever civil servants accommodate themselves only too easily to a system that, at least until 1954, amounted to manifest defrauding of the Quebec taxpayer."[53]

By the mid-1950s Trudeau had become a close student of Canadian federalism and a defender of provincial rights. At the same time, he remained a social reformer who believed that the federal government was responsible for economic growth and stability and for promoting equity among regions and peoples. Nor surprisingly, he attracted the attention of English Canadians, who saw in him a perfectly bilingual and articulate opponent to the "reactionary" Duplessis government in Quebec. Through his friend Frank Scott, Trudeau met leading CCF intellectuals as well as Eugene Forsey and others associated with the Canadian Labour Congress. These English Canadians immediately recognized his political usefulness. Trudeau did not believe in a major constitutional revision and did not deprecate the influence of British institutions in the development of democratic habits. His attitudes infuriated conservative Quebec nationalists, such as the historian Robert Rumilly, who attacked him as a French Canadian who "goes to Toronto to hurl abuse against French Canadians, in English, before the English, for which he is celebrated as a grand spirit, a genius." Rumilly's harsh description of Trudeau's arguments did not greatly distort them: Trudeau believed that the French Canadians had foolishly subordinated their politics and economics to the defence of their ethnicity. Moreover, their strong Catholicism made them too respectful of hierarchy, resulting in an attitude, in his words, that "combines political superstition with social conservatism."[54]

Rumilly, a Duplessis supporter in Canada and a monarchist in France,[55] dismissed Trudeau as a leftist but did not deny the sincerity of his Catholic beliefs. Trudeau's writings, while reflective of the progressive social tradition of Catholic personalism, drew increasingly on contemporary social science as it was developing in the United States and, to a lesser extent, in Britain. For that reason, his voice and his sources resonated in English Canada. Yet Anglo-American social science alone does not explain the character of his analysis and discourse in the mid-1950s.

After the encounter with Archbishop Léger, the rebuke from Father d'Anjou, and his many quarrels with official Catholic voices, Trudeau became more determined to challenge the sway of the official Catholic Church in Quebec. His writing becomes more openly secular; his determination to challenge church conservatism more marked; the willingness to call himself anti-clerical much greater. He lost interest in debates within the church and concentrated on arguments about the church. Sylvia Ostry, then a young economist and later an eminent scholar and public servant, recalls how Trudeau would become animated and emotional in the mid-fifties when he spoke with her in cafés about the church's oppressive presence in Quebec.[56] When he was attacked in *L'Action catholique* because he said that clerics should withdraw entirely from politics, he repeated the argument at greater length in following issues of *Le Devoir*.[57] Increasingly, he became a public presence, along with his *Cité libre* colleagues. He loved debates on topics such as "Does Canada need other political parties?" (Trudeau feared a new nationalist party would be conservative); "Does Canada need a stronger military?" (No, said Trudeau, who pointed to "the futility of a good part of our military efforts"); or "Do Canadians need identity cards?" (Trudeau was firmly opposed). One television program, "Idées en marche," attracted Duplessis's wrath when Trudeau supported Louis St. Laurent's statement that Quebec was not a "different" province "from a constitutional point of view." Television captured attention, and so, increasingly, did Pierre Trudeau.[58]

These days, he had a new determination and direction. When he left on a trip in 1954, he took a long list of friends to whom he would write, many of them women. The despair he had expressed about himself and the future to Pelletier and, earlier, to Helen Segerstrale had disappeared. In August 1955 he wrote to Helen, who was now married in Europe. The tone was markedly different. "I have been doing the expected," he noted, "practising law with the trade unions in Canada, but I also manage to do a lot of writing, radio & television work. It is all very satisfying, especially because I can satisfy my wanderlust from time to time."[59]

Pierre Trudeau was finally home.

CHAPTER 7

—

EVE OF THE REVOLUTION

The 1949 Asbestos Strike in the Eastern Townships was a decisive moment in the history of Quebec—and in the life of Pierre Trudeau. The strike actually defined Trudeau more than it changed the province. The victory of the Catholic unions, which was achieved through negotiation, was surprising, but it proved difficult to build upon. The Duplessis regime did not crumble, and the Catholic Church retained its dominance. Trudeau quickly discovered that he could not get a position at the Université de Montréal, but he at least had independence—the product of his inheritance and his own will. He remained determined to learn from the experience of the strike.

The international unions had strongly supported the strike and sought to take advantage of it. Some of the strike leaders, including Gérard Pelletier, Jean Marchand, and Canadian Labour Congress (CLC) activists, decided that a book should be written to describe the diverse experiences of the strikers, their clerical and intellectual supporters, and the labour unions—which, for the first time, had shown exceptional resolve in confronting the Duplessis government and the multinational companies connected with the mines. Two years later,

Recherches sociales, a group funded by the Canadian Labour
Congress to strengthen socialist sentiment among francophones, commissioned a book that would analyze how the strike
represented "a turning point in the social history of Quebec"
and "inform the general public of the cruel or reassuring lessons we had learned."[1] F.R. Scott, the McGill law professor and
socialist activist, was the director of the project, with Gérard
Pelletier as editor. When Pelletier's schedule became too busy,
his *Cité libre* co-editor, Pierre Trudeau, took on the task.
Trudeau had not edited a book before, nor had he ever written
a sustained analytical essay of the type needed here for the
introduction and the conclusion. The project had significant
potential—but would prove a challenge.

Trudeau was now thirty-two years old and arbitrating
labour disputes, researching the brief for the Féderation des
unions industrielles du Québec (FUIQ) for the Tremblay
Commission on Federal-Provincial Relations, writing articles
for *Cité libre* and various newspapers, teaching courses for little
or no money to workers during the summer, and, of course,
travelling.* Most of the authors who had agreed to write the
other articles for the book on the Asbestos Strike worked closely
with the labour movement: Maurice Sauvé was the technical

---

* Unfortunately, Trudeau did not keep detailed notebooks in the fifties as he
had on earlier travels. Nevertheless, his brief notes show that he used travel
to develop his political views. In Europe in the fall of 1951, he draws the
lesson from the study of different party systems that bureaucrats should be
more effective and concludes that Quebec's greatest need is an independent
and competent public service. He did keep a laundry list of his extended
1951–52 travels that broke down items into nine fascinating categories: cities,
architecture, adventure, national traits, theatre, music, art, antiquities, and

adviser for the Canadian and Catholic Confederation of Labour (CCCL); Pelletier edited *Le Travail* for the CCCL and was its director of public relations; Jean Gérin-Lajoie worked for the United Steel Workers; and Charles Lussier, like Trudeau, practised labour law. Other authors included Father Gérard Dion of Laval University, the editor of *Relations industrielles*; Réginald Boisvert, a television writer who specialized in working-class dramas; and the brilliant young Laval sociologist Fernand Dumont, who agreed to explore the historical forces that "prepared the scene for the Asbestos Strike."[2] F.R. Scott would write the foreword. A disciplined worker, Scott soon despaired as the editor and the authors continually missed their deadlines.[3] There was additional delay as Trudeau tried, unsuccessfully—and with the help of author Anne Hébert, on whom he had an unrequited "crush"—to find a French publisher in the fall of 1955. To his chagrin, he discovered there was little interest in contemporary Quebec in Paris.[4]

Progress on the book was further delayed when Trudeau departed for Europe in the winter of 1955–56, but he tried, with the assistance of Laval political scientist Jean-Charles Falardeau, to stitch the volume together while he was away. Still manuscripts did not arrive, and promises went unkept. Falardeau himself

---

scenery. The architecture category was brief and peculiar: Italy's elegant Villa d'Este and Le Corbusier's work in Moscow and Paris. More interesting was music: *Der Rosenkavalier* at the Berlin Opera, Pablo Casals at the Prado, a Sudanese ensemble in the desert near Khartoum, and pygmy drums in the Congo. Adventure was typical and amusing: "sleeping outdoors in equatorial forest and raging baboons; tracking elephants & buffaloes; riots in Cairo; swimming [in the] Bosphorus; and contradicting Politbureau." Voyage 1951–1952, TP, vol.12, file 4.

apologized abjectly just before Christmas: "I repeat to you, Pierre, that I understand, that Frank [Scott] understands, that Gérard [Pelletier] understands your impatience, [we understand] even the disgust of which you spoke some time ago. You accepted, and you fulfilled your responsibility, to edit this volume to completion, you carried out these chores briskly and, with good reason, you already had enough of it in the summer." Falardeau was astonished that Trudeau "in these circumstances and despite all, remained so patient." When something mattered, however, Trudeau could be patient indeed.[5]

Finally, in 1956, a complete text came together, and the *Cité libre* press became the publisher. Trudeau wrote two major essays for the book: a long introduction describing the social, economic, and cultural context of the strike, and an epilogue reflecting on the effects of the strike and on developments in Quebec after 1949. Polemical, angry, eloquent, these essays remain his finest analytical writing.

Through the prism of the Asbestos Strike, he illuminated the calamity of Quebec in the twentieth century, a time of "servile and stupefied silence" in which the social doctrine of the Catholic Church was "invoked in support of authoritarianism and xenophobia" until, in Asbestos in 1949, "the worm-eaten remnants of a bygone age" finally came apart.[6] The many drafts among his personal papers and the delays confirm that Trudeau chose these and other inflammatory words and sentences carefully. What separates these essays from other of his writings is their detailed research, especially on the economic history of Quebec, and the extensive presentation of facts in support of his arguments. In social scientific terms, he sought to rearrange the "facts" of Quebec's historical experience and then establish new norms for behaviour in that society. Although nearly all the arguments had already appeared in Trudeau's earlier writings, they are presented here more clearly and consistently in a brilliant attempt to convince "a whole generation, [which] hesitates on the brink of commitment," to smash old totems and "examine the rich alternatives offered by the future."[7]

Trudeau organized his introduction meticulously, beginning with the "facts," followed by the "ideas," and then the "institutions." The facts established that Quebec had benefited from industrialization and modernization, although the riches had not flowed as bounteously to the francophone population as to others because "we fought [modernization] body and soul." Ideas had mattered: "In Quebec . . . during the first half of the twentieth century, our social thinking was so idealistic . . . so divorced from reality . . . that it was hardly ever able to find expression in living and dynamic institutions." Nationalism became a system of defence that "put a premium on all the contrary forces" to progress: "the French language, Catholicism, authoritarianism, idealism, rural life, and later a return to the land." At a time when French Canadians confronted a materialistic, commercial, and increasingly democratic North America, nationalism became a "system of thought" that rejected "the present in favour of an imagined past."[8]

The institutions of a modern state were either stunted or stillborn in Quebec, he argued, principally because of the predominance of the Roman Catholic Church, with its conservative and nationalist doctrine. Labour unions were feeble, the press servile, and political parties corrupt. The fault lay with the leaders, not the people, because the church had never encouraged the political education of the masses. Votes were sold on election day for a bottle of whisky by citizens who spoke righteously after Mass on Sunday about the common good of society. Yet these same leaders simply "rejected any political action likely to result in economic reforms" because "liberal economic reforms were proposed by the 'English'" and "socialist reforms by 'materialists.'" Instead, they pursued quixotic dreams of a return to the land and of corporatism, an economic philosophy "which had the advantage of *not requiring any critical reflection.*" Church and state combined to exclude or condemn those who challenged this consensus, whether they be Communists, the Co-operative Commonwealth Federation (CCF), the left, or the English. The universities, under the heavy hand of the clergy, also avoided not only critical reflection but also modern technology and social science. In these collective failures lay the importance of the Asbestos Strike, which "assumed the proportions of a social upheaval."[9]

Trudeau went on to make scathing attacks on the principal exponents of nationalism and Catholic social doctrine in Quebec. He condemned the Jesuit scholar Father Richard Arès and the Montreal economist Esdras Minville as ignorant of both modern social science and the contemporary world itself. He linked Abbé Groulx with authoritarianism and xenophobia. He accused André Laurendeau of fearing any social reform initiated by the federal government because of the threat it represented to "Catholic morality" and the dreams of corporatism, in which individualism would disappear and elites would be organized to manage society. He criticized the conservative and nationalist economist François-Albert Angers for his support of corporatism, his opposition to state action, and his condemnation of socialism. He attacked various church leaders for their opposition to socialism and the CCF, including Father Georges-Henri Lévesque, even though he admitted that Lévesque had recently demonstrated more liberal ways as the dean of the Faculty of Social Sciences at Laval. And he even condemned his earlier friend and mentor François Hertel for a 1945 essay that spoke wistfully of the need for corporatism.[10]

Although Maurice Duplessis remained the main target, few escaped Trudeau's relentless attack. Paul Gouin, Thérèse's uncle, merited praise for creating the Action libérale nationale in the 1930s, but he was also criticized for his alliance with Duplessis. The exile of Bishop Charbonneau to Victoria became a symbol of the oppressiveness of the church and its antipathy to free speech. Grudgingly, Trudeau gave credit to the church for its efforts in charitable associations, welfare organizations, and adoption agencies, but, in truth, he concluded, the church's "heart and mind were certainly not in it, but longed for the golden age when an obscure rural people was accustomed to hide behind the skirts of the clergy."[11] Not surprisingly, Jean-Charles Falardeau and Frank Scott worried about the impact Trudeau's comments on these individuals would have.*

The essay is an incisive, often bitter, social and political analysis that defines Trudeau's beliefs more sharply than ever before. It sets out the outline for what he would later term the "just society," one in which legal protections assure democratic participation in the development of public policy. He was firmly anti-nationalist—not simply an opponent of conservative Quebec nationalism but wary of a doctrine that closed borders to ideas, people, and goods. Because of the church's link with

---

* Falardeau wrote a long letter to Scott saying he had asked Trudeau to "make more accurate and historically objective his references to P. Lévesque and to the Faculty of Social Sciences [at Laval]" and to "tone down the aggravating accent of his statements concerning such people as M. Minville etc." Scott and Falardeau both emphasized editorial perfection because of the difficulty they had experienced in finding a publisher, and because they expected the book to be severely criticized. When it was finally finished, Falardeau wrote to Trudeau that they should learn important lessons from the whole affair: "That would require another book in itself." Falardeau to Scott, Sept. 7, 1955; and Falardeau to Trudeau, July 27, 1955, and April 13, 1956, TP, vol. 23, file 16.

conservative nationalism in Quebec and its opposition to "progress," he believed it should retreat from the socioeconomic realm and occupy only the spiritual heights, where its presence was fully justified.

Here Trudeau was very much a "modernizer," one who believed that material needs were important in a democratic society and that contemporary social science and Keynesian economics were essential to the creation of the "good life." He was also a socialist cast in a British-Canadian mould. The essay treated the CCF as a great opportunity lost. Despite later claims that Trudeau was never a party person, this piece made it clear that the CCF closely reflected his views, just as the receipts for CCF dues for 1955 in his papers prove his participation in CCF campaigns.* Indeed, at a conference sponsored by *Le Devoir* in February 1955, Trudeau—in elegant suit and tie, with pocket handkerchief perfectly placed—scandalized his listeners by strongly urging socialism for Quebec. "M. Elliot-Trudeau," as the newspaper wrongly named him, "reproached *Le Devoir* for having no philosophy of economics. A kind of schizophrenia," he declared, "exists among the editors of *Le Devoir* on these questions."[12]

Like many of its leaders, Trudeau thought that the best hope for the future of the CCF lay in the trade-union movement, whose earlier gains in the forties had not been built on during the Cold War fifties. He rejected the "proletarian messianism" of the

---

* So do the comments of CCF activist Thérèse Casgrain, who wrote to Saskatchewan premier Tommy Douglas on April 16, 1955, asking if "Pierre Trudeau, whom you have met and who is one of our extremely promising young Canadians," could attend the federal-provincial conference with the Saskatchewan delegation. Saskatchewan Archives, Douglas Papers, collection number 33.1, vol. 671.

Communist left, but he saw alternatives in the democratic socialism of Western Europe. He ended his epilogue to the book: "The only powerful medium of renewal is industrialization; we are also aware that this medium will not provide us with liberty and justice unless it is subject to the forces of an enlightened and powerful trade-union movement." Finally, Trudeau looked beyond the Quebec border with a generous description of North America and English Canada. Quebec, he argued, could not stop the world and seal itself off, just as "nationalistic countries like Spain, Mexico, Argentina, etc. have learned that bloody revolution eventually topples archaic structures." Fortunately, "we," the French Catholic people of Quebec, "have a safety-valve in a continental economy and in a federal constitution, where pragmatism, secularism, and an awareness of change are the predominant attitudes."[13] For the first time, Trudeau had clearly defined the value of Canada for himself and for his province.

Beneath the clarity of the vision, beyond the rhetoric of debate and the flow of statistical evidence, Trudeau's essays expressed a deep-seated anger. Not surprisingly, they generated anger in return, and they continue to do so as modern historians reassess the dramatic events of the fifties and sixties in Quebec. At the time, François-Albert Angers devoted six essays in *L'Action nationale* to Trudeau's attacks on nationalism and his promotion of socialism, fearing it would lead to homogeneity with English Canada. More troubling to Trudeau was the response of Father Jacques Cousineau, a highly respected Jesuit who had mediated the strike in 1949 and was considered a supporter of the rights of unions and workers. The priest pointed to the role of the Catholic-affiliated unions in the strike and the activity of some important elements of the church in its mediation and resolution—all of which Trudeau had ignored. It was a just criticism, but Cousineau went too far in claiming that Trudeau simply reflected the views of the CCF and its Quebec branch, the Parti social démocratique (PSD). Father Richard Arès, the editor of the Jesuits' *Relations*, refused to publish Trudeau's reply to Father Cousineau or even a letter to the editor from him. If Trudeau was disappointed, he was not surprised by his former Jesuit mentors' disavowal of their prize student.

Trudeau expected the neo-nationalist André Laurendeau— whom he had met in the thirties, fought with in the forties against conscription and Canadian war policy, and debated in journals and on television in the fifties—to attack him in *Le Devoir* for his views. Laurendeau did, but indulgently. While agreeing that the conservative nationalism of the Duplessis government and the social thought of the church created a barrier to social reform and essential change, he argued that Trudeau oversimplified and ignored the genuine challenges to the survival of a French-speaking people in a modern North America. Nevertheless, he deemed the essay a brilliant and evocative ode to liberty: in its argument, ideas, and prose, it presented "a remarkable personality" to Quebec public life.[14] Still, Laurendeau rebuked his colleague for his anger and for his personal attacks on those who had fought the same battles and endured similar blows. At the very least, he said, Trudeau was rude, especially to many of his early mentors and teachers.

If Trudeau's essays on the Asbestos Strike are significant for the intellectual history of Quebec, they are fundamentally important in his own intellectual biography. In them we sense that Trudeau, the student who fiercely cherished his individuality, the adolescent who chafed against authority, and the young lover who dreamed of a haven from the deadened hand of Catholic morality, believes he has finally broken free. His own past has become another country, one he has largely abandoned and whose monuments he no longer honours. Those long nights and days at Brébeuf College where he pored over the texts of Abbé Groulx, French religious philosophers, and assorted papal encyclicals now seemed like wasted time. His interpretation of historical change focused in quasi-Marxist terms on economic forces, rejecting the role of social thought that, in Quebec, did not reflect reality.[15] Like many of his colleagues on *Cité libre*, he dismissed his early studies as useless, unrelated to the real life of workers or the contemporary needs of Quebec.*

The passionately idealistic yet traditional anti-Communist Catholic youth who had demonstrated against André Malraux, supported Marshal Pétain, and possibly thrown stones through Jewish shop windows had, by his early thirties, become a socialist who used Marxist dialectics to understand economic change and now notoriously claimed that priests had no more divine right than prime ministers or anyone else. Just over a decade earlier, Trudeau had vigorously supported the nationalist Bloc populaire canadien, had funded the conservative nationalist *Notre Temps*, and had even had nationalists muse about him leading an independence movement. In the mid-forties, François Hertel was his close companion, Catholic and nationalist thought a preoccupation, and Abbé Groulx an admired counsel. Now, in the mid-fifties, he had begun to form his own independent opinions and to break from his roots: he chided his mentor Hertel, attacked his friend Father Richard Arès, and derided François-Albert Angers, who had supported him against Father Braun after his trip to the Soviet Union.

—

---

* Gérard Pelletier asked Jean Marchand, who had attended Laval, where Father Lévesque was establishing a school of social science, what he had learned in university: "He gave me the shortest possible answer: 'Nothing.'" For his part, Pelletier described his college education as "rather anemic." Gérard Pelletier, *Years of Impatience, 1950–1960*, trans. Alan Brown (Toronto: Methuen, 1984), 75.

Trudeau's time in Ottawa had bred a strong resentment against the second-class status of French-speaking Canadians within the Canadian public service. The fifties in Montreal now provided him with a practical education that made him a bitter opponent of the conservative and nationalist government of Duplessis and a resentful critic of the church that tried to silence him and his colleagues. And, through Frank Scott, the CCF, the Canadian labour movement, and his participation in the Canadian Institute of International Affairs (through which he attended two international conferences in Africa and in Asia), Trudeau would increasingly develop relationships with English Canadians who had considerable respect for his credentials from Harvard and the London School of Economics.[16] With his effortless and often eloquent English and his liking for foreign travel, he was sought out for conferences and media appearances in English Canada. His striking appearance, whimsical yet elegant taste in clothes, and unpredictability of views made him a well-known figure in Montreal cultural and intellectual circles, and television carried his name and views to a broader audience. While some of his previous characteristics changed significantly in this decade, others remained constant. He was still elusive, a mystery to those around him. And he continued to pursue his ambition for public life, even if its object was not yet clear.

The Asbestos Strike [La Grève de l'amiante] appeared in the fateful fall of 1956, when Britain, France, and Israel conspired to attack Egypt and brought the world to the brink of war. Soviet troops, meanwhile, crushed the Hungarian uprising, exposing the brutal disregard of democratic and individual rights within the Communist bloc. In France and elsewhere, Communist intellectuals were abandoning the Communist Party, but they remained disillusioned with the West because of the conspiracy among the French, British, and Israeli governments to smash

Arab nationalism. By 1957 the United States, the Soviet Union, and the United Kingdom, which was clinging desperately to great-power status, had tested hydrogen bombs that had the capacity to destroy humanity in minutes. The Soviets tested an intercontinental ballistic missile that could not be intercepted, and President Nikita Khrushchev admitted the crimes of the Soviet past.

In Canada the Liberal government felt the changing winds of international politics, and Prime Minister Louis St. Laurent condemned the British-French collusion, declaring that the age of "supermen" had passed. Although his remarks offended many English Canadians, they recognized an important truth: the old colonial empires were quickly collapsing. At Bandung, Indonesia, in 1955, Prime Minister Jawaharlal Nehru and other leaders of new or emerging states declared a position of neutrality in the Cold War. "Sisters and Brothers," Indonesian president Achmad Sukarno intoned at the opening, "how terrifically dynamic is our time! . . . Nations and States have awoken from a sleep of centuries . . . We, the people of Asia and Africa, far more than half the human population of the world, we can mobilize what I have called the 'Moral Violence of Nations' in favour of peace."[17]

Trudeau quickly accepted the justice of this cause. His travels had made him suspect frontiers—the dangers they created and the damage they did to people who lived around them. He worried about nationalism in the developing countries as much as in Canada. In 1957 he joined a Commonwealth group under the auspices of the World University Service that travelled to Ghana, the first decolonized African member of the Commonwealth. While he welcomed the liberation, he worried about what the future held for Ghanaians. In discussions, he presented the case that "culture can exist only if people are able to provide themselves with [the] instruments of government."[18] He was already worried that those instruments in the developing world were weak. And he was right.

This onrush of world events stirred Trudeau and others like him in Quebec. Increasingly, the conservative nationalism of Duplessis and the leaders of the Roman Catholic Church was on the defensive, as Trudeau and his colleagues championed the concept and principles embodied in the United Nations 1948 Universal Declaration of Human Rights. These principles in turn influenced a series of important judicial decisions in Canada in the fifties. Trudeau, drawing on his legal training, began to work closely with the Canadian Civil Liberties Association and, especially, with F.R. Scott in asserting the importance of individual rights. In 1957 the Supreme Court of Canada finally struck down Duplessis's notorious 1937 Padlock Law, which permitted the state to "lock" down any facilities where it believed "Communist or Bolshevik" activity had occurred. Scott was the principal lawyer in that case as well as in the Roncarelli case. In 1946 Duplessis had denied Roncarelli's tavern a liquor licence because he had paid bail for some Jehovah's Witnesses who insisted on their right to free speech. Roncarelli sued Duplessis, and the case made its way through the courts and through the elections of 1952 and 1956, where Duplessis made effective use of it:

> The Liberals were not going to take the side of the Witnesses any more than they were ready to declare any partisanship for the Communists, so Duplessis was free to disport himself as the indispensable rampart of democracy and established Christianity . . . against enemies that had no audible spokesmen. It was like hunting; it was good sport. Duplessis was a great nimrod, hunting subversive rodents, and the federal game warden kept interfering with him.[19]

The Liberals remained silent when Duplessis passed a preposterous law in 1953 that authorized the provincial government to ban any religious movement that published "abusive or insulting attacks" on the established religions. Such legislation horrified and embarrassed Trudeau. In 1959 the "federal game warden"—the Supreme Court of Canada—finally decided in favour of Scott and Roncarelli and against Duplessis, who was ordered to pay damages of $46,132. That he did—not from his own pocket but from funds advanced by the Union nationale.

Although historians first treated the fifties as a "return to normalcy," much as the twenties had been, closer scrutiny has revealed the strong dynamic for change that emerged from unlikely places—from suburbs and urban slums, coffee houses and country music. Just as Jean Marchand had sung Monique Leyrac's "Les lumières de ma ville" during the 1949 Asbestos Strike, in the 1950s Félix Leclerc gained international celebrity as he spun his musical folk tales of Quebec life. As a popular Québécois musical culture developed, it faced powerful competition from the blues and the rock rhythms of Elvis Presley, Bill Haley, and the first Motown beats that bellowed from the Impala hardtops that "cruised" St. Catherine Street. Trudeau treasured Leclerc, Leyrac, and the other chansonniers, but he found rock an alien dialect, even though his lithe body followed its beat in the late fifties on the dance floor. And, when his mother sorted out some of the Trudeau real-estate holdings, she asked Pierre if he wanted to take over some space at 518 Sherbrooke West, in the heart of the new nightlife district. While he retained his Outremont home address with her, the downtown "pad" brought him close to the new excitement on Montreal streets as the sixties approached. It also gave him independence, just as his appeal to and interest in women was strong.

Madeleine Perron, for example, wrote a note praising *Cité libre*, but especially its editor. She asked if he had time between "two conquests" to send her a copy of the latest issue and concluded, "My admiration to the author, my hommage and respect to the prince, and my biggest peck to Pierre." Doris Lussier, who was gaining fame as an actor in the new television hit *La famille Plouffe/The Plouffe Family*, in both English and French Canada, supported his attack on clericalism in *Cité libre*, ending her message with the words "Long live your liberty! Sacred Pierre. You are peerless, like a Greek god." Lionel Tiger, a McGill professor who also enjoyed Montreal's nightlife, sent "regards to the exquisite woman with whom I occasionally see you living the good life with."

Carroll Guérin, an artist and occasional model to whom he likely referred, certainly was exquisitely beautiful, and she became one of Trudeau's most frequent companions in the late fifties. In her elegance, dress, and appearance, she strikingly resembled Grace Kelly, the American movie star who married Prince Rainier of Monaco and dominated the tabloids of the day. And indeed, Trudeau did pursue women very much as the Greek gods did—or, for that matter, Prince Rainier. When a student in England did not return his calls during one of his visits, he wrote:

> Perhaps I am beginning to look ridiculously like the running gentleman harassing the perfect woman . . . Still for a short while yet it remains that "spring is a 'perhaps' hand in a window," and as I am leaving for France shortly I will have one more go at this perhaps business. And I invite you to tea, or dinner, or to the theater, or to the cinema, or the concert on Wednesday, the 26th. If you want to bother refusing or accepting, you can phone me at Dominions Hotel . . . Otherwise I will be waiting for you outside the Academy, 65 Gower St., between 5:15 and 5:45 on Wednesday.

Alas, we don't know if she showed. But there were many others who did.[20]

In a time marked by conformity, Trudeau was different, and the difference charmed. He took a major role as a lawyer in the fifties in challenging orthodoxy, as the courts broke down the layers of prejudice that had formed around private clubs and social groups. This burst of "civil rights" cases reactivated Trudeau's legal instincts and recalled his outrage in the previous decade with the internment of both Camillien Houde (for his opposition to conscription) and Adrien Arcand (for his fascist sympathies). The dramatic 1954 United States Supreme Court decision on racial segregation in schools, *Brown vs. Board of Education*, raised the bar for previously smug Canadians who had criticized Americans at the same time as they ignored segregation in Halifax and southern Ontario schools or overlooked clubs and universities that barred Jews.*

The newspaper *Vrai* became a crusading voice for those whose rights were destroyed or undermined, whether Jehovah's Witnesses, mental patients, or Wilbert Coffin, a backwoods guide who, editor Jacques Hébert believed, had wrongfully been convicted of murdering three American hunters. Trudeau joined with his close friend Hébert in these campaigns and wrote long

---

* In his study of race and the Canadian courts, James Walker has clearly shown that Quebec was not out of step with other Canadian jurisdictions in restrictions on the rights of Asians, Jews, and Blacks. In 1954, when the federal government revised the *Immigration Act*, Minister of Finance Walter Harris explained that "the racial background of our people would be maintained within reasonable balance; and . . . we would avoid an influx of persons whose viewpoint differed substantially from that of the average, respectable, God-fearing Canadian." The *Globe and Mail* thought Harris went too far but, revealingly, dissented weakly: Who are we being protected from, it asked, "Arabs, Zulus, or what? No one seriously proposed taking immigrants from any part of the world save Western Europe." Quoted in James Walker, *"Race," Rights and the Law in the Supreme Court of Canada* (Waterloo: Wilfrid Laurier Press, 1997), 248.

articles for him explaining the origins of democracy and liberty. When Duplessis called an election for June 20, 1956, Trudeau decided to stay in Quebec that spring to be an active participant in the campaign—active, but not Liberal. The Liberal Party was not yet a palatable alternative for him, even though its leader, Georges-Émile Lapalme, had restructured it and sought out better candidates. But the party was broke, while Duplessis's Union nationale was awash with funds that it used shamelessly to favour friendly newspapers, buy gifts for voters, and reward constituencies that elected its candidates. Duplessis's decisive victory seemed to confirm that, in Quebec, provincial election success could be bought. During the election, the sixty-six-year-old four-term premier faced a coalition of opponents ranging from the labour unions to the Social Credit "Créditiste" movement. Still, Duplessis managed to capture headlines, especially in his favoured rural areas, with inflammatory charges that the federal government, and Cabinet minister Jean Lesage in particular, had intervened by importing—of all things—"Communist eggs" from Poland to Quebec. By the time the Liberals recovered, the Union nationale "had already saturated the province with pamphlets and newspaper advertising conjuring up the lurid spectacle of the imminent arrival of a new communist armada flying the hammer and sickle, bringing more federally procured eggs for the unsuspecting breakfast tables of the province."[21]

Meanwhile, the CCF had remade itself into the Parti social démocratique (PSD) under the leadership of Trudeau's friend Thérèse Casgrain—the daughter of a millionaire French-Canadian stockbroker, and herself a remarkable and strikingly attractive woman—who had headed the campaign for women's suffrage in Quebec for many decades. Grace Trudeau reported the name change to Pierre in the late summer of 1955, while he was driving his Jaguar in Europe: "Did you know that the CCF party name had been changed? Mrs. Casgrain was invited on the

TV last week to give *her views*—as she remarked to me on the phone today—this was no doubt only because of changing the party's name." She also wrote in October that "Mrs. Casgrain" had called to discuss an article about her that had appeared in *Le Devoir*. She generally liked it, except for a "remark on her figure 'taille haute *et robuste.*'" In Grace's opinion, the photograph beside the article denied the adjective "robuste."[22] Trudeau supported Casgrain in her whimsical quest to reposition the party, but we do not know whether, in the privacy of the polling booth in Outremont, he voted for Lapalme (who stood for the Liberals in the riding and won overwhelmingly) or he was one of the 726 souls who cast their ballot for the PSD candidate (who finished last behind the Communist contender).

We do know that Trudeau joined with several other left-leaning personalities, including René Lévesque, in writing a letter to *Le Devoir* attacking the Liberal Party for its phoney "nationalist" attack on the PSD for being centralist and controlled by English Canadians.[23] Overall, the PSD won only 0.6 percent of the vote, while Duplessis triumphed with 51.8 percent and seventy-three seats—both figures slightly higher than in 1952.[24] It was a stunning defeat for the Liberals, who took only twenty seats, three fewer than before, with 45 percent of the vote. The results provided vivid testimony to the ineffectiveness of the opposition and the unfairness of the electoral system.

—

What did Duplessis's triumph mean? Did all those carefully crafted articles, those brilliant analyses of the inevitable emergence of Quebec from an authoritarian, priest-ridden past, and the engagement in opposition of so many of the finest minds of the media and the university count for so little? How did it all happen? In his first article in *Cité libre* in 1950, Trudeau had called on those who opposed the current regime in Quebec to be "coldly intelligent." Perhaps they were not.

The election results, as well as the refusal of the Liberals to integrate the *Cité libre* program into their own platform, suggest that Trudeau and his colleagues were sowing a lot of seed on very barren ground. *Cité libre* has loomed large in history because its principals later became eminent in Quebec and in Canadian public life. At the time, however, the journal merely exasperated Duplessis and was usually ignored. It was not compulsory reading among Quebec City politicians or officials.[25] Moreover, its range was surprisingly narrow and its publication irregular. In the final four years of the Union nationale, 1956 through 1959, *Cité libre* published a grand total of nine irregularly spaced issues. The subscription records also fail to impress. In February 1954 *Cité libre* had only 444 subscribers, of whom 115 had not paid or had disappeared. The remainder were sold by the directors or in bookshops. In 1957–58 the print run was approximately 1,500 copies, compared with almost 15,000 for the Jesuit-controlled *Relations* and over 2,000 for *L'Action nationale*.

In addition, *Cité libre*'s range and character of subscribers in the mid-fifties was disappointing. There were only six subscriptions from France, and few outside Ottawa or the province of Quebec. The grand hopes of a journal that would complement or even rival France's politically influential and socialist *Esprit* had been abandoned. The French, as happened too often, did not reciprocate the warm embrace of the *Cité libristes* and, by the end of the 1950s, Trudeau, Pelletier, and others grumbled about *Esprit*'s ignorance of Quebec. Members of the journal's editorial board constantly reminded friends to renew, carried issues to conferences, and extracted a few dollars from those who could afford it. Trudeau sent mocking letters to friends, saying that, if they were truly poor, they need not pay the $2 subscription cost; otherwise, they should pay up. Pierre Vadeboncoeur, whose "share"

Trudeau initially subsidized, compensated by enthusiastically selling copies wherever he went. For Guy Cormier, who had moved to New Brunswick, the pressure to peddle and personally subsidize the journal was too much, and he tried to resign in 1958. Maurice Blain attempted to escape as well. Finally, in 1960, after the fall of Duplessis, the review was reorganized under the leadership of Jacques Hébert, fully funded, and suddenly began to prosper. Ironically, its best times lay in the past.[26]

It's easy to mock a bunch of intellectuals talking to themselves, having long dinners and debates over wine in living rooms or basements furnished with cracked-leather couches, their wives and girlfriends mostly silent or pouring the drinks, and the men warily testing the newcomers or arguing over where commas belong.* Despite its infrequency and limitations, however, *Cité libre* mattered enormously to Trudeau at the time—and later. He had no university position, no regular

---

* The writer Jean Le Moyne was invited to one meeting with eighteen participants in Charles Lussier's basement. "In the dim light I could see two small bottles of wine at each end and a Dominican priest, a man both austere and paternalistic, sitting in their midst . . . The discussion was extremely mature but it was so solemn and ponderous I wanted to escape. Our meetings [at *Le Relève*] were very different. We would have a wonderful dinner with much laughter and talk about books. The end of the evening would find us under the table replete with good wine and great ideas. I was thinking about this [contrast] when the Dominican suddenly asked me where I was coming from, and I answered him facetiously, 'From under the table, Father.' Nobody knew what I was talking about, of course, but if they had known, I had the feeling they wouldn't have laughed." Jean Le Moyne, quoted in Stephen Clarkson and Christina McCall, *Trudeau and Our Times*, vol. 1: *The Magnificent Obsession* (Toronto: McClelland & Stewart, 1990), 64–65.

column in a newspaper, no affiliation with a major political party, no seat on corporate boards, and, unlike René Lévesque with his regular program, he appeared only intermittently on the sensational new medium of television.

Trudeau seemed to resent Lévesque's celebrity, particularly when he became the exciting new voice of the French-language media after his dramatic coverage of the Korean War. The anecdote about their first meeting in a CBC cafeteria is revealing. "Hi, guys!" Lévesque said as he spied Trudeau and Pelletier at a table planning a new issue of *Cité libre*. But before Lévesque could sit down, Trudeau retorted: "Hey, Lévesque, you're a hell of a good speaker, but I'm starting to wonder whether you can write." Lévesque had failed to deliver some promised piece for the journal. "How can I find the time?" Lévesque shot back. But Trudeau would not relent: "Television's all very well," he said, "but there's nothing solid about it, as you know . . . Now, if you knew how to write, maybe with a little effort now and then—" "If that's what you think, you can go peddle your potatoes, you bloody washout of an intellectual," Lévesque exploded.[27] *Cité libre* gave Trudeau the finest potatoes he could peddle at the time.

The subscribers might be few, but they talked a lot and eventually they mattered. Frank Scott congratulated the editors on the first issue, in which he found "the socialist spirit was present even if it was well hidden." Senator Charles "Chubby" Power, a powerful Quebec City minister in the King government, wrote to Trudeau in 1953 congratulating him on the journal but, interestingly, dissenting on his strong criticism of Quebec nationalism. Father Georges-Henri Lévesque took notice of Trudeau's ideas in *Cité libre*, as did young students who would later make their mark in Quebec intellectual and political life. Pelletier complained that although the journal had an enormous impact in religious colleges, that influence meant only two or three subscriptions because tattered and clandestine copies were passed around almost like sexy French postcards. The author Roch Carrier recalled how a young priest would quiz him about *Cité libre*, and he soon began to realize that it was not to rebuke him but to discover what the sensational but forbidden publication had recently said.[28] At a time when Trudeau's responses to criticisms of his writings were denied publication by Catholic reviews or newspapers, *Cité libre* provided him with a platform from which to respond.

The readers included Guy Favreau and Lucien Cardin, both future justice ministers in the Pearson government; Eugene Forsey, the research director of the Canadian Congress of Labour; many Canadian diplomats, including Jean Chapdelaine, Pierre Trottier, and Trudeau's future undersecretary of external affairs, Marcel Cadieux; as well as the Union nationale politician Daniel Johnson, the eminent journalist Blair Fraser, the poet Earle Birney, the young philosopher Charles Taylor, and Canada's renowned political philosopher C.B. Macpherson. As the editor, Trudeau dealt directly with submissions from authors, and he now had the opportunity to work closely with the finest young minds in Quebec, including the political scientist Léon Dion, the sociologist Guy Rocher, and the essayist Jean Le Moyne (who would be his French speech writer when he became prime minister). The relationships that he forged as editor lasted—and they mattered.[29]

Still, the criticisms of the journal stung. The 1956 devastating election results revealed how politically ineffectual not only *Cité libre* but also the other critics of the Duplessis government had been. The Liberal performance in Quebec deeply disappointed; and, alarmingly, the Liberal government in Ottawa had also begun to stumble. St. Laurent slumped in his Commons seat in depression as the Conservatives and others ferociously attacked his government for arrogance. Well past the biblical three score and ten, St. Laurent seemed incapable of reacting imaginatively to the challenges of Canada and Quebec. The government drifted and, in 1957, it was defeated by the Conservatives under John Diefenbaker. The Conservatives lost the popular vote because Quebec remained overwhelmingly loyal to the Liberals and St. Laurent, yet they won the most seats and formed the government on June 21, 1957. The unilingual Diefenbaker won only nine seats in Quebec but managed to take power by ignoring Quebec in his electoral strategy. St. Laurent soon resigned, and Pearson became his inevitable successor as Liberal Party leader. In Montreal, Jean Drapeau, who had been elected as mayor on a reform platform in 1954, lost his position in 1957. It was, for the reformers, a bitter loss and a bad year.

—

This rapid shift of the political terrain left Pierre Trudeau and his colleagues much less surefooted, so in the summer of 1956 he and others organized Le Rassemblement, a grouping of intellectuals, professionals, and labour officials with the specific goal of promoting democracy. It refused to affiliate with any party, but, instead, announced it would work for progressive approaches to Quebec politics. Trudeau had always admired popular movements and their leaders—men such as Paul Gouin, Henri Bourassa, and, in the city of Montreal, Jean Drapeau. They had rejected the special interests embedded in the traditional parties and set out to create their own parties—groupings based on a popular movement with a clear program. He hoped to do the same with the Rassemblement.

At its founding convention on September 8, the noted scientist and academic Pierre Dansereau from the Université de Montréal became its first president, with Trudeau as vice-president. Among the directors were his friends and colleagues André Laurendeau, Jacques Hébert, and Gérard Pelletier. The

Rassemblement mingled *Cité libre* modernizers with neo-nationalists like Laurendeau who believed that traditional nationalism's link with the church was dangerously misguided, and that Quebec's social and economic system needed rapid change. Few members had direct political experience, and most were suspicious of political involvement. The new organization existed uneasily somewhere between a lobbying group and a fledgling political party. Not surprisingly, it was politically ineffective.[30]

Laurendeau, who had worked with the Bloc populaire canadien in the forties, soon lost interest as the members began to bicker.* The Laval political scientist Gérard Bergeron, an early member, identified the problem in his 1957 description of the "Rassemblement type" as one who had originally disdained direct political action, then become involved in social action, and, suddenly, in the mid-fifties, realized that the solution to social problems must come through the "politics" he continued to despise. In his memoirs, Trudeau claimed that he turned to the Rassemblement because the major parties in Quebec remained unacceptable and the CCF's Parti social démocratique was weak, its policies too centralist and too reflective of the concerns of English Canada. The only alternative was the Rassemblement, a "fragile and short-lived body . . . [created] to defend and promote democracy in Quebec against the threats posed by corruption and authoritarianism."

---

* Trudeau regularly jousted with Laurendeau and *Le Devoir*. In 1957 he was invited to a conference of "Amis du Devoir" and asked to be a keynote speaker. He began by citing André Gide's response to the question, Who is the greatest French poet? "Hugo, hélas!" If one were asked what is the best French newspaper in Canada, he continued, the answer should be "Le Devoir, hélas!" *Le Devoir*, Feb. 4, 1957.

Throughout its brief history, its members quarrelled about membership, possible affiliation with the Parti social démocratique, and the role they should take in direct political action. Trudeau persisted in his belief that the Rassemblement was the best political choice available, and he became its third and final president in 1959. By then, Laurendeau had resigned, saying that he found the group's intellectualism too remote from the everyday voter, who, in the end, would decide the nature of social change.[31]

Laurendeau's complaints about the Rassemblement were cause for concern, but Jean Marchand's opposition was much more serious. After meeting with "Comrade Marchand" in late August 1957, Pelletier told Trudeau that Marchand wanted to reflect on matters before proceeding further with the group. He specifically wanted "a self-examination about what we are and what we are doing about the R and what the relationship between the R and the real world is." Marchand always insisted that Pelletier's and Trudeau's intellectual activities should have a direct connection to the "real" world, where workers woke at 6 a.m., earned barely enough to send their children to school, and lacked the pensions that would have protected them in their old age. The Conféderation des travailleurs catholiques du Canada (CTCC) was divided on the usefulness of the Rassemblement, and the other unions had merged to become the Quebec Federation of Labour (QFL). This new organization was directly linked with the Canadian Labour Congress, and its leaders were urging workers to support the CCF. Where did that leave the Rassemblement?[32]

In the end, Marchand did abandon the Rassemblement, but it lingered on in political limbo. Although Trudeau remained active, the organization was feeble, with membership fees arriving intermittently and a bank balance of only $71.13 on August 15, 1958.[33] In *The Asbestos Strike* in 1956, Trudeau had argued for a just society based on socialist principles, but one year later he was already recoiling from the Parti social démocratique, the Quebec socialist party, and claiming that "democracy" must come before the social revolution. Quebec, he urged, must have democracy before it could change its social and economic institutions.

Despite his frustration with the political scene in Quebec, Trudeau split with his reformist colleagues on one provocative issue—his argument that Duplessis was correct to refuse federal grants for universities. Yet here, too, he was being consistent, for he had already expressed this view in the brief he had written in 1954 for the Tremblay Commission. He had been overruled by the research director, Eugene Forsey, so the draft was altered, but Trudeau's mind was not.[34] He had recommended a clear division of responsibilities between the federal and the provincial governments, along with restraint by the federal government in using its taxing authority to invade provincial fields. When, in 1956, Louis St. Laurent allowed Quebec's grants to be held in trust by the National Conference of Canadian Universities until Duplessis relented, Trudeau's opposition seemed inexplicable to some and infuriating to others.

Trudeau responded in *Cité libre* the following January, arguing that the federal government had no right to take excess tax revenues and create devices by which it could then invade provincial jurisdictions. The crisis of the universities, which, in the fifties, were becoming the motors of modernization, was real. Between 1945 and 1953, the enrolment at Laval had grown by 109.6 percent and, in the same period, the Quebec government's budget had increased by 194 percent. Yet the provincial grant to Laval had gone up only 7 percent. Professors, whose salaries had exceeded those of most other professionals in 1940, had, by 1951, seen their average earnings rise by only 17.4 percent to $3,850 per year, while other professionals saw an increase from $2,502 to $9,206 in the same period.[35]

Understandably, some university teachers who had fought the battle for increased funding in *Cité libre* now complained that the independently wealthy Trudeau did not understand their personal plight. As tempers flared, traditional nationalists and, of course, Duplessis warily accepted the support of their often bitter antagonist, but Trudeau shunned their embrace. If Quebec universities were poor, he said, the fault lay within Quebec, specifically within the provincial government that had refused to fund universities adequately. At a student congress at Laval in November 1957 he urged professors and students to begin a general strike to force Duplessis to become more generous.* An outraged editorial writer at *Le Soleil*, Quebec City's leading newspaper, countered with a lead editorial attacking his irresponsibility.[36]

—

Trudeau might be unpredictable, yet he was usually consistent as he carefully honed his political identity. In *Vrai* he wrote a series of articles on democracy, liberalism, politics, and political thought.[37] In other writings, principally in *Cité libre*, he defined his stand on particular themes. On radio and on television he took part in numerous debates on contemporary issues, often stirring criticism. One radio program caused much controversy: he asked when it was right to assassinate a tyrant. Given that many critics called Duplessis a tyrant, Trudeau surely knew he would provoke a response. In an article in *Vrai* he had already written that if the social order was perverse, citizens

---

*A year later, Trudeau debated the question on radio and argued that the grants were "against the constitution and the spirit of federalism." TP, vol. 25, file 4.

should follow their conscience rather than any authority: "And if the only sure means to re-establish a just order is to wage a revolution against a tyrannical and illegal authority, well, then, do it." On radio, the qualifications that appeared in print—"personally I dislike violence"—were lost. A municipal politician jumped into the debate and declared *Vrai* and Trudeau more dangerous than the "yellow press" that the religious authorities had condemned. Pierre Trudeau's article, he fumed, was "a direct call for sedition." It was a serious offence "to preach revolution."

Jacques Hébert, the editor, replied on Trudeau's behalf in the sarcastic and personal tone increasingly common in Quebec political debate in the mid-1950s: "Brave M. Lauriault, you thought you read: 'Is it necessary to assassinate an imbecile?' and you became terrified. But rest assured; it is only about tyrants. Therefore, you are not endangered. Sleep quietly. The revolutionaries won't waste their cannonballs on wet noodles like you."[38]

To escape this parochial and disputatious environment, Trudeau sought new intellectual outlets. In March 1957 the *University of Toronto Quarterly* had invited him to write an article on political parties in Quebec. He refused, saying that "the orientation of my actions within the next several months hinges upon a series of decisions which are still being collectively pondered and are still in the making. It is fundamentally a question of what is going to happen to a new democratic ["political" is crossed out] movement we have founded—the Rassemblement." He did, however, begin to prepare an article for a book to be edited by Mason Wade, author of the standard history textbook *The French Canadians*. When the book was delayed, Trudeau submitted his piece to the *Canadian Journal of Economics and Political Science (CJEPS)*, which published it in August 1958 under the title "Some Obstacles to Democracy in Quebec."

Trudeau's arguments flowed from a familiar stream of analysis of Quebec's political development, and echoed other voices, such as recent work by Michel Brunet, a nationalist historian at the Université de Montréal, which claimed there were three dominant themes in French-Canadian social and political thought: "l'agriculture, l'anti-étatisme et le messianisme." But to most English Canadians at the time, these views were new. *CJEPS* was read by virtually every economist, political scientist, and historian working in the English language, and some politicians and journalists also subscribed. In common rooms, cocktail parties, and even a few Muskoka cottages, Trudeau's article caused a stir.[39]

In forceful prose and polemical argument, Trudeau made his case that, "in the opinion of the French in Canada, government of the people by the people could not be *for* the people, but mainly for the English-speaking part of that people; such were the spoils of conquest." French Canadians had democracy but did not believe in it: "In all important aspects of national politics, guile, compromise, and a subtle kind of blackmail decide their course and determine their alliances. They appear to discount all political or social ideologies, save nationalism."

Although he criticized English Canadians who believed in democracy for themselves but not for others, his critique of the authoritarianism of the Quebec past, the corruption of contemporary Quebec politics, and the blend of nationalism with a conservative Roman Catholic Church and a weak Quebec state resonated widely in English Canada—too widely in some cases. John Stevenson, a veteran Ottawa journalist for *The Times* of London, praised the article generously in a letter to Trudeau: "For a French-Canadian to make such an arraignment of his racial compatriots required great moral courage, and you certainly showed it in your article." He even asked for some offprints to send to the Queen's private secretary.[40] The following year Trudeau's article won the prize sponsored by the president of the University of Western Ontario for the best scholarly article in English. Grace Trudeau reported that the award received prominent mention in the English press of Montreal but not in the French press.[41]

Wherever he could, Trudeau pressed his case for greater democracy in Quebec. He covered the provincial Liberal convention in May 1958 for both *Vrai* and the CBC and concluded that the party and the convention were anti-democratic:

> It would be unjust to impute to the Liberal Party alone an anti-democratic tendency which is the characteristic of our people as a whole. To be sure, a party that has dominated the political life of our province for so long bears a major responsibility for our political infancy. But other factors also make a significant contribution: the authoritarianism of our religious and social institutions, the insecurity complex deriving from the Conquest, the systematic degradation of our civic life under the Union nationale, and many other factors as well.

Trudeau condemned the Liberal Party Congress as undemocratic not because of party officials or even party rules but because the Liberal Party itself failed to realize that a party cannot be built from above. The congress had been given little time for policy discussion; its purpose, after all, had been to choose the leader. He recognized that the new leader, Jean Lesage, a federal MP for thirteen years, was "a fighter, an energetic organizer and a charming and ambitious man," but there was no evidence, he said, that he was a democrat or that a party under his leadership would become the mass-based political movement essential to obliterating the forces of reaction and authoritarianism in Quebec.[42]

On a copy of Lesage's acceptance speech, Trudeau underlined Lesage's call for the party to seek the active sympathy of "all honest citizens who want to serve the democratic ideal," and for those groups that wish to "pursue their action from the margins of existing political parties" to rally under the Liberal banner to defeat Duplessis. At this point in the document he scrawled, "Drapeau?"[43]

In 1954 Jean Drapeau had won the Montreal mayoralty as the head of the non-partisan Civic Action League. Might not the mayor and his movement be an alternative to Lesage if it were to spread its democratic embrace beyond Montreal? Drapeau, who perhaps shared the dream, invited Gérard Pelletier, Trudeau, and the activist Jean-Paul Lefebvre to the basement of his home in the Cité-Jardin. The talk went badly when, according to Pelletier, Trudeau and Drapeau fought over the nature of democracy and "Trudeau invoked principles that were very disturbing to the practical mind of Drapeau."[44] Trudeau truly believed a popular movement based on the young and an educated working class could achieve genuine social change in Quebec. Drapeau thought he was unrealistic.

Trudeau's consistency of views was becoming the enemy of compromise—and he increasingly antagonized his former colleagues and friends. In the minutes of meetings of the Rassemblement, he is central in defining its purpose and direction. He took the lead in steering the group away from the Parti social démocratique, to the distress of Thérèse Casgrain and its new leader, Michel Chartrand, who had hoped that Trudeau's socialism would bring about his definite commitment to the party. He had worked closely with Chartrand in the anti-conscription campaigns of the early 1940s and through all the labour actions of the 1950s. Now they were becoming antagonists.

But if Trudeau disappointed Drapeau, Chartrand, and others, he thrilled an eighteen-year-old Ottawa student who met him at a Rassemblement meeting in Ottawa in April 1957. Madeleine Gobeil, who was to play a major part in his personal life, had read *Cité libre* and the book on the Asbestos Strike.

Carroll Guérin: Pierre admired her feminine beauty, her boldness, and her wit.

Carroll, an artist, sometimes worked as a fashion model too.

Carroll and Pierre enjoyed an idyllic summer holiday in Europe.

Carroll often changed her hair-
style—blonde, dark, short, long.

The beautiful and intelligent Madeleine Gobeil was a close companion for well over a decade.

The young intellectual, 1950s.

In the fifties, Trudeau gave over much of his time to the labour movement in Quebec. Note the shirts and ties, typical of the quest for respectability at the time.

Pierre and Frank Scott with the aircraft that transported them for their Mackenzie River Valley trip. Even going into the wilderness, Frank wore a hat.

Pierre relaxes on the Mackenzie River trip, 1956.

The Canadian Delegation in Mao's China, 1960. From left to right: Pierre Trudeau, a Buddhist monk, and Jacques Hébert.

Three men in a boat: The Cuba Escapade, 1960.

Trudeau sets out to row to Cuba.

Now, she wrote, she would like to know more about the myths surrounding Pierre Trudeau.[45] He responded to her letter with a serious discussion about politics, but he remained elusive about himself. Nevertheless, her interest charmed him, and they stayed in contact with each other until his marriage in 1971.

Gradually, television also contributed to the myth that was developing about Pierre Trudeau. Although he appeared much less often on the magic screen than Lévesque or Laurendeau, sometimes, he stole the scene. On one occasion on his program *Pays et Merveilles*, Laurendeau taunted him about being a young millionaire touring the world. "Did you use a rickshaw, the Chinese vehicle where 'coolies' pull the rich?" he demanded, archly. "Yes," responded Trudeau, "but I put the coolie in the seat and pulled the rickshaw myself."[46] The quick repartee that was the mark of the public Trudeau was already apparent.

—

By the fall of 1958 it was clear that Jean Lesage was having some success in rallying the opponents of Duplessis behind him, but his arguments did not convince Trudeau. Rather, in the October 1958 issue of *Cité libre*, Trudeau announced the creation of yet another new grouping—the Union des forces démocratiques—a movement that aimed to bring together everyone who shared a belief in democratic principles. Those who committed themselves to its Democratic Manifesto were not allowed to be members of political parties that refused to support the new Union. With the lowest cards in the deck, the Union bluffed and pretended it had the highest trump. The Rassemblement continued to exist, but the Union became the new vehicle for popular political reform—primarily through the accumulation of signatures that were intended to indicate political strength.* Trudeau signed the document as the president of the Rassemblement, but there were few other prominent or inspiring new faces.[47]

Over at *Cité libre*, Gérard Pelletier was becoming uneasy regarding the finances, the gaps between issues, and, increasingly, the divisions within the group. The directors gathered on November 11, 1958, in the grand Outremont home Trudeau still shared with his mother—the first time since a sparsely attended meeting in May. The minutes bear a strained sense of humour: "Mr. Pierre Vadeboncoeur's absence was regretted by no one; Mr. Gilles Marcotte's, whose sympathy for *Cité libre* was notorious, was lamentable. The absence of two directors, Messieurs Charles Lussier and Roger Rolland, whose commitment to *Cité libre* has become more and more intermittent, has been noted." Trudeau began with a complaint about the funding of the journal, pointing out that, in the past, a few of the directors had been obliged to pay personally for the publication of some of the issues. How the other directors reacted as they sat in a room with a famed Braque and a startling Pellan painting on the walls, elegant china in a cabinet nearby, and Grenier, the chauffeur, outside was not recorded in the minutes. They agreed to prepare another issue, for which the missing Vadeboncoeur was given major responsibility. They did not accept Guy Cormier's

---

*Historian Michael Behiels was scathing in his criticism: "The procedural strategy had a bad taste of boy scout amateurism and a large dose of political naïveté. When a public manifesto was signed finally by twenty-one 'eminent' political personalities in April 1959, only one Liberal, Marc Brière, endorsed the document, and he had not been mandated by the party." See his *Prelude to Quebec's Quiet Revolution: Liberalism versus Neo-Nationalism, 1945–1960* (Montreal and Kingston: McGill-Queen's University Press, 1985), 254.

suggestion that the journal should add a statement on its cover page that "the articles published in the review do not reflect the opinions of *Cité libre* but only the authors themselves." Pelletier argued that such a statement would "separate" the journal too much from the opinions expressed in it.

The directors met again just before Christmas at Gérard Pelletier's more modest home at 2391 Benny: "One doesn't know whether it was the approaching Christmas season, the Jingle Bells on St. Catherine Street, the Santa Clauses in the store windows that stirred the spirits of the participants, but the assembly was a wild one." At one point, Pelletier, who was chairing the meeting, pointed his index finger at Trudeau and told him to shut up because, for once, he was not the chair, so couldn't talk whenever he wished.* Trudeau, the minutes recorded, refused to heed the chair's rebuke. Once again the meeting went badly. Pierre Vadeboncoeur, who was absent again, had told Trudeau that he had no time for an issue on "peace" that he had earlier proposed. They were left with a few potential articles, most of them already overdue. Trudeau would see if a December 1958 conference in Ottawa on the anniversary of the Universal Declaration of Human Rights had any useful material. Réginald Boisvert promised a piece on three university students who were protesting outside Duplessis's office, including Laurendeau's daughter Francine and the future Trudeau minister Jean-Pierre Goyer. Before long, however, Boisvert resigned from *Cité libre*, declaring he had lost interest.[48]

---

*A few weeks later Trudeau's garrulous behaviour caused one real loss. According to *Nouvelles illustrées* on December 27, 1958, Trudeau was an "excellent combatant" in a judo competition, but he was disqualified because he "talked too much"—a characteristic not expected of a brown belt in judo.

The two groups—the Rassemblement and the Union des forces démocratiques—had brought attention to Trudeau's belief that a broad democratic mass movement was necessary to defeat the Union nationale and the forces of reaction. Now another new argument became strongly identified with Trudeau in these years: that participation in the democratic process and individual rights took precedence over the collective rights of the group and the authority of leaders, whether of church or state. He became a crusading lawyer for the cause, taking on cases that supported the rights of aggrieved individuals against both the state and the church. His clients ranged from the Canadian Sunbathing Association, which was violently raided by Quebec provincial police officers bearing cameras as well as guns, to the inmates of asylums and hospitals. The sunbathers seemed to intrigue him—he spent considerable time researching their case. He also vigorously supported Jacques Hébert's defence of the accused murderer Wilbert Coffin and, after Hébert was convicted for contempt of court, he successfully took his appeal to the Quebec Court of Appeal. He became even closer to Frank Scott, after the law professor moved directly from the classroom into the courtroom to win victories in the Supreme Court in the Roncarelli case and the Padlock Law case. Trudeau made sure to attend some of the sittings for these historic cases.

These decisions, along with Prime Minister John Diefenbaker's announcement of a Canadian Bill of Rights, intrigued Trudeau and drew his attention to the courts outside Quebec. At the December 1958 conference on the Universal Declaration on Human Rights in Ottawa, he encountered Bora Laskin, the future chief justice, who was emerging as the major legal academic in English Canada. Laskin, like Frank Scott, had begun to argue strongly for a Canadian bill of rights in the mid-1950s—Laskin, in particular, believed that the debate over the bill raised fundamental issues of Canadian federalism. His approach was highly layered: "The most fundamental civil liberties (freedom of association, speech, and religion) were exclusively assigned to federal authorities," while others, including those associated with legal process or economic entitlements, might be either federal or provincial, depending on the precise right.

Scott differed from Laskin on this issue by arguing for the constitutional entrenchment of all important rights. Trudeau sided with Scott: he looked on the Constitution not only as a protector of political rights but as a means of placing limits on "the liberal idea of property" that was "hampering the march toward economic democracy." It was a debate in which Trudeau, who had already argued for a bill of rights encompassing "the most fundamental civil liberties" in his presentation to the Tremblay Commission four years earlier, was to become an important participant and, ultimately, the most significant one.[49] The debates linking federalism and civil liberties flowed directly into discussions about the future of Quebec—once Maurice Duplessis was out of the way. Moreover, Trudeau's increasing participation in these debates and the publication of his article in the *Canadian Journal of Economics and Political Science* made him much better known among English Canadians.

No person was more important in Trudeau's introduction to English Canada than Frank Scott—a foremost literary talent, legal scholar, and socialist political activist. Trudeau recalled first meeting Scott when he came to the Université de Montréal in 1943 to speak understandingly of French Canadians and their opposition to conscription. Scott, for his part, believed that he first saw Trudeau at an anti-Semitic and anti-Communist rally in the late thirties. He was deeply concerned by what he termed "fascism in Quebec" and became a leader in the transformation of Canadian socialism from the authoritarianism evident in the Regina Manifesto to a Western European democratic socialist party. Despite his loathing of fascism, he had initially been opposed to Canadian participation in the Second World War, and was the most prominent English-Canadian voice arguing the case of Quebec opposition to conscription.

Scott and Trudeau met each other frequently as they worked on civil liberty questions in the early fifties and became active in the Canadian Civil Liberties Association. Scott was Trudeau's anglophone ideal: a highly intellectual man whose ideas were balanced by the practical needs of everyday politics; a constitutional lawyer who sought to protect individual rights within a bill of rights; and a poet who was also an eminent social scientist. A large man whose ubiquitous pipe created a pensive presence, Scott intimidated gently. Women adored him, and he responded generously—to his artist wife Marian's considerable dismay. Trudeau welcomed invitations to Scott's parties at his country house in the Eastern Townships, where beautiful young anglophone students clustered about the professor. He also gained access to leading European socialists through Scott's introduction. Here was a man of considerable substance—and he intrigued Trudeau.[50]

In the late winter of 1956, just as the book on the Asbestos Strike was finally to be published, Trudeau heard that Scott was planning a trip to learn first hand about the North. As an experienced voyageur, Trudeau apparently called Scott to ask if he could join him on the adventure. Initially Scott was taken aback, but he respected Trudeau's ability in the wilds and, perhaps, Trudeau also intrigued him. Once in the canoe together, they got along well. Both were physically strong, although Trudeau, the smaller man, typically took on challenges that seemed reckless to Scott. Ever the poet, he described one occasion when Trudeau entered a tremendous surge of water at the point where

the Peace River and Lake Athabasca merged. He yelled, "You
can't go into that," but Trudeau ignored his pleas and forged on:

> Pierre, suddenly challenged,
> Stripped and walked into the rapids,
> Firming his feet against rock,
> Standing white, in white water,
> Leaning south up the current
> To stem the downward rush,
> A man testing his strength
> Against the strength of his country.[51]

Just as Trudeau's journeys in the early 1940s had traced the
path of the nationalist hero, so the journey into the Canadian
Northwest also seems to have been a nationalist experience, one
that made Scott and Trudeau understand the vastness of the
land, its harsh demands, and its endless rewards. In another of
his poems on the trip, "Fort Providence," Scott wrote:

> We came out of Beaver Lake
> Into swift water,
> Past the Big Snye, past Providence Island
> And nosed our barges into shore
> Till they grated on stones and sand.
> Gang planks, thrown to the bank,
> Were all we had for dock
> To drop four tons of freight.
>
> A line of men were squatting
> Silently above us, straight
> Black hair, swarthy skins.
> Slavies they call them, who left
> Their name on Lake and River.

None of them spoke or moved
Just sat and watched, quietly,
While the white man heaved at his hardware.
Farther on, by themselves,
The women and girls were huddled.

They saw from far off the fortlike school where a Grey Nun
from Montreal was in charge, and they spoke French to the
priests and nuns who taught the native Slaveys in their own
broken English.

We walked through the crowded classrooms.
No map of Canada or the Territories,
No library or workshop,
Everywhere religious scenes,
Christ and Saints, Stations of the Cross,
Beads hanging from nails, crucifixes,
And two kinds of secular art
Silk-screen prints of the Group of Seven,
And crayon drawings and masks
Made by the younger children,
The single visible expression
Of the soul of these broken people.

Upstairs on the second storey
Seventy little cots
Touching end to end
In a room 30 by 40
Housed the resident boys
In this firetrap mental gaol.

The natives learning English from French priests, the missing maps, and the haunting reference to the residential school

surely left a deep imprint on Pierre Trudeau's mind, one that would later influence his own and his country's future.[52] For now, however, the adventurers returned home safely, bonded by their challenge to the Canadian North and their common understanding of Canada's possibilities.* Just as he had at the Ontario camp long before, Trudeau had tested his strength against a foreign physical world and discovered he could conquer it easily.

—

Trudeau began to participate regularly in English-language television programs, including coverage of the 1958 election with his old family friend Blair Fraser on the CBC, and he took part in other activities organized by English-Canadian groups. In 1957, for example, at the World University Service of Canada summer program in Ghana, other delegates included Douglas Anglin, a Carleton University specialist on Africa; James Talman, from the University of Western Ontario; Don Johnston, Trudeau's future lawyer and Cabinet minister; Robert Kaplan, another Trudeau

---

* Scott's biographer Sandra Djwa says, correctly, that Scott had a considerable influence on Trudeau. She also suggests that Scott's use of the term "just society" was the source for Trudeau's later political slogan. She admits, however, that tracing the influence is difficult. She points out that in his memoirs, Trudeau refers to T.H. Green and Emmanuel Mounier as important influences in the forties but does not mention Scott. Moreover, she continues, "There is no reference to Scott's role in Quebec in the Memoirs, nor to their joint Mackenzie River trip. Scott's name appears only once in a brief paragraph on the CCF." Although Trudeau admired Scott, his papers suggest that Scott's influence was perhaps more personal than intellectual. Sandra Djwa, "'Nothing by halves': F.R. Scott," *Journal of Canadian Studies* 34 (winter 1999–2000), 52–69.

minister to be; Tim Porteous, a future Trudeau staff member; and Martin Robin, who was to teach Margaret Sinclair before Trudeau married her. In the discussions about Canada in Ghana, Anglin and others argued that federalism should be highly centralized, but Trudeau countered that federalism, even in an "industrial age" that needed strong government, should be seen as a counterweight to the deadening effect of bureaucracy and a tool to bring government "closer to the people." Porteous, who was one of the creators of the wildly successful McGill revue *Spring Thaw*, recalls that Trudeau was shy but completely unpredictable. He insisted on breaking the anglophone monotony by taking a side journey to neighbouring francophone states.[53]

Trudeau's activities among English Canadians attracted little notice at the time in the intense debates going on in Quebec, where the Rassemblement and the Union des forces démocratiques were now cast to the side as the forces of opposition to Maurice Duplessis gathered behind Jean Lesage. Trudeau's position became more difficult. Political scientist Léon Dion criticized the negative tone of Trudeau's analysis of Quebec politics and his excessive reliance on arguments about the past. Others were less polite. The *Nouvelles illustrées* began to make Trudeau a regular target. Its gossip column mocked his "election" to the presidency of the Rassemblement, implying with considerable truth that the organization was elitist and its elections meaningless. In an anonymous letter to the editor of the same journal on April 25, 1959, the author urged that Trudeau should be sent on the first interplanetary journey so he could establish his new party on the moon, where "it would be more useful."

Trudeau's efforts seemed increasingly quixotic and even a waste of his considerable talent. In the *McGill Daily* of October 31, 1958, "Jean David" commented on the Democratic Manifesto. "Generally," he wrote, "the author is considered to be a brilliant man but to many [he] still remains a dilettante. This means that Trudeau himself has a limited influence but his ideas are usually taken into account." The effect of the manifesto, he continued, would be tied to the reaction of Quebec political leaders. At McGill a few months later, Trudeau once again said that because the "people" have not been taught democracy, they should create a completely new party. It was, he said, "the only way out."[54] A few days later in a debate on Radio-Canada, Jean Drapeau firmly rejected the Union des forces démocratiques as an effective tool to bring down Duplessis.[55] Trudeau could brush off student complaints and even Drapeau, but now he received a blow that troubled him more: his friend from childhood, Pierre Vadeboncoeur, attacked his Democratic Manifesto.

Vadeboncoeur had worked closely with Trudeau on all his projects, hailing his return to Quebec in *Le Devoir* in 1949 as a giant step towards a new day in Quebec. His anti-nationalism was even stronger than Trudeau's in the early 1950s, and both spoke regularly, if vaguely, of revolution. He was the butt of Trudeau's pranks, which he fully reciprocated. You remain, he wrote in 1955, "the one guy in the world I love, with whom I love to laugh and be reckless." Although Vadeboncoeur was a lawyer by training, a labour activist by profession, and a successful essayist by nature, he was perpetually short of money. Trudeau lent him funds when he needed them, as he had since they had both begun classes at Académie Querbes decades before. From the beginning it had been a strong, mutually supportive friendship.

In 1959, however, Vadeboncoeur became exasperated with his old friend. First in a labour-socialist publication and then in *Le Devoir*, he gently attacked the Union des forces démocratiques and Trudeau. "You'll find," he began, "that the analysts who are too clear-sighted sometimes make the greatest errors. The famous options that are proposed by that deeply penetrating spirit—that is my oldest friend, Pierre-Elliott Trudeau—are of such a kind." Soon after, in *Le Social Démocrate* and then in *Le Devoir* on May 9, he denounced the Union as "le Club de M. Trudeau," an elitist bunch who were undermining the possibility of socialism while ineptly promoting the Liberal Party. It was a hard punch, and it hurt Trudeau.[56] However, old friends can take blows, and Trudeau took it in good spirit.

When Pierre Vadeboncoeur made his attack in *Le Devoir,* Trudeau was away on another long trip around the world. Then events in Quebec moved quickly in his absence: the strike by producers at Radio-Canada in mid-1959 resulted in a political earthquake that turned René Lévesque and others into neo-nationalists. Trudeau himself later identified Radio-Canada as the strongest force in breaking through the media monopoly and the elite's fears, both of which had protected Duplessis's autocracy. The strike, therefore, had dramatic implications for the flow of free political information in the province. During this crisis, on September 7, Maurice Duplessis died unexpectedly after a series of strokes. The tattered remnants of the Rassemblement, along with critics such as Vadeboncoeur and Casgrain, accused Trudeau of departing just as the battle lines formed, but, in truth, he was not ready for further battle. His letters and his papers at the time suggest that he was eager to escape the infighting and quarrels in Quebec as the various factions jostled for position and the old fortresses of church and tradition began to crumble. Moreover, he had not expected Duplessis to die. After all his years in power, few did.

—

When Trudeau left Quebec at Easter 1959, he hoped to enter China once again, though he also intended to revisit old haunts and discover new vistas. Unlike his journey a decade earlier, he did not set off this time to be a vagabond student wandering the world with a knapsack. He was forty years old now and he travelled first class most of the way, staying in fine hotels such as the St. James in Paris and Hotel Mount Everest in Darjeeling. Yet, in spirit, he remained a passionate observer and a curious student. In Vietnam he noted the presence of police on every corner and despaired that the country might remain forever divided. In India he discovered a passion for politics among the people, and the historic Hindu openness to sexuality. He visited the gorgeous, erotic friezes in Kathmandu, Nepal, where the women are portrayed with their limbs spread apart and their "sex open," and animals bear "the perfect replica of the human sexual organs of normal size." He marvelled at the "ménages à trois" or even four. The "glorification du sexe" was part of their life, he wrote, perhaps with some envy. On one street he saw men walking with their hands on their genitals and wondered what it meant. The secular Congress government of India was trying to promote birth control, but the Catholic Trudeau questioned whether it would "modernize" the country or simply create neuroses.

Moving on to Persia, he noted how the forces opposed to the Shah detested the Americans, whose discreet presence as consultants there was considerable among the military. But he was most impressed by the changes in Israel, a country he described as a miracle. From the deserts of the Middle East, the Israelis had created a land of "greenness, of gardens, flowers, wheat fields, cotton, and corn" and a society of healthy children and well-dressed citizens. Although he detected a touch of chauvinism among the Israelis, he compared them favourably with the surrounding Arabs. He noted in his diary that he believed they were not expansionist and were willing to accept the status quo.[57]

Trudeau later attended an International Socialist Congress in Hamburg, Germany, where he met Moshe Sharett of Israel and Guy Mollet of France. Throughout his trip he called on prominent individuals in business, politics, and academic life. Before he left, he had asked his numerous contacts for appropriate letters of introduction. One of the most curious was a letter from Rex Billings, the general manager of Belmont Park in Montreal, who, on April 9, 1959, wrote: "The bearer of this letter, Mr. Pierre E. Trudeau, is a director of Belmont Park, and is travelling abroad on a combined business and pleasure trip. He will be visiting various amusement parks in the course of his travels, and any courtesy extended to him will be appreciated."[58] He was not able to visit China, although two prominent English Canadians who were sympathetic to Chinese Communism—Margaret Fairley, a Toronto intellectual, and James Endicott, a controversial United Church minister—attempted to obtain an invitation for him. His mother was pleased they did not succeed. She worried throughout the trip: Don't stick "out your neck to reach China—and have your passport confiscated or get into an international mess," she warned. "You have seen enough excitement in your life—besides you won't be able to run as fast as you once could—remember your sore foot."

In the end, he spent most of the time in Europe, where he bought a new Mercedes for the family. He also bought gifts: pearl earrings for Carroll Guérin, amber earrings for "Alice," pearls for "Ada," a silver pin for "Nicole," an unspecified gift for Mireille G., a pin and scarf for "Kline," and some perfume and a "pin" for Grenier, the family chauffeur. He bought a black and gold brocade jacket in Hong Kong for himself, and then spent 225 dollars or pounds for a suit made by William Yu at the celebrated Peninsula Hotel. On September 9 his mother wrote to him that the Mercedes had arrived in Montreal missing one door.[59]

Back home, his oldest friends were puzzled; his colleagues, often frustrated. Who is Pierre Trudeau? they asked during the political ferment of the summer and fall of 1959. Who were his friends? What did he want? His mother knew how much he wanted what she termed "success." She resented Alec Pelletier when she told her in May how "*her* husband" kept Pierre informed during his absence—"not that I know of anything very important," she added, as "my entourage is the passive kind I suppose." In fact, Gérard Pelletier was rarely in touch with Trudeau* and seems not to have known what occurred in his personal life all that well.[60]

Meticulous as always, Trudeau kept a record of the letters he wrote during his long absence. It appears that he wrote ninety-two letters. Pelletier and Jacques Hébert received two each, one less than his mother and the same number as Suzette and her family. Carroll Guérin, his most frequent but far from exclusive female companion, received eleven. Numerous other women, including Nicole Morin, Micheline Legendre, Marie Sénécal, Madeleine Gobeil, and others whom he met in Europe, received a single letter. The rest of the list intrigues because it illustrates how Trudeau had forged new ties with English Canadians and Americans who were almost completely absent in his lists from the late forties and early fifties. Among them are John Stevenson of *The Times*, Morris Miller of Saskatchewan, Lionel Tiger of McGill University, Ron Dare of the University of British Columbia, and the historian Blair Neatby.[61]

Trudeau arrived home in the fall just before Maurice Duplessis's promising successor, Paul Sauvé, unexpectedly died. He was succeeded by the unimpressive Antonio Barrette, who set off a stampede among the reformers to support the Liberal banner. Trudeau seemed at a loss as René Lévesque, journalist Pierre

---

* In his memoirs, Pelletier says that Trudeau "barely read daily papers." Yet his papers are crammed with clippings from all the major newspapers, and he found even obscure references to himself in the tabloid press.

Laporte, constitutional lawyer Paul Gérin-Lajoie, and several reform leaders announced they were joining Jean Lesage to fight the next election. While others prepared for this stunning political change, Trudeau happily busied himself with plans for an astonishing canoe trip from Florida to Cuba. As Lesage began to electrify audiences, and René Lévesque dazzled viewers on television, Trudeau set off from Key West for Cuba with two friends. According to the Florida newspapers, Trudeau, Valmor Francoeur, and Alphonse Gagnon, a millionaire businessman from Chicoutimi, had developed "a unique method of propulsion. While one man paddles in conventional fashion, the second lies on his back and paddles with his feet. The third rests and they switch off after two-hour hitches." Unique it surely was, but wildly dangerous too: three-foot waves drenched them thirty miles out and a shrimp boat pulled them back to the Florida shore on May Day, 1960. Although the trip had no ideological connection, it became part of the lore of Trudeau's links with Fidel Castro, whose rebels had recently taken Havana. In interviews, Trudeau said nothing about politics, but he apparently told the *Miami Herald* he was thirty-nine, then dropped the age to thirty-six for the *Key West Citizen*. Like the trip, it was all good fun.[62]

But his absence was not whimsical—it may have been deliberate. The platform of the Lesage Liberals had become increasingly neo-nationalist during the first months of 1960. Jean Lesage's campaign emphasized provincial autonomy and began to speak of a special status for the province. Trudeau became very troubled as the rhetoric of nationalism, which he had so long deplored in *Cité libre*, became the lifeblood of the Liberal campaign, particularly in Lévesque's television appearances. The Liberals tried to woo Marchand, but there is no evidence they asked Trudeau—the president of the Rassemblement, the co-editor of *Cité libre*, the author of the Democratic Manifesto, and the founder of the Union des forces démocratiques—to become a candidate. He was, perhaps, wounded—or maybe he sensed it was wise to bide his time. Certainly, he made himself difficult to contact—a small canoe in the middle of the ocean could not have been more impossible to reach—as the forces of opposition to Duplessis swelled behind Lesage and his team.

Once the Cuban canoe escapade was over, Trudeau returned to Montreal and wrote an editorial in *Cité libre* that appeared just before the election of Jean Lesage on June 22, 1960. It argued, grudgingly, that the Liberals were to be preferred to the Union nationale, but he persisted in claiming that his Union des forces démocratiques would have been a better alternative than the Liberal Party in the creation of a new government. He was especially scornful of the Parti social démocratique and the Civic Action League for their refusal to join actively with the Union. He debated with his young friend Madeleine Gobeil whether it would be "complicity" to support the Liberals.[63]

On June 22 Lesage won a surprisingly narrow victory over the battered Union nationale. It was, and remains, a landmark in the recent history of Quebec, one that opened dams that had been long closed. Unlike most of his colleagues and friends, Trudeau was not taken at the flood.

CHAPTER 8

—

A DIFFERENT TURN

I'm confident French Canadians will once again miss the turn," Pierre Trudeau wrote in *Le Devoir* at the beginning of 1960, the year of Quebec's historic "Quiet Revolution." "At least, they'll miss it if their political authorities continue to cultivate mediocrity, if their ecclesiastic authorities continue to fear progress, and if their university authorities continue to scorn knowledge."[1] Many in Quebec and elsewhere did miss the turn that, in the sixties, became a social and political revolution in the West. The decade began in North America with leaders who had been born in the nineteenth century. Canada's John Diefenbaker adored the monarchy, disdained alcohol, spoke fractured French, had served in the First World War, and was formed by the devastation of the Great Depression. President Dwight Eisenhower, whom he greatly admired, was, at seventy, older than Diefenbaker but, like Americans generally at that time, more modern in his tastes and demeanour. Yet both seemed old in 1960 as the American Democratic candidate for the presidency, John Kennedy, began his successful campaign, at the age of forty-two, with a call to pass the torch to a new generation of Americans who faced new challenges and dreamed new dreams.

Montreal had shared the remarkable prosperity enjoyed in this continent during the postwar years. Historian Paul-André Linteau ranks the period with the 1850s and the beginning of the twentieth century as the most prosperous in the city's history. And prosperity brought its physical and cultural rewards, such as the boulevard Métropolitain that channelled the expressway to the city's heart and allowed Trudeau's Mercedes to change lanes swiftly as he sped southwards to a party at Frank Scott's summer home in the Townships, or northwards to the sophisticated resorts of the Laurentians. The number of automobiles in Montreal more than quadrupled from 229,000 vehicles after the war to over a million in 1960—far beyond the wildest dreams of Charles Trudeau with his gas stations in the twenties. With its skyscrapers culminating in the symbolic cruciform of Place Ville Marie in 1962, Montreal seemed a thoroughly North American and modern city.

In the clubs of the city centre, Trudeau saw Oscar Peterson emerge as the finest jazz pianist of his age and Félix Leclerc as one of the great chansonniers. After the nationalist riot of 1955, when the National Hockey League commissioner suspended the local hero Maurice "the Rocket" Richard, the Montreal Canadiens inspired francophone pride by winning five consecutive Stanley Cups. By this time Trudeau cared less about hockey, which he had once played well, than about culture, but here, too, a new spirit appeared, with the creation at the end of the fifties of Gratien Gélinas's Comédie-Canadienne, a host of smaller theatres, and Ludmilla Chiriaeff's Les Grands Ballets Canadiens. Trudeau no longer had to rely on touring companies to bring him ballet, the art he treasured most. But prosperity assured that the best touring companies came as well, and he heard the great Maria Callas and the New York Metropolitan Opera, which performed in Montreal five times between 1952 and 1958.[2]

Trudeau savoured these changes, just as he did the new restaurants where he and his various dates—he seems to have had several companions at this time — enjoyed ever finer cuisine and wines.* Montreal was the international city he had dreamed it might be in the thirties. Yet there is a wistfulness to his tone at the time, a sense that the heavy hand of the past had not lifted after Duplessis's death in September 1959. He feared that Quebec would miss the turn essential to its competing success-fully in the North American economy and realizing its full human potential, if its francophone universities remained immersed in their sacramental heritage and if its political debates shunned the cosmopolitan flavour that marked other Western capitals at the beginning of the sixties. His own efforts to open the political system through the development of new political groupings had won little success, and that failure no doubt affected his vision as he watched the real changes occur-ring about him.

Trudeau, of course, was not alone in underestimating the changes in Quebec that had occurred in the fifties. By 1960 his voice was heard in the debates in *Le Devoir*, on television news programs, and in public meetings, especially those organized by the Institut canadien des affaires publiques. He also became a familiar figure at meetings where Laval or Montréal students protested against the meagre provincial government support for the universities, and the young filled the admittedly small ranks of the Rassemblement as well. At his best in debate, his scintillating, quick wit scored with an astonishing range of literary, philo-sophical, and exotic allusions. He was particularly active in

---

* His frequent companion of the 1960s, Madeleine Gobeil, describes Trudeau as a gourmand who, when in Paris, went to Michelin-starred restaurants and ordered Bordeaux from the fabled châteaux. However, he drank little and wine lingered long in his glass. Interview with Madeleine Gobeil, May 2006.

public debates on civil liberties issues, which often focused on the use of an identity card. Trudeau strongly opposed the idea.[3]

Despite all his political activity, his writing, his networking of the previous decade, Trudeau remained an outsider. He was both "the most fascinating and disappointing intellectual of the 1950s" in Quebec, according to the Laval University professor Léon Dion. There was a "bewitching magnetism" around him, an envy of his intellectual and physical prowess, and admiration for "his charm and his wealth. He had the reputation of possessing the most cultivated and the most progressive spirit of the times."[4] None of his contemporaries offered more, even though some, like René Lévesque, were better known. However, he chose to walk away when the Liberal troops stormed the barricades, and he was not a player in what Lévesque dubbed the "spring cleaning of the century" that began in June 1960. Lévesque was there with Jean Lesage as he assembled his team, took office, and began to sweep away the barriers to speech, thought, and social change. As others took up the brooms Trudeau had so long advocated, he, strangely, remained at the sidelines.

But was it so strange? By all accounts, Trudeau's feelings and his prospects were uncertain at this critical moment. Although Lévesque later claimed that Trudeau, Gérard Pelletier, and Jean Marchand all turned down the chance to become candidates in the 1960 election (Marchand certainly said no to Jean Lesage, who considered the celebrated labour leader a prize candidate), Lévesque's biographer Pierre Godin argues convincingly that Pelletier and Trudeau were not even asked. At the time, Trudeau welcomed Lévesque's last-minute decision to enter politics and, after the Liberal victory, his appointment to the Cabinet. Later, he admitted he was envious that Lévesque had "made a jump into politics at a time when it was crucial." "I felt a bit sorry for myself," he said, "because I'd never be asked to get into politics . . . I was against the party he had joined." But he also told Lévesque's

Liberal Cabinet colleague Paul Gérin-Lajoie that he was "lucky" to have "Liberal beliefs": "This permits you to get into politics," he said. For his own part, a wistful Trudeau believed he "would always be on the outside writing articles about what the politicians should be doing and weren't." It was the price he paid for trying to create viable new parties—the Rassemblement and the Union des forces démocratiques—and for condemning vigorously the traditional political parties. Still, for all his talk, he had never doubted that he should be on the inside. He had told a union meeting in 1957, for instance, that "it was much better to have men standing up in the legislature in Quebec than marching on it." But when the reformers finally took their place on the front benches in 1960, a disappointed Trudeau wasn't there.[5]

Yet bliss it was in that summer of 1960 to be alive, democratic, and liberal, even if not Liberal, in Quebec. Despite Trudeau's differences with the leaders of the new regime, he shared with them "a common understanding on a range of subjects such as the urgency for the modernization of Quebec or the sad awareness of the loss created by 25 years of Duplessisism in the province."[6] Trudeau's post-election article in *Cité libre* treated the Lesage election as heaven-sent—his mood contrasting sharply with his previous hesitations about the election and the Lesage Liberals. "We must first salute those who delivered us from the scourge of the Union nationale," he wrote. "It is the Liberal Party and none other which waged the decisive battle for our liberation, and it is to them that today I doff my hat." In particular, he saluted "the incorruptible Mr. Lapalme and . . . the indefatigable Mr. Lesage," who had built piece by piece an army from a group that, then years before, had only eight members in the legislature.[7]

But Georges-Émile Lapalme and Jean Lesage did not doff their hats to Trudeau for helping to build the army that triumphed in June 1960. In his superb memoirs of his political career, Lapalme dismissed the role of *Cité libre* in defeating

Duplessis. And the former premier, had he been alive in 1960, would surely have agreed. The reasons behind their grudging reservations were all too clear in that same article Trudeau published immediately after their election victory. Some of the new Liberal politicians had only recently begun to oppose the Union nationale, he said, and he still had doubts about the past, present, and future of the Quebec Liberal Party:

> For sixteen years, the Province has wallowed under an incompetent, tyrannical, and reactionary government. This regime, resting on lucre, ambition, and a fondness for the arbitrary, would not have been possible, however, without the cowardice and complacency of almost all those exercising authority, commanding influence, or leading public opinion . . .
>
> Whether chancellor of a university, principal of a school, union leader, director of a professional corps, head of a company, militant nationalist, or administrator of any institution, each used the particular arrangement he had come to with the power of government as a pretext to justify not denouncing this power when it systematically harmed the common good in the domain for which each was responsible: industrial relations, natural resources, well-ordered economic development, civic honour, respect of intelligence, education, autonomy, justice, and democracy.

Trudeau also defended his absence from the political front ranks in his article. He disingenuously omitted mention of his central role in the formation and leadership of the Union des forces démocratiques. He pointed to the close results in many constituencies as well as Lesage's narrow victory. He argued, accordingly, that if all anti-Duplessis forces had united behind a coalition such as the Union, the majority would have been larger and the mandate for change stronger. He criticized the socialist party—the Parti social démocratique (PSD)—which had joined the Liberals in refusing to rally behind his Union, and claimed that the dismal results it received were deserved. In Trudeau's view, the PSD would "probably disappear from the provincial scene for a long time." In this judgment he was correct. Finally, he pointed out that the Liberals had only recently united effectively against Duplessis: in the past, under the domination of Mackenzie King and Louis St. Laurent, they had acquiesced too often to Duplessis's anti-labour policies, on the one hand, and Ottawa's centralization, on the other. While the Liberals had remained in thrall to the forces of reaction, others had fought for justice "with vehemence, courage, and persistence."[8] In other words, he claimed, the editors and authors of *Cité libre* had been on the thin front lines when the Union nationale was intimidating almost all the others. Trudeau's argument fundamentally and correctly asserted that the party politicians had determined the outcome in the present, but that the thinkers and the students, the ones who cared about *Cité libre*, had been equally important in what French historians call the *longue durée*.

Trudeau had other reasons, too, for his reservations about the Liberal government. The Radio-Canada strike had made Lévesque into a nationalist angry with the government of Canada, though he remained a secularist modernizer and became part of a group identified as neo-nationalists—a group that included André Laurendeau, the journalist Pierre Laporte, and the academic Léon Dion. Trudeau dissented ever more strongly from the neo-nationalist position, and the presence of many neo-nationalists in the new Lesage government bothered him. These differences divided Trudeau and Gérard Pelletier, who tended to follow Trudeau's lead, from those who became the Quebec intellectual mainstream after June 1960.

There had been signs of the future division earlier in *Cité libre*. In 1957 Léon Dion had issued a mild dissent from the general tone of Trudeau's analysis of Quebec society. He criticized the "pessimistic nationalism" of Michel Brunet and the so-called Montreal school of historians in a *Cité libre* article that did not mention Trudeau. Correspondence makes clear, however, that Trudeau, who at the time shared some of Brunet's analysis, was also a target. Trudeau published the article after considerable editorial debate. The following year, in another journal, Dion criticized Trudeau in more detail, arguing that he ignored the existence of some democratic institutions within Quebec while being too vague about what democracy itself represented. He wrote that Trudeau's bleak assessment of the dominance of the clerical and conservative elite and of the obstacles to democracy in Quebec ignored moments in Quebec's history, such as the Rebellion in the 1830s and responsible government in the 1840s, when democratic tendencies were strengthened. Trudeau's focus on unions and democracy was too narrow, his despair too sterile, he charged.

Earlier, Pierre Laporte, *Le Devoir*'s senior political reporter, had also reproached Trudeau, "my good friend," for his pessimism after hearing a presentation he made to the Institut canadien des affaires publiques. Laporte claimed that Trudeau went too far when he said that "French Canada had produced nothing, not a thinker, a researcher, a man of letters or a professional worthy of the name." Trudeau, moreover, was dead wrong when he claimed that English Canadians had given democracy as a gift to French Canadians. Like Dion, Laporte asked what they should make of the blood spilt and the battles won by the patriots in the 1830s and 1840s once representative and responsible government came to Quebec.[9] "A gift from the English?" Hardly.

These emerging divisions were reflected within the *Cité libre* team itself. Although some of the younger writers and their supporters were at loggerheads with the founding fathers, the fall of the Union nationale suddenly drew enormous attention to the journal. Despite sporadic publication and limited circulation, they all knew it had played a major part in expressing and disseminating intellectual dissent throughout the 1950s. Dion might have had differences with Trudeau, the editor, but he recognized the journal's significance in a February 1958 letter to him: "It is here that I see the immense usefulness of 'Cité libre'—it allows us to express our thoughts with ease before and for our contemporaries."[10]

In the summer of 1960 *Cité libre* was reorganized under the business leadership of Jacques Hébert, who had experience running *Vrai* as well as a successful new publishing house, Éditions de l'homme. By broadening the journal's group of supporters, he turned it into a financial success: its subscriptions increased dramatically from under one thousand to over seven thousand at one point. English-Canadian subscriptions soared as the intelligentsia in the rest of Canada struggled to understand what was happening in Quebec. Yet, as so often occurs, this success bred even more dissension as Trudeau's hesitations about the Lesage government, on the one hand, and his criticisms of the Parti social démocratique, on the other, created friction with earlier sympathizers such as Paul Gérin-Lajoie and René Lévesque, who were themselves ministers in the new government, and Pierre Vadeboncoeur and Marcel Rioux, who were becoming ever more strongly socialist and nationalist.

Then, suddenly, the spectre of separatism began to disrupt their deliberations. The first but still minor explosion came on September 10, 1960, when about thirty mostly young Quebec francophones in a Rassemblement pour l'indépendance nationale (RIN) issued a manifesto that called for the "total" independence of Quebec.

—

As the newspapers reported the RIN manifesto, sometimes dismissively but often with curiosity, and the Lesage government began its fundamental reforms of Quebec's educational and social system, Pierre Trudeau and Jacques Hébert were flying over the

Atlantic with the hope of visiting China. Hébert and Trudeau obviously enjoyed each other's company, even though they were very different: Hébert, an extrovert who laced his life with wry but regular humour; Trudeau, essentially an introvert whose pranks were invariably ingenious. They shared a love of the unexpected and the mysterious and a distrust of the mighty and the meretricious. By the sixties, they had forged a partnership based on their love of exotic travel and their sometimes playful but often deadly serious attack on the establishment—whatever it might be.

Both men, but especially Hébert, were outraged when Wilbert Coffin was hanged on February 10, 1956, on questionable evidence, for the murder of three Pennsylvania hunters. The American secretary of state, John Foster Dulles, personally contacted Quebec authorities on the case, Duplessis responded as requested, and the conviction came quickly after the judge charged the jury with the words "I have faith that you will set an example for your district, for your province, and for the whole of your country before the eyes of America, which counts on you, and which has followed all the details of the trial." This disgraceful charge, the fawning government response to American intervention, and the flimsiness of the evidence outraged the lawyer Trudeau and the crusading civil libertarian Hébert. For a decade, their demand for posthumous justice for Coffin bonded them in their mission.[11]

This commitment also made them defiant in the face of American and conservative Canadian challenges. China intrigued them, both in itself and as a challenge to orthodoxy. Except for a photograph, Trudeau omitted mention of this six-week trip from his memoirs, even though he and Hébert had written a book, *Two Innocents in Red China*, describing it. Three others accompanied them: Denis Lazure, a psychiatrist and future separatist politician; Micheline Legendre, one of Canada's great puppeteers; and Madeleine Parent, a leftist union activist.

They were a peculiar quintet encountering an enigma. Although Canada had begun trading with Communist China in mild defiance of the Americans, there were no formal diplomatic ties between the two countries. The group formed a "delegation" whereby they all officially visited sites appropriate to their particular background. In Trudeau's case that meant courts and related institutions.

The Chinese had invited one hundred French Canadians to visit their country, but only twenty, according to Trudeau and Hébert, "dared to answer." Most of those invited feared for their reputations should they accept. The authors, however, felt they were "pretty well immune to reprisals." Both "had been generously reproved, knocked off, and abolished in the integralist and reactionary press in consequence of earlier journeys behind the iron curtain." Thus, "the prospect of being assassinated yet again on their return from China was hardly likely to impress" either of them.

In the Shanghai chapter, Trudeau ruefully complained that his mischievous companions had told his solicitous hosts that he loved sea slugs. As a result, every day they served him the "quite repulsive beast which lives in slime and looks like a fat, brownish worm covered with bumps." Trudeau had fled Shanghai in 1949 as Mao's armies neared. He found it "strange to come back after eleven years to a city that used to embody all the fascination, all the intrigue, all the violence and mystery that could arise from the collision of East and West." Now the beggars and wounded soldiers were gone; the streets were clean, and no one wore rags. The bars and brothels of earlier days had disappeared; the city went to bed at 11:30; and "Shanghai has become an industrious city." One night Trudeau escaped from his insistent and sometimes imperious guide, Mr. Hou, and wandered through the streets at midnight. He found nary a bar or a café but, in the city's parks, saw "several young couples

[with] their arms round each other's waists [who were] kissing." The sight appealed to his warm, romantic side and broke the monotony of the too "industrious" city.

On October 1, the anniversary of the Communist victory, the Canadians and the other guests stood atop the gate at Tiananmen Square in Beijing and witnessed tens of thousands dancing and celebrating below them while fireworks turned the heavens into daylight. As Mr. Hou began to escort the guests back to their hotel, Trudeau hid behind a pillar, then suddenly darted away into the crowd and disappeared. "What happened," Hébert wrote, "we shall never know exactly, nor are we convinced that Trudeau remembers it clearly himself. He took part in weird and frenzied dances, in impromptu skits, in delightful flirtations." Later, he described "exotic orchestras, costumes of the moon people, strange friendships and new scents . . . dark tresses, inquisitive children, laughing adolescents, brotherly and joyful men." The memory lingered of lights dimming and faint footsteps in dark alleys, and a long walk back to the hotel in the early dawn.[12]

In his epilogue, Trudeau said that his purpose in writing the book was to dispel the notion of "the Yellow Peril." The real threat, he concluded, is "not the Yellow Peril of our nightmares; it is the eventual threat of economic rivalry in the markets of the world, and the nearer threat of an ideological success that is already enabling China to help . . . the even poorer countries of Asia, Africa, and Latin America."[13] He said that the "two China" policy of recognizing China and Taiwan as sovereign entities was unacceptable and dangerous. It was American "prestige" that prevented the acceptance of China in the international arena, but, in a thermonuclear age, "innocents" must ask whether Taiwan is "worth the trouble of setting off the final thermonuclear holocaust." Trudeau himself did not worry about the "China threat" during his own lifetime. China had too much to do internally; its history was not that of an aggressor, unlike the nations of the West. Hébert and Trudeau did get to meet Mao, "one of the great men of the century," who possessed "a powerful head, an unlined face, and a look of wisdom tinged with melancholy. The eyes of that tranquil face are heavy with having seen too much of the misery of men."[14]

A largely handwritten draft of the book is preserved in Trudeau's papers, and it indicates that Hébert was the principal author and Trudeau mainly the editor. Trudeau's most substantial contribution is the chapter on Shanghai and the epilogue, although Hébert claimed that Trudeau made constant changes to drafts of other sections. Perhaps because of this shared authorship, the two friends wrote in the third person in their book.

Hébert published the volume and launched it at the Cercle Universitaire on Sherbrooke Street in Montreal on March 28, 1961. Fortunately for them, the anticipated attacks on their "innocent" presentation of "Red China" were few. Indeed, several priests came to the elegant book launch and eagerly sought the authors' autographs. In his speech that evening, Trudeau called for Canadian recognition of China and again predicted, accurately, that China would someday challenge the West not only in ideology but also in trade.[15]

Almost half a century later, Trudeau's prediction of the economic challenge of China is fulfilled. Yet today we also know that the misery the travellers saw in Mao's eyes was very often of his own dictatorial making. In their well-received biography of Mao, Jung Chang and Jon Halliday strongly criticized Trudeau and Hébert for their naïve views of China. The "starry-eyed" travellers, they wrote, ignored all the evidence of famine that refugees in Hong Kong reported in detail to anyone who would bother to listen. In their own book, Trudeau and Hébert did dismiss these reports. Pre-Communist China, they said, was a place "where unspeakable misery and deadly famine were the lot of the unemployed and their whole families. Unemployment meant death by hunger and cold." With Communism, in contrast, all Chinese had work: "This means precisely that it has been able to guarantee them the right to live. Before this fundamental fact, all our Western reflections on the arduous nature of work in China, on female labour, on the wretched standard of living, on the totalitarian régime, appear as ineffectual quibbles."*

Today, these reflections are clearly no longer "ineffectual quibbles." As Trudeau, Hébert, and the other Western guests participated in long banquets where wine flowed and food abounded, over twenty million Chinese died in the great famine of 1960. While Chinese starved, Mao showered funds on Indonesia, Africa, Cuba, and Albania, seeking to become the "model" for the post-colonial world that Trudeau and Hébert had heralded. But in the epilogue, Trudeau appeared to have some premonition of what was to come: "It is true that, if the authors . . . are guilty of anything, it is naïveté. We had the naïveté to believe that what we saw with our own eyes did exist; and the further naïveté to think our readers capable of

---

* Trudeau's enthusiasm for China pervaded his letter to his friend Carroll Guérin. She wrote when she received a note from him at the time: "It was fascinating to receive word from China, particularly since you praise it so much. Pierre, you are so lucky to have met Mao Tse-tung . . . I imagine everyone will react to your favourable reports as they did towards your previous ones about Russia in '52." Guérin to Trudeau, Oct. 18, 1960, TP, vol. 39, file 6. China continued to intrigue Trudeau. Years later, when asked by Thérèse Gouin Décarie and Vianney Décarie who had impressed him most among world leaders, Trudeau answered immediately, "Chou En-lai." Conversation with the Décaries, June 2006.

making the necessary adjustments in the often outrageous claims made by our Chinese informants."[16]

Indeed, the Canadians became part of a theatre directed by Mao without realizing that they were players. Yet Trudeau was perceptive in early recognizing that China was forming the base for a strong industrial society and correct in his assessment that the majority of Chinese themselves had more confidence in the regime than they had had in the ramshackle and corrupt quasi-democracy of 1949. Even if the travellers failed to learn about the horrible events in the countryside simply because they did not ask enough questions (and would likely not have received honest answers if they had), they were correct in their analysis that the increased literacy in the cities and in large areas of the country would be a powerful and positive force for future transformation.

Trudeau was not alone in his overly sanguine view of China. In a review of the book the following year, the writer Naim Kattan observed that the authors exhibited no ideological bias. "Some readers," he wrote, might find it "a negative description of China"; others might declare it uncritical. "It all depends on the colour of the glasses a person wears. Jacques Hébert and Pierre Trudeau did not wear any." They reported what they saw, and they did not know that so much was concealed from them — their myopia was shared by many others at the time. Chang and Halliday denounced not only Trudeau and Hébert but also the future French president François Mitterrand, and the former head of the Food and Agricultural Organization, John Boyd-Orr, who commented that China was feeding its people well. Even Field Marshal Bernard Montgomery, the hero of the Battle of El Alamein, denied reports of widespread famine and dismissed criticisms of Mao. China, he declared, "needs the chairman," who must not "abandon the ship."[17] Others followed in this same positive vein for many years, including the quintessential realist Henry

Kissinger, who bantered most banally with the Chinese leader about sexual appetites.*

Given Trudeau's response to other leaders and nations around this time, it's fair to ask a broader question: Was he generally too sympathetic to authoritarian regimes of the left? Trudeau's comments about China under Mao followed not long after his optimistic assessment of the Soviet Union during the last months of Stalin's madness. He also became an early advocate of Fidel Castro, visiting Havana after his failed canoe trip to Cuba. There he met "Che Guevara, with his cigar, mingling with the guests and everything else." He did not meet Castro, although he attended a huge rally where Castro "made a great speech . . . and

---

* Western views of China and Mao were much more generous than views of the Soviet Union and Stalin. Journalist Edgar Snow's book *Red Star over China* romanticized Chinese Communism, and, by the 1960s, Mao was a cult hero among the radical young who clung to his famous Red Book. By the 1970s even American Republicans had succumbed. Although Mao did not praise America, Nixon told Mao at their first meeting that "the Chairman's writings moved a nation and have changed the world." He said Mao was a "professional philosopher"; in return, Mao spoke admiringly of Kissinger's success with women. Unbelievably, the transcript reads: Mao—"There were some rumours that said you were about to collapse (laughter). And women folk seated here were all dissatisfied with that (laughter, especially pronounced among the women). They said if the Doctor is going to collapse, we would be out of work." The Chinese took extraordinary pains to cut off locals from foreigners. During the Nixon visit, which occurred at Chinese New Year, thousands of rural youth were sent back to their villages lest they encounter the American president—an encounter that security had already made impossible. Jung Chang and Jon Halliday, *Mao: The Unknown Story* (New York: Knopf, 2005), 584, 587–89.

people were just mesmerized by him."[18] And in 1976 he became the first NATO leader to visit Cuba. At home, in his long battle with Duplessis in Quebec, Trudeau had been a strong proponent of "democracy," "civil liberties," and "individual" rights—yet it was obvious that the Communist regimes of Stalin and Mao in particular were guilty of abundant human rights abuses. Trudeau did change his views of the Soviet Union and Stalin after Khrushchev's dramatic revelations in 1956. Yet even if he saw little state oppression in China, no objective observer would suggest that the values of democracy and human rights were cherished in the Chinese Communist state—or, for that matter, in the Soviet Union and Cuba. While acknowledging that many others failed to penetrate the thick curtains concealing famine, human rights abuses, and brutality, we have to admit that Trudeau, despite Kattan's review, did have some rose colour in his glasses.

There are a number of reasons for his seemingly contradictory approach. To begin with, Pierre Trudeau often reacted against conventional views, and, when he visited the Soviet Union in 1952 and China in 1960, stern anti-Communism was the dominant political current in North America. Already it had caused numerous abuses of civil rights in North America itself. Trudeau's travelling partner Madeleine Parent and her husband, Kent Rowley, had endured the fierce sting of irrational anti-Communism from the Quebec police, the RCMP, and the press. These events establish a context for Trudeau, who loathed the careless anti-Communism of Duplessis, the anti-Soviet diatribes of Conservative leader George Drew, and the McCarthyism that tainted American public life in the 1950s. They pricked him towards contrary actions. As Robert Ford, Canada's ambassador to the Soviet Union, later remarked, Trudeau was by nature "anti-establishment" and the Soviets were never the establishment—even on the left.[19]

A complex and peculiar incident that occurred during the 1960 Quebec election campaign illustrates Trudeau's sensitivities on this score. Abbé Gérard Saint-Pierre, in dismissing one of Trudeau's election comments, called him "the Canadian Karl Marx" in a Trois-Rivières newspaper sympathetic to the Union nationale. A Quebec court had recently held that calling someone a Communist was libellous. Trudeau decided to take action but, interestingly, followed Catholic canon law rather than pursuing the case in civil court. Accordingly, he asked Georges-Léon Pelletier, the bishop of Trois-Rivières, to demand a retraction from Saint-Pierre; otherwise, he threatened to turn to the secular courts. Bishop Pelletier answered on June 20, noting that Trudeau had once said that Lenin was "a remarkable sociologist." He added: "In common parlance, Karl Marx personifies socialism whether it be political or economic. It is difficult therefore to prove that one can associate this description with heresy, much less communism." Pelletier cleverly concluded that "the label 'communist' actually preceded Karl Marx." Trudeau therefore deserved no retraction.

On June 30 Trudeau appealed, although he agreed that the spirit of Bishop Pelletier's reply reflected certain papal encyclicals. When he received no apology, he wrote again on August 26. Pelletier quickly replied on September 3 and authorized Trudeau to go ahead with a suit in civil court. But it was too late. Quebec libel law required that any action had to proceed within three months of publication. The Pelletier letter had arrived precisely at the point when the legal remedies were exhausted.

A later debate on the issue took place in the pages of *Cité libre* and the conservative Catholic *Notre Temps*, in which "Jean-Paul Poitras" said that Trudeau had not needed to turn to canon law but could have gone directly to the courts. In a reply entitled "The Inconvenience of Being Catholic," Trudeau denounced Poitras for his ignorance, adding wryly that "for a long time, *Notre Temps* has accused *Cité libre* and its editors of being bad sons of the Church. Today *Notre Temps* and M. Poitras accuse me of holding the laws of the Church in too high regard."[20]

By the summer of 1961, however, when Trudeau wrote this attack on clericalism and the church's conservatism, he was tilting at windmills. The debate belonged to the past, not to the intense present of Quebec after June 1960. What remains remarkable is the time he spent on the matter when so much else of political significance was developing in Quebec. The denunciations of the "Soviet sympathies" of his LSE mentor Harold Laski, the Union nationale's use of the Padlock Law, and the wild exaggerations of the "menace" of Communism all played a part in his attitude, as did, perhaps, his long-forgotten thesis on the reconciliation of Communism and Catholicism. Trudeau rightly despised this McCarthyism of the North, especially when the church was involved. These experiences and this attitude formed part of the baggage he carried to China.

A second explanation for the authors' naïveté in their reaction to China lies in Trudeau's understanding of international politics, an area where Harold Laski, Emmanuel Mounier, and the eminent French newspaper Le Monde had all had considerable influence on him. He believed, like many other intellectuals of the time, that, in the nuclear age, all possible effort should be made to break down the differences between the East and the West. André Laurendeau and Le Devoir shared his views, as did Gérard Pelletier, particularly in the late fifties and early sixties when the superpowers began testing ever more potent hydrogen weapons and the Western anti-nuclear movement grew rapidly. On June 24, 1961, he clipped a piece from Le Devoir in which his former fiancée Thérèse Gouin, by then a highly regarded academic psychologist, wrote of the terror she felt for the fate of her children in the thermonuclear age. Trudeau shared Thérèse's fears, and his beliefs bonded him to the young, a tie he cherished. But it was not only the young: Maryon Pearson, Lester Pearson's wife, boldly joined the Canadian Voice of Women, an organization whose rallying call at the time was opposition to nuclear weapons. In those anxiety-filled times, Trudeau, like many of his students, wore a peace symbol on his lapel.

Furthermore, Trudeau reflected contemporary social science in its belief that, especially in recently decolonized countries, nations could achieve economic gains more quickly by central planning than by democratic means. He concluded a CBC "post-news talk" on Valentine's Day with some reservations, saying that what he saw in China "was not the neat economic planning of our textbooks," and he spoke of the "bottlenecks" that planning caused. But, he concluded, "only a fool would fail to see that . . . it was the clumsy awakening of what in years to come . . . may turn out to be the world's most powerful industrial giant."

For many observers in the late 1950s, the Soviets seemed to have grown economically at rates far beyond that of the United States and Canada. They had launched the first earth satellite and, according to John F. Kennedy in the 1960 presidential campaign, had managed to produce far more missiles than the United States had done. In a world where missiles counted, the Soviets had apparently become the greatest military power. China, for its part, seemed much superior at the time to its obvious democratic comparison, India, in terms of literacy, economic growth, and infant mortality. Eminent social scientists such as Samuel Huntington noticed the results and concluded that democracy might not be the best path for the newly independent African and Asian states to follow.

In 1959 Michael Oliver, the McGill professor and socialist activist, had asked Trudeau to comment on an article by George Grant, the well-known Canadian political philosopher. Grant was critical of contemporary capitalism but argued that social priorities were "more advanced" in North America than in the Soviet Union. Trudeau placed a question mark beside that claim, though he agreed with Grant that North American capitalism did not produce the "right services"—there were too many cars and garages and not enough classrooms.[21] Trudeau was willing to give the Soviets, the Chinese, and, later, the Cubans much credit for getting their "social priorities" correct. While acknowledging the limitations on civic rights in these authoritarian societies, he emphasized their social achievements, especially when others in the church and in Quebec and Canadian politics so vigorously denied them.

Finally, Trudeau and Hébert were more troubled about the intellectual and cultural development in China than their critics suggested. After one of the endless "factory" tours where they saw how "Soviet experts" had helped production—as an official delegation they had no choice but to go where their hosts took them to showcase the Chinese accomplishments—the Canadians longed

> to dream awhile before the tomb of an emperor, or the tranquil Buddha of some pagoda lost in the mountains. But that's the past, and Mr. Hou, like all the Mr. Hous in China, thinks only of the present, dreams only of the future. When we ask our hosts to identify some modern building, they reply enthusiastically: "It's a hospital, it's a library—built *after* the Liberation."
>
> "And that lovely temple, on that little hill over there?"
> "I don't know—some temple . . ."
> "Buddhist?'
> "Perhaps."
> It doesn't interest them.[22]

The earnestness and ignorance of the Chinese universities also bothered them: "Trudeau asks the economists if they know some of the Western economists who have studied socialist economics: Schumpeter and Lerner, for instance, or even the Polish economist Lange? They don't know them." The Canadians "can't help wondering" if the students "ever take time for a little fun." Apparently they don't, and if a foreign student from a "brother"

Marxist country is caught redhanded in a "harmless flirtation," he will be considered a "degenerate, a bad Marxist," and sent home. As one who flirted constantly, Trudeau's condemnation was severe![23]

—

When Trudeau returned home from China in November 1960, he found that Quebec's politics and classrooms were becoming very different from those he had excoriated in the fifties. His fears that the Lesage government would be hesitant and too beholden to traditional political interests had been unwarranted. The "team of thunder," as the Liberals called their government, moved forward with breathtaking speed as it secularized education, began to redefine social security, and even considered an international role for Quebec. René Lévesque became a symbol of this dynamism and, increasingly, its nationalism. The Catholic Church reeled from the impact of change, and its priests began to notice that the faithful now came much less often to mass. Cardinal Paul-Émile Léger, as he had now been promoted, struggled to meet the forces of modernization. He implored Le Devoir not to break its historical link with the Roman Catholic Church and agreed to restrict church interference in the universities—a decision that opened academic positions to church critics such as Marcel Rioux and, of course, Pierre Trudeau. In Trudeau's case, the cardinal personally intervened to remove the ban, and Vianney Décarie played a major part in securing a position for his wife's great admirer.[24]

In January 1961—a decade after the historic meeting between Léger, Trudeau, and Pelletier over Trudeau's article questioning the "divine right" of priests—the cardinal once again invited them in for a discussion—this time to his home in Lachine. It was, Pelletier recalled, "a friendly encounter"—a mood that would colour their relationship through the momentous Vatican II reform process and in many other meetings until 1967. Then Léger, the prince of the

Quebec church, left his province for Cameroon, to become once again a simple parish priest.[25]

What had happened in Quebec was that the positions of Pelletier and Trudeau, on the one hand, and the cardinal, on the other, had converged. True, there were still some flourishes from the past, as in Trudeau's battle with the bishop of Trois-Rivières. Another occurred when Jean-Paul Desbiens anonymously published *Les insolences de frère Untel*, a strong condemnation of Catholic education in Quebec. André Laurendeau wrote the preface and, in the fall of 1960, he received a severe rebuke from Cardinal Léger for his efforts. The book sold an astonishing 150,000 copies, but, by then, Desbiens had been excommunicated by the church. Here was a cause Trudeau and his colleagues could champion, as in the dark days of the fifties, and *Cité libre* gave Desbiens its "prix de la liberté" to express its solidarity with him.[26]

Unlike many of their now openly agnostic or atheist colleagues, however, Trudeau and Pelletier remained believers. Pelletier admitted as early as October 1960 that he had not realized how weak the Quebec church had become behind its imposing physical structures and powerful traditions. In *Cité libre*, where Quebec Catholic ways were often deplored, Pelletier lamented that "we are proceeding, I believe, towards a spiritual void and a religion without a soul similar to North American Protestantism." Pelletier and Trudeau were not admirers of Abbé Groulx, but they shared his opinion, to some degree, that the spiritual aridity of the Quiet Revolution had created a confusion of ideas and an aggressive secularism.[27]

Trudeau also shared with Pelletier a growing admiration for the reform movement in the Roman Catholic Church that began with the election of Pope John XXIII in 1958.[28] The historic encyclical *Mater et Magistra*, issued on May 15, 1961, reflected many of the intellectual streams, including personalism, which had animated the first meetings between Pelletier and Trudeau as young men in postwar Paris. The Pope's own rhetoric, including his references to the importance of the individual within society and, above all, his call to "open the windows" of Catholicism to the world, bore a strong resemblance to Trudeau's beliefs and writing. And Trudeau found little humour in the mocking of the church that became increasingly common in Quebec in the sixties. However, it was not the blasphemy of the artist or the young, with whom he was otherwise closely allied in spirit and style and concern, that perturbed him most during the winter of 1960–61: it was the increasingly assertive nationalism of Quebec political debate, a nationalism that he came to regard as a substitute for the religious zealotry of the past.

—

Since its November 1960 reorganization under Jacques Hébert, *Cité libre* had become a monthly publication. It had been refinanced with seventy-five shareholders and had created a large administrative committee, including an auditor and an archivist. The larger grouping meant, of course, greater diversity of views. Trudeau and Pelletier, as editors, were troubled as neo-nationalists and separatists on the committee became increasingly vocal and, they believed, too influential.

Curious about what the young thought, they organized a gathering of the "friends" of *Cité libre* at the Université de Montréal on a Saturday morning in the fall that year. The crowd looked much different from those of earlier days. The suits were few, the women far more numerous, beards were everywhere, and separatist slogans were on the notice boards. The students challenged directly, showed little regard for formalities, and clearly demonstrated that the sixties belonged to the young and that those over forty, like Trudeau, would have to prove themselves before they got any respect. His own turtlenecks, sandals, open shirts, and casual jackets no longer seemed bohemian and shocking—even though he often asked his young companion, Madeleine Gobeil, for sartorial advice.[29] There, at the university, Pelletier immediately "noticed the first unequivocal signs of a nationalist renaissance among our juniors." One young woman heckled him and accused *Cité libre* of disregarding French culture in Quebec. He replied that the journal had been culturally nationalist from its first issue but had rejected political nationalism as retrogressive.

Pelletier and Trudeau responded quickly to the charges against them in the pages of *Cité libre* and elsewhere. After he returned from a holiday in Europe, Trudeau drafted an article on nationalist alienation, "L'aliénation nationaliste," which appeared in March 1961 as the lead. He began by declaring that the journal had always displayed a tendency to consider Quebec nationalists as alienated. He replied, at least implicitly, to the young woman at the university that memorable Saturday morning:

> The friends of *Cité libre* were suffering—as much as anyone else, I guess—from the humiliations which afflicted our ethnic group. But as great as the external attack on our rights may have been, still greater was our own incapacity to exercise those rights. For example, the contempt shown by "les Anglais" for the French language never seemed to rival either in extent or in stupidity that very contempt shown by our own people in speaking and teaching French in such an abominable way! Or again, the violations of educational rights of French Canadians in other provinces never seemed as blameworthy or odious as the narrow-mindedness, incompetence, and lack of foresight that have always characterized education policy in the province of Quebec, where our rights were all nevertheless respected. The same could be said for areas where we claimed we were being wronged: religion, finance, elections, officialdom and so forth.

Trudeau went on to castigate separatists who, in the past, "called on the people for acts of heroism . . . on the very people who did not even have the courage to stop reading American comics or to go see French movies." Separatists wanted to close the borders and hand back power to the same elites who were responsible for the "abject state from which separatists were boldly offering to free us." The young separatists might "make fun of the cowards at *Cité libre*" who would not endorse separatism or extreme nationalism. Yet it was they who were unrealistic in not recognizing that they were aligning themselves with the most conservative "interests in the heart of the French-Canadian community." Separatism and neo-nationalism would close off that community, cut off the breath of true freedom. In a conclusion that became a later slogan, Trudeau declared ringingly: "Open up the borders, our people are suffocating to death."[30]

—

In the spring and summer of 1961 the atmosphere in Quebec and in Canada worried Trudeau, especially the attraction of separatism to the young. Even his most frequent female companion, Carroll Guérin, wrote to him: "What do you think of the separatist motion? Do you think it will eventually succeed. You probably will disagree, but I have a feeling that it might—so necessary is it for the French Canadians to find an identity and so strong is their conviction that this identity cannot exist interspersed with the English factor." Disagree they did, but on nuclear disarmament they shared the view that it was the greatest problem of all. The times might be exciting, but crisis loomed close by.

In Ottawa, John Diefenbaker's Conservatives were beginning to stumble badly, and they seemed particularly inept in facing the challenge of the new Quebec Liberal government. Diefenbaker's stunning electoral victory in 1958 (in which he won 208 seats, the

Liberals 48, and the CCF 8) had forced the other parties to serious reconsideration of their own position. The Liberals began a policy review in 1960 in which Maurice Lamontagne played a major part and Jean Marchand a minor one.

Trudeau, however, was not drawn to those discussions; his ties on the federal level were far closer to the Co-operative Commonwealth Federation, which had now decided to re-establish itself as the New Democratic Party. Trudeau's ties with English Canada politically were almost exclusively with CCF intellectuals, notably Frank Scott, Eugene Forsey, Michael Oliver, and, in the 1960s, the philosopher Charles Taylor. He developed further links after he met the historian Ramsay Cook at a friend's wedding, and Cook soon invited him to contribute to the CCF-leaning *Canadian Forum*. The purpose in creating the NDP was to connect the party more closely with organized labour, an objective Trudeau had supported in both the Quebec and the Canadian context throughout the fifties. Yet, when that merger occurred, he hesitated to make an open commitment to the new socialist party.[31]

Jean Marchand later claimed that he had dissuaded Trudeau from this tie in the fifties because there were more immediate problems, such as "to get rid of Duplessis." After Maurice Duplessis fell and the CCF transformed itself into the more urban NDP, Marchand said it became a problem of conscience for them. Normally, he and Trudeau, as labour champions on the left, would support the CCF-NDP, but, he explained: "It's useless to start building a party with your neighbour and say, 'Well, maybe someday in twenty or twenty-five years we'll have a good party representing exactly our ideologies.' We thought that the NDP could not achieve power even if we had joined the party because a large portion of Quebec would have been opposed to us." He was pragmatic—and no doubt correct.[32]

Trudeau, like Marchand, also knew that Tommy Douglas, the pioneering socialist premier of Saskatchewan and the first NDP leader, was not likely to attract Quebec voters. Moreover, although he admired the intellect and ethics of his fellow voyageur Frank Scott, there were real differences in their approach to the Canadian Constitution and in their understanding of the role of Quebec within Canada. Trudeau was always most generous in acknowledging Scott's influence on him, but, after analyzing some of Scott's theories, he often reached his own, sometimes opposite conclusions. For his part, Scott, much as he respected Trudeau, did not like his acclaimed article "Some Obstacles to Democracy in Quebec."[33] Trudeau was too much a decentralist for Scott's very centralist taste, and his criticisms of the British tradition did not have the approval of the professor—a man of proud Anglo-Canadian heritage and bearing. In debates with Scott in which other francophones participated, Trudeau rejected nationalism in the same breath that he expressed doubts about the centralizing policies of Canada's socialists.

Despite these disagreements, Frank Scott and Michael Oliver had asked Trudeau to contribute an article to *A Social Purpose for Canada*, a book sponsored by the CCF.[34] Trudeau joined the editorial committee of the project in 1958, along with Frank Scott; Eugene Forsey, the research director for the Canadian Congress of Labour; George Grube, a University of Toronto professor; and David Lewis, an official with the CCF. Like the Asbestos project, the book dragged on; Trudeau was the laggard this time, with his essay on the practice and theory of federalism finally arriving in May 1960.

Michael Oliver, who was the editor for the volume, did not like the essay and commented harshly. He accused Trudeau of overstating his argument and of being imprecise, because he often "used" politics rather than political science.

The complaint has some merit, for Trudeau's writings are not those of the academic political scientist or university intellectual. He wrote for broader audiences and avoided the heavy apparatus of scholarship, a fact that his academic foes often criticized.[35] Moreover, Oliver claimed that Trudeau's argument in favour of decentralization was contradicted by his call for an activist state. He was especially puzzled by Trudeau's statement that he was an "outside observer" of the CCF. In fact Trudeau was,* even though he participated in campaigns and, occasionally, held party membership cards. He regarded the CCF, correctly, as the federal party that had consistently advanced civil liberties and argued for greater economic equality. Those views he shared. Yet the party was too English, and his approach to federalism was different, particularly after the NDP began to flirt with Quebec nationalism and the "two nations" approach to Canadian federalism in 1963.[36]

The NDP was one example of how, in 1961, Trudeau was generally wary of committing to any binding ties. His *Cité libre* articles betrayed his general discontents. He was now over forty years old—in a decade that the young tried to dominate. Most of his friends were married with children. His hair was thinning, and his worried mother told him to try the remedy of

---

* Trudeau, along with Frank Scott's son Peter, did not demonstrate the earnestness of many socialists in the fifties. Their efforts in one of Thérèse Casgrain's campaigns consisted of "driving recklessly around Montreal in Trudeau's open sports car with a bull horn. They regaled passers-by with CCF slogans in two languages, vying with each other in a public display of witty bilingualism, with Scott concocting the French sentences and Trudeau embellishing the English." Stephen Clarkson and Christina McCall, *Trudeau and Our Times.* vol. 1: *The Magnificent Obsession* (Toronto: McClelland & Stewart, 1990), 88.

standing on his head.[37] His plans for the political role he had so long desired seemed to have misfired, while others among his friends, such as René Lévesque and Paul Gérin-Lajoie, were dominating headlines as political actors and changing their society. He often felt disenchanted and at loose ends.

In the winter of 1961 he busied himself with publication of the book on the China trip. He dithered over the invitation list to the March launch and personally wrote out the addresses of more than two hundred people he and Hébert invited. This invitation list provides insight into his connections and friendships at the time.[38] The invitees were overwhelmingly francophone, with a few anglophones such as Michael Oliver of McGill University and the writer Scott Symons. Frank Scott, interestingly, was missing. René Lévesque was the major politician invited, but apparently he did not come. Thérèse Gouin Décarie and Vianney Décarie did. The old *Cité libre* crowd, including Réginald Boisvert, Maurice Blain, and Guy Cormier, were on the list, and most of them attended. There were new names associated with television and the cultural community. And there were also many single women.

Carroll Guérin, the hopeful artist and occasional model who was now Trudeau's most frequent companion, was there for the celebration. Her candour and liberal lifestyle had immediately attracted Trudeau when he met her in the late 1950s. He was encouraging her to go to Europe to study, promising to join her there in the summer. (When she went to England and applied to the London School of Economics, Trudeau asked his former Canadian classmate Robert McKenzie to assist entry. He did not, and Trudeau learned from Caroll that McKenzie disliked him.) At the book launch, Trudeau also spent time with another invitee, Madeleine Gobeil, who had matured into a brilliant young woman in the four years since Trudeau first encountered her as a teenage student at a meeting of the Rassemblement in Ottawa.

Ambitious, forthright, and visibly young, her beauty, sometimes blonde, at other moments darker, impressed Trudeau's friends whether they saw her on a beach or at the symphony.[39] Their friendship developed into a romantic relationship that endured for well over a decade.*

As the sexual revolution began in the early sixties, women were becoming a preoccupation for Trudeau, but now he shunned the intense relationships of earlier years in favour of multiple involvements. He preferred, in the jargon of the age, "to play the field" or, in Jean-Paul Sartre's description of his own involvement with women, "the theatre of seduction." His female friends complained that he still held back much of himself. One of them

---

* Madeleine Gobeil, who would become Trudeau's most frequent companion until his marriage to Margaret Sinclair in 1971, took part in a *Maclean's* roundtable chaired by Gérard Pelletier in the spring of 1963. The young journalist Peter Gzowski described her on that occasion as fitting "neither the cliché about the shy, family-dominated young *canadienne* who wants only to be married and have a dozen children or the one about the gay, champagne-drinking flirt. She is serious, clever, frank and, above all, emancipated. She is, for example, unafraid to say publicly that she no longer believes in her church." She was, however, the most unambiguously "Canadian" in her comments, saying: "Maybe it's because I come from Ottawa, but I feel I'm more Canadian." However, when asked how they "felt" about English Canadians, she agreed with another participant: "I find [English Canadians] boring too. They have nothing interesting to present. They aren't really very good conversationalists." Peter Gzowski, "What Young French Canadians Have on Their Minds," *Maclean's*, April 6, 1963, 21–23, 39–40. Madeleine claims that she and Pierre rarely discussed religion. He insisted that his faith was a private matter. Interview with Madeleine Gobeil, May 2006.

said his "interior" was closed, but, to Carroll, the shyness that was in itself so attractive made him "emotionally withdrawn."*

Trudeau still officially lived with his mother in the Outremont family home, though he kept his "pad" on Sherbrooke Street. Grace was becoming forgetful and, when he was away, their letters were fewer than they once had been. Her decline had begun, and it saddened Pierre even more than the state of politics in Quebec. They celebrated Christmas and other festive times together with Tip, Suzette, and their families, and, as always, Trudeau entranced the children with his shy charm and endless athletic tricks—jackknife dives, headstands, and dramatic leaps. Suzette still lived close to her mother and was devoted to the family.

The summer of 1961 brought huge changes in their careers for Trudeau and his friends. A surprised Gérard Pelletier eagerly accepted an offer to become the editor of *La Presse*, and Jean Marchand agreed to become the head of his union, the Confédération des syndicats nationaux (CSN). The outsiders were moving inside. While Trudeau had been in China, the rector of the Université de Montréal had called Grace, "terribly anxious" to speak with him about a teaching position there. Ironically, although he had long complained about his enforced exile from

---

* Carroll herself was not shy, and her lively exchanges with Pierre capture his charm for women as well as his weaknesses. After she called him in Montreal, she wrote to him on June 18, 1962: "How thrilled I was to speak to you a couple of hours ago! I am still under the effect, and practically phoned you back to tell you how glad I was but thought that you probably would not appreciate it if I reversed the charges again."[40] She advised Trudeau on the furnishing of his flat and often joined him as he carefully selected his stylish clothing. She also persuaded him to buy his exquisite Mercedes 300SL convertible. Conversation with Carroll Guérin, Dec. 29, 2006.

the Université de Montréal by the Catholic Church and now had the opportunity he craved, he did not really welcome it. The times had changed. The classroom, which had earlier beckoned, no longer seemed an attractive haven. Initially he turned down an appointment to the Institute on Public Law there, but then half-heartedly accepted an associate professorship at the law school itself (with a cross-appointment to the Institute)—an institution he had scorned as a student and as a lawyer. Once the arrangements were in place, he promptly left for Europe.

Trudeau ran with the bulls in Pamplona—a mad and daring act—met Carroll Guérin in Rome, and went to the jazz festival at Juan-les-Pins on the Riviera, where he and Carroll heard the young star Ray Charles and the jazz legend Count Basie.* They stayed in a small hotel somewhere on the Mediterranean. The days were unforgettable; the parting difficult. "When you said goodbye to me this morning," she wrote later that day, "do forgive me for asking you to go, but as you know, I felt so very sad at the thought we were going to be separated again that I did my best to avoid a scene on the street—without too much success. Funnily enough, the little maid who opened the door was in tears herself, so we happily skipped the ladida." After giving Carroll some funds to purchase some art for him as she returned to student life, Trudeau

---

* In 1968 the celebrated Canadian artists Michael Snow and Joyce Wieland organized a "Canadians in New York for Trudeau" meeting in that city, where they were living. They had a jazz trio with the drummer Milford Graves. Snow introduced Graves to Trudeau as "the greatest drummer in jazz today." Trudeau shook Graves's hand, saying, "Oh! Well, what about Max Roach." Graves was not insulted but astonished at Trudeau's knowledge of jazz. Michael Snow in Nancy Southam, ed., *Pierre* (Toronto: McClelland & Stewart, 2005), 125.

travelled eastwards alone and visited the massive palace in Split, Yugoslavia, where Diocletian went to escape the declining, decadent Rome. Like Diocletian, he grumbled to others about the state of his homeland and even mused about staying in Europe.[41]

Back at home, Grace Trudeau worried about her son. On September 5, 1961, she wrote: "By now your peregrinations are finished, or coming to an end—it was labor day yesterday—schools reopening—so the professors are expected to take their duties." On September 25 she wrote again, pleading for him to come home: "Four months is a long stretch! Your Mercedes is raring to go."[42]

Obviously, Trudeau had prepared little for his classes, with the inevitable result that he had to work very hard when they began. George Radwanski later described Trudeau's work habits in his pre-political years: "He laboured intensely at whatever he happened to be doing and he did quite a variety of things, but—with the exception of *Cité libre*—he always gave the impression of doing it with one foot in and one foot out, poised to move on to something else."[43] Certainly Trudeau was not ready to settle in the classroom. A few years later he said that when he arrived at the university, he "found a rather sterile atmosphere; the terminology of the Left was now serving to conceal a single preoccupation: the separatist counter-revolution."[44]

Through the winter of 1961–62 he began to seethe as the Lesage government became more neo-nationalist and the young called the founders of *Cité libre* dinosaurs. *Cité libre* itself was not immune, as both the younger and older members of its expanded board challenged its traditional aversion to nationalism, its criticism of socialism, and its virulent opposition to separatism. In April Trudeau complained to a friend that he was often working till midnight at the university and was mostly unhappy. He wanted to be in a warm country in the sun with the sea nearby: "Truly," he said, "everything is detestable in Quebec."[45]

That spring Peter Gzowski came to Montreal to experience

the new excitement and discovered the remarkable "engaged intellectual" Pierre Trudeau. (The photograph on this book's cover was included with the article.) In a profile of Trudeau that he published in the French- and English-language *Maclean's*, he described him as an "angry young man" who directed his eloquent scorn at the separatists' "dead causes." Trudeau gave credit to the reforms of the Lesage government, he said, but declared how much better it would be if they had more government members like René Lévesque with energy and talent. And, Gzowski continued: "He was caught tossing snowballs at Stalin's statue—*before* stoning Stalin was fashionable." Here Trudeau becomes a turtle-necked, intellectual celebrity: a millionaire professor with an exquisite sense of fashion, a classic Mercedes sports car, an apartment on elegant Sherbrooke, and a pied-à-terre at his mother's "large house" in Outremont. Trudeau was also an excellent athlete, orator, and "a connoisseur of fine wines and women. He created a sensation," Gzowski continued, "when he decided to swim in the pool when it snowed at one of the meetings of the Institut des affaires publiques at Ste-Adèle." The articles attracted considerable public attention to Trudeau in Quebec and in English Canada. He later claimed that he was offered an English CBC television position at this time, perhaps as a result of the article.[46]

—

That same month, Trudeau published another article in *Cité libre*, "The New Treason of the Intellectuals"—probably the most influential essay he wrote in the 1960s. His target was direct: Quebec separatism and nationalism and their prophets, "the clerks"—the Quebec intellectuals. He took his title from a 1927 polemic by Julien Benda, who had fought the trend towards conservatism and nationalism in the 1920s in France, as Benda opposed Maurras and other authoritarians Trudeau had once admired. His anger spilled over as he made five fundamental arguments that became central to his stance in political debates in the 1960s.

First, he wrote, "it is not the concept of *nation* that is retrograde; it is the idea that the nation must necessarily be sovereign." Second, he responded to the best-selling 1961 book *Pourquoi je suis séparatiste* by Marcel Chaput, a federal government employee, which resulted in Chaput's dismissal and a political fury among Quebec nationalists. Chaput, Trudeau argued, was dead wrong in suggesting that the experience of decolonization in Africa and Asia had relevance for Quebec. Chaput himself had admitted that "French Canada enjoys rights these people never did." Many of these newly independent states were poly-ethnic, as was Canada. They were not homogeneous nations but multi-ethnic countries where minorities dreamed of the rights French-speaking Canadians had long possessed. Woodrow Wilson's "Principle of Nationality," just like the decolonization movement itself, had never been intended to create a wave of nationalist secessions.

Third, Trudeau continued, for most of history there had been no nations; however, since the rise of the nation-states in the previous two hundred years, the world had witnessed "the most devastating wars, the worst atrocities, and the most degrading collective hatred." There would be no end to wars "until in some fashion the nation ceases to be the basis of the state." Fourth, history taught that "to insist that a particular nationality must have complete sovereign power is to pursue a self-destructive end . . . every national minority will find, at the very moment of liberation, a new minority within its bosom which in turn must be allowed the right to demand its freedom." Fifth, Anglo-Canadians "have been strong by virtue of our weakness," not only in Ottawa but also in Quebec City. In both places, the politicians had been marked by political cynicism and the political system by "the pestilence of corruption." Had English-speaking Canadians "applied themselves to learning French with a quarter the diligence they have shown in refusing to do so, Canada would have been effectively bilingual long ago."

Too much energy had therefore been wasted on worthless quarrels. The "treason of the intellectuals" arose from their propensity to fight such quarrels and to waste hours of each day discussing separatism. These discussions amounted to no more than an aimless flapping of the arms in the wind. Nationalism in Quebec was reactionary. In a battle, the right-wing nationalists, from the village notary through the small businessman to the members of the Ordre de Jacques Cartier, would always triumph over the new left-wing nationalists, who dreamed of nationalizing and using the state to secure benefits for the emerging French-Canadian bourgeoisie. The existing Canadian Constitution already gave full scope to Chaput, or the young separatists, to carry out the reforms they wanted and to have the "inspiration" they craved. To a young poet who had said that a new state of Quebec would make him "capable of doing great things," Trudeau replied: "If he fails to find within himself, in the world about him and in the stars above, the dignity, pride and other well-springs of poetry, I wonder why and how he will find them in a 'free' Quebec."

The "nation" guards a heritage, he continued; it does so principally through a Constitution and a federal system that protect a pluralistic and "poly-ethnic society." Those matters with "ethnic" relevance—education, language, property, and civil rights—were already within the power of the province of Quebec under the existing Constitution. So, he concluded, "French Canadians have all the powers they need to make Quebec a political society affording due respect for nationalist aspirations and at the same time giving unprecedented scope for human potential in the broadest sense."[47]

These arguments remained at the core of Trudeau's response to Quebec separatism and neo-nationalism for the next three decades. Some items changed: he moved away, for example, from his status quo approach to the Constitution. But most fundamentals—bilingualism, a reverence for the role of law, more franco-phone presence in Ottawa, a suspicion of nationalism attached to economic policies, and a stronger state at provincial and federal levels—endured in his speeches, his writings, and his actions. In the spring of 1962 he reiterated them publicly in a debate among André Laurendeau, René Lévesque, Frank Scott, and Jean-Jacques Bertrand, the Union nationale politician and future premier. When Bertrand asked whether Trudeau opposed a project to open up the Constitution and create a "special status" for Quebec, Trudeau answered quickly and unambiguously, "Yes." He believed that the Constitution should be patriated, but he opposed any special status for Quebec that would diminish the other provinces and ultimately lead to the break-up of the federation. In his interview with Peter Gzowski he was scathing: "A nation or people has only so much intellectual energy to spend on a revolution. If the intellectual energy of French Canada is spent on such a futile and foolish cause as separatism, the revolution that is just beginning here can never be brought about."[48]

Trudeau's argument that nationalism reflects bourgeois aspirations at the expense of broader working-class economic interests developed partly from conversations with two young brothers, the sociologist Raymond Breton and the economist Albert Breton—ideas they went on to present in *Cité libre* and elsewhere. Trudeau became particularly attracted to their claim that the new Quebec must focus not on nationalist diversions but on "real" solutions to economic problems—reforms that would improve the lot of all, and not the bourgeois elite alone.

—

Trudeau's anger was real, and his ideas had become more focused. That focus intensified in the course of regular debates that began in the fall of 1961 when René Lévesque, now minister of natural resources in the Lesage government, asked André Laurendeau to organize a group to meet with him every second Friday over the winter (which in Montreal stretches from October into May). Laurendeau in turn invited Jean Marchand, Gérard Pelletier, and Trudeau. Pelletier's Westmount home was the usual meeting place; there, dinner was casual and incidental to the conversation. Trudeau and Marchand usually departed first and left the voluble Lévesque and Laurendeau arguing long into the smoke-filled night. The meetings began with René Lévesque describing events that had occurred during the previous two weeks in Quebec City. Trudeau would await his moment, then pounce on the errors in the stream of consciousness that flowed from Lévesque.

Nevertheless, Trudeau and Lévesque shared many views on the need for Quebec's modernization and, by the mid-winter of 1962, Trudeau had come to respect what Lévesque was doing as a member of the government. However, this amity shattered quickly when Lévesque pressed forward with his campaign to nationalize the hydroelectricity companies, which had long been the symbol of English-Canadian economic dominance in Quebec.[49]

The issue was old; its political impact, new. Neighbouring Ontario had state-owned hydroelectricity, but the rich water resources of Quebec were still largely in private hands. The case to nationalize private electricity production and distribution outside Montreal was clear: rates would be made more uniform throughout the province and the ever-growing needs of industry and consumers would be met. The enormous cost to meet these demands would be shifted to the government, to the society as a whole. Nationalization had both political and economic significance. Even though it had been mentioned briefly in the elaborate Liberal platform of 1960, it had remained dormant. Lévesque became impatient with the constant divisions within the Cabinet over the issue and, in February 1962, went out on his own and launched "Electricity Week"—a public campaign in favour of nationalization. Laurendeau enthusiastically supported it; Lesage, however, was wary and at one point stopped speaking to Lévesque because he had breached Cabinet solidarity. Lévesque became "René the red," a role he played brilliantly during the summer as he struck out against the economic elite. His antagonists inevitably became the Anglo-Canadian business barons, and his arguments ever more nationalist.

In exasperation, Lesage finally organized a Liberal retreat at a chalet at Lac à l'Épaule. He asked George Marler, a minister without portfolio who, in Lévesque's words, spoke "French as well if not better than us . . . [and] represented with exquisite courtesy the most upper-crust of the dominant minority," to put forward the case against nationalization. In striking emotional and physical contrast, the excitable and passionate Lévesque presented the opposite view, with cigarette and hand gestures animating his talk. When they finished, "all eyes were on the premier, only the twiddling of his pencil belying his air of quiet composure." To the astonishment of all, Lesage decided to call an election to settle the issue. The election slogan quickly and historically became "maîtres chez nous"—masters in our own house.[50]

Trudeau immediately dissented on the policy and, especially, the nationalist slogan. At their Friday night meetings, he strongly attacked Lévesque's plans. Both have left an account of their confrontation. Lévesque reconstructed the exchange in his memoirs:

"You say it's going to cost something like $600 million," Trudeau would argue, inviting others to register the enormity of the thing. "$600 million, and what for? To take over a business that already exists. It's just nationalist suspender-snapping. When you think of all the real economic and social progress you could buy with a sum like that!"

"Yes," I'd reply, "but a sum like that doesn't just drop out of the sky for any old project. In the case of electricity, the present assets and the perpetual productivity stand as security. Try to find an equivalent to that."[51]

Lévesque further argued that the control of "such a vast sector of activity" would be "a training ground for the builders and administrators we so urgently needed."

Trudeau's memories are similar. He recalled one night when Lévesque launched into his dream of nationalizing Shawinigan Power just as Premier Godbout had nationalized Montreal Light, Heat and Power during the war years. "I asked," Trudeau recalled, whether it would not be better to spend the money on education: "He said that it would allow us to create managers and to double employment. But I told him I saw the priorities differently, and the argument began about the use of the term nationalization and I said, at least if you can do it, you ought to speak of socialization, not nationalization." Trudeau, unlike Marler and the capitalists, did not object to state ownership of hydroelectricity. Indeed, an article he published that June in the *McGill Law Journal* on "economic rights" went far beyond any of Lévesque's "socialist" appeals in his campaign that summer to have state ownership in the hydroelectricity sector. Trudeau's problem was the nationalist rhetoric surrounding the hydro debate. "What he was afraid of," Lévesque later wrote, "was the mobilizing potential of the word and its power of acceleration, a force one felt might be able to go very far in a society that took a stormy turn." Lévesque had a point.[52]

But Trudeau did too. Trudeau also believed that the highly emotional arguments of the Lesage government were increasingly diminishing both the social scientific and rational analysis of what was best for all citizens in Quebec. Maurice Lamontagne, probably the best-known Quebec economist of the time, shared Trudeau's views: education was a far better investment than the bricks and mortar of a power plant. Albert and Raymond Breton were also opponents who did not accept Lévesque's arguments about the creation of a "cadre" of franco-phone professionals. In their view, the poor, the workers, the shopkeepers, and the widows who also spoke French would pay the price for the creation of that cadre—and so would their children. Nor, in Trudeau's view, was the Lesage government's "politics of grandeur," with its "red carpets in Paris" and pretentious titles and trips, more than a diversion from its proper tasks in improving Quebec's education and infra-structure. Trudeau looked on anxiously as Lesage welcomed the French culture minister, André Malraux, to Quebec like a princely emissary and, in return, accepted invitations to the French presi-dent's palace, where de Gaulle treated him as a honoured and cherished head of state. Trudeau knew Lord Acton's maxim well, and he saw again how power could corrupt.[53]

When Trudeau was asked whether these arguments with René Lévesque broke up the Friday night meetings, he replied, "No, because I was the only one who made them." Gérard Pelletier and Jean Marchand apparently were largely silent. André Laurendeau, the neo-nationalist who had called for simi-lar nationalization two decades earlier, supported Lévesque. The meetings came to an end after two years in November 1963, but, as Pelletier later wrote, it was not because of any particular con-tention at the time. The differences were fundamental, and they had been present at the creation of the meetings in the fall of 1961. But as Lévesque's nationalist fervour grew, the gap became too great to bridge.[54]

In discussing their different points of view, Lévesque's biographer has argued that Trudeau's heart was on the left but his stock portfolio made him fall on the right.* Others, including Frank Scott, Stephen Clarkson, and Christina McCall, believe that Trudeau moved towards free-market liberalism in the 1960s in reaction to nationalism, pointing to the fact that Albert Breton's "public goods" arguments are associated with the free-market neo-classical Chicago school economists. However, Trudeau's public and private writings at the time as well as Breton's contemporary association with the federal NDP undermine such claims. Trudeau's article in the *McGill Law Journal* was a vigorous attack on the liberal concepts of property, and drew on the economist John Kenneth Galbraith and even the Marxist C.B. Macpherson, not on Milton Friedman and Gary Becker of the University of Chicago. Moreover, based on Trudeau's own comments, Gzowski called him a "millionaire

---

* Pierre Godin raised the charge in support of his belief that Trudeau's "portfolio" affected his actions. He pointed out that Trudeau was, frankly, a cheapskate when it came to paying entertainment bills or tipping. Evidence suggests the charge has some validity. Margot Kidder, who dated Trudeau in the 1980s, recalled how she pretended she was going to the washroom after the dinner ended so she could return to the table and leave some additional cash for the waiters—to whom Trudeau had given just a couple of dollars. The bartender at the upscale Troika Restaurant in Montreal in the 1960s remembered an evening when Trudeau came in alone. An apparent friend joined him at the bar. When they appeared ready to leave, the bartender gave the bill to Trudeau, assuming that he was the host. He paid, and both customers left. However, Trudeau quickly returned and rebuked the bartender: "Never again give me a bill unless I ask for it." Yet there are also abundant examples of Trudeau generosity, from his treatment of "poor boy"

socialist." In November 1962 in *Cité libre*, Trudeau described himself as a "man of the left," but one who deplored the lack of realism of the NDP. In the upcoming crucial election, he said, the provincial party was not uniting behind the Liberals and was even considering a candidate to oppose René Lévesque, the voice of the left in the provincial government.

Despite his own opposition to the nationalization of electricity, Trudeau could not understand how any democrat could consider voting against the Liberals, given the unthinkable reactionary alternative. Indeed, he was more supportive of the Liberals in 1962 than he had been in 1960. His major regret after the election was that Lesage would have no "man of the left" to reinforce René Lévesque. He ended with the hope that, after the election, a new Liberal government would express, with more "realism," a genuine politics of the left in Quebec.[55]

—

Gaby Filion in the early forties at school, through François Hertel and Pierre Vadeboncoeur in the fifties. This mixed behaviour does not seem unusual. In a television docudrama aired later, Pelletier asked Trudeau why he was so parsimonious. Trudeau replied that, even when he was a schoolboy at Brébeuf, kids wanted him to pay because they knew he was rich. Trudeau's defensive analysis was almost certainly correct. The biographies of millionaires are replete with similar stories, such as the payphones for guests in Jean Paul Getty's castle. Thérèse Gouin Décarie describes Trudeau's attitude towards money as "confusing," while Madeleine Gobeil says he was an intellectual who was troubled by his millionaire status. Pierre Godin, *René Lévesque: Héros malgré lui* (Montreal: Les Éditions du Boréal, 1994), 118; interviews with Margot Kidder and Jacques Eindiguer; and "Trudeau, the Movie," CBC Television, Oct. 2005.

On November 14, 1962, René Lévesque won his gamble, and Jean Lesage his election. These were fateful, terrifying months. In October the world probably came closest to its destruction when John Kennedy and Nikita Khrushchev went "eyeball to eyeball" over the presence of Soviet missiles in Cuba. When Khrushchev "blinked" and backed down, the Canadian federal government began to come undone. Not a minute too soon, thought Trudeau, Marchand, and Pelletier. Marchand had considered joining the Lesage team for the 1962 election, but, unlike in 1960, Lesage did not extend an invitation this time. One reason may have been an angry televised debate between Marchand and Réal Caouette, the Quebec Social Credit / Créditiste leader, who, in the June 1962 federal election, had won an astonishing twenty-six seats in Quebec and reduced John Diefenbaker's Conservative government to minority status. Jacques Flynn, the Quebec Conservative organizer, correctly analyzed the Social Credit success: "No one had foreseen it . . . it was a protest, period—a vote against."[56] Caouette's success was the strongest pillar in Trudeau's argument that every democrat must vote Liberal in the Quebec election: Caouette represented the broader forces of reaction that threatened to undo the Quiet Revolution that had begun in 1960.*

---

* Indeed, Trudeau's fears were justified. The Gallup polls showed strong Social Credit support in Quebec. Union nationale politician Daniel Johnson wrote to Diefenbaker at the height of the 1963 election on March 8, 1963, predicting that if an election were held that day, the Social Credit party would win "50–55 seats." The letter suggested the continuing support of some Union nationale politicians for Diefenbaker, on the one hand, and Caouette, on the other. Johnson to Diefenbaker, March 8, 1963, Diefenbaker Papers, XII/115/F/281, Diefenbaker Library, University of Saskatchewan.

In the fall of 1962, Jean Marchand, perhaps wounded by Lesage's failure to enlist him for the November election, began to talk quietly with Trudeau and Pelletier about running for the Liberals in the next federal election. It would not be long in coming. John Diefenbaker had quarrelled with Douglas Harkness, his defence minister, who had upbraided him for his hesitation as prime minister to support President Kennedy during the Cuban Missile Crisis. Harkness then set off a Cabinet revolt that, at a meeting around the dining-room table at 24 Sussex Drive, nearly forced Diefenbaker from office. Instead, the government fell, an election followed, and Lester Pearson became prime minister—though in a Liberal minority government.[57]

Lester Pearson's government took office on April 22, 1963, but Jean Marchand, Gérard Pelletier, and Pierre Trudeau were not part of it. In the election, Trudeau had firmly supported the federal NDP because of Pearson's January statement that Canada should respect its previous commitments and accept nuclear warheads from the United States. This stand probably won seats for the Liberals in Ontario and accelerated the demise of Diefenbaker, but it hurt the Liberal cause in Quebec. In Ontario, the historically Tory *Globe and Mail* and Toronto *Telegram* swung behind the Liberals. In Quebec, however, *Le Devoir* and *La Presse* (which Pelletier edited) both supported the NDP opposition to nuclear weapons.

The most vitriolic attacks, however, came in *Cité libre*, where Jean Pellerin, Pierre Vadeboncoeur, and Trudeau condemned Pearson's stand "as part of a nefarious scheme to sell Canada down the river in return for American campaign funds." Trudeau's attack has become legendary, and its virulence has not been exaggerated. Contrary to popular lore, however, he was not the first to describe Pearson as "the defrocked prince of peace." That derisory gem mocking Pearson's Nobel Prize for Peace had been coined by his friend Vadeboncoeur, but Trudeau used it to begin his own essay. "Pope Pearson," he wrote, had decided one morning when eating his breakfast to embrace a pro-nuclear policy and thereby defrocked his own party:

> It mattered little that such a policy had been renounced by the party congress and excluded from its program; it mattered little that the leader acted without consulting with the national council of the Liberal federation, or its executive committee; it mattered little that the Leader forgot to speak to the parliamentary caucus about it, or even to his main advisors. The Pope had spoken; it only remained for the believers to believe.

The nuclear policy itself was contemptible; the "anti-democratic" character of the Pearson decision, intolerable.[58]

Trudeau came close to a conspiracy thesis in interpreting the Pearson action and the fall of the Diefenbaker government. The "hipsters of Mr. Kennedy" had decided that "Diefenbaker must go." You think I dramatize? Trudeau asked.

> But then how do you think politics are done? Do you think it's as a mere tourist that General Norstad, the erstwhile supreme commander of the allied forces in Europe, came to Ottawa on January 3 to publicly summon the Canadian government to respect its commitments? Do you think it's by chance that Mr. Pearson, in his speech on January 12, was able to rely on General Norstad's authority? Do you believe it was by mistake that the State Department passed on to the newspapers, on January 30, a communiqué reinforcing Mr. Pearson's position, in which Mr. Diefenbaker was bluntly treated as a liar? Do you think it's by chance that this communiqué provided the leader of the opposition with arguments he liberally peppered throughout his

speech in Parliament on January 31? Do you believe it was by coincidence that this series of events ended in the fall of the government, on February 5? Well then, why do you think the United States would proceed any differently with Canada than with Guatemala, when reasons of state required it, and circumstances lent themselves to it?

Although Diefenbaker largely supported this interpretation, neither Basil Robinson, his foreign policy assistant at the time, nor Denis Smith, his definitive biographer, agrees. As so often, coincidence and error explain most of what happened. But not all.[59]

The Kennedy administration made its detestation of Diefenbaker known publicly. The contempt for the prime minister's hesitation to endorse Kennedy's ultimatum to the Soviets—a response that was, in Smith's words, "honestly ambiguous in the Canadian tradition"—pervades the reports sent from Ottawa by the American ambassador, W.W. Butterworth. When Trudeau wrote his attack on Pearson, he was troubled about the American influence on Canada. Vadeboncoeur was horrified: he identified "Americanization" with the deadening impact of modern technology on the human spirit. In the April 1963 issue of *Cité libre*, he and Trudeau joined in a virulent attack on the Liberals and, in particular, on Lester Pearson. Trudeau had long considered the prime minister a too willing supporter of American international arrogance.

—

On the nuclear issue, Trudeau's views were shared by Pierre Vadeboncoeur, André Laurendeau, Claude Ryan, René Lévesque, Michel Chartrand, and virtually all his allies and friends of the forties and early fifties. But nationalism and separatism were another matter. In the early sixties, different attitudes on the "national" question were fraying and ending many old friendships. Trudeau's correspondence and writings of the period reveal an erosion of the shared confidences and principles that had long marked good friendships. Sometimes, however, separatist sentiments did not break off relationships. When Carroll Guérin, for example, told Trudeau she thought the "French people" (she was "half French") had an innate need to separate, her views did not affect their summer weeks of cherished intimacy. With men, however, it was different, and Trudeau remained troubled about the number of break-ups that occurred.

On Remembrance Day 1992, Trudeau met with Camille Laurin, an old friend and an Outremont neighbour with whom he had shared long walks in the fifties. Laurin, a psychiatrist, had been the "father" in the 1970s of the Quebec language legislation that made Quebec officially unilingual and deeply offended Quebec federalists. Now, as they sat together again, Laurin recalled that he and Trudeau had once shared "the same goals of modernization and declericalization" and had fought a common "battle for liberty against dictatorship, cynicism, and political immorality." As late as November 1961, Laurin had described separatism in *Le Devoir* as an illness. Using Freudian terms, he claimed that French Canadians saw the English as fathers and, thus, separatism was a form of revenge. Trudeau now asked Laurin what had made him change his mind. Lesage's "revolution," he answered. It had made him realize that federalism would not give Quebec the necessary tools to modernize. Trudeau replied that a strong team in Ottawa would open Quebec to the world while assuring modernization at home. Laurin demurred and pointed to the fate of the francophones in other provinces.[60] It was an old debate, but one that was largely stilled among the young professionals and intellectuals in the fifties by the common political cause they pursued. In the sixties, their common goals dissolved in political difference.

Pierre Vadeboncoeur and François Hertel had been closer friends to Trudeau than either Pelletier or Marchand. Their increasing disagreements on the "national" issue, however, shattered the ties of friendship as Vadeboncoeur began to embrace nationalism, then separatism, and an ever more militant socialism. Vadeboncoeur placed the break in 1963–64, as the slogans of Quebec separatism burst out of university classrooms and bars, where students and fringe politicians met, and exploded into the mainstream of public debate. He recalled the moment when he decided that Trudeau and Pelletier were blind to the forces animating the young and the future. They were, he wrote, not "brutes" but simply blind: "Mr. Pelletier responded to me when I spoke of the existence of a current leading to independence: 'But what current?'"[61]

Vadeboncoeur believed that he and Trudeau took different paths mainly because Trudeau's approach to political understanding drew so much on the law. In the 1940s, at law school, they had both regarded the law as a conservative force. They despised the law even as they dreamed of revolution, staged political theatre, and searched the streets at night for poetry and romance. Trudeau, he said, failed to understand the new world after 1960, one that was infected with "a massive contagion of political ideas, notably among the poets, the artists, and the best intellectuals of the country," a contagion so powerful that the general population caught its exceptional strain. As they drifted apart, Vadeboncoeur was initially sad, wistful, and respectful of his friend's integrity.

In 1970, as criticism of Trudeau's intellectual honesty abounded, Vadeboncoeur came to his defence, stating that he "did not have the least hesitation in affirming that Trudeau had not betrayed his beliefs . . . but, to the contrary, he had remained scrupulously faithful to his beliefs." Inevitably some bitterness came later, when he began to write bluntly about Trudeau, the destroyer of so many dreams. Trudeau himself was mostly silent, but he placed exclamation marks beside a 1963 press clipping that described Vadeboncoeur as by far the most radical member of a panel on separatism and socialism. As they parted ways, Vadeboncoeur paid back the money his closest friend had lent him over the years. Two middle-aged men were left with their memories of a shared childhood on the streets and alleys of Outremont, of the terrifying first days at Brébeuf, of the hilarious moment when Vadeboncoeur threw his law notes into the air and declared he was free, and of the secrets they shared when Trudeau came back from Europe in 1949. Thirty years after they separated, Trudeau paid a final personal tribute to his old friend, by then a major literary figure. He wrote in his memoirs that it was Vadeboncoeur who had taught him to write good French.[62] It was a lasting gift that estrangement could never efface.

If Vadeboncoeur had been one of Trudeau's closest male friend of adolescence and youth, François Hertel was his principal mentor in those days. Later, they had met frequently in Paris, where Hertel edited a journal on the writings of the French diaspora to which even Grace Trudeau subscribed. The rise of separatism after 1960 stirred Hertel's old sympathies and aroused new hopes. In the winter of 1963 he wrote an essay, "Du séparatisme Québécois," in which he recalled for readers his statement in 1936 that "one day, separation will come." Now, finally, Quebec was preparing to leave Canada and was creating "a solid bloc" in which its intellectual, artistic, and social life would flourish "in a rediscovered security and serenity." There was no serenity as Trudeau marked the essay with nine exclamation marks, one question mark, numerous underlined passages, and one illegible comment that reacted to Hertel's statement that even a Swiss-style decentralization, which he had held out as a last option thirty years before, was no longer possible.

The essay displeased Trudeau immensely, but he was outraged when students at the Université de Montréal published an article by Hertel in *Le Quartier Latin* in April 1964. André Laurendeau, a nationalist but also an eloquent opponent of separatism, had agreed to co-chair the Royal Commission on Bilingualism and Biculturalism that Pearson established soon after he took office. Laurendeau's new role was too much for Hertel. He wrote: "If you want to assassinate someone, assassinate a traitor, someone who is celebrated among us—that would be the perfect blow. For example, deliver from existence poor, bored Laurendeau, a prematurely old man who is also obscene." In *Cité libre* in May 1964, Trudeau lashed out against Hertel. He accused him, in a biting comment, of being a Torquemada about to begin an inquisition. He profoundly regretted that Hertel, whom he had long respected for his refusal to conform, had chosen to enter "into the separatist chapel." In a Quebec where terrorists were becoming heroes and the collectivity was once again being idolized, Hertel's words were thoroughly "irresponsible," as was *Le Quartier Latin* for publishing them.[63]

Hertel protested to Trudeau and others—ingenuously, given the tensions of the times—that he was being metaphorical and that he actually detested violence. Yet a chill had entered his relationship with Trudeau and, eventually, it froze nearly all contact. Like Pierre Vadeboncoeur, Hertel later came to Trudeau's defence when others questioned his sincerity. While dismissing Pelletier derisively as a "boy scout," Hertel echoed Vadeboncoeur in suggesting that Trudeau's failure to share their beliefs derived from his excessive focus on the law: "In the case of Trudeau, whom I know well, it's another matter. He's a jurist, one who, in my view, has become imprisoned in a formula that he would do well to enlarge. A little British by birth too."

The last comment no doubt further infuriated Trudeau. In fact, while favouring independence, Hertel did later became concerned about some of its violent physical and verbal expressions, and he loathed the "Communism" of some of its most vociferous supporters. As they drifted apart, he and Trudeau still apparently exchanged casual notes. When Hertel returned to Canada in the eighties, he was wistful about the past and suspicious of the direction the young had taken in the 1960s in literature and in life. He died in 1985 and, to the surprise of all, had a religious funeral, which Camille Laurin and Pierre Trudeau attended together.[64]

Hertel and Vadeboncoeur were correct in their sense that Trudeau's interests were no longer strongly literary, as they had been in his early forties.* The strong literary preoccupation of his youth had waned. As a professor at the Université de Montréal he had joined the Groupes des Recherches Sociales, and his own writings reflected his increasing interest in social science and law, especially the intersections between the two. In June 1963 he wrote to an Ontario friend in reply to a letter sent a year earlier. The delay, he said, resulted from the strain he had been under. He declined the friend's request to "tour" Canada to explain the "French-Canadian point of view" because he was leaving for Europe and North Africa: "The past year has been a mad one: lectures & research at the University, my office, *Cité libre*, civil

---

* Trudeau and Vadeboncoeur continued to share their enthusiasm for labour matters. Although Trudeau, unlike Vadeboncoeur, was not a full-time labour organizer in the 1960s, he spent untold hours drafting a brief that incorporated labour's views for the constitutional committee established by the Quebec National Assembly in May 1963. The brief reflected Trudeau's hesitation about "opening up" the Constitution as well as his support for instituting a bill of rights. This work prepared him exceedingly well for the debates about the Constitution in the following decade. For his overall opinions on these issues, see his essays "We Need a Bill of Rights" and "Quebec and the Constitutional Problem" in Gérard Pelletier, ed., *Against the Current: Selected Writings, 1939–1996* (Toronto: McClelland & Stewart, 1996), 214–16, 219–28.

liberties, peace research, and all that. It is not too serious that I do not answer letters; but it is serious when I find no little time for legal studies. I hope to find a way next fall to barricade myself up in the University."[65]

He did not barricade himself, not least because it was the leftist and separatist students who were building barricades he wanted to tear down. Far more satisfying was the time he spent at cafés near his Sherbrooke apartment with Madeleine Gobeil, who was now teaching at a Montreal classical college where she found, to her dismay but not to Trudeau's surprise, "a whole generation of people my age who, instead of working and becoming competent in their own field, sit around discussing things like separatism." Albert Breton, the most impressive young francophone economist of his generation, with links to some of the leading international economists of the age, was present when Madeleine made that comment. Now, when asked whether his first allegiance was to Canada or to Quebec, he always described himself as a "North American." And although Trudeau was critical of American politicians, he was increasingly attracted to American social science and intellectual debates. In the early 1960s his social thought increasingly reflected the arguments about countervailing powers and the poverty of the public sector set out by John Kenneth Galbraith, whose book *The Affluent Society* was a bestseller.

Over the winter of 1963–64, Trudeau joined with the Breton brothers, Montreal lawyer Marc Lalonde, sociologist Maurice Pinard, lawyer Claude Bruneau (who had worked for Conservative Justice Minister Davie Fulton), and psychoanalyst Yvon Gauthier to investigate why, in Trudeau's words, separatists wanted "the whole tribe [to] return to the wigwams." That, Trudeau further argued, "will not prevent the world outside from progressing by giant's strides; it will not change the rules and facts of history, nor the real power relationship in North America."

In May 1964 *Cité libre* published their manifesto "Pour une politique fonctionelle," which appeared simultaneously in a translation by Montreal lawyer Michael Pitfield in the *Canadian Forum* under the title "An Appeal for Realism in Politics." The authors revealed their legal and social scientific training as they deplored the lack of realism in Quebec politics, the absence of political leadership, and the government's refusal to deal with economic problems. In making their case for "the free flow of economic and cultural life," they rejected "the idea of a 'national state' as obsolete" and announced their refusal "to let ourselves be locked into a constitutional frame smaller than Canada." Trudeau's new friends helped him find a different approach through "functional politics." As so many old friends marched off under a new nationalist banner, Trudeau took a different turn.[66]

CHAPTER 9

—

POLITICAL MAN

On an early spring morning in Westmount in 1963, René Lévesque, Gérard Pelletier, and André Laurendeau were still at the Pelletiers' table at 2 a.m. Trudeau and Jean Le Moyne had left earlier. Out of cigarettes but still brimming with thoughts, Laurendeau and Lévesque had a last cup of coffee. Suddenly, an explosion ripped through the silence outside. "It's a FLQ bomb," said Laurendeau, blaming the Front de libération du Québec, a loose organization created earlier that year to bring about an independent Marxist state through violence. "No, no," Lévesque retorted, "it's an explosion in the Métro," the subway system then under construction in Montreal. Laurendeau disagreed: "I recognize the sound. They planted one not far from my place last month." Alec Pelletier descended the stairs and was decisive: "It's a bomb." Another explosion, and this time even Lévesque began to doubt his Métro explanation. The FLQ found mailboxes an easy target—where else could they drop a package and not look suspicious?

The three journalists—one now a Cabinet minister, another an eminent editor, the third a political and media icon—set out in search of a big story. With Alec still cloaked in her elegant dressing gown, they soon found a grocery store whose windows had shattered, leaving a wall of cigarette packages completely exposed: "What luck, René," Alec declared. "Just help yourself."

With the scent of smoke and the thrill of the chase intense, the men set off to find the source of the other explosion. Oblivious to danger, they drove close to a mailbox where another bomb lay, but, fortunately, that explosion would come later in the morning. As crowds milled around the splintered glass, Pelletier kept an astonished silence. Lévesque was divided in his response, critical, yet admiring: "You've got to hand it to them—they're courageous, those guys." Laurendeau became reflective: "It's incredible," he mused. "When I was twenty I used to call on a girlfriend in this part of town. I never dreamed that such things could happen here. Absurd, isn't it?"[1]

In fact, 1963 was often an astounding year—of mailbox bombs, the rising FLQ, and the assassination of John F. Kennedy. After Kennedy's death in the Dallas afternoon of November 22, Laurendeau, Trudeau, Pelletier, Lévesque, and Marchand had the last of their meetings that evening. Lévesque mourned the president's death profoundly, "as if the crime had wiped out a member of *his* family." Trudeau was analytical, pondering other American presidential assassinations, while Laurendeau deplored the violence that, in the argot of the 1960s, seemed as American as apple pie. Their different reactions to Kennedy's death reflected their varying reaction to the equally stunning changes in Quebec. Throughout the year, René Lévesque had been making explosive comments about the future of Quebec within Canada. He had begun to reflect publicly about Canada being composed not of ten provinces but of two nations. He often mused about the possibility of separation if the federation failed to reform itself. He startled an admiring Toronto audience when he described Confederation as an "old cow" that had to change or Quebec would leave. When asked by the television host Pierre Berton whether he would be greatly troubled if Quebec left the Confederation, Lévesque replied: "No, I wouldn't cry long." The controversial comments and casual quips that boldly flirted with separation did not escape the notice of Laurendeau and Trudeau.[2]

Laurendeau was deeply troubled. Though nationalist in his views, he was nevertheless becoming identified as a "federalist" committed to the reshaping of the Canadian Confederation. In September 1961 he had bluntly stated his position in *Le Devoir*: "Independence? No: a strong Quebec in a new federal Canada." Soon after, as John Diefenbaker's Conservative government crumbled in Ottawa, Laurendeau called for the creation of a commission that would study and report on the creation of a new bilingual and bicultural federation. Diefenbaker said no, but Liberal opposition leader Lester Pearson endorsed Laurendeau's proposal in one of his speeches.

When Pearson took office in April 1963, he moved quickly to create the commission. After some fumbling, as his weak Quebec colleagues recommended people who commanded no support in Quebec, Pearson turned to Laurendeau and asked him to co-chair the commission he had originally proposed. Laurendeau hesitated at first but consulted widely. Lévesque gave him many reasons to refuse and one odd reason to accept—the "big bang" that Laurendeau's quick resignation from the commission would cause. Still, after a shouting exchange in which Laurendeau declared he was not a separatist and Lévesque replied, "Neither am I," Quebec's most popular politician resigned himself to Laurendeau's chairmanship. In July, Laurendeau met Pearson and accepted the position. He also convinced Jean Marchand to join him as one of the commissioners.[3] The commission hired Michael Oliver of McGill University and Léon Dion of Université Laval as co-directors of research, and they created an ever-swelling research team* for, perhaps, the most significant royal commission in Canadian history.[4]

Trudeau watched these events warily, particularly since he worried about Laurendeau's avowed nationalism. The commission asked him to undertake a study of the role of a "Bill of Rights" in protecting cultural interests.[5] He accepted initially but put it aside as the demands of his university courses, his journalism, and the family business increased after 1963. His mother's health was deteriorating, the manager of the family's business had died, and Tip was now often absent abroad or at his country retreat. He had developed a reputation as a fine architect, but he and Pierre do not seem to have been close after they left Brébeuf. When Trudeau was abroad, his list of correspondents indicates that he seldom wrote to Tip although their affection was still obvious to all when they were together. He saw Suzette often at their childhood home in Outremont, and they bantered as they always had. She was a shrewd financial manager, and Grace and Pierre both valued her advice. Her role at the centre of the

---

* By the fall of 1964, the Royal Commission on Bilingualism and Biculturalism, chaired by André Laurendeau and Carleton University president Davidson Dunton, was, in historian Jack Granatstein's words, "far and away the largest research organization in the country," with eight divisions, forty-eight full- or part-time researchers, and a small army of consultants and students. Besides Marchand and Laurendeau, Trudeau knew well Frank Scott and journalist Jean-Louis Gagnon, who were committee members. The commission's eight members were evenly balanced between francophones and anglophones and included one francophone and one anglophone "ethnic," Professors J.B. Rudnyckyj and Paul Wyczynski (who is, coincidentally, the father of the archivist directly responsible for the Trudeau archive). There was one female member, Gertrude Laing of Alberta, but no Aboriginal member—the cause of much complaint during committee hearings.

family intensified as her mother's health began to fail quickly in the sixties. Trudeau took over more responsibility for the management of finances and, when he was in Montreal, met weekly with his advisers. They included the lawyer Don Johnston, who later joined his Cabinet. Trudeau's "office" was a spare room with a metal desk, filing cabinets, and bare floors located on the burgeoning rue St-Denis. No doubt Trudeau enjoyed lunch in the nearby bistros much more than the accounting details.[6]

Pelletier's demanding work as editor of *La Presse* meant that he had less time to devote to *Cité libre*. And the journal's troubles were many. In the 1950s Trudeau had been a rare voice on the left; now many others had leapt over him, shouting Marxist slogans and scrawling revolutionary mottoes on school corridors and street signs. The intellectual boundaries that *Cité libre* had established in the early 1950s expanded quickly in the early 1960s, to the great distress of the founding editors. In 1963 these boundaries burst. Young members of the *Cité libre* team quit to establish the strongly leftist and nationalist journal *Parti pris*, but not without bitter farewells. In *Cité libre* itself, the twenty-five-year-old journalist Pierre Vallières argued that the founders should realize that the torch should be passed to a younger generation. The original team recognized the strength of the sentiment and, despite Jacques Hébert's doubts, made Vallières "editor" of *Cité libre* in 1963.[7] In the summer issue, not long after the night of the mailbox bombs, Vallières wrote an article on *Cité libre* and his generation. He began with the journal's stirring 1950 declaration of purpose. Those once-young men who had made that declaration were, he cruelly pointed out, "now forty or over." They had fought worthy battles against Duplessis and for the workers in the dark 1950s, but now they felt no need to engage in a "dialogue with the younger group."[8]

In February 1964 Pierre Vallières published another article in *Cité libre* which discussed a speech Walter Gordon, the federal finance minister, had given in Toronto alerting the audience to the "revolution" in Quebec. Vallières scorned this term as a description of events in the province since 1960 because, he argued, there could be no revolution without the destruction of bourgeois capitalism. It was time to choose the streets instead of the salons of Westmount, to prefer action to dreams. Gérard Pelletier, who had known Vallières in 1960 when he was "a member of the Little Brothers of Jesus, a mystic, something of a dreamer," deplored this revolutionary rhetoric. He recognized the creativeness of the revolutionaries, the seriousness of their work, and the important literary efflorescence occurring on the left. Their aims, however, were unacceptable: "a separatism wholly secular and anti-religious, a totalitarian socialism installed by violence, with the inevitable civil war provoked by the systematic agitation of a revolutionary party."[9]

Trudeau was not as polite as Pelletier in his rejection of the incendiary new dreams of youth. A generation earlier, he had mused about revolution himself. When the Catholic Church and Senator Joseph McCarthy excoriated and pursued Communists with terrifying and destructive zeal, he had dared to visit Russia and China and to declare himself a socialist. Now, in May 1964, he rejected any link with the *Parti pris* editors, who had, in their first issue, declared the founders of *Cité libre* "our fathers." He refused to acknowledge these self-declared offspring and attacked Vallières and the new nationalist socialists as separatist "counter-revolutionaries." Deep "upheaval" was characteristic not only of revolutions but also of counter-revolutions, he warned. Think of fascism and Nazism, of Hitler, Mussolini, Stalin, Franco, and Salazar:

> It cannot be denied that they all claimed to be serving the destiny of their respective national communities; further, three of them called themselves socialists. But who would call the whole of their work revolutionary? They upset a

great many institutions, they even opened the way for some material progress; but they abolished personal freedom, or at least prevented it from growing; that is why history classes them as counter-revolutionaries.

And so I get fed up when I hear our nationalist brood calling itself revolutionary. Quebec's revolution, if it had taken place, would first have consisted in freeing man from collective coercions: freeing the citizens brutalized by reactionary and arbitrary governments; freeing consciences bullied by a clericalized and obscurantist Church; freeing workers exploited by an oligarchic capitalism; freeing men crushed by authoritarian and outdated traditions.

That revolution had never occurred, although "around 1960, it seemed that freedom was going to triumph in the end." There were the victories of Roncarelli in the freedom-of-speech case, the retreat of the church from dogmatism, and the entry of previously barred professors into universities. In 1960, he exulted, "everything was becoming possible in Quebec."

A whole generation was free at last to apply all its creative energies to bringing this backward province up to date. Only it required boldness, intelligence, and work. Alas, freedom proved to be too heady a drink to pour for the French-Canadian youth of 1960. Almost at the first sip it went at top speed in search of some more soothing milk, some new dogmatism. It reproached my generation with not having offered it any "doctrine"—we who had spent the best part of our youth demolishing servile doctrinairism—and it took refuge in the bosom of its mother, the Holy Nation.

But the dogmatism of the cleric was giving way to the "zealots in the Temple of the Nation," who, like the authoritarians of the past, "already point their fingers at the non-worshipper." Indeed, in its April 1964 issue, *Parti pris* had acknowledged that there was "a necessary totalitarianism," while attacking Trudeau not for his ideas but because he was rich. Trudeau responded angrily.

He began with a discussion of his own previous and contemporary writings that had praised revolutionary figures in Russia, Algeria, and Cuba. "Genuine revolutionaries" such as Lenin, Ben Bella, and Castro had stressed "collective freedom as a preliminary to personal freedom" in situations where personal freedom had "scarcely been protected at all by established institutions." That was not the case in Quebec: "True, personal freedom has not always been honoured in Quebec. But, I repeat, we had pretty well reached it around 1960." Those who now talked of revolution had not been in the vanguard: "Thanks to English and Jewish lawyers (ah, yes!), thanks to the Supreme Court in Ottawa, personal freedom had at last triumphed over the obscurantism of Quebec's legislators and the authoritarianism of our courts."

Every week, Trudeau complained, "a handful of separatist students" told him they were "against democracy and for a single-party system; for a certain totalitarianism and against the freedom of the individual." Like the most traditional and reactionary individuals, they believed that they possessed "the truth" and all others must follow them. When others didn't, they turned to violence, all the while claiming persecution. In their privileged places "in the editorial rooms of our newspapers . . . at the CBC and the National Film Board," he said, "they lean with all their weight on the mass media." Others went underground to plant bombs and became "fugitives from reality." The separatist "counter-revolution" served mainly to protect the interests of the francophone "petit-bourgeoisie" and the professional classes, who would have diplomatic limousines, offices in the new national bank towers, and tariffs to protect their fragile businesses. "Rather than carving themselves out a place in [twentieth-century industrial society] by ability," Trudeau sneered, "they want to make the whole tribe return to the wigwams by declaring [their] independence."

As this privileged minority gained more status, he warned, society would lose. Algerian rebel Frantz Fanon's *Wretched of the Earth* was a book that militant separatists "kept beside their bed." Trudeau cleverly turned to Fanon to support his assault on the nationalist separatists. In Fanon's own words, "A national *bourgeoisie* never ceases to demand nationalization of the economy and the commercial sectors . . . For it, nationalization means very precisely the transfer to the native population of the favours inherited from the colonial period." Trudeau acidly concluded: "Separatism a revolution? My eye. A counter-revolution; the national-socialist counter-revolution."[10]

Trudeau's angry eloquence erupted not only in this article but also in *Cité libre*'s editorial meetings, where he directly confronted the nationalist and often separatist tendencies of the new editorial team. Pierre Vallières, whom Pelletier also employed at *La Presse*, was a particular target as he became more vigorously separatist and flirted romantically with revolution and the FLQ. In his remarkable autobiographical tract, *Les Négres blancs d'Amérique*, written after he became an FLQ leader committed to the violent overthrow of the state, Vallières described his encounters with Pelletier and Trudeau. Although they rejected his article for a special 1962 issue on federalism, he said, they encouraged him to write for *Cité libre*. Pelletier may even have believed that hiring him in 1963 to write for *La Presse* and later to edit *Cité libre* would restrain his separatist inclinations. Vallières also believed, probably correctly, that his references to the French liberal philosopher Emmanuel Mounier appealed to them and that they did not really understand his broader arguments.

Vallières's views were initially opaque. They became more transparent and unacceptable during 1963, and his efforts to reach out to earlier *Cité libristes*, notably Pierre Vadeboncoeur, who had become a champion of the literary separatists, upset the founders. Then, in March 1964 Vallières and other new voices used *Cité libre* to attack the journal's former editors directly. Some articles mocked them, including a clever satire by the poet and future separatist politician Gérald Godin comparing federalists and separatists to Hurons and Iroquois. In Vallières's opinion, Trudeau and Pelletier believed they had created "a monster." The young, for their part, suddenly realized that "their former idols had become old so quickly." Vallières and several others resigned immediately after this issue appeared. He founded a new review, *Révolution québécoise*, that embraced socialism, separatism, and violence. Two years later, he was in jail charged with terrorism.[11]

Trudeau might quarrel with the young, but he himself remained youthful in his taste and demeanour. He wore turtle-necks at the university, raced his Mercedes through the streets, and sought out younger friends. He was an active member of the anti-nuclear movement and an early opponent of the Vietnam War. On campus, he wore the dove peace symbol as early as 1962, long before it became ubiquitous. Yet he did not share the eccentric François Hertel's fascination with, and approval of, those "who play with dangerous and different ideas" because he believed that the ideas of Vallières and his colleagues were irresponsible and destructive. Perhaps he had once had such notions, as Hertel insinuated in his reply to Trudeau's 1964 attack on him in *Cité libre* after the priest seemed to call for the assassi-nation of André Laurendeau. But the mingling of separatism with nationalism and, more recently, with violence represented to Trudeau a horrid return to an earlier world of extreme nation-alism that had thankfully disappeared. Where Vallières saw echoes of the streets of Algiers or Hanoi, Trudeau saw the Munich beer halls of the twenties and the Nuremberg rallies of the thirties. The gulf between them widened quickly in 1964. His long-time companion Madeleine Gobeil, now living in Paris but still fully engaged in Quebec debates and making a name as a writer, told Trudeau that she would publish in *Cité libre* because it would identify her as anti-separatist. To publish in *Parti pris*, which was much more strongly literary in character, would lead everyone to believe she was a separatist.

Both journals had drawn the line. Trudeau, along with Pelletier and others, once again reorganized *Cité libre* with the intention of making it a journal of opinion that was leftist, secularist, but most decidedly not separatist. The journalist Jean Pellerin remained as editor after Vallières left, and the McGill philosopher Charles Taylor, for whom Trudeau had worked in the 1963 federal election when Taylor was an NDP candidate, became very active in the journal. Yet serious divisions remained: Charles Taylor, Jean Pellerin, and others were sympathetic to nationalist arguments and to the NDP's support for the concept of "two nations." Pelletier and Trudeau were increasingly not.

—

These passionate debates and differences shaped later understandings of what happened in Quebec in the sixties. Was there a profound rupture from the past at the time? What happened to the French Canadian and when did the Québécois appear? What was the meaning of the Catholic past and the socio-political culture of the thirties and forties for the new society that emerged in the sixties? And, above all, what was Quebec's place in Canada?

On the last question, Trudeau had become increasingly clear: Quebec's place lay within a Canadian federal state where individual rights were well defined and the cultural rights of French-speaking Canadians were guaranteed. He differed from André Laurendeau and from his New Democrat friends in his vehement opposition to the concept of "two nations"; he, in contrast, emphasized constitutionally guaranteed individual rights.

While accepting the existence and importance of the French language and culture in North America, he rejected a political definition of "nation" based on "ethnicity." Toronto historian Ramsay Cook, who knew him well in the early sixties, recalled that Trudeau came to believe that democracy in Quebec—a goal he had long cherished—faced one huge danger after the Lesage victory: nationalism. "For Trudeau," Cook wrote, "nationalism was conformist force founded upon conservatism and insecurity. At worst it was totalitarian. Moreover, in the Quebec context, nationalism acted as an emotional substitute for reasoned solutions to real problems." It was, therefore, the young who would lose the future as they sought out some "imaginary Jerusalem" rather than more immediate and useful goals.[12]

In his study of memory and democracy in Quebec, social critic Joseph-Yvon Thériault insists that Trudeau, as an intellectual and a politician, must be understood in the context of Lord Durham's famous report that described two different "nations" in the 1830s. Of Trudeau, he wrote, "His thought as much as his political deeds is structured as a critique and a transcendence of French-Canadian nationalism." In this respect, Pierre Trudeau was very much "a Quebec man of his generation." Like Durham, he identified the quarrel of the French-Canadian people as "a debate about principles between the defence of nationality and liberal values." He believed that the "defence of nationality" had prevented the development of "a true political pluralism" among French Canadians.[13]

In the 1960s Trudeau's thinking on nationalism and politics was increasingly framed in the language and concepts of political science, although he resisted academic and intellectual straitjackets. He became even more interested in what a new friend, the French journalist Claude Julien, termed "the American challenge"—and, indeed, there were echoes of Julien and American social science in the call for functional politics that Trudeau and several other Montreal intellectuals issued in 1964. Julien, a foreign correspondent for *Le Monde* who had been educated at Notre Dame University in Indiana, believed that the technological achievements of contemporary America threatened to leave Europe a fading, second-class continent. On his frequent trips to Paris, Trudeau visited Julien, who—like him, a Catholic on the left—kept wondering what the leftist and statist doctrines would mean for economic progress.

In his attack on the "separatist counter-revolutionaries" that year, Trudeau lamented the price the young in Quebec had paid for ignoring "the sciences and the techniques of the day: automation, cybernetics, nuclear science, economic planning, and whatnot else." Instead of facing the future, a few built bombs, others wrote revolutionary poetry, and the world moved past them. The poets, painters, authors, and songwriters were once again raising the banners of revolution in the coffee houses, the clubs, the streets, and in literary reviews, but, Trudeau believed, many of the younger generation were dangerously closing both their borders and their minds. While he welcomed the progressive reforms of Vatican II, the youth around him mostly ignored the changes and rejected religion itself in favour of alternative secular substitutes.

To get a better perspective on what was happening, Trudeau sought out new voices. The University of Montreal economist Albert Breton shared the same concerns as he and Julien did. They had lunch almost every week in a campus restaurant, where Trudeau revealed a "sweet tooth" along with his extraordinary knowledge of federalism. He could quote *The Federalist Papers* verbatim. Breton, who went on to become one of the world's leading economists in the study of federalism, claims that he "first learned about federalism from [Trudeau] during those lunches." Trudeau began to attract other young intellectuals—such as the lawyer Marc Lalonde and the public servant Michael Pitfield—because of his generosity in expressing his own ideas.

They also had their good times and laughed easily together: on one occasion as a few of them journeyed to the annual meeting of the Canadian Political Science Association in the Maritimes, they decided to indulge in the local delicacy and ordered lobster at a roadside restaurant. Bitter was their disappointment when it came in sodden lumps from a can.[14]

Separatism itself did not lead immediately or always to a break in personal relations; when Trudeau visited Paris, for instance, he always saw François Hertel, who had openly embraced separatism at the beginning of the sixties. He even welcomed the new nonconformism of the youth in Quebec, which expressed itself in a riotous abundance of facial hair, T-shirts, and mini-skirts in Montreal's lively bars and bistros. Moreover, like the rebellious young, he retained a Parisian's disdain for American foreign policy and materialism, particularly the Vietnam War and nuclear policy. The problem was not the non-conformity of the young—he relished and personally represented individualism in taste—or the sixties amalgam of sex, drugs, and rock and roll. He much enjoyed the first, tolerated but did not participate in the second, and danced superbly to the third. Rather, it was the conformity of the young that bothered him enormously, particularly at the university, where the students were overwhelmingly separatist. Most serious, in his view, was their unwillingness to consider alternative views and, in the case of the FLQ, their deadly seriousness. "Would Quebec miss the turn?" he had asked in 1960 on the eve of the Liberal victory. As he listened to students with their dreams of an "imaginary Jerusalem," he feared that, once again, it had.

Trudeau therefore shared Julien's sense that American energy and technology were transformative and that Canada was fortunate to share a continent with such a dynamic force for change. In the same vein, Quebec was blessed to be part of the prosperous and vital Canadian federation. Despite doubts about the influence of

American investment that he had first expressed in the 1950s, he even accepted parts of Julien's strained argument that Canada, with its openness through that investment to American technology and creativity, was "Europe's last chance."[15]

Trudeau no longer read much Quebec fiction—which increasingly played to Quebec nationalism. Gérald Godin, Hubert Aquin, Michel Tremblay, Jacques Godbout, and others who formed the cultural base of the nationalist and separatist efflorescence of the mid-sixties all annoyed Trudeau in their use of the colloquial "joual," their polemical rejection of the past, and, above all, their profound political irresponsibility, as he saw it. Although chansonniers like Gilles Vigneault and Félix Leclerc touched his romantic core, he reacted uneasily to the marriage of the cultural avant-garde to separatism and its flirtation with violence. In a different sense, he opposed the attempt by academic sociologists, notably by his old friend Marcel Rioux (now a separatist), to treat francophone Quebec residents sociologically—a path that led directly to the distinctiveness that, in his view, found political expression in separation.[16]

Following the "purge" at Cité libre and the publication of the statement on functional politics, Trudeau became increasingly distressed about the more explicitly nationalist direction of the Lesage government. He simultaneously worried that Lester Pearson's government in Ottawa was badly advised on constitutional matters and too weak to respond to the aggressive demands for jurisdiction and dollars from Quebec City. In his articles and in letters or comments to some of his closest friends—Carroll Guérin and Madeleine Gobeil, both now in Europe, and Marc Lalonde and Jacques Hébert—he expressed despair about the state of Canadian affairs and fretted over the best way to respond. Although he had never much admired Pearson, he had come to believe that Lesage was actually a weak leader who had lost control of his government. What should he do in these circumstances?

Trudeau realized that columns in *Le Devoir* or rants in *Cité libre* reached few of the workers in shops, in factories, or on farms who would make the final choice on the issue. Confrontations with his students in the classroom were also unsatisfying. He began to place his hope in television, which was entering a golden age of public affairs broadcasting. In 1964 he tried to negotiate an agreement with the CBC to become a host for the *Inquiry* series. The negotiations failed. Carroll Guérin summarized his sad lot in the early winter of 1965: "Correcting exams must be a huge bore; but I guess it is part of the price one has to pay for teaching. What a pity the TV thing proved to be a flop. It goes to show that our apprehensions were not without reason. It is a pity that entertainment is placed before *ideas*—but what can you expect from Toronto."[17]

Laurier LaPierre, a McGill University historian, became the Quebec intellectual who charmed English Canadians in 1965, alongside Patrick Watson, on *This Hour Has Seven Days*, a Sunday night program that shocked both the government and its audience. But Trudeau became a frequent participant in seminars and other academic gatherings as Canadians tried to understand what the tempests of change would bring. In 1964 the federal Parliament bitterly debated a new flag for Canada, one that would not bear the traditional British symbols. Carroll Guérin detested the design; Trudeau dismissed it as a trifle. In October 1964 riots broke out as the Queen made the last royal visit to Quebec City, not long after another English institution, the Beatles, made a more successful imperial progress across North America. The times, the American folk artist Bob Dylan rightly declared, were "achangin.'" But not always happily, it sometimes seemed, for Trudeau. His enemies appeared to be multitudinous, and Malcolm Reid summarized their reasons in his book about the literary and political radicals of mid-sixties Montreal:

What *Partipristes* could not forgive Trudeau, what seemed to them false and treacherous in his demolition of theocracy, was his cool, assured tone. How could he live in the smothering of liberty and not cry, not scream, not scribble on walls, not take to drink or dynamite? Such calm could come only from a basic cosiness with the very English money which paid for this reign of darkness, an Anglo-Saxon confidence that all would be straightened out when the French-Canadians learned engineering, business administration and behaviorist labour relations.[18]

The critique was unfair, but not entirely incorrect. Even if Peter Gzowski had described him—admiringly—as an "angry young man," Trudeau had learned to control his internal rage and to present himself to the world with a "cool, assured tone." In his self and in his politics, he was determined to be "functional," just like the architectural style—lean, international, and modern. And that style increasingly impressed those who came into contact with him, in person, through the press, or on television. Trudeau, a leading francophone professor told Ramsay Cook in 1964, was "the most talented intellectual in Quebec," but, alas, one whose talents were not fully exploited.[19] That situation was about to change.

—

The fourth year of the Quiet Revolution began with the Armée pour la libération de Québec, one of the several fringe separatist groups, announcing its intention of liberating the province by force within two years—a declaration punctuated on January 30, 1964, when an ALQ group stole a truckload of arms and ammunition, including anti-tank missiles, from the armouries of the Fusiliers de Montréal. Further raids on defence installations occurred on February 15 and February 20.

Editorialists debated whether the Queen should stay home as rumours of a murder plot circulated. "Are we savages?" Lorenzo Paré asked in *L'Action*. During the royal visit, the police struck the separatists down with truncheons. The *Globe and Mail* reacted as the separatists hoped when it declared that "Canada has walked to the edge of crisis and in many ways its performance has been appalling." Trudeau had no love for the British monarchy, but he agreed: events were spinning out of control.[20]

In 1964 Abbé Lionel Groulx, one of Trudeau's early mentors, published *Chemin de l'avenir*, "the road to the future"—a future that he claimed lay somewhere between outright independence and associate-state status. Immediately, the Société Saint-Jean-Baptiste came out in support of an associate state in a document written by the well-known historian Michel Brunet. Such a tract would likely have gathered dust in the archives except for its endorsement on May 9, 1964, by René Lévesque, who declared that associate-state status should be negotiated "without rifles and dynamite as soon as possible." Lévesque did not back down, and soon even Jean Lesage seemed to affirm most of his arguments. Such demands can easily be dismissed today as empty political rhetoric, but Trudeau and others recognized that the Lesage government had gathered together an impressive group of bureaucrats who were more than a match for their federal counterparts. The Ottawa men were reeling under the continual expansion of Quebec City's demands.

The Pearson government had come to office committed to creating a European type of welfare state in Canada. Unlike Europe and even the United States, Canada had no "social security" system in 1963. Only a fraction of high school graduates went to university, compared with the system of mass university education that had developed in the United States after the Second World War. Pearson's ambitions, which were inscribed in the Liberal Party platform after the historic "Thinkers'

Conference" at Kingston, Ontario, in September 1960, directly challenged the distribution of powers in the *British North America Act*, in which health, education, and social welfare generally were the responsibility of the provinces. Despite the opposition of many provinces, including, of course, Quebec, the Pearson government, once elected, decided to press forward with a fundamental restructuring of the role of the state in Canadian life. The Lesage government proposed the same for Quebec.[21] Not surprisingly, the governments clashed.

The clash, however, was sometimes productive—in many ways a justification of Canadian federalism, as Trudeau argued at the time. The province of Quebec had independently developed a strong proposal for a social security or pension system. The federal government was compelled to react. After difficult and bitter negotiations, the Canada Pension Plan and the Quebec Pension Plan were created through a system in which Quebec was allowed to "opt out" and receive a larger share of "tax points." Judy LaMarsh, Pearson's minister of health and welfare, threatened to resign over the issue, but pleas to her that invoked "national unity" concerns obtained her silence—for a while.* Trudeau welcomed the new social spending, but was disconcerted by the clumsy and irregular character of the decision-making and by the precedents being set.

---

* Judy LaMarsh was excluded from the final meeting when the deal was made to create the pension plans. She wrote in her bitter memoirs: "I felt that I had been shamefully treated by my Leader. Pearson did not then, nor has he ever, even acknowledged what a dirty trick he played. I admit that circumstances may have forced his hand, but I will always maintain that he did not need to do it that way." Later, LaMarsh became a strong opponent of "special deals" for Quebec and, eventually, of Pierre Trudeau, even though he largely shared her opinion. Judy LaMarsh, *Memoirs of a Bird in a Gilded Cage* (Toronto: Pocket Books, 1970), 281.

What astonished Trudeau more were the moves by the Quebec government to obtain an independent presence in international affairs. What had begun, sensibly, as the creation of a francophone Canadian presence in the French world, with the establishment of Quebec offices in Paris and elsewhere, had become a path whereby Quebec would attain an independent right to sign treaties and to conduct international relations in areas of provincial competence. More troubling was the presence in Charles de Gaulle's government of numerous officials who encouraged Quebec in these ambitions. Trudeau's old acquaintance Paul Gérin-Lajoie, a leading constitutional scholar, was the political and intellectual leader of the Quebec foray onto the international stage, and others, notably *Le Devoir* journalist and nationalist Jean-Marc Léger, rallied intellectual opinion behind the government's ambitions.

In January 1965, while the two men were both relaxing in Florida, Lesage told Pearson he had lost control of his government: he felt like a man holding on to the tail of an enraged bear. Public opinion polls indicated that Quebec separatism was no longer an idle dream but, potentially, a political movement with the support of somewhere between one-fifth and one-third of Quebec voters. As the Royal Commission on Bilingualism and Biculturalism travelled through the country, commissioners heard tales of francophones who had lived in Ontario, Manitoba, or elsewhere who had been denied jobs and told to "speak white." These incidents sparked many comments and bred resentment. André Laurendeau's diary of the commission's tour included such details as the young francophone living near Windsor, Ontario, who told how her French accent caused her problems even in an area with a historic and substantial French presence. When she was trying to rent an apartment, a friend told her not to make the calls because of her accent. Across Canada, the Commission rubbed against old scar tissue from the earlier wounds of conscription during the war, school language battles, and the rebellion of Louis Riel. Laurendeau also recounted how one commission member, Gertrude Laing, spoke with a young "Anglo-Canadian" who admitted that "he hated the French, that several of his friends felt the same way," and that he did not "believe at all in the task we are involved in." When pressed why, he said he had the impression that Quebec was "destroying the Canada he loves."

Polls taken by the *Calgary Herald* and the *Winnipeg Free Press* indicated that their readers believed the commission's work was harmful—an opinion Conservative leader John Diefenbaker shared. Not surprisingly, the commissioners decided they must sound an alert by issuing a "preliminary" report. Published in February 1965, that report declared, memorably, that "Canada, without being fully conscious of the fact, is passing through the greatest crisis in its history."[22]

After the commissioners rang this alarm, *Cité libre* published an anonymous attack on the report and on Laurendeau himself. Laurendeau was convinced that Trudeau was its principal author. He learned his suspicions were correct when Jean Marchand confirmed them and Trudeau later "partially" agreed. Trudeau's papers do contain a draft of the text.[23] It was primarily the commission's method that concerned Trudeau. As historian J.L. Granatstein observed, "the commissioners had gone beyond the traditional role of a royal commission in collecting data and offering recommendations; instead, they had involved themselves in the process and had become, in fact, *animateurs*." Trudeau, Marc Lalonde, and the others who had called for a functional politics thought that Laurendeau remained trapped within the nationalist womb—especially given his musings about a special status for Quebec. They feared that the federal Liberals' Quebec representation was simply too weak to counter the challenge from Quebec City and, at the same time, deal with the commission's demands.

In the spring of 1965, however, national public opinion

polls began to shift towards the Liberals. John Diefenbaker's protracted and histrionic opposition to the maple-leaf flag had angered many Canadians, and the Quebec Conservative Party had disintegrated. Despite some doubts about the bi and bi commission, there was a general expectation that its report would work to the Liberals' advantage. Many in the party therefore pressured Pearson to call an election

Unfortunately, at this moment, scandals and corruption were dogging the Quebec Liberals.[24] The weak Quebec ministers were a problem in Ottawa. Guy Favreau, the minister of justice, had been unable to secure provincial acceptance for the Fulton-Favreau proposals on the reform of the Canadian Constitution. Now his health was quickly failing and, in the spring of 1965, he became embroiled in a scandal surrounding a notorious drug dealer, Lucien Rivard.* Pearson had already lost his parliamentary secretary, Guy Rouleau, because of the scandal and the firebrand Yvon Dupuis because of an apparent bribe.[25] Now two more Quebec ministers, Maurice Lamontagne and René Tremblay, had become major political liabilities because of their alleged failure to pay for furniture from a bankrupt Montreal furniture dealer. The scandals, the astute journalist Richard Gwyn wrote in 1965, "resulted from a series of compromises made in the name of political expedience, which

---

* Lucien Rivard was a drug dealer whom the United States wanted to extradite. In fighting the extradition, he managed to gain the assistance of Guy Masson, a prominent Liberal, and, more important, Guy Rouleau, the parliamentary secretary to the prime minister, as well as Raymond Denis, the executive assistant to the minister of citizenship and immigration and the executive assistant to Favreau himself. Denis, it appeared, offered a $25,000 bribe to the lawyer representing Rivard. Favreau should have submitted the case to Justice Department legal advisers rather than deciding himself that no charge should be laid.

permitted what *Le Devoir* memorably termed 'the Montreal Liberal trashcan' to stand outside the back door of Parliament a good half-decade after it should have been removed."[26]

At the very moment when Quebec had become the Liberal government's most challenging issue, its francophone voices were discredited. Gérard Pelletier declared that Pearson's path led him into a "perpetual cul-de-sac," no matter what direction he turned. Journalists in French and in English cruelly portrayed Lester Pearson, who had privately impressed André Laurendeau and the other commissioners with his sensitivity and shrewdness, as a hopeless bungler. In January 1965 Pearson had met with Lesage and implored him to come to Ottawa, suggesting that the post of prime minister would be his reward. Lesage told him the timing was wrong: he was in the third year of his mandate in Quebec, and an election would normally fall in the fourth year. Pearson knew that the federal Liberals could not wait so long. Their sophisticated American pollster Oliver Quayle told them they must call an election in the summer of 1965, while Diefenbaker was still the Conservative leader. Moreover, in July 1965 Pearson managed to get nearly all the premiers to agree to a "medicare" plan, thereby giving the Liberals the progressive issue they needed to attract NDP votes. Despite strong opposition from

---

Favreau offered his resignation, Pearson refused it, but then appointed him to a new portfolio. He remained bitter for the remaining few years of his life because so many had abandoned him. Tellingly, Pearson responded to a letter from the eminent historian A.R.M. Lower, who had complained that there was too much "rot" in Canadian politics, by saying: "I do not agree that the conduct of Mr. Favreau, Mr. Lamontagne, and Mr. Tremblay, however inept and ill advised, represents any form of corruption or lack of integrity on their part." Lower had neither mentioned the three ministers nor referred specifically to Quebec.

many prominent Liberals, including Defence Minister Paul
Hellyer and the wily political veteran Paul Martin Sr., the Liberals
had already raised expectations of an election.

Pearson, who stood accused of indecisiveness, could hold off
no longer. After a late-summer tour of the West, he returned to
Ottawa on September 7, 1965, and called an election. Three days
later, at a Montreal press conference in the Windsor Hotel, the
three friends Pierre Trudeau, Gérard Pelletier, and Jean Marchand
together announced that they would stand as Liberal candidates.
For the Liberals, it was a coup; for Quebec politics, a shock.

—

Jean Marchand was the prize: a trade union leader as Liberals
battled with the NDP for labour votes; a bare-knuckled debater who
could go "toe to toe" with Réal Caouette's Créditistes; and a popular figure with the Lesage government, including René Lévesque.
But the fall of 1965 was Trudeau's time too, just as it was Marchand's
and Pelletier's. Marchand's role in the labour movement had
become more difficult, and he had resigned as the head of the
Confederation of National Trade Unions (CNTU) in the spring,
knowing that politics offered an alternative. In that same spring, the
board of directors of La Presse had fired Pelletier as editor.[27] Politics
beckoned all three men to the Liberal fold almost at once. Trudeau
was elated—his mood reflected the excitement of his new venture,
his sense of mission at this troubled time in Quebec's and Canada's
history, and the realization, at last, of his plan to be a political man.

Jean Marchand had considered running provincially or
federally with the Liberals since 1960. When he decided not to run
in 1963 because of Pearson's stand on nuclear weapons, he stepped
aside quietly. Such was not the case with Pelletier, whose editorial
opinions at La Presse denounced the decision and continued to
criticize the scandals that plagued Pearson's minority government.

It was Trudeau, however, who rankled Liberal veterans most. They forgot neither his bitter denunciation of Pearson's decision to accept nuclear weapons nor his frequent attacks on Liberal MPs as "imbeciles" or "trained donkeys." Accordingly, Pearson was informed that Vadeboncoeur, not Trudeau, was the author of the notorious phrase "the defrocked prince of peace." Technically, the explanation was valid, although Pearson apparently was not told that Trudeau liked the phrase so much that he had chosen it to introduce his own caustic essay on Pearson in *Cité libre*. Fortunately, there were no copies of the review in Pearson's library. According to Jean Marchand, the powerful national party organizer Keith Davey tried to convince him that he should run alone only days before the election was announced. But he stood firm and insisted that the others must run too. He had "great confidence," he told Davey, "in Mr. Trudeau's mind and in Pelletier's judgement."

On September 9 the decision could be delayed no longer. At Guy Favreau's request, Marchand, Pelletier, and Trudeau met with him at a suite in Montreal's Windsor Hotel, along with Maurice Lamontagne and party organizer Robert Giguère. Maurice Sauvé apparently came without invitation. The meeting began at 8:00 p.m. and lasted until 3:00 a.m. Lamontagne frankly argued against the candidacy of Trudeau and Pelletier, telling them that things would be "very tough" and they would receive a cold welcome in Ottawa. But Trudeau maintained his "jolly mood" through it all. At 4 p.m. the next day, September 10, the three, quickly dubbed the "Three Wise Men" by the English press and "Les trois colombes"—the Three Doves—in the French press, announced that they had suddenly become Liberals and would stand as candidates in the next election.[28]

Trudeau remained the coy political mistress and took some time to find a constituency. According to journalist Michel Vastel, Trudeau dreamed of representing Saint-Michel de Napierville, where his ancestors had dwelt. It provoked uproarious laughter in the editorial rooms as journalists pondered the image of "the intellectual of *Cité libre*, the bourgeois of Outremont" going from door to door among the farms on the South Shore of the St. Lawrence. More astutely, the young Liberal Eddie Goldenberg realized Trudeau's remarkable political appeal when he came just after the announcement to speak to students at McGill University. He reflected on Greek philosophy, analyzed democratic thought, and, to Goldenberg's initial consternation, spoke unlike any politician he had ever heard. But the students were entranced. With Trudeau, it seemed that politics at last might be different.[29]

After much commotion, the party finally found Trudeau a seat in Mount Royal, a constituency that was rich, strongly Liberal, largely anglophone, and with a significant Jewish population. McGill University law professor Maxwell Cohen had positioned himself to run there, so Pearson intervened himself to persuade a disappointed Cohen to step aside. The excellent House Speaker Alan Macnaughton, who had held the seat since 1949 with remarkable majorities in recent elections, gracefully made way for Trudeau. However, the popular physician and veteran Victor Goldbloom was unwilling to allow the party's favourite a clear run at the nomination. His reluctance may have emerged from Trudeau's casual appearance when he came to a meeting with Liberal organizers driving his Mercedes sports car and wearing "an open-collared sports shirt, a suede jacket, a beat-up old peaked hat, muddy corduroy slacks, and sandals." He was sent home to change before the sceptical party faithful could encounter this strange new political beast. Trudeau mused about dropping out, claiming he did not want to run against Goldbloom, who was a "good man." The result, Marchand said, was "the most awkward convention I have ever seen, with Goldbloom saying that Trudeau was the best candidate, and Trudeau saying that Goldbloom was the best candidate." At the insistence and with the blessing of Pearson's organizers, Trudeau became the candidate.[30]

In 1962, as the international anti-nuclear movement spread, Gérard Pelletier and Trudeau read a peace movement pamphlet. Trudeau wears the "ban the bomb" lapel pin to identify his commitment.

"The Three Wise Men": Gérard Pelletier, Jean Marchand, Pierre Trudeau, 1965.

Pelletier, Trudeau, and Marchand announce their candidacy for the Liberal Party, September 10, 1965.

The Big Attraction.

The inevitable tea party for the new candidate in Mount Royal, 1965.

The candidate's storefront office: first campaign, Mount Royal, 1965.

Trudeau's first campaign poster, 1965.

Trudeau as a candidate in Mount Royal, 1965: note the
Fleur-de-lys and the Star of David in the background.

Lester Pearson and his successors: Pierre Trudeau,
John Turner, Jean Chrétien.

A forceful Trudeau at the Quebec Federal Liberal Party Conference, 1968.

Suddenly Everyone Looks a Little Older.

Pearson featured his minister of justice at the federal-provincial conference in 1968.

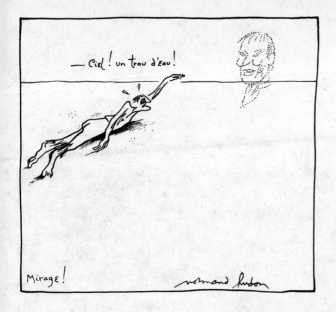

A Mirage!

The Swinger.

The candidate surrounded by his supporters at the leadership convention.

The early gunslinger pose: Liberal Party leadership race, 1968.

Some members of the Trudeau team at the leadership convention, 1968. From left to right: Jean Marchand, Mitchell Sharp, Pierre Trudeau, and behind with a pipe, Edgar Benson.

Trudeau kissed women, not babies: leadership convention, 1968.

Playing with a flower to break the monotony during the four ballots of the leadership race. Edgar Benson looks on.

Candidate for the Liberal Party leadership, 1968: sliding down the bannister at the Château Laurier Hotel, Ottawa.

Marchand had to calm Trudeau once more when he learned that his friend Charles Taylor, for whom he had campaigned in 1963, would be his NDP opponent. Taylor had participated in a joint attack in *Cité libre* in reply to Pelletier's and Trudeau's October 1965 explanations for their decision to run for the Liberals. Their argument for joining the Liberal Party amounted to a blunt statement that they wanted to be politicians to carry out their policy aims, and only the Liberal Party offered them the possibility of placing their hands on the levers of power. "There are two ways in which one can become involved in public life," they wrote: "from the outside by critically examining the ideas, institutions, and men who together create political reality; or from the inside itself by becoming a politician oneself."[31] It was, as Taylor pointed out, the type of expedient argument that Trudeau and Pelletier had so often condemned.

Moreover, they were both self-declared voices on the left, and their decision weakened the NDP, whose popular leader, Tommy Douglas, was attracting much new support. Their sudden switch to the Liberals stunned the Canadian left, but it also encouraged many. Ramsay Cook, who had been an eloquent voice interpreting Quebec politics and thought among English-Canadian intellectuals, wrote to Trudeau on September 10, 1965: "Today's announcement of your intention to seek a nomination in the next election astonished me . . . While my heart is with the NDP, I would gladly do anything I could to help you." He, too, had become disillusioned by the NDP's two-nation policy. Trudeau's old colleague Maurice Blain—not so willing to help—was disappointed that they had abandoned the political left to work in "a traditional party subservient to capitalism, identified with anti-democratic institutions, and committed to electoral opportunism."[32] These comments worried Trudeau, but Marchand convinced him he should not let them get to him and simply knock on doors to win the votes.

On November 8 Trudeau won Mount Royal with a margin

of 13,135 votes, less than half of Macnaughton's margin of 28,793 in 1963. It was not a smashing victory, but he had a safe seat for the remainder of his long political career, always with large margins of victory. The government also won re-election, but once again the cherished majority eluded Lester Pearson as Diefenbaker's campaign skills carved up the Liberal vote, especially in the West, and scandals continued to plague the Liberals in Quebec.* It was, Liberal organizer John Nichol later said, "a long, long way to go for nothing." Marchand entered the Cabinet immediately as the minister of citizenship and immigration, with the promise that he would soon become the minister of a new Department of Manpower. Once Pearson named him his senior Quebec minister, Marchand relished the task of "cleaning up" the Quebec wing of the Liberal Party.

Pelletier and Trudeau took their place on the back benches, probably because some penance was appropriate before the other Liberal MPs could be expected to accept the freshly minted Liberals. Politically, it was wise to dampen expectations because the trio had caused a whirlwind in Quebec, especially in intellectual circles where there was, in Blain's words, "an emotional reaction."

---

* The final results were 131 Liberal (129 in previous Parliament); 97 Conservative (95); 21 NDP (17); 9 Créditistes and 5 Social Credit (24 combined). There were two independents. The Liberals took 40 percent of the popular vote; the Conservatives, 32 percent. In the pre-election polls and election polls, the Liberals were in the 45 percent range and stood at 44 percent in early November, just before the election. The Liberals actually had a higher percentage of the popular vote (42%) in the April 1963 election. The Liberals did gain 12 seats in Quebec, but lost three to the Conservatives despite the party split before the election. The NDP, despite the leadership of the popular Robert Cliche, did poorly, increasing its vote to 11.9 percent only because it ran many more candidates in Quebec.

As he perceptively remarked just after the election, the three "had not so much embraced a new career as set out on a mission." Detested by separatists, distrusted by neo-nationalists and the left, they came to represent a shift in the political landscape in Quebec and, perhaps, in Canada. For Pierre Vadeboncoeur, this mission slowed the swelling momentum leading to an independent socialist Quebec. Laurendeau, who approved of their switch, nevertheless believed that "their decision dealt a major blow to 'democratic socialism' in Quebec, and killed a lot of hopes." Years later, Bob Rae, the former federal NDP member of parliament and Ontario premier, said that their emergence on the federal scene as Liberals "ended the dream of a socialist Canada under a New Democratic government."[33]

Such judgments belonged to the future in the fall of 1965 when, in Pelletier's words, "many people thought that Trudeau and I would cross the aisle in Parliament after a month." Of course, they did not. In 1992 Trudeau told Michael Ignatieff, who had supported his campaign for the leadership in 1968, that he had decided "not to make party options too soon." Rather, he advised, you should complete your philosophical formation first because, "once you join a party, it's hard to switch. You have the whole history of friendship and everything else."

Even before the supposedly decisive meeting on September 9, 1965, Trudeau had told Madeleine Gobeil that he was making "the big jump."* More tellingly, his confidante Carroll Guérin wrote to him in October, just before the election. She regretted leaving him at the airport, "though I am quite glad

---

* When Madeleine Gobeil met Grace Trudeau on election night, the proud mother declared: "Now he might amount to something." Interview with Madeleine Gobeil, May 2006.

that you are engrossed in politics now; probably because I'm safely removed from the front now! But I felt I was leaving you to something very vital (to put it mildly), and not walking off while you returned to a way of life that you must admit was something of a dead end." She summarized so many intimate conversations in those two brief sentences. Pierre, whom she loved profoundly, had found his place. "With hugs," she concluded her letter, "even if you are in the Liberal Party."[34]

—

The Liberal Party was scarcely congenial for a backbencher arriving in Ottawa in the winter of 1965–66. Walter Gordon, who had strongly urged Pearson to have an election, offered his resignation after the defeat. To Gordon's surprise, Pearson accepted it. With Gordon's departure, the left or reformist wing of the party was suddenly weak, particularly when the more conservative Mitchell Sharp became the new minister of finance and the decidedly conservative Robert Winters, after he had divested himself of his numerous company directorships, minister of trade and commerce.

What this reorganization meant, the eminent journalist and editor Claude Ryan wrote in *Le Devoir*, was that the Cabinet had "two tiers"—the first a group of senior ministers who were "the real masters," and the second a group of juniors, who would have to prove themselves. The "masters" came almost entirely from Ontario; in Quebec, only Marchand might be called upon "to enter the 'inner sanctum' where the big decisions are made." Ryan was correct in his assessment that nearly all the Quebec ministers were on the lower tier; what he did not realize was the extent of the mandate Pearson gave Marchand to "do that [clean-up] job" in Quebec they both deemed essential. Trudeau and Pelletier, in Marchand's words, supported him but "were not directly involved or personally involved" in the political house-cleaning. They were backbenchers "like the others," though already an aura surrounded them.[35] There were also the doubters and the believers.

The influential Toronto *Globe and Mail* greeted the entry of Marchand, Pelletier, and Trudeau as potential bulls in a Liberal store filled with fragile china. For his part, Pearson's lead Quebec minister Guy Favreau, though willing to accept their entry, was so upset that he took "a long ride on his motorcycle at high speeds" to work off his frustration—no doubt something Pierre had done in the past himself.[36] Of the three, Trudeau was the least well known; the firing of Pelletier from *La Presse* amid rumours of plots by Lesage and large business interests had attracted attention even in English Canada. Trudeau was not listed in the English-language *Canadian Who's Who* for 1965, and almost none of his writings were available in English. When he first arrived in the fall, Ottawa reporters treated him as an exotic species whose sartorial tastes as much as his intellectual prowess set him apart from his parliamentary colleagues.* Not for the first time, the media attributed to him a lower age.

Yet difference and mystery intrigue. In a book on Canadian nationalism published in 1966, the well-known University of Toronto historian Kenneth McNaught famously

---

* The young Albertan political assistant Joyce Fairbairn first met Trudeau at the Parliamentary Restaurant, where he often had breakfast after the short walk from his room at the Château Laurier Hotel. He brought, she claimed, a reputation for being eccentric "because of his initial casual attitude toward wearing apparel. In a House of Commons filled with suits and ties and socks and laced shoes, he showed a shocking tendency toward sports jackets, cravats, and sandals—sometimes worn without socks." After "a lengthy succession of

drew attention to Trudeau: "It was to stem the now common habit of looking upon and treating Ottawa as a foreign power that this brilliant and essentially non-political sophisticate plunged into the icy waters of federal politics in Quebec." McNaught, a leading socialist activist and the biographer of J.S. Woodsworth, feared Trudeau's impact on his NDP but welcomed his voice in Ottawa and Quebec:

> For his pains he has been smeared as a *vendu*, and there is little doubt that he shares what I have called the English-speaking view of Canada. His political fate will likely be the political fate of Canada. Nor should anyone question the agony of his decision, for it involved further crippling the struggling Quebec wing of the NDP, which is the party that best represents Trudeau's social thought. His decision that the Liberal party—the party which flirts most openly with American continentalism—is yet the party which alone might avert the imminent culmination of racial nationalism was the measure of his fears for Canada.[37]

In Quebec, Jean-Paul Desbiens, whom Trudeau and *Cité libre* had honoured in 1960 for the publication of his notorious attack on the Quebec education system, similarly declared in a letter to

---

boiled eggs," she warmed to Trudeau, who made little of the "light political conversation" that marks "the Hill," and she grew to respect him enormously. And to like him: "From the very beginning I sensed a shyness in him that was hooked on to an element of kindness that I came to know well over the years of work and friendship." The shyness sometimes came through—wrongly in her view—as arrogance or lack of interest. Joyce Fairbairn in Nancy Southam, ed., *Pierre* (Toronto: McClelland & Stewart, 2005), 39.

Trudeau that he and his colleagues represented for Canada its "last hand of cards."[38]

Trudeau, wisely, appeared eager to lower expectations. During the election campaign he told reporters that when he became a candidate, he was not offered a Cabinet post. Moreover, he said, "I made it clear I did not want such a post before anyone had the chance to offer me one." Blair Fraser, the national reporter Trudeau had known well since his youth, wrote profiles of Trudeau, Pelletier, and Marchand shortly after the Cabinet was formed in December 1965. The article rightly identified Marchand as the key player. "Trudeau and Pelletier," Fraser wrote, "are quite content as backers of Marchand, with no special ambitions." He reported that Trudeau found the all-candidate debates surprisingly enjoyable and that "his wry humour went down well." He also rightly identified some of the baggage that Trudeau carried with him to Ottawa: he had "never been obliged to work for a living"; his "English-speaking mother (*Le Devoir* insists on spelling his name Elliott-Trudeau)"; and, "gravest of all . . . his habit of speaking his mind." Some details aside, the article, oddly, has one wildly-off-the-mark analytical flaw — Fraser's assertion that "the fact that he is a well-to-do bachelor" was something "which women voters seem to resent."[39]

Immediately after the election, while others flew to Ottawa to pursue positions, Trudeau, true to form, went off to Europe on a ski trip. While he was there, Pearson decided to offer him the post of parliamentary secretary to the prime minister. Trudeau promptly declined, probably because he was wary of working closely with Pearson when he had little knowledge of him and his office or simply because he worried — correctly — that too rapid promotion breeds jealousy.

Marchand was livid. He had promoted Trudeau for the position of parliamentary secretary to the minister of finance and was pleasantly surprised to learn that Pearson wanted him for the Prime Minister's Office. Never close personally to Trudeau and exasperated with his moral dithering about running against Victor Goldbloom for the Liberal nomination and then against Charles Taylor in the election, he called Trudeau in Europe. In the sanitized version of the heated conversation that appears in his memoirs, Trudeau says that he told Marchand: "Give me time to get settled, to do my homework. You know I don't like to go into anything unprepared." Marchand responded caustically: "We didn't come here to refuse to work, Pierre. What brought us here is that there's a job to be done, and we have to grab every opportunity to do it."[40] Trudeau could not refuse his colleague, and so he became parliamentary secretary to Lester Pearson—the man he had criticized regularly since his first encounters with him as a young bureaucrat in Ottawa in 1949.*

What he saw of Pearson in the first months of office confirmed some of these doubts. The failure to win a majority government profoundly depressed the prime minister: on election night his face seemed frozen when he spoke on television; he took no questions and told reporters, "It's been a hard two months—I think I'll go home and go to bed." Probably he slept little that early morning of

---

* When asked why he appointed Trudeau his parliamentary secretary, Pearson said: "I had read his pieces for years, and was impressed by them, particularly by his detailed technical knowledge of economics and constitutional law. We're into a period where that's very important, and we'll be dealing a lot with Quebec. Pierre is a Quebecer and seems the kind of qualified person we need." It is unlikely that Pearson had read his pieces for years, and Trudeau did not have "technical knowledge of economics." Yet, in a period when the Quebec government had many highly sophisticated constitutional specialists, such as Claude Morin, Paul Gérin-Lajoie, and Jacques-Yvan Morin, and "technical economists," such as Michel Bélanger and Jacques Parizeau, Trudeau was a precious asset in Ottawa.

November 9 as he contemplated the resignation he would offer to his Cabinet in the morning. It was, as expected, rejected, but he left the meeting determined to have a new team. Walter Gordon left quickly, along with prominent party officials such as Keith Davey and Jim Coutts. Tom Kent, a dominant intellectual presence in Pearson's office, became Jean Marchand's deputy minister in the new Manpower Department. Pearson insisted that different faces were essential, even if the old ones were, in some cases, those of friends or of politicians wrongly caricatured as corrupt. Maurice Lamontagne, who had been Pearson's major Quebec adviser since opposition days, was an early casualty as Pearson told him personally that it was time for him to "get out." René Tremblay suffered the same fate, and Guy Favreau was retained in the minor post of president of the Privy Council. There his health continued to weaken, his East Block office remained empty, and his secretaries rarely saw him until he died in 1967. Maurice Sauvé, correctly distrusted by his colleagues as the source of "leaks" to the press about the government's internal troubles, retained his minor Cabinet post of minister of forestry, but his influence was much diminished. Apart from Jean Marchand, the sole important francophone was Minister of Justice Lucien Cardin—and, as another scandal would soon reveal, his task was beyond his capabilities.[41]

Later, when asked about these times, Trudeau said that "what surprised our little gang . . . is how easy it was to get yourself in a position of importance in a . . . historically established party . . . We knew that if we could get the people to support our ideas, some of the old guard would say: 'Well, these guys can win with new ideas, so let's win.'"[42] What made their success possible were two major factors: the discrediting and disappearance of the "old guard" (Lamontagne dated from the St. Laurent era, and Favreau and Tremblay from 1963); and the priority that Pearson and the Canadian public gave to the Constitution and the Quebec issue after the election of 1965.

Trudeau sensed the opportunity immediately. André Laurendeau, who did not "feel" like congratulating Trudeau on his victory, met him at two cocktail parties in early January. He remained the jolly soul he had been in November in the Windsor Hotel, and Laurendeau "was struck by his good spirits, and his energy: it's been a long time since I've seen him so up." Marchand told Laurendeau that the Liberal MPs were finding it difficult to accept Pelletier, whose barbs they remembered well and whose column on being a candidate during the 1965 campaign reflected extremely poor political judgment. Trudeau was different: he was "wonderfully successful. He astounds English Canada." And, Marchand concluded, "I'm willing to bet my shirt that within a year Pierre will be their big man in French Canada, eclipsing all the others."[43]

—

Fortunately and fortuitously for Trudeau, the first big issue he had to address was the Constitution. Already, before he entered politics, he had worked intensely on constitutional questions with his friends Marc Lalonde, Michael Pitfield, and groups affiliated with the Canadian Labour Congress in Quebec. Now, the unwillingness of the Lesage government to support the Fulton-Favreau process for constitutional revision in 1965 and 1966 brought deadlock and crisis. For Lester Pearson, it was a bitter disappointment. In February 1965, for example, he had confided to his close friend the journalist Bruce Hutchison that his greatest accomplishment was in the area of "Canadian federalism" and that he was now "totally devoted to national unity." This issue became the bond between Trudeau and his political chief: he could grasp the bloom of fresh opportunity from this nettle of failure. And, as he gained success, his respect for Pearson slowly grew.

The opening came from Premier Jean Lesage, who, antici-
pating a provincial election, separated the provincial Liberals
from the federal Liberals. The federal Liberals immediately
arranged a convention for their Quebec branch, where constitutional policy became the central issue. Jean Marchand, realizing
he must establish his authority at this convention, turned to
Trudeau for assistance on policy questions. Already Lesage's hesitancy had cast doubt on the federal government's earlier
approach to Quebec, and the January 20, 1966, Throne Speech
in Ottawa had set out a "harder" line in its approach to constitutional revision and to provincial demands, stating that it would
"exercise great care in agreeing on joint programs with the
provinces in which all provinces do not participate."

Now, at the convention, Trudeau, under Marchand's tute-
lage, brought forward resolutions for the Quebec Liberal
Federation that reflected his own similar hesitations about "any
kind of special status for Quebec." Intellectually, he dominated
the gathering. His argument that no major revision of the *British
North America Act* was needed was generally accepted, as was his
rejection of "an independent Quebec, or associate status, or special status, or a Canadian common market, or a confederation of
states." He also argued for bilingualism within the federal government and the importance of a Bill of Rights that would enshrine
individual rights across the country. Although Claude Ryan in *Le
Devoir* dissented from Trudeau's "honest but dubious" proposi-
tions and his "cold logic," the power of Trudeau's ideas and the
centrality of his role in federal politics in Quebec were firmly
established within months of his arrival in Ottawa.[44]

Trudeau's early success in federal politics occurred at a time
of chaos in Ottawa. The CBC's popular television series *This
Hour Has Seven Days* (which had considered Trudeau as a host)
had introduced a confrontational form of interviewing that
caught most politicians unprepared. In one program just after

the election, Justice Minister Lucien Cardin revealed the name of George Victor Spencer, a postal clerk who had been fired because he was suspected of spying for the Soviet Union. Ruffled, he went on to say that Spencer would not be charged but would be under surveillance for the rest of his life.

With those careless words, Cardin upset both civil libertarians and anti-Communists and made himself a target for John Diefenbaker, who fancied himself, with some justice, as the advocate of both. When the House returned in January, Cardin faced Diefenbaker's relentless attack. Quebec Liberals already detested Diefenbaker and blamed him for the destruction of Favreau, Lamontagne, and Tremblay—again with some justice. The Cabinet had decided in January that there would be no inquiry into the charge, but Diefenbaker and the NDP demanded that George Victor Spencer's curious case required investigation. Some members of the Liberal caucus, including Trudeau and Pelletier, began to question the government's stand. Bryce Mackasey, an outspoken Montreal MP, rose in the Commons to call publicly for an inquiry. On the way to Pearson's office, apparently to offer his resignation as parliamentary secretary, Mackasey encountered Trudeau, who, in Mackasey's recollection, told him, "I'll go with you [to Pearson's office] and I'll resign as well, because I felt what you felt." Pearson gave them a "good tongue-lashing," telling them if he wanted their resignation he would ask for it.[45] It was, for Trudeau, a good lesson.

More lessons soon came as Spencer's case magnified the government's and the prime minister's weaknesses. On March 2 David Lewis of the NDP told the House that Spencer himself wanted an inquiry—a clear repudiation of Pearson's statement the previous day that no inquiry was needed. Diefenbaker went for the jugular as only he, the most effective parliamentary debater of his generation, could do. Two days later, sensing that the beleaguered justice minister stood alone, he pressed the attack, hinting that the government was concealing various security breaches in the past and the present. It was mudslinging at its worst, and Cardin responded in kind, warning Diefenbaker that he was the last person to give advice on security cases. Pearson, who had come into the House, strongly applauded his minister. Diefenbaker pointed at him and shouted: "Applause from the Prime Minister. I want that on the record." Cardin misunderstood, thinking that Diefenbaker was demanding the name of the security case, and he stupidly blurted out "Monseignor." He had meant to say "Munsinger." Gerda Munsinger was a German immigrant to Montreal who had carried on affairs simultaneously with a Soviet diplomatic official and Pierre Sévigny, the associate minister of national defence in Diefenbaker's government. Pearson and Favreau had threatened Diefenbaker earlier with revelation of the Munsinger affair if he persisted in his bitter personal attacks on Quebec ministers.* Thus began the only serious sex scandal in Canadian political history and, more significant, the departure of Lester Pearson from Canadian politics.[46]

In a minority government and with his major advisers of the past now absent, Pearson made the fatal error of reversing his position and agreeing to the inquiry, even though three senior ministers, including Marchand, had defended Cardin's stand against an inquiry in the House.[47] Once again it seemed that Pearson had abandoned a Quebec minister under siege. Jean

---

* In one disgraceful episode when Pearson repeated the threat, Diefenbaker responded by shaking his fists at Pearson and saying that "he had a scandal" on him. Diefenbaker, in Pearson's words, said that "he knew all about my days as a Communist." Pearson laughed in his face and said it was the testimony of a "deranged woman," Elizabeth Bentley, who had been a dubious but major source for J. Edgar Hoover and other Americans pursuing Communists.

Marchand, according to one account, went over to Pearson's desk after he announced the inquiry and said: "If you ever do to me what you've just done to Cardin, all hell will break loose." It soon did. Lucien Cardin went home to Sorel for the weekend, decided he must resign, returned to Ottawa, and handed a letter of resignation to the prime minister. Pearson refused to open it. On the Tuesday, Trudeau attended the Quebec caucus. The members were furious with this abandonment of Cardin and almost voted for a motion of censure directed against Pearson, an action that would force the prime minister to consider resignation. Marchand told Cardin that he would resign with him, as would some other francophone Quebec ministers. Under pressure, Cardin stayed on; and Pearson stumbled through a sordid inquiry into the security risks of Gerda Munsinger's lively sex life.[48]

Trudeau shared the anger of his Quebec colleagues. He drew important impressions from the political chaos he experienced during his first three months in Parliament. First, he confirmed his impression that Lester Pearson was a weak but well-meaning leader. Second, he agreed with his Quebec francophone colleagues that their ministers did not receive the support they needed to confront the challenges of Quebec nationalism and separatism. Third, he strengthened his opinion of the House of Commons as a chamber where "trained donkeys" brayed and "imbeciles" roared. One day when Trudeau appeared for a vote wearing leather sandals and a foulard, Diefenbaker thundered denunciations at him for showing such disrespect for the ancient sartorial rules. He paid little attention to the House in the remainder of his first year and never developed the affection for the Lower Chamber that parliamentarians ranging from Wilfrid Laurier to Henri Bourassa to John Diefenbaker had done. In later years, Trudeau made some memorable speeches in the House, and his quick repartee made him highly effective in Question Period. But he was not a born gladiator in the political arena of the House of Commons.

After Trudeau's death, Pierre Vadeboncoeur defended his old friend, with whom he had bitterly disagreed since the mid-1960s, against charges that he was haughty and conceited. Quite the contrary, he said, Trudeau was often unsure of himself and was not "a natural tribune." As a politician, he became successful through his talents, but even more through a determined will to control "with precision, his actions and his attitudes." Because he was not a natural in the political battle, he sometimes adopted a pugnacious approach that was "contrary to his own more simple and authentic character." These thoughtful comments illuminate Trudeau's unusual political persona when he went to Ottawa in 1966—one exuding strength while simultaneously retaining a deep reserve that could become a beguiling shyness or, unexpectedly, a burning anger.[49]

Although Trudeau became Pearson's parliamentary secretary, they seldom worked together that year. In his own memoirs, Pearson admits that "Trudeau had neither very much to do nor the opportunity to learn very much in my office." Trudeau, in his own memoirs, states that he expected "some modest parliamentary chores and some pencil-pushing." Instead, Pearson sent him "running around the world."* In April he attended a meeting in Paris of the newly created Canada-France Parliamentary Group, one of the forums that allow backbenchers to travel and be

---

* With a minority government, the House sat long into the summer of 1966. As a summer student working on Parliament Hill that year, I regularly saw Pearson and Paul Martin, whose External Affairs office was in the East Block. Even Guy Favreau made occasional appearances, but, except for a few votes in the House, Trudeau was rarely in Ottawa. I first learned about him when some friends of mine met him at a Laurentian resort in mid-summer. They found him serious with them but very flirtatious with the women.

rewarded. Herb Gray, a young MP from Windsor, also attended the Paris meetings, where, he recalls, Trudeau startled the Canadians and the French alike with his detailed knowledge of Paris, Europe, and Africa, and with the stunning blonde woman who accompanied him to some of the formal events. Trudeau seemed at home in Paris, a perception validated by the "contact" list from his 1963 trip, which bears over forty names, including such eminent intellectuals as Jean Domenach of *L'Esprit* and the distinguished and currently fashionable philosopher Paul Ricoeur—and, inevitably, numerous single women.[50]

This parliamentary association was important because of the French and, more particularly, President Charles de Gaulle's interest in Quebec nationalism and separatism. Many French journalists travelled to Quebec at this time, attracted by the liveliness of the political debate, the literary and musical efflorescence of Montreal and Quebec—Michel Tremblay and Marie-Claire Blais, Félix Leclerc and Monique Leyrac were suddenly receiving raves in the French press—and their own government's increasing willingness to deal directly with a Quebec administration that had completely lost its suspicion of republican and atheist France. Quebec responded warmly to this embrace, establishing a "délégation générale" in Paris and undertaking a series of ministerial visits where Lesage and his ministers received treatment normally reserved for representatives of the most important sovereign states. Meanwhile, the Canadian ambassador, Jules Léger, Trudeau's old friend from Ottawa days, was treated contemptuously by de Gaulle, whose government signed a Quebec-France cultural entente in February 1965 that *Le Magazine Maclean* termed "the entry of the state of Quebec on the international scene."

Although the struggle between Ottawa and Quebec City to limit Quebec's "international" activities had many comic aspects, including the measurement of flags and even battles between limousines to lead processions, there is no doubt that some French officials, principally in the president's office, joined in intrigues to promote the independence movement in Quebec. Just as Canada had gained independence through its signature on fishing treaties and its appointment of "ministers" to foreign countries, so Quebec's international activities in Paris and, increasingly, in the former French colonies could well have led to political sovereignty. On this matter, Pearson and Trudeau strongly agreed. Trudeau therefore represented Canada at an international convention of French jurists and, later, wandered through five African countries to promote Canadian interests in the new "Francophonie"—a French Commonwealth being promoted by Senegal president Léopold Senghor, a poet who very much impressed Trudeau.[51]

Before he entered politics, Trudeau had criticized Quebec's efforts in the international arena, and he agreed to chair a group of legal experts who were considering how Canada should respond to these challenges. Two Pearson advisers whom Trudeau admired greatly, Marc Lalonde and Michael Pitfield, were part of the group, along with the undersecretary of state for external affairs, Marcel Cadieux, and the head of the department's legal division, Allan Gotlieb. This brilliant group of lawyers tested Trudeau, honed his intellectual skills, and shaped his response to Ottawa as well as Quebec. They shared the fear that Quebec's international ambitions could cut away the legal ties that bind a nation together, and these fears intensified when the Lesage government endured a stunning defeat in the election of June 5, 1966.

The new premier, Daniel Johnson of the Union nationale, promised to be much more nationalistic than Lesage, who in the final weeks of the campaign had ferociously denounced separatism. Johnson, whom Trudeau had met in the 1940s and who had been an early subscriber to Cité libre, campaigned on the slogan of his 1965 book, "equality or independence," and promised in the first plank of his party's platform to make Quebec "a true national state" through an extension of the province's powers and its sovereignty, especially on the international level. On election night, Johnson ominously remarked that, when you subtracted the Jewish and English Liberal vote, 63 percent of the French "nation" had rejected the Liberals. "Too many people," Johnson opined, "treat the *BNA Act* like a sacred cow, even though it's been violated many times in closed committee sessions and even in hotel rooms. So why not get rid of it and draft a sixth constitution?"

Trudeau, of course, personally rejected all these premises: the need for a new Constitution, the equation of the French-speaking population of Quebec with a "nation," the need for special status for Quebec, and the right of Quebec to have separate international representation. His group, together with Al Johnson, who had joined the Department of Finance from the Saskatchewan bureaucracy, began to elaborate a strong federal response to Premier Johnson's demands, which were presented by Finance Minister Mitchell Sharp to the federal-provincial conference on tax and fiscal affairs in September. Firmly rejecting special status for Quebec and further "opting out" by Quebec alone, Sharp asserted the essential need for the federal government to maintain the taxing authority necessary to meet Canada's fiscal needs. Claude Ryan in *Le Devoir* accurately noted the influence of Trudeau and Marchand in the federal approach, particularly in the firm rejection of "special status for Quebec."[52]

For much of the fall of 1966, Trudeau himself was absent from Ottawa because he was a member of the Canadian delegation to the United Nations. There he infuriated Paul Martin Sr., Canada's minister of external affairs, who at the time was leading all the polls as the most likely successor to Lester Pearson. In the late 1940s Pearson had established the practice of sending promising MPs of all parties to the UN as a way of building support for his foreign policy, and it proved to be an effective tool. Trudeau, however, took an immediate dislike to the elaborate rituals of the UN and to the policies Canada espoused there, particularly its tortured approach to the admission of China. He openly dissented from Paul Martin's "two China" approach, which called for both mainland China and Taiwan to have representation and was doomed to failure.

The Vietnam War now dominated the headlines as American involvement deepened and international opposition to the war grew. Yet the UN was at the sidelines, unable to give leadership in ending the conflict. Gérard Pelletier later recalled that Trudeau often spoke about the war in these times and, like Ryan, Laurendeau, and most Quebec intellectuals, strongly opposed American involvement. Vietnam, which had charmed him so much on his 1949 voyage, disappointed him when he returned in 1959. It no longer had "charme" or "classe." He noticed the police everywhere and the presence of the International Control Commission members, including many Canadians. Sadly he noted: "The country will perhaps be divided forever." More disturbing was the evidence that the government in the South depended entirely on the support of the Americans, who were ubiquitous.[53] However, Marcel Cadieux from External Affairs, who had served in Vietnam in the 1950s and detested Communist North Vietnam, discouraged Martin from criticizing American war policy. Trudeau, therefore, cast an increasingly wary eye towards the External Affairs Department and its minister, especially after he learned from Cadieux that Paul Martin favoured a conciliatory approach to the romance blooming between the government of Daniel Johnson and France. With Lalonde and others, he became sharply critical of Martin and warmly welcomed the January re-entry to the Cabinet of Walter Gordon, a vocal critic of American foreign policy.[54]

Gordon's return would be fundamentally important to Trudeau's future, although he barely knew Gordon at the time. Gordon was an ardent economic nationalist, an outspoken opponent of the war in Vietnam, a critic of Canadian membership in

NATO and in NORAD, and an increasingly strong critic of Pearson, whose political career he had financed and nurtured more than anyone else.[55] And the times increasingly favoured the left. *Canadian Dimension,* a magazine founded by one of the Vietnam "draft dodgers" from the United States who took refuge in Canada, polled many leading intellectuals in the winter of 1967 and discovered that most expected a "nationalist and socialist" government to rule Canada very soon. Pearson sensed the change and—in an astute political move—began to tack to the left.[56]

Gordon had expected that Maurice Lamontagne would join him in the Cabinet. When he did not, Gordon asked Pearson for an explanation. Pearson replied that Jean Marchand had vetoed the appointment—information Gordon immediately passed on to Lamontagne, who then confronted Pearson. The prime minister confirmed the story and invited the two men to his residence to sort it out. There Marchand told Lamontagne that the Quebec caucus would not accept his reappointment to Cabinet. It was a brutal blow and pointed both to Marchand's pre-eminence in federal Quebec politics and to the opportunity open to new Cabinet members from Quebec. Not surprisingly, on April 4, 1967, Trudeau succeeded the battered Cardin as minister of justice. In a single, quite brilliant stroke, Pearson appointed the most out-standing constitutional specialist in the party just as Quebec and the Constitution were becoming the major issues facing the government, and he strengthened the left of the party just as the NDP threatened the Liberals in English Canada. On both fronts, Trudeau acted quickly to reinforce his strengths.[57]

The times appeared to be perfectly tailored to fit Pierre Trudeau. In 1967 the very foundations of tradition seemed to be col-lapsing as John Lennon declared the Beatles more popular than Jesus Christ, the pill broke down ancient sexual taboos, and the young cheered for revolution. Canada finally seemed ready to abandon its reserve as television broke through restrictions in its treatment of sex, politics, and religion. Above all, it was Canada's Centennial Year, which began quietly but, by late spring, had become a noisy celebration of a North American country that was suddenly and unexpectedly "cool." Expo 67 in Montreal became a wildly successful world's fair that gave a sophisticated and modern face both to Quebec and to Canada.[58]

In English Canada, even *Canadian Business* magazine welcomed Trudeau enthusiastically and declared that the "swinging millionaire from Montreal who drove sports cars and wore ascots into the House of Commons" represented "the best traditions of the *engagé* intellectual." The French press was more restrained, including Claude Ryan in *Le Devoir*, who complained that Trudeau did not reflect Quebec opinion in his constitutional orthodoxy. Trudeau brushed off the complaints, quickly organized his office, and embarked on an astonishingly ambitious agenda that would transform Canada. Justice Department officials who had heard of Trudeau's "playboy" reputation were astounded to encounter a remarkably disciplined worker with great intellectual ability and an unusually retentive memory. Years later, when asked what was most impressive about Trudeau, staff members matched each other with tales about his "elephantine" memory for detail, to the point where he could recall memoranda by date and even by paragraph. Nicole Sénécal, a press secretary, said she never had a "boss" so difficult yet so wonderful.[59]

Initially, he focused on two major items: the Canadian Constitution and the reform of the Criminal Code. It was the latter that attracted the public's interest as the forty-seven-year-old bachelor announced plans to legalize homosexual acts between consenting adults, permit abortion when a mother's health was endangered, and broaden greatly the grounds for divorce. "Justice," Trudeau told Peter Newman, then a journalist for the *Toronto Star*, "should be regarded more and more as a department planning for the society of tomorrow, not merely the government's legal advisor . . . Society is throwing up problems all the time—divorce, abortions, family planning, pollution, etc.— and it's no longer enough to review our statutes every 20 years."

Within six months, in the late fall of 1967, Trudeau introduced these historic amendments to Canada's Criminal Code, and just before Christmas the House unanimously approved the first divorce reforms in one hundred years. A senior NDP member, H.W. Herridge, praised Trudeau for creating a "precedent in Canadian history." Where other governments had avoided divorce reform as "politically dangerous," Trudeau himself had moved forward and had shown he was "a very sensitive, humanitarian individual." According to one correspondent, "Trudeau blushed."[60]

Lester Pearson had announced his resignation a week before Herridge spoke. The Centennial had brought much satisfaction but also considerable grief. In late July Charles de Gaulle made his official visit to Canada aboard the French warship *Colbert*. After landing at Quebec City, the French president made a royal progress along the historic North Shore to Montreal. There, on July 24, from the balcony of Montreal's Hôtel de Ville, the greatest French leader of the century made his infamous declaration, "Vive le Québec libre," before a huge and enthusiastic throng. Lester Pearson was livid; Paul Martin Sr., who was in Montreal, counselled caution. When the Cabinet met on July 25, both Jean Marchand and Robert Winters were reluctant to rebuke de Gaulle.

Trudeau disagreed: according to the Cabinet minutes, the minister of justice "said the people in France would think the Government was weak if it did not react." Moreover, he pointed out, de Gaulle did not have the support of French intellectuals, and the French press was opposed to him. Despite the hesitations of Martin, his most senior English Canadian minister, and Marchand, the leading Quebec minister, Pearson heeded Trudeau's advice and his own instincts. With the help of the Quebec ministers, he drafted a harsh rebuke to de Gaulle, who responded by cancelling his plans to go to Ottawa. The incident strengthened Trudeau's role within the Cabinet.[61] It also raised the debate about Quebec's future to a new intensity.

During the summer, Trudeau and Marchand consolidated their hold on the Quebec federal Liberals. The provincial party was debating a historic resolution that René Lévesque had placed before them, calling for Quebec independence followed by negotiations for an economic union with Canada. It was, Claude Ryan correctly wrote, "a new step towards the moment of truth." For Trudeau and many of his colleagues, it was proof that Lévesque had long been a closet separatist. When the resolution was defeated, Lévesque and others left the Liberal Party and formed the Mouvement souveraineté-association—the base from which the Parti Québécois took form. At the MSA's first meeting, Lévesque promised the triumph of a party committed to Quebec sovereignty, a party he would lead. The battle of Canada had begun.[62]

Lester Pearson had fought his last fight, and he knew his successor would face new battles on more difficult terrain where his skills were poor. So did Walter Gordon, whose influence in the party remained strong because he had mentored so many MPs and retained his close links with the *Toronto Star*. Gordon called Trudeau in mid-November and invited him to his Château Laurier suite to meet with two of his Cabinet allies, Edgar Benson and Larry Pennell. All four men agreed that they were not excited about "any of the leadership candidates."[63] Pearson had let it be known that the next leader should come from Quebec, and he initially turned towards Marchand. But Marchand's flaws were many: his English was not good; his voluble personality was attractive but politically risky; and his judgment was not always sound. During the de Gaulle incident, he had been offside with Cabinet opinion, and his plan to allow public servants to unionize and strike was unpopular on editorial pages and among many of his colleagues.

Trudeau, in contrast, was attracting increasing attention, which he shrewdly did not exploit. The plan he had developed in the late 1930s, when he first determined he wanted a public and political life, remained in place. He would cloak himself in mystery and be the friend of all and the intimate of none. Moreover, the extraordinary discipline he revealed in bringing the Criminal Code legislation forward while simultaneously acting as the federal leader on constitutional matters dispelled most of the criticisms about the swinging playboy who had never worked.

Many friends commented that they had never seen Trudeau as happy as in the summer of 1967. True, there were some disappointments. His mother, who had nurtured his dreams of a public career, was no longer able to appreciate his success. The last note from her in his papers is a couple of tragically broken sentences from Florida written in the spring of 1965 as Alzheimer's disease began to infiltrate her once lively, curious, and considerable mind. Her decline created a gap in his life that none could fill.

In Ottawa he was still frequently seen with Madeleine Gobeil, who taught at Carleton University and attracted great attention with an interview she did with Jean-Paul Sartre for *Playboy* magazine in 1966. They dined together regularly, talked long into the night, and shared their excitement about the new world unfolding before them. She introduced Trudeau to Sartre and Simone de Beauvoir, and, probably more meaningfully, to the first James Bond movies—which, not surprisingly, Pierre relished.

Pierre's most intense relationship during this decade appears to have been with Carroll Guérin, who now lived mostly in Britain. But after she and Trudeau spent that memorable summer together on the beach at St. Tropez, sharing an intense affair, she became ill with a serious virus. He saw her the next summer, although she was, in her own words, no longer fully a woman. They met again in 1964, when she was very ill and any physical activity was impossible. It was, she wrote, "very generous of you to want to meet me under these circumstances. I realize only too well what a burden I am, even to myself."[64]

Guérin never forgot Trudeau's kindness. He also persuaded her mother, who regarded her artist daughter's European residence as expensive whimsy and her illness as primarily psychological, to become more generous. Like most of Trudeau's female friends, Guérin was emotionally voluble and poured out her feelings freely and passionately. She, too, found Trudeau "emotionally withdrawn" and sought to turn the keys that locked his core. In the summer of 1967 he disappointed her when she hoped to meet him in Corsica. Instead, he left the Buonaparte Hotel before she arrived for the rendezvous, without informing her and without leaving a forwarding address. She admitted he had not "really sounded very enthusiastic over the phone in Montreal" when they planned the meeting. But, she wrote, "maybe it was all for the best . . . Anything you do, Pierre, will always be very close to my heart; but it would seem that as far as living together is concerned we are not able to manage . . . With all my heart, dearest Pierre, I wish you all the success that you so rightly deserve." She would retain her deep affection for Trudeau despite being "stood up."[65]

At Christmas that same year, it was Trudeau's turn to be stood up. He decided that December to escape Canada's winter and the increasing attention of politicians and the press by flying with two friends, Tim Porteous and Jim Domville, to Tahiti's Club Méditerranée, where he intended to read Gibbon's *Rise and Fall of the Roman Empire* and think about whether to seek the leadership of the Liberal Party. There, one afternoon as he was waterskiing, he attracted the attention of an alluring nineteen-year-old college student who was lying on a raft. Stunning in her bathing suit and with eyes that immediately entranced, Margaret drew crowds around her. Pierre came over to her and began to talk about Plato and student revolution—Plato, he knew well, while she was intimate with student revolt. She told him that her name was Margaret Sinclair and she was attending the new Simon Fraser University in British Columbia, where student radicalism was in full flower. She was, in her words, drinking it all in—"the music, the drugs, the life." She "jibed only at opium, scared off by Coleridge." Yet she "did try mescaline one day, and spent hours sitting up a tree, wishing I were a bird."

Margaret's parents were holidaying at the Club Med with her. Her mother, the wife of the Honourable James Sinclair, a war veteran who had been a minister in the St. Laurent government, told her daughter that the man she had met was Pierre Trudeau, Canada's minister of justice and the "black sheep" of the Liberal Party. Entranced by Margaret, Pierre joined the family at the long Club Med table for dinner each night. Margaret remembers she was not "particularly impressed," even though her parents were increasingly aware of his growing attraction to their daughter. Later, when he, so very "shy" and polite, asked her to go deep-sea fishing, she initially said yes but went off instead with "Yves," a handsome young French waterski instructor who was also the grandson of the founder of Club Méditerranée. He danced like a Tahitian and loved long into the night. But Pierre persisted, "old and square" though he might be. Margaret's vitality, her astonishing beauty, and her refreshing candour left a deep impression on him as he flew home. When he next saw her, at the Liberal leadership convention three months later, the black sheep of the Liberal Party was about to become its "white knight." At that moment, suddenly, he recalled Tahiti.[66]

—

CHAPTER 10

A TALE OF TWO CITIES

érard Pelletier was grumpy as he arrived for dinner in a small private room at Montreal's Café Martin on a cold Sunday evening on January 14, 1968. Jean Marchand and Pierre Trudeau, his dinner companions, were "hale and hearty, in wonderful shape" after vacations in the sun, while he was "as pale as a grub." Marchand had summoned his colleagues to discuss the fate of the Liberal Party as it faced an imminent leadership contest. The three had met in mid-summer and decided that it would be best if there were no francophone candidate because "the man to govern Canada was inevitably a conciliator, and in the present situation, francophone Canadians were in no mood for compromise." But Marchand had changed his mind in December. There had been almost no francophone presence when the Progressive Conservatives chose Robert Stanfield as their new leader in September 1967. If there were no francophone candidates for the Liberal convention in April 1968, what would Quebec conclude? "That the Canadian government and the big federal parties are run by English Canadians, and we have nothing to do with it." The logic seemed impeccable, but the real surprise was Marchand's decision about his own future. He would not be a candidate—it must be Trudeau.[1]

Pelletier immediately realized that he would have "a ringside seat" for a historic political battle, and, the following day, he began a diary to record the Liberal leadership contest of 1968. Simultaneously Richard Stanbury, a newly appointed Toronto senator and the principal organizer of the leadership convention, also began a diary. Back in the fall, Lester Pearson had confided his intention to resign as prime minister to Stanbury and to John Nichol, the president of the Liberal Federation, and had correctly predicted that the leadership race would be hotly contested. Pearson hoped for a strong Quebec candidate—Marchand was his favourite—and he worried about Paul Martin Sr., the external affairs minister, who he believed belonged too much to the Liberal past at a time when new voices were essential.

As Richard Stanbury began preparations for the convention, he shared these worries. In early January, when he scheduled his meetings with the candidates, he began with Martin. "Who's your candidate?" Martin demanded. "Of course I'm impartial," Stanbury replied. "Oh, you and I know that, but who's your candidate?" Stanbury said he thought it was a "fine wide-open race and that anyone might win." Martin "harrumphed," and the conversation ended. Stanbury already knew that Martin, who had stood first in the polls, was failing to find his expected support. Toronto, which had been a Tory bastion for most of Canada's first century, was now a dynamic centre of Liberal intrigue, dreams, and fears.[2]

In the sixties, Toronto shucked off its conservative raiments and customs and donned the more colourful garb of its hundreds of thousands of immigrants. The formerly staid citizenry began to drink wine, open nightclubs, and play professional sports on Sunday. Stanbury still taught his Bible class every week, but the dense Protestant, British, and Conservative atmosphere surrounding the city was quickly lifting. Those traditional forces continued to hold sway on Bay Street, which, since the 1950s, had vanquished all its economic competitors. But Montreal remained Canada's largest city and a very sexy one too, as the elegant modernity of Expo 67 and the swinging new night life in the old city testified. Pierre Trudeau's path to 24 Sussex Drive would pass through the political heart of Canada's two largest cities. As they set out to persuade him to run, Pelletier and Marchand told Trudeau they would "handle" Quebec; the rest of Canada was his concern. He barely knew "the rest," but English Canada was quickly learning about Trudeau who the wily young political operative Keith Davey had not even considered as a possible candidate two months earlier.[3] He cleverly borrowed *Globe and Mail* editorialist Martin O'Malley's statement "The state has no place in the bedrooms of the nation" and, in a December 22, 1967, television interview made it famously his own.[4] It caught precisely the new spirit of the times.

On January 13, 1968, the Gallup Poll revealed that the Liberals had gained on the Conservatives, who had moved ahead in the polls after they chose the Nova Scotia premier, Robert Stanfield, in September. The Liberals now trailed by only six points. That same day Peter Newman reported that a group of Toronto academics were "rallying the forces" behind Pierre Trudeau. He described the instigators—Ramsay Cook, John Saywell, and William Kilbourn—as three of the academic community's brightest young men, although he wrongly described these historians as political scientists.* Their petition imploring Trudeau to consider the Liberal leadership quickly

---

* Ramsay Cook was instrumental in organizing these petitions, but William Kilbourn got only one signature: Pierre Berton's. Saywell, apparently, took little part in the campaign. At the University of Toronto, radical student activists Michael Ignatieff and his friend Bob Rae also rallied behind the Trudeau candidacy

gained signatures from hundreds of English-Canadian academics who were fascinated by the possibility of a Trudeau candidacy.[5] Peter Newman linked the petition and its "assault on smug old-line thinking" with the forthcoming publication of Pierre Berton's book *Smug Minority*, which, in Berton's words, asserted that "the kind of political leadership we've had has been the wrong leadership, because it has been restricted to a cosy little group." Trudeau, Berton claimed, would save Canada from this coterie:

> Trudeau is the guy who really excites me; Trudeau represents a new look at politics in this country; he is the swinging young man I think the country needs. What we need is a guy with ideas so fresh and so different that he [is] going to be able to view the country from a different point of view. He has many weaknesses—inexperience, inability to project on the platform and all this. But they said these things about Kennedy too.

These comments from Newman and Berton, English Canada's most influential journalists, appeared one day before Marchand, Pelletier, and Trudeau gathered for the fateful dinner at the Café Martin. Yet when Marchand said after the first aperitif that Trudeau should run, Trudeau was, in Pelletier's words, "stunned." He left his boeuf bourguignon untouched on the plate.

Why was Trudeau stunned? His close friend Jacques Hébert had been urging him to run for the leadership for months. In the fall he had met with Walter Gordon and other English-Canadian MPs and mused about leadership. Pelletier and Marchand were probably unaware of this meeting, but Trudeau surely recalled the important encounter. Pearson had told Marchand that there must be a Quebec "French" candidate, and there were only two possibilities—Marchand or Trudeau. In Montreal, Pearson's aide Marc Lalonde did not take a Christmas vacation because he was busy organizing the potential Trudeau candidacy. Trudeau's own assistants, Eddie Rubin and Pierre de Bané, helped Lalonde put the details in place—and Trudeau knew what they were doing. Just before New Year's Eve, Lalonde persuaded Rubin and Gordon Gibson, the executive assistant to BC minister Arthur Laing, to rent an Ottawa office for the campaign. Rubin found the office, gave Gibson $1,000 to pay for it, and Gibson signed the lease—all to conceal the office's true purpose. By that time Walter Gordon had told the *Toronto Star* that he favoured Marchand for the leadership, but, if Marchand did not run, Trudeau would be his choice.[6] All this had happened before the dinner at Café Martin.

As usual, Trudeau's coyness was deliberate and wise. He knew that Marchand's support was crucial, but he was not yet certain that his colleague did not want to run. In Tahiti, he told Tim Porteous that he believed Marchand would eventually run. When Trudeau, Pelletier, and Marchand met again on January 18, Trudeau said he would be a candidate if Marchand refused, and then he listed his own weaknesses. Pelletier, who was much closer to Marchand than was Trudeau, believed that Trudeau "really wanted to be sure that Marchand's refusal was final." It was. Marchand privately and publicly attributed his refusal to his health—a serious drinking problem was already developing—and to his limited English vocabulary and heavy French accent. In December he had already told André Laurendeau that he had no desire to succeed Pearson, as Davidson Dunton had suggested to him. He told Laurendeau that he didn't enjoy living in Ottawa: "I don't like to have to speak English all the time; it diminishes me by 50%. It's a crazy job, worse even than being a trade unionist— there at least you've got roots."[7]

A second reason for Trudeau's seeming reluctance was that he had several opportunities to gain exposure in the forthcoming few weeks, and they would be lost if he declared his candidacy.

The Quebec Liberal Federation was meeting in Montreal on January 28, and Trudeau could advance his views there on law reform and constitutional review. Even more important was the constitutional conference that Pearson had promised after the "Confederation of Tomorrow" conference organized by John Robarts, the Ontario premier, in the fall of 1966. Trudeau and Pearson had responded by expressing a new willingness to discuss constitutional change and, in particular, a Canadian Bill of Rights that would form part of a revised Canadian Constitution. Trudeau had promised that he would consult the premiers before the constitutional conference. If he was a candidate, he would have to resign as minister of justice, a move that would imperil the chances for a breakthrough at the constitutional talks.

Finally, Trudeau was genuinely fearful of the intense glare of media attention on his private life. As reporters began to cluster about him, and his photograph appeared regularly in newspapers, he recognized that celebrity brought political gains, but at the expense of the inner core he had long and jealously protected. Madeleine Gobeil, who saw him often, recalls his intense need for a private space, away from other people. Right from the start of his time in the spotlight, he never bothered to correct the many stories that stated his age as forty-six during the leadership race.[8] Moreover, he told Margaret Sinclair before they married that in recent years he had prayed every night for a wife and a family. He was now forty-eight, an age when fatherhood becomes difficult and a first marriage rare. Would the prime minister's office end those hopes forever?

—

On January 18 Trudeau set out on his tour to meet the provincial premiers, and an increasingly curious press followed him. Accompanied by Eddie Rubin, who openly promoted his minister, and the eminent constitutional specialist Carl Goldenberg, Trudeau's tour was unexpectedly eventful and successful. W.A.C. "Wacky" Bennett, British Columbia's Social Credit premier, ignored Trudeau's statement that the two of them would not meet the press during the course of their confidential discussions. To everyone's surprise, Bennett told the assembled journalists that Trudeau impressed him so much that "if he ever decides to move to British Columbia, there's a place for him in my Cabinet."

More important than Bennett's praise was the endorsement from the equally eccentric Liberal premier of Newfoundland, Joey Smallwood. Observers expected that Smallwood would support Trade Minister Robert Winters, whom he knew well and who came from the Atlantic provinces. However, Winters had dithered about his candidacy, and this indecision exasperated Smallwood. When Smallwood met Trudeau on January 25, he immediately took him and his party to his private dining room, brought out a vintage Chambertin, asked Trudeau how to pronounce Chambertin properly, demanded that his colleagues try to match Trudeau's elegant accent, and proceeded to entertain his guests with a breathless monologue ranging over many topics but centred on himself. When Trudeau's assistants became anxious because the late hour meant that Trudeau would miss his visit to Nova Scotia, Smallwood called Nova Scotia premier G.I. Smith and asked him to join the party, where the wine— Smallwood called it "syrup"—was flowing freely.

Smith refused, and eventually the federal party took its leave. As he was departing, Carl Goldenberg, who knew Smallwood well, told the premier that Trudeau was the finest political philosopher in Parliament. Smallwood no doubt fancied himself as the finest on "The Rock" and immediately called a press conference so that Trudeau and he could match thoughts and wits. There in the lobby of the Confederation Building in St. John's, a city Trudeau scarcely knew and with a premier he had never met before,

Smallwood appeared to endorse Trudeau. He was, Smallwood declared, "the perfect Canadian" and the "most brilliant" MP of all. This bizarre performance was of fundamental importance to Trudeau because Smallwood controlled the votes as no other provincial premier did. His support for Trudeau in the leadership race would eventually provide the margin needed for the victory of Pierre Trudeau and the defeat of Bob Winters.[9]

After a brief visit with Premier Louis Robichaud of New Brunswick, Trudeau went directly to the Quebec Liberal Federation meeting in Montreal, where Marchand and Lalonde made sure that Trudeau would play the central role. Even in the absence of the leadership contest, he would have attracted attention because of the constitutional issues that Lester Pearson and Quebec premier Daniel Johnson identified as the principal concerns of their governments. Moreover, the proposed Criminal Code revisions, particularly those respecting abortion and homosexuality, were causing increasing criticism in rural Quebec and within the Roman Catholic Church. Both the Constitution and the Criminal Code were Trudeau's responsibility, and both created dangers and opportunities for him in his bid to become the Canadian prime minister.

The "committee" to elect Trudeau met for the first time at the home of the thirty-seven-year-old Marc Lalonde on January 25, just as Smallwood was giving his major endorsement of the Trudeau campaign. Donald Macdonald, an Ontario MP three years younger than Lalonde but close to the powerful Walter Gordon, reported that seventy Ontario delegates were already assured. Pelletier said that Quebec would provide "at least 450." Trudeau's committee members were young, eager to bring their generation to the party's forefront. Seniors had long prevailed there—Louis St. Laurent was sixty-six when he was chosen in 1948, and Lester Pearson was sixty-one in 1958. The sixties were different: in the United States, John Kennedy called for the torch to be passed to a new generation, while in Quebec, forty-five-year-old René Lévesque was wooing the youth into a swelling separatist force. Trudeau's new voice needed to be heard to win this essential Quebec support. Lalonde and Marchand made sure that Trudeau was the only respondent to questions about "special status" on the panel on Canadian federalism sponsored by the Quebec Liberal Federation on Sunday, January 28—just in time for the Monday media.[10]

The newspapers the following morning reported how Trudeau had brilliantly outlined the federalist option and how the delegates jumped to their feet, applauded, and sang, "Il a gagné ses épaulettes." Even Claude Ryan of *Le Devoir*, who was increasingly critical of Trudeau's rejection of the concept of special status, admitted that Trudeau had been most impressive. Where delegates had expected a cold, distant, and abstract intellectual, they heard a remarkable communicator "capable, without oratorical artifice, of raising to a degree of lucidity and simplicity, an accomplishment that is perhaps the apex of eloquence in our times."[11] This surprising reaction, given Ryan's doubts about Trudeau's constitutional views, surely gave Trudeau more confidence, but he was not yet ready to declare.

Events were moving fast—too fast, it seemed to some. On January 30 the Canadian Press ran a story, which appeared across Canada, that "professional politicians" were asking, "Has Justice Minister Trudeau, without even declaring candidacy for the Liberal leadership, peaked too soon?" The next day a "Mrs. R.A. King" responded to the story in a letter to the *Montreal Star*: "Last summer, John Diefenbaker chided Mr. Trudeau for appearing in the House of Commons in casual clothes. As far as I am concerned, if this brilliant Canadian chooses to run for the Liberal leadership and becomes prime minister, he can preside over parliament in a bedsheet!" Such responses infuriated the other candidates, and the Canadian Press reported that there was "naturally some ill-feeling . . . at Mr. Trudeau's jet-propelled rise to national prominence."[12]

The reports were true. Convention organizer Richard Stanbury, who in his diary had described the Montreal meeting as a "good launching pad" for Trudeau, learned that Mel McInnes, the special assistant to Allan MacEachen, the minister of national health and welfare, was complaining that the party hierarchy favoured Trudeau. Stanbury wrote to MacEachen offering to resign if the minister truly believed he was not impartial. MacEachen accepted the reassurance. However, it did not help that his relative and close friend Bob Stanbury, a Toronto MP, announced at the end of January that he was organizing a committee to "draft" Trudeau. Moreover, Bob Stanbury told the press that a poll in his riding indicated that Trudeau was already the frontrunner, even though not formally a candidate.

Gérard Pelletier, who, unlike most journalists, had not been impressed by Trudeau's performance at the Quebec Liberal Federation,* now faced constant pressure from Paul Martin, to whom he was parliamentary secretary. First Martin demanded to know if Trudeau was running; then, within days, he was so obsessed with the subject that, four times, he called

---

* Pelletier believed that Trudeau spoke well, but he confided to his diary that Trudeau's "tasteless jokes about France-Quebec relations" irritated him. He wondered whether they indicated a broader problem: "Making jokes (and Lord knows they're easy to make) implies, after all, that France-Quebec relations are unimportant. Knowing what he actually thinks on the subject, I'd be happy if he spoke seriously. But I don't understand the lack of sensitivity he puts on this matter, nor his apparent lack of respect for others' feelings on the subject. Perhaps it's a sign of his impatience." Gérard Pelletier, *Years of Choice,* 1960–1968 (Toronto: Methuen, 1987), 264–65.

Pelletier "Pierre." On January 23 he even sent his son, "Paul Martin *Junior*, as he calls himself," to tell Pelletier that his father wanted to be identified with the "leading wing of the [Quebec] party and not with the *old guard*." However, members of "the leading wing" refused to sign up with Martin because they were waiting for Trudeau. They would continue to wait.[13]

Trudeau had one more event he and his supporters did not want to miss: the opportunity to challenge Daniel Johnson at the constitutional conference of February 5–7, 1968, in Ottawa. There, Lester Pearson, barely concealing his preference for a francophone successor, seated Trudeau next to him. He had already ceded the intellectual ground to Trudeau, who, on February 1, had issued a booklet, in Pearson's name, entitled *Federalism for the Future*, which outlined the federal government's stance and Pearson's own views.[14] After its release, Trudeau gave interviews outlining how the federal government would approach both the conference and the demands from Quebec. The booklet rejected special status and the "two nations" policy espoused by Daniel Johnson, the federal Progressive Conservatives, and the NDP because Trudeau believed that special status would lead inevitably to separation. Instead, it emphasized the linguistic rights of francophones throughout Canada, placing them on an equal basis with anglophones in Quebec.

Trudeau had known Daniel Johnson since the 1940s, when they were both conservative young Catholic nationalists in Quebec who strongly opposed conscription and the war policies of the federal Liberals. In the close world of Montreal legal, religious, and academic circles, Johnson and Trudeau had frequently encountered each other, but their relationship soured after Johnson was appointed Maurice Duplessis's assistant. In that role he became the target of nasty cartoons by Hudon in *Le Devoir*, where he was depicted as a court jester, and of scurrilous jibes by opponents who labelled him "Danny Boy." As a Union nationale member of the National Assembly since 1946, however, Johnson was often underestimated, certainly by Lesage. It came as a shock, then, when he stunningly defeated the Quebec Liberals in 1966 and began to consolidate his victory.

Johnson was highly intelligent and a shrewd politician, yet he was not ready for Trudeau at the constitutional conference. He expected Pearson to lead the debate with his customary diplomatic skill, and the other premiers, who shared some of his doubts about the Trudeau program, to accept the recommendations on linguistic equality proposed by the Royal Commission on Bilingualism and Biculturalism. Indeed, he had welcomed the initiative in the preceding weeks. What he did not anticipate was the major role Trudeau would play. Before the conference, Trudeau spoke derisively of "the little empire" the Quebec provincial government sought to build. He told Peter Newman, his ever more enthusiastic promoter, that he wanted to "take the fuse out of explosive Quebec nationalism by making sure that Quebec is not a ghetto for French Canadians—that all of Canada is theirs."

To Johnson's satisfaction, on the Monday morning in the historic West Block, Pearson opened the conference in expansive, optimistic but dramatic words: "Here the road forks," he said. "If we choose wrongly, we will leave to our children and our children's children a country in fragments, and we ourselves will have become the failures of Confederation." Reassuring speeches followed from the other premiers. Johnson spoke third, after Pearson and Ontario's John Robarts. He was dour and direct in stating that only the "adamant few" denied that Canada was made up of "two nations." It was essential that a two-partner Canada be created to ensure the maintenance of the "ten-partner" Canada. Other premiers responded, some comically (W.A.C. Bennett and Joey Smallwood) and others icily (Alberta premier E.C. Manning, who warned of a constitutional "Munich" whereby Quebec would be appeased at the cost of Canadian unity). Outside the

West Block, a lonely protester took up this theme on a placard: "Another Munich. Another Appeasement."

On the Tuesday morning, Johnson lauded the premiers' general acceptance of linguistic equality but then reiterated his demand for fundamental constitutional change. As he listened, Trudeau was sitting beside the genial and casual Pearson. The intense television lights sharpened all the participants' features but were particularly favourable to Trudeau's chiselled face and striking eyes. Johnson, in contrast, appeared uncomfortable under the glare. In his response to the Quebec premier's speech, Trudeau bluntly expressed his strong opposition to special status and his belief that these proposed changes to the Canadian Constitution would only undermine the position of Quebec's MPs in Ottawa. He further emphasized the importance of a Canadian Charter of Human Rights to enshrine linguistic rights, a proposal that Manning and Johnson had dismissed the previous day. His tone ever more biting, his voice metallic, Trudeau responded to Johnson's reference to him as the "député de Mont-Royal" by describing the premier as the "député de Bagot."

Sensing the tension and worried himself about Trudeau's tone, Pearson called for a coffee break. During the break, Trudeau curtly nodded at Johnson and muttered that the Quebec premier was seeking to destroy the federal government. Johnson sneered that Trudeau was acting like a candidate, not a federal minister.

Reporters rushed from the room to file their stories. The federal government has finally found its own voice, they stated, as they ignored the complicated substance of federal-provincial relations and focused on Trudeau's articulate attack on Johnson. English Canadians who had been troubled by the weak federal response to Johnson's demands for equality or independence were impressed, perhaps because they were weary of the protracted debate about the Constitution and probably because Trudeau had confronted Johnson so effectively. French-speaking Canadians had been given a rare opportunity to hear an important national debate in Ottawa in French. More could have been achieved, but the conference did have two notable results: the acceptance of linguistic equality for both official languages in the government of Canada, and the creation of a formal structure for review of the Constitution through regular conferences. They were no small accomplishment.[15]

"At the beginning of February," Jean Marchand later recalled, "Pierre Trudeau was really created." After the hesitancy that had seemed to mark the response of the Pearson government to Quebec's demands for greater legislative powers, Trudeau came to represent clarity, novelty, and strength. While Claude Ryan and many Quebec editorialists lamented both the tone and the substance of Trudeau's remarks, English-Canadian editorialists welcomed his approach. Quebec sociologist Stéphane Kelly later described how Trudeau's "virile performance" at the conference made him a Hamiltonian candidate, "a strong and authoritative leader, capable of establishing order after ten years of political instability."[16]

After the conference ended, Trudeau joined his assistant Eddie Rubin and other members of his prospective campaign team. They were probably worried about the intensity of the exchange and its impact, but youthful organizer Jim Davey, who had been assessing Trudeau's support across Canada, reported that the effect was electric. He concluded: "Trudeau should be presented as he really was, as himself, both for his own personality and his own ideas about Canada, its problems and its great opportunities." Once the analysis was done, Trudeau walked down Parliament Hill to the Château Laurier, where he stayed when he was in Ottawa, and swam in the elegant art deco pool in the basement of the grand hotel. As he methodically did his laps, he realized the prize might be his. But it was not certain.

—

Trudeau's opponents were already in the field, and delegates were making commitments. Paul Martin began his phone calls before breakfast and continued late into the night, in complete disregard of Canada's varied time zones. Pelletier and Marchand thought that the bilingual Martin would take at least half the Quebec delegates if Trudeau did not run. Mitchell Sharp, Canada's finance minister, was constantly in the news, and his elegance and authority had considerable influence in both the Canadian public service and corporate boardrooms. Paul Hellyer, the defence minister, was already at forty-four a multi-millionaire and a seasoned political veteran. Through his historic if controversial unification of the defence forces during the Pearson government, he had stood up to the generals and never retreated. John Turner, at thirty-eight, was even younger and already a junior minister. He had grown up in British Columbia, won a Rhodes Scholarship to Oxford, danced with an enchanted Princess Margaret, learned French and practised law in Montreal, and had invited Trudeau to his wedding to Geills Kilgour, the daughter of a leading Winnipeg businessman. This impressive and handsome young politician, Peter Newman wrote, "jogged into the race . . . with a list of professional and personal attributes that made him sound like a story-book prime minister, or at least a story-book prince."

Other candidates included the brilliant albeit idiosyncratic Eric Kierans, who had been a minister in the Lesage govern-ment; Joe Greene, a lawyer from eastern Ontario, who con-sciously appealed to the boys and girls from back concessions; and the Nova Scotian Allan MacEachen, the craftiest parlia-mentarian of his times. It was already a remarkable field when Gérard Pelletier and Pierre Trudeau drove together to Ottawa on Sunday evening, February 11, 1968, and tried to sort out Trudeau's confused thoughts.[17]

Trudeau told Pelletier that he was close to a decision, but uncertainty persisted. Marchand was working hard in Quebec, but

Claude Ryan, the editor of *Le Devoir*, was preparing to endorse Sharp; Maurice Sauvé was leaning towards Martin; and Maurice Lamontagne had become a bitter opponent of Trudeau. After the constitutional conference, André Laurendeau criticized Trudeau and expressed his support for Johnson, while René Lévesque, now organizing a separatist party, dismissed Trudeau as the new Nigger King (roi-nègre) of Quebec. Jean Lesage also made known his displeasure with Trudeau. Two impressive young francophone ministers, Jean-Luc Pepin and Jean Chrétien, had committed to Sharp, as had the powerful C.M. "Bud" Drury, whom Trudeau much admired. Although Quebec Liberal Party president Claude Frenette, who had won a decisive victory over a Hellyer candidate in January, was an enthusiastic Trudeau supporter, he and Marchand needed a decision from Trudeau soon. But Trudeau refused to decide. He told Pelletier that Sunday evening that he had two major considerations, which Pelletier summarized in his diary:

> Has he the right to run for the highest position in the party after only two years in Parliament and barely ten months in the Cabinet? Why is it that no one thought of him in November, and two months later his name is all over the press? Why is there all this agitation in the party, by all those who want to see him leader?

Always wary of the press, Trudeau found it "ironic and disquieting to be hoisted onto the shoulders of the media." His second consideration followed from the first:

> Even if he was convinced of the legitimacy of becoming a candidate, he would still take into account a "visceral resistance," a diffuse anxiety, "something" in him that counselled himself against the undertaking.

Pelletier responded to Trudeau at length on the first point as they continued their drive to Ottawa. Trudeau should not worry about his hesitations, he advised. If he did not hesitate, he would be presumptuous, but presumptuous he had never been. He would have to trust the judgment of others about his capacity to govern and the risks it involved. In Pelletier's view, the media attention, which was already dubbed "Trudeaumanie" in French and "Trudeaumania" in English, was in some ways a "spinoff" of the Kennedy legend that had so profoundly affected North American politics—and would again, in March 1968, as Bobby Kennedy began his historic and tragic quest for the American presidency. Trudeau should not worry, Pelletier insisted. "If that myth settled on the shoulders of an incompetent, a candidate without vigour, he would be crushed. But it happened that Trudeau had a certain stature. He would never be crushed by the myth. On the contrary, he had what was needed to sustain the myth and make it reality. Chance, but not only chance, had chosen Trudeau."

Pelletier then turned to the second objection and asked Trudeau, "Do you sleep well?" Yes, he replied, "very well," but it was in the mornings that he began to worry about feeling unhappy as prime minister. He would lose the *joie de vivre* and "never accomplish anything worthwhile." Pelletier again rejected Trudeau's fears and said that this resistance would disappear once he made a decision. He had seen what had happened since the three friends came to Ottawa. Unlike Marchand and himself, Trudeau took to Parliament and government "like a duck to water—every minute of it, or almost." Then Pelletier made the crucial point that the press did not know: Pierre, he said, "your whole life has been a preparation for politics." The car became silent. When they arrived and Pelletier shut off the engine, Trudeau remained seated. Finally he spoke: "I think you've convinced me," he said quietly. "I'll see, tomorrow morning."[18]

Finally, the die seemed cast when Pelletier, Marchand, and Trudeau met for lunch on February 13 in Marchand's office. Yet Trudeau still refused to make a commitment and demanded reassurance. They met again in the evening, but "the conversation slipped into the same old ruts." Earlier, on the weekend of February 9, Trudeau had gone to the Ontario Liberal convention, where his brief appearance resembled that of a rock star as young women squealed and grabbed at him while reporters thrust microphones into his face. He told an insistent crowd that he would decide within ten days. Bob Stanbury, Donald Macdonald, and many others who organized the Toronto meeting were becoming increasingly impatient as their political futures became hostage to Trudeau's delays. The same was true of Marchand and Pelletier after they met Trudeau for dinner on that Tuesday night. The conversation convinced Marchand and Pelletier that Trudeau probably would not run. They then went to a meeting of the Trudeau "team" without Trudeau and, in Pelletier's words, felt as though they were living "in a bad dream" as Trudeau's many Ottawa supporters plotted a Trudeau campaign that would likely die before birth. Trudeau apparently did not tell Marchand and Pelletier that he had met with Pearson earlier, before the dinner with them, and that the prime minister, whose common sense he had come to admire, had encouraged him to run. Later, he shared his thoughts with Marc Lalonde and Michael Pitfield before he walked slowly back to the Château Laurier and decided his fate that cold winter night.[19]

The next morning, Valentine's Day, Trudeau surprised Marchand and Pelletier in the Parliamentary Restaurant by telling them he would run. Marchand immediately announced that he would step down as Quebec leader at the Wednesday morning caucus and that Jean-Pierre Goyer, a fervent Trudeau supporter, would help him organize the Quebec caucus for Trudeau. Trudeau was not yet ready to go public with his decision, and he wanted proof of support. Goyer, accordingly, promised a crowd of over fifty Quebec MPs and senators for a noontime gathering on Thursday, February 15, but only about twenty showed up. It was disappointing, and also an indication that Trudeaumania might have swept the media but had run into some resistance on Parliament Hill. Trudeau fretted; Marchand fumed. Pelletier and others worked the phones and determined that caucus support in Quebec was strong. At 6:30 that evening the Trudeau team of Marchand and MPs Edgar Benson, Jean-Pierre Goyer, and Russell Honey met with assistants Eddie Rubin, Pierre Levasseur, Jim Davey, and Gordon Gibson. They carefully counted the potential support and concluded that Trudeau already had 675–700 votes on the first ballot. That number was not enough to win, which required about 1,200 votes, but it was enough to convince Trudeau that he should announce his candidacy the following day.[20]

On February 16, 1968, Trudeau walked across the street from his West Block office to the National Press Club and declared himself a leadership candidate. It was a remarkable announcement, unlike that of any leadership hopeful before. He drew the press into the conspiracy that he and his friends had created, and it captured them—for a while:

> If I try to assess what happened in the past two months, I have a suspicion you people [the press] had a lot to do with it. If anybody's to blame, I suppose it's you collectively. If there's anybody to thank, it's you collectively. To be quite frank, if I try to analyze it, well, I think in the subconscious mind of the press . . . it started out like a huge practical joke on the Liberal Party. I mean that, because, in some sense, the decision that I made this morning and last night is in some ways similar to that I arrived at when I entered the Liberal Party. It seemed to me, reading the press in the early stages a couple of months ago, it seemed

to me as though many of you were saying, you know, "We dare the Liberal Party to choose a guy like Trudeau. Of course, we know they never will, but we'll just dare them to do it and we'll show that this is the man they could have had as leader if they had wanted. Here's how great he is."

The press, Trudeau continued, then said that the Liberals did not have the guts to choose the "good guy." Now, the joke had blown up in the media's many faces and in his own face:

> You know, people took it seriously. I saw this when—not when the press thought I had a chance, and that I should go, and so on—but when I saw the response from political people, from members of the party and responsible members of parliament. This is when I began to wonder if, oh, you know, this whole thing was not a bit more serious than you and I had intended. And when members of parliament formed committees to draft me, and when I got responsible Liberals in responsible positions in different parts of the country telling me seriously that I should run, I think what happened is that the joke became serious . . . So I was stuck with it. Well, you're stuck with me.

Stick to Trudeau they did, until he finally became prime minister of Canada less than two months later.[21]

—

Trudeau's hesitations had irritated many friends and puzzled the other candidates. The pattern was familiar to some, such as Pelletier and Marchand, who recalled earlier examples of Trudeau's reluctance. Yet the stakes were higher and, as Pelletier told Trudeau, he had spent a lifetime preparing for the political career now within his grasp. This time Pelletier could not "guess what was going on in the conscience, the emotions, the inner depths of a friend, even when one had known him for twenty years." His friend had refused to peel away the carefully constructed layers that shielded his emotional core. But despite his supporters' concerns, Trudeau had good reason to consider his decision carefully.

To begin, the one person whose consent he valued most had fallen silent. On weekends he would return to the family home, see his mother with her polished nails, perfect coiffure, elegant but conservative dress, take her hand and speak softly, but now she had no answers. Alzheimer's disease or some other form of dementia had closed Grace Trudeau's excellent mind at the very moment when her fondest dream was about to be realized. Trudeau was more alone than ever before.

Moreover, he was rightly wary of the media enthusiasm for his campaign. He knew that this embrace could chill quickly, as it had for Diefenbaker or Lesage, whose charisma had lasted but a fleeting moment. Journalist Leslie Roberts, a supporter, feared that the media's "constantly repetitive use of that idiotic word 'charisma'" could cause a counter-reaction through which Trudeau "could easily be laughed back to seventh place in the twelve-man league of leadership contenders by his own best friends."[22] Trudeau himself worried that he was simply an "epiphenomenon," a phantom floating above the reality of Canadian politics—a reality he barely knew. He also knew that his past had secrets that could quickly capture the front pages of all the dailies. Already, the maverick Toronto Liberal Ralph Cowan was passing around translations of Trudeau's bitter 1963 attack on the "defrocked prince of peace" Lester Pearson, and he promised more revelations. Trudeau, the scourge of separatists and the most eloquent supporter of a secular state in the sixties, had endorsed an independent, Catholic "Laurentie" in the early 1940s. He had championed Pétain and urged violence.

Many who now loathed him knew his past. Would they reveal it? How would it affect him?

In fact, he didn't appear to care. When asked on a Radio-Canada late-night comedy show to name his favourite author, he answered "Niccolò Machiavelli"—a startling choice for a democratic aspirant. But it amused him and, apparently, his audience.[23] Politics, he seemed to be saying to himself and to others, could be playful.

Finally, Trudeau valued his privacy and often reacted to attacks in a decidedly personal manner—as in his protracted dispute with Father Braun in the early fifties over his trip to the Soviet Union. When he became a political celebrity in the winter of 1968, the gossip, jealousy, and suspicion that invariably attach themselves to prominence quickly abounded. Christina McCall, who knew Ottawa well in those days, remembered the Conservative candidate in the Beauce who, in denouncing Trudeau's legislation regarding homosexuality, said that the bill was "for queers and fairies," adding, gratuitously, that Trudeau was a bachelor. Walter Gordon told McCall that, when he confronted Trudeau in the House of Commons lobby about the many rumours of his own homosexuality, Trudeau reacted angrily and suggested that the men making the charge should leave him alone with their wives for a couple of hours. According to one reliable source, Pearson himself asked a close associate of Trudeau whether the justice minister was a homosexual. The infamous Canadian Intelligence Service, which had linked Pearson with Communist spy rings, began to transfer its attention to Trudeau, who had already made appearances in its pages.[24]

To these largely personal concerns, Trudeau now added a shrewd political assessment: it was by no means certain that he would win the leadership and the election to follow. The Progressive Conservative lead in the polls was 6 percent, and the Liberal leadership campaign was already proving divisive.

Moreover, the "draft Trudeau" campaign could identify only seven hundred supporters; he would need to attract about five hundred more to win the leadership. Neither he nor Marchand knew the party beyond Quebec, and they had to rely on the assessment of others to estimate his support. Surely all those church suppers, summer barbeques, and favours rendered over thirty-three years of Liberal service meant something for Paul Martin's candidacy! Was the party a largely hollow shell waiting to be filled with enthusiastic newcomers? Did it matter that his most eminent academic supporter in English Canada, the historian Ramsay Cook, had been a longtime supporter of the CCF-NDP and, in a 1965 private letter, had criticized Trudeau's affiliation with the Liberals while welcoming his presence in Ottawa? The political times were not normal or predictable. And it was fortunate for Trudeau they were not.

Trudeau announced his candidacy on Friday, February 16, and, three days later, the Liberal government was defeated on a budget item in the House of Commons. In the House, Finance Minister Mitchell Sharp and Acting Prime Minister Robert Winters had decided to go ahead on a third-reading vote against the advice of Allan MacEachen, the Liberal expert on House rules. The bells rang, the Conservatives rounded up members the Liberals thought were absent, and the Liberals lost the vote. Normally, that would mean the defeat of the government and an immediate election, presumably with Lester Pearson leading the Liberals in the campaign.

Pearson was holidaying in Jamaica, and three leadership candidates were absent. Pearson, "shocked and enraged," flew home and berated his colleagues for their irresponsible actions. He then persuaded Robert Stanfield to agree to a twenty-four-hour adjournment of the House. It was a fatal error for the Conservative leader, one the highly partisan John Diefenbaker would never have made. As Walter Gordon later said, all "Stanfield had to do . . . was to get up and walk out of the House [saying]: 'The Government is defeated; there is nothing more to do here.'" But Stanfield hesitated and lost. Pearson counterattacked, managed to delay the vote of confidence on the narrow item of the Monday night vote, and convinced the Créditistes to reverse their vote. Throughout the crisis, Trudeau gave constitutional law advice to Pearson and the Cabinet and performed coolly in the House of Commons in defending the government's stand. Immediately, he benefited most from the whole dramatic event.[25] The leadership race continued, but Mitchell Sharp's campaign had been mortally wounded.[26]

The press reacted sharply to the chaos in Liberal ranks. It confirmed for Trudeau the grumbling of his supporters Marc Lalonde and Michael Pitfield about the poor organization of the Pearson government and validated his belief that a more rational approach to politics was essential. Rationality in government became a major theme of the Trudeau campaign. The sudden weakness of the Sharp campaign caused a stir among conservative Liberal supporters, especially in the business community. At the 1966 Liberal policy convention, Sharp had successfully presented himself as the opponent of both Walter Gordon's nationalism and left-wing tendencies in the party. The rapid expansion of Canadian social programs in the mid-sixties had taken a toll on the government's finances, and Sharp had proposed postponing the inauguration of medicare for one more year. After the week of February 19, it was difficult to imagine Sharp becoming leader, and the conservative and business faction of the Liberal Party began to worry.

Suddenly a movement developed in the Senate to draft Robert Winters, who had dismissed a run for the leadership in early January and had himself been implicated in the disastrous decision to hold the vote. His role there appeared to be forgotten, and Winters responded to the draft, offering his resignation to Pearson on February 28 and announcing his candidacy the following day (February 29 in this leap year). He spoke in terms his supporters understood: "I have always believed that if you don't agree with the policies of a firm, you either get out or take it over."[27] He would be the candidate for fiscal rectitude and against government excess.

—

The first polls that appeared in early March were taken in early February. They showed Paul Martin in the lead, but Trudeau, who had not then even announced, stood a remarkable second. The results were very encouraging, but Martin had a strong organization, while Trudeau's was still informal. Trudeau's campaign team was decidedly amateurish, with Pelletier as the policy coordinator, Jean-Pierre Goyer in charge of convention arrangements, Jim Davey as leadership campaign coordinator, Pierre Levasseur as the Ottawa operations manager, and Gordon Gibson, the son of a wealthy British Columbia political legend, as Trudeau's handler and travelling companion. Though short on political experience, they were bright, ambitious, and willing to try novel approaches, in part because they didn't know the traditional ones. But who could be sure the new approaches would work? Moreover, on March 1 the Trudeau campaign fund had collected only $6,500.

After Winters's announcement, the characteristically pessimistic Pelletier wrote in his diary on March 6: "Trudeau's victory seems to me most uncertain." He was repelled by "the high degree of *fabrication* and mythology" that surrounded Trudeau as a candidate, a "personage" who bore "no resemblance to the fellow I've know for twenty years under the name of Pierre Trudeau." Yet what peeved Pelletier astounded and intrigued others. And there was another factor: the candidate Pierre Trudeau was not the man Pelletier had so long known.

Pelletier had worried about Trudeau's bitter sarcasm and unexpected cruelty in debate. What he saw once the campaign began was a "cool" Trudeau, slow to anger and amused and tolerant when journalists attacked. When television interviewers Pierre O'Neil and Louis Martin unfairly accused Trudeau of having no support in Quebec, he "stayed cool" and "replied that we should wait and see." When they rudely interrupted him before he answered, he simply smiled. Moreover, the timidity that Trudeau usually exhibited at social events disappeared in the midst of the adoring crowds that greeted him during the leadership tour. At the launches for the two books hastily assembled by his supporters from his previous writings, *Federalism and the French Canadians* and *Réponses,* Trudeau astounded both his old friends and reporters as he kissed the numerous beautiful women present as enthusiastically as traditional politicians bussed babies. At least, in this new political phenomenon of kissing adult women, he did bring much experience.

Out on the campaign trail, reporters vied with each other to spin the tastiest tales. A desk clerk at a Sudbury hotel was so stunned by Trudeau's handshake that she forgot to make change. A MacEachen supporter declared, on seeing Trudeau, that rather than meeting him she wanted to marry him, forgetting that her husband stood nearby. A middle-aged woman in a meeting at the National Library became so nervous in asking her question that she placed the microphone in her ear. A playful Trudeau answered with the microphone in his own ear. In British Columbia the wife of the president of the Liberal Federation, a Hellyer supporter, told reporters that the party needed a new leader who was not stodgy. "And anyway," she continued, "I think he's sexy." Everyone knew she meant Trudeau. Soon Trudeau was dubbed the candidate of the Age of Aquarius—he wore a rose in his lapel just as hippies wore flowers in their hair. He promised he'd open 24 Sussex Drive to parties and, when asked who would be the hostess, he replied: "Why should there be only one?"[28] Woodstock was not far away.

Trudeau's new "personage" carried the message that he would be different. He ran for office among the finest group of politicians ever to contest a party leadership in Canada, and he stood out above them all. The issues identified with him—specifically, the reform of the Criminal Code, the Constitution, and Quebec—reflected the spirit of a country that wanted to change and, in the case of Quebec, knew it must change. His high-contrast campaign posters, which, against the advice of the campaign executive, were commissioned by two remarkable young women, Alison Gordon and Jennifer Rae, were also strikingly different. Years later they were "the most coveted souvenirs of the leadership race."[29] In the *Toronto Star*, Peter Newman recognized the significance of Trudeau's announcement the very day it was made: "Two years ago, in pre-Expo Canada it would have been almost impossible to imagine [Trudeau] as a serious contender. Now, we don't have to go on muttering hopefully, 'the times they are achangin.' The times *have* changed."

Trudeau's Criminal Code amendments and, more important, his clear explanations of the reasons for the changes—"the state has no business in the bedrooms of the nation" and "what may be sin to some is not law for all"—contrasted strongly with the ambiguity with which his opponents approached the same issues. Norman Spector, then a left-leaning McGill student, expressed the view of youth and the spirit of change when he wrote a letter to the *Montreal Star* on January 12:

The reforms which have been instituted in recent weeks by the Hon. Pierre Elliott Trudeau should meet with the approval of all thinking Canadians. Without a doubt our minister of justice is an intellectual of the first order.

To those of us who have reached the conclusion that the Liberal party had grown staid and stodgy, the reforms of the Criminal Code come somewhat as a surprise. Is this the same Liberal party which is procrastinating so needlessly

before inaugurating medicare? Is this the party which ele-
vates Robert Winters and ostracizes Walter Gordon? Have
the Liberals finally seen the light?

For many of the young, the unorthodox and stylish challenge of Pierre Trudeau had become the light that illuminated a
new Canada.

—

For others, such as his old acquaintances Daniel Johnson and
Claude Ryan, Trudeau's accession to the Liberal leadership
would thrust Canada into a new darkness. The first spat came
with Johnson soon after Trudeau announced his candidacy. The
Quebec premier focused on a flippant comment Trudeau had
made that the French taught in Quebec was "lousy"—there was "a
state of emergency as regards language" in Quebec which its government ignored. This remark contrasted strongly with the politeness that Trudeau exhibited in challenging his Liberal leadership
opponents. Johnson replied acidly, claiming that the election of
Trudeau would mean the death of Canada. Trudeau encouraged
English Canadians to retain "backward and retrograde attitudes"
towards Quebec. He called Trudeau "Lord Elliott" and compared
his remarks to those of Lord Durham, who had famously encouraged the assimilation of French Canada in 1839.

Trudeau responded quickly and pointed out that his goal, in
contrast to Durham's, was to gain equality for the French language
throughout Canada. He challenged Johnson directly: "I think this
shows how afraid he is of the people of Quebec becoming interested in federal politics. If they do, then he knows he won't be lord
and master over all Quebec." For good measure, he added that
"calling me Lord Elliott when his name is Johnson is . . . a sticky
wicket." To another critic, he simply and effectively replied: "When

the king is naked, I say that the king is naked." Trudeau not only won the debate with Johnson but also gained attention and support in English Canada. A poll of Alberta delegates revealed a surge of support for Trudeau, who was increasingly seen as the best candidate to confront Quebec separatism and nationalism.[30]

The clarity of purpose that impressed many Albertans troubled others. Claude Ryan began to criticize him daily in *Le Devoir* for his rigidity. The dispute with Johnson infuriated Ryan, who warned English Canadians that they were mistaken in believing that Trudeau was a "Messiah" who would lead them out of the constitutional wilderness. He argued against Trudeau's constitutional stand and emphasized that the two provincial parties were united in their support for special status. Another international issue with serious implications for the special status of Quebec appeared with the invitation from the African state of Gabon for Quebec to participate in an educational conference among francophone states. Trudeau took a hard line, pointing out that foreign affairs was a federal responsibility, and he even provoked Pelletier, who wanted a compromise in which Quebec could form part of the Canadian delegation to the conference. Nevertheless, his strong statement against "French interference" so soon after Charles de Gaulle's "Vive le Québec libre" speech reinforced his image as the key opponent to special status and special rights for Quebec.

The other candidates noticed the swelling opposition to Trudeau in Quebec ranks and began to criticize him. Mitchell Sharp, for example, attacked Trudeau's harsh exchange with Johnson, while Paul Martin Sr. argued that a prime minister must be "a man who has not clouded relations with any prominent government or provincial premier." Once again, Trudeau benefited from the simplicity of his constitutional stand: linguistic equality enshrined in a charter of human rights. In the classic formulation of the French scientist and writer Comte de Buffon, the style became the political man.[31]

Gérard Pelletier was finally convinced of the political worth of Trudeau's new personage when his old friend visited his riding of Hochelaga. His previous appearances there had been listless, but this time Trudeau was confident, poised, and the object of adoration. It proved for Pelletier the "American" maxim that "nothing succeeds like success." The excitement in Hochelaga reminded him of what Trudeau had said to him after he was mobbed in Victoria. There, when his campaigners asked him how he managed to smile all day long, he did not dare tell them the truth. But he confided to Pelletier: "It would have been harder not to smile. I found it all so odd, grotesque, almost hilarious."

Odd and hilarious it may have been, but it was working. Thanks to the efforts of Marchand, the Quebec support finally materialized with thirty-one MPs agreeing to support him publicly after a March 6 meeting. In a confidential survey of MPs carried out in mid-March, Trudeau received support from thirty-eight of the eighty-seven MPs who replied. Hellyer, who had won the first delegate-selection meetings in Toronto, had the support of fifteen; Winters, thirteen; Martin, eleven; Turner and MacEachen, four each; and Sharp and Greene, one each. Trudeau, moreover, was the second choice of nineteen, followed by Winters, with fifteen. In the last week before the convention, the campaign became, very simply, Trudeau against the rest.[32]

Walter Gordon finally endorsed Trudeau on March 26, although he admitted he was troubled by Trudeau's opposition to economic nationalism. And Joey Smallwood officially supported Trudeau, a fact he had confided to almost every journalist in Newfoundland. Members of parliament Bryce Mackasey and Edgar Benson took the leadership in his campaign and provided valuable political experience for the last days. Then fortune fell unexpectedly in Trudeau's path: Mitchell Sharp withdrew from the campaign and threw his support to Trudeau.

A complex string of events lay behind this move. Sharp had tried to reinvigorate his campaign in the last half of March, but the crowds were meagre and his heart was weak. As his well-financed organization polled the delegates, it quickly learned that Sharp's support had evaporated. After the budget crisis in February, Sharp had spoken with Pearson about withdrawing and asked the prime minister what he thought of Trudeau. Pearson said he was impressed but puzzled, a factor that persuaded Sharp to stay in the race. Rumours of this discussion leaked to the Trudeau camp. Marchand, in a gesture that betrayed considerable naïveté, then approached Sharp to say that he and Trudeau should run a joint campaign, with the caucus deciding who should become leader. Although Sharp was identified with the conservative and business wing of the party, he had lost respect for Robert Winters. When Winters indicated in January 1968 that he had no intention of contesting the leadership, he gratuitously added that the finances of Canada were in bad shape and poorly handled. Sharp, as finance minister, took the remarks personally and asked for an apology. Winters apologized in a private letter, but then destroyed its political impact by refusing to allow Sharp to release it.

Sharp met Pearson again in late March and told him that he now had a higher opinion of Trudeau. Pearson said he did too. So, on April 3, the convention's eve, Sharp endorsed Trudeau, and Sharp's supporters Jean-Luc Pepin, Jean Chrétien, and Bud Drury also joined Trudeau's team. All three were political gems—Pepin because he was an elegant and charming orator, Chrétien for his extraordinary campaign skills, and Drury for his ties with business.

The news fuelled a wild Trudeau rally at the cavernous Chaudière nightclub across the Ottawa River. There the irrepressible Joey Smallwood declared that "Pierre is better than medicare—the lame have only to touch his garments to walk again."[33]

—

On Thursday, April 4, the convention's first day, James Earl Ray shot Martin Luther King in a Memphis motel and riots swept through large American cities as his murderer fled to Toronto. The tragedy provoked sombre thoughts but did not deaden the excitement surrounding the policy workshops in Ottawa. Trudeau's crowds were the largest, crammed with mini-skirted youthful enthusiasm. The tribute to Lester Pearson that evening ended with the bizarre gift of a puppy and, to the retiring leader's embarrassment, Maryon Pearson's strong hint of affection for Trudeau.

The next day came the speeches. Ottawa's Civic Centre was crammed, television booms and cameras were everywhere, and streamers dangled from every rafter. Two fringe candidates, the Reverend Lloyd Henderson and Holocaust denier Ernst Zündel, were not permitted to speak in the regular workshops but were restricted to a short session in which the trilingual Zündel condemned the historic mistreatment of French and German Canadians. On Friday evening, Trudeau was the target of the other speakers, who largely disappointed except for Joe Greene, who gave a populist "barnburner." Paul Hellyer's poor performance had a major impact later as voting delegates remembered his bland words.

With a speech drafted mainly by Tim Porteous, with French translation by Gérard Pelletier, Trudeau spoke well; Richard Stanbury thought only Greene was better, and none doubted that the Trudeau crowd was the largest and noisiest. He spoke for only nineteen of the permitted thirty minutes because his supporters demonstrated so long and vigorously. They continued to cheer him as he declared: "Liberalism is the only philosophy for our time, because it does not try to conserve every tradition of the past; because it does not apply to new problems the old doctrinaire solutions; because it is prepared to experiment and innovate and because it knows that the past is less important than the future." The message was typically clear: the Liberal future lay with Trudeau. It was both a promise and a warning.[34]

Trudeau began Saturday, the final day, with a pancake and maple syrup breakfast at the Château Laurier which six hundred delegates attended. As he left, he slid down the hotel's grand staircase banister, to the delight of photographers and delegates alike.

Balloting began at 1:00 p.m. At 2:30 Senator John Nichol announced the results:

Greene	169
Hellyer	330
Kierans	103
MacEachen	165
Martin	277
Trudeau	752
Turner	277
Winters	293

Trudeau had met his team's expectations; Paul Hellyer's face began to drip with perspiration; Maurice Sauvé immediately bolted from his seat beside Paul Martin and pushed through the crowd towards Trudeau. Young historians Robert Bothwell and Norman Hillmer were shocked to see Claude Ryan begin to shake with rage in the press booth.[35]

Lloyd Henderson received no votes and was automatically eliminated, and Ernst Zündel had withdrawn before the ballot, but that meant the other candidates had to decide individually if they would step aside. Kierans and Paul Martin, who had led the leadership polls for so long, both withdrew graciously. MacEachen intended to withdraw but failed to notify Senator Nichol by the deadline, so, to the disappointment of the Trudeau camp, he remained on the second ballot. On that ballot, Trudeau moved up to 964, as he picked up most of MacEachen's left-wing support. Winters finished second with 473 votes, Hellyer won a disappointing 465, while Turner rose to 347 and Greene fell to 104. The beneficial impact on Trudeau's campaign of Mitchell Sharp's withdrawal suddenly became obvious.

The two successful businessmen Hellyer and Winters conferred on what they should do to stop Trudeau. Despite Winters's entreaties, Paul Hellyer refused to drop out—which would have cast the weight of his votes behind Winters. Winters then asked Judy LaMarsh, who supported Hellyer and loathed Trudeau, to have a word with Hellyer. Television and boom microphones were new to Canadian politicians at the time. Unaware she was being overheard, a tearful LaMarsh, now wearing a Winters button, shouted at Hellyer: "It's tough, Paul, but what the hell. Do you want that bastard taking over the party?" He didn't, but, crucially, he did not withdraw.[36]

On the third ballot, Winters took 621 votes; Hellyer, 377. Trudeau, at 1,051, was only fifty-three ahead of their combined vote. Turner held onto 279, and Greene, at 29, was dropped. Had Hellyer spoken better on Friday evening, had Sharp not endorsed Trudeau, Paul Hellyer probably would have become Liberal leader. These are the "what ifs" of history, which intrigue but remain wistful dreams for losers. Hellyer did keep his promise to Winters that he would endorse him if Winters moved ahead on the third ballot. Enthusiastically waving a Winters banner, he began to chant "Go, Bob, go." Joe Greene joined the crowded Trudeau box, where Trudeau coolly amused himself by tossing grapes in the air and catching them in his mouth as they fell. John Turner stubbornly refused to withdraw, and, as the final voting began at 8 p.m., most of the crowd erupted in shouts of "Trudeau. Canada. We want Trudeau."

When Nichol began to read out the final results—Trudeau 1,203—the crowd exploded, drowning out the announcement of

Winters, 954, and Turner, 195. Trudeau's face momentarily and exuberantly beamed, then froze in silent contemplation.

What images swirled in Pierre Trudeau's mind as the crowd swarmed around him as he moved slowly to the podium? Certainly he recalled the moment two days before when he spied in the crowd the beautiful young woman he had met on the beach in Tahiti, and he immediately broke away from his handlers to speak a few words to her. He probably thought of Thérèse Gouin Décarie, who, with her husband, had organized the academic petition for his candidacy at the Université de Montréal. And there were surely memories of those nights in Pelletier's basement, drafting tracts that few read and many resented; of days in Paris dreaming of a Quebec that might be, and of summers at Old Orchard Beach with the family; of long nights when Papa brought home his political friends who argued long into the night, and of a mother who, in silence, still radiated her endless love for him. He reached the stage at the front of the convention hall, mounted the steps—and, suddenly, he smiled.

NOTES

—

Unless otherwise specified, all references to the Trudeau Papers are found in MG 26 02 at Library and Archives Canada.

CHAPTER ONE: TWO WORLDS

1. Isaac Starr, "Influenza in 1918: Recollections of the Epidemic in Philadephia," *Annals of Internal Medicine*, Oct. 1976, 516.
2. Quoted in Jean-Claude Marsan, *Montreal in Evolution* (Montreal and Kingston: McGill-Queen's University Press, 1981), 256.
3. The population of Montreal in 1911 was only 25.7 percent English. The third largest group, the Jews, at 5.9 percent, tended to affiliate, nervously, with the English minority while building their own institutions to maintain their religious identity. See Paul-André Linteau, *Histoire de Montréal depuis la Confédération* (Montreal: Les Éditions du Boréal, 2000), 162. The English group had fallen from 33.7 percent to 25.7 percent between 1901 and 1911.
4. Zweig is quoted in Gérard Bouchard, *Les deux chanoines: Contradiction et ambivalence dans la pensée de Lionel Groulx* (Montreal: Les Éditions du Boréal, 2003), 38. Earlier, in 1904, the renowned French sociologist André Siegfried had visited Canada and declared Canadian politics corrupt, unable to rise above "the sordid preoccupations of patronage or connection." How long, he asked, could Canadian politicians suppress the crisis that loomed before them? André Siegfried, *The Race Question in Canada*, trans. E. Nash (1907; Toronto: McClelland & Stewart, 1966), 113.

5. Terry Copp, "Public Health in Montreal, 1870–1930," in S.E.D. Shortt, ed., *Medicine in Canadian Society: Historical Perspectives* (Montreal: McGill-Queen's University Press, 1981), 395–416; and Martin Tétrault, "Les maladies de la misère: Aspects de la santé publique à Montréal, 1880–1914," *Revue d'histoire de l'Amérique française* 36 (March 1983): 507–26.

6. Grace Trudeau to Pierre Trudeau, March 30, 1948, Trudeau Papers (TP), MG 26 02, vol. 46, file 16, Library and Archives Canada (LAC).

7. The Clio Collective, *Quebec Women: A History*, trans. Roger Gannon and Rosalind Gill (Toronto: The Women's Press, 1987), 254–55.

8. "Philip" was the surname of Trudeau's maternal grandfather. "Baby's Days," Baby Book 1919–1929, TP, vol. 1, file 14.

9. Ibid. In a contest in 1988 when members of the Prime Minister's Office were asked to give his full name, Trudeau wrote "Joseph Yves Pierre Elliott ? Trudeau"—and lost the prize. See Nancy Southam, ed., *Pierre* (Toronto: McClelland & Stewart, 2005), 64.

10. The Baby Book indicates that Trudeau held his head erect at two months, crept at eight months, and stood alone at eleven months. He had his first tooth on August 6, 1920, and his second on August 10. His first outing on a sleigh was on December 8, 1919, and his first trip to St-Rémi on December 13, 1919, when his grandfather, Joseph Trudeau, died. He had his tonsils removed on October 16, 1921. TP, vol. 1, file 14.

11. Charles Trudeau to Grace Trudeau, Aug. 17, 1921, TP, vol. 53, file 30.

12. Pierre Trudeau's assessment of Charles is found in George Radwanski, *Trudeau* (Toronto: Macmillan, 1978), ch. 4. Other notable biographies of Trudeau that contain important family material, often drawing on the interviews Trudeau gave to Radwanski, are Stephen Clarkson and Christina McCall, *Trudeau and Our Times*, vol. 1: *The Magnificent Obsession* (Toronto: McClelland & Stewart, 1990), vol. 2: *The Heroic Delusion* (Toronto: McClelland & Stewart, 1994); and Michel Vastel, *Trudeau: Le Québécois* 2nd ed. (Montreal: Les Éditions de l'Homme, 2000). See also Pierre Trudeau, *Memoirs* (Toronto: McClelland & Stewart, 1993).

13. Radwanski, *Trudeau*, 43.

14. Victor Barbeau, quoted in Claude Corbo, *La mémoire du cours classique: Les années aigres-douces des récits autobiographiques* (Outremont, Que.: Les Éditions Logiques, 2000), 33.

15. These comments and records are found in TP, vol. 1, files 1–6.

16. Trudeau, *Memoirs*, 6; Radwanski, *Trudeau*, 47.

17. Trudeau, *Memoirs*, 10–13.

18. Vastel, *Trudeau*, 22–23. Clarkson's recent comment is in John English, Richard Gwyn, and P. Whitney Lackenbauer, eds., *The Hidden Pierre Elliott Trudeau: The Faith behind the Politics* (Ottawa: Novalis, 2004), 33. For the friend's recollection, see Clarkson and McCall, *Trudeau and Our Times*, 1: 30. Max and Monique Nemni also doubt that Charles was abusive and paint a similar portrait to the one presented in this book. See Max and Monique Nemni, *Trudeau: Fils du Québec, père du Canada*, vol. 1: *Les années de jeunesse, 1919–1944* (Montreal: Les Éditions de l'Homme, 2006).

19. Paul-André Linteau, René Durocher, and Jean-Claude Robert, *Quebec: A History, 1867–1929*, trans. Robert Chodos and Ellen Garmaise (Toronto: James Lorimer, 1983), 345–47.

20. Charles Trudeau to Grace Trudeau, Aug. 17, 1921, TP, vol. 53, file 30.

21. Trudeau, *Memoirs*, 13. Also Radwanski, *Trudeau*, 44, and TP, vol. 53, file 31. On his club memberships and directorships, see *Le Devoir*, April 11, 1935.

22. Interview between Pierre Trudeau and Ron Graham, April 18, 1992, TP, vol. 23, file 3. In this interview, Trudeau said that he thought the majority of the customers were the French elite. That probably was not the case, although the evidence is elusive.

23. Pierre Trudeau to Charles Trudeau, nd, TP, vol. 53, file 33.

24. Charles Trudeau to Pierre Trudeau, Sept. 28, 1926, and Charles to Pierre, May 1930, ibid., file 31.

25. Pierre Trudeau to Charles Trudeau, nd, and Charles to Pierre, July 19, 1929, ibid.

26. Pierre Trudeau to Charles Trudeau, ibid.

27. Pierre Trudeau to Charles and Grace Trudeau, March 10, 1935, and Pierre to Charles, April 8, 1935, ibid., file 33.

28. Trudeau, *Memoirs*, 30; Radwanski, *Trudeau*, 54.

29. Radwanski, *Trudeau*, 55.

30. Trudeau, *Memoirs*, 30.

31. Père Jean Belanger to Pierre Trudeau, April [12?] 1935, TP, vol. 41, file 1.

32. Trudeau gave this information to the painter. TP, vol. 23, file 6.

33. Radwanski, *Trudeau*, 55.

34. *Le Devoir*, April 15, 1935. The names are overwhelmingly francophone.

35. Pierre Trudeau to Grace Trudeau, April 28, May 2, and June 10, 1935, TP, vol. 2, file 5.

36. Vastel, *Trudeau*, 27.

37. Clarkson and McCall, *Trudeau and Our Times*, 1: 31.

38. Ibid.; Radwanski, *Trudeau*, 55–56.

39. TP, vol. 1, file 22.

40. Grace Pitfield wrote these comments to Christina McCall-Newman on October 26, 1974. Quoted in McCall-Newman, *Grits: An Intimate Portrait of the Liberal Party* (Toronto: Macmillan, 1982), 65.

41. Richard Gwyn, *The Northern Magus: Pierre Trudeau and Canadians* (Toronto: McClelland & Stewart, 1980), 23.

42. "Notes sur la succession JCE Trudeau et la Cie Trudeau-Elliott," TP, vol. 5, file 17.

43. TP, vol. 1, file 25.

44. Conversation between Trudeau and Suzette, his sister, TP, vol. 23, file 5.

45. "Cahiers d'exercices," TP, vol. 2, file 8.

46. Fernand Foissy, *Michel Chartrand: Les vois d'un homme de parole* (Outremont, Que.: Lanctôt, 1999), 29.

47. The files on his Querbes period are found in TP, vol. 1, files 16–22.

48. The three essays are "Dévouement de Dollard," "Danger des armes à feu," and "L'enfant poli." Ibid., file 22.

49. Trudeau, *Memoirs*, 25, 31–32.

50. Radwanski, *Trudeau*, 36. Bernier confirms the character of the political discussion on page 37.

51. The best description of the origins of Groulx's nationalism is in Bouchard, *Les deux chanoines*, 38ff. Also, Pierre Hébert, *Lionel Groulx et L'appel de la race* (Montreal: Les Éditions Fides, 1996), 20–21.

52. Frédéric Boily, *La pensée nationaliste de Lionel Groulx* (Sillery, Que.: Les Éditions du Septentrion, 2003), 50.

53. Lionel Groulx, *L'appel de la race* (Montreal: Bibliothèque de l'Action française, 1922). See the account of the reception of the novel in Boily, *La pensée*, ch. 5.

54. Quoted in Donald Horton, *André Laurendeau: French-Canadian Nationalist, 1912–1968* (Toronto: Oxford University Press, 1992), 82.

55. See Louise Bienvenue, *Quand la jeunesse entre en scène: L'action catholique avant la révolution tranquille* (Montreal: Les Édition du Boréal, 2003), 42–44.

56. Trudeau, *Memoirs*, 21. For the water incident, see Trudeau to mother, April 14, 1937, TP, vol. 2, file 8. On friends, see Radwanski, *Trudeau*, 53; and Clarkson and McCall, *Trudeau and Our Times*, 1: 36–40.

57. Personal Journal 1938, June 8, 1938, TP, vol. 39, file 9.

58. Interview with Alexandre Trudeau, Feb. 2006.

59. François Hertel, *Leur inquiétude* (Montreal: Les Éditions de Vivre, 1936), 14.

60. See Louise Bienvenue et Christine Hudon, "'Pour devenir homme, tu transgresseras . . .': Quelques enjeux de la socialisation masculine dans les collèges classiques québécois (1880–1939)," *Canadian Historical Review* 86 (Sept. 2005): 485–11. See also their "Entre franche camaraderie et amours socratiques: L'espace trouble et ténu des amitiés masculines dans les collèges classiques (1840–1960)," *Revue d'histoire de l'Amérique française* 57 (spring 2004): 481–508.

61. Trudeau, "My Interview with King George of England," Feb. 17, 1935, TP, vol. 2, file 5.

62. The comment is found ibid., file 10; for the underlining, see TP, vol. 37, file 9.

63. TP, vol. 2, file 8. On the incident with the other Catholic youth groups, see Nemni and Nemni, *Trudeau*, 131–32. This book indicates that Trudeau and Pelletier had not met at the time; however, his Journal entry for November 12, 1939, shows that he met Pelletier at a student conference in Quebec City. TP, vol. 39, file 9.

64. TP, vol. 2, file 8.

65. Ibid., file 10.

66. Ibid.

67. Ibid., file 8. Story "L'aventure."

68. Vastel makes the comment in his April 8, 2006 "blog": http://forums.lactualite.com/advansis/?mod=for&act=dis&eid=1&so=1&sb=1&ps=10. The Nemnis' account of the 1937 speech is found in their *Trudeau*, 83–85.

69. The comments on Maritain are in TP, vol. 2, file 8. See also Nemni and Nemni, *Trudeau*, 308ff.

70. The "Semaine sociale" program is in TP, vol. 4, file 6. The Fordham letter is in vol. 2, file 10.

71. TP, vol. 2, file 9.

72. Personal Journal, TP, vol. 39, file 9.

73. Ibid., Aug. 18, 1937.

74. Ibid., Jan. 2–5, 1938.

75. Ibid., Feb. 2, 1938.

76. Letter to mother, Dec. 19, 1936; undated poem, TP, vol. 2, file 8.

77. Ibid., Oct. 1937.

78. Ibid., Feb. 5, 1938.

79. François Hertel, *Le beau risque* (Montreal: Les Éditions Fides, 1942), 130.

80. The draft of the play is found in TP, vol. 1, file 29.

81. The original text reads: "Une des qualités du genre epistolaire est le tact. C'est à dire que celui qui écrit doit prendre ton proportionné aux circonstances et adapté aux sentiments de celui qui lira la lettre."

82. Pierre to Grace Trudeau, TP, vol. 2, file 10.

83. TP, vol. 39, file 9.

CHAPTER TWO: LA GUERRE, NO SIR!

1. Pierre Trudeau, Personal Journal, June 19, 1938, Trudeau Papers (TP), MG 26 02, vol. 39, file 9, Library and Archives Canada (LAC). The original French reads: "Je me demande quelque fois si je pourrai faire quelque chose pour mon Dieu et ma patrie. J'aimerais tant être un grand politique et guide mon pays."

2. See Farley Mowat, *And No Birds Sang* (Toronto: McClelland & Stewart, 1979).

3. Debate transcript in TP, vol. 2, file 10.

4. Corriveau to Trudeau, Sept. 7, 1939; Trudeau to Corriveau, Sept. 12, 1939, TP, vol. 45, file 4.

5. "Entrevue entre M. Trudeau et M. [Jean] Lépine, 27 avril 1992" [Lépine interview], Trudeau Papers, (TP), MG 26 03 vol. 23, file 2, Library and Archives Canada.

6. J.L. Granatstein, *Canada's Army: Waging War and Keeping the Peace* (Toronto: University of Toronto Press, 2002), 180. More detail is found in Jean-Yves Gravel, ed., *Le Québec et la Guerre* (Montreal: Les Éditions du Boréal, 1974), especially Gravel's own contribution, "Le Québec militaire," 77–108.

7. Trudeau to Grace Trudeau, Nov. 26, 1935, TP, vol. 2, file 5.

8. In an influential work on the mid-1930s, political scientist André Bélanger argued that the period is marked by the intellectuals' turning away from direct political action as they responded to the "mêlée" by concentrating on religion, nationalism, and economic organization through corporatism. There was, in his view, "a major turning" in 1934–36. Bélanger, *L'apolitisme des idéologies québécoises: Le grand tournant de 1934–1936* (Quebec: Les Presses de l'Université Laval, 1974). Of course, ideas do matter, and the political retreat of the intellectuals does not mean that their writings and thoughts failed to affect the actions of their students or their readers. Trudeau's claim that he paid little attention to politics is valid in the sense that he and his classmates apparently did not participate in elections.

9. "Propos d'éloquence politique," Feb. 10, 1938, TP, vol. 2, file 10.

10. Interview between Pierre Trudeau and Ron Graham, April 28, 1992, TP, vol. 23, file 3. Max and Monique Nemni have not seen this document or the reference to Trudeau's participation in demonstrations against Communists cited in chapter 1. They assume, correctly, that Trudeau did take part in the numerous demonstrations against Communism by Catholic students. See their *Trudeau, Fils du Québec, père du Canada*, vol. 1: *Les années de jeunesse, 1919–44* (Montreal: Les Éditions de l'Homme, 2006).

11. No title, note of Oct. 6, 1937, TP, vol. 2, file 10.

12. Lucienne Fortin, "Les Jeunes-Canada," in Fernand Dumont, Jean Hamelin, and Jean-Paul Montminy, eds., *Idéologies au Canada français* (Quebec: Les Presses de l'Université Laval, 1978), 219–20.

13. Quoted in John Herd Thompson with Allen Seager, *Canada 1922–1939: Decades of Discord* (Toronto: McClelland & Stewart, 1986), 313–14.

14. Douglas Letson and Michael Higgins, *The Jesuit Mystique* (Toronto: Macmillan, 1995), 143.

15. Quoted in Louis-P. Audet, *Bilan de la réforme scolaire au Québec, 1959–1969* (Montreal: Les Presses de l'Université de Montréal, 1969), 14.

16. "À l'aventure," nd [1936?], TP, vol. 3, file 8.

17. Personal Journal, entry of April 10, 1938, TP, vol. 39, file 9.

18. Pierre Trudeau, *Memoirs* (Toronto: McClelland & Stewart, 1993), 22. For a later appreciation of Hertel's impact on students, see J.-B. Boulanger, "François Hertel: Témoin de notre renaissance," *Le Quartier*

Latin, Feb. 14, 1947, 4. See also Trudeau, *Memoirs*, 23–24. On Hertel more generally, see Michael Oliver, *The Passionate Debate: The Social and Political Ideas of Quebec Nationalism, 1920–1945* (Montreal: Véhicule, 1991), 130–35; and Jean Tétreau, *Hertel: L'homme et l'oeuvre* (Montreal: P. Tisseyre, 1986).

19. Boulanger, "François Hertel: Témoin de notre renaissance," 4. Trudeau saved this article in his papers. TP, vol. 38, file 30.

20. Tétreau, *Hertel, L'homme et l'oeuvre*, 64–65.

21. Lionel Groulx, "La bourgeoisie et le national," *L'Action nationale* 12 (1939): 292–93.

22. On Groulx and democracy, see the discussion in Gérard Bouchard, *Les deux chanoines: Contradiction et ambivalence dans la pensée de Lionel Groulx* (Montreal: Les Éditions du Boréal, 2003), 91–93.

23. See H. Stuart Hughes, *The Obstructed Path: French Social Thought in the Years of Desperation, 1930–1960* (New York and Evanston: Harper and Row, 1968), 67.

24. *Brébeuf*, May 27, 1939.

25. TP, vol. 39, file 9.

26. Jerome Kagan, *Three Seductive Ideas* (Cambridge, Mass: Harvard University Press, 2000), 138.

27. TP, vol. 39, file 9, July 1939.

28. Trudeau to Camille Corriveau, Jan. 11, 1939, TP, vol. 45, file 4.

29. Personal Journal, Jan. 28, 1938, TP, vol. 39, file 9.

30. Ibid., April 12, 1938.

31. Ibid., July 7, 1938. Also in his notebooks, July 1, 1938, TP, vol. 2, file 10.

32. Clarkson and McCall argue that, throughout his life, Trudeau identified with Cyrano, the romantic poet and protector of the weak whose "life dream took on a particularly dramatic form . . . He would yearn, as he openly admitted, to climb alone to the heights." Stephen Clarkson and Christina McCall, *Trudeau and Our Times*, vol. 1: *The Magnificent Obsession* (Toronto: McClelland & Stewart, 1990), 44. Max and Monique Nemni disagree with the Clarkson-McCall interpretation and argue that Cyrano was a favourite of most French adolescents. However, the strength of Trudeau's admiration for Cyrano's individualism in 1938 is clear in the journal entry and seems to support the interpretation of Clarkson and McCall.

33. Interview quoted in George Radwanski, *Trudeau* (Toronto: Macmillan, 1978), 35. For a different view, see Nemni and Nemni, *Trudeau*, 89ff. They did not see the journal containing these remarks.

34. Personal Journal, July 29, 1938, TP, vol. 39, file 9.

35. Ibid., Aug. 1, 1938.

36. Ibid., Sept. 1, 1939.

37. Ibid., Sept. 3, 1939.

38. Ibid., Sept. 6, 1939: "J'ai peu lu, mais j'ai baisé une femme."

39. Ibid., Oct. 9, 1939.

40. Ibid., Oct. 20, 1939.

41. *Brébeuf*, Nov. 11, 1939.

42. Personal Journal, Oct. 9–31, 1939, TP, vol. 39, file 9.

43. Alex Gourd to Rhodes Committee, Jan. 8, 1940, with enclosure of Trudeau's record; "Recorder-en-chef de la cité de Montréal to Rhodes Committee," Jan. 10, 1940; and Trudeau, "Statement of General Interests and Activities," Jan. 7, 1940, TP, vol. 5, file 7.

44. Gérard Pelletier, then a leading figure in Jeunesse étudiante catholique, asked student journals to express their opinion on the war, but *Brébeuf* did not respond. See Michel Vastel, *Trudeau: Le Québécois*, 2nd. ed. (Montreal: Les Éditions de L'Homme, 2000), 34, for background on this incident.

45. Quoted in *Catholic Register*, May 30, 1940.

46. Kagan, *Three Seductive Ideas*, 145–46.

47. Max and Monique Nemni, who wrongly believe that Trudeau had not encountered Jacques Maritain, describe Maritain's liberal democratic view and indicate that Trudeau opposed them. In fact, both Hertel and Trudeau had expressed agreement with elements of Maritain's individualistic thought. It is a measure of the change during the Vichy years. Maritain was identified with the personalist movement, and it is clear that Trudeau, who first read Maritain in the mid-1930s, had learned about the personalist approach long before he studied in Paris—the time when the Nemnis assert he assumed its outlook as the core of his Catholicism. In his biography of Trudeau "le Québécois," Michel Vastel points to 1940 as the decisive year when Trudeau decided to go to law school in Montreal and to move more deeply into the "French" world. His argument, which was new when it was presented in 2000, is based on a careful and, to my mind,

accurate reading of Trudeau's pieces in the school newspapers: *Brébeuf* and *Le Quartier Latin*. Vastel, however, did not have access to the full evidence on Trudeau's political involvements—evidence that would have strengthened his argument. In their biography of Trudeau, Clarkson and McCall emphasize that Trudeau was "contradictory," but they argue, much too strongly in light of the evidence of Trudeau's own papers, that his father's death was the principal explanation for his behavioural patterns. His own record suggests that he was not so ambivalent towards his father but much more reflective of the nationalist ethos as it developed at his school— Brébeuf. See Nemni and Nemni, *Trudeau*, 308–13; Vastel, *Trudeau*, 27–41; and Clarkson and McCall, *Trudeau and Our Times*, 1: 39–46.

48. Trudeau to Corriveau, March 30, 1940, TP, vol. 45, file 5. The Nemnis describe Trudeau's favourable reception to Carrel and are justifiably critical. Nemni and Nemni, *Trudeau*, 98–103.

49. Personal Journal, June 19, 1940, TP, vol. 39, file 9.

50. Kenner to Trudeau, March 17, 1940; Trudeau to Kenner, May 1, 1940, TP, vol. 49, file 37.

51. Esther Delisle has argued that Trudeau became a strong nationalist in 1937 and pushed that agenda through membership in a secret society and, later, by intense political action with other strong nationalists during wartime. This account exaggerates Trudeau's nationalism, especially before 1940, although it does add much detail to the existing record. It also refutes Trudeau's own arguments that he stood outside politics and beyond the wartime controversies, except for a couple of eccentric interventions. See Esther Delisle, *Essais sur l'imprégnation fasciste au Québec* (Montreal: Les Éditions Varia, 2002), 20–50. The sources she uses are an interview with François Lessard and Lessard's book *Messages au "Frère" Trudeau* (Pointe-Fortune: Les Éditions de ma grand-mère, 1979), 122; and an interview with Hertel in *La Presse*, July 9, 1977. Dr. Delisle has kindly given me some of her original material, including Lessard-Trudeau correspondence.

52. Delisle, *Essais sur l'imprégnation fasciste au Québec*, 42; and Sandra Djwa, *A Life of F.R. Scott: The Politics of the Imagination* (Toronto and Vancouver: Douglas & McIntyre, 1987), 170–76.

53. The question was asked by René Matté on April 5, 1977. Trudeau did not

respond orally, but the Speaker indicated that Trudeau had nodded his agreement. Hansard, April 5, 1977.

54. Personal Journal, June 15, 1940, TP, vol. 39, file 9.

55. The trip is described in Personal Journal, June–July 1940, ibid. The draft of the letter to Camille in which he speaks about the family is found in his papers, vol. 41, file 2. It is undated but, obviously, July 1940.

56. *Toronto Daily Star*, April 8, 1968. Robert McKenzie and Lotta Dempsey interviewed Raymond Choquette, a Trudeau family accountant.

57. *Brébeuf*, Oct. 30, 1941.

58. *Le Quartier Latin*, March 3 and March 15, 1939.

59. He began classes on September 18, 1940. His notes indicate that Groulx was very detailed in his explanations and that he commented frequently on the physical attributes of the individuals he mentioned. TP, vol. 6, file 13.

60. TP, vol. 5, file 23.

61. Corriveau to Trudeau, Nov. 21, 1940; Corriveau to Trudeau, Dec. 30, 1940; and Trudeau to Corriveau, Dec. 31, 1940, TP, vol. 45, file 5.

62. Trudeau to Corriveau, Feb. 4, 1940 (1941 by content), and March 18, 1941, ibid., file 9.

63. This description comes from an interview with Charles Lussier. See Clarkson and McCall, *Trudeau and Our Times*, 1: 41.

64. Archibishop of Montreal to Trudeau, April 9 and April 17, 1941, TP, vol. 4, file 8.

65. Hertel to Trudeau, Aug. 27, 1941, TP, vol. 49, file 8.

66. Stephen Clarkson and Christina McCall, *Trudeau and Our Times*, vol. 2: *The Heroic Delusion* (Toronto: McClelland & Stewart, 1994), 35, based on an interview with Rolland.

67. Hertel to Trudeau, Aug. 25, 1941, TP, vol. 49, file 8.

68. Trudeau to Hertel, Oct. 18, 1941, ibid.

69. Ibid., Nov. 15, 1941.

70. Tétreau, *Hertel*, 70; Delisle, *Essais sur l'imprégnation fasciste au Québec*, 58–59.

71. Delisle has provided me with several letters from d'Anjou to Lessard which mention Trudeau. Most are referred to in her *Essais sur l'imprégnation fasciste au Québec*, 59.

72. TP, vol. 5, file 21.

73. Nemni and Nemni, *Trudeau*, 230ff. See Trudeau's comments in his *Memoirs*, 24.

74. Trudeau to Corriveau, Feb.17, 1942, TP, vol. 45, file 6.

75. TP, vol. 5, file 12.

76. Hertel to Trudeau, Dec. 1941, TP, vol. 49, file 8; Trudeau to Hertel, Jan. 13, 1942, ibid.

77. *Le Quartier Latin*, March 20, 1942.

78. *Montreal Daily Star*, April 8, 1942. Delisle, *Essais sur l'imprégnation fasciste au Québec*, 61. Trudeau has the clipping in his files. Riel did not remember that event when Delisle asked him about it. Lessard confirmed that Trudeau was a witness at the trial.

79. Nemni and Nemni, *Trudeau*, 243.

80. Hertel to Trudeau, April 17, 1942, TP, vol. 49, file 8.

81. Much of the letter is quoted in Nemni and Nemni, *Trudeau*, 216ff. The letters to Boulanger are in TP, vol. 44, file 6.

82. Trudeau, *Memoirs*, 26–27; Nancy Southam, ed., *Pierre* (Toronto: McClelland & Stewart, 2005), 66–67. A note in Trudeau's papers, vol. 3, file 5, describes what he took on the trip. He had $70 in traveller's cheques and $25 in cash—a fairly large sum for a motorbike trip.

83. *Le Devoir*, Nov. 26, 1942, found in TP, vol. 5, file 19.

84. Ibid., Nov. 28, 1942.

85. Trudeau to Roméo Turgeon, Dec. 9, 1942, TP, vol. 53, file 45.

86. *Le Quartier Latin*, Nov. 29, 1942.

87. Roger Rolland to John English, June 7, 2006.

88. Trudeau, *Memoirs*, 36–37; Lépine interview, TP, vol. 23, file 2; Claude Bélanger, "The Resignation of Jean-Louis Roux," Nov. 1996, www2.marianopolis.edu/quebechistory/events/roux.htm. See also Delisle, *Essais sur l'imprégnation fasciste au Québec*, 43; and, especially, Jean-Louis Roux, *Nous sommes tous des acteurs* (Montreal: Éditions Lescop, 1998), in which he describes his membership in a secret "cell."

89. Roux later said that he was a member of Les Frères Chausseurs but left the secret organization because of parental opposition. A personal letter sent to Father Marie d'Anjou indicates that he intended to pursue cultural projects for the future state. The letter, with the heading Ville-Marie rather than

Montreal, says he continues to share the goals. Delisle claims, with some supporting evidence, that the play *Le Jeu de Dollard* was organized by two Les Frères members. Trudeau appeared in numerous theatrical events during his university years, and his presence in this performance is not necessarily political. In the same sense, those who played in Brecht were often not Communists. Delisle, *Essais sur l'imprégnation fasciste au Québec*, 63; Roux to François-J. Lessard, Nov. 5 [nd], Lessard Papers, privately held.

90. Radwanski, *Trudeau*, 60. Program in TP, vol. 5, file 10. *La Presse* reported the debate on January 16, 1943. Delisle has another account of the debate, claiming that it occurred in 1942. Lessard says that he participated, but the program does not confirm his presence there. Delisle, *Essais sur l'imprégnation fasciste au Québec*, 60. See also the description in Nemni and Nemni, *Trudeau*, 344ff.

91. *La Presse*, June 25, 1943. File on results is found in TP, vol. 5, file 24. On the prizes and the medals, see ibid., file 25.

92. Suzette to Pierre, July 1, 1943, ibid.

93. Vastel, *Trudeau*, 56.

94. Clarkson and McCall, *Trudeau*, 1: 44–45.

CHAPTER THREE: IDENTITY AND ITS DISCONTENTS

1. Trudeau to Corriveau, Sept. 24, 1940, Trudeau Papers (TP), MG 26 02, vol. 45, file 5, Library and Archives Canada (LAC).

2. Freud received seven mentions, one more than Aquinas and, interestingly, Emmanuel Mounier, but fewer than eleven other individuals. No Canadian other than Groulx (9) exceeded three mentions. Although Groulx ranked higher than Freud, he stood below two other Catholic philosophers, Teilhard de Chardin and Jacques Maritain (11), two writers, Georges Bernanos and Dostoevsky (11), and the French Catholic writer Charles Péguy (10), and he tied with the existentialist and novelist Albert Camus and the novelist Honoré de Balzac. The choices of Trudeau's political colleagues Gérard Pelletier and Jean Marchand were typical of others of their generation: Pelletier—Pascal, Mounier, Bernanos, Malraux, and Claudel; Marchand—Pascal, Berdiaeff, Péguy, Dostoevsky, and his own contemporary and Trudeau speech writer Jean Le Moyne. The list and an excellent analysis are found in Germain Lesage, *Notre éveil culturel* (Montreal: Rayonnement, 1963), 135–48.

3. The original lists are found in "Qui avons-nous interrogés et qu'ont-ils répondu?" *Le nouveau journal*, April 7, 1962, III; but the lists and discussion in Lesage, *Notre éveil culturel*, are much more useful.

4. Louis Bouyer, *Newman: His Life and Spirituality*, trans. J. May (New York: Meridian, 1960), 226.

5. Lesage, *Notre éveil culturel*, 143–45.

6. E.-Martin Meunier and Jean-Philippe Warren, *Sortir de la "Grande noirceur": L'horizon "personnaliste" de la Révolution tranquille* (Sillery, Que.: Les Éditions du Septentrion, 2002), 108.

7. Charles Taylor, *Sources of the Self: The Making of the Modern Identity* (Cambridge, Mass.: Harvard University Press, 1989), 40, 51–52.

8. Personal Journal 1939–40, Feb. 5, 1940, TP, vol. 39, file 9.

9. Trudeau to Corriveau, Sept. 24, 1940, ibid., file 5.

10. Trudeau to Corriveau, March 18, 1941, ibid., file 9.

11. Corriveau to Trudeau, March 21, 1941, ibid.

12. Personal Journal 1939–40, Feb. 5, 1940, ibid.

13. Hertel to Trudeau, Sept. 1941, TP, vol. 49, file 8.

14. Hertel to Trudeau, Oct. 1941, ibid. The letter appears to have been sent with the previous one.

15. Grace Trudeau to Trudeau, Feb. 4, 1940, ibid.

16. Gustave Beaudoin to Honourable Hector Perrier, provincial secretary, May 25, 1943, TP, vol. 7, file 3.

17. Trudeau to Pierre Dumas, May 18, 1943; Dumas to Trudeau, July 30, 1943, TP, vol. 41, file 4;Trudeau to Donald Watt, director of Experiment in International Living, May 8, 1943, TP, vol. 15, file 7; and Trudeau to Grace Trudeau, nd [Aug. 1943], TP, vol. 53, file 34.

18. Pierre Trudeau, "Pritt Zoum Bing," *Le Quartier Latin*, March 10, 1944. See also Max and Monique Nemni, *Trudeau: Fils du Québec, père du Canada*, vol. 1: *Les années de jeunesse, 1919—1944* (Montreal: Les Éditions de l'Homme, 2006), 364–65.

19. For the lease and other documents, see TP, vol. 7, file 2.

20. For Marcil, who was Speaker in Laurier's last government (1909–11), see www.parl.gc.ca/information/about/people/key/SP"-BC/hoc-cdc/sp_hoc-e.asp?SP=2734.

21. The *Bulletin d'Histoire Politique* 3 (spring/summer 1995) devoted an entire

issue to "La participation des Canadiens français à la Deuxième Guerre mondiale." It remains the best account of the complex story of war participation. The essays by William Young, Robert Comeau, Béatrice Richard, and Jacques Michon are especially valuable.

22. The badge is found in TP, vol. 5, file 12. The file also has a press clipping from *Le Devoir* indicating that a speech by the pro-war Abbé Maheux had been disrupted by Bloc members. Trudeau underlined the part about the disruption, emphasis that may indicate his own participation.

23. "Inaugural Speech," in Michael Behiels and Ramsay Cook, eds., *The Essential Laurendeau*, trans. Joanne L'Heureux and Richard Howard (Toronto: Copp Clark, 1968), 123.

24. Trudeau to Donald Watt, May 25, 1944, TP, vol. 15, file 7; and National Service Separation Notice, ibid., file 12.

25. This information is found in the Hertel Papers held at the Archives nationales du Québec (Montreal), file P42.

26. François-Marc Gagnon, *Paul-Émile Borduas: Biographie critique et analyse de l'oeuvre* (Montreal: Les Éditions Fides, 1978), 108. Hertel's review, "L'actualité: Anatole Laplante au vernissage," is found in *Le Devoir*, May 19, 1941. Oddly, Gagnon identifies Trudeau as being present at only one Borduas exhibit—in October 1944. It is very unlikely he was there because he was then a student at Harvard. However, he did attend other openings, as the Borduas correspondence indicates. He also bought a Borduas painting.

27. Drafts of letters to Gabrielle Borduas, Sept. 1942, TP, vol. 43, file 31; and Gabrielle Borduas to Trudeau, Dec. 14, 1943, ibid. When I asked Senator Laurier LaPierre whether he knew Madame Borduas, he replied, unprompted, that he did and that she loved Pierre Trudeau.

28. Camille to Pierre, March 22, 1941, TP, vol. 45, file 6. Interview with Alexandre Trudeau.

29. Interview with Thérèse Gouin Décarie, June 2006.

30. Ibid.

31. George Radwanski, *Trudeau* (Toronto: Macmillan, 1978), 66.

32. Pierre Trudeau, *Memoirs* (Toronto: McClelland & Stewart, 1993), 38.

33. "Tip" to Pierre, April 18, 1945, TP, vol. 53, file 26.

34. Trudeau, *Memoirs*, 39.

35. He wrote to the vicar general, Monsignor Hickey, who replied that "in

view of the circumstances, [the archbishop] grants you permission to read even on vacation" whatever books were required. Hickey to Trudeau, Nov. 20, 1944, TP, vol. 7, file 5.

36. Interview with John Kenneth Galbraith, Feb. 28, 2005. See his similar remarks in Nancy Southam, ed., *Pierre* (Toronto: McClelland & Stewart, 2005), 208–9.

37. On Keynes, see TP, vol. 7, file 11; on Haberler, ibid.; on Schumpeter, ibid., file 13; on Galbraith, Southam, ed., *Pierre*, 208.

38. The comments are from Trudeau's notes on their writings in TP, vol. 7, file 16.

39. See ibid., for the comments and the details.

40. Ibid., file 21.

41. Trudeau to Thérèse Gouin, May 1, 1945; Gouin to Trudeau, May 24, 1945; and Trudeau to Gouin, May 25, 1945, TP, vol. 48, file 13.

42. Radwanski, *Trudeau*, 62.

43. Trudeau, *Memoirs*, 37.

44. Conversation with Gerald Butts, close family friend, April 2006. Trudeau used the word "chaff."

45. Friedrich was of German aristocratic background. He emigrated to the United States in the 1920s and became a leading authority on constitutions and democracy. He was an adviser to the American military government of Germany. McIlwain was a specialist in intellectual history, notably medieval political thought. His publications also had a strongly constitutionalist and institutionalist focus.

46. TP, vol. 7, file 18.

47. Ibid., files 19 and 22.

48. Ibid., file 19.

49. Trudeau, "A Theory of Political Violence," ibid., file 23.

50. Christina McCall and Stephen Clarkson, *Trudeau and Our Times*, vol. 2: *The Heroic Delusion* (Toronto: McClelland & Stewart, 1994), 42–44.

51. Edith Iglauer, "Prime Ministre/Premier Ministre," *New Yorker*, July 5, 1969, 41.

52. Andrée Trudeau to Pierre Trudeau, July 18, 1946, TP, vol. 53, file 26.

53. Pierre Trudeau, "College-Jean de Brébeuf—Notes prises durant la semaine sociale 1937," TP, vol. 4, file 6.

54. Trudeau to Gouin, April 19, 1945; Gouin to Trudeau, April 21, 1945, ibid., file 2.

55. Trudeau to Gouin, July 5, 1945, ibid., file 14.

56. Trudeau to Gouin, Sept. 26, 1945, ibid., file 15.

57. Ibid.

58. Trudeau to Gouin, Oct. 11, 1945, ibid.

59. Trudeau to Gouin, Oct. 17, 1945, ibid.

60. Trudeau to Gouin, Nov. 15, 1945, ibid.

61. Trudeau to Gouin, Nov. 19, 1945, file 3.

62. Charles Trudeau to Pierre Trudeau, April 18, 1945; and Wedding Invitation, June 20, 1945, TP, vol. 53, file 26.

63. Trudeau to Gouin, Dec. 8, 1945, TP, vol. 48, file 16.

64. Iglauer, "Prime Minister," 38. See also Radwanski, *Trudeau*, 48–49.

65. Clarkson and McCall, *Trudeau and Our Times*, 2: 36.

66. Gouin to Trudeau, Feb. 25, 1947, TP, vol. 48, file 10.

67. Trudeau to Gouin, Jan. 3, 1946, ibid., file 17.

68. Trudeau to Gouin, Jan. 23, 1946, ibid.

69. Trudeau to Gouin, March 15, 1946, ibid., file 18.

70. Trudeau to Gouin, April 1, 1946, ibid.

71. Trudeau to Gouin, April 29, 1946, ibid.

72. Trudeau to Gouin, April 25, 1946, ibid.

73. Trudeau to Gouin, May 22, 1946, ibid., file 19.

74. Conversation with Alexandre Trudeau, Feb. 2005.

75. Trudeau to Gouin, July 14, 1946, TP, vol. 48, file 8.

76. See TP, vol. 8, files 1 and 2.

77. Trudeau to Gouin, July 20, 1946, ibid., file 8.

78. Interview with Thérèse Gouin Décarie, June 2006.

79. Gouin to Trudeau, nd [July 1946], ibid., file 5.

80. Gouin to Trudeau, Sept. 29, 1946, ibid., file 8; and Agenda 1946, TP, vol. 39, file 1.

81. TP, vol. 8, file 11.

82. Trudeau to Gouin, Oct. 9, 1946, TP, vol. 48, file 20.

83. Trudeau, *Memoirs*, 42–43.

84. Antony Beevor and Artemis Cooper, *Paris: After the Liberation, 1944–1949*, rev. ed. (London: Penguin, 2004), np.

85. Hertel, "La quinzaine à Paris," *Le Devoir*, May 12, 1971. The hotel is currently the Esmeralda, a one-star hotel of considerable reputation which has attracted celebrities ranging from Serge Gainsbourg to Terence Stamp. The quotation is found in a review posted in the hotel window at 4 St-Julien-le-Pauvre.

86. *Brébeuf*, Oct. 7, 1946.

87. Linda Lapointe, *Maison des étudiants canadiens: Cité internationale universitaire de Paris. 75 ans d'histoire 1926–2001* (Saint-Lambert: Stromboli, 2001), 80–84; interview with Vianney Décarie, June 2006.

88. Found in TP, vol. 8, file 7. Viau wrote a review of the show "Reconnaissance de l'espace" in *Notre Temps*, July 12, 1947.

89. Trudeau, *Memoirs*, 23.

90. The evidence is in his Agenda 1947, TP, vol. 39, file 1.

91. Trudeau to Gouin, TP, nd [1947] vol. 48, file 11.

92. Trudeau, *Memoirs*, 40.

93. For Index letter, see TP, vol. 8, file 6; Chartres, ibid., file 7; Renouvin and Siegfried, ibid., file 13.

94. Trudeau, Agenda 1947, TP, vol. 39, file 1.

95. Trudeau had seen the great film by Marcel Carné soon after he arrived in France. Trudeau to Gouin, Oct. 9, 1946, TP, vol. 48, file 20.

96. Trudeau, *Memoirs*, 44–45; Marcel Rioux, *Un peuple dans le siècle* (Montreal: Les Éditions du Boréal, 1990), 49.

97. The letter is dated Sept. 16, 1946, and on Senate of Canada stationery. TP, vol. 8, file 6.

98. Trudeau to Gouin, Oct. 21, 1946, TP, vol. 48, file 20.

99. Ibid.

100. Trudeau to Gouin, Nov. 5, 1946, ibid., file 21.

101. Gouin to Trudeau, Nov. 14, 1946, ibid., file 9.

102. Trudeau to Gouin, Nov. 22, 1946, ibid., file 21.

103. Gouin to Trudeau, Nov. 24, 1946, ibid.

104. Trudeau to Gouin, Dec. 3, 1946, ibid.

105. Trudeau, Agenda 1946, TP, vol. 39, file 1; Gordon Elliott to Trudeau, Dec.16, 1946, TP, vol. 46, file 1.

106. Trudeau to Gouin, Dec. 12[?], 1946, TP, vol. 48, file 2.

107. Trudeau to Gouin, Dec. 29, 1946, ibid.

108. Interview with Thérèse Gouin Décarie, June 2006.

109. Gouin to Trudeau, Feb. 15, 1947, ibid., file 10; and Trudeau to Gouin, Feb. 22, 1947, ibid., file 22.

110. A brief biography can be found at www.aejcpp.free.fr/psychanalysefrancaise5.htm. It contains this reference.

111. Trudeau's notes are found under the heading "Journal personnel thérapie, fév.–juin 1947," TP, vol. 39, file 10.

112. Gouin to Trudeau, Feb. 25, 1947, TP, vol. 48, file 10.

113. Journal personnel thérapie, TP, vol., 39, file 10.

114. Ibid.

Chapter Four: Coming Home

1. Gouin to Trudeau, March 3, 1947, Trudeau Papers (TP), MG 26 02, vol. 48, file 10, Library and Archives Canada (LAC).

2. The school had an impressive budget of $50,000 and would draw 150 students from the broken European countries. Professors from Harvard would participate. Trudeau to Gouin, March 19, 1947, ibid., file 22.

3. Trudeau to Gouin, March 6, 1947, ibid.

4. The schedule is found in Trudeau's agenda. TP, vol. 39, file 1.

5. Gouin to Trudeau, nd [received in Paris apparently on May 1, 1947], TP, vol. 48, file 10.

6. Trudeau to Gouin, May 21, 1947, ibid., file 11.

7. Trudeau to Gouin, April 7, 1947, ibid.

8. He dreamed that Desautels, Rolland, and Hertel were at the table with him and he urinated. He was afraid that he had scandalized the others, but Desautels dismissed the thought, saying that she had already seen sailors in a similar predicament. TP, vol. 39, file 10.

9. Trudeau to Gouin, June 7, 1947, TP, vol. 48, file 23. Also, Journal personnel thérapie, fév.–juin 1947, ibid.

10. Christina McCall and Stephen Clarkson, Trudeau and Our Times, vol. 2: The Heroic Delusion (Toronto: McClelland & Stewart, 1994), 45.

11. Michel Vastel, Trudeau: Le Québécois (Montreal: Les Éditions de l'Homme, 2000), 47.

12. Trudeau to Lomer Gouin, July 10, 1947, TP, vol. 48, file 24.

13. Interview with the Décaries, June 2006.

14. In her acknowledgments to her *Intelligence and Affectivity in Early Childhood: An Experimental Study of Jean Piaget's Object Concept and Object Relations* (New York: International Universities Press, 1965), Thérèse Gouin generously thanked Father Noël Mailloux, who, in her words, "made her love Freud" (xvi). As her analyst, he had appeared frequently in the Trudeau-Gouin letters.

15. Vastel, *Trudeau*, 46–47.

16. McCall and Clarkson, *Trudeau and Our Times*, 2: 88–89.

17. Gouin to Trudeau, nd [1969], TP, vol. 48, file 1.

18. An account of the trip is in TP, vol. 11, file 12, including photographs.

19. For the note on the *Empress of Canada*, see TP, vol. 7, file 17.

20. Trudeau, Agenda 1947, TP, vol. 1, file 39.

21. Lomer Gouin to Trudeau, nd [Nov. 1947], TP, vol. 48, file 1.

22. Quoted in Clarkson and McCall, *Trudeau and Our Times*, 2: 47–48.

23. Trudeau to Thérèse Gouin, Good Friday 1947, TP, vol. 48, file 11; and Trudeau to Lessard, nd [April 1947], Lessard Papers, privately held.

24. On *Notre Temps*'s conservative and Catholic stance, see Jean Hamelin, *Histoire du catholicisme québécois: Le XXe siècle*, vol. 2: *De 1940 à nos jours* (Montreal: Les Éditions du Boréal, 1984), 138. According to Hamelin, the journal was inspired by the French rightist publications. Conrad Black wrote in his biography of Maurice Duplessis: "Léopold Richer, former Bloc Populaire hothead, had rallied to become one of the more obsequious members of Duplessis's journalistic clique. He became the editor of *Notre Temps*, which styled itself 'the social and cultural weekly' and was owned by Fides, the publishing house of the Pères de Ste. Croix in Montreal. Richer himself, a nationalist and hostile ab initio to the Liberals, once converted to Duplessism, did so with the passion of conversions." He was not fully converted when he dealt with Trudeau in 1947. Conrad Black, *Duplessis* (Toronto: McClelland & Stewart, 1977), 566.

25. *Notre Temps*, Nov. 15, 1947; and H.P. Garceau, *Notre Temps*, to Trudeau, Dec. 27, 1945, TP, vol. 22, file 28, in which Garceau asks Trudeau to send some articles and tells him that they miss him in Montreal and that the promoters of economic liberalism will soon get their just retribution.

He said he sees several of their "friends" who are trying to do their part, notably the nationalist historian Guy Frégault.

26. Emmanuel Mounier, "L'homme américain," *Esprit*, Nov. 1946, 138–40; and John Hellman, *Emmanuel Mounier and the New Catholic Left, 1930–1950* (Toronto: University of Toronto Press, 1981), ch. 10.

27. Trudeau to Gouin, April 1947, TP, vol. 48, file 11.

28. Gérard Pelletier, *Years of Impatience, 1950–60*, trans. Alan Brown (1983; Toronto: Methuen, 1984), 19.

29. Ralph Miliband, "Harold Laski," *Clare Market Review* (1950) on www.spartacus.schoolnet.co.uk/TUlaski.htm; Pierre Trudeau, *Memoirs* (Toronto: McClelland & Stewart, 1993), 46.

30. TP, vol. 2, file 26.

31. Trudeau, *Memoirs*, 47.

32. Letter from Trudeau to John Reshetar, quoted in Clarkson and McCall, *Trudeau and Our Times*, 2: 46.

33. Harold Laski, *The State in Theory and Practice* (1935; New York: Viking, 1947), 3.

34. Max Beloff, "The Age of Laski," *The Fortnightly*, June 1950, 378.

35. Harold Laski, *Authority in the Modern State* (New Haven, Conn.: Yale University Press, 1919), 74–75; and Bernard Zylstra, *From Pluralism to Collectivism: The Development of Harold Laski's Political Thought* (Assen, The Netherlands: Van Gorcum, 1968), 75.

36. Trudeau had met often with CCF intellectual and McGill law professor F.R. Scott. He was more interested in Scott's strong civil libertarian stance in wartime than in his CCF activity. He certainly voted CCF in the 1949 federal election when he was the agent for the CCF candidate in Jacques Cartier riding in Montreal. TP, vol. 2, file 6. Trudeau also met with Scott and Canadian Labour Congress (CLC) researcher Eugene Forsey in May 1949. TP, vol. 11, file 18. He applied for a job with the CLC in April 1949. One of his law professors at the Université de Montréal, Jacques Perrault, a prominent CCF activist as well as the brother-in-law of André Laurendeau, wrote a letter of introduction for Trudeau on April 28, 1949, to the CLC. He said that Trudeau had stood first in his class at law school and recommended him as "an ideal research man in general for your movement in Canada and more particularly for

the province of Quebec." Perrault to A. Andras, assistant research director, CLC, April 28, 1949, ibid., file 23. It is tempting to contemplate Trudeau's fate had he worked for the CLC in the early 1950s. He would have been more definitely linked with the CCF and, almost certainly, would have been a CCF candidate—probably a losing one in a Montreal constituency. Most likely, he would never have become a Liberal Party leader.

37. Claude Ryan to Trudeau, Sept. 25, 1947, TP, vol. 8, file 30. Other clippings in the same file indicate other activities.

38. Trudeau attended the LSE Canadian Association, which had its first meeting on February 19, 1948. Among the attendees were Robert McKenzie, later an eminent British political scientist; John Halstead, a future Canadian diplomat and writer; and John Porter, Canada's most celebrated sociologist when Trudeau entered politics in the 1960s. Ibid.

39. Trudeau Agenda, 1948. March 20, 1948, TP, vol. 22, file 20.

40. Trudeau to "M. Caron," nd, ibid., file 23.

41. Interview with Jacques Hébert, Feb. 2006.

42. Laski wrote: "The bearer of this letter, M. Pierre Trudeau, is well known to me. He has been a member of my seminar in this School, and has won both my regard and respect for his vigour and tenacity of mind, and for his power to arrive independently at his conclusions. I recommend him with warmth and respect." Trudeau later responded by naming Laski as one of the five greatest intellectual influences upon his life. He named no other teacher and, in this respect, Laski was a mentor as no professor at Paris, Harvard, or Montréal had been. TP, vol.11, file 23.

43. Léger letter, June 15, 1948; and Beaulieu letter, June 23, 1948, ibid. They said Trudeau was a journalist for *Notre Temps* and *Le Petit Journal*.

44. Suzette to Trudeau, March 10, 1946, TP, vol. 3, file 40; and Trudeau to Charles Trudeau, Oct. 20, 1948, TP, vol. 53, file 36.

45. Trudeau, *Memoirs*, 48.

46. Agenda 1948, Aug. 28, 1948, TP, vol. 11, file 20.

47. Trudeau, *Memoirs*, 49–51.

48. Ibid., 53–54. The journals of the trip are in TP, vol. 11, file 21.

49. Trudeau to family, Oct. 23, 1948, ibid., file 22.

50. Trudeau to family, Dec. 2, 1948, ibid.

51. The record is confused. Although Trudeau was enrolled in a doctoral program at LSE and had asked Laski to supervise his thesis, he now regularly
said that the thesis was for Harvard. Having completed his general examinations at Harvard, he was eligible to proceed on to the thesis stage.
However, there is no record at Harvard or in Trudeau's records that he had
found the required supervisor or had undertaken the necessary registration
of the thesis. Harvard was very loose in thesis supervision. As a student
there in the 1960s, I learned of one Canadian academic who had been
working on his thesis for twenty years. In any event, Trudeau's thesis was
really a pretext for travel, and his journals of the trip are more appropriate
for journalism than for thesis research.

52. Trudeau to family, Dec. 2, 1948, TP, vol. 11, file 22.

53. Trudeau to Suzette, Dec. 27, 1948, ibid.

54. Trudeau to Grace Trudeau, Jan. 18, 1949, ibid.

55. Trudeau to Grace Trudeau, Jan. 28, 1949, ibid.

56. Ibid.

57. Trudeau to Grace Trudeau, Feb. 11, 1949, ibid. Also, Agenda 1949,
Feb. 11–12, 1949, ibid., file 18.

58. Trudeau to Grace Trudeau, March 10, 1949, ibid.

59. Trudeau to family, March 20, 1949, ibid.

60. Ibid.; Trudeau, Memoirs, 60. Norman had been contacted about Trudeau
earlier and was the ranking Canadian official in Japan.

61. Trudeau, Memoirs, 61.

62. George Radwanski, Trudeau (Toronto: Macmillan, 1978), 69–70.

63. Ibid., 69–72.

64. Pelletier is quoted in Edith Iglauer, "Prime Minister/Premier Ministre,"
New Yorker, July 5, 1969, 44.

65. "Réflexions sur une démocratie et sa variante," Notre Temps, Feb. 14, 1948.

66. Trudeau to Lise and François Lessard, Oct. 19, 1948, Lessard Papers.

67. Trudeau, "Des avocats et des autres dans leurs rapports avec la justice," in
TP, vol. 22, file 31.

68. See the Canadian John Humphrey's Human Rights and the United
Nations: A Great Adventure (Dobbs Ferry, NY: Transnational, 1984), in
which Humphrey, an author of the 1948 Declaration of Human Rights,
points to the centrality of the 1940s in defining human rights.

69. Trudeau to John Reshetar, as quoted in Clarkson and McCall, *Trudeau and Our Times*, 2: 46.

70. *Notre Temps*, Feb. 14, 1948.

71. Letter to the editor, *Le Devoir*, July 6, 1949.

72. Agenda 1949, May 19, 1949, TP, vol. 11, file 18.

73. Paul-Émile Borduas, "1948 Refus Global," in Ramsay Cook, ed., *French-Canadian Nationalism* (Toronto: Macmillan, 1969), 276–84. Also, François-Marc Gagnon, *Paul-Émile Borduas: Biographie critique et analyse de l'oeuvre* (Montreal: Les Éditions Fides, 1978), ch. 13.

74. *Le Devoir*, Sept. 28, 1948.

75. Pierre Vadeboncoeur, "Jean Marchand, autrefois," www.scn.qc.ca/Connaitre/Histoire/Vad/Vad2.html.

76. Douglas Stuebing, John Marshall, Gary Oakes, *Trudeau, l'homme de demain!* trans. Hélène Gagnon (Montreal: HMH, 1969), 44. Interview with Jacques Hébert, Feb. 2006.

77. Marchand is quoted in Radwanski, *Trudeau*, 74.

78. Monique Leyrac and 1949 film in http://www.thecanadianencyclopedia.com/index.cfm?PgNm=TCE&Params=U1ARTU0002065.

79. Pelletier, *Years of Impatience*, 14–15, 76.

80. Trudeau, "Quebec at the Time of the Strike," in Pierre Trudeau, ed., *The Asbestos Strike*, trans. James Boake (1956; Toronto: James Lewis & Samuel, 1974), 66–67.

81. Pelletier, *Years of Impatience*, 86ff. On asbestos and its significance as a product in Quebec, see William Coleman, *The Independence Movement in Quebec, 1945–1990* (Toronto: University of Toronto Press, 1984), 113–15.

82. Black, *Duplessis*, 528.

83. Trudeau, ed., *The Asbestos Strike*, 329.

CHAPTER FIVE: HEARTH, HOME, AND NATION

1. Gérard Pelletier, *Years of Impatience, 1950–1960*, trans. Alan Brown (1983; Toronto: Methuen, 1984), 85–86.

2. See Paul-Emile Roy, *Pierre Vadeboncoeur: Un homme attentif* (Montreal: Éditions du Méridien, 1995).

3. Quoted in Robert Rumilly, *Henri Bourassa: La vie publique d'un grand canadien* (Montreal: Les Éditions Chantecler, 1953), 777.

4. *Le Devoir*, April 13, 1949.

5. The notes for "Où va le monde" are found in Trudeau Papers (TP), MG 26 02, vol. 12, file 1, Library and Archives Canada (LAC).

6. Pierre Vadeboncoeur, letter to the editor, *Le Devoir*, July 14, 1949.

7. "Entrevue entre M. Trudeau et M. [Jean] Lépine, 27 avril 1992 [Lépine interview]," Trudeau Papers (TP), MG 26 03, vol. 23, file 2, Library and Archives Canada.

8. Interestingly, in his history of the London School of Economics, the German sociologist Ralf Dahrendorf suggested that the school's influence had been great on the democratic and liberal left in the postwar era. Some would describe the influence as Fabianism, others as socialism, and a few as the welfare state, but what the diverse voices expressed was, in Dahrendorf's words, "the combination of Westminster-style democratic institutions with a benevolent interventionist government guided by a view of the good or just society." For much of the West and even the developing world, what it meant was "a little Laski, so to speak, a little Beveridge, some Tawney and a lot of Pierre Trudeau, the long-serving Canadian Prime Minister with an LSE past." Ralf Dahrendorf, *LSE: A History of the London School of Economics and Political Science, 1895–1995* (Oxford: Oxford University Press, 1995), 405.

9. Marcel Rioux, *Un peuple dans le siècle* (Montreal: Les Éditions du Boréal, 1990), 50.

10. François Hertel, *Méditations philosophiques* (Paris: Éditions de la Diaspora, 1963), 26. The continuing affection for Hertel is found in Roger Rolland's tribute to him in *Le Petit Journal* in 1948. Hertel possessed, Rolland claims, an extraordinary verve. The article, "François Hertel," is found in TP, vol. 38, file 61. Trudeau had learned from his mother about Hertel's discontents and his desire to return to Paris. Grace Trudeau to Pierre Trudeau, Oct. 31, 1948, TP, vol. 46, file 15. Hertel's own description is found in "Lettre à mes amis (15 août 1950, Paris, France)," *Cité libre*, Feb. 1951, 34–35.

11. Grace Trudeau to Pierre Trudeau, Feb. 20, 1948, TP, vol. 46, file 16.

12. E.-Martin Meunier and Jean-Philippe Warren, *Sortir de la "Grande noirceur": L'horizon "personnaliste" de la Révolution tranquille* (Sillery, Que: Les Éditions du Septentrion, 2002), 115; see also footnotes 27 and

28, which describe the appeal of Paris intellectual life to Gérard Pelletier and Jean-Charles Falardeau.

13. Grace Trudeau to Pierre Trudeau, Jan. 8, Jan. 13, Jan. 11, Jan. 17, Jan. 26, Feb. ?, and Feb. 20, 1947, TP, vol. 46, file 15.

14. Ibid., Feb. 27, 1947.

15. Ibid., July 16, 1947.

16. Ibid., Oct. 31 and Nov. 20, 1947.

17. Ibid, Feb. 1 and Feb. 20, 1947.

18. Ibid., file 20, Feb. 24 and March 28, 1952.

19. Ibid., June 4, 1948, and Feb. 4, 1949. The estimated conversion of $700 in 2005 dollars is $5,600.00. See http://www.eh.net/hmit/ppowerusd/dollar_answer.php.

20. Ibid., Nov. 6, 1948.

21. Ibid., July 2, 1948.

22. Ibid., file 17, Feb. 4, 1949.

23. Ibid., file 18, Oct. 18, 1950.

24. Kristin Bennett in Nancy Southam, ed., Pierre (Toronto: McClelland & Stewart, 2005), 253.

25. Grace Trudeau to Pierre Trudeau, Nov. 28, 1951, TP, vol. 46, file 18.

26. Interviews with Thérèse Gouin Décarie, June 2006; and Madeleine Gobeil, May 2006.

27. Margaret Trudeau, Consequences (Toronto: McClelland & Stewart, 1982), 77–78; and Henry Kissinger in Gerald Ford Papers, Gerald Ford Library, Memorandum, Dec. 4, 1974, MR 02-75.

28. Grace to Pierre Trudeau, May 11, 1948, TP, vol. 46, file 17.

29. On Hébert and MacEachen, see Allan MacEachen, "Reflections on Faith and Politics," in John English, Richard Gwyn, and P. Whitney Lackenbauer, eds., The Hidden Pierre Elliott Trudeau: The Faith behind the Politics (Ottawa: Novalis, 2004), 153–60. On Kidder, see her remarks in Southam, ed., Pierre, 256. On Cattrall, see Line Abrahamian, "Taking Choices, Making Choices," Reader's Digest, April 2005, 70–71. Also, conversations with Marc Lalonde, Margot Kidder, Allan MacEachen, and Margot Breton.

30. Pierre Trudeau, Memoirs (Toronto: McClelland & Stewart, 1993), 64. On the salary, see R. Gosselin to Trudeau, Aug. 31, 1949, TP, vol. 9, file 7.

31. Pierre Trudeau, *Federalism and the French Canadians* (Toronto: Macmillan, 1968), 5. On the Department of External Affairs and the Royal Commission, see Gilles Lalande, *The Department of External Affairs and Biculturalism*, Studies of the Royal Commission on Bilingualism and Biculturalism, Number 3 (Ottawa: Information Canada, 1970), 42–46; and J.L. Granatstein, *The Ottawa Men: The Civil Service Mandarins, 1935–1957* (Toronto: Oxford University Press, 1982), 6. For an excellent description of the character of Ottawa at the time, see Stephen Clarkson and Christina McCall, *Trudeau and Our Times*, vol. 2: *The Heroic Delusion* (Toronto: McClelland & Stewart, 1994), 59ff.

32. See, for example, TP, vol. 9, file 13. Gordon Robertson's later comments on Trudeau may be found in his autobiography, *Memoirs of a Very Civil Servant: Mackenzie King to Pierre Trudeau* (Toronto: University of Toronto Press, 2000), 88–89.

33. Trudeau to Gordon Robertson, Oct. 28, 1950, TP, vol. 9, file 23.

34. Robertson to Trudeau, Jan. 6, 1951, TP, vol. 10, file 4. The other documents referred to are found in this file, as is the reference to Diefenbaker. On January 24, 1951, the Cabinet considered the question of internal security controls which Trudeau had been studying. RG 2, PCO, Series A-5-a, vol. 2647, LAC.

35. Registration quotation is in a Memorandum to R.G. Robertson, March 17, 1951, with attachment to "Mr. Eberts." The comment is in the attachment, not in the memorandum, which would have received wider circulation. TP, vol. 10, file 27.

36. Vadeboncoeur's comments are in *Le Devoir*, Oct. 20, 1965; and Hertel's comments are in *La Presse*, Sept. 17, 1966.

37. Trudeau's comments are in TP, vol. 9, file 10. On the complexities of the fiscal and social security questions, see R.M. Burns, *The Acceptable Mean: The Tax Rental Agreements, 1941–1962* (Toronto: Canadian Tax Foundation, 1980), ch. 5.

38. Draft of "Theory and Practice of Federal-Provincial Cooperation," nd, TP, vol. 10, file 5.

39. Memorandum to R.G. Robertson, March 13, 1951, ibid., file 3.

40. Draft of letter to Léger of Aug. 31, 1950, ibid., file 11.

41. Grace Trudeau to Pierre Trudeau, Feb. 28, 1947, TP, vol. 46, file 17.
42. Marginalia on Pearson's speeches of Dec. 5, 1950, and April 10, 1951, TP, vol. 10, file 11.
43. Trudeau to LePan, April 28, 1951, ibid.
44. Trudeau to Robertson, June 6, 1951, ibid., file 1.
45. Interviews with Trudeau staff. Meeting organized by Library and Archives Canada.
46. He saved the clipping in TP, vol. 38, file 70.
47. Segerstrale to Trudeau, Nov. 6, 1951, TP, vol. 53, file 1; Trudeau to Segerstrale, nd [Jan. ? 1952], ibid.
48. The notes to the East Block have no dates. Letter about her mother is November 10, 1951, and letter responding to Trudeau complaints is December 21, 1951. Letter about Gibraltar is January 2, 1952. Ibid.
49. Helen Segerstale to Trudeau, Jan. 26, 1952, ibid.
50. Trudeau to Segerstrale, March 17 [?], 1952, ibid.
51. Trudeau to Norman Robertson, Sept. 24, 1951, TP, vol. 10, file 1.
52. Trudeau to Norman Robertson, Sept. 28, 1951, TP, vol. 9, file 2. Trudeau's immediate supervisor, Gordon Robertson, treats Trudeau's departure briefly and has not responded to the account of the final conversation between the two presented in Trudeau's memoirs. See Robertson, A Very Civil Servant, 88–89.
53. Quoted in Michael Behiels, Prelude to Quebec's Quiet Revolution: Liberalism versus Neo-Nationalism, 1945–1960 (Montreal and Kingston: McGill-Queen's University Press, 1985), 62.
54. Pelletier, Years of Impatience, 114.
55. Ibid., 112–13.
56. Accounts are found in TP, vol. 20, file 2.
57. TP, vol. 21, file 2.
58. "Faites vos jeux," Cité libre, June 1950, 27–28.
59. Pierre Elliott Trudeau, Against the Current: Selected Writings, 1939–1966, ed. Gérard Pelletier, trans. G. Tombs (Toronto: McClelland & Stewart, 1996), 27–28. Original, "Politique fonctionnelle," Cité libre, June 1950, 20–24.
60. Draft of letter to Jean Marchand, nd [1951], TP, vol. 15, file 8.
61. Quoted in Pierre Godin, Daniel Johnson, 1946–1964: La passion du pouvoir (Montreal: Les Éditions de l'Homme, 1980), 77.

62. Paul-André Linteau, René Durocher, Jean-Claude Robert, and François Ricard, *Quebec since 1930* trans. Robert Chodos and Ellen Garmaise (Toronto: James Lorimer, 1991), 254–57.

CHAPTER SIX: NATIONALISM AND SOCIALISM

1. "Entrevue entre M. Trudeau et M. [Jean] Lépine, 27 avril 1992" [Lépine interview], Trudeau Papers (TP), MG 26 03, vol. 23, file 2, Library and Archives Canada.

2. Michael Behiels, *Prelude to Quebec's Quiet Revolution: Liberalism versus Neo-Nationalism, 1945–1960* (Montreal and Kingston: McGill-Queen's University Press, 1985), 70.

3. Ibid., 60. On Korea, only 21 percent of Quebecers (both French and English) approved of the proposal to send forces to Korea (41% in the rest of Canada) on August 3, 1950. On July 23, 1952, only 32 percent thought it was not a mistake to send troops to Korea (59% in the rest of Canada). See Mildred Schwartz, *Public Opinion and Canadian Identity* (Scarborough, Ont.: Fitzhenry and Whiteside, 1967), 80.

4. Arès to Trudeau, March 2, 1951, TP, vol. 21, file 9.

5. D'Anjou to Trudeau, Feb. 21, 1951, ibid.

6. Ibid., March 2, 1951.

7. Gérard Pelletier, *Years of Impatience, 1950–1960*, trans. Alan Brown (1983; Toronto: Methuen, 1984), 119.

8. On Johnson, see Pierre Godin, *Daniel Johnson, 1946–1964: La passion du pouvoir* (Montreal: Les Éditions de l'Homme, 1980); Pelletier is quoted in Michel Vastel, *Trudeau: Le Québécois* (Montreal: Les Éditions de l'Homme, 2000), 105; Pelletier quotes the critical friend in his *Years of Impatience*, 87; Thérèse Casgrain, *A Woman in a Man's World* (Toronto: McClelland & Stewart, 1972), 139; comments of Jean Marchand from an interview in Stephen Clarkson and Christina McCall, *Trudeau and Our Times*, vol. 1: *The Magnificent Obsession* (Toronto: McClelland & Stewart, 1990), 70; and Duplessis in Conrad Black, *Duplessis* (Toronto: McClelland & Stewart, 1977), 559. Vastel is especially good on the 1950s and spends considerable time dealing with the image and the reality of Trudeau in that decade.

9. Fournier in Stephen Clarkson and Christina McCall, *Trudeau and Our Times*, vol. 2; *The Heroic Delusion* (Toronto: McClelland & Stewart, 1994), 65.

10. Conversation with Sharon and David Johnston, Dec. 2004; interview with Donald Johnston, June 2004. Johnston, Trudeau's lawyer and a Cabinet minister in the eighties, describes Trudeau with the family in his memoir *Up the Hill* (Montreal: Opticum, 1996).

11. Pierre Trudeau, *Memoirs* (Toronto: McClelland & Stewart, 1993), 69.

12. Paul-André Linteau, René Durocher, Jean-Claude Robert, and François Ricard, *Quebec since 1930* (Toronto: James Lorimer, 1991), 287.

13. Curiously, Trudeau told Helen Segerstrale on August 21, 1952, that he had been offered a position in political science at the Université de Montréal but had turned it down. This information conflicts with various other accounts, but it does suggest that Trudeau did not believe then that Duplessis had blocked his appointment. It may be that he referred to an offer that had not been approved by senior university officials. TP, vol. 12, file 53.

14. *Marshall McLuhan: The Man and His Message*, co-production of CBC Television and McLuhan Productions produced and directed by Stephanie McLuhan, 1984; Marshall McLuhan, "The Man in the Mask," quoted in W. Terrence Gordon, *Marshall McLuhan: Escape into Understanding. A Biography* (Toronto: Stoddart, 1997), 235. McLuhan's enthusiasm for Trudeau was evident in a 1968 *New York Times* book review of Trudeau's essay collection *Federalism and the French Canadians* (Toronto: Macmillan, 1968).

15. "Portrait de P.E. Trudeau à Radio-Canada, 1950," TP, vol. 11, file 27.

16. Interview with Marc Lalonde, April 2004.

17. Pelletier, *Years of Impatience*, 27.

18. At the time he wrote the article opposing the Korean War, Trudeau had debated with his *Cité libre* colleagues whether he should use a pseudonym that could be easily recognized, such as "Pierre d'Ecbatane." "Trudeau, citoyen," to "citoyens libres," [1951], TP, vol. 21, file 28.

19. Ben Rogers to Under-Secretary of State for External Affairs, April 1, 1952; Robert Ford to Under-Secretary of State for External Affairs, April 3 and April 17, 1952; and Trudeau to Norman Robertson, dated March 17 but sent April 17, 1952, from Moscow. All are in Privy Council Records, RG 2, C-100–4, LAC. I would like to thank Paul Marsden for drawing my attention to these records.

20. "Au Sommet des Caucases," broadcast *CBF au réseau français*, Sept. 18, 1952, TP, vol. 12, file 16.

21. Interview between Pierre Trudeau and Ron Graham, May 12, 1992, TP, vol. 23, file 12.

22. "J'ai fait mes Pâques à Moscou," broadcast *Réseau français de Radio Canada*, Sept. 4, 1952, ibid.

23. "Aux prises avec le Politbureau [sic]," broadcast *CBF au réseau français*, Sept. 25, 1952, ibid.

24. Trudeau to Laurendeau, draft of letter, Nov. 17, 1952, TP, vol. 12, file 12.

25. Braun, "Apparences et réalités religieuses en U.R.S.S.," *L'Action catholique*, Nov. 19, 1952.

26. The articles in *Le Devoir* are June 14 and June 16–21, 1952. The Braun attack may be found in *L'Action catholique*, Nov. 17, 1952. Also, *Nos Cours* 14 (13) (Jan. 10, 1953): 19–32. Correspondence with J.-B. Desrosiers in TP, vol. 12, file 12, including Trudeau letter of Dec. 4, 1952; letter to Father Florent, Jan. 23, 1951, ibid., file 14.

27. TP, vol. 12, file 18.

28. "Retour d'URSS: Le camarade Trudeau," *Le Quartier Latin*, Oct. 23, 1952.

29. Ibid.; and "Staline est-il poète?" broadcast *CBF au réseau français*, Sept. 11, 1952, TP vol. 12, file 16. On the Moscow conference, see the report by the economist Alec Cairncross, "The Moscow Economic Conference," *Soviet Studies* 4 (Oct. 1952): 113–32. Cairncross saw value in the conference as an occasion for Western economists to meet their Eastern counterparts. He noted that "the delegations from the West were drawn mainly from left-wing or radical groups and no voice was raised at any time that could be said to be really representative of right-wing opinion. The speeches, therefore, gave a rather one-sided impression and were uniformly complimentary to the USSR, but often extremely hostile to the USA" (114).

30. Susan Trofimenkoff, *The Dream of Nation* (Toronto: Gage, 1983), 285. See also Gérard Laurence, "Les affaires publiques à la télévision, 1952–1957," *Revue d'histoire de l'Amérique française* 6 (Sept. 1952): 213–19.

31. For a description of Lévesque's style, see Paul Rutherford, *When Television Was Young: Primetime Canada, 1952–1957* (Toronto: University of Toronto Press, 1990), 175–77; and Pelletier, *Years of Impatience*, 27–28.

32. Jim Coutts, "Trudeau in Power: A View from Inside the Prime Minister's Office," in Andrew Cohen and J.L. Granatstein, eds., *Trudeau's Shadow: The Life and Legacy of Pierre Elliott Trudeau* (Toronto: Random House Canada, 1998), 149.

33. Trudeau to Segerstrale, Aug. 21, 1952; and Segerstrale to Trudeau, Dec. 18, 1952, TP vol. 53, file 1.

34. The election was closer than the number of seats indicated. The Liberals won 46 percent of the vote compared with 50.5 percent for Duplessis, but they won only 23 seats compared with 68 for the Union nationale. This imbalance became a major political issue in Quebec in the 1950s, although it occurs frequently in the British parliamentary system.

35. Black, *Duplessis*, 362–63.

36. Pierre Eliott Trudeau, *Against the Current: Selected Writings, 1939–1996*, ed. Gérard Pelletier, trans. George Tombs (Toronto: McClelland & Stewart, 1996), 29–33. Also, "La Revue des Arts et des Lettres," broadcast *CBF au réseau français*, Jan. 27, 1953, TP, vol. 25, file 5.

37. Pelletier, *Years of Impatience*, 131–33. On the political neutrality, see Roch Denis, *Luttes de classes et question nationale au Québec, 1948–1968* (Montreal: Les Presses Socialistes Internationales, 1979), 157–58.

38. Draft of remarks to Couchiching Conference, 1952, TP, vol. 25, file 41.

39. Trudeau, "Techniques du voyage," "Moulin à vent," Jan. 17, 1954, TP, vol. 12, file 17.

40. See, for example, Clarkson and McCall, *Trudeau and Our Times*, 2: 69–71.

41. Quoted in Pelletier, *Years of Impatience*, 110.

42. Paul-André Linteau, *Histoire de Montréal depuis la Confédération* (Montreal: Les Éditions du Boréal, 2000), 483.

43. *Le Devoir*, Oct. 15, 1952; Denis, *Luttes des classes*, 136ff; Donald Horton, *André Laurendeau: French-Canadian Nationalist* (Toronto: Oxford, 1992), ch. 8; and, for the description of Laurendeau's anti-Duplessis sentiment as it developed within his family, see Chantal Perrault, "Oncle André," in Robert Comeau and Lucille Beaudry, eds., *André Laurendeau: un intellectuel d'ici* (Sillery, Que.: Les Presses de l'Université du Québec, 1990), 34.

44. Trudeau, "Réflexions sur la politique," *Cité libre*, Dec. 1952, 65–66. On unionism and the *Cité libre* group, see Behiels, *Prelude to Quebec's Quiet Revolution*, ch. 7.

45. Trudeau, "La Revue des Arts et des Lettres," broadcast *CBF au réseau français,* Jan. 2, 1953.

46. André Malavoy, "Une recontre mémorable," in Comeau and Beaudry, eds., *André Laurendeau,* 20.

47. George Radwanski, *Trudeau* (Toronto: Macmillan, 1978), 83.

48. "École de la metallurgie, Cours de P.E. Trudeau, le 23 janvier 1954," TP, vol. 15, file 6.

49. Maurice Lamontagne, *Le fédéralisme canadien: Évolutions et problèmes* (Quebec: Les Presses de l'Université Laval, 1954).

50. Father Lévesque made contact with Trudeau through Doris Lussier, a friend of Trudeau who worked with Lévesque. She had given Lévesque the text of one of Trudeau's speeches. He said it was a strong address "whose vehemence equals its truth." He hoped to meet Trudeau soon and to have him speak at Laval.

51. Behiels, *Prelude to Quebec's Quiet Revolution,* 191.

52. "Mémoire de la F.U.I.Q.," TP, vol. 16, file 2.

53. See Black, *Duplessis,* 485; and Trudeau, "De libro, tributo et quibusdam aliis," in Trudeau, *Federalism and the French Canadians,* 66–69. Original in *Cité libre,* Oct. 1954, 1–16. On the grants specifically, see Trudeau, "Les octrois fédéraux aux universités," *Cité libre,* Feb. 1957, 9–31.

54. Robert Rumilly, "Pierre E. Trudeau honoré pour avoir insulté les Can.-Français," TP, vol. 14, file 38.

55. On Rumilly's background and attitudes, see Jean-François Nadeau, "La divine surprise de Robert Rumilly," in Michel Sarra-Bournet and Jocelyn Saint-Pierre, eds., *Les Nationalismes au Québec du xix au xxi siècle* (Québec: Les Presses de l'Université Laval, 2001), 105–16.

56. Conversation with Sylvia Ostry, Feb. 2003.

57. Erasmus, "À propos de 'Cité Libre,'" *L'Action catholique,* June 22, 1953.

58. Accounts of these programs are found in TP, vol. 25, files 3 and 4. Confidential interview with female friend about the Roman Catholic Church.

59. Trudeau to Segerstrale, Aug. 6, 1955, TP, vol. 53, file 1.

CHAPTER SEVEN: EVE OF THE REVOLUTION

1. Frank Scott, "Foreword," in Pierre Trudeau, ed., *La Grève de l'amiante* (Montreal: Les Éditions Cité libre, 1956), ix. Further references are to the

English edition, *The Asbestos Strike*, trans. James Boake (Toronto: James Lewis & Samuel, 1974). The background to Recherches sociales is described in David Lewis, *The Good Fight: Political Memoirs, 1909–1958* (Toronto: Macmillan, 1981), 456. Gérard Pelletier describes the financing arrangements and the "foundation" that would finance it. Frank Scott, Eugene Forsey, Jacques Perrault, and Jean-Charles Falardeau were the trustees, and they met to finalize the arrangements on February 11, 1951. Trudeau Papers (TP), MG 26 02, vol. 25, file 15, Library and Archives Canada (LAC).

2. Fernand Dumont, "History of the Trade Union Movement in the Asbestos Industry," in Trudeau, ed., *The Asbestos Strike*, 107. Gilles Beausoleil, then a graduate student at the Massachusetts Institute of Technology, was the other author. Many others were considered as possible authors, including Jean Marchand.

3. The project was nearly abandoned in 1953 because of the delays. Jean Gérin-Lajoie to Trudeau, March 11, 1953, TP, vol. 23, file 16.

4. Ibid., Nov. 23, 1955.

5. J.-C. Falardeau to Trudeau, Dec. 20, 1955, ibid., file 15. The problems with the printers are discussed in Grace Trudeau to Pierre Trudeau, Oct. 6, 1955; she sympathized with his difficulty in finding a publisher on Dec. 1, 1955, TP, vol. 46, file 23. Falardeau strongly opposed trying to publish in France in a letter of June 17, 1955, TP, vol. 23, file 16.

6. Trudeau, ed., *The Asbestos Strike*, 345, 14, 67.

7. Ibid., 348–49. Trudeau's earlier articles that contain the seeds of the essay include "La démocratie est-elle viable au Canada français?" *L'Action nationale*, Nov. 1954, 190–200, and "Une lettre sur la politique," *Le Devoir*, Sept. 18, 1954. On the church, see his "Matériaux pour servir à une enquête sur le cléricalisme," *Cité libre*, May 1953, 29–37.

8. Trudeau, ed., *The Asbestos Strike*, 6–9. An excellent analysis of Trudeau's argument can be found in Michael Behiels, *Prelude to Quebec's Quiet Revolution: Liberalism versus Neo-Nationalism, 1945–1960* (Montreal and Kingston: McGill-Queen's University Press, 1985), especially chs. 4 and 5.

9. Trudeau, ed., *The Asbestos Strike*, 16–21, 25, 37, 64–65.

10. Trudeau said, correctly, that Hertel advocated a corporatist version of personalism in 1945. Ibid., 24. On the politicians, see ibid., 51.

11. Ibid., 44.

12. *Le Devoir*, Feb. 2, 1955; *Vrai*, Feb. 12, 1955.

13. Trudeau, ed., *The Asbestos Strike*, 346–49.

14. François-Albert Angers, "Pierre Elliott Trudeau et *La Grève de l'amiante*," *L'Action nationale*, Sept. 1957, 10–22, and Sept.–Oct. 1958, 45–56; Father Jacques Cousineau, *Réflexions en marge de "la Grève de l'amiante"* (Montreal: Les cahiers de l'Institut social populaire, 1958); and Pierre Trudeau, "Le père Cousineau, s.j., et *La grève de l'amiante*," *Cité libre*, May 1959, 34–48. Laurendeau's articles are found in *Le Devoir*, Oct. 6, 10–11, 1956. The files on the Cousineau case are in TP, vol. 20, files 20–21.

15. The dismissal of Catholic and nationalist thought was a characteristic of many of the *Cité libre* group. Trudeau's own comment that the strike was purely the product of industrial forces and that ideas such as those of nationalism and religion could play no part brought later rebuke from Fernand Dumont, Trudeau's collaborator in the fifties: "An event which bears historical meaning without an ideological character, one that is produced solely by the forces of production, isn't that the greatest marvel?" Trudeau's implicit dismissal of the value of his own education and, of course, his years in law school was not unusual on the part of his generation. Fernand Dumont, "Une révolution culturelle," in Dumont, Jean Hamelin, and Jean-Paul Montminy, eds., *Idéologies au Canada français, 1940–1976* (Quebec: Les Presses de l'Université Laval, 1981), 19.

16. On Scott and Trudeau, see Sandra Djwa, "Nothing by Halves: F.R. Scott," *Journal of Canadian Studies* 35 (winter 2000): 52–69.

17. Quoted in J.D. Legge, *Sukarno: A Political Biography* (London: Allen Lane, 1965), 264–65.

18. Report of World University Service of Canada tour, TP, vol. 13, file 4.

19. Conrad Black, *Duplessis* (Toronto: McClelland & Stewart, 1977), 389.

20. Perron to Trudeau, Sept. 9, 1950, TP, vol. 20, file 2; Doris Lussier to Trudeau, May 21, 1953, TP, vol. 21, file 12; Lionel Tiger to Trudeau, Aug. 28, 1958, TP, vol. 18, file 1; Trudeau to "Jennifer," nd [1954], TP, vol. 53, file 38.

21. Black, *Duplessis*, 372–73; Paul-André Linteau, René Durocher, Jean-Claude Robert, François Ricard, *Quebec since 1930* (Toronto: James Lorimer, 1991), 269–70.

22. Grace Trudeau to Pierre Trudeau, Sept. 6, 1955, and Oct. 22, 1955, TP, vol. 46, file 23. When Casgrain had stood as a candidate in Outremont in 1952, Trudeau had worked for her. Ibid., vol. 28, file 14.

23. *Le Devoir*, June 1, 1956. Trudeau's drafts are in TP, vol. 22, file 12.

24. These results are taken from the official site of the Quebec National Assembly: www.assnat.qc.ca/fra/patrimoine/votes.html.

25. André Carrier, "L'idéologie politique de la revue *Cité libre*," *Canadian Journal of Political Science* 1 (Dec. 1968): 414–28.

26. Trudeau had many files on *Cité libre*. See also Yvan Lamonde and Gérard Pelletier, eds., *Cité libre: une anthologie* (Montreal: Stanké, 1991), for a more general history. A comparison of the journal's circulation is found in Pierre Bourgault, *La Presse*, Nov. 11, 1961; he gives the figures. Cormier's attempt to resign is found in TP, vol. 21, file 5. For the general files, see TP, vol. 20, files 1–45. The exchange with Vadeboncoeur occurred on January 22, 1955, TP, vol. 21, file 29. See also *Time*, Jan. 19, 1953.

27. Quoted in Pelletier, *Years of Impatience*, 1950–1960, trans. Alan Brown (1983; Toronto: Methuen, 1984), 26.

28. Lamonde and Pelletier, eds., *Cité libre*, 16.

29. These lists are drawn from files in the Trudeau Papers, especially TP, vol. 21, file 36. Scott to "Reginald [Boisvert]," July 7, 1950, ibid., file 26; Léon Dion to Trudeau, April 26, 1957, ibid., file 12; Jean Le Moyne to Trudeau, March 9, 1955, ibid., file 12; Rocher to Jean-Paul Geoffroy, May 20, 1951, ibid., file 25; Blair Fraser to Trudeau, nd, ibid., file 3; and Rocher to Trudeau, Jan. 21, 1953, ibid., file 2.

30. See Behiels, *Prelude to Quebec's Quiet Revolution*, 250–51, for a description of the Rassemblement platform and organization. For the constitution and principles of the Rassemblement, see *Le Devoir*, Sept. 14, 1956.

31. Pierre Trudeau, *Memoirs* (Toronto: McClelland & Stewart, 1993), 70; Pierre Dansereau, "Témoinage," in Robert Comeau et Lucille Beaudry, eds., *André Laurendeau: Un intellectuel d'ici* (Sillery, Que.: Les Presses de l'Université du Québec, 1990), 184; Gérard Bergeron, *Du Duplessisme au Johnsonisme* (Montreal: Éditions Parti pris, 1967), 132–35; Behiels, *Prelude to Quebec's Quiet Revolution*, 253–56; and André Laurendeau, "Blocs-notes," *Le Devoir*, Dec. 3, 1957.

32. Pelletier to Trudeau, Aug. 29, 1957, TP, vol. 27, file 13.

33. Ibid., file 9.

34. Pierre Trudeau, "Les octrois fédéraux aux universités," *Cité libre*, Feb. 1957, 9–31; Forsey to Trudeau, Feb. 26, 1954, TP, vol. 16, file 7.

35. Figures from Jean-Louis Roy, *La marche des Québécois: Le temps des ruptures (1945–1960)* (Montreal: Éditions Leméac, 1976), 273.

36. *Le Soleil*, Nov. 6, 1957. Trudeau debated the question on October 10, 1958, on radio and argued that the grants were "against the constitution and the spirit of federalism." TP, vol. 25, file 4.

37. They were later published as Pierre Trudeau, *Approaches to Politics* (Toronto: Oxford University Press, 1970).

38. Ibid.; "Faut-il assassiner le tyran?" *Vrai*, March 15, 1958; and Hébert's defence in *Vrai*, March 22, 1958.

39. The correspondence with Wade began on November 3, 1955, and included letters of October 5, 1956, and October 30, 1956. The *University of Toronto Quarterly* letter was written on March 12, 1957, and Trudeau's draft reply was April 17, 1957. He wrote on January 13, 1958, to offer the article to the *Canadian Journal of Economics and Political Science*, TP, vol. 24, file 1. See Trudeau, "Some Obstacles to Democracy in Quebec," *CJEPS* 23 (Aug. 1958): 297–311, republished in Pierre Trudeau, *Federalism and the French Canadians* (Toronto: Macmillan, 1968), 103–23. See also John Dales to Trudeau, Feb. 11, 1958, TP, vol. 22, file 1.

40. John Stevenson to Trudeau, Oct. 15, 1958, TP, vol. 53, file 13. The quotation is from Trudeau, "Some Obstacles," 106–7.

41. Clippings and the notification of the prize from James Talman, a historian at the University of Western Ontario, are found in TP, vol. 22, file 1. *Le Devoir* did report it. Flavien Laplante to Trudeau, Dec. 26, 1959, vol. 13, file 8.

42. *Vrai*, June 14, 1958.

43. The Lesage speech with Trudeau's annotations is found in TP, vol. 22, file 38.

44. Pelletier, *Years of Impatience*, 168.

45. Madeleine Gobeil to Trudeau, April 7, 1957, TP, vol. 47, file 32.

46. *Le Petit Journal*, May 29, 1955.

47. Trudeau, "Un manifeste démocratique," Cité libre, Oct. 1958, 1–31; and Behiels, *Prelude to Quebec's Quiet Revolution*, 254.

48. "Rapport d'un assemblée de Cité Libre tenue le 11 novembre 1958," and "Rapport d'une assemblée de Cité Libre tenue le 6 décembre 1958," TP,

vol. 21, file 41. On the university protest, see Jacques Hébert, *Duplessis Non Merci!* (Montreal: Les Éditions du Boréal, 2000), ch. 7.

49. Edward Sommer to Jacques Hébert, Feb. 15, 1961, TP, vol. 14, file 5. On the sunbathers and other files, see ibid., file 2. Trudeau appears to have had a friend who was an American nudist. On Laskin, Scott, and the relationship of federalism and civil liberties, see the excellent account in Philip Girard, *Bora Laskin: Bringing Law to Life* (Toronto: University of Toronto Press, 2005), 210–21. On Trudeau's views, see his "Economic Rights," *McGill Law Journal* 8 (June 1962): 121, 123, 125.

50. Letters of introduction by Scott in TP, vol. 13, file1. On the anti-Semitic and anti-Communist presence, see Sandra Djwa, *The Politics of the Imagination: The Life of F.R. Scott* (Toronto: McClelland & Stewart, 1987), 173. On the effect of the 1930s, see Sean Mills, "When Democratic Socialists Discovered Democracy: The League for Social Reconstruction Confronts the 'Quebec Problem,'" *Canadian Historical Review* 86 (March 2005).

51. The account is drawn from Djwa, *The Politics of the Imagination*, 322–27. F.R. Scott, "Fort Smith," in *The Collected Poems of F.R. Scott* (Toronto: McClelland & Stewart, 1981), 226.

52. Scott, "Fort Providence," ibid., 230–31.

53. Interview with Tim Porteous, May 2006.

54. The clippings with these comments are found in TP, vol. 25, file 28.

55. The Drapeau-Trudeau debate is found in TP, vol. 28, file 9.

56. For the notes that indicate the close friendship, see TP, vol. 21, file 29. The copy of *Le Social Démocrate* is found in vol. 28, file 9. The description of Vadeboncoeur teaching Trudeau to write is in Trudeau, *Memoirs*, 20.

57. For Trudeau's notebook describing the trip, see TP, vol. 13, file 5.

58. The Trudeau family profited from Belmont during the fifties, and Trudeau took the major responsibility for handling family investments. Ibid., file 6.

59. Ibid., file 6; and Grace Trudeau to Pierre Trudeau, June 1 and Sept. 8, 1959, TP, vol. 46, file 26.

60. There is scarcely a reference to Trudeau in the newspapers I consulted that is not neatly clipped in his own papers. Pelletier also claims that Trudeau had to be "coaxed" into television. In fact, he sought out appearances, kept press clippings about them, and urged his mother to watch his

performances. Pelletier explains that "it was understood between us that friendship had its limits." In terms of personal feelings and ambitions, the limits were significant. Pelletier, *Years of Impatience*, 187–88; Grace to Pierre Trudeau, Nov. 24, 1958, TP, vol. 46, file 25; and *The Canadian Intelligence Service* (July 1959): 2.

61. Michel Vastel, *Trudeau: Le Québécois* (Montreal: Les Éditions de l'Homme, 2000), 109. The list of addresses is found in TP, vol. 13, file 7.

62. TP, vol. 13, file 11. The stories on the trip are found in *Miami Herald*, May 2, 1960; and *Key West Citizen*, April 29 and May 2, 1960. There is a long story in the Canadian *Star Weekly*, Jan. 14, 1961, about Gagnon and the canoe technique.

63. Gobeil to Trudeau, May 18[?], 1960, TP, vol. 47, file 32.

CHAPTER EIGHT: A DIFFERENT TURN

1. *Le Devoir*, Jan. 29, 1960.

2. The account comes mainly from Paul-André Linteau, *Histoire de Montréal depuis la Confédération* (Montreal: Les Éditions du Boréal, 2000), ch. 16. Comment on the Metropolitan Opera and other cultural matters is in Paul-André Linteau, René Durocher, Jean-Claude Robert, and François Ricard, *Quebec since 1930*, trans. Robert Chodos and Ellen Garmaise (Toronto: James Lorimer, 1991), 304–5.

3. Some of the debates on the subject are in Trudeau Papers (TP), MG 26 02, vol. 22, file 16, Library and Archives Canada (LAC), including a strong denunciation of his television efforts on identity cards by Dr. J.S. Lynch which appeared in *Le Devoir*, Nov. 20, 1959.

4. Léon Dion, *Québec, 1945–2000*, vol. 2: *Les intellectuels et le temps de Duplessis* (Sainte-Foy, Que.: Les Presses de l'Université Laval, 1993), 195ff.

5. On the Liberal victory in the political arena, see Pierre Godin, *René Lévesque*, vol. 1: *Un enfant du siècle, 1922–60* (Montreal: Les Éditions du Boréal, 1994), 403–5. The information is repeated in Dale Thomson, *Jean Lesage and the Quiet Revolution* (Toronto: Macmillan, 1984), 85–86. Trudeau's comments are from interviews with Ron Graham for his memoirs in TP, vol. 24, file 15. His statement on the need for men in the legislature is in *Le Travail*, Feb. 22, 1957.

6. Pierre Godin, *René Lévesque*, vol. 2: *Héros malgré lui, 1960–1976* (Montreal: Les Éditions du Boréal, 1997), 118.

7. Pierre-Elliott Trudeau, "L'élection du 22 juin 1960," *Cité libre*, Aug.-Sept. 1960, 3. The article was written in July. Trudeau occasionally used a hyphen in his name at this time.

8. Ibid., 6. Georges-Émile Lapalme, *Mémoires: Le vent de l'oubli* (Montreal: Éditions Leméac, 1971). On Duplessis, see Godin, *Lévesque*, 1: 290.

9. Dion, *Québec, 1945–2000*, 2: 195–96; Léon Dion, "Le nationalisme pessimiste: Sa source, sa signification, sa validité," *Cité libre*, Nov. 1957, 3–18; Léon Dion, "L'esprit démocratique chez les Canadiens de langue française," *Cahiers*, Nov. 1958, 34–43; and Pierre Laporte, "La démocratie et M. Trudeau," *L'Action nationale*, Dec. 1954, 293–96.

10. Dion to Trudeau, Feb. 27, 1958, TP, vol. 21, file 12.

11. The case continues to find its place on lists of major injustices. Prominent Canadian criminal lawyer Eddie Greenspan has cited it as an argument for the abolition of capital punishment. See http://www.injusticebusters.com/2003/Coffin_Wilbert.htm.

12. Jacques Hébert and Pierre Trudeau, *Two Innocents in Red China*, trans. Ivon Owen (Toronto: Oxford University Press, 1968), 71–72.

13. Ibid., 150.

14. Ibid., 150–52. The comment on Mao is on page 71.

15. On the launch, see TP, vol. 24, file 3. Also, *Montreal Star*, March 29, 1961, which has the photograph of Hébert with the priests.

16. Trudeau and Hébert, *Two Innocents in Red China*, 61, 152. Jung Chang and Jon Halliday, *Mao: The Unknown Story* (New York: Knopf, 2005), 460.

17. Chang and Halliday, *Mao: The Unknown Story*; and Naim Kattan in *The Montrealer*, June 1961, 4.

18. Interview between Pierre Trudeau and Ron Graham, May 12, 1992, TP, vol. 23, file 12.

19. Interview with Robert Ford, Oct. 15, 1987, Robert Bothwell Papers, University of Toronto Archives.

20. Pierre Trudeau, "De l'inconvénient d'être catholique," *Cité libre*, March 1961, 20–21; and Pierre Trudeau, "Note sur le parti cléricaliste," *Cité libre*, June/July 1961, 23. The correspondence is in TP, vol. 21, file 35.

21. On the Soviets and the perception of strength, see Michael Beschloss, *The*

Crisis Years: Kennedy and Khrushchev, 1960–1963 (New York: Edward Burlingame Books, 1991), ch. 2; Trudeau's broadcast "China's Economic Planning in Action" is found in TP, vol. 25, file 26; Samuel Huntington, *Political Order in Changing Societies* (New Haven: Yale University Press, 1968); Trudeau, "De l'inconvénient d'être catholique," 20–21; and Michael Oliver to Trudeau, Oct. 29, 1959, TP, vol. 24, file 4.

22. Trudeau and Hébert, *Two Innocents in Red China*, 47.

23. Ibid., 111, 113.

24. Interview with Thérèse Gouin Décarie and Vianney Décarie, June 2006.

25. Gérard Pelletier, *Years of Impatience, 1950–1960*, trans. Alan Brown (1983; Toronto: Methuen, 1984), 120n12.

26. Desbiens and Untel are described in Dion, *Quebec, 1945–2000*, 2: 224–25.

27. Gérard Pelletier, "Feu l'unanimité," *Cité libre*, Oct. 1960, 8. The section on Groulx draws from a list of objections taken from various writings of the fifties and sixties found in Gérard Bouchard, *Les deux chanoines: Contradiction et ambivalence dans la pensée de Lionel Groulx* (Montreal: Les Éditions du Boréal, 2003), 22–23. In a 1962 letter to Raymond Barbeau, Groulx strangely echoed Trudeau in suggesting that Quebec was not ready for democracy; quoted in Bouchard, *Les deux chanoines*, 222.

28. Trudeau, "De l'inconvénient d'être catholique," 20–21, in which he clearly asserted his Catholicism while criticizing its restrictive aspects.

29. Interview with Madeleine Gobeil, May 2006.

30. Gérard Pelletier, *Years of Choice, 1960–1968*, trans. Alan Brown (Toronto: Methuen, 1987), 56–62; Pierre Trudeau, *Against the Current: Selected Writings, 1939–1996* trans. George Tombs (Toronto: McClelland & Stewart, 1996), 143–49.

31. Ramsay Cook to Trudeau, April 1962, TP, vol. 21, file 3; Trudeau to Cook, April 19, 1962, Ramsay Cook Papers, privately held.

32. Marchand, quoted in George Radwanski, *Trudeau* (Toronto: Macmillan, 1978), 260.

33. Sandra Djwa, *The Politics of the Imagination: A Life of F.R. Scott* (Toronto: McClelland & Stewart, 1987), 332–37. Scott told Djwa that he considered refuting the article in a 1980 letter.

34. The file dealing with *A Social Purpose for Canada* is found in TP, vol. 24.

35. A collection of attacks on Trudeau's writings and actions was published in 1972. Among the authors are the erstwhile friends Marcel Rioux and Fernand Dumont. André Potvin, Michel Letourneux, and Robert Smith, *L'anti-Trudeau: Choix de textes* (Montreal: Éditions Parti pris, 1972).

36. "The Practice and Theory of Federalism" is republished in Pierre Trudeau, *Federalism and the French Canadians* (Toronto: Macmillan, 1968), 124–50.

37. Grace Trudeau to Pierre Trudeau, Sept. 14, 1960, TP, vol. 46, file 26.

38. The book launch list in in TP, vol. 24, file 5.

39. On Gobeil, see *La Presse*, April 6, 1966.

40. TP, vol. 39, file 6. Sept. 21, 1961.

41. Trudeau to Guérin, Sept. 21, 1961, TP, vol. 39, file 6.

42. The travel file with ticket stubs and bills and a few letters is found in TP, vol. 13, file 13. Also, Grace Trudeau to Pierre Trudeau, June 14, July 26, Sept. 5, and Sept. 26, 1961, vol. 46, file 26.

43. Radwanski, *Trudeau*, 83–84.

44. Trudeau, *Federalism and the French Canadians*, xxi.

45. Trudeau to Marie-Laure Falès, April 22, 1962, TP, vol. 53, file 39.

46. Peter Gzowski, "Portrait of an Intellectual in Action," *Maclean's*, Feb. 24, 1962, 23, 29–30; and "Un capitaliste socialist: Pierre-Elliott Trudeau," *Le Magazine Maclean*, March 1962, 25, 52–55. Note the considerable difference in title.

47. Pierre Trudeau, "The New Treason of the Intellectuals," in Trudeau, *Federalism and the French Canadians*, 151–81.

48. "Faut-il refaire la Confédération?" *Le Magazine Maclean*, June 1962, 19; Gzowski, "Portrait of an Intellectual in Action," 30.

49. Godin, *Lévesque*, 2: 118; René Lévesque, *Memoirs* (Toronto: McClelland & Stewart, 1986), 172–73; and Pelletier, *Years of Choice*, 128–30.

50. Paul-André Linteau, René Durocher, Jean-Claude Robert and François Ricard, *Quebec since 1930*, 340; Gérard Bergeron, *Notre miroir à deux faces* (Montreal: Québec/Amérique, 1985), 48–50, on the emergence of Lévesque in the public; Thomson, *Jean Lesage and the Quiet Revolution*, 117, for an account of the Cabinet meeting; and Lévesque, *Memoirs*, 172ff.

51. Lévesque, *Memoirs*, 173. In *Memoirs*, the footnote to this quotation states: "These quotations are not meant to be textually accurate but serve only to reconstitute the correct context."

52. Trudeau in "Entrevue entre M. Trudeau et M. [Jean] Lépine, 27 avril 1992" [Lépine interview], Trudeau Papers (TP), MG 26 03, vol. 23, file 2, Library and Archives Canada. It is interesting that Trudeau omitted these comments in his memoirs. Also, Pierre Trudeau, "Economic Rights," *McGill Law Journal* 12 (June 1962): 121–25.

53. Lépine interview, TP, vol. 23, file 2; Albert Breton, "The Economics of Nationalism," *Journal of Political Economy* 72 (Aug. 1964): 376–86.

54. Stephen Clarkson and Christina McCall, *Trudeau and Our Times*, vol. 2: *The Heroic Delusion* (Toronto: McClelland & Stewart, 1994), 79–81; and Pelletier, *Years of Choice*, 137–38.

55. Trudeau, "Economic Rights," 121–25; Clarkson and McCall, *Trudeau and Our Times*, 2: 79–81; Godin, *Lévesque*, 117–19; and Pierre Trudeau, "L'homme de gauche et les élections provinciales," *Cité libre*, Nov. 1962, 3–5.

56. Flynn's comments are quoted in Michael Stein, *The Dynamics of Right-Wing Protest: A Political Analysis of Social Credit in Quebec* (Toronto: University of Toronto Press, 1973), 87n33.

57. The account of Diefenbaker's dining-room revolt and the nuclear weapon issue is found in Denis Smith, *Rogue Tory: The Life and Legend of John Diefenbaker* (Toronto: Macfarlane Walter & Ross, 1995), ch. 12. Trudeau's views are found in Lépine interview, TP, vol. 23, file 2. Pelletier later claimed that Lévesque and Lesage blocked Marchand when an organizer's report indicated that his candidacy would result in Créditiste votes being lost in rural areas to the Union nationale. It was a reasonable assessment. Pelletier, *Years of Choice*, 138–39.

58. John Saywell, ed., *The Canadian Annual Review for 1963* (Toronto: University of Toronto Press, 1964), 31; and Pierre Trudeau, "Pearson ou l'abdication de l'esprit," *Cité libre*, April 1963, 7–12.

59. Trudeau, "Pearson ou l'abdication de l'esprit"; Smith, *Rogue Tory*, ch. 12; and Basil Robinson, *Diefenbaker's World: A Populist in Foreign Affairs* (Toronto: University of Toronto Press, 1989).

60. Interview with Laurin is found in TP, vol. 24, file 13. *Le Devoir*, Nov. 28, 1961, offers the Freudian analysis. Interview with Graham Fraser, April 2005.

61. Pierre Vadeboncoeur, "Les qui-perd-gagne," in his *To be or not to be: That is the question!* (Montreal: Les Éditions de l'Hexagone, 1980), 101.

62. Ibid., 102; and Pierre Vadeboncoeur, *La dernière heure et la première* (Montreal: Les Éditions de l'Hexagone, 1970), 53. See also Pierre Vadeboncoeur, "L'héritage Trudeau: La fracture," *L'Action nationale*, Nov. 2000 (http://www.action-nationale.qc.ca/00–11/dossier.html).

63. The essay is found in *Rythmes et Couleurs*, Feb.–March 1964, 1–13. Trudeau's comments are in TP, vol. 38, file 30. The remarks about Laurendeau are made in "Un extraordinaire document de François Hertel," *Le Quartier Latin*, April 9, 1964. Trudeau's comments are in "Les Séparatistes: Des contre-révolutionnaires," *Cité libre*, May 1964, 3–4.

64. Hertel's comment on Trudeau is found in *Le Devoir*, Sept. 18, 1966. The article is entitled "Le bilinguisme est un crime." Grace Trudeau to Pierre Trudeau, Sept. 13, 1961, TP, vol. 46, file 26; and Jean Tréteau, *Hertel, l'homme et l'oeuvre* (Montreal: Pierre Tisseyre, 1986), 131–32, 211, 223, 232, 258, 320. Tréteau indexes Trudeau under "Elliott Trudeau."

65. The correspondence with the Ontario friend is found in RG 32, file 4, Archives of Ontario.

66. Gobeil and Breton are quoted in Gzowski, "What Young French Canadians Have on Their Mind," *Maclean's*, April 6, 1963, 21–23, 39–40; "Pour une politique fonctionelle," *Cité libre*, May 1964, 11–17; "An appeal for Realism in Politics," *The Canadian Forum*, May 1964, 29–33.

CHAPTER NINE: POLITICAL MAN

1. The accounts are from Gérard Pelletier, *Years of Choice, 1960–1968*, trans. Alan Brown (Toronto: Methuen, 1987), 130–33; Patricia Smart, ed., *The Diary of André Laurendeau* (Toronto: James Lorimer, 1991), 21; and Trudeau's discussion with Pelletier, June 9, 1992, Trudeau Papers (TP), MG 26 02, vol. 23, file 16, Library and Archives Canada (LAC).

2. Pelletier, *Years of Choice*, 136–38. Lévesque's statements are taken from the account of his changing attitude in Pierre Godin, *René Lévesque*, vol.2: *Héros malgré lui, 1960–1976* (Montreal: Les Éditions du Boréal, 1997), 290–92.

3. Laurendeau, Sept. 1961, quoted by Pierre de Bellefeuille, "André Laurendeau face au séparatisme des années 60," in Robert Comeau and Lucille Beaudry, eds., *André Laurendeau: Un intellectuel d'ici* (Sillery, Que.: Les Presses de l'Université du Québec, 1990), 159; Smart, ed.,

Laurendeau, 24; and J.L. Granatstein, *Canada 1957–1967: The Years of Uncertainty and Innovation* (Toronto: McClelland & Stewart, 1986), ch. 10. The so-called language issue, which is at the core of the changes, is described in Paul-André Linteau, René Durocher, Jean-Claude Robert, and François Ricard, *Quebec since 1930* trans. Robert Chodos and Ellen Garmaise (Toronto: James Lorimer, 1991), ch. 41.

4. Members are described in Smart, ed., *Laurendeau*, 13–17. The founding and development of the commission are described well in Granatstein, *Canada 1957–1967*, ch. 10. Well-chosen excerpts of testimony and commentary are available on http://archives.cbc.ca/IDD-1-73-655/politics_economy/ bilingualism/.

5. The commission of Trudeau's study is described in the Royal Commission files in Fonds Laurendeau, June 18, 1964, document 324E, Fondation Lionel Groulx, Montreal. There is no apparent evidence in Trudeau's own papers that he worked on the study.

6. Interviews with Donald Johnston, May 2004, and Sophie Trudeau, Feb. 2006.

7. Interview with Jacques Hébert, Feb. 2006.

8. Pierre Vallières, "*Cité libre* et ma génération," *Cité libre*, Aug.–Sept. 1963, 15–22.

9. Pierre Vallières, "Sommes-nous en révolution?" *Cité libre*, Feb. 1964, 7–11; and Gérard Pelletier, "*Parti pris* ou la grande illusion," *Cité libre*, April 1964, 3–8. On *Parti pris*, see Pierrette Bouchard-Saint-Amant, "L'idéologie de la revue *Parti-pris:* Le nationalisme socialiste," in Fernand Dumont, Jean Hamelin, and Jean-Paul Montminy, eds., *Idéologies au Canada français, 1940–1976* (Quebec: Les Presses de l'Université Laval, 1981), 315–53.

10. This text of "Separatist Counter-Revolutionaries" is taken from Pierre Trudeau, *Federalism and the French Canadians* (Toronto: Macmillan, 1968), 204–12. It was originally published as "Les séparatistes: Des contre-révolutionnaires" in *Cité libre*, May 1964, 2–6. The translation here is from the *Montreal Star*, which, along with other English-language outlets, published it in the late spring of 1964.

11. Pierre Vallières's account is found in his *Les Négres blancs d'Amérique: Autobiographie précoce d'un terroriste québécois* (Montreal: Éditions Parti pris, nd [1968]), 291–96.

12. Ramsay Cook, *The Maple Leaf Forever* (Toronto: Macmillan, 1971), 36.

13. Joseph-Yvon Thériault, *Critique de l'américanité: Mémoire et démocratie au Québec* (Montreal: Québec Amérique, 2005), 310–13; Trudeau to Hertel, Jan. 13, 1942, TP, vol. 49, file 19.

14. Breton in Nancy Southam, ed., *Pierre* (Toronto: McClelland & Stewart, 2005), 35. Many discussions with Breton about Trudeau.

15. Trudeau, "Separatist Counter-Revolutionaries," 206. See also Claude Julien, *Le Canada: Dernière chance de l'Europe* (Paris: Grasset, 1965); and Jean LeMoyne, *Convergences* (Montreal: Éditions Hurtubise, 1961), 26–27.

16. A good account of the cultural renaissance is found in Linteau et al., *Quebec since 1930*, ch. 53. See also Michel Vastel, *Trudeau: Le Québécois*, 2nd ed. (Montreal: Les Éditions de l'Homme, 2000), 123; and Guérin to Trudeau [Feb. 1965], TP, vol. 49, file 8.

17. On Trudeau and the CBC, see Eric Koch, *Inside This Hour Has Seven Days* (Toronto: Prentice-Hall, 1986), 45; and Carroll Guérin to Trudeau, Dec. 16, 1964, TP, vol. 49, file 8.

18. Malcolm Reid, *The Shouting Signpainters: A Literary and Political Account of Quebec Revolutionary Nationalism* (Toronto: McClelland & Stewart, 1972), 59–60.

19. Cook, *The Maple Leaf Forever*, 41.

20. John Saywell, ed., *The Canadian Annual Review for 1964* (Toronto: University of Toronto Press, 1965), 46–49, includes the Paré quotation; and *Globe and Mail*, Oct. 14, 1964.

21. Saywell, ed., *The Canadian Annual Review for 1964*, 52–54; *Le Devoir*, Sept. 18–19, 1964; and John English, *The Worldly Years: The Life of Lester Pearson, 1949–1972* (Toronto: Knopf, 1992), 218ff.

22. Smart, ed., *Laurendeau*, 73, 90. The polls are described in John Saywell, ed. *The Canadian Annual Review for 1965* (Toronto: University of Toronto Press, 1966), 44. See also A *Preliminary Report of the Royal Commission on Bilingualism and Biculturalism* (Ottawa: Queen's Printer, 1965), 13.

23. Patricia Smart's introduction discusses Laurendeau's discovery of Trudeau's authorship of the critical article. Trudeau admitted "partial paternity" to Laurendeau. Smart, ed., *Laurendeau*, 6–7, 154.

24. English, *The Worldly Years*, 300–4; Claude Morin, *Le pouvoir québécois en négociation* (Montreal: Les Éditions du Boréal, 1975), 137.

25. Pearson to Lower, Dec. 22, 1964, Pearson Papers, MG 26 N3, vol. 3, LAC.

26. Richard Gwyn, *The Shape of Scandal: A Study of a Government in Crisis* (Toronto: Clarke Irwin, 1965), 244. In *The Worldly Years*, 278ff, I discuss the reaction of Pearson to these scandals.

27. Vadeboncoeur described how unionists realized that Marchand had lost his earlier élan and how "many militants" believed that "he had become too uncompromising in his actions and beliefs." See the official site: www.csn.qc.ca/Connaitre/histoire/Vad/Vad2.html. Pelletier describes his firing in *Years of Choice*, 138–39; see also Saywell, ed., *The Canadian Annual Review for 1965*, 483.

28. For the best account of the negotiations, revealing the deep tensions among the Quebec Liberals, see the interviews conducted by Peter Stursberg in his *Lester Pearson and the Dream of Unity* (Toronto: Doubleday, 1978), 255–60. See also Vastel, *Trudeau*, 129–32, which draws on interviews with Marchand conducted later by Pierre Godin.

29. Interview with Eddie Goldenberg, Sept. 2004.

30. Lamontagne in Stursberg, *Lester Pearson and the Dream of Unity*, 258; Pelletier, *Years of Choice*, 176; Vastel, *Trudeau*, 130; Peter Newman, *The Distemper of Our Times: Canadian Politics in Transition* (1968; rev. ed. Toronto: McClelland & Stewart, 1990), 360, on Macnaughton's "skill" as a Speaker; and George Radwanski, *Trudeau* (Toronto: Macmillan, 1978), 90. On Cohen, see Pearson to Cohen, Aug. 5, 1965, Pearson Papers, MG 26 N5, vol. 45; interview with Robin Russell, Macnaughton's assistant, June 2001.

31. "Pelletier et Trudeau s'expliquent," *Cité libre*, Oct. 1965, 3–5.

32. Ramsay Cook to Trudeau, Sept. 10, 1965 (thanks to Ramsay Cook for this letter); and Maurice Blain, "Les colombes et le pouvoir politique: Observations sur une hypothèse," *Cité libre*, Dec. 1965, 7.

33. Election results from Pierre Normandin, ed., *The Canadian Parliamentary Guide 1972* (Ottawa: Normandin, 1972), 382. Nichol quoted in Stursberg, *Lester Pearson and the Dream of Unity*, 274; Blain, "Les colombes," 8; Smart, ed., *Laurendeau*, 153; Pierre Vadeboncoeur, *To be or not to be: That is the question* (Montreal: Les Éditions de l'Hexagone, 1980), 91–109; and interview with Bob Rae, July 2003.

34. Gobeil to Trudeau, Sept. 8, 1965, TP, MG 26 02, vol. 47, file 35, and Guérin to Trudeau, Oct. 25, 1965, vol. 49, file 8.

35. Ryan in *Le Devoir*, Dec. 18, 1965; and Marchand in Stursberg, *Pearson and the Dream of Unity*, 261.

36. *Globe and Mail*, Sept. 14, 1965. On Favreau's motorcycle, see Pelletier, *Years of Choice*, 177.

37. Kenneth McNaught, "The National Outlook of English-speaking Canadians," in Peter Russell, ed., *Nationalism in Canada* (Toronto: McGraw-Hill, 1966), 70.

38. Jean-Paul Desbiens (Frère Untel) is quoted in Newman, *The Distemper of Our Times*, 512.

39. *Montreal Gazette*, Oct. 23, 1965; and Blair Fraser, "The Three: Quebec's New Face in Ottawa," *Maclean's*, Jan. 22, 1966, 16–17, 37–38.

40. Pierre Trudeau, *Memoirs* (Toronto: McClelland & Stewart, 1993), 78. See also the account in Stephen Clarkson and Christina McCall, *Trudeau and Our Times*, vol. 1: *The Magnificent Obsession* (Toronto: McClelland & Stewart, 1990), 93–94; Smart, ed., *Laurendeau*, 154; and Pearson as quoted in Radwanski, *Trudeau*, 91.

41. *Globe and Mail*, Nov. 9, 1965; English, *The Worldly Years*, 310–12; and Lester Pearson, "Election Analysis," Dec. 10, 1965, Pearson Papers, MG 26 N5, vol. 45.

42. Interview between Pierre Trudeau and Ron Graham, April 29, 1992, TP, vol. 23, file 4.

43. Smart, ed., *Laurendeau*, 154.

44. Bruce Hutchison, "A Conversation with the Prime Minister," Feb. 11, 1965, Hutchison Papers, University of Calgary Library; John Saywell, ed., *The Canadian Annual Review for 1966* (Toronto: University of Toronto Press, 1967), 52–53; *Le Devoir*, March 29, 1966; and *Toronto Daily Star*, April 2, 1966.

45. On Spencer, see Newman, *The Distemper of Our Times*, 534–53; House of Commons, *Debates*, Feb. 25, 1965; Saywell, ed., *The Canadian Annual Review for 1966*, 9–11; and, especially, Stursberg, *Lester Pearson and the Dream of Unity*, 291–94.

46. Diefenbaker had the materials in his papers. J.G. Dienbaker Papers, box II 008386–92, Diefenbaker Centre, Saskatoon. Pearson's account is in an interview with Bruce Hutchison, Feb. 11, 1965, Hutchison Papers.

47. House of Commons, *Debates*, March 2–4, 1966; and Newman, *Distemper of Our Times*, 540–42.

48. Newman, *Distemper of Our Times*, 540–42; Marchand is quoted in Stursberg, *Lester Pearson and the Dream of Unity*, 294; his resignation threat is described on page 297. Interview with André Ouellet, May 2001.

49. Pierre Vadeboncoeur, "À propos de Pierre Elliott," *Le Devoir*, Dec. 8, 2005.

50. Newman, *The Distemper of Our Times*, 604; Trudeau, *Memoirs*, 78–79, where Pearson's comment in his own memoirs is quoted, presumably indicating agreement. Interview with Herb Gray, June 2005.

51. *Le Magazine Maclean*, Jan. 1965, 2; and English, *The Worldly Years*, 319ff. The fullest account is given in John Bosher, *The Gaullist Attack on Canada* (Montreal and Kingston: McGill-Queen's University Press, 1999). See also Trudeau, *Memoirs*, 78–79.

52. Clarkson and McCall, *Trudeau and Our Times* 1: 99–101; Johnson's quotation on the Constitution is in Newman, *The Distemper of Our Times*, 445; Saywell, ed., *The Canadian Annual Review for 1966*, 57–73; and *Le Devoir*, Sept. 15, 1966. Interview with Mitchell Sharp, Jan. 1994. Sharp first noticed Trudeau during a discussion of the proposed tax structure at a Cabinet committee meeting where he represented Pearson and where he expressed his strong opposition to special status. See Mitchell Sharp, *Which Reminds Me . . . : A Memoir* (Toronto: University of Toronto Press, 1994), 139.

53. Comments in notebook, April 25, 1959, in TP, vol. 13, file 5.

54. Interview with Paul Martin Sr., Sept. 1990; interview with Marc Lalonde, Oct. 1990. John Bosher had access to Marcel Cadieux's diary, in which he fiercely criticized Martin, particularly on the French issue. See Bosher, *The Gaullist Attack on Canada*. Before his death, Cadieux spoke to me about his strong feelings against Pearson for his criticisms of American policy on Vietnam and against Martin for his "gimmicks," which he believed were a means to use foreign policy for electoral gain.

55. Gordon took the lead in the late 1940s in creating a fund, the "Algoma Fishing and Conservation Society," in honour of Pearson's Northern Ontario constituency. He was also the principal organizer of his leadership campaign and of the party reorganization in the late 1950s and early 1960s. He introduced Pearson to Keith Davey, Richard O'Hagan, and

many others who played a major role in the Pearson governments, and he was an important recruiter of candidates in the Toronto area. His relationship with Pearson never recovered after the prime minister accepted his resignation after the 1965 election. He wrote angry memoranda about their relationship, claiming that he had raised $100,000 in private funds for Pearson, and he remained deeply distrustful of Pearson, who, he wrote after his meeting in January 1967, "will renege [on the deal] if he can." Walter Gordon, "LBP," Dec. 5, 1965, Gordon Papers, MG 26 B44, vol. 16, LAC; and Memorandum of Jan. 18, 1967, ibid.

56. Gad Horowitz, "A Dimension Survey: The Future of the NDP," *Canadian Dimension* 3 (July–Aug.): 23, 24.

57. Lamontagne and Gordon told their stories to Stursberg, *Lester Pearson and the Dream of Unity*, 374–76.

58. Clarkson and McCall, *Trudeau and Our Times*, 1: 102; and Saywell, ed., *The Canadian Annual Review for 1966*, 34, 52–53.

59. Interview, Library and Archives Canada, March 5, 2003.

60. William Robb, "Trudeau Up Front," *Canadian Business*, May 1967, 11–12. Newman in *Toronto Daily Star*, April 25, 1967. The correspondent who saw Trudeau blush is Robert Stall, *Montreal Star*, Dec. 20, 1967. On Trudeau's early argument that natural justice must be observed, see RG 2, Privy Council Office, Series A-5-a, vol. 6323, April 6, 1967.

61. RG 2, Privy Council Office, Series A-5-a, vol. 6323, July 25, 1967.

62. *Le Devoir*, Sept. 20, 1967. The text of the Lévesque address calling for sovereignty was published in *Le Devoir* between September 19 and 21, 1967.

63. Gordon, Memorandum, Nov. 17, 1967, Gordon Papers, MG 26, B44, vol. 16.

64. Guérin to Trudeau, July 4, 1964, TP, vol. 28, file 8; interview with Madeleine Gobeil.

65. Guérin to Trudeau, Sept. 15, 1967.

66. Margaret Trudeau, *Beyond Reason* (New York and London: Paddington, 1979), 28–29; interview with Margaret Sinclair Trudeau, Feb. 2006.

CHAPTER TEN: A TALE OF TWO CITIES

1. Gérard Pelletier, *Years of Choice, 1960–1968*, trans. Alan Brown (Toronto: Methuen, 1987), 254–55. Pelletier's account seems to suggest that the dinner took place on January 7, 1968, but Donald Peacock's

more contemporary *Journey to Power: The Story of a Canadian Election* (Toronto: Ryerson, 1968) has the accurate date and a fuller account of the meeting at Café Martin (185ff). Trudeau's own memory has Pelletier making the first remarks. "Entrevue entre M. Trudeau et M. [Jean] Lépine, 30 April 1992," [Lépine interview], Trudeau Papers (TP), MG 26 03, vol. 23, file 5, Library and Archives Canada.

2. Richard Stanbury Diary, property of the writer. Mr. Stanbury also responded to my questions about specific diary entries. The Martin exchange took place on January 31, 1968. The best account of the Toronto Liberals remains Christina McCall-Newman, *Grits: An Intimate Portrait of the Liberal Party* (Toronto: Macmillan, 1982). John Nichol's recollection that only he and Liberal Federation official Paul Lafond knew about Pearson's resignation before it happened is contradicted by Stanbury's diary and by other interviews on the subject conducted by Peter Stursberg. See his *Lester Pearson and the Dream of Unity* (Toronto: Doubleday, 1978), 405–6. Interview with John Nichol.

3. Minutes of the meeting of Sunday, October 22, at 580 Christie Street, Keith Davey Papers, box 17, file 15, Victoria University.

4. O'Malley had written the phrase in the *Globe and Mail* on December 12, 1967. Trudeau was obviously taken with it and repeated it in an interview ten days later. See Richard Gwyn, *The Northern Magus: Pierre Trudeau and Canadians* (Toronto: McClelland & Stewart, 1980), 64.

5. *The Montreal Star*, Jan. 13, 1968. To my knowledge, the French press did not report on the petition.

6. Peacock, *Journey to Power*, 183–85; Martin Sullivan, *Mandate '68* (Toronto: Doubleday, 1968), 274; interviews with Marc Lalonde and Jacques Hébert; and *Toronto Daily Star*, Jan. 3, 1968. See also the account in John Saywell, ed., *Canadian Annual Review for 1968* (Toronto: University of Toronto Press, 1969), 17ff.

7. Laurendeau's diary entry of Dec. 3, 1967, in Patricia Smart, ed., *The Diary of André Laurendeau* (Toronto: James Lorimer, 1991), 170. Marchand's drinking caused Trudeau personal concern and he raised it with him. Interview with Alexandre Trudeau. Also conversations with Pauline Bothwell and Tom Kent, who were, respectively, Marchand's assistant and deputy minister. Interview with Tim Porteous, May 2006.

8. In the *New York Times* story, April 7, 1968, reporting his leadership win, Trudeau is described as a "46-year-old Montreal lawyer." Later, Jean Lépine challenged Trudeau on the ambiguity about his age, but he denied that he had lied. He placed the blame on journalists who did not check the facts. Lépine interview, TP, vol. 23, file 5.

9. On Smallwood, see Peacock, *Journey to Power*, 190–92. Smallwood's own comments are found in Stursberg, *Lester Pearson and the Dream of Unity*, 421. J.W. Pickersgill, who had been the Liberals' principal Newfoundland minister, eventually left politics because he could no longer deal with the eccentricities of Smallwood. As his summer tenant in the mid-1970s, I was often regaled with tales of Smallwood's increasingly bizarre behaviour. He included this support for Trudeau as one of the examples of such behaviour.

10. Pelletier, *Years of Choice*, 264. Peacock describes the tortured negotiations with Lamontagne over the Sunday session in *Journey to Power*, 195–96. Interviews with Donald Macdonald and Marc Lalonde.

11. *Le Devoir*, Jan. 29, 1968. See also Saywell, ed., *Canadian Annual Review for 1968*, 18–19.

12. *Montreal Star*, Jan. 30–31, 1968.

13. Stanbury Diary, Feb. 9, 1968; *Globe and Mail*, Jan. 30, 1968; and Pelletier, *Years of Choice*, 261, 27.

14. L.B. Pearson, *Federalism for the Future* (Ottawa: The Queen's Printer, 1968).

15. Cook in Saywell, ed., *Canadian Annual Review for 1968*, 82.

16. Marchand quoted in Stursberg, *Lester Pearson and the Dream of Unity*, 425; Stéphane Kelly, *Les Fins du Canada selon Macdonald, Laurier, Mackenzie King et Trudeau* (Montreal: Les Éditions du Boréal, 2001), 205.

17. Peter Newman gives the best summary of the candidates in his *The Distemper of Our Times: Canadian Politics in Transition* (1968; rev. ed. Toronto: McClelland & Stewart, 1990), 596–601.

18. Pelletier, *Years of Choice*, 272–74.

19. Ibid., 274–76; and Peacock, *Journey to Power*, 222–24.

20. There are differences in the accounts of the meetings with Pelletier. Some claim that Trudeau told them on Valentine's Day, but others (Saywell, ed., *Canadian Annual Review for 1968* and Peacock, *Journey to Power*) suggest the 15th. Pelletier's account is based on his diary and therefore is probably correct. See his *Years of Choice*, 276.

21. The quotation is from Saywell, ed., *Canadian Annual Review for 1968*, 21.

22. *Montreal Star*, March 9, 1968.

23. Tim Porteous in Nancy Southam, ed., *Pierre* (Toronto: McClelland & Stewart, 2005), 65. The answer may have been serious. Trudeau, along with many academics, considered that Machiavelli had been misunderstood and distorted.

24. Christina McCall-Newman, *Grits*, 113–15. Confidential interview. Trudeau saved copies of the *Canadian Intelligence Service* in his papers. The March 1968 issue features "revelations" by a former RCMP intelligence officer about Trudeau's trips to China and Russia and his failed jaunt to Cuba.

25. However, some journalists criticized Trudeau for following "old-style politics" in so vociferously defending the government. The *Globe and Mail*, which had been friendly to his candidacy but was hostile to the government, pointed out that "that man of principle, Justice Minister Pierre Trudeau, fell obediently in line with party discipline and voted with the government. Or is that *erstwhile* man of principle?" Feb. 19, 1968. Peter Newman rightly said that Trudeau benefited most because he, Turner, and Kierans "alone project a new style that dissociates them from the blunders of the Pearson administration." *Toronto Daily Star*, March 3, 1968.

26. Gordon interview in Stursberg, *Lester Pearson and the Dream of Unity*; *Globe and Mail*, Feb. 20 and 28, 1968. An excellent account of the Liberal manoeuvres is found in *Toronto Daily Star*, Feb. 26, 1968. Constitutional authorities were divided on the question of whether the government had the right to bring forward a vote of confidence. Eugene Forsey, for example, believed that it did. See Saywell, ed., *Canadian Annual Review for 1968*, 12–13. Sharp's analysis is found in his *Which Reminds Me . . . : A Memoir* (Toronto: University of Toronto Press, 1994), 159ff. Trudeau's comments are in Hansard, Feb. 27, 1968.

27. On Winters, see Newman, *The Distemper of Our Times*, 602–3. The February polls are found in the record of the Canadian Institute of Public Opinion, MG 28 III 114, file 89, Poll 327, LAC.

28. Pelletier, *Years of Choice*, 290–91; Peacock, *Journey to Power*, 255–58. The hostess comment is in *Toronto Daily Star*, March 4, 1968.

29. Tim Porteous in Southam, ed., *Pierre* , 61.

30. There is a full account in Peacock, *Journey to Power*, 251–53. See also *Le Devoir*, Feb. 16–17, 1968.

31. *Le Devoir*, March 6–7, 1968. The criticisms of Trudeau are found in Saywell, ed., *The Canadian Annual Review for 1968*, 24–25. On Johnson and Gabon, see Pierre Godin, *Daniel Johnson, 1964–1968: La difficile recherche de l'égalité* (Montreal: Les Éditions de l'Homme, 1980), 329–33.

32. Pelletier, *Years of Choice*, 293–300; *Montreal Star*, March 23, 1968.

33. Sharp, *Which Reminds Me . . .* , 155–65; interview with Mitchell Sharp. The Smallwood quotation is found in Newman, *Distemper of Our Times*, 628.

34. Stanbury Diary; Peacock, *Journey to Power*, 283ff. Interview with Tim Porteous, May 2006.

35. Conversation with Robert Bothwell, Feb. 2006.

36. The account follows Peacock, *Journey to Power*. However, slightly different wording is found in Newman, *Distemper of Our Times*, 638. The substance is the same.

NOTE ON SOURCES

—

T he source for this volume is the remarkable collection of personal papers that has been transferred from the Trudeau home in Montreal to Library and Archives Canada in Ottawa. These papers were assembled in minute detail by Grace Trudeau and by Trudeau himself.

The most interesting item in the preserved papers is the Gouin-Trudeau correspondence of the mid-1940s. When the relationship between Thérèse Gouin and Trudeau ended, she returned his letters. They later discussed the correspondence, and he promised it would not be released in her lifetime — although he mentioned to Madame Gouin Décarie that he had recently read the letters once again. Having now been privileged to read the correspondence myself, I can understand Trudeau's wish that the letters be kept complete. They are remarkable and, eventually, when they are published, they will take their place among the most illuminating and important exchanges in Canadian letters.

Although Trudeau made little apparent use of his papers for his memoirs, there is considerable indication he read much of the collection later in his life. There are notations, question marks, and identification of individuals whose full names are not given in the originals. His papers also contain the excellent interviews conducted for the memoirs by Ron Graham and Jean Lépine, as well as some interviews with family members and others as diverse as Michael Ignatieff and Camille Laurin. Again, very little use was made of this material for the memoirs. We now know that Trudeau's memoirs concealed much of his private thoughts and activities, but he did maintain the integrity of his papers, which fully disclose them all. We can only speculate on his reasons, but there is evidence in the Trudeau papers that, as early as 1939, he expected that he would, one day, have a biographer. Moreover, he admired confessional literature, from Saint Augustine through to Proust. Ultimately, he has allowed others to bare the soul that he so carefully concealed in his lifetime, and he apparently did so deliberately.

Some documents seem to be missing in his papers. For example, there are almost no letters from Father Marie d'Anjou or François Lessard, although we know that both corresponded frequently with Trudeau about nationalist and religious matters in the forties. There are also few letters from Jean Marchand and Gérard Pelletier, and none of substance from Trudeau in their papers—all of which suggests (especially in the case of Pelletier) that the correspondence relating to their political and literary work in the fifties and sixties is either lost or in some abandoned filing cabinet. Still, Trudeau's private papers are an exceptionally rich lode for a biographer to mine, and valuable nuggets appear in virtually every box.

This book has full endnotes indicating primary sources and secondary works. The majority of the secondary works dealing with Trudeau will be relevant for the second volume of the biography, which will deal with his political career and its aftermath. It is impossible to separate the sources for the two volumes because interviews relating to his later life, for instance, can also be relevant in discussing his earlier years. A full bibliography, including manuscript sources and interviews, will be available on the web at www.theigloo.org after the publication of this volume, and it will grow as I write Volume Two. The site will also provide an opportunity for others—students, scholars, and all interested readers—to offer their own information that might be relevant for Trudeau's later life.

ACKNOWLEDGMENTS

—

I n the Preface to this book, I thank the Trudeau family and the executors of the Trudeau Estate—Alexandre Trudeau, Jim Coutts, Marc Lalonde, Roy Heenan, and Jacques Hébert—for their invitation to write this biography. I also thank them for issuing the invitation without, for a moment, thinking to impose restrictions on me, and for entrusting me to write a full and objective account of Pierre Elliott Trudeau's life. I would also like to thank the Trudeau family for their encouragement, not only Alexandre and Justin, of course, but my friends Margaret Sinclair Trudeau and Sophie Grégoire, who is married to Justin Trudeau, for their invaluable feminine view on Trudeau's family.

There are many others whom I must thank greatly for expanding my understanding of Pierre Trudeau. Three individuals in particular, who not only knew Trudeau well but also greatly affected his life in this period, offered me assistance in clarifying the story. The remarkable Thérèse Gouin Décarie, Trudeau's close companion over many of these years, agreed to cooperate with this biographical project and gave me access to material that was essential. (Her husband, Vianney Décarie, also provided important information about Trudeau's early years.) Roger Rolland, the friend in many of Trudeau's early pranks (and later his speechwriter), corrected tales that had been told wrongly in the past and provided new ones. Madeleine Gobeil, who knew Trudeau intimately in the sixties, when his personal files are thinner, offered unique, intelligent insight into his habits, tastes, and friendships.

I met two of Pierre's close friends when I attended Harvard University. Ramsay and Eleanor Cook came to Boston in the fall of 1968, just after Pierre became prime minister—in part because of their efforts. After Ramsay's lecture on Canadian history to Harvard undergraduates, a few of us Canadian doctoral students ruminated with him about the fate of the Trudeau government, which had already begun to lose some of the aura that surrounded it during the summer months. The following year I met Albert Breton, Trudeau's former colleague at the Université de Montréal, who followed Ramsay as the Mackenzie King Professor at Harvard. I was Albert's teaching assistant, and, when my wife, Hilde, and I formed an enduring friendship with Albert and his wife, Margot, they gave me a view of Pierre that was marked by immense personal warmth and respect. Ramsay and Eleanor have read this manuscript, and both have saved me from many errors of fact and interpretation.

I have also benefited from interviews about Trudeau that I conducted when I wrote a biography of Lester Pearson and, with Robert Bothwell, a book on postwar Canadian history. The bulk of these interviews with leading political and bureaucratic figures of the sixties and seventies are in the Bothwell Papers at the University of Toronto Archives and at Library and Archives Canada, and in my own papers at the University of Waterloo Archives. Bob has shared research notes from his work on Canadian foreign policy and Quebec and, in the United States, in the Nixon and Ford Papers. I owe an enormous debt to him for his generosity. I also owe a debt to many who have written perceptive articles, books, and essays about Trudeau. A full critical bibliography will accompany Volume Two of this biography and, in the meantime, the titles will be listed on the website for this book.

Library and Archives Canada has provided extraordinary assistance for this work. Under the expert guidance of Christian Rioux, a team organized the Trudeau Papers quickly and wisely. Peter de Lottinville, Michel Wyczynski, and George Bolarenko were also helpful, and I would particularly like to thank Michel for responding at short notice to my requests for visits. Paul Marsden, now at the NATO archives in Brussels, pointed me towards some important documents on Trudeau's work at the Privy Council in the 1950s. At every stage, Ian Wilson, the national archivist, has assisted me in my work with his exceptional attentiveness to the record of Canadian political history. Through his auspices, I was able to interview in small groups during 2002 and 2003 the following individuals (all with Honourable in their titles) who served Trudeau well: Jack Austin, Jean-Jacques Blais, Charles Caccia, Judy Erola, Herb Gray, Otto Lang, Ed Lumley, Allan MacEachen, André Ouellet, John Reid, Mitchell Sharp, and David Smith. Other Trudeau assistants and colleagues who participated in these interviews were Gordon Ashworth, Jean-Marc Carisse, Denise Chong, Ralph Coleman, Marie-Hélène Fox, Bea Hertz, Ted Johnson, Michael Langille, Mary MacDonald, Bob Murdoch, Nicole Sénécal, Larry Smith, Jacques Shore, Courtney Tower, and George Wilson. These interviews will be made available on my website when permissions are given.

I received many letters from both opposition and government members of the Trudeau years after the Canadian Association of Former Parliamentarians placed a notice in its newsletter asking former parliamentary colleagues of Trudeau to contact me about their experiences. Edward McWhinney, the distinguished constitutional authority, had not been a parliamentary colleague of Trudeau, but he, too, sent me a very helpful and long letter.

The Social Sciences and Humanities Research Council has supported this project through its research grant program, principally through funding for graduate research assistants. Several of these assistants were my doctoral students at the University of Waterloo, and they have simultaneously worked on dissertations examining various public policy issues of the Trudeau years. Their efforts will make regular appearances in the notes to the second volume of this biography. They also assisted in research in the important collections at Library and Archives Canada relevant to Canadian public life in the 1950s and 1960s. For this invaluable help I would like to thank Stephen Azzi, Matthew Bunch, Jason Churchill, Andrew Thompson, and Ryan Touhey. My former student Greg Donaghy, now in the Department of Foreign Affairs, helped with many inquiries. Marc Nadeau carried out research in Quebec archives, at Brébeuf College, and the Université de Montréal. Esther Delisle shared with Marc and me the evidence of the young Trudeau's involvement in a nationalist cell. Her exceptional research skills first found the trail that pointed to the proof presented in the early chapters of this book. The Hon. Alistair Gillespie and his biographer, Irene Sage, have shared their research in British and American archives, and Mr. Gillespie allowed me to read his own notes, which begin with the leadership convention. I would also like to thank the Hon. Richard Stanbury for giving me copies of his diary, which I have used extensively in the final chapter.

The University of Waterloo and its Department of History have provided a highly supportive atmosphere for scholarship and collegial activity. The department's chair, my friend Pat Harrigan, was the first reader of many of the chapters of this book (and the first to report victories of the Detroit Tigers, a passion we share). There are too many colleagues to mention who have contributed in some way to the book, but I would like to thank Dean Bob Kerton and President David Johnston at the University of Waterloo for their assistance during the past few years. In particular, they negotiated an agreement whereby I became executive director of the Centre for International Governance Innovation, a Waterloo-based think tank studying international affairs, which resulted from the imagination and financial generosity of my friend and former neighbour Jim Balsillie.

At the centre, Lena Yost has been my superb assistant, with support from Jenn Beckermann in the summer months. Research director Daniel Schwanen has not only taken on many tasks I should have done but has put his flawless bilingualism to the task of translation. Kerry Lappin-Fortin translated many of the quotations in French, and Alison de Muy helped with translation and some other questions. Trudeau's friend and close collaborator on his memoirs, Ron Graham, also translated some of Trudeau's letters. I would like to thank several colleagues at the centre, especially Andy Cooper, who did the bulk of the work on some books we co-edited; Dan Latendre and his staff, who helped with technical questions; and Paul Heinbecker, whose affection for Brian Mulroney provided the countervailing influence that Trudeau always deemed essential. Balsillie fellow Victor Sautry has helped with many tasks, and several excellent undergraduate students also provided research assistance. Alex Lund and Eleni Crespi worked for me during the summer months; and Jonathan Minnes has been the major organizer of the papers, the assistant "on call" throughout the year, and a reliable sleuth when endnotes were missing. Joan Euler gave me some useful articles I would not otherwise have found. Nicolas Rouleau, a brilliant young lawyer, volunteered to help me with the project. He brought a lawyer's mind to the manuscript, a historian's skill to research, and his bilingual facility to the project.

Once again Gena Gorrell, a proofreader who has an excellent eye for detail, has saved me from many errors and omissions. At Knopf Canada, Michelle MacAleese has assisted with the illustrations, and, with constant cheerfulness, Deirdre Molina has sorted out the various drafts of the manuscript, maintained the bulging files, and brought the scattered parts together. However, my greatest debt is owed to two exceptional women in Canadian publishing: my publisher Louise Dennys and my editor Rosemary Shipton. Louise received the Order of Canada this year because of her extraordinary contribution to Canadian publishing. She has brought to this biography boundless enthusiasm, stylistic elegance, a keen wit, and a devotion to understanding Canada. Her award is richly deserved. Next spring Trinity College at the University of Toronto will bestow an honorary doctorate on Rosemary Shipton, a recognition of her outstanding work as an editor. Trudeau took over Rosemary's life this winter, and, through the spring and early summer, she has shaped this book with remarkable skill and care. Like all prose she so expertly and graciously touches, mine has become clearer and better. My faults remain, but they are fewer because of Louise and Rosemary.

On a late September afternoon in 2000, my fifteen-year-old son, Jonathan, came home from school and said, "Adam and I are going to Montreal tonight." Two French-immersion students who were born the year after Pierre Trudeau left office, they had decided they must go to Trudeau's funeral. As the coffin travelled by train from Ottawa to Montreal, they left the old Kitchener station for the long ride that ended, fortunately, with seats in a remote corner of Notre Dame Cathedral, where they were present for one of Canada's greatest state occasions. Jonathan and his mother, Hilde, have endured too many absences from me while I wrote this book. I thank them both for their generosity and support, especially Hilde, who wanted so much to fight off her cancer until this book was published. She could not. I now mourn her deeply and dedicate this life story to her.

PHOTO CREDITS/PERMISSIONS

—

If not otherwise specified, all photos and images come from the Trudeau Papers

CP
Pierre in Middle East, Peter Bregg; Canadian delegation in China; Trudeau slides down bannister, Ted Grant.

LIBRARY AND ARCHIVES CANADA
Trudeau in 1950s, Walter Curtin PA-144330; Pelletier, Trudeau and Marchand announce candidacy, Duncan Cameron PA-117502; Pearson and his successors, Duncan Cameron PA-117107; Trudeau speaking, Horst Ehricht PA-184613; Trudeau at Federal-Provincial Conference, Duncan Cameron PA-117463; Trudeau at leadership convention, Duncan Cameron PA-206324; Trudeau team, Duncan Cameron PA-206327.

McCord Museum
The Big Attraction, M965.199.1451; Suddenly Everyone Looks a Little Older, M965.199.6529; A Mirage!, M997.63.37; The Swinger, M965.199.6647.

Don Newlands/KlixPix
Pierre Elliott Trudeau (cover); Three men in a boat; Rowing to Cuba. Early Gunslinger; A kiss for good luck; Flower in mouth.

TRUDEAU FAMILY

First baby picture; Grace Elliott Trudeau; Pierre with packsack.

PERMISSIONS

The author has made every effort to locate and contact all the holders of copy written material reproduced in this book, and expresses grateful acknowledgment for permission to reproduce from the following previously published material:

Lévesque, René. *Memoirs* (Toronto: McClelland & Stewart), 1986.

Pelletier, Gérard. *Years of Impatience, 1950–1960*, trans. Alan Brown (Toronto: Methuen), 1984.

Pelletier, Gérard. *Years of Choice, 1960–1968*, trans. Alan Brown (Toronto: Methuen), 1987.

Saywell, John and Donald Foster, eds. *Canadian Annual Review for 1968* (University of Toronto Press, Toronto), 1969.

Scott, F.R. *The Collected Poems of F.R. Scott* (Toronto: McClelland & Stewart), 1981.

Trudeau, Pierre Elliott. *Against the Current: Selected Writings, 1939–1996*, trans. G. Tombs (Toronto: McClelland & Stewart), 1996.

Trudeau, Pierre Elliott and Jacques Hébert. *Two Innocents in Red China* (Toronto: Oxford University Press), 1968.

INDEX

—

JOHN ENGLISH is the General Editor of the *Dictionary of Canadian Biography*, a professor of history at the University of Waterloo, and executive director of the Centre for International Governance Innovation. He is the author of the acclaimed two-volume biography of Lester Pearson, *Shadow of Heaven: The Life of Lester Pearson, Volume 1: 1897–1948*, and *The Worldly Years: The Life of Lester Pearson, Volume 2: 1949–1972*, along with several other books on Canadian politics. He lives in Kitchener, Ontario.